John Cowper Powys, novelist, poet, critic and philosopher, was born in 1872, the eldest son of the Rev C. F. Powys. On his mother's side he was descended from the families of the poets Donne and Cowper, and his two brothers, Theodore Francis and Llewelyn, also achieved literary fame.

Educated at Sherborne and Corpus Christi College, Cambridge, he was a lecturer in America for many years, and many of his most famous novels were written away from the England he loved so much. He died in 1963. His other books include *A Glastonbury Romance*, *Wolf Solvent*, *Maiden Castle*, *Porius*, *Autobiography*, *The Brazen Head* and *Weymouth Sands*.

By John Cowper Powys in Picador

A Glastonbury Romance
The Brazen Head

John Cowper Powys

Owen Glendower

published by Pan Books

First published 1941 by John Lane, The Bodley Head
This edition first published 1974 by Cedric Chivers Ltd
First published in Picador 1978 by Pan Books Ltd,
Cavaye Place, London SW10 9PG
All rights reserved
ISBN 0 330 25371 9
Printed and bound in Great Britain by
Richard Clay (The Chaucer Press) Ltd, Bungay, Suffolk

Dedicated
to
Huw Menai
of the
Rhondda

TABLE OF CONTENTS

HISTORICAL NOTE

Readers who would prefer, before reading
OWEN GLENDOWER, to refresh their memories
on the history of the period, will find the
historical setting outlined by the Author in an
Argument at the end of the book.

CHARACTERS OF THE NOVEL

MENTIONED IN HISTORY

Owen ap Griffith Fychan (commonly called Glyn Dŵr or Glendower)
Margaret Hanmer, "The Arglwyddes," Owen's wife
Griffith, his eldest son
Meredith, his youngest son
Catharine, his youngest daughter
Tudor ap Griffith, his brother
John Hanmer, his wife's brother
Rhisiart ab Owen, Owen's secretary
Henry IV
Prince Henry, afterwards Henry V
Henry Percy, commonly called Hotspur
Thomas Fitz-Alan, Earl of Arundel and Lord of Chirk
Reginald Grey, Lord of Ruthin
Lord Grey of Codnor
Lord Talbot of Goodrich
Sir John Oldcastle
The Archbishop of Canterbury
Lord Bardolf
Rhys Gethin, Owen's Chief Captain
Lewis Byford, Bishop of Bangor
Griffith Young, Owen's Chancellor
Hugh Burnell, Sheriff of Salop
Francis de Court, Lord of Pembroke
Henry Don of Kidwelly
David Gam of Brecon
Hywel Sele, Baron of Nannau
Crach Ffinnant, Owen's Prophet
Walter Brut of Lyde, Hereford, a Lollard
Alice, his wife
Griffith Llwyd, Owen's Bard
Iolo Goch, Owen's bardic friend
Hopkin ap Thomas, Prophet of Gower
Sir Edmund Mortimer, Owen's son-in-law
Rhys Ddu of Cardigan
Elliw, his daughter

THE ARCHDEACON OF BANGOR

JOHN AP HYWEL, Abbot of Llantarnam, Caerleon

PATROUILLART DE TRIE, a French hero

ROBERT DE LA HEUZE, " Le Borgne," a French Commander

ROBERT WHITNEY, Knight

KINARD DE LA BERE, Knight

WALTER DEVEREUX, Knight

THOMAS CLANVOW, Poet, Author of *The Cuckoo and the Nightingale*

BROTHER EDDOUYER, Emissary from the Avignon Pope

UN-MENTIONED IN HISTORY

FFRAID FERCH GLOYW, the Prophetess of Dinas Brân

LOWRI FERCH FFRAID, her illegitimate daughter

TEGOLIN FERCH LOWRI, Lowri's illegitimate daughter

MISTRESS SIBLI, a dwarf

LUNED, a lady-in-waiting

RAWLFF, a page, subsequently knighted

IAGO, a page, subsequently a sailor

ELPHIN, a page, subsequently a herald and late a priest

GLEW THE GRYD, Owen's Porter

FATHER PASCENTIUS, a Cistercian monk

FATHER RHEINALT, a Cistercian monk

ABBOT CUST OF VALLE CRUCIS

PRIOR BEVAN OF VALLE CRUCIS

PHILIP SPARROW, champion of the peasantry

BROCH-O'-MEIFOD

MORG FERCH LUG, his wife

DENIS BURNELL, Constable of Dinas Brân

ADDA AP LEURIG, Seneschal of Dinas Brân

SIMON THE HOG, married to Lowri

EFA FERCH TUDOR OF MÔN

RHISIART AB EDMUND, a grandson of Owen's

GILLES DE PIROGUE ⎫
⎬ Ambassadors from Charles VI of France
JEAN DE PIROGUE ⎭

Time of the Novel: A.D. 1400 TO A.D. 1416

I

THE CASTLE

Don quixote might well have recognized in the gaunt piebald horse that carried young Rhisiart down that winding track towards the river Dee a true cousin of Rosinante's. Like Rosinante he was as much of a personality as his master; and like Rosinante he was burdened with a strange assemblage of unusual objects.

One of these objects was a heavy crusader's sword, at that time completely out of date; while another, contrasting oddly with this old-fashioned weapon, was a trim leather case such as Disputants at the University of Oxford were wont to carry, packed so full with parchment—covered manuscripts that any inquisitive stranger under the excuse of caressing Master Rhisiart's steed might, had he been able to read, have deciphered between the gilded straps, fragments of a Latin that clearly was not the Latin of the Church.

Master Rhisiart had also burdened his powerful but odd-looking steed with a huge bundle of a young man's changes of raiment, wrapped up in what might have been taken for—and in actual truth *was*—a thick bed-cover of well-worn sheepskin, better adapted to a scholar's wintry nights at Oxford than to the hot June sun that just then beat down upon it.

But this was not all; for firmly attached to the sheepskin bundle was an object that flung back the blazing sun in a thousand fiery points as the horse moved, an object that needed no very close inspection to reveal itself as a light mail-jacket of polished metal formed of a number of loosely-riveted links.

Rhisiart was certainly not a good-looking or a particularly sociable-looking youth, and yet neither at Oxford nor on his slow journey north-west had his extreme self-consciousness, though a far touchier medium for impressions than superficially appeared, suffered many rebuffs from strangers. This may have been due to something dangerous about the gleam of his dark eyes, but it was no doubt also the effect of a large aquiline nose, a feature which the rank and file of that epoch had come by bitter experience to regard as a sign of noble, if not predatory blood.

Save for the antique sword and the coat of chain-armour fastened to his sheepskin bundle, the youth's appearance would have passed for that of a well-born scholar, a novice perhaps of some religious house, though this latter possibility was made unlikely by the fact that in his leathern belt, next to what was clearly a well-filled wallet, was stuck a rather vicious-looking dagger.

"How soon, how soon shall I see it?" had been the refrain of Rhisiart's thoughts ever since he left behind him the towering battlements of Chirk. This desire of the young scholar's heart had nothing to do, as might have been expected, with his first sight of the sacred river. It was a more personal and more inflammable craving than could be satisfied by any merely historic encounter.

Ever since his earliest childhood he had longed for the moment that was now approaching—the moment when with his own eyes he would see that ruined castle on the sharp-pointed hill, where his traitor-ancestor had died, the besiegers baffled, but the man's own heart broken by his fearful remorse. His own particular ancestor had been this princely traitor's bastard; but for several generations his immediate family, oblivious to this double "bar sinister," had been devoted servants of the Sheriff of Hereford in a semi-legal, semi-official role.

This old piebald horse, of which he had been permitted by his mother to take possession, was the last of a sequence of such beasts on which it had been the fancy of the pageant-loving sheriffs of Hereford to mount their clerkly assistants; and it had needed all that Rhisiart's hooked nose and flashing eyes could do to quell in mid-speech many broad-mouthed jests at the expense of this pride of Hereford town.

Indeed, so peculiar did the horse look that the prentices of Welshpool, encouraged by the presence of a group of idle bowmen from Lord Charlton's Castle, had raised the cry of "Mummers" as he stopped to buy a capful of strawberries in that pleasant market.

It was clear that Master Rhisiart's mind was agitated by more than one emotion as he followed his sinuous path through the scattered patches of hazels and the verdurous park-glades with their clumps of freshly-green beeches, and through all the ferny hollows full of rabbits and grass-snakes, that the ruling Fitz-Alan in his grandiose way was wont to speak of as "our Forest of Chirk."

The young man kept swinging round in his saddle, causing the more warlike portion of his baggage to jingle so sharply that any horse but Griffin would have been seriously disturbed. Then he would bring him to a complete standstill, and with his own neck so twisted round that he resembled those unfortunates in the Inferno, upon whom the humorous ferocity of the Emperor of the Universe had worked its will, he would stare backwards.

Having listened intently in this manner for some minutes he would swing himself round again and spur Griffin on, his whole soul straining and stretching forward in single-hearted intensity to meet whatever it was that lay behind the next curve.

"I must see it alone," he said to himself, "at least I must see it *for the first time* alone."

And then when the next curve of that pastoral road had revealed nothing but another clump of beeches hiding the horizon he would pull up Griffin again and once more twist himself about with jingling and discomfort.

"If that heretical fellow overtakes me at this minute," he thought, "just when Dinas Brān may be round the next corner, I'll completely forget myself. I'll do him a damage!"

Rhisiart had neither spurs nor whip. He and the old horse needed no such intermediaries. At the slightest touch Griffin would quicken his jog-trot. But these motions of haste in the young man were always the unconscious expression of his feelings in response to some irresistible mental vision of Dinas Brān; and the moment his mind returned he reined back the obedient creature, whose weariness was apparent.

A moment soon came, however, when something had to be done; for during one of his nervous pauses he became aware, beyond all mistake, of the sound of voices behind him.

"The Lollard has found another victim," he thought. "What the devil am I to do?"

It was only too clear that unless he went on at a cruel pace he would soon be overtaken. All manner of wild ideas rushed through his head. Should he turn round and ride back, pretending he'd lost something on the road? But that unconscionable heretic would no doubt think he was doing God service by riding back with him!

And who was the fellow's companion? Very likely some henchman of the Earl of Arundel, the last kind of person before whom he'd care to betray his feelings when he first saw Dinas Brān. He flung down his reins on Griffin's neck and groaned aloud.

Up went the old horse's ears, and its nostrils expanded, wide and quivering. Then very slowly and to its rider's complete astonishment it began leaving the road and ascending a grassy slope that led to a small patch of woodland.

Tightening his knees about the piebald sides he knew so well, Master Rhisiart, getting his cue from the horse, began eagerly urging him forward; and to his delight, when they did finally reach the wood, there presented itself to them an overgrown narrow path totally invisible from the road below, but obviously leading clear through the little copse to whatever it might be that lay behind.

Into this leafy path, while the young man on his back bent low down to avoid the swishing hazels and the brittle sharp-smelling elders, Griffin forced his way.

Wisps of trailing parasitic tendrils, bewildered caterpillars and grubs, feeble brown moths and flimsy white butterflies clung, as he moved, to his hot panting bulk. The vegetable waifs, among these disturbed natives, entangled themselves in the woolly sheepskin and between the links of jingling armour; while the living insects, including little armadas of drifting midges, seemed ready to drug themselves to death in the sticky equine sweat, or to risk a more violent end between impatient human fingers, so long as they could taste, for one paradisic instant, the inebriating nectar of mortal blood.

Once safely escaped from all danger of evangelical interruption young Rhisiart drew rein and fell to listening. How curiously satisfying to hear those manly tongues in lively discussion and their owners so completely unaware of this ambush above their heads!

The wood was too thick, and he had already plunged too far into it, to have any chance to see what kind of a fellow-pilgrim the Lollard had picked up, but the tone of the unknown's voice, when at last he got the ring of it clear of the other's eloquence, made him rise very straight on his saddle and, with a gesture he was quite unconscious of till after he had made it, jerk towards himself by the middle of its worn-out sheath his crusader's blade.

But he soon let the sword sink back to its place beside the sheepskin, and with a sigh he plucked a twig from a sycamore branch at his side and began stripping it of its leaves and counting them as they fluttered down.

"One . . . two . . . three . . . four," he counted. "In four years I'll have shown them what Rhisiart ab Owen can do!" But the voice that had so disturbed him still went on, and our friend couldn't prevent a stir of malicious pleasure at the thought of his eloquent acquaintance being fairly out-harangued.

"*Out-chanted* I ought to put it," he said to himself. "This is clearly Welsh poetry, and my gentleman has found his match!"

It certainly was an extraordinary sound that reached them in that wood; and Griffin seemed as fascinated by it as his master.

"That's Welsh poetry, Griff!" murmured the boy, stroking the gaunt shoulder beneath him. "We'll hear plenty of that from now on. So you'd better get used to it, old friend!"

But the horse, feeling the reins slack on his neck, bent down and began tasting some wood-sorrel that attracted him amid the moss and rubble. Though both the heretic and the poetry-declaimer, who were apparently riding at a swinging trot, were soon out of hearing, our traveller sat on there on his horse's back absorbed in a bottomless sea of thought.

The sound of that Welsh poetry had brought back all those particular memories of his early life from which he had built up the main outlines of the narrow imaginative cult by which he had come to live.

Upon Modry his nurse, a handsome young Welshwoman who had married before he was capable of grasping all she had taught him, lay the responsibility for this unbalanced idealism. He had learnt Welsh from Modry much more quickly than he ever picked up French or Latin from the monastic schools in the city; and along with her native tongue she had inspired him with a frenzy of patriotic feeling for his ancestral country, especially for that portion of it that surrounded Dinas Brān. A person would only have had to give a cursory glance at Rhisiart's appearance to gather the fact that he would be just the very one to get lodged in his brain some obstinate and passionate obsession.

As he let Griffin search about for something more to his taste than wood-sorrel and allowed his own fingers to follow idly the pattern made by sun-flicker and leaf-shadow upon that stooping neck, he recalled how Modry's teaching had thrown him at Oxford into the society of an ardent group of Welsh scholars. He felt ashamed now as he thought how crudely he had patronized these evasive eccentrics on the strength of his mother's proud Norman blood, and how mockingly he had cajoled them and led them on, till one by one they had secretly confessed to him that at any clear call from their native hills they would sell their books, get themselves arms and horses and gallop westward.

His closest friend among them, Master Morris Stove of his own Exeter College, had already begun practising with the long-bow for this unlikely event. The learned man's convulsions of pride when by some chance he killed a wild-duck on the banks of the Isis came back to him now and he found himself comparing his own more fanciful and complicated motives with this heroic simplicity.

Master Stove had no long-cherished shame to purge, no dark old treachery to obliterate, no Dinas Brān lifting its mystic battlements against indescribable spiritual horizons.

All *he* possessed was the plain downright imperative, one that had already got him into many a street-brawl in Oxford town, to hold the call of Cambria above everything in the world.

From his earliest childhood under Modry's influence Rhisiart had hugged to himself a vague fairy-story hope that he might be the one destined by fate to restore the lost glories of the old chiefs of Powys or at least make Dinas Brān what it had been in the days of Griffith ap Madoc.

Modry had got it lodged in his earliest consciousness that his name Owen carried with it some mystery of prophetic significance; and she had talked to him *sans cesse* of the great Owen Red-hand, in the Black Prince's time, who had fought for the king of France. Many a night by his dying fire, with this very sheepskin over both their legs, he had heard Master Stove express the view that the elderly Baron of Glendourdy, or Glendower, who was a cautious and law-abiding subject of the late unhappy king and a great patron of poetry and scholarship, might have been the Owen of all these prophecies had he been a younger man, or a man prepared to live a dangerous and desperate life.

"But he's old," Master Stove would add with a groan. "He must be nearly fifty. Besides he's related to half the Border, and his daughters have all married English barons."

Rhisiart could remember one particular interruption when Stove was speaking like this and they were both drawn to the window by a sudden uproar and saw some terrified town-official extricating himself from an angry mob and heard great shouts going up: "We want King Richard! Give us back King Richard!" He could hear now, as he stared at a clump of late bluebells, that looked in the shadow of the underbrush as if they were purple rather than blue, the bitter curse with which Stove came back to their wretched students' fire and began accusing this peace-loving Glendourdy of having betrayed the unfortunate King.

"It was old Fitz-Alan who came between them. He always hated Richard; and Owen was his squire." Up and down that small green clearing among the hazels Rhisiart let his horse carry him, while one after another of the sights and sounds of this little wood—certainly a very modest portion of the "Forest of Chirk"—mingled with his thoughts.

He saw what he supposed to be a black-cap singing passionately on the branch of an oak-tree. He could see the outline of its throat as it heaved up and down under the long-drawn notes of its whistling. He could see its feathers ruffled at the same time by a faintly stirring wind.

"I'll let my friends down there get well to the river. If I give them a little longer they'll be across the ford and lodged at the Tassel, unless they're going on to the Abbey to-night."

Thus he talked to himself; seeking in reality any excuse to postpone the great moment to which he had looked forward almost as long as he could remember.

Was he afraid that the sight of the real Dinas Brān would make the ideal one—that mystic terminus of every vista of his imagination—dissolve into air?

Always vague but always dominant, the secret channel which his under-life had worked for itself had adopted Griffith ap Madoc's hill-fortress as the ultimate symbol of its direction.

In some confused and tortuous way he had come to take it for granted that he, plain Master Rhisiart, descendant of a traitor's bastard, would be accepted by the invisible spirits of all his ancestors as the destined restorer of their lost glory. Years ago the patriotic Modry had told him of this Baron Glendourdy or, as the Welsh called him, Glyn Dŵr; but she, like Morris Stove, had always spoken of him as too absorbed in scholarship, too rich, too peaceable, too closely connected with the English Court, to be in any sense the man of destiny who would people with free warriors—like fiery shapes from a vasty deep —the towering battlements of the old castle of their race.

As he listened to the black-cap's self-absorbed singing, and watched Griffin's leisurely movements among the cool-rooted woodland growths, he began to realize two things; first that he had deliberately thrust the idea of this "Glendourdy" into the background of his mind from an obscure prejudice against a person so lucky as to be the recognized heir, not only of his own chieftains of Dinas Brān but also of the ancient rulers of South Wales, and with all this to have played his cards so well as to have won renown in Richard's wars without being implicated in the ill-starred monarch's ruin; and secondly that hidden out of sight, down deep behind his own boyish ambitions, had lain all the while a shrewd and practical resolve to introduce himself, with his piebald horse, his crusader's sword, and his coat of chain-armour, to the notice of this powerful kinsman of his—and see what happened!

His horse was bending so low now over a large patch of wood-spurge, amid whose foliage he had apparently discovered some especially succulent leaves, that Rhisiart was forced to lay his hand on a hazel-branch beside him to keep himself and his heavy load from a tendency to slide forward.

Normally he would have dismounted during this pause; but his mind was in such a state of abstraction that it was like the mind of a person under a drug. He had grown unconscious of the ordinary significance of material bodies. He had ceased to be a lean youthful figure, in a dark scholar's dress with a leather belt and a velvet cap, mounted on a piebald horse. He had become a bubble of complicated thought, a bubble that floated beside the sheepskin bundle, a bubble devoid of weight or substance.

"Will it spoil it all?" he thought. "Will it break to bits the only ideal I've got in life, when I see Dinas Brān?" So wayward and so self-lacerating was this Hereford boy's nature that as he looked at the sun-and-leaf flickerings on Griffin's back and listened to the queer sounds the animal was making as he tasted those leafy juices, he felt already the ice-cold waters of disappointment. Dinas Brān *couldn't* be what he had, all his days, imagined it!

And with this feeling that he was approaching the worst catastrophe that could befall him—the loss of his life-illusion—there came over him in an accumulated weight of released emotion his jealousy and envy of this lord of Glyndyfrdwy, this legitimate heir to Dinas Brān, who was such a friend of Thomas Fitz-Alan and such a traitor to the murdered King.

Rhisiart stared and stared at a flimsy currant-moth that was now fluttering feebly through the twigs of a thick-growing elder. He felt as though, with the panicky distaste of those slender antennae, he himself was cursing the raw pungency of that rough foliage.

It was King Richard's wistful face, as he had seen it once at Hereford, that hovered about those sharp-smelling boughs, and when he thought of his murder he confused those delicate features with those of a man he had seen put to death in his childhood, an unforgettable, abominable sight, taking the heart out of all the June woods of England!

And it was an imaginary Cousin Glendourdy, crafty, grey-headed, portly, full of punctilious fussiness about nice heraldic points, only anxious to be left in peace to his bards and his women, who was the bitter-smelling elder-branch against which that moth fluttered!

"He's not the Owen of the prophecies," thought the obsessed youth, "any more than was Owen Red-hand! There's been no 'Owen of Wales' since they buried Owen ap Griffith ap Cynan in Bangor Church."

The lad's nostrils dilated and his whole face changed its appearance as he sucked in his lower lip. In a sudden spasm of angry vision he saw the diplomatic Glendourdy drowning their disgrace in drink and song while the Fitz-Alan ensign floated from the fortress of Griffith ap Madoc.

Impatiently he dropped the hazel-branch, snatched up the reins and rode on. Stinging sprays of trailing branches brushed against his mouth and rustled against his knees, but he bent his head low and pushed forward, while the piebald horse kept shaking his mane and champing on his bit, as if the taste of some woodland weed had turned sour in his throat.

At last there appeared a free open space at the end of their path; and at the sight of this both man and horse strained eagerly forward, the young human body and the old equine body fusing themselves together, in that excited rush, as if they were one creature.

There it was! There before him, towering up beneath a great bank of white clouds and against a jagged ridge of bare and desolate rock, rose the castle of his imagination.

For some minutes he remained spell-bound, absolutely caught out of himself, lost to everything but that majestic sight. It was not less, *it was more,* than the picture he had in his mind.

All ramparts ever built, all towers, all fortresses, all castles, seemed to him mere clumsy reproductions of the ideal perfection of Dinas Brān. It wasn't that it was so large—and he could see clearly, even from this distance, that it was in a battered, broken condition—but it took into itself that whole hill it was built upon! Yes, that was the thing. Dinas Brān was not the stones of its human walls, not the majestic out-lines of its towering battlements, not its soaring arches and turrets and bastions; it was an impregnable mountain called up out of that deep valley by some supernatural mandate. Its foundations were sunk in the earth, but they were sunk in more than the earth; they were sunk in that mysterious underworld of beyond-reality whence rise the eternal archetypes of all the refuges and all the sanctuaries of the spirit, un-touched by time, inviolable ramparts not built by hands!

Oh, it was far more than the image of his long hope, far more than what he had prayed for in the audacities and desperations of his long desire!

The season of the year, the climax of June's lavish greenery, had undoubtedly something to do with it. It was this that gave it that apocalyptic look; as of some far-away fairy-tower in some old pre-druidic Book of Revelation.

And the late afternoon light too, under which our traveller saw it, contributed to this enchanted effect. Out of green pastures, in which might have wandered flocks upon flocks of fairy sheep, rose that mystic, castellated mountain, and the horizontal sun-rays falling at their lowest possible angle, ere the crest of the Berwyns beat them back, threw a rose-bloom upon its towers. And if the sunset threw such light upon the stone ramparts, it gave to the grassy precipices from the brink of which the masonry ascended such a glow of incredible greenness that the first thing that came into Rhisiart's head when his trance relaxed was a green shield he had seen a workman painting once in the illumination of a tomb in the cathedral for one of the dead King's beautiful and fatal minions.

Rhisiart's old horse seemed at first, as often happens with animals, to be contemplating that astonishing stretch of landscape with an interest hardly less than his master's; but when the youth jumped off his back and proceeded to go through a ritualistic performance that he had been rehearsing for many years, Griffin gave his bony frame a vigorous shake, causing the armour he carried to jangle loud and clear, and began sniffing about again in the sweet-scented herbage of the wood's edge.

But Rhisiart ab Owen took his crusader's sword from the creature's back and drawing it from its embossed and enamelled sheath planted it firmly in the greensward. Then, kneeling on one knee so that the cross-handle of his weapon rose between him and Dinas Brān, he gave vent to a series of solemn ejaculations; not so much praying to his Creator, or even to the Mother of Christ, as uttering a string of incoherent vows, the drift of which was that he dedicated himself to the super-human task of restoring the honours and glories of his ancestors.

As he made these vows his curious physiognomy lost its sullen self-concentration, and an innocent and childlike look took possession of it. But it must be added that when he leapt to his feet again, and plucked the great sword out of the grass, this look completely vanished, its place being taken by an even more pronounced scowl of truculence and secretiveness than it had previously worn.

Ingrained and obstinate was the pride in the lad's face as he clambered back, not very elegantly, upon his saddle; and even the gaze he kept turning upon his ideal castle as he rode down the hill, letting Griffin choose his own path through the bracken, retained little of that moment of inspiration.

Nor indeed, if the truth must be told, were the thoughts that crossed Rhisiart's mind any more admirable than the expression worn by his hooked nose, his sallow cheeks, his sucked-in under-lip. They were images of fantastical domination, images of himself exercising arbitrary power over multitudes, images of himself revenging himself upon multitudes; and revenging himself not only for every rebuff he had suffered from his Hereford relations, who regarded him as a fool and a failure, but even upon his mother, who never ceased teasing him for his equivocal ways and calling him her "little monk," her "begging friar," her "catch-penny pardoner."

Rhisiart had only a few indistinct memories of his father; but from certain scenes that *had* impressed his childish mind he had conceived the notion that he too had been despised, frustrated, ridiculed and misunderstood.

"You wait!" he shouted in his heart, addressing the whole of Hereford City, *"you wait!"* And in his mind he saw himself surrounded by an applauding host of rebels, as he rode down from Dinas Brān, leaving the "Lion, rampant, gules" of the old Griffith ap Madoc banner floating from its battlements!

Once in the road, with the sinking sun behind him, he began making a few hurried re-adjustments both in his personal accoutrements and in his somewhat singular baggage.

The piebald horse regarded these manœuvres with cynical lethargy. "For God's sake," he seemed to say, "ride on to the stable; or leave my harness alone while I see what grows here."

But Rhisiart had been seized with a fear lest his precious piece of chain-armour might slide off when they moved at a greater speed, and being but a clumsy squire-at-arms it took him some while to adjust it, and the great sword with it, to his satisfaction.

While thus employed, and while Griffin was chewing the grass, he caught sight of a little patch of moschatel, whose small green flowers, thrown into delicate relief by the horizontal sun, brought to his mind many a stroll at vesper-time in the Oxford meadows when Master Stove had astonished him by the noble simplicity of his Welsh heart.

"No," he thought, as he pulled Griffin's head round and threw back his own, "no, if I weren't of the House of Dinas Brān, if I were a poor nameless 'legitimate' like Morris Stove, I'd get my Doctor's gown and serve this crafty king.

"But they say he's too mean and miserly to use men of birth; the devil take him! They say he lets the Percies fight for him at their own charges. Well, if the worst comes to the worst I must turn clerk and scrivener and copy these new-fangled verses—what did they call them?—'*Cywyddau*'—for Cousin Glendourdy."

The old horse, who now began anticipating better nourishment than wayside grass, had quickened his pace to a fast trot; and it wasn't long before not only Dinas Brān but the much-frequented river-ford leading to the Tassel appeared in full sight.

Our traveller had been recommended as he came through Chirk to take lodging that night at the Tassel or Tercal, and the recommendation had imprinted itself on his mind owing to the fact that his informant, who was a Salopian humourist, chaffed him on his personal resemblance to the sullen-looking bird whose raptorial beak adorned that famous hostelry's sign-board.

To Griffin's chagrin Rhisiart pulled up for a minute or two, when he saw, half-a-mile below him, the sacred river winding through its sun-illumined valley. From his present position he could see a great many interesting things; and he wanted to gather his wits together and decide on some clear line of action.

There was quite an assemblage of travellers waiting on his own side of the ford, and on the further side there seemed to be some kind of country-fair going on round the entrance to what looked like a farm-house.

Nearly a mile further on he could make out a much larger group of buildings, the central one of which was evidently built of more solid material than the rest.

"*That*," he thought, "must be the Tassel; but what's going on down there by the river?"

And then he remembered that to-day was the Eve of Saint John; when in many of the more old-fashioned districts of the country it was the custom to hold local fairs, to which not only the peasants came but to which the castles and monasteries of the neighbourhood were accustomed to send their stewards and caterers. Automatically and perfunctorily our young man decided that before making any move towards an encounter with "Cousin Glendourdy" he would have to attend High Mass somewhere or another; and it crossed his mind that the natural thing to do would be to hunt up the Abbey which his Dinas

Brān ancestors had founded in these parts. He knew it was called Valle
Crucis; but that was all he knew. "But at least I'll see their tombs," he
said to himself; and this secular thought quickened his languid piety
into a lively intention.

"But where shall I sleep to-night?" was his next thought, as the
piebald horse, with erect and twitching ears, strained at his bit.

"On the Eve of Saint John every room in the Tassel's sure to be
taken; and probably the monks' guest-house will be packed too. Well!
I'll have to go to some farm or sleep in the woods. Think of having
forgotten Saint John! How that damned Lollard would chuckle!"

The obsessed youth had indeed been grievously slack about his religious duties since he left Oxford. His mother had dragged him to
church before she would let him say goodbye; but since then, till his
childish prejudices had been roused by the Lollard's challenge, he
hadn't given the thing a thought.

"I suppose those Chirk people keep a troop of their lazy devils in
Dinas Brān," he said to himself, as he rode down the hill.

"Will the Earl go to the Abbey to-morrow? I'd rather like to set
eyes on him—and on Lord Grey of Ruthin, too." And the lad's mind
reverted to the few famous personages he had had the luck to see
in the late King's time.

With less trepidation than many young men would have felt—but his
nearness to his ancestral fortress seemed a stronger armour than any
that Griffin could carry—Rhisiart boldly advanced to the agitated
group of persons who were arguing and disputing at the brink of the
ford.

Two dismounted riders, leading their horses, approached him at
once, and one of them, greeting him in a pleasant manner by name,
introduced him to the other.

"He gave me the slip, this young gentleman," he remarked in English with an indulgent smile. "Rhisiart ab Owen his name is, if I get
it right; but yours, Master, if you'll pardon me for saying so, hardly
seems—"

"Seems or not seems, Master Brut," cried the Lollard's companion,
"the young gentleman will have to call me what all Powys and Yale
and Cynllaith Owen and Glyndyfrdwy and Maelor and Bromfield and
Chirk-land call me, or he may call me King of the Fornicators. 'Yr

Crach,' the Scab, is my name, born in Ffinnant near little Llanfechain, where every maid is my cousin and every old trot my god-mother! No, you needn't blush to look at 'em, young master. Birth-marks all, birth-marks all! And by whom were they put on me, think ye? Every jack one of them, by Holy Derfel, when I came out of Sister's belly! Sister Mallt she was, my blessed mother, God give her peace; and 'Yr Crach,' of Ffinnant near Llanfechain, I am, young master! Every man born knows Llanfechain where the great hanging oak is, and where Sheriff Burnell's grandmother, he who now's so hot for the new King, were drowned in green pond for a whore of Satan. And there's no Welshman, nor no Englishman neither, between Chester and Chirk that doesn't know 'Yr Crach,' the Scab. Listen to me, young gentle-man," and to Rhisiart's disgust the fellow laid a hand on his black sleeve. "How do I manage it, so as to have no enemy in all the Marches? Is that what you're asking? Well!" and he lowered his voice, "I'll tell you! 'Tis these here rose-petals as does it," and with a wicked grimace he tapped his shocking facial disfigurement, which certainly had the effect of intensifying the halcyon blue colour of his one remaining eye to such a point that Rhisiart found it hard to keep his eyes away from it. "But that's not all," and the Scab proceeded to close this bright window to his roguish soul with a cyclopean wink. "First and last, 'tis all Holy Derfel's work. He put these rosy-posies on me afore I came out of my poor mother; and do 'ee know who *her* were? Her were a dedicated nun; and to bear a *baban* to Derfel were too much for the maid. They didn't have to do nothing to her. She died in peace. She died smiling and whispering to her *baban* and calling on Derfel. That's who she called on, young man, Blessed Saint Derfel; and seeing you're a friend of Master Brut here, who's the best Christian poor old Scab have met for many a year, I thought it best to tell you who I were and who, in a manner of speaking, me parents were, so that there'd be no mistake. Presently if, as I hope God wills, we'll pass the night together I'll compose a poem for you. I've already composed five for Master Brut; and if he writes them down later, as he says he's a mind to, maybe he'll do the same for yours. 'Tis one thing, young gentleman, to be an inspired bard; 'tis another to understand reading and the art of—"

But Rhisiart, who had already dismounted and left his horse to make friends with the Scab's Welsh pony and the Lollard's mare, interrupted the poet's discourse by enquiring of Master Brut where he intended to sup and to sleep.

"From the look of things over there," he added, "there's a market going on.

"And what are those monks making such a disturbance about? That Prior, or whoever he is, seems to be reading his missal as if he were alone in his cell."

"Prior?" broke in the Scab in high glee. "Where have you come from, Mr. Scholar, not to know a Lord Abbot when you see him? Your Prior's the great John ap Hywel, Abbot of Caerleon, where the Round Table is. See the horse he's riding, my good sir! *He* don't have to haggle for a lift in a ferry-boat! It's his Chamberlain, his Almoner, his Kitchener belike, or just a pack of his lay-troop who're raising hell. Long Thomas of the Tassel puts his price up, and small blame to him—on such days as these. The ferry's his ferry and the boat's his boat; and though the ford goes with the Barony he's the one they have to pay. *I* haven't learnt law for nothing in cloister."

"Why doesn't the Abbot intervene? Why don't these Almoners or lay-brothers, or whatever they are, go to him and complain, if that rascal's asking too much?"

"Tell your friend why they don't, for God's sweet bones!" cried the Scab, turning to Master Brut.

And the Lollard explained that Abbot Hywel was known all over Wales for his piety and his passionate temper. "No man dares," he said, "especially when that book's in his hands, approach him with any secular matter!"

The Scab fixed his solitary blue eye upon our young man and winked solemnly. "Temper, you see! That's what *he* calls it. *He* thinks a Christian should have command over his high blood. Don't'ee listen to him, young master! If I wasn't a prophet of Derfel he'd be a dangerous companion for a poor bard. Wait till Hal Bolingbroke gets hold of him! He'll truss him up like a partridge. He'll baste him to a crisp. He's a great baster of hèretics is your King Hal. God griddle his—" And the Scab ended with one of the foulest oaths our traveller had ever heard.

The altercation over the ferry-boat rose now to such a pitch that it became incredible to Rhisiart how that formidable-looking Abbot could sit so quiet on his great black horse.

"Here! Catch hold, master, for a minute!" and snatching at Griffin's bridle he tossed it to the Lollard and ran down the slope straight to the abstracted dignitary.

What the impulse was that forced him to do this he would have been hard put to it to explain. No thought he could define, no intention he could describe, made him do it: and yet he would have done it had Abbot John looked ten times more formidable.

"My Lord!" he cried, laying his hand on the black horse's trappings. "My Lord! My Lord!"

Walter Brut watched his friend's audacity with no little concern. "Jesus help him!" he muttered, and then he added, "and help us all, and forgive us our sins, our most grievous sins!"

But the Abbot of Caerleon broke from his trance with a start that made his horse rear. "What? Eh? Who? A messenger from *him* are ye?"

"My Lord," the young man repeated, "I'm a messenger from no one. I'm riding, my Lord, from Exeter College, Oxford, to my cousin Owen, Lord of Cynllaith and Baron of Glendourdy."

The Abbot of Caerleon gave the excited intruder one searching look. "And who's this?" he asked. "Is he from Oxford, too?"

Rhisiart, who was in the act of making the formal gesture of kissing the Abbot's hand, swung round and beheld Master Brut blamelessly advancing towards them with a serene countenance, while a few paces behind him, as if not to be out-done in this daring move, came the irrepressible bard, trailing in his rear all their three steeds.

"And who's *that?*" asked John ap Hywel. "*He* at any rate isn't from Oxford."

Rhisiart stood politely aside as the Lollard came up. "The peace of Jesus be with you, John ap Hywel," he said; and Rhisiart as he heard him couldn't escape a shock of interest at the difference between the two men. Deeply indented with furrows of thought and passion was the ap Hywel's swarthy face; whereas the fair placid countenance of the learned Hereford squire had the angelic smoothness of a Saint Michael in a church window.

And it was the same with the tones of their voices. The Abbot spoke

English painfully and with a perceptible Welsh accent, but every word
was charged with a smouldering intensity of emotion; whereas Master
Brut expressed himself casually, easily, quickly, almost as if he regarded the whole business of using words at all as something un-
essential and irrelevant.

"You know my name so well," replied the churchman gravely, "that
you won't be surprised if I ask you, before we go further, why, in
greeting me like this, you make such a point of omitting the first and
the third Person of our most Holy Trinity?"

"Forgive me, my Lord Abbot," returned the other, completely unabashed. "I should have supposed that to any high-placed apostle of
our faith the name of Jesus was sufficient."

The lines in the dark-visaged monk's face deepened and he seemed
on the verge of an angry retort; but to Rhisiart's astonishment, in
place of anything of the kind, a sad and tender smile crossed his lips.

"In the name of the Father and of the Son and of the Holy Ghost,"
he murmured in Latin, "may both the peace He brought and the faith
He revealed be yours, my son. And now," he went on in English, "may
I ask you your name, and the name of this young gentleman and the
name of—" But the piebald horse's desire to reach his master gave the
Bard of Ffinnant an opportunity of answering for himself; and before
his rapid flow of extremely colloquial Welsh, sprinkled with poetical
bardic tags, had subsided, an interruption occurred which altered the
whole situation.

The excited crowd of monks who so gallantly had followed their
Abbot from Caerleon were displaying now a less agreeable aspect of
their nature. "It must come," thought Rhisiart, "from their secluded
lives that they haggle like this over a penny."

But matters by this time had reached such a point that the ferry-man,
who was a powerfully built, grim-looking peasant, was now obstinately
pushing his way through the midst of them and making straight for
the Abbot.

With a heavy sigh John ap Hywel thrust his breviary into his leather
pouch and rode towards the crowd, followed closely by Rhisiart, leading Griffin, while the Scab, detaining Master Brut by his arm, tried to
explain in clumsy English the gist of what he had just said to the

great man and his assurance that his remarks had met with uncommon appreciation.

"It's always the same," he gave the Lollard to understand. "The higher-placed these fellows are the better they understand me. It's the rag-tag of them, like those idiots over there, that see nothing but the devil in the bardic art."

Rhisiart was almost as astonished as the angry monks at the rough manner in which the ferry-man addressed their Superior; but John ap Hywel received him with courtesy, and helped him, for the fellow was too indignant to be very articulate, to explain the cause of the uproar.

The explanation, though our traveller could make nothing of it, apparently satisfied the Abbot, for searching in the wallet that held his psalter he handed him a large silver coin, the receipt of which produced an immediate change in the man's demeanour.

"What do they call you, my friend?" the churchman asked him.

"Philip Sparrow, your reverence. I be herdsman, your reverence, to Long Thomas of Tassel; but being Saint John's Eve like, I've a-took ferry-boat in place of Mother Kench who be selling she's pasties and bride-cakes yonder."

The fellow paused, glanced at the silent and sulky monks with a revengeful scowl, and then looking across the river set himself to listen to the confused uproar that was coming from the further bank.

"I wish, your reverence—" he began uneasily.

"Speak up, man," said the Abbot, who also had been listening with some concern to the sounds that were reaching them. "Out with it! It seems to me there is something more than ale-drinking and cake-eating going on over there."

"I wish, your reverence—"

"Speak up, man! The Brothers and I were hoping to be at Valle Crucis to-night; but if there's anything here needing the—"

He was interrupted by an agitated movement towards him of all his monks. Troubled by what they were hearing from across the Dee, their natural instinct, as with a pack of startled animals, was to draw close to their leader.

Walter Brut and the Bard of Ffinnant came forward too, the latter having deemed it wise, in case of accidents, to be on his pony's back.

For a space they were all, churchmen and laymen alike, awed into silence by the sounds they heard and the mysterious tumult that was rapidly increasing. One wild, resonant voice kept rising above all the rest, and they heard too, and this was curiously agitating to Rhisiart, certain desperate cries for help evidently proceeding from a feminine throat.

"Your reverence—" began the heavy-browed ferry-man and then hesitated again, looking nervously at the crowd of silent faces.

"Speak up, Philip Sparrow," murmured the Bard, pushing his pony forward while his eye grew bluer and his birth-marks redder in his desire to win favour.

"He's a simple man, my Lord, a poor, simple ignorant man. Perhaps if you allowed *me* to have a few words with him I should be able—"

But ap Hywel waved him aside. "Come close to me, Master Sparrow —that's it!—you needn't be afraid of me—I'm only a poor priest. Closer still, my good friend! That's it! Now then, tell us what's going on over there. Is it the King's justice? Are they hanging those people? Is it a man and a woman? Are they adulterers caught in the act? Have they committed sacrilege? Under whose lordship is this fair? Chirkland? Valle Crucis? And where's the seneschal of Dinas Brān? Speak quietly. Take your time. No one's going to hurt you."

While the churchman was speaking Rhisiart could see his fingers busy with the trappings of his great horse.

"He'll be across the river in a second," he thought, "and Griffin and I with him! They're torturing those two over there! Oh damn this· fellow! Let the slave go, and find out for yourself, my good lord! Oh hurry, hurry, you holy idiot, for God's sake! That woman'll be past helping in a minute or two."

But the low-bent swarthy head of the ecclesiastic and the up-raised equally swarthy face of the ferry-man were so close to each other now in their exchange of deep-throated whispering that though Griffin was licking the neck of the Abbot's horse Rhisiart couldn't follow— for all his nurse's lessons—the rapid Welsh they were using.

Their conversation was drawn out to such a length and the cries, if such they were, of victimized man and woman across the river grew so violent that not only the nerves of young Rhisiart but the more seasoned ones of Master Brut and the Scab began to grow strained.

As for the monks, they were staring at their leader with such anxious faces that no one could have guessed the crude simplicity of the thoughts that rushed through their tonsured heads as they pressed forward. One worthy brother had been occupied all that morning in wondering whether there would be wine as well as beer provided by the Valle Crucis caterer on their arrival. Another had been weighing in his mind many casuistical reasons why, in honour of Saint John's Feast, it would be advisable to give himself a plenary indulgence in the matter of a small and private vow against eating flesh.

They were all hungry and tired; and this new obstruction to their journey on the top of the exorbitant demands of the ferry-man seemed the last straw. Curiously enough—possibly from their own self-mortifications and daily broodings upon death and judgment—they were less disturbed by the sinister events across the river than were the three secular persons.

There trembled through Rhisiart's young body the strangest tinglings of emotion. He could hardly be called a normal youth in his relations with women. Rarely had he had the faintest flicker of natural lasciviousness towards them. In fact, the only woman except his mother and Mistress Modry who had ever infringed upon his life at all had been an ex-harlot in Oxford, married to an elderly water-man, whose outrageous tales of her first experience of men's desire, related to him on a sunny bench by the Isis in her husband's garden, he did remember with a certain glow of unholy pleasure.

But that woman's voice across the Dee excited in him such a turbulent flood of sympathy that he could hardly restrain himself from urging Griffin into the river. Her voice seemed to conjure up her figure, her look, her spirit, her whole being! Something in its tone made him convinced that she had eyes like Modry's, very dark, but of a queer greenish tinge, and that her body, like Modry's, was exceptionally long and slender.

And how strangely the towers of Dinas Brān as he saw them still, straight before him though illumined no more with the rosy glow of the setting sun, became part of that woman's cry!

For some reason, as he listened, he arrived at the conclusion that the outcries of neither of them were the expression of physical pain. If it *were* so, the man's, at any rate, were triumphing over what he suffered.

Still that everlasting whispering! Would it *never* stop, so that he could show them how a Herefordshire horse could ford a river and how a Hereford lad could rescue a girl?

In the sinking of the sun a faint grey haze, too delicate to be called a mist, had risen from the water, and had stolen imperceptibly over the whole landscape. It was only very dimly, though he knew exactly where to look, that he could any longer make out the castle's walls. But this mist had the effect of endowing that reiterated double cry with something almost supernaturally disturbing.

Perhaps that was why the Caerleon monks bothered so little about it! They were so much *on the inside* of the supernatural that the little accidents of daily life, the harshness of a superior, a hole in somebody's sandal, the substitution of wine for beer, a chilly draught in the choir-stalls, a leak in the gutter-pipe, caused them more actual worry than any glimpse into the dark vistas, full of howling devils, of death and pain.

But for Rhisiart and for Master Brut, and in a measure even for the Bard of Ffinnant, these reiterated cries became something that swallowed up everything else.

Rhisiart could see that the Lollard at any rate was deeply disturbed and as anxious as he was himself to ford the river and solve the mystery.

The man had the clearest complexion he had ever seen and the most open countenance. His smooth unwrinkled face, his full red lips, his closely-cropped fair hair struck our friend—for all his prejudice against the tediousness of the fellow's talk—as making a most agreeable impression, along with the modesty of his well-fitting country-gentleman's attire. He felt indeed, as they now exchanged glances in which their mutual impatience was revealed, that he had done injustice to the power of character behind the man's stolid calm and theological prolixity. He went so far as to decide that if they *were* destined to share any perilous or reckless adventure he couldn't wish for a more trustworthy companion.

Thus much young Rhisiart took in; and it had needed those terrifying cries from across the river to rouse even this insight, as he sucked in his upper-lip and turned his narrow Norman face towards the object of this unusual perspicuity.

But he was finding those double cries more and more disturbing. They made a landscape within the landscape, tragic, fatal, full of ominous premonitions.

In the man's voice was all the desperation of the terrible power of the soul to resist, to defy, to repeat its challenge, against the force of overwhelming odds.

But the feminine voice affected him even more. Yes, all the mystery, all the lawless pity of a woman's soul, all the deadly sweetness of a woman's body were being thrown out upon that summer twilight!

The liquid and tender greenness of the evening seemed to be gathered into it. The cry was richer, fuller, closer to Nature, than the one with which it alternated, and to which it echoed.

To Rhisiart it was more than a sound among other sounds, more than a normal cry for help above a normal tumult. It had in it the curves of a woman's neck, the softness of a woman's breast, and as it reached him out of the green sap of the long darkening of that summer day it had a mystery of appeal that was like the sob of the night-dews upon a thousand hills. Master Brut was in his saddle now and his sturdy grey mare was addressing the piebald in a low whinny, as much as to say, "What's the matter with these young men of ours?" while to the jangle of his heavy accoutrements the Abbot's old war-horse, lifting his head and snuffing at the air, might have been taken as retorting, "Wait a second longer, my innocent friends, and you shall see what life is!"

But the whispering was over now at last. "Get the Brothers across!" cried John ap Hywel, while his eyes began to burn like bivouac flames through thick smoke. "Fall into procession when you're all across and follow us!

"Chant the *'Illumina, Domine Deus, tenebras nostres!'* while you're looking for us; but don't leave the river till every one of you is safe over. Now, Master Rhisiart, now Master Brut, as fast as you like!"

II

RHISIART DRAWS HIS SWORD

THE SACRED Dee, or Deva, or Dyfrdwy, whose name in Welsh signifies "divine water" or "the water of the divinity," is not always as easy to ford as its firm, un-muddy, pebbly channel would lead a stranger to suppose.

Such a stranger were well-advised to obtain local advice ere he makes the crossing; since many quite historic fords are, within a limited distance, inconstant and variable.

On the present occasion the laconic Philip Sparrow was so busy getting his late antagonists across the river that he lacked the opportunity to show the horsemen the best place for *them* to enter the stream.

Thus the old black charger and the piebald were soon up to their bellies in the swift current, while the pony and his rider seemed in actual peril. The Scab's small animal was quite as high-spirited as the big horses, but the Bard himself was considerably agitated and incommoded; especially as the little creature displayed a lively desire to resort to swimming before the occasion required it.

The gurgling of the water now quite drowned those appalling cries; or it may have been, Rhisiart said to himself, that death had ended it and the victims were out of reach of all human help. He was in less of a fury of impatience, therefore, when the Abbot reined in his big horse almost in mid-stream to watch the success of Master Brut's benevolent manœuvres to assist the disturbed prophet of Derfel. This process meant the return to shore of both Lollard and Bard, for Philip Sparrow was now calling to them from his crowded boat and directing them to a shallower spot.

But the old war-horse and the elderly piebald seemed so much to enjoy the swirl of the water that the Abbot had time to explain to Rhisiart what the ferry-man had revealed.

Rhisiart listened spell-bound to this account; and as ap Hywel got excited in what he was telling him the youth noticed two things: first that he referred to Glendower with a curious reserve, and secondly that he quoted the ferry-man's speech with the rough gusto of a native.

The ferry-man had evidently small respect for his employer, the landlord of the Tassel, whom he had described as a cringing and contemptible time-server. He had explained that two great Welsh notables, who were notorious Bolingbroke men, Hywel Sele of Nannau and David of the Squint, or David Gam, had been staying for a week at the Tassel and had filled the place with riot.

"It seems," the Abbot went on, "that they wanted to see Glyn Dŵr, and when he refused to see them they fell into a rage and swore they'd stay at the Tassel at his expense. They've been treating all-comers to drink; they've been drunk themselves; and to-day in honour of Saint John, they've been giving prizes for archery and spear-throwing.

"But it appears that Mad Huw, the Grey Friar from Llanfaes, a man all Welshmen know, though I doubt if his fame has reached Oxford, has also come to the fair. He goes about the country, declaring that King Richard's still alive. Of course, for all we can tell in this part of Britain, what he says may be true; though they say some kind of a corpse was shown in London.

"But he tells me a girl from Dinas Bran, a mere child, but comely and kindly, follows the fellow everywhere. He says she's still a maid for all her following a man by night and by day, through wet and fine, in sickness and in health.

"He tells me the Friar puts thorns of the rose between them when they sleep, or else thistles and nettles; and at times he says he makes her tie him wi' ropes afore they lie down.

"But these aren't tales for a young man's ear," and the Abbot gave a grim smile, "save that this black water keeps our erring flesh cool! Oh you're there, Master Brut? You're there, Master Bard? On with us then! We'll let the Brothers pray for us. 'Tis Mad Huw they've got hold of; Christ and Saint John be his help!" And crossing himself seven times the Abbot of Caerleon slipped his right hand under his cloak and rapidly numbered as many beads.

Rhisiart was amazed at the change in the great man's manner and tone. His speech had lapsed into something similar to the peasant's he was quoting, and in place of a mystical ascetic he saw at his side an excited warrior, his eyes shining with the glow and glory of battle.

The young scholar remembered to the end of his days every impression both physical and mental of that eventful moment. The dark swirl of the sacred river, its noisy foaming over its rocks, the blood-streaked rack of jagged clouds that now completely hid the real Dinas Brān only to lift in front of him once more, as he had seen them since his boyhood, the enchanted battlements, towering to heaven, of the citadel of his secret thoughts; these things became like a spiritual body, larger, freer, more porous than his fleshly one.

He hadn't troubled to kick loose his stirrups, as the other three riders had done, and he was wet to the knees; but as they struggled up the bank he fancied he heard that woman's cry again and all manner of confused imaginings surged through him.

He couldn't resist, in his boyish way, as he kept Griffin's head close to the tall flanks of the Abbot's steed, telling himself one fantastic story after another.

He told himself that it was none other than Princess Myfanwy of Dinas Brān to whose rescue he was riding! He told himself that the moment was actually at hand when he would strike his first blow to redeem from purgatory the arch-traitor of his race.

They were riding into the fair-crowd now, straight between the booths. There were wooden trestles outside the rough tents, piled up with every sort of merchants' wares. There were men's accoutrements, women's ornaments and raiment; there were tanned skins, there was dressed leather; there were every kind of homespun woollens and every variety of horse-trappings and stable-gear.

The Abbot drew rein only once; and that was to enquire of an old Salopian herdsman from over the border whether it was the Lord of Nannau's men who were ill-using the Grey Friar and his virgin.

"They be joined up wi' 'em, your reverence," the man replied. "But 'tis my Lord's Steward from Chirk, Simon the Hog we call 'un, tied the man up to burn 'un, and a' said he'd burn the wench too if her didn't stop hollering. She be quiet now, I reckon; so maybe them's given her a finisher. Two companies of the Earl's bowmen be up there. 'Tis them have tied Mad Huw to cart-tail; and them's sent to Valle Crucis for a priest to shrive 'un. Simon swore a' wouldn't turn the Devil himself into Hell without a bald-pate to bless the deed. But what I says, saving your reverence, is that the holy man must look sharp if he's to do his good work. Simon be buying so much for the Earl and be drinking so much for 'isself that them who've got aught to sell don't know he from God Almighty; and seeing he bides at Chirk and holds it for the Earl, I reckon them at Valley Crucis 'ud wink at his wickedness were his lads to start burning the man afore priest do come. They say the Maid's mother, from Castell Dinas Brān, be at market, along with Denis Burnell the Constable, who do hold she for's 'ooman, and they do say—"

But ap Hywel had heard enough already—and so indeed had young Rhisiart, who got no joy from learning that the keeper of Dinas Brān had the English name of Burnell. Simon the Hog, Denis Burnell the Constable, Simon the Constable, Denis Burnell the Hog, he repeated under his breath and, "O great Spirits of the Dead, help me, help me!"

"Blessed Jesus!" he heard the Lollard mutter.

"John Baptist!" he heard the Abbot exclaim.

"Saint Derfel!" cried the Scab; and they all rode forward.

They passed close to one market-counter at which in the warm twilight a large company of men were drinking, and Rhisiart tried to imagine that he could single out among them the unpleasant face of Simon the Hog.

But blessed be God's Mother! There was the Grey Friar himself and still alive! They'd fastened him to the cross-plank of a small dung-cart, his arms tied tight behind him, and both the dung-cart and the defiant man were exposed to the jeers of a crowd of bowmen on the summit of one of those mysterious mounds that in Wales are to be found everywhere.

The warlike churchman took in the situation with one shrewd glance. There was a motley crowd assembled in front of the bowmen, and many members of it were clearly in a threatening mood.

One of these went straight up to the Abbot and began telling him something that Rhisiart couldn't catch; but he did catch the name

"Meredith ab Owen," and he noticed that both the man and the rider turned their heads towards the wooded slope above the valley.

Ap Hywel was the first to arrive on the scene; Rhisiart followed; while the Lollard and the Bard brought up the rear. Our friend could feel that the approach of four horsemen, when everyone else, including the archers, was on foot, produced a considerable stir among the crowd.

But for himself he had no eyes for anyone except his imaginary Princess from Dinas Brān. She was dressed more like a boy than a girl; but her doublet had been torn at the throat and her girl's neck showed bare. She was running wildly round the half-circle of archers, imploring first one and then another in every tone of vibrant feminine appeal to let her ascend the mound and join the Friar. In several cases she actually pulled some of the younger and more susceptible, or it may be *less* susceptible, of these fair-haired lads—for many of them came from the Fitz-Alan estates in the south—a few paces up the slippery mound, till the mockery of the others or a rough command from the oldest of the troop made them draw back.

But it was evident that the whole company was deriving an unholy pleasure from the mingling of beauty and desperation in this girlish figure; and it struck even Rhisiart's inexperienced mind that while only the most depraved among them would have hurt her *if alone,* there was no denying the fact that a dark salt tide of cruelty was stirring in them *as a crowd.*

Both the girl and the Friar showed signs of lively excitement upon the arrival of the four horsemen, but it was clear to our friend that the Abbot had decided to postpone his interference for a time. "He must have heard something," thought the boy; and he turned Griffin's head a little so as to take a closer look at both the Friar and his Maid. "She's younger than me," he said to himself.

As for Mad Huw, there was something about him that reminded Rhisiart of his friend, the Lollard. The Friar's face was much thinner than Master Brut's and it wasn't nearly so fair; but it had the same kind of spiritual calm; nor, as far as a stranger could detect, did it betray the remotest sign of mental derangement.

It was true that when the man uttered his prophetic declaration about the late King his features lost this serenity. At these times his eyes grew so praeternaturally large that they became as beautiful as

a woman's. They became in fact, the lad said to himself, so dangerously
hypnotic, that it was no wonder the girl followed him everywhere.

But the Friar's Maid—for Rhisiart had no other name for her save
his own secret Dinas Brân one—no sooner caught sight of the four
horsemen, if the Scab on his pony could be called a horseman, than
she burst through the ring of archers and throwing her bare arms
round the pummel of the Abbot's saddle, while her braided hair
swayed and swung against the war-horse's belly, begged and implored
him to release her idol.

"They've got the faggots to burn him!" she cried in that clear
childish voice that had already pierced Rhisiart's heart. "They've got
the faggots to burn him! And they're only waiting for a priest! Save
him, Father! Save him, sweet Father!"

Some of the soldiers burst into brutal laughter. Others muttered
obscene jests. The crowd of common people grew thicker every
moment as more and more marketers, pouring up the slope from
the sale-booths of the fair, pressed forward towards the great black
horse and its priestly rider.

The four new-comers were in danger of being separated from one
another by the impact of the people, and Rhisiart had all he could
do to keep Griffin steady and hold him with his head against the
big charger's flank.

Ap Hywel was now bending down over his horse's head and asking
the distracted girl a number of grave questions, the bulk of which,
because of the tumult surging round them, Rhisiart couldn't catch.

But as he let his eyes linger on her figure he fancied he felt gradually,
slowly, irrevocably—the dew of destiny soaking that moment. She
was still clinging to the Abbot's knees and the crowd about her was
already uttering dangerous cries, some of which were hostile to the
man in the dung-cart and some to the bowmen; but when the Grey
Friar himself lifted up his voice Rhisiart was astonished at his own
response.

Even from his present distance he could see the light in the man's
abnormally large eyes, and as he looked to see how Master Brut was
affected he wasn't surprised to see a twitching in those plump cheeks
and a contraction of those calm lips, indicating in no uncertain manner
that the self-possessed heretic was equally stirred.

The Grey Friar in his emotion used the late King's name as if it
had been hardly less potent and precious than the name of Christ.
From that dung-cart on the mound there kept rising into the air, and
floating away over the weapons of the Chirk men and over the
agitated fair-folk, the same reiterated cry; and the fact that the ropes
that bound him were cruelly tight and that they'd even fastened
some kind of cord round his neck gave to each repetition of the words
a vibrant intensity, as though they were projected by some supernatural force in the man through a body that was suffering martyrdom.

So no doubt he would have cried had they been actually burning
him, and the fact that his bonds were causing him such pain gave to
his reiterated appeals a quivering force that was evidently piercing
the soul of that poor Maid. "Our dread and puissant Prince, Richard,
is alive! Richard, the friend of the poor, is alive! *Richard,* the son of
the Black Prince, is alive! *Richard,* God's wounded rose; *Richard,*
Cambria's bleeding heart; *Richard,* the sweet passion-flower of love;
Richard, the oblation and sacrifice of love—*Richard is alive!"*

"How miserable, how base, how cynical," thought Rhisiart, "these
modern days are! Damn this usurping Bolingbroke with his mock-
piety and his heresy-hunts! This Friar's a saint; and saints see more
than common men. Perhaps—perhaps—" And with his upper-lip drawn
into his mouth till his hooked nose became the image of a falcon's
beak, Rhisiart turned from the dung-cart to the girl.

In her desperate and pitiful pleading her torn boy's doublet had
slipped down, displaying her shift beneath it and laying bare part of
her shoulder.

Simultaneously with this, some abrupt decision among themselves—
or it may have been an order from the one who seemed older than
the rest—caused the bulk of the Chirk archers to swing round and
face the Abbot, while the rest moved a few paces up the mound
towards their prisoner. They had other weapons than their long-bows,
but it was by their bows that they made themselves feared, and
Rhisiart once more cursed the levelling science of this modern weapon.

"Why doesn't the Abbot tell them who he is?" he thought. And
then he thought, "But I suppose in these degenerate days the Church
has no power except to burn heretics. They'd put an arrow through
him, I expect, if he tried to talk to the Friar as he's talking to that

girl. It's these curst long-bows that have spoilt everything. In Grand-father's time, on Griffin's back, and with my sword, I'd have soon cut the Friar's cords and cried 'Long live King Richard!' and made these English serfs kiss a Welsh Abbot's shoe; but these new-fangled long-bows bring everything down to a common—what *is* ap Hywel going to do? Why *doesn't* he stop talking tó that girl and tell the soldiers who he is?"

But watching the Abbot closely—a proceeding which gave him an excuse for watching the girl—he decided that the man *must* be in possession of some piece of knowledge that made the situation less critical than it seemed.

But it certainly seemed as ominous as it could well be; and there was proceeding now from the dung-cart a cry that resembled the croak of a half-strangled bird. "He's coming to us again! Richard, the friend of the poor; Richard, the enemy of the rich; Richard, the sweet rose of Britain!"

But from the half-choked Friar it was always back to the girl that Rhisiart's agitated feelings rushed. That bare shoulder had begun seriously to trouble his senses. His whole soul was in a turmoil. He couldn't himself understand the conflicting feelings that were whirling up from the obscure depths of his being and struggling with one another in his nerves and brain.

He hadn't failed to notice that what most upset the Friar's Maid— and small wonder!—was the horrible regularity with which an evil-looking camp-follower of the Chirk men kept heaping up faggots and brushwood in a great pile round the stump of a dead thorn on the southern side of the mound.

And along with this it hadn't escaped him that the archers them-selves, whose leader in the absence of the Steward seemed to be merely the oldest among them, were always slipping aside to take a pull from a great barrel of liquor. "It's stronger than beer," he said to himself. "It must be metheglin."

Unbelievably brutal were the jests each archer shared with the villainous bonfire builder every time they had to pull at that barrel; and it was doubtless this furtive tippling that accounted for the in-creasing interest they took in the Friar's girl; and as the lad watched them he decided that it was the expression of some of the older ones, who weren't openly taunting her as she clung to the black horse, that was the most ominous thing.

Some of these silent ones had an air as if it would be the greatest pleasure to shoot arrows at that bare shoulder. They were well-disciplined men; they were good-natured men; but, even so, with that barrel at their disposal it was disconcerting to see the way they flicked at their taut bow-strings.

Some would point the tip of a long, polished arrow straight at our friend himself; others at the Lollard, but most of them seemed to take their chief delight in aiming at the girl, as if she had been a tantalizing hare or deer.

"The Abbot must have something on his mind," thought Rhisiart, "that he's keeping dark; or surely he'd ride straight up the mound. I pray to God he won't draw that breviary from his wallet!"

Our friend could see the unwarlike Bard of Ffinnant making obvious attempts to back his pony a little, a manœuvre that was entirely unsuccessful, for a mob of bare-legged spearmen from the hills kept pressing him forward.

From several snatches of speech that reached him from these people Rhisiart got the impression that there were some in the crowd who knew nothing of the immediate locality and who thought that the Grey Friar was none other than the late King himself, and that the four horsemen had come from London to arrest him.

He prayed that this incalculable Abbot realized the ticklishness of the situation and that any rash move might bring the discharge of those terrible new-fangled bows. Oh how he hated the look of them!

And how he loathed the power their technical efficiency had of making a man's heroism of small value! He'd been studying the *Itinerary* of Giraldus de Barri in his college library, and recalled what the Archdeacon had said of the yew-tree bows of *that* epoch. What would the good man have thought could he have seen these soldiers of Fitz-Alan with their murderous engines of destruction?

Such were the lad's reasonable thoughts; but all the while below these thoughts there was going on a strange ferment in the depths of his nature. Feelings totally unknown to him, sensations that he would have denied were possible to him, rose up and strove for the mastery.

The sight of that girl with her long braid of reddish hair and her bare shoulder roused more than a simple protective instinct in him. He *did* long to protect her; and yet in this surge of unwonted feeling he felt a dark, hot, secret sympathy with the arrows that were aimed at her.

"I musn't look at her," his heart cried; and yet he kept looking at her, and the sight of her, always with those arrows, made him feel as if he could shoot her and protect her, protect her and shoot her, at the same moment, and get wild pleasure from doing both these things.

And he knew too in his heart—for Rhisiart was no self-deceiver— that it was all due to the way her boy's doublet had slipped.

"I musn't look at her!" one voice in him protested; but, even while it was uttering the words, not only *was* he looking at her, but he was being swept away on a dark tide that save for certain puzzling moments in his early youth he had never known before.

Below the disturbing whiteness of that soft flesh throbbed a living soul that he longed to guard and protect; but something else in the youthful beauty her torn doublet exposed had a fearful power in it that turned this pity into its extreme opposite and the object of it into a dedicated victim of arrows and spears!

The actual girl over there, pleading so passionately the cause of her idol, the breathing, living girl who had a life of her own as vivid as his life, excited melting pity in him; but this mysterious *other* one, the maddening prey of his dark urge, was something abstract and impersonal.

What did he *want*? That was the question. He wanted to protect the owner of that bare shoulder; and yet he wanted to see that shoulder pierced. He wanted to protect against all the world that red braid of twisted hair; and yet he wanted to see it cut off by a sword!

He had once heard the late unhappy King cry aloud at a lost tournament in Worcester a wild and strange oath, the strangest he had caught on any lips: "By the nails of the Cross!" and something about the feelings this girl roused in him brought back that cry.

But how pearl-white, how smooth, how polished that shoulder was, and how daintily twisted was the red wisp that fell across it! To save his soul from instant damnation, he couldn't stop himself from imagining one of those terrible modern arrows quivering in that tantalizing flesh.

There would be no blood. No, not one single drop. Between the fluttering wild-goose feathers and the flesh in which their burning head was buried there would be only the long yew-shaft.

"Richard is alive, the lovely rose of Britain! Richard, our sweet sacrifice, is alive!"

But the girl suddenly drew away from the side of the horse, and covering her shoulder stood erect with her head high as if to face a new danger. Rhisiart saw at once what brought this about. It was the appearance on the scene of a personage he felt at once to be none other than Simon the Hog. The fellow was evidently further gone in drink than any of his men; and seeing this quickly enough the archers instinctively unstrung their bows and relaxed their alertness.

Still absorbed in the girl, who was now standing alone, Rhisiart noticed that it wasn't only the appearance of the Hog of Chirk that had reduced her to this intense quiescence. He could see that she had caught sight of some other figure in the crowd. Yes, she was actually lifting her arm now, in a childish gesture of recognition, to someone on the outskirts of the tumult.

Following her gaze the lad became aware of a richly-dressed woman's form forcing a way through the press, and from something in her appearance, all alert as he was to anything that affected his "Princess Myfanwy," he jumped at once to the conclusion that the two were mother and daughter. He could even see the girl making an attempt to meet the woman, but this she evidently found to be quite impossible, but being both of them tall, he could catch the way they greeted each other, and their exchange of looks confirmed, to his impetuous judgment, his idea of their relationship.

The Hog of Chirk advanced straight towards the black horse; but the Abbot's complete indifference to his authority, for the great churchman surveyed him as if he were unworthy of notice, seemed to sober him a little. He muttered something about being interrupted in his duty to the King; but it was clear to our friend that the look of indignant contempt that the girl fixed upon him was almost as disconcerting as the Abbot's haughty stare. He went on with sulky protests, but his eyes began wandering uneasily over the rapidly-increasing crowd, and all at once Rhisiart saw his expression change to a look that was totally beyond the boy's power of interpretation.

It was a look in which pain, fear, rapture and humiliation seemed all mingled together.

Rhisiart followed the man's glance. Ah! So *that* was it! It was at the woman our friend had decided was the girl's mother that the wretch was now gazing; and as he gazed all his tipsiness seemed to leave him and his first expression was followed by one of tragic and despairing obstinacy.

Still taking no more notice of the now strangely-transformed Steward than if he'd been a nonentity in the crowd, the Abbot uttered some low-voiced command to his monks who at once began chanting, just as naturally as if they were in their own choir-stalls, the well-known psalm, *"In exitu Israel de Egyptu."* They were monks from the banks of the Usk, and they had no authority on the banks of the Dee, but our friend was amazed at the calmness they showed at this agitating moment, keeping the rhythm of their chant as if it were losing itself amid familiar aisles and arches, instead of in the angry murmur of a menacing crowd.

When the psalm died away Rhisiart wedged Griffin still closer between the black horse and the Hog of Chirk. "Hold your peace," he whispered bending down towards Simon. "It's the Abbot of Caerleon!"

But the fellow didn't seem to understand his words. He turned on him a face so distorted with conflicting emotions that it resembled the face of one of the damned in Dante's Hell; and shrugging his shoulders began pushing his way through the crowd towards two new persons who were approaching the scene.

Rhisiart's heretical fellow-traveller had by this time got his mare quite close to Griffin, and the two animals were happily flirting.

"Do you know who those two are?" enquired our friend; and he wasn't greatly surprised to learn that they were the Lord of Nannau, a cousin of Owen Glyn Dŵr, and his bosom-crony, David Gam, the notorious swordsman from South Wales, each of them ferocious Anglophiles and devoted champions of the House of Lancaster.

Both the rider on Griffin and the rider on the mare watched with interest the complaint that Simon was evidently making to these newcomers about the attitude of the mounted intruders.

As the group approached, the crowd surging away from them with respectful hostility, Rhisiart could see the Hog of Chirk directing their attention to both the Friar, whose voice was still audible though very weak, and also to the sinister scarecrow who with inhuman obstinacy continued his task of piling up brushwood round the stump of the dead thorn.

During the temporary relaxation among the archers which had followed the emotional trouble, whatever it was, that had for a moment paralysed Master Simon, our friend observed with relief that his "Princess Myfanwy" had succeeded in ascending the mound, and was now engaged in ministering as best she could to the victim in the dung-cart.

The Lord of Nannau, a tall, powerful figure with a smooth, sleek, handsome face that made Rhisiart think of a vicious bully he had known in his Hereford school, speedily detached himself from his companion and approaching the Abbot began protesting against this delay in "the King's justice" which he and his monks were causing.

The man on the black horse listened to what he said, and watched grimly the hurried recovery of their discipline by the Chirk archers; though none of them seemed to have the heart to separate the Maid, now once she had reached him, from the condemned man.

But what an extraordinary figure the notorious David Gam was! Rhisiart had heard of his prowess as a soldier of fortune attached to the House of Lancaster, but it was a surprise to find him a bosom-friend of this Lord of Nannau, who was at least a distinguished-*looking* person.

Anything less distinguished, anything less of a gentleman, than the famous swashbuckler from South Wales, could hardly be imagined!

Gam was of abnormally short stature but with arms so muscular and so long as to resemble those of a gorilla. He had the peculiarity of always keeping these simian appendages bare, though they were covered, as indeed was his head and his frequently exposed chest, with red hairs of an animal-like thickness.

It was with one of these arms that he was now barring the way, as the richly-dressed stranger, of whose relationship to his "Princess" our friend was more assured than ever, tried to approach the Hog of Chirk.

Aye! but how beautiful her face was—and young, too, perhaps *too* young to be the Maid's mother. "But I think she *is* her mother all the same," said Rhisiart to himself.

The lad too could even catch the glint of the cajoling smile with

which she protested against the monstrous arms that barred her way.
But she made no attempt to circumvent them. All she did was to flash
a look at the Steward of Chirk, so full of what seemed to our young
friend the most *devouring* emotion he had ever seen, that he wasn't
surprised at the man's tragic discomfiture.

Beneath that Medusa stare the fellow seemed as paralysed as a rat
before the eyes of a snake. He made an attempt to speak, and Rhisiart
thought he *would* have spoken if a sudden shout from the crowd and a
stir among the archers hadn't turned the attention of everyone to the
mound.

And there, ascending the mound and moving straight to the dung-
cart, was a cowled figure that our friend for a moment took to be one
of the Caerleon monks, till a repeated cry of "Valle Crucis! Valle
Crucis!" undeceived him.

The archers showed a respect for this plain monk from their own
religious house that they had refused to the mitred Abbot from South
Wales, and from our friend's "Princess," as she greeted the new-comer,
there came ringing down the slope an exultant cry. "It's Father
Rheinalt, Mother! It's Father Rheinalt!" This curious name—for from
the vantage-height of Griffin's back it could be seen that the cowled
figure was bending over the man in the dung-cart, either shriving his
soul, or assuring him of his safety—had an instantaneous effect upon
both the girl's mother and the Hog of Chirk. They exchanged one
look, that to our agitated youth was as startling and inscrutable as a
blow in the dark, and immediately turned hurriedly away, the latter to
have another word with the red-haired Gam, the former to speak to the
Lord of Nannau, who had just retreated with a vicious leer on his
smooth face from the imperturbable Abbot.

Rhisiart couldn't hear what this second pair were saying, but he
could hear Simon make a boon-companion appeal to the little red
monster, reminding him with a forced attempt at jocularity of some
savage escapade they'd had together in Ireland.

Of this brutal tale our friend could only gather that it had to do with
some revolting treatment of certain Irish girls; but the little red man
refused to be cajoled.

"Peace, good Simon," Rhisiart could hear him say. "Enough, worthy
Simon! If you're serving the Lord of Chirk.

"I'm serving the Lord of Nannau, the King's best friend in these parts. Your plain Davy's on the road, I tell'ee, to be Sir David Gam at your service, renowned for generations. So hush, gentle Simon; be at peace, honest Simon; and let's see how you do your duty to that Richard-loving traitor. Burn the man, good Simon, and without any more dilly-dally. Is that shaven poll up there a-shriving of him? 'Tis for that, I tell'ee, and not to gabble about Irish maidens, that I came here. I came here for a burnin'. Burnin's be rarer to old Davy than the prettiest maidenheads. Oh, a mighty man for burnin's is King Hal, a grand man for burnin's. So get on with the job, sweet Simon; or lend *me* one of your big bows, and I'll give him 'Richard's-come-back'!"

Whether encouraged by these words or rendered desperate by the Medusa-looks of the woman, Master Simon now moved in among his archers and directed them to tighten their ranks.

Rhisiart exchanged a glance with the Lollard and both of them drew their horses as near as they could to the Abbot's charger, so as to form a solid phalanx of mounted men.

As they did this the lad glanced at the imperturbable expression with which the Abbot grimly and quietly waited upon the course of events. "I expect he's heard something," he repeated to himself; but he couldn't help thinking how helter-skelter and casual a real battle must be, if it took so long for a single event, like the burning or the release of this Friar, to come to a decisive climax.

"Are all the events in the great world like this," the boy thought, "so different from what the historians say?"

But at this moment, and Rhisiart knew very well that it wasn't *this* the Abbot was expecting, the Scab's mountaineers, waving their spears like savages, began pushing their way towards the spot where the Lord of Nannau and David Gam, for the woman had withdrawn into the crowd, were standing alone.

The Scab and his pony were thrust forward, surrounded, and then left behind by these excited men.

"Saint Derfel! Saint Derfel!" they cried as they brandished their spears; and even in that tense moment Rhisiart was amused by the mixture of alarm for his own skin and pride in the excitement he'd stirred up that was displayed by the one-eyed Bard, though the intrepid pony showed no sign of any emotion save the joy of battle.

The Abbot called out to his monks to draw back; and he himself did the same, for the old war-horse was growing unruly. Rhisiart and the Lollard followed with *their* steeds; and as the three horsemen backed away it became clear to our friend that if the Lord of Nannau and his precious companion didn't also beat a speedy retreat he would have the satisfaction of seeing them spitted like a couple of wild boars who have no avenue of escape.

It must be confessed that for one single second our young friend—for, after all, this would have been his first skirmish with real bloodshed— hoped heartily that the two bullies *would* escape those gleaming points; but whether this automatic prayer, which he might have uttered had they actually *been* wild-beasts, had or had not anything to do with it, out of that closing circle they did manage to skip; and that was the last seen of either of them that night.

The Medusa-like woman in the rich garments had also vanished; while the Valle Crucis monk, whose name, as the girl had shouted it down the slope, had had such a startling effect, must have succeeded in loosening the condemned man's bonds, for that monotonous and intolerable reiteration about King Richard, though much weaker than formerly, was no longer in the voice of a man who was being choked.

The now quite sober Hog of Chirk had got his archers into good order by this time, all along the slope of the mound; while the Scab's spearmen, gathered now in front of the crowd, were suffering something of a reaction in the presence of those drawn bow-strings.

And there fell upon the scene one of those inexplicable silences that occur sometimes at a crisis. The shouts died down. No one stirred or made any movement except to gaze anxiously at the wooded hills around them. Had Rhisiart's light-hearted mother, now taking her pleasure in the gaieties of Hereford town, caught sight at that moment of the frowning intensity of her son's narrow face, with its abnormally high forehead and big nose, she would most certainly have teased him unmercifully and called him, as was her wont, her "baby Chancellor."

But just as it was an upsetting discovery to him that he could fall in love with a girl simply from imagining her being pierced through the shoulder by a new-fangled arrow, so it was a sinister enlargement to his knowledge of life to see how a place of execution could act like a magnet upon human nerves.

Modry used to tell him that there was a magnet in all Welsh souls that always pointed north, to where the mouth of Hades was; and this perpetual cry, "Richard is alive!" seemed to act just in that way: drawing that whole motley assembly towards the mound, towards the dungcart, towards the towering pile of brushwood prepared for the burning.

The Abbot showed no sign that he intended to ride his charger through the archers, or to dismount and climb the slope on foot. "Would I risk it in his place?" our lad thought. And then he thought, "We're all waiting—on this Eve of Saint John—for a miracle to happen. There! He's staring up at those hills like everybody else! Do they expect the King and his army back from Scotland?"

A fearful turmoil now began in young Rhisiart's heart. He felt that if he didn't ride forward, straight into those fifty arrow-shafts, he would be burnt too, burnt slowly to the end of his days, by a remorse worse than his ancestor's in Dinas Brân.

Still the man in the cart kept crying, "Richard! Sweet Richard!" but his face now, which was like an angel's, and Simon's face, which was like a lost soul's, were both turned towards the bare-legged spearmen at the foot of the mound.

Rhisiart heard the Lollard whisper something to the Abbot of which he could only catch the word "madness"; but the Abbot's reply struck him as a strange one. "He won't let the man be burnt," he heard him mutter. "He'll come at the last moment."

Rhisiart's brain began to grow dazed under his desperate interior struggle. *Who* would come at the last moment? Wasn't fate beginning to lay it upon *him* to be the one to act at this crisis, be the result what it might? And if such *was* his destiny it was useless to dodge the logical conclusion; namely that if he did fling himself upon these deadly modern weapons not a soul would ever know that the treachery of Dinas Brân had been redeemed!

It was through a blood-red mist that he heard the hoarse voice of the Bard of Ffinnant invoking Saint Derfel. Modry had told him queer things about Saint Derfel; and he could see from his position on Griffin's back that a mysterious wave of feeling had begun to pass over the people like the wind at Pentecost.

Master Simon appeared to be having an angry dispute with the repulsive individual who was now engaged in pouring some imflammable oil upon the pile he had made. But what the devil was that extraordinary Abbot doing now? Was *he* expecting a miracle? Did he, a learned Cistercian, have faith in this mad Derfel cult? "By God, I believe the old chap's going to bestir himself! What's he calling to his monks about in Latin? Are they the ones who're going to march upon the arrows?"

"Richard, our sweet sacrifice, is alive!" Never in his life had the young Rhisiart felt more at the mercy of uncontrollable events than he felt at that moment. His brain seemed stunned, his senses drugged, his powers of action atrophied. He suddenly felt very young. He even felt like crying.

In spite of the familiar piebald back on which he sat and his big crusader's sword and his sheepskin bundle his nerves became like those of a child whose pretence had suddenly, to his intense bewilderment, *come true.* He did his best afterwards to forget his weakness at this particular moment; but those wildly-brandished spears and those wilder cries of "Derfel! Derfel! Saint Derfel for Edeyrnion!" approaching him from one side, while those terrible modern weapons menaced him from the other, gave the poor lad a paroxysm of sheer panic.

Instead of thinking of Dinas Brān or even of his red-haired "Princess" he thought of the kindly streets of Hereford, and he thought of his mother.

And fate seemed resolvèd to put him to shame; for what must his fellow-traveller, this cool-blooded heretic, do at this juncture but slip down from his mare, hand her bridle to him to hold, and completely unarmed as he was, walk calmly up to the pile of faggots on the southern slope of the mound, and taking Master Simon by the arm, begin, to the man's amazement, uttering some eager, long-winded conjuration.

Rhisiart began to feel a curious darkness stealing over his senses. Was he going to faint? But summoning up all the spirit that remained to him he did manage to urge Griffin forward about three yards, dragging the mare behind him. There he stopped, for he saw the glittering point of one particular arrow directed straight to his heart and he caught the cold, resolute, measuring eye of the bowman who was extending the string.

Thankful to be still alive, he tore his gaze from that arrow's point, and half turning his head tried to catch what the Abbot was saying to his monks. It sounded like a mixture of Latin and Welsh, but neither his lessons with Modry at Hereford nor with his teachers at Oxford had given him a clue to the words he heard.

In any case the Abbot was taking no notice of him; and there he was with Master Brut's mare on his hands, the only remaining person in the open space between the arrow-heads and the spear-heads!

To relieve their feelings the bare-legged followers of Derfel were now tossing their weapons in the air and catching them as they came down. From both sides there arose, and in no very gentle terms, extremely blunt advice to the boy on the piebald horse to get out of the way.

It had been, however, young Rhisiart's custom, during the solitude of his long ride through the woodland paths, to pretend to himself that he was rescuing Dinas Brân, and though the only eyes that saw his exploits were those of rabbits and sparrow-hawks it had been his delight to draw his crusader's sword out of its scabbard. So accustomed to these heroic pastimes had old Griffin become that the moment his bridle was jerked he would lift his head, advance far enough to satisfy his rider's impulse, and then, realizing that it was all pretence, begin quietly cropping the grass, well-assured of at least ten minutes of peace.

And now, not in the least affected by either spears or bows, being accustomed as a sheriff's state-beast to every sort of warlike pageant, he displayed only a reproachful astonishment at the antics of the Lollard's mare, who was rapidly getting out of hand.

"Richard, our sacrifice!" The Friar's voice was growing very faint, and the yells of the Scab's mountaineers almost drowned it, but through all the turmoil of thoughts and images that made the boy feel as if he were being drowned in a black tide, the thought kept coming to him: "I wonder if, when it's over, they'll take as many arrows out of Griffin as out of me."

And then he thought—but it was rather a flash of electric vision, running like a tongue of fire through his body, his nerves, his brain, his heart, than any definite thought—"If I just stay where I am it'll be a quick death; and I'll have died for Myfanwy if not for Dinas Brân. But a gentleman always rides forward!" So strong was his conviction that his end *had* come that he already felt the arrows piercing his flesh; and though the feeling it gave him had nothing of that dark trembling he had felt when he thought of the arrow in the girl's shoulder, it did bring with it a wild and desperate exultation that seemed to hover in circles above his terror as a hawk might hover over a heron.

But the thought, *"Will it hurt?"* and the thought, *"I mustn't cry out,"* wrote themselves in letters of fire upon the wings of this exultation.

And then there fell on him "like a clap of thunder and a fall of mist" a curious cessation of all movement of time. Time stopped; and something else, another dimension altogether, took its place; and in that deep time-vacuum, with an absolute naturalness—helped doubtless by the calm assumption of his horse that he was doing what he always did —he drew his crusader's sword out of its sheath and lifting it high into the air rode forward.

III

MOTHER AND DAUGHTER

It must have been a spectacle evocative of many various impressions, the sight of this tall, dark lad on the piebald horse brandishing his old-fashioned weapon in the face of the best archers in England.

"Why, each one of those fellows," the more practical onlookers must have thought, "holds that boy's life on his bow-string!"

To some it must have seemed the very top of idiotic folly, to others the limit of theatrical bravado, to others just the old pitiful tale of youth's throwing its life away on the chess-board of human wickedness.

To a few it may even have seemed an action prompted by cunning craftiness, timed to a nicety, and calculated to win a particular kind of notoriety at the minimum risk.

There must have been some among the archers, on the other hand, to whose south-of-England humour the whole episode was simply comic. This humorous attitude to it was certainly encouraged by the bad behaviour of the Lollard's mare who not only plunged and dragged, but did her best in every possible way to make Griffin and his master ridiculous.

It was indeed the necessity of using both hands to restrain this roguish animal that brought the lad to his senses; but he had no sooner recovered his normal wits and had even begun, in a natural human reaction, to congratulate himself that he was still alive, than he realized that the whole situation had completely changed.

Intoning the chant, *"In toto corde meo,"* and led by their Abbot on his great steed, the monks of Caerleon were moving in procession between the opposing ranks. But it wasn't because of the bravery of the monks that a great cry was now going up from all the people. As it rose, and rolled away over the hills, it was echoed by what sounded to Rhisiart's ears like thousands of deep voices, all crying the same name, and it was as if the river itself had caught it up, and as if the long-sighing summer night-wind were carrying it, and as if the high invisible battlements of Dinas Brān were sending it back!

"Owen! Owen! Owen!" it repeated; and then, while the lad gazed in astonishment at the figure approaching him, "Meredith ab Owen! Meredith ab Owen!" was the acclamation he heard around him.

What Rhisiart saw now was a slender young man, plainly dressed save for some kind of hawk's feather in his cap and totally unarmed, coming straight towards him down the slope of the mound while the Chirk men lowered their weapons to let him pass. His hands were bare, his throat and neck were bare, and he walked as easily and leisurely as if he were in the circuit of his own sylvan halls. Round his neck, suspended by a silver cord, hung a richly-decorated hunting-horn, with which every now and again his fingers would toy, a trick that struck the manly taste of our Hereford friend as bordering upon the effeminate.

But Rhisiart forgot all tricks of manner when Meredith ab Owen came up to him and spoke to him; forgot everything but his face and its expression which made him feel as if he were confronted by his own favourite Knight of the Round Table, the enigmatic Gwalchmai!

But Meredith ab Owen was a sad not a gay Gawain. In form he was a dark, slim youth, not so tall as Rhisiart himself though some five or six years older; but what struck our traveller most about his face was the quality of its wistful disillusionment. He had never seen such a depth of gentle life-weariness as looked out at him from this young man's dark eyes.

There was a softness, like that of a glossy dusky brown of certain time-dimmed royal velvets, about his hollow cheeks, while his features, in that gathering dusk, were all soft and nebulous, as if their human flesh were only partially solidified after being called up from the vasty deep by some enchanter.

It very soon became apparent why the Chirk men had lowered their arms. And they were doing more than that now. They were piling them into a great heap beside the unused bonfire, while Master Simon himself, with his hands tied behind his back, was directing this symbolic proceeding!

The whole mound was surrounded by Glendourdy's men. They had descended like an elfin host out of that Midsummer Eve greenness. Especially had they appeared from that particular direction beyond the mound where Master Simon, in his private griefs, had forgotten to place a guard.

Rhisiart instinctively doffed his scholar's cap to this young man as he had not done to anyone but the Abbot all that long day; and feeling ashamed to address him from Griffin's back, he swung his leg over his saddle, extricating it with some difficulty from his big bundle and bigger sword, and slid to the ground.

Here, holding both the horses, he made with some awkwardness his best Hereford obeisance, looking, as his mother had taught him to do when addressing a great personage, not at the young man's face but at his feet.

"May I ask," the new-comer earnestly began, while beyond them against the darkening sky the monks of Caerleon chanted their *in-convertendo,* "When the Lord turned again the captivity of Sion," "may I ask whether it was on behalf of Henry Bolingbroke, or on behalf of King Richard, that you drew your sword and kept the peace?" And then in a much lower and more youthful tone he added quickly, "What a perfectly lovely horse! I've never seen anything like him. Do you come from London? Are you on a pilgrimage to Valle Crucis? May I have the pleasure of knowing the name of one who has faced the Earl's best bowmen? But I see you're wrought-up. My curiosity is ill-timed. But if you're *not* expected at Valle Crucis I know my father will want to thank you in person; and perhaps you will allow me—I'm expressing myself clumsily—but I keep thinking of how you looked just now—and how *you* looked—" and with a smile full of a most wistful tenderness he stroked Griffin's heavily-loaded back—"I mean, I beg you'll allow me to take you both to Glyndyfrdwy to-night?"

Rhisiart lifted his eyes and then dropped them, turned his hook-nosed profile first towards the chanting monks, and then towards the jubilant crowd. He acted like some agitated young falcon upon whose perch an eaglet has suddenly alighted. Embarrassed though he was it didn't escape him how respectfully the excited crowd kept aloof, leaving a clear open space about the two of them.

But his first duty as a man of honour was to disillusion his new friend as quickly as possible. "I did nothing," he stammered. "I—I just happened to be where I was. It's all a mistake. I wasn't—what you think. It was—my horse "

"I'm sure it was your horse," said Meredith ab Owen with a smile of almost girlish sweetness. "Well! you must bring your horse for my father to thank. Will you tell me his name?"

Rhisiart murmured the word "Griffin" and then once more plunged into a long and incoherent explanation of how he'd become so panic-stricken that he'd been afraid to move, and how— "And this fine old sword came out of his sheath of his own accord?" said the other with perfect gravity. "Well, we'll have anyway to take your sword and Griffin to my father; and since you're the owner of these independent beings I'm afraid you can't very well refuse—"

There was indeed something so engaging about this young man, with his dark well-fitting tunic, his bare brown knees, his cap with its hawk's feather, and his puzzling air of belonging neither to court nor camp, neither to cloister nor college, that Rhisiart gave up the attempt to explain his behaviour. "It's fate," he thought. "I've told him; so if he *won't* believe, it's his own fault! I'm not going on proclaiming my childishness!"

But the young man was now, in his delicate, indirect, and almost feminine fashion, asking him who he was. "My father will want to know; and it'll save you the bother of explaining if I can tell him in advance."

"Rhisiart ab Owen is my *real* name," replied our friend eagerly. "I'm descended on the bastard side from Madoc ap Griffith of Dinas Brān. *Your* father's the Baron Glendourdy, isn't he? I thought that's who you were, when you came so sudden, and I'm glad you've asked me to come, because—though only on the bastard side, of course—I am, unless I'm mistaken, a sort of connection of your honoured house."

Meredith gave him at that the most radiant smile he'd ever seen, and bending forward with his cap in his hand kissed him tenderly in the Norman manner on both cheeks.

"Why then we're cousins," he cried, "and cousins well within the ninth degree! I had a queer feeling there was *something* about you. What do they call you at home?"

"Rhisiart's what I usually call myself," answered Griffin's rider, doing his best to soothe both the horses, for the mare's restlessness was beginning to fret the old piebald. "I've been at Oxford; but I thought—I thought—"

"You thought you'd like to see your Welsh cousins! And so you shall. You shall see us all. I won't tell you yet which you'll like the best! But I *know* very well indeed. And I'll tell you afterwards if I was right. On second thoughts I think you'd better sleep here to-night—here or at Valle Crucis—and come on to Glyndyfrdwy to-morrow. My father's at Sycharth just now. Our old friend Iolo Goch's lying ill in our place there; and I can tell you when *he's* ill my father won't stir or think of anything else. But he's better now and we're going to move him to-morrow to Glyndyfrdwy. Father's had a special conveyance made for him out of withy-wands; and our own people will carry him. They *may* stop for High Mass at the Abbey; but I doubt it. The poet's not over-pious. Few of our bards are. Their religion is like the Scab's yonder, with his Derfel. By the way, I hear another cousin of ours, along with that cut-throat, David the Squint, is stopping at the Tassel. Have you seen anything of *him* here?"

Delighted to have something easier to talk about than his own conduct, Rhisiart launched forth into a vivid description of the two traitors, a description that was spiteful enough and boyish enough to afford their young enemy no small satisfaction; but all the while he was talking his eyes were searching for the red-haired Maid, whom he finally discovered not very far away and looking anything but radiant.

The girl wasn't with her Friar. She was talking to the richly-dressed woman; and now when he saw them side by side he felt certain of their relationship. "Yes, she's younger than I am," he thought. "I don't believe she's sixteen!"

"Well," said Meredith, "I must pay my father's devoir to John ap Hywel now. She's lovely, isn't she?" he added quickly, causing our friend's startled blood to rush to his cheeks. "I don't wonder you were relieved when I asked you to come to us *to-morrow* instead of to-night. Well, good luck! See you to-morrow at Glyndyfrdwy." And he ran lightly up the slope of the mound.

Impatient to get rid of the Lollard's horse, Rhisiart now looked about him to try to discover Walter Brut. Yes! There he was, still talking in his obstinately-tender manner to the unhappy Simon.

"Did he think *I* was unhappy when he talked to me? Does he talk

like that to all the unhappy people he meets? God! I couldn't stand it
if I were the Hog of Chirk." And for some reason, just as it gave
Rhisiart a curious pain to watch the wretched Simon submitting to the
spiritual consolation of Master Brut, so it troubled his mind to see the
Friar's Maid listening to her own mother!

"Why don't people leave each other alone?" he thought, as he saw
the girl's head hanging down under what was evidently the handsome
woman's bitter tongue. He glanced towards the exhausted Friar, by
whose side was still standing the heavily-cowled monk from Valle
Crucis, and he couldn't help noticing that this same monk kept turning
round to stare at the two women; and, unless the twilight misled him,
the fellow was as uneasy under what he saw as he was himself.

Master Simon too, he noticed, stole many a furtive glance at the
mother and daughter; but the scolding to which the girl was submitting didn't appear to worry *him* very much.

"I believe there's some trouble between them all," our lad thought;
and he tried to pretend to himself that he had had an inkling of this
from the first moment he'd seen them. He remembered an occasion in
his childhood when his frivolous Norman mother had observed his
interest in a complicated social situation. "The little monk's got his
eyes about him," she'd said to Modry. Yes, he began to feel sure that
between these two men and these two women there was a mysterious
bond. And how did the mad Friar come into it?

The whole problem provoked him; for if there was one thing he
prided himself upon it was his social acumen. And how could there be
any link between that tragic-looking Cistercian and this richly-dressed
woman? Or, for the matter of that, between such a woman and the
Hog of Chirk?

"I wouldn't give any of them a thought," he decided irritably, "if it
weren't for that girl."

But how the monk was staring! "Blessed Mary!" Rhisiart said to
himself, "if I were Master Simon, afraid of that over-dressed sorceress,
and afraid of that scowling priest, I wouldn't be so patiently listening
to a gospel-man! I'd hit out. I'd do somebody a mischief!"

The Maid's head, grown dusky in the twilight, was sinking lower
and lower under her mother's words. But what a long braid she had,
as she clasped her hands across it behind her back!

Suddenly the woman seemed to lose all patience, vexed rather than appeased by the girl's quiescence. With one last word, obviously as cruel as a blow, she turned impatiently from her and moved off towards the slope of the mound.

Rhisiart's heart beat fast. Now had come the chance he had been passionately desiring, ever since he had first set eyes upon this girl. But he was burdened with two horses, both of them heavily loaded, both of them restless and hungry, both of them in as ill a humour as it is possible for elderly horses to be. She still stood there by herself, biting her lips and watching her mother make her way towards Simon; and Rhisiart felt he *must* snatch this precious moment, or she would be whirled out of his path and out of his life forever! His knees shook, a hollow emptiness in the pit of his stomach began throbbing like the tap-tap of a sickening drum.

Desperately he dragged the two unwilling beasts towards her, Griffin every now and then turning his head and twitching an ear as if to say, "I know what you're feeling, Master; but I would like to bring my feed of oats before your enamoured intelligence."

She turned her head when she saw him coming, and their eyes met. Then looking down she ran the palms of her hands over the folds of her boy's dress. Reaching her side, where Griffin, either out of an old servant's instinctive tact or because of his gnawing belly, induced the mare to drop her head along with his own and crop a few grass-blades, he suddenly found that something had deprived him of the gift of speech. There she was, and here he was, but not a syllable could he utter. All the moisture seemed to have left his lips, his palate, his throat. Nor did the power that had taken away his speech even allow him to look at her.

Luckily it didn't make him shut his eyes, and never has there been a patch of earth so microscopically stared at as the one between her feet and his. In this small radius of midsummer vegetation, great creative Nature had caused to spring up an exceptionally early meadow-orchis, and following Griffin's example the boy deliberately stooped down, and plucking this spike of soft petals, whose colour was lost in the falling night, thrust it hurriedly, and as if he were just giving it to her to hold while he adjusted the bridle of his horse, into the maiden's hand.

The crafty old piebald seemed to take a sly pleasure in making what the youth had to do to this bridle as difficult as possible. "Take time, Master," he seemed to say. "It's better not to rush them at the beginning. Pardon me if I taste that bit of clover!"

No classical Pandarus could in fact have been kinder to young Rhisiart than his hungry old horse, and before, as they say, he realized he was in the water, lo and behold! he found he could swim.

While their four young hands were disentangling the confusion of reins, which the immortal fingers of Eros, helped by old Griffin's artfulness, were twisting as fast as they untwisted them, it was Rhisiart who found it easiest to talk; and he talked rapidly, saying things that astonished himself a good deal more than they did the Friar's Maid.

He told her that he had heard her voice as well as the Friar's before he crossed the river. He told her what a power over him her voice had had, and how wonderful it was that it could carry so far and yet remain so clear and sweet.

"What's your name?" he finally blurted out, stealing a glance at the curve of her cheek.

"Tegolin," she answered, stroking Griffin's neck. "It's a funny name, but I've got used to it."

He now realized that she had stuck the meadow-orchis into her red-gold braid, where it swung as she moved as naturally as if it were growing there.

But if it was Rhisiart whose tongue was free when they were busy over the horse, the moment their eyes met *she* took the lead.

"I saw you drawing your sword," she said in a low voice, pressing a finger against the one of her cheeks which felt less cooled than the other by the damp on Griffin's neck. "I've never seen a gentleman's sword drawn before. They use spears and bows in my *cantref*. How beautiful it looked as you held it up, and you sitting so lonely in front of them all! You looked like Pwyll, Prince of Dyved, riding against Hafgan, crowned King of Annwn."

Poor Rhisiart! If she had never seen a gentleman's drawn sword before she had certainly never suffered from a gentleman's touchy conscience before.

It now became necessary for the boy to enter at full length, with his profile turned sharply away, into every detail of that wretched predicament in which *panic,* according to his furious pride of self-depreciation, played the part of courage.

She heard him gravely, watching him intently, her blue eyes growing wider and wider as he went on. But when he came to Griffin—how in the midst of his dazed and desperate thinking the old horse shook himself and lifted his ears, thus hypnotizing the man on his back into the automatic playing of *his* part in their familiar game—a faint smile flickered across her lips.

"I was thinking so hard," he said, "that everything seemed only half-real, everything swayed and heaved and melted; and I suppose I'd so mixed up drawing that sword with vows and resolutions to *be* worthy of it that in my weakness and cowardice it *drew itself,* if you know what I mean."

He turned upon her so suddenly that he caught that tender half-smile; and for some reason instead of making him angry or making him more ashamed of himself, it was just the one thing he needed, and the words that followed it became only a roundabout commentary upon the effect it produced and the knowledge it revealed.

"I'm just like you," she whispered. "I'm always begging the Friar not to come to these places and not to cry his message where there's such terrible danger; but when we *do* come I seem to turn against all I've said and something in me pushes me on, and I push *him* on, and so it happens."

They were both stroking Griffin now and she looked Rhisiart straight in the eyes. "When these moments come," she said, speaking slowly and very emphatically, "I don't think it's ever *we* who're brave. I think it's something inside us."

The fact that he was understood in his deepest weakness, and also in this "something" which was in him and yet outside him, brought the tears suddenly to his eyes, and he made such a pathetic effort not to break down and, in doing so, screwed up his queer physiognomy so absurdly that Tegolin, with her own mouth distorted, bent suddenly forward and, snatching up his hand as it rested on the horse's neck, pressed it tightly for a fleeting second against her breast.

This impulsive gesture established no new relation between them.

Indeed, ignorant of the ways of women, our friend accepted it as the natural behaviour of a young girl who wanted to comfort him; but from the unconscious way they both acted it was as if their hands had been independent entities for whose behaviour they were in no sense responsible.

"How old are you?" she asked him. "I was sixteen on the first of this month."

Rhisiart smiled proudly. "I was seventeen on the first of this month. So I'm a year older than you."

"Draw the sword again for me," she begged him. "Only a little way! I don't want anyone to see you do it. But *please* draw it!" And then she added, evidently reverting to his pride at being a year older, "Seventeen isn't much."

Rhisiart obeyed her at once, and in the hay-scented twilight that seemed as if it would last till dawn, he pulled from the ancient sheath about three inches of that exquisitely-chiselled blade.

"May I touch it?" she asked.

Rhisiart hesitated and pondered in silence. Did the girl know all he would be giving her if he let her do that? But her long twisted braid had already fallen sideways against his sheepskin bundle and against his ancient tunic of chain-armour, and though it was too dark to see much difference in colour between her hair and the meadow-orchis, a blur of paleness at one spot in that dusky braid showed him it hadn't yet fallen.

There was a broad, expansive yellowish light above the mountains to the south-west, but the river below them was of a cold, metallic whiteness; and the fragment of steel he had laid bare took to itself, as she bowed her head over it, the cold grey of the water of the river rather than the warm tint of the sky.

There were no longer any wild sounds or desperate shouts coming from the people. He could see that the Grey Friar had fallen peacefully asleep and that the tragic monk from Valle Crucis was kneeling by his side. The Chirk bowmen were sprawling on the ground, disarmed now and helpless, but joking in their careless English manner with their captors, and perfectly content at the turn which events had taken.

Glendourdy's son was standing alone on the slope of the mound, evidently waiting till the Caerleon monks had finished their evening psalms.

The indefatigable Lollard, who was still sticking fast to the Hog of Chirk, was leaning against the faggots; and it was across the great heap of surrendered weapons that he was murmuring his evangelical consolations.

With the constant smell of new-cut hay there came to them on the soft wind occasional waftures of other pleasant fragrances. Some of these Rhisiart took for the scent of honeysuckle; but there were others that may have been exotic foreign perfumes that merchants from overseas had brought to the fair; and once he was sure he smelt a whiff of wood-smoke from the Tassel Inn.

The bare-legged Derfel-worshippers had now lighted a bonfire of their own, and round it, with their spears stuck in the earth, they were reclining at their ease, listening to some bardic composition of the inspired Scab.

Thus the Latin of the monks and the Welsh of Derfel's prophet answered each other across that misty expanse, uplifting in pure haphazard an antiphonic hymn to the powers of the night. Most of the crowd had already vanished and the silences and mysteries of Nature resumed their ancient sway. The sacred "Gorsedd" mound, covered with the same unbroken turf as had covered it before rumour of either Christ or Derfel had reached this place, rose to its proper dignity and claimed its indestructible inheritance.

All these things did Rhisiart feel, but only vaguely and indistinctly, as he pondered in his mind whether to let her touch the sword. Conscious of the boy's hesitation Tegolin lifted her head, and it was now too dark for him to see her flushed cheeks.

"If you'd rather I didn't touch it," she said, "of course I won't. *Would* you rather I didn't?"

Her renewed question forced Rhisiart to make a decision. But oh, it was so hard! To let her touch his precious sword at this turning-point of his life would be to commit himself to her in a way far beyond the flower in her braid or his hand against her bosom!

Hit in her pride by his continued silence she drew away from him and began tightening the leather collar of her boyish doublet. He caught the movement and it brought back a rush of that dark unholy emotion that had swept through him when he had envisaged the imaginary arrow.

It was therefore with the most dangerous thing in him, as well as with the depths of his secret mania for Dinas Brān, that he tore the hesitation out of his heart. It was as if the imaginary arrow had been in him instead of in her, so much did it cost him; but he whispered hoarsely, "Yes, Tegolin, you *may* touch it!"

All her sweetness, all her submissiveness returned to her as she came close to him and leaned across Griffin's back. But instead of touching the exposed steel with her fingers she bowed her head over it and pressed upon it her open lips.

Rhisiart drew a deep breath.

"How cold and damp it is!" she murmured.

He gave a queer little chuckle. "Steel's always like that," he said. "But it's not wet with blood." And then, in a low eager voice, "When shall I see you again—Tegolin?"

Her reply was a double question. "Where are you sleeping to-night? Are you squire to Owen?"

"You mean the Baron Glendourdy? No, I'm not his squire *yet;* but I'm his cousin, and I'm going to see him. No, I don't know where I'm going to sleep. Meredith said I couldn't see him till to-morrow night."

Tegolin looked at him with increased interest, and as she looked at him something about his innocence and un-worldliness touched her to the heart.

For all his crusader's sword and his chain-armour and his hooked Norman nose, she suddenly saw him as very young and very lonely and not a little helpless.

"You heard what the Abbot over there said about taking us to Valle Crucis?"

Rhisiart murmured a gloomy assent. "Oh don't be afraid. We're not going there. Brother Huw and I have a cow-stall to ourselves at that farm near the ferry. It belongs to the Tassel, but it's quite different. If you come later and ask for us— Only don't tell anyone else; for I can't have the Father disturbed any more to-night, and if people follow us he'll preach till his heart breaks."

Rhisiart had strained his spirit of independence to such a point of late that it was like a sweet immersion in a bath of warm and fragrant water to place his will entirely at her disposal. He thanked her earnestly and gravely; and in that obscure light she smiled at him with a smile of such protective strength that a wave of relaxed peacefulness flowed over him and he drew a long happy sigh.

"I must get Brother Huw away now," she said. "I can see he's awake and listening to Father Rheinalt. Father Rheinalt is good and kind— I'll tell you about him—another time—but I don't want—" She paused and looked round them. "It's my mother who's on my mind now! She's gone up there"—and Tegolin pointed to the dead tree and the faggots and the pile of arms—"to gloat over Master Simon; and I can't bear it when she gets like that. Brother Huw would forgive anyone; even if they were burning him alive. He says King Richard would too, but I don't know! You see I don't believe *everything* the Friar says! But will you do something for me? Will you get my mother away from Master Simon and find someone who's going to Dinas Brān? She's living in the castle up there with Denis Burnell, the son of the Sheriff of Shropshire. Mother tells everybody Father Rheinalt married them; but, oh dear, *I* don't know! I was a baby when she married Master Simon; and the nuns brought me up. But it was her going to Simon—I know *that*—that drove Father Rheinalt into the monastery. But I'll tell you all I know about them another time. But I don't know much. The nuns wouldn't let me see her, and since I've been with Brother Huw—but do get Mother off to Dinas Brān! There *must* be some of Denis Burnell's people here. The Chirk men will tell you where to find them. Don't *go* with Mother, mind. Not under any condition! Come to the farm and ask for *us*. But oh! go quick! Get her away from Simon and find Burnell's—" she stopped abruptly. "Do you mind if I ask you *your* name? Mother's a distant relation of Owen's; but he doesn't like her, though she's useful to him. My Lord of Arundel's very fond of her, too; so she has two strings to her bow. What *is* your name?"

No story our friend had ever told himself about his romantic future was as full of conflicting emotions as Rhisiart's face when the words Dinas Brān fell from Tegolin's lips. There flashed across his brain a memory of a summer evening by the banks of the Wye, when he had prayed desperately to the Virgin that some tremendous event might transform his life. And now—"My name is Rhisiart ab Owen," he said hurriedly. "In Hereford they call me Rhisiart."

Tegolin turned away her head, and laying her hand on Griffin's mane began twisting its hairs round her fingers. "What shall *I* call you?" she enquired. Her shyness communicated itself to him, and he too looked away.

"Modry used to call me Gwion Bach," he brought out with a wry smile. At that she turned sharply upon him.

"Who was Modry?"

"My nurse," he said; and she gave a little laugh; and then it became his turn to ask a question. "Have *you* ever been up to Dinas Brān, Tegolin?"

"Never!" she confided. "Mother would hate to see me there. Besides, Denis might treat the Friar as Simon tried to do."

"But why don't you go alone?"

"And leave Brother Huw? How on earth would he get on? And anyway Mother wouldn't want me up there in these clothes. Don't you see, Gwion Bach, I've got hosen like you? I'm the Friar's page. He often forgets that I'm a woman at all! Oh you've no idea—" she broke off. "Please go quick, Gwion Bach, and take her to the Constable's people. I can see—" Hurriedly she helped him to get the bridles of both horses round his wrist. "Goodbye," she cried, giving him an anxious push. "And ask for us at the farm—Gwion Bach!"

It was a strange scene he encountered when finally he'd got the horses to the top of the slope; and he arrived there hot and exhausted and very irritable. Both animals had been a great trouble. The mare had pulled violently at her halter in her desire to get quickly to her master, while Griffin, sulky and hungry, had hung back, knowing that his only chance for oats and hay lay to the west rather than to the east.

Dragging one beast therefore, and dragged by the other, Rhisiart skirted the circle of disarmed bowmen, who, seated on faggots from the stake-pile, were playing cards and drinking and singing and chatting to their captors, till he came to where his Lollard friend stood in the background, looking baffled and nonplussed, listening with an expression of growing apprehension to the ambiguous and cruel words poured out upon his convertite by Tegolin's mother.

The heretic's eyes were wide open and his full lips considerably apart, while upon his smooth face there had formed at least two noticeable lines that Rhisiart had never seen there before. Everything about him, down to the way he was fidgetting with his feet, seemed absorbed in one overwhelming sensation, the recognition of evil of a kind he had never met before!

What a handsome woman she was, this mother of Tegolin, and what a terrifying one! Her hair hadn't a touch of grey in it, but it was much duskier than her daughter's, and was indeed of so dark a tinge of chestnut as to look black in that obscurity.

But no shadow of night obscured the terrible glint in her eyes. It was clear to our friend that the student of the Gospels was spell-bound by what he heard. He stared at the woman as if the wicked emotion she displayed were a conjured-up trick rather than a revelation of reality.

Absorbed in the miserable mind of the Hog, Master Brut had been struggling for hours with profanity and despair, but from the eyes and lips of this beautiful woman there jetted forth a passion so weird as to produce the feeling that it came from a fount of evil infinitely deeper and more dangerous than anything in her wretched victim.

All this after Tegolin's hint was easy enough for Rhisiart to read in the Lollard's face, as he placed the mare's bridle in his hand. "He's been struggling with an *ordinary* devil," the lad thought, "but with this witch he'll have to change his weapons!"

Master Simon was sitting hunched-up on one of the highest faggots, with his back against the dead tree, and he looked to our friend like a man who was deriving some horrible satisfaction from being beaten to death. His lower lip hung loose as if his jaw had dropped. In the dying light you could see that the corners of his mouth were dribbling. His heavy head drooped sideways upon his chest. His hands, as they dangled helplessly across his knees under the torment of the woman's tongue, looked as if they had been cut off in the pillory and unskilfully replaced, so white and leaden-like they hung.

"You've come from my daughter," was the woman's greeting to Rhisiart. "I saw what she was up to! I could almost hear her words. I suppose you're from Sycharth, eh? I wish you *would* go and tell my Dinas Brân people that I'm ready to go. That *was* what Teg told you to do, wasn't it? She's always looking after her mother. It's touching, but it's very awkward. You saw how simple she is? She and her Friar are a

fair pair. They're shining candles in this naughty world; but *you* look
shrewd enough. Are you one of Owen's scribes? Can you write a good
Latin letter? No, no, I'm serious, young man! I must see more of you.
I'm in want of just such a— But *there* they are! Lawnslot! Cys-tennin!
Rhy-dderch! Well, lads, it's time we set out. They'll think we're mur-
dered as it is. Throw down those bows, my boys. I'll explain to the
Constable. Yes! you can keep your other things. I'll explain *that* to
Meredith."

While our traveller was contemplating the strong and athletic appearance of these lads from Dinas Brān, who were evidently like so
many others in Wales "serving two masters," he felt old Griffin give
a sudden jerk and make an attempt to swing round. Turning rapidly
himself, while the three stalwart young "traitors" gathered close to their
mistress's side, he saw a great war-horse approaching, bearing on his
back a most formidable-looking personage, armed in grander and
more modern armour than Rhisiart had ever seen, but with no weapon
in his hands and his hands themselves ungauntleted and bare.

This awe-inspiring individual had a weather-beaten, battle-scarred
face, piercing grey eyes, an aquiline nose, a grey moustache, and
grizzled hair beneath his steel helmet. Though both the man and his
horse looked travel-stained and weary, his whole presence breathed an
air of proud, habitual and impatient authority.

Everybody present, including Master Simon, the Chirk bowmen and
the three lads from Dinas Brān, straightened themselves and uncovered
their heads.

Rhisiart pulled Griffin back a little, and took the opportunity, while
the horseman turned with a series of angry gestures upon Master
Simon, to enquire of the lady who he was.

"Hush, you young fool! He'll hear you," she whispered. And then
in a tone of bitter sarcasm, "It's the great man himself. It's Thomas
Fitz-Alan, Earl of Arundel and Surrey, Lord of Oswestry, Chirk-land,
Bromfield and Yale! He's come post-haste from the King. The Scottish
war must be over."

Rhisiart mechanically followed the example of the rest and removed
his cap. Then he led Griffin as close as he could to the Lollard's side.
It was a relief to him to observe the calm dignity and unabashed composure of that revolutionary scholar.

But the magnate in armour took no more notice of the two young men than if they'd been pedlars from the market. His whole attention was directed to his unlucky Steward, whom he proceeded to rate unmercifully for the predicament into which his men had fallen.

"I've seen Glendourdy's son," he said, "and he's given me a safe-conduct for your idiots to go back whence you came. But look at all these good bows—all lost by this madness! Who told *you* to take on yourself to burn heretics and rouse the countryside? This is the very thing I've been trying to avoid. I warrant my Lord Grey's hand's in this, the obstinate numskull! This is exactly the kind of thing young Percy was warning us against. It's all *wrong*. I've told the King over and over again he should follow Percy and not Grey. Grey thinks only of himself and his damned red castle. Well! off with you all! Back to Chirk by the nearest road! And don't touch those bows, or I can't do anything for you. If the whole country's not up, it's not *your* fault. Simon, Simon! I've a great mind, Simon, to tie you up, head and foot, and leave you to our Welsh friends. You've done more harm than you wot of, my little Simon! Oh, I've a mind to leave you. God's holy teeth! I've a mind to leave you to the wolves!"

What struck Rhisiart as so queer, and what made him terribly embarrassed too, was the way the Earl kept turning from Simon and addressing his remarks upon these matters of high state policy to himself and Master Brut. He might have been addressing them to Griffin and the Lollard's mare as far as any recognition of their existence as personalities went; but without acknowledging their presence as separate human entities he evidently required some sort of sounding-board for his quirks and his sallies.

"Oh, it's you again, is it, Mistress Lowri?" and he made a courtly but ironical bow. "How is your gracious mother? I see your daughter has got her Friar safe back. Tired already of our little Constable, eh? Gone back to brave Simon, gentle Simon, faithful Simon, ha?"

This was the first time Rhisiart had heard the woman's name. "Lowri," he repeated to himself in a whisper, while he watched her press close to the Earl's saddle and lay her richly-gloved fingers on the trappings of his horse.

"So you've made it up, have you, Mistress, you and Simon? You've got tired of Dinas Brān and our little Denis? Somebody must lend you a mount then, I suppose, if we're to have you back in your old bower in our unworthy domain!" And he cast a hawk's eye upon Griffin and the mare as if their owners had not been present.

The Earl's style of address as he talked to Tegolin's mother was something quite new to Rhisiart's experience. It was an indulgent tone—with an under-current of ribaldry—and it was extremely intimate, too. It was such a different thing from the impersonal obliviousness with which he treated our two young men that there was something indecent about it. In fact our friend, who had already taken an extreme dislike to this handsome and shameless lady, decided in his blunt Oxford manner that she was a whore and that the Earl was treating her to a mocking parody of the French Courts of Love.

He came to the conclusion, however, a moment later, though quite likely with gross injustice, that there was an ardent sensual passion behind this mock-chivalric tone. "Oh it's all dying," thought the startled lad, "the high romance of the old days! If this battered, cynical old tyrant were like the Black Prince, *how* different! He'd at once have spoken to Master Brut and me. Mistress Lowri would have told him how I drew my sword between spearmen and archers; and he would have offered to make me his squire! I wouldn't have accepted; but I'd have liked to tell Tegolin he'd made me the offer."

The Earl was bending down over his saddle now listening to Lowri's whispers.

Master Simon hadn't changed his besotted look of maudlin submission since the woman had first appeared on the scene. Rhisiart concluded that he took for granted that her appearance was his doom, that she had come, like the Erinyes, to hound him to his death, and that there was nothing for him to do but accept the worst and hug it to his heart. Indeed, while Lowri whispered like a she-devil in the Earl's ear, our friend watched Simon with curious interest. He saw him replace his cap on his head and squat down at the foot of the Friar's tree and fold his arms. The fellow seemed to know by instinct that the end of this whispering would be the end of his life. Indeed, he seemed half-dead already.

Rhisiart himself could hear quite enough to gather that the woman was giving the great man lurid and abominable details of Master Simon's behaviour to her.

Every now and then the Earl would interject some indignant and horrified exclamation; such as: "Impossible!" "Did he do *that?*" "Oh monstrous, monstrous! Such a man pollutes the air!" "Not *that,* Mistress? No, no! He couldn't have done *that,* and to a woman as—oh vile! oh most vile!"

At last she finished her tale and drew away; and she made Rhisiart think of a deadly snake uncoiling itself from a formidable beast it had poisoned.

"Here, you fellows! Come here a minute!" cried Fitz-Alan hoarsely; and all the archers crowded round him. "I'm going straight to Chirk now, my lads, and I want you to come with me. My horse is tired so I shan't leave you in the lurch. But *you* and *you*"—and he named the two most brutal-looking of the band—"stay behind and string up this unspeakable devil! Hang him to this very tree where he was going to burn the Friar; and when you've done it come straight after me! Nobody'll touch you if you don't touch them!" He paused, and once more fixing his eye—without seeing them—upon our two friends, "If only," he muttered, "that fool Grey hadn't put in his damned voice, and the King had left Percy and me to settle things. It makes me sick to see the King led astray as he is! I've told him from the beginning that what we want in all these Islands is simply a wise application of the Conqueror's Feudal System. Let 'em all do homage to the King—just as I do myself—and remain masters within their own provinces. This Glendourdy of yours—you call him a wizard—but I know a wizardry that would settle him and settle all his sons too, from Griffith to Meredith—simply the old-fashioned Feudal System properly applied, with our Norman Primogeniture, in place of this mad splitting-up of estates! But Grey of Ruthin's a fool. That's what *he* is, a damned fool, and, as Solomon says, 'The Fool will end by begging his bread'!"

Rhisiart found it impossible to lend more than half an ear to this political sermon preached to the air and the darkness through his non-existent form; but it struck his mind that the man's only excuse for his inhumanity would be if he really *were* enamoured of Lowri.

So indignant did he feel at the injustice of the whole thing that he couldn't resist a murmured protest.

"My Lord Earl, may I be allowed—as one who has studied law at the

University of Oxford—to inform the prisoner of the charges brought against him?"

"*Gorge de Dieu!* And who in the wide earth told *you* to lift up your voice? I don't know who your are, and I'm in Glendourdy's power here or I'd soon find out; but this you *shall* have, young malapert, you shall have the privilege of selling me your horse, to take this lady—" And he actually began fumbling beneath the pommel of his saddle to find Griffin's price.

But Mistress Lowri came close to him again and whispered something else. Rhisiart presumed she told him she was going back to the Constable of Dinas Brān, and he fancied she *may* have told him of his cousinship with Owen, for he let the gold-piece drop back into his wallet, gave her a stiff but courteous obeisance, and gathered up his reins.

"Is that your old confessor, Father Rheinalt, over there talking to the Friar?"

"Yes, my Lord. He's praying with him."

"Well! let him stop praying with him and come and pray with your Simon! He prayed too long with one person I know, once upon a time; till that person grew too heavy to go to confession. . . . Well, well, I mustn't tease you, my pretty; but I should have thought it would exactly suit your particular kind of humour to have your Rheinalt absolve your Simon. However! Do as you like."

He turned to the two archers. "Oh you've found a rope, have you? Very good! Now remember I shall ask you to tell me how Simon died. *Gorge de Dieu!* There goes the Abbot; and I *must* have a word with him. Tell all your Welsh friends, you lovely one, that I hanged my steward *to make them bread.* Au revoir!" And he rode off in pursuit of the monks of Caerleon.

"Gently, Mëaster! Coom, Mëaster!" cried one of the two archers, approaching Simon as if he were a tethered beast. He was a Wessex man, and Rhisiart, even at that horrible moment, couldn't help noticing how queer his English sounded. "Out o' the way wi'ee! Us must heave up rope to hang'ee, Mëaster, to thik wold tree!"

The wretched Steward struggled with difficulty to his feet and cast a confused look round him. Rhisiart fancied that there came a kind of comfort into his face when he saw that the Lollard was still there.

But the other archer—a great hulking South-Saxon from Lewes—began roughly and clumsily putting the rope about the man's throat.

"*Stop!* I won't stand by and see this iniquity done!" Rhisiart had no time on this occasion to get his crusader's sword into action, but he snatched his dagger out of his belt and in the darkness this looked dangerous enough.

The Sussex man drew back, but the Wessex man caught the boy, dagger and all, round the waist, and pinned both his arms against his sides.

At that point the Lollard sprang forward; and without drawing his sword delivered such a shrewd blow with his fist at the Sussex man's head that it sent him reeling.

"Cystennin! Rhydderch!" cried Lowri in a voice of hysterical fury. "Oh, and there's Lawnslot, too!" she added with hideous exultation. "Come lads, every one of ye! Help to swing him up, or I'll tell your master you failed me."

The three Welshmen came forward, and the noose was soon round the unhappy man's neck.

"Catch hold of the other one, lads, priest or no priest!" And the Lollard, whose religious exhortations had misled her as to his quality, was seized and secured in the same manner as Rhisiart.

"One minute!" she cried; and the two young men, struggling help-lessly against the powerful arms that held them, saw her approach the extemporized gibbet and begin whispering to the man and even caressing with her fingers the rope round his neck.

"Help! Help!" shouted Rhisiart, while Griffin to the mare's astonish-ment uttered a shrill whinny.

The hanging of the Hog of Chirk now seemed only to await the moment when the woman should choose to stand out of the way. Rhisiart peered desperately through the darkness to catch sight of Tegolin; but she had gone, and the Scab and his spearmen were gone, and monks and the market-people were all gone.

Save for a couple of repulsive-looking old women who had come like vultures to the scene, the mound was completely deserted. Nothing remained but the dung-cart, the faggots, the heap of long-bows and the dead tree converted into a gallows.

"One minute!" cried Lowri again; and this time she came so close to Master Simon that their figures, to Rhisiart's disturbed vision, mingled together. Her words seemed to burn the darkness into smouldering holes.

Rhisiart struggled desperately in the arms that held him. "It's murder! It's damnable murder!" he cried; and his heart felt as if it would burst under his ribs.

"Jesus forgive you! Jesus receive you!" prayed the Lollard hoarsely.

"Mine'll be the last face you'll see, Simon," she whispered. "The last voice you'll hear! Hell is deep, but you'll know I'm thinking of you. You'll know—"

"*Off with you, every one of you!*" It was as if his voice came out of the dark substance of the mound itself, but he must have come round it in the darkness. "Off with you!" he repeated, addressing the two bowmen, "and tell your Lord to hang his servants within his own walls. Tell him that my father—do you hear?—that *my father* makes himself responsible for this man. And now, Mistress," and he turned to the woman, "I hope you're satisfied. The man's half-dead with the fright you've given him. I don't really know"—this he said very much slower and emphatically, and Rhisiart was delighted to see the woman wince —"I don't really know what my father will decide about you." Then he turned to the Dinas Brān Welshmen. "Take your mistress back to the Constable," he said, "and tell him from Meredith ab Owen that he'd better hear Mass to-morrow *at Valle Crucis!* Don't forget, you three! Have you got that? Very good. Well, off with you, Mistress! My father will keep his eye on your girl and on her Friar. Remember me to the Constable. And if I were you, I'd keep to the direct highway!"

Rhisiart cursed the darkness that had fallen now, thickened by mists rising from the river; for he was obsessed by an almost sensual desire to *see her face in its defeat* and for her to *know* he was seeing it. But this unholy wish was totally denied him; for the lady said not a word to anyone, looked at nobody, gathered up the skirts of her green-embroidered gown, laid her hand on the arm of the tallest of her three Welsh servants, and hurried away in the direction taken by the monks.

Rhisiart and the Lollard were left alone with Master Simon and his rescuer. The first thing Meredith did was to sigh such a world-weary sigh that it came near to being a groan. Then he moved towards our friend and began caressing Griffin.

"We couldn't get our sword out in time, eh?" he murmured; and Rhisiart was so close to him that he caught upon that disillusioned young face one of the strangest smiles he had ever seen. It was a smile that flickered, wavered, faded and vanished, like a candle-flame falling for a moment on a ghostly portrait.

"I didn't like—I didn't dare—till I knew—" stammered our pilgrim in shame and embarrassment.

"Do you know *now?*" returned the other, while they heard the Lollard's voice muttering some religious exhortation as he bent over the prostrate Steward.

"I know nothing. I've seen too much to-day. But by degrees—do you think, Arglwydd"—he had the wit to use the Welsh word, though they both were speaking in English—"that your father could find some employment for me about his person? I know a little Latin and French and—and a good deal of law. And I'd like to be—I'd like to be *where you are*—and I'd like to serve—"

It may be seen from these impulsive words how much the events of that day had affected our traveller's feelings. In place of any "Princess Myfanwy" he was now compelled to link the mystical fortress of his desire with this Medusa-like mother of Tegolin; and in place of a rich, idle, selfish "Glendourdy" he now visualized as the background of all that was going on in these regions an unapproachable, mysterious figure whose power seemed palpable at every turn but whose personality remained evasive and obscure.

"He wouldn't like me to say too much now," returned the young man gently. "But I do think he might find a use for you. Anyway I know my mother would like to see you. So come to Glyndyfrdwy to-morrow—not *too* early—somewhere about four o'clock, let's say, if that'll suit you. Have you anywhere to sleep to-night? The Abbey guest-house will be full; and I wouldn't try the Tassel if I were you."

"I have a place," murmured Rhisiart, thankful enough that the darkness hid the way his cheeks burned. "But may I—" he paused while they both listened to the Lollard's murmurings over the man on the ground. "May I beg you"—and he lowered his voice to a whisper—"if you're really going to take this unfortunate man with you, to let my fellow-traveller, Master Brut, go too? *He* hasn't anywhere to sleep to-night, and his horse'll be a help to you in carrying this fellow."

"You know something else, it seems," returned the young chief, "beyond Latin and French! You know our Welsh tongue uncommonly well, and you speak it with the true Powys Fadog accent. Your teacher must have come from these parts. I'm going to sleep with my foster-parent to-night, who is a swine-herd half-way to Wyddgrug, and I'll leave our prisoner there till my father decides what's to be done with him. Your friend must please himself of course." He politely lowered his voice to a whisper. "Brut, did you say his name was? Why, that's as though we said 'Master Divination.' He acts like a priest but I can see he's a *gwr bonheddig,* and I expect—" He stopped suddenly, for he didn't miss the droop of Rhisiart's whole body and that it had become an effort to the boy the moment he leant against Griffin to keep his eyelids from closing.

"But you're dead-tired, lad! Up with you! I'll explain everything to your friend; and I'll let him finish his prayers. I'll tell him he can find you at Glyndyfrdwy. Here's a hand now. Up with you! That's the way! And listen, comrade"—Rhisiart bent low over Griffin's neck—"the next time you draw that sword of yours, it mayn't be to *separate* Welsh and English! God 'ild you."

Though the darkness grew perceptibly more dense as the old piebald cantered down the slope towards the river, carrying a rider whose eyelids soon ceased to droop as he rode, neither horse nor man made any question about the way.

Griffin must have tasted in advance the delicious refreshment, composed of all that the heart of an old horse could most desire, that the practical Tegolin had obtained for him, along with a heavenly bed of clean straw.

Not less sweet, indeed much sweeter, was the soft hay upon which the young man stretched his limbs in the farm's most retired cow-shed. By his side, under his own sheepskin—which indeed proved somewhat too hot for that June night—lay Tegolin in her white smock; while in another part of the shed the Friar slept his deep untroubled holy man's sleep, with his back against the back of a sleeping heifer.

Between himself and this girl—the first feminine being by whose side he had lain since his infancy—was nothing but her linen shift and his own woollen shirt; but they were both so tired out that though his left arm was beneath her head and his right above her breast, their clipping and kissing soon ended in a deep and almost simultaneous sleep.

A maid she lay down, and a maid she rose up; and neither of them flickered an eyelid when, in the first light of dawn, the Grey Friar stood over them before repeating, to the murmur of the river and the breathing of the cattle, his morning office.

All through that short summer darkness he too had slept an untroubled sleep; and when he awoke to whisper his psalms and to extinguish the smouldering wick in the lantern above his head, it seemed to his crazed wits as if the lost King whose return he confused with everything in life that *is* and yet is not, and with everything in death that is not, and yet that *is,* were present with them in that shed. He mingled King Richard with the sound of the river, with the scent of the hay, with the awakening of the swallows, with the cool dawn-airs that stole into their shelter like the forerunners of an exultant host, but above all with those youthful heads lying side by side! The Maid was his, and this young soldier of his King was the Maid's, and therefore *his* too; and the great John Baptist whose day was dawning was carrying them all three forward, forward where the river was flowing, forward where the mists were lifting, forward into a new Valle Crucis, a new Wales, where there were no burnings and no Bolingbrokes, no hearts that would not heal, no loves that could not be satisfied!

IV

HAND IN HAND

NEITHER BROTHER HUW nor Tegolin, when it came to the point, showed much desire to visit the monastery on a crowded feast-day, and since the lad himself was anxious to enjoy their society as long as possible, it was decided that they should all three seek, for the next night at any rate, the hospitality of his formidable kinsman at Glyndyfrdwy.

Tegolin, however, with a woman's feeling for what was meet and right on such a day, persuaded her two companions—for the half-witted Friar seemed as forgetful as Rhisiart about ordinary religious observances—to pause for early Mass at the little church of St. Collen, which lay directly in their path. They found only children and a few very aged men and women entering this small edifice; for it seemed as if the whole countryside was tricking itself out in gala attire to attend the High Mass at Valle Crucis.

There was an atmosphere of undisturbed peace brooding over the small churchyard as they led Griffin up the path to the door; and Tegolin was soon pretending to be gravely absorbed in helping Rhisiart to tether the old horse where it could best enjoy the uncut grass. The Hereford boy was in a state of exuberant high spirits, and he began at once, in his blundering youthful way, teasing her about the manner in which, with a view to baring her head without betraying her sex, she had squeezed her twisted braid of red hair under the collar of her tunic.

His infatuation grew moment by moment; but the thrill of being attracted to a feminine creature was so new to him that he had no idea how to steer his emotion into the channel where it would give him the greatest pleasure. And indeed, if the truth must be told, he had even less of an idea how to steer it so as to give the object of it the corresponding pleasure!

Thus there arose all manner of trifling but disconcerting awkward-nesses between the Friar's young companions. Such sensual feelings as the boy had kept showing themselves in clumsy, indirect ways. They were so fresh to his experience that he lacked the power of focussing them on the particular differences between a boy and a girl where they would be provocative of delight to both.

All he seemed able naturally and spontaneously to do was to tease her, and to tease her in that particular way that young girls especially dislike because it makes them feel as if they'd become children again.

But Rhisiart was no fool; and when he found that such things as making fun of her red hair and of her blunders when she tried to speak English only brought a flush to her cheeks and a quiver to her lips, while at the same time they produced a discord in his own feel-ings, he cast about in the depths of his consciousness for the cause of this atmospheric disturbance.

What troubled him was that there seemed such a queer gulf between the delicious thrill that *the idea of being in love* with a real, actual girl gave him as it diffused itself through everything, and these blundering attempts he kept making to establish a humorous brother-and-sister rapport between them.

Luckily for him, the romantic part of Tegolin's nature was so absorbed in the service of the Friar that she could afford to treat these boyish lapses—all except those that had to do with her braid and her broken English—with a detached maternal indulgence; and she had enough subtlety to surmise that it was because his sensual feelings were all disturbed and bewildered, and because he had not discovered his destined way of love, that he behaved as he did.

But it was all different from last night. Last night it had been so sweet and natural when they lay in each others' arms, overcome by exhaustion. What Tegolin didn't realize was that it was just this innocent sleeping together that had destroyed her strangeness to him without initiating him in the art of love. He wanted to assert himself with her but he didn't know how to do it.

He wanted to touch her, to ruffle her, to disturb her, just as a boy wants to do something—he knows not what—to a bird or a butterfly whose beauty troubles him.

All this ridiculous teasing sprang from the exciting trouble into which she threw him; but had it not been that so much of her nature was already absorbed in her devotion to the Friar, it is likely enough that the difference between what he had been last night and what he was now would have made her seriously unhappy.

Rhisiart indeed, though it would have given him small pleasure to know it, had been placed by fate in an especially favoured position for the enjoyment of Tegolin's identity just because he was *not* the object of her ideal romance; nor was he without some dim inkling of this when he began to notice certain arbitrary injustices and even cruelties into which her romantic love betrayed her where Brother Huw was concerned.

They had hardly got clear of the environs of the Tassel, and they took care to make a wide circuit to avoid meeting any of the Lord of Nannau's followers, when the Brother began to grow uneasy in his conscience about their decision to avoid Valle Crucis.

Rhisiart, who had at last got her to mount his old horse and was watching with intense delight the engaging curves of her limbs as her body clung in womanly fashion to Griffin's mottled back, was shocked when, instead of humouring the Friar by piling up every sort of reason against this visit, she insisted on dragging out of the poor wretch the tragic and touching weakness of the flesh which was the real secret cause, as she knew well, of his dislike of going near the place.

"Why on earth can't she," thought Rhisiart, "leave this human frailty in her hero alone? Why must she compel him to confess it and acknowledge it? How does she dare to risk arousing in him just the sort of righteous obstinacy that might well ruin us all?"

But now that she was off Griffin's back and all flushed and flurried about this business of going bare-headed into the church, what must Rhisiart do but, forgetting his recent resolution to stop these boyish impulses, begin teasing her again—this time about her page's dagger, an ornament which, according to what she evidently considered the latest fashion, though even in Hereford it had long been given up, she had ostentatiously suspended at the point where her tunic covered her hip. At this she came near to really losing her temper; and giving him a reproachful look she turned indignantly away.

At his wit's end to appease her—for he saw that this was the worst of his blunders—he began a confused apology, when she suddenly softened of her own accord and, touching his elbow, signed to him to note the conduct of their companion. She did this with a smile of such intimacy and an air that linked them so closely in tender amusement at Mad Huw's peculiarities that the boy was astonished.

Indeed he was so absorbed in this novel privilege of being allowed to be one with her in her protectiveness towards Mad Huw that he could only take in very cursorily what it was that she found so touching in the Friar's present proceedings. What she gave him was the look that one girl might give another in the presence of an eccentric man they were both in love with, and if our friend's response was half-hearted to this it was because he found bitterness in it as well as sweetness.

All that Mad Huw was doing, as far as Rhisiart could see, was interfering not very effectively between an aggressive little boy—hardly more than an infant—and a flock of geese.

It had evidently fallen to the child to look after these creatures in the absence of their proper guardian, who was no doubt at that moment putting on her gala-dress before the family mirror in view of the Feast of Saint John.

The child was a mere baby, but of extraordinary sturdiness and resolution. Nature had not only given him the legs of a giant but also the countenance of a dictator. But Nature had also bestowed on his enemies, the geese, the power of exciting awe; so that what Mad Huw had taken upon himself to meddle with was a war between two irrational thunder-storms, neither of which was able to use lightning.

The child was evidently swayed by the opposite emotions of aggression and panic; and so were the geese. And these emotions came and went in periodic alternation. The infant was armed with the lid of an iron pot and with the leg of a milking-stool. The geese had their voices and their elongated necks. The child stamped at the geese. The geese hissed at the child. Sometimes panic seized the one side and sometimes the other. When the signal "advance!" was sounded at what might be called "headquarters" in the child's head, he would strike the iron against the wood and rush to the attack; whereas when nature gave the signal "retreat," it was in the blind confusion of his flight that these objects jangled together.

"Retreat" had been the order of the day when Brother Huw inter-

vened; and the geese had followed in their thin line of battle so hard
on the track of the little boy that he was fain to cling to the Friar's
habit and hide his face behind it.

The Friar's countenance, as he faced these outstretched loud-screech-
ing necks, was like that of a boy of seven who is protecting a boy of
six. He made them debouch in the direction of the river; but they
didn't scatter, nor did they draw in their necks. Their instinct told
them that these substitutes for the goose-girl who was before her
mirror were of negligible authority.

"What's your name, little one?" asked the Friar gravely.

"Caswallon," the child replied without emerging from his refuge;
and it was impossible to tell at that moment whether it was by accident
or by intention that the spear and shield clashed together behind the
Brother's back.

"What are you doing, Caswallon?"

"Driving the Saxons!"

"Who is your general, Caswallon?"

"Me," said the child, peeping out at the screaming geese.

"Who is your king, Caswallon?"

"Me," confessed the infant, emerging into the open.

"Who is your abbot, Caswallon?"

"Me," admitted the little boy.

The Friar bent down. "Do you know who's coming back?" he
whispered.

But "advance" must have sounded just then so loudly in that crowded
tent of king, abbot and general that there was no time for other
thoughts. With a terrific beating of wood upon iron the geese were
now triumphantly driven, flapping and screaming, out of the church-
yard.

The combatants had hardly disappeared when the old parish-priest
emerged from a wooden hut near-by, a hut that looked as if Saint
Collen might well have built it with his own hands. He passed close
by our three friends on his way to the sanctuary, and glanced at them
in some surprise, giving them each a quick searching look; then
muttering a hasty blessing in reply to their salutation, he hurried into
the building.

They were all three a trifle upset as they followed him, for Rhisiart unthinkingly must needs tell Tegolin that a wisp of hair was still visible; and the Friar received a sharp word from the Maid because of the reluctance he showed to leave the free sunshine.

But when once the Mass began all these troubles ceased. Indeed our friend had never been moved so much by the magic of the supreme mystery of his faith as he was that Midsummer Day, kneeling there between the two wanderers. The sky above them indeed was but a neutral sky. It was neither over-clouded nor was it clear. But it was one of those days when a delicate film of faint mist, floating in diaphanous diffusion between earth and heaven, seems to bring these divided regions close together, while at the same time it endows them both with a curious element of unreality.

The voices of the parish-priest and his solitary server seemed to merge, as they intoned, into the quiet breath of the whole umbrageous valley, while the scent of the hayfields, which flowed in through the open door behind them, mingled as pleasantly with the smoke of the censer, as the diffused sunlight filtering down upon that small grey building through a motionless filigree of leafy twigs itself mingled with the pallid light of the altar candles.

Brother Huw had behaved reverently, but he had soon grown rather restless; and it was a relief to Rhisiart when Tegolin allowed them to rejoin their horse and pursue their way. The girl had possessed herself of several St.-John's-cakes and a pat of fresh butter at the farm; and as soon as they got well out of sight of the small wooden homesteads scattered about St. Collen's Church, they began to look round for some suitable spot where they might break their fast.

Rhisiart had had considerable difficulty in persuading the Friar's Maid to make use of Griffin. Indeed, most of the way from the Tassel-farm to Llan-Collen, they had all walked by the horse's side.

But the Mass had sobered them all, and as they moved slowly along, following the river up-stream, Tegolin sat silent and pensive on the horse's back. They found a spot at last exactly suited to their purpose, and letting Griffin wander as he pleased, they seated themselves on a dead ash-tree by the edge of a small brook. It was a spot eminently suited to all that Rhisiart was feeling. The little stream made a faint tinkling as it descended into the river. Its banks were covered with ferns and moss; and the St.-John's-cakes and the fresh butter tasted more delicious than any repast he could remember.

"Have you ever seen my cousin, the Lord of Glyndyfrdwy?" he enquired of Tegolin. "I've always thought of him as a time-serving grey-beard, who spends his days tagging bardic rhymes, like that chattering Derfel-idiot, not as a person who'd take any real risk for Wales and her people."

Tegolin smiled. "You've got him wrong, Gwion Bach; though I've no doubt that's exactly what he intends you English should think of him. No, I've never seen him. Have *you* ever seen him, Brother Huw?"

"Seen whom, my daughter?"

"Owen Glyn Dŵr."

The Friar nodded. "I saw him at Flint when the King was taken. The King looked at him. I can see his eyes now, my daughter. And I saw the look Glyn Dŵr gave him in return. It was a strange look. It wasn't the look of a Judas; and yet it wasn't a pitying look. But I think the King got comfort from it." The Friar paused and muttered something to himself. Then he went on. "I saw him turn and follow him with his eyes as he rode away. And I saw the King fall into a muse, so that he seemed scarcely to notice the evil tongues about him. The man must have said something with that look. But it was a strange look."

"What was it like, Brother Huw?"

The Friar took a sip from the little silver cup the girl passed to him, and handed it on to Rhisiart.

"I've often asked myself that very question, child," he murmured, letting his own gaze wander up the course of the little stream, "and I've told myself sometimes that it was the sort of look that a traveller in Jerusalem might have given *Him* when they were leading Him to Golgotha. A traveller—a traveller—"

Rhisiart and the girl exchanged glances.

"A traveller," repeated the Friar.

"Did he seem—I mean did he seem to you—*old?*" asked Rhisiart eagerly. "Was his hair grey when you saw him?"

The Friar's sensitive countenance took on such a stricken expression that the boy added hurriedly, "I know you can't catch a very good likeness from a distance—so don't trouble yourself. I expect you can't bear to think of what happened then. It was only that I wanted—to find out something—about my kinsman—before the moment of meeting him. He seems to be extremely difficult to meet. The Scab told me he was much more genial and much easier to get on with before they crowned the new King."

Tegolin was balancing herself now on a portion of the fallen tree a little higher than her companions. She was unceremoniously licking the butter from her fingers and in the process making a little whistling sound.

Rhisiart, who after the experience of the last twelve hours felt that feminine psychology held few secrets for him, said to himself, "She's thinking how nice it is to be a beautiful girl and to be with two men on Saint John's Day."

But Tegolin soon sacrificed these agreeable thoughts to a confession of curiosity; and she begged Rhisiart to tell them about his friend the Lollard.

At the word "Lollard" the large dark eyes of the Friar narrowed ominously, and a cold hostile film came over them. As Rhisiart watched him he realized that the enlightenment he had received about women hadn't extended to madmen. To this heroic fanatic—himself in mortal terror of all ecclesiastical restraint—the word "Lollard" was like the word "sodomy."

"What on earth," thought our philosophical youth, "is going on now in this fellow's brain?" And then as he tried to recall what his own vague feeling had been about Lollards before he met Master Brut, he couldn't conceal from himself that obscene images of ravished nuns and violated virgins, of monstrous outrages upon consecrated wafers, of goats dressed up as apostles and the rumps of apes substituted for holy relics had inevitably flitted across his mind.

But Tegolin—and this only confirmed certain conclusions he had come to about his mother and Modry—seemed able to speak of Lollard quite easily without a thought of bestiality or the Black Mass. Quite calmly she now proceeded to enlarge upon her question, though our friend was convinced she saw—as how could she not?—that forbidding expression on her hero's face.

"Didn't you *like* him, Gwion Bach? You told me he was a Lollard,

and then you stopped! I thought he had a *lovely* face as he talked to
the Hog; and how straight he sat on that beautiful-coloured horse!"

It was our friend's turn now to look less than noble. "Have you
ever confessed a Lollard, Brother?" he enquired.

The monk shook his head. "But our Prior," he remarked after a
pause, while his lustrous eyes transformed themselves into the glazed
windows of a condemned cell, "our Prior told one of the lay-brothers
that he once had to fast for three days after hearing a Lollard's confession—just to conquer the evil thoughts it aroused in him."

"Have you ever seen a Lollard burnt, Brother?" asked Rhisiart
viciously.

But Tegolin intervened at this with a quick girlish gesture. *"Don't,*
Gwion Bach! No, Brother Huw, I won't let you tell him. You ought
to be ashamed of feeling like that, and you so nearly burnt yourself!
Blessed Virgin! Can't you leave these wickednesses to King Harry?"

A curious puzzled look came into the Grey Friar's face, and he
fixed his eyes on a great clump of pink campions, near which Griffin
was searching for some more dainty growth. That he should be caught
sharing any opinion with Richard's enemy was appalling to him; but
his gorge rose in equal disgust at the abominations he had come to
link with the word "Lollardry."

Tegolin snatched off her page's cap, and began leisurely unplaiting
her red braid. But suddenly a troubled look came into her face, and
her eyes darkened. She glanced nervously at Rhisiart and asked him
whether the Bard of Ffinnant was also on his way to Glyn Dŵr's
place.

"God! I hope not!" laughed the boy. "But is he really a Bard? Is
he really the son of a nun? He's a comical kind of Merlin if he is!"

His words had a surprising effect upon the girl. She jumped down
from her perch, her loosened hair flowing over her shoulders, and
stood erect in front of him, her hands behind her head. Her position
threw her youthful breasts into prominence under her boy's tunic
and added height and dignity to her figure, but her eyes were flashing.

"Why did you say that?" she asked in a low intense voice. But before
Rhisiart could reply the Friar hurriedly intervened.

"Don't'ee mind him, child, don't'ee mind him! He doesn't know
what he says, He speaks like a Saxon."

But the girl was seriously upset. In his bewilderment and remorse as he stared with open mouth at her white face and mass of blood-coloured hair she made him think of a Salome in a church-window.

"I only said," he stammered, "that if the Scab *was* the son of a nun he wasn't much like Merlin."

His words brought Mad Huw to his feet, and both the Maid and the Friar stood looking down at him as if the ground had suddenly opened between him and them.

Rhisiart began to feel really troubled. What on earth had·upset them so? "But he's such a conceited fool," he stammered uneasily, making a sorry pretence at a laugh. What the devil was the matter now? Into what new blunder had he fallen?

"There are three names, my son," said the Friar sternly—and Rhisiart, even· in the midst of his confusion, noted with interest that while the man spoke he kept his expressive eyes tight shut, a proceeding which gave to his hollow cheeks and the quiet outlines of his face the look of an image carved on a tomb—"there are three names which we of North Wales never allow ourselves to utter lightly: the name of Our Lady, the name of Derfel, and the name of—"

"Hush, Brother!" interrupted Tegolin, actually clapping her fingers in her nervous excitement over the man's mouth. "Don't say any more to him! I should have thought a gentleman like him would show better taste! But it's ignorance, of course. You have to be born and bred a Welshman to understand these things, and perhaps you don't know, though someone *must* have told you by now, that I'm myself the unlawful—there's no—no! there's *no* reason why I shouldn't tell him, Brother!—the unlawful child of that Father you saw yesterday—the one who covered his head when David the Squint put his arms round Mother—the one Simon was so afraid of! So you see when you poked fun at Yr Crach just now for having a nun for his mother it made me feel—it gave the same shock—as if you were teasing me about Father Rheinalt."

She took a long breath, dropped her hands, and stared frowningly, just as the Friar had done a little while ago, at the wealth of pink campions beside which Griffin was feeding.

But the Friar came up close to her and, drawing her head towards him so that all its torrent of hair fell over his sleeve, began whispering in her ear.

Rhisiart could see her face as she listened, and he was struck by its abandonment against Mad Huw's shoulder and by the way her fingers plucked at the cord round his waist. She made a gesture of assent at last, and then with a gentler look than she had given our friend for some while, she came, and the monk came with her, a step or two nearer. They both made this step—or so the boy in his bewilderment fancied—as if he'd been something under an evil spell.

"Gwion Bach," she said slowly and earnestly, "the Brother thinks, and I think too, that you ought to know before you see your cousin that we're on the verge of great events. Our Lord Owen has just called all the bards and all the leading men round here to come to his house at Glyndyfrdwy for some secret purpose. Brother Huw believes—and I've never known him wrong in things like this—that Owen intends to defy this cruel King, to throw off—what do you call it in English?— his *allegiance,* and raise the flag of— No, stop, Gwion Bach!"—these words were in answer to the excited cry with which Rhisiart leapt to his feet—"for there's more to—"

She paused, bent her head, and began toying uneasily with the embroidery sheath of her page's dagger. "The truth is the Brother doesn't like all he's heard about what your cousin's doing. The Brother hoped he would tell them of King Richard's return and gather the *cantrefs* together in *his* name. Instead of this he's using these Derfel prophets to stir up the people. You English don't understand these things; but in these parts Derfel's held to be more than a saint. Many people think he wasn't a saint at all, but something else— something beyond what is—"

She dropped her dagger and let it swing against her side again. Then she moved still nearer to him, laying her hand on his belt. "We girls," she whispered, "girls like me at any rate, are always being warned by the priests to have nothing to do with these Derfel men. They tell us"—she lowered her voice to a whisper—"that there have been cases when—when children have been born—whose mothers— girls like me—have cried out in their pains—that it was Derfel's! So now you see, Gwion Bach"—and she raised her voice again and glanced proudly at the Friar with the air of a pupil who has said her lesson correctly—"why we wish our Lord Owen would put more trust in the Friars, who are all friends of King Richard, than in heathen Bards like the Scab. Of course I know the way the Scab boasts, and what a fool he is, and what a drunkard and coward he is, and all the rest—but you know, Gwion Bach"—here her voice became almost inaudible—"very cunning and wicked people can wear a mask like that, and it isn't only Brother Huw who's told me of girls taken by Derfel. You won't find a maid in all Edeyrnion who doesn't beg her lover to marry her quick, and all for fear of Derfel. It's maids in love they say he visits, not the others. He always knows when a girl's in love because his Horse begins neighing when he rides round the house. It's when the wind's in the west and rain's coming that he rides; and when a girl hears Derfel's Horse she knows she's found out."

Rhisiart's countenance, while he was listening to these surprising matters, was a picture, but Brother Huw, when his King was in his thoughts, became oblivious to what went on in the minds of others, while Griffin, who might have been disturbed if his head had been directed towards his young master, had wandered off between the pink campions and the bracken.

Our friend had attended lectures on Aristotle at Oxford, and had even been led, by one of the magnates at his own Exeter College, who was of a bold and sceptical turn of mind, to an investigation of the arguments against occult superstitions in Cicero's *De Divinatione*. And so, while his senses were stirred to their depths by the girl's words and the nearness of her soft body to his own, and while only the Friar's presence prevented him from hugging her to his heart and swearing that he would guard her from a thousand Scabs and a thousand Derfels, he felt it was only just to himself and to his University to bring the light of a little modern rationalism to bear on this ticklish subject.

"I have given much time," he began gravely, "to the study of Incubi and Succubi; and though many authorities hold the view that they are descendants of Lilith, the writers most to be trusted argue with convincing force that they are a creation *sui generis* and are only to be feared when—"

Though these bold words brought Mad Huw several steps nearer to Tegolin's side, and caused a shiver to pass through his frame and his beautiful wild-deer eyes to peer nervously among the thickets around them, Rhisiart felt that it would be childish not to put at his friends' disposal the results of his scientific research. "Only to be feared," he went on in a high-pitched rapid tone, for he was fearful lest his mind should suddenly become a complete blank, "when the normal animal spirits have been debilitated. Master Morris Stove— a learned Welshman with whom I lodged—told me he had studied the works of eleven Doctors of Divinity on this point and not one of them but demanded in such cases the word of more witnesses than the victim's; that is to say, of the woman visited by the Incubus or of the man visited by the Succubus. Master Morris Stove assured me, as the result of his studies, that if the girl visited by the Incubus could prove that it was impossible at the time referred to and according to the reasonable sequences and progressions of nature, for any masculine being other than a supernatural one to have had access to—"

But his discourse was interrupted, not by the Friar, for he was too agitated to speak, but by the approach of Griffin, who with the armour and the sword jangling on his back came hurriedly trotting up and incontinently thrust his heavily-breathing nose into his master's bosom.

To the unphilosophical mind of Tegolin there was something comical about this interruption of what promised to be a topic of more legality than liveliness; and she gave vent to a little laugh. Our friend tried not to feel hurt by this, and all would have been well if the Friar, thrust unceremoniously backward by the horse's bony flanks, hadn't nearly fallen.

Now Mad Huw had been compelled ever since. he escaped from the hands of the Hog of Chirk to struggle with the demon of jealousy. With the help of his Guardian Angel, for we may believe that to madmen as well as to children are such special protectors granted, he had until now restrained his feelings.

But although as a saint it had been possible to repeat his psalms while the outward form of Tegolin lay by his rival's side, it was as a man impossible to bear a jostling from the rump of this rival's horse. Giving way therefore to his long-suppressed feelings, when the mottled rear of this young rationalist's steed thrust itself between him and his Maid, he snatched at the nearest weapon that presented itself to his hand, which was nothing less than the great sheathed sword lying across the offending back, and with the heavy handle of the old weapon struck the animal several violent and vicious blows.

A dangerous flash shot for a second out of Rhisiart's eyes; but Griffin only swished his tail and blinked, while Tegolin rushing to the Friar's side pulled him quickly away.

"They didn't mean it!" she cried in her penetrating voice. "They didn't mean it!" and many a time long afterwards Rhisiart remembered those words. They seemed to him like an appeal from the heart of the whole round earth against the blind folly of men's childish quarrels.

What exactly Tegolin had implied in them the lad never knew. Did they include all three of the girl's masculine companions or only himself and the horse? At any rate he felt ashamed of his momentary fury and thanked Heaven it had done no harm. Removing his cap he advanced humbly to the offended man and began with a charming earnestness making excuses for Griffin's clumsy movement. "In fact, he thought I was reciting a lesson," he concluded, "and perhaps," and this he added with a smile that would have disarmed a harder heart than the Friar's, "perhaps I *was!* For indeed this question of children born without human fathers is one about which Master Morris Stove and I have had long disputations. Master Stove made it the subject of one of his official theses when he was studying for his Doctor's—"

"Hush!" interrupted Tegolin, pushing back her hair and listening intently. "I thought I heard something."

It appeared that Griffin heard something too, for he swung round and raised his head. They all instinctively moved nearer to each other and then stood transfixed, staring nervously down the path up which they had come. Presently Rhisiart, noting his horse's quivering nostrils and erect ears, began making the warlike preparations, such as loosening his great sword in its sheath and adjusting more conveniently the dagger in his belt, that a lad brought up as he had been upon tales of less civilized epochs would naturally make when he found himself the sole protector of a woman and a priest.

"They're not riders, whoever they are!" whispered Tegolin at last, "and I don't think they're armed either. Listen! Do you hear?"—and she drew a deep sigh of relief—"I'm sure they're bare-footed!"

They all listened; and even to Rhisiart's city-bred ears it seemed as if the low murmur of the human voices that he now could hear approaching were unaccompanied by any footfalls at all! It seemed to him as if they were being approached by the ghosts of voices travelling along a familiar path.

"They're only herdsmen from the mountains," whispered the girl, "coming back from Saint John's Mass."

But Mad Huw shook his head, or rather, to be exact, he nodded his head like a person who congratulates himself upon his own secret perspicuity. "Those men are religious men," he said. "Those tones are the tones of religious men debating a fine point of doctrine."

"Impossible!" replied the girl. "Your ears mislead you, Brother. No religious men could possibly be walking away from Valle Crucis at *this* hour. No, no! Don't be so absurd, Brother Huw. You know yourself it *can't* be what you say. Those are neat-herds or swine-herds coming back from Mass."

A flickering smile crossed the Friar's face at this positive declaration from his young disciple. But as the murmur of voices drew nearer he began to show signs of alarm.

"Don't give me up to them, young gentleman!" he whispered anxiously. "I'm sorry I hit your horse. They want to shut me up in Valle Crucis. That's what they've come for—to shut me up!" He paused with his hand on Rhisiart's belt, while his great, beautiful hunted-deer's eyes fixed themselves beseechingly on the lad's face.

"Of course he won't give you up!" cried Tegolin. "Not one of them shall touch you. Gwion Bach! let him get up on Griffin! *That'll* give him faith in you—more than anything else."

Our friend obeyed her without hesitation; and bending his knee to serve as a stirrup-stone he helped the Friar, who had never mounted a horse in his life, to seat himself somehow on Griffin's broad back.

The old piebald turned his head with a peculiarly human gesture, as if to investigate the temper of this new burden; but he was evidently satisfied by what he saw and made up his mind to forget those unfortunate blows.

Thus, with the Friar in the saddle, Tegolin holding the bridle, and Rhisiart with a shining dagger-blade clutched in his hand, our three friends and their sagacious companion awaited the arrival of the strangers. Yes, Mad Huw was right. It was unmistakeably the figures of two Cistercians that were now advancing towards them.

Their own appearance on the summit of that small eminence was evidently no surprise to the two monks. Either they had heard of their movements as they came through Llan-Collen, or they had been to the Tassel-farm to make enquiries. All they did as they came forward was merely to cease their animated discussion, exchange a quick word or two, and accelerate their pace.

"It's Father Rheinalt!" cried Tegolin in high excitement, and without a thought of the others she ran eagerly down the slope to meet the two monks.

Rhisiart hurriedly replaced his dagger in his belt, and rather shame-facedly began concealing his big sword under the edge of the sheep-skin.

"Don't let them—" whispered Huw in his ear, and then, with an evident moral effort, the poor madman straightened himself on the back of the piebald; and though Rhisiart could feel he was trembling —a weakness that all Simon's piled-up faggots had been unable to produce—he began proclaiming to the new-comers, just as if they had been a procession instead of a couple of pedestrians, that King Richard was still alive.

So loud and resonant was this challenge that Rhisiart, though he was all ears to catch what his red-haired Maid was saying to the man she had admitted to be her earthly parent, couldn't overhear a syllable of their dialogue. He did notice, however, that while the girl knelt to receive the man's blessing the other monk—out of delicacy perhaps— moved aside and began absorbing himself, or pretending to absorb himself, in the examination of some wayside plant.

Tegolin's father seemed so stirred by the girl's pleasure in seeing him, and so moved by her tenderness, that he paid not the smallest heed to the familiar cry, "Richard, our sweet sacrifice! Richard, the chosen of God!"

But the other monk, whose appearance, though our friend only gave it a glance, was indeed sufficiently striking, did make a curious little gesture of assent, or at least of sympathy, raising for a second his great shaven poll and making a gentle, half-acquiescent, half-deprecatory movement with one of his plump hands.

Having been brought up by his mother to behave with courtesy to all ecclesiastics, Rhisiart made an effort to lead Griffin down the slope, so as to meet the Cistercians. But after each of his official pronouncements about the late King Mad Huw clutched at the boy, imploring him pitifully not to give him up. Then, as if not content with these appeals, he straightened himself in the saddle and thrust his feet, and the stirrups along with them, as far forward as he could, while he made desperate pulls and tags, sometimes at the reins, sometimes at anything he could lay hold of on the horse's back. These frantic movements, which resembled those of an obstinate and sulky child, struck Rhisiart as so pitiful that he threw politeness to the winds and remained where he was. He was afraid that if he left the Friar for a moment the fellow would slip off the horse and in his wild fear of losing his liberty make a bolt up the mountain; and so, though it hurt his sense of proper behaviour and even made him feel a fool, standing there like a sentry guarding a prisoner, he patted Griffin's neck and tried to recall his feelings when he had first listened to this man uttering his mad cries.

But Father Rheinalt and his daughter had now overtaken the other monk, and in a few seconds they were all standing together, with Griffin in the centre, asking questions, exchanging news, and discussing that mysterious summons to Glyndyfrdwy.

It soon became clear that the Friar was more afraid of Father Rheinalt than he was of the other Father, and, to confess the truth, our friend shared this feeling.

"It's all getting beyond me," he thought, as he watched that white face in its blood-coloured frame turning from her begetter to this madman she idealized. He noticed how whenever she spoke to the man on the horse she kept her fingers in contact with the monk, either upon his shoulder, or his wrist, or upon some fold in his raiment. Was it before he became a monk that this man begot Tegolin? And how with such a past—for he could never have been married to Tegolin's mother—could he have risen to the high honour of being sent to represent their foundation at Glendourdy's conclave?

The two had no physical resemblance that he could see. The monk was as swarthy as a Moor. Rhisiart had never seen such black hair or such dark flashing eyes. One thing was quite clear: the man was a volcano of smouldering and tragic passion. His burning eyes seemed to drink up Tegolin, as if she had been a water-spring in a boundless desert.

No wonder Mad Huw was afraid of him! How could a father with such a passionate feeling for his child let her wander about like this with a vagabond hedge-preacher?

"I suppose," the boy thought to himself, "it's what old Stove at Oxford used to call a case of mass-obsession. All the country holds Mad Huw for a saint and her for an innocent; and this dark monk— God comfort his soul!—gains glory with the other Fathers, if not with the Abbot, by being known as her begetter."

But the lad sighed as he looked at the three of them. What place could he hope to have in the heart of such a girl? Oh, how deep he had got landed in the drama of life! He could well remember an occasion when, on his way to his elegant school under the newly decorative wing of the big church, he had cried aloud for something *real* in life, cursing the monotony of the conventional pageants and gaudy processions of which his mother was so fond, with the same fashionable colours always repeating themselves and the same ever-lasting flags and banners! He could remember catching sight of an old-fashioned, brown-robed begging friar under a heavy Norman arch amid the flamboyant modern buildings and thinking how much and more simple, more honest, more close to Nature life must have been in the old days.

"Oh life, life, bring me something real!" he had cried out on that occasion; and *now,* here he was, actually in love with a vagabond girl whose mother was the mistress of the Constable of Dinas Brān and her father a Valle Crucis monk! Here he was, drawing nearer and nearer every moment to the presence of this mysterious kinsman, whose character—even more than the problem of Incubi and Succubi —had been the subject of interminable discussions with his Oxford friend.

Rhisiart roused himself from his reverie to find that Father Rheinalt and Tegolin between them, by the simple process of asking him to tell them the whole story of his encounter with the late King, had already succeeded in allaying Mad Huw's fears. With our friend's help they now persuaded him to descend from Griffin's back; while Father Rheinalt explained that it was due to the powerful intercession with their Prior of Father Pascentius—here the other Cistercian made a smiling bow—that at the close of High Mass he had been allowed, on condition that Father Pascentius accompanied him, to obey an urgent summons he had received from the Lord of Glyndyfrdwy.

The man told them all this in abrupt short sentences. It was evidently a nervous trouble to him to use words at all. He was like one who has been rendered hoarse from solitary confinement. "Father Pascentius is a great authority on Saint Thomas," he finally blurted out; a statement that was received by this authority with what Rhisiart soon found to be his most characteristic gesture—an expressive wave of his heavy hands which seemed to wipe out from the scroll of destiny every certainty that man could desire and every assurance that prophetic foresight could reveal.

Mad Huw opened his great beautiful eyes to their fullest extent and gazed upon this marvel of erudition with renewed comfort. He had, it appeared, in his experience at Llanfaes, found that the learned among the Brothers were kinder to mental eccentricities than the more wordly and bustling.

As for Rhisiart he gazed upon Father Pascentius with awe. He had learned at Oxford to respect theological learning beyond everything else except proficiency in civil law. The great metaphysician, however, was now discoursing to Tegolin about the flower he had seen; and it was evidently a more stimulating experience to him to talk to a girl about the nature and properties of plants than to his usual pupils about the mystery of the Trinity.

Father Rheinalt meanwhile was trying to discover from Mad Huw how far the Franciscans of Llanfaes were actually prepared to go in their opposition to the usurping monarch. Thus the field was clear for our young friend, as he mechanically plucked the grass at his feet and offered it to Griffin, to take a good look at the commentator upon Saint Thomas.

Rhisiart's own teachers in the fashionable monastic-school at Hereford had been inclined to mock at the Cistercians as an unpolished and rustic Order, as negligent of scholarship as they were averse to the enterprise of great cities, and he had suffered so much from those modish and foppish people, cringingly obsequious to their wordly rulers, that it filled him with malicious joy to contemplate this great imposing theologian whose presence, before he spoke a word, would have made those sychophantic Hereford priests look like sleek little mice.

But all the same Father Pascentius was an enigma to our traveller. He had an enormously fat body, unwieldy and awkward, huge gross hands, unnaturally large feet, while his great tonsured head was remarkable for nothing but the gleam of his eyes. He might have been compared to a clumsy trireme carrying at its bows two burning lanterns.

But what puzzled our friend about the man as he watched him talking to Tegolin—and at one point he saw him take a wisp of her hair in his coarse fingers—was the feeling of distaste his eyes excited. Rhisiart didn't feel in the faintest degree afraid of him, nor apparently did Tegolin or Mad Huw. But he certainly had insatiable eyes. They were as radiant as small globes of transparent jet, in the heart of which Nature had placed inextinguishable flames.

Rhisiart's knowledge of human character had hardly less than trebled itself in the last four-and-twenty hours, not to speak of the insight he had won into the darker aspects of his own nature, but Father Pascentius was too much for him! Those little insatiable eyes seemed like astronomical spheroids that possessed devouring intensities and absorbing interests of their own, completely unconnected with the corporal frame of the man and indeed only remotely connected with the undistinguished countenance they transfigured. Other human eyes, especially with persons of character, tend to resemble deep holes descending into subterranean worlds; but though the eyes of Father Pascentius were far too intense to be called shallow, they didn't seem to lead into his personality. They were things in themselves. They were like that solitary eye of the daughters of Phorkys that could be transferred from one Phorkyad to another.

Nor, our friend decided, could the eyes of Father Pascentius be said to express either good or evil. He couldn't imagine himself demanding tenderness from them; and yet he could very well imagine himself appealing to them for help, as he might appeal to a philosopher's stone or to an inanimate magic crystal. They certainly were the most intelligent eyes he had ever seen. Immortal intelligence shone out of them! They were *undying eyes*. After a thousand years they would be still shining in Father Pascentius's sarcophagus amid the ashes and the dust; but they would be no more human then than they were now!

Rhisiart began at first by feeling uncomfortable when he saw these singular luminaries fixed upon Tegolin's loosened hair, for it seemed to him that the intellectual voracity in them transformed itself then into another sort of voracity. But by degrees this look the man was fixing on Tegolin became the lad's own look! There was nothing that it communicated comparable to the dark emotion he had felt when he thought of the arrow in the girl's shoulder; but it *was* an exultation of the senses; and it struck him as amazing that he could feel like that under the influence of another person, especially when his own feelings when she lay in his arms had been so very different. His cheeks grew hot—lightly as the man did it and lightly as the girl took it—when the theologian toyed with that wisp of blood-red hair.

A fierce liberation of free desire such as he had never known before rushed through his nerves. And the strange thing was that this feeling didn't bring with it that sense of remorse which had seized him after conjuring up that image of the arrow. It seemed to carry with it its own justification and an immense sense of freedom, springing from the release within him of an interior urge that gave him a new and reckless strength.

And in the rush of this strength he suddenly felt a rebellious hostility not only to that smouldering passion of Father Rheinalt but even to the pathos of Mad Huw. It was against both the tragic possessiveness of the father and the clinging helplessness of the Friar that this new feeling rose; and it seemed to him as though those undying Phorkyad eyes in that undistinguished head were liberating both himself and Tegolin from some enslaving fatality.

And mixed with all this, as he kept furtively glancing at that negligible mask with those burning eye-slits, was the curious feeling that, without a word addressed to him since their original greeting, Father Pascentius was not only giving him the courage to be himself, but revealing to him a self that it would certainly need some courage to be!

Yes, the wretched modelling of the man's shapeless features gave our friend the sense of surreptitiously consulting some inanimate wooden idol, whose wonder-working eyes—brought from some far-off prehistoric shrine—possessed an older and more formidable authority than the image into whose sockets they had been irrelevantly thrust.

It was Father Rheinalt who finally gave the signal that they should move on. It was clearly a passionate excitement to him to be taking his daughter for her first visit to Owen, and the girl's nervousness made him unusually loquacious. He was the only one of the party who had been to Glyndyfrdwy before, and he explained that they should aim at making their appearance an hour or two before the chief meal of the day, which took place, he told them, soon after four o'clock.

"Owen is peculiar in certain things," he said. "He likes to keep up the old customs; and though our young friend here"—and he gave a friendly nod towards Rhisiart—"must expect neither the grandeur of a castle nor the ceremony of a court, he will, I think, be impressed by what—"

"But, Father!" interrupted Tegolin. "You don't mean that Gwion— I mean that Master Rhisiart—will be asked to sit at the high table with—"

The monk's swarthy face relaxed in the first smile that our friend had seen upon it that day. "My good child!" he protested. "We're in Edeyrnion, aren't we, where you and I were born, and where Father Pascentius was born? Where have you and Brother been in your travels that you've forgotten how things are done at home? We shall all, of course, every one of us, sit at the high table; and if we had servants— which, being what we are we haven't—you'd see *them* being well-feasted not so far away! Yes, and you too, my good friend"—and he patted Griffin's neck—"will have *your* entertainment within a bow-shot of where we're all sitting. Owen's own horses will be further off; but the house-stable is close by, and he keeps it free for his guests' beasts."

"But Father," the girl murmured, and our friend noticed that she instinctively began braiding her long hair, "I'm not dressed for— There'll be the Arglwyddes and the young ladies—oh, I should die with shame to be seen among them like this. You don't understand, Father! When we were in Mona—"

"Hush, silly child!" said the monk sternly. "You've made your bed and must e'en lie in't. All Gwynedd, all Powys, know our Friar and our Maid. The Arglwyddes is a sensible woman. Does she think a girl can do what you do, and go where you go, and be the plague to Hal Bolingbroke that you are, and be dressed up like a court-lady? Besides, if it shames you to sit at meat with Owen's people in your tunic and hose, you can get tricked out to your heart's content in their women's chambers. The Arglwyddes has better serving-maids at Glyndyfrdwy, and bigger robing-rooms, I warrant, than any you'd find at Chirk or Ruthin or Chester! You speak like a gipsy-wench, child—not like the Maid of Edeyrnion that all Wales wots of!"

Tegolin bit her lip and hurriedly finished braiding her hair; but Rhisiart could see she was by no means re-assured.

He himself began wondering with a good deal of nervous anxiety when and how he would be able to snatch an opportunity to put on some of the fine things he'd got concealed in his sheepskin bundle. Until Tegolin expressed her fears this disconcerting aspect of the matter had never occurred to him; and now as he helped the girl to mount Griffin, and persuaded the Friar to add his small bundle to the horse's burden, it flashed through his mind how calmly he had assumed that his attendance upon this famous Maid of Edeyrnion and her notorious friend would be accepted by everybody in the same light as it appeared to himself!

And how *did* it appear to himself? How far was his own heart irrevocably committed? And what would happen when the Maid and the Friar set out on their travels again? Was he intending to accompany them, mounted on Griffin, wherever they went, with his crusader's sword at their disposal?

"What's the matter with you, daughter?" enquired Father Rheinalt after the four men had walked some distance in silence by Griffin's side. "You haven't spoken a single word since I told you about the high table at Glyndyfrdwy! Are you *still* fretting over your clothes? I tell you it's the fashion now among noble ladies to dress as you're dressed when they travel. And when they're hungry and thirsty—you should see them at our refectory!—they don't mind *us* seeing them like that.

Why should you be more particular about the Arglwyddes of Glyndyfrdwy than about the Abbot of Valle Crucis?"

"It's quite different, Father!" the girl retorted. "But what's the use of arguing? You could *never* understand! Master Rhisiart knows what I feel."

Never had there fallen from feminine lips a more ill-advised retort than this. The monk turned upon Rhisiart with a smouldering flash of instinctive hostility.

"I've no doubt," he remarked sarcastically, "that this young gentleman has seen a great deal more of the world than I have. It is true I've only lived very briefly in Rome and Paris and Padua and Verona. It is true I wasn't lucky enough to see Constantinople when I was in the land of our Redeemer. It is true I never visited Toledo when I was in the household of Don Alvares in Salamanca. But I've seen what I've seen; and I tell you this, you proud wench—and you can pout as you like! When at our Prior's advice I didn't interfere with you following the Brother across the country—no! excuse me, Father Pascentius, I *must* speak to her now or forever hold my peace!—it was because I knew what honour it would bring to Edeyrnion. And you've done nobly, Daughter, and all Edeyrnion is proud of you! I'm right, aren't I, Father Pascentius? My little girl's a famous figure in North Wales. Isn't that so?"

Father Pascentius made his characteristic gesture; and with a wave of his plump hand reduced to metaphysical equality all feminine achievements.

Then he turned quickly to Rhisiart who was looking at Father Rheinalt with a defiant and threatening stare.

"He's never been to Oxford anyway," he remarked, "nor have I! And I doubt if he's ever—in all his travels—seen a city as sophisticated as Hereford. You must remember, Father," and he turned to his fellow-monk, "that young people are much more sensitive about their appearance than we old recluses. You who've seen the great world in Paris and Rome and Padua and Verona, and have been in what's-his-name's household in Salamanca, should know young people better than to speak to them like that! Our daughter here doesn't follow the Brother to win glory for Edeyrnion, or even for Wales. She follows him because he needs her and because she believes in him. I'm afraid some of our clever politicians"—he lowered his voice so that Mad Huw couldn't hear him—"have been using both the Maid and the Friar as pawns against Hal Bolingbroke. But we'll see what Owen ap Griffith says. It *may* be—" Here he murmured something into the monk's ear, and drew him forward a little, keeping a heavy hand on his shoulder.

Mad Huw had picked up a stick and was amusing himself with it in the most youthful manner. He kept digging it into the ground and leaning his weight on it and making grotesque little jumps.

Tegolin signed to our friend to come to Griffin's head. "I ought to tell you more about me and *him*," she whispered, nodding towards the Cistercians. "It *is* true he's been in all places. He wasn't boasting, so you mustn't be angry with him. He's jealous about Oxford and he hates England. He was a *Boneddwr*—what do you call it in England? —a small landowner—when he met Mother. She was the same as she is now! She was his—how do you say it, Gwion Bach?—his paramour —when I was born; and then she left him for the Earl, under cover of marrying Master Simon. It was then he took the vows. But he loves her to distraction still. The sight of her drives him mad. Sometimes I think she's afraid he'll kill her. And I believe once—"

"For sixteen years?" threw in Rhisiart in an incredulous tone. "Can men feel like that for sixteen years?"

"Hush!" the girl whispered and touched his lips with her finger. "Perhaps they can't in Hereford, Gwion Bach; but they can in Edeyrnion."

They were both silent. She trying hard to imagine what the hooknosed lad at her side would look like in fifteen years, and he telling himself a story about breaking into Dinas Brân at the head of a Welsh host, and giving Denis Burnell his life at the piteous supplication of both herself and her mother.

The sky had grown a little more cloudy, though they were still only thin, filmy clouds, when our party of friends arrived at the outskirts of Owen's manorial abode.

The first intimation they had of the approach of their journey's end was a somewhat startling one.

They were following a narrow path between the river and some heavy over-hanging woods when they were aware of the shrill notes of a horn among the trees above them. This sound was answered by another of the same kind higher up the mountain, and then by another, sounding more faintly, from the opposite side of the river.

"Come on, Brother Huw! We must keep together!" cried Rhisiart; and he himself was astonished at the instinctive authority with which he spoke.

But he seconded his words by dragging Griffin hastily forward, while with his other hand he clutched at the Friar's habit and unceremoniously pulled him along. The monks in front were at first too engaged in their conversation to catch these sounds; but the horn in the woods above them soon approached so near that they couldn't help hearing it, and they at once swung round and waited for the others to come up.

They were hardly together when two figures burst from the brushwood about five hundred yards above them, one pursuing and one pursued, and began leaping and scrambling down the slope. The fugitive was evidently at the end of his tether and must have been hunted for some time, for his clothes were stained and torn and he was both bare-headed and bare-handed. He was rushing down the hill so desperately, and was in a state of such panic, that for a moment he didn't notice the group of people gathered round the girl on the piebald horse.

But it may be believed that all our friends noticed *him;* and for a moment or two they remained spell-bound, lost in that curious state of mind, at once complex and very simple, with which human beings contemplate a life-and-death chase.

As for Rhisiart, his heart beat wildly, beat more than it had done since he lifted his sword between the archers and the spears. The infinite duration of time crumpled itself up into a little round ball. He looked at those two figures, the pursuer and the pursued, in a throbbing trance. There was something in the sight that seemed to arouse instincts in him old as the world. The fleeing figure was himself. The pursuing figure was himself. To escape, to keep his life, *only* to keep his life, was the spinning, dizzying, hurling, crashing bolt of his blinded passion. Into water, into fire, down precipices, into oblivion—so that somehow he might escape!

But to overtake, to have the prey at his mercy, to overcome in this

straining, groaning, panting contest, to break his heart in one frantic
sob, but to have him down, down at last, down beneath his feet!

In Tegolin, however, there was no such division of feeling. Long
before the other watchers came to their senses the heart within her was
calling out, in a tongue older than thought, older than justice: "To
me—to me—to my breasts, hunted! Here, here! Here to me! No, not
there! *Here* to my heart, here to what doesn't question, doesn't judge,
doesn't waver, doesn't think! Here to what is life merely, life only,
life beyond all dispute, all argument, all justice, all reason!"

And all the while in the shining black eyes of Father Pascentius,
those little black eyes of the everlasting blessing on *the event,* gleamed
burning interest. Would he catch him? Would he escape? Yes, no—no,
yes? Double sixes again! Being, Not-Being, Not-Being. Being; so runs
the world away!

As soon as the fugitive noticed our group of onlookers he stood for
a second stock-still, just as an animal might have done, who, hunted
by another animal, is suddenly confronted by human beings, and stares
at them, gasping, panting, desperate.

Then, as he recognized the familiar Cistercian dress, the man
swerved in his flight and began scrambling and stumbling, in the same
wild-beast haste, straight towards them. But he was still more than
three hundred yards away when his enemy, who was leaping after him,
overtook him.

Had the wretch continued his descent uninterrupted he might possibly have gained the river, but his moment's delay was his ruin. He
stretched out his arms in wild supplication when he saw that the monks
had seen him, and uttered a cry for help, but the cry was soon turned
to a piercing and heart-rending scream, when feeling his pursuer to be
just behind him he tripped on a rock and rolled over in the bracken.

It was now the other man's turn to catch sight of the group of people whose appearance had given his enemy into his hand; but all he
did was to wave haughtily with his left hand for them to remain where
they were while he proceeded to despatch his victim. In this process
he evidently didn't intend to hurry himself.

The victim was disarmed, exhausted, done for, and the pursuer
apparently felt justified in keeping him waiting for his death until he
had regained his own breath. Thus both the man crumpled up upon

the bracken and the man holding the spear above him panted out their long-drawn gaspings in a fearful unison and in complete disregard of five strangers.

It must be confessed that Rhisiart's first instinct was the law-abiding Hereford one—more than natural in the scion of a legal family—the instinct to assume that a man in such haste must be a malefactor and that the death held over him was a lawful execution.

Tegolin, however, who had been brought up in a less well-ordered society, felt nothing of this. All she felt was the spear of the hunter at the throat of the hunted; and jerking Griffin forward she lifted up her voice in a shrill cry of protest. The sound of her cry made Mad Huw recall his own recent predicament and he began leaping up the rocks with such agility that it was soon clear he would reach the scene of the killing before she could.

Meanwhile, the man with the spear, who was a tall personage with a heavy protruding forehead, deep-set eyes and shining teeth, seemed determined to get his own breath before despatching his panting enemy.

He kept lifting up his spear as if pondering where to strike, but he was clearly reluctant to waste his stroke, and the memory must have come to him of some unpleasant recent occasion when he couldn't draw out his weapon from the victim's body.

So, panting still, he deliberately bent down, and pulling the man round by the hair of his head, shortened his grip upon his weapon, and experimentally, but without breaking the skin, pressed the spear-point against the man's throat.

It was more with the feeling that he must, right or wrong, support Tegolin and her Friar, than that he ought to interfere in what was probably a mere deer-stealing execution, that Rhisiart followed his friends to the spot.

Meanwhile, what might be called a double-spouted jet of ultimate human emotions rose up from the green hollow where the man lay under the spear-point. It cannot often happen between slayer and slain that such a vivid exchange of consciousness takes place as occurred between those two breathless men.

The man with the heavy brows and gleaming teeth had become unconscious of everything else but of the ecstasy of thrusting his spear into this human throat. He felt the throat with his thumb and the point of his spear with the same thumb. An intensely vivid foretaste of what in a second he would feel, when, rising from his knees, he leaned his full weight upon the spear and pinned the man to the earth, came over him mingled with the extraordinary sweetness of crushed bracken.

And then he forgot everything in the expectation of having that throat under his spear, and of pressing his full weight upon it. The actual words, "I pinned him down like an eel!" came into his mind; and he thought of the gurgling sound the soul would make as it left. the body.

"Down, down!" his pulses drummed. "You below; I above." And side by side with this up-jetting emotion on the part of the slayer rose a parallel spurt of mortal feeling on the part of the victim. Are there perhaps invisible students of such ultimate human feelings whose business it is to make notes of the varying degrees in the gamut of this music?

If there are such, and if these parallel vibrations had been weighed in some psychic balance, it would have been found that the expectation of imminent death was less intense on this occasion than the rapturous expectation of inflicting it.

The truth is that for the man panting on the ground the bitterness of death had already passed. It had come in a crescendo of despairing sobs when he had felt his pursuer gaining on him. And when he stumbled and fell on that slippery stone it reached its consummation. *Then* it broke and ebbed; and though he could suffer still, he couldn't suffer with an intensity equal to the other's triumph.

An infinite weariness had come upon him as he lay supine on that pungent-sweet bracken, while the other pricked at his throat. His thoughts took physical shapes. They took the shape of a neck-bone bending under iron; and he even began to confuse the bone which was his life with the iron which was his destruction. The idea of pain no longer existed. The fear of death no longer existed. The humming in his ears and the panting of his lungs became the grinding of the iron which was his enemy upon the bone which was himself.

"Stop! Stop!" shrieked Mad Huw, as he came leaping like a wild goat up the steep ascent. "It's Richard you're killing! Hold your hand, you murdering slave!"

The man's answer was to bring down his spear with the full weight of his body upon the fragment of space occupied a pulse-beat ago by a naked throat.

But Mad Huw's cry, though unheard by the prostrate man's benumbed reason, was heard by the life-impulse of his body. And his body, making a movement like a galvanic fish, twitched out of the way, so that the flashing spear-head pierced nothing but the earth; and at that point Mad Huw flung himself upon him.

"It's Richard! It's Richard!" he kept repeating, as he wound his lean arms round the tall man's person. "Don't—you– know—that—he's— the sacrifice—for us all!"

It took more than a moment even for the fellow's immense strength —and his spear still quivered in the earth—to free himself from the madman's clutch; and no sooner was he free than he found himself confronted by a girl with a swinging braid of blood-red hair, to whose knees his victim was now clinging.

The shock of this combination of events catching him at the moment when the electric explosion of his savagery had run like lightning down the shaft of his spear into the ground dissolved the magnetism of his mood. A struggle took place in his distorted lineaments that was most curious to see. He bit his lip till the blood ran down his chin.

"Who in Holy Mary's name—" he began, then, shaking himself free from the Friar's grip, he saw Rhisiart by Tegolin's side with an ugly-looking dagger in his hand.

"Mercy! Mercy!" cried the hunted man. "Don't let him kill me, my sweet people! I'm a priest of God!"

"A priest of God? You scurvy scrivener! Lady, he's a spy of Bolingbroke's. He's a filthy parchment-eating lawyer, lady. He'd have taken service with Owen to damn us all! And he'd have done it too, if I hadn't chased him out like a stinking fox. Look at him, the mangy cur! Does he look like a priest?"

The wretch at the girl's knees made Rhisiart think of a criminal he had once seen hanged in Hereford for coining the King's money.

"Get up, man!" he cried, with the air of a sheriff's procter, pulling the kneeling suppliant to his feet. "Here are those who'll know whether you're a priest or not!"

It was then that to everybody's surprise Father Pascentius stepped forward.

"Haven't I seen you before?" he asked.

Rhisiart, who was still supporting the culprit with the grandiose air of a pillar of Hereford justice, felt it proper to repeat the monk's question as if his prisoner had been an idiot. "He's asking you if he's ever seen you before!"

But the fellow took no notice of anybody except Tegolin, upon whom he continued to cast desperate and appealing looks.

"I'm *sure* I've seen you before," repeated the commentator upon Saint Thomas; and then, while a gleam of something like amusement lit up his heavy face, he made his characteristic gesture; and remarked with a finality of authority that seemed indisputable, "This man is no spy. He is—"

But the personage with the spear interrupted him. "I don't care *who* he is! The point for you, my good Father, is who *I* am!" And at this he unslung his horn from his neck and blew a resounding blast.

Rhisiart dropped his prisoner's arm so suddenly when he saw and heard this blast of the horn that the poor wretch—staggering, as the psalm says, like a drunken man at his wit's end—reeled close up to Tegolin, who was now standing with her arm across Griffin's neck, and clutching at the belt round her waist swore to her by Saint Tysilio, by Saint Collen, by the majestic Festival of Saint John, *per festum Sancte Johannis Baptistae,* that he was a priest of God!

"A parish-priest, dear lady, a respected and learned priest, sweet lady, and though it is true not altogether unknown at the court of the King, a good Welshman at heart, and above everything else anxious to lay all my legal learning at the feet of the rightful Prince of Wales!"

Rhisiart who now held the savage stranger's hunting-horn in his hand, for seeing his interest in this symbol of romance the man allowed him to examine it, heard this tremendous and fatal utterance— "the rightful Prince of Wales"—with a curious shock. It struck him in a double way. In the first place it awed and moved him profoundly; as if with the impact of an oracular word, a word that the tossing wind of destiny had only after long hesitancy brought itself to pronounce.

In the second place, falling as it did from the white and twitching lips of this runaway lawyer, the word had an artificial sound, an unnatural sound, a sound smelling of parchments and sealing-wax, rather than of chariots and horses.

It would sometimes come back to him, all his life after, when he heard that magic title, "Tywysog Cymru," this unpleasing memory of a hunted lawyer's frightened, reckless, unscrupulous, and infinitely crafty face!

Father Pascentius was now talking rapidly to the man with the spear, while Rhisiart, after a friendly nod of permission from its owner, was himself trying to blow the horn. He would have got on better at this job if he had been able to keep his eyes, as their gaze wandered here and there above his distended cheeks, from focussing upon the psychic encounter that was going on between the girl and her "respected parish-priest."

This encounter, which at first had been a matter of clinging looks and then had become—when he clutched at her belt—a matter of clinging hands, had now become a curious exchange of words.

After some extremely quavering notes, that made the spearman smile as he listened to Father Pascentius, Rhisiart took the horn from his lips and under pretence of polishing its silver rim retained it in his hand, while under his bent brows he spied upon Tegolin and the fugitive. A woman's power of pity—Christ and God, he had never realized it before. But what a world of secret treacheries this hinted at, what a world of yieldings, sweet and furtive, that not the most jealous love could guard against!

"She's got a look in her eyes," he said to himself, as he licked his fingers and polished the horn's rim, "that she's never had for me, or Rheinalt or Huw. And why the devil does she keep her lips open as she listens to him? And she's got her knuckles pressed against one of her breasts now, as if it was just there she felt the pity—this damned unfair pity for a sneaking lecherous scrub whose soul ought to be in Hell! Yes, and I swear there's a tear on her cheek, too. What a little goose she is! A fool, that's it; just a silly fool!"

In truth it did almost seem as if the man's narrow escape from death and that heart-rending scream he uttered when he tripped had really, as girls love to say, "done something" to Tegolin. It seemed as if the fearful vibration of the life-and-death struggle he'd been through had projected a charge of magnetism, quivering and irresistible, that was seducing her innermost nerves.

"Why had she followed Mad Huw?" our friend thought, as he watched this subtle process going on. "Out of pity! And why did she let me take her in my arms last night? Out of pity!"

But the boy soon realized that he wasn't the only one of their party hit to the quick by the girl's concern for this runaway scribe. He soon became aware that both Father Rheinalt and Brother Huw were watching the pair as jealously as he was himself. This at once consoled him; and even brought a slight reaction in her favour!

Wasn't the girl free to extend her pity—granting that it *were* a sort of vice—in any direction she pleased?

But the tension came to end now, and in a surprising enough manner. Father Pascentius had at last, it seemed, quite won over the impulsive warrior with the spear. Both of them came forward; and the man, who a few minutes ago had been fumbling at the fellow's throat, now stretched out his hand to him and made the sort of blunt and bluff apology that he might have offered had he killed a dog or brought down a horse.

The person he addressed pulled himself together, moved away from Tegolin, swept a guarded reproachful and defiant look round the assembled company, and clasped his hands behind his back.

At his pursuer he didn't look at all, nor make the least acknowledgment of his apology.

"I remember you now perfectly well," said Father Pascentius. "You are Master Young, Incumbent of Llanwys in Dyffryn Clwyd, and Canon Elect of Bangor. No, listen to me, Master Young! Your name was mentioned I understand in the new King's Court as a candidate for the Archdeaconry of Ardudwy. But it was over a point of canon law that I had the honour of your acquaintance, Master Young; nor do I think you will have forgotten the occasion quite so completely if I remind you that you took up a position, in regard to the Bishopric of Bangor, and the Holy Father's consecration of Lewis of Aber, that was somewhat contrary to our Welsh hopes. No, hear me out, Master Young! This worthy gentleman, deceived by your appearance, misunderstood your business here. He was mistaken; at least let's hope he was mistaken! But all this can wait till we reach Glyndyfrdwy. It will be in our company that you'll come to Baron Owen; and this gentleman assures me he'll give us his escort and the benefit of his—"

Rhisiart had all this while been closely watching the face of their ambiguous captive, and the longer he had looked at it the less he had liked it. It was a flat face with very small features and a mouth whose thin lips accentuated the prominence of a narrow, projecting, and extremely pointed chin.

The man's eyes were pale, and had a wandering, restless, furtive look; but what puzzled our friend in his prolonged scrutiny, and confounded his analysis, was a certain indescribable air of formidable power and self-possession.

"He's no common customer," thought the lad, "and he's no fool, but I don't like him."

Liking or disliking, however, had now to give way to obvious humanity, for what interrupted the Cistercian's remarks was nothing less than the sudden collapse of Master Young, who fell, as a dead man might have fallen, with a decidedly unpleasant thud, upon the grass at their feet.

To our friend's vexation, and to the equal annoyance of Father Rheinalt, it fell to Tegolin's lot, with the aid of her silver flask and some water from the stream, to recover him from this well-timed swoon; and the end of it was—the very issue that Rhisiart had been for some while dreading—that it became his destiny to hoist the fellow up upon Griffin's serviceable back, and even to remain by his side when once they'd got him mounted.

By this time our friends had found themselves surrounded by quite a number of wild-looking spearmen, whom their leader's horn had brought to the spot; so that when the party finally moved forward again on their way, their company was a large and formidable one. Father Rheinalt took exclusive possession of his daughter during the rest of their march, so that our friend had at once to support Master Young and listen to Mad Huw's incoherent rhapsodizing.

At one point indeed the commentator upon Saint Thomas was thoughtful enough to come to the lad's side and explain to him, and to the man he was supporting, the identity of the impulsive huntsman.

"He's a friend of Iolo Goch," the theologian explained, "and a land-owner from Cwm Llanerch in the Vale of the Conway. He heard that the old bard was dying, and he heard of this gathering at Glyndyfrdwy. So he came with his tenants, and Owen has kept him. He seems to have become a kind of outlaw since"—and he lowered his voice so as to be unheard by Mad Huw—"since Richard's death. His name is Rhys. They call him Rhys Gethin, Rhys the Savage; and my own impression is"—and he spoke more kindly than he'd done before to the man on the horse—"that the less you yourself make of what happened just now, Master Young, the more likely it'll be that your over-zealous pursuer will get a shrewd rebuke! Owen doesn't like tale-bearers. But you may be sure our rough friend won't hold *his* tongue; and *your* discretion will win all the more favour."

With these politic remarks—and Rhisiart began to think that if Father Pascentius was as good a philosopher as he was a diplomat the Cistercian Order would certainly hold its own—the discreet sage drew back to the rear of the company and fell to botanizing.

For several miles Rhisiart had all he could do to keep Master Young from slipping from Griffin's back. The nervous reaction from what he'd gone through, combined with complete physical exhaustion, produced intermittent spells of extreme sleepiness, at each access of which he would lose his balance and sway violently to one side or the other.

However, by degrees, he recovered himself, and as his strength revived his normal intelligence revived too, and he began to question his young escort.

Rhisiart replied at first in unsympathetic monosyllables; but few young men can for long resist talking of themselves to an ingratiating listener and it wasn't long before the crafty lawyer-priest had heard all he wanted about our friend's life in Hereford and Oxford.

Rhisiart grew in fact more and more disarmed by the man's tact as a listener; and the next stage of their conversation took the form of a brilliant disquisition, to which the lad listened with absorbed interest, upon the nicest and most delicate points of Welsh politics.

The astute cleric was at pains to make clear to the young Oxonian that Father Pascentius's tone towards him was due to the bitter rivalry that existed in Wales between the regular and the secular clergy. The

Friars, he told him, were all for Richard, whereas the Cistercians were struggling to retain a diplomatic neutrality between the House of Lancaster and its enemies.

And then, while his curiously *level* face with its round toothless mouth and projecting chin grew animated with frank confidence, he began without shame to confess to the young man that he was in the greatest personal quandary whether to range himself openly with the new nationalist movement among the Welsh, or to return to Henry's court and content himself with advocating the Welsh cause in the councils of its enemies.

This frankness in an obviously formidable man of affairs was exquisitely flattering to our friend's vanity. He found himself even going so far, under the stimulus of the other's confidence, as to speak freely of his own secret ambitions. It must be remembered that this was the first time in his life he had presumed to discuss public affairs with a man who could boast a personal acquaintance with the reigning monarch; and as he walked by Griffin's side, watching the subtle play of Master Young's mobile face—which he kept mentally comparing to a certain recently-carved gargoyle, through whose mouth the roof of his College Chapel drained itself of the rain—he began to feel a sense of worldly superiority to his recent companions, none of whom, he felt sure, was capable of following Master Young's statesman-like thoughts.

Of his own ambitions he began to speak more and more freely; avoiding, however, with an instinctive shyness, any reference to Dinas Brān. He questioned the archidiaconal candidate very closely about the character of the Lord of Glyndyfrdwy, and was delighted to find that his own suspicions about his famous kinsman, as being more addicted to poetry than politics, were fully shared by this virtuoso in human character.

"No, I've never met him," Master Young declared, "and to tell you the truth I am exactly in your own position with regard to him. Indeed, the chief purpose of my journey—so rudely interrupted by that uncivilized brute—was to judge for myself the chances that this cousin of yours would have, in case these Burnells and Arundels and Greys *did* drive him into revolt."

"Shall you," enquired our young friend impulsively, warming to a man whose opinions jumped so closely with his own, "shall you, do you think, follow Father Pascentius's advice, and say nothing to my kinsman of this murderous attack? And what, by the way, if I have an opportunity of talking privately with him, would it be best for *me* to say about the matter?"

Master Young didn't reply for a moment. His eyes wandered thoughtfully over the slopes of a bracken-covered range of hills that now appeared on the right of their winding track.

"I think I must leave all that," he said at last, with a melancholy sweetness, "to the natural discretion of an Oxford scholar. No, I think the good Father *was* right, absurdly prejudiced as he is! No, I shall say nothing to Owen myself, unless— No, I shall say *nothing.*"

He paused a moment and then, leaning his hand against the edge of Rhisiart's little bundle of books whose parchment-covers were protruding from the sheepskin, he twisted himself round, as if to assure himself of the whereabouts of Rhys the Savage, and remarked lightly, "Of course, if I hadn't been a priest I should have stood up to that ruffian. It's the first time in my life I've had to take to my heels. Holy Mary! And I'd be a dead man now, if I hadn't bestirred myself."

In spite of his mental affinity with the would-be Archdeacon it did cross Rhisiart's mind that though the fellow had indeed "bestirred himself," and done so with the agility of a hunted rabbit, it was the intervention of Mad Huw rather than his personal activity that had saved his skin.

Master Young must have divined the drift of his new friend's thought, for he now remarked that he had only recently heard of the wandering Friar of Llanfaes. "I'd like to thank him though, for his assistance just now."

Once more Rhisiart couldn't restrain a fleeting thought that the word "assistance" was a somewhat modest one for what the Friar had done while Master Young panted on the ground; but anxious to further this laudable duty he raised his voice and speaking authoritatively and loudly, as if to a deaf child, called the Friar to their side.

"I almost believe, Brother," whispered Master Young, "yes, I really almost think, that I owe you my life."

Mad Huw contemplated him in astonishment, his beautiful eyes wide open. "It's the blessed King," he replied in awe-struck tones; "it's he who's come back and will be with us soon, who saves all our lives.

That's why we're all going together. That's why you and the Maid and that man with the shining teeth who wanted to make your death a quick one, and the Father who tears up flowers to put under his vest, and this young man who draws his sword and puts back his sword are going to beg Owen to deliver the land from this enemy of Christ, this scourge of innocence, this plague-spot Bolingbroke!"

Rhisiart had already grown so accustomed to treat Mad Huw's words with tender solicitude that it made him think of the legal parchments in the sheriff's office at home when he saw Master Young's pragmatic mind curl up like bonfire shavings under these fiery words.

But he was really shocked when the priestly lawyer thrust his hand into the stout wallet he carried at his waist and fishing up from its recesses a couple of silver groats held them out to Mad Huw, with the words: "For your little necessities, Brother! I am not a rich man, or—"

But the lad never supposed that the Friar would have had the wit, or indeed the gall, to do what he did with these two glittering coins. A couple of Rhys Gethin's somewhat ragged followers were trailing their spears at a little distance; and the Friar, calling out to them in the rustic idiom of the Vale of the Conway, flung the coins towards them and chuckled like a mischievous boy when the men nearly fell into the Dee in their struggles to pocket these precious pieces.

The sight of Master Young's disconcerted face and the way the small, well-modelled features of its oblong expanse contracted, as if they had received a smart fillip from the back of a lean hand, lessened considerably our friend's disgust. But he did make a mental note that it is possible to be a great statesman and a very questionable gentleman.

Tegolin from her position in the little cavalcade by Father Rheinalt's side must have noted with indignation this offer of money to her hero, as if he'd been an ordinary begging friar, for she came hurrying up to them, and Rheinalt followed her. It was impossible for our friend not to feel a certain amount of malicious joy when he heard his intellectual acquaintance receive some lively home-thrusts from the impetuous and impulsive girl.

"So you pay for your life with silver groats, Master Young?" and her tone had a texture of delicate fury in it that made the boy think of the polished slipperiness of his mother's voice when she came upon his father and Modry in the rose-garden.

What, however, puzzled the boy about it, and by no means pleased him, was the manner in which Master Young received his punishment. His curious pale eyes seemed to darken in a kind of withdrawn and abstracted delight and out of his thin-lipped toothless mouth, that seemed to round itself in sensual expectancy, came a faint purring sound. It was an intense relief to Rhisiart when Father Pascentius enquired politely of the would-be Archdeacon what his view was about Owen's chance if there were a rising. Master Young replied at once with grave authority.

"The worst," he remarked, "of a gathering like this, with all its ridiculous mystery and its bard-business and its bandits from the Conway and its"—he lowered his voice with a glance at Mad Huw— "its Franciscan fuss about Richard, is that it's all local and provincial! The stage is set for great events—*that* I grant ye; but it's a bigger stage than your bards and bandits realize. I'm as good a Welshman as any of you, but I can tell you this, if the red dragon comes back it'll be because the lions and leopards have fallen out among themselves. There must be trouble in Ireland, trouble in Scotland, and all Northumbria rising; yes! and a war-cloud from France too, before the House of Lancaster's shaken. I know the Prophecies of Merlin as well as any of you; but if Owen ap Griffith thinks he can drive the English out of Wales by magic and sorcery, he's—"

"Richard, sweet Richard, will do it by his blood!"

The Friar's voice rang out so loud that Rhys the Savage with a couple of his followers came hurrying down upon them through the bracken from the higher path they'd been following; and at his enemy's approach Master Young fell silent.

Indeed they all fell silent; and the murmur of the river and the chirping of a small bird in the undergrowth and the harsh croaking of a raven poised above the high rocks were the only audible sounds, save when Griffin's hooves struck against an unseen stone.

Then Tegolin's voice became audible; though it seemed as if the girl were rather talking to herself than to any of the men round her.

"Only a terrible, only an intolerable wrong, worse than any I've heard of yet, would justify the lifting of the red dragon, and all the burning and all the spoiling and all the torrents of blood that would follow a struggle between Welsh and English. Baron Owen must die one day, as we all must, and how will he feel if, for some paltry quarrel with my Lords of Chirk and Ruthin, he has covered our land with blood, and blackened it with fire, and made—"

"Hush, girl!" interrupted Father Rheinalt, his features distorted with the intensity of his feeling. "Hush, or you're no daughter of mine! As John ap Hywel said to us in the guest-house last night, it is the Lord Himself who is sowing dissension between Henry of Lancaster and the Percies; and what I say is, if all Gwynedd, and all Powys, and all the *commotes* of Deheubarth were soaked in the blood of their children, it would be a small price to pay for a Wales free and united as it was—"

"As it *never* was!"

The words fell harshly and brutally from between the gleaming teeth of Rhys the Savage. "Pardon me, Gentles and Fathers all," he went on, while his two shaggy-haired, bare-foot followers glared at the man on Griffin's back as if at the least stir of contradiction they would wring his neck, "but when I hear these Lollardy-words about peace and unity and all Welshmen linked in love, and think of the proud warriors of old and the free princes of Gwynedd, who'd as soon see a scurvy South-Walian on the banks of the Conway as they would a dirty Saxon, I could spit on the earth! In those old times," he went on while his followers' eyes flashed in sympathy, "there were *real* saints among us! Saint Derfel, Saint Tysilio, Saint Collen—wouldn't any of *them* as soon fling a spear at a Gwyddel from Ireland, or a Silurian from Gwent, as at any serf-Saxon or bastard-Norman!"

Rhys the Savage uttered these words in furious jerks, rolling his eyes and baring his teeth. Like spouts and jets and flukes of hot blood they whistled about that little company's ears.

What with the spear he held in his hand and kept toying with, and what with his followers' barbarous looks, neither the cloistered monks nor the secular cleric uttered a word.

But Mad Huw cared nothing for this beastly chatter, nothing for this brandished spear.

"Holy Saint Francis!" he cried. "What talk is this? Was Blessed Francis a Lollard? Was the Son of Mary a Lollard? Is sweet King Richard, who gives his life for us all, a Lollard? Yes, go on! Gnash your teeth and roll your eyes at me, Rhys Gethin! I snap my fingers at you. Haven't I read the secret of the years in sweet Richard's eyes? And it *is* love that will conquer, in spite of your teeth and your spear! King Arthur wasn't born in Conway nor Dewi Sant in Edeyrnion. It wasn't in Mathrafal that Merlin found the red dragon for Gwyddyrn the Goidel! Holy Saint Francis! what Devil's coil is this, Rhys Gethin? Not a word will King Richard say through me for Owen; not a word will poor Huw say for himself, unless Owen is out to bring all Wales together!" He stopped breathless and let the lean arm he had stretched out sink to his side.

The irresponsible chief from Cwm Llanerch lowered his spear and stared frowningly at the earth; and it seemed to Rhisiart as if his ferocious tribalism really had received a shock. Inspired, however, by a not unnatural delight at seeing his enemy discomforted, Master Young deemed it a propitious moment to thrust in *his* diplomatic oar; and he proceeded in carefully-chosen words to bring forward the legal aspect of the subject.

"And if Owen," he said, "did bring all Wales together, as Brother Huw desires, his success could never be lasting until he made peace with England. And the only way he could make peace with England would be by paying homage to the King in London. This, just this, and nothing less than this, has been the wise policy of all our greatest princes. A free Principality—and I would even go so far as to say a Principality with a Parliament—rendering without question that geographical, that legal, that historical homage to the crowned King in London that has been paid since the days of King Alfred—that is the line to follow!"

For one beat of his agitated pulse Rhisiart felt sure the lawyer's end had really come this time. The spear was raised, and he could see it actually quivering in the Conway man's reckless hand. He himself was moved by no rush of automatic impulse to defend Master Young, but he did, as soon as he had taken breath, lay a firm hand on the hilt of his crusader's sword which offered itself so easily to his hand.

But Tegolin *had* moved by an instinctive impulse—and it can be believed how our friend went over this incident again and again in his mind—and if Rhys Gethin hadn't held back just in time the spear would have passed through her body rather than Master Young's.

It was a toss of the dice, too, whether the fellow's uncivilized henchmen would do what Tegolin's rush forward had prevented their master's doing; but with an angry oath in which he included the whole party, Rhys the Savage called off his men as if they'd been a pack of dogs, blew his horn as a sign to his little army on the upper path, and scrambled up the rocks to rejoin them. Half-way up he paused upon a platform of stone for a final word, and pointing at Griffin's rider—for the whole party had stopped to follow his ascent with their eyes— "Wait till you find yourself," he shouted, "you scurvy Carmarthen spy, in Owen's prison at Carrog! You'll only come out of *that* like a trapped rat—to be baited by Conway puppies!"

They were now actually in sight of the tall flagstaff in the centre of the enormous circular stockade which surrounded Owen's dwelling. This flagstaff, made out of an untrimmed spruce-fir of exceptional height, was planted on the top of one of those ancient mounds, centres in Wales, as doubtless in ancient Greece, of mystical entombings for the dead and of magic enchantments for the living.

They could see the patrimonial pennon of Owen's ancestors floating from that fir-pole top, bearing, though from that distance the whole flag showed smaller than a butterfly, the solitary "lion rampant" of the chiefs of that ancient princedom. It wasn't long—for at the sight of the mound and its flagstaff they instinctively quickened their speed— before they saw much more of this fortified palace. It was built mostly of gigantic planks of wood, but of wood supported and foundationed upon a system of massive stonework.

It was clear that none of our friends, even if they had been ten times more numerous than they were, would be without shelter that night. Owen's domain was indeed a "Llys," as the old romances call such a place, worthy to be compared with those primeval ones of the ancient Welsh myths, mentioned so constantly in the "Four Branches of the Mabinogi."

Like the Homeric palaces it was two stories high, the upper one devoted to the women of the family and their feminine attendants and the lower occupied almost entirely by one enormous hall, strewn with last year's bracken, with an open fire in the centre, round which at night, when the tables had been cleared, the whole company of warriors and their retainers could sleep.

But this was by no means all; for quite clear of the main edifice there were out-buildings and guest-houses and extensive stables, not to speak of bakeries and kitchens and laundries and cattle-sheds. The place, in fact, could offer food and shelter, and frequently did so, to a population much larger than many villages.

Unlike the great Norman castles, however, and unlike such purely Welsh castles as Rhisiart's Dinas Brān, Owen's "Llys" would have been at the mercy of a body of foes formidable enough to defeat its defenders. *That* indeed was its essential character. It could extend a more lavish hospitality than the largest castle; but its strength lay in its warriors, not in its walls.

Rhisiart's emotions as they approached the main entrance to the place, the general effect of which rather resembled an immense stockade than an embattled fortress, were so deep and overwhelming that he kept sucking his lips into his mouth and tightening his belt, and twisting the hairs of Griffin's mane between his fingers, in complete unconsciousness of anything but the romance of the moment.

With a gesture that touched Tegolin far more than anything he had done since he held up his crusader's sword between the archers and the spears, he finally slipped his hand into hers, and in complete oblivion of the fact that Master Young had descended from Griffin's back and was supporting himself or pretending to support himself by leaning upon him, he clutched her fingers and pressed close to her side, much more as a child with an elder sister might do than an armed lover with a timid maid.

The summer afternoon had by this time clouded over and the wind was beginning to rise; but this only stirred the folds of the pennon, which he could still see waving from its mound, into that occasional slow unrolling on the air, which gives to a flag the appearance of being woven of some rich, heavy heraldic stuff.

In an instinctive movement of awe and excitement the whole of their little company advanced close together, Tegolin holding Griffin's bridle, Rhisiart holding Tegolin's hand, and Master Young leaning heavily, like a sick or wounded man, on the lad's other arm.

On arriving at the barred gate of the enclosure they found two horsemen waiting patiently on their respective steeds, one of which was coal-black, and the other of a dark roan-colour.

Rhisiart was in too deep a trance of excitement to take in anything save a vague impression of patient men upon patient horses. His inmost being kept saying to itself, "With my girl's hand in mine I've come to the palace of my fathers."

One ridiculous little thing did, however, considerably bother him, disturbing in a measure his ecstatic trance; namely, that across the illuminated parchment of the one among his books that protruded itself from beneath his sheepskin bundle there hung down in full view—probably because of the fidgety movements of Master Young—a considerable portion of a stout pair of knitted drawers, with which his mother had insisted upon providing him when he left Hereford.

Nothing would have induced him to release Tegolin's hand in order to thrust this domestic object out of sight, but the image of that curst underwear might have taken to itself quite monstrous proportions if Tegolin hadn't whispered in his ear, "Mother of God! if it isn't the Abbot and the other one!"

She had hardly uttered the words than the impetuous Father Rheinalt rushed forward and boldly greeting the Caerleon prelate, and kissing his hand, introduced to his notice the less presumptuous Father Pascentius.

Luckily for the harmony of the occasion it was only the girl and our friend himself who knew that the calm smooth-faced layman in the dark clothes of a scholarly country squire was the notorious Walter Brut, whose trial for heresy before his bishop had already made him infamous to the orthodox.

Whether the warlike Abbot from Caerleon knew the identity of his companion, Rhisiart had no idea; but the great man kept it to himself if he did, and the whole company of them were soon greeting one another with the happiest friendliness, Master Young assuming a prominent part in the exchange of courtesies, and taking stock of Master Brut with a lively and interested curiosity.

The Abbot from the banks of the Usk was indeed in his most genial mood, his powerful features more animated than our friend had ever seen them; and though he had evidently been wiling away the time in his usual manner, his Psalter was no longer open and he was soon waving it in the direction of a taciturn and heavily-armed Porter, who was seated with his back against the closed gates, polishing a murderous-looking battle-axe.

"I suppose you Valle Crucians," he remarked with a chuckle, "are well known to that surly gentleman over there; whose name I gather is Glew the Gryd. And, if you are, you'll doubtless also know how impossible it is to disturb him. He *has* revealed to me, however, that Owen is at the death-bed of Iolo Goch, whom he's just brought over here from Sycharth; and until the old Bard wakes from the coma into which he's fallen everything must fain be at a stand-still. It's a blessing my almoner isn't here. The man's such a stickler for the proprieties that what he'd say to see his Superior, and his Superior's worthy friends, waiting the pleasure of Glew the Gryd is more than I dare imagine.

"But here's our brave Brother Huw; and if I mistake not, this pretty lady is the famous Maid Tegolin. Give me your hand, daughter! The last time we met we had a worse reason for possessing our souls in peace than we have to-day.

"And how goes it with my silent lad of the big sword and Hereford horse? If we can't see the great Owen yet a while, we must e'en make the best of his cousin."

The formidable Abbot of Caerleon was evidently in one of his relaxed moods when nothing could upset him, and when, as long as he could speak Welsh and not Latin, and there were none of his convent at hand, he was free with everybody.

Rhisiart's acknowledgment of his greeting—and the boy wasn't too dazed to notice Master Young's astonishment at the broad rustic dialect in which the Abbot's sallies were expressed—was interrupted by the necessity of distracting Griffin's interest from the Lollard's roan mare.

There was a huge horse-block before the entrance to the "Llys," adorned with ancient bronze rims and rings; and to one of these rings our friend proceeded to fasten the piebald's bridle, remembering, as he did so, that other horse-block at the gate of another Welsh palace, upon which, as his Modry loved to relate, the great goddess Rhiannon, in the tale of "Pwyll Pen Annwn," had to sit for penance!

Meanwhile, as behind him, and he noticed it with extreme displeasure, Tegolin was taking the opportunity of introducing Master Young to the Abbot, in front of him the indignant Father Rheinalt had walked straight up to Glew the Gryd.

"What do you mean by this? Is Welsh hospitality gone forever? I thought Owen's gates were never shut. Have you *no* respect for a Lord Abbot?" Such were a few snatches of the monk's observations that reached Rhisiart as he fastened the piebald to the horse-block.

"*You* come here and talk to him, lad!" cried the Cistercian at last. "He's always been a brute," he whispered when our friend with some reluctance drew near. "Owen spoils him because he saved his life in Scotland. He's a great—"

He raised his voice so as to pierce the Gryd's inflexible ears—"I'm telling this young scholar from Oxford, who is studying how to drive out devils, what skill you have with the battle-axe!"

"She wants sharpening," was all the answer he got.

Then Rhisiart shot *his* bolt. "Why have we to wait till your master can leave his friend?" He raised his voice till he could feel it penetrating every crack and cranny in that obstinate gate. "Couldn't one of his sons open the door, or his High Chamberlain, or his Chief Butler, or even one of his cooks?"

"It's sharpening *she* wants," repeated the Porter.

"Don't you think," the boy shouted, raising his voice still louder and using a pitch that had always had great success at his Hereford school, "that you could just slip in for one little moment, and tell the Arglwyddes that her kinsman from Hereford waits outside?"

"Her be blunter nor the mischief," said Glew the Gryd, "but I'll sharpen the bitch yet or starve for't!"

Rhisiart gave vent to a blunt English oath; but the imperturbable Glew only shrugged his shoulders, and continued applying the sharpener to the edge of his weapon.

The lad looked hopelessly round. He was aware of plenty of people coming and going among the out-buildings. Sometimes a group of them would stop to stare for a moment, talking and gesticulating to one another; but when either the Lollard or Father Pascentius began cautiously moving towards them, they disappeared like rabbits into their burrow.

He went back to the old horse-block and began stroking Griffin. Mad Huw had already seated himself on a bench under the wall and was contentedly watching a flock of pigeons, several of whom, doubtless recognizing him as a creature nearer themselves than normal humanity, seemed on the point of alighting on his knee.

All at once the lad's impatience vanished from his mind like a puff of smoke. He suddenly remembered another of Modry's tales, where the porter at Arthur's gate refused admission to Kilhwch the son of Kilydd. "The knife is in the meat," he repeated to himself, "and the drink is in the horn . . . and none may enter therein save the son of a king or a craftsman bringing his craft."

"Can it be possible," he thought, "that in this civilized day and age, when life has become so scientific and safe, and men question every-thing—even the existence of Incubi and Succubi—and when free-thinkers like this Lollard read the Scriptures in place of the Missal, that I should see with my own eyes a figure like this porter?"

And then as the Lollard rode up and began explaining how he had left the unhappy Simon in the herdsman's hut in order to appeal per-sonally to Owen on his behalf, Rhisiart found himself thanking all the saints in his heart that Tegolin had braided her hair again before expos-ing herself to the gaze of so many! The Lollard smiled as he watched the lad thrust his offending under-clothes carefully into hiding; but catching sight of the bundle of books that now emerged, as a result of these adjustments, he asked him in a friendly tone what they were.

Our friend replied courteously but a little vaguely, for the works in question were more classical than scriptural; but as he equivocated and muttered something about old school-texts, his mind became more and more concerned about the welcome he would receive from his kinsman, and whether, if he *did* get employment under him, it would mean a temporary separation from Tegolin.

"If it does," he thought, "*can* I stand it? And what may not happen to her without my protection? Oh, how hard and terrible life's great decisions are!"

And then as he watched the girl standing there between Master Young and the Abbot, "What I'd like," he thought, "would be just simply to marry Tegolin, and live quietly with her here under my cousin's roof; making excursions now and then against Chirk and Ruthin, and perhaps, with the help of that savage knight and his men, assaulting Dinas Brān in some surprise attack, and being met by Tegolin with her hair all unloosed, when with Burnell dead and her mother a captive I return at this very—"

His reverie was interrupted by the sound of some considerable stir going on inside the great gates.

Master Brut ceased talking, and both the piebald and the roan pricked up their ears.

Rhisiart turned hurriedly round to see if Tegolin had heard anything, but she was too deep engaged with the Abbot and Master Young.

As for Father Pascentius, he had calmly seated himself by the side of Mad Huw, and with his garments hitched up above his great unseemly legs was examining a fragment of moss.

"Iolo Goch must be dead," said the Lollard suddenly; but Rhisiart was silent. *Death?* Well! it had to come; as he'd seen it so nearly come to Mad Huw and to Master Young; but that was death in its violent form. What of dying in a closed chamber with only a little square hole to let in the air and the whole outer world?

And Rhisiart suddenly realized, as he stood by the old horse-block and in preparation for the opening of the gates began to loosen Griffin's bridle from the bronze ring, what it meant for Iolo Goch to be dying. Till this moment the Bard's being at the end of his long life had been no more to him than if they'd been waiting there for the death of a cow or an ox. But now, as he watched Tegolin's delicate figure in her page's dress and noted its soft curves and the slenderness of her neck compared with all these men, a vague obscure thought that he couldn't have put into any words took possession of him. It was something so passive, so receptive—but there was no real word for it!—in Tegolin's pose, something that suggested, compared with the compact and concentrated energies of all these men, the deep, soft, yielding, silent-growing potency of Nature herself! Yes, there was an aura about her, an aura that even those monks were feeling—the greatest mystery in the world! And between the old Bard's death inside the gates and this young girl's life outside the gates there seemed to the lad then—only it was all vaguer than words and subtler than thought—a magical reciprocity, a reciprocity between two things that were both of them deeper and more real than any waving in the wind of that "lion rampant."

What was this? Surely he heard the sound of iron bars being drawn and of iron chains clanging and jangling as they were unfastened!

But the imperturbable axe-sharpening of Glew the Gryd didn't cease; and it was an obvious supposition that obstinate though the Porter was he could hardly remain seated in the centre of the gateway when the gates were thrown open!

"This gate must lead into a court-yard," our friend thought, "where there must be stables for our horses. I shall certainly see where they put Griffin. But not at once. I'll let my cousin's servants take him away when we *first* get in. Will my cousin be on the steps of the great hall to welcome me? Will he perhaps have heard rumours already about how I lifted my sword?

Ah! the axe-sharpener *had* skipped aside like a great disturbed goblin and the gates were opening! They opened very slowly; so slowly that Rhisiart fancied he detected some ritual-motive; for surely the natural thing after all this delay would have been to fling them wide in one grand burst!

But opening they were; and the Abbot got down from his black charger and with great dignity advanced alone, allowing Father Rheinalt to lead the horse behind him. After Father Rheinalt came Father Pascentius supporting Master Young, and after them came Master Brut with his mare.

Thus it was that Mad Huw, made aware of a rich concourse of people—suddenly revealed like a sumptuous picture between the posts of the great gate—fell to crying out that Richard was alive, that right would now prevail over wrong and that the oppressed would be comforted. And as he proclaimed this message at the top of his powerful voice he pushed eagerly forward, squeezing himself between the mare and one of the gate-posts, in a desperate attempt to overtake the Abbot.

Thus, by what seemed to the boy a special providence, he and Tegolin, with Griffin pulled along by his bridle behind them, were enabled to enter the "Llys" of Owen side by side; and it may easily be believed how spontaneously their hands sought each other and clung tight together, as they followed the rest into that crowded court-yard.

V

GLYNDYFRDWY

THAT HE was taller than the rest of them, that his legs were bare above his high, tightly-fitting, chamois leather shoes, that he had a dark tunic with broad purple belt and a purple mantle over his shoulders clasped by a massive gold brooch, that his yellow-grey beard was forked and carefully trimmed, that round his head was a twisted golden thread and from his belt hung a short two-edged sword of antique shape, were all things that Rhisiart only took in after several minutes had passed.

What he noted at once about Owen ap Griffith's appearance were his eyes. These were of a flickering sea-colour, sometimes grey and sometimes green, yet always with an under-glow of light in them that had the effect of an *interior* distance.

And something else Rhisiart noticed very quickly about his kinsman's eyes, and indeed about the whole expression of his face, and this was a sudden change that would every now and then bring a kind of paralysis of all animation, not so much as if he were engaged in thought as if his consciousness had been transferred to an interior plane.

Owen's forehead was low and broad, the hair thick and wavy; but his locks were so neatly trimmed, and the thread of gold so carefully disposed across his brow, that the general effect was courtly and regal rather than shaggy or leonine. His nose was of the type sometimes called Roman, but it had nothing of the aquiline, and its nostrils were unnaturally large. His cheek-bones were decidedly prominent, his cheeks hollow and curiously white against his yellow-grey hair. His skin was obviously of the texture that responds to exposure by growing freckled rather than tanned.

But it was the curious change that kept coming over his lineaments

120

as he turned to greet first one and then another of his guests that arrested our friend most. It seemed to occur quite independently of the person he was addressing, and it didn't effect either the flow of his own words or the politeness with which he listened to the words of others.

To our highly-strung traveller it seemed there was something startling and rather troubling about this phenomenon. He told himself several times that he must be imagining it, for none of the man's interlocutors, as the boy watched them, showed the slightest awareness of these curious psychic withdrawals.

"I *must* be imagining it," he repeated to himself. But then, as Owen turned from Master Brut to Master Young, it seemed to him that this intermittent paralysis—just as if the man's soul had left his body altogether—descended so palpably that he found himself making an instinctive movement forward as if the chieftain might suddenly reel and stagger.

Rhisiart had never in his life concentrated such a mental intensity of scrutiny as he concentrated during those first brief moments upon Owen Glyn Dŵr.

Apart from these queer "attacks," for so our friend regarded them though nobody else seemed to notice them at all, the lad was amazed by the courtly manner in which Owen handled his guests, greeting them rapidly one after another, and yet leaving each of them obviously delighted with his reception.

Another peculiar of Glyn Dŵr's which interested Rhisiart was the man's way of talking in so low a voice to the person he was addressing that no one else, however closely they were standing, could hear what he said. This especially struck the lad because all the English magnates he had known in Hereford were wont to prove their importance by the high pitch of their voices.

All these impressions, though he could have put them into words at his leisure, passed through his brain in that rapid mental sequence which resembles the flow of images rather than of thought; but what startled the lad most was not the nature of any particular observation he made as a surprising upheaval in his whole emotional attitude.

In his secret feeling about Dinas Brān, that feeling into which he had thrown all the shy and obstinate idealism of his furtive pride, he had deliberately thrust away the image of this lawful head of his tribe as an unworthy inheritor of the high tradition; but now that he stood there watching the man's every movement with such passionate interest he was conscious to his absolute astonishment of a mounting feeling towards him, the quality of which disturbed him to the centre of his soul. And the curious thing was that the dominant strain in this feeling was neither admiration nor awe. It was an up-welling of fierce protective pity.

Owen's presence affected him with the tremulous heart-beating feeling such a young savage might experience who finds that the god of his race—upon whose rough image he had long cast a negligent and even critical eye—has suddenly appeared to him in the wistful and helpless beauty of his real identity out of that familiar and neglected shrine. It was partly the scrupulous delicacy of the man's forked beard and of the thin gold thread round the brow that evoked this feeling, for in some curious way these details bore an infinitely pathetic look, as if the figure thus adorned and tended had been prepared or had prepared himself for some mysterious sacrificial rite.

Rhisiart never again got quite the impression he received that mid-summer afternoon, and there came moments when its memory grew blurred. But it never altogether left him; and the Owen he saw that day took his place, easily, naturally and with a fatal inevitableness, on the ramparts of Dinas Brān and gathered into himself their mystic enchantment.

All this while Rhisiart had been clutching tightly the hand of the red-haired Tegolin and waiting patiently till the chieftain thought fit to approach them. Once or twice the girl made an effort to free herself, and the boy knew perfectly well that she was growing anxious about Mad Huw who was behaving rather oddly.

The sight of Glyn Dŵr evidently brought back to his distracted mind a lively remembrance of the fallen King at Flint; and indeed it was clear that the Friar's mind was grievously confused. Rhisiart expected him every moment to lift up his voice about the late King as he always did in the presence of any new group of people; but in place of doing this he was standing in troubled amazement, sometimes gazing intently at Glyn Dŵr and sometimes staring wildly about him, as if he expected to see Richard himself.

In her concern lest the Brother should make a scene and prejudice their host against him, Tegolin now implored Rhisiart in a loud whisper to let her go to him. But Rhisiart took no more notice of her appeal than of the voices of a group of starlings who in that crowded court had begun to show agitation.

But at last Owen himself went up to the Friar and both Rhisiart and the girl gazed with astonishment at the scene which took place. Mad Huw must have known that the man was *not* Richard, but the fact that he had seen them together on the only occasion when he had ever set eyes on the King evidently had a bewildering effect on his troubled wits. Down on his knees he sank and began kissing the hand with which Owen tried to lift him up; and when Glyn Dŵr did at last get him to his feet the poor man fell to blubbering like a child.

At this Rhisiart did let go of Tegolin's fingers, and the girl shot off like a released arrow to the Friar's side while our friend followed more slowly, leading Griffin with him. He paused out of politeness when he was about a dozen yards away; for he saw that the chieftain had addressed the girl, and was now speaking to her in that same low voice in which he had conversed with the rest. He could see what a comfort it was to the Friar to have her at his side again; and he noticed the touching pleasure with which the man watched her as she replied to Glyn Dŵr's questions.

Presently he saw that the chieftain must have said something that concerned both Tegolin and the Friar, for the girl turned and evidently repeated his words, at which Mad Huw, now quite calm and happy, nodded a vigorous assent.

This seemed to our friend the moment for which he had been so patiently waiting; and with a heart that beat in an emotion that it was impossible to conceal and still leading Griffin by the bridle, he went straight up to his kinsman, and dropped down on one knee just as his mother had made him to do in his childhood.

"Why, Cousin Rhisiart, you put us all to shame with your pretty manners! No, no, dear boy, you mustn't do that, even though I *am* old enough to be your father!"

Thus speaking Owen raised the lad to his feet and kissed him tenderly on both cheeks. For a second our friend's lip quivered, and he could easily have followed Brother Huw's example and burst into sobs; but he pulled himself together, blinked a little, swallowed the lump in his throat, bit his lip, and stammered something about his mother sending her respects and about his father being many years dead. "And I thought perhaps, my Lord, that you might—that I could—that there might be—"

"Something you could do for me, cousin, eh?" said the other kindly. "Certainly there is; and not only one thing! There aren't so many Oxford scholars drifting about Wales that we can afford to miss the help of one who is of our own blood. We must talk more of this, later, lad, and about Hereford too. But meanwhile—no, keep your horse! We must introduce him to your cousins. And we must present our Maid of Edeyrnion too, and this good Brother of Saint Francis."

As Rhisiart followed the chieftain towards the steps that led up to the main building, his heart was so over-brimming with emotion that everything and everyone he set eyes on showed like visionary shapes in the translucent depths of a magic crystal. He never forgot that moment. Moving behind Mad Huw and Tegolin, who were both at Owen's side, the twisted braid of the girl's hair, as it hung below the bottom of her tunic, became to him in his exultant mood like a blood-red ladder up which he was climbing into a Jack-and-the-Beanstalk felicity.

With each step he took there seemed to fall away from him a great segment of his past identity. The image of his pleasure-loving, frivolous mother, calling him her "little monk," appeared for a moment and was swallowed up. The image of Morris Stove bending over their Oxford fire and pouring forth disparagements of Owen materialized for a second, like a bubble on a stream, and was lost forever.

Before he knew where he was he found himself confronted by the assembled group of all his fellow-travellers. The Abbot was talking earnestly to a portly lady dressed in a thick green mantle over which fell a crimson scarf; Master Brut was being politely questioned by a dark anxious-looking man of about thirty who bore an obvious resemblance to the matron in the green mantle.

A servant was leading away the Abbot's charger while another had just laid his hand on the bridle of Master Brut's mare. But stroking the roan's silky flanks, and being talked to by the commentator upon Saint Thomas across the animal's back, was a startling vision of girlish loveliness.

Rhisiart's politeness altogether deserted him under the shock of this apparition, so that in place of falling on his knee as he had done before, he merely lifted the fingers of the portly Arglwyddes to his lips and responded as vacantly as any Hereford clown to the stiff greeting of the lady's eldest son.

"Come here, Catharine," cried her father, "and don't stare at our cousin as if he were a Legate from the Pope."

"I think Cousin Rhisiart finds more to look at in Catharine than he does in Mother or me," remarked Griffith ab Owen in a penetrating high-pitched voice that was totally at variance with his stocky figure.

"Answer that question, Catharine, that Father Pascentius asked you," said the Arglwyddes, "before you run away."

"You see," said Owen quickly laying his hand on Rhisiart's shoulder, "you're a member of the family already! We're scolding you and our little Catharine as if you'd been brought up in the same nursery! No, no! Kiss your cousin properly, my pretty! You give him as cold, shy, and distant a cheek as if he were young Grey of Ruthin!"

"Catharine has answered my question already," said the theologian placidly, and Rhisiart, as the blood receded from his flushed face, enquired with studied ceremony of the Arglwyddes whether he might accompany the servant to the stable so that he might know where to find his horse.

"Our cousin doesn't trust you, Gwalchmai," said Griffith to the man who was waiting at the mare's head and had already possessed himself of Griffin's reins. "He thinks your Welsh oats will be thin fare after his English ones."

The fellow evidently got the drift of this speech, though it was deliberately spoken in English, for he cast upon this bastard relative of his master a look of such hostility that Rhisiart resolved that he *would* see what was done with the horse.

He found it difficult to move, however, and quite impossible to retort, as he would have liked, to the Arglwyddes and her eldest son.

Everybody seemed talking at once, and yet all their voices seemed faint and far away. He knew very well what he wanted to do himself. He wanted to say something, something important; something that had just come into his head. But he couldn't think—and the man they called Gwalchmai was already leading off the mare and Griffin. He felt like a traitor to the old horse.

But the Arglwyddes was speaking again. "When you've stopped staring at your cousin, Catharine, I wish you'd run upstairs and tell Nurse—"

"This is our Maid of Edeyrnion," interrupted Owen, addressing his wife in a sterner voice than Rhisiart had yet heard him use. "Mistress Tegolin! Come here, child. Yes, and bring the Brother too! The Friar must have that little room upstairs, near the women, so that the Maid can look after him. They've been together so long that he'd feel—"

The Arglwyddes came forward and greeted Tegolin more warmly than Rhisiart had expected, and the way she spoke to the Brother too was a surprise to the lad. "She's nicer than I thought," he said to himself, "though she's taken a dislike to *me*. Did she see me holding Tegolin's hand? Does she think I'm her lover?"

He still felt that the many voices round him, as he stood at the bottom of that flight of steps, kept receding into the distance, and he still felt that he had something important to say, something that it was absolutely necessary that he should hear himself say.

And there was still that long blood-coloured braid of Tegolin's as she leaned forward with bowed head listening humbly yet proudly to the Arglwyddes; and he could even see a small withered flower twisted into it where its plaits were knotted. "And we'll put you, my Lord Abbot, in the blue chamber," Owen was saying, "and Father Pascentius and Father Rheinalt with you—and I think, with your leave, Arglwyddes," and he smiled at his wife, "we'll put Master Brut under the care of Cousin Rhisiart in the 'Saracen's chamber.' Some of my good men are subject to silly superstitions, Master Brut; otherwise I'd tell them to give you the guest's place by the hall-fire. But the nights are warm now; and I daresay you young men will be glad enough to be out of the heat and smoke. The Saracen's chamber isn't often slept in, but there are no lack of warm rugs and I— What's that, little one? Oh, no! Cousin Rhisiart won't be afraid. Besides he won't be alone."

These last words were addressed to Catharine who had whispered something to her father. Having re-assured the young girl Owen paused for a moment with an arm round her waist and his eyes fixed on Rhisiart; and even though the boy and Catharine were still staring at each other the lad felt that one of those curious attacks had seized the chieftain and that the look the man fixed upon him had no "speculation" in it.

A great rack of clouds, that had been sending several advance-guards across the sun, now swept in its whole bulk completely over it; and it seemed as if this palpable darkening of the earth had a psychic effect upon the group of persons standing there.

The Abbot who, with Father Rheinalt and Father Pascentius, was waiting, half-way up the steps, for the Arglwyddes to tell someone to show them where the "blue chamber" she'd referred to was to be found, proceeded calmly to take out his psalm-book.

"He'd read that," the lad thought, "if he were dying on a battle-field or sinking in a ship."

The omnivorous intelligence of Father Pascentius was, however, totally unaffected by this solar lull in the movement of events, and he proceeded to break the spell by approaching the Arglwyddes and begging her in a series of rapid plausible sentences to allow Master Young to share the Saracen's chamber with Rhisiart and the Lollard.

"If Owen is afraid," he remarked, "of letting Master Brut sleep by the hall-fire, he surely will see that it would be unwise to allow an unattended clerk in Orders with such an English name to sleep in so public a place and be at the mercy of any dissension that might arise?"

"But I don't believe there are enough rugs for *three* guests, Father, in the Saracen's room," replied the lady, a little disturbed. "*Catharine!* Haven't you gone *yet?* Didn't you hear me tell you to go and see Nurse, and explain to her what your father— No! wait, child! You'd better take Mistress Tegolin and the Friar straight up to Nurse and tell her that Griffith Llwyd ap Dafydd ab Einion—and don't forget to repeat his full name, if he's up there now, for he doesn't like people to take liberties with him—will have to sleep in the hall to-night. But tell Nurse he can bring his harp down and that if he plays it *very quietly* he can even refer to Iolo Goch. Oh yes, and tell Nurse—"

But the young girl had already gone up to Tegolin and taken her by the hand; and it was our friend's destiny to see the blood-coloured braid passing through the gate into the hall, side by side with Catharine's slender figure.

"Is it white samite she's wearing?" Rhisiart asked himself, "or is it that stuff Modry used to talk about, called *pali,* that Branwen ferch Lyr, and Kicva ferch Wyn Gloyw, and Rhiannon ferch Heveyd Hēn always wore, and that Modry said was really French silk?"

When the girls and Mad Huw had vanished, Rhisiart felt as if the figure in *pali* had diffused itself like a spiritual essence through every object he looked at. The heraldic stone-pedestals on each side of the steps shimmered with silvery gleams. The velvety darkness of the interior of the building contained a flickering perspective of *pali*-wearers.

Owen himself was talking to the Arglwyddes now. They were evidently debating the point raised by Father Pascentius about Master Young; and, while this went on, Master Young himself with diplomatic indifference was asking Tegolin's father about the antiquity of certain great stones that had been built into the masonry of the steps.

How the man's countenance managed to convey such a feeling of power, when every feature of it, especially the toothless mouth, was so negligible, puzzled our friend a good deal; but he tossed the problem aside, and going up boldly to Griffith, asked him whether he might see where his horse had been put.

Owen's eldest son gave him a hostile glance, almost as vicious as Gwalchmai's had been; but when Master Brut, to whom Griffith was speaking, seconded this request and made some joke about Hereford horses being more brittle than others they received a sulky nod of assent, and the young chieftain went so far as to offer to show them the way.

The Lollard's unfailing sweetness of temper did, however, by degrees work a change in the young man's tone; and though Rhisiart continued to feel ill at ease with him, his boyish interest in the stables, and in the Welsh ponies they were shown, clearly mollified the man's unfriendly humour.

Rhisiart was glad enough too that they had the son of the house with them when he found that his precious bundle had been taken into the hall instead of into the Saracen's chamber; and when at last the fellow-travellers found themselves safely established there with all their belongings, and with a promise from Griffith to come himself and conduct them into the hall when the proper moment came, the boy felt that he had been spared just that particular nervous discomfort in strange quarters that he had been dreading as they approached Glyndyfrdwy.

He was gratified, too, to find that in spite of its being Midsummer Day the Arglwyddes—or that mysterious potentate of the upper floor who had been referred to as "Nurse"—had caused a small wood-fire of birch-logs to be lighted in the great open hearth of the Saracen's chamber, for the place certainly had the chilly air of a long-unused apartment in a great house.

The Lollard's travelling equipment turned out to be a good deal more extensive as well as more carefully packed than his own, and Rhisiart found himself several times thanking Heaven that the duty of being tactful in social matters formed an obvious part of this person's evangelical principles.

Both the young men—for it turned out that Master Brut, though he looked older, was only twenty-five—set themselves to wash and dress before taking much notice of their accommodation.

Rhisiart did, however, observe, as after dipping his face in a silver bowl of clear water he rubbed it violently with a linen napkin, that above their fire, where the smoke disappeared through a blackened aperture leading into the central hall, there stood on an elaborately-carved stone bracket a large, headless crucifix. He observed too, as he pulled on his tight scarlet hose, and thrust his head through his black armless tunic, that the walls were hung with faded tapestry in which, though the figures had long ago become discoloured with smoke, he could make out several episodes from Virgil's story of Eurydice.

Master Brut's change of garments proved a good deal more fashionable than our friend's, for the Lollard assumed, in place of the lad's sleeveless tunic, a long loose gown of dark blue velvet, caught up at the waist by an enamelled belt, trimmed at the skirt by a thin band of twisted silver.

Master Brut carried no weapon, and Rhisiart fancied he caught him looking with an amusement he couldn't quite conceal at the meticulous care with which our friend arranged his rather pretentious ivory-handled dagger; not dangling it, however, in the fantastic style that Tegolin had affected, but fastening its sheath with two short cords to a slit in his tunic.

When they were dressed they took care to throw more logs on their fire, agreeing that they would retire from the banquet as soon as the potations of mead began and enjoy themselves in peace, exchanging their impressions of Glyndyfrdwy.

"They must have disposed of our lawyer-friend somewhere else; and I must say I'm glad of it," remarked Rhisiart, contemplating the two comfortable beds, each of them raised about a foot from the ground and covered with soft rugs, that filled most of the space beneath one of their walls.

"I hope the poor man *won't* have to sleep in the hall," murmured the other uneasily; and his silence after this remark somewhat disturbed our friend, for knowing the Lollard's reckless good will he felt afraid he would get it on his conscience that he ought to exchange places with Master Young!

To distract his companion's mind from such evangelical qualms he began examining their quarters. A rough painting of what looked like a decapitated turbaned head, held up by a mailed arm, and wearing an expression of undying ferocity, hung from the wall opposite their fire; and the young men soon discovered that the Saracen's chamber had two windows, both mere slits in the wall, and so deeply set that, though they were unglazed, it wasn't possible to see much through them.

One of these, no larger than an arrow-slit in a castle stairway, led into the open air, and the other, though the young men could only see a tiny segment of what it revealed, opened directly into the hall.

"Let's see where we are, and whether they keep guards in these passages," urged our impatient friend, placing his fingers on the bolt of the door with the intention of opening it.

At first Master Brut showed lively signs of disapproval of this bold enterprise—even going so far as to lay a restraining hand upon the boy's arm—but when the door was flung open, he took as much pleasure as his companion in the various mysteries it concealed.

They found themselves in a low-roofed, narrow passage-way, which at night must have been lit up, for they could see the iron brackets for the torches; but by day, even on a day like this, it was very dark and gloomy.

"Wait a moment," Master Brut said. "I always make a mental map of a strange place before advancing," and on Rhisiart's giving him an impatient and puzzled frown, "I saved my skin," he added, "in my heresy trial, by making a mental map of the Bishop's mind!"

"We'll talk about that later," said Rhisiart. "Shall we explore *this* way a little? I think it was *that* way Griffith brought us here."

"Listen!" cried the Lollard; and the two tall young men, in their rich dark attire, the light from the Saracen's chamber falling dimly on our friend's scarlet hose and on the other's enamelled belt, stood side by side, hushed and intent.

A low faint sound, like the sound made by a deeply-convoluted shell when held to the ear, became audible to both of them. It began very low and as it increased in volume it no longer resembled that initial shell-murmur, but became more like "the rushing mighty wind" of Pentecostal visitation. Then it changed again and it seemed to the two listeners that it was the sound of distant voices, in fact a confused whirl of voices, voices in different keys and tones, voices of lamentation, voices of supplication, voices of wild and terrifying triumph.

"What the hell—" whispered Rhisiart; and then with an access of sheer childish panic he clutched Master Brut's wrist.

But following the same graduations of sound in its dying down as it had followed in its mounting up, the noise now subsided into its original sea-shell whisper and soon ceased altogether. Absolute silence followed. They could hear each other breathing. It was as though they were in a tomb.

"Why the devil can't we hear any stir of life in this place?" murmured Rhisiart; and to his considerable dismay a distinct echo came down the passage towards them, repeating "in this place"—"in this place." Boy-like he must needs revenge himself upon his own trepidation by a clumsy challenge to this phenomenon. "Who are you down here?" he murmured, as loudly as he dared. "Down here! Down here!" replied the echo.

"You don't suppose that damned Griffith has forgotten to call for us?" whispered our friend.

The Lollard smiled at him. "If we were really shut up here," he said, "with that sound and this echo, I should certainly beg you to stop cursing like that! Don't you remember how Griffith had to get a great key from somebody, to open the door we came through? It was when you were asking him where Owen himself slept."

"By God, you're right, Master! I can see him now as he shut it and put the key in his pouch! I'd forgotten. Shall we go *that* way and bang

at the door? I'd sooner go that way than the other after hearing that
noise."

The Lollard made no reply. What Rhisiart could now detect upon the
blurred countenance beside him was a completely new expression.
Master Brut's calm features had tightened into the technical intensity of
a man of science. He made various grave motions with his hand, drawing lines and angles in the air; and then proceeded to regard this
invisible map with his head a little on one side.

"What the—what is it?" enquired our friend regarding these proceedings with some uneasiness. "You're not doing anything, I hope,
that's—"

But Walter Brut straightened himself briskly and replied with eager
precision. "As we stand now, with our backs to our chamber, we are
looking due north, that is to say, at right angles to the entrance of the
palace. *That* direction," and he pointed down the passage whence the
noises had proceeded, "leads directly towards the mound where we saw
Owen's banner. That way," and he pointed into the gloom where in
his imagination Rhisiart could see a veritable dungeon-gate, "leads to
the great hall. Do you remember where he told us Owen slept himself?"

Rhisiart shook his head.

"Well I *do* remember," and in the light of that open door a look of
the most childish complacency came into the heretic's face. "He said it
was up the passage leading out of the north end of the hall, that's to say,
over *there!*" and he pointed at the wall opposite their door. "I see it all
now like a map! Have I made it clear to you?"

Rhisiart shook his head. He found it difficult to interest himself in
these architectural plans of Owen's abode. His mind kept running on
two things; the unpleasant thickness of the door that made this passage
so silent, and the inexplicable sound they had just heard.

"Our passage led out of the hall due west," continued the Lollard,
"and, as I said, at right angles to the one leading to where Owen sleeps.
You noticed, I suppose, that great latrine we passed before we came to
the locked door? It must drain into some stream outside. We're lucky
in our chamber, I mean to have one of our own! And I hope you
noticed what a modern one it is? I've never seen such a neatly-made
disgorge. It must drain into the same steam as the common one. Owen
must have had it cut in the wall when he came back from Scotland. I've

always heard that the nobles in Scotland disposed of their excrement
more scientifically than—"

"Pardon me, Master," interrupted Rhisiart who had begun to say to
himself, no wonder this chap became a Lollard! "I'd like to ask you one
little question. What will you do if this sulky Griffith—damn his soul!—
doesn't come for us? Our window's too narrow; and nothing would
make me go a step down there!" and he indicated the passage from
which those sounds had come.

Master Brut smiled. "Let's have a look at that door he unlocked," he
said. "He may have left it open and we're disturbing ourselves for
nothing."

With more uneasiness than he would have cared to confess Rhisiart
followed him. Huge rafters, dark with the smoke from the torches,
crossed the roof of the passage, and the walls, as far as they could make
out in the gloom, were partly of blackened oak and partly of rough
stone.

They soon came to the door, which looked, as they approached it, as
though it might easily be four or five feet thick and which soon proved
as unyielding to their united weight as if it had been a wall. Rhisiart put
his ear to the crack where the hinges were.

"I think I can hear *something,*" he began. "No, I can't! It's a humming in my own ears. Mother of God, Walter Brut, but I believe we're
prisoners!"

The Lollard laid his hand on his shoulder. "Nonsense, lad," he said.
"And you a Welshman, too! I would be less surprised to hear that Prince
Hal was preaching to Gospel than that Owen's hospitality—" But both
the young men stepped suddenly backwards, for, even as they were
staring at it, the door began to open.

It opened towards them, and with its opening such a confusion of
sounds emerged that Rhisiart felt dazed. But almost immediately it
closed again, and left them in the same tomb-like silence.

"Come back to our room," said Master Brut. "I don't want him to find
us here shivering like a pair of thieves!" They hurried back, closed their
door, pulled a bench in front of their fire and sat down.

"What would this place be like in winter," our friend remarked, "if a
fire is as nice as this on Midsummer Day?"

"It's our nerves make us chilly," said the other. "When I was in our

Bishop's prison it was mid-August, and yet I was always bribing my gaoler to bring me logs."

Rhisiart was silent. That iron-studded, sound-proof door had imprisoned his imagination.

"Do you often think about death, Master Brut?" he suddenly enquired. "What would you have felt, what would you have done, if that door *had never opened again?*"

The Lollard smiled and laid his hands on our friend's scarlet-covered knees. "I should have prayed for the spirit," he answered.

"*I* should have prayed for a miracle!" cried the other.

"The spirit *is* a miracle," retorted the heretic.

"How old do you think Catharine is?" enquired our friend.

The Lollard removed his hands from the boy's knees. "Catharine?"

"Owen's daughter—the girl in that shimmery dress."

The Lollard half-rose from their bench and at some risk to the long skirt of his decorous dark blue gown threw on the fire another log.

"That tall little child? Oh, I don't know; I didn't look at her particularly— About twelve I should think— Yes, that tall fair little thing; yes, I saw her. I expect the Arglwyddes has her hands full correcting Owen's spoiling! She looked a capricious little baggage to me. But I daresay in ten years she'll have grown into a sensible and beautiful girl."

"Don't you think she's beautiful now?"

Master Brut shrugged his shoulders; and after turning to glance at the window began making calculations with extended forefinger over the spluttering logs.

"Making another map?" our friend enquired.

The man lowered his hand and contemplated Rhisiart with a grave frown. "I believe I misled you just now," he remarked, " but the truth is—"

"You *did* admire Catharine?"

"The truth is, this palace of Owen's isn't built *even* with the points of the compass. Owen's sleeping-place—I believe the Arglwyddes sleeps upstairs with the women—isn't due north of the great hall but northwest *by* north, and this of course means—"

But both the young men now jumped simultaneously to their feet for there was a low but very distinct knock on their door.

"Come in!" cried Rhisiart in Welsh; and in his excitement he added an old-fashioned greeting that Modry used in her fairy-tales, "and God be with you!"

To their immense relief, in place of the sulky elder brother, it was Meredith who entered their room. He was in the same plain hunting garb that he'd worn when he came to Mad Huw's rescue; but he was perspiring and out of breath, and his clothes were stained, muddy, and disarrayed. He flung down a bundle he was carrying, shook hands warmly with Master Brut, and after a second's hesitation kissed Rhisiart shyly.

"Look after the fire for a while, will you, you two!" he said. "I want to use your conveniences for a moment and wash and change. Griffith and I sleep in the ante-room to my father's chamber, but my mother has put some lawyer-priest there to-night, a fellow they say Rhys Gethin nearly killed. Griffith swears he'll read all my *englyns,* and eat all the Moorish sweet-meats Catharine bought from a pedlar for us. He certainly looks as if he hadn't teeth for much else! But look after your fire —I'm as finicky as my father over being watched at my toilet!"

The two guests proceeded to obey him to the letter, and, returning to their bench, fell for politeness' sake into a low-voiced rather forced conversation between themselves. Meredith seemed to take an unconscionable time over his ablutions and his change of clothes and long before they heard his voice again they had lapsed into silence, Master Brut even nodding a little in the aromatic heat of the burning logs.

"Now, gentlemen, we're ourselves again!" The young men rose to their feet. Turning to face him it was all Rhisiart could do not to utter an audible cry of admiration.

Meredith's banquet-attire was cut after a style the lad had only seen once in Oxford among a group of students who had been to the University of Paris. The tunic was quite short, leaving the limbs in their tight-fitting yellow hose uncovered half-way up the thigh. His neck and chest were bare save for the links of a heavy gold chain, and his tunic, which was of a rich moss-green, had wide loose sleeves, showing a white satin lining.

In place of the dagger worn by our friend in the manner he regarded as so much more *à la mode* than poor Tegolin's, Meredith ab Owen wore nothing but an exquisitely-embroidered velvet pouch with a golden clasp, hanging from a belt that was fastened beneath, not above, his moss-green tunic. Round his dark hair, which fell in wavy curls upon his shoulders, was a thick gold "torque" of antique design, clearly a family heirloom; and his feet, like those of his father, were slippered in some sort of soft light-coloured skin, drawn-out, however, beyond his toes, into curious narrow points.

"Don't laugh at my finery, coz," the youth cried hurriedly. "You mustn't think I dress like this often. It's only to do honour to the Abbot of Caerleon. Mother has made Griffith, as the eldest son, put on King Eliseg's belt, given him by Arthur. They say Merlin made it for Arthur's sword. Father's never worn it. He thinks it would be sacrilege. But Griffith cares for none of these things! I hope it won't bring us all bad luck. Mother made him do it. Mother's half-English you know, and I sometimes think—she—doesn't—quite— You see it was meant for a belt but Griffith doesn't care, and Mother doesn't understand; and he's going to wear it round his neck! Father looked at me when they were talking about it—the way he does! But he said nothing."

Rhisiart could see that all this flow of talk was chiefly to conceal the youth's embarrassment at his extravagant attire. The young man had blushed deeply when they first turned round; and he hadn't finished speaking before he began prodding the birch-logs with the iron-prong as if to cover his discomfort in a blaze of sparks.

"How did you leave the prisoner?" enquired Master Brut.

"Oh, I ought to have told you before," burst out Meredith eagerly. "He's getting better. I sent my foster-father to find the Scab, and the Scab bled him and gave him a sleeping-draught, and my foster-mother's looking after him. He clings fiercely to that little psalter you gave him. The Scab tried to take it away when he bled him, but he couldn't open the fellow's fingers. What spell did you work, Master, to turn the Hog into a scholar? Scholar! he can't read or write! It's only because you gave it to him. What did you do to the fellow, Walter Brut, to get this power over him? I believe he'd do murder for you! You'd better take him as your disciple, Master, if my father doesn't want him, and somehow I can't see—"

"Oh my Lord," interrupted the Lollard, catching sight of the stained and torn clothes the youth had thrown down on one of their beds. "I ought to have left my horse with you! You've been—"

The man's concern was so spontaneous and sincere—and certainly to see Meredith as he was now it did seem hard to imagine him struggling and panting and covered with mud and blood—that Rhisiart was shocked by the flash of cold steely anger with which he received these friendly words. His face went hard and hostile and his dark eyebrows under his golden torque twitched like a haughty girl's.

"We Welshmen don't need to depend on our guests' horses, fine as they are," he muttered; and Rhisiart thought to himself, "I know exactly what you felt just then! Master Brut will have to learn that kindness and simplicity aren't enough when you're dealing with *us*."

He found himself glancing at the Lollard with malicious curiosity while Meredith, trembling with the effort of controlling himself, folded his dirty clothes and carried them to the other side of the room.

Our friend was absolutely amazed, and to confess the truth caught by a spasm of sheer terror when he saw Master Brut step with complete aplomb across the chamber and pat the aggrieved son of Owen familiarly and coaxingly on the shoulder.

Meredith jerked himself up, and presented to the well-meaning intruder a countenance so convulsed with fury that Rhisiart could see the Lollard draw back as if he'd trodden on a snake. In a flash our friend saw the two men locked together in a deadly struggle. But no! Nothing of the kind occurred.

Meredith drew back a step, with a movement—in his rich dress—like a turn in a dance; and then in place of leaping at the other's throat he made very deliberately a low obeisance before him, so low that the golden torque around his head fell with a metallic ring on the stone floor.

The young man retained this pose of hysterical emotion, or of vibrant malice, or of inspired restraint, for it was totally beyond our friend's fathoming to decide which it was, for quite a few beats of the younger guest's pulse; but when he straightened his back, with a flutter of his loose green sleeves, it was with one of the sweetest smiles that Rhisiart had ever seen.

The Lollard picked up his fallen torque for him and an interchange of looks beyond our friend's comprehension passed between them.

"Could *I* smile at anyone like that," thought Rhisiart, "and still hate him?" for curiously enough it never entered the lad's proud head to suppose that Meredith *didn't* hate the man still; though from the easy way the two of them talked, as they left the Saracen's chamber, it was as if they were better friends than before the incident occurred.

As soon as they were all three in the passage, Master Brut spoke of the strange sound they had heard.

Meredith showed a lively interest at once. "I'm glad you mentioned this to me," he said, "and to nobody else. We're all rather touchy about those sounds; and on the whole, if I were you, I wouldn't refer to them —except with *me,* of course! You've been to the end of the passage? No? Well, there's nothing to see; not even a closed door! The passage ends in a block of stone. Long ago, in my great-grandfather's time I believe, it was closed up. It used to lead—I expect they've told you—to somewhere below the mound. My brother knows more about it than I. They tell the eldest son, whatever there *is* to be told, in each generation. No! I've never heard those sounds. I expect," and in the dim light from their door our friend caught a look of complicated sadness on his face, "I'm too *modern* to hear such things. But Catharine's often heard them. *She* says—but I mustn't tell a young girl's secrets!

"May I shut your door, gentlemen? You'll find it easily enough after the banquet, for the torches will be lit then. Well? Are you ready? Shall we go?"

But when they reached the door at which the young men had recently stood their guide turned. His face was now a mere blur in the darkness and all that was visible of his dress was the white lining of his sleeves.

"I brought the Scab with me," he remarked. "Please be civil to him! And I brought bad news for us all. The King is on his way from Scotland; and Grey is back at Ruthin."

Though Rhisiart could see that he'd lifted his arm by the moving gleam of his white sleeves, he couldn't see what he did to make that huge oaken mass swing towards them on its hinges. When it closed behind them, however, the visitors found themselves in a vaulted stone vestibule into which a confused rumour of movement and voices reached them from the hall beyond.

There were narrow window-lights here through which the daylight entered, making pale the flames of a couple of torches against the wall, and adding a queer effect to the wisps of fragrant smoke that floated up among the arched mouldings of the roof.

"Sit down a minute, will you?" said their guide, pointing to a rough smoke-blackened bench.

Here he left them and disappeared between some heavily-hanging curtains into the tumult of voices.

"Did you notice what he said," whispered Rhisiart to his companion, "about Catharine's hearing those sounds? What a strange life it must be for a young girl in a wild place like this! But I think he's a favourite of hers, don't you, from the way he spoke?"

Master Brut nodded. "As we're sitting *now*," he remarked, "we're undoubtedly facing the entrance to the hall. *That* must mean just as I thought, that the building faces—I hope," he interrupted himself, "that that lawyer fellow *is* being looked after! It would be easy in all this up-roar for someone—"

But at that moment the green sleeves and yellow stockings of their elegant friend reappeared, accompanied by none other than Owen himself.

The young men rose. Rhisiart bent his knee and the Lollard his head. Owen approached them with a smile of recognition and laid his hand on our friend's shoulder.

"How nice you look," he said. "*Both* of you!" he added, including the young heretic with an appraising eye. "I'm afraid you'll think, with your English taste, that we're too fond of gaudy colours in Edeyrnion. Well, it's not every night we wear such fine feathers, is it, son? What I came to settle with you two"—and his tone changed to something almost apologetic—"is a small point of family punctilio. You won't be offended, I hope, Master Brut, if I put you *just*—only just—below the dais? You'll be within our reach, so to speak. In fact you'll be just below us, and close to our Bard. But as we must have the good Fathers with us up there, and we know the little points of variance between you and them, the Arglwyddes thought you'd feel more at your ease—"

Rhisiart, upon whose shoulder Owen was still resting his hand, didn't dare to look at the Lollard's face. His own face, he knew, was flushing darkly and deeply. Oh, this was an insult—and an insult to *him* as well as to his room-mate! How differently would his mother, for all her frivolous snobbishness, have acted! These were French ways, like those of the flaunting nobles that Richard brought to Hereford! Master Brut was a truer gentleman, as he was a far nicer man, than any of those insolent priests. And what about Master Young? *He* would no doubt be on the dais, to make up for his cowardice, and because he was a canon in a cathedral!

But the Lollard's own easy and friendly words—for he spoke at once, assuring his host that he had never sat on a dais in his life, that he was a simple farmer, who always avoided such state-occasions, that his trial for heresy had got him far more notoriety than he deserved, and finally that he would have felt extremely awkward and embarrassed among the monks and the ladies—considerably soothed our friend's mind.

He caught Meredith, however, watching the man as he spoke with intense concentration and with a curious little flickering smile on his lips.

"He's thinking what a simple fellow he is," was what passed through Rhisiart's mind, "and how silly it was to get so angry. No, by God, I'm wrong! He's looking at him as if he can't understand him, as if he's completely puzzled by him!

When he had finished explaining why he would prefer not to be on the dais, Master Brut turned upon them all an open countenance of such serene friendliness that Rhisiart felt puzzled himself. "Can he *really* be a simple farmer?" he thought. Then he noticed that a pause had arrived in which they all stood waiting in silence—waiting presumably for Owen to make some move.

But Owen, though no one but Rhisiart seemed aware of it, had been seized by one of his "attacks." Doubtless to the rest of them the chieftain looked merely like a statesman-like warrior, pondering some nice point of court etiquette, and plucking as he did so first at one side of his forked beard and then at the other; but to Rhisiart he looked like some delicately-carved statue, hung with sacrificial wreaths, awaiting the ritual-dance. The man's soul, so it seemed, had left his body altogether and carried its consciousness into a different region.

But now with what to our friend was quite a startling shock Owen threw off this lethargy, and lowering his fingers from his beard extended them to Master Brut and shook him warmly by the hand.

"Well done, sir," he said, "you're a magnificent liar, a triumphal liar, an heroic liar! You shall sit wherever you want to; but you must come and see me when the banquet's over"—and he turned to the puzzled Meredith—"you'll bring him, son, won't you?—for I'd like to ask the advice of such a liar as you, Master Brut, on a great many questions!"

To this unexpected command the Lollard only turned the same serene unruffled face, acknowledging it with a glance into the chieftain's eyes, but without even a nod of acquiescence as far as Rhisiart could see. He wasn't surprised, however, as they followed Owen to the door of the hall, to overhear Meredith whisper in the "simple farmer's" ears, "I'll look out for you as soon as he leaves. He won't stay when the drinking begins. You must have made an extraordinary hit with him. I've never heard him speak to an Englishman like that before."

"But I'm *not* an Englishman," Rhisiart heard Master Brut reply; "and your father seems the only one here to know what 'Brut' means!"

As the three young men stood back to let Owen enter the hall alone, they heard him being greeted with a cry that made the blood rush tingling through Rhisiart's veins. "Owen ap Griffith, Prince of Powys!" they heard again and again; and then, in words that were yet more applauded, and in which our friend thought he recognized the shrill voice of the Bard of Ffinnant, "Owen, the Elect of Saint Derfel!"

Nor was our friend greatly surprised, when the clamour had subsided and Meredith was ushering them in, to catch the familiar voice of Mad Huw. Not even in such a gathering as this could they persuade the Friar to relinquish his allotted task on earth; but he was not quite oblivious of the spirit about him. "Owen," Rhisiart heard the Friar shout, "Owen, the friend of King Richard! Owen, the friend of the sweet sacrifice of God!"

The first thing Rhisiart did, when Meredith, having safely disposed of Master Brut in a snug position just below him, placed him in a seat at the end of the dais, side by side with Master Young, was to choke and sneeze. The hall was thick with fragrant birch-wood smoke from the fire in its centre, round which what looked as many as fifty men-at-arms were grouped, some seated on rough stools, some lying on heaped-up bracken, into which every now and then gleaming sparks from the fire would drift down, to be extinguished as soon as they fell.

Up and down among the banqueters serving-men and serving-maids were already circulating, filling the guests' wooden bowls with steaming stew, and piling their earthen-ware plates with meat and hot cakes. Through the high, narrow windows a pale diffusion of the mellow afternoon light of that Midsummer Day fell upon the scene, but not in sufficient strength to make pallid or negligible the bright flames that shot up amid the smoking logs. Jugs of beer and of light wine followed the meat and stew, in the hands of lively and chattering boys, all dressed for the occasion like little pages in the black and yellow of Owen's ancestral livery, and carrying on their breasts the single lion, "rampant and sable," of the old princedom.

As he had been promised, Master Brut had as his neighbour below the dais the striking figure of Griffith Llwyd, Owen's private Bard, whose harp was suspended from a bracket in the wall just above the Lollard's head.

All the privileged assembly on the dais sat facing the body of the hall, Owen himself in the centre, with the Arglwyddes on his right and his eldest son on his left. Rhisiart, as he sat with the lawyer-canon of Bangor at the end of the long table, was able to scan the figures of the whole company; and his swarthy face darkened in a hot excited flush when he simultaneously caught the eyes of both Tegolin and Catharine who were seated side by side.

And what was this? In place of her page's attire the Maid of Edeyrnion was dressed in a rich green gown, almost as sumptuous as Meredith's tunic, while her blood-red hair, free of its braid, flowed long and loose about her shoulders. Mad Huw was safely ensconced by the girl's side, and Rhisiart could not help being touched by the appealing way the man kept glancing at her, just as though he were a child at some grown-up ceremony for which he had been carefully schooled.

"How much brighter the dresses are," thought our friend, "than those at home. And yet," so he commented in his mind, "they're worn much more carelessly, much less as if their wearers were conscious of them, than ours are."

For himself he was most uncomfortably conscious of his new suit; and he found himself wondering whether Catharine had noticed his scarlet hose before he sat down, and whether Tegolin had seen the *real* way, in modern civilized circles, that young men wore their daggers.

Every now and then he would steal a furtive glance at the two girls; and almost always when he did so Tegolin would give him a frank, brave, encouraging smile, while Catharine would hurriedly look away.

Feeling that it was incumbent upon him as a relative of the family to make the Canon of Bangor feel at his ease, Rhisiart interrupted the good man's absorbed enjoyment of a slice of savoury meat-pasty by remarking to him how like a prince of the old days Owen looked as he sat at the board with a great silver flagon at his side and the hilt of his sword gleaming above the dark oak of the long table.

"He'd be fitter for the part," murmured the legal expert hoarsely, "if he would listen more and think less."

"Think less?"

"Look at him now. He's not listening to anyone, or noticing anything! I believe that half the time he's composing these damned *cywyddau*."

"Look at the Abbot, Master Young! Is that the place of honour by the Arglwyddes's side? How fast he's drinking that red wine! Will he make a speech to the company, do you think? Look! He's telling her a story now, but she's only half-listening. She's watching over her shoulder that old witch with the black wand."

"King Harry," commented the world-wise Canon, washing down his pasty with a draught of beer, "won't have a woman near him when he's at table; but our good natives here are so gross in their cups, that if it weren't for the sharp eyes and sharp tongues of an old beldam like that they'd be drunk before the harp-playing!"

Rhisiart followed the old woman's movements with interest and wonder. Every now and then she would hobble up to the Arglwyddes and whisper something; then she would return to the back of the hall and point out to the serving-men with her staff some group among the warriors by the fire whose platters or flagons needed replenishing.

She wore an amazingly tall stiff cap, from which a long white wimple descended to her shoulders, and her spotless gown, made of some grey woollen stuff, hung about her form in stiff creases.

"She must be the Nurse," thought Rhisiart; and then as his eyes, which were always hovering about the two girls, met Tegolin's glance again, and again were evaded by Catharine's, he was arrested by the sight of Rhys Gethin, who appeared to be narrating some murderous personal encounter with the most irreverant and reckless abandon to none other than Father Pascentius. The Father's expression of lascivious interest in what, from the warrior's gleaming eyes and flashing teeth, must have been a tale of blood and rapine, was the more noticeable because of the expression full of a disgusted loathing of what he heard upon the passionate countenance of Father Rheinalt.

Indeed, it was clear to the lad that Tegolin's begetter was completely out of his element, and sitting there, separated from his daughter, was angrily brooding upon one single wish, to get safe back to his cell!

"Is the poor monk," thought Rhisiart, "reminded of the Hog of Chirk by these blood-thirsty tales?" Regarding it as a dedicated topic of conversation with a man of the great world, and a topic to which he himself could display some degree of penetration, our friend commented to his companion upon this angry aloofness of Father Rheinalt and compared it with the almost liquorish interest displayed by the theologian.

"I'm afraid the man's an idealist," responded Master Young; and then with a tone of weary acquiescence in the aberrations of the human race, he added, "I have always found that idealism gets more in one's way than actual wickedness; but the only thing to do is to expect it, allow for it, and discount it. You are beginning life, Master Rhisiart, and will have to learn these things by experience but I can assure you—"

He was interrupted by a disturbance just below where they sat, and Rhisiart saw his friend, the Lollard, pushed unceremoniously from his place by the side of the Bard by none other than the loquacious Scab.

Derfel's prophet was already a little drunk, and in his whimsies and humours had taken it into his head to give personal advice to Griffith Llwyd as to the direction his bardic impulse should take when the moment arrived.

The Lollard himself only smiled agreeably, and found a place on the bench behind; but our friend felt such indignation on his behalf that he couldn't resist calling out to the intruder and telling him, in no unsparing language, that he was taking a better man's seat.

The Bard himself acted like one whose sole concern was to keep his flowing beard from coming into secular contact with the foaming beer and the broken morsels of meat and pastry from which he was selecting his long-anticipated feast.

Rhisiart had always been told that Welsh Bards were insatiable trencher-men; but he had never seen such a zest for the flesh of sheep and cattle as was manifested by the descendant of Einion.

The Bard had a wizened, puckered little face, like that of a harp-player among pigmies. His pinched nose, pale blue eyes and twitching lips peeped out from his tangled mass of hair like a squirrel from an ivy-tod; and it appeared to our friend, as after a reassuring nod from the dispossessed Lollard he gave himself up to the amusement of watching the little hairy man's reception of the Scab's advice, that his vanity was so impenetrable that not only Derfel's prophet but Derfel himself would have had no effect upon him.

Like an owl under its feathers the Bard seemed to be of so small and brittle a frame that it was incredible to our friend not only how he could dispose of so much bodily nourishment, but *upon what,* in that wrinkled nut of a skull, any kind of *awen* or inspiration could find scope to work! The prophet of Saint Derfel, drunk as he was, recognized at last that it was harder to make headway with a bard at table than with spearmen in the field and began to become abusive. So noisy did he become—and Rhisiart could see that the rougher element among the warriors by the fire were entirely on his side—that it became necessary for Owen himself to intervene; and Meredith was sent to pacify the disturbers.

Our friend noticed with satisfaction that it was from the Lollard that this ambassador from the dais tried to arrive at the cause of the fracas, and he also noticed how oblivious he was to the rough usage that his green sleeves and yellow hose underwent as the Scab's supporters jostled him, and squeezed him against the greasy trestles and benches.

Rhisiart long remembered one particular moment of this scene. It was when Meredith was being more hustled than the lad had supposed could be possible under this roof, and when the sagacious Master Young had whispered in his ear the opinion that the Bard being a virtuoso was naturally unpopular with the rabble, whereas the Scab was a born demagogue, that the picture that arrested him so limned itself upon his mind.

Meredith was being hopelessly shouted down. More and more of the rougher warriors were leaving their seats by the fire and crowding forward. The Bard, afraid that someone would meddle with his harp, had drawn an ugly-looking knife.

And it was then that all Meredith did was to raise his arm, which in its loose sleeve rose above the tumult like the flag of a sinking ship, towards his father. And Rhisiart caught, as he watched the father and

son, a look pass between them of such weary amusement that everything else in that smoky hall faded away, and the man with the forked
beard and the man with the black curls created between them a gulf
of intellectual detachment into which all the fever of life sank.

A wordless conclusion was evidently reached between the two, for
Owen said something to the Arglwyddes and something else—across
the lady—to the Abbot; while Meredith, extricating himself from the
press, returned to his place on the dais.

"He's got more sense than I thought," whispered the worldly-wise
Canon in Rhisiart's ear. "He's going to get up and speak."

Our friend shook his head. Master Young might know the ways of
King Henry. It needed a returned native to know that a Welsh
chieftain never rose up at a feast, but always left the art of oratory to
his bards and his prophets.

But what actually happened was different from what either the
gentleman from London or the gentleman from Hereford expected.
Owen *did* rise to his feet—"And Blessed Virgin!" thought Rhisiart,
"I'll be damned if he doesn't look like Modry's Pryderi!"—but instead
of making any attempt to forestall his prophet or his bard, he stretched
out his great two-handed cup at arm's length away from him, and leaning forward over the table dipped into it the fingers of his other hand.

His rising was the signal for a great wave of silence to flow over
the company. It was like enchantment. Where each man stood or
crouched or sat—*there* he remained. But when he stretched out the
silver flagon and dipped his fingers into it a second silence followed
the first silence, like a soft volcanic cloud following a tidal wave; and
at this, and Rhisiart himself felt it, all the petrified human shapes in the
hall—those tragic, laughable, fevered shapes whose tumult had been
swallowed up in a hush deeper than the mere negation of sound—drew
their breath with an audible sigh. It was at that moment that he met
Tegolin's eyes and clung to them for an instant; an instant of tension
so vibrant that it resembled the tinkling fall of the hands of time's
clock upon the marbly base of space.

Then he turned back to Owen and saw him sprinkle drops from the
cup in every direction; and he was aware of a shiver of consciousness
in the people, mounting up and up, until it became one universal living

nerve suspended in the air. Then Owen let his left hand fall to his side and with his right lifted the flagon high above his head.

And as he held the cup he raised his head so high and tilted it back so far that Rhisiart, from where he sat, could see the soft white flesh of his neck under his grey-yellow beard. Then, not in a loud voice, indeed in a voice that was almost like a whisper, he uttered some words that were totally unintelligible to the Hereford boy. They sounded like Welsh; but they were no Welsh that Rhisiart knew. But whatever the words were, their effect was electric. Every man in the hall, following Owen with the rhythmic consentaneousness of a familiar ritual, repeated the words he had used; and, after that, with a movement as spontaneous as if it had been practised for a thousand years, they lifted their cups to their lips.

And if it had been an extraordinary experience to our traveller to sink, with Tegolin, into that underworld of silence, it was hardly less of a shock when, on Owen's resuming his seat, the hall became filled with a confused uproar of excited voices.

Derfel's obstreperous representative had already pushed his way back to the fire and the descendant of Einion had already risen to take down his harp, when Rhisiart noticed the old lady with the tall head-dress and black wand go shuffling in an evident fever of excitement to the Arglwyddes's side. Between these two there then ensued a long and intense discussion, to which it was plain that both Owen and the Abbot were listening with absorbed attention.

Rhisiart couldn't see Owen's face, but he saw the face of his eldest son, as the torch-light in that midsummer twilight gleamed on the belt of Eliseg, and what he read there made it clear to him that something of very serious moment had happened or was on the verge of happening.

And then, as was natural enough, the news was passed along the dais till it reached Rhys the Savage and his theological neighbour. "What is it? What is it?" our friend whispered to Master Young.

At first the Canon of Bangor was too occupied in straining his own ears to reply; but presently he turned and, with that smile of egoistic satisfaction with which the imparter of important news betrays his advantage over the recipient, announced to Rhisiart that the aged Iolo Goch had expressed a desire to attend the harp-playing.

Whether Master Young's words were overheard by the harpist himself the lad couldn't tell; but he had never seen any human being isolate himself so completely from all contact with his kind as the Bard did then, pushing back his masses of hair from his ears, touching one harp-string after another as if they had been the lips of the dead, and literally drinking up the faint sounds which he evoked as if they had been sound, touch, sight, smell, taste, and ecstatic spiritual absorption, all in one!

The smoke from the fire was now so thick that the noise of loud coughing became audible from many quarters, and when the "Nurse" had retired from the scene Rhisiart could see the Arglwyddes giving a new set of instructions to one of the men-at-arms.

The upshot of these last orders became manifest almost at once, for the great oaken doors of the hall were presently flung wide open, revealing, in the blue-grey twilight, a large throng of peasants of all ages who had been attracted by the prospect of Griffith Llwyd's famous performance. Master Young sighed heavily when he perceived this addition to the audience.

"I understood," he whispered to our friend peevishly, taking unnecessary care that the Bard should not hear his words, "I understood that this was to be a serious council, what in Wales we call *cynghor,* but evidently it's going to be a country fair. Didn't I tell you," and his voice and manner were full of a bitter contempt, "how *he over there* misses every opportunity? The man's a fool, I tell you, even if you *are* his cousin. He's a play-acting fool! Where, I'd like to know, does all this bard-business and Derfel-business lead? Here is news just arrived —did they tell you?—that the King's back from Scotland. Lord Grey back at Ruthin, and Fitz-Alan—you told me yourself—at Chirk, and what's Owen doing? Pouring out libations to Merlin, and setting up one Bard on his death-bed against another Bard in his dotage! Listen, Master Rhisiart, you're one of this extraordinary family; can't you manage—"

Our friend's heart bounded. In a flash he saw himself in the rôle of a trusted intermediary between this cosmopolitan statesman and a newly-proclaimed Prince of Powys. But he soon found that the would-be Archdeacon's final words had a more immediate significance.

"Can't you manage," Master Young insisted, "to get that old trollop

over there to bring us some French wine? I can't last out these mum-
meries much longer. Bah! and what a chilly air they've let in! I *must*
have something more wholesome than this sickening-sweet mead!"

But another and more serious reason now presented itself for the
shutting out of the peasants and the night-air. There were sudden cries
in the court-yard, and loud agitated voices, and the high-pitched
clamour of women; and while Owen and Griffith rose to their feet and
the warriors by the fire clutched at their weapons a jostling body of
men hurled themselves into the hall, and behind them, against a yell
of protests from outside, the great doors were shut and barred.

Everyone in the place—except the descendant of Einion—made a
hurried movement to see what had happened and who had entered;
and in a moment the cry rose up, "A spy! a Ruthin spy! Kill him,
kill him! Throw him in the fire!"

Rhisiart saw the Abbot of Caerleon hasten round the top of the dais,
as if to intervene; but Rhys Gethin was too quick for him. With a
bound the man vaulted over the table, leapt down into the hall, pushed
his way through the crowd, and presently his abrupt, hard voice could
be heard giving hurried and drastic orders.

To see what was going on our friend instinctively climbed up upon
his seat and from this point of vantage he could make out the figure,
bound and helpless, and with blood streaming down his face, of a
powerful, fair-haired man in the dress of an English archer.

"Kill him! Throw him into the fire!" rose a howl of innumerable
voices.

"My Lord, my Lord," came the deep voice of the Abbot, "this man
must be heard, lest his immortal soul—"

"He won't speak! He won't speak! To the fire with him!"

Then came the murderous voice of Rhys Gethin, and Rhisiart could
see through the smoke that he had taken hold of the wretched captive
—"*Now* will you speak?"

Rhisiart glanced at Owen expecting some intervention, and to
balance himself on his stool he pressed his knee against the neck of
Master Young. But it seemed to him as if Owen's soul had fled far away
from the whole tumult.

"He's got one of his attacks," he said to himself. "But *I* must do
something. *I* can't stand this."

"*Now* will you speak?"

"Stop, stop!" came the ringing tones of Mad Huw, while he could be seen forcing his way towards the victim. "Stop! he may be Richard!"

But at last there came a sign from the victim himself, and it came in the familiar accent that brought back all his Hereford childhood to our friend's mind.

"God save King Harry!" cried the Englishman, "and may his—" but his voice ended in a long-drawn death-cry.

There was a moment's appalling hush; and then, over the whole assembly, there rose, more piercing, more pitiful, even than the man's last breath, the rending shriek of a young girl; and Rhisiart, stumbling down from his stool, saw Owen lift up his daughter in his arms and carry her out, while scream after scream, cutting into the smoke and cutting into the murkiness of that murder like a knife, quivered back into the hall as she was carried away.

VI

BARDS AND HERETICS

THE DEATH of the spy and the collapse of Catharine broke up the first part of this midsummer banquet. But more was to follow. Owen had carried the girl away; and his absence was a signal for a wild clamour of voices from every part of the hall. But Rhisiart was amazed at the presence of mind and calm authority displayed by the Arglwyddes. Leaving the dais she called first one retainer to her side and then another, giving them abrupt and decisive orders. There ensued a general clearing away of boards and trestles. Water was brought to wash away the blood of the dead, while fresh supplies of green bracken were strewn on the flag-stones round the fire.

Then he saw her approach her elder son and give him what were evidently careful and explicit instructions as to the nature of the Bard's performance.

"She's told him, I warrant," said the lad to himself, "that he'd better confine himself to playing on his harp and not attempt any improvisation in words."

He watched the lady follow Griffith with her eyes as with Eliseg's great belt twisted so absurdly round his neck the chieftain's son made his way to the harp-player. And he noted how as soon as the self-centred artist had understood her commands and was prepared to obey them she despatched one of the little pages to fetch Rhys Gethin to her side.

Since the monks and the Abbot with them had followed Mad Huw into the body of the hall, and since the legal-minded Canon had slipped down from his seat to discourse to the Lollard, Rhisiart found that Tegolin and himself were the sole possessors of the dais. The girl was standing up, following Mad Huw with her eyes, but evidently uncertain what to do. Her tall figure in its green robe, with the mass of blood-coloured hair framing her white face, brought in a flash to the lad's mind one of the few Homeric passages—and this was only a quotation in a Latin manuscript in his college library—that he had ever seen.

It was a description of the ill-fated Cassandra; and it only came back to him because it was connected with over-turned goblets and a desolated board and with blood and wine spilled together on the floor; but it returned to him often, this impression, and whenever it returned it wasn't only the girl he saw, standing alone in front of that tenantless table. He saw a vision of the strange beauty that could rise—but it was all vague and blurred in his brain—out of the very depths of tragedy.

It came and went in a moment, the impression he got then, but when it passed he found himself already at the girl's side. His approach decided her. "Come," she whispered hurriedly, "let's go to the man they killed. I want to see—"

How cold her fingers were as he took her hand! He glanced quickly at her face; but her smile re-assured him; and they made their way without difficulty to the scene of the killing. The men-at-arms fell back with a murmur of awe and admiration to let the Maid of Edeyrnion pass.

They found Mad Huw on his knees by the head of the corpse whose wide staring eyes gazed frantically at the ceiling; while standing at the victim's foot were the two Cistercians and the Abbot of Caerleon, intoning in low antiphonic alternation certain solemn verses over a soul that had perished without the rites of the Church.

The Maid fell on her knees by Mad Huw's side; but in place of bowing her head in prayer she began at once closing with her fingers the dead man's staring eyes, wiping the blood from his face with a handkerchief she drew from her own bosom, and with deft womanly touches smoothing away all she could of the distortion and horror of such an end.

The only dead bodies Rhisiart had seen hitherto had been the unhappy mangled remains of victims of Hereford justice, and as he stood looking down on this youth, obviously only a few years older than himself, and saw the girl's hair cover the lad's breast as she folded his dead hands, a recurrence of some half-forgotten night of childish fear, fear of the tumult and the violence of life, came over him, the shouts of the street, the howlings of the wind, the patter of the rain, and the ineffable safety of Modry's presence and the flickering fire-light and the warm bed in which he lay; and for a second he became this stranger laid to rest under Tegolin's soft hair.

But the girl rose up now and roused Mad Huw from his trance. She must have known what was on the Brother's wild brain for she whispered to him something about the dead being alive, and Rhisiart saw a strange swift smile pass between them, as though, by reason of some secret confederacy with Rhys Gethin's victim, it had become unnecessary just then to name the late King's name.

The Arglwyddes herself and her son Griffith now appeared on the scene, and our friend noticed that Rhys Gethin, with five or six of his men-at-arms, was unbarring the door of the hall to let himself out.

This was a relief to our friend; for it seemed better for the dead and better for them all that the corpse should be carried to the house-chapel without having to pass that man of blood.

The Arglwyddes herself, when this had been done, carried off Tegolin and the Friar to their rooms on the floor above, and Rhisiart was consoled for the Maid's departure by being treated as sufficiently one of the family to help Griffith and the pages in arranging the benches and composing the audience in preparation for the harp-playing.

He found himself finally reclining by the Lollard's side on a fresh heap of bracken, the fragrant smoke from the fire quieting his pulses, while he listened with half-dazed senses to what struck him even in his benumbed abstraction as a fantastic dialogue between the tipsy Scab and the inquisitive Master Young.

The Abbot and the two monks having returned from the chapel— the exact geographical position of which, in the corridor leading to Owen's chamber, was now being demonstrated to him by the Lollard with the aid of sundry little fragments of firewood—and having been comfortably installed within a convenient distance of the harp-player and an equally convenient distance of a capacious bowl of steaming metheglin which stood between the fire and the empty dais, Griffith gave the signal to the Bard to begin.

As Owen's eldest son it was evidently this young man's privilege to sit by the Abbot's side in the state-chair, and to represent the chieftain at this traditional performance. In the absence of both Lord and Lady, and freed, as the night fell and more torches were lit, from the formidable presence of Rhys the Savage, the company disposed themselves in easy relaxed postures to give themselves up to what—as far as the majority were concerned—was the great event of the evening.

Rhisiart could see that Griffith was abstracted as he sat in his father's chair, and it was clear that the impatient Abbot was chafing for something to happen more germane to the cause for which he had come so far; and as for Father Rheinalt our friend felt that like himself the unsociable monk was struggling against a strong tendency to fall asleep. Like himself too, Tegolin's parent kept casting furtive glances at the particular door that led in the direction marked on Master Brut's invisible map as north-west by north.

Both the monk and the youth had evidently come to link this "northwest by north," as they sat in the hall, with the apparition of desirable shapes, and the more the birch-tree smoke and the heady, sweet, hot mead drowsed their senses the more did they hope against hope that this blessed quarter of the compass would repeat its beneficence.

Rhisiart indeed, as he stretched himself out in the fire-light by the Lollard's side, soon reached such a point of confused expectancy that the dusky portals of this particular exit managed at once to shimmer like *pali* and to gleam like blood-red hair.

But the son of Dafydd ab Einion had now really begun to play, and though the Scab might criticize and the Canon of Bangor might groan at such irrelevance, the mass of the audience, soldiers, servants, and pages alike, were caught up into an ecstasy of response.

Large as the place was it was crowded from wall to wall. New groups of people had been slipping in all the while ever since the murder of the spy. Almost the whole of Owen's enormous household must have been present, together with a considerable percentage of countryfolk from the vicinity, who possessed friends at court to smuggle them through the kitchens.

At first the Bard played very low and almost timorously; but as he warmed to his task his fingers seemed to gather strength and swiftness and his whole personality seemed to melt into the instrument and become an organic part of it, so that it appeared to Rhisiart as if that little wizened head, small and brittle as a nut under a mass of foliage, were a physical portion of the harp, and as if the harp itself, endowed with a figure-head of its own, were plucking at its own breast and making music of its own heart-strings.

The man was so little and the harp was so large, and he threw himself with such absolute abandonment into every motion he made, that another impression our friend received was that of an aged "atomy," or fluttering insect, clambering at intense speed up and down the shining strings, and, as it moved, evoking all manner of subtle halftones and fractional modulations such as are audible to the sub-human ears of the creatures of the air, but until touched by this winged scarab of divination inaudible to the ears of men!

And then without leaving behind these hummings and dronings, these wailings and whimperings, these gnat-cries and shard-borne moans, this singular virtuoso began invading the sky and plundering from its invisible registrations such sounds as the screaming of eagles, the croaking of ravens, the quiverings of larks.

But the spirit of the descendant of Einion was not content with these limited regions of naturalistic vocalization; though even by this time, as our friend gazed at him through the smoke, the little head with its hairy burden had vanished completely, and a towering, formless, shapeless personality had taken its place, an irresistible, non-human personality that shook the notes out of the frightened harp as a god might shake music out of a shell.

But it was Nature's more grandiose reservoir of sounds that the spirit dominating these obedient strings now began to ransack. Sweeping the instrument with stronger fingers, till it seemed as if more than a mere framework of strings responded to his touch, he began to evoke the winds in their voyagings, the cataracts in their crashing falls, the wild rains in their torrents.

The Hereford boy was sitting straight up now, hugging his knees. All lethargy had passed from him, as apparently it had from that whole crowded assembly. He ceased turning his glance "north-west by north." Even the tipsy Scab had been reduced to silence and Owen's eldest son had stopped fidgetting in his chair. The Abbot had pulled out his psalter and put it back again many times, not knowing what he did.

The Lollard had risen to his feet. Master Young himself had allowed the fate of nations to recede into the background, while his toothless mouth became as round as a wood-pecker's hole.

A queer sensation began to invade Rhisiart's nerves, as if not the harp alone but the whole torch-lit hall were the instrument the obsessed player was using, and as if his own secretest fibres, and those of all the company about him, had become the strings at which the man was tearing.

But what was this? Lost in his blind inspiration, the player had forgotten the Arglwyddes's command that *the harp only* was to speak. At first with low sounds that seemed hardly human syllables, and then, as he went on, with words that took their meaning as well as their music from the notes that accompanied them, he began a celebration of his Lord's prowess in battle. "With a broken sword," he said, "the son of Griffith Fychan mowed down the enemies of King Richard! With a red flamingo's feather in his helm he flamed through the battle, and the sound of his onslaught was like the sound of the waves of the sea when they roar over the sand-dunes! The dead, the dead fight for the son of Griffith Fychan, and the spirits of the air gather about the rush of his onset, like the winds out of their dark pavilions in the track of the hurricane!"

As the man's voice rose in his wild excitement the notes of the harp seemed sometimes to follow, sometimes to lead his utterance; but what Rhisiart, as he listened, found most extraordinary was the way a certain hard, clear, conscious, almost cold *intention* continued to retain in the midst of the wildest excursions of his frenzy the symphonic unity of his performance.

He went back upon himself, he gathered up his earlier motifs, he reverted to those hummings and whisperings, like the vague stirrings in the air of thousands of summer afternoons. He reverted to the screaming of eagles, to the pipings of curlews, to the cawings of rooks.

Into the rhythm of the hooves of Owen's war-horse, into the rush of the flying track of that flamingo feather, into the cleaving of skulls under that broken sword, he tossed the roar of the falling cataracts he had plundered, he flung the wailing of the journeying winds he had invoked.

Rhisiart couldn't follow all the words he used. Many of them were old archaic words, words borrowed from Taliesin, from Aneurin, from Llywarch Hen. Some of them he suspected to be words coined for the occasion by the Bard himself. Nor could he follow all the strange rhythms of the accompaniment. Many of these seemed to him to be conjured up out of the very abysses of prehistoric time. He heard the crashing of ice-floes in the glacial era; he heard the moaning of winds in forests roamed by mammoths; he heard the hissing of the lava in prehistoric volcanoes as it was drowned in the tidal waves of nameless seas.

There came a point when the lad actually couldn't see the form of the man who was playing. A cloud of conjured-up shapes, like the shapes of the first day of creation, blotted him out. The descendant of Einion had ceased to be a harpist in a smoky hall. He had become the beating of immortal wings in a great void! He had become the breath of the ultimate spirit moving on the face of the waters.

"The poor little hairy man!" Rhisiart heard Master Young exclaim with a gasp of wonder to Derfel's prophet. "He'll fall down in a fit soon. He ought to be stopped."

"Hush! for Christ's sake!" responded the Scab. And our friend, rising like a deep-sea fish, or descending like an empyrean-bird, from the regions into which he had been transported, said to himself that a player who could make Master Young sentimental and the Scab cry, "Hush! for Christ's sake!" must indeed be an artist.

"But what in the Virgin's name—" The startling, indeed it might be called the *shocking,* effect of the sudden cessation of the Bard's performance was felt by everybody in the hall.

Owen's son jumped up from his chair and stood transfixed. The Abbot and the two monks crossed themselves as if in the presence of something supernatural. Rhisiart himself leapt to his feet, and the Scab and Master Young rose so hurriedly that their bench fell with a thud on the flag-stones.

Borne in on a litter, upon which rugs and cushions had been hurriedly flung, appeared a tall lean figure, with a drooping red moustache, hollow eye-sockets in which burned a pair of literally blazing eyes, a high, bald, unwrinkled brow, upon which the torch-light as it flickered shone like pallid gold, and a thin elongated neck, whose veins and muscles, as the man lifted his head, seemed to be almost anatomical, so naked of flesh they were!

Straight up in his litter the man heaved himself, leaning on his own wasted arms, and it seemed as if his blazing eyes swept round upon every separate person in the company as if they were searching for someone in particular. The dying man was carried slowly and carefully by four men-at-arms, while Owen himself, his face cold and hard with the emotion he was at pains to control, walked by the side of the litter, every now and then bending down with his hand on the man's shoulder, rather, it seemed, to catch the murmur of his wishes than to prevent him from rising.

They carried him straight towards the fire but very slowly; and he might have been Owen's father from the impassioned solitude the chieftain displayed, holding back with difficulty, as must have been clear to all, the tempest of emotion he felt. Soldiers, archers, servants, guests and pages—all crowded round the dying man. Many fell on their knees. There was the sound of the weeping of women, and harsher and stranger than that the hoarse heart-shaken sobs of battle-scarred veterans.

Rhisiart in an impulse of shyness and awe fell back as the cortège advanced, and so did his friend, the Lollard; but the Scab and Master Young moved forward to meet the litter, and even tried to draw some notice to themselves from the absorbed Owen.

When the bearers reached the fire they put down the litter, which was really a sort of wooden couch, and themselves drew back, leaving Owen alone by the dying man's side.

The great Bard—and our friend was near enough now to see that he was much older than his red moustache implied—was evidently struggling desperately to make clear to the chieftain something that he wanted done; but though he had the physical strength to hold himself erect his voice came in feeble sighs, weak and faint, and was accompanied by a curious whistling sound that was distressing to hear.

Rhisiart could see that Owen couldn't catch the import of what he was struggling to say, and the scene grew more and more painful, great drops of sweat appearing on the chieftain's brow and unmistakeable flashes of angry impatience in the Bard's burning eyes.

At last Owen straightened himself and glanced hopelessly round. He caught Rhisiart's eye and beckoned to him.

"Where is Meredith?" he murmured when the lad approached.

Griffith ab Owen, who was standing near by, caught this whisper, and as Rhisiart turned to look for Meredith, he saw the elder brother's face grow suddenly distorted with passion and saw him snatch Eliseg's belt from his neck and fling it upon the foot of the litter.

Owen himself seemed totally oblivious of his son's anger and he stared at the sacred belt as if it had dropped down from the ceiling.

To Rhisiart's immense relief he now caught sight of Meredith's green tunic and yellow hose, and he called out to him that he was wanted.

Owen was still staring at Eliseg's belt as if he had never seen it before.

"It's one of his attacks," our friend said to himself; and when his eyes met those of the dying man he caught such a desperate appeal in them that he couldn't bear it.

"Perhaps, my Lord," he cried impetuously, facing that forked beard in his rashness, "the other bard would understand him!" He could see that Iolo the Red understood his words for the great bald head was slightly shaken, but Owen mechanically obeyed his young cousin's hint and summoned the harp-player to his side.

Griffith Llwyd ap Dafydd ab Einion, oblivious of everyone and everything, was just then meticulously wiping every separate string of his harp with a piece of cloth; but to our friend's surprise he obeyed his lord's summons and came forward, his slight frame staggering under the weight of his instrument.

"Put that down!" commanded Owen sternly, but the Bard took no more notice of his words than if they had been addressed to the smoke. Dragging the great harp towards them he finally balanced it against the knee of the dying Iolo, and then bending down kissed one of the poet's knotted hands as it pressed against the side of the litter.

Pantingly and feebly came another desperate gust of whistling words; but it was clear to Rhisiart that though the harp-player was able well enough to follow the first wind of creation he could make nothing at all of this same mystic breath, when in its sighings and groanings it expressed the heart's desire of a dying man.

Meredith was with them now and it was obvious that with *his* failure to understand what Iolo was trying to say Owen gave up all hope.

The old man was getting more and more desperate. He kept rolling his eyes from one to another in frantic supplication, and Rhisiart could see that his long moustaches were actually dripping with foam as he struggled to give to these death-whistlings some sort of coherence.

The Scab had already been pulled away twice from Iolo's side; though it seemed to our friend as if the dying poet himself had a stronger hope of being understood by this disfigured scaramouch than by any of the others.

As for the Abbot and the two Valle Crucians the dying Bard wouldn't allow them to come near him. Rhisiart already had received hints of Iolo Goch's dislike of ecclesiastics. Scraps and tags attributed to him, containing the most blasphemous animadversions upon both the regular and the secular clergy, had spread as far as the Hereford border, and no doubt many scurrilous quips and jibes from the controversies of a much earlier epoch were attributed to this modern enemy of the Church.

There was one moment, and the spectacle of it sent a quiver of agitated though not altogether unpleasant awe through our friend's nerves, when even the powerful soul of the Abbot of Caerleon met its match, in a collision of eye-glances that was like the bandying of buffets at a spiritual tourney.

"Priests and bards!" the boy said to himself, as he watched not only the Abbot, but even the simple-minded and patriotic Father Rheinalt draw back defeated from this heathen death-bed; "priests and bards— aye! but they'll be enemies to the end of the world!"

The whole assembly, gentle and simple, men and women, were now crowding round the singular death-bed, and an awed silence held them as they listened to the incoherent sounds that came from beneath that red moustache.

Rhisiart was struck by the popular reverence that left a clear space round the litter where Owen stood alone with big unnoticed tears running down his set face into his forked beard; and he remarked too how not one of the soldiers and servants, however eager they were, pushed forward into the circle of the family and their guests.

The harp they had been listening to still remained propped up against the litter, and at the feet of the dying man still lay the belt of King Eliseg, untouched since Griffith had flung it down.

Every eye was fixed upon the face of Iolo, and though not a sob was heard, Owen's tears weren't the only tears that fell. The two Valle Crucians mechanically told their beads but did not lower their heads, and Rhisiart was conscious of a certain discomfort as if in the presence of something indecent as he caught the look of devouring interest with which Father Pascentius stared at the great bald head before them and listened to those whistling sounds.

Suddenly the dying man seemed inspired by a new hope. He lifted one of his hands to his face and covered his eyes, and it was clearly a relief to most of the onlookers to escape those wild supplicating glances.

Owen made a movement to support him but he shook off the offered hand. It was plain to them all that the man was desperately, quietly, passionately exerting his will-power in some intense interior concentration. A faint gasp, a perceptible murmur, arose, as from one man, from the whole of that spell-bound crowd. But an audible word broke from one of them.

"He is calling upon Derfel!" cried the irrepressible Scab. The bald-headed figure before them, supporting itself in that erect sitting-posture by one lean muscular arm, swayed backwards and forwards in the intensity of the will-power he was exerting.

"He is praying to God!" sighed the Abbot of Caerleon. "Into thy hands, O Lord, I commend—"

But to the amazement of all present the passionate tension of the dying man suddenly relaxed. He removed his hand from his eyes. He accepted with a nod, and even with something like a smile, the support which Owen offered him. Thus he remained for quite a considerable passage of time, with every feature of his face as completely relaxed as was his body.

"Jesus receive him!" murmured the voice of the Lollard.

Rhisiart too thought that the end had come; but that terrible whistling sound still continued, and the great head, though the tension of the neck was eased, didn't droop or sink.

Suddenly he made a slight movement to the left—towards that direction which Master Brut had so carefully designated as "north-west by north," and our friend following that movement with his own eyes gave so lively a start that the watchers in front of him turned their heads, too. There in the doorway, in a long child's night-gown, and with her fair hair tied back from her bare shoulders, stood the young Catharine! The girl was struggling to free one of her wrists from the grasp of the old woman they called "Nurse"; and even while she struggled she lifted up her voice and cried in tones that rang through the hall, "They're killing someone! I know they're killing someone! Where are you, Father? I *must* go to my Father. They're killing some-one!"

Owen signed to Meredith to take his place and swung round. "Let her go, Nurse!" he cried. "Come here, child! No one's being killed. Be a brave girl and come here."

The crowd parted in silence to let that white figure with its staring feverish eyes rush into his arms. He hurriedly unclasped the brooch that held his great purple mantle and wrapped its thick folds round her.

"Say goodbye to your friend, Catharine. His spirit's struggling to get free." For a second the girl hesitated, as well she might, for the eyes of the dying man burnt more feverishly than her own; but his whole face was illuminated as she bent over him.

"What do you say, Uncle Iolo? Say it again, slower! Whisper it, Uncle Iolo. *I can hear you.*"

Owen raised his hand for silence. But there was no need. The whole hall had become silent as death. From the Abbot to the youngest page, everyone held their breath. Not a soul present but knew this was the man's supreme moment, his last chance of being understood.

And she did understand him! *How* she did was a mystery to Rhisiart. But it may have been that the girl's instinct in making him *whisper* was the secret of it. Perhaps all the while if someone had held their face close to his lips that terrible whistling wouldn't have drowned his words.

"Oh women, women!" thought our young psychologist. "It's you we want, *and only you,* at such a moment!" The lad was astonished at Catharine's calm. Sinking down by the man's side on the litter she pushed her brother away and let the full weight of that heavy torso fall against her young body. And balanced there, her father's mantle brushing the strings of the harp and her own white gown touching

Eliseg's belt, she resolutely and clearly, in a voice that didn't even tremble as she spoke, repeated after him in her own words all he whispered to her.

Rhisiart could hear some little page behind him struggling pitifully not to cough as the smoke from the fire got into his throat, and some serving-wench at the end of the hall sneezed once or twice; but except for that every word the girl uttered fell like a smooth stone into the unrippled pond of absolute silence.

"He says he *willed* someone to come," she interpreted. *"Me* to come," she corrected herself. "He says you must all swear on the king's belt to be his men against the English. He says September the—" Here she paused and Rhisiart could see the frown of intense childish trouble with which she struggled to catch the difficult word. "September the— the fifteenth—no! the—the *sixteenth—* He says on September the six-teenth you must all come here and—and—and proclaim my father Prince of Wales. He says on Saint Matthew's Day we must—"

She broke off for a long tense moment while it became clear that the pressure of the gaunt shoulder against her had suddenly grown too much. Then in something almost like a cry of pain she repeated the single word "Ruthin," and sank sideways under his dead weight.

That word "Ruthin," the name of their bitterest enemy's stronghold, must have been the last word uttered on earth by Iolo Goch, and so closely involved was the girl's body with the man's death-spasm, that when Owen and Meredith had lowered his head on the cushions of the litter, Rhisiart could see the Nurse, into whose arms the exhausted child flung herself, wipe from the front of her night-gown a smear from the red froth that had come from that desperate mouth.

What, however, chiefly worried our young adventurer's mind, as the old woman in the tall head-dress disappeared "north-west by north" with her young charge, was whether the final glance that Catharine flung back towards them included himself in its farewell.

Her father had clearly forgotten her as he bent over the corpse of his old friend, while he himself saw nothing save her vanishing figure; but *had* her eyes met his, as he gazed after her, or was it an illusion? She still had Owen's purple mantle wrapped round her as the Nurse took her away; took her down that corridor which was now fraught for our friend's mind with all the perfumes of Arabia, but the image he retained of her, the image that remained in its cloudy niche in his soul all the while he was staring at Eliseg's belt lying at the dead man's feet, was the image of her as she had appeared when the crowd divided to let her pass, her flaxen hair all braided for the night and her eyes so wide and staring.

There was now a surge and clamour of voices, loud as the roar of the surf when some heavy postern door looking seaward is suddenly opened, and there was a general rush forward.

Owen was still standing by the Bard's head. Without his purple robe he looked like a statue carved in gold, and he looked younger, too; though his forked beard stood out more clearly than it had done before. Rhisiart could see he was totally absorbed in his grief. He seemed to have grown oblivious to everything in the world but Iolo's death; and our friend asked himself whether that final request or command or prophecy uttered by the dead man was going to be obeyed or not. "Probably not," he thought, as he watched Owen's distraction. But he was counting without the impetuous Abbot and without the reckless monk who'd begotten Tegolin.

Both these men now advanced to the foot of the bier, and their deep rich voices, trained to the intoning of ritual, rose simultaneously above the hubbub. "I swear by the belt of Eliseg to be true man and liege servant to the puissant Prince Owen ap Griffith Fychan as long as my life shall last!"

The rolling resonance of these two patriotic priests' voices hadn't died away before they made room at the litter for Father Pascentius. He uttered this formidable vow in the same words but quite slowly and quietly; and Rhisiart observed that he didn't hesitate to take hold of the sacred heirloom and examine it with curiosity and that as he moved away he made that characteristic gesture with his hands that had become a habit with him and that seemed to absolve all the makers of vows from all the vows that they had made since the beginning of the world!

The clamour and shouting in the body of the hall had now become so vociferous that it was evidently a trouble to Owen; for he kept frowning vaguely, and staring round; but there was a film over his eyes as he did this, and since he neither spoke to quiet them nor raised his hand for silence the shouting grew louder and louder.

"Make the pretty cousin swear!" Rhisiart heard one voice bawl out. "Make the little Hereford calf give a kick at his King!"

"Make the damned Lollard swear, my Lord Abbot!" cried another, "so us can see how one of these heretic dogs takes an honest Christian oath!"

"My Lord Abbot," cried a third, "make the lawyer swear! Don't let the lawyer sneak off without risking his neck!"

With that natural human instinct that causes the persecuted to cling together both Master Young and Master Brut now came forward to our friend's side.

But the Lollard only paused to give Rhisiart a humorous smile and to whisper hurriedly, "Here we are following John ap Hywel again!" before he boldly advanced to the litter.

But in place of touching the king's belt as he made *his* vow, he laid one hand on the thigh of the dead man and the other on the hilt of Owen's sword. The action startled the chieftain, and even for a second seemed to anger him, but when he saw who it was who had touched his sword a faint smile crossed his lips. "You too, Master Brut? Well, well! Don't go to bed to-night without coming to see me!"

Aroused by the Lollard from his trance, Owen embraced the situation in a moment with Rhisiart and Master Young hesitating as liege subjects of King Harry about committing such an overt act of treason.

"Make the Hereford cousin swear, my Lord!" shouted a voice from the rear as soon as it was seen that Owen's consciousness had come back to earth.

"Make the Canon of Bangor swear, my Lord!" came the harsh voice of the Scab. "If an Abbot can be a good Welshman, a Canon can!" But Owen was himself again.

"No need for any of *our* family to swear!" he said easily and with careless dignity. "And we shall want Master Young," he added gravely, "to represent us at Henry of Lancaster's Court. So it would be a mistake to narrow his freedom by oaths and vows. But it would be a great comfort to me and my family, too," and he raised his head with a gesture so princely that it filled our friend's eyes with tears, "if everyone here to-night will vow with me, by Our Lady of Valle Crucis and Saint Derfel of Edeyrnion, that we will not sheathe our sword in this righteous cause till Henry of Lancaster—"

He was interrupted by a thunder of voices and a savage clatter of arms, as every hand and every weapon that was to hand was raised in the air.

"Saint Derfel for Edeyrnion!" cried the Scab in an ecstasy, and not only that great hall but the whole of the palace seemed to rock and sway to the shout that arose: "Saint Derfel for Edeyrnion! Saint Derfel for Owen Glyn Dŵr!"

Rhisiart never forgot the conflicting tumult of his feelings at that moment. He longed to have Tegolin's hand tight in his. He longed in some queer way for the Modry of his childhood. Along with all his emotion at the sight of that tall, grief-stricken, golden figure, and along with all his response to this high moment, he was aware of an obscure stab of homesickness for the familiar faces and voices of the old Hereford streets; and deep in his heart he was grateful to Owen for saving him just then from the irrevocable plunge of taking the Abbot's vow.

"And now," Owen was saying, "the Arglwyddes and I have only to tell you all that there will be mead and wine in this hall till midnight. Griffith Llwyd ap Dafydd ab Einion will remain with you. He will sing for you of the dead and of the living, of our wrongs and of the day of our vengeance. He will sing to you the glory of Iolo; he will sing to you the destruction of Mathrafal; he will sing to you of the rise and the fall of Dinas Brān. He will sing to you of the great king of our house upon whose belt we have sworn." He paused, while throughout the hall there was a general movement of relaxation, the spearmen and men-at-arms resuming their places about the fire, and the great gate being unbolted to admit the villagers and to relieve the guard.

Then appealing once more for silence he reminded them how the dead Bard had named with his last breath the sixteenth day of September as the day of their re-assembling.

"Let the word go forth," he concluded, "to the north and south and east and the west; but let it be a word *for our people only*. If a Saxon from Ruthin or Chirk or Castell Goch ask you, 'What is this September? What is this sixteenth?' say in answer that it is the day of the threshing of the wheat and the day of the burning of the weeds!"

While Owen was uttering these final words, Rhisiart watched how the young man Griffith sat down gloomily on a heap of bracken close to the fire, where he bent forward and stared at the burning logs. The fragrant smoke swept over him and hid him from our friend's sight; but, when it swept away, there he was still, his powerful shoulders hunched up, and his big hands rubbing first one shin and then another, as he felt through his hose the scorching heat.

What *were* that young man's thoughts, our lad wondered. Did he hold all this business of swearing by Eliseg's belt as arrant tom-foolery? Did he despise his father for his womanish grief over Iolo? Did he hate Meredith as an obsequious popinjay in his green sleeves and yellow hose? He *couldn't* surely hate Catharine? But he certainly hadn't looked at her, as she bent over the dying Bard, with a very tender eye. "On my soul," our friend concluded, "I believe both he and the Arglwyddes are critical of all this Welsh enthusiasm. The Arglwyddes comes from the Hanmers, a good solid border family, and no doubt Griffith takes after her. If these damned lords of Marches had had the least tact, the Arglwyddes and her son between them would never have let Owen go so far. Yes! that fellow warming his shins hates his Welsh blood. He wore that belt round his neck just to mock them; and he flung it at Iolo's corpse as you'd fling down a glove!"

Our friend was so absorbed in his attempts to pluck out the heart of Griffith's mystery that the Lollard had to address him twice.

"The Abbot's speaking to you, Master!" he repeated.

But when Rhisiart turned round, the impatient autocrat from Caerleon had hurried on with the matter in hand and was giving directions to the pages for the transporting of Iolo to the chapel.

Owen had already disappeared and the hall was now full of bustling servitors of both sexes, dispensing the new supply of mead in a manner so lavish as to reduce to positive niggardliness all that our lad had ever seen of baronial hospitality.

"*Beati pauperes spiritu!*" began the Abbot in his great bass voice; Father Rheinalt who was clearly a mighty intoner of penitential passion, answering at once with the next beatitude, while Father Pascentius, his eyes roving wantonly, so Rhisiart fancied, towards the serving-wenches and the mead-cups, followed their lead more leisurely and mechanically.

"What are *we* supposed to do now?" enquired Master Young of the

Lollard and our friend, when the corpse had been carried out. There was in the man's tone such a mixture of querulous grievance, of amused and indulgent disapproval, and of philosophical patience, that our friend felt quite drawn to him. After all he *was* from that great civilized world, of London and Paris and Rome, the skirts of which he himself had touched in Oxford, but of which, except Owen, nobody here knew a single thing!

"I believe Meredith will come back for us in a moment," Rhisiart replied. "For there's to be a sort of council in Owen's private chamber; and I fancy we—" He spoke in his grandest Hereford voice, picked up in the sheriff's court; but the Canon of Bangor had had occasion to propitiate too many proud young men in his time to allow the faintest smile to cross his diplomatic features.

"Hasn't everything been decided already," he said, "by my Lord Abbot? I don't see what's left to hold a council *about!* Though I confess it was to be present at some kind of a meeting of that sort that I risked my life with our friend, *le Capitaine sauvage.* By the way, Master Brut, don't you think our young patron here, who as one of the family has already been so kind to us, had better warn the gentleman in the yellow hose when he *does* come back that all the guards from the base-court are *in here,* getting drunk, and that none—for I've been watching these little arrangements very carefully—have been sent out to replace them, and if Grey or Burnell or Fitz-Alan *happen* to be on the prowl—and we know that at least one of their scouts has been caught already—this feast-night of Saint John would make a perfect psychological moment for an attack! One good bonfire would bring the yard-gates down, and another would bring *those* down, and where would Glyndyfrdwy be then? Up in smoke, my young master; up in good pine-log smoke, and all these sinful Christian souls with it; though I daresay they wouldn't take *the life* of that little girl we saw just now. They certainly wouldn't if they came from Chirk!"

And the Canon gave vent to a cavernous "hee! hee!" out of his toothless mouth. The fellow was addressing Rhisiart, but he looked at the Lollard; and our friend, too outraged by the allusion to Catharine to meet his eye, also looked at the Lollard, and it was a deep satisfaction to him to see the expression of stern disgust on the heretic's face. There followed an uncomfortable silence between the three of them, but a distraction offered itself in a comical dispute hard by, between the Scab and the nervous harp-player, in the course of which the tipsy prophet presumed to lay hands on the precious instrument, actually drawing sacrilegious fingers across the strings.

While the three visitors were watching this clash between prophet and musician, and observing how the indignant artist wiped each string the other had touched, as if it were a living creature, they heard a loud and prolonged battering at the bolted door.

"Just what I said!" whispered Master Young. "By the Baptist I believe it *is* Grey or Fitz-Alan!"

As he spoke, Rhisiart saw him thrust his hand into his doublet, as if to make sure of the safety of some secret packet that he kept hidden there.

But even while our friend was wondering what line he ought to take if there *were* a rush of Englishmen into the hall, a man-at-arms deliberately unbarred the door and let in none other than Rhys the Savage. Rhys was followed by quite a large company of spearmen, many more than the few who had left the place with him, and by the manner in which these fierce warriors stared round them it was clear they were unaccustomed to scenes of such courtly revelry.

Upon Master Young's face might be read the struggle between two emotions: immense relief at this timely addition to their defenders, and a natural dislike of being under the same roof with the man who so recently had made him bolt like a rabbit.

"Pray God," he whispered to Rhisiart, "the brute is no drunkard, and will keep the liquor away from those ruffians of his! Well, at any rate, Owen's palace is safe 'pro tem'; and if it gets known outside that the place is manned to such a tune, those Ruthin fellows will clear off, even if they *are* on the prowl. Yes, they've lost their chance, the fools; just as Owen has lost *his* by telling the world what he's going to do—oh, my dear young man, I sometimes feel as if the whole human race is so brainless that it *deserves* to suffer what it does! But here's your handsome cousin; and, by cock, he'd make a pretty Lord Chamberlain to the little Dauphiness of France! Where do you suppose he picked up that pattern for his tunic? It's the very mate to the one my Lord Beaufort wore at the King's coronation!"

Rhisiart saw Griffith ab Owen get up with an impatient gesture when his brother approached them, and walking round the fire enter into conversation with Rhys Gethin.

"Father wants you all in the 'magician's chamber,'" Meredith began hurriedly. "Oh, there's my brother talking to Rhys! That's just what I hoped he *wouldn't* do at this juncture. Rhys is our perdition in council, as he is our salvation in the field. Griffith is angry about the oath, and angry with my father for mentioning September the sixteenth. He never liked Iolo. He thinks my father was infatuated. He'll do what we decide, but he thinks it's silly to break with the King just because of Grey. He thinks the Abbot's a hot-headed firebrand, and of course"— here the dark youth smiled his weary and whimsical smile—"that's just what he *is!* But Father feels, and I daresay he's right, that if Wales is ever liberated it'll be through hot-heads and madmen, through bards and Derfelites, through Rhys Gethins and Father Rheinalts, rather than through the counsels of the prudent."

Master Young's eyes narrowed in his flat, featureless face and the muscles around his mouth twitched so much as to cause hairs on a wart on his chin to emerge into an emphasis that hitherto had escaped even the observant Rhisiart.

"Wise counsellors," he remarked in a whisper, "must use all weapons; but *they need not keep them!*" The tone in which he uttered these last words was so sinister and formidable that our friend had a vision of Rhys the Savage and John ap Hywel and poor Father Rheinalt being handed over to their enemies.

But he caught Meredith looking so anxiously at him that he asked if there was anything he could do for him.

"Perhaps, if you," Meredith began, with a pondering look at his elder brother whose saturnine countenance was evidently responding heartily to the savage Captain's discourse; "perhaps, if you were to—" They were interrupted by some new disturbance going on outside the bolted gate.

Rhisiart even thought he could detect the sound of a woman's voice. Rhys Gethin leapt from Griffith's side and rushing to the door shouted some unknown Welsh words through its thick resistance. These must have been a password of some sort; for apparently satisfied by the response, he pushed back the iron bolts. A couple of his spearmen entered at once dragging a woman with them. She was a young woman of a pleasing figure but somewhat plain face; and the poor thing was weeping so wildly that many in that hall half turned to see what was the matter. But a woman in tears who was neither a pretty girl nor a Welsh girl excited little interest; especially as Einion's grandson had begun to play a mournful and tender dirge over Princess Myfanwy of Dinas Brān.

A certain number of the Captain's spearmen did, however, put down their flagons and lurched towards the new-comers and their wretched captive.

"From Ruthin, from the castle," our friend heard Meredith murmur with a sigh, and in a tone that certainly showed more weariness than commiseration. "They're always finding sweethearts outside the walls and then they get caught. She'll be put to work here or married to one of our men. You needn't waste pity on her. But pardon me, gentlemen, this is my chance to get hold of my brother."

"Shall we try to find this astrologer's cell he speaks of?" suggested the Canon after a pause. Rhisiart hesitated. Meredith had already taken his brother by the arm and led him aside. Instinctively he followed the Lollard, who had already advanced a step or two towards the group round the English girl, for he said to himself, "After all *I* haven't been invited to this council any more than you, you clever rogue; but Master Brut I *heard* being invited! I wish I knew whether I *am* expected or not. I would hate—Christ! how women *can* cry! And she doesn't look hysterical either. She looks a sensible, sturdy kind of wench—I suppose she doesn't *want* to be married to one of Rhys's men *or* to serve under that old woman with the head-dress! But I expect these women of the people don't feel things as Tegolin or as Catharine would."

With this unsympathetic thought in his head he caught, as he was advancing still nearer, a glimpse of such wild trouble in the woman's face that it was worse to see than her weeping was to hear; and the idea suddenly seized him, "What if it's that dead Englishman who was her lover?"

Rhisiart was standing near the Lollard, but still a little way behind, and he noticed that Master Brut was clasping and unclasping the fingers of his right hand, as if he were about to use his fists. "He may be a Welshman," our friend thought, "and he may be a heretic, but I'm damned if he's not going to give that savage a good Herefordshire clip!"

"Well, I'll swear to it then," Rhys Gethin was snarling through his wolfish teeth. "I'll swear to it on my honour."

"Come off that, Captain!" cried one tipsy spearman. "Honour ain't naught on Saint John's Day!"

"On *this* then, you scoundrel!" and he held up the cross-hilt of his dagger.

"Not good enough, Captain!" cried a burly archer from Conway. "*Here!* Here's me own mother's death-cross! Swear on *this,* Captain, and then Hell-fire'll have'ee if a don't keep word!"

There was a dead silence in that portion of the hall save for the woman's sobs, while Rhys Gethin stretched out his hand and took the little iron crucifix.

Rhisiart saw the fingers of the Lollard's right hand clench themselves and remain closed. A rush of wild thoughts raced through the lad's brain. "I don't care if it *is* the finish of me here," he thought. "If Master Brut goes for him, I'm with him, Owen or no Owen!"

"I swear on my Saviour," cried Rhys hoarsely, "that the man who hands over a good silver groat—a good one, mind you, no Scot counterfeit!—shall have this woman, ring or no ring, from this day forward; and the man who lifts a hand to take her from him will have to deal with *me!*"

Rhisiart heard the Lollard draw a deep breath while his shoulders stiffened. There was a low murmur of voices among the group of men gathered round the sobbing woman.

One of the men who had brought her in kept his hand on her wrist, or, as Rhisiart saw by her face, she would have rushed across to Owen's sons who were now pacing to and fro on the other side of the hall, absorbed in some heated argument. "*They* don't care!" he thought. "I suppose this sort of thing's always happening."

Meanwhile there must have been something about that little iron object in their Captain's hand that made those dare-devils hesitate. And in addition to this, as our friend quickly divined, a murmur of protest had begun to arise among a group of the Arglwyddes' serving-maids who had been drawn to the scene.

"Well," repeated Rhys Gethin, "if none of you white-livered mothers' sons have the guts to take this bitch—and she's a plump wench though she's not as well-favoured as some I know—I'm damned if I won't throw down the groat myself! I deserve one night of—"

But at that the Lollard walked straight up to the man, our friend at his heels. But it was a great silver piece he held out to the ruffian, not a clenched fist.

"It's more than a groat!" thought Rhisiart as the resplendent coin, fresh from the King's mint, flashed in the torch-light.

Rhys Gethin took it, tossed it in the air, caught it again, bit it between his shining teeth, and thrust it into the pouch in his belt. "Take her then, Master Scholar," he said. "She's yours, such as she is! And if any of you staring fools try to meddle with Master Scholar's property, you know what I've sworn! There she is, Master; and there's your mother's death-cross, my son!" and he returned the crucifix to the man who'd produced it.

Then he turned to the woman who was swallowing her sobs and staring at the strange gentleman in the dark velvet gown as if he were an angel.

"What's your name, my pretty?" he jeered.

Rhisiart couldn't catch the girl's murmur; but apparently her questioner did.

"*Alice!*" the outlaw roared. "Her name's Alice!" And then he burst into a tavern song:

> *What matter her name, Clerk Waters said.*
> *With books at my feet and books at my head,*
> *There's room for the doxy who makes my bed!*

"But off with her, Master Student, or she'll have no tears left to cry to-night. And bring me drink, my kittens, and stop that giggling!" And he turned to one of the girls who were carrying the mead and possessed himself of a double-handled flagon.

"Here's to Alice of Ruthin and her Hereford scholar!"

Rhisiart felt a more murderous desire to stick his dagger into the fellow's ribs than he had felt with regard to anyone in his whole life. He glanced hurriedly at the Lollard, but that worthy had laid his hands already on the woman's shoulders and was murmuring something he couldn't hear.

"Bring her away," he whispered, going up to them. "Let's take her to Meredith."

The kindly servant-girls had made room for them, and they were crossing the hall, the Lollard still whispering God-knows-what in the woman's ear, when Master Young intercepted them.

"What madness is this?" he protested. "Those sons of Owen have no time just now to dispose of camp-followers. Are we *never* to reach this council-chamber? Let the woman go, for Christ's sake! She'll look after herself all right, now that Savage has forgotten her. Let her go to the kitchen as Meredith said. She isn't such a great beauty. The scullions won't draw blood over her."

Thus protesting, but to no purpose, the Canon of Bangor followed them as they went up to the brothers.

"The crusader's sword again!" laughed Meredith. "There, there, my girl! You're all right now. The gallant Captain's fully occupied. Nurse will find you a place to sleep upstairs, unless—" and he glanced with a sly questioning look at the two Herefordshire youths.

"I don't want her to be—" began the Lollard. "I mean I don't want to lose sight of her till I have—"

Meredith smiled while Griffith gazed gloomily upon the silent woman, as if she were a window into a receding corridor of trouble.

"Till you have decided what to do with her, eh? All right, Master Brut! Our guests' belongings are as sacred as our guests' heads. Well, bring her along. We'll get hold of Nurse. She'll look after her for to-night. My father wants you both in the magician's chamber—and you too, Canon! I'm sorry we've kept you waiting; but Griffith and I had a certain little point to settle," and he gave his elder brother the same half-tender, half-mocking smile that he had given the Lollard.

" 'Twas lucky," he whispered to Rhisiart, as they all moved to that "north-west by north" door that our friend had come to know so well, "that you settled it without blows with the Captain! If this woman comes from *inside* the castle she may be useful to us. But don't let your friend worry about her. I don't want to disturb my mother; but Nurse will look after her."

They came to an arched door carved in stone that struck Rhisiart as the oldest piece of masonry he'd yet seen in the place. Here, a flight of steps, lit by a couple of dimly-burning torches, led up to the women's quarters. The same sluggish door-warden they had seen guarding the outer gate sat nodding on the lowest step.

"Nurse!" cried Meredith over this sluggish person's head. "Nurse! Nurse!" he repeated, when only a faint feminine titter sounded in the distance, "Nurse!"

Then they did at last hear the tap, tap, tap of the ebony wand and the shuffle of the rabbit-skin slippers, as the old crone, with an extremely irritable face in the smoky torch-light, came feeling her way down.

"Will you take this woman—" began Meredith. "Her name's Alice!" threw in Master Brut, and there was something about the Lollard's in- sisting on her name at this moment that gave our friend a very queer feeling. For one thing it seemed like a humanizing seal set upon this helpless creature's form, and for another thing it aroused an obscure pulse of sensuality in him.

It suddenly made the anonymous body of this "woman from Ruthin" something precious and desirable, the neck, the bosom, the waist, the limbs, of a nameless victim of chance becoming the sentient personality of Alice.

And indeed it seemed that the woman herself was struck by the tone in which the Lollard had said "her name's Alice," for, with a hurried glance at the wrinkled unsympathetic face under the tall head-dress, she laid both her hands on Master Brut's velvet sleeve. "Come here, girl!" commanded the Nurse out of the gloom of the staircase.

But Alice only hid her face against the sleeve of her protector.

"Leave it with me, Masters!" cried the old woman hobbling down the remaining steps, and laying her bony hand on the girl's shoulder. "It will soon learn its place with me." She spoke in broken English, apparently for the benefit of Alice, but the effect of her words was clearly the reverse of re-assuring.

The girl began to cling frantically to Master Brut's arm; and over her bowed head the heretic appealed to Rhisiart.

"Perhaps your friend, the Maid—" he murmured.

"May I call Tegolin?" asked Rhisiart of Meredith.

"Make it let go of the gentleman," repeated the Nurse, "and leave it with me!"

"*Tegolin!*" Our friend had anticipated Meredith's consent, and his voice rang loud and clear up that dark stairway.

Griffith muttered something about disturbing the Arglwyddes, while Master Young shrugging his shoulders edged away from this meddlesome boy and gave vent to an ostentatious sigh of disapproval.

"Hush!" cried the Nurse indignantly; and pointing at Alice with her stick she uttered some querulous instructions to the lethargic porter who scrambled stiffly to his feet.

But at that instant there were voices and lights and laughter and hurried footsteps above; and down the stairs came Tegolin, her red braid coiled round her head, a blue mantle thrown over her night-gown, and her eyes shining with excitement and high spirits.

To Rhisiart's romantic mind there was something annoying in the fact that he had caught the Maid of Edeyrnion thus revelling in the society of girls of her own age. "She wasn't with the Friar at all," he thought in a spasm of reproach. "She was laughing and enjoying herself with those hussies!"

It was clear that the lad's masculine objection to such a waste of sparkling eyes and panting bosoms was fully shared by the old woman in the head-dress. She pointed her stick again at Alice, who now had lifted her head and was staring at the Maid. It was evidently a profound surprise to this English girl to find anybody in this stronghold who was different from Rhys Gethin.

But our friend was now speaking hurriedly to Tegolin while Meredith with a movement of his hand reduced the porter to his normal sluggishness.

"And don't let her out of your sight for a moment, for the Blessed Virgin's sake!" he implored the girl. "Master Brut saved her from the Captain. She's from Ruthin and her name's Alice. Don't let anyone get her away from you till Master Brut's seen her again."

Never had our lad felt such complete trust in any living creature as he felt in this red-haired apparition smiling down upon them from those dim stairs. Tegolin seemed to absorb the whole situation in one laughing glance.

"How clever she is!" the boy thought. "No, there's no one like her." And then he sighed; and this sigh of his, like so many motions of the perplexed human heart, had more causes than one.

One of its causes was that he had seen the Maid so radiant as she was at that moment, coming fresh from that circle of young girls and the warmth and glow of their admiration. "Neither Mad Huw nor I," he thought, "can make her happy like that." But another cause of that sigh was the discord in his own heart brought about by the vision of Catharine and by the queer spasm of sensuality which his pity for this Ruthin girl had excited. This latter feeling still subsisted after Tegolin, followed by the old woman, had disappeared with the girl up the dark steps.

It was still with him when a moment later they passed the open door of the little chapel, in which he got a glimpse, under the red lamp of the Sacrament, of two black-draped forms lying motionless before the altar, with lighted candles at head and feet. "It's because the beauty of her figure," he thought, "is so insulted by the plainness of her face! But am I so much more depraved than these Welsh people that I can't feel *pity* for a girl without this *other* feeling?"

He set himself, as they went down the long passage, imagining how that dead boy, if he were indeed her lover, must have forgotten the plainness of her face when he embraced her, these warm summer evenings, under the Ruthin walls; and he rubbed his fist against his forehead in the darkness as he followed the sons of Owen. His brain felt so dizzy with all impressions he had received this day of Saint John that he began to envy old Griffin who had nothing to adjust himself to except the smell of Welsh ponies and a strange bed of Edeyrnion straw.

A very different kind of porter stood at the door of the magician's chamber when they came to the end of the passage. He was a youth of short stature but of singularly athletic build, and his bare arms rested, as he stood there, on the cross-handle of a long naked sword, not unlike the old crusading one that now lay at the foot of our lad's bed.

"Well, Madoc ab Ieuan," said Meredith, "we've come at last! Has he got tired of waiting?"

Madoc smiled as he moved aside. "You know what he is," he answered. "If you hadn't come till midnight he wouldn't have known it, Masters! He's deep in his books."

"Are you sure it's his books?" returned Meredith. "I was afraid from your tone that it might be—"

But Griffith ab Owen had already knocked impatiently at the door, and at a word from within they all entered, while Madoc entering with

them took up, as was the custom in that court, the same position inside
the room as he had occupied outside.

As the young man had warned them Owen rose from a massive
reading-desk so arranged that the light of no less than three brightly-
burning torches fell full on the parchment page he was deciphering.

"In God's name, welcome!" cried the Baron of Glyndyfrdwy, "and
be seated, every one of you! Welcome to all, and welcome to each, and
may the Holy Virgin and all the Saints be with you! But where is
our good Abbot and the Fathers?"

Griffith muttered a Welsh proverb about the best council being a
council without a priest; and Rhisiart caught Master Young scrutin-
izing Owen with a very sly and searching look. "He believes it's all
put on," thought our friend. "He believes he's dodged having the Abbot
here on purpose! He believes he's playing the sort of game King
Harry must usually play."

"They must have gone to their sleeping-place to chant the night
office," said Meredith. "I heard them in the chapel an hour ago, but
they weren't there just now."

"Go and fetch them, son, will you? It would be wrong to the Abbot
to begin our discussion without them."

"Shall I fetch Rhys Gethin and the Scab, too, sir?" enquired
Meredith.

But Master Young hurriedly intervened. "Wouldn't it be wiser, my
Lord, to come to our decision *first,* and then call the Captain and the
prophet? Indeed, I submit to you, sir, that we might make—what might
be called a—a *tentative* decision—and *then* call the Abbot and the
good Fathers? I'm a churchman myself, but I've sometimes found—"

"You're quite right, Canon, you're quite right," interrupted Owen
hurriedly. "We'll leave Rhys and the Scab to their cups and we'll leave
Griffith Llwyd to his harp. But I think, my boy, you *must* fetch the
Abbot and the Fathers. They came especially for this, and if they
found—"

But Rhisiart noticed that when Meredith had departed on his errand
Owen made Master Young sit down by his side on the Oriental divan
that extended along the whole length of one of the walls, and entered
at once into a low-voiced consultation with him.

Griffith ab Owen began nervously pacing up and down the chamber;

while the Lollard proceeded to examine with a scholar's interest the vast shelves of folios that rose on either side of the hearth. Above the divan with its Arabian rugs there hung from the ceiling an arras of some richly-woven stuff that gave the room a curiously sumptuous look, more like the apartment, Rhisiart thought, of some effeminate Saracen than a warlike Christian prince; while under the lancet window, through which, in the summer darkness, could be seen several glittering stars, stood two mysterious objects which suggested the abode neither of a Gothic baron nor of a Paynim knight but rather of some Nostradamus or Albertus Magnus engaged in the arts of black magic.

These two objects excited our friend's curiosity so much that he couldn't resist approaching them, although as he did so he noticed that the young squire with the sword watched him with suspicious alertness.

One was an enormous crystal globe supported on an ebony pedestal; while the other was a great square board of ancient wood-work, upon which, on a white ground, were inscribed a series of astrological symbols that our friend supposed, in his complete ignorance of such things, to be the signs of the zodiac.

The lad knew well that it was only the effect on his own mind of that orb of crystal, upon whose equivocal depths the bright torch-light from the neighbouring reading-desk was shining; but the thing certainly did have the power of materializing his thoughts, for the longer he stared at it the more vividly did his imagination conjure up in its orbic depths the three feminine forms of his recent experience. In truth he was still pondering, just as if they had been really imaged in that crystal, upon the red braid of Tegolin and the shining *pali* of Catharine and the simple garment that covered the alluring figure of Alice, when Madoc flung open the door of the chamber to admit the Abbot and the two monks.

Owen rose at once and greeted them as ceremoniously as a King might greet an Archbishop. Rhisiart tried to stand as humbly, as patiently, and yet with as much self-possession as Madoc ab Ieuan; but not having a sword to lean upon, he felt awkward and embarrassed. He envied Master Brut his calm, frank, unabashed aplomb; but he thought to himself, "I should never dare to behave as he does."

He couldn't help glancing at Master Young while these high-flown greetings, almost Chinese in their ritualistic courtliness, passed between

chieftain and the churchmen, and he felt a pang of innocent and youthful envy at the flawless manner of the learned lawyer.

The Canon was leaning a little forward, as if in habitual reverence
to all the potentates of Christendom. His face was contracted into an
expression of alert and confidential gravity. His thumbs were in his
belt, and his thin shoulders, discreetly raised, indicated a supercilious
indifference to all earthly considerations except that of obeying the
caprices of the great without infringing the law of the greater.

To reduce his respect for this perfect demeanour, which was indeed
beyond anything he had seen in Hereford or Oxford, our friend was
driven to recall the headlong, scurrying speed, mad for dear life, with
which this consummate courtier had bolted into their arms when Rhys
the Savage was about to rip him up.

The Lollard in his easy unabashed manner had already asked an
eager question of Meredith concerning some particular book he had
found which contained, so he declared, certain daring free-thinking
speculations which went much further than those of which he himself
had been accused in the Bishop's court.

Griffith ab Owen, interrupted in his sullen perambulations by the
Abbot's entrance, silently pulled out from beneath a pile of folios an
ancient duskily-painted chair, upon whose back was carved an elaborate
coat-of-arms, and in this the Abbot was now installed.

Owen still continued to address John ap Hywel in what struck our
friend as rather excessive propitiation, but by degrees he realized that
this was the chieftain's Welsh way of leading up to a very ticklish
question, the delicacy of which, following so hard upon all this effusive
ceremony, evidently discomposed the worthy man.

As far as the lad could make out, and Owen's courtly Welsh was
interspersed with several French phrases that clearly confused the Abbot
as much as they did our friend, he was enquiring now in some subtle
and roundabout way as to the possibility of Masses being said for the
soul of Iolo Goch, and incidently whether the Abbot of Caerleon would
use his influence with the Abbot of Valle Crucis—in spite of the Bard's
having behaved so obstinately on this death-bed—to get permission for
his entombment within the Valle Crucis precincts.

Turning hurriedly, as if to consult a living register as to the drift of
these high politics, the Abbot instinctively glanced at Master Young,

who was beginning to strike our friend as the kind of man who by his mere presence had the power of compelling great personages to appeal to him.

The Canon answered the Abbot's look by a few hurried words in ecclesiastical Latin, and then himself with indescribable deference appealed humbly to Father Pascentius, who promptly replied—fixing his insatiable black eyes upon the book under the three torches—in such a stream of scholastic "buts" and "ifs" and "in-as-much-as-we-mights" that the bewildered Abbot, after producing and replacing his old battered psalter, had nothing to do but to nod gravely several times with his tonsured head.

"What," he enquired hastily of Owen in obvious anxiety to let the soul of the obstreperous Bard rest in peace, "what are the royal arms against which I am now resting my poor mortal back?"

Owen with a deep sigh of relief, and with the first smile our friend had noticed on his face since Iolo's death, hastened to explain that they were the arms of the old princedom of Powys before King John burnt the palace of Mathrafal; and no sooner had he offered this explanation than Master Young, snatching at such a heaven-sent opportunity of plunging *in medias res,* rose to his feet, and while all the company, except our friend who played nervously with his dagger and Madoc ab Ieuan who leaned abstractedly upon his sword, found seats for themselves, began a lively and vivid statement of the present political situation.

The Abbot frowned, Father Rheinalt fidgetted, Griffith rested his arms on his knees and covered his face with his hands, Meredith stretched out his shapely yellow-stockinged legs and toyed, as a woman might have done, with one of his green sleeves, while the Lollard smiled sweetly and innocently into the devouring black eyes of the commentator on Saint Thomas.

"I am, as Lord Owen knows, a Welshman with a bar sinister," the lawyer began. "He knows the secret of my birth. He knows the great family from which I spring. He knows too, I think, that though I serve in my official capacity the House of Lancaster, my heart is always with the land of my fathers, and when the moment comes I shall be at his side.

"But the moment—and this, my Lord Abbot and reverend Fathers, is the point I wish to make to-night—the moment *has not yet come*. France is not ready to help us. Scotland is still divided against itself. The Holy Father at Avignon"—here all the ecclesiastics gazed at him in consternation—"though recognized by two powerful nations, is still weak compared with the Holy Father in Rome. The Tudors in Mōn, though restless and dissatisfied, are not yet strong enough, or indeed united enough, to be of much help; while above all, my Lords and Fathers, the rift between the Percies and the—the King *de facto*—has to grow wider before the break comes. The break *will* come—I can assure you of that from the highest possible authority—indeed from the lips of my Lord of Northumberland himself—but *they are not ready yet*. The Earl of March is in Henry's hands; and though by his marriage-link with Hotspur, who by the way has expressed to me over and over again his admiration for 'our brave friend Glendourdy,' as he is pleased to call you, sir, my Lord Edmund is committed to their side, the great House of Mortimer is still in need of re-assurance as to what would happen to their Welsh estates in case—well, in case we were successful! My conclusion, therefore, gentlemen, and I have risked much and travelled far, as Lord Owen knows, to lay this humble view before you, is that we have everything to gain by delay and everything to lose by being hasty and precipitate. I heard, as did we all, those noble and inspired words from lips that are now silent, but in justice to our great cause I must say—"

"You made a mistake *there,* my friend!" thought Rhisiart, when Owen, with a stern gesture and with less courtesy than the lad had ever seen in him, motioned the speaker into silence. "Why the devil must you drag in the Bard?"

But the Abbot was speaking now, and though he was no orator, and though from that old Powys throne his words came in crude jerks and angry spasms, and though before he had gone far he relapsed into the rough peasant dialect that was natural to him, there was an intense moral fervour in his words that moved everybody present. Griffith sat up straight. The Lollard ceased to smile. Father Rheinalt's swarthy countenance gleamed with delight. Owen himself leant forward, plucking nervously at his forked beard.

"Does the God of battles wait," cried the passionate churchman, "till all the wretched pawns on the chess-board of human politics think the

right moment, the safe moment, the crafty son-of-Belial moment, has
come for striking for the right? No man, I say *no man,* can predict the
future, can calculate the issue, can foretell the event. All we can do is to
obey our consciences and strike boldly at the oppressor. It is God, Owen
Glyn Dŵr, it is the God of our race, who will give us the victory, not
the nice calculations of clever mortal men! The great rising we intend
is the rising of the oppressed against the oppressor! It is the rising of—"
here he stammered for a word, and then groaned angrily and forgot
what he was going to say. "I mean," he added with a noble simplicity,
"if we remain pure in our motives, if we remain righteous and Christian in our lives, if we strike for justice and liberty and not for malice
and revenge, we shall need no Percies or Mortimers, or French kings
or false schismatic Popes; we shall need only our good Welsh spears
and our good Welsh Prince, we shall need only our"—his voice became
hoarse, and he bent forward, clutching the arms of his chair and bowing his forehead over his knees, while his powerful shoulders shook
with emotion—"our trust in the God of our fathers, our faith in the
Blessed Virgin and all the—"

Here his voice broke, and so overwhelming was the man's feeling
that even so young a lad as Rhisiart couldn't fail to see that he was putting into these simple and even commonplace words the accumulated
passion of a life-time.

But Father Rheinalt could no longer contain himself. "My—my—my
Lord Abbot," he stammered, leaping to his feet, "and my Lord Owen,
I never—I never thought to hear such words spoken in Powys Fadog
as those I've heard from the Canon of Bangor. Our land is stirring with
the breath of a new hope. From Bangor to St. David's, from Llanfaes
to Strata Florida, the clergy of our race, regulars and seculars, friars and
monks alike, are crying aloud to the Holy Father to free us from the
yoke of Canterbury. With a Prince of our own blood and Bishops of
our own blood, and Abbots like—like thee, my Lord—the Holy Father
will be brought to know the truth, that—that at the last Day—when
the Souls of the Faithful rise to meet their Judge—Wales will be—will
be—of all the company of blest—the land nearest to—nearest to—the
heart of—of the successor of Peter, of the Vice-Regent of Christ upon
earth! But oh, my Lord Abbot, we must strike them down, these oppressors! With fire and sword we must smite them! We must burn

their habitations, for they are of Satan! We must tear down their castles! We must kill and kill and kill in this holy cause. It is a Crusade,
my Lord Abbot; it is a new Crusade—to smite and burn and kill till
there isn't one of these accursed English left alive—no, not in Ruthin,
not in Chirk, not in all Powys, not in all Wales, from Mona to Deheubarth!"

He sank back exhausted, and there fell a troubled and embarrassed
silence over the whole company.

Then Owen spoke; and his words came slowly, gravely, sadly. "He
has been deeply wronged. His heart burns. Out of its cruel burning he
utters these things. Aye! and there are many hearts between Mona and
Gwent that burn as his does. But if the Lord Abbot will allow me, I
would like to ask Master Brut here, for he is a good Welshman—a
Britonibus ex utraque parente originem habens—as he declared when
tried before an English court, what *his* impressions are of our chances.
Master Brut, my Lord Abbot gives you permission, and we ourselves
ask you as a favour—"

Rhisiart noticed that the chieftain's astute use of the Latin tongue
had its intended effect, but he noticed also the obstinate frown with
which the Abbot gave his curt nod of assent.

The Lollard, however, turned upon them all his calm and unperturbed smile; and after a time, so frank and conciliatory was his manner and so gentle was his tone, even John ap Hywel began to contemplate him with a relaxed indulgence. The gist of his speech, as far as
Rhisiart could make out, was that it was the destiny of the Welsh race
to give a new and more spiritual significance to the Catholic Faith, a
significance in closer harmony with the actual words of Jesus as reported in the Gospels than anything at which the unimpassioned and
worldly temper of the English prelates could possibly arrive.

The general feeling he got, before the man's hopeless long-winded-
ness made him feel drowsy, was that any real practical success of Owen
would be to the advantage of this new spiritual revival, this escape from
materialistic superstition into the "glorious liberty of the children of
God."

But the Lollard's arguments were so monotonous, and so garnished
with tedious quotations from the Scriptures, that our friend's mind began to wander. His eyes began to wander too from the placidly argu-

ing countenance of his room-mate. They fixed themselves upon that mysterious crystal; and the moment they did so his sleepiness passed away and all manner of troubling images obsessed his brain.

He thought of how Alice had looked when she hung her head and wept so pitifully in the hands of Rhys Gethin. He saw again with an irresistible stir of his senses that contrast between her rounded figure in its scanty woollen garment and her uncomely face.

But *was* her face so uncomely? Her eyes were heavily-lidded, and had an expression, for all her tears, that suggested to him—he couldn't have explained why—a nature disturbingly amorous and passionate, a nature dedicated to every kind of sensual response. The longer he stared at that crystal globe the further his thoughts carried him and the more shameless they became. He imagined—but in the heat of his imaginings this unconscionable crystal thrust before him those two black-covered forms he had glimpsed in the chapel! Dead, stone-dead and mortuary-cold they were, the great Bard and the unknown spy, and the merciless crystal seemed to force the lad, full as he was of the hot sweet shame of filling those heavy-lidded eyelids with fresh tears, to lie down there, before that very altar, in direct physical contact with the deadly chill of mortality.

Still, still the Lollard went on; and at last Griffith actually got up from his seat, and going over to the young man with the sword began whispering to him.

"It's his spirituality," thought our friend, "that Griffith can't stomach; but why doesn't he make us *feel* this spirit without so much sermonizing? That's his damned heresy I suppose!" And into our friend's youthful brain the obscure question insinuated itself whether all this spirituality, so logically defended, was "meant" for a race that produced people like the Scab and Rhys the Savage.

"The Church," he thought, turning his eyes to Owen's signs of the zodiac, "knows what it's doing when it keeps these preachers in their place."

But Griffith's restlessness had now spread to the whole company, and Master Young who had sat since his rebuff with an expression of protesting innocence, his toothless mouth open and his reproachful eyes staring into vacancy, permitted himself an ostentatious yawn followed by a resounding sigh.

Owen alone preserved his pose of concentrated interest in the Lollard's discourse.

"Good luck to him if he understands all this!" the boy thought. But suddenly he decided that his wise kinsman was deliberately letting the man go on so as to clear the air from the electric bloodthirstiness of Father Rheinalt's "burn, kill and slay."

Back to the crystal wandered Rhisiart's eyes, and while the Abbot brought out his psalter, and Father Rheinalt groaned aloud, and Madoc ab Ieuan, pressed his lean stomach so heavily against the handle of his sword that its point made an audible scraping upon the stone floor, the images in the boy's mind were accentuated by a red wave of hair falling over one corpse and a shimmer of silk *pali* over another; and so impishly did the crystal go to work that in some outrageous manner he was actually making Alice cry while that burning hair lay upon one cadaver and those warm childish breasts pressed softly upon the other.

But the Lollard sat down at last, and if Rhisiart had been amazed at the tedious arguments with which he defended his sublime notion of the unimportance of all sublunary happenings compared with the life of the eternal spirit, he was still more amazed at the incredible good temper and complete lack of injured vanity with which he smiled upon them all, and even went so far, so it seemed to our friend, as to direct towards him a boyish wink as he resumed his seat. Were all epoch-making councils of all history as undecided and confused as this one, the lad wondered; and then at a nod from Owen Father Pascentius stood up.

"By God and Christ," thought Rhisiart, "what eyes the man's got!" And there was Griffith arrested in his pacing, and there was the Abbot eagerly clasping his bony knees with his great hands, and there was Master Young coming to life again and sniffing the air like a badger who smells a fox. "If he manages Saint Thomas as he does all these people," thought our friend, "he's the greatest philosopher the Church has ever had."

But why wasn't Owen caught by the fellow's black eyes and magnetic talk? It was natural that the Lollard wasn't; for even Rhisiart had the wit to recognize that in Father Pascentius's words the pure clear air of the spirit, which the heretic's earnestness had evoked, disappeared as completely as the tedious arguments with which he had supported it.

Every mortal object of human interest, Welsh independence, revenge upon the English, the reign of justice, the advisability of burning Ruthin, the sweetness of slaughtering every living soul in Chirk, all fell into their places, all became parts and parcels of the complicated nature of the unknowable First Cause!

Everything was allowed for, every event, every emotion, every human possibility. A united Wales under Owen was allowed for, to be followed, as far as our spell-bound friend could make out, by a united England, Scotland, Ireland, if not France too, under some problematical descendant of Owen—"A child of Catharine's!" rushed through our friend's mind—and as for the Lollard's appeal to the words of Jesus, it became Rhisiart's destiny to learn how these also, even these, must be regarded as relative to the limited comprehension of the human mind; while in the universal stream of the Church's tradition the Absolute revealed itself.

All the tags and scraps of scholastic training the lad had accumulated at Oxford fell into an illuminated synthesis as he listened to this amazing speech. And the wonderful thing was it really *did* seem to have its connection with the problem of whether or not to defy the House of Lancaster!

How far the Abbot and Father Rheinalt understood what the man was saying it was hard to tell, but they were deeply impressed; and the legal intelligence of Master Young was evidently fascinated too. It was like being present at some miraculous creation, out of the air, of the veritable *tree of faith,* extending its branches, all relative but all rooted in the Absolute, over every aspect of human controversy!

Our friend was startled, and indeed, to confess the truth, a little shocked, by the attitude of Owen to this masterpiece. The chieftain smiled at the Lollard, glanced at his astrological map, caressed his beard, and finally went so far as to take down from a hook beside his desk a long, dark satin gown ornamented with strange hieroglyphs and slip his arms into its sleeves! He then laid his hand upon the crystal globe; and in this position, wrapped about in that dark mantle, he made our young man think of Elymas the Sorcerer listening to the inspired metaphysics of Saint Paul!

When the theologian at last sat down, making quite unconsciously with his plump hands his usual gesture of universal futility, his black eyes seemed to drink up at one gulp every person in the room.

But Master Young was on his feet again now. "It is clear," he said in his most insinuating and velvety voice, using his lips as if they were teeth, "that the learned Father feels exactly as I do about this rising; feels in fact that for my Lord Owen to commit himself to lift his standard as soon as the Feast of Matthew would be one of the worst mistakes he could make. I don't mean," he went on hurriedly, for Owen had made a dangerous movement forward, "I don't mean to underrate the wrongs we've suffered. But if we can only wait till more nations have joined the Holy Father at Avignon; if we can only wait till the Percies break with the King; if we can only wait till France—" And he went blandly on, introducing the little Earl of March again, and Sir Edmund Mortimer's link with Hotspur again, and the Mortimer estates again.

"He'll come to Ireland soon," thought our friend. But Rhisiart's mind wandered off before he came to Ireland. And what abominable speculations that crystal kept calling up! It even set him wondering which of the corpses in the chapel—the great Bard or the unknown spy—would begin to *stink* first. In veritable shame he turned away from this heathen globe, turned away hurriedly, before it had time to lead him back to Alice of Ruthin and her salt tears. Then, for Master Young still hadn't got to Ireland, he began wondering why the Lollard's speech was so dull and Father Pascentius's so arresting. He felt a glow of pride at his penetration when he decided it was because Father Pascentius included so many evil things in his clue-word "relative." It was, Rhisiart impiously decided, just as if God had burning black eyes that enjoyed *everything as it was* on the easy ground of its being all "relative."

Suddenly, and not without wicked pleasure, he caught sight of a wasp moving gingerly and tentatively around the top of the Canon's pointed slippers; and a shameless desire seized him that this great Doctor of Decrees might be stung ere he reached the question of Ireland!

To distract his attention from the wasp's explorations he boldly took upon himself to carry a log to the fire and lay it down as quietly as he could upon the now smouldering embers. When he turned from doing this he was astonished to see the young Madoc regarding him with a look of uncontrolled fury.

"Heavens!" he thought, "what have I done now?"

And then he remembered how in one of Modry's tales there was a young knight whose special privilege it was—and his alone—to replenish his lord's fire.

"This is the third enemy I've made," he thought, "Gwalchmai the stable-man, Glew the Porter, and now this young fool!"

But he soon lifted his head and looked at Master Young, who had not only reached Ireland but had passed it and the Mortimer estates, too. Then he heard the Canon say: "And so, my Lord Owen, and so, my Lord Abbot, I think I have made it plain to you why the death-bed words of our venerated friend and his allusion to the sixteenth of—"

"Enough, sir!"

At these words from the indignant chieftain, the Canon's toothless mouth closed on what it was uttering, half of the sentence hanging in the air, and the other half, like a creature decapitated by the spring of a trap, disappearing down the man's throat.

Glyn Dŵr's sea-green eyes flashed ominously. He made a quick movement with one of his hands, but it wasn't a weapon he drew but the great signet-ring from off his finger.

As Master Young stepped back in consternation, he moved straight up to him and pressed the ring into his hand.

"Return," he said in a low vibrant voice, a voice audible to everyone in the room, "return to Henry of Lancaster and tell him he may raise the devil in every shire in England and burn every heretic and every friar; but never shall he— But keep my ring, Master Canon, keep my ring; and when your hour comes, your 'relatively suitable' hour"— and he gave Father Pascentius a look like a flung dagger—"you may use it to claim free access to our presence, whether it be here or in *some other place!*" He drew back from the abashed lawyer and glanced at the Abbot whose eyes shone in sympathy like an old war-horse who hears the trumpet; and then he said in a gentler voice, "Stay with us here for a day or two longer, Master Young; and be assured of this, that when you *do* return, that ring of mine will be a safe passport wherever Welsh is—" He was interrupted by the sound of hurrying feet in the corridor and a tumult of excited voices.

Madoc ab Ieuan gripped his sword and stood listening intently, his head on one side like a blind-folded hawk. Rhisiart moved impulsively to the young man's side, and everyone in the room, including the Abbot, rose to his feet.

"Open the door," said the chieftain quietly. As soon as he was obeyed there stumbled into the room, panting, indignant, perspiring, and yet full of pompous authority, a little, stocky, swarthy foreigner, dressed in a rider's garb of outlandish pattern.

With the point of his sword Madoc drove back the revellers who had followed, and in spite of many angry and tipsy protests bolted the door in their faces.

Then the pompous stranger, glancing hurriedly round the room, saluted the Abbot, gave Owen a formal little bow, and drawing a heavily-sealed document from his cloak waved it in the air as if it had been an enchanter's wand.

"From Rome," he said, with the solemnity befitting an emissary from the Metropolis of the Universe, "from the Holy Father, in his Holiness's own hand and seal!"

Our friend caught the eye of Master Brut; and in a moment, for some deep instinctive reason, all the three English-bred travellers, Master Brut, Master Young and Master Rhisiart, moved close to one another and remained apart from the rest.

The Abbot advanced with dignity but with a reverence that struck our friend as almost comical. After a second's hesitation the squat little man, whose shrewd inquisitorial eyes had narrowed at the sight of the great crystal globe and the zodiacal map and whose dark eyebrows had lifted a little at the array of questionable folios, allowed the respectful churchman to inspect the document he held.

"It is as he says, gentlemen," the Abbot reported solemnly. "I have seen it before and I know it," and falling humbly upon his knees and with a touching expression of awe on his rugged face the burly prelate reverently pressed the Pope's superscription to his lips. Father Pascentius first, and then Father Rheinalt, imitated the Abbot in this pious recognition of the papal missive.

As soon as they had risen to their feet the aggrieved Italian burst into an indignant account of what he had undergone from the drunken revellers in the hall. Dogs, caitiffs, insolent and ignorant serfs he declared them to be; and worst among them all—this he made very plain—was the blasphemous "Capitano Rossi."

At this Italianating of Rhys the Savage, our three visitors from over the border couldn't help exchanging a smile; though in the lawyer's case it was a somewhat wry one.

But the extravagant airs assumed by this bearer of the Pope's sign-manual didn't seem to arouse any mirth in the rest of the company. Even Meredith looked grave and thoughtful; and the sulky Griffith appeared as abashed with awe as he might have been had this comical little official been an angel of God.

As to our three travellers, however, whatever traditional piety the word "Rome" might conjure up within them, they had imbibed for too long the humorous independence of the shires to feel anything but amusement in the presence of this grandiose messenger from the papal city.

The whole incident was of absorbing interest to Rhisiart; not from any respect for the touchy little Italian, but as a revelation of the imaginative quality of his fellow Welshmen. He was conscious himself of an irresistible up-welling of malicious detachment. He could hardly bear to see the dignified old Abbot and the heroic Father Rheinalt looking like respectful school-boys before a fellow who after all was only a fussy mountebank, and who looked like the leader of a band of Tuscan Mummers whom one of King Richard's favourites brought in his train to Hereford! He felt a wanton longing to jump up and down in front of the Pope's ambassador, making jeering faces and calling out, as the Hereford prentices had done, "Blanco! Neri! Blanco! Neri! Punchinello! Arleguini!"

It was quite evident that Master Young, who had been many times to Rome, and knew in person several of the Papal Secretaries, would soon intervene if this prating little man didn't stop repeating over and over again to the Abbot, in his Tuscan accent, *"Troppo avem sofferto!"* —Too much have we endured!—and come to business; for he whispered loudly to Master Brut that it was the custom at baronial houses all over Europe for a messenger from Rome to present his credentials to none but the person designated, and above all not to reveal them to local ecclesiastics!

"You can see," Master Young whispered to the Lollard, evidently hoping that Owen would hear, "how necessary such a rule is when you realize how often His Holiness must wish to communicate with some noble foreign gentleman without the knowledge of the local clergy."

Rhisiart was vastly entertained to note how this well-timed rebuke from a personage who might have been an archbishop's secretary changed in a trice the tune of the querulous Tuscan. "But I am forgetting my duty," the fellow now murmured, "I am much to blame— but Capitano Rossi has upset me and I am not myself yet." Then at last he did move across the room to where Owen was standing and gave him the document.

Owen took it with a bow and raised its seal to his lips, and though he didn't bend his knee as the monks had done his face remained solemn and reverential.

Master Young at that point glided like a well-meaning and serviceable ghost to Owen's side. He didn't offer to interpret the scroll, but he gave the fabric of its parchment an appraising pinch with his finger and thumb, as if to indicate that there was nothing in this document, not even the kind of calf-skin used with which he was unacquainted.

But Owen *did* ask Master Young to read and interpret the missive to the company. "I have nothing to keep secret from these friends of mine," he assured the Tuscan.

As Master Young began to read, Rhisiart said to himself, "It's just like the old days! Here are we Celts and Saxons disputing over our tribal feuds and suddenly the long finger of Rome is stretched out into our midst and we all bow down and cry, 'To Rome be the power and glory!' On my soul, the Canon's perfectly right to remind us of that anti-Pope at Avignon. A Benedict for a Boniface and Britain for herself!"

Whether it was the heresy emanating from the unruffled countenance of his friend, or whether it was his youthful reaction to the dangerous new ideas which had buzzed about his ears in Oxford, it seemed to our lad that there was something pathetic about the way these Welshmen cringed before the emissary from Rome.

"I suppose their women," he pondered sententiously, "intermarried with the Roman legionaries." And he decided that over his fire that midsummer night in the Saracen's room he would introduce this illuminating thought to the notice of Master Brut. "But oh dear," he sighed, "our fire will be out!"

"This document," Master Young was saying, "is what we call an indult; and I will now proceed to translate it into the vernacular. 'From his Holiness, Pontifex Maximus, Servant of the servants of God, Boniface the Ninth, under our paternal hand and seal, to our beloved son in Christ, Owen ap Griffith, armiger baron in tenure of Sycharth and Glyndyfrdwy. By the authority given to us by Almighty God we do hereby permit and allow the aforesaid Owen ap Griffith's ordained Confessor to give unto the aforesaid Owen, and unto Margaret his wife, not only in the hour of their death, *but at any other time,* plenary remission from all their sins.'"

It may have been the weight of conclusive legality that Master Young gave to his paraphrase of this imposing document or it may have been that the solemn words "remission of sins" carried a personal poignancy for all present; but there certainly fell a grave hush upon that group of men, and our young friend himself experienced a definite reaction from many of his recent thoughts.

Owen himself seemed the least moved of them all; and Rhisiart noticed that he and the Lollard exchanged a long enigmatic look; full of God-knows-what unholy reservations.

But the Pope's messenger seemed to recover his spirits and began to assume an air of almost indecorous levity. He approached the hearth, where the logs, thanks to our friend's interposition, were blazing high, and expressed his wonder at the disappearance of the smoke.

"I've heard of these new-fangled chimneys," he said, speaking in French with a broad Italian accent, "but the Holy Father is afraid to tamper with his walls. How rich you Welsh gentlemen must be, how *very* rich, to afford—hee! hee!—such luxuries as chimneys!"

Owen gave the man a curiously haughty look and made a gesture with his hand as if to dismiss as irrelevent and even indecent this homely topic; but Rhisiart could see that the chieftain was listening to a second hullabaloo that had arisen in the passage. He himself fancied he could detect the drunken voices of both Rhys Gethin and the Scab out there, and Madoc ab Ieuan had assumed once more that intent expression, with his head a little on one side, that made him resemble a blind-folded buzzard.

The Abbot and Owen's sons were also listening with some nervousness to the tipsy voices outside, and the irrepressible Tuscan was beginning some jest about the folios, when Master Young, who had been standing by himself lost in thought, suddenly confronted the fellow with an outstretched menacing forefinger and said to him in sharp clear French, "May one enquire, sir, if the message you're bearing from his Holiness to the King of England has to do with the new statute? I refer to the recent royal edict entitled *'De Heretico Comburendo.'* "

Owen swung round on his heel; and the Lollard, as if to bear off some tragic mental image, began making one of his architectural maps in the air.

But our friend, watching the Pope's messenger closely, saw the colour leave his face as he began gesticulating and protesting and denying. "You've got him, Master!" Rhisiart said to himself; and he looked hurriedly down at Master Young's pointed shoes to see if the wasp was still in view.

"May you *never* be stung till the end of your days!" he prayed. "And I wish to God Owen would take *your* advice, in place of those drunkards' outside there!"

Owen now stepped up to the lawyer's side and, taking not the least notice of the agitated and protesting Italian, said curtly in Welsh, "I thank you, good Master Young! I hope *your* time will come before any of us expect it. I shall remember there *is* another Pope."

Rhisiart's impression was that the noise outside had risen to such a pitch that the Abbot didn't catch this last remark; but he fancied he caught the black eyes of the theologian gleam with an ominous comprehension.

"Open the door!" commanded Owen Glyn Dŵr.

Madoc surlily obeyed; and there appeared in the entrance, both of them hopelessly drunk, the figures of Rhys Gethin and the Scab.

"This fool says—says, my Lord—this fool says," cried *il Capitano Rossi,* "that it's on the Saint Matthew's Day we're to raise our flag—but I tell him its on the sixteenth we're to do that, and on Saint Matthew's Day we're to burn—"

"Listen, you two; listen, both of you!" interrupted Owen, tearing off his mantle and drawing his sword; "if I hear any more of this, if I hear a word more of this babbling and bragging, by the head of my father, it won't be on Saint Matthew's Day but on the night of Saint John ·hat I'll raise my flag and burn—*and burn Nannau!* Yes, by Saint Derfel, Master Scab, I've a mind"—and he lifted his sword and pointed it at the drunken prophet—"I've a mind to raise my flag now and march you both across the Dee and across Ardudwy till we see how you'll stand up against Cousin Sele's arrows! Get back to the hall, both of you, and tell them all, all who're not too drunk to listen, that we've decided in council—*yng nghgngor,* do you understand?—to burn my cousin's house to the ground, and David Gam's too, tell them! Now off with you both—and no more of this.'"

Totally bewildered, reduced indeed to a sort of drunken stupefaction, but muttering the words "Nannau" and "Hywel Sele" as they went off, the two revellers retreated and the door was shut.

Meredith dragged his brother aside and began whispering to him, while the Abbot and Father Rheinalt stared blankly at Owen as if he had lost his wits.

"You shall sleep in *this* chamber to-night, sir," the chieftain remarked quietly to the messenger from Rome. And then, as he put up his sword, "You'll find Henry of Lancaster on the Scottish border if you ride fast, and if the Douglas doesn't catch you! What you heard just now has to do with a family feud; and you'll have to ride hard if Henry's to save *Nannau*—can you remember that word?—on Saint Matthew's Day. A family feud, good sir, a family feud! But remember, Scotland looks to Avignon, not to Rome; so if the Douglas *does* catch you—a family feud, my good sir!"'

Master Young who was still holding the indult now handed it to Owen, who received it gravely.

"The Abbot of Caerleon," he said, looking significantly at the puzzled group of churchmen, "is my confessor, and if Nannau *is* burned on Saint Matthew's Day, it will be one of the sins he must remit." And he laid down the indult beneath the crystal.

VII

VALLE CRUCIS

RHISIART KNEW at once, when he awaked on the following day, that he had slept late. The first thing he realized was that his room-mate had already dressed and was sitting, so as to get the benefit of the light from the window, on his big sack-cloth bundle, reading a small unbound book.

Our friend soon interrupted this peaceful orison. "Why the devil didn't you wake me?" he cried indignantly.

Master Brut closed his book and jumped to his feet. "For a purely selfish reason, my good lad," he replied with his everlasting smile. "I like to read the Gospel in absolute quiet the second I'm dressed."

Our friend stared at him. "The office for the day you mean—like a priest?"

Master Brut's smile deepened. "No, my friend, the sayings of Jesus which put priests in their place!"

"Is that a whole *Novum Testamentum?*"

"No, my boy, it's not. It's an abbreviated translation of Saint Luke's Gospel in the original."

"Wasn't Latin the original?" enquired Rhisiart.

"Well, lad, well, not *exactly* the original," replied the Lollard as tactfully as he could. "*Some* authorities hold the view that the Greek is earlier."

"Don't they say the same thing?"

"Not always, son, not always."

"But in *essentials* they do; they *must!*" protested our friend, tossing off the rugs and sitting on the side of his bed and hugging his bare knees. His pride was hurt by having slept so late, and he felt the righteous anger of orthodoxy burn in both his cheek-bones.

"Is the proclamation to the world by 'multitudes of the heavenly host' of the birth of a Redeemer an essential thing?" enquired the Lollard with Socratic deliberation.

"Of course," growled our friend, "if it was a miracle attested by the Church and recognized by the Holy Father. It is reported by Saint Luke."

"Well? What then? What are you driving at? Some damned trick of devil's logic I warrant!"

He rose, as he spoke, and began, without thinking what he did, to pull on the scarlet hose he had worn the night before.

"You're not going to wear *those?*" protested his friend. But Rhisiart, standing like an irate long-legged heron, with one white shank and one red one, seemed to tell him by his glaring scowl to get on with his argument.

Master Brut hesitated. He was evidently torn between his passion for theological discussion and his inherent good-nature. But the worthy man's conscience must have helped his disputatiousness to overcome his tact by persuading him that "he owed it to the truth" to enlighten his stubborn friend.

"What Saint Luke in his Greek," he went on, "makes the angels say is, 'Peace on earth; good-will to men,' whereas what the Church's Latin makes them say is, 'Peace on earth to men of good-will.' Now it is clear that there *is* an essential difference here. In the one case—"

"Come in!"

Rhisiart uttered this permission with unnecessary violence; but his relief in escaping his friend's logic was so great that he turned quite a cheerful face to the page who entered. This was a boy about twelve, pretty as a maid, with clear-cut features, white skin, and long eyelashes, which, when he shyly cast down his eyes, pencilled themselves with exquisite delicacy on his soft cheeks. His limbs in their tight hose were certainly modelled more beautifully than any maid's, and the "lion rampant and sable," embroidered on his tunic, set off to perfection his ivory-soft neck and coal-black curls.

Rhisiart, under the warm glow which the beauty of this boy evoked, became anxious at once to make his own person as manly and well-accoutred as possible, and hastily removing his scarlet hose began pulling on his student's breeches and tunic and even went so far as to draw from its sheath, in order to inspect its edge in a careless and martial manner, his formidable Toledo dagger.

But the dark-eyed page, after giving each of them a timid smile, took no more notice of the dagger than if it had been a brush or a comb. He set up a rough table which he had brought with him; and then, going several times to the open door, where from certain suppressed gigglings that entered the Saracen's room it appeared that he had colleagues of both sexes, he placed upon the table an enormous flagon of foaming beer, a substantial joint of cold beef, a rabbit-pasty, and a platter of hot newly-buttered scones.

Finally he carried in and set by the table two rough three-legged stools, polished smooth by use, but bearing on their shiny surface not a few neatly-cut inscriptions, the amusement probably of many a long winter evening in the Glyndyfrdwy kitchen. Not content with this, having lifted his long eyelashes and shown his bright teeth to explain to our friends that the wind was easterly and the weather unseasonable, he carried to the hearth a bundle of straw and a faggot of sticks, and made for them, to their great comfort and cheer, a blazing fire.

Before he left them to themselves, Rhisiart, anxious for any excuse to keep so attractive an attendant by their side, and with a delicious feeling that he had been transported into one of Modry's romances, called him to their table, and pledging him in a draught of ale and playfully drawing him to his side with an arm thrown about his waist, as he had seen one of Richard's followers do with a wine-bearer at Hereford, he began asking him various questions.

One question led to another; and it wasn't long before such singular revelations began to fall from the boy's diffident lips that Master Brut felt it his duty to dismiss the coy prattler.

Our irascible friend was on the point of making this into a new grievance, if not into a mortal insult, when the Lollard began, in so grave and gentle a tone that it was impossible not to be disarmed, a direct appeal to his honour. Very tenderly and with such real affection and concern that it touched the lad to the heart, especially as Master Brut deliberately used the rustic Herefordshire dialect, giving a touch of nostalgic homeliness to his elder brother's tone, he warned the boy of the danger of these fashionable flirtations with beautiful pages.

"I know the temptation only too well," he said. "It has many times overcome me, and will no doubt do so again—God help us all!—but I swear to you, lad, there are no cunning whores in Paris more treacherous and dangerous than these pampered pages; and it's just because"—and he spoke with such frank earnestness that the ribald feeling Rhisiart was indulging, that the whole thing was a bagatelle, subsided a little—"just because it's such a temptation to me that I can speak with knowledge about it. It begins with just such toying and dallying as you indulged in a minute ago, which no doubt was perfectly harmless; but after a time, if the Blessed Christ doesn't help you, the thing becomes an obsession. Think of Edward the Second! I've no doubt that at your age he played harmlessly enough with the pages of the court, but you remember to what it led? Do you know, Rhisiart"—and he lowered his voice—"certain things, like what the chronicles say of the shrieks of Edward the Second, have come near to making me an atheist. But of course lots of men who're not kings have known— But pain like that, my lad, when it comes to the shrieking point, is what I can't— Do you know, Rhisiart, there've been times when I've *cursed* God, yes, cursed him, for making a world where such things can be; and if it wasn't for—" He stopped suddenly, and a strange wild look that alarmed his companion crossed his placid face. Then he said quietly and in his ordinary voice, "But I needn't have dragged in Edward— Christ give him pardon and peace!—our poor late King, Mad Huw's Richard, ruined himself in just the same way. These unhappy men's minions—all fatal, all treacherous—are only grown-up pages. Oh, my dear lad, if I could only tell you all I've seen—"

Our friend was moved beyond his wont. It wasn't so much what the man said; it was the revelation of the feeling that lay beneath that calm exterior. He stretched his arm across their wooden table and grasped the other's hand and their eyes met in embarrassed sympathy.

Then Rhisiart raised the great two-handled flagon to his lips. "To Wales and Owen Glyn Dŵr!" he cried, and gave it to his comrade.

"To Wales and Owen Glyn Dŵr!"

Their meal went on after that in desultory talk about last night's events; but as they rose from the table Rhisiart said abruptly. "What do you suppose that boy meant by saying that Griffith and Meredith have left the palace and that Rhys Gethin has gone back to Conway? Do you think Owen was upset by the way things turned out? And did you hear what he said about giving up his room to that ridiculous Italian?"

"And the way he lied about Nannau?" responded the other, as they moved to their bench by the hearth. "He wanted to keep the man from questioning the servants, I fancy. What puzzles me about it all," the Lollard went on, "is Owen's attitude to Master Young. How could he be ready to let the man go back to Henry, with that ring of his on his finger and without any security? I don't know what *you* feel, lad, but it struck me the fellow must hold some sort of commission from Avignon. Did you notice how he was always coming back to that?"

Rhisiart bent forward over the fire, turning his Norman profile to his friend as he drew in his lips. "He's a clever man," he remarked after a pause. "He knows more about state-affairs than anyone I've ever met. Maybe it *would* be a wise move to play off Avignon against Rome."

Master Brut smiled. "Oh, you orthodox believers!" he burst out. "Can't you see how it upsets the whole system for there to be *two Popes?*"

Rhisiart waved this aside. "Owen must know more about him than anyone else. I heard someone say in the hall that he's the bastard of one of the greatest of our Welsh families. Anyway, Owen trusts him; and I don't believe he'd do that if he didn't know something that we don't. Do you think Rhys Gethin's in disgrace that he's going back to Conway? You should have seen how he ran the bastard to earth! If it hadn't been for Brother Huw, Avignon would have had to find another champion. But wasn't it amusing the way he exposed that Roman? He talked better French—that's how he did him down—that and his lucky guess that the chap was going straight to Bolingbroke and that he had—"

But Master Brut begged his friend not to forget what he was going to say next; and retired for a minute or two to make use of their new-fangled latrine invented by the Scotch nobility.

While he was thus engaged there came a soft knock at the door; and Rhisiart, thinking that at any rate for that moment he could tease the pretty page without interference, hurried to open it himself.

But in place of the white cheeks, long eyelashes and delicate limbs of

young Elphin, there stood Meredith ab Owen in full warlike array!
He wore a steel breast-plate, sharp-pointed steel greaves and a small
steel helmet, without any visor, fitting tight to his head. Even as he
stood there he began fidgetting with his helmet to conceal some straggling dark curl, and in a flash our friend was reminded of the peevish
way Tegolin had struggled with *her* locks at the door of the Church of
St. Collen.

"They call us bare-foot savages," Rhisiart thought, "but on my soul,
that boy Elphin would suit the court of Constantinople!" And he
allowed Meredith to take all the time he needed over his military adjustments, so as to give Master Brut an opportunity to regain a strategic
position by the hearth before their entrance.

Meredith had brought his fighting-spear to show his young allies;
and it was upon this weapon, when they were all three sitting on the
bench by the fire, that the general interest concentrated.

"Do you ever use it as a javelin?" enquired our friend.

"I've always heard so much of Welsh spear-throwing, but I've never
held a real Welsh spear in my hand before. This must be the sort of
thing that our ancestors, the Trojans, used, isn't it? With such a spear
as this"—and our friend couldn't resist getting up from the bench and
brandishing it—"Hector must have wounded Patroclus!"

"Who was Patroclus?" asked the son of Owen; and then with a sad
little smile that contrasted quaintly enough with his flashing armour,
"I'm not like my father. I never went to Oxford; and they've got only
a few scraps of Homer in the Valle Crucis; and I don't believe even
Father Pascentius can translate what they *have* got!"

Our friend was quite prepared to enter at some length—as the headless crucifix looked down upon them and a chilly draught descending
the new-fashioned chimney made the birch-logs smoke—upon the inexhaustible learning of his teacher at Exeter College; but Meredith in
a quick change of mood stirred the fire with the point of his spear and
confessed to them he had brought bad news.

Both the young men looked anxiously at him.

"That Roman?" they exclaimed simultaneously.

Meredith propped his weapon against the side of the hearth and
laid his helmet down beside him. "You've hit it, lads!" he said. "That
smug rogue's let the devil himself loose, and the fat's in the fire with a

vengeance. You know he went off last night? Yes, he wouldn't stay half-an-hour after we broke up. Our lawyer-friend's attack on him burst his bubble. He *had* a message to the King from Rome, had it under his vest all the while! In a fit of panic when the noise in the hall grew worse he confessed as much to my father, claiming immunity as King's messenger; and then, calling for his horse and his servants, off he rode—straight to Valle Crucis.

"As luck would have it, the guest-house there was full of our enemies. Grey and Fitz-Alan had dined at the refectory and were staying for the night. *They* sent down to the Tassel for Cousin Sele and Davy Gam; and young Burnell from Dinas Bran was brought down, too. I wonder Lowri let him come; but at any rate there he was. Not one honest Welshman among them! They must have stayed up, plotting trouble for us, half the night. That curst Roman was at the bottom of it. I think he'd have made trouble anyway, but Master Young's attack on him set the gunpowder off! And now, quite early this morning— Griffith and I were still asleep, but father was awake: I think he'd been in the chapel all night praying over Iolo—what must arrive but a nice little set of demands from old Abbot Cust. It's the Prior of course who composed this precious document. He's the master there, and a worse enemy we've never had. But at any rate, what they demand is:

"*One,* that your friend Alice, whom they call a house-serf at Ruthin, though the gossip in our kitchen is that she's young Grey's paramour, be carried over there and delivered to her master;

"*Two,* that Mad Huw and the Maid be brought before the Abbot's court; and

"*Three,* that one Master Brut, of the Manor of Lyde in the County of Hereford, be also handed over to the aforesaid court to answer why, how,.and on what authority he, a declared heretic, should travel at large through His Majesty's fiefs of Ial, Bromfield, Glyndyfrdwy and Edeyrnion, to the danger, peril, risk and injury of His Majesty's faithful and pious subjects of the aforesaid manors, baronies and jurisdictions!"

It would be hard to say which of his guests was more staggered by this blow; and harder still to say whether it was of Tegolin or of Alice or of his friend, the Lollard, that Rhisiart first thought. But they both kept silence, waiting to learn more before committing themselves to any comment.

"Well," Meredith continued, bending down to ease the clasps of the steep plate that covered one of his knees, you can imagine what *I* said when Father came and told us. But I could see Father had made up his mind before he gave us a chance to speak. He said we must give way on every point except in the matter of giving *you* up, Master Brut. To that, he said, nothing would make him consent. But he thinks his submission about the Friar and the Maid and about that girl was the only thing they *hadn't* counted on.

"He said our reputation for hospitality and their knowledge of our touchiness about the honour of our house and so on was what set them—Prior Bevan especially—on making these demands.

"He thought the whole thing was only to give colour and excuse to a move on which they'd already decided. He said the only alternative to submission was to leave this place, and leave our place at Sycharth, and take refuge in the mountains of Snowdon. But he said this would ruin our plans for the rising in September. You see he's got those unlucky dates—the sixteenth and the eighteenth—lodged like a doom in his head! It's what we call a fate or a *tynghed* on him. He loved old Iolo so much that he makes everything depend on carrying out his prophecy. Griffith and the Arglwyddes are very upset about it. They don't care, I'm afraid, what happens to your Alice, Master Brut; but the idea of giving up the Friar and the Maid seems monstrous to them. And, of course, it *is* monstrous; but so is the idea of giving up that unlucky girl!

"But Father's got it into his head that nothing worse than temporary captivity could possibly happen to the Friar and the Maid, though I don't suppose *he* gives the fate of Alice much thought—but, as I say, his absolute conviction is—since his night with the dead Bard in the chapel—that if we hoist our standard in September, as Iolo prophesied, every victim of those monks and every prisoner in Ruthin and Chirk will be set free!

"Well, having decided on submission, except in *your* case, Master, the next thing he decides, since they won't dare to attack such obedient servants of Holy Church as we shall be then, is for Rhys Gethin to scour the Conway country till he gathers a regular army of spearmen, and for Griffith to rush to Mona to get help from the Tudors, and for me to hurry off to our place at Sycharth and bring over here all the money"—he lowered his voice in what might have been a mock-imitation of a Jewish usurer—"about five thousand silver groats, that he's got hidden there. Some of this sum Rhys Gethin will want for his new army; but the bulk of it Father will hide in the mound, where, if Grey *does* burn this place, it'll be absolutely safe."

"But what about the Arglwyddes and Catharine?" our friend enquired.

"Oh, we'll have our scouts round here! We shan't take *them* away; and at the first news of danger in the offing the ladies'll ride across Moel Goch to a perfectly safe hiding-place."

"And your father?" asked the Lollard.

The youth smiled. "Oh, *he* can be left to take care of himself!" And then, seeing an expression of shocked amazement on his hearers' faces, he burst out laughing.

"You think I'm frivolous and callous, do you? Well—you'll soon feel just as I do when you see more of him! Everybody here feels the same; even the Arglwyddes, even Catharine."

"What do you mean?" asked Rhisiart.

"Oh, it's not a thing you can easily put into words," replied the young chieftain, rising from the bench and picking up his helmet. "It comes from living with him. I don't say it gives you any especial confidence in his success—I mean in his triumph over our enemies—but it makes it impossible to imagine him—*him himself* I mean—helpless in their hands."

Master Brut looked up at the face of the young warrior, who now towered above them, the fire-light flickering on his breast-plate. One dark lock from beneath his steel cap crossed his forehead and the glint of the metal made his eyes even more animated than their wont.

"Pardon the question if it seems impertinent," said the Lollard gravely. "But is your father a religious man? Does he *pray* more than most of us ordinary people?"

Owen's son smiled his sad ironic smile. "If he *wasn't* praying last night I don't know what he was doing. Our Porter told me he was on his knees for hours."

"Christ have mercy on him and on us all!" murmured the other.

"But I don't want to give you a wrong impression," Meredith went on. "He's always reading that crystal you saw, and he's always studying astrology. Our old wives consider him a necromancer. Nurse told Catharine once, when she caught her listening at the mound-stone, that she was going the way of the master. *She* thinks he's sold his soul to the Devil; but I know— Rhisiart's a relation and you, sir, are"—he hesitated a moment—"an honest man, so I needn't be squeamish—but I know Griffith and the Arglwyddes sometimes think—"

He stopped and listened. "I thought I heard it—the mound I mean— but it was only the rain—that he's committed to Saint Derfel." He paused again; and once more he smiled that sad ironical smile. "There! I've said enough, and too much, my lads! Saint Derfel means nothing to you, and why should he? God! why should he? *Why should he?*"

His voice, as he repeated this, had a wild, high-pitched, hysterical note that troubled his hearers not a little. But his mood changed in a flash. "Blessed Mary!" he cried, "what nonsense I'm talking! It's this midsummer rain. Well, comrades, wish me luck with that damned silver! It's the sort of job I hate. I wish I were going to Mona, and Griffith to Sycharth. But when Father makes up his mind—well, good-bye, my lads!"

But the Lollard was on his feet now. "Just one little thing," he said quietly. "Will you tell your father, before you go, that I shall accompany the Friar and the Maid and—and the other. It's a small point, among all the rest, but I'd like him to know it. In this way *all* their demands will be satisfied. But in any case, tell him, I've decided to go. I can leave my horse, eh? and my clothes and books?—and then, if I don't come back—"

It was Rhisiart's turn now to jump to his feet. "And tell Cousin Owen," he announced emphatically, "that, with his permission, *I* would like to go, too. It might make his obedience, *our* obedience, more clear and definite if his"—and he gave a little forced laugh—"if his hostages were accompanied by a—by a sort of relative of the family."

Meredith fixed upon them both a grave and absent-minded stare. He had turned at the door, and they could see from the abstracted look that he was still listening to something outside the room. At last he shrugged his shoulders.

"It's a pity," he said. Then, after a moment or more of listening, "A pity," he repeated. Then, while his face took on a hard, rigid, mask-like look, "Up in smoke it goes then, my chance of having someone to talk to. I must play chess again with Madoc ab Ieuan and hide-and-seek with Catharine! So you've decided, have you, Master Brut? And you too, Rhisiart? Well, I think your idea of a member of the family bringing our—what did you call them?—our 'hostages,' may appeal to my Lord. I'll send you word, anyway." And with a stiff little bend of his steel-clad head the gleaming figure was gone.

Then our friend turned peevishly to his companion. "What made you do that?" he said. "Owen wanted you to stay."

"Tu quoque!" retorted the other. "What do *you* know about Welsh etiquette and honour? A member of the family! A member of *my* family of combustible heretics is what they'll make of *you,* lad, riding with Master Brut along the King's highway and drawing your sword against the archers of Chirk! But there it is. We've both done it now; and there can be no going back. Meredith knew Owen would agree, or he wouldn't have looked like that at the last. Poor lad, I expect he *does* pine for someone to talk to, with only that spoilt child and her taciturn brother."

Rhisiart made no reply. He walked across the room to where his sheepskin bundle lay and pulled out his crusader's sword. "No, I must leave *you* behind," he said to himself, "just as I must leave Griffin."

Following one of his little private rituals he drew his dagger and laid its blade for a moment across the blade of the old sword. Then, replacing this latter, he straightened himself, tightened his belt, brushed away some crumbs from his doublet and remarked rather peevishly to his friend, "No one'll meddle, I hope, with our things here while we're away?"

The Lollard, who was transferring his precious Gospel manuscript from *his* bundle to some hidden receptacle about his person, hastened to point out how extremely unlikely it was, at this particular juncture, that any other guests would be put in the Saracen's room. "But if you're fussy about your things, I'd say a word to that old woman. She's the one—"

"Gentlemen! gentlemen!" the interruption came in a high-pitched tremulous voice from outside their door, and upon the door itself fell sundry vigorous blows from something harder than human knuckles.

"Talk of the devil—" cried Rhisiart. "By Gis! if that's not the Nurse!"

"She's come to tell us they're ready to start," said Master Brut; and both the young men, standing there in their neat students' garb, cast that curious look round their chamber that most human beings and many animals throw round the already familiar outlines of their lair of the past night. Then they flung open the door and slipped out side by side. Yes! there was the tall head-dress. There was the white wimple suspended from its grotesquely elongated peak, and there was the black staff.

"Oh Masters, what goings-on!" the old woman cried. "Oh gentlemen, sweet gentlemen, what a coil is here! 'Tis my precious Missy that be the cause; for the pretty honey-bag has shrieked and battered at my Lord's door, where 'a be turning wet to fine with crystal-gazing, and calling up of spirits from below, and now, seeing he won't open to her, or change his hard heart, dost know, honey-gents, what's gone and done? 'A's gone and barred herself up, along with they naked men, and them ready to stink too afore sun-down, and all in chapel-vault! I've never let her blessed little knees touch they cold stones all her days, no! not at Holy Mass, and there my sweet lamb be—for I've squinnied through door-crack and seed'un—along wi' they naked dead—and crying her heart out! She do think the world of *thee,* Master Rhisiart, though I shouldn't say it, and the man that gets her, oh, my daisy-gents, the man that gets her! will know what I alone do know, who've washed her and combed her since her first cry."

Rhisiart felt too nervous, too agitated, too puzzled, in short too young, to do more than stare blankly at the old woman and fumble awkwardly with the wallet in his belt. There did just enter into the shrewd sheriff's-officer portion of his youthful consciousness that what the old lady was really after was a tactful, casual, discreet and timely-offered half-ducat or even a silver crown; but since like the Lollard his whole stock of funds consisted of a few fresh-minted gold nobles and a quantity of king's pennies, neither of which seemed appropriate to the occasion, he contented himself with allowing his fingers to remain in contact with the wallet in his belt.

His companion, however, was less tongue-tied. "Go and tell your

silly child," he said, "that her cousin is going along with the Maid—
if that's what's bothering her—and you can add, if you like, that I'm
going along with her cousin and that I've got great influence! Influence *at Court,* you may say; and you needn't tell her that I speak
of the King of Heaven; but will you please tell me, my good lady,
where the Abbot's room is, for I would dearly like to have his venerable
blessing before we all set out."

"John ap Hywel are you speaking of? Bless my stars, young man!
Let me see; let me see. . . . So that wench is going with you to Abbot
Cust's court, is she? And you gave the Captain a whole groat for her?
Marry of God! Enough to make a grand lady unpin her smock, not
to name a poor Ruthin girl! Abbot John, do you say? Why he rode off
on his black horse before 'twas light. They say he's gone to raise men
for my Lord from Usk to Dynevor! But if you want a holy man's blessing on your dear face there's Father Rheinalt left. He's going to monk
it no more, 'a says! We've never had a shaved priest in hall since old
Father Jenkyn died. *He* were a one, Father Jenkyn. Couldn't abide
sour wine nor sharp-tongued women. And 'twere the poor gentleman's
sweet tooth, I reckon, in this sad world what took him off at the last.
I mind well his end. There weren't a dry eye in kitchen or bower. And
when I laid him out—Marry of God, what didn't I see! And him that
couldn't abide sour wine or stand-off women. 'A wore against his poor
skin what must have tormented him night and day! Us don't know
nothing of a man, that's what I tells the maids, shaved or unshaved,
till us lays him out! So go to Father Rheinalt, young man. He'll bless
your kind face and absolve your sweet sins!"

Our friend all this while had been listening with only half an ear to
the Nurse's chatter; for it seemed to him that he too—just as Meredith
had done—heard something out of the darkness by the mound-stone
that was *more* than rain or wind. But he was surprised at Master Brut's
affability to the bawdy old trot, and still more surprised when he saw
him put into her hand some loose silver from his pouch, with the
words, "Well gossip, whether your confessor be Jenkyn or Rheinalt
don't'ee forget with all your 'Paternosters' and 'Hail Marys,' to say a
prayer to the Saviour now and again, in plain Welsh."

"Where is Father Pascentius, Nurse?" our friend enquired abruptly.

"Him? Don't you talk of *him* to me, Master Rhisiart. He went off last night with that false proud priest who brought all the trouble on us; and before he went what must he do but come up to me where I stood by the stairs, listening to the harping, and ask me more questions in five blessed minutes than I've heard all my days. You can believe he got God's truth! He got as much truth as a fish of the sea gets air. That's what *he* got for his pains!"

By this time, hearing the Nurse's voice and seeing in the light that issued from the open door of the Saracen's chamber her familiar figure in close colloquy with the two guests, a group of inquisitive pages had arrived on the scene, and among them the pretty lad who had brought them their meal.

The Nurse was now relating to the Lollard a new story about the deceased Father; so that Rhisiart in that dim light, feeling himself a reckless soldier about to risk his life, hesitated not to pull the boy to him, and while he fondled him, to ask him whether Master Young had yet gone off.

The boy replied that the Canon was at present closeted with their Lord in the astrologer's room, but that a considerable band of spearmen under the command of Madoc ab Ieuan had been deputed to conduct him to the border. He also whispered to our friend in that conspiring dimness that Mad Huw was already in the hall.

The mention of the Friar brought about a remorseful reaction in Rhisiart's impulsive blood and, changing his manner abruptly if not rudely, he packed Elphin off to find out if the ladies had come down. The boy, sulky and loitering, had scarcely reached the entrance to the vestibule when Mad Huw himself came hurrying past him. The door of their chamber had been closed by this time and the remains of their meal had been divided with a good deal of suppressed squabbling among the pages. The Nurse herself was locking the shut door with one of the great keys that jingled at her side, and the Lollard was watching this performance with an interest that even a student of the Greek Testament might legitimately feel where the bulk of all his worldly goods was in question, when Mad Huw came down upon them.

Our friend detected at once that the man's sojourn in a civilized abode, short as it had been, without fear of molestation or of mockery, had had some deep psychological effect on him. He had ceased, at least under *this* roof, all noisy proclamations of Richard's return, and in place of these vociferous outcries he had acquired a trick of hurried, secretive, mystic communications.

This new form taken by his ruling passion may have been due to the hours he had spent among the lively and sympathetic maidens of the Arglwyddes's entourage, or to some deep impression made on his mind by the presence of the two dead men in the chapel, or even, it may be, to his consciousness of the great conspiracy in the wind. He certainly acted now as if he were in the midst of some dramatic secret transaction and in the presence of a perpetual audience of spies from whom this transaction must be concealed.

"He's being moved across Wales," he whispered in our friend's ear as soon as he emerged out of the darkness, "and it's because he's expected at Valle Crucis that that Roman came here last night. Richard loves the Grey Friars just as Owen does; and that's why the Pope is so spiteful. The Popes have been jealous of them from the beginning. And every house, every wall, every tree, has a spy in it now; and that's why we have to be so careful what we say and whom we talk to. And there's another thing, my son, that we mustn't forget. *Not all Grey Friars are Grey Friars.* Skulking wolves some of them are, and cunning foxes! You have to look out all the time. You have to look for their pointed ears and their sharp teeth."

"Have the Maid and the woman from Ruthin come down yet, Brother?" enquired the Lollard.

"No, no, no, Master Brut; they're waiting, just like we are. We're all waiting, so that Bolingbroke won't hear a sound when He's brought across Wales."

At that moment the pretty page, Elphin, came back, and in order to punish Rhisiart for his abrupt dismissal he remained, in spite of the passage being so dark, proudly and coyly out of our friend's reach.

"Hist!" cried the old woman fixing the key of the Saracen's chamber to her girdle. "There's Derfel making his moan! He's asking for a new maidenhead! Who was that last Derfel-bride in Edeyrnion, Brother Huw? Can'ee remember her name? 'Twere'nt Gwen were't? No, *her* bastard were Tom Ifan's. Nor it weren't Sibli ferch Rhys either; for her man was Davy Ddu of Bonwm. Which *were* the last Derfel-imp, Brother? I can mind when Crach Ffinnant were born;

but her what bore he were a convent-maid. Were it Sara Llwyd of Trawsfynnydd? But she—"

"Come, Masters! Come, Masters!" interrupted Mad Huw. "The Maid must be down by now. I always know when she's near. No, daughter, I can't remember the last one's name any better than your-self; but I know the unhappy licence that God, for his own mysterious purpose, has allowed to Satan in the name of Derfel. *Saint* Derfel"— and the Friar crossed himself devoutly—"is in the company of the Blest; but there are those, in the heathen places of this land, who con-jure up terrible evil in that blessed one's name! Would that Lord Owen relied, as our Richard does, upon the humblest Brother of Saint Francis, rather than upon all the powers of the air! But come, Masters, come! The Maid is calling." He paused for a moment, and then turning towards mound-stone drew himself up, a tall grey figure in the gloom, no longer—so it seemed to Rhisiart—a poor distracted half-wit, but a formidable priest of God. *"In nomine Christi et omnium sanctorum,"* he cried sternly, "be silent, unhappy spirits!"

His words were responded to by a sound that Rhisiart, with his sceptical Norman blood, took for a receding wail of discordant echoes; but a dead silence undoubtedly succeeded this, a silence that was only broken as they followed that grey figure towards the hall, by a plaintive, "Marry of God, sweet men!" from the bewildered Nurse.

An hour later, with the two girls, mounted upon Welsh ponies, and a boy from the stable, who was to bring back the animals, following after them, all five hostages were making their way, and doing so quite leisurely, towards the famous monastic house.

Rhisiart's nature was stirred to its depths by what was happening. Tegolin and Alice exchanged casual and friendly remarks as they rode along together, with the Friar at the Maid's left and the two young men on the other's right, while their youthful escort, humming and whistling to himself and throwing stones at the rabbits, loitered care-lessly in the rear. Luckily for them all the rain had ceased, and though the wind was still in their faces and blowing fresh and chill there was a feeling in the air as though the sun might break through at any mo-ment, and the yellow and green of gorze and bracken stretched away up the slope above them and down the slope beneath them, with a rich re-assuring welcome.

They were all of them young, and the rain-washed air of that summer afternoon, and the spacious curves of the great mountains above them, over-lapping each other like prone giantesses, and the fox-gloves in the hollows beneath them, and the yellow trefoil under their feet, made it hard for them to believe they were heading for pain or disaster.

"I've been thinking out," said Rhisiart to Master Brut; "the exact line I'm going to take. I'm going to make a lot of being one of the family. So for God's sake, don't contradict *anything* I say! And I'm going to make a lot of being a law-student—do you understand?—from Oxford. What do you think's become of our Abbot's monks? I take it *they're* not rushing after their leader half across Wales. And if they're still at the Abbey—well! we've got *some* friends at court."

The Lollard chuckled. "I doubt if even the monks of Caerleon would stand up for a sworn gospel-man like me! But Abbot Cust knew me as a child. So I can't believe— But it's Prior Bevan who's my danger, and our Friar's too, I'm afraid. From all I hear about *him,* and they tell me he's a bullying Salopian and has got the old man under his thumb, you'll need your best forensic eloquence—especially as everybody saw us together on Saint John's Eve."

Rhisiart's thin Norman face contracted with a spasm of boyish arrogance. "You wait, partner!" he announced proudly. "I've been thinking it out; and I'm not at all sure Father Bevan won't find himself check-mated!"

The Lollard watched a rain-ruffled brown butterfly pursuing his less heavily-winged mate across the patches of yellow trefoil. "I hope you're right, comrade," he said, "but it'll be a bad look-out for us if Hywel Sele and Davy Gam are still on the scene. That rascal from Rome must have done his worst. Oh, these Papalists! These Papalists!"

Mad Huw caught the trouble in his tone and peered back at them over the pony's mane. "Mum's the word, Masters!" he murmured. *"He* may be there by this time. But he'll be disguised. If you see him you must take no notice. I shall know him and he'll know me; but neither of us will make a sign! Mum's the word, my lads, till we've got him safe to London."

Both the young men nodded respectful assent to these instructions; but the Ruthin girl, whose desirable figure as she rode by Tegolin's side had shared with the swaying red braid and with the yellow gorze they were passing not a little of our friend's concentration, turned her head quickly and self-consciously now from the Maid to the men and back to the men, and said with some embarrassment and with hot cheeks, "Will you tell them about me, Mistress, please? I want them to know; especially the lawyer-gentleman from Oxford!"

"Won't you try and tell them yourself, Alice?" protested the Maid.

But the girl gave Rhisiart a heavy-lidded enigmatic look from her pony's back and shook her head. "I can't do it," she said. "I'm not ashamed, and I know the gentlemen are kind. But I just can't do it. The words cling to something in here"—and she indicated her bosom—"and I can't drag them out."

Tegolin frowned. Rhisiart could see that the self-consciousness of her companion irritated the Maid and that she hadn't any overwhelming sympathy with her in her present predicament.

"Alice wants you to know," she said, speaking hurriedly and rather brusquely, "that she lives with her parents in the English quarter of Ruthin. Her father's a master-baker, from—Coventry didn't you say, Alice?—yes, from Coventry, but her mother's Welsh. Her father wanted her to marry the lad we saw murdered last night, and Alice had to consent, and they were betrothed, but she never loved him; so that his death last night was—what did you say it was, Alice?—not a Providence, for that would have been too heartless—well, an *escape* anyway! But Alice has been working every day since she was a child in Ruthin Castle; and she thinks Lord Grey's son Ambrose wants to— how do you say in in English?—*treisio,* to violate her; and she would much rather—that's what you said, Alice, wasn't it?—leave Ruthin altogether than risk such a thing. She says her parents don't believe that Ambrose would hurt her, and short of that—stop me if I'm wrong, Alice!—she says they're rather proud he notices her and gives her presents."

The Maid paused; but Alice turned quick towards her. "Tell them what I said just now; for I *did* mean it, and I *do* mean it!"

"Alice said just now," repeated the Maid in an almost mechanical tone, "that she'd like above everything else to be my servant and to go about with me and Brother Huw; and when I told her that we both have now sworn to support Owen and join his household, she said—

stop me if I'm telling them wrong—that she *still* wanted to be my servant. She says she hates kitchen-work and is very good with her needle."

"And what did *you* say to this, Tegolin?" our lad sharply enquired. He had noticed all the way through her speech that she felt anything but really friendly towards this girl, and in his secret heart he attributed this entirely to jealousy. "She has the Friar," he said to himself, "and yet she won't let a person think of anyone else!"

"I told you—didn't I, Alice?" replied the Maid gently, "that I've never had a servant since I was little and I'm too old to begin now."

"Mistress! Mistress!" protested the other, "when you know you're not seventeen! I shall be nineteen come Michaelmas. All born ladies like you have their tire-woman, if it's only to comb their hair." And with a tender protective gesture the Ruthin girl extricated from the plaited coils so near her hand a couple of dandelion-seeds.

Watching this slight movement, Rhisiart suddenly wondered if the Maid of Edeyrnion had kept that meadow-orchis he had given her when she wanted to touch his sword. It wasn't, of course, in those plaits any more. She had loosened her hair last night. But had she preserved it, or just forgotten all about it? And did she ever think now, after so much had happened, of how honourable he had been when she slept in her smock under his sheepskin?

The tale of Alice's troubles must have made her hearers think of their own, for all that youthful company fell now into gloomy silence, from the influence of which Mad Huw found it necessary to escape by turning repeatedly to watch their childish escort throw stones at the rabbits.

It gave Rhisiart a very queer feeling when at last, through a gap in the mountains, the bases of which were now heavily wooded, he caught a glimpse of Dinas Brân. How much had happened since he had planted his sword in the earth at the first sight of that extraordinary stronghold!

He still gazed at those towers with reverence and awe, but with how much more knowledge of life than when from old Griffin's back he had first observed them! He thought of Modry. What would *she* have felt if she could have looked into the future and seen the young listener to her wild tales riding beneath those battlements with a mad priest, a reckless heretic and these two disturbing young women?

And then he thought of his light-hearted Norman mother. How she would have laughed could she have foreseen to what use he was going to put the expensive legal education she had given him! "She would think I'd been just a fool to let Tegolin get up from that straw the same as she lay down. And she'd say it was all in the game and *à la guerre comme à la guerre* if I stole Alice away from Ambrose Grey!"

But they were getting near the monastery now, and it wasn't long before they reached a grassy hill-side, flecked with patches of yellow trefoil, and interspersed with grey rocks and a few ancient, solitary-growing birch-trees, from which the walls and pinnacles of the Abbey itself were visible in the vale below.

The girls brought their ponies to a stand-still; and the young rabbit-chaser came running hastily to their side, panting and excited, to inform them in rustic Welsh that he had been forbidden to go any further.

His tone struck Rhisiart as more perturbed and imperative than was suitable to the occasion. He seemed almost rudely anxious to get the ladies out of their saddles; nor did the three big copper coins bearing the bearded countenance of Edward the Third which our friend rather nervously thrust into his hand lessen his feverish desire to be off.

When he *had* mounted one of the ponies and got a firm hold of the bridle of the other he barely stayed to acknowledge with a word their final salute. Off he went at a wild gallop, and it was only after watching him disappear round a bluff of the hill-side that they realized the cause of his haste. They had been so absorbed in their first view of the Abbey that it had escaped their notice that in a narrow defile just below them, under a group of tall chestnuts, was a party of men-at-arms, upon whose helmets and spears the sun, as it fell through the wet branches in the fresh breeze, cast a proud flicker of lights and shadows. There was nothing for them to do but to advance as boldly and calmly as they could; but the path having narrowed itself between slippery banks, they were compelled to proceed in single file, Rhisiart leading the way and the Lollard bringing up the rear.

Partly in order to display his calmness to Tegolin who came behind him, and partly because the presence of danger brought his kinsman to his mind, Rhisiart turned when they were half-way down the declivity and asked the Maid in an easy, casual whisper why it was that Owen hadn't come out to see them off.

"I saw him at the foot of the stairs," she returned hastily. "They said he was so upset about Master Brut going that he couldn't bear to meet him. He was in a strange mood. He stood and stared at me just as if he didn't know me, and then just bowed like a man in a trance and went back to his room." She paused; and then, in a low hurried tone, "Gwion Bach," she whispered, "you won't forget me, if they separate us?"

"They *shan't* separate us!" he replied boldly; but she shook her head, and although he turned too quick to see it a sad little smile crossed her face as they went on.

They were soon confronted by the armed men, who turned out to be fewer in number than the gleam of their armour under the chestnut-trees had suggested. Not more than half-a-dozen they were; but they straddled across the path, while their leader, a singular-looking young man, advanced a few steps alone.

"It's Master Ambrose!" whispered Alice to Tegolin, plucking her by the arm. "Tell the young gentleman to leave him to me; and get quick into the precincts! He can't touch us in the precincts."

Tegolin caught Rhisiart by the belt. It was his crucial moment, when he was straightening his shoulders and collecting his wits for the encounter; and he turned impatiently, frowning crossly. It was just like a girl to go and disturb a person when it was all worked out in his mind exactly what to do.

"It's young Grey," the Maid dutifully whispered. "She says to leave him to her, and for us to get quickly into the enclosure where they can't touch us!"

"All right," said Rhisiart brusquely. Her words made him suck in his lips till they were as queer-looking as Master Young's. But to have a couple of girls deciding what was to be done at a crisis like this!

"Who are you?" he asked in blunt Hereford fashion, just as if he were interrogating some fancy-foreigner in the old law-office in Worcester Street.

"Grey of Ruthin," replied the young man haughtily. "Are you Glendourdy's cousin or are you his secretary?"

"I'm his cousin *and* his secretary, and I happen to have just taken my degree in civil law at Oxford and I have come to represent my cousin in the Abbot's court, and it is at my advice that he has acted so legally and so properly in the sending of Master Brut of Lyde in the County of Hereford, of Mistress Tegolin, commonly known as the Maid of—"

"Tut! Tut! Master Cousin Legality! Didn't you hear who I am? I'm Ambrose de Grey de Ruthin 'commonly known' as the son of my father, and I've not come here to be lectured on law, but to possess myself of—of—of the person— How *could* you frighten me so?"

The discontinuity of this curious young man's speech was due to the fact of Alice's slipping hurriedly past both the Maid and Rhisiart and spiritually—though not actually—throwing herself into his arms.

It must be admitted in our friend's favour that he didn't allow this grievous shock to his self-esteem to interfere with the working of his intelligence. He was angry, he was humiliated, he was ashamed of himself, and he felt extremely young, but his wits seemed to work all the quicker for this, and to work quite independently of his irritable and outraged dignity.

Beckoning to Master Brut, who either had caught the Ruthin girl's shrewd whisper or was acting in accordance with evangelical principles, for he remained amenable to every ripple in the stream of events, he hurried them between the Ruthin soldiers who were staring with absorbed interest at Ambrose and Alice, and led them through a small wicket gate into the precincts of the monastery.

Here a diminutive little monk, with his robe tucked up under his belt, was gathering herbs for some culinary or medicinal purpose, and he advanced tentatively and politely towards them.

Rhisiart, however, took no notice of this friendly advance on the part of the monk, for all his interest—like that of the Ruthin men-at-arms—was absorbed in the conversation between Ambrose and his runaway girl.

The heir of Ruthin was certainly one of the queerest-looking youths Rhisiart had ever seen. He was well above middle-height, indeed of much the same stature and build as our friend himself, but his face was sickly-white, and his mouth oddly twisted awry. He had been disfigured by a sword-cut in his boyhood; and this disfigurement, though he wore on his upper lip a small black moustache, could not be concealed. His chin was abnormally long and pointed, and this with a pair of protruding ears, which stood out grotesquely from beneath his steel cap, gave him the look of some kind of animal—our friend couldn't decide *what* animal—that had been endowed by an impish freak of Nature with a human form.

But whatever animal it might be that Ambrose Grey resembled it was, Rhisiart felt, not only a sick animal but an animal obsessed by a veritable demon of desire. He had hollow eyes of a pale blue tint, and the fact that they seemed, at the distance our friend now stood, to be entirely devoid of eyebrows, increased the besotted craving, as if he could drink her up, body and soul, with which he gloated over Alice.

For some reason the very strength of the youth's desire, unholy and carnal though it was, had a poignancy that made it hard for our friend to despise him, much less to hate him. There was something at once grotesque and tragic in such unbalanced emotion, which resembled that of an infatuated beast for its mistress, rather than the passion of a seducer for his victim.

The Ruthin girl had said "leave him to me," and it was clear that she was justified in her confidence. By gestures and whispers and low-voiced murmurs, like a crafty white pigeon fooling a demented jackal, the girl led him nearer and nearer to the wicket, and just as one of the men-at-arms, more on the alert than his master, was on the point of intervening, she slipped through the gate and closed it in the young man's face. Even then, it seemed to our friend, as the herb-gathering monk approached them, that the obsessed youth had no idea of what this meant, or of the fatal barrier which that flimsy trellis-work offered.

Automatically, all armed as he was, young Grey pushed the gate open, and heedless of the astonishment of Mad Huw who was whispering to the Lollard, he took the girl by the arm and made an attempt to drag her back.

But the little herbalist indignantly intervened. "Sacrilege! Sacrilege!" he cried, and our friend had never seen such a transformation. From every feature and from every limb of that slight figure there emanated the spiritual authority of a thousand years. "Holy ground! Holy ground!"

"Get back, Master Ambrose, or I'll—" And, with that, waving his bunch of weeds as if they were the "bell, book and candle" of an outraged Christendom, he hustled the bewildered Ambrose outside the precincts, and closed the gate.

But it wasn't only the little Cistercian who was transformed; for no sooner was the man outside, with the indignant monk guarding the closed gate, than the Ruthin girl sprang to the fence and began in viciously honeyed tones a series of mocking taunts.

These taunts, in her rich sensual voice, were uttered without the least tremor of anything hysterical. She didn't seem bitter, or even angry. There was a voluptuous unction in her tone.

"Better luck, next time, stupid! Why don't you try it with Molly Price again who was born blind? Or with Sibby Saunders who'd let a toad do it? Or with Polly Walker who says you waggle your ears when you get anyone down? Do you know what Mother Pusey who keeps the whore-house calls you?—Monsieur Point-du-Tout! And do you know what—"

But the monk intervened. "Come away, woman," he said sternly. "You shall go to the Prior! And you, Master Ambrose, take your men off at once and never—"

But something in the young man's livid and ghastly face made him stop abruptly. Skilled as a good priest in sounding the depths of mortal passion he recognized that this was no ordinary case of sexual brutality.

"If you or my Lord of Ruthin," he said in a gentler tone, "have anything against this young woman, you can take off your armour, lay down your weapons, and come now, at once, to the Prior's court. Is it your pleasure to do this?"

But the youth in armour seemed hardly to understand what was said to him. In a curiously helpless manner, and stumbling a little as if some vital contact between his brain and his limbs had been severed, he moved to the gate again. His eyes had never left the face of the woman, and he now began fumbling with the wooden catch of the gate as if his fingers were paralysed and his wits drugged.

But his men came crowding round him and, though Rhisiart couldn't catch their words, it was clear they put some pressure upon him that was more than he could resist. With his head hanging in a curious sideways manner over his steel gorget, as if he'd received some wound in the gullet and was bleeding internally, he let himself be led away; not, however, before one of his men had flung a threat into the girl's face of so shocking a character that Tegolin made a protective movement towards her and the monk indignantly lifted his hand.

But the Ruthin girl merely narrowed her eyes under her heavy lids and smiled contemptuously.

Rhisiart was conscious as he looked at her of a wild drumming in his pulses and of a sensual stir that made his eyes darken and the pit of his stomach turn dizzy. He had hated her when she said those things to that stricken youth in armour, and he hated the way she was smiling now under that ruffian's appalling threat; and yet something about those heavy-lidded eyes and those rounded flanks made this hatred quiver and vibrate with a craving to hug her till she cried out under his grip.

But Mad Huw had come over to him now. "Not a word, not a word of *him!*" the Friar whispered. "This Prior's court is a trick. They know we know where *he* is. But if they torture us we mustn't breathe a word." Then he glanced anxiously at the Lollard. "Does *he* understand? Will he *be* silent?"

Rhisiart assured this innocent conspirator that if anyone understood *anything* it was Master Brut; and they all followed the little monk, as walking by Tegolin's side with eyes modestly cast down upon his bunch of herbs he led the way towards the Abbey.

They soon arrived at the imposing west front, where, above the rich Gothic entrance, several delicately-carved windows seemed calling upon the sun with a beguiling and living welcome to mingle its rays with the smoke of the incense and the rhythm of the sacred chants. Here their guide paused. "You must pardon me, gentlemen," he said, addressing the two young men, "for *you,* Brother," and he turned to Mad Huw, "will understand how it is, but I must call for Sister Cunlap to take the ladies to the women's guest-house." Thus speaking he took hold of a rope which dangled from an orifice above the gate and gave it a gentle pull.

There was a faint tinkle from inside the building, and a small iron-grated shutter in the frame-work of the door was shot back disclosing a tonsured head and a pair of inquisitive eyes.

"Is Brother Jenkyn there?"

"Yes, Father."

"Is he free for a moment?"

"Yes, Father."

"I want him here."

There was a brief pause during which Tegolin came close up to our friend and whispered hurriedly, "Don't believe any message you get from me unless the messenger says, *'Crusader.'* Do you understand?"

He nodded assent.

"Kiss me, Gwion Bach!"

Their lips met. His were hot and dry, hers cold as a stone. She drew back to Alice's side; and our friend, though he felt her gaze was upon him, and he wanted to meet it, was aware of a sensation like the pressure of an iron bar across his forehead which compelled him to turn away.

Then the gate was cautiously and partially opened and an elderly lay-brother squeezed himself out, crossed his arms upon his chest, and bowed to their guide.

"Tell Sister Cunlap I want her, Brother. Tell her to come at once. And tell her there are some visitors for the women's guest-house."

The lay-brother glanced at the two girls. "For the night, Father? Or just to lie down, Father?"

The monk frowned and shook his head, as if by this introduction of the image of night combined with the image of the lying down of ladies Brother Jenkyn had gone too far.

"Tell the Sister to come at once, Brother! Tell her we're waiting."

Although that queer bar of iron still weighed on his eyelids, our friend spent most of his time during the uneasy interval that followed the Brother's leisurely disappearance in trying to catch Tegolin's eyes; but Alice was holding her in eager whispered conversation, and he had no success.

Meanwhile, through the chink of the great door which had been left ajar, but was now crossed by a heavy chain, there came the sound of chanting.

"What office can *this* be, Father?" enquired the Lollard. "I thought in the Cistercian Order—"

"It's choir-practice, Master Brut," replied the monk with a smile. "No, no! As I said just now, the Prior receives complaints in his cell to-day; but to-morrow, owing to his age and ill-health, the Abbot's court will be held in the chapter-house. I believe"—and he lowered his voice so as not to be heard by the door-keeper—"that to-day the Prior will only request you to submit to a few questions in the library. That is his usual procedure in cases of—in cases like yours. And then—after the Librarian's report—"

"But I hope," interrupted Rhisiart, trying in vain to remember a particular Latin phrase that was always used in the sheriff's office to denote privilege, "I hope you'll explain to Prior Bevan that I've come as Baron Glendourdy's emissary, I may say as his representative, to show his pious observance of the wishes of Abbot Cust by placing at his disposal—"

But here Mad Huw, breaking in with what he evidently considered the most diplomatic of casual gestures, caught our friend by the arm and murmured portentously, "Hush! Hush! Mum's the word, sweet sir, and don't forget it!"

It was while he was re-assuring Mad Huw with vigorous asseverations of his constant discretion that he caught sight of a little drama between Master Brut and the Ruthin girl that sent the hot blood to his cheeks again and disturbed his senses. He heard the Lollard suddenly request the Father to pardon him, and quite calmly and naturally as if he were saying goodbye to a well-intentioned pupil he walked up to the girl and deliberately tearing a page out of his precious Gospels and folding it up very carefully, and indeed with some difficulty, for the parchment was unyielding, he thrust it into her hand.

And the Ruthin girl never lifted her eyes while he did this. *That* was what absorbed and startled our friend so. She dropped her eyes when she felt him near and kept them lowered. Rhisiart was in front of her, so he couldn't be mistaken. She didn't look at Master Brut all the time. She held her eyes down while her hands kept fumbling and twitching—our friend was sure of that too—at the rough clasp of her dress. He saw her take the bit of paper the man gave her—she raised her eyes enough for that—but the Lollard's sturdy back intervened just then, so that he couldn't see what she did with it. Did she unclasp that pin she was fidgetting with, and slip it into her dress?

But through the monotonous reiteration of conspiring whispers breathed into his ear by the Friar he heard her now; and though the Lollard's back hid her face her voice was so rich and clear that he could catch every syllable, especially as she spoke in English. "I'll burn, before they get it from me!" he heard her say; and he surmised that the Lollard uttered a startled protest and made an attempt to get the paper back; for there was certainly some sort of struggle between them which was ended by Tegolin; but whether Tegolin made her give back that gospel-page Rhisiart couldn't tell, for Master Brut's broad back hid them both at the crucial point.

"Sister Cunlap says, Father," began lay-brother Jenkyn as soon as he reappeared. The fellow's eyes were gleaming with excitement. What he'd caught of the Sister's orders to her subordinates had evidently quickened his lively imagination. But he wasn't allowed to finish his report, for rapidly behind him, wearing a heavy veil, came the Mother of the guest-chamber herself. Sister Cunlap was clearly an amiable woman and not less clearly a very simple one, and her countenance, when she lifted her veil to speak, reminded Rhisiart of their old cook at home. He could see that both the girls were extremely relieved by the unveiling of that ruddy face and those homely grey eyes.

"The Lord be with you, Father, and with you, gentlemen," she began at once; and though a little out of breath her voice had a pleasant ring. "And the Lord be with *you,* my daughters!"

Mad Huw stepped up to Tegolin and laid his hand on her wrist. "The password's 'mum,' child, till we meet again; and the same *here,*" and he tapped his forehead with an air of theatrical cunning.

"The Maid of Edeyrnion will be all right with me, Brother," said Sister Cunlap re-assuringly.

"I know it, I know it, I know it!" chanted the Friar in childish spirits, "but we walk among pitfalls and our paths are beset by evil men!"

"Forgive my question," enquired the Lollard, "but how comes it that you all know us by name?" And he looked with his frank dis-arming smile from the Father to the Sister and back to the Father.

"Everybody round here knows Friar Huw of Llanfaes," said the good-natured woman, looking as she spoke so much like his mother's cook that Rhisiart had a vision of that cheerful, friendly English hearth, with its turnspits and burnished pots, its smoky roof and brown flitches of bacon, "and everybody knows our brave Maid! Be you her serving-wench, my pretty daughter?"

Alice laughted outright at this. "I *hope* to be, Sister," she broke in eagerly, "but Mistress Tegolin—"

"I have come from the Baron of Glyndyfrdwy," interrupted our friend, "in obedience to—"

But Sister Cunlap's blank and bewildered face cut short his words. Feeling something of a fool he turned to the monk for corroboration, and once again searched his mind for that curst legal phrase about privilege; and then it seemed—as he went over it afterwards—as if the two girls had been whisked away under the voluminous wing of the worthy Sister with such discreet rapidity that, however much he'd been on the alert, no final glances could possibly have been exchanged.

As soon as they were well inside the nave of the Abbey church, which seemed full, at the same time, of a rich quietness and of a warm stir of sacred movement, their guide, after passing by with a searching glance several of his fellows, selected for his purpose a monk with the face of a happy but stupid child, and handed over Mad Huw to his care.

The choice was a singularly good one; and indeed, as our friend looked about him in this muted fragrance, where the afternoon sun as it fell through the high windows was so mellowed by the incense and the candles as to become something dim and sacrosanct, as if the great heathen orb itself had been lured into obedience, he came to the conclusion that this kind of ascetic fraternal life evoked a sort of "sixth sense," a sense by which, without any overt instruction in worldly diplomacy, a certain exquisitely subtle and sagacious handling of intruders from the outside world was practised. It was almost, he felt, as if some invisible cocoon of sanctified silk, impalpable as the surrounding incense, was made to encompass the recalcitrant motions of normal humanity, under the power of which such visitors from outside became docile and pliable, losing, without realizing what was happening, the vital urge of their natural self-assertion.

It was a great comfort to him—for in Tegolin's absence he felt responsible for Mad Huw—when he saw the respectful wonder, and even awe, with which this childlike Father went off, with the Friar's hand on his shoulder and all those obscure hints concerning Richard's movements hovering about his ears.

Yes, under this high carved roof and in this atmosphere where the very beams of the sun fluttered down like the locks of a shorn Samson before the altar candles, he felt as if there existed between all these silent, muffled, mysteriously busy Fathers a wordless understanding; an understanding that fathomed all, directed all, assuaged all, and no doubt could punish all, without the exchange between them of so much as a sign!

His instinct was justified when, after a merest whisper, in passing, with one of his colleagues, their guide informed them that he would leave them to their own devices for a few minutes while he went to inform the Prior of their arrival.

The fact that the chanting that was going on had no connection with any particular office made it possible for our two friends to wander where they pleased; and the first object of note they stumbled upon after making their formal genuflexion to the high altar was the pulpit.

Rhisiart made a gesture of wanton boyish hostility in the presence of those narrow steps and that carved rostrum. Aye! how he had hated the sermons in the Cathedral, and more still the laboured logic of the dean of his College! But the Lollard entered at once into a careful and scientific calculation of the acoustic properties of the screen above the preacher's desk.

"I believe you'd enjoy haranguing the whole establishment," Rhisiart whispered to him. "I warrant you'd make the Abbot squirm!"

But the face of his friend showed nothing but a sad earnestness. "I *would* like once, just once," he murmured, "to preach the Gospel of the Saviour up there!"

But leaving the pulpit and following side by side one of the narrow transept-aisles, they came upon a tomb that moved our friend to unforeseen excitement. It was his turn now to show emotion; and Master Brut was astonished to see him fall on his knees and even close his eyes in prayer. When he got up he pointed out to his companion the word "Madoc" carved on the great stone, above a two-edged cross-handled sword.

"Think of his having actually lain here," he whispered, "under this very stone, for nearly two hundred years!"

"Who is?"

"Why, man, he's the founder! He's everything! And he's my ancestor, too. It's *his* blood that was in the blood of that traitor—" The lad stopped, overcome by his emotion. Like an avalanche of rubble all the lesser impressions that had been absorbing his mind fell away, and the towers of Dinas Brān, as he had seen them that first moment from the edge of the wood, rose up in undiminished magic before his eyes.

But he swallowed his tears. "I must come here again," he thought, "and I must come alone!"

Respecting, though they were completely obscure to him, the feelings of his friend, the Lollard moved on. But Rhisiart, already a little ashamed of his agitation, soon followed him and found him puzzling over the inscription upon a most striking effigy, the like of which neither of the young men had seen before.

It was the figure of a woman, lying supine as if in a bed of granite; and what especially struck the two friends was that her form was *hollowed out,* not superimposed upon the stone in raised relief.

Once more it was Rhisiart's destiny to interpret to his well-meaning but unenlightened friend the historic treasures of Valle Crucis.

"Read! Read, man! Can't you read what it says? It's Myfanwy herself!"

"She has a lovely name," murmured the Lollard cautiously, "but I don't think I recall— Is she mentioned in Giraldus?"

But Rhisiart waved Giraldus aside without a word. Bending reverently down he kissed the effigy's chilly feet in its hollow coffin.

"Princess," he recited, when he rose, as if the syllables were an incantation that could only be uttered in a special tone, "Princess Myfanwy of Dinas Brān; and *that*"—and he pointed to an effigy at her side—"is her husband. The story is that she loved—but *you* don't want to know the story. But she's been my ideal ever since I was a child. She must have come down from up there every Sunday for Mass! I expect her lover came too—"

No! you can glare at me all you like, Jennap ab Adam! If you couldn't do it while she lived you can't do it now. You can lie by her side, Monsieur, with the sword that killed him. But he's lying in her heart; and he'll lie there for ever! You can't cut love out of a girl's heart, Monsieur! *You* by her side, *he* in her heart—that's how things are. And that's how they'll be at the Judgment Day, though she goes to Hell for it!

They were moving towards the Lady chapel now when the herb-gathering monk who'd brought them in suddenly appeared as if out of the wall.

"He's ready to see you," he said. "But he won't keep you long. Father Pascentius will then see you in the library. Will you come this way? He's in the cloisters."

He led them half across the entrance to the Lady chapel on whose altar was a gleaming array of candles evidently newly lit. The fellow stopped and began muttering under his breath so many "Hail Marys" that the suspicious and touchy Rhisiart began to feel as if everything that happened to them here was part of a deliberate plan to guide their souls into the way of peace.

"Would you like to go nearer?" said the monk when he rose. "It's a beautiful altar. Edward the son of Yeo is buried beside it. Some of us think that our Blessed Lady is already beginning to work miracles there. She certainly protected Edwardus *filius* Yeo with special favour when he took sanctuary here. He gave very liberally to our necessities. We pray for him daily. Won't you come nearer to the altar?"

But Rhisiart suggested that they mustn't keep Prior Bevan waiting any longer, while the Lollard enquired what crime Edwardus *filius* Yeo had committed that he had to pay so heavily to the servants of Our Lady. The monk had got them as far as the little passage leading into the sacristy before he replied to Master Brut.

But at this spot, well out of hearing of both Our Lady and her protégé, the man seemed automatically to assume a totally different tone. He now expressed nothing but natural horror at the nature of the crime committed by this subject of heavenly intervention. "Our Lady of Valle Crucis," he said, "has melted many hearts, black with appalling sins, but her power has never been more miraculous than in the case of Edwardus *filius* Yeo."

Rhisiart was too much perturbed by the extreme stuffiness of the sacristy, and by wondering whether what was obviously woman's work being done there upon these embroidered vestments was a

penance, to feel much inquisitiveness about the bones in the chapel.
"God forgive us all!" he murmured watching the exquisite measures
being taken to mend and clean a certain pontifical garment, through
whose embroidered purple, to all appearance, Caesar himself might
have been stabbed to death.

"Those poor fellows!" he thought. "They must feel like those
wretched moths Modry used to catch and kill in my blankets at home."

But the Lollard was totally unaffected either by the mustiness of
the place or by the patience of the men doing that women's work. He
still went on sounding the monk about the sins of the son of Yeo.
"Do you mean to tell me that Our Lady protected a rascal like that by
a miracle?"

The monk's face lit up. To be permitted—and in the presence of
these penitential colleagues—to argue with a heretic in defence of the
maternal clemency of the Mother of God was an unlooked-for gift
from Heaven.

"Surely all good Catholics must feel that the greater the sin the more
wonderful the divine mercy?"

"Blessed is the intercession of the Holy Virgin," said the Lollard,
"but the Son of God alone, in the power of the Father and of the
Spirit, can give absolution."

The brow of the little monk beneath his big tonsured head knitted
itself into wrinkles of incontrovertible logic as he set out to explain
that just as the Vicar of Christ and the Priests of Holy Church have
power on earth to forgive sins, so it is impossible not to suppose that
the same power—

But our friend could think of nothing but these sacristy monks.
"They're like those pictures in our new Cathedral window," he said
to himself. No, they didn't once raise their eyes while this dialogue
proceeded, though there was a faint shuffling of sandalled feet on the
stone floor. "They'll chatter about it like magpies, I warrant, as soon
as they get to their dormitory."

But a great booming voice interrupted the colloquy, and there in the
doorway leading from the sacristy to the library stood Prior Bevan himself! He was a big, burly middle-aged man of over six feet, with a
large, plump, unruffled visage, small searching eyes, and a jaw like the
prow of a river barge.

Rhisiart made a little stiff obeisance and went boldly up to him. "I am the Baron of Glyndyfrdwy's cousin," he began, "and in obedience to Abbot Cust's message I have brought—"

But the Prior's deep voice intervened. "Just so, just so, *exactly* so," he bellowed. "*You,* sir, are Rhisiart ab Owen of Oxford, and *you,* sir, are Walter Brut of the Manor of Lyde, near the City of Hereford, lately under trial for heresy by your Bishop." He paused for a moment, while his piercing, screwed-up little eyes moved from person to person among everybody in sight.

"Abbot Cust·is in bad health, in bad health," he went on. "It is to be feared he may have to leave to-morrow's court as well as to-morrow's chapter to me, leave 'em to me. We must pray that it may not be so; but it looks as if it would be so, as if it would be so." Prior Bevan's habit of repeating the final words of every sentence struck our friend as curiously disconcerting. It was as if he were dragging in to his support, to crown his most casual utterance, a great thundering echo from some invisible judgment-seat. You might presume to contradict that barging jaw and those imperative eyes; but there would still remain this portentous echo to bring you down.

"Father Pascentius," he proceeded, "though engaged with a novice in his cell, engaged with a novice in his cell, is ready to receive you both. He will prepare you for the court to-morrow with a few little necessary questions, little necessary questions; and after that you will retire to the guest-house for sleep, for sleep. The Lord be with you, Master Rhisiart, and the Lord be with *you,* Master Brut—*ne forte offendas ad lapidem pedem tuum!*" And with this rather ambiguous last word for the benefit of the Lollard, and some low-voiced instructions to their guide, the Prior walked solemnly past them and entered the church.

Their guide now led them past a little alcove at the end of the stuffy sacristy which served for a library. Master Brut allowed his unruffled countenance to relax into a sly smile in our friend's direction and even into a profane wink; for the collection of folios presented to their eyes was very meagre, not a twentieth part of the books they'd observed in the astrologer's chamber at Glyndyfrdwy.

One young monk, who cast down his eyes at their approach just as the sacristy ones had done, was engaged with a camel's hair brush and a pot of glue over a volume in worse condition even than the vestment they had just seen.

Their guide, in the quick subtle manner acquired by living so long and so silently cheek by jowl with other men, detected in a second what they felt and hurried to explain that all the real treasures of their collection had been conveyed to Father Pascentius's cell to assist him in his labours upon Saint Thomas.

Out into the cloisters the little man now led them; and since these pleasantly-vaulted promenades occupied only two sides of a spacious lawn with a clear fountain in its centre both our travellers paused in admiration. On a stone bench, covered with a piece of well-worn matting, sat a couple of monks, who had evidently just come in from working in the fields and were contentedly resting themselves; and the sight of these men gave our friend a much happier impression of Valle Crucis than anything he'd yet seen.

Quick as ever to catch their mood their guide approached these men who rose at once and greeted them with frank, easy, natural simplicity. "He's not had time to give them the least hint," thought our analytical friend. "It must be the open air."

But after the conversation had drifted to the special devotion to agricultural pursuit of the great Cistercian Order, the thought did begin to insinuate itself into our lad's suspicious brain that it was *not* by a mere accident that these tonsured farmers should at that exact moment have been resting in the cloisters. Receiving an easy and almost secular farewell from these new acquaintances they were now led up a narrow flight of steps to the monks' dormitory. Through this they passed quickly, all *too* quickly for Rhisiart's taste, for he was beginning to compose in his mind a more succinct and effective address to their friend with the Phorkyad eye than he had as yet been able to deliver, and those agreeable cubicles each with its own especial window and breviary-shelf pleased and attracted him not a little. "How glad I would be," he thought, "when the bell rang for bed in this busy place!"

But they now reached a doorway at the head of a much smaller and more secretive-looking flight of steps than the one they'd come up, and at this door their guide deserted them; only turning to inform them, as he disappeared down this narrow descent, that it led directly into the church.

The cell of Father Pascentius, who was evidently a favoured personage, was of considerable size, and, as their guide had hinted, contained more books than the whole of that collection at the end of the sacristy. He was seated at his desk before a beautiful transcript of the works of Saint Bonaventura, and by his side stood a handsome boy of about fifteen for whom he had obviously been translating, and no doubt criticizing, the work before them. He greeted them warmly enough, but didn't rise from his seat. Indeed, instead of doing so, he put his arm round the boy's waist and asked him a question about the passage they had been studying.

The boy, naturally enough, found it embarrassing to be thus catechized before two strange young men, and blushed and blundered in his reply; but instead of releasing him in the presence of these signs of nervousness, the Father seemed to take pleasure in his discomfort, and pressed him with further questions.

Finally, just as Rhisiart had reached in his mind the climax of what he was about to say, the theologian asked the boy why he was in such a hurry to be gone.

This time the lad answered earnestly and to the point. "There's an archery-match at the Tassel to-night, Father, and Davy Gam is giving a new bow to the winner, and I promised to go."

"To go with whom?"

"With Sieffre of Dyffryn Clwyd, Father."

"With *that* young rogue; eh? Well, I'm sure—I don't—know. Didn't I say I was afraid I might have to keep you in to-night?"

"Yes, Father."

"Well, I'm sure—I don't—know."

The boy's lips trembled. Like a wild bird he glanced at the narrow window and then down at the great book on the desk.

"What do you think these gentlemen would say if they knew *why* you may have to give up the archery-match to-night?"

The blood rushed to the boy's cheeks and he hung his head.

"Look at me, Griff!"

But Griff only bent lower.

"Well, off you go! But remember—"

Rhisiart moved aside to let the lad reach the door, and when he was gone Father Pascentius gave utterance to a heavy sigh.

"Well," he repeated, motioning his visitors to be seated, "well—I'm sure—I don't know. But now to business, to business, as the Prior would say. *Your* case"—and he turned his black eyes on our friend—"is more simple than *yours*"—and he turned them on the Lollard—"but it's clear you both have come into this country at the same summons as brought Father Rheinalt and me to Glyndyfrdwy the other night. Now, of *that*, my sons, I would say nothing, if I were you, when we meet at the court to-morrow. Owen has his friends here, of which as you know I am one, and he has his enemies, among which, as you may *not* know, is our good Prior. But Owen's quarrel won't come up at the court to-morrow, unless either of you are unwise enough to bring it up. But you, Master Rhisiart, will have to defend yourself from the charge of breaking the King's peace in the matter of Brother Huw. That's the charge that the King's friends at the Tassel and my lord Fitz-Alan of Chirk will bring against you; and considering that Hugh Burnell and his son Denis and the yeomen of a couple of shires are encamped only half a mile away, it's a serious charge." He paused and, lifting up one of the vellum covers of the great book under his hand, produced a paper of notes, which he proceeded to scan.

"The line I would suggest you take in your defense, my son, is that you were moved by your zeal for Holy Church to protest against the impiety of Master Simon in taking it upon himself to put to death a Brother of Saint Francis without trial before the proper authorities. Our house has already many points of litigation against the Earl of Arundel, and if you steadily repeat in court, 'I drew my sword for the rights of Valle Crucis,' and refuse to discuss anything else, our Abbot—I should say our Prior—will be forced to defend you."

Rhisiart bowed, swallowed with an effort the eloquent speech he had been composing, and expressed his becoming gratitude.

"And *now*," said Father Pascentius, referring again to his notes, "having decided that we'll keep our Welsh controversy out of it altogether, and in the matter of Brother Huw that we appeal to the privileges of the Church, it remains, Master Brut, to arrange *your* line of defence.

"Now I would suggest," and he settled his unwieldy form more comfortably in his seat and stretched out his legs, "that you answer me, here and now, a few crucial questions and that—when we've prepared your answers—I write them down. Is that your pleasure, my son?"

"Hereafter as may be," replied the cautious heretic.

"I have before me," continued Father Pascentius, "the opinions of certain followers of the deceased Master Wycliffe, and I will take the most questionable of these opinions in due order. Firstly, John Becket of London holds and maintains that Christian baptism is of no value if done by a priest living in mortal sin. Do you, my good son, separate yourself entirely and absolutely from this unphilosophical and crazy notion? For what parent anxious to save the soul of his child would think of bothering himself about the life of the officiating priest—the mere medium of the divine mercy?"

"I certainly *can*, Father," replied the Lollard, "absolutely and entirely separate myself from this opinion."

Rhisiart looked out of the window, feeling as weary of all this as the youthful Griff. And since the window opened upon the deep well-stocked fish-pond and since standing in a flat-bottomed boat, his clothes fastened about his waist and his legs bare, was an excited monk with a rod and a great net, his thoughts were agreeably distracted.

But Father Pascentius continued. "Secondly, we have the opinion of one John Purvey, a friend of Master Wycliffe, that decisions of Popes and councils have no value unless they are grounded expressly on Holy Scripture or on reason and should be publicly burnt as heretical. Now, Master Brut, do you absolutely and entirely separate yourself from this un-Catholic view, which, as you can clearly see, destroys the tradition of the Church, the authority of the Fathers, the unity of our communion with the departed, and the faith once for all delivered to the Saints?"

Rhisiart was drawn back sharp from the window by the abrupt tone of his comrade's anwer. "I do *not!*" said the Lollard firmly.

Father Pascentius was not in the least perturbed.

"Quite right," he said. "I can see you are a cautious student of the necessary antinomies and contradictory truths in our Holy Faith! I can see that you recognize the profound danger of emphasizing any single aspect of Catholic Doctrine lest other aspects, no less important, should be disparaged. There *have* been, and no student of history can deny it, local councils and individual Pontiffs whose arbitrary and capricious decrees have been implicitly, if not explicitly, burnt as heretical by a more universal authority. *Securus judicat orbis terrarum,* and it is only by the patience of the Holy Spirit and by the patience of Rome in holding back her decisions till the *orbis terrarum* has spoken that this grave danger of arbitrary caprice in local councils and individual Popes is avoided. You see, Master, my question concerning this man's heresy was designed to test your theological balance. Had you replied too hastily in an unqualified dissent from Master Purvey's opinion I would have felt anxiety lest you might fall into the opposite heresy of judging truth by vulgar majorities. The Catholic Faith is the great sublimator and subsumer of the inevitable contradictions and paradoxes of the human mind. To balance her *orbis terrarum* she has her *Athanasius Contra Mundum* She is at once the centre and the circumference wherein the pendulum of our poor fallible reason swings.

"I know well, Master Brut, that with your well-balanced nature you are fully aware of the ferocious and fanatical extremes into which reason and logic can lead us. Isn't it much more likely that the critical thought of so many generations of wise and learned men, giving articulation to the inspired piety of the people, should be in the right of it rather than the arbitrary opinions of John Purvey?"

Rhisiart nodded at his obstinate companion with such a frown on his narrow Norman visage and his lips sucked in to such an extent that his face took in the appearance of the handle of a carved walking-stick.

"Surely," his look said, "you cannot follow a Jackanapes Purvey against the shrewd legal wisdom of universal common-sense?"

But the Lollard was unshaken. "I cannot separate myself," he repeated, "from Master Purvey's opinion that in the Holy Scriptures, reasonably interpreted, is to be found the Truth."

"But not the *only* truth, my son! And not the most important truth. The Church as the Bride of Christ can answer you, my dear lad, in Christ's own words. Was He referring to our poor, crazy, logical faculty when He said, 'I am the Way, the Truth, and the Life?' But let me pass to another opinion of this disciple of Wycliffe— No! no— I beg his pardon!—we return again here to John Becket who certainly disgraced his martyred namesake when he maintained the following amazing thesis: that his own teaching—the teaching of this worthy citizen of London—was more likely to be edifying to others and pleasing to God than all the teaching of the Church in all previous times."

The Lollard smiled at this. "Not having heard Master Becket's discourses, Father, I cannot say; but I confess I think the good gentleman's tone *does* smack a little of self-conceit."

Father Pascentius, without a movement of his great heavy body, turned his burning eyes once more upon his notes.

"Do you, my son," he began again, "utterly and absolutely separate yourself from the opinion of William Chatrys, otherwise called Sawtry, priest of Kings Lynn, when he maintains that after the words of consecration the bread remains bread and nothing more? This, my son, I needn't point out to you, is an opinion which cuts at the very root of our Holy Religion. Surely, surely my dear child, you cannot subscribe to such a denial of the supreme article of our Faith?"

To Rhisiart's amazement Master Brut hesitated before replying. This was a serious shock to our friend, who thought that only Mohammedans, Turks and Chinamen refused to believe in the Miracle of the Mass. Then very slowly, word by solemn word, as if he were sealing each syllable with his blood, the Wycliffite answered. "It remains bread, but bread *plus* the body of Christ. It does not cease to be bread, but it remains holy, true, and the Bread of Life. *That* I believe to be the very body of Christ."

Never had Rhisiart seen such dark fire in any human eyes as that which shone from the eyes of Father Pascentius as he gazed at and through the pale but unruffled countenance before him.

But he spoke gently and even tenderly. "You have weighed your words well, my son, and if you will allow me I will make a note of them exactly as you uttered them." He bent over his desk and wrote, and when he'd finished he repeated the words to the accused and asked him if they were correct.

Master Brut, with a faint smile, inclined his head.

Rhisiart began to feel extremely uncomfortable. Matters were getting out of control and he was being carried out of his depth. He stared at the paper in the monk's hand as if it had been a death-warrant, while a rush of confused images swept through his brain of historic occasions when a few scrawls upon a bit of parchment had meant life or death.

"Thank you, my son," murmured Father Pascentius, folding up the paper; "and now I will tell you frankly what I think. You weighed your words so well that I think it depends entirely upon the prelate who judges your case. In the same hands as those in which the unfortunate Master Sawtry was found himself you would be condemned. Henry Spencer, the Bishop of Norfolk, has declared his intention as is well known, of making all you Gospel-men 'hop headless,' as he is pleased to put it, 'and fry faggots,' and Archbishop Arundel is of the same kidney. *Our* good Bishop, however, Bishop Trevor of St. Asaph, is totally averse to such unintelligent harshness. He's a theologian, not a bully; and he would at once remember all the profound metaphysical issues involved, relative to the change of 'substance' and the continuity of 'accidents' to which your words obviously refer.

"The unlucky thing is—I speak to you two lads as a fellow-Welshman—that our good Prior is looking for the Archbishop's word with the Holy Father in regard to filling our Abbot's place when he leaves us. With Abbot Cust, who also is a theologian and well read in the metaphysic of the schools, you would be perfectly safe. But I doubt—" He hesitated and pondered. "However," he went on, with a quick glance at door and window, and with the flicker of a conspirator's smile, "we three are sworn adherents of Owen, and Owen has taken a very natural fancy to you both, and, after all, the bread *does* retain, to our relative and fallible senses, the 'accidents' of bread, and if our old gentleman"—he paused and, folding his hands on his great belly, gazed at the vaulted roof—"could, perhaps, see you to-night, he *might,* sick as he is, be persuaded to give our ambitious Prior"—here he unclasped his hands and leaned heavily forward over the great book—"a *very* considerable—shock."

There was a deep silence among them for a second or two, while there came through the narrow window the brooding voice of a distant wood-pigeon. Then Father Pascentius lifted up the vellum cover of Saint Bonaventura and dropped it, and again lifted it up and again dropped it, and while the wood-pigeon, in a voice soft as the divine afflatus of a scholastic philosophy as yet unrevealed to the wisest, was answered by the voice of its mate, he leant back once more in his chair. He now appeared to be surveying an alien speck upon the noble parchment before him, a speck that may have been the result of a sneeze of his own but more probably was caused by Griff's distress over the complexities of seraphic argument.

Touching this speck upon the great tome as if it had been a fairy's seal he now addressed his visitors with an air of such pensive casualness that it made them feel as if the arrival of a hundred heretics from Hereford was less important than the dropping of a single tear upon Saint Bonaventura.

"Suppose somebody," he murmured, looking down at the tip of the plump finger he had placed upon this small speck, "suppose somebody *should*—as is of course quite easy in a community like ours—have been whispering for several days in a certain old gentleman's ear that since he *has* to die anyhow he might just as well spend his last breath check-mating the English? Isn't it possible that when to-morrow comes such an old gentleman might decide to hold his court in person? I ask you, isn't it just possible he might?"

Though to all appearance it was of the mark left by Griff's tear that the Father asked this question, Rhisiart hastened to prolong the topic by boldly enquiring how it came about that with such a patriotic influence at Abbot Cust's elbow this drastic document from the Abbey had reached Owen that morning.

The burning Phorkyad eyes *were* raised at this, and there was a significant pause.

"Well, I'll be frank with you, son," said the theologian. And after what seemed a suspicious glance in the direction of an eaves-dropping wood-pigeon, he went on gravely. "The King must have heard something in Scotland. And after our experience of Owen's discretion last night can we wonder at it? At any rate, here is Hugh Burnell, a sturdy Shropshire squire and, let me tell you, a man worth a dozen of these border-barons, encamped at Oswestry. It was from *his* camp and with a guard of *his* bowmen that this Italian arrived, not only a go-between, as Master Young guessed, between Rome and King Hal, but, as our Prior soon discovered, between Rome and the Archbishop.

"The Prior snatched at this grand chance. He was up all last night sending messengers and letters; and there was nothing for the Abbot to do but to implore Owen to yield on every point. I myself added a note to Father Rheinalt with a hint about Huw and the Maid and this Ruthin woman—aye, my lads, but there's been a fuss about *her*: Grey's people were over here before dawn making their complaint—but now that he's sent you two as well—and I never thought he'd wit enough for *that*—we may, if the old man can be brought to the scratch, give Owen the breathing-space he needs."

Rhisiart's thin face had grown by this time dark red with excitement. Here he was, playing a living, nay! a leading part in momentous, in historic transactions!

"Father!" he burst out. "Was Master Young right in thinking so strongly that Owen ought to wait?"

But the wily theologian evidently felt he had gone far enough in his talk with these simple young men. He rose ponderously from his seat.

"By my confession!" he cried in Welsh, using a phrase familiar to Rhisiart in Modry's tales, "I'll chance it! Come along, Masters. We'll pay a visit to the old man!" Thrusting his notes into the pocket of his habit, and opening the door with caution, he conducted them down a short passage-way to an airy platform, where half-a-dozen winding steps led up to the private rooms of the Abbot of Valle Crucis.

Without knocking, and moving as quietly as his great bulk permitted, the monk opened the door of his Superior's ante-room. Here they were met by an intelligent-looking lay-brother who seemed less surprised at their appearance than might have been expected. "He's intended to do this all the time!" thought our astute friend.

"Brother Gerald is studying medicine," remarked the theologian, introducing the man in a series of low whispers. "How is he to-night?"

The lay-brother shook his head. "He *will* get up," he whispered. "You'll find him reading by his fire. He's eaten nothing. He can't sleep. Does"—he paused and jerked his head in the direction of the dormitory—"he know you've brought them?"

Father Pascentius made his characteristic gesture of wiping out all human follies and reducing the whole troublesome drama of existence to kindly nothingness. "Who knows what he knows?" he murmured. "At any rate, *here we are!* May we go straight in?"

Brother Gerald glanced quickly at the young men as much as to say, "You see what he is! You see what little good it would do for *me* to protest!" and moving straight across the ante-room, opened the inner door.

Rhisiart was quite taken aback by the simplicity of Abbot Cust's cell. It was much smaller than Father Pascentius's study. A good many books, however, chiefly of an antique devotional nature, though our

alert Oxonian did notice a delapidated and evidently much-studied
Virgil, occupied two sides of the little room. Next to the window,
which was filled with dark reddish-coloured glass, hung a large wooden
crucifix, of somewhat ghastly realism, upon the rude features of whose
victim flickered the light of a couple of rustic candles both of which
were dripping upon their iron sconces.

Unlike any ecclesiastic our friend had ever seen, the frail figure that
rose from the hearth to greet them wore a straggly beard. This beard
was of a reddish tint, and combined with the extreme pallor of the
man's emaciated countenance and the fragility of his diminutive frame,
it gave him the appearance of a small fish, an holy and red-finned
roach, the Abbot of the Fish-Pond. It was his enormous learning and
his mystical piety that had been the cause of his rise to an Abbot's
throne; but his appointment had been much more popular with the
Welsh than with the great barons of the border. Chirk and Ruthin
and Dinas Brān were all delighted when the formidable Prior, as well
adapted to this difficult world as Abbot Cust was ill-adapted, began
to harry and drive and dominate and overawe this gentle creature of
another element.

"What a contrast to our old friend of Caerleon!" thought the young
men; but they both knelt down with unsimulated humility before
this abject little figure, not so much because he was reported to be
the most learned Abbot in Wales as because there was something about
him suggesting that his days were near their end.

"This is going to be," said our friend to himself, "the most important
conversation I've ever had in my life!" But Father Pascentius had
barely seated himself opposite the Abbot, with the medical lay-brother
and the two visitors established on wooden stools between them, when
a sound that caught the quick ears of Brother Gerald caused him to
jump to his feet and hasten through both the doors into the little
passage from which they had entered.

The Abbot showed so much anxiety over this new disturbance that
Rhisiart wondered if he didn't fear the intrusion of the formidable
Prior, and he noticed that even Father Pascentius fell silent.

"Is it the Prior?" seemed indeed to be what they were all thinking;
and for several minutes, as people do when something menacing is
threatened, they all swung round and stared at the door.

The general tension was increased rather than relaxed when Brother Gerald hurriedly returned with a grave face.

"It's Mistress Lowri," he announced, bowing quickly to the Abbot and glancing at Father Pascentius. "I told her my Lord Abbot was too ill to see her in his reception-room and I told her it was against our rule for her to see him here; but she says it's a matter affecting the honour of the house and a matter too, if I understood her correctly, relating to to-morrow's court." He now turned point-blank to the sick man. "She refused to be satisfied until I told you, my Lord, that the news she brought was of such importance that—"

Rising with some effort from his chair Abbot Cust looked appealingly at Father Pascentius.

"Where is she now?" the latter enquired of the messenger.

"In my Lord's reception-room."

"Have any of the Fathers seen her?"

"I don't think so, Father. She came straight through the garden to my Lord's postern, and Brother Jorwerth let her in."

"Are all the Fathers in the church?"

"I think so, Father."

The theologian turned to the Abbot. "It almost seems to me, my Lord," he said, "that this *would* be an occasion for relaxing our rule. If you were well enough you would certainly go down to your reception-room. And since it's an affair for your court to-morrow—" He paused, as Abbot Cust sank back with a nervous spasm into his chair, and then added, "You remember you saw the Lady Charlton here once, and we all felt grateful to you for stretching a point when so much depended—"

"But Mistress Lowri!" gasped the sick man.

Father Pascentius rose. "I will take the full responsibility, my Lord, and if the Prior—"

The mention of his troublesome subordinate seemed to rouse the old man and he spoke in a tone of defiant authority. "Go and fetch her yourself, Father. My days are numbered." And then as if the fact of having asserted himself in the small matter of breaking a monastic rule gave him courage for a bolder plunge, he looked challengingly at his medical attendant and announced in a trembling voice, "If it kills me, Brother, I shall preside over our court *myself* to-morrow."

Father Pascentius gave a quick glance at the Lollard and left the room. In his absence, Abbot Cust seemed to become a different person. He sighed, he shrugged his feeble shoulders, he rubbed his face with his thin hands. And then he glanced almost humorously at his visitors.

"Mistress Lowri," he said, "is a good Welshwoman and a true ally of Owen's. She is living—*miserere nobis!*—in venial, though let us hope not in mortal, sin; but I am not without hope for her. Her daughter is a good girl—a very good girl—and I don't want—I don't want when I'm so near my own last account—to break the bruised flax!"

"My Lord," began Rhisiart boldly, "I don't know if they've told you that it was to save Brother Huw from being *burnt,* burnt illegally, burnt contrary to your own jurisdiction by Master Simon of Chirk, that we, in company with the Abbot of Caerleon—"

Abbot Cust raised his hand to stop him. "I know," he murmured, "I know, my son." And then with a heavy sigh, "This burning for heresy is a new thing in our land. There *have* been cases—I suppose there *are* cases—but I don't like it, I don't like it!"

"Are we to blame the present King, my Lord," interjected Master Brut eagerly, "or is the Archbishop—"

The Abbot gave him a long, sad, weary look. "These are dark times, my son, dark and cruel times; and I can well see that if our rulers resort to such methods it is natural that violent and godless men like Master Simon will take upon themselves—"

"But in *some* matters, my Lord," broke in Rhisiart, full of boyish pride at being permitted to talk freely with a mitred Abbot, "our ways are better, aren't they, than our fathers' before us? We saw just now in the church, my Lord, the tomb of Edwardus *filius* Yeo; and our guide informed us—"

Abbot Cust's withered face brightened perceptibly. It was clearly an immense relief to him to pass from modern persecution to mediaeval crime. "Ah, my dear child!" he said, assuming the joyful expression of a scholarly historian, "we are dealing here with a most interesting subject!" He moved in his chair as he spoke and leaning forward from its edge warmed his bony fingers over the fire. He forgot the chapter-house, he forgot Master Simon, he forgot Mistress Lowri. He became a passionate Welsh archaeologist proud of the darkest secrets of his country's mythical past. "From what I can gather," he began, "it seems that this particular benefactor of ours was one of these curious disciples of our great Saint Derfel. I suppose you lads have never heard of Saint Derfel and his Horse? Well, for many hundreds of years this curious Being has been the object of what to my mind is undoubtedly a most interesting heathen cult. The Church of our ancestors, as I always say, was wise in assuming the canonization of this queer figure, though I doubt myself whether the Holy Father had anything to do with it!'

"I have myself—but alas! I shall die without finishing my notes— made some slight investigations into this extraordinary subject, and it appears," and he quoted a Latin author unknown to either of his hearers, "it appears that not only was the deflowering of young virgins a definite part of the worship of this ancient Welsh god, but that certain unscrupulous men made use of this dark tradition to satisfy their unholy desires under the guise of priests—no! I mustn't say priests—under the guise of *disciples,* of this singular Personage and his Horse. It was, I understand, as one of the worst of such offenders that this 'Edwardus,' who later was privileged to decorate our Lady chapel, was found guilty. And the curious thing is, my dear boys, that there still survive, in out-of-the-way districts of this country, ignorant and simple people who—"

But Master Brut could contain himself no longer. For some while now Rhisiart had been aware that though the Lollard's eyes were fixed with absorbed interest on the aged antiquary, he had begun scraping the floor with his feet and muttering "um-um-um-um" without knowing he was doing it.

"Pardon me, my Lord," he cried, his eyes eager and stern and grave under his smooth brow, "but how can the Church tolerate such evil superstitions? How can *you,* my Lord, tolerate them?"

"I don't—quite—follow you, my son," and the old man sighed and leaned back in his chair.

The Lollard began afresh: "Isn't all this making of saints out of devils part of the same concessions to evil as the selling of Indulgences and the preserving of relics and the tyrannical claims of messengers from Rome like that Italian last night?"

"But, my son, my son," murmured the old man, "Saint Derfel and his Horse are like Brān and his Crow, and like Rhiannon and her Birds. The Church in her wisdom has always sought to consecrate rather than to destroy; and as Father Pascentius writes in some notes upon Saint Thomas that I've had the benefit of reading, the ultimate nature of the Deity, what He is Absolutely in Himself, must be forever unknown to our finite intelligence. Every good Catholic is, in this absolute sense, in the dark, and must ever be in the dark, about God. But the Church has always been tender and indulgent to the instincts of awe and worship, even where—"

But in a voice vibrant with emotion the Lollard interrupted him. "With humble submission, my Lord," he said, "it remains that—whatever the Church teaches—*we* possess, as Saint Paul says, the mind of Christ."

The Abbot sighed heavily; more, Rhisiart was certain, from anxiety as to the fate of this audacious free-thinker than from any personal irritation. Evidently desirous of dodging any further allusion to the desperate psychologizing of Saint Paul, the old man now changed his tone. "But apart from theology," he pleaded, "surely you, my son, as a good Welshman, must feel that these old legends have played, and will play again, an important rôle in the preservation of our national spirit?"

Rhisiart, thinking of all that Modry's tales had done for himself, threw in his word at this: "Yes, surely, Walter! Yes, surely!"

But Master Brut, undeterred, flung out his deepest thought. "Not in our superstitions," he cried, "but in our *language* is the salvation of our race; and I hope a time will come when in our own tongue and in our own mountains the Gospel of Christ will so stir Wales that once again as in the days of Saint David—"

The Abbot lifted his hand. "My son, my son!" he groaned; and for a moment he closed his eyes, and Rhisiart was sure he was praying for this misguided and unbalanced soul. But once more, while Brother Gerald glared indignantly at the presumptuous heretic, the old man returned to his favourite topic. "It must be my blundering exposition of this old Derfel cult," he said, "that leads you to speak as you do. I have gone very deeply into it and I can assure you—"

But to our friend's disgust, though to the obvious relief of the lay-brother who evidently regarded these antiquarian predilections as a sign of his patient's approaching end, the door now opened to admit, not only Father Pascentius and Mistress Lowri, but a roughly accoutred burly gentleman whose genial and brusque manners over-rode every soul present. It was pitiful to Rhisiart to see the collapse of the old prelate to whom he had been listening with such rapt respect.

Abbot Cust fell back in his chair without the heart to do more than make a weak, faint gesture with his hand to bid them all be seated.

But the Englishman, standing erect in his cross-gartered hose, his great leather-jerkin, his muddy shoes with their gleaming spurs and his broad leather belt with its couple of hunting-knives, took complete possession of the situation. He was certainly one of the most good-natured magnates that our friend had ever seen. His broad red cheeks, big nose and shrewd grey eyes were quite spoilt from the point of view of good looks by certain noticeable small-pox scars, but the honest friendliness of his smile, in spite of the fact that most of his front teeth had been knocked out in quarter-staff, made him a person— Rhisiart felt at once—whom even as your enemy you *couldn't* hate!

He had been talking to Mistress Lowri as he crossed the ante-room, and now having bent the knee to the silent Abbot whose bearded chin had sunk down upon his chest, he went on with what he'd been saying to her, though out of respect for the sick man in a much lower tone of voice.

The lady's dark eyes, after her quick obeisance to the Abbot, flashed provocatively at Rhisiart, and her red lips parted in a mocking smile; and all the while she was listening to the Salopian Sheriff's words she concentrated upon our friend, disregarding everybody else. These beguiling advances, although lips and eyes were alone employed, were anything but wasted. Our friend's inner consciousness went promptly whirling off upon an imaginary future in which he was the cause of sundry desperate and distracting quarrels between a mother and a daughter. Sheriff Burnell was, it seems, half-rallying and half-threatening the lady. He kept chaffing her about his son's infatuation, he kept chaffing her about *her* infatuation for Owen, and all the while he kept referring to her purpose in coming so secretly to the Abbey, which apparently concerned the fate of her husband, Master Simon.

"But you know where he is," Burnell was saying. "And you could

lay hands on him if Denis gave you the men and my Lord here gave
you the licence. But what would you do with him when you got him?
He's your lawful husband, isn't he? Starve him to death at the foot of
Denis's bed? That's the point, isn't it, my Lord?" and he turned to
the comatose figure in the chair. "That's the point, isn't it, Father?"
and he warded off with unruffled aplomb the black fire that was being
shot at him from beneath the brows of the theologian. "King Harry
wants his liege subjects to live in peace, and you, reverend Fathers,
want all of us husbands and wives to consort amiably and piously
together for the procreation of loyal, faithful, baptized and Christian
souls! But the point in this case, it seems to me, is that the King's
justice, of which Hugh Burnell, not *Denis* Burnell, is the custodian,
has a claim upon the body and goods of Master Simon, commonly
called the Hog, that must precede the claim of his espoused wife,
even though she burns to have the custody of him, and even though
she *is* the friend of the Constable of Dinas Brān. What do *you* say,
Father?"

Father Pascentius began his wily handling of the situation by imploring the Sheriff to sit down.

And the man *did* sit down, with a great deal of creaking of his
leather attire and not a little scraping of his spurs on the floor; and
he sat down opposite the comatose Abbot, upon whose narrow forehead, white as ivory, the firelight was flickering.

But having very sagaciously got the sturdy Salopian into a deep
seat by a warm fire and opposite a nodding old man, with knuckles
that clutched the arms of his chair like gleaming bones, Father Pascentius whispered something to Brother Gerald, who darted to a
little cupboard in the wall and brought out a small gold vessel, which
he filled from a larger vessel in the same recess and presented to
Sheriff Burnell.

The Salopian smiled benevolently at the whole company, raised
the gold vessel to his face, smelt it, held it up towards the unnoticing
head opposite him, and disposed of half of it in a gulp. But so strong
was the wine that even this seasoned drinker spluttered a little as it
went down and spilled a few purple drops upon his brown leather-
jerkin.

"Malmsey?" he chuckled, smiling at Father Pascentius.

"The oldest in Wales," replied the commentator upon Saint Thomas. "The King has no better. The Archbishop none so good."

The Sheriff glanced at the two young men. "Once in a way—to the Lord Abbot of Valle Crucis—English or Welsh—guilty or not guilty—will you fill for the lads?"

At a nod from the Father the troubled and outraged Gerald refilled the gold beaker; and between them the Lollard and Rhisiart drained it to the dregs.

"To my Lord Abbot!" they cried in turn.

Something in their warm heart-felt youthful tones reached the old man in his prostration, and raising his hand with an effort, *"Pax vobiscum, filii carissimi!"* he whispered.

While this was going on, Mistress Lowri with a burning spot in each of her white cheeks, but with her beautiful head modestly cast down, had seated herself on the floor close to the old man's feet; and the Abbot now, with a gesture that was evidently spontaneous, laid his hand for an instant on her bent head.

"Be as good a woman, daughter," he murmured, "as your child is a good girl." The head he had touched with its dusky weight of fragrant hair sank still lower.

Rhisiart couldn't see her face but he was bewitched by the manner in which, as her dark riding-cloak fell back, the folds of her green-and-gold gown settled themselves about her crouching limbs.

"Pray for all—for all the"—murmured the old man softly—"for all the faithful departed—*et videbit omnis caro salutare Dei."*

In the silence that fell upon them after this Rhisiart could catch, far away in the Church below, the deep-voiced intoning of the monks.

The rich wine had already begun to go to the boy's head, for he had had nothing to eat since their meal in the Saracen's chamber; but as he sat there on his stool close to his comrade, while Father Pascentius, on one side of the fire and Brother Gerald on the other, looked from the Abbot to the Sheriff and from the Sheriff to the Abbot, and the ghastly face upon the wooden cross stared reproachfully upon them all, a deep quiescence fell upon him, and an indescribable feeling possessed him that was profoundly sad and yet in some strange way comforting and sweet.

Abbot Cust was lying back in his chair now with his eyes closed and his hands folded, breathing softly.

"My Lord sleeps," whispered the careful Brother.

"Come, Father," said the robust Salopian, looking up at the theologian, "you are a sensible Welshman as I am a sensible Englishman. We're not young hot-heads like these lads here; and we're no—God rest my poor Bessy's soul!—no avengers of injury!" Saying this he glanced at the woman on the floor, whose own eyes were fixed on those of the dazed Rhisiart who was trying to defend himself from them by calling up the image of Tegolin.

"Well, Father," he went on, "putting aside all the Norman legalities so dear to your good Prior, what's to be done with all these hostages Glendourdy's given up? I would suggest, as a plain servant of His Majesty, that we pack them all off to-night before my Lords of Chirk and Ruthin arrive, and before little Davy at the Tassel gets wind of it, straight to my son in Dinas Brān. *There* they'll simply be prisoners *at the King's pleasure;* and not Welshman in the hands of Lord Marchers. I had definite authority from the King to raise these troops from his loyal county of Salop; and I had orders to use them *at my own discretion.* Grey and Fitz-Alan are as jealous of each other as wolf-hounds. Grey had the King's ear in Scotland and has now posted home with the hope of catching your friend Owen off-guard. But Owen by his submission to my Lord Abbot, and by handing over these people, has dished him neatly, and cut the ground under his feet. These lads are here"—and he glanced humorously at Rhisiart and the Lollard—"and your daughter and her Friar are here"—he looked at the lady on the floor—"and the Ruthin hussy's here, too. Now wouldn't the best thing for all concerned be to hurry off the whole lot of them under a strong guard of my Salopians, who care for none of these things, to my son at Dinas Brān? They'd be His Majesty's prisoners then under the care of His Majesty's Constable; and our good Prior down below will be as neatly cheated of his precious court-trial, which *might* end," and he gave the young men a shrewd and significant glance, "most unpleasantly; and Grey, with his friends at the Tassel, will be cheated of their revenge on Owen."

His long speech ended, the robust Englishman made an instinctive motion of his hand towards the golden beaker which either the

Lollard or Rhisiart had placed on the floor between them; and Father Pascentius made a sign to Gerald to refill it.

While the Brother was thus engaged, Abbot Cust, to everyone's astonishment, opened his eyes and leaned forward. It was clear to them all that he had formed some definite resolution. But he sighed heavily before speaking, and murmured sadly, *"Usque quo Domine, sanctus et verus, non judicat et vindicas sanguinem nostrum?"* But after that, he straightened himself in his chair; and as if to re-assure the perturbed Brother Gerald he deliberately twitched the end of his beard with his finger and thumb.

"If I agree to your demand, Sheriff," he said, "and allow you to take them to your son, will you swear on your word as a Shropshire gentleman and before all these present that you'll write to King Henry of Owen's submission, and that none of these people will be given up, save into the King's own hand, or into that of his Lord Deputy at Chester?"

The faithful Gerald was so agitated by this miracle of energy in his master that he spilled quite a quantity of the precious wine as he handed the cup to the Sheriff.

"Brother! *Brother!* Be careful!" pleaded Father Pascentius; and it struck Rhisiart's mind as quaintly characteristic of the commentator that at what was perhaps a life-and-death moment to some of them he should be fussing over spilt Malmsey.

But Hugh Burnell rose to his feet with the cup in his hand. "The King!" he murmured, tilting it to his lips. And then, with a wink at Mistress Lowri, *"Heddwch!"* he cried, using the historic word with which the bards proclaimed peace.

"And now," said Abbot Cust, with a faint smile, as his head sank against the back of his chair and his hands, too weak to pluck his beard again, lay like used-up gloves on his lap, "we won't torment our medical brother here any more. I know he has been long impatient to get us to bed."

The Sheriff bent one of his steel-protected knees to the ground, while our two friends knelt down completely.

"Bless us, my Lord!" prayed Rhisiart hoarsely.

"Gratia Domini nostri Jesu Christi cum vobis nobisque in saecula

saeculorum!" whispered the old man, raising his fingers with an effort.

As he got up Rhisiart became aware that the smell of spilt Malmsey was mingled with the heavy fragrance of feminine hair. Mistress Lowri had risen to her feet and was standing by his side.

The Sheriff was asking Master Brut about the price of a yoke of oxen at Hereford fair and Father Pascentius was bending over the old man, so that the lady was able to whisper anything she pleased in our friend's dazed ear.

The Malmsey-fumes in our lad's head were still at work, and he thought to himself, as she drew off her glove and let her fingers rest for a second on the sleeve of his tunic, that he'd never seen such a slender waist. Certain unchaste words from some old voluptuous ballad about loosening a lady's zone came into his head.

"How *can* she be Tegolin's mother?" he wondered, as the image of the maid's boyish figure in her page's dress opposed itself to this Circean form, whose green-and-gold gown seemed to cling like a serpent's skin to her sides and to her flanks. All this while, as he was wondering what kind of fabric it could be that had the trick of displaying all the charms of her body with such tantalizing completeness, she was whispering to him that he need have no fear of Denis Burnell. "It'll just be a pleasant adventure for a brave boy like you," she said; "nor need your friend have any fear. The King is much more easy-going than any of these monks. They say he'd have let off these London heretics if it wasn't that the Archbishop keeps edging him on."

She paused and, with a gesture that made Rhisiart think of some woman in the tale of "Math fab Mathonwy," slipped her fingers under her warm belt, as if to ease for a second its pressure against her waist.

"My daughter's such a little nun," she sighed irrelevantly. *"Her* only trouble'll be the nearness of her mother. I hope *you* aren't as virtuous as all that! What kind of a girl is this pet of young Grey's? They say he's half insane about her. Some men *are* like that. It's curious, isn't it? While a lad like you—"

"Mistress!" interrupted Hugh Burnell, "you'll have seen plenty enough of this young gentleman by the time the King pardons him. But remember—there's one thing that *I* won't allow—never mind what the Fathers say—and that's that you should get Master Simon

into your hands. *That* I won't have! I'm not so simple as not to know
what you're after." He moved up quite close to her as he spoke. "Give
me your fingers!" he commanded.

She obeyed him, meek as a maid.

"Burning—burning!" And he pretended to drop hastily and in
horror the hand she'd given him. "You've been thinking of nothing
else, you pretty one, day and night—*I* know you, if Denis doesn't!—
of what you'll do to this husband of yours when you've—"

The Abbot's voice broke in at this juncture, and to Rhisiart's mind
there was something at once awe-inspiring and grotesque about the
look of that straggling beard and extended neck as he peered round
the stooping figure of his attendant. "If you torment that wretched
sinner, woman, or cause him to be tormented, to whom by your own
will you were united, I swear to you, on the word of an old man
about to meet his Judge, your soul shall burn in unquenchable fire!"

Our friend couldn't help glancing at Mistress Lowri's face when
these terrible words had made a silence in the room; but not a feature
quivered as she slightly inclined her head. "Her lips must be as hot
and dry as her hands," the boy thought; and as the idea of burning
lips transferred itself to burning limbs, even if it *were* in the fire of
Hell, his pulses beat to a yet wilder tune.

"What's the matter with me?" he thought, as Father Pascentius
came forward to usher them out. "Am I as wicked as this woman?"
And all the way through the monk's dormitory, and all the way down
the stairs into the cloisters, till the chanting from the church reduced
even Hugh Burnell to silence, our friend tried desperately to fathom
this wickedness in himself. Why was it that when Tegolin slept with
him under his sheepskin his feelings had been so gentle? They had
been amorous feelings, too; but amorous with a tender, sweet, diffused sensation that seemed hardly more intense than what the girl
herself must have felt!

But now, just because this woman's fingers were so dry and hot
and the nerve of cruelty in her was so quivering, he was stirred to
such a point that his knees knocked together as he helped her to
descend the stairs.

When they reached the cloisters, however, and paused to listen to the chanting in the church, all the boy's feelings, both good and bad, vanished in a pressing physical need. He perceived that the Lollard made no bones about this natural necessity, but boldly retired—chanting or no chanting—behind a stone buttress that buried itself in the dark and dewy obscurity of that enclosed lawn, but our friend was far too shy to do this, and it was only when emerging from the cloisters into the paddock between the men's guest-house and the women's guest-house that he had the courage to leave them and seek the latrine in the former place.

It had struck his mind before, but never so much as now, how queer it was that a pressing physical need of this simple sort should be able to obliterate everything else. " 'Twould be the same," he thought, "if I were on my way to be executed, or to see Lowri have her husband executed! It shows how Nature comes first. Comes before the most agitating drama, before all good and all evil, before *everything!*"

Returning to rejoin the others, who were waiting for the appearance of Tegolin and Alice, he passed—with his interest in life fully restored—the chief kitchen of the Abbey. He was surprised to find this building a good deal smaller than the one in his Oxford College; but how convenient it was, compared with that! He couldn't resist entering this place for a moment, the practical Norman in him being fascinated by such curious inventions. There were no less than three shining spits against the furnace, connected by an iron bar in such a manner that they could be turned at the same time by any small boy. This boy could stand, too—Rhisiart noticed—well out of the way of the cook when he was basting the meat. But the polished containers for disposing of the refuse were of such a scientific kind that our friend longed for Modry to see them. His mother had never taken any interest in such things, but he had listened to Modry, and watched her too, and he knew as well as anyone what modern contrivances in such a place meant!

There was nothing very much going on at that moment in the Valle Crucis kitchen. Rhisiart indeed found it deserted except for an elderly lay-brother from Scotland who was engaged in preparing a special kind of Scotch griddle-cake. This he laconically explained was for the supper of Prior Bevan who came from the Scotch border; "And he's a true man, young Master, and honest, and that can't be said of many!"

While our friend was regarding with wonder the singular iron plate, like a small tin shield, upon which the Scotchman was at work, there came a voice at the door, and swinging hastily round Rhisiart saw the most unhappy simulacrum of a human being he had ever seen in his life. He was a man half-naked, with a face so emaciated that little remained of any recognizable personality except the misery in his eyes. This misery was neither passionate enough nor recent enough to be called despair. In a sense it was sadder than that; for despair had ceased to be concerned with the necessities of life and this unhappy one was kept alive by the momentary relaxations of suffering that occurred in his daily hunt for such necessities.

Rhisiart could see at once he was a stage below the level of the outcasts that in Hereford were known as vagabonds. He certainly wasn't a beggar. All the beggars he'd seen before had been "characters," characters of a sort! But in the man who now stood mumbling in the doorway there was nothing left but physical craving. He lacked the heart even to lift his curse, still less his hand, against *anything*, human or divine. He had no love, no hate, no wrath, no grievance. He hadn't even self-pity. His abasement was so complete that it was beneath humility, below resignation. His need was so dominant that it had obliterated the last human emotion—the emotion of gratitude. Either he had once been flung a scrap from that kitchen-door or had managed to pillage some garbage from one of those neat recepticles for refuse before it reached the pigs, for he now hovered in that entrance in his rags and his nakedness with an air that partook at once of a migratory bird and of a starving cat.

But the Scotchman no sooner set eyes on him than he snatched up a skewer from a hook by the fire and drove him away with a volley of obscure curses. Rhisiart would have left the place in disgust; for the last thing he wanted was for the Sheriff to think he was skulking off.

But the image of his friend, the Lollard, suddenly presented itself to his consciousness. Like a younger boy with an older one he had come by this time to divine pretty well how at any crisis his comrade would act. "I'm not afraid of a scurvy Scot," he thought, and snatching up one of the Prior's half-cooked cakes and a repulsive bone that had a quantity of red meat still clinging to it, he pursued the outcast, crying out, "Stop! Stop!" 'Twas a wonder the wretch didn't only run the faster; but either Rhisiart's tone was different from the curses he was used to, or the boy's high-pitched Norman accent had a magnetic authority, for he stopped and turned and gathered his rags about his nakedness.

Thrusting the cake and bone into his hands the lad waited, panting. He felt no great spasm of pity, for the distressing stench that emanated from the wretch blotted out such feeling; but like a child feeding an animal he was curious to see what he would do.

But the creature looked at nothing, saw nothing, understood nothing except the wet raw meat adhering to the bone. This he began hastily devouring, until his white lips and even his hollow cheeks became greasy and bloody; and while he gnawed he pressed the Prior's cake tightly against the hairs on his chest, and every now and then, over the bone, Rhisiart could see the whites of his eyes as he glanced suspiciously round him.

And it was lucky for Rhisiart that he *did* glance round him, for the Scotchman, skewer in hand, was obstinately limping after them, and our touchy friend would certainly have expressed his shame and disgust in some disgraceful act if the bone-gnawer hadn't fled away.

"Foul fa' your thievish hand!" panted the cook. "I'm na sae muckle of a puir kitchen-knave that ye can gar me gang to nourish such as he. Do ye ken who'a be, ye thieving Jackanapes? Ye might as well give scraps to Judas Iscariot!"

Anxious though he was to rejoin the others, Rhisiart reduced his pace to the Scotchman's limp, as they returned, and listened to a lurid description of a creature he had taken upon himself to champion.

It appeared that the man had been caught making love to a plough-boy, and though there was no question of actual sodomy, the women had hunted him out of his home, the Church had excommunicated him, Lord Grey had had him flogged almost to death, while the children of any hamlet he tried to enter were encouraged to drive him away with curses and stones. And, as the Scot explained, "When ilka bairn in his kelpy Welsh tongue cries *droog* at a man when 'a shows his face ye'll ken a critter's best dead than alive. Why, laddie, the very dogs maun hae their spit at him; and yet the man lives! He just canna dee, I reckon, till the Deil carries him awa'."

Our young man experienced not a little personal uneasiness as well as indignant pity when he heard the cook's story. His mind reverted most uncomfortably to that dusky corridor at Glyndyfrdwy. But what would the Lollard have done? Refused to go a step towards Dinas Brān till he'd got the fellow clothed and fed and given a fresh start?

With his hand in his belt he wondered whether he should offer this moral Scotchman a small piece of silver, but instead of doing so he confined himself, as he bade him farewell, to enquiring his name.

"Gibbie Saunders I *were,* young Master," was the reply, "free born by the braes of Annan. Brither Jock I be now; but aye! I wad gie the banes from my ribs, laddie, to be auld Gibbie Saunders at hame among the lavrocks!"

But it wasn't of Brother Jock's troubles that our friend thought as he hurried to rejoin his companions in bondage. A deep shame such as he had never known in his life took possession of him. No wonder that ghastly head on the Abbot's crucifix had hung so heavy! "What luck," he thought, "to be mad like the Friar! What luck to be as good as Tegolin!"

But he soon had occasion to test the sincerity of this new feeling, when among the whole crowd of his friends—all the "hostages of Glendourdy" as they were called by the bluff Salopian—he sat down with the Sheriff's men by a bivouac fire at the foot of that eminence he knew so well. There were blazing torches there as well as the fire; and from all sorts of odd angles, in the dusk of that summer evening, the red-glancing lights and flickering flames fell with strange effect upon moving faces and shifting garments as he shared, hungrily enough, that solid soldiers' meal.

Mistress Lowri had made no effort to refuse on behalf of her Constable's "hostages" this timely refreshment. "She's saving her man's larder, the cunning bitch!" Rhisiart heard one trooper whisper to another with yeoman maliciousness—and indeed it had crossed his own mind to wonder what kind of repast, if any at all, would be awaiting him in that half-ruined fortress.

But in his present mood it was with a singular relief that he answered Tegolin's quick concern as she handed him the bowl of sweet mead and the platter of ox-tongue. He tried hard not to look at the tightly-buckled cincture, above which the breasts of Lowri ferch Ffraid seemed to draw the fire-light and drain the twilight.

But the treacherous thought slipped somehow into his mind as to whether the points of those breasts under that green-and-gold gown were as burning as her limbs, as her fingers, as her lips.

The Ruthin girl seemed to be in radiant spirits and kept edging herself closer and closer to Tegolin's side. *Her* heavy-lidded eyes he didn't scruple to catch, as she sat munching that good Shropshire fare and plaiting and unplaiting the end of her companion's braid as it lay across her lap.

But the sweet mead he kept drinking, although, after that heady wine, it tasted like pure milk and honey, didn't tend to diminish the excited conflict going on between his senses and his conscience. As he listened to the deep voice of Hugh Burnell, still talking to Master Brut about the price of beasts in Hereford fair, and to the jerky whispers of Mad Huw who had got into his head that he would surely find his King safe and sound in the great keep of the fortress, the lad tried desperately to fix his mind on the red braid of the Friar's Maid.

But the more he drank the more did the red braid seem to melt into the Ruthin girl's lap. "I must be losing my wits," he thought, "or is the Abbot's curse working on me as well as on Mistress Lowri?"

The Salopian conscripts, most of them yeoman-farmers with a sprinkling of journeymen-craftsmen, were evidently thoroughly enjoying their trip across the border. Rhisiart caught snatches of a lively conversation going on where a young springald from Shrewsbury, upon whom this good mead appeared to have the same effect as it did on himself, was asking a veteran of thirty, who had been in the Irish wars, as to the precise number of maidenheads that had fallen to his prowess.

The Lollard and Hugh Burnell on the other hand were now engaged in a heart to heart talk about border politics, from which, as he listened, he gathered that they were practically of the same opinion, namely that Wales ought to be liberated from the Norman castles and their oppressive occupants, and ought to have a prince of her own and even a parliament of her own, but that this prince should do homage to the King in London and that, as against France or Scotland or the Turk, England and Wales should be staunch allies.

It was perhaps this absorption of her protector's parent with Master Brut that brought it about that our friend now found himself in close juxtaposition with the gold-and-green gown, and divided by the whole blaze of the fire from Edeyrnion's chaste Maid; and it was likely enough that the complete disappearance of the red braid, which had already been melting into the Ruthin girl's lap, was what at that juncture made his conscience throw up its hands. For the red braid had become a kind of heraldic symbol to him, like a red lily on his shield, and now, in the place of this pure token, there were only the fiery tongues of flame!

And Mistress Lowri was talking to him now, talking in a low intense voice about what his future was to be, and what a great part he might be destined to play in Owen's revolt. Her words were the words of a mature woman encouraging a young man's most secret ambitions, but behind her words there was a quivering caress, a furtive, flickering caress, as if with electric finger-tips she were searching for the very passion-pulse of his naked being!

"Denis knows, and *he* knows," was one of the things she murmured as she tossed her head in the direction of Hugh Burnell. "Yes, they know and so does Fitz-Alan, what I feel about Wales and about Owen. But they think it's just a woman's folly. Owen himself—and he knows I know it—thinks that I'm just their spy, their agent, their bought and treacherous tool! But I'm like you, Richard"—this was the first time anyone had called him "Richard," and it gave him a curious thrill—"I've got Norman blood—well! to tell you the truth, Angevin blood—but it only makes what's Welsh in me more dangerous and more deadly! Has anyone told you about me, Richard? How my father deserted my mother; and how I've played the whore to keep the old lady in comfort and peace? Well, never mind that! But I'm a bastard— just as Tegolin is—and she takes after *her* father, just as I do after *mine*."

While she spoke, and she soon returned to what Rhisiart's future would be when the revolt broke out, he could see her playing with one of her silken gloves, drawing it off and drawing it on, and finally letting her bare hand lie between them, like a lovely little white bird only waiting to be caught. Nearer and nearer to that fatal white hand his fingers kept hovering, but she suddenly made the mistake of speaking of Tegolin and her Friar in a tone that made it possible for him to clapse his own knee with both his hands, and to utter a wordless prayer to that ghastly-drooping head he had seen on the Abbot's wall.

And it was then, in the tension of the struggle within him while her voice mingled with the leaping and lapping and licking of the flames in front of them, that he had a curious hallucination. The smoke of the bivouac fire as it swept away into the darkening sky had been for some while taking strange shapes, but now it took definite and recognizable shapes. It took the shape of a gigantic figure, in the armour of the ancient days, mounted on a huge war-horse, and the word "Derfel" came into his mind, coupled, however, not with the word Saint, but with the word *Gadarn,* the Mighty, and following Derfel Gadarn was the wraith of the old poet he had seen die so hard, and the grotesque figure of the preposterous Scab; and along with them, leaping and bounding, was the wolfish apparition of Rhys the Savage.

Nor was this all; for as that bivouac smoke broke into the substance of his secretest trouble, he seemed to see the shape of Owen himself, hesitating there, his hand raised to his forked beard, and his eyes fixed, in one of his strange seizures; while, over against those others, and as if offering him an alternate destiny, the whirling smoke began to take the form of the mysterious Brān himself. Yes, in the strange mood in which he was now, with the corporealizing of those smoke-wisps, he felt he knew, as he had never known before, what he really felt about the man these English called "Glendourdy." There was something subtly tragic about him, something that really did approach —as he recalled how he stood by the Bard's side in his golden array— a figure decked and adorned for sacrifice.

And the lad remembered how, in one of Modry's tales, when Brān the Blessed brought his army into Ireland to avenge Branwen's wrongs, the only way of crossing the dangerous river was that his people should pass over the body of their lord.

There was one sentence Modry always used to quote in the old tongue; and because it was one of the few moral tags she ever did quote it had remained in his mind. *"A vo pen bit pont,"* she would say —He who is the head, *he* will be the bridge.

No! he hadn't touched yet those burning fingers lying at his side, though he felt them there through all his bones, and he knew that the yielded willingness of her whole body was in them and every one of its quivering nerves!

But now as the sign came from Hugh Burnell for the ascent of the castle-hill he couldn't have sworn—no! not on the handle of his crusader's sword—whether he was sorry or glad he hadn't done it!

How steep that ascent was! All manner of irrelevant questions kept coming into his head. How *had* they dragged the stones up here to build this place? His back hurt him as he thought of the serfs who must have done it. No! he hadn't taken thought enough of these things! Would the all-enduring common people *really* gain if Owen were victorious?

He could see some red lights at one spot in the great circular ramparts above him. Was that where the entrance was? But more arresting to his mind was a single yellow light he could see, high in some turret up there. "I warrant Mad Huw thinks the sad face of his King is watching us from that window!"

The nearer they approached the castle, the less he could see of anything but those encircling ramparts. But his imagination built up corridors, passages, buttresses, stairways, balconies, courts, towers—a vast, intricate world of masonry under the twilight sky. "It's a real Welsh fortress," he thought, "built before Edward's time; built, I daresay, when John destroyed Mathrafal.

But what, he wondered, was it *before that?* And the idea arose in him that there was probably a peaceful hill-city up there, before there was a castle at all. But *whose* city? And vague memories came back to him of Modry's tales about Brān, how he was so huge that he could cross the Irish Sea on foot, so huge that no roofed abode could contain him. "The City of Brān the Blessed," he said to himself, and he tried to imagine that somewhere within those walls was to be found a secret chamber, where, older than Caesar, older than Derfel and far more majestical, was the gigantic head of Brān the Blessed, immortal, indestructible, pitifully smitten, but able to give surcease to all human sorrow!

Aye! it came back to him, as he climbed this hill of his long desire—a "hostage" not a conqueror now—the way Modry had comforted him with the thought of Brān the Blessed, as they listened awestruck one summer night to the wild weeping of his frivolous mother!

He had been walking now for some while in silence a few paces behind the Lollard—for Hugh Burnell had taken chivalrous possession of his son's ambiguous lady—and he was watching how the green and the gold of that gown mingled with the buff of the man's jerkin and the glint of his steel, when suddenly Tegolin appeared at his side.

"Gwion Bach!" she said gently, laying her hand on his arm, "don't'ee forget the Tassel-farm."

He made an effort to look straight into her face as they paused in the ascent, but his eyes sank upon that boy's dagger of hers, swinging so gallantly in that absurd out-worn fashion against her hip. Something like a groan came from him; and then he suddenly felt an unaccountable rush of anger.

"Why did you refuse that girl?" he cried irrelevantly. "She wanted to serve you. She hates young Grey."

"I've *not* refused her, Gwion Bach," she replied softly. "She *is* going to serve me!" And then with one more attempt to meet his eyes, but the wind swept the torch-flare down so that they were left in darkness, she drew away from him and was gone.

It was by the light of several smoky flambeaux, gleaming and red like the eyes of a dragon above the entrance, that they reached the castle gate.

Tegolin had gone ahead, with the Friar and the Ruthin girl, and had already passed under the archway. The Lollard, after his evangelical custom, had fallen into the rear. Hugh Burnell was giving instructions to his men. So that it came to pass, as if by a deliberate intention of chance, or, shall we say, of Derfel Gadarn, that our friend entered Dinas Brān side by side with its lawless chatelaine.

And Mistress Lowri in that dark archway did at last possess herself of his hand. "Shall we burn *together*, Rhisiart?" she whispered. And for answer he pressed those hot fingers in a clasp as feverish as their own.

Thus did Rhisiart ab Owen cross the threshold of the fortress of his ancestors.

VIII

THE SWORD OF ELISEG

It was much darker inside than outside the walls of Dinas Brān; and it was characteristic of the divided rule under which the already half-ruined place raised its battered head that there was a great scarcity of torches and lanterns.

Having succeeded in troubling the most deadly nerve in Rhisiart till his whole nature was in a turmoil, the lady of the castle completed his discomfiture by taking no more notice of him than if he had been one of the English troopers who were now handing over their prisoners to the Constable.

Having been embraced by her "protector" with a solicitude as tender as if she had returned from a pilgrimage to the Holy Sepulchre rather than from the Abbey at the foot of their hill, Lowri led her daughter and her daughter's new attendant across the wide-stretching grassy court, which although empty now looked big enough to contain the tents of a squadron of troopers, towards her rooms on the further side, the side which faced the precipitous slopes of the Eglwyseg Rocks.

Into such neglect for several hundreds of years had the fortress fallen that many of the upper chambers upon which the outer walls abutted had sunk forward into the court, leaving the lower ones, which were in most cases more strongly vaulted and buttressed, to be reached through scattered heaps of ruins. The only chambers in Dinas Brān which were habitable were those ranged round the huge circle of the outer walls. The ancient banquet-hall was still sometimes used; but of the chapel and the castle-library nothing but heaps of stones remained, some of them still carved and moulded, others shattered out of all recognition.

Rhisiart stared inquisitively at these pitiful stones, for they lay in heaps in every direction, and he tried in vain to imagine how the place

looked in the heyday of its glory, before the treachery of his own ancestor had left it to alien hands.

One curious effect these ruins had upon him as he waited in the
draughty damp-smelling darkness, along with the Lollard and the mad
Friar, was to evoke such a different Dinas Brān from the one he had
imagined that it was no longer a rival to the imaginary one and no
longer mingled with it or impinged upon it. All the while he had been
approaching the real Dinas Brān, that other, that mystical one which
he had created in his childhood, had kept blending with it, had kept
rising out of it and beyond it into more fabulous, more enchanted
towers. But now as he stood in that dim guard-room, listening to Mad
Huw's irrelevant whispers and quiveringly conscious of the dark nerve
which Lowri had set twitching in his inmost being, these two Dinas
Brāns *separated completely*. The imaginary one lifted itself clean out
of this draughty mad-house of broken stones, of which Lowri was the
evil spirit and wherein he must meet "burning" with "burning," and
limned itself on those flying cloud-wracks of the mind's horizon that no
madness could touch and no burning blacken!

That Dinas Brān, painted with mystic pigments upon a spiritual canvas, rose up still in its immortal air, clear of all these tumults.

But they were no pleasant moments, these first moments of his treading that deep-indented stone floor that had been trodden by Princess
Myfanwy and by Madoc ap Griffith. Obsessed by the adder-tongue of
lust, of that particular lust drugged with cruelty that he had come to
recognize as his master-devil, he recalled how a Russian student at
Oxford, a youth who had come in the train of Chrysoloras, the tutor of
the Emperor Manuel, always used to say, when he went to a bawdy-
house, "My insect wants a bite," how deeply he himself had been
shocked by this expression! But now he began to feel that this Russian
knew what he was talking about! It seemed to him that he could
actually feel an "insect" of lust within him, that was only connected
with his brain by a thin corridor, and that had no connection at all
with his heart or his soul.

He was looking at this moment through an archway, where there was
a light gleaming from the wall, and where the modern long-bows of
the Sheriff's men as they lounged about, chattering with the Constable's

servants, gave him a very queer sensation. He could hear the familiar English jokes, with their customary allusions to the Scotch wars and the Lollard heresy and the doubtful loyalty of the Percies and high price of French wines.

"How different," he said to himself, "from the old days, when people treated serious things seriously, and there was none of this modern cynicism that spoils the romance of everything! And God! how draughty it is in here and how cold for midsummer!" The cold indeed seemed doubly unnatural; not only unnatural at that time of year but as if the very walls themselves of this lost fortress had died with its defenders and were now corpse-walls, riddled with the smell of decomposition.

Even that evil desire, which existed in him apart from his will and which was like a devouring insect in his deepest nerve, ceased to give him any pleasure. He knew he would obey it. That woman had touched him with her dry hot fingers and he *must* obey it. But what he longed for, as the noisy laughter of these Shropshire intruders mixed with the high-pitched broken English of the natives, was to feel again all he had felt when hand in hand with Tegolin he had first set eyes on Owen's forked beard!

He tried to catch the Lollard's eye, but the worthy man was giving his full attention to Mad Huw's excitement which seemed to be plunging into the deep patience of that bland countenance like hail into a pond.

Rhisiart shivered, and thrust his hands—they were cold enough now! —into the folds of his jerkin, while through the stone doorway and over the heads of the soldiers he could catch a glimpse of the mountains away towards the north. And a strange feeling came over him. It was a feeling of the vanishing away of all things, the absorption of all things; the rushing down in a cataract of annihilation of loves and hates, of bodies and the bones of bodies, of souls and the thoughts of souls, all of them swallowed up like unreturning ripples in the great ocean of Being.

It was the physical sensation of *cold* that brought this feeling. He was sure of that. It was the death-chill wafted against his face from the damp stones; and as the four winds of heaven ambuscaded one another and wailed at one another, and mowed and mumbled and mewed at one another along the grave-stone indentations and hollow channels of that gusty floor, he felt that he would never be warm again, never be naturally happy again. The infernal ice was closing in on him and his twitching nerve. Oh it wasn't ordinary cold! It was a particular *kind* of cold. He knew *that* well enough. It was a cold that had a shiver in it that came from some deeper level than mere damp, or mere stone, or the mere teeth of the wind. It was a shiver that had something metaphysical in it. He had felt it once at Hereford, when he was a little boy, down by the bull-baiting field in winter, when there was frozen mud and ice everywhere, and the servant who was with him had gone to help in the killing.

There were great blocks of ice in the river that day, and some of them, drifting down from the slaughter-ditch, had blood on their surface. He hadn't wept but he had pressed his forehead against an iron post with a ring in it, and *had felt glad* that those blocks of ice were being carried away, and had wished that the animal they were killing and the men who were killing it and his mother's servant who was helping, yes and himself too who was there to look on, might *all* be carried away.

He wished now that it could be suddenly five hundred years hence, be at the opening of the twentieth instead of the opening of the fifteenth century, with his bones lost and Lowri's bones lost, and the shard of that insect within him, that was now goading him to his perdition, lost, too!

"No, I haven't *seen* him, Master. I never told you I'd *seen* him," Mad Huw was saying to the Lollard. "But I know he's here; and I know he's here because my head doesn't ache any more, and I don't hear voices any more. And shall I tell you something else? And *you* can hear this too, lad, if you like."

But his voice was almost inaudible though he had been speaking low enough before. "*I'm no trouble to the Maid any more!*" he declared. "Yes, I do what she tells me. She's like the Mother of God to me, now that *he's here*. She'll be sending for me soon and I shall go. I sha'n't cry out. I shall do what she says without a word. If she told me to go back where she first found me I should obey. *With him here* I'm let off everything! I haven't to think what to do or what to say. It's all happiness now, because I know he's safe. He's safe and waiting his—"

But at that moment they were confronted by an apparition. An old man, grey as a ghost, stood before them, solemnly bowing to each of them in turn and with every bow introducing himself with stately politeness. "Adda ap Leurig ap Coel," he said, and repeated it three times.

Grey as a ghost he was, this formal little man, and so lean and so upright that he resembled one of the pillars of the groined roof under which they stood. His garments were grey and his head was grey and his countenance was grey.

Mad Huw broke into the pleased laugh of an infant who had been offered a bauble. The Lollard gave him a polite smile. Rhisiart scowled. But the apparition went on. "Seneschal Adda. And my Lord has sent me to show you your rooms."

"A dungeon! A dungeon!" cried Mad Huw in extreme delight. "And you've got chains for us?" and he stretched out his hands towards the official, the folds of his old travel-stained habit looking almost black against the other's neat garb.

"I'll come back for you, Brother," said Seneschal Adda quietly, "and for *you,* Master Rhisiart. Will you follow me, Master Brut?"

"No, no, it's all right!" cried the Lollard hastily, laying a restraining hand on his companion's impetuous arm. And then to the other: "I shall be able to see my friend later, eh, Seneschal?"

Adda ap Leurig bowed without speaking; but in spite of the darkness his prisoners caught a suggestion in his look that he didn't regard the sight of Rhisiart's scowling face as an unmixed advantage.

But the Lollard moved up close to our friend and paused for a moment till he caught his full attention. Then with an unruffled face and his usual flickering smile, a smile that was neither gay nor sad, a smile that always made Rhisiart a little uneasy, for it seemed to rise to the surface of that placid countenance from a psychic level different from that of most human smiles, he uttered the following enigmatic words:

"If you're called upon to make any decision, lad, make the *negative* one! I'm quick at catching the aura of a place; and I tell you I've never felt so many mixed currents of good and evil as there are here. Everything in this castle's confused to a point of insanity—*embrouillé à la folie!* So look to yourself, gossip. *Prenez garde à cela."*

"You heard what I told Master Brut?" whispered Mad Huw as soon as they were alone.

Rhisiart assured him that he had heard every word. He felt at that moment that the merest mention of his royal namesake would be more than he could bear. But a new burst of bawdy camp-merriment reached them from the lighted guard-room. "The English are enjoying themselves," he muttered vindictively in Welsh.

"They are good-natured lads," remarked the Friar quietly. "Our quarrel isn't with them, and never will be. No, not even if Owen raises the dragon."

Rhisiart gave him a wicked look. "They'd have burnt you, all the same, that other night."

"No, no, my son. Not they, not the soldiers! And even Master Simon wouldn't if he hadn't been tormented in his mind. It was *her*," and he lowered his voice and made a motion with his head towards the interior of the castle. "She's in league with the Scab, and if you don't know what *that* means, you don't know the power of Satan round here. Why they tell me"—and his voice sank to a yet more solemn whisper—"that those two are plotting to give Derfel another bride. They say there's a maiden in this castle— Yes, and they say when her men have caught Simon that she'll—"

"Your precious Simon would have burnt you!" interrupted Rhisiart savagely; and then he added out of pure malice: "But our Lollard must have felt like you about him, for I've never seen a priest of God take more trouble than he did to drive the evil spirit out of a man!"

Mad Huw's generous temper vanished in a flash; and in its place came a harsh professional austerity. "To drive out devils by Beelzebub, the Prince of Devils," he began angrily; but remembering the context of these words, he sighed deeply, and in a tone that had less bigotry in it, a tone that reverted to the purer disciples of his Order, he said gravely: "Lollardry is the first step to atheism, my son. Your friend may be a good man. I daresay he is. But he is opening the flood-gates to the tide that will sweep everything away."

One of the Shropshire yeomen was carolling a bawdy stave; and Rhisiart could catch through the illuminated arch an indecent refrain he had often heard on summer evenings, floating out from the beer-houses on the warm air, along the river-wharves of Hereford.

"What tide, Brother?" he asked mechanically.

"The tide of *reason!*" cried the Friar fiercely, "the tide of mad, wicked reason!"

The loudness of his tone attracted into their dusky alcove a couple of young pages who had been listening to the troopers' song, and with the quick instinct of their tribe these lads soon perceived that their intrusion was not displeasing to Rhisiart.

"Please, sir," the taller of the boys shyly began, "are *you* the Oxford astrologer who's come to help Owen drive out the English?"

"Run away, there's a good child!" murmured the Friar. "We're waiting for the Seneschal and can't listen to you now."

But Rhisiart, who liked the lad's appearance, disregarded this admonition. "If I *were* an astrologer," he said, "what would you like me to predict? That Owen *should* become Prince of Wales? Or that your Constable's father should give him up to King Hal?"

"The Crow's going to put you in the Princess's Bower," announced the boy irrelevantly. "I heard my Lady tell him; and the one the King's going to burn for spitting on the Blessed Sacrament he's putting in the 'Traitor's Tower,' where the Friend of the English died of shame."

"And, please, sir," threw in the smaller page, "the Crow's cross to-day because my Lady has sent Lawnslot and Gerallt to bring Simon the Hog up here. Please, sir, 'twas me, not Rawlff who heard she's sworn to chain him to the 'Old Skeleton'! Rawlff says such doings will bring down the Blessed One's curse upon us all. Be you afeared of the Blessed One's curse, Master?"

Rhisiart's pinched Norman face had had a troubled frown upon it ever since her mother had carried Tegolin away; but it relaxed now into the first smile he had smiled since entering the castle. He seized the last speaker's arm above the elbow. "Let's feel your muscle," he murmured, "and you'll soon know if I'm afraid or not! They say in Hereford, where I come from, 'A lion's gamb and a deer's heart,' but who the devil do you mean by 'the Crow'? No secrets now! Tell me of whom you're talking?" And he tightened his bony fingers round the arm he held till the boy screwed up his face and struggled to escape.

The older boy contemplated his companion's predicament with a mixture of complacency and jealousy. "*I'll* tell you, sir," he interjected, "for no one can make *him* speak—not even my Lady!"

Rhisiart released this young hero and turned to the taller one. "Well! you tell me," he said.

" 'Tis Adda ap Leurig we call 'the Crow,' " the latter replied eagerly.

"He's the oldest man in the place. He was born here and has lived here all his life. He's the only one, except my Lady, who durst go near *Ysgerbwd Hēn,* the 'Old Skeleton,' where my Lady'll chain up the Hog when Lawnslot and Gerallt have caught him. Under the 'Traitor's Tower' *he* is, by the nettles and burdocks, where the men's latrine drains out. Gurrr! But there's a filthy smell down there, Master, when the wind's in the quarter. Luned says my Lady often goes down there to hear *Ysgerbwd Hēn* rattle; but the Constable doesn't like her going, Luned says, because of the nettles and the smell, and because it's where the men's latrine runs out."

"Who's Luned?" enquired Rhisiart. Save for the grail-messenger the only possessor of this name he'd ever known was a silly relative of his mother's.

"She can climb better than *him,*" said the boy, indicating his friend. "She's older than me," he went on. "She's eighteen. But in a few years I shall marry her, and we shall have seven sons and three daughters. She's very *nearly* nineteen. She waits on Ffraid ferch Gloyw."

"Who's Ffraid ferch Gloyw?"

"My Lady's mother. She never comes down the Tower. And *that's* where Efa is! Efa waits on her, too."

"Who's Efa?"

"Efa's *his* friend"—and he indicated the younger page—"and *she's* younger than Luned. They say Ffraid ferch Gloyw makes her sleep every night in a bed that's older than the castle. They say it has a piece of the Blessed One's cauldron worked into it."

"Why does she make her sleep in that?"

"So that Crach Ffinnant can't touch her. Crach Ffinnant wants her for Derfel."

Rhisiart was aware of a distinct stirring of excitement with regard to this Efa who was "wanted" by Derfel. In Luned on the other hand he seemed able to feel very little interest. So, to divert the boy, he enquired who it was, or whose bones they were, that bore the name of the "Old Skeleton."

The lad looked hurriedly at the younger page as if to make sure that it was right and proper to reveal these secrets of Dinas Brān; but since his friend was listening awestruck to Mad Huw's revelations he was forced to test Rhisiart's reliability by his unaided wit.

"You're the one, aren't you, sir?" he said, "that the bowmen of Chirk tried to kill and who'd have done it if the Scab hadn't thrown an illusion over you so that they couldn't see you?"

Rhisiart suppressed his natural reaction to this, and contented himself with enquiring whether such was the version of things given by the Bard. There was something all the same peculiarly irritating in the idea that his defiance of all the scientific archery of Chirk should be attributed to the black arts of the Scab!

"I am Owen Glyn Dŵr's cousin," he added sternly; and he took the opportunity, in a casual and nonchalant way, of toying with his antique dagger and of surveying it from every possible aspect before he replaced it in his belt. But the name "Owen" was enough without the dagger. "*Ysgerbwd Hēn* is the skeleton of Hywel the Bard," whispered the lad.

"I only found that out myself last winter. *He,*" and he indicated the younger page, "only knows it because I told him. Hywel the Bard loved Princess Myfanwy and she used to let down a rope from her window when the Prince was away; and the Prince heard of it and came back suddenly. The Prince chained him where she could see him from her window. That's what they say my Lady will do with the Hog."

"Did you tell me," asked Rhisiart, "that this Ffraid ferch Gloyw is the Lady Lowri's mother?"

The boy glanced about him and spoke in still lower tones. So low indeed did he speak that Rhisiart was forced to draw him very close before he could hear.

"Yes, yes, her mother," he said, "and we're all afraid of her except my Lady; and my Lady's a *little* afraid of her. Luned says it was to give her a home that she consented to live with the Constable."

"Does Luned like her?" asked Rhisiart; and as he bent down to catch the reply the boy's breath reminded him of some forgotten day in his childhood when he had scrambled through a briar-rose hedge. But though the lad was panting with excitement something seemed to prevent his replying.

"Well?" Rhisiart repeated; and then, quite sharply, "I want to know whether Luned likes her."

"Luned—won't—say," the boy brought out with an obvious effort. "She tells me it's not right to ask her."

Rhisiart began to feel as if this unknown maid's discretion were a rebuke to his own curiosity; and to change the subject he asked the boy his name.

"Rawlff ap Dafydd ap Llwyd," replied the youngster proudly, "and *he's* Iago ap Cynan. We're Owen's men," he added, "though we wear the Constable's livery. But the Constable knows it. Nobody can deceive *him,* not even my Lady!"

Rhisiart didn't miss this remark, and it made him thoughtful. "I must be careful," he said to himself, and he became aware that something in his colloquy with these two boys had a little cooled the response of his itching insect-nerve to Lowri's beckoning.

But it would be certainly awkward if the Constable knew as much as the boy hinted he knew. It would not be very nice to share the fate of Hywel the Bard. "I must be careful," he thought.

Meanwhile the younger page, catching his own name, had turned for a second from the extraordinary revelations Mad Huw was disclosing to him, so that Rhisiart was enabled to make further use of this antidote to his worser devil by clutching the boy's arm again. The older lad, however—perhaps because of the insight into life he was learning from the sagacious Luned—snatched from this casual gesture a hint that if he didn't make some swift self-assertive move, it would be the son of Cynan and not the son of Dafydd who would be the Oxford scholar's friend; and pretending that he had heard a summons from the guard-room he begged Rhisiart's pardon, and pulling his friend after him ran off beneath the lighted arch.

It may be imagined how astonished Master Adda the Seneschal was when, returning from disposing of the Lollard in the Traitor's Tower, he discovered his sulky hostage loitering at the entrance of the guard-room and listening with the utmost good-humour to the troopers' revels. He was still more surprised when, as they made their way to that chamber in the wall from which to an accustomed eye the "Old Skeleton," could be seen among the elder-bushes, he heard this uncompromising young Norman—for in his long life on the marches he had come to know well enough that type of profile—begin talking to him with friendly assurance.

"How comes it, Master Adda," was one of Rhisiart's questions, as he and the Seneschal crossed the court, "that you, a Welsh gentleman of high birth, should be serving the son of the English Sheriff?"

The base-court of Dinas Brān was as draughty as it was dark; and our friend, as he pulled his cloak about his ears, made no effort to discern the effect of his words upon his companion's countenance. But at all events the old man's *tone* was neither shocked nor hurt.

"I might retort, young gentleman," he said, "by enquiring how you yourself, a Hereford *Bonheddwr,* have come all this way to join Owen, to whom I understand you're only very distantly related. But why should either of us ask such foolish questions? Welsh and Norman, Welsh and Saxon, we have mixed with each other now for at least three hundred years. Though not of the House of Madoc ap Griffith, I *am* of the blood of the old Talaith of Powys, and it is my privilege to possess, for my family has lived at Meifod since John burnt Mathrafal, a bronze sword which goes back to the days of King Eliseg."

"King Eliseg!" cried Rhisiart. "But he was of Arthur's time; and it was long before Arthur's time that swords were made of bronze."

The Seneschal was silent. He had shown so many visitors to Dinas Brān this old Bronze-Age weapon and had told them so often it belonged to King Eliseg that it was distasteful to him to be reminded of the gap between the sixth century B.C. and the sixth century A.D. He consoled himself by remarking that Eliseg of Powys possessed in his time as cunning a magician as Arthur of Caerleon, and that his bronze sword was as enchanted as the other's steel one. "But I wish," he said, "Owen Glyn Dŵr and Harry Bolingbroke could settle their account alone, like Gwydion and Pryderi, for to speak frankly I think a war between the two races is absurd." He laid his hand on Rhisiart's arm and spoke with grave earnestness. "Owen possesses the belt of Eliseg; and I possess his sword; and there's an old *englyn,* "When the sword of Powys goes back to the belt of Powys it will reach across all Wales."

They were passing just then close to a certain aperture in the ramparts, where the constant rain working upon some original flaw in the masonry had caused an enlarged opening to appear, a jagged and sorrowful opening, that gave the impression of something desolately ruinous. Through this aperture Rhisiart could see nothing but darkness; but the night wind as it blew damp and chill between the crumbling stones evoked such a feeling of exposure and discomfort that it took the heart out of Master Adda's *englyn*. The old Seneschal, however, was so accustomed to these rebuffs to his antiquarianism from across the border that he was only made more intent upon impressing the Oxonian with his knowledge.

"*There's* Myfanwy's Bower," he now announced, "where the Lady Lowri has arranged for you to sleep. And this is *my* chamber, as it was my father's and my grandfather's, and I would be honoured"—and Rhisiart saw his erect old figure bend in a courtly obeisance—"if you would enter for a moment."

There was nothing to be done but to obey; and our friend was well rewarded for his affability; for when the Seneschal had taken him by the hand and made him bend his head to avoid the lintel he was ushered into what was—though it was of small dimensions—the most perfect example of a twelfth-century chamber he had ever seen.

While the old man was engaged in lighting three large iron lanterns that were suspended from the roof, Rhisiart walked gingerly to the window. The room was more remarkable for its twelfth-century carving than for its furniture, but our young friend did notice one heavily-embroidered chair whose appearance reminded him of a certain Lombardy merchant's shop in Hereford where his mother used to meet her fashionable gossips and, while the obsequious Italian unrolled his Moorish fabrics and dusted his Venetian curios, would chatter about the latest town scandal. Thrusting his shoulders with some difficulty through the narrow window at the end of this low-roofed chamber, Rhisiart gazed downwards, both to the left and the right, in an eager endeavour to catch a glimpse of that audacious lover's skeleton, but the night was much too cloudy, and all he could see was a thin stream of light, emerging from what seemed to be a larger room than this, where the dark walls curved away to the northward.

A pungent scent of elder-blossom did, however, reach him from the darkness, mixed with a vague sourness on the air which suggested the pollen of nettle-flowers and perhaps also the presence of that latrine of which the page had talked. The combination of these smells with the thick darkness, a darkness which in a manner he couldn't define, suggested that the whole castle was suspended in a void rather than founded on a hill, held him at his post of observation for an unpardonable time. He behaved indeed as if Master Adda were his private attendant rather than his indulgent jailer.

But he was reduced to a blush of shame over his impoliteness, when, on withdrawing his head from the window, he not only found that the Seneschal had already extracted his bronze relic from its hiding-place and was holding it as if it were a piece of the True Cross, but that the figure of a young girl had suddenly materialized, like an apparition of Myfanwy herself, and was standing at the Seneschal's side, swinging at arm's length a little silver lamp. Either from the lamp or from the girl there now spread through the vaulted chamber a queer Oriental perfume that brought to Rhisiart's mind a dark-eyed, indeed devilish-eyed, pedlar, who used to come to their house in Hereford and talk for hours in the kitchen.

And as the light of her lamp threw its rays upwards, every aspect of her personality seemed emphasized by this Saracenic odour; and it was on this undulant wave of Sabean incense that her personality sank into his confused consciousness. He guessed at once that this was the discreet young hand-maid of whom the page had spoken; and though her extreme pallor was mitigated by the way the light she carried mingled with that of the lanterns above her head, Rhisiart could see that her coils of dark hair fell on either side of features that were more striking than beautiful. Luned's nose was the reverse of delicately moulded. Her upper lip protruded beyond her lower. Her chin was too prominent. And though her neck and throat had a warm, soft, disarming appeal, not only were her breasts too womanly for her years, but they seemed to our friend unnecessarily emphasized by the broad band beneath them.

"*The sword of Eliseg!*" murmured Master Adda, holding out the weapon towards him, as if it rested on a royal cushion.

But Rhisiart merely nodded at him. "Let me introduce myself, Maiden," he cried eagerly, and approaching the girl with the sort of obeisance that he had seen the Hereford nobles offer, when they singled out a particular tradesman's daughter from among the spectators at some public joist, he made as though he would lift her unresisting left hand, for she held the lamp in her right, magnanimously to his lips.

"*The sword of Eliseg!*" repeated the Seneschal; and then it became evident to our impetuous friend that the girl's dark eyes were wide-open in a strange, defiant, excited gaze, and were fixed, not on him at all, but on the rusty bronze weapon, with its double edge and simple cross-handle.

"Put it away! Don't let him touch it!" she cried indignantly. "You know perfectly well, Master Seneschal, what my Mistress feels about the Blessed One alone being reverend in this castle. *Eliseg's magician was Saint Derfel.*"

Rhisiart let her hand drop. He recognized that her excitement was so great that she was totally oblivious of the fact that he had taken it at all. She was completely absorbed in her emotion; and her eyes, as they confronted that rusty weapon, were bright with anger. The lad received the impression that she regarded it as she might have regarded something that was an obscene threat to her girlhood. The old man drew back.

Rhisiart could see that Luned's tone cowed him. He muttered something that the boy couldn't catch and, hurriedly bearing away the weapon to the further side of the chamber, replaced it reverently in a wooden chest that stood against the wall.

Meanwhile the girl did look at Rhisiart. She looked at him with a friendly surprise. He was not sure whether he liked this surprise. It was clear she was astonished as well as pleased to find him so youthful and inexperienced.

"My Mistress has sent me to bring you to her," she said gravely; and then smiling at Master Adda as he returned from concealing his precious relic, "I didn't know," she said gently, though with a faint suspicion of reproach, "that Rhisiart ab Owen had not yet seen his room? It's to be Myfanwy's Bower, isn't it?"

Master Adda hastened to explain that he was even then on his way to guide the young gentleman to Myfanwy's Bower; and leaving his lanterns burning in the vaulted roof and accompanied by Luned with her silver lamp he hurriedly proceeded to escort his hostage to what might have been called the tragic heart of Dinas Brān.

But no sooner was Rhisiart in the air and in the obscurity of the court, where the sandal-wood fragrance that emanated from the girl was carried away by the wind and where her lamp only caused a pale-flitting watery moon to glide along the flag-stones, than the riotous sound of the troopers in the guard-room reached his ears, and this virile revelry made him feel rebellious.

"I wish I'd taken Eliseg's sword in my hand," he remarked aloud, addressing no one in particular; and as he spoke he swung round and looked at the faint light issuing from the chamber they had left.

"Luned says our Lady's mother has forbidden me to show it to any-one," interposed the Seneschal; "otherwise I'd not only have let you take it in your hand, but I'd have let you stretch it out of the window and *hear the skeleton rattle.*"

Rhisiart couldn't help glancing, and dark though it was, at Master Adda's face as he uttered these vicious words. Their tone, as they emerged from that sedate grey figure, was startling. " 'T was my an-cestor," the Seneschal went on, "who lent it to Jennap ab Adam when he killed him and exposed him to the crows; and they say that at sight of it, especially when the stars are in their midsummer position, those adulterous bones—"

But the girl startled them both at that point by the suddenness with which she lifted her lamp and swung it full upon Rhisiart's face. Then she turned to the old man.

"You'd better let him do what he wants," she said, letting the light slowly sink down. "If he doesn't do what he wants now he'll want to do it worse when he's thought of it at night." She paused for a moment. "I speak for the Lady Ffraid," she added in a low tone.

Rhisiart gazed at her through the darkness in bewilderment, but all he saw was her small, dark, obscure figure, round whose indistinct garments, caught up below her full bosom, the lamp she carried was making bizarre patterns on the stones.

The Seneschal, however, was far too anxious to have his treasure appreciated by an Oxford scholar to care greatly how the opportunity was stored to him. "Come then," he said. "It was my young Lord Mortimer who last held the sword. Meredith ab Owen, when I showed it to *him*, said he was no friend to Saint Derfel."

The girl's voice rang out at that; and Rhisiart was aware of a new note in it. "My Lady says that Meredith ab Owen is the only one of all the Welshmen she knows who has remained true."

"True to *what*, young Mistress?" murmured Adda ap Leurig.

"True to Brān the Blessed!" she cried excitedly. This display of emotion about what, after all, was only superstition, irritated young Rhisiart.

"She just repeats what the old woman tells her," he thought; and he couldn't help raising his shrill Norman voice in a high-picthed argumentative tone, as they retraced their steps. "Brān wasn't any móre a saint than Derfel. Master Brut and I have just heard the Abbot talk of these things. He didn't say it in so many words; but I gathered his drift, and I'm sure he implied that Derfel and Brān were both—"

"Not a word of *him!*" cried the young lamp-bearer. But she added more gently, "I'll wait for you here. What you do, Master Seneschal, do quickly! My Lady—" she stopped and turned away.

But Rhisiart, as he entered for the second time that vaulted chamber, was uncomfortably aware of her figure in the darkness outside, standing tense and taciturn, her face towards the rising wind and her lamp making a flickering pool upon the ground.

As he stood there nervously waiting, while the Seneschal crossed the room to his precious chest, a thing he did as reverently as a priest approaching his altar, he realized that the girl's attitude had roused in him a surge of complicated feelings. He felt in some odd way as if the indulgence she had given him to handle Derfel's sword was a greater restraint than her opposition. And he rebelled fiercely against this restraint. He experienced an uncomfortable sense of being as young as Rawlff ap Dafydd! He had the feeling as he stood there, with drops of sweat bursting out on his forehead, as if this whole great mass of half-ruined masonry were isolated from the rest of the world and were growing more isolated every moment!

It was as if Dinas Brān were really in some extraordinary manner not as solidly *material* as other places. And why shouldn't there be spots like this on the surface of the earth where the electric currents of good and evil have clashed and contended for so long that they had drawn the opacity out of "matter," showing it to be, what Aristotle said it was, entirely malleable by mind?

He felt just then that Dinas Brān had become like an enormous meteorite without any planetary gravitation, drifting up and away towards the northern constellations and carrying with it all its good and all its evil!

"How old is this castle?" he asked suddenly; and in immediate reply to this, though it meant leaving his sacred chest unbarred, the Seneschal promptly brought over to his visitor a parchment-covered volume from which, as they stood side by side, he proceeded to read.

As if in order to concentrate the stranger's attention on the antique text, the old man insisted upon touching with his finger-nail each single word in the line as he pronounced it; and the nervous Rhisiart was only just able, by wrinkling his hooked nose and drawing in his lips with an audible sucking sound, as if someone were tickling him, to endure at all the movements of that ancient human claw under the lantern-light.

A drop of sweat from his forehead finally just missed falling on the page, and he became so irritated by the courtly polish of that ridiculous finger-nail that he was driven to cry aloud; "Allow me! Allow me!" and incontinently drawing his dagger proceeded to use its sharp point as a substitute for that moving finger.

Though he heard with his ears the words the man was reading, he only responded to them with half his mind. What he was thinking now was that though his "insect-lust," to use the Russian's expression, had a cruel and wicked aspect, it was also connected with the preservation —perhaps the "insect" itself had the gleaming shard of a fire-fly!—of his independent identity against forces that were fain to swamp it and swallow it. There did come to him all the same, though muted and muffled, certain nursery memories as he watched that dagger-point; and of these he recalled enough to be conscious of a suspicion that the "Crow," was applying to Dinas Brān details that belonged to a quite different stronghold.

"And they did not any of them know the time they had been there; and it was not more irksome to them having the head with them, than if Brān the Blessed had been with them himself . . . but one day. . . . 'Evil betide me if I do not open the door to know if that is true which is said concerning it.' . . . So he opened the door and looked towards Cornwall . . . and when they had looked they were as conscious of all the evils . . . as if all had happened in that very spot . . . and because of their perturbation they could not rest, but journeyed forth with the head towards London. And they buried the head in the White Mount—"

It had clearly become a ritualistic performance with the old man, this reading from the life of the Blessed Brān; but he carried the book away now, and moved back to the iron-bound chest.

Our friend could see how his hands shook with eagerness as he opened this receptacle; and there was a moment, when he rose from his stooping position with the blade in his hand, that Rhisiart fancied he heard those old bones creak, much as the Bard's bones outside were said to creak under the power of Derfel's sword! The lad's thoughts came thick and fast as the old man held out the rusty relic, presenting it once more just as if it lay on a velvet cushion.

Rhisiart's desire was to treat the whole thing lightly, as a casual whim that he wanted to satisfy before his introduction to Tegolin's grandmother; but there was something in the old man's excitement, in the aloofness of the girl outside, in the thought that it was actually this very weapon that had been brandished in Jennap ab Adam's hand as he rose from Myfanwy's side, that stirred up once more the tumult in his conscience. He stood there irresolute, staring at that rust-covered brazen blade, but feeling a curious childish longing to rush out into the court and rejoin the wise Luned!

But what a fool he would appear to the expectant old man! What a weak, un-manly, fool! Besides he *couldn't* disappoint him now. But why did his wrist feel like this, feel just as if it had been suddenly turned to lead? The whole thing was the silliest trifle. Why then was his forehead damp and his heart pounding? Master Adda was evidently disconcerted by this protracted pause. Fortunately the light from the lanterns in the roof fell in such a way as to leave the agitation in the face of the tormented young man partially concealed.

"Don't be afraid," said the Seneschal with tender consideration for what he regarded as a spasm of religious awe. "Even if King Eliseg's magician *was* none other than Derfel Gadarn the sword has brought no ill-luck to Mortimer who was the last to whom I showed it. I'm speaking of Sir Edmund of course, not of the young Earl."

Rhisiart bit his lip. Why the devil didn't Luned come rushing in and give him an excuse for avoiding this curst elongation of clotted rust that looked so like a stalactite of blood?

"So Meredith refused to touch it?" he found himself murmuring; though so little had he *intended* to hesitate any longer that he actually felt the wind already bringing in through the window the rattle of the Bard's bones as he brandished the "pitiless bronze." It was just as if it were his physical body hesitating, and not himself at all! Why *had* Meredith ab Owen refused to touch it?

But Master Adda was once more quoting his ridiculous jingle about the sword and the belt. Rhisiart felt at that moment that he completely understood Griffith ab Owen's attitude to all these devilish superstitions. When one's nerves were on edge and one had serious matters on one's mind these absurdities were too much! "After all," he thought, "I'm a Norman as well as a Welshman; and I like clear issues. I like to be honestly wicked and I like to be honestly good.

"Embrouillé! Embrouillé! What cursed things decisions are!" Oh why didn't that girl make some sign and end this wretched scene? Or why didn't this old man with his shaky hands get weary of waiting, and put that piece of rust away! Why when you'd committed yourself to some fantastical caprice couldn't you just stop and without giving any reason *change your mind?*

But what was this? His legs had suddenly begun to move, apparently of their own volition, and he was walking hurriedly towards the window, and *without* the bronze sword! As he went he found he was uttering the words, "One minute—one minute—one minute," over and over again.

Arrived at the window he once more squeezed his shoulders through its narrow orifice and peered out into the darkness. He *felt* rather than heard that Master Adda had followed close behind him with that rusty abomination. By God, if there hadn't appeared some kind of rift in that cloudy sky! Yes, and *there*—right under that protrusion from the wall which no doubt was the balcony of Myfanwy's Bower—he *could* catch a glimpse of something that wasn't nettles! Was it the white blossoms of elder-bloom or was it— He had a curious feeling, as he stared downward, as if the whole castle, yes! with the whole mount that bore it, were surrounded by a dizzy, precipitous gulf, not a slope he could climb, but a gulf, a gulf that sank down and down and down, with that white thing at the bottom!

But his body, and by Christ his tongue too, were playing their tricks once more and behaving in a way that was not only beyond his will but unpredicted by his mind! He was back under those lights in the vaulted roof again, and he was eagerly, almost cajolingly, begging the Seneschal to replace the sword of Eliseg in its chest.

"The time hasn't come," he was saying, "for me to hold it. In a year perhaps, if I can be of use to Owen, I may be worthy . . . but not yet—" This reference to Owen and indeed the whole line he took of being "unworthy," whether it were an inspiration reaching him from the figure outside, or some atavistic reversion to crafty Norman diplomacy, had an effect upon the old man that was beyond anything he could have calculated.

The Seneschal nodded his head several times gravely and feelingly and then, with complete satisfaction and without the least demur, proceeded to do exactly what had been required of him. Thus for the second time that night was the sword of Eliseg thrust back into darkness.

Once out again in the open air of the court-yard Rhisiart experienced an access of shyness with regard to the girl with the lamp. He was profoundly thankful that the stars in that midsummer sky were obscured by clouds so that Luned couldn't notice how embarrassed he was.

And it certainly *was* enough to make a person look a fool, this silly relinquishing of a natural caprice for absolutely no reason! But Luned spared his feelings; and the sword being relegated to temporary oblivion, she at once became younger, gayer, more girlish. She even began teasing Rhisiart about sleeping in Myfanwy's Bower, assuring him, in a tone that was almost mischievous, that Mistress Lowri was very particular about the men who had that privilege; and that Efa said whenever a young man with the heart of a bard slept there he wasn't allowed to sleep alone, but that an *Ellylles* slept with him.

"And the *Ellylles* who slept with him had two peculiarities. In the first place her body and all her bodily ways were what he loved best in the whole world. But in the second place her head was the head of a skull! And Efa said that this was because in grievous pity for what was chained at the foot of her tower Myfanwy's flesh *died before she died*. Efa said that after the bard's death Myfanwy never left her Bower; and that though they kept burying her in Valle Crucis her body always returned at night. Efa said that her head was as bare as the head in the chains before they could make her lie quiet; and 'twas only when she stopped having any lips at all that she would sleep by Jennap ab

Adam. That's what she says; but *I* think she didn't mind him having her *body,* because her spirit never left the *Ysgerbwd Hēn!*"

The patient Seneschal lent the same benevolent ear to these tales of the lamp-bearer, as they reached him through the darkness, as he would have lent to the confidential talk of Efa and Luned themselves, had he come upon them on the battlements.

And as for Rhisiart, it was far more important that his foolish behaviour over the sword should be forgotten than that the wise Luned should be rebuked for chattering. The girl was indeed in the liveliest spirits when they entered for a moment that fatal Bower. She went so far as to sink down laughing on the pile of last year's bracken, covered with a thick blue rug, which was to be the young man's bed.

Since it was she who held the light, Rhisiart was unable to catch more than a glimpse of her face as she lay on his couch, but the faint outlines of her form on that blue coverlet brought back to his mind with a sweet shiver of romance the feelings he'd had in the cattle-shed by the river when Tegolin shared his rest. He took but scant notice of anything in Myfanwy's Bower save that blue rug with the damsel's form upon it, but he saw enough to realize that the chamber had been recently garnished with all the modern decorations of the flamboyant epoch which had just ended. There was nothing here of that twelfth-century dignity and simplicity that hung about the faded embroidered chair and the carved chest in Master Adam's room. How his modern-minded mother would have adored these fantastical decorations! The very window, jutting out from the castle-wall, was full of foliated tracery. And as he glanced at these things all manner of sophisticated Oxford discussions floated at the back of his mind and he resolved that he would take the first opportunity that offered itself of indicating to the ladies of Dinas Brān that their passion for these fourteenth-century novelties was a vulgar innovation and quite out of keeping with the atmosphere of the place.

As they came out into the court he became aware of a sudden change of sound in the guard-room at the castle-entrance. The tipsy laughter and riotous snatches of song had ceased, and an intermittent clamour of surprised voices had taken its place. This was followed by the passing across the court of a silent band of men, not more than half-a-dozen in number, carrying on a hurdle some unfortunate captive, whose tightly-bound figure, as the group drew near, was thrown into prominence by the yellow blaze of several streaming torches.

The man himself, as far as Rhisiart could tell, as he was hurriedly borne past them, was unconscious though still living; but what caused Rhisiart's most dangerous nerve to start pulsing within him was the fact that before the bearers bore their load away to the northern extremity of the court, he was certain he recognized the features of the unlucky Master Simon, the Hog of Chirk.

So those monks were right in their surmise; and right in their priestly estimate of Lowri's nature. The woman *had* managed to get into her power the man she was ready to risk Hell for the pleasure of torturing. As the flare of the torches vanished he heard the great sentinel bell of Dinas Brān striking midnight, and each stroke of this solemn announcement sank into his soul.

Instead of following the men, however, who were carrying the unfortunate Master Simon, the old Seneschal, who had stood still to watch the passing of that cortège, now proceeded to conduct his young hostage to the eastern side of the castle's base-court. Luned's lamp still flickered around them like an *ignis fatuus;* but the figure on the hurdle had taken the heart of the girl's liveliness, and not a word did she utter until they arrived at the foot of what was called the Ladies' Tower. Here she whispered something to the Seneschal; and the old man turning gravely to Rhisiart intimated that at this point he would bid him good-night.

But he turned to the girl again before he left him. "I suppose your pages, young Mistress, will be all asleep when he comes out? Will he be able to find his way to the Bower alone? I don't want him to get into any trouble with the Sheriff's people. They're evidently making a night of it over there."

"My Lady will arrange it," replied Luned, "and if not," she added quickly, "I'll show him the way!"

Our friend had himself begun to speak, and had got as far as the words, "I know exactly," when his cheeks suddenly got hot. Was there in the whole of Oxford, he thought, a greater fool than he?

IX

THE LADIES' TOWER

Rʜɪsɪᴀʀᴛ's ʙʟᴜsʜ of shame and abrupt pause caused no astonishment to the bearer of the lamp. She was asking the old gentleman some practical and indeed domestic question. At any rate the lad caught the word "brisket" and the word "venison" as he frowned gloomily at the entrance to the Ladies' Tower, wondering whether Lowri, as well as the old woman, was awaiting him up there, and whether it was here that they'd put Tegolin and the Ruthin girl.

"I don't care for her," he said to himself as he glanced at his guide. "She's too dark, and her figure's not like the figure of Owen's daughter. Perhaps she's got Saracen blood! She looks lovingly at me; but she certainly doesn't admire me! What a man wants, when he's left his horse and his sword behind him, isn't patronizing love but some sort of respect." And the Norman mind of our friend, aware of a midnight reaction against everything *embrouillé,* went so far as to clear up the difference between a man and girl by deciding that nothing was easier than to make a woman love you but nothing harder than to make her admire you!

"Besides," he thought, "love imprisons a person. Brut talks nonsense about not making friends with boys. *They* do admire anyone!"

Having returned old Adam's farewell bow and having cordially thanked him for his kindness, Rhisiart now followed the girl through a narrow archway and up a winding flight of stone stairs. So small was the circumference of this spiral ascent that Luned would have disappeared completely every third or fourth step had she not made a habit, as they mounted, of swinging completely round and, with one arm clinging to the surface of the great column round which the steps circled, stretching the lamp down with the other till it illuminated every step he took.

This precaution, as he quickly discovered, was by no means a work of supererogation, for some of the steps were almost completely worn away in the centre, and he had to place his foot sometimes on their extreme right side and sometimes on their extreme left.

He caught a glimpse, at several points in the ascent, of various rough carvings on the stone column round which the steps revolved, one of these, a gross love-knot intertwined with two initial letters, brought with a sudden rush to his mind a philosophical illumination he had once had on a staircase in Oxford as he contemplated a similar mural design.

He nearly missed one of the dangerous steps as he tried to recall the exact nature of the intellectual truth revealed to him on that occasion. It was after attending a lecture on Virgil, and it had to do with that poet's bold passage about "mind animating matter" which the lecturer associated with the Aristotelian view of the nature of God. It gave him, he remembered, some sort of intimation as to the presence of the divine *Nous* in the very lowest forms of the inanimate, even in a stone wall, for instance, like this very one, against which, by her flickering lamp, he could see his guide's rounded arm!

At last they reached a small closed door with a little stone platform in front of it. There was a cord dangling down from the top of this door with a piece of lead tied to the end of it, and at this cord Luned vigorously pulled, waiting at each pull to hear the result; and Rhisiart thought he *could* just catch, though far away and as if at the end of an unseen corridor, a faint tinkling response.

A long pause ensued after this, during which they listened intently for the sound of steps, and though they neither of them heard anything resembling steps, heard nothing in fact but each other's exhausted panting, it gave them an opportunity to draw closer together, and Rhisiart laid the tips of his excited fingers upon the wrist that held the lamp.

The girl gave her dress several little violent jerks with her free hand, brushed some dust from her skirt, and pushed back a wisp of heavy dark hair that had fallen across her cheek.

"You mustn't be surprised," she began, gently repulsing his fingers, "if my Lady talks to you in a whisper and makes *you* talk in a whisper. Efa always goes to bed earlier than Sibli and me, and my Lady won't let her out of sight, even when all the doors are barred. My Lady makes her sleep in the Tower bed."

"Why is that?" enquired Rhisiart, wishing that he had the courage to snatch the light from his all-knowing guide.

"For a very good reason," replied Luned, and her face, as the lamp threw the curve of her chin and the contours of the cheek into relief, assumed the expression of a resolute nun.

"For *what* reason?" he insisted, trying to take a commanding and dominating tone.

Luned hesitated. Then, with a gesture that he had already remarked as characteristic of her, she stiffened her short frame to its full height, jerked back her dusky head in a movement which threw forward her bosom, and with a bold and gallant rush of words, though speaking with an obvious effort, "You've heard, I suppose," she said, "of the brides of Derfel."

Rhisiart nodded.

"Well, Efa has been chosen to be the next one!"

"Chosen?" he protested. "But hasn't he been dead for a thousand years?"

Luned gave him a reproachful look as if this stupid levity were ill-timed. "They want to give her to him on the night they proclaim Glyn Dŵr. They say that the people of Ardudwy will rise in greater numbers if Derfel has a new bride."

"Why did they choose this particular girl?" enquired Rhisiart.

Luned was silent; and then disregarding his question she brought out in a quick burst of words, while her dusky cheeks darkened still further, "Efa *wants* to be given! She *wants* to be the one! We can only hope, my Mistress says, that her child—if she has one—*will burn Derfel's image and his Horse with it!*"

These last words were spoken with so much feeling that our friend's predatory desire received a shock; and once more it was made clear to him how right the Lollard was in his use of the word *embrouillé*. He contented himself, however, with a humble enquiry as to the origin of this "Efa" who alone among the maids of North Wales actually *wished* to be the bride of a devil.

Luned showed no hesitation in satisfying his curiosity. "She's a niece of Rhys ap Tudor of Môn," she explained. "She's a cousin, therefore, of Owen's; and I suppose in some degree a relative of your own. But you won't see anything of her to-night, unless we wake her by talking *very* loud! She sleeps sounder even than Sibli."

"And who is Sibli?" and he raised his hand to his mouth to conceal a yawn. It began to present itself to his mind as a discouraging certainty that he was not destined to enjoy any sort of love-making that night.

But before Luned had time to answer his half-hearted question they both heard little tapping steps behind the closed door; not by any means quick steps, but steps that dragged and tapped, steps that were presently accompanied by the sound of a high-pitched voice muttering to itself. Luned lowered her lamp and they both gazed in silence at the dark outline of the barrier in front of them.

Presently the door was opened inwards, very cautiously and very slowly; but nothing appeared where Rhisiart expected to see a human head. A hoarse sound, however, made him look much lower; and there, only a yard from the ground, between the iron-clamped wood-work and the stone door-post, flickered what seemed a woman's features. Towards this face Luned directed her lamp, and Rhisiart stared down at it in astonishment. The face showed unmistakeable signs of having been roused from deep slumber. It had still about it the nameless scum of the wharves of Lethe; and it kept wavering up and down in that narrow crack as if its owner were repeatedly rising on tiptoe and repeatedly sinking back again upon her heels.

"It's all right, Sibli!" cried Rhisiart's guide. "Let's in, for Jesus's sake. We're tired."

The personage addressed opened the door a few inches wider but still barred the way. "She says 'we,' " she muttered in a kind of malicious chant as she opened the door an inch or two further; and her tone had a gloating mischief that made Rhisiart feel extremely uncomfortable.

He glanced quickly at the dusky profile of his companion. Had she betrayed him? How did he know that this mysterious Ffraid ferch Gloyw was not in the habit of sacrificing young men to Brān the Blessed, just as report said that the Scab sacrificed young women to Derfel Gadarn?

"She says 'we,' she says 'we,' she says 'we'!" chanted the woman, while her head bobbed up and down in the aperture, like the quick-silver in a barometer. "We're tired, we're tired, we're tired. To bed, to bed, to bed!"

But Luned thrust her back, and squeezing herself through, began whispering hurriedly, evidently explaining to the woman, whom Rhisiart thought to be the loathliest creature he'd ever seen, exactly who the visitor was. "*She* thinks a lot of him," Rhisiart heard her whisper; "and I wouldn't wonder if he doesn't enter her service. He got into trouble about the Hog of Chirk. He defended the Hog when *she* was hanging him. Lawnslot was there and he's told me all. In the guard-room they call him Master *Leap-before-you-look,* because of the way he faced the archers of Chirk."

It was Luned herself and not this malicious porter who now pulled the door wide-open; but Rhisiart only found himself in a round, low, stone vestibule, with three steps leading up to an arch on the opposite side, and nothing in it but filthy straw, scattered heaps of what looked like human excrement, and three extremely menacing rusty chains attached to iron rings in the wall.

"Tell my Lady we're here and ask her whether we're to come in."

Before obeying these orders Sibli rose and fell several times on her high shoes, which gave vicious little clacking sounds as her heels came down. She was a dwarf, but not a particularly small dwarf. But her chief peculiarity, and what had formerly earned her many a silver groat from the inquistive whores and wanton wags of Chester was a birth-mark on the tip of her sharp chin, from which a long tuft of hair protruded. This tuft of hair had been dyed on one occasion by a couple of lively prentices in that rowdy town with an indelible pig-ment of a brilliant purple colour; and it was on the strength of an appendage of so unusual an aspect that this gnome-like creature had earned her living till she entered the service of the ladies of Dinas Brān.

The dwarf now tapped her way on her high shoes up the stone steps and disappeared through the arch, leaving Rhisiart and Luned alone. Both the young people had regained their composure and they proceeded to contemplate each other with shy interest. There was an antique lantern suspended from the roof by a twisted iron chain, and the girl tried to extinguish her own little lamp by vigorous puffs of her breath. In this she was unsuccessful; and as the lad bent down to try the force of *his* lungs on the obstinate flame, she made no attempt to prevent her dark tresses brushing against his forehead.

From her whole person there still emanated that fragrance that reminded him of a certain Moorish jewel-box of inlaid cedar-wood that his light-natured mother used to unlock on festival mornings, and there was such a glow about her ripe lips and warm-breathing bosom that he felt a longing to quench the fever in his nerves, caused by the sight of the figure on the hurdle, by playing, without further restraint, that rôle of a lean hawk seizing upon a soft-plumaged pigeon to which he considered his Norman blood entitled. Hotter and hotter did this blood in his veins grow as he hovered over her.

He was staring now at the extinguished lamp clasped against her body and covering, as she pressed it to her, the embroidered band that was tied so tightly under her bosom. As for the discreet damsel herself she had certainly become shy and silent; but she displayed no token of alarm or any sign of repugnance. In fact, if instead of frowning at the lamp he had glanced at her face, it is possible that he would have detected the quiver of the faintest approach of a smile upon her lips.

This was the first time in Rhisiart's life that he had been the cause of a girl's becoming shy and silent. Tegolin of course had taken the lead from the beginning, and Tegolin's mother had carried him off his feet, and with neither of *them* had he felt in the least formidable.

But the hint he'd had in Valle Crucis of a certain nerve in Lowri that fatally corresponded to the same nerve in himself had had the effect of making him a different person from the lad who had been so horrified at his thoughts when he allowed them to run riot about the imaginary arrow in Tegolin's bare shoulder.

The wickedness excited in him by Lowri's burning fingers, and by the picture she had conjured up of letting him make love to her in the presence of her victim, had been accentuated to such a pitch by the sight of the man on the hurdle that he felt now as though he were a lost soul, a soul for whom the seduction of a discreet and nun-like maid could be the occasion for nothing but cynical satisfaction.

Looking round with the idea of finding a place to deposit the girl's ubiquitous lamp, which he had already come to regard as possessed of an annoying identity of its own, he caught, through an arrow-slit in the wall, a glimpse of the sky. "Ah!" he thought, "the stars, the stars! If only I could see the stars I would be a man. I would dominate this girl and beguile her mistress like a real adventurer! But there are *no* stars! This damned Tower has blotted them out! Yes, if I could see only one single tiny star I'd be a man!"

Unfortunately for our friend he had no practical experience as to what measures a man took to make a sensible girl yield up her virtue. All he had discovered in himself was a will to be unscrupulous. All he had discovered in her was a prejudice against Saint Derfel. So he decided that he must just wait and see what opportunity the devil would give him! There was no doubt as to what he *wanted* to do. He *wanted* to twist his lean limbs and his fiery spiritual desires, like the glittering scales of a snake, round every curve of Luned's struggling form; conquering her not only physically, but also spiritually, so that there should be no part of either her body or her soul that did not cry out. "Rhisiart, I'm afraid of you! Rhisiart, I can't resist you! Rhisiart have mercy!"

It *may* perhaps have been, though in such crises one can never be sure, only the rapidity of the dwarf's return that saved Luned from the ultimate test of a maid's discretion; but as it worked out, her hook-nosed companion lacked even the courage to take her hand in his own, as together they ascended the steps and passed under the arch and the two lanterns.

Here they were confronted by a pair of heavy curtains, between which the little Sibli, turning towards them like a jubilant fiend, bent low in a mocking curtsey. As the little creature did this she raised one of her bird-like claws to her chin and made a motion as if directing, in an obscene wish to humiliate both them and herself, its tuft of purple hairs towards them. But she swung round and with all the force of her small arms pulled aside the curtains and held them apart while they passed through.

Rhisiart was at the first moment far too overpowered by the Lady of the Ladies' Tower to take any definite notice of her surroundings; but, as time went on, his impressions of the singular apartment in which Mistress Ffraid now spent her life gathered weight and clarity.

One thing our friend had at once to admit; and that was that in place of resisting the influences of the elements the chief peculiarity of the Tower-chamber was its exposure to them. In one part of it indeed the roof was entirely uncovered to the sky; and in order to dispose of the rain when it entered there was a deep groove cut in the flag-stones, leading to an aperture through the outside wall.

The Lady Ffraid passed most of her hours seated or reclining on a dais at the southern end of the chamber from which, by a nice calculation, she was able to watch the particular segment of the sky with its changing constellations, where appeared those celestial bodies with whose influences she was especially concerned. Immediately below this opening the apartment was hung from roof to floor with the biggest piece of tapestry Rhisiart had ever seen, upon which could still be detected—though many of the colours and some of the forms were very dim—a striking representation of a deadly combat between a yellow and a red dragon.

Rhisiart's artistic Oxford friend would have been hard put to it to find any trace in this extraordinary apartment either of the flamboyant modern style, so dear to their parents, or of any conscious reversion to the austere beauty of the twelfth century, so treasured by themselves. The place contained indeed hardly any furniture at all; and what it did contain were such huge, rough, clumsily-carved objects as might well have been unearthed from the ruins of Mathrafal or left here from the days when Eliseg built the castle, or even have reverted to a still deeper level of antiquity, to nothing less than the sacred hill-city of the Blessed One himself!

But these details were only revealed to the young man by degrees. At the present moment as he advanced towards the southern extremity of the chamber, which resembled more than anything else the narrow platform with its wide altar-space of an ancient Greek stage, all he had eyes to see was the Lady Ffraid ferch Gloyw, whose name the little Sibli was now mockingly informing him meant nothing more than "Bridget, the daughter of Claudius." He climbed the two or three easy steps that led to the place where the Lady Ffraid was sitting, and in his desire to approach with a dignity becoming a cousin of Owen's he stumbled over the edge of a heavy Moorish rug, which among several others of a similar kind was spread out upon the dais. This stumble gave something grotesque to his approach. Indeed he was enraged to hear Sibli utter, without an attempt to suppress it, a high-pitched scream of pure delight.

But he was relieved to notice, as he recovered from this shock and dropped, as he'd seen his mother's noble admirers do, on one knee before her footstool, that the Lady Ffraid was totally devoid of any irritable punctiliousness. What he found disturbing about her, though neither Luned nor Sibli seemed in the least troubled by it, was not that she was exacting or particular or in any conventional way terrifying, but that she possessed a brain about five times more penetrating than the one with which he himself at that epoch of his life had been endowed.

"But she oughtn't," he said to himself, "to make me *feel* the superiority of her mind. That's not what women were intended to do. However, I'm not as frightened of her as *some* would be, or as stupid with her as some. Brut would be conceited enough to interrupt her. But I wish she *would* let me talk a *little* more!" And he went on to decide that if she did let him speak he would tell her about his meeting the great scholar Chrysoloras who taught Greek to the Emperor of Constantinople.

But it certainly was not about Chrysoloras, or the Emperor of Constantinople, that he found himself discoursing now, as he stood like a sulky school-boy in his dark Oxford tunic, with his thumbs dug deep into his belt. In fact he was completely tongue-tied. Tegolin was his good angel; Lowri his evil one. But this old woman— No, it was impossible to say what effect she *was* having on him. Was she throwing a "veil of illusion" over him? Was she trying to bewitch him? "I must say to myself," he thought, *"Rhisiart is Rhisiart,* over and over again. That's the best way when you're being bewitched. But what a lot of wrinkles she has! And they all seem *aiming* at me. I must pull myself together. Rhisiart is Rhisiart—Rhisiart is Rhisiart—Rhisiart is Rhisiart! —and I'd better not listen to what she's saying. It's with their *words* they do the damage. I can't stop up my ears, but I can look about."

He did realize that the old lady was speaking of Owen and giving him elaborate instructions as to how to use his influence over Owen; and the gist of her words, as far as he permitted himself to catch it, was that he must detach Owen from Crach Ffinnant and Derfel Gadarn.

In pursuance, however, of his drastic resolution to hear without listening, he forced his eyes to wander in the direction of little Sibli; and what he saw there was disagreeable enough to counteract any spell; for the dwarf was positively wriggling with pleasure at the embarrassed stupidity of his appearance. As she met his wandering stare she pressed her tiny knuckles against herself in an ecstasy of vicious satisfaction and swayed to and fro, poking her chin at him.

It is clear that Ffraid ferch Gloyw, for all her cleverness, underrated the childish cunning of the youth before her. She must have thought that his wandering attention was simply unmannerly curiosity. That he was deliberately resisting her instructions with an interior effort of will cannot have occurred to her. Living isolated in that Tower-room, pondering day and night on the Influences of the stars, the old lady had correctly divined Owen's need of a devoted young scholar; and the moment she heard of our friend's presence in Dinas Brān the thought must have come to her that if this devotion could be steered in a direction hostile to Derfel, Owen's destiny would gather momentum; and would revert, in fact, to the pure cult of the Blessed One from which these Derfel superstitions had diverted it.

At this point, however, there arose in Rhisiart's consciousness such a vivid memory of what Luned had told him about this singular young maid who "wanted to be given to Derfel" that he had less difficulty in keeping his response to the great lady's instructions cautiously mechanical. Rhisiart *was* Rhisiart now in the most primitive sense, as he contemplated the great piece of furniture near the warm peat-fire which he had heard spoken of as the Tower bed. So it was actually into the old, black, oaken boards of that archaic structure that there had been inlayed, perhaps a thousand years ago, a real fragment of Modry's favourite "cauldron of renovation" which Brān had given to the King of Ireland!

"Is she asleep now in that bed?" he thought, while his latest "Certainly, Madame!" sounded more intelligent than before. "And where would her head be? Just behind where that modern shield was leaning against the thing?"

Whether the sleeping girl's head was behind it or not, this polished shield became at once interesting to Rhisiart because it *was* so bare of every device. A deep, dark mirror it was, this plain shield, and the longer he stared into it the stranger, the more impossible, grew the reflections he saw in it. For instance, he fancied he could see within it, *not,* as was to be expected, Sibli's lantern or Luned's freshly-lit lamp, but the actual movements of the voyaging clouds across the bare space in the roof, and what looked like the journeying of the stars themselves in and out of the moving clouds! He even assured himself—though he knew such a thing was totally out of the question—that he could see the flutterings of dark wings mingled with those clouds and with those stars.

"Has my coming here," he thought, "disturbed the crows of Dinas Brān, or is this shield, like Owen's crystal, a mirror of the future rather than of the present?"

And then while the Lady Ffraid was still formulating an elaborate schedule, just as if she were never going to see him again, as to the methods by which he should turn the heart of Owen from serving Derfel, he suddenly realized that the sleeper in the Tower bed was peeping at him over the top of the shining shield! Yes, it was here, like a mermaid in a sea-shell, that the mysterious Efa had been sleeping all this while. She wasn't asleep *now,* however! On the contrary, with her elbows on the top of that shining shield, she was straining towards him with her whole body, straining with a wordless cry, "Take me! Take me!"

If our friend had already been lending no very attentive ear to the great lady's instructions, it may be well imagined that he now became entirely oblivious of them. His being was absorbed in that bright shield-rim, over which those pleading eyes, disheveled curls, and warm, soft neck were outstretched towards him, like the very figure-head of the Cyprian Barge emerging from the haven of Love!

"How young she is!" he thought. "She's a lot younger than me!" And incontinently he gave himself up to the most reckless and wanton interchange of glances. His narrow skull, with its predatory beak and snatching lips, must have looked to the Lady Ffraid, as she bent above it, like the human cranium of a man-headed kestrel. Taught by nobody but Nature herself how to prolong this eye-dalliance, Efa instinctively pretended to be struggling in vain to resist the sweet rape of his hawk-pounce.

But the Lady Ffraid suddenly turned her head towards the Tower bed. "Lie down, child, at once," she commanded sternly. "Bring that light nearer, Luned! It gets in her eyes over there. Lie *still,* child! You *musn't* lift your head from the pillow! Come nearer, Luned! Come nearer, Sibli! And, Luned, you're too hot in that gown. Take it off, girl! Master Rhisiart has seen maidens in their shifts before. He's a gentleman. You needn't be shy of him. Take it off for her, Sibli! Do you hear, woman?"

It may be imagined that our visitor's gentility didn't prevent him from turning his eyes from the Tower bed to the sight of the dwarf's helping Luned to disrobe; and when the girl's figure was disclosed in her white smock, he certainly did feel less curiosity as to how far the wanton Efa had obeyed her mistress. Of one thing our young man was certain; namely, that Luned's shyness in laying aside her gown was quite unaffected; was, in fact, something altogether different from the self-conscious shrinking of the younger girl.

When the dwarf had folded up Luned's dress and they had both brought their lights to their mistress's side, Ffraid ferch Gloyw spoke again.

"Listen, you three! I'm going to do something *now* that will keep Efa quiet, even if it doesn't send her to sleep. I'm going to tell our young friend's fortune. Sit down here by my side, Master Rhisiart, and show me your hands. *There!* No; like *that!* Nearer with the lamp, Luned; you'd better kneel down, girl, and hold it close."

Rhisiart now became aware of a most eager excitement among all the feminine beings in the Tower-room. From the invisible Efa to the great lady herself there was projected into that peat-warmed chamber the particular vibration that any beating of the great wings of Destiny always arouses in the daughters of men. But for himself during this moment of tense expectation, as he laid his hands with their palms upward upon that prophetic lap, the lad couldn't help glancing at the voyaging clouds and the apparently voyaging stars, as they pursued each other across that opening in the roof. And he began to wonder if there *could* be any real connection between the influence of those remote splendours and the snail-track hieroglyphs in his ape-like palms. And then from that starry hole in the roof he proceeded to look down at these same monkey-human hands of his! And as he looked at them he fancied he could feel a queer tickling in them, as if his "line of life" and "line of heart" *were* actually responding to the far-off influence of those splendours in the firmament!

"I believe," he said to himself, "she *made* Luned take off her gown. I believe she wants me to fall in love with Luned." And then as he stared down at his hands, while the Lady re-arranged the cushions that supported her enormous bulk, he seemed to grow aware of the twin orbs of her vast bosom bulking larger and larger upon him, as if in some superhuman vitality of maternity, they were irresistibly drawing him towards them!

"It would be like falling into the Pontic Sea to fall into *her* arms," he thought and he hardened his heart like a child when it stiffens its body. He suddenly began to feel suspicious of the whole atmosphere of this Tower-chamber. He felt as if some secret core of free egoism and masculine profanity was in danger of being submerged and lost in this super-feminine place. He felt obscurely hostile to all four of them. Up here together they seemed too powerful! He felt as if his only defence—the only way he could beat off this influence—would be by unscrupulous love-making. He felt now as if even his eye-encounter with Efa hadn't resulted in the pure, irresponsible conquest he had intended!

It was as if every feminine presence here—and he began to feel as if the Tower-room itself were a colossal feminine entity—were doing her best to absorb and drain out of him the very fount of his manhood.

With a savage self-insight, such as he had never known before, he recognised this core of his nature to be something free, hard, shameless, untamed, uncaught; and *this* it was that all this feminine sorcery—yes! even Efa's pretence of resistance over the rim of the shield—was bent on swallowing up!

He even found himself turning in his helpless desperation towards the disinterested viciousness of Tegolin's mother. *She,* at any rate, that depraved and shameless creature, had turned her sex into a lust that was *motiveless,* that was *impersonal,* that led nowhere, except perhaps to Hell, and that left him *as he was,* a free, uncaught, independent adventurer!

He even began to experience a malicious sympathy with his princely cousin's association with Crach Ffinnant. The Scab wouldn't let him be swallowed up as he himself was now in danger of being.

But the fortune-telling was on the point of starting in earnest; and our friend assured himself that less astute intelligences than his own—the well-meaning Lollard for instance—would by now have been absolutely bamboozled! "Rhisiart is Rhisiart," he repeated like a charm. "And I expect," he said to himself, "it takes the kind of *legal* mind that would have made me resemble Master Young, if I'd stayed at Oxford, to cope with situations like this."

But now that Sibli was holding a taper close to his extended palms, while Luned, kneeling at her mistress's feet, was pressing so close in her lively curiosity that her warm breasts touched his knees, Rhisiart had an admirable opportunity to take in detail the appearance of Ffraid ferch Gloyw. She certainly had a figure of terrific proportions. Not only was she a very tall woman, quite as tall as himself, but her person was so enormously stout that her height was lost in the mountainous curves of her form. Her face, which our friend decided may once have been beautiful, was now covered with a multitude of little wrinkles. These wrinkles even descended to her double chin; while the creases about her nose and about the curves of her cheeks were accentuated by a certain habit she had acquired of twitching her nostrils and screwing up her eyes.

But her hair was the chief wonder of her appearance; and had our friend been less absorbed by the expectant itching in his palms, little Sibli would have had further opportunities for bursting into malicious derision at the sight of his naïve astonishment.

As it was, whenever he *did* glance at the wrinkled countenance bending over his hands, he was filled with amazement, not only at the monumental enormousness of the woman's face, but at the masses of hair, thick and curly, which, as in that vision of the Ancient of Days in the Book of Revelation, were whiter than that whitest wool.

"Let us all repeat a 'Hail Mary,'" whispered the Lady, closing her eyes; and without a moment's hesitation two, if not three, feminine voices joined her in the words, *"Ave gratia plena, Dominus tecum . . . benedicta tu inter mulieres . . . benedictus fructus ventris tui."*

Rhisiart crossed himself, and bowed his head over that portentous lap. The words brought Modry to his mind. She too upon uncanonical secular occasions could often be caught murmuring the consecrated words. It must, he thought, be a habit of the Welsh; and he couldn't help wondering what the difference was between the tone of his friend, the Lollard, in such matters and the way the thing sounded in these rich feminine murmurs, as if it were an incantation!

But though his own lips moved in familiar response, there stirred, deep within his nature, a protest of reckless and impious defiance. Call it his wickedness, call it what you like, he felt he *must* keep the central core of his identity from being drugged, swamped, dissolved, in this Tower-room piety. The Blessed Virgin reinforcing the Blessed Brān was too much! He was once more conscious of a reaction in favour of the scurrilous Scab. The shameless thought actually crossed his mind that he would be ready himself to represent the demonic Derfel in the sacrifice of Efa's virtue to Owen's success!

But Luned's soft breasts were pressing closer still against his knees as she and Sibli stretched forward. The dwarf, as he could feel, was actually squeezing her purple chin against his shoulder; while over them all the great waves of fragrant warmth kept flowing from the burning peat-sods behind the Tower bed.

"It is in your line of heart, child," the old lady was proclaiming now. Her voice had precisely the same rich, low, chanting cadence as when she murmured, *"Ave Maria, gratia plena,"* and Rhisiart was reminded of that deep-toned wood-pigeon he had listened to in the theologian's cell in Valle Crucis. "Yes, it is in your line of heart—*there,* just at that point!—where I can see the crux of your destiny. Strangely enough, though, the point I mean—do you see that protective square?—has nothing to do with any woman. Do you remember, girls, the night Owen himself came to me? This square upon Master Rhisiart's heart-line corresponds almost exactly to what I found in Owen's. Your hands are quite different, child—well! I musn't tell you how they're different— but you and my Lord your cousin have at any rate *that square* in common! But you have a more unusual line of heart, child, even than Owen's. I've never seen one quite like it; and I confess it looks to me as if you would never be happily married. At this moment, as far as I can make out, you are being offered the love of several ladies; but though you will take some minor advantage of their feelings—*that* is indicated quite clearly—you will not be united in any serious manner to any of them! In fact, my dear child, from what I see *there"*—and she indicated that portion of his palm from which the four out-spread fingers diverged—"the curious thing is that unless an element of—of something I don't like to see at all is allowed to enter, it is impossible for you to get involved with any woman. On the other hand, you have a sensitive conscience, capable of causing you a great deal of acute distress; and so it looks to me as if—"

But at this point the little Sibli could restrain herself no longer. She uttered three shrill screams of elfin merriment; and Rhisiart became aware that the small creature, in her vicious interest, was actually digging her sharp chin into the back of his neck.

"Could I not, Lady Ffraid," he murmured, "overcome this—this influence in my stars—if I used"—he hesitated a second—"if I used all my will, and even"—he stopped again in a still longer pause while his cheeks grew hot—"even prayed to the Blessed Saints?"

The huge head with its animal-like covering bent in silence over his hand. The dwarf's guttering candle spilled a trickle of grease over his jerkin. Luned's soft bosom pressed so hard against his knees that it must have hurt her. And there arose in that Tower-room a faint whispering and rustling as the summer wind passed through it on its devious and spiral way; stirring the thick curls of the great lady, agitating the dead reeds on the floor, causing the fighting dragons on the arras to bulge and swell.

Sometimes it sounded as if it were sighing down the Tower-steps, with long-drawn broken gasps, longing to snatch at love-messages engraven there, longing to carry them across the valley and hide them in the lonely cracks and crevices of the Eglwyseg Rocks.

Sometimes it swept up to the roof of that Tower-room, and went eddying on, softly and sadly, like a messenger whose message none had understood, into the vast air-spaces that separated Dinas Brān from the northern constellations.

"It looks to me," murmured Ffraid-ferch Gloyw at last, "that your real danger, child, the supreme danger of your life, lies in yourself, and springs from your obstinate fear of committing yourself to *any* woman's love."

These conclusive and final words had an instantaneous effect in that warm, yet draughty chamber. They seemed to suck up in an arctic void all the magnetic currents that were rocking and lulling our friend, as if he had been a sturdy infant passed from one lap to another.

The little dwarf revealed her feelings at this anti-climax by a portentous yawn, followed by a grumbling apology to the visitor for the candle-grease she had spilt on his doublet. Luned rose stiffly to her feet and stretched herself with a deep-breathed sigh; while the old lady, returning his hands to him with a gesture of aristocratic indifference, enquired in an abrupt tone whether he was comfortably lodged for the night.

"The Seneschal has put me in Myfanwy's Bower," our friend explained, "but, as Mistress Luned knows, I haven't had much opportunity as yet of enjoying this privilege." As he spoke he also rose to his feet, and stepping backward a pace or two took the opportunity of once more fixing upon his mind—for somehow her talk *had* given him the impression of a last interview—the extraordinary personality of this mother of Lowri and grandmother of Tegolin.

Ffraid ferch Gloyw's face looked nobly monumental as he surveyed it from this distance, but screwing up her dark eyes she met his boyish stare with an amused smile.

"Do you see my daughter in me?" she asked him, "or do I remind you of our dear red-haired Maid?" And then, without giving him time to reply, "My daughter and *her* daughter," she said lightly, "take opposite sides as to your cousin's future. Lowri holds by Derfel; while our Maid follows me in remaining faithful to the Blessed One."

Now it must be admitted that Rhisiart's experience of intellectual woman, whether old or young, was extremely slight, in fact might have been called nil; nor had Providence—when it caused the most frivolous lady in Hereford to give birth to a son who was as grave when he made love as when he said his prayers—chosen to compensate him for this peculiarity by any exceptional "insight," as it is called, "into human nature." Insight into the complications of jurisprudence, both civil and canonical, he did possess; and since he had gone to Oxford he had struggled to apply the niceties of Aristotelian metaphysics to the vagaries of human reason.

But he had of late begun to feel that even *this* was like fishing for minnows with a salmon-net. The strands were perfect; but the stream flowed through them, and the minnows followed the stream. In plain words the events of life—although they did have a certain resemblance to Aristotle's ideas—had the peculiarity of tumbling down upon him in impish disorder, as if they desired, without quite losing their labels, to behave as unlike philosophical events as they possibly could.

It had been no small shock to Rhisiart when he found his senses were more stirred by the wicked lust of the mother than by the sweet fidelity of the daughter. And now there seemed to be absolutely nothing in what he had learnt at Oxford that accounted for the fact that when Ffraid ferch Gloyw tried to lure him to the Blessed One by the naughtiness of Efa and the shyness of Luned he still should resist!

And he had by this time got a shrewd inkling that the methods of the Blessed One in the liberation of Wales were ttle to his taste. Had he become a hostage for Owen in Dinas Brān only to have it softly suggested to him on every side that his compatriots could get their freedom without drawing a sword? The proud, unscrupulous Norman blood in his veins rose in revolt as he stood there, sulky and sleepy, among these women. He found himself thinking with relief of that old warrior, Abbot Hywel, on his black horse, and of Father Rheinalt and his savage maledictions upon the Saxon.

Nothing would make *them*—holy men though they were—talk of liberating Wales without the sword! He began to curse himself for letting Luned come between him and King Eliseg's "pitiless bronze," and full of this sulky reaction against the great lady, to whom he seemed to find it all the same so hard to say farewell, he told himself that he was entirely glad that the daughter of Rhys ap Tudor had resolved to be Derfel's bride!

"If I weren't so sleepy," he said to himself, "I'd ask the old lady to let Luned show me the way to Myfanwy's Bower." But it wasn't only sleepiness. He recalled how clear and simple his purpose had been when he dug his crusader's sword into the turf at his first sight of Dinas Brān. "Something's gone wrong with me," he said to himself. "These women have confused my mind. I wonder if life was as mixed up as this to King Richard when he was my age?"

What was Ffraid ferch Gloyw whispering to Luned now? Had she forgotten he was standing there, waiting to be allowed to go? Well, he must make the move himself. To fall into unfathomable gulfs of delicious oblivion in Myfanwy's Bower seemed at that moment the only paradise in the world! He fancied that he caught a sudden darkening of Luned's cheeks as he did at last make his good-night bow, but though he saw the girl's eyes turn to her mistress, it was clear that Ffraid ferch Gloyw took for granted that an Oxford scholar could find his way about a castle without assistance.

Overcome by this access of sleepiness there might have been an awkward moment as he stood blinking at the great lady like a hook-nosed owl. And awkward it evidently did seem to Luned and the dwarf; for, as if inspired by a simultaneous desire to throw off some uncomfortable oppression, they carried the lights they held to a large iron chest at the back of the dais. Here they deposited them; and the effect of this move, for the lights on the walls were burning low, was to leave all the three feminine faces in deep shadow as the young man moved away.

But before he reached the curtain leading to that littered vestibule, the voice of the Lady made him turn round again; and sleepy as he was, he was relieved that she *did* speak, for he felt that his sudden departure was not falling out as a triumph of good manners.

She spoke quietly, so as not to disturb Efa. "You will have to choose, my dear child!" she said. And as if to emphasize her words she rose portentously from her couch, letting the mighty robe she wore sink down from her shoulders. Though still in shadow, her huge bulk in that peat-warmed chamber began to tower up before him, till it became a shape of superhuman proportion, its vast girth accentuated rather than diminished by the plain grey garment she wore, bound at the waist by a dusky cincture.

"Yes, you'll have to choose," she said, "between the one path or the other if you're to be intimate with Owen. The stars are predicting a fatal encounter; the invisible powers are gathering; and upon the alternative, whether his course will be guided by Brān the Blessed or by Derfel the Accursed, his whole future and the future of Wales will depend."

Muttering some rather feeble remark about a hope that the Lady Ffraid would pray for them all Rhisiart bowed low before the whole group of women and, parting the curtains asunder, passed out of their sight.

He had only just crossed the evil-smelling vestibule, however, and was standing under the lighted archway surveying the dark stone steps, when the curtains behind him opened and closed; and behold there was Luned, with a cloak thrown over her white smock, carrying her silver lamp.

"My Lady told me to lend you this because the stairs are so dark," she whispered, "but my Lady would rather I didn't go any further. She thinks we might meet the Sheriff's men and there'd be talk." She paused and half-turning round gave the curtains behind her a quick apprehensive glance. But they had fallen back in their heavy folds and formed a massive barrier between the two of them and the chamber they had left. "It isn't that my Lady," Luned went on—while our suspicious friend assumed that she was only making what in a military language is called a "covering movement"—"it isn't that my Lady would mind our own people, who're all Welsh, seeing us, for they would understand. It's only that these English soldiers—"

And as she continued whispering, in the vein so shrewdly interpreted by our friend, enlarging upon the intelligence with which the Welsh would "understand" while the English would only indulge in ribald grossness, he himself, with a design that was no less clear to *her,* was engaged in taking the lamp from her hand. "It isn't that my Lady doesn't know," she murmured, "how entirely to be trusted you are, and how you are an Oxford scholar and Owen's cousin. It's only that in a place like this there's such a lot of gossip that one has to be careful. And it isn't as if my Lady didn't trust me with anybody, and especially with—"

Whether the discreet Luned heard *herself* uttering these final sensible words it was hard to say, but certain it is that, even before she ceased to have the breath to go on, the no longer sleepy Rhisiart had arrived at that point in masculine sensation where a girl's words mean no more than the beating of the wings of a moth against a panther's ribs. He had got the lamp away from her without extinguishing it, and had managed, without letting her go, to balance it, along with her cloak, upon one of the stone-mouldings; but what he couldn't do was to cleanse the fetid air of this vaulted place, which certainly was, with its damp walls and its human excrement, the most inharmonious spot for such an encounter as could well have been selected.

On that night with Tegolin at the farm all had been in keeping with .his romantic feelings. The mad monk, the sleeping cattle, the scent of hay, the sound of the river, the presence of his crusader's sword, the flower in the Maid's red braid, everything had worked in with his mood. But in this vile-smelling vaulted chamber he found, as he twined his bony frame about his not unwilling captive, that a totally new feeling took possession of him. For the first time in his life he realized the nature of pure lust.

They were both on their feet—indeed nothing else was thinkable in

that foul alcove—but as her response increased and her breath came in
gasps he had no desire for anything else than to press her more and
more tightly against him.

There was a narrow window behind her, through which, as he held
her, he could detect a group of those pale northern stars in which destiny had written so much. The sky was clear where those particular
stars receded into a gulf of blue-black space, and what a queer pattern
they were making! He found a curious satisfaction in observing those
points of light as he strained her softness against his hardness, for they
helped him to escape from the malodorous atmosphere of the place, and
especially from the presence of one particular faecal entity which had
already arrested his attention and that might well have been formed in
the bowels of the Blessed One himself, as by the flame of that iron-
socketed torch it took to itself the role of a reproachful witness.

The girl was shivering a little in his arms now as they swayed to and
fro in front of that narrow aperture; but our friend was too absorbed to
consider whether this was due to any weakening response of her nerves
or simply to the contrast between this draughty evil-smelling spot and
the fragrant peat-fire she had just left.

But Rhisiart was throwing into his caresses all the pent-up masculine
irresponsibility which the matriarchal aura of the Tower-room had
drained out of him. He hadn't forgotten the words of Rawlff ap Dafydd,
but in his present temper it only heightened his sensuality to think that
he was stealing a march on that sturdy page. The ecstasy he was enjoying was shot through, like radiant parti-coloured silk, with the flickerings of his savage imagination.

Unlike the desire of some lads whose wantonness might have led
them into "making love" to a maid with whose personality they weren't
in love, Rhisiart's feelings were mental rather than physical. His caresses
were electric and intense rather than violent and gross, but they were
completely devoid of that fiery passion that redeems the senses. What
he felt most definitely was a thrilling wonder at the pure mystery of
feminine response.

Wonder too at the intensity of the feelings which he himself was
experiencing! These feelings, as they increased, seemed to grow more
and more *general*. It was no longer the conscious personality of the

little lamp-bearer that he held in his arms. They were not Luned's breasts any more that came to life under his touch. They were the breasts of girlhood in the abstract. And as he contemplated those distant points of light through the narrow aperture beyond her head they ceased to be what human custom called *stars*. They became flame-points of quivering angelic desire plunging into the dark coolness of uttermost space.

It is true that his ecstasy in rocking her to and fro and associating his feelings with those shivering points in the ether was not entirely unalloyed. The "Hail Marys" which she had repeated just now kept tolling their muted reverberation like a bell-clapper muffled in black velvet.

But the fact that his emotion was more imaginative than personal seemed to give him a sort of license to be unscrupulous; and his consciousness that the girl was responding to him with her body, even resisting him with her will, increased this unscrupulousness. But that concerted feminine appeal to the Mother of God—"Hail Mary! Hail Mary!"—didn't grow less. And for some strange reason, though it troubled his conscience, it increased his lust. Out there, with those distant stars, it seemed like the cry of the ultimate darkness, of the primordial femininity of original *matter,* ravished by the energy of light.

But what was *that?* Could it have been only a frantic croak from some nocturnal bird? *There!* He heard it again! And it seemed to him that across the form he was embracing, and into that narrow window through which the stars had become his accomplices, there came from the base-court below several deep-throated human groans.

The Russian's "insect" in him was alert in a second. Had Lowri even now, while her infatuated Constable slept, slipped down to her victim's side? Had she taken with her one of her unscrupulous Welsh attendants; that Lawnslot, for instance, whom he'd seen with her on Midsummer Day and who certainly had the look of a born executioner? God! There was the sound again! And as he lent his ear to it, instead of releasing the now quite docile girl, he began to play with the monstrous fancy that he was holding Lowri; Lowri who was calling upon him to love her more, *more,* while in a frenzy of satisfaction her eyes devoured the helpless Simon.

And it happened to Rhisiart that the more these outrageous thoughts mounted up in him the more did that bell-clapper sound—"Hail Mary! Hail Mary!"—mount up with them. *"Ave Maria, benedicta tu inter mulieres!"*

Oh, he had known evil before; but he had never known it was so *embrouillé;* that it held in its depths such varieties of deadly sweetness!

Luned had forgotten to shiver now, though she still had the wit to cast a glance now and then in the direction of the curtains. She was apprehensive, no doubt, of seeing a lifted candle, and beneath it the dwarf's illuminated chin!

But the stars through that window were all Rhisiart could see— *"benedicta tu inter mulieres"*—and *they* seemed to be growing larger and larger! Burning angels of the spheres they were, moving so rapidly in their eternal circles that their very speed made them motionless. And as Luned responded more and more to him, and playing upon her nerves he drew from her response what seemed to him like dark vibrant music, he began to feel as if all those enormous burning Beings were projecting in ever-widening circles a dazzling and glittering spray of desire as they plunged and dived and floated, and then rose up again, following the great astral wheel of super-mundane life that is encircled by the *Primum Mobile* of the cosmos!

Yes, he was sharing, he was sharing the high translunar impulse of those celestial creatures as they drew sweeter and ever sweeter music from the dark bosom of eternally receding space!

In the exultation of these moments all manner of wild heresies that he had heard of at Oxford returned to his mind, gathering a new and fearful meaning. He recalled how one young scholar from Italy had confessed to him that he knew a man at Padua who denied that the earth was the centre of the universe! He recalled how it was whispered that a student from Prague, who had recently arrived to study the doctrines of Master Wycliffe, had promulged the blasphemous thesis that all the stellar heavens, including the *Primum Mobile* and the *Empyrean,* were the material body of God Himself.

"Does God, then," came the bold thought into his head, "hold infinite space to his heart as I am holding this girl?" And all the while, as he kept wondering how far this ecstasy of his could stretch without breaking, those glittering stars in that blue-black gulf grew larger and brighter. They were no longer little round pin-pricks in a great black tent. They were alive. They were enormous Beings. They were quivering with feelings akin to his own. He was one of them! He could feel the vast hollows of ether about him, wafting breath after breath of dark, delicious, primordial coolness against his burning face.

What did love matter to that abysmal coolness on his face and to those flashing fires that were now whirling about him? "No, no! I *don't* love you," he thought, "You're not going to catch me *that* way! If you *want* love-making you shall *have* love-making; but my fate's free, my fate's my own!" And it rushed into his mind that what Owen wanted was a man who could save him from himself, save him from all these superstitions; a man who knew Roman Law and Church Law and Common Law, a man who couldn't be fooled by wizards and bards and priests and women!

What did she say? That Wales can be free without fighting for it? Shiver, shiver in your black air, you burning stars! Yes, yes, my sweet one—but it's those proud glitterers I must follow—and take Owen and Wales with me!"

But his ecstasy was over now; and with a gasp that was half sob, half sigh, he let her go. Aware for the first time that in his excitement his dagger had fallen from its sheath, he bent down to pick it up; glad enough at the excuse for avoiding her eyes. A strange shame, an intolerable shyness, took possession of him; and a heart-felt wish formed itself in the depths of his consciousness that neither to-morrow nor the next day, nor the day after that, need he see her again, nor breathe that sandal-wood fragrance!

But his punishment was only beginning; and the first stroke of it came as a direct result of his discourtesy in averting his eyes from her. For what must his gaze fall upon as he shook his belt and dagger into place, but that repulsive faecal entity whose loathsome presence had so outraged him at the start. And then—alas, for masculine resolution!— the Tower-chamber began again to exercise its soft, sweet, maternal influence.

How calm the girl was as she slowly and languidly repossessed herself of her mantle! That protracted embrace, in which he thought he had been spiritually ravishing her, in which he imagined he had played the part of those high stars plunging into the yielding ether, though it had left her submissive and docile, had given her a power over him that

made him feel like a helpless child! He had expected to suffer remorse,
but he had expected also to be able to look at ᴧer like a hawk looking
at a captured linnet!

But here she was, as she cheerfully adjusted her mantle and pushed
back her heavy hair from her ears, meeting his eyes with an effortless
triumph that was like the unrippling, undeviating upheaval of a wave
that had sucked down a ship. The Welsh word for fate—*tynghed*—came
into his head. Modry had taught him that word before he was six, in her
tale of Arianrod.

Yes, he had used those softly-panting breasts for his impersonal pleasure. Now it was their turn; and *they* would be more personal! Those
soft eyes that watched him from above that gently-heaving bosom had a
look in them that he had seen before. He had seen a little girl he used
to play with in Hereford with exactly that look when she cuddled a
tiny toy-soldier. He was that toy-soldier now. "I've put a *tynghed* on you
for good and all," that look assured him. He glanced furtively, wearily,
at the arrow-slit in the wall through which his soul had voyaged into
space.

But the stars he had identified with his free ecstasy were smaller,
paler, feebler, further away. They seemed to be weeping for his defeat;
while the excremental entity upon the floor grinned at him.

And now, in a tone as rich and mystical as the voice of Mistress
Ffraïd herself, there issued from that warm, happy, care-free throat, as
she handed him the lamp and lifted her face to be kissed, words that
were the seal of his responsibility. "I'll be feeding the crows at the foot
of our Tower to-morrow," she said, "when the castle-bell strikes noon.
I shan't expect to see you—but if you *are* by any chance on this side of
the court—"

She said no more. Nor had she need to say more. An indescribable
weakness, as if the hard core of his independence had turned into a
warm-flowing sluice, reduced him to silence. Tenderly she smiled back
at him as she parted the curtains; and he fancied he could hear the
derisive chuckle and could glimpse the painted beard of the dwarf, as
the words of Mistress Ffraid returned to his mind. "If you want to help
Glyn Dŵr you *must* choose between Brān and Derfel." *Brān? Derfel?*
What had he known of either of *them,* when with a free heart he
planted his crusader's sword in the grass above the river, while Griffin—

Yes! What were those stable-men at Glyndyfrdwy doing with old Griffin now? Were they feeding him properly? Were they making sure that he had his bucket of water?

He unbarred the door at the head of the stairs and closed it behind him. He turned Luned's light upon the dark-winding steps. He felt as if his old adventurous, reckless, free heart were rolling down those steps in front of him, tapping the damp flag-stones in the darkness. "Griffin would be no good to me here," he thought, as he followed his heart down. "A prisoner doesn't want a horse."

But the image of the old piebald at that moment was too much for him. By the time he reached the place where the steps were worn away the twitching of his mouth increased; and before he arrived at the bottom his throat was swelling with the sobs of a little boy.

X

RHISIART LOOKS ON

THE FOLLOWING three months of our friend's incarceration in Dinas
Brān passed in a manner so different from all he had expected that
he decided that the only thing he could count on in the great world
both with regard to himself and with regard to the events that happened was that no prediction was possible! To his bewildered surprise,
and, we may add, to the relief of all the more normal elements in his
nature, the very next day after his escapade with the dwarf he was
informed by his young acquaintance, Rawlff, that the Constable had
left the castle to go on some secret errand of the King's and had taken
the Lady Lowri with him.

It was now three months since these two had vanished; and not
even the all-knowing Luned had been able to satisfy his curiosity about
them. Rumours of the wildest kind kept spreading through the castle.
Some said that Denis had interrupted, on that first night of Master
Simon's captivity, a scene between his mistress and her former husband
which had shocked him so that he punished her by carrying her off,
no one knew whither! Another rumour went so far as to declare that he
had forced her to journey with him all the way to the great Nunnery at
Shaftesbury, and had caused her to be shut up there.

Certain it was that since her departure the unhappy Simon had made
several unsuccessful attempts to escape. Rawlff gave it as his opinion,
based on something Luned had let fall, that in spite of her cruelty to
him the man was actually pining for her; and if he had escaped would
have risked his life in pursuit of her!

This in Rhisiart's opinion was a fantastic view, founded on the romantic illusions of youth, and he had on several occasions held both the
son of Dafydd and the son of Cynan spell-bound for a whole summer
afternoon, while he revealed to them certain cynical truths about human

nature and about the relations between men and women. Listening to
him on the battlements with either the fertile plains of Bromfield and
Iāl stretching beneath them to the eastern horizon, or the rugged moun-
tain-ranges of Saint Tysilio mounting up towards the west, the page-
boys not only displayed an intense interest in these' ideas but a lively
admiration for the brain that entertained them; for they could not help
reflecting that only experiences of a most startling character could have
led to conclusions so drastic.

These frequent and intimate parleyings between our friend and the
two pages did not pass unnoticed. Rawlff himself admitted to Rhisiart
one day that Lowri's servants, Lawnslot and Gerallt, had asked him
point-blank what it was that Master ".Leap-before-you-look" was always
talking about.

"What did you say?" Rhisiart asked.

"I said bull-baiting in Hereford and bear-baiting in Oxford," replied
Rawlff.

"You said well," commented our friend; and he thought, "At his age
I wouldn't have answered like that. That's where they're cleverer in
Wales than in England."

But these warm late summer days had not only been completely different from what he had anticipated; they had been also very much
happier. The castle hadn't yet—as he had been sure it would—married
him off to Luned. Besides, he had got fond of Luned, and he *would*
have got more than "fond" of Efa if she hadn't, one hot August day,
slapped his face so viciously that his cheek hurt him when he lay on
his left side at night.

Tegolin, it seemed, preferred the company of her mad Friar to that
of Luned and Efa. She had known them from their childhood. But
with neither of them, though for very different reasons, could anything
have persuaded her to be confidential.

Alice of Ruthin, too, seemed rather to avoid than to cultivate the
society of the Tower-chamber ladies. This was partly, as Rhisiart knew,
a matter of race and class. No English girl of such humble extraction
could feel at ease with high-born maids of the Welsh aristocracy. But
it was also, he decided, a matter of personality, for the further his acquaintance with Alice grew the less he liked her; while her attendance
on Tegolin proved a serious obstacle to his getting the Maid to himself.

Did Tegolin, he wondered, chafe at all under this restraint? Did she
miss the romantic excitement of their first companionship? He couldn't
tell! He had never fancied she was in love with him. But he had felt
from the start that there was an unbreakable link between them; and it
seemed strange she should have settled down so easily to this queer confined life without making any move to enter into closer touch with him.
As a matter of fact they hadn't had one really intimate conversation
since they had been together in Dinas Brān.

But it wasn't that he gave any deep thought during these peaceful
months to Tegolin's feelings. She was always the same to him, always
kind and natural. She had never been a demonstrative person save in
her heroic championship of the Friar; and if she was a little more reserved than formerly, and now and then a little abstracted. he attributed
these things to the moods of Mad Huw, who seemed to be growing
more and more dependent upon her.

In the absence of the Constable and his mistress the management of
the castle reverted to old Adda, though there was a general awareness
of the obscure influence of Ffraid ferch Gloyw in the background. The
Seneschal's position during this momentous time was by no means an
enviable one. But Adda ap Leurig was a self-assured old man, of great
dignity of deportment, and of no small diplomatic experience. He was
proud of his post; and on one occasion when the famous Welsh robber,
Gruffydd ap Dafydd ap Gruffydd, who had had trouble with Lord
Grey, was brought in duress to Dinas Brān, he managed to uphold so
vigorously the jurisdiction of the Sheriff of Shropshire against that of
the Bishop of St. Asaph that, in the course of the legal debate as to who
should have the privilege of hanging him, Gruffydd ap Dafydd escaped
scot-free.

But trouble was in the air; and that it was a trouble much more
charged with dangerous electricity than the case of the notorious robber was proved by the fact that hardly a day passed after the first of
September without messengers of some sort arriving at the castle, agitated and excited, bringing tales of movements of English troops or of
Welsh insurgents.

It was no doubt the absence of Denis Burnell that made the place a
centre for the intrigues that were going on; for Adda ap Leurig had for
so long followed a policy of drawing the two races together that every-

one on the Marches knew that if anyone *could* patch up a quarrel between a Welshman and an Englishman, that one was the old antiquary
of Dinas Brān.

It was so long, too, since Wales had fought for her independence that
there were a great many Welshmen on the Marches who, without losing anything of their racial traits, had won for themselves, among the
King's officials, positions of great responsibility.

Hitherto old Adda had ostentatiously refused to believe that Owen
was plotting to strike for anything more important than a tract of
bracken-covered upland between Gwyddelwern and Derwen of which
Lord Grey had robbed him.

But as September advanced the rumours that kept reaching the hill-
fortress grew so wild and startling that it became hard for the Seneschal's prisoners to believe that the old man knew as little about the trend
of events as he publicly averred.

During July and August he had evidently enjoyed his position of
authority and the chance which the border-situation of his impregnable
fortress offered him in his rôle of peace-maker. But when September
came, and the fatal day drew near to which the dying words of Iolo
Goch had pointed, it was clear to everyone in the castle that their
Seneschal had become a changed man. He kept his counsel, but his
countenance grew daily greyer and more taciturn; and Rhisiart noticed
that there was a perceptible tightening in the discipline in the place, and
that a closer guard was kept, not only upon the unlucky Hog of Chirk
but even upon his own movements and those of his friend, the Lollard.
He kept wondering whether, after all, the astute old man wasn't in
constant touch with both the Sheriff and the Constable. Was he playing
some complicated and double part, intending all the while, when the
returning army was near enough, to hand his hostages over to the
King?

Our friend had his moods of considerable nervousness. A pretty end
it would make to the grand adventure of his life to be hung, drawn,
and quartered with every circumstance of Lancastrian cruelty before
he had struck a single blow for the cause! Night by night as the days
wore on—each more lovely in its autumnal peacefulness than the last
—he communicated these apprehensions to Master Brut; but nothing
that he said could destroy the heretic's aplomb.

"I may have to suffer in the end," the Lollard would say, "and I daresay neither of us will live to be as old as Master Adda; but I feel a stronger confidence than I can describe to you that the Lord Jesus intends to use us for the cause of Wales and her religious liberty, before our hour comes. If Henry of Lancaster were as near as Shrewsbury, and all his host with him, I should still feel the same. If I could only persuade you to let me read—" and the man's discourse would swing off to those interminable theological points, illustrated by his Greek text, which Rhisiart found so unbearably tedious.

And there was still another worry to our friend, as those lovely September days went by, arising from the missionary zeal of his fellow-prisoner. It seemed to Rhisiart that the Ruthin girl was up to some shameless game with the worthy man. Master Brut had an innocent habit, or at least it seemed innocent to Rhisiart, of relating to him at night every detail of his patient attempts to initiate this languorous hussy into the mysteries of the Christian Faith.

It was not, of course, concealed from our astute friend that when the good Wycliffite did this he had an eye to killing two birds with one stone, and by appealing for intelligent sympathy in his struggle with the soul of this tantalizing baggage to instil sideways a drop of evangelical truth into the careless heart of his comrade in arms.

But Rhisiart discounted all this in his growing suspicion that Alice was leading her teacher a fine dance. His own regard for Master Brut, quite apart from the man's mania for making convertites, had increased steadily all this summer. He had never met a person, certainly not another young man, so considerate to his moods, and so interested—and our friend had many of these and loved to express them—in his ideas.

One aspect of the Lollard's nature, however, suited Rhisiart less well; and that was his sociability. Master Brut was always coaxing the young people of the castle—and the man seemed to have no prejudices either with regard to sex or class—into joining in various open-air games. Certain ball-games he especially loved to organize, for these were adapted to women as well as men; and though he always explained the rules of these games, as if they were old traditional country sports, Rhisiart secretly suspected that the best of them were invented by himself and invented solely to give the girl from Ruthin an opportunity to enjoy herself with her social superiors.

Rhisiart in his own heart despised and hated all games. It was one of his quarrels with what he called the garish vulgarity of modern times that young people were no longer content with the old-fashioned pastimes of mumming and miming, jonglerie and joisting, all of which had about them an aspect of the poetic, but must needs play at some hit-or-miss sport with a Jack-in-the-Pulpit solemnity, such as made a man feel a complete zany.

But Walter Brut was a difficult person to turn aside when he had once set his hand to a thing; and one by one his little group of players at Ting-a-Ring, at Hit-and-Run, at Shuttle-Cock, at Bob-Bunting, at Save-your-Saucer-Sally, at Spy-Fox, increased and increased; until before hay-time was over and harvest begun, not only Rhisiart himself but Lowri's two henchmen, Lawnslot and Gerallt, and the pages Rawlff and Iago, together with Tegolin and Alice and Luned and Efa, got into the habit of meeting at the foot of the Ladies' Tower every fine afternoon, thus to disport themselves. Here, divided into opposing sides that generally assumed the names—to avoid touching modern politics—of Greeks and Trojans, the Lollard would elaborate such unexclusive sports that the high-born had no advantage over the low-born, nor the men over the women!

It was upon an occasion of this kind, on the fourteenth of September, in the year of grace fourteen hundred, that Rhisiart, having grown weary of comparing the movements of Tegolin with those of Efa, and of Luned with those of Alice, sat down upon a stout-backed bench by the old Seneschal's side and tried to disperse both his own dislike of games and his hearer's dislike of war.

"May I ask you, sir," he began, "a rather delicate question?"

Adda ap Leurig sighed. At the first sound of the young man's breaking silence, his grey face had lit up, for he believed that at last he was to be asked for another sight of Eliseg's sword. But the word "delicate" dashed this hope to the ground.

"Well?" he groaned, watching Efa leap up from the flag-stones like a young deer and intercept a lightning-like fling of the ball, thrown by Lawnslot to Gerallt, "what is it, lad?"

"You haven't heard anything," enquired our friend, "to suggest that people in this castle think there's something—I mean any kind of plighted troth—between Mistress Luned and me?"

The old gentleman couldn't restrain a smile. "Dear me, no!" he responded hastily. "Certainly not!" Then more gravely, after clapping his hands to indicate appreciation of a piece of brilliant play by young Rawlff, "I have recently discovered," he remarked, "that many round here hold the view that it would be a good thing if Owen gave his remaining daughter to someone with Welsh blood. It has gone against the grain with many, though I approve of his policy myself, to see him with so many sons-in-law who have nothing Welsh about them except their lands!"

Our friend's eyes shone, and his swarthy cheeks darkened with pleasure. "Would I really—" he began.

The sly old antiquary was delighted with the effect of this casual suggestion; for it is certain that whomever else he may have considered as a partner for Owen's child, he had never thought of Rhisiart.

"I only hope," he went on hurriedly, "that when this foolish war-scare has blown over—for of course we know in our hearts that Providence has intended our two races to live side by side—you'll be able to make your cousin see that the policy of all wise people must be the unity of Ynys Prydain! Why, in that old book of mine from which I recall reading to you a passage on your first night here, it is always assumed that the rulers of Wales do homage for their lands to the King in London. You must remember, lad, that *we* gave London her kings in the old time; and who knows whether in future times we shan't do the same! The great thing is for the two races to intermarry."

"But, sir!" interrupted Rhisiart, proud to think he was discussing affairs of state. "Didn't you say that people round here blamed my cousin for marrying his daughters to—"

The old gentleman gave him a shrewd glance. "I said his *daughters,* lad. What *I* would like to see would be a marriage between Meredith ab Owen and a little princess of the House of Lancaster. *Then,* if there were a child, for you must remember that Owen through his mother is as much the rightful heir to South Wales as he is through his father to Gwynedd and Powys, that child would be, I tell you, successor to both Edward the Third *and* Rhodri Mawr! That *is,"* he added with a frown, "unless the Percies dethrone King Harry to put the little—bravo! well caught, Mistress Efa!—the little Earl of March in his place."

While they were thus conversing Rhisiart observed the familiar figure of Mad Huw approaching them. Now it was well known to every gossip in the castle that the Grey Friar was always careful to avoid the sight of his devoted Maid when she was engaged in these youthful sports. Some scandal-mongers maintained that it was a carnal temptation to the worthy man to see her fling herself about in the ardour of the game. Others attributed it to a cloistered prejudice against any mingling of the sexes. Whatever its cause, Rhisiart felt an uncomfortable sense of foreboding when the man broke his custom and came hurrying up to them.

"They tell me in the guard-room," he began at once, taking no notice of our friend and addressing the Seneschal, "that there have been three messengers to-day asking for Master Denis. I listened while the men at the gate were talking; and I heard them say that it *was* true the Usurper had returned from Scotland. I heard one man say he'd got his whole army with him and had·already reached York. Of course *we* know"—here he turned to our friend and gave him a significant and exultant look—"what this lost soul is after, and that God has already defeated his devil's design— But I've come to suggest to you, Master Seneschal, that the castle-beacon should be lit at once. *We* know where God's Richard is; but it might be wise to warn the people that the enemy of God is on his way."

The mingling of native shrewdness with maniacal fantasy in Mad Huw's remarks struck Rhisiart deeply. As he looked from this prophetic figure standing there with its outstretched arm pointing towards the gate, while the game before them grew momently more absorbing, it struck him that it was a curious thing to see all these lovely young creatures so oblivious of the larger game of which the more responsible minds in Dinas Bran were so gravely aware.

Of course it was absurd of the Friar to suggest lighting the castle-beacon of an English out-post to warn the Welsh of the approach of the English King. But if the Constable chose to be absent when events of such importance were in the air anyone in Dinas Brān had a right to make suggestions.

"Master Seneschal must be wishing more than any of us," Rhisiart now blurted out, contemplating with his swarthy narrow face and sucked-in lips both the Friar and the old man, "that Denis Burnell would return."

Adda ap Leurig directed towards the young man a dull unresponsive stare. "That is as it may be," he replied laconically. And then added, "But I trust you and Master Brut, and you too, Brother Huw, aren't tired of the manner—inadequate as I admit it is—in which the Constable's responsibility has been carried on in his absence?" Nothing in any king's court could have surpassed in dignity the bow and smile with which Mad Huw received these words.

But Rhisiart was less polite. "You won't hand us over to Bolingbroke, I trust, sir, whatever demands you receive from the English camp?"

The old man's face stiffened; and he gave a quick glance at the Friar, evidently afraid lest the allusion to Richard's enemy should produce an outburst. But Mad Huw was following at that moment some rather severe test of his Maid's skill so intently that he didn't seem to have caught our friend's words.

Rhisiart followed the Friar's gaze. Certainly the Maid of Edeyrnion looked by far the most athletic of the four girls and by far the best proportioned. Alice's figure was more voluptuous; but the boyish resilience of Tegolin's muscles struck our friend's mind as more beautiful. But just now he was not only concerned with beauty. He found a peculiar and special pleasure, though it could hardly be called an aesthetic one, as he watched these girls at play, in their appealing *awkwardness*. How funnily they threw the ball when they got hold of it! Was that due, he wondered, to the natural softness of the upper portion of a girl's arm where it touches her bosom, or was it due to some inescapable pliability in her bones that forbade the stiffer purchase necessary for a powerful fling? And if their awkwardness pleased him, another thing that afforded his satisfaction was to watch their self-consciousness increase as they began to get hot and dishevelled, and to note how in any pause their fingers would fly to their heads or to their belts.

From these philosophical contemplations our friend, turning his attention to his neighbour, found the Seneschal sitting bolt upright upon the bench, his thin figure erect, and his eyes fixed, not on the crisis in the match, but on the ground at his feet. It was at once evident to Rhisiart that the man was making some important decision; so that it did not surprise him when lifting his head and speaking with a grave deliberation he uttered the following words:

"I may as well tell you, young Master, that there is to be a conclave to-night, over our supper-board, at which your presence, and that of your heretical friend over there, will be required. My Lord of Nannau and his friend, David Gam, arrived at the Tassel last night. Father Rheinalt is expected this afternoon at Valle Crucis, and as soon as the Prior has received him, he and Father Pascentius will come up here to meet these gentlemen."

Rhisiart's countenance fell. The last persons he desired to meet in Dinas Brān were Hywel Sele and the notorious David. He was faintly re-assured by the thought of Tegolin's father being present; but towards Father Pascentius his attitude was only a little less nervous than towards the brutal pair of Anglophiles.

But the Norman blood in his veins did him a wise turn at this juncture. While he was debating legal niceties in the Oxford lecture-rooms this same Norman blood had often stood him in good stead; and now it enabled him to turn upon the Seneschal a frank, disarming, and almost stupidly ingenuous face. It enabled him in fact to open his eyes and mouth with modest astonishment. It enabled him to express the hope that in his meeting with Sele and David he would bear himself as befitted a cousin of Glyn Dŵr's; and he concluded by expressing a puzzled and almost childish wonder that the impetuous Rheinalt should dare to meet these dangerous and remorseless free-booters; and that he hoped the patriotic Cistercian wouldn't say anything to excite their fury The tone he took completely re-assured the old man.

"To tell you the truth, Master," the Seneschal said, "I had this morning a message from Owen himself proposing to come and meet these men. But I replied at once begging him not to run such a mad risk. I told him that it would be very difficult for me to protect him. I warned him that it wasn't only Welshmen who knew about the date prophesied by Iolo Goch, and now so near."

All sorts of agitating ideas rushed through Rhisiart's head at this piece of news. But he forced his narrow face to grow almost square in its simple ardour, while his indrawn lips fell apart in a look of gaping trustfulness.

And Adda ap Leurig went on making the mistake that sly old men make when they underrate the subtlety of youth. He added yet more to his revelations; for he was clearly anxious for reasons of his own not to keep his prisoner in the dark, as long as such enlightenment could be, as it were, brought about inadvertently and without too great a shock. So, like a butterfly whose antennae are delicately feeling the plant it hopes to use for its purpose, the Seneschal lingered upon his words, ready to shear off the moment their implications produced trouble.

"I knew," he went on, "from Owen's message, that he was growing anxious about your fate and that of your friend. I could see he fully understood *my* dilemma, being, as I am, the Constable's representative here. And it seemed to me that in his consideration for both parties—for myself as responsible for you to the King, and for you as his hostages with the King—he was prepared to take a very serious personal risk. It was to avoid this risk—for Hywel Sele, in spite of their relationship, which is, I understand, much nearer than your own, hates Owen with a murderous hatred—that I took the course I did; for I was sure that both of you honourable young gentlemen would have bidden me to do so. I refer to the course of strongly dissuading him from such madness. In fact I went so far as to *forbid* him, in the name of the Constable, and of the Sheriff, and of the King, to come near Dinas Brān at this dangerous moment! As to his further plans, I told him I wished to hear *nothing* of them, and indeed refused to hear anything. I told him bluntly that I held Dinas Brān for the King, and that if he approached it in the present tension of feeling, I should man the walls and hoist the Royal Standard."

The old man drew breath, and sank back on the bench, exhausted with his effort. But this didn't prevent his directing towards his hearer, through half-closed eyelids, a long searching look.

Our young man, however, promptly turned away his head, leaving Master Adda to close his eyes to the warm autumnal sunlight, and to subside, or pretend to subside, into a peaceful sleep. But Rhisiart's face now took on its narrowest Norman intensity. He sucked in his lips till his mouth became like a crack in a sun-baked ridge of sandstone, and he fixed his frowning stare not upon the game, which was reaching its close with the victory of Tegolin's side, but upon the scarred and broken terraces of the Eglwyseg Rocks.

Ever afterwards, thinking of this moment, he associated these jagged precipices and cosmogonic bastions with the grim thoughts against which his spirit was beating like a wounded bird. Was it the old man's intention, he wondered, to make an indirect appeal to him, and through him to the Lollard, to be ready, *for Owen's sake,* to be handed over to Henry of Lancaster?

A horrid vision came between him and those blood-streaked jagged rocks. He saw himself in the position of an unhappy traitor he had once seen on the scaffold in Hereford; and the pit of his stomach turned at the thought. He saw Master Brut bound with chains to a bull-baiting stake while men in leather jerkins and with bare hairy arms piled faggots round him. His lips just then were not available for smiling; but a sardonic self-mockery crossed his mind when he recalled the dark emotion with which he had thought of making love to Lowri while her eyes met those of the victimized Simon.

"There's nothing," he thought, "like being put through it oneself to see one's blood-lust in its true proportion!" And then he thought, "What a thing that it should be *my* life that will probably end now and not anyone else's! And except for the ordinary execution-crowd no one will know! The crowd will disperse, each to his home; *but where will Rhisiart be?*"

He was so absorbed in his dark thoughts that he was hardly aware that the match was over and that the players were either standing about discussing the game or moving slowly away. Seeing their outward forms with only a very faint consciousness of their identity, he now noticed the Friar and Tegolin advancing to meet each other. With this same lacklustre eye he watched them meet. With this same lack-lustre eye he watched the childish pride with which the Friar congratulated the girl on her victory.

Mad Huw and Tegolin, after all, he had only known for a few months; but *himself, his* consciousness, Rhisiart's feeling about Rhisiart, he had known as long as he could remember, and it was *this* that now faced its end! That punctilious little grey man at his side, no longer pretending to sleep, talking quite naturally to Luned just as he might have done if it had been *someone else,* had been hinting that the youth called Rhisiart was destined to be hung and quartered! *Then* there would not be anyone in the world to say, "Rhisiart is Rhisiart—*that is, I am I.*"

Our friend had got as far in his thoughts, when once more he felt physically sick. He couldn't forget certain particular circumstances of what he had seen in Hereford. Barrels of burning lime, or bubbling tar, rose up before him; into which certain shapeless and bloody objects, that five minutes before had been the limbs of a living man, were plunged by the help of iron prongs. "I mustn't begin to spue," he thought, for he suddenly felt in his vitals the nausea that comes to mortal men when they *really take in* that what has happened to someone else is likely to happen to themselves.

Instinctively he turned his gaze to his friend, Master Brut, resolving that he would ask him in a moment to accompany him on a walk round the battlements. He felt he *must* tell Master Brut what peril they were in, and tell him at once. The excellent man would probably preach him a sermon about trusting in the Lord, and expound to him where the doctrine of Master Huss in regard to death differed from that of Master Wycliffe, but for some reason he felt just now that such a discourse would be a comfort.

But just as he was going to summon his friend, young Efa came running up to the Lollard to implore him to accede to some caprice that had suddenly entered her lively head.

Rhisiart was actually on his feet now; but he hung back, watching Efa's coquetry. The young girl was certainly the loveliest creature, save Owen's daughter, that he had ever seen, and he felt that for light-hearted love-making, as intense in its concentration as it was remorseless in its dodging of responsibility, he and Efa were exactly suited to each other. They were indeed, he now decided, *too* suited to each other; for ever since she had slapped his face in the ruined chapel, where they had come much nearer to cheating Derfel than they had intended, he had shown himself as haughty with her as she was haughty with him.

It *had* entered his head once or twice that this mutual pride was silly, since, like himself, she had no heart, that organ he so especially dreaded in women! But a slap in the face *was* a slap in the face; and it wasn't very nice to have to sleep on his right side for nearly a week!

All the same, as he watched her now, leaning forward against the Lollard's stout figure and twisting between her fingers one of the buttons of his tunic, while her curls brushed his shoulder, the doubt did penetrate our friend's consciousness as to whether he'd been wise in doing nothing but sleep on his right side. Suppose he *had* given his dignity to the devil and made love to her again? Would a couple of months spent in irresponsible pleasure have enabled him to regard those bubbling barrels and iron prongs with equanimity; or would they—

But Efa had left the Lollard now—apparently with his consent to her plan—and was racing from Luned to Tegolin, and from Tegolin to Alice.

Not only the hang-dog Lawnslot—whose ugly visage had from the start brought bloody executions into Rhisiart's mind—but quite a large group of troopers from the guard-room were still hanging about, some no doubt with the hope of an assignation with the Ruthin girl, others just content to stare as long as they dared at the irresistible Efa. Rawlff and the other boy, however, had clearly had enough of feminine society. They had both been on the losing side; and Rhisiart saw them now hurry off with obvious relief upon some private enterprise of their own.

But Master Brut now approached the Seneschal with a bland and smiling countenance.

"With your permission, sir," he said, "our four lasses propose to give us a round or two from an old Welsh dance. Mistress Alice knows it quite as well as our young ladies here, and little Efa swears to me that there is nothing in it that could offend."

Adda ap Leurig seemed at first unable to catch his meaning. "Offend?" he repeated as if thinking aloud. "Offend? It must need be that offences come, but woe to that man by whom—but quite right, quite right, though for myself you'll have to excuse me. I've got to make certain—arrangements—we're expecting various important guests to-night to what poor cheer our kitchen and buttery can provide, and I must bestir myself. Master Rhisiart will tell you that I hope to have"—he spoke with a deliberate gravity and emphasis—"the honour of the presence of you both at our little—banquet. And you, Brother," and he turned to Mad Huw, who was evidently undergoing some interior emotional struggle, "must beg Mistress Tegolin to excuse you, too; for I have a wounded man on my hands in need of spiritual consolation."

There was something about this direct appeal to his divine office—an appeal which, owing to his eccentricity, the poor man had not received for years—that touched the Friar to the heart. His whole face lit up. "Certainly I will come," he responded. "At once, at once! Let us not linger a moment. Even now it may be too late!"

Rhisiart did not fail to notice, as the two went off together, the fine politeness with which the Seneschal refused to give to any of them that

look of sly complicity with which normal human beings tend to con-
spire together to make sport of the abnormal. "The Welsh," he said to
himself, "are certainly the most civilized people in the world."

But the Lollard wanted his help now to spread upon the ground long
strips of brightly-coloured ribbon, making squares and angles and ob-
longs upon the flag-stones.

"At home," the Lollard said, "our ribbons are fastened to the pole;
and the dancers hold them in their hands. But in this dance, which is
called the *Dawns Gwymon* or Sea-weed Dance, the girls pick up the
ribbons from the ground and exchange them with one another. It must
have been danced originally upon the sea-sand; and like all extremely
ancient dances it has a number of inflexible rules for every movement,
and nothing is left to chance or to personal mood or caprice." He now
turned to the four young dancers who were talking eagerly together,
and began clapping his hands in a monotonous beat. The troopers who
had drifted to the scene immediately followed his example, as also did
Lawnslot and Gerallt. By degrees, under a few signs from Master Brut,
all the men present formed themselves into an extended circle around
the dancers, every one of them keeping up this monotonous beat of
hand-clapping.

Rhisiart was quite startled by the peculiar sensation that came to him
as he joined the other men; a feeling as if in some odd fashion he were
joining a musical accompaniment that had had no beginning and could
have no end! He felt as if he and all his companions were *intruding*
upon some unearthly ritual that had always been going on, though only
as they began to share it had it become visible and audible to them; and
as he clapped his hands in rhythm, he felt as though the stiff, mechanical
movements which the four girls now began to make, as they stooped to
pick up the ribbons and raising them above their heads wove them into
a swaying pattern as they danced, were inescapably forced upon them
by this monotone of beaten hands.

Where he stood he was facing the Lollard, and though the man's face
was often concealed by the weaving and unweaving of the dance, when
he did catch sight of it, it wore an expression that completely puzzled
him. It was a religious expression, and might have been called a mystical
expression, and yet it was full of a kind of ecstatic sensuality. Its ex-

pression reminded him of the look he used to catch in Hereford Cathedral on the face of a certain choir-boy when he was singing the *"tantum ergo."*

For himself Rhisiart was surprised at the difference of his feelings from those he had when he was watching the game of ball. "It must," he thought, "be those barrels and prongs." But it *couldn't* have been the barrels and prongs; for that vision of unspeakable frightfulness had already sunk away to the far background of his mind, where it lay like a blood-red bruise. No, it was something different. While that game had gone on he had watched each one of these girlish forms with satyrish interest. But now in some strange way the natural appeal of bodies and limbs struck him with a piercing sense of pathos. "It's for the bearing of children," he thought, just as if he had never seen a woman before, "that their hips are formed like that!"

The truth was that all the mechanical movements they were making now, as their arms rose and fell and their bodies bent and straightened with the weaving and unweaving of the ribbons, and all in obedience to the unceasing beat of the hands that encircled them, emphasized this curious pathos. Those soft arms, those tender bosoms, those curved limbs, what could be more unlike the complicated series of clear-cut, doll-like, automatic gestures into which they were being forced under the mandate of that monotonous clapping?

At any rate, as he went on beating his hands, he felt as if he could hardly distinguish one girl from another! The voluptuous limbs of Alice seemed forced into a frieze-like purity of outline as they followed these scrupulous measures, while the luxuriant breasts of Luned seemed to tighten and dwindle into Artemisian maidenliness as she spasmodically lifted and lowered her arms.

Tegolin's red braid, not content with tapping against her own shoulders, seemed sometimes to resemble a fiery shuttle that passed in and out of the flaxen curls of Efa, and the dusky tresses of Luned. At certain moments in the dance, under rules so automatic that the gesture reminded Rhisiart of priests at an altar, each pair of dancers formally and lightly gave each other a mechanical kiss.

From where Rhisiart stood, beating his hands together, he could see further than the stiff movements of these soft creatures hypnotized out of their natural capriciousness by the imperative of an archaic tradition. He was tall enough to see through a gap in the battlements the whole plain of Maelor spread out before him.

And as he gazed he was aware that a peculiar and emerald-coloured light had obliterated all impertinent and teasing details, leaving intact only the universal aspects of the world—the earth, the air, and the water. Yes, stretched out before him in that curious Homeric light, for the girls were dancing close to the battlements, Maelor melted into Bromfield and Bromfield melted into the pastures of Shropshire. The light was indeed so green that it was as if the fiery sun had changed into a huge translucent emerald. The rich aftermath of meadow grass broke the distance into a vast chess-board of the Immortals, and so enchanted in its windless calm did the scene look that the smoke that rose from the plain and kept forming itself into filmy wreaths took the shape for him of god-like Beings moving across an emerald stage.

And then he thought of the thunderbolt that was to fall on all this when Owen raised the red dragon. Instead of soft blue wreaths of delicate vapour there would be vast-rolling clouds of black smoke, and shrieks and tumult and blood and flames! Beat—beat—went his hands, along with hands of his companions; and the more tired the men grew of clapping the more obstinately they clapped.

The girls themselves were well-nigh spent by this time, but Rhisiart knew in his heart that until they actually fainted away nothing would induce them to stop till the men stopped.

But suddenly the men *did* stop; and instantaneously the girls sank back against the battlements; sank back so entangled with ribbons that they might have given Rhisiart, or anyone else who had the heart to think of such things, the idea of tangles of sea-weed and iridescent sea-spray clinging to a flotsam of stranded Nereids!

But the thoughts of our friend, as well as the thoughts of every other man there, had left both the dance and the dancers. A burst of trumpet-blasts had reached them from the gate of the castle, and as they all turned towards the guard-room they saw the emblazoned pennon of the Royal Arms flutter slowly to the top of the flagstaff. There was a general rush across the court towards the guard-room; and Rhisiart and the Lollard heard several shrill bugle-calls summoning the castle-servants to appear at the gate.

Never had our friend seen Mistress Lowri look prouder or happier than when on the arm of Denis she came up the steps that afternoon! The misty autumn sun fell upon her rich dress, for she had been riding, according to the fantastical new fashion, in plum-coloured velvet and a sweeping crimson sash, but it fell too upon that indescribable radiance that emanates from women when they feel that the stars in their courses are fighting their battle!

Old Adda was far too discreet to ask any questions at their first encounter or to reveal any of his own difficulties. He held his black wand of office very straight and bowed with a low and separate bow to both Denis and Lowri.

Nor did Denis ask any questions of his Seneschal. He began to converse easily and leisurely with the old man, almost as if he were deliberately giving his lady time to greet the Lollard and our friend; and when Rhisiart, struggling to steel himself against the woman's fascination, turned to look at Denis, he found that in spite of Lowri's magnetic appeal he continued staring at him for a considerable time.

Denis Burnell had a small clipped beard which had turned so prematurely grey that when he and his father were together strangers who caught the likeness between them took them for brothers. He had the same affable manner as his father and the same quizzical hazel eyes; but there the likeness ended. Nor would it have been easy for Rhisiart to say what *did* arrest him so about the man. It was some kind of personal power; but exactly where it lay he would have been puzzled to define. One quality Denis obviously possessed and that was an unruffled calm; but along with this calm Rhisiart got the impression that the man suffered from a perpetual absent-mindedness, just as if his mind were forever functioning on two levels.

One of these levels was a world of practical necessity, in regard to which he was quick and competent; but the other was a world of inner vision which apparently reduced the former, for all his competence in it, to something as futile as it was frivolous.

Rhisiart was fully aware that in his desperate temptation he was frantically trying to put his interest in the Constable between himself and the Constable's lady. His whole nature suffered so much from the contrast within him that just as in the case of that accurst bronze sword his narrow forehead became wet with sweat.

Lowri kept addressing faintly ironical questions to the Lollard, but certain little twitchings about the corner of her mouth which was nearest to Rhisiart, accentuated by a drop of saliva left there by the tip of her tongue, seemed to convey to him a wordless intimation.

"I'm still holding you," that electric communication seemed to say. "Wait till our hands meet, and *then* you won't resist any more!"

And the cruel thing was that this tantalizing profile, with that quivering corner that so disturbed him, seemed as youthful as Tegolin's own.

But what was she saying to the Lollard? It seemed incredible to our friend; but she was actually asking Master Brut questions about the miserable Simon, questions about his attempts to escape, questions about the treatment he had received from the Seneschal.

To these questions the disciple of Wycliffe answered with an eloquent appeal on behalf of the wretched prisoner and with reiterated asseverations about what he described as "his change of heart."

Our friend was so disturbed that all manner of subtle impressions forced themselves upon his mind that ordinarily he would have lacked the wit to catch. He noted, for instance, as Denis gravely commented upon the startling news that the old Seneschal *was* at last freely imparting, how the young grey-bearded man was alluding as casually to such troublesome intruders as Hywel Sele and David Gam as if they were figures on a pictured tapestry only brought into momentary life by a suddenly-risen wind! And even while he struggled against Lowri's fatal appeal something in him exulted in vibrant spasms of sympathetic devilry as she led the Lollard on to describe in detail the various spiritual transformations that the grace of the Redeemer had worked in the desperate soul of the Hog of Chirk.

"*We*'ll see," the corners of her lips seemed to whisper in our friend's ear, "what this conversion amounts to when *we* visit him to-night!"

"I mustn't look at her! I mustn't look at her!" Rhisiart's better angel kept repeating; and he even went so far as to try to thrust between himself and those burning white fingers—for she was deliberately slipping off her riding-gloves now—that image of himself mounting the scaffold where stood those barrels of pitch.

But the stress of his feelings seemed to have turned his mind into such a sensitive plate that, while every little outward thing about him was mirrored upon it, those hooks and prongs failed to materialize. He noticed every detail, for instance, of the heavy accoutrements of certain Salopian yeomen; for quite a number of English levies had followed Denis up the hill.

It was indeed while his demon was forcing him to observe the fantastic belt of one worthy trooper, that was ornamented with the white skulls of stoats, that he became aware that a wild-looking body of Welshmen armed with spears were parleying with the gate-keeper. Something made him fix his gaze upon these men, whom the official at the gate was evidently admitting on the condition that they piled their spears against the wall; and in a flash his mind rushed to the bed in the Tower-chamber and its tantalizing occupant.

Yes, standing under the raised portcullis was none other than Crach Ffinnant himself! The prophet of Derfel was, as the Scripture says of another tricky idolator, moving "delicately." He ostentatiously laid down a not very dangerous-looking weapon by the side of the others, and while pleading with the Porter and holding up his arms so that his clothes might be searched, and turning his birth-marked cheek and scavenger's eye to everything in sight, it soon became clear that he *was* going to be allowed to skulk in. When he did get in, Rhisiart watched him wrap his heavy mantle discreetly round him and hurry off, with his head bent and with furtive glances to left and right, straight in the direction of the Ladies' Tower.

"He looks like a stoat," thought our friend, "entering a rabbit's burrow. I shall certainly tell Luned to warn Ffraid ferch Gloyw. I wonder if they'll let *him* have a share of this damned banquet? I'd wish him luck if he'd throw his evil eye on Cousin Sele's smug face!"

It was with an ice-cold shiver at his heart and a rush to his lean cheekbones of blood that pricked and burnt that he now gave Lowri a nod, for he couldn't force his lips to utter a sound, when she asked him to come to her presence-room in an hour's time. "Knock three times slowly and then three times quickly," she told him, "and if I don't open at once *go away at once.*"

Never in his life had he experienced, never was he destined to experience again, any hour like the hour that came upon him then. The Russian's ravening "insect" had now possessed itself entirely of his will; and whenever he thought of how hotly twisting her fingers would be as she let him have his pleasure while her eyes clung to the eyes of her victim, his knees shook under him and everything round him darkened and receded.

But though the Russian's "insect" *had* to be fed, and all questions of deciding against feeding it had come to an end, the strange thing was that the rest of his nature, his ordinary sensitized being, instead of feeling atrophied by this horrible obsession, this fact that his will was *all insect,* seemed to have become abnormally porous to every kind of impression. His senses felt praeternaturally alert, just as they had been three months ago, when he was hypnotized by the voice of Ffraid ferch Gloyw.

He accompanied the Lollard back to the Traitor's Chamber, conveying to him in brief and unnecessarily pessimistic words all he had learnt from the Seneschal. "They may call it a banquet," he assured the good man, "but what it is for us is a gallows' supper. It's simply a conclave of our executioners. You mark my words, Brut. Hywel Sele and David Gam will insist bluntly that we should be given up."

"Given up, lad?" questioned the other. "Given up to whom?"

"To King Harry," Rhisiart blurted out fiercely, "who'll burn *you* and hang and quarter *me!*"

The psychological disciple of Wycliffe gave his friend a very straight look. He seemed to divine that all was not well with the boy's nerves. His face assumed its most irritating look of smiling aplomb; but all he actually said was that the spirit of Christ was as powerful in the English camp as it was within the walls of Dinas Brān.

This reference to something in the castle that it *couldn't eat* kept the Russian's "insect" and its perambulating shard in sulky silence.

The Lollard was consequently extremely relieved when he got the obsessed young man to sit down by his side on his bed. The Traitor's Chamber was a good deal more draughty and very much damper than Myfanwy's Bower, and it was furnished more like a guard-room than a guest-room. Master Brut, however, had made his little arrangements. He had moved his straw-pallet under a portion of the roof that still kept the rain out. He had got his Greek Testament and his *Consolations* of Boëthius neatly spread out on a battered chest at the head of this unpromising couch; and as they had done almost every evening during these months the two young men sat down together there and talked without turning their heads, as naturally as if they were talking to themselves.

"You've got something on your mind," said the Lollard at last, after trying in vain to interest his friend in the latest development of the spiritual growth of Alice of Ruthin.

But instead of answering him Rhisiart jumped to his feet. "God in Heaven!" he cried. "I'd forgotten the news I've got for the Ladies' Tower! Our friend the Scab is here; and the Lady Ffraid ought to be warned of it at once."

"What are you going to do?" And the Lollard, also risen to his feet, bent down and very deliberately placed the Greek Testament on the top of Boëthius.

Rhisiart turned on him when he reached the door. "Find someone who *can* be trusted in this damned place!"

The Lollard's smile vanished. "You're beginning to forget, my friend," he said sternly, "that I'm no more an Englishman than you are. There's no race in the world more trustworthy than the Welsh; *when they're properly handled*. To put your own head on the block isn't trustworthy: it's insane."

"Oh shut up, for Christ's sake! Sometimes I think there's no bigger fool on either side of the Dyke than you are, Walter! You may understand Greek; but you don't understand *me!*"

With this our irascible friend slammed the oaken door of the Traitor's Chamber and made off in a blind huff. "I'd like to take a glance at that presence-room of hers," remarked the hungry "insect" within him while its hollow shard rattled huskily. "I feel as if the mere look of the place would help me to bear the delay!"

Rhisiart knew well enough where this room was, but he had instinctively avoided it during the last three months. As he approached it now, however, whom should he meet, returning from their bird's-nesting excursion, but the two pages! The boys stopped at once. They had much to tell him. But he cut short their confidences. "Want an excuse to climb the Ladies' Tower and be sure of a welcome?" he craftily said addressing Rawlff.

"And me too?" put in the younger boy.

"Certainly, sonny, if Rawlff lets you! But the message, remember, is only to be given to the Lady Ffraid herself."

"Tell me what it is, Master Rhisiart; and I'll decide whether under the circumstances it would be wise or unwise to take a kid like this into our confidence."

The son of Cynan flushed fiery-red; but professional shrewdness, even in the smallest of all the pages of Dinas Brān, enabled him to be patient. "It's no good getting angry," he must have said to himself. "The great thing is *not to be left behind*. I can settle with this conceited ass later."

"It's a perfectly simple message," Rhisiart said, "and since you're both friends of Luned and Efa you'll realize its importance. It's to tell the Lady Ffraid that Crach Ffinnant's *already in the castle*."

The boys exchanged a quick glance of full understanding, and without another word or sign darted off towards the Ladies' Tower. Rhisiart paused to watch them disappear; and then, urged on by his obsessed will which dragged his conscience, his soul, his senses, his nerves, like a row of captives tied together by the neck, he advanced towards the fatal door. "It can't be more than thirty minutes," he said to himself, "since she said 'come in an hour,' but I may as well have a look at the place."

A couple of Salopian troopers strolled past in the September twilight. They were engaged in political discussion. "What *I* say," one of them was remarking, "is that the sooner it comes the better. I don't give a damn for this chatter about bardic predictions. What *I* say is that these Welshies need a lesson. And they'll get it too—you mark my words! They say in Chirk that the Earl told Grey to keep his people within the walls, so as to lead on that braggart Glendourdy. And who *is* Glendourdy anyway? Only a whoreson bandid! Let the beggar revolt *I* say! What we want is an excuse to scotch the sly snake once and for all. I wish the Welshies *would* come out. But they won't! You mark my words; they *won't*. They won't give us a chance. Christmas will see things just as they are now. A few fines, maybe. But you know what the King is. He's too lenient. He'll fine 'em, and let 'em go. If I had *my* way he'd burn the beggars out, once and for all, whether they rose or not! Burn 'em out! That's the only way to give these whoreson bards a lesson. Let 'em skip for their own whoreson skins and you'd soon see. Of course the King ought to call up the Staffordshire folk as well as we.

Why should *we* always bear the brunt on the Marches? If I were Harry do'ee know what I'd do—" but the voice died away before our listener could learn this nice point.

He walked straight towards the door and the curious thing was that his knees knocked together as he moved and he kept jerking his dagger half in, half out of its sheath. The nearer he approached the half-ruined mass of masonry on this north-west side of Dinas Brān the more hungry beccame the Russian's "insect." But if it possessed the power of dragging an individual's reason and conscience after it, it possessed no flicker of authority over the antics of the great goddess Chance. And Chance bestirred herself now.

For *what was that?* His obsessed eyes had been so absorbed in that closed door, a door which was easy enough to recognize by reason of its new-fangled modernity and the way some tricky craftsman had carved all manner of Frenchified levities above its lintel, a door which he knew better than any other door in the castle, just *because* for three months he had refused to turn his head towards it, that it was with a startled shock, a shock so great that it made him feel physically dizzy, that he now caught sight of the repulsive little figure of the Tower dwarf, standing with her impish back to him and lost to the whole world as she gazed through an upper light of one of those flamboyant foliated windows.

The little creature had climbed up upon the exterior ledge of the window through which she stared; and her thin extended arms clutched mechanically at the newly-chipped mouldings of the tracery. In this position she resembled, to our friend's abnormally acute senses, a female crucifix turned back-to-front. What was she watching there with such intensity? It was indeed more than intensity. The dwarf's whole being seemed to be resolving itself into the masonry of the stone-work to which she clung! So death-still was she that her motion-lessness made him think of a chrysalis; though as he stared at what was a symbol of *more than staring* he felt that if he could have seen this crucified chrysalis from the *inside* there would have been some-thing frightful about the expression on its face.

But the Russian's "insect" now decided that it was not fair—and what a sight that purple beard would be, squeezed against the pane, if the persons within the chamber were to glance up!—that a demented dwarf should gloat alone in solitary ecstasy at such interesting spectacles.

And so our friend, under its guidance, with exquisite caution, and moving like a creature who possessed the cunning of the insane, climbed up the stone-work till he was just behind Mother Sibli. There, bringing his hand in absolute silence to within an inch of the back of that grotesque cranium, he clapped it on her mouth and lifting her from the window and pressing her like a helpless infant against his ribs, he took her place at the small broken window-light. For *that* was, he discovered, the reason why this peeping-hole was so ecstatically satisfying. The coloured glass in that particular pane had been broken. You could hear as well as see what was going on.

Rhisiart was soon made aware that he wasn't crushing the life out of the dwarf, by reason of the sharp teeth that began at once to draw blood from his hand; but what he was watching and listening to inside the presence-room held him so transfixed that it was a wonder he didn't break the small creature's bones in absolute unconsciousness.

The presence-room was luxuriously furnished in that fashionable end-of-the-century style that Rhisiart's mother loved so well and which his aesthetic Oxford friends regarded as the height of ostentatious vulgarity.

Huddled upon the edge of the spacious bed, his arms tied tight behind him and his feet manacled together, so that he could only have moved, had he been compelled to do so, by a series of grotesque jumps, crouched Master Simon, while before him, coolly and calmly putting the finishing touches to her toilet for the banquet, was the Lady Lowri, looking so deadly lovely, with her white cheeks and scarlet lips, her long curved eye-lashes and arctic-ice eyes, that with the same hand that was closing the dwarf's mouth Rhisiart, in feverish emotion, began twisting the creature's beard into stiff little horns. These horns he continued to make constantly stiffer and more pointed; for his fingers were hot and moist and the beard was naturally adhesive.

"Will you love me just the same when that ugly little boy comes," he heard the Lady say to the Hog of Chirk, "and I let him do anything he likes? Will you love me *then?*"

Shockingly husky and hollow was the man's reply. "If you kiss me," he said, "like you did just now I could bear anything. But why should the boy die when his life's only beginning?"

"You don't think I'd let him live—*afterwards,* do you? But I won't poison him. You needn't look like that! I'll just hand him over to the worst devil in Wales, that traitor who's coming here to-night, Sele of Nannau! Nobody will ever hear of him again. Let him tell Sele all he likes. He won't tell anybody else."

And then the husky voice began again; and Rhisiart could now catch a glimpse of the man's eyes which seemed to him *all sockets,* as if two diminutive glow-worms of glittering fire swam in two circular bottomless cavities!

"Will you kiss me—like you did just now—*when he's gone?*"

"You liked that, did you?" she whispered, hovering above him so that he could breathe her breath.

But what Rhisiart had already not failed to miss was the way these strange creatures clung with their eyes to each other's eyes, all the while they were talking. Not for one second did their eyes cease from this feverish clutch; and it seemed to the eavesdropper that it was because their eyes were clinging in this particular way that their words sounded like the broken speech of people who are dancing, or of people who are riding in a boat, rocked by the undulating waves. That was indeed, he found out afterwards, what sank most deeply into his consciousness, the sense that this manacled man, whose gleaming eye-candles floated in such dark cavities, and this dazzling creature in yellow satin *were* actually dancing some strange mad love-dance together, such as might easily turn into a death-dance for anyone who meddled with it! And that was to have been *his* rôle! In the dusk outside that window he felt such a wave of gratitude at his escape that he positively murmured three "Hail Marys." He also became so conscious of the inconvenience he was causing little Sibli that he bent down and whispered in her ear.

"We're in the same galley, Mistress," he breathed, "and we've got to keep this to ourselves—do you understand?"

The sharp teeth ceased biting his hand and a sound that resembled suppressed giggling issued from the living bundle he was pressing against him.

"Will you still love me whatever I let him do?" repeated the woman in yellow satin.

"In chains," retorted the man on the bed, "and without my hands, how can I know *you* still love *me!* Oh, if I only had you back at Chirk, if I only had you back at Chirk—"

"What would you do? Not *that* again—not what I told Fitz-Alan?"

"Yes, yes! just that!"

"You'd never dare!"

"Try me!", and those sockets became like lanterns in a pair of mephitic wells. "You'd have hung me if Meredith ab Owen hadn't come."

"Listen, Simon. Would you love me still if I brought *him* in here and let *him* have me?"

"You don't mean young Rhisiart now?"

"Of course not! I mean Rheinalt."

The Hog of Chirk, after an unpleasant struggle to rise to his feet, during which she never put out a finger to help him, turned back to her and hopping towards her on his chained legs made frantic clutches at her body with his bound hands.

But she twitched her dress out of his fingers and clasped him round the head, blinding those obsessed eyes. "I *know* you," she cried. "You won't believe me that I hate him until I've driven him mad. But why should I do that?

"Tegolin loves him."

Then it was permitted to Rhisiart—who, after a little more whispering had lifted up Sibli so that she could share with him the broken pane—to behold a queer sight. For the satin-gowned lady turned this shocking figure of a half-clothed ruffian round about in her hands, till the two of them were facing each other. His chains clanked as she turned him; and she did it just as if his coarsely-garmented hairy torso had been something inanimate. Then she forced him backwards, compelling him to make half-a-dozen grotesque leaps, until she got him against the wall. Then she flung her whole weight upon him, clutching his hair with her fingers while she assaulted his scarred face with a rain of burning kisses.

"*Order* me to send him mad! *Order* me to send him mad!" she gasped, and tugging at his hair she shook his great haggard face to and fro, as if she had been a lurcher-bitch worrying a rabbit.

It was only when she paused for a second to take breath, letting her hands sink down that Rhisiart had an opportunity to catch the look in the man's face, and it was a look he remembered all his days. It was a look of beatified bliss. It was the look Saint Stephen must have had when they were stoning him and he saw the heavens opened.

Master Simon was now propped helplessly against the wall; and indeed, if it had not been for an unevenness in the stone floor against which he pressed his heels, he would have sunk down under her weight. For oblivious of the effect upon her thin satin gown she cuddled close against him, quivering and twisting like a mesmerized serpent.

Rhisiart, as he watched them, forgot to suck in his lips. His mouth for some seconds remained open like the mouth of a gudgeon. He found himself treating the little monster who shared his eavesdropping as if she had possessed a normal feminine shape. It was upon the emotion of Lowri that the Russian's "insect" was now concentrating; and he had cause enough to open his mouth! He was witnessing just then for the first and last time in his life what few men have been privileged to contemplate; namely, the writhings of a lust-demented lady on the breast of a man whose arms were tied behind his back.

Strangely enough it was with the woman and not with the man in this singular scene that our friend was identifying himself. It was into *her* nerves, not into those of the Hog of Chirk, that his demon passed. Each convulsive shudder of that beautiful form under that satin robe was like a spasm of his own; and the tension between her and that unsightly torso was like the tension between the most reckless, the most desperate, the most instinctive desire in him and something, some Person, some indescribable Reciprocity that had been escaping him ever since he set out on his quest. His thoughts soon became completely inarticulate. A power, an impulse, was stirring into which his conscious mind could give no rational form. Of one thing, however, he *was* aware. The Russian "insect" was submerged, drowned, lost! Had it perished of surfeit?

He suddenly felt *physically light,* as if no material obstacle could resist him. The fancy rushed through his brain that this whole scene was taking place *in his mind,* as he watched, light as a feather, the dipping of his own limbs in those barrels of pitch! He was dying for Owen. He *had* died for Owen. It was against the majestic torso of Owen that his soul, now quivering in spasms like hers, would soon be at rest, untroubled, dissolved, satisfied!

He had quite ceased from treating the dwarf he was supporting as if she were a woman. *He* in some extraordinary way was the woman now. No! not a woman; a spirit, light as a feather! Was he going off his head? Those barrels, those prongs, had vanished altogether. The scaffold had vanished. He was no longer Rhisiart ab Owen. *Who* was he? He was Efa. He was Efa giving herself up for Owen's triumph. But not to the Scab. To Owen himself! Owen was his own prophet. Owen was his own high-priest of Derfel. Light as a feather, *that's* what he was! And the golden torso of Owen had now transformed itself, horribly transformed itself. It was the torso of that image of misery he had fed with the bone. It was the torso of that crucifix he'd seen in the Abbot's cell. His eyes had grown blurred. In his ears was a sound like the sound of Tegolin's cry when they were strapping Mad Huw to the cart on the gorsedd-mound.

It was through a mist now, like the mist through which he had ridden between the spears and the arrows, that he tried to see them. A wave was rocking him, so light had he become; a tidal wave that could neither sink him nor salvage him. And it was on this wave he was resting now. No, it wasn't a wave; it was Owen's breast.

Lowri's shudderings had quite ceased. She was clinging to Simon's body like yellow sea-weed to a rock. Had she fallen asleep? Was the silence that had descended upon the two of them, like the silence of the sculptured dead, like the silence of King John's tomb in Worcester Cathedral? "I mustn't disturb them," he said to himself; and he suddenly became aware, in his half-bodiless state, that he dreaded *to hear himself* knock at that fastened door. A panic seized him. What if he couldn't descend from his perch? What if he heard himself knocking and couldn't get away?

Tightening his hold on Sibli he made a few tentative movements. Oh, thank God, he wasn't paralysed! Hurriedly he clambered down to the ground. And then forgetting entirely to put the dwarf upon her feet, he ran with her, pressed tightly against his chest, till he reached the foot of the Ladies' Tower.

Here, moved by God knows what sudden impulse, he actually imprinted his lips upon the little creature's contorted visage; and, only after having done so, gently put her down.

The autumn twilight had darkened the whole sky; but there was a lantern swinging above the stone archway; and by its light, in spite of the confusion in his mind, he saw enough to be shocked by the effect of what he had just done. The little creature stood for a moment like a bird transfixed by an arrow, too dazed to die. Then without a second's warning her twitching face melted in a tempest of tears such as Rhisiart would never have supposed such a grotesque little skull could contain.

He did all he could think of to console her. He knelt down before her and stroked her hands. He called upon the Saints, upon the Holy Virgin, upon the Blessed Brān himself. He invoked Saint Bride the patroness of the Lady of the Tower. He called upon God to bear witness that he had meant no insult to her, no affront to her dignity.

" 'Twas as if you were my—as if you were my—my aunt!" he stammered.

But she gasped out some words of her own now, mixed with the sobs that shook her from head to foot. "No—one—has—ever—kissed me—before!"

Something in the tone of this made him stop referring to his aunt. He even began to discover that there was a sensation at the back of his eyes suggesting that if he couldn't comfort her quickly, he would begin to cry too. All he could do was to pick up one of her tiny hands, that seemed to be loose and lifeless as a jointed doll's at the end of her thin arms, and very gravely and very formally, in his best Hereford manner, lift this small object to his lips.

"I beg and implore you, Mistress Sibli," he murmured, as reverently as if she had been a princess, "to forgive me what I did, and to allow this night, and all that has befallen us, to be a solemn and sacred secret between us two, binding us together in a covenant, in a pledge, known to no other living soul!"

Never had Rhisiart's Norman blood stood him in better stead. As a

Welshman he would have been far too imaginative to have thought
of using a word like "covenant" or "pledge." As a Saxon he would have
been too realistic to put so much emphasis upon a point of such nice
legality.

But it was just this legal turn to the matter, as if he had given her
a document signed and sealed, that was the one thing needful. In her
in-grown, convoluted self-pity the idea of a *bond* between herself and
this impulsive young gentleman was something upon which she could
live for months and years. It was as if he'd handed her her marriage-
lines after "taking advantage" of her.

Her tears dried up, her sobs ceased. Since he was still on his knees
before her their faces were very close. But she had suddenly become
a normal woman, a woman *who had a man,* and her first instinct was
not to kiss him but to scold him.

"You ought to be dressing yourself for the banquet," she said crossly,
straightening as she spoke the collar of his tunic. "I can't think how
you'll be in time as it is! You saw how *she* was dressed. You'd better
go first to the Traitor's Room and see what your friend is putting on.
Have you a black velvet doublet with black hosen to match? If you
have, put *that* on. If you haven't— Well! you must ask Master Brut.
He's seen more of life than you."

Rhisiart rose to his feet. It was extremely disagreeable to him to be
told he had seen less of life than his devoted friend. From their first
encounter on the highway he had regarded Master Brut as a complete
ignoramus in anything that had to do with polished society. He decided
to regain his diminished prestige with his new ally by turning the conversation to the deeper psychology of love; that sphere of philosophy
in which his insight had proved so startling to the page-boys. He had
not yet learnt that although women love to exalt the intelligence of their
man to the outer world, to the man himself they dole out this admiration in a less wholesale manner.

"I thought she hated Master Simon to the death," he now began,
looking down frowningly at the lifted purple chin beneath him. "I
saw her myself trying to hang him. She seemed to want to caress the
rope that was doing it. He was only saved by Meredith ab Owen."

The small upraised visage, to which he addressed this startling
revelation, carried upon its features in the flickering lantern-light a

mysterious kind of lustre. This lustre was no mere outward phenomenon, such as a purple reflection from the creature's outraged chin.
It proceeded from a feminine heart stirred by the emotion of first love.

But Rhisiart looking down upon it from above was only anxious to
regain, what he feared he had lost, her respect for his searching intelligence. With the knitted brow of a thinker, therefore, he laid before
her the following disturbing question: "Is it possible for a woman to
order the man she loves to be hanged; and not only so, but to watch
him being hanged; and not only so, but to caress his body while it
swings? I tell you, Mistress, I saw her, I heard her! She told him she
would think of him burning in Hell whenever she drank a sip of
water!"

While he spoke in this manner, and indeed went into yet more horrid
details, Rhisiart couldn't help noticing the lustre that shone from the
dwarf's face. It crossed his mind that Sibli's actual features weren't
displeasing at all. If it weren't for the purple beard her face might even,
by *some* people any rate, be called a comely face.

But the more he was forced to confess that the countenance looking
up at him was not completely ugly the more inclined he grew to take
cold-blooded precautions. He set himself to withdraw every sort of
magnetic reciprocity from the expression with which he looked down
upon her. He tried to throw into his stare the abysmal indifference of
a cold-hearted cat to the perverse advances of a dog. He began reiterat-
ing his puzzled indignation at Lowri's behaviour. "I tell you, Mistress,
I *saw* it with my own eyes! I would be obliged if you could tell me
what has changed her since then? Or *isn't* she changed? How, from
hating him so, has she come to love him like that? But perhaps you'll
say it never was love, except on *his* side. But, Sibli, *surely* it was love!
Wasn't it love, Sibli?"

The dwarf evidently derived profound emotional satisfaction from
being appealed to decide this delicate point. She paused before replying,
not because she didn't know well what she wanted to say, but because
it was a precious moment to her to be the arbitress in this solemn Court
of Love. At last she nodded her head so vigorously that, considering the
thinness of her neck, it was hard not to feel as if her little doll-like skull
might suddenly slip out of its socket and roll to the ground.

"Then why did she want to hang him that day?" he protested.

"And why didn't she untie his hands to-night? Master Brut sees him every afternoon and always unties his hands. Lawnslot must have tied them when he brought him to her room. But why didn't she untie them?"

The Presiding Judge of the Court of Love considered this problem with a radiant countenance. "She did it afterwards—after we went away. She was in a different mood then."

"Then you *do* say she loves him? Loves him as much as he loves her?"

Once again there took place that alarmingly vigorous nodding of the small head. "As much as *he* loves *her?*" repeated Rhisiart in frowning amazement; for it seemed to him that if amorous phenomena of *this* kind were frequent in the world, neither he nor the Lollard knew much about life.

"As much as *he* loves *her?*" he reiterated stupidly.

"More!" and with this she gave her newly covenanted friend such a sharp rap with her tiny knuckles that he stepped back a pace. "More!" she repeated, her tone rising to that familiar pitch which he hadn't heard for so long. And then, making him, with a chuckle of hilarious glee, a low mock-curtsey, "More! more! *more!*" she screamed at the top of her voice. as she disappeared up the Tower-steps.

XI

ROOM FOR THE PRINCE!

THE BANQUET-HALL of Dinas Brān had fallen, by the year of grace fourteen hundred, into so ruinous a state that it was very seldom used. Indeed, if the truth must be told, the last Lord of Bromfield, Iāl and Maelor to use it regularly was that treacherous representative of the old *Tywysiog* who before betraying his province to the English had become the ancestor of our friend Rhisiart.

It was clear enough to all the guests that evening why it was that the hall was rarely used. Several wild birds that had entered the place before it was dark still fluttered about among the stone arches, arches whose particular type of masonry resembled that of the sacristy of Valle Crucis. In many places the roof had such great jagged holes in it that it must have been evident to all that had the night been stormy the banquet would have had to have been held elsewhere.

One advantage of the hall's ruinous condition was that the great volumes of smoke, which rose from more fires and larger fires than Rhisiart had ever seen in a manorial chamber, were enabled to escape into the cloudy night. The stars, as he hadn't failed to notice before he entered, were completely invisible. It wasn't possible from where he and Master Brut were seated to detect anything through those jagged apertures but thick darkness.

Rhisiart couldn't help thinking of Ffraid ferch Gloyw, tended by little Efa, alone up there in her tower; for both Luned and his friend Sibli could be seen along with the other ladies not far from where he sat. And thinking of little Efa left alone with the old lady it was a considerable relief to Rhisiart to notice among the group of Welshmen at the lower end of the hall the unmistakeable facial disfigurement and the solitary roving eye of Crach Ffinnant. Hung at intervals on the walls—though the columns of swirling smoke prevented our friend from

341

seeing more of them than the one just above his head—were large, rough, imaginary representations of former rulers of north-eastern Wales before the days when violence and treachery together brought down to the ground the mystic towers of Mathrafal.

These crudely-limned figures, darkened by smoke, dimmed by damp, had become no better than forlorn eidolons in faded torques and desecrated armour! "Slain in battle" had been their epitaph; and what was left of their once commanding presences had become like the half-ruined hall round which they hung: a rumour, a memory, a long-reiterated sigh upon the flickering streamers of the torches and the undulant eddies of the wind.

The one figure Rhisiart *could* make out, though between him and its sorrowful lineaments the smoke from a great crackling fire kept rolling, was that of a dark-bearded man with an expression of resigned desolation. Was that face, he wondered, the face of the famous traitor who was his own ancestor? "Shall *I* have that look one day," he thought, "when I have dodged the executioners of Bolingbroke by betraying Owen?"

The Lollard was talking to him earnestly and quietly all this while. No one else could hear them, for the uproar from all sides, now that the honey-hearted mead had begun to flow, was deafening, and all tongues, and all souls too, seemed loosed in a torrent of excited speech.

But the Lollard was talking about the inevitable power of Master Wycliffe's ideas when once the common people understood them.

"The common people!" thought Rhisiart sadly and bitterly. "Doesn't he realize that there's no more chance of the common people understanding such things than of their understanding Saint Thomas Aquinas?"

But Master Brut's arguments were so forcible that our sceptical friend began trying desperately to imagine a Wales wherein every serf and every serf's wife and daughter were alive to the metaphysics of the Redemption. He couldn't imagine it! "This Lollardry," he thought, "is a thing for the few; and must always be for the few! You can't put the philosophy of religion into simple brains. You can only give them the images and the symbols that have been worn smooth by the handling of centuries!"

Lending, therefore, but half his mind to the discourse of his companion, Rhisiart allowed his attention to wander at large over the torch-lit spectacle of that ruined hall.

The women were all seated together; and he was hard put to it, as his gaze scanned their faces, to convey to each particular pair of eyes, as his own encountered them, the appropriate recognition of a special understanding. With Tegolin this was easy, and with Tegolin alone. The Maid was dressed in blue, and with her flaming hair falling loose and unbound over her shoulders she looked more beautiful than he had ever seen her.

But she met his glance in the old spontaneous manner, with a direct comprehensive smile; and he had the wit to see that his startled admiration at the transformation of her appearance pleased as well as amused her. She was seated at the end of the row of ladies and had Mad Huw at her side; nor was it hard to detect that the poor man was in a seventh heaven of happiness.

Her floating hair brushed against his grey habit, and Rhisiart could see that she made signs to the pages who carried round the sweet-smelling mead to leave his goblet empty. She herself, he noticed, did every now and then share a two-handled loving-cup with the good man, a cup that our friend suspected contained some very mild home-made wine.

Rhisiart's own mood was just then a chastened and tender one; and something about the poor Friar's beatitude as he permitted himself to sip this innocent beverage touched him to the heart.

"He must feel that his King is safe," the boy thought; and then he thought, "I know what he feels; for I feel the same about Owen."

Entirely at ease with regard to Tegolin, between whom and himself there seemed to have fallen away, whenever their eyes met, every trace of misunderstanding, Rhisiart was rendered considerably uncomfortable by his fear of any direct glance from Tegolin's mother. This latter lady, by whose side sat the Constable, seemed, however, too absorbed in a contest of ironical wit with Hywel Sele of Nannau, who held the place of honour on Denis's right, to have time to exchange any sort of devilry with himself. He did notice, however, that she wore that same tight-fitting gown of yellow satin; and he couldn't resist a startled emotion that was almost like *awe,* as he caught amid the turmoil of voices the airy accents of her jests with Owen's worst enemy.

"I should think that dress would burn her flesh," he thought, "like the robe of Nessus!"

But it was in meeting the eyes of Luned and little Sibli that he actually suffered most. He was too proud to dodge their glances, in which there seemed to him to be a sort of mischievous conspiracy to make him feel a fool. He was certain the dwarf was murmuring remarks about him to Luned, remarks at whose nature he could make no guess, but the purport of their conversation, as he saw it go on, was something that filled him with uneasiness. It wasn't that he didn't trust Sibli absolutely in the matter of their vigil at the presence-room; but he suspected that the little creature was bringing down by as many pegs as she could whatever admiration for him and awe of him the wise Luned might have succeeded, during all these months, in hiding away in her spacious bosom.

He couldn't see Lowri's face during her wit-contests with the Lord of Nannau; but what he *could* see was the face of Father Rheinalt, and this concentrated image of fatal obsession revealed everything. It was clear that whenever she flirted with Hywel Sele across the Constable she took a devilish delight in throwing some significant look at the agitated monk—and well he knew what her looks could be! She threw these looks at the man just as a cruel boy might throw stones at some wretched pond-newt that refused to quit rising to the surface in obstinate but helpless defiance.

Yes, it was easy enough to read in the passionate features of Tegolin's father the desperate trouble into which these looks threw him. Our friend decided that Master Simon must have ended that strange meeting of theirs with the command, *"Drive him to it!"*

Father Pascentius was seated near Father Rheinalt, but between them there was an old silent lay-brother, of huge proportions and with an enormous beard, so that the two monks had clearly no opportunity to exchange confidences as they devoted themselves to the highly-seasoned meats and the heady drink.

Rhisiart's diplomatic mind was teased by this; for the longer he watched Tegolin's father, the more nervous he became lest the man should burst out into some violent patriotic indiscretion, the rashness of which would prove a vent for the turmoil into which Lowri was throwing him.

And what a fool the Lollard must be so blandly to go on explaining to him the precious "difficulties"—all pretended no doubt!—which the Ruthin wench found in Wycliffite doctrine when matters were so crucial!

"The baggage has got hold of *you* sure enough, you poor idiot!" was our lad's secret comment as he muttered his mechanical surprise at what his friend was so eagerly revealing. For it was not concealed from Rhisiart that the tension, as this strange banquet went on, was growing moment by moment more perilously acute.

How should it not be so with that cold-blooded jeering devil from Nannau just come to make trouble and supported by that little red monster, who as he gulped down the mead looked more and more like one of those Pictish aboriginals that were supposed to linger still in the Plinlimmon mountains!

"Well," thought Rhisiart, "it's clear that I'll get scant help from *you,* Master Brut, if I'm to manage to keep our honour and yet save our skins!"

He could see that the Seneschal, who kept whispering across the board to Denis, was as worried by the look of things as he was himself. The old gentleman had a couple of Welsh men-at-arms of his own— our friend knew the fellows by sight but knew no more of them— stationed at his elbow; and every now and then he would despatch one or other of these men on some discreet errand, either to the end of the banquet-hall, where Crach Ffinnant and his mountaineers were already growing uproarious, or to the entrance of the great ruinous hall, where a considerable number of Shropshire yeomen were keeping an attentive eye upon Denis Burnell.

Men-at-arms from the guard-room kept joining and leaving this stationary group, perhaps merely to share their flagons; but perhaps also, for Rhisiart soon became aware of considerable excitement as these new-comers went and came, to bring further disquieting news from the castle-gate.

At one point our friend was sure he heard, carried across the court-yard on a sudden gust of wind, the sound of trumpets from outside the walls. At any rate it soon became clear to him, as for the twentieth time he put down his own cup untasted, that, trumpets or no trumpets, *some* very grave and momentous news had just now reached Master

Adda and had been hurriedly passed on by him to the imperturbable Denis.

As he gazed at the forlorn features of the historic personage—could it really be his ancestor?—whose crudely-depicted lineaments looked down at him through the smoke, he couldn't help recalling the sinister old tale of that banquet between the British chiefs and the heathen invaders that had been suddenly interrupted by the cry of *"Knives!"* and the plunging into unsuspicious Welsh hearts of a double score of hidden Saxon blades. Yes—trumpets or no trumpets—some event of a startling and unexpected kind must have occurred. There was an ominous stir among the Shropshire troopers and the flirtation between the Lord of Nannau and Mistress Lowri stopped as suddenly as if it had been interrupted by a flight of arrows.

Both Luned and the dwarf, after staring with wide-opened eyes upon the Constable, turned spontaneously towards Rhisiart; and he could see Father Rheinalt speak hurriedly to the old grey-beard at his side, while Father Pascentius fixed upon the Constable's face what looked like two burning points of black fire.

Hywel Sele, making a quite obvious effort to compose his great, sleek, clean-shaved countenance, bent down to the little ruffian at his side and whispered something to him that caused the man to turn his head and throw a most murderous glance at the three clerics from Valle Crucis.

The Scab alone and his friends from the mountains seemed oblivious to this new development. They were either too far gone in their cups, or they were so used to dramatic surprises and tensions, that twenty trumpets might have sounded without their turning their heads.

Denis Burnell's expression alone betrayed no flicker of surprise, or astonishment, or agitation. Once as he sat there with the whole banquet-hall, except those preoccupied mountaineers, watching him in awed silence, he deliberately turned to our friend and gave him a pleasant re-assuring smile.

As for old Adda, he had clearly reached a point when things had become too much for him. All he appeared to want to do was to efface himself completely and leave the progress of events to take their pre-destined course.

Suddenly Rhisiart found himself trembling violently from head to foot. He wasn't conscious of any definite cause for alarm, beyond the awareness he had had all the evening that his life along with Master Brut's was in extreme peril. But what afterwards struck him as significant was the manner in which he forced this trembling to stop. He stared at Tegolin in a sort of desperation, concentrating all his will to make her meet his eyes. *There!* She met them. She gave him a deep steady understanding look, a look like the one he had had from her that Midsummer Eve when they told each other their ages!

Nor did she smile this time as their eyes clung together. She just stared at him and he at her. Indeed he was the first to look away. But when he did so, drawn by something arresting in the Ruthin girl at her side, his trembling fit had gone.

But the Ruthin girl's manner held him fascinated for several seconds. His prejudice against this young woman was maliciously deep. He couldn't get out of his head her tone to that unlucky young son of Lord Grey. He couldn't forgive her for leading his comrade such a dance.

But now, as he turned to her from his eye-encounter with Tegolin, he was suddenly aware of something in her nature such as he had not realized before. The girl was now gazing at Tegolin with an intensity of regard that startled him. It was a look of a kind such as he had never seen in any woman's face directed towards another woman. It was more than affection; it was more than admiration; it was a look of *worship*. Illuminated by this look the heavy, uncomely countenance of the girl was absolutely transfigured! He couldn't help glancing quickly at his companion. Had Alice's spiritual instructor, that besotted dupe, seen what he saw?

But no! The Lollard, like everybody else at that tense moment, was looking from the Seneschal to Denis, and from Denis to the Seneschal.

What was that? It seemed to him that there now reached them all, carried on the far-drawn breath of the autumnal wind, blowing the flames of the fires and the flames of the torches into long red streamers, an obscure sound of enthusiastic cheering. Was Owen already in possession of the castle? Were all its Lawnslots and Gerallts and Jorwerths going over to his side?

"I think the Constable will be on his feet in a second," he thought. And then drawn once more to the Ruthin girl, whose whole being seemed melting into that of the red-haired Maid, he said to himself, "I could never love as much as that!"

Yes, Denis *did* rise now to his feet and whisper something to the Seneschal. But as he moved slowly down the hall between the trestles and the torches, to pass out of sight among troopers, his whole air expressed no more than a mild concern.

But there rose at once an uproar of excited tongues, under cover of which Rhisiart announced to the Lollard that in his opinion Owen's revolt had already begun. "It may even be," he assured his friend, "that news has come that the castle is captured!"

But the Seneschal must, by now, have given some special orders; for from the further end of the vaulted chamber, from behind the place where the adherents of Derfel were revelling, there came, clear and distinct, the sound of a long-drawn sequence of penetrating pipe-notes. These notes produced an instantaneous hush—as Homer would say— "throughout the shadowy hall."

Even the Scab's friends held their peace. Gently and slowly with one last faintly-receding note, the pipe-music died away.

Glancing towards the entrance Rhisiart realized that the Shropshire troopers were as puzzled as he was himself. Some moved uneasily forward. Those who had been surreptitiously drinking sneaked hurriedly to the nearest trestle-board to replace their beakers. Others straightened their belts and jerked their weapons into position. All stared at one another in amazement; their broad-mouthed mutterings being the only sounds audible from end to end of the whole time-worn place.

"What is it?" whispered the Lollard, turning towards him a face of such childish and simple wonder that Rhisiart sucked in his lips in irritation.

"He took it calmly enough," he thought, "when I told him the war had begun. But at the note of a flute he looks as if he'd seen an angel. I shall never—"

But his irritation with the childishness of his comrade was interrupted by an outbreak in chorus, without a word uttered to start it, from every male Welsh throat in that smoky hall.

Our friend tried in vain to catch the full meaning of what was sung. It was in old Welsh; and though Modry had taught him many antique words, they were mostly the names of domestic objects.

But as far as he could put the words together now, what he heard was an archaic Welsh rhyme that ran roughly like this:

> *Woe for us! Woe for us! The embers are dead.*
> *The Birds of Rhiannon are all flown away.*
> *Beauty has gone with the Blessed Head.*
> *We are left to the sword and the wind and the clay!*

It was not only the Lollard who was moved how. A wave of emotion ran down the whole length of that ruined hall as every Welshman joined in these enigmatic words. The monks from Valle Crucis alone refrained: Tegolin's father whispering conspiracy into the ear of the bearded lay-brother, while Father Pascentius wore the air of one who was ostentatiously detaching himself from everything in the world save the *Summa Theologica*.

But the moment the words ceased, all the women in the place rose up from their seats and with the same spontaneity as the words had been chanted moved in procession towards the door. Two by two, they moved, with a gravity like the gravity of some automatic religious ceremony.

Mad Huw hesitated a second, and it was clear to Rhisiart that the Maid was giving him his choice to go or stay, but when he saw that cloud of fiery hair drifting off between the tables, a look of terrified desolation came into his face and he hurried after her with the forward-flung concentration of one who sees his very soul escaping from him.

Master Brut was now expressing to Rhisiart his evangelical distaste for the chant the men had just sung. He declared it was a survival of a heathen celebration of the Earth-Goddess. "It is this sort of thing," he assured our friend, with a harsh expression in his guileless face not unlike Mad Huw's when he indicated the perils of Lollardry, "from which our study of the New Testament will free the Church! This sort of thing *is* in the Church but it is *not* in the New Testament. There is nothing for instance in the New Testament to suggest—"

But Rhisiart's mind had voyaged far from the New Testament. He was recalling the feeling he had had as he watched Lowri and Simon; that vision of himself weeping like a lover upon the golden breast of Owen. He associated this pure emotion now with what had been revealed to him of the Ruthin girl's feeling for Tegolin. "When I made love to Luned," he thought, "my soul was hard as a bit of marble. But when I thought of Owen, as I watched those two, I felt I could lose myself in that man's soul. I felt I could melt and dissolve away, as long as I melted into *him!*"

The Seneschal had moved now into the place of the absent Denis, and was engaged in a heated but whispered argument with Hywel Sele. Meanwhile Sele's friend David was clearly itching for something to happen that would end all this suspense. "What an unpleasant little man!" thought Rhisiart, contemplating the scarred face and great naked hairy arms of this famous swashbucklering servant of the House of Lancaster.

Every drop of the lad's Norman blood turned physically sick at the primitive brutality, just like what one might imagine emanating from some squat skeleton of the Bronze Age, that the figure of this famous soldier of fortune revealed. Teased by the whispering in front of him, which must have been, in some special way, curiously irritating to his type of nerves, David Gam deliberately drew from within his clothes an evil-looking knife and began sharpening it against the edge of the trestle-board.

Every now and then, however, he would lay down this dangerous weapon upon the table and glare round him with an expression of such murderous intention that Rhisiart said to himself: "The moment a blow's struck, if it's at the other end of the hall, this hairy wretch will leap up like a little wolf and go stabbing right and left among the Scab's Welshmen!"

It became impossible for our friend to stop himself from murmuring a few "Hail Marys," so extremely unpleasant he felt it would be to engage in a struggle with this goblinish assassin. There was something about his gnome-like stature combined with those gorilla-like arms that made the idea of any physical contest with him singularly distasteful. "I would far sooner," he thought, "stand up to Hywel Sele. At least he wouldn't tear out your liver with his own hands!"

And in imagination Rhisiart found himself with his teeth imbedded in one of those hairy arms as the little monster held him down on the ground and kept stabbing him with heavy sickening thuds, while each time the blade was lugged out and the blood spurted, his mind thought clearly and distinctly, *"That's* the last!"

He couldn't help a small but very cold shiver running down his spine, for this time he had no Tegolin to meet his look, nor was the expression of Hywel Sele, under what old Adda was whispering to him, at all re-assuring.

"At least that's what *I* think," concluded Master Brut, turning his bland countenance towards the Scab's followers, who, under the influence of what they'd drunk, were breaking into song.

"And now what do *you* feel?"

Rhisiart made no reply. He had begun to be puzzled by the manner in which both the Cistercian Fathers were now appealing to their long-bearded companion. Where had he seen this majestic old man before? He tried to recall the various persons who had crossed their path in Valle Crucis three months ago. No! This old man escaped him; and yet there was something about him—

But a great gust of wind, bringing a palpable suggestion of rain and rain-soaked earth, made him turn his face to the entrance. Such a moan did this wind make, as it swept torch-flames and fire-flames before it, that even the Scab's people were awed into silence. And on the wind there now came, and the thing was all the more impressive because of the choking clouds of bitter smoke, an unmistakeable sound of trumpets. The feelings that whirled through our friend's consciousness swayed and eddied, gathered and dispersed, like wind-swept flocks of starlings. He knew now, by the movements and gestures of the troopers in the entrance, that it was not Owen who had possessed himself of Dinas Brān.

He could hear the wind still moaning through the broken masonry of the walls and through the fragments of stone-vaulting in the roof, where the ancient sleeping-places above the hall had crumbled during the centuries and now lay in scattered heaps on the hill-side. The taste of the thick aromatic smoke that filled his mouth made him feel that he was once more twisting his bony limbs round the soft cedar-wood-scented body of Luned while he cried to the stars to witness that he had *her* while she did not have *him!*

But to die for Owen. Never to be Rhisiart again! And for death to come to him so soon! To come to him when he hadn't even taken his degree. When he had never killed a man, never ravished a girl, never struck a single blow for the land of his fathers! Would Tegolin cry when she heard of his execution a *little* more than the Ruthin girl when she heard of the burning of Master Brut? And the shameful wish stole over him, as he and the Lollard choked in the smoke and watched Father Rheinalt and Father Pascentius get up from their seats and move towards the entrance, while their long-bearded lay-brother bent himself forward over the board, pressing upon it with his elbows, and covering his eyes with his hand, that he had done what his mother always said would suit him best—become a monk!

How happy to be Father Pascentius and sit in your cell all day long, listening to the wood-pigeons, and thinking up objections to every single interpretation of Saint Thomas that was not by a Cistercian!

But this hot thunder-wind blowing the choking smoke into his face, combined with the superstitious silence of the men of Derfel and the high expectation of the guards at the entrance, produced finally a most curious impression. He had the feeling that his fate was advancing upon him in the form of a vast pair of dusky feminine breasts, each with a crater where the nipple should have been out of which proceeded fire and smoke!

He felt that to be Rhisiart still, to be Rhisiart free and independent, to be Rhisiart who *could* climb the steps of that scaffold, or who *could* fall sobbing on the breast of Owen, it was necessary that he should embrace, oh! relentlessly embrace, the fragrant darkness that thickened and deepened below that advancing vision!

"Give me your hand, my friend," he found himself gasping out to the Lollard. "I believe it's *the King!*"

The Lollard not only accepted the proffered fingers and held them fast; he bent forward and in full view of the great, plump, white, sneering face of Hywel Sele, that leered like a comfortable sword-fish surveying the antics of a couple of mackerel, kissed our friend on the forehead.

"Fear not!" he whispered in Welsh. "Christ is greater than any—"

"Room for the high and mighty Prince, Henry of Lancaster, Prince of Wales! Room for the noble and puissant Baron, Henry Percy, Warden of the King's Marches! Room for the most noble Knight and most Honourable Member of the King's Privy Council, Thomas Fitz-Alan, Earl of Arundel!"

Everybody in the place, from one end of the hall to the other, rose to his feet; and from the Shropshire yeomen, who were a good deal more excited than the Seneschal's Welsh retainers, a deep-voiced cheer went up.

"Long live Prince Hal! Long live Harry Hotspur!"

Not a voice was raised for the grizzled Lord of Chirk. The Earl was hated by the Welsh, in spite of his conciliatory policy, even more than was Lord Grey; while the stout Salopians, of the old Mercian breed, nourished in their rustic hearts deep resentment against both these Norman barons.

Rhisiart stared with wide-open eyes at the slender figure of the little Prince, as he paused in his courtly Lancastrian fashion to receive the blessing of Father Pascentius.

Father Rheinalt drew up his swarthy tonsured head and folded his arms with such a forbidding air that our friend could see the boy cast on him a quick puzzled look as he made his way between the tables to greet the Seneschal. That diplomatic old Welshman was completely in his element; and Rhisiart felt proud of his Welsh blood when he saw the perfect tact with which he bent his knee to this alien Prince and made some easy jest that brought at once a frank response from the boy.

With something that looked like exaggerated and sarcastic diffidence Hywel Sele bent *his* proud knee, but our friend couldn't help remarking that it was rather upon his companion with those hairy red arms that the royal child gazed with more interest. The elderly lay-brother, who had been left alone, now himself came forward; and if Rhisiart had been impressed by the courtly dignity of old Adda he was amazed at the natural ease with which this humble retainer of Valle Crucis bent his tall frame, lifted the child's hand to his great beard, and then modestly stepped backwards into the covering smoke of the nearest fire.

Before he knew what was happening it was his own and his companion's turn. The Lollard was in front; and Rhisiart could see that his frank smile and kindly blue eyes made a favourable impression on the little Prince. But it was a complete surprise when, in the midst of his own obeisance, the young Harry began speaking to him as if to another boy, and a greater surprise still when, after a puzzled nod in the direction of the Bard of Ffinnant, who with his birth-mark ablaze and his solitary eye gleaming like a bewitched gem was uttering unintelligible words, the royal child, evidently feeling that he had completed his duty, deliberately sat down at our friend's table.

The Prince once seated, all the rest of the company found places as chance dictated; but Rhisiart for a few minutes saw nothing in that smoke-darkened hall but the unnaturally long, strangely wistful countenance of the Usurper's heir, his dark steady gaze, his troubled nervous mouth.

But the boy was chatting freely and naturally to him now, giving no sign that he knew him as a prisoner, only delighted, it seemed, to discover someone not so remote from him in age, and someone too— it may be believed how *this* delighted Rhisiart!—who could describe to him in detail how boys lived when they became students at Oxford.

What an extraordinarily long face the child had! And how naturally and hungrily, having once made sure that the great Hotspur was satisfied with his behaviour, he devoured the venison-pies that Lawnslot and Gerallt were privileged to set before him, and only frowned a little, but made no protest, when Master Brut, treating him like an infant, mixed water with his wine!

He was dressed in plain black and white; and had no colour at all about him except a scarlet ribbon round his neck from which hung a little silver medallion of the Blessed Virgin.

The only weapon Rhisiart could discover about his person was the hunting-knife on the opposite side from the hunting-horn, in his black leather belt. It may be believed that it was not very long before our good friend—who habitually used this antique treasure to win favour with younger boys—produced his own wonderful-looking dagger.

The Prince's eyes gleamed with delight when he saw it, and with so much more delight when Rhisiart let him handle it, that our friend had a troublesome pang lest his chivalrous civility should compel him to make him a present of it.

"Is it sharp?" enquired the child, flashing a swift penetrating glance at the lucky possessor of such a treasure. And then, "May I try it?" he asked; and immediately began searching in the pocket of his tunic for some letter or document to practise upon.

Rhisiart couldn't help glancing aside to see whether Hotspur saw him hand over this murderous weapon to the heir of Lancaster. But the crafty border-chief was fully occupied in propitiating the wild Welsh of Cadair Idris and Llyn Tegid. He prided himself on the fantastic estimate with which the uneducated all over these islands accepted his military prowess.

As a matter of fact Percy was a far more brilliant diplomatist than he was a formidable fighter. Indeed it was actually *because* of a certain temperamental distaste for desperate single combats that the front he assumed to the world was such a rough and brusque one!

And as Rhisiart glanced at him now and noted how his impassioned gestures, gleaming dark eyes, and rich deep-throated voice were casting a spell over the Derfel-men, he couldn't help thinking, as he marked the popular hero's unwieldy bulk compared with flexible muscles of the young Prince, that in a couple of years he would far sooner face Harry Hotspur in the field than Harry of Monmouth.

Turning his attention to Fitz-Alan, who now sat between the Constable and the Seneschal, he seemed to detect from the mere look of the back of the man's head that he was in a towering rage. Unscrupulously eavesdropping, as the Prince after some hesitation began cutting and stabbing with the borrowed dagger a voluminous document to which was attached the royal seal, Rhisiart was certain he caught the syllable "she" dropped more than once from the Earl's lips. He was talking about Lowri; *that* was it! He was complaining to Denis, with the peculiar irritation that men of a certain type feel towards the philosophical companion of a desirable woman, that it was very early for the ladies to have left the banquet.

It was clear to our friend, who could see old Adda's face, but not the face of the Constable, that the latter was taking the whole blame upon himself for this discourtesy; and it was plain that such coolness under the Earl's wrath excited the wonder of the old diplomatist. Denis must have jested about the little Prince, for Rhisiart quite distinctly heard the Earl protest in his harsh voice that he couldn't imagine the lady in question being shy of meeting a mere child.

Meanwhile the boy in question having proved to his lively satisfaction the sharpness of Rhisiart's dagger upon the paternal letter, and having succeeded in quaffing a deep draught of red wine before the Lollard had time to dilute it, was now engaged in a dangerous game of his own, which consisted in throwing the dagger into the air above his head and catching it by the handle as it came down.

Master Brut was evidently not a little troubled at this proceeding, and so indeed was Rhisiart, for he doubted very much that he would escape serious trouble if the heir to the throne injured his right hand with a blade borrowed from himself. But something in him was so sympathetic with the owner of that long white face and tense wrought-up nerves that he kept avoiding the Lollard's eyes; and thus, unworthily and meanly, put upon that conscientious man the responsibility of interfering.

Turning his head a little in this mischievous process, to the end that at least he shouldn't *see* the boy wound himself, he met the sub-human glare of David Gam, and became conscious that Hywel Sele was slowly rising to his feet with the obvious intention of stopping this dangerous game with his own hands.

But the Lollard had already interfered. *"God's teeth!* What d'ye mean by *that?"*

The boy's shrill cry of pain and rage rang through the hall; for the well-meaning scholar in snatching at his arm had brought it about that the descending dagger, which had been flung higher than usual, grazed, as it fell clattering among the cups, the Prince's bare wrist, breaking the skin and drawing blood.

Everybody leapt to his feet. The troopers came rushing forward. The Scab set up a peculiar howl of his own which sounded like the neigh of Derfel's Horse; and before either the Constable or the Earl could swing round, David Gam's hairy arms were about our friend's body, while Hywel Sele was clutching Master Brut by the throat.

"Kill the murderers! Kill the assassins!" cried the excited troopers, jostling even Fitz-Alan and Denis as they thronged forward to protect the son of their King.

But the little Prince, hurriedly mounting his chair and stepping from thence upon the table, raised his hand high in the air and made his youthful voice ring through the hall. "I'm all right, good people! I'm all right! It had nothing to do with these gentlemen. I was"— he paused nervously and then added very slowly and distinctly—"I was playing a game of my own."

The anxious troopers raised a thundering cheer and, laughing and

jesting, obediently drew back; but so occupied with the safety of the
child, who was now sucking his wounded wrist while he still stood
erect on the table, were both the Constable and the Earl that the
Lollard might have been strangled and Rhisiart's ribs cracked if chance
or Providence hadn't intervened.

As it happened it was our friend who suffered most. In fact he
suffered a great deal worse than Master Brut; for the latter, being
harder to get at had more time to defend himself, and though dedicated for a skilful torturer Hywel Sele wasn't a born killer with his
hands. But the friends were in evil plight. Crowding about the boy
on the table nobody seemed to care what was going on behind the
table, nor was there any sound down there save the heavy panting
of four human throats.

Our friend went through what to him seemed like several hours of
desperate contest. The little red man had got hold of him round both
his elbows; and having seized him like this, he began, with heavily
drawn breathings, to tighten his hug.

When the two Anglophiles were alone together, later that night,
and Hywel Sele was almost dead drunk, he so far forgot the character
of David Gam as to enquire about his feelings as he was hugging
"that young fool."

"I suppose," he remarked, "you thought you'd just go on squeezing
the little devil till you'd squeezed the Holy Ghost out of him?"

But David Gam could only return an extremely fatuous grin to this
question; for the truth was he had simply given way to a whole-
hearted joy in the power of his hairy arms.

"You're an idiot," was his patron's comment upon this grin. But
Gam wasn't an idiot. He was a person whose identity could only be
fully realized when he was squeezing the life out of another person.

But if Gam's feelings on this occasion were simple ones, Rhisiart's
were extremely complicated. Thought after thought rushed headlong
through his consciousness. "He'll break my arms first," he said to
himself, "and then my ribs." And in his breathless pain he was surprised to find himself becoming two Rhisiarts. One Rhisiart was
savagely biting the bare shoulder of the ruffian who was hugging him.
The other Rhisiart, quite cool and collected, was looking on as if he
were totally uninvolved. "I am being obscurely murdered," thought

this other Rhisiart. "And no one except little Sibli will care very much. But I'm not going to call for help, however it hurts. *Go on!* Break my bones. You can't *make* me call for help! No one will ever know about this except Owen. But Owen *will* know about it. No! you *can't* make me call out!—Owen—will—know—about it. No! I'm *not* crying because of the pain. I'm crying—because—Owen—will know about it."

But suddenly the pain ceased to be the kind that required all his will-power to bear it without calling out. In place of murmuring, as he had been doing from the beginning, "He'll break my arms if he goes on!" Rhisiart began to find something in the pain itself that gave him a strange exultation, an exultation akin to but not identical with the old dark trembling of the "nerve perilous" that Lowri had played on. "It's for Owen," he thought. And then he thought, "Am I going mad?" For the pain had begun to take a palpable form; and the form it took was the form of a corpse, which was himself, and yet not himself!

With this corpse he was wrestling; and as he wrestled he kept crying out, "I know your name! I know your name!" And sometimes the corpse had an evil stench, and sometimes it had a lovely heavenly smell like lilies of the valley.

And he kept crying out to it, "I know your name!" though how it could *have* a name when it was only himself remained one of those problems that often confront a mind under some cracking tension.

Less occupied with anxiety about the little Prince than the Earl and the Constable, and by reason of their holy office more alert to the *back-washes* of events, the two Valle Crucis Fathers and their burly attendant pushed their way past the absorbed magnates. Father Rheinalt took Hywel Sele completely by surprise and sent him reeling, while the lay-brother, plucking the little red man from *his* victim like a maggot from a tasteful nut, hurled him with the force of a catapult straight into the substantial figure of Harry Hotspur, reducing that genial hero to a state of breathless speechlessness!

The first thing that Rhisiart himself felt when he recovered his senses was a fit of violent nausea. Humiliating though it was in the presence of all these notables he was forced to go down on his knees beneath the Prince's table, and vomit there like a sick dog. He knew that the kindly hands that were patting his shoulder, as he retched his heart out, were the hands of Master Brut; and when, pale and exhausted, he regained his seat he knew it was the same hands that were offering him a drink of water.

Father Rheinalt and the bearded lay-brother had moved away, and he could dimly make out their two cowled forms standing in the smoke by one of the fires; but Father Pascentius had remained on the scene and was now engaged in giving a detailed account of the whole occurrence to the ruffled Earl, while the Constable, taking care to send old Adda to intercept any false rumours that might be spreading through the castle, was preparing to bind up with his own hands the child's bleeding wrist.

But the little Prince, waving aside Denis's help, jumped lightly down from his perch, and Rhisiart caught the dark eyes in that long white face turned half-reproachfully and half-sympathetically towards himself and the Lollard. The temper of the scene changed rapidly now, from tragic tension to amused relief, a change that was accelerated by the noisy and humorous invective which Harry Percy, to recover his own aplomb, began pouring upon the head of David Gam.

In the reaction from the shock neither our friend nor Master Brut was in much of a mood to exchange confidences. Rhisiart was aware of two physical sensations, one unpleasant and one pleasant: the smell of his own vomit rising up from the darkness and the pressure upon his fingers of the Lollard's hand. Resignedly fatalistic though his mood was he did retain enough vitality to watch with fascinated interest the proceedings of Hotspur.

Though so conceited about his legal acumen our friend really *had* it in him to be, whether he knew it or not, a formidable novice in the art of diplomacy. It was therefore very natural that he should be so fascinated by Hotspur who was a living example of all that he most instinctively reverenced.

And he watched Hotspur now with growing amazement! The man still kept turning to the Scab and his fellow-Derfelites, treating them as if they were an independent Welsh tribe whose attitude of mind it was essential that he, as the Warden of the Marches, should be able to follow with intelligent sympathy.

But what it was impossible for Rhisiart not to notice was the haughty attitude of Fitz-Alan to both Hywel Sele and David Gam. This evidently meant little to the red-haired adventurer, who, as a mercenary free-lance, expected nothing else, but that it was a surprise and a shock to the Baron of Nannau was very obvious.

It was also plain to Rhisiart that what especially hurt the self-respect of this complacent and sardonic Anglophile was the fact that the Lord of Chirk regarded him and behaved to him as if he were, socially-speaking, on a level with David Gam.

"Shall we all move, my Lords and Masters"—it was Denis himself speaking—"to the further end of our poor hall, where our good friend here, the Bard of Ffinnant"—and he made a courtly bow in the direction of the Scab—"is anxious to give our gracious Prince Henry a specimen of his curious and interesting art?"

The young Henry, who had been for some while regarding the disfigured countenance and the cyclopean eye of the prophet of Derfel with excited wonder, brightened up at those words, and at once cast such an appealing and self-accusing glance at our friend, whose unlucky dagger was now safe back in its sheath, that the Constable hastened to ·add—"Oh yes, my Prince, Master Rhisiart and Master Brut will join us; and so I hope"—and he raised his voice so as to be heard by Father Rheinalt and the formidable lay-brother—"will our Fathers in God from Valle Crucis."

It was a blessed comfort to both Rhisiart and the Lollard to leave the spot from which they might so easily have been carried away dead; and when, following the Constable and the Prince, the whole company re-gathered about the fire at the end of the hall, our friend's spirits rose so considerably that he began to take a more hopeful view of their fate.

"I hope to God," he said to himself, "the Scab won't go and spoil it!"

But encouraged by Denis, who by this time seemed to have got the situation well under control, the representative of Derfel confined himself to a series of bardic improvisations, to which, since they seemed to know by instinct the drift of his *Awen,* the rich bass voices of his mountaineers extemporized a kind of vocal accompaniment.

The artful monotony of these ancient melodies from the slopes of Cadair Idris soon began to have a more than soothing effect upon the less musical in the audience.

The red-haired David, who treated the occasion as if it were a bivouac in the desert, soon slipped from his seat to a couch of bracken, where neither the sparks that showed signs of igniting his bed nor the noise of his own snores were able to disturb his oblivion.

The little Prince too, though with no other movement, allowed his head to sink against the Lollard's shoulder; while the great Lord of Chirk, whose experience of life had not included Welsh minstrelsy, occupied himself in puzzling out word by word, for he was a poor scholar, a despatch which he had received that morning from the King's camp.

By the time the performance was at an end and the old Seneschal had returned from his errand of counteracting false rumours, Denis hastened to put the royal child into his care, with instructions that he should be given a bed, under a responsible guard of Shropshire troopers, in the warmest guest-room in the castle. As the sleepy little boy put his hand in the old man's hand everyone rose to their feet.

Hotspur, however, stroke up to the child, whose long white face in the torch-light had something phantom-like about it, and bending down whispered in his ear and placed a coin in his hand.

"I would—like—to—bestow," the boy repeated at once, bravely straightening his shoulders and holding his head high, "this—little— token—upon—so—upon so gifted a poet." There was no need for anyone to push the Bard of Ffinnant forward, for that worthy fully comprehended, none better, what it was proper for princes to do when they were impressed by the inspirations of genius.

With the natural grace of a born courtier the rogue now went down on his knee.

"I—bestow—on you," said the little boy, losing his sleepy stare as he encountered the burning eye which was fixed upon him, "this—poor piece—of gold." He paused a moment, keeping the outstretched hand waiting, and then added, "I shall tell—my father—of—of your kindness —to me."

The hand of the prophet of Derfel had closed upon the coin and he was retiring in discreet haste, when suddenly a voice that made Rhisiart quickly turn his head, though it was only the voice of the lay-brother, called upon the mountaineers to acknowledge this gift to their leader.

The tumultuous shout that followed was so loud that the unre-

sponsive Fitz-Alan turned upon the men with a menacing scowl. But
the diplomatic Hotspur intervened. " 'Tis a royal gold 'noble' of the
Prince's great-grandfather," he announced in his rich hypnotic voice,
"Edward the Third of Crécy and Poitiers, where the Welsh archers
helped us to conquer France. You'll see upon it, my good friend"—
this addressed to the Scab who certainly by this time had seen all there
was to be seen—"the image of King Edward sailing in a galley. I'm
sure you all wish for his great-grandson as many more happy nights
in Wales as—as there are—" But the allusion to prowess of the Welsh
at Edward's battles was enough to start a vociferous acclaim, and as,
to the tune of it, old Adda led the boy away, Rhisiart gazed with renewed respect at Harry Percy. "It isn't by the sword," he thought,
"it's by the tongue, that the world is ruled." As he thought of this, a
bold and startling idea took possession of him, an idea so agitating
that it caused the pit of his stomach to feel as if it contained a flapping
sail. Why shouldn't he make an oration to these great lords, defending
Owen against the treacherous machinations of Lord Grey, and indicating that if there *were* any sort of rising it would be solely and entirely due to the brutal selfishness of that unworthy sycophant.

Once having come into his head this awe-inspiring idea took such
possession of him that he found it hard to give polite attention to anything that was spoken to him. On the little Prince's departure the
sagacious Hotspur expressed the view to the Bard of Ffinnant that it
would be comfortable for him and suitable to the late hour if he should
follow the example of the heir to the throne and retire to rest. This
advice jumped well with the wishes of the prophet, who longed to
devote himself to an uninterrupted study of the king crossing the sea;
and so rapidly did he leave the hall that his followers were put to it
to keep pace with him.

When the Welshmen were gone our friend's trembling resolution
to make his first political oration was defeated by Hywel Sele, who,
already more than a little drunk, launched into a rambling attack upon
his cousin Glendower. He complained openly to Hotspur that neither
the present Lord of Chirk nor his predecessor took a strong enough
line with the son of Griffith Fychan. "I know him through and
through," Hywel Sele affirmed. "He's just like his father. He never
forgives and never forgets. He caught me once, in pure boyish sport

of course, when we were serving the late King, cutting off one of the forks of his beard, and do you think, my Lord Warden, that he has ever forgotten that boyish jest? *You* can bear me out in this, Constable! His pride and touchiness and his ridiculous gravity where his personal vanity is concerned are fantastic. The man's got no sense of—" He wanted to say "sense of humour," knowing Hotspur's genial reputation, but he was too drunk to remember the English word—so he concluded with the French word *esprit*. "And what's worse," he blundered on, "he's a dabbler in—" He wanted to say "black magic," but the phrase escaped him: "You saw that rascal who snatched at your gold noble? Well, everyone on the Marches knows that this precious cousin of mine who's so finicky about his beard—they say he washes the hairs of it every morning with liquid gold!—hires that one-eyed buffoon to pimp and pander for him under cover of—under cover of— you know!—that holy Saint's holy Horse! I should like to ask"—here a peculiar leer of drunken cunning crossed his face—"how these Valle Crucis Fathers reconcile it with Holy Church to defend such a devil-worshipper! What have they got, I should like to know, either from Griffith Fychan or from Owen? Not a groat! And yet in your own presence, my Lord, here were these Fathers meddling with—with the King's justice! This drunken beast here"—and he contemptuously touched the oblivious Gam with his foot—"was only doing what I told him. He's a brute of course"—and he viciously disturbed the bracken under the sleeping man's head—"but he was doing his duty. But honest men doing their duty are to be meddled with, are they? Meddled with by Valle Crucis! Meddled with by the Lord of Chirk!"

Hywel Sele was getting confused or he wouldn't have made the blunder of expressing his spleen against the Earl in this appeal to Hotspur.

It was Fitz-Alan who now interrupted him, and he did it without a word. He did it by taking up in his hands the thin-stemmed silver beaker out of which he'd been drinking and after bending it between his fingers as if it had been made of tallow instead of metal flinging it into the fire.

It was Denis who now intervened. Leaning forward a little, and addressing Hotspur, but fixing his grey eyes on some remote point in space, "My Lord," he said, "there has been in this castle to-night, and

I may remind our friend of Nannau that it is under none but the King
that I am Constable here, a series of misunderstandings that will have
to be unravelled. These two gentlemen now with us, Master Brut and
Master Rhisiart, are *not* here as guilty of treason. They are here as
hostages for Glendourdy. It was under a misapprehension, my Lord,
that our guests from the Tassel attacked these gentlemen; and as for
Valle Crucis, as long as I am Constable of Dinas Brān *I shall welcome"*
—here he turned to the two monks and the bearded lay-brother, who
were now seated under the wall just beyond the man on the floor—
"all the assistance I can get in the performance of my duty."

"May I say—" began the Lollard. But to Rhisiart's relief, for he felt
that the last voice he wanted to hear just then was that of his friend,
Harry Percy himself broke in.

"Pardon me a moment, sir. Pardon me, Constable. As far as I understand this situation, the Baron of Nannau, and his loyal but at the
moment inarticulate ally, are here as representing the policy of Lord
Grey of Ruthin. To the regret of Fitz-Alan and myself, Lord Grey has
at the moment much influence at Court. But I will be quite frank
with you, my Lords and Masters. It was to counterbalance this influence that I found a way of putting pressure on the King to trust me
with the person of his eldest son. The Prince is to hold—and he'll be
soon able, in spite of his tender age, to justify my confidence—a Court
of his own in Chester. In that Court Harry Percy's, and not Lord
Grey's, will be the determining voice.

"It is to protest against this that Grey has, even now, posted back
to the King; and to despatch Glendourdy's hostages to the royal camp
at this moment would be simply to give them up to Grey, a course
entirely contrary to the policy of conciliation the Lord of Chirk and
myself are resolved to apply to Welsh affairs. The King's army is
marching south. The royal presence is required in the south. And if
by making Glendourdy see that his quarrel is a *private one*—with
Grey and not with England—we can smooth over this present trouble,
there will be no need for the royal army to delay its return south."

There was a long silence after these words. Hywel Sele was too drunk
to gather their import; but he felt things were going against him, and
he drew closer to the man on the floor; bending over him and prodding

him. His whole attitude towards David Gam from now on was curiously revealing of the relations between them.

Rhisiart contemplated in awed admiration the rugged countenance of the heir to the vast Northumbrian estates. There was a single black lock falling across the Percy's forehead, and his straggling dark moustache only seemed to accentuate his full, red, Viking-looking lips. And as our friend gazed at these massive lineaments, and actually dared to meet the man's warm, irresistibly magnetic eyes, he decided that he would postpone his first public speech until he had conversed with a few more really enlightened statesmen like this Hotspur, and a few more really great legal authorities like Master Young.

One thing he would never do. He would never interrupt a group of formidable rulers with a blunt outburst like the Lollard's. He would turn on everybody present, before he said a word, a warm, glowing, disarming, ingratiating *look,* like that which Hotspur had turned upon him. "If the tongue," he said to himself, "is stronger than the sword, a certain kind of look is stronger than the tongue."

Meanwhile Hywel Sele, who had imbibed so much that he was forced to withdraw himself for a moment—indeed to our friend's ideas of propriety he might have withdrawn himself further—proceeded, as he re-took his seat, to indulge in a series of angry fumblings with his great silver-mounted belt which had become unhooked. It was clear that the man missed the bodily services just then, like those a "gentleman in attendance," which David Gam habitually performed for him; for he now began viciously kicking his slumbering friend, evidently with the intention of suggesting their departure to the Tassel Inn.

But at this point Father Pascentius suddenly left his companions, and deliberately sat down, without so much as a "by your leave," in the empty space that had been left unfilled between the Lord of Nannau and the Lord of Chirk. As he did this he gave our friend a shrewd glance with his black eyes, as much as to say, "We'll drive this nail home."

Rhisiart was now in excellent good spirits. The only thing that worried him was the teasing question as to just *where,* as his friend and he loitered in the monastery three months ago, he had met that powerful-looking lay-brother.

"I know I *must* have seen him down there," he thought. "Is he one of the men who spoke to us in the cloisters?"

But apart from this trifling puzzle he had a delicious feeling of lying back, calmly and recklessly, on the great wave of destiny. He hadn't drunk much since he had vomited so violently; but the little he *had* drunk, and indeed was still drinking, seemed to have a wonderful effect on his nerves. He began to experience a tender and almost tearful regard for everybody about him. Even towards the great, handsome, evil, mask-like visage of Hywel Sele, down whose unwrinkled expanse big drops of perspiration were pursuing one another, he felt nothing but pity.

As to his would-be assassin on the floor, he even found himself vaguely concerned when a burning wisp from the fire, falling on one of those great hairy arms, caused the fellow to swing over in his sleep. "What's *making* me feel like this?" he wondered; and he decided that it had to do with Owen. An indescribable sweetness seemed to flood his soul whenever he thought of Owen.

The man's figure bulked larger, fairer, more majestic, more fraught with a strange diffused glory than anything he had ever known. "If Mad Huw feels like *this*," he thought, "for the late King, he and I are in the same boat." And letting his imagination run riot he imagined all four of them safe back at Glyndyfrdwy, himself happy with the live Owen, Mad Huw happy with the dead King, and Tegolin holding both their hands!

He felt so elated that he longed to catch a glimpse of at least one of those Northern constellations whose magnetic influence through so many summer nights had calmed his soul. "But they'd be all different to-night," he thought, "all changed. It's autumn now."

He cast his eyes along the cornice of the broken roof. Yes! there were certainly many ragged gaps in the unrestored crumbling masonry. And yes! he *could,* through one dark aperture, make out a fragment of the sky. But how dark it must have grown out there since they sat down to the banquet! There were certainly no stars to be seen that night.

When his mind returned to itself after this attempt to escape into stellar space, he found that Father Rheinalt had left the lay-brother to his own devices and was seated close to Father Pascentius.

What was the lay-brother doing now? Rhisiart saw him walking slowly up and down, examining closely the various places where the walls had fallen outwards, and where the pitch-dark patches of sky were visible. How black and mysterious those patches looked—just as if space were a palpable substance rather than a hollow negation of all substance! And backwards and forwards across these apertures in roof and walls rolled the smoke of the fires, as if, like himself, the warm interior soul of Dinas Brān were seeking to cover up its blind track through the dark by wisps of comfortable thought!

Both Master Brut and he had their backs against the wall, whereas all the others were leaning forward over a long refectory-table, some resting their chins on their hands, and some sitting bolt upright, like figures on a pack of cards.

What on earth *could* it be that caused the restlessness in that big lay-brother, wrapt up so close in his monastic cowl? Up and down the whole length of the hall the fellow kept wandering. Was he interested in the smoke-darkened fancy-figures of those bygone heroes? Or was he, like Rhisiart himself, longing to steady his soul by a glimpse of the stars? But there were no stars. *That* was certain. The night had grown pitch-dark and the wind had dropped. Dinas Brān might have been a lonely galley, like the galley on the king's gold noble, carrying the fate of the "Isle of the Mighty" from darkness to darkness.

There! He thought *that* would happen soon. The Lollard's chin had sunk down upon his chest, and the man was sleeping peacefully. The great magnates before him, that noble Hotspur, that sad, withdrawn Denis, that battle-scarred Earl, were all listening gravely—everybody was listening, except the now quite tipsy Lord of Nannau—to the steady low-pitched voice of Father Pascentius.

How like a picture it had become! "All the history of this island," Rhisiart said to himself, "could be read, if I had the knowledge of Master Young, in those faces!"

And what would his mother say if she could see her "little monk" now? "Oh I wish I could make an impression on these great men! I wish I could say something to them now, so penetrating, so original, that they would all look at each other and think to themselves: 'How lucky Glendourdy is to have a relative like that!'"

But instead of saying anything at this propitious moment that would force these makers of history to recognize that they had a fellow-spirit among them, our friend could do nothing but impress their faces on his attentive mind. Still lying back on that curious sweetness that the thought of Owen brought, he felt as though in some odd way his identity had lapsed, and he had become a disembodied spectator of some pause in the march of events, when Destiny itself was treading water or marking time, and when as with a full moon in an eclipse the solemn shadow of the weight of life's procession dimmed with a coppery mask the revolution of the spheres!

Some kind of enchanted interlude had fallen upon this group of people, like that of the mysterious vigil with the head of the Blessed Brān, when a similar group of warriors were lifted up into a beatified timelessness! All it needed now, our friend thought, as his imagination struggled to disregard the commonplace attire of the men about him and to envisage them as they would have looked in the majestical days of old, was that strange singing of the Birds of Rhiannon, which, like Helen of Troy's nepenthe, swallowed up all sadness.

"Will there ever come a time," he said to himself, "when the art of painting will immortalize such countenances as these men have; not just in fancy-trappings, like those old Princes mouldering on the walls, but with such living details as that scar across Fitz-Alan's cheek, that dark wart above one of Hotspur's eyebrows, that impeccable forward-pushing point of the Constable's clipt beard, and, above all, the life-draining, in-sucking gleam of Father Pascentius's eyes!"

It was Father Pascentius who was addressing them all now; and as far as Rhisiart was concerned he might have been talking to a consistory of Alexandrine Fathers; for this was Theology, the Queen of Wisdom, and how the heroic Hotspur managed to throw back that dark lock from his forehead and respond to such abstractions was a marvel to see.

Denis too, under the Father's discourse, appeared actually to come back to earth, while even the battered face of the Lord-Marcher Earl, across which in the fire-light could be seen the ineffaceable red mark left by his steel visor, wore the same expression of intelligent attention that it might have worn in the stables had his head equerry been explaining to him the points of a new charger.

It did, however, gradually dawn upon the legal mind of our friend that the crafty theologian had taken advantage of the Lollard's slumber to make it clear to these important personages that the worthy man was *not* the type of obstinate heretic whose soul it was the peculiar joy of Henry the Fourth and his bustling Archbishop to save by the anguish of being burnt alive.

"For God's sake sleep on, Master Brut!" was the prayer our friend sent up now; and he even strengthened it by more "Hail Marys" than he had ever strung together in all his days; for though he couldn't understand a word of Father Pascentius's theology, he knew too well the spirit of his camerado and how the reckless man would disperse in a second all this convoluted logic by some aphorism from the mouth of his Saviour.

"Where our too zealous Bishop of Hereford," Father Pascentius was now arguing, "was led astray in accusing Master Brut of a schismatic bias was in relation to the order of perfection among immaterial substances. Now in my examination of Master Brut three months ago I found that where the learned Bishop had become confused, and indeed had approached a grave heresy himself, was in this most equivocal, most ambiguous, most dangerous matter of *plurality* in the Divine Persons, otherwise than according to the order of origin.

"For if the Holy Ghost were not from the Son they would be equally referred to the Father in point of origin; wherefore either they would not be two Persons, or there would be *order of perfection* between them as the Arians pretend or there would be a distinction of matter between them; which is impossible. Consequently it is impossible that the Son and the Holy Ghost proceed from the Father except in such-wise that from the Father alone one alone, that is, the Son, proceeds, and from the Father and Son, inasmuch as they are one, the Holy Ghost proceeds. Anselm was quite correct in saying that the Son and the Holy Ghost are distinct from each other by this alone, that they proceed in different ways; but, as Saint Thomas had clearly shown, they cannot proceed in different ways unless the Holy Ghost proceeds from the Son; wherefore if it be denied—and it is at this point that the learned Bishop of Hereford must have lost his bearings, quite simple as the point is, and, as you, my Lords and Masters, must clearly perceive it is—if, I say, it be denied that the Holy Ghost is from the Son it must likewise be denied that he is distinct from the Son.

"The conclusion being thus, as the angelic Richard of Saint Victor makes entirely plain, and as you, my Lords, are so clearly perceiving, it lifts the learned Bishop out of his perplexity and at the same time lifts this honest and loyal gentleman, out of all neighbourhood to heresy; for as I have made clear to you, my Lords and Masters, the difference of properties, when we speak of the Divine Persons, consists merely in the number of persons producing, in that the first has being from no other, the second from one only, the third from two."

"I would like to ask you, Master Theologian," broke in Fitz-Alan, "whether in the dispensations of divine wisdom there is any special provision made for separate *races?* I am a plain soldier. I serve the King. But I have found it sometimes"—here Rhisiart caught a quaintly humorous expression flitting across the man's scarred face—"tedious and stupid when I come home tired with chasing my Welsh thieves to listen to my Chaplain, though he's a worthy man enough, God comfort him, and a stout drinker, preaching to me that all men are equal in the eyes of God, and have souls of the same Substance, to be haled out of Purgatory or damned in Hell! You, Father, let me tell you, are the first scholar I've ever met who can quote your Anselms and your Ariuses; and I'd like to ask you the plain question, how without any damned Lollardry I could shut the mouth of this good priest of mine?

"What I'd *like* to tell him would be that the Blessed Creator when he made the soul of an English gentleman made it out of completely different stuff from the soul of a Welsh thief, just as one of my grand old wolf-hounds has a different nature from a skulking, fish-eating otter. Doesn't your angelic Saint Richard of Somewhere, or your angelic Saint Thomas of Something, have anything pat to this matter, with which I could give my smug cleric a wholesome jolt? I'll take your word for it, Father, that the decent lad nodding over there is no curst heretic. But I tell'ee 'tis no joke for a man like me, keeping the King's peace by day and by night, to be told that these sons of whores are no better than honest men when it comes to the Last Judgment!"

A silence followed this unexpected outburst. "I believe," thought our friend, "all these magnates are drunk. I believe Father Pascentius himself is drunk."

Glancing at the two monks, however, he recognized that it was from Tegolin's father, not from the theologian, that indiscretions were threatening.

The dark-swelling vein on Father Rheinalt's forehead looked as if it might suddenly burst and spout black blood over them all!

"I cannot sit here and listen," the monk began, but the theologian clapped his hand over his mouth. Rhisiart feared an outburst would follow this; but Cistercian discipline prevailed, and the man obeyed his superior. It was clear that Father Pascentius was deriving huge satisfaction from the whole situation. His voracious eyes looked as if they were actually swelling with the joy of mental contest. They looked as if they were sucking up the sacredest quintessence of these human souls into which they were thrusting their insatiable proboscis.

Hotspur shook himself now like a great friendly school-boy when an awkward scene in the class-room has taken place; and for the second time our friend caught his eye.

"Now if Owen ever sent me," he thought, "as a special envoy to *you,* Harry Percy, we'd soon come to a perfect understanding. What a pity it isn't you instead of this bigoted Bolingbroke who's on—"

But he caught himself up, for he thought of that white-faced boy. But quite beyond his will what should slide into his head now but a picture of himself, dressed in the garb of a chancellor, signing in Westminster Hall an eternal treaty between Prince Owen and King Hotspur!

"The question you have raised, my Lord of Chirk"—it was the theologian speaking—"is one of profound importance. My good friend, Father Rheinalt here, completely missed its point; which was not, of course, the unphilosophical, uncanonical, un-catholic error of the superiority of one race over another, of the Welsh over the English, for instance, or the Saxon over the Norman, but the natural tendency to the cardinal virtues in *some* souls compared with the natural tendency, for it does, as you well say, seem *almost* to amount to this in other souls to the cardinal vices. And while we're talking of these moral differences I would like to express a hope, good my Lord, that when the Most High chooses to take our beloved Abbot from our head, which may—God preserve him long!—happen any hour, you will feel the importance of refusing your support to Lord Grey's choice of a successor, which has only to be named to be seen in all its absurdity—our well-meaning but hopelessly incompetent Prior!"

That same flickering smile that Rhisiart had noticed before did at that moment cross the face of the Earl; but instead of pressing his original point, or making any comment upon the blunders of Lord Grey, he leaned across and gave Hotspur a rude nudge with his fist, directing his attention as he did so to the solemn antics of the tipsy Hywel Sele.

That gentleman was now gravely and absorbingly occupied in seeing how long he could scorch the hairs on his friend's bare arms without causing him to awaken. As he bent down over this task his great, handsome, sardonic physiognomy assumed an expression of frivolous but intense concentration, like the concentration of a person who plays a card-game by himself. The placing of his foot upon the arm of the sleeping man, to hinder his turning over, seemed as much part of this quiet game as did the ignition of various convenient wisps of bracken to serve as tapers.

A protracted series of these extempore tapers were now applied to the hairs on the sleeper's bare arm; but a rule of the game seemed to be that the assiduous scorcher was forbidden to approach a scarcely-healed wound on the curve of the man's elbow.

Hotspur's reaction to the spectacle thus called to his attention struck Rhisiart as a somewhat singular one; for across the hero's ballad-like physiognomy passed an unmistakeable contortion of extreme fear, a contortion that was accompanied by all those palpable manifestations of a childish shivering-fit that are indicated in the phrase, *a goose walking over your grave*.

The great warrior recovered himself immediately; and Rhisiart was confirmed in his admiration of him as the first of English gentlemen, when he heard him begin at once, without the least shame, explaining to Fitz-Alan that from infancy he'd had a horror of torture; and that these curious antics of the Lord of Nannau hit for some reason that vein of weakness in him.

"Well, Lord Percy," said the Earl, with more sympathy than Rhisiart expected, "I'll give my troublesome confessor a dozen groats next feast-day to say a thousand 'Hail Marys' that you and I, when *our* time comes, may die a clean death in the field."

"Amen!" murmured Hotspur from the bottom of his heart.

For some while Rhisiart had been aware, as he sat by his sleeping friend's side, and he had already induced Master Brut to stretch himself out on the bench and use him as a pillow, that Denis had been listening to the murmur of voices from the outer end of the hall. Thus it was no surprise to him when Lowri's protector rose to his feet.

"With your permission, my Lords," he said, "I'll dismiss our guard. The men must be tired; and though I'm loth to interrupt our conversation, there seems no need to keep them in attendance any further."

"Surely, surely, Constable!" Hotspur responded at once. And then with a friendly glance at the two young men, "And if these gentlemen—"

But Rhisiart hurriedly shook his head and murmured something about the great privilege it was to be in such exalted company.

"Well, off with those poor troopers, Constable!" Hotspur repeated. "We won't keep any of you *very* much longer; but I don't often get a chance to discuss matters with my Lord here, nor"—and he smilingly stretched himself in his seat and loosened the great sword in his sheath —"nor with our famous Valle Crucis scholar."

"One word, Constable!" interjected Fitz-Alan. "I've no suspicions under your roof. But I'm an old soldier and have my humours and my habits. If you don't mind, you might send Trenchard and Hardy to me. You've only to mention their names, *Trenchard and Hardy*. Even in my closet, even in my chamber, I keep those two. They're more than servants. They're companions in arms. Chirk ain't Chirk without 'em. They can sit down behind us here."

"Trenchard—Hardy," repeated the Constable, and with a bow to his feudal superior he moved away.

Rhisiart soon heard the grateful shout, not loud but heart-felt, with which the Shropshire yeomen welcomed the permission to seek their rest; and when Denis returned, there came, striding heavily behind him, the Earl's two attendants.

"All right, Trenchard? All right, Hardy?" was Fitz-Alan's laconic greeting. "There you are, my men. Sit ye down! Here's some marrow left in this good pasty. And here—drink out of this!" And moving stiffly to where the men had seated themselves, the Lord-Marcher conveyed to them without spilling a drop his own deep flagon of mead.

"Dorset men, both," he whispered, as he and Denis resumed their places. "I have a parcel of good grazing land down there, and those fellows suit me better than any of my Arundel lads. King Richard always used to say, 'To fight for me when I'm awake give me Yorkshiremen, but to keep my bed when I'm asleep give me men from Dorset.' But if the Constable will forgive my returning to our present business—" He paused and gave Denis a look that caught our friend's eye at once, for it was a look that was like an armorial seal!

It was a look at once imperious and cajoling, the look of a born master in the nicest points of feudal relationships. "For the truth is, my Lord," and he turned to Harry Percy, "we are exceptionally fortunate to-night."

These last words were spoken with so much emphasis that everyone present—except Hywel Sele who, with his great bland face wearing the same tipsy solemnity, continued scorching the hairs on his friend's arm—leaned forward to catch what was coming.

"I am only revealing," he went on, "what you two Fathers, for we soldiers are children—and don't think I don't know it!—compared with you churchmen, must have detected already, that Percy's brought the Prince to the Marches to cut the ground under Grey's feet! Never mind how he got the child. The point is, *having* got him, *and* the King's Writ with him, the boy's Court at Chester will turn that great beggarly castle at Ruthin into a castle of sand! What, dear my Lord," and he gave the great Hotspur a most quizzical glance from under his bristly eyebrows, "you *don't* know yet is that this Father," and he nodded in the direction of Tegolin's parent, "is our friend Glendourdy's private confessor. I dare warrant he's not so stern with Owen as my terrible Father Talbot is with me! You *are* Owen's confessor, Father, eh?"

Father Rheinalt's brick-red face darkened ominously; but he bowed an unhesitating admission, while Father Pascentius murmured hurriedly in legal Latin, "It is allowed."

Rhisiart's eyes were glued on the great Hotspur now. Would he spoil this scene of perfect diplomacy by some brusque North-Country blunder? Fitz-Alan had gone too far, telling him about Father Rheinalt.

Not at all! Pushing back his dark forelock and crossing his iron heels, the famousest warrior in Britain only smiled his most winning smile at the embarrassed monk.

" 'Tis nigh as good," he cried, "as seeing Owen himself, and see him I can at this moment, Father, just as he rode like a madman into the hottest prick of the Douglas spears! 'Twas splendid—though of course not war, as a wily old borderer like me regards it. But tell Baron Owen from me—" but he caught himself up; and with an easy deprecatory chuckle turned to Fitz-Alan.

"Tell him from Lord Percy and me," threw in the latter, "that we recognize his quarrel to be with Grey—with Grey and not with King Hal—and you can even hint to him, if you like, that if he chased Grey back into his Red Burrow like a fox into his earth—" He stopped short and glanced, Rhisiart thought, a little nervously at Hotspur. But that border-chief to our friend's culminating delight only clapped his great hands over his ears and murmured with a chuckle, "The King's Warden of the Marches, tell him, suffers from a whoreson deafness!" And Rhisiart saw that it was all the reserved Denis could do—philosopher though he was—not to display his simple Saxon disgust at these frivolous Norman ways.

But having made their point, both the great men now relaxed in the most amiable manner; and Hotspur enquired of Father Pascentius whether he possessed a complete copy of the *Summa* of Saint Thomas. "In my father's library when I was a child," he said, "the good Father who tried to teach me—well! to write my own name—used to take down—".

But Father Pascentius required no further encouragement. In exactly the same tone of ironical patience that he had used to his pupil in his cell he scrupled not to plunge into an elaborate explanation of the superiority of the Cistercian libraries, and especially his own at Valle Crucis, over those of the other religious houses.

But Rhisiart turned his attention now to a lively conversation that was going on behind him between Master Trenchard and Master Hardy.

" 'Tis our wold Corfe, looks'ee," the elder of the two men was now remarking, "that do coom into me vancy as us do sit here. Do'ee mind how Mëaster Cob, down Bere way, used to mention 'un? 'A said his granfer, or summat, were from they parts. But I've a seed 'un me wone self. Ees, 'tis wold Corfe to the image this toomble-down pleace, 'sknow?"

"So't be, Jimmy Mummer, so't be," acquiesced the younger man.

" 'Twere well for I, Tom," went on Trenchard, "if thik were the worst o't. What do taunt me poor mind be thik reverend man what be now a-marching up and down, back and forth. Don't'ee look behind'ee, Tom! But to tell'ee true I be worritted lest 'un be the Wold Un his wone self!

" 'Twere conjurer Long John to Fordington who told I of me last end, and how 'twould be. 'A said 'twould coom to I in a girt wambly pleace, same as this pleace be! 'Tis no common man, Mëaster Trenchard, 'a said, what I do see as thee's doomster. 'Tis a tall man I do see, a proper tall man, but 'a do glower at I, as the Sperrits bring un up, like a holy man, Mëaster Trenchard."

"Don't'ee utter such words, Jimmy Mummer, don't'ee utter 'em," protested the younger man. "What would Mary Elizabeth say, an her heard such dimsy words?"

Trenchard sighed heavily. "Ees, lad, ees, lad," he groaned. " 'Tis of she I be frettin, Tom. Ye'll be leal to me little wench, Tom, wunna, when I be gone? Ees, lad, 'tis of she I be frettin! I do see she cryin' her heart out over me death-mound time one of they every shaven-polls do act as 'a were spyin' at I. 'Taint that I be afeared for me wone self, looks'ee! Jim Mummer have had his day and have served his lord, and have kept Mary Elizabeth in twine and hosen, in smock and fairing; and now be ready to let his wold bones rest in peace. 'Tis of Mary Elizabeth I do thinky and thinky. Swear to I, lad, over thee's 'dirk-handle, that thee'll be a true man to me sely child? Her thinks the world of 'ee, Tom, and that's the blessed truth. And though she be only sixteen come Martimas her can beake a ceake crisp as any wold wife in Wareham."

Our friend's attention was now diverted by the two monks rising simultaneously from their seats. But he caught one more remark of the man called Tom, apparently commenting on the care with which Jimmy the Mummer had placed his long-bow on the board beside him with an arrow across its string.

"With your pardon, my Lords," said Father Pascentius, "Father

Rheinalt and I must be descending the hill. The hour is late; and, as it is, we shall have to enter by the Abbot's postern. Brother Glyn over there, Master Constable, may with your good leave have to stay the night in the castle. There are some little trifles of church-tribute due to the Almoner that he has instructions to collect. We bid ye good-night, gentles all! *Dimitte populi tui, Deus, et ostende eis viam bonam per quam ambulent—et da gloriam in loco isto."*

"*Et da gloriam in loco isto,"* repeated Father Rheinalt; and they moved quickly across the hall to give their final instructions to the restless lay-brother.

The two noblemen emitted the unconscious sigh of relief that the departure of the learned commonly evokes, and moving nearer to each other began consulting in whispers.

Denis kept his eyes fixed on his accustomed point in space; while Jimmy Mummer's hands, as he listened to Master Hardy's re-assuring voice, kept fidgetting uneasily with that long-bow string, as if, beyond all rationality, he would dearly have loved to discharge its deadly missive clear at the heart of this perambulatory cleric.

"I have a notion"—it was the Constable's voice directly addressing our friend—"that this dark night may end in a storm. Perhaps this would be, therefore; a good moment—"

"Do you mean a thunder-storm, sir?" interrupted Rhisiart. "I've been thinking myself, sir, that there's something queer about the darkness that has rolled up in the last hour. It has fascinated the lay-brother over there, too. Look, sir! He's talking about it to Father Rheinalt; and it seems clear to me—"

It must have seemed clear to the philosophic Constable that like other young persons when the moment for rest is mooted, the Oxonian was saying anything that came into his head, behaving in fact like a child who hopes to make its elders forget the fatal motion of the clock.

But something so startling had just then met the lad's eye that his childish babble was changed to an intense desire to turn away the Constable's attention from the talk between Tegolin's father and the lay-brother. As for Father Pascentius our friend hadn't failed to mark the undignified haste with which, jerking up his habit like an impatient old woman, he had scuttled out of the hall.

"I must wake Brut! I must wake Brut!" was Rhisiart's chief thought now; and he found himself trembling with excitement as he shook the Lollard by the wrist, waving that object up and down and taking care to hide the man's face while he did so. Oh! he could feel the Constable's steady gaze watching him; and he couldn't help becoming cognizant too of an intense interest taken in his proceedings by Hywel Sele.

The drunken idea had evidently entered the Lord of Nannau's head that he might pick up some new manner of tormenting a sleeper by watching Rhisiart's roughness to his friend.

But Walter Brut was fully awake now; and our Oxonian got a glimpse into the instinctive sagacity of the Hereford squire that astonished him not a little. For the Lollard, having drawn a deep breath, and having stretched himself by throwing back his head, as a dog does when it is rudely waked, gave one slow meditative look at everyone in the hall, ending with a concentrated stare at what our friend had seen, and hurriedly rose to his feet, pulling up Rhisiart with him.

"*Garde à toi!*" he whispered. "*It's Owen himself!*"

Now what our friend had seen, when he realized that he must turn the Constable's attention away from the lay-brother's attention, was an actual slipping down, by several inches, of that great beggarly beard, and the appearance beneath it of the familiar forked beard of shining gold.

Nor had this been all. He had noticed that before Tegolin's father left Owen's side and hurried out of the hall, just as rapidly, though with a bolder stride, than Father Pascentius, he had received from beneath Owen's voluminous robe a thick and newly-woven coil of rope!

"*My Lords!*" It was Owen himself speaking. And there he was— standing with his back to the only entrance, his right hand thrust through the handle of a sword he must have been concealing as well as the rope, so that the bare blade was now swinging from his wrist like a giant's trinket, while in his free hands was one of the Salopian long-bows that had been left by the weary troopers when they were dismissed.

Standing thus, like Odysseus confronting the suitors and tossing away his habit and his false beard, Owen emptied a full quiver of arrows upon the table in front of him.

"*My Lords!*"

Hotspur and Fitz-Alan were on their feet in a second, the former drawing his sword, the latter buckling his belt. Quicker than a flash of lightning could have burst did that bare blade appear in Harry

Percy's hand; but not less quick—for the brain, even of an Oxford student, can move faster than lightning—the queerest side-way impression rushed through Rhisiart's consciousness.

"What a friendly weapon," he thought, "that sword of Hotspur's is!" It was certainly an old sword; and it fitted the man's hand like a glove. Its ancient cross-handle in some fantastic way conveyed to the lad's mind the notion that it was a *kind* sword! It certainly had a homely look, and a proverbial, mellow, North-Country anvil-look. It looked like an heraldic sword, and yet it looked like the sword of a "good giant" in a fairy-tale.

Indeed before this rush of unexpected suggestions had been whirled out of the boy's head he actually found himself contemplating the gleaming object as if it weren't a death-dealing thing at all, but something which you could use for homely usage—almost like a spade!

"My Lords!" And as Rhisiart stared at Owen standing there under a great sconce of flaming torches, slowly and deliberately fitting an arrow to his string, it seemed to him that not only the forked beard and the princely torque and the gleaming breast-plate were all of gold, but that from the man's figure itself emanated a supernatural light!

Rhisiart's nerves, as may be imagined, were in a state of hyper-tension, and this tension was rather increased than diminished by the fact that a real flash of lightning, which was followed immediately by a startling burst of thunder, interrupted Owen's words. The lightning lit up for a second the entrance to the hall, but its cessation, for it was not repeated, made the dense darkness behind that golden figure more Tartarean than before.

Rhisiart had, as we know, a sturdy and un-mystical soul; but Modry's imagination had dominated his childhood, and though his intelligence assured him that it needed no magician to conjure up a storm on a night like this, it was impossible to suppress an exultation in the feeling that when his hero, his god, *did* show himself at last, the age-old tokens of the conspiring elements were there at his side!

"My Lords! I have only one request to make of you, and then I'll trouble you no further. You are Peers of the Realm of England, and I am Owen ap Griffith Fychan. But I have to ask you, as I stand here in this hall of my ancestors, to permit me, with all due courtesy and according to the laws of chivalry, to take away with me to-night Rhisiart ab Owen, my Secretary, and Walter Brut of Hereford, my Librarian; which same learned and honourable persons were hostages for me in this castle of Dinas Brān for as long as I didn't appear to claim them."

Hotspur began pushing back the refectory-table, in his heavy, easy-going fashion. He clearly intended to walk straight up to Owen and enter upon a friendly discussion with him. Neither the dramatic stir in the elements nor the fantastical strangeness of Owen's appearance—as if the man really were the necromancer people accused him of being—seemed to impinge on his consciousness at all. He had told Father Rheinalt he wanted to see Owen; and here the fellow was. A few direct and friendly words together, and what waste of life and property might be avoided!

"One minute—one minute—Baron Owen," Rhisiart heard him say, as he stamped with one of his armed heels on the stone floor to get rid of a trifle of cramp. But before he could advance a step the explosion had occurred.

Rhisiart hadn't even time to turn his head, but it crashed through his brain, as if he'd been hit by the arrow himself, just what had happened. Without warning, without a nod from his master, old Jimmy Mummer of Puddletown had drawn his bow-string and drawn it by no means, as Scripture says, "at a venture." In fact he had smitten the transfigured lay-brother through the upper part of the very arm that was holding the Salopian's bow. Through the man's arm the well-aimed arrow sped, close to the shoulder, and there it stuck fast, the barb having passed clean through, and the feathers remaining quivering and shivering on the hither side.

Hotspur must have stepped back a pace, recognizing the possibility that a sudden shock of pain might make so impetuous a chieftain start shooting indiscriminately at them all; but with the arrow still piercing his arm and obviously biting pretty sharply, for our friend could see his face twitching, Owen lifted his own borrowed weapon and, as it seemed without giving himself a second to take aim, discharged an arrow full into the throat of his assailant.

This done, and Jimmy Mummer falling choking into Master Hardy's arms, the ex-lay-brother was seen deliberately to fit another arrow to his string. His appearance certainly had for our Oxonian at that moment a more striking air than even the flash of lightning had given it.

He seemed to resemble at the same time a sacrificed god and an avenging god; for, with every movement he made, the arrow-point which stuck out of him and the arrow-feathers which stuck out of him *moved with him,* giving to his appearance a ghastly element of the grotesque.

As he watched him and wondered when he would have to leap to his side there came into our friend's mind a monstrous picture of Saint Sebastian which had followed the Eastern Emperor to Oxford.

The Russian gentleman who spoke of the "insect" had shown it to him and had explained to him that it answered to some special craving in Byzantine piety.

But in Owen's case the effect was further enhanced by the manner his short sword—of the kind known on the Marches as "Roman"— swung from his wrist.

But Owen was speaking again now. "I am sorry, my Lords, this thing happened. I shall pray"—and the man actually had the gall, burdened as he was, to cross himself as he stood there—"for the soul of this unhappy person. I should be as he is now, if his hand hadn't shaken; for my throat, like his, lacks a gorget. Will you be pleased, my Lords, to give me your word as gentlemen that Master Rhisiart and Master Brut may depart with me? If you will, this painful scene shall end at once! And let me repeat again—I am sorry to have killed that man; and I promise his friend that I will have Masses said—"

"Damn your Masses, your girt conjuring devil, you whoreson by-blow of a Welsh whore!"

At this Fitz-Alan, who was now kneeling over the dead man, and taking no more notice of Owen than if he'd been one of the pictures on the wall, rebuked Master Hardy; but Master Hardy went on. "What wold Jimmy said to I just now, clear as Sturminster-bell, be enough to crack the heart in I, Mëaster. 'A said, 'Mary Elizabeth,' clear and sensible, as if 'a were in Sarum choir. Ees! Durn ye! I beant afeared of 'ee, ye girt glittering Warlock, and I do pray for thee's whoreson sake thik arrow be *adder-'nointed!*" And Tom Hardy of Milborne Port spat on his fist and shook it fiercely at Baron Owen of Glyndyfrdwy.

But Owen was speaking again. "The first man of you," he shouted, "who makes a movement towards me will get my second arrow. Let

Master Rhisiart and Master Brut come here to me. I don't ask for a safe-conduct out of this castle. I came without permission and I shall go without it. But these two gentlemen must go with me!" But Fitz-Alan took no more notice of Owen than he did of Hotspur. His whole attention was absorbed in the pitiful attempts made by Master Hardy to pull the arrow out of the dead man's throat.

He now said to him in a husky voice, "Shall *I* do that, or do *you* want to do it, Tom?"

"Do't thee wone self, Mëaster!" And Rhisiart was destined to see a sight he'd never seen before, and a horrible sight it was. For the Earl had put his heel on the Mummer's body, and pull with his whole strength, to get the barb of the arrow out of the man's neck; and when the thing did come, the black blood that followed was a grievous sight. It was a sight, however, that caused nothing but lively interest in the Lord of Nannau.

Rhisiart was too occupied with wondering whether he ought to rush to Owen's side to pay much attention to the two gentlemen from the Tassel. But once when by chance he did turn his head it was to discover that the drunken Sele was actually on the floor by his friend's side, shouting into his ear that the Devil had come to take him to Hell in the person of Owen Glendower.

Rhisiart couldn't help a moiety of his attention being arrested by what the smooth-faced gentleman was saying. "He's come for you, Gam, and you'd better go quietly; and I'll go home to bed. I shall miss you in the morning, Gam, but it can't be helped. Better go quietly with him, Gam; and I'll to the Tassel. Say goodbye, Gam! It may after all suit you better than Purgatory. You'll find a wondrous company of whores down there, Gam. When you see those Irish girls we killed, ask 'em which they like best, *us or the devils.*"

Master Brut by this time, heedless of the blood, was on his knees by Fitz-Alan's side. His eyes were tight shut; but he wasn't telling his beads or muttering anything in Latin. He was, to Rhisiart's amazement, addressing the Son of Mary in plain English and as if He were standing a few paces away.

Hotspur, meanwhile, leaning on his "kindly" sword, kept his puzzled but quite self-possessed gaze fixed on the strange figure at the end of the hall.

"That arrow ought to come out," Rhisiart heard him mutter. But Denis addressed the Northumbrian without turning his head. He too kept his eyes on Owen.

"With your permission, my Lord," he said, "I think I *will* let these lads go. They're his hostages. And he's come to claim them."

"Let 'em go," muttered the other. And again he repeated, "That arrow ought to come out."

But the Constable moved to Fitz-Alan's side. "I may tell him he can have them, my Lord?"

"Them?—*us*—*all!*" groaned the Earl, staring at his dead servant; but immediately after and with a flicker of a grim smile, "Parley with him, parley with him, Constable. Didn't you hear what he said? *She'd* never forgive me if he shot you too!"

It was clear that neither of the great noblemen felt impelled at that juncture to disregard Owen's threat.

But Denis Burnell, who had nothing but Saxon blood in his veins, and whose great-grandfather was a Shropshire shepherd, appeared to feel that the son of the King's Sheriff had certain duties to perform which were unavoidable. So without a weapon in his hand, or a word in his mouth, he strode hurriedly up the hall, neither holding his head high nor holding it low, but keeping his eyes, as usual, fixed on some remote point in space that was neither bounded by Owen's golden beard nor by the black darkness behind it.

Slowly, as he came near, the solitary figure beyond the trestle-board allowed his transfixed arm and his dangling sword to sink down.

Rhisiart with his eyes screwed up into burning, glittering points, out of which the soul of the lad rather than his intelligence gleamed, watched while the two whispered together, with nothing but the table between them; but presently Denis turned round and easily and naturally beckoned to him.

After muttering he hardly knew what to the two Lord-Marchers, and literally dragging his friend from his knees, Rhisiart advanced up the hall.

"That arrow ought to come out!" was the last word he was privileged to hear from the lips of Harry Percy.

"A keepsake, Constable!" he caught in a hoarse murmur from Owen, and with a gasp of consternation he saw his hero hand over to Denis his precious "Roman" sword.

Well! It was all over now, and into the heart of the scriptural "outer darkness" Glyn Dŵr led his youthful hostages from that lighted hall.

"We are going the wrong way," our friend heard the Lollard mutter, as they moved through the impenetrable obscurity. "This isn't the way to the gate!" he repeated.

"We're not going to the gate," their guide replied. "We're going by the ramparts. Father Rheinalt is there with our rope." *With our rope?* Was this astonishing man assuming that a monk, a scholar and an Oxford student had the knowledge and courage of sailor-boys.

Presently they heard the deep-throated voice of Tegolin's father. And the voice came from the precise direction towards which they were hurrying. All they had to do was to increase their speed. How on earth had their guide known which way to go? Was the substance of this extraordinary man's nature actually porous in some way, like that of animals and birds, to the chemistry of the elements? Or was he *really,* as his enemies were always hinting, a black magician?

"I don't care," our friend thought, as with his fingers in Master Brut's belt he hurried after his hero, *"what* he is! I shall never leave—"

But suddenly with a deep interior shiver came the thought of that rope! Ah! here were the ramparts—all broken and jagged at this point —and here was the dark form of Father Rheinalt!

The monk was tugging with might and main to make his great coil sure and fast round the abutment of a massive and unbroken stone.

Rhisiart shuddered when he peered into the black gulf into which that rope descended. How high did the wall just here rise above the ground? A sickening sensation seized him, like fingers of ice clutching at his vitals. He could feel his torn and bleeding hands slipping, sliding, losing their hold.

"Can *you* do it?" he whispered to Master Brut; and he knew the Lollard was smiling by the familiar tone of his response.

"Of course, lad, if the monk can! Twist your legs round it, that's the great thing; and take it hand under hand. Don't let it slide through your fingers. We used to do it to get crows' nests. Kick yourself clear of the wall as you go down."

But Rhisiart suddenly knew that *nothing* could make him trust himself to that rope. And with this knowledge there came upon him the worst moment he had known in his whole life. The wildest, maddest ideas rushed through his mind. "For his sake," he thought, "I could jump down there! But swing over that blackness on that—"

"Who goes there?" And the blaze of a lantern, whose shade had suddenly been removed, flashed upon all four of them.

Luckily it wasn't a trooper. It was one of Denis's regular watchmen. And the worthy man, an elderly ex-forester from Chirk, was more startled than the men he'd stumbled on. This sudden uncovering of his lantern upon such a group, one of them with an arrow through his arm, was such a shock to him that Master Brut who was nearest had no difficulty in pinioning his arms to his sides and throwing him to the ground. There was a brief struggle, during which the fellow kept crying out, "Help! Murder!"

But it ended with the Lollard getting his light away from him and kneeling on his prostrate form, while the lantern, lying on its side, threw weird horizontal rays upon the monk's sandals.

All this while Rhisiart kept saying to himself, "I can jump and I can die, but I can't—"

A black dizziness was attacking him now. He felt as if he had *already* jumped, and was lying dead beneath the wall. As he fought against this blackness he was aware of the monk deliberately untwisting the girdle of his habit and binding it round the prostrate man, while the Lollard did what he could to stifle his piercing cries.

But what was that? Oh, Hail Mary! Hail Mary! Hail Mary! Weren't those shouts? And weren't they answering the cries of the man on the ground?

"I can jump and die, but I can't—" But the blackness was over him now, O the blackness. . . .

Not dead? Hadn't he jumped then? Where was he? What was that light in his eyes? Tree-trunks? There were no trees in Dinas Brān!

"There, lad! A drop more of this, and you'll be all right."

It was from Owen's own little silver phial that this choking fire-water was bringing him back. They were in the midst of a thick coppice of birch-trees, on whose white trunks the lantern was flickering.

He began at once babbling the most childish questions; and he saw it was Owen, his face twitching with pain, who was answering him with grave amusement.

"Did I jump?" he gasped.

"*Jump,* lad? You wouldn't be alive if you had! You *climbed* down —like the rest of us!"

He shut his eyes. He began to feel that "blackness" again. No, no! He *couldn't* have done that.

"You came down just as I told you to!" threw in Master Brut. "You came down faster than my Lord, faster than the Father."

And then he remembered how he had ridden forward on Griffin that far-off Midsummer Eve, between the bows and the spears. He'd been in a trance *then,* a trance of "blackness," like this time! It must have been Owen who willed him to do what he *couldn't* do!

"*But*—" he began.

"There are no 'buts,' " said the Lollard. "Down you came, like any ship-boy. Best not think about it any more, lad!"

But our friend seemed unable to stop thinking about it and asking questions about it. He was in that soft, melting tearful mood, with which young people return to consciousness after some crushing experience, and he couldn't help blurting out, with his eyes fixed on his hero:

"How did *you* learn, sir, to climb down ropes so easily?"

Owen was on his feet now, passively submitting, though with many suppressed groans, to Father Rheinalt's blundering attempts to loosen the arrow.

"Much as—your friend *did!*" he cried; but the final word emerged from his mouth with something so like a scream that the Lollard could no longer contain himself.

"Excuse me, Father," he cried, thrusting the monk away. "I am more of a doctor than you. In these things we need to be pitiless. Please kneel down, Lord Owen, and cling to the tree as fast as you did to that rope. I must hurt you *very sore* so you'd better bite on this." And the calm blooded Wycliffite, while Owen obediently though with a wry face sank down and gripped the tree, searched about with the watch-

man's lantern till he found a fragment of not too rotten wood. Clenching his teeth upon this object the Lord of Glyndyfrdwy prepared to
bear what was coming.

Our friend stumbled to his feet. He longed to share his master's
suffering. He longed to press himself against that noble form and sob
out his devotion.

The monk meanwhile was glaring at the self-constituted doctor as if
he could have killed him.

"Stand back, Father!" cried Owen; and then to the Lollard: "Get
birch-lichen if I bleed—*birch-lichen*—do you understand?"

The Lollard nodded. And Owen turned to Rhisiart. "Hold the light
for him, cousin!"

After examining with the utmost care both the head of the arrow and
its feathers, which latter were now clinging close to the shaft owing
to the hot hands of the nervous monk, the first thing the Lollard did
was to take out his knife and sever this feathered end of the dart, as
close as possible to the wound. The next thing he did was to cut away
every strip of clothing from the man's shoulder.

"Hold it *steady*, lad!" And Rhisiart, clenching his own teeth, did at
least succeed in preventing the light from skipping about like a will-
o'-the-wisp, anywhere but on the hurt arm.

"*Now*, my Lord!" And Owen's teeth sank into the block of wood,
while the Lollard, bending low over the man's shoulder, and gripping
the arrow-head and the few inches of shaft that had followed it through
the flesh threw all his spirit into one clean, straight, unshrinking pull,
till—while the lantern suddenly flung its rays at the sky—he lifted up
the whole weapon, bloody, but unbroken, safe in his hands!

Owen uttered a long, gurgling sigh, like the release of water from
under a lifted weir, and loosening his grip of the birch-trunk sank
down beneath it, while from his mouth the piece of wood, bitten
clean through, fell with a just perceptible sound upon the wet moss.

The Lollard promptly snatched the lantern from our friend, and
its rays instead of tremblingly searching the zenith fell upon the dark
stream of red blood now issuing from Owen's flesh.

"Birch-lichen!" whispered the wounded man. "Press it against the
place and bind it tight! And give me my phial."

But our friend Rhisiart, to use the expressive Homeric phrase, "took other counsel."

Within the narrow but astute cranium of his Norman skull there had just repeated itself that ominous word uttered by Master Hardy—"adder-'nointed." He waited till the Father had held the phial to Owen's lips; but he refused to wait till Master Brut returned with the lichen.

"*Cousin Owen,*" and it was only the intensity of his feeling that made him use that word, "I heard the man's friend speak of adder's poison. I want to suck your hurt before he binds it up!"

The chieftain's eyes opened wide, and a very strange look flickered up into them. "If you will, child," he murmured faintly, "but my blood is dangerous."

Rhisiart didn't wait for further permission. Kneeling down by his hero's side in the darkness he had no difficulty in finding the wound in his arm and pressing his lips to it. Then he sucked and swallowed and sucked and swallowed.

"Spit it out, coz! Spit it out! A man's blood's a man's soul. Do'ee want to share—"

But in spite of this protest, our young friend knew well that the unhurt arm had been lifted, and that his master's fingers were stroking his head.

The Lollard had nothing but praise for his fellow-hostage's behaviour when he returned with the lantern and the lichen; but Father Rheinalt, from that moment till they reached Glyndyfrdwy, uttered not one single word.

"I oughtn't to have let him do it," thought Glyndyfrdwy's lord. "*I* know those Wessex men-at-arms! They're the same to-day as they were in King Alfred's time. *Adder-'nointed!* They all talk like that; but they'd no more poison one of their weapons than they'd trust a Welshman with one of their daughters. Why did I let him do it then? Why didn't I make him *know* how it commits him? Ha! old conjurer, at your tricks again! Well, if it *has* been, it *was* to be, and if it *is* to be, it *will* be. You don't know what you've done; and I don't know what I've let you do, Rhisiart ab Owen. But I know *this* well enough. I've got what I wanted!"

XII

MATHRAFAL

It was about dawn on September the sixteenth, in the first year of the fifteenth century, that Owen Glendower threw off the heavy wolf's skin beneath which he had slept, and looked about him in that familiar room at Glyndyfrdwy, the room that his jesting family had long nicknamed "the magician's chamber."

The coals on the open hearth were still red, and in the grey light that seemed pressing like a sorrowful face against the narrow window he could see lying still open upon his desk the old parchment-covered folio—the most precious of all his books—which he had been championing the night before. It contained poems and prophecies reputed to have been uttered by Taliesin, Llywarch Hēn, and others—one or two claiming to be from the actual mouth of Merlin himself!

Even his friend Iolo had confessed himself unable to interpret more than a line here and there of these *ogyrvens* as he had called them. The old Bard had done much better with Taliesin. But that great pilgrim of incarnations, whose special genius for imaginative metempsychosis made the human soul seem like an unwearied traveller down the ages, was still as much of a riddle to him as was the obscurer Merlin.

Before he slept last night he had summoned his impassioned harp-player, Griffith Llwyd ab Einion, and had spread out the mystic pages before *him;* but Griffith had explained at such length, and with so many technicalities, how the whole art of poetry had been revolutionized by Dafydd ap Gwilym, that Owen had been seized with an unscholarly rage; and had, he now remorsefully remembered, seriously hurt his faithful Bard's feelings by declaring roundly that these fashionable modern *cywyddau,* lovely as they were, totally lacked the terrible grandeur of the earlier inspiration.

Justly irritated by this outburst, the worthy man had grown vehement in his defence of modern poetry, maintaining that it dealt with living realities, in place of parables and symbols and mythic fables; and had finally so warmed to his subject as to challenge his lord and master to prove by some actual quotations from the book before them the superiority—in anything but oracular obscurity—of the old over the new.

This challenge—and Owen smiled in that grey light as he recalled how it had confounded him—he had unworthily dodged in a manner more proper to a touchy baron than a patient scholar, merely muttering something about its being better for a great bard to write of magic cauldrons and mystic castles and the Lords of the Under-World than of the arching of ladies' eyebrows and the curves of their breasts.

Standing there staring at that narrow window and thinking of the ceremony before him and of the dragon-beflagged pavilion that had been erected for it in the field by the river, an anger against his fate greater than he had ever known before, though something akin to it was a recurrent mood with him, swept over his soul. He glanced at the red coals of his fire. He glanced at the couch from which he'd risen, and he gave vent to a sigh that seemed to come from depths below his consciousness.

He suddenly felt like someone who has been dragged back from levels of life far more satisfying than any outward events, levels where he could lose himself in the unlabouring flow of the tides of Being.

He loosened one or two of the galling hooks of his mail-shirt, and kicking off the fur slippers in which he'd been sleeping began hurriedly pulling on his silken hose and his new-fashioned deer-skin garters. Then he struggled into his upward-twisted boots with their fantastical curve. Thus accoutred but still unwashed and uncombed he went to the iron-barred door and listened. *Tramp—tramp—tramp,* up and down the whole length of the corridor. Yes, his faithful door-man was on guard as usual.

He hesitated for a moment, contemplating in the grey light a couple of curious marks that had been cut in the wood-work of the door. They were clearly meant for some sort of lettering—the initial letters of some child's name—but it was a calligraphy so different from the kind used now that neither his father nor *his* father had known whose initials they were. Lost, lost, the hand that made those marks.

And so would this day be lost—at least *as it was to him;* though no doubt in the chronicles kept at Valle Crucis future pupils would have to learn by rote for their tedious novitiate, "On the sixteenth of September, in this aforesaid year of grace, Owen, son of Griffith the younger, was unanimously proclaimed Prince of Wales by a gathering of the men of Gwynedd and Powys." He stood listening to the lad's marching steps.

"Shall I call him in," he thought, "to make up the fire? No, better not!" and turning to the heap of logs he proceeded to do it himself.

He had certainly awaked in a mood wherein the least encounter with any mortal person was something from which he shrank. Watching the leaping flames throw flickering rays on his ridiculously up-curved shoes he thoughtfully stroked his beard.

And then, as he crossed the room to his chamber-latrine to relieve himself, "Did Bolingbroke feel like this when he first got them to cry 'God save the King!'"

Stepping gingerly now to an arras-hung aperture in the wall he extracted a silver tray of toilet-articles whose dainty appearance would certainly have pleased the heart of Mad Huw's Richard. Conveying these objects to the window, along with a mirror of polished steel, he discovered that the dawn was still too dim for his purpose.

"I suppose it's nothing to you," he thought, apostrophizing the grey slit in the eastern wall, "whether a Prince anoints himself or doesn't anoint himself!" and he impatiently lit one of the great sweet-scented flambeaux that stood above the oracular crystal globe. Then he set himself to comb his beard and arrange with the utmost nicety one of his ancestor's tarnished circlets of gold about his forehead. If he didn't take as much trouble over all this as Hywel Sele had told Hotspur he did, he certainly took a good deal of pains to enhance his princely.appearance; making use of various courtly devices to this end that would have reminded his new Secretary of the fantastical fol-de-rols of Richard's entourage, when that unhappy King kept his Easter Jousts at Hereford.

From his childhood he had had this mania for a meticulous care of his person. How well he knew every curve, every contour, every mark, every hair on his face! It was always a puzzle to him how essentially careless about their appearance all his children were. "They must," he thought, "have got this peculiarity from the Arglwyddes, who—noble and loving creature!—leaves her gown, her head-dress, the fashion of her hair, entirely to her tire-women."

He had often thought, "I don't know *why* I'm so fussy about my appearance. My father wasn't, nor *his* father." But at this moment, as he went on combing his beard and trimming it across his fingers, he was in a mood to carry his self-analysis further.

"I've never been *ashamed*," he thought, "of anything I find I am. I wish to Blessed Mary I hadn't hurt old Griffith's feelings by attacking this clever modern poetry in comparison with the old great bards; but I'm not *ashamed* of it—because that's how I am! I shan't be ashamed of getting a vicious joy in beating down every enemy I have, especially Grey and Sele and Gam and that sly wolf, Fitz-Alan! I'm not ashamed of using one brave man's love, and another brave man's conscience, another's ambition, another's patriotism. I'm not ashamed of using Saint Derfel his holy self!

"No, old cloven-beard"—and he regarded his soft, yet rugged countenance with grave satisfaction—"I'm not even ashamed of my whoremongerings or of lying to the Arglwyddes! And yet, old conjurer"—and he stared long and deeply into his curious-coloured eyes—"you *are* ashamed, really and ultimately *ashamed* of; of something that you habitually do. And 'tis the custom, my tricky cloven-beard"—and the man distorted his face out of all recognition—"for a sovereign prince before his coronation to confess himself to the uttermost!"

Relaxing his visage to its normal form he dipped his fingers in an ointment-pot and managed without removing the bandage to anoint the wound in his arm. "The Arglwyddes," he thought, "will want to dress it, but it'll be too late. The Prince of Wales provides his own holy oil! But *is* there anything to confess? Owen confessing to Owen!"

And then he drew a deep and bitter sigh. And as if fishing for his own self-treachery in his fluctuating eyes he spiked with his spirit a terribly glittering fish, and as he caught it he thought, "That's my reward for knowing you so well, old cloven-beard. I can detach myself from you till my soul *isn't in you at all,* till my soul is there, or there, or *there*"—and he made motions with his head—"till my soul's so independent of you that it can make you do anything—*perhaps even live after you're dead!*

"Yes, old conjurer, there's a soul watching you that by petting you and cossetting you and humouring you has got all your secrets out of you, and has caught now, on your declaration day, the most slippery one of all. Listen, forked-beard! Listen, treacherous eyes! You want to do it—all you're going to do—not as the elements do things, not as the Spirit of the elements does things, but as priests and druids and magicians and fortune-tellers go to work, *by meddling with the future!*"

Had the gargoylish head that the monkish scribe had caused to emerge from the letter "M," with which the unintelligible prophecy in the open folio began, been endowed as some have fancied such entities are with the power of vision, it would have been startled at that moment to see the prospective Prince of Wales grimly and with some physical distress hook up his mail-shirt and when this was done fall on his knees.

Had this angel-demon head been also—as a child might pretend—possessed of thought-reading powers, it would have been further startled by hearing the following voiceless prayer:

"Oh Unknown Spirit of the Universe, build up before me, before the soul of Owen ap Griffith Fychan, like the rampart of an unassailable fortress, the unbroken, the undisturbed, the absolute darkness of your impenetrable purpose!"

Rising to his feet, after this, Owen replaced his mirror, put away the various utensils of his toilet, and going to the door listened to the marching steps of his sentry. Then, as soon as he knew that the man was at the remotest end of the corridor, he rushed to the wall where his ancestral weapons hung and took down a mighty battle-axe of antique design. The next thing he did was to fling over the magic globe, which now reflected the first real light of the rising sun, the wolfskin from his head. Then after a moment's pause he raised the great axe in both hands and brought it crashing down upon the hidden crystal. Three times he raised the axe and struck. At the first blow the thing cracked; but with such a strange sound that it came near to relaxing his nerve. At the second blow the crack sank deeper into the darkened object. At the third the crystal fell into fragments! He stood listening intently, leaning on the handle of the weapon and surveying the wolf-skin.

Tramp . . . tramp . . . tramp! His sentry's steps drew near. No! thank the Mother of God—they receded again. The fellow was surly and faithful; but, even so, he felt at that moment as if he would shriek like a woman at the shock of facing another, *any* other, human soul.

There, the sun had risen! A thin spear-head of golden rays flickered upon the crumpled skin that now lay almost flat upon the massive oak support. He stared at the ruffled pall, as if he expected to see blood-stains of some sort—blood-stains of the eidola of the future—staining that grey pelt.

Making a painful effort, he switched off the covering; and the golden light, now no longer a mere spear-head, bathed the illuminated fragments. He counted them mechanically. There were seven of them. Half-mechanically he cast his mind forward. "Fourteen hundred and—" but he brusquely curbed *that* thought, and carrying back the old war-axe to its place hung it up as it was before. Then he gathered the seven fragments together and conveyed them to a chest over against his books, removing and replacing all that the chest contained till the fragments were concealed. This done, he pushed the oaken stand, still intact but badly dented, to the same spot, and lifting it up in his arms, not without consciousness that his shoulder was giving him some vicious pangs, placed it on the top of the chest. Then he went to the window, and facing the sunlight, all grandly accoutred and anointed as he was, became—had there been eyes peeping through that arrow-slit to see—a figure of gleaming gold.

His countenance, however, had suddenly grown strangely stupid and dull, like the drugged and helpless countenance of a sacrificial animal. And thus he lapsed, even as he stood, into one of those singular trances that had caught Rhisiart's attention when they first met.

Had the continuance of this queer coma, like the sleep of a beast who sleeps as it stands, been threatened by the familiar knock of his surly sentry he might not have been roused; but a lighter, though hardly less familiar tap took him to the door, and it was against the girlish breast of his youngest child, warm from her bed, that his soul came back from its fathom-deep recession.

It was much later on that eventful morning—that morning in the middle of the first September of the new century—when the self-anointed Prince of Wales—for this was a declaration not a coronation—the long fantastic ceremony over, stood alone on his high platform in the pavilion by the river to listen to the voices of his subjects. Old Griffith, the family Bard, had already recited, to his own accompaniment on the harp, a carefully prepared poem in the manner he had defended so vigorously, and he had just begun, what struck the new Prince as a far more inspired performance, an improvised chant in the older style, when the irrepressible Scab, clearly determined that prophecy on this occasion should supersede poetry, burst into a Derfel-celebrating series of dithyrambic howls.

As was always the case, the extraordinary waves of magnetism that vibrated in the voice of this singular person soon began to release emotions which the solemnity of the ceremony had hitherto held in check. Glendower himself, however, as he watched that crowd of upturned faces extending far beyond the entrance of the tent grew sadder at heart.

"Long live Owen, Prince of Powys!"

"Blood," he said to himself, "blood and ashes! That's what *this* means."

"Long live Owen, Prince of Gwynedd!"

"I'll do it," he thought. "Nothing can stop me now. *But to what end?* There won't be a castle in Wales in Harry's hands when I've finished with him. *But to what end?*"

"Long live Owen, Prince of Deheubarth!"

He raised his hands to his forehead and adjusted more comfortably the old coronet of his race, made of heavy gold, that Hywel ap Madoc, Dean of St. Asaph, had unearthed from his cathedral's crypt.

"Will they stop shouting," he thought, "when I sit down?" And the grotesque idea rushed into his head: "Suppose that old oak throne from Meifod breaks down under my weight? What did William the Norman say when he fell on his knees at Senlac? But I shouldn't fall on my knees!"

"Long live Owen, Prince of Wales!"

He let his eyes move slowly from face to face among the figures in front of him.

How proud and happy the Arglwyddes looked! *She* at any rate wasn't thinking of blood and ashes! He turned from his wife to his brother Tudor, who was standing between her and *her* brothers, Griffith and Philip Hanmer; and there shot into his brain the memory that this kind-hearted man, younger than himself by a year and a half, had once carried him up the last lap of Snowdon on his back. *He* looked exultant and happy too. *He* wasn't thinking of blood and ashes. And then he caught the eye of his new Secretary, as the lad stood by Meredith's side holding in his hands the new standard, a golden dragon on a white ground, about which he was weary of hearing his women talk. It was the Arglwyddes's choice. He knew it was all wrong. It ought to have been a red dragon, not a yellow one. But what matter? It would soon be red enough! But that boy was *his;* body and soul he was *his.* That's what he'd wanted, and that's what he now had.

"Only I wish," he thought, "that little Catharine wouldn't stare at him so!"

He lowered himself cautiously into his ricketty "throne." It creaked, but didn't collapse. "Meredith must have had it tinkered up," he thought. "He remembers everything. How sulky Griffith looks! But the rest of the boys"—and his eyes swept hurriedly along the line of tall lads, come at his call across the mountain from Sycharth and now grouped behind their mother's chair—"Mother of God! they look as if this were in Westminster Hall! What do they think, the brave children? That their sisters have only to embroider golden dragons, and their dad only to put a gilded bit of iron round his head, and Bolingbroke will send heralds of peace? How many of *you,* my bright-eyed lads, will live to see the *real crowning* of Owen? Blood and ashes—but I shall do it. But oh! how sad Meredith looks!"

Crach Ffinnant had fallen into a monotonous chant now; and Owen, settling himself in his ancestral chair, had plenty of time to let his thoughts wander where they would. It was even unnecessary for him to keep a responsive eye on the prophet of Derfel, for the sole concern of that magnetizer of souls seemed to be to make an impression on the Arglwyddes and the ladies who surrounded him!

And it was, as he turned his own eyes upon the mother of his children, touching enough to him—for he knew her so well!—to see the attempt she was making to look sympathetic towards the Scab,

when in reality she was both puzzled and horrified. But there was a
pair of bright eyes near the great lady that showed no such weakness.
Twice already during that interminable ceremonial had he caught the
lively and wanton gaze of young Efa from Dinas Brān.

He knew Efa well. He had seen her when she first came to these
regions; he had seen her as a maiden when he visited the Lady Ffraid;
and he had heard rumours of the shameless, or was it the miraculous,
notion that had obsessed her since she'd grown up of being chosen as
Derfel's bride.

What completely puzzled him was how the girl had got out of the
old lady's keeping. Had the Scab kidnapped her? No—impossible!
Even he wouldn't dare to presume as far as that. Besides—oh, the
whole thing was unthinkable. One of the least fatal aspects of it would
be a blood-feud to the death with the Tudors of Mōn..

But what an amorous little wench she looked! Owen gravely raised
his left hand—for the right one held the golden-hilted sword of Madoc
ap Meredith, his family's best substitute for the prehistoric treasure in
the hands of Adam of Dinas Brān—and tugged, as was his habit when
exercised in his nerves, first at one and then at the other of the points
of his forked beard. He couldn't keep out of his mind another shameless girl's face—and yet it was a shamelessness different from this—
that had looked up at him once, when before going to Richard's wars
he had let the Scab twist to a lecherous purpose his mystical interest in
Derfel Gadarn.

"No, I *won't* smile at you, you tormenting minx!" he thought. And
then he became aware that the Scab's madness was spreading rapidly
through the whole host of spearmen who crowded round that richly-
decorated pavilion on the southern bank of the Dee.

He knew their habits of thought so well and he knew their local
dialects so well that, though many of them used the slang of Ardudwy
and of the regions round about Mur-y-Castell and Penllyn, he could
catch from their excited comments upon the prophet's oration that
they were beginning to indulge in the hope that the wild scene of three
years ago, when under the "holy madness" they had forced him into
the mound-chamber, as if he'd been Derfel himself, and the wantonest
maid of the *cantref* with him, was going to be repeated.

He ceased tugging at his forked beard. He was suffering a curious physical pain just then, the cause of which he alone of living men knew.

It was old Iolo who had set him upon this trick. The old man had sworn not to die, had sworn to linger on in a half-death like a corpse-god, if he weren't obeyed. He could hear him now assuring him with oracular earnestness that he would never free Wales if he didn't wear day and night, as monks do their hair-shirts, a coat of chain-armour under his clothes.

In these last months—and he couldn't have kept the secret from the Arglwyddes, if they hadn't ceased sleeping together after Catharine's birth—he had only taken the thing off when his door was barred and not always even then.

But to-day when he had to wear Eliseg's belt in addition, he couldn't relax when the mail-coat, separated only by a silk shirt from his ribs, began to chafe and bruise him. His arrow-wound troubled him much less; but it too was a discomfort, because in the natural process of healing and under the weight of all these ceremonious robes it had set up a lively tickling.

One of the few things he had over-heard of his enemy's talk to Hotspur and Fitz-Alan was Sele's statement that he had no sense of humour. His malicious relative had bawled this out in a tone that was meant to emulate the coarse camp-jesting of Norman barons. But it alone, of all the fellow had said, had pierced Owen's chain-armour.

"*Am* I," he said to himself, as he fidgetted on his princely chair under this combination of pain and tickling, "am I devoid of a sense of humour? I'm certainly not devoid of something resembling it. But I just notice such things and let them go. I suppose humour's a thing that bubbles up, like loving-kindness, out of a person's soul. No, cousin; you're right. My soul can't send up bubbles like that, any more than yours can, sweet coz—even when it's drunk!"

And as Owen sat on there, growing less and less at ease both in mind and body, and even while a portion of his brain had begun to devise methods and schemes to side-track this mounting mob-excitement, there came over him a vision of the one man he had met whose English humour—and English it certainly was; and yet what profound wisdom lay behind it!—had impressed him as a thing of genius. How well he could see it now, that portly form of the famous Lollard, Sir Thomas Oldcastle! Instinctively he looked about him for the evangelical countenance of his new Librarian. Yes, there he was, evidently more aware than his friend with the Norman nose of the sinister electricity that the prophet was conjuring up.

But Owen looked in vain for any Oldcastle humour in those gently worried lineaments. Master Brut evidently was, as he perpetually claimed with somewhat pedantic emphasis, a Welsh heretic, not an English one! No, there was nothing in *him* of that deep fountain of philosophy which in "the old man of the castle" took the form of humour.

"There's something formidable in the fellow," Owen concluded, "and I must find out what. But it isn't what Sir Thomas had!" And then it came to him with what a quizzical eye the great Oldcastle would regard the present scene, and himself seated in this ricketty old chair, aching under the pressure of Eliseg's belt! But he mustn't think of these things; he mustn't think of the monstrous grotesquerie of human affairs. Action—*any* action—hadn't he learnt that?—meant evil as well as good. Save a man's life? And what will he do with it? Starve his serfs; murder his friend; drive his woman into despair, and then die a death far worse than the one you've saved him from!

"Yes, what I'm doing now, and what *nothing* can stop me from doing, won't only mean ashes and blood. It'll mean mumming and miming and play-acting and masquerading, till a man's heart turns sick! Well—well"; and he shifted his fingers from his ancestral sword and pressed them—he hadn't let himself do *even that* before—against his bandaged arm, "I've got to save those shining eyes and that baby-mouth *somehow*. How the devil did she get here? What these children *can* do, when the life-lust gets into their little—"

"Long live Owen, Prince of Wales!"

The Scab had now collapsed in complete exhaustion; but matters were looking unpleasant. The Arglwyddes had risen; and the gentlemen were all crowding round, to protect her and the other women. How madly they were pushing forward, that wild host he had called up from nothing! Well! from the caves and camps and homesteads and forests of Edeyrnion and Ardudwy!

He rose to his feet and straightened his shoulders. Both these movements were so painful that they made his mouth twist a little under his beard.

"We want Derfel's bride! We want Derfel's bride!"

Owen raised his left arm with a gesture of authority. "Let Rhys Gethin come to me," he shouted. "Let no man of you move a step till I've talked with Rhys Gethin."

He saw that his brother and his wife's two brothers and his eldest son and Rhisiart and Brut and half-a-dozen more of the gentlemen there had formed a circle round the women; and he saw that Meredith had forced his way out of the pavilion. He let his arm sink down; but raised his voice again.

"I, Owen ap Griffith Fychan," he cried in a clear voice, "swear before you all, and before Derfel Gadarn and his prophet, that I will not sheathe my sword, or cease from battle, till there's not a castle in Wales under any flag but the dragon!"

But the *vivats* for "Owen, Prince of Wales," came fainter now, till the hideous howls, "We want Derfel's bride!" began to drown them completely.

"How do they know that silly child's here?" he thought. "But Griffith's getting angry. *That* won't do. God! if he isn't flinging them back already!"

And then an inspiration came to him. Thrusting his unbandaged arm beneath his robes, he drew forth a parchment-scroll to which was attached a formidable red seal that swung in the air as he raised and straightened the document.

"A moment, my men—a moment!" he cried; and then raising his powerful voice to its fullest pitch so that his words might be heard outside the entrance to the tent, "I have here," he began, "the last will and testament of Iolo Goch, the illustrious Bard of our ancient Princedom! Iolo Goch leaves to me, and through me to you, the greatest host raised in this land since Llewelyn, all the gold which in his long life he stored up! Iolo foresaw by the celestial signs and the sacred constellations just what was to happen on this historic day. I propose, therefore, after talking with Rhys Gethin, to open my old friend's iron chest, referred to here, under his hand and seal, and now in my possession; and although the gold he speaks of in this will and testament"—his word rose to its fullest compass at the word "will" and the word "gold"—

"may be in the ancient coinage and therefore of uncertain value in the Usurper's realm, it were only in accordance"—here he made as if he were reading from the parchment he held—"with Iolo's bequest to me, and to you through my hands, that we delay our march upon the Red Castle until this gold, spoken of in Iolo's will—"

But Rhys the Fierce was now at his side; and it soon became clear to Owen, when the man began explaining a new plan of campaign that had come into his head, that it *was* a hundred times more likely to succeed than the one they had all agreed upon and worked out in such careful detail in their recent council of state.

"Saint Matthew's Fair," Owen kept repeating to himself; and the words called up many enchanted memories. Saint Matthew's Fair wasn't on the morrow for which their march on Ruthin had been planned; it was on the day *after* that, but the delay gave them time to gather round the doomed town in such strength that resistance would be out of the question.

"I've been thinking," Rhys Gethin said, "that Grey when he sees our numbers will be scared to show his nose out of doors. We haven't the engines and we haven't the time for a siege, and we'd only blacken his ruddy walls and then decamp, with no real blow struck at all. If we burnt the town on market-day 'twould be something; but to burn it on Saint Matthew's Day—why 'twould be remembered forever! And that's—oh, damn those men and their blasted Saint!—what *I* suggest. And you see, dear my Lord, 'twould hurt Grey more than anything we could do *except take him prisoner. That* would hurt him most— more than to kill him! I heard his own son, the one who loves the wench I sold for a groat to Master Brut, say that his father'd sooner be dead than in Glendourdy's hands. But to burn Grey's great Fair— think of it, my Prince! Why the news'll travel all over England; and the big merchants of Winchester and Gloucester and Sarum and Exeter will send their pedlars to Chirk or to Castell Goch at Welshpool instead of Ruthin! Why 'tis one of the old devil's chief sources of revenue, this Saint Matthew's Day. He'll howl like a black dog when he smells the smoke going up! I'll see that my people bring plenty of oil. Mother of God! but we'll have a bonfire! The burghers of Chester'll shiver like novice-nuns when the herdsmen of Moel Fammau light their beacon. I know the houses at Ruthin well, my Lord; and I tell you—oh

damn you, you brainless, lecherous Derfel swine! I'll Derfel you! I'll
bridle you! Frighten the ladies, will you, you mountain-hogs? You
wait, my squealers, till Rhys Gethin takes you where you'll get something to squeal for!—I tell you, my Prince, apart from the booths of
the Fair half the roofs of the Ruthin houses are reed-thatched. We'll
light them their candles for sweet Saint Matthew! We'll sell them
Hereford saddles for silver bells! We'll make maidenheads cheap at
Ruthin Fair! We'll give them red flames for their red gold!"

"We want Derfel's bride!"

"Oh, for Mary's sake, hold your peace, you Tegid thieves! I'll give ye
a bride, you bare-foot scavengers! I'll give you gold, you rogues!"

And then, while Rhys explained other advantages of not making the
attack-till the day after to-morrow, Owen thought, "If I don't do something with this fellow, now that I've got him here, I shall deserve—"

And beyond the spear-points, and beyond the ladies' head-dresses,
and beyond the fluttering of the pennons, and beyond the cries for the
Saint's bride, Owen saw the glittering baubles of Saint Matthew as
they were when he and his brother Tudor as little boys came across the
Berwyns on sumpter-mules to the great Fair. He saw the embossed
trappings, the shining shields, the wax figures, the nodding hobby-
horses; and all the enchantment of that early vision came over him with
such force that these crazy shouts about gold and Derfel seemed like
voices in a madhouse.

In a flash he began identifying himself with one particular harness-
merchant of those old times whose glittering wares had fascinated his
imagination. There'd be salesmen there in a couple of days just like
Master Peter of St. Albans. There'd be quaint old travelling pedlars
from Shropshire and Hereford—and then—whirling down upon them
in a moment—shouts and screams and rape and murder and blood and
ashes—and the sly, white face of that fox, Grey, peering out, as the
smoke rose, from some arrow-slit in those inaccessible red walls!

"We want Derfel's bride!" But there were now—thanks be to the
Blessed Mother!—other and equally excited shouts: "The will! The
gold! Iolo's will! Iolo's gold!"

Ah! Meredith had brought in with him now his own special troop
of spearmen from Sycharth, picked men, well-disciplined and well-
armed, old retainers of their house, who would perish, there in the

tent, rather than yield an inch to this mutinous crowd from the mountains.

He took the opportunity of explaining to Rhys in as blunt and clear a manner as was possible in that tumult what insanity it would be to allow the Lady Ffraid's ward to suffer any hurt. "The girl's a Tudor of Mōn," he kept repeating, "and you know, man, what *they* are. They'd go over to Harry to-morrow if a hair of her head was touched! As it is—but they won't believe *that*—it's too wild a tale."

The chieftain from the Conway nodded. Then he listened to the hubbub outside the tent and smiled grimly. "Your gold *nearly* did it, my Lord," he remarked laconically, "but not quite. Can't you think of something else? Can't you take the wench away yourself, as if you were— The old Red Head used always to be talking of Mathrafal. Couldn't you tell them—"

Owen stared at him. Then his face cleared. "Right, as usual, Gethin!" he muttered. "My wits seem dull this fine noon. Owen of. Glyndyfrdwy's a cleverer man than Owen, Prince of Cymru! Well, go out to them, my friend, and tell 'em I'm going to give Derfel his bride. But tell 'em Iolo said it must be done at Mathrafal this time—and *done alone!* Tell Meredith I'll want his troop with me and *only* his! Don't be afraid. I'll send them back and be back myself in plenty of time."

It was one of the rarest and most perfect September afternoons when Owen and Rhisiart, the former on a powerful grey horse, with little Efa, almost invisible in a big mantle, perched behind him, and the latter on his old piebald, rode up the bridle-track that led across the solitary uplands of the Berwyn Range. Owen rode slowly, partly so as not to out-distance his troop, and partly that he might not tire the horses at the beginning of so long a ride. Whether the small creature behind him kept her head turned towards Griffin and *his* rider Owen had no notion. It certainly wasn't necessary for her to cling tightly to him, for if there was one craft in which his river-side adherents excelled it was in saddle-making, and he had had this particular saddle especially designed so that he could take little Catharine with him from Sycharth and back without incommoding her.

He was indeed so little aware of the childish arms that encircled his steel-clad waist that, as he pondered on the events of that momentous morning and on their dubious issue, he caught himself more than once forgetting that there *were* two living souls mounted on that grey steed.

For more than an hour the cavalcade moved forward in silence. What a comfort it was to have a boy like this! Whenever he turned his head to make sure their followers were in sight he caught nothing but a quaint mixture of grim resolution and exultant happiness on his squire's face. The young people certainly weren't chattering to each other! In fact, as mile after mile of fading heather, red whin-patches, and masses of bracken, still green, but sombrely and heavily green, fell behind them, the new Prince might have been riding completely alone so little was there to interrupt his thoughts.

"I must keep those men with me," he thought, "till we get across the mountain. But once across I'll let them wait our return. I'll get to Mathrafal by that path through the forest, where there'll be absolutely no chance of meeting any large body of men; and armed and mounted as we are"—again he forgot the feather-weight at his back—"we needn't worry about ordinary encounters."

He had long since decided that at all costs he must get this ticklish little encumbrance, butterfly-light though she was, back safe to the Lady Ffraid, with all her fragile Tudor "honour"—as hard to preserve, it seemed, as a lily's gold-dust!—intact as when she came.

"I shall take her," he thought, "to Broch-o'-Meifod. Nobody, not all the English in Shropshire, would dare to meddle with her in his mill under *his* protection! She can sleep in his mill to-night. *That'll* be an adventure for her to talk about to her friends on the hill—and Cousin Ffraid will *know* it's been all right."

"Do you like riding over a mountain like this, child?" he asked gently at last, fearing that his absorbed silence might be troubling her.

"Oh yes, my Prince," came the answer. "I've never been so happy."

Her voice rang out so firm and strong that it quite startled him. It was like the sudden ringing of a clear little bell just behind his head.

"I suppose I ought to say something," he thought, "now that the ice *is* broken, to get this 'bride of Derfel' business out of her head." But he was puzzled how to begin. In the elaborate and fantastical code of courtesy in which he had been brought up, and for which the late King's dissolute but punctilious court had been famous, it was one of the basic principles of chivalry to assume that a maid's thoughts were as chaste as those of the Blessed Virgin.

But it had given him an unexpected thrill of pleasure when she said "my Prince" in the tone she did. The Arglwyddes had called him so, and so had all his tall sons when they kissed his hand in the accredited feudal fashion; but these formal ceremonies had been for so long a family jest between them all that when he was about to kiss little Catharine on his departure, and was interrupted by Rhys Gethin's addressing him as "Prince," he heard the child eagerly clap her hands and cry out, "It's begun! It's begun!"

Heaven help him! It had indeed "begun"; and it was in part to blot out the picture of Ruthin market in flames that he plunged into this unchivalrous discourse to Efa.

"I ought to tell you, Demoiselle," he began with unprincely hesitation, "that the great Iolo, whose memory I so revere, directed me—by his occult knowledge of the stars—if I wished to make my revolt a success, to find—to find a bride for Derfel."

Clear and firm, without the least trace of the shyness he was displaying, rang out that little silver bell behind his half-turned head.

"I know—I know! I *want* to be Derfel's bride!"

"But Iolo also said"—may the Saints forgive me for all my lies this morning!—"that it was to be—"

"Yes, my Prince?"

"That lad is perfect," thought Owen. "Bless my soul, if he hasn't pulled up that old horse of his, so as to be out of ear-shot!"

"—to be a *spiritual* union . . . like that of Saint Ursula with Our Lord."

Had he announced to this little Tudor that she must have her feet cut off, she couldn't have been more upset.

"*I don't—want—to—be a nun.*"

And Owen again blessed the tact of his new squire; for he became conscious that from the butterfly-weight behind him there was proceeding a series of bitter sobs. He flung down the reins and half-turned in his saddle.

"I—don't—want—to be—a nun! I want to go back to Luned and Sibli!"

With some discomfort to his bandaged arm he turned far enough round to catch sight of that outraged and miserable little face. It struck him like the face of a wax image he'd seen once, half-melted by the heat of a torch! He patted with his gauntleted hand the only portion of her small person he could reach, which must have been one of her knees.

"Then you shall *not* be a nun," he whispered, with all the emphasis he could throw into the words. "And I promise you on my word of honour I'll send you back to Dinas Brān to-morrow night!"

"On—your—word—as—as a Prince?"

"On my word as a Prince!" and he crossed himself with the utmost gravity.

"May I tell Rhisiart?"

He swung round and picked up his reins.

"Rhisiart!" he shouted.

The old piebald came cantering to their side.

"I've promised the Demoiselle Efa that she shall be back in Dinas Brān by to-morrow night; and back, too, without being anybody's bride."

"Yes, my Prince." And Owen noted how careful the lad was to keep his eyes on his.

"Am I to escort her there, my Prince?"

"No, no, lad! We're going to get Broch-o'-Meifod's blessing on our business. We'll stay with him to-night and *he'll* be her escort to-morrow. You and I will have our hands full." He could see the boy suck in his lips and frown doubtfully.

"You don't know, either of you children, who Broch-o'-Meifod is. He's the safest man, to trust a lady with, between the Orkneys and Land's End. *Can you hear what we're saying, Efa?"*

"I—wanted—to see—a battle—my Prince." There was still a hint of tears in her voice.

"You'll see what you want then—won't she, Rhisiart?—if the stars fight for us. You'll see the red dragon—I mean the golden dragon—flying from your tower, before we've finished with these English! She will, won't she, Rhisiart?"

Rhisiart bowed in silence over Griffin's neck, drew rein, and fell back once more, so that the big grey horse could have the track to him-

self. Comforted, but feeling obscurely in some portion of her consciousness that she had been cheated of the dramatic role she had planned
for herself as she lay night by night telling herself stories in the Tower
bed, Efa resigned herself to destiny.

The motion of the grey horse, in her present mood of relaxed submission, caused her to nod; and very soon a new sound from behind
his back reached the Prince's ears, the soft and even breathing of a
butterfly-maid asleep!

The September afternoon as they rode on grew more and more
golden. Here and there even the foliage of the bracken bore faint traces,
like the shadow of the passing of years over the locks of a proud queen,
of the mountain's response to the sinking of the vernal sap; while so
far had the rich tints of the bell-heather already yielded to the paler
hue of the ling that in place of the imperial purple of the high summer
the tender lavender of this latest of the mountain children bloomed
amid a bleached and rusty obscuring.

And yet the bracken was green still, and the autumnal gorze had an
even yellower glow than its vernal predecessor. It was only that, over
the whole mass and roll of the Berwyns, the year's decline was beginning to be revealed in what might have been a sprinkling of scarce-
visible cosmic ashes, ashes imponderable in any earthly balance, and
thinned out by their descent through space, and yet perceptible, as they
reached the earth, through the diffused sun-rays.

It was one of those days, peculiar to September, when the whole
landscape seems resting; resting and waiting in spell-bound patience
for the passing across the earth of powers and presences beyond the
normal, powers that could only present themselves when the forces of
life and death, of growth and dissolution, were held in motionless
equilibrium.

To the faithful troop of retainers who followed them the riders on
the grey and the piebald horses must have appeared at that hour, if
not quite the unearthly beings the season demanded, at least separated
from the common run of men and things, heightened, consecrated,
dedicated to some unusual quest, as that golden haze floated round
them and moved with them as they moved!

Owen wore round his helmet, as was the custom of a hundred years
earlier, the golden circlet of a ruling Prince in Cymru. Slung in front

of his saddle was his two-edged Roman sword, a deadly weapon when handled with skill, and one of which he'd already proved the value in the Scottish wars.

But what gave his faithful Sycharth men the greatest satisfaction as they watched it moving before them in that golden haze was their Prince's great lance, bearing on a long streamer, now scarcely fluttering in that still air, the single lion rampant sable of the ancient realm of north-eastern Wales. This lance, heavy though it was, he could support with a careless touch, for its handle rested in a deep leather groove in the front part of his saddle.

Over his breast-plate, upon which this same black lion ramped, he wore a flowing moss-green mantle, richly embroidered with silver.

As for his new squire, that resolute young man—not it must be allowed without some embarrassment and difficulty—had put on his ancient coat of chain-armour and had refused to leave behind either his great crusader's sword or the handsome Toledo dagger that had drawn blood from the wrist of the Usurper's heir. If it had not been for these menacing antiquities Rhisiart's attire was more adapted to the council-chamber than the camp, but he had consented, under pressure from the ladies of Glyndyfrdwy, to place a red feather in his student's cap, and this, against his black locks, had an appearance of no little distinction.

According to his pre-arranged plan Owen dismissed his troop as soon as they descended into the valley. Here our three riders were confronted by a dense forest of oak and sycamore; the young woman—now fully awake and with eyes shining eagerly for adventure—couldn't help exchanging with the young man behind her several exclamations of delight. She had allowed her cloak to fall back from her head, and her bright curls, loosed from control, caught so magically the slanting sun-rays that fell between the branches that to Rhisiart's eyes she resembled some little fabulous princess from one of Modry's stories.

There was so little wind stirring that the warm fragrance of this mass of tresses, thus loosened just behind him, reached Owen's consciousness like the floating essence of its owner's reckless youth; and if the flickering sun-motes that had turned themselves in those tangles were an enchantment to the boy, the sense that he was riding in a moving cloud of fragrant hair was not without its power to relax the strung-up nerves of the man.

How far little Efa in her childish excitement had an inkling of the spell she had so lightly cast upon that mossy track it would be hard to say; but all manner of wayward fancies, airy and wanton, fluttered like butterflies in and out of her small head.

Griffin alone, as he followed step by step the movements of the other horse, seemed to be thinking rather of bodily refreshment than of romantic vistas. But the spell the girl had thrown upon them was entirely impersonal. Man and boy would have been immune at that high moment to the most perilous temptation.

But it was as if a mute wax image of a little maid, carried along behind an armoured figure, had suddenly come alive, and the leafy path itself with all its ferny tendrils had begun to respond to a kindred presence.

The two young people soon began to exchange low-voiced murmurs of wonder and admiration at the manner in which their leader—who from his boyhood had known every path and track of this umbrageous region—urged the grey horse forward.

Turn after turn he took. Mossy glade after mossy glade he followed. Often had little Efa to press her forehead against his broad back lest her curls should be caught in the switching branches.

At last they came to a rushing stream, and Owen guided his grey horse along the southern bank of this obstacle, a course which presented more difficulties than they had yet experienced. In the first place the stream's bank was strewn with the dead branches of old trees, trees that had flourished and drooped and sunk into lifelessness years before the new prince was born. In the second place the branches of the living trees on that little river's side had a tendency to grow nearer the earth, as well as to sprout more vigorously than the rest, owing to the watering of their roots.

But the grey horse was thoroughly accustomed to such uneven going and old Griffin, though reared in a city and inured to social pageants, had always been one to relish a woodland track; so that it was really—for Rhisiart soon removed his cap with its red feather—only a matter of dealing with Owen's great lance, which he was forced to hold horizontally, as if in readiness for an attack, and with Efa's curls, which she was driven to cover once more with her cloak. There came at last a moment when their guide drew rein.

"Slip down, both of you children," he said gently, "and stretch your legs. But keep an eye, each of you, on *some* kind of wood-marks to bring you safe back here, in case you want to wander alone. But you needn't be frightened," and he smiled at Efa who was already on her feet, "even if you *do* get lost, for I could find you in five minutes anywhere round here!"

"Shall I tie up Griffin, my Prince?" asked Rhisiart.

"God! *no,* lad," and Owen, jumping down from his horse, planted his spear in a bed of water-mint, "I'll look after both of them. They'll be quieter together. Off you go, children! I'll give you as long as you like. But if I whistle don't come back till I whistle *like this,*" and he imitated the thin shrill cry of the water-ouzel.

"That boy'll have the sense to leave her to herself for a minute," he thought, as with his wounded arm through both bridles he proceeded to ease himself. "Between me and God that boy's *perfect!* Oh, I hope I shan't drag him to his death. I'll keep him busy with pen and parchment—and then—" And leading the horses to a spot where they could crop the lush-growing grass, he fell into one of his prolonged reveries.

He would have been puzzled to explain in intelligible words—indeed he had never attempted it, save once to old Iolo, and even *he* had only stared at him in silence and shaken his head—what happened to his conscious soul when these fits took him. He knew one thing about them, however. They always left him with a feeling of power and confidence and serenity. His own vague notion was that his soul "went somewhere" at these times. But where could it go in a world like this, to come back refreshed, strengthened, fortified? Where could it go, for instance, to come back with such absolute assurance as to the success of his revolt?

On this occasion he found himself dallying with some nameless clue that he had caught as he stared with unseeing eyes at the flow of the little stream. It was a clue—he felt sure of *that,* though he had long given up any attempt to force his soul to remember what happened to it or where it "went" at these times—that concerned what he would do for Wales when the English *were* driven out. He had always known vaguely what he would do, but on this particular return to consciousness he retained an obscure intimation that his soul had come back from an interview with none other than the Holy Father! The odd thing was that he was convinced he hadn't been thinking of Rome.

"Can it be," he said to himself, "and didn't that man Griffith Young hint at something of that kind—that I'm destined to grow enough of a Lollard to follow the sly French King and have a Pope, or at least a half-Pope, of my own?"

A pair of late wood-butterflies, linked together in love, came fluttering past; and in a mood of languid superstition, giving the fancy no more weight than the insects themselves possessed, as they drifted awkwardly by on their double set of wings, he told himself that if they settled on a patch of ragwort near the path it would be to Avignon he would go, and if on the loosestrife by the water it would be to Rome; whereas if they drifted away without settling at all it would mean a church of Wales independent of them both.

The pair of airy lovers, however, did none of these things. Naturally enough they fluttered down to the ground. But the Prince's reverie, whatever its nature may have been, must have lasted longer than he supposed, for with the subsidence of the butterflies, the last golden rays of the sun sank also; and he was aware of a premonitory chill in the air, rising, like the breath of some great hidden water-beast, from amid the roots of the mint and the burdocks.

He pulled his green mantle closer round him. "Strange," he thought, "if these fits I get should one day leave me as dead-cold as a corpse! I wish I'd told those children not to be away *too* long."

But he'd scarcely breathed this wish than *there* they were; Efa looking flushed and radiantly happy, while Rhisiart struck him as sulky and embarrassed.

"She's been teasing him," he said to himself. "She's been making him treat her in *her* way—not in his!"

Mounted as before, they rode on awhile, still following the little stream.

Suddenly Owen brought his horse to a stand-still, and the lad's piebald stopped too without need of a word or the least pull on his bit.

Their leader called their attention to an extremely aged oak-tree, still green, but reduced to little more than a gigantic torso save for one outstretched arm.

"The old north-way to Mathrafal," he told them, "begins here. It runs for a mile along the stream. You'll see a lot of these old stumps presently."

Rhisiart and Efa exchanged awed and bewildered glances. The boy had recovered his spirits. The girl looked grave and slightly pale.

Moving forward again, the young people were soon staring in wonder at what they saw; for the brushwood had quite disappeared, and parallel with the course of the little brook, which now ran smoothly between mossy banks, a broad avenue of immemorial turf stretched before them, flanked on either side by these gnarled and misshapen relics of what a thousand years ago must have been majestic oak-trees.

In place of the striking of hooves upon stones, the snapping of fallen twigs, and the swishing of the under-growth, the feet of the two horses now fell in a strange awe-inspiring silence upon that soft turf; while in place of exchanging any youth-and-maiden signals, whether of war or peace, Rhisiart and Efa gazed about them as if they had crossed the leafy threshold of an enchantment older than the forest itself.

But Owen drew rein again. "I think," he said, turning round in his saddle, "just *in case* some of the Sheriff's people should have taken it into their heads to encamp round here, 'twould be a good idea if you slipped down now"—he addressed himself to Efa—"and rode with Master Rhisiart. I'd be freer then to use my lance."

"Shall I take her in front of me, my Prince, or—"

But the agile little maid was already on the greensward and, pulling herself up by the help of Griffin's saddle and the quick pressure of a light toe on the rider's instep, she soon had her arm round the boy's waist and her body adjusted to the old horse's rump.

"Well done, child!" cried the chieftain in a relief that his chivalry couldn't altogether conceal. "I can account for a troop of them now!"

But the first use the Prince made of being the sole burden upon that grey back was to bring the two horses neck to neck, and as they rode on to begin an impassioned discourse to his two listeners concerning the place they were approaching. Something about that verdurous and mossy track between perishing relics of an antiquity that staggered comprehension seemed to shake off from the man's mind every pressure of modern transactions.

But there was another cause for Owen's excited, low-voiced murmur to those two. Save when, under rare conditions, he had got Meredith and Catharine together by the log-fire in his "magician's chamber" he had rarely enjoyed the heavenly liberation of a perfect audience. With old Iolo he had always been the one to listen, and with the Bard Griffith it was not hard to grow restless and argumentative. The strain of the morning's interminable ceremony had driven his soul inwards till everything on earth had seemed of little moment. But the place, the hour, these grave and eager listeners, set free elements in his nature such as he had only vaguely realized were there at all.

"I tell you," he was saying now—and his voice took on a solemn intonation that seemed to his hearers as if it came from far away; from over the ruins of these ancient trees, from beyond this long green twilight-vista, from across the dim grey stones that they now began to distinguish in the distance—"I tell you, children, there's no name in this land of mystical names, no! not Caer-Dathyl, or Caerleon, or Narberth, or Dynefor, or Harlech, that can compare with Mathrafal. Those of our fathers' fathers who before both Christ and Caesar journeyed towards the setting sun and paused in this place must have mingled with the Caer-builders and the Mound-builders and the Circle-builders who possessed this land from the beginning.

"And, in the process of this mingling, the souls of the people who were here from the beginning conquered our fathers' souls even while our fathers' swords smote them down! And these first people must have known secrets beyond the understanding of our fathers. But our fathers were bards as well as warriors, and though they understood not the hidden meaning of the words, and though the words seemed to them like the motions of winds and motions of waters, they gathered up their ignorance into the most magical names ever invented by man. Who can tell, my little ones, what hidden power over life, over nature, over the ways of men, lies bound up, as with a living scroll, in the syllables of this name? Our fathers flung into this name all their beating against the gates of the mystery that bowed them down, as it bows us down!

"What high and fatal secret, lost—and yet perhaps not quite lost—awaits, in this destiny-charged name, its final revelation?

"Do you see those stones, children?" And he held back his grey horse and laid his hand upon his squire's hand to slacken the piebald's stride. "Whenever I pass those stones at an hour like this, do ye know what I feel? I feel as though in the dust of Mathrafal there lives forever, indestructible I tell you, children, *indestructible,* all the pilgrim-prayers, all the journeying longings, all the voyaging desires, all the cravings and the cryings, older than the wind, deeper than the sea, of the people of this land. Let them burn Mathrafal into cinders; let them grind Mathrafal into dust; I tell you, Cousin Rhisiart, I tell you, Cousin Efa, as long as *this name* lasts on the lips of the people of this land there will be one beat, one pulse, one motion left in our blood that neither the good nor the bad nor the worst nor the best of our crafty conquerors can ever blot out or destroy!"

His hand by this time was pressing so heavily upon Rhisiart's hand that old Griffin was growing uneasy, though the grey horse, more accustomed to his rider's peculiarities, seemed prepared to accept any unusual gesture without surprise.

"Ought I to stop while I *can* stop," he said to himself, "or dare I say *everything* to them?" For there was now pressing upon him, like a wave mounting up from some unknown chasm in the soul, a wild torrent of suppressed feeling.

"I *must* yield to it," he thought. "It's only fair to *them!*" And pulling back the grey horse till it almost fell on its haunches he swung his great lance into the air till the black rampant lion fluttered against the rose-coloured sky.

His face was blurred to his hearers in that dim light, but he *felt* as if its features were melting, and as if his whole torso were melting and turning into a dissolving tower of mist. He felt as if he had sat on that spot on his grey horse for a thousand years, while the rains and the dews and the days and the nights passed over him, telling to all who came what was the secret of the place. He couldn't really utter it —he knew *that* well enough—for the meaning of it belonged to the ancient people, not to his own proud race—but he felt as if he'd been appointed—had a *tynged* or a "fate" put on him—to sit on his horse forever at the gate of Mathrafal!

Strange that even at that moment his self-consciousness should be so active, feeling itself so vividly into the consciousness of that boy and that maid. But, as his brain moved now like summer-lightning from point to point, he noted in a flash how powerful the spell upon him must be, if he could so calmly envisage himself in those eyes—his forked beard, his lion rampant, the golden circlet round his helm—and yet submit, like an inanimate mask, to the wild stream of words that the spirit of the place poured through him!

"Sometimes, children," he went on, "I've felt as if in the early days, in the days when merchants from Tyre and Sidon and the mouths of the Nile visited these Isles, there was a great city with granite walls and marble towers here. Iolo once revealed to me that in that book of mine—you know the one, Rhisiart?—it says that the people *before* the mound-dwellers worshipped the Great Serpent, and built their cities to the Great Serpent, and were wiser even than the mound-dwellers! I can't speak of these things myself. I'm sure of one thing, though— that in Eliseg's time, or before Eliseg, there were great ways leading to this place from the four quarters of the horizon. The remains of the oaks are all covered up now, save only here; but wasn't it once between *stones* and not between *trees* that pilgrims approached Mathrafal? Approached kneeling, it may be, when the Great Serpent gave his peace to—"

His voice died away and a long, shivering convulsion seized him. Rhisiart urged Griffin forward. The girl uttered a cry like an injured squirrel. The heavy lance fell from the man's grasp and lay on the ground, with the rim of a red toad-stool, like a broken fairy shield, lying beside it.

But Owen's soul returned to him almost at once, and returned to strange effect. He let his reins go as his lance had gone, and he even shook his mantle away from him. But he lifted up both his hands above his head, and not looking towards his companions, not looking even towards the entrance to Mathrafal, but looking no doubt, as he felt in his coldly self-conscious brain he was actually doing, into another dimension of life, he gasped out the words: *"The Past is the Eternal!"* and then, as he lurched, toppled, crouched, huddled, and almost fell from the saddle, across the grey mane of his steed, he tried

to mutter, and thought he *had* muttered; but he never knew whether
they heard him:

"The Past . . . is . . . the . . . is the . . . for which we . . . and I
give you a . . . a new . . . a new war-cry—*Mathrafal!*"

Efa was on her feet and at his side, even before Rhisiart; but it was
the lad's arms that raised him and propped him up in his seat and
obeyed his murmured instructions to give him the little silver phial
from the pocket of his saddle.

Whatever the contents of that phial were, a few drops seemed
enough to send back the blood to his brain and heart as the two young
people watched him. "Shall I carry your spear, my Prince?" the boy
asked him then; but the look of infatuated sympathy with which both
the youthful creatures were regarding him was as restorative as what
he'd drunk.

"No, no, cousin!" he said in his normal tone. "You've got the lady.
I must have the spear."

Moving on now at a slow walking-pace and keeping their horses
neck to neck they were soon actually passing between the ruined pillars of the western gate of Mathrafal, that very heap of broken and
scattered stones—some of them of megalithic size—which they had
seen afar-off, awaiting them at the end of the mossy avenue. It was
clear to Owen that Rhisiart and Efa would have much more enjoyed
the spectacle if they hadn't been nervous of his losing control of himself
again.

"Aye, the darlings!" he thought. "How *can* I re-assure them? How
can I make them understand that I never lose control of myself; that
everything I did just now, even to hugging my horse's neck, even to
letting myself collapse, was deliberate? Efa ought to understand; for
it's only what Nature teaches all women." He pondered for a while in
silence leading them between such a chaotic mingling of old rocks and
old masonry and old mounds and perhaps yet older subterranean passages, marked still, or the roofing of them marked, by undulant eleva-
tions in the grassy turf, that the imagination was at once excited and
baffled.

"I *must* go on talking about it," he thought, "or they'll get into their
heads that I can't speak of the place without getting hysterical."

So he drew rein and turned; and at once little Efa hid herself so completely behind the boy's back that all he could see of her was one terrified wide-open eye and a single wisp of bright hair, objects that normally would have had an endearing effect, but that had an irritating effect just then as he contemplated them between the crusader's sword and the coat of chain-armour.

But the young descendant of two generations of sheriff's clerks in the aristocratic City of Hereford was once more a match for a delicate predicament.

"You're a perfect wonder, lad," thought the Prince, as he looked in vain for the faintest trace of apprehension or embarrassment in the narrow features of his new squire. "I only wanted," he began, in the most practical and matter-of-fact tone, "to show you two how that little stream follows every wall and buttress and angle of the ruins. *There,* if I'm not mistaken"—and he pointed down to the water from the edge of a steep bank, the surface of which was still faced with massive stone-work—"was the north entrance. Think of it, my cousins! Five hundred years ago there must have been a postern here; and I suspect there's a secret passage here still, only King Eliseg, or King Brockwel, or King Cyngen must have blocked it for safety against the English.

"It's getting dark, Rhisiart, and we mustn't tire our little maid; but I *must* just tell you one thing more, and it's something I've never— careful, Seisyll! careful, old horse!—told any living soul. Sometimes, cousin, when I've stood here on this rock above this stream, I'm certain I've felt the rush of the souls of the dead, whirling past me like leaves on the air! I call them the dead; but what do we know? In the ancient times, long before Eliseg, long before the coming of our people, the souls of the living must have thronged these ancient ways. I mean that from their mounds and their camps and their caves living men and women, as they poured out their mead and broke their bread, must have felt over miles of forest and moor the call of Mathrafal, felt it until in their longing and craving their souls came crowding to these gates, jostling, as they rushed through a twilight like this, the souls of the free dead! I *would* like—if you're not too exhausted, Cousin Efa —just to show you—"

But his words were cut short by the sound of a horn and several sharp words of command reaching them over the darkened meadows. There wasn't enough light to see the nature or the number of these intruders; but though they were still too far-off for it to be possible to distinguish the words, both Owen and his companions recognized at once that they were uttered in an English voice.

"Come," whispered Owen. "It's not the moment to take risks. We'll be as safe in Broch-o'-Meifod's as in Valle Crucis. Most likely they're only Chirk foresters, and I'm behaving like a fool. But I'd be unworthy of to-day if I didn't show some caution. Turn your horse, lad, and follow me close. It's all right, Ffa—only for Christ's sake hang on to him with both arms!"

Owen's tall Seisyll—and it was the first time Rhisiart had heard that historic name—set off at so fast a gallop that Griffin, with his double burden, was hard put to it to keep up with him. As it was, the old pageant-horse stumbled once or twice in the darkness; and it was a lively comfort to his young rider when, passing through a clump of beeches, a warm red, glowing light could be discerned shining from the open door of a substantial wooden building.

Owen himself breathed no small sigh of relief when, extricating himself and his great lance from Seisyll's complicated harness, he heard the clatter of the piebald and saw his distended nostrils and panting sides.

"This is my cousin, Master Broch, the Demoiselle Efa ferch Tudor of Môn. And this is my cousin too, Rhisiart ab Owen, from the University of Oxford. This is Master Broch-o'-Meifod, cousins; and here is Mistress Morg ferch Lug, his good lady, and these are Morgie, Orlie and Mair, the prettiest girls in the Paradise of Wales!"

By the time the horses had been fed, watered and stabled, and Efa had been brought back from the women's quarters, refreshed and radiant, it was certainly around a noble supper-board and over against a noble fire that the party assembled. Loud, gay and unrestrained was the chatter that broke out as soon as the collation began.

Neither the gigantic Miller nor his sprightly lady showed the faintest sign of embarrassment in the presence of the newly-proclaimed Prince. The little Mistress even rallied him and made jokes at his expense, to which Morgie, Orlie and Mair listened with round-eyed bewilderment.

The three girls certainly were strikingly pretty, but not one of them as pretty as their mother; and it was clearly this astonishing little being who made the deepest impression on Efa. Not only did she look as young as any one of her three daughters; but it was the blending of such authority and decisive despotism, with such fairy-like grace, that Efa found so fascinating.

Mistress Broch looked quite as young as Morgie, her eldest daughter, not to speak of being more vivacious and sprightly than *any* of her daughters; but what so intrigued little Efa was the extraordinary combination, in this frail creature, of aggressive despotism with delicate beauty. It was as if the three girls who were the most soft-hearted maidens in Meifod had been doomed to pay for their pretty faces and good-natured hearts by heavy and unwieldy figures, whereas the mother was as light as a feather on her feet.

Little Efa, who from her life at Dinas Brān was more interested in other women than in anything except imaginary seductions, was fascinated by watching the queer relations between this elfin mother and these heavily-built nymphs. They didn't seem at all afraid of her, which was a surprise to Efa, who missed nothing of the deadly sarcasms shot here and there from between those beautifully curved lips. Perhaps they were too simple-minded to catch these jeering jibes, or perhaps having been, by reason of their enormous stature, spared the usual corrections of children, they had grown by custom and habit completely immune to this darting tongue.

As he sat enjoying the honey-hearted mead, and swallowing the well-cooked morsel of meat not un-garnished with spicy herbs from the mill-garden, Owen fell by degrees, though he responded friendly enough to the elfin lady's airy teasing, into a train of thought that soon made his retorts a little perfunctory.

"It's no good going back on this business," he said to himself, "even in my thoughts. There *was* a time for that—but that time is over. To drive out the English—well! and what then? Iolo used to say that he found in the old books hints that the way of life of the first people was far wiser, far freer, than anything suggested in good King Hywel's Laws. It seemed, Iolo said, that there were no princes, no rulers then, but only the men of the land, living at peace together and worshipping peaceful gods without sacrifices and without blood. Prince? Prince of Powys? Prince of Gwynedd and Deheubarth? What is Prince? A word! And what does that word mean? Blood and ashes! What does it mean in *this* house and in all the other houses in Wales? It means the strong men, the brave men, it means the men I love best as Owen Glyn Dŵr, dragged after me to God knows what fate, for Owen the Prince! What do the spirits of Mathrafal care that Owen should be— But no more of that. There *was* a time for that. But *now* the hour, the flood of the tide, the stars in their courses—these *are* Owen, Prince of Wales! These are what I am; and like the tide, like the stars, I must take the men I *must* take, though the event is not theirs or—"

His thoughts became confused at that point, and in an obscure and even blasphemous desperation he began to think of himself as if he were a blind portion of the life-force itself, and as if his struggle with Grey and Fitz-Alan and Bolingbroke and the English found its justification as part of the resistless process of the cosmos.

But while the new Prince pondered in this way and while little Efa watched intently the girls and their mother, the youthful Rhisiart found himself unable to remove his eyes from the Master of Maen-y-Meifod. This was the first time he had met any human being with a personality of equal weight to that of his hero, and to see and hear these two great men at close quarters and on such natural terms was an absorbing experience. The Master of Maen-y-Meifod was a person of Herculean proportions—indeed physically speaking he was the most powerful human being Rhisiart had ever seen—but his rugged countenance was rendered more striking, if not more grotesque, by the fact that his great head was completely devoid of hair.

If he was the biggest and strongest man Rhisiart had ever seen, he was also the most comical-looking. He was in fact like a combination of the Show-Giant and the Show-Dwarf in Hereford Great Fair.

Rhisiart hadn't failed to notice how his Prince had said that no one on either side of the border would dare to meddle with Broch-o'-Meifod or with anyone under his protection; and as he listened to the Miller now at the head of his board, by that spacious and blazing hearth, he was able to realise the full truth of these words.

It wasn't only the man's enormous size. There was something even more awe-inspiring about his colossal bald head and about the cavernous pits out of which his eyes peered forth—and so deeply set in his skull were these same eyes that it was hard, if not impossible, to distinguish their colour.

It was only by asking him a series of point-blank questions that Owen succeeded in drawing him out at all; and he was baffled by the

despotic little fairy at the head of the table long before he was able to
make him talk in the way he hoped for; that is to say, in a manner
that would really satisfy his young squire's curiosity.

"Between me and God," said the Prince to himself, "if I can't do
better than this as a diplomatist I'll never be a match for Bolingbroke."

But it was in vain that he tried to imagine even the King of England
out-facing Morg ferch Lug at her own table. The little lady had indeed
got the look now that Owen especially dreaded. It was a look so bright,
so sparkling, so scintillating with domination, that it always gave him
the feeling that he himself was some inanimate object in the process
of being cut by a diamond!

"She doesn't like me," he thought, "and she's prejudiced against
Rhisiart. But Efa dotes on her already." Up went his hand to his
beard as he heard her begin rattling off one of her liveliest most
vividly-told tales about the Miller, the only point of which seemed to be
the big man's lack of the most human intelligence.

There were sitting "below the salt" at that commodious board three
stalwart labourers and as many robust house-girls, and it was to these,
quite as pointedly as to her guests, that this imperious little woman
directed her sallies. Roars of laughter from the three men and more
restrained gigglings from the three wenches made up the politic response from that end of the table, but the heavier-witted daughters
turned their beautiful heads in puzzled protest towards their gigantic
begetter.

"You know how he always wears his axes, my Lord, stuck in his old
leather belt? He's only got three of 'em on now; but I've seen him
come down to his morning ale with half-a-dozen of 'em round his
waist. Well—what must he do when Fitz-Alan's archers came here a
hundred strong to take that old robber Griffith, who was hidden all
the time in Broch's corn-bin our Orlie sitting on the lid, but forget to
put his belt on! And there was his belt, with all his axes in it, hanging
on a peg by the hearth, and he with nothing but his naked hands. And
do 'ee think, my Lord, he made any bones about what he said to 'em—
and they, with their bows and spears and clubs, all crowding in at our
door?

"If I hadn't told him what I thought of him before them all, so's
to make a booby of him, and sent our lads for the mead-barrel, he'd

have been a real 'badger in the bag,' as the saying is, and the lasses and me, what about *us,* with hot devils like them let loose?"

"Tut, tut, pretty," responded the bald-headed giant. " 'Twas to give harvest-home kisses and thy cider-press cuddlings that I took off the belt that warm day; and wondrous it were, Owen ap Griffith Fychan, to see how bashful the pretty was because our girls were only a loft's steps away! How could I know, Owen ap Griffith, that the slipperiest thief on the border and the smartest troop in the province would choose the same afternoon to visit Maen-y-Meifod?"

In vain did Owen follow up this protest from his friend by putting some hurried question about the harvest to one of the labourers at the foot of the table, a man whom Rhisiart had already recognized as none other than that same surly Philip Sparrow who had played ferry-man for the Tassel's landlord on Midsummer Eve.

Master Sparrow was evidently quite prepared to respond to this question at some length; but Morg ferch Lug seemed to have the power of carving pasties, filling goblets, handing round sweet-meats, without any intermission in her brilliant talk.

"What a sly elf she is!" thought Owen. "Morgan le Fay couldn't be slyer. She's going to keep this up till Broch and I are too heavy with food and drink to think of anything but sleep. *Can* there be anything in the tales about this creature that her father had traffic with a water sprite? I mustn't forget to tell Rhisiart the whole story." And as he bowed his head before this silvery stream as it eddied round the table it struck him how extraordinary it was that this woman should have realized what he'd come for, before he'd realized it himself!

He'd told those two, and he'd believed it when he told them, that it was simply to ask Broch to take Efa back to Dinas Brān that he'd come to Meifod; but he now saw that he had *really* come with the hope of persuading the Miller to join him in his dangerous adventure.

It was a relief to Owen—and at first it looked as if he'd been totally unfair in all his suspicions—when Morgie and Orlie and Mair came gravely up to their father and held up their heads to be kissed prior to their retirement for the night. The Prince lifted each particular hand of these young giantesses to his lips, and it was touching to him to see how moved their lovely faces became under this perfunctory courtesy.

They carried off Efa with them; and Owen was interested to see how eagerly she went. "She's really a girl's girl, that little thing!" he thought. "And that's why she worked up all this Derfel business. No normal child would get pleasure from imagining herself ravished by a goblin. She's about as queer for a girl as Rhisiart is for a boy."

While the handmaidens were clearing the table Master Broch requested his friend's permission for Philip Sparrow to join them round the fire.

"And tell Llewelyn and Rhys, Philip, that they can broach a fresh cask in the kitchen in honour of Owen, Prince of Cymru."

Glendower liked the way his friend brought this in. The words came so easily that they gave him, more than all the ceremonies of the morning, that sweet shock of romantic realization that his own thoughts seemed set upon spoiling.

He was pleased, too, by the spontaneous grace of those unlettered men; for each of them before retiring to the kitchen dropped on one knee and uttered in Welsh in a goodly and clear voice, "May our Lord the Prince overcome his enemies!"

Morg ferch Lug had led the way when her daughters took Efa from the room; but Owen kept expecting her re-appearance every moment. She had bidden him a formal good-night; and yet it would be an unusual proceeding, and one quite contrary to Welsh custom in these things, for her to come back later.

But, for all that, it was so much too good to be true that he and his friend were destined to have this deep fire and this deeper barrel of mead entirely to themselves that Owen could *not* believe it.

"No, no!" he thought, "she'll come back." And indeed as he went on asking Master Sparrow various social questions and getting from that sturdy enemy of the gentry some extremely uncompromising replies he had a disagreeable sensation of the surprisingly near presence of the darting and glancing daughter of Lug.

Perhaps it was this discomfort that made his defence of the regiment of princes a little feeble and querulous as he brought down on his head the clear-cut revolutionary notions of Master Sparrow. The hired harvester from the Tassel had for so long been accustomed to alternate between sardonic silence—when his mouth fell at the corners and a savage sneer distorted *his* features—and a dogmatic brow-beating of any interlocutor that to be listened to as Owen listened to him was disturbing and exciting.

The Prince himself felt it incumbent upon him in his new rôle to make various mental sorties into regions from whose austere landmarks he had hitherto shied away; but it was entirely against his idea of himself as a magnanimous ruler to show stiffness and prejudice in the presence of startling modern ideas. His acquaintance with the great Oldcastle had done more than shake his orthodoxy; it had destroyed at the root that unquestioning acceptance of the existing class-system which makes every innovator a criminal.

But he was, as we have seen, hardly what could be described as an altruist. And it is one thing to be free from prejudice, and quite another thing to have the spirit of a revolutionary!

Master Sparrow was an egoist too, deriving, it is to be feared, quite as much satisfaction in the logical defeat of an opponent as in any feeble effort such an one might be persuaded to make to grope his way towards the light.

Broch-o'-Meifod looked on with an expression of absent-minded wonder as the dispute proceeded; whereas Rhisiart didn't know whether to admire the more the good-humour of his Prince under Master Sparrow's sarcastic dogmatism, or the actor's skill, for such he took it to be, and a thing quite in his own vein, with which Broch summoned into his face a look of childish simplicity.

"You Lords and Gentles," Master Sparrow was now saying, "will do everything else for the people except the one thing that lone would change all."

"What is that, Master?" enquired Glendower, while the bald-headed giant's innocent stare met the knitted eyebrows of the observant Oxonian.

"Get off their backs!"

The harvester flung this word forth with such vehemence that Owen's hand went up to his beard.

"But what method would you use," he said, trying to keep all irritation out of his voice, for he felt sure his sagacious squire was observing him carefully to see whether he would escape from this with his dignity intact, "use, I mean, as a substitute for the system that gives us our present rulers?"

"Gives us *yourself,* that is, my Lord," commented the free-spoken fellow.

"Myself—perhaps," said Owen, "but many others, too."

"Grey of Ruthin?" interjected the harvester with a sneer.

Owen forced himself to smile. "We needn't quarrel over the nature of the *status quo,* my man," he said. "The custom is a common one, and I admit an imperfect one. But what do you propose to substitute for it?"

"Whose hands till the soil, my Lord? Whose hands sow the grain and gather the harvest? Who herd the sheep and shear them in their season? Who feed and water the cattle?"

"Damn that mischievous elf!" thought the harassed Prince irrelevantly. "She's here *somewhere*—I feel her—glancing and dancing!" And he inserted a finger between his bandage and his wound, as if the daughter of Lug were the cause of the tickling that now began to trouble him.

"Who weave the cloth for your garments, my Lord," went on the triumphant harvester. "Who build your castles, and are slaughtered by the hundreds on your private wars? Who are hanged by your Manor-Courts if they kill one of your deer?"

But Owen was staring at the unshuttered window. He was sure he had seen a small white hand emerge from the darkness and point derisively at him with out-stretched fingers. "I must come to business," he thought, "before this gets worse."

"I admit the injustice of our system, Master," he said. "And I would willingly talk further with you on how to remedy it. But just now I have only this to say—you are a powerful man of your hands, Master Sparrow; and I am sure you deserve the silver you've earned by gathering in our friend's harvest. What I would like to know now is, whether you would consent to come with Master Broch as his body-servant if *he* consented," he gave his friend a steady, shameless, penetrating glance, "to leave his mill for a time and help me drive the English out of Wales?"

This point-blank question did alter for a moment the habitual scowl on Master Sparrow's visage; but it made a much more perceptible disturbance in the corrugated countenance of the bald giant, and not only in his countenance.

Broch-o'-Meifod gravely and heavily rose to his feet from the stool on which he was sitting and unhooking his leather surcoat began brushing with his hands, or rather beating with his hands, the rough woollen garment he was wearing beneath it. This garment, girded up at the waist under his belt, was what he'd had on all that day at the mill; and as he struck it now with his fists, clearly without the least consciousness of what he was doing, a cloud of flour-dust drifted away from it, and floated off with the log-smoke.

"I believe," thought Owen, "he did *that* in an automatic impulse of obedience to Morg!"

It must have been at the very instant when the man was thus, without knowing what he did, dusting his miller's garment, that he made the supreme decision of his life; for by the time he sat down again on his oak stool his face had resumed its normal composure.

On Master Sparrow's face, too, habit reigned again; but it did strike Owen as if that familiar sneer of contempt at the blindness of human valuations had been lightened a little by a natural lust for adventure.

Owen exchanged a quick glance with Rhisiart, and it struck the Prince as strange that the hardly perceptible nod the young diplomatist gave him—as much as to say, "You've got them, both, my Lord!"—should have so greatly re-assured him. He himself gave a deep sigh of relief. He found he'd been counting much more than he'd known upon the aid of his indomitable friend, and he felt profoundly comforted when he stole a glance at his face.

But now, lest the man should think he was pressing him too hard, he deliberately let his eyes wander over that spacious chamber. How clean it was! The Maen-y-Meifod house-girls must use better mops than *his* maids used at Glyndyfrdwy.

And could all those boards and panellings and rafters, black as night, and yet glowing, gleaming in the firelight, be just ordinary oak? And what a clever device *that* was—Broch must have thought of that himself—to let the smoke out through a wide hole above the door, instead of by these tricky smoke-vents behind the—

But all of a sudden, tug at his beard as he might, sharpen the points of it as he might, till they resembled the beard of a prince of Nineveh, he found that an ice-cold shiver was running up and down his spine, and that his legs were growing cold. Mother of God! he couldn't even *feel* his feet any more. They were numb; they were as dead as if they had been amputated!

Turning his head to the window he now felt sure that he saw a slender wrist and a white finger pointing directly at him. It had vanished in a second; but this new vision of it, more definite than the first, was a deadly shock to his nerves. He tried to recall an incantation that Iolo had given him as a sure protection against *Ellyllesan* or female demons, but not a word of it could he remember!

He began to feel as if his blood were turning to ice. Instinctively he had recourse to his old mental trick; and never had he used it with such a desperate effort! Instead of trying to move hand or foot he threw every ounce of will he possessed into an imaginative *exteriorizing* of his soul. He forced himself to visualize himself, sitting there, exactly as he was, facing the Miller and the harvester, but he struggled and strained with every fibre of his being to imagine—just to imagine—that *It,* the inmost Self of Owen, was watching the whole scene like one of the Birds of Rhiannon from the top of a conventionalized picture of Tysilio, the patron saint of Meifod.

In imagining the exteriorization of his soul he was forced to concentrate on Tysilio's face—and what an ugly face it was!—and Tysilio saved him. His blood began to circulate again and he forced himself to meet his squire's anxious and puzzled gaze.

"I think, cousin," he said quietly, relaxing the tenseness of his will as he might have unstrung a bow, "we might leave Broch and Master Sparrow for a minute to talk over my suggestion. I'd like to show you those old shields over there, of my friend's ancestors. They were barons in Meifod before John burnt Mathrafal; but all their lands, except the mill-farm, were forfeited to the English."

He rose as he spoke, breathing a sigh of unspeakable relief to find that his limbs obeyed his intention; and resting his hand on Rhisiart's shoulder moved across the hall. They were approaching the entrance, on both sides of which hung the ancient shields, when the dark, polished doors flew open, and Mair ferch Broch, the youngest of the three girls, stumbled awkwardly into their presence. The girl was in her night-gown; and her agitation was so great that she hadn't even waited to throw a cloak over her shoulders.

"Father! Father!" she was crying; and then, finding herself confronted at such close quarters by Glyn Dŵr and Rhisiart, she staggered backwards and nearly fell.

But Broch was at her side in a moment. "Mair, child? Mair, Mair, what *is* it?" And lifting her up in his arms as if she were a creaking stiff-jointed doll he carried her to the fire.

Owen made a sign to Master Sparrow to leave them together, a sign which the sarcastic champion of the people obeyed with tactful discretion.

"It's about *her*," the fellow whispered as soon as he reached them. "I heard what the damsel told the master. It's about *her* going out to the mill-pond to set the mill-wheel working."

"Mill-pond, mill-wheel? I can't understand you," protested the Prince. "She meant, Owen ap Griffith," replied the other, "that Morg ferch Lug *has gone to turn the wheel.*"

"I still don't understand," said Glendower gravely.

"Twice already," explained the other, "since Broch brought her to Maen-y-Meifod has the Mistress run wild like this. When she runs wild, the wheel goes round of itself! The first time she did it 'twas to be-devil her own mother anent the poor lady making a stir over her marrying a man old enough to be her grand-dad. *That* were sixteen years agone, afore the Mistress had cruddled her first-born."

"Well, Sparrow—for Heaven's sake tell us, good Master Sparrow—" But the fellow sneered like a devil. "Punctual Sparrow!" he sneered. "Serviceable and useful Sparrow! Convenient and appropriate Sparrow!" and he mimicked the Prince's accent with a savage unction.

Owen bit his lip. He had never been treated like this before. But something was "upon" him to make him act according to the most fantastical code of magnanimity. "Richard's father, the Black Prince," he thought, "let himself be insulted by the rudest of his French prisoners; and between me and God, old conjurer, you've got to make this fellow a test of your self-control."

"Pardon my impatience, Master," he enquired, "but what was *the second time* she turned the wheel?"

"You'd be wiser, Owen ap Griffith, and 'twould be more to the point to ask me what the result'll be of her turning it the third time! But— let that go—her mother died the day after she'd turned it on *her;* and the second time she turned it was when King Richard laughed at her complaint about the Chirk foresters killing her pet deer. So she turned it on *him;* and a year later, just about the time when she'd run wild, *he* was a dead man."

"What do you mean by running wild, Master Sparrow?"

"Just what I say. Broch and the young ladies dursn't move from their beds nor from wherever else they may be when she be out at mill-wheel. If'ee was to peep into kitchen now, ye'd see Jock Efan and Dick Lloyd hugging themselves over fire, just as the Master and Mistress Mair be doing yonder, and if ye went upstairs—though God forbid your noble lordship should see such sights!—ye'd find Mistress Morgie and Mistress Orlie twisted together like silver eels; that is, if ye saw them at all; for 'tis like enough they'd have the blankets over their heads!"

Owen fixed upon him an un-hearing, un-seeing look that brought down the corners of Master Sparrow's mouth into his taciturnity. Then the Prince glanced at his friend by the fire, who was still rocking his daughter on his knee; and finally he met the untroubled gaze of Rhisiart, who boldly inquired if he should take his sword from the porch and go down to the mill-pool.

But it was to Master Sparrow the Prince turned. "She's the mistress of the house," he said, "and we mustn't meddle with her; but if you *could* stop her from rushing in on those two without warning it would be a good thing, and if you could persuade him," he lowered his voice, "to carry the child back to bed before her mother sees her it would be wise. I leave it to you. Only I do hope, Sparrow," and he deliberately gave the man a particular smile of intimate confidence such as he had found seldom failed of its purpose, "that you *will* decide to accompany us to-morrow. You're not likely, Sparrow"—here he spoke very earnestly—"to find such a chance of seeing *some* of your ideas put into practice, as you are with me."

Then he turned to his impatient squire. "And now, cousin," he said. "We'll have a look at the mill-pool together!" The bald-headed giant

at the fire turned towards them at that moment; for Owen had deliberately uttered his last words in a penetrating tone. But all the man did
was to lay his finger on his lip.

"He's getting her to sleep, Sparrow," Owen whispered. "Make him
take her to bed fore *she* comes in. And if you *do* go with us to-morrow,
remember your only job will be to look after him—to see he doesn't
leave his belt behind him when he goes into battle. And remember too
that I know what belongs to my men—before I take them to be
slaughtered!"

"I believe," he said to himself, as he and Rhisiart left the hall, "that
the man will come. And it's just what we need among us, a few all-or-
nothing champions of the people. If my dragon-standard—whether it
be yellow or red—isn't a rallying of the people, what is Owen?"

"May I take my sword, my Prince?" enquired Rhisiart, watching
eagerly to see whether his chief would touch his great lance with its
leonine streamer.

"Surely, lad, surely. No, no—not your chain-armour! And you can
lend me your dagger if any pinch comes; but how chilly it is with all
this water about!" Saying this he wrapped himself round in his green
mantle.

"It's other weapons than spears I'll need tonight," he thought.

Rhisiart too remained bare-headed; but the rush of autumn air that
blew in through the great doors when he unbarred them induced him
to snatch up a coat of sheep's wool that hung against the wall. Thus
attired, with the crusader's sword bare of its sheath, the Prince and his
companion set forth to meet whatever awaited them.

They found a different sky, a different atmosphere, a different feeling in the air, from what they had been experiencing all that warm
September day. It was partly the mill-pond and the mill-stream that
accounted for the death-like chill they felt; it was partly the warmth of
the great fire they'd left; but to the Prince's mind at any rate there was
something else abroad, something that made him shiver as they moved,
even under his heavy mantle.

Did Cousin Rhisiart feel what he felt? He'd have given a good deal
to know. But a certain shame, and a desire not to put ideas into the
boy's head, made him keep his feelings to himself.

What he liked least of all about the look of things in those obscure purlieus of Meifod mill was the appearance of the waning moon. Rack after rack of yellow-tinted unwholesome clouds kept voyaging across it, not so much borrowing its radiance, for it had little radiance, as borrowing its illness, its sick desolation, its malady, its maniacal unease.

What a shapeless thing of leprous whiteness it was, this journeying deformity, on the distorted surface of which could still just be detected the floating ends of the tumbled hair of the moon-maiden!

And there it was again, as they approached the mill-pool, swaying and tossing, rising and sinking, in those reedy depths! Their own figures, as they moved, threw dim, misshapen inhuman projections upon those livid ripples, more like the motions of monstrous fish *beneath* the surface than of shadows passing across it.

Save the tall reeds nothing but a few ancient willow-stumps, most of them dead, were to be seen by the water's edge, and those that were *not* dead were even less auspicious, so ghastly were the twigs, in that sick light, that protruded from them!

At last, as they went tramping side by side through the moist grass, across which every now and then came fungus-odours from half-submerged and time-blackened roots, they could see before them, where the out-flow of the water narrowed and deepened, the vast form of the mill-wheel. They had to cross a couple of half-open weirs before they reached the wheel, weirs that opposed or released the rush of subsidiary channels into the mill-pool, and it was as they were crossing the second of these, listening, as they clutched the wooden rail, to the hollow gurgling beneath the dam, that they realized that the towering form of the great wheel before them had slowly begun to turn.

It turned silently at first; but as soon as they were both on firm ground again, and quite close to it, there arose from beneath its vast rondure a strange, multitudinous sound, a sound not loud enough to be called a roar, but too loud to be described as a murmur.

Beside the wheel, and above the wheel, extended the dim shape of the mill itself, along the outer wall of which, high up from the ground, higher even than the topmost curve of the wheel, ran a narrow, balustraded platform, and standing upon this platform, with all the wild-tossed intermittent light of that ghastly shapelessness in the sky falling full upon her elfish figure, hovered the form of Morg ferch Lug.

She was evidently expecting them; and the moment she realized they'd seen her she waved to them to stay where they were and disappeared into the mill.

"She's going to stop the wheel," whispered Owen to his companion, "and then she'll come back and curse us!"

Rhisiart nodded but seemed not the least disturbed by this prospect. Catching the lad, a moment later, observing with calm and untroubled interest the way the water dripped and lingered and fell with diminishing force from the wheel's subsidiary revolution, Owen thought to himself, "God! he's got the nerve of a Norman!"

But there she was again, poised above their heads, above the now motionless wheel, and drawing to herself the full ghastliness of that phantom sickness in the sky.

Owen's mind was working fast now, and noting all manner of irrelevant details. What in Christ's name had the woman got round her? A robe of white foxes' skins? No, her form shimmered in that fevered light too much for that.

But the moon and she were cousins-german; and it was as if she couldn't toss forth the hectic sparkles of her marsh-fire hate quickly enough, before the next onrush of rolling clouds covered her confederate!

Her voice, when it did come, was hardly human. It wasn't easy to catch all her words, so wrought up was she. And yet it wasn't a wail, or a scream, or even a series of marsh-bird's cries. It was like the voice of a creature that has leapt out of one element into another and was using ordinary human words with a difference. They were Welsh words; but they were old Welsh words, many of them words that Owen had only met in that ancient folio of his.

"Take him away!" shrilled this voice, wherein seemed to shiver all the gurglings of the weirs and all the drifting sobs of the moon-wane, "take him away and murder him, my man, my marrow, my life! You shall have him, Owen the Accurst, Owen, the Bane of Cymru! But take this with you. As long as you destroy you will succeed. But try to build up again what you've torn, what you've burnt, what you've ravaged—and *then* will be the end! New-comer you are to this land, Brython the Accurst, with your spear of iron and your sword of brass; and I tell you to-night that the wheel has turned against you. You conquered *us* by your force and your cunning and your talk of the good and the evil; and so shall the English conquer *you!*

"Evil is the King in London, evil and cunning; and he talks of the good while he burns and tortures. And as you fight against him, Owen ap Griffith, you will grow like him! As long as you *destroy* you'll succeed; but try building up again, Owen ap Griffith, try building up these homes and these lives you've laid waste, and you'll see what you've done! For this land, Owen the Accurst, Owen, the pure-blooded Brython, belongs *not* to you, to your evil strength and your weapons of steel, belongs *not* to your talk of the good and the evil. It belongs to us, to us who have been here from the beginning, to us the *old people!*

"Out of the old rivers, out of the old hills, out of the moons who know us and the deep night which is our beginning and our end, I lay upon you, Owen the Destroyer, the curse of the turning of the wheel! Take him away, my life, my marrow. Take him away, the prop of my children. I lay upon you the oldest curse in the world, the curse that is stronger than iron or brass; the curse of the water and the wind!"

Her out-stretched hands which had been pointing at the motionless figures beneath her now sank down; while she herself, like one of the last drops of water, sliding from the wheel she'd turned, vanished as suddenly as she had appeared!

Owen shivered, pulled his green mantle round him and became as motionless as any of the dying willow-trunks that leant over the pool's brink. What his wandering soul was doing during these moments was curious enough when the nature of the place and of the occasion be considered. It had gone labouring back through the heavy years like an underground mole till it came to a critical day in his boyhood when his younger brother Tudor had jumped over a sandy stream by the edge of the sea, and not all the encouragement of their father nor all the repeated rushes Owen himself made to the brink of this obstacle were strong enough to conquer his fear of jumping. He could see now, as he tugged at his beard, just what he saw then, an old massive spar of ship's timber, with barnacles and sea-weed clinging to it, that was stopped from getting back to the sea by a bank of sand, and yet was forced to ride on the tide and ride on the stream and forced to push before it and drag after it masses of sea-wrack and river-drift.

For no reason, to no purpose, for no intelligible motive, this piece of timber endured the rush upon it from one side of the salt streams and from the other side of the fresh streams; and it was with this object that Owen had identified himself.

In his boyish shame at not daring to jump, and at hearing his father say, "If you can't jump, Owen my boy, you'd better give it up," he had, rather in the way he did still, tried to fling his soul into that ancient fragment. "It just follows the tide," he had said to himself. "For it *has* to float. *It can't jump.*"

"I think," he now remarked quietly to his companion, "we'd better start at dawn to-morrow; and you and I had better wait as near to Dinas Brān as we dare, till Broch gets that child safe back. I promised her she should go. We'll let him have Seisyll. He won't take long. And then we'll have to decide whether to go straight to Ruthin and meet our people, or go home first. But if we go straight to Ruthin we must warn Rhys not to wait for us. Ayē! aye! aye!" He sighed, but not too heavily, a little weary physical sigh, like that of a man who picks up a burden; a burden he knows he can carry, but a burden that'll give him small ease or comfort.

But he felt that the boy was staring at him, puzzled and anxious in that dim light, and he turned his face away. It was then that he noticed a piece of rotten wood, with what looked like a living plant growing on it, gliding towards the pool of darkness under the wheel.

"Lend me your sword, cousin!" he said; and bending over the pool, without much difficulty he steered the floating derelict to their feet.

He gave no reason to the boy for this proceeding, as he thrust the bit of wood with its wisp of plant-life among the roots of a willow-stump. "You can never tell with these Normans," he said to himself, as he returned Rhisiart his sword; but he couldn't help a quickening of his pulse as they crossed the weirs.

"*That* anyway," he thought, "won't go under the wheel of Morg ferch Lug!"

XIII

THE COMET

SOMETHING LIKE a year and a half had passed over Wales, and the excitement among its people created by the hoisting of their old dragon-standard had increased to an extent that was stirring up the wildest rumours on both sides of the border.

Following no advice but that of his friend Broch-o'-Meifod and his chief captain Rhys Gethin, Owen had decided to do what so many of the wisest patriots of his race had done before him, namely, to leave his patrimony—in his case both Glyndyfrdwy and Sycharth—and retreat to an inaccessible and unapproachable citadel among the rocks and mountain-lakes at the foot of Snowdon.

He had therefore taken possession of a half-ruined fortress of unknown antiquity; and with the aid of stone-cutters and craftsmen from Gethin's domain in Conway had converted it during the summer and autumn of 1401 into a quite spacious stronghold with halls and chambers capable of sheltering not only a large household but a considerable bodyguard of devoted and well-armed adherents.

These latter kept increasing all through the winter of 1401; neither the snow-choked passes of that wild district nor the dangers and difficulties of leaving the England of Henry of Lancaster being able to deter thousands of patriotic Welshmen from deserting their studies in the universities and their avocations in the great merchant-cities and plunging into this desperate struggle to drive the stranger from their land.

Owen had gathered all his own family and all his closest personal friends round him in his mountain retreat. Important changes had taken place both at Valle Crucis and Dinas Brān which further enlarged the circle of what had now become quite a princely court in that inaccessible region.

The one event which those starry revolutions upon which she was always brooding had *not* predicted had befallen Ffraid ferch Gloyw, for she had died in her sleep; with the result that Lowri had fled with Simon to Owen, bringing not only Luned and Sibli and the two page-boys, but her daughter Tegolin, still accompanied by Alice of Ruthin and Friar Huw. As for little Efa, she had long since returned to her home in Anglesea.

Fate had chosen to delay the death of the Abbot of Valle Crucis until, when this event did occur, there was no question as to his successor; and the pro-English Prior, now the new Abbot, made it so uncomfortable for Father Pascentius, who had long intrigued against him, that the sly theologian, one dark providential night, brought not only his own casuistical intelligence to the Prince's mountain-court, but, packed securely on a sure-stepping Welsh pony, his famous unfinished Commentary upon the *Summa Theologica*.

It had been left, amid all these alarms and excursions, to the common-sense of the Arglwyddes—for the excellent lady steadily refused to use any other title—to suggest to the Prince to get Father Rheinalt out of the way before the arrival of the dangerous Lowri and her chastened Hog of Chirk. The patriotic monk had been therefore despatched with a letter to the warlike Abbot of Caerleon begging him not to send to the Snowdonian fastness any more long-bows from the Usk; but in place of this to get together as much *gold* from his monastery's treasury as he could lay his hands on!

The outlawed Prince wrote to him that it was gold to pay the troopers he *had* that he wanted, not more hungry mouths to feed; and it was the reply to this communication that he was now impatiently awaiting, while his Lady hoped and prayed that it would be by another hand than that of their passionate messenger that the response would come.

It was a clear evening in early February of the year 1402, when Owen, having returned from a fortnight's raid into Lord Grey's now far-off Vale of Clwyd, found himself, the great meal of the day well over, alone with his Secretary Rhisiart in his own private chamber.

Rhisiart was engaged just then in making fresh drafts of two important communications that the Prince had despatched during the winter, one a letter in Latin to the native chieftains of Ireland, and the other a letter in French to King Robert the Third of Scotland.

News had reached the little court during its Christmas celebrations that the messengers entrusted with these epistles had fallen into the hands of the Usurper; and it was with a view to making another attempt to get them to Ireland and Scotland that the young Oxonian was copying his original rough drafts.

The room was a low square chamber with a spacious enclosure in its centre to serve as a fire-place and a wide vent above the iron-barred door to create a sufficient draught of air to carry away the heaviest portion of the smoke. Three deep lancet windows pierced the thick outer walls, and at one of these Owen now stood, contemplating the twilit expanse before him with more satisfaction than he had felt for some months; for it had needed as many as two score of sturdy ponies to convey to their over-crowded stronghold all the plunder his raid had carried off.

There had been a persistent thaw during the last couple of weeks and though the snow still lay on the ledges and ridges along the higher slopes, in many quite considerable open spaces and level terraces lovely stretches of fresh emerald-coloured grass were now apparent.

But just because the fatal law of contrariety can play more devilish tricks with an introspective soul than with one of a simpler kind, no sooner did he feel this surge of spring-sap mounting up in his veins than almost automatically, by reason of his unremitting self-consciousness, a certain recent occurrence, consorting ill with any kind of self-complacent well-being, presented itself in all its revolting and shameful details, and called upon him to watch the unrolling before him of a Hell-scorched scroll of memory.

The diplomatic Dean of St. Asaph, prompted he now suspected by that fanatic for peaceful settlements, the old Seneschal of Dinas Brān, had induced him to cross the frozen hills on the Feast of Stephen to try and patch up some sort of family truce with his cousin of Nannau.

The Arglwyddes had been fiercely opposed to the whole proceeding. "I shall never trust that man," she kept repeating; and when he had argued that with such high dignitaries from the cathedral present at their encounter Hywel Sele's hands would be tied, she had only shaken

her head and given expression to one of those teasing feminine retorts
that offer nothing to lay hold of, but carry about them all the same an
atmosphere of imponderable truth which can penetrate the joints of
the most rationalistic armour.

It was the Arglwyddes who had insisted on his taking Rhisiart with
him, and it was to this precaution combined with old Iolo's chain-
armour that he owed his life. His treacherous cousin had indeed so
skilfully arranged matters that in a little excursion round the Nannau
deer-run the peace-making ecclesiastics were left in the lurch, and Owen
and his squire found themselves alone with their host and a couple of
his game-keepers.

As he now listened to the scratching of Rhisiart's pen behind him,
and the tinkle of goat-bells and the murmur of spring-floods in the
valley before him, the whole foul business came back. Whether there
had appeared some wild creature of the forest that gave the assassin
his excuse he never knew. Rhisiart averred he saw nothing of the
kind. But it wasn't till he caught the swing-round of that calmly-aiming
figure, and felt the shock against his heart of the man's arrow, that he
realized what had happened. He himself had been totally unarmed,
but he could now see the red fires that danced before his eyes as he
leapt on his assailant and grappled with him before he could draw his
sword.

But oh, how clearly he could recall the way his first burst of fury,
giving him super-human strength, changed, as he felt the man's bulk
yield under his attack, to an ice-cold cruelty of vengeance.

What had he said to him as he bent his body backwards across a
fallen tree and watched his contorted face grow whiter and whiter,
while he heard the keepers break away, first one and then the other,
from before Rhisiart's flashing dagger? What *had* he said to him?
'Twas queer he'd forgotten just that; but he knew well what he felt
as he drew back from the dying man and straightened himself and
wiped his forehead and panted like a beast.

He had felt a cold anger against God, against Fate, against Death,
for taking his enemy out of his hands before— Before what? Before
he had made him lick the dregs, before he had made him eat the
mandrake, before he'd made him say: "My master, my master!"

He left him lying there with his back broken, and stood for a moment watching Rhisiart chase the keepers down the hill. How the lad ran! And how those terrified men, who evidently thought the magician's familiar spirit was after them, ran faster than their pursuer!

And then he caught sight—and it was only a few furlongs away—of a vast upstanding oak-trunk, hollow as a gigantic reed, though its diameter must have been at least a yard wide, and raising its great jagged mouth like a dragon's maw towards the sky.

He walked up to it. Yes, its mouth was about a man's height from the ground; and it was hollow, clear down to the root, for there were several large holes in its lower surface through which the light showed. It was then, *as he realized what he was going to do,* that he began trembling with an unholy excitement. His desire that the man should *know* before death snatched him away that he was mastered, his desire that there should be the exchange of realization, "You have lost" and "I have won," was now replaced by a totally different feeling, a darker, more inhuman, and much more agitating feeling.

But curiously enough the agitation of this new feeling came near to destroying his hatred of his dying enemy! He was going to do something now that he might have done to someone he didn't hate at all, someone who only happened—

He looked into the valley. Rhisiart and the keepers were out of sight. He looked towards Nannau. Not a living soul visible! He returned to the man whose back he had broken. The man's eyes were open and they were watching his enemy intently; but he was unable to speak, and there was a queer pulse beating beneath one of his staring eyes, a pulse that caused the skin to move up and down, as though there were a miniature mole at work below it.

The dying man's sword was still half-way out of its sheath, and when he lifted him up it fell completely out, clattering down. *That* was the most curious and shocking thing of all, the look the man gave him, as with infernal care he replaced the weapon in its sheath. But he lifted him up again and carried him to the tree. It was only then that he realized that to hoist this living corpse in his raised arms and plunge it into that gaping mouth was beyond even the unholy strength which the devil at that moment was pouring through his muscles.

Ah! there was Rhisiart! "Here, lad," he gasped. "We must *bury* him in this tree!"

Not a sound, not even another look; and the body was so limp in their hands that he said to himself, when it was done, that it *was* a corpse, as Rhisiart supposed. But the two of them at last, panting and sweating, were free to leave him behind, alive or dead, in his upright grave. "The shock must have killed him, broken as he was," he kept repeating to himself, as they hurried back for their horses.

It wasn't easy to get Seisyll and Griffin out of the stable without word reaching the hall, but they managed it somehow; and Owen could now see, as he watched the soft spring-darkness descend on Snowdon, the geir-falcon profile of his adherent as they spurred their steeds over the frozen passes and up the slippery ascents.

"The . . . shock . . . must . . . have . . . killed . . . him" was the tune to which those eight hooves thudded over the sunlit ridges and clanged against the blocks of ice in the glittering streams.

But he listened to Rhisiart's legal advice all the way home—for the young Oxonian enlarged on several astute alternatives—as to what they should write to St. Asaph to explain Sele's disappearance and their own precipitate departure.

But the worst of having a soul like his which could *exteriorize* itself, or at least could imagine it could, was that ever since that Feast of Stephen this wandering soul of his kept sending him messages from its perch on the hollow tree.

The one thing that he wanted to know—whether the man *was* killed by the shock of being flung into the tree—his wandering soul couldn't reveal. In place of which it kept sending him back all sorts of ghastly details of what was happening to the corpse.

Not a single piece of news that was of practical importance did his soul report, save one only; namely, that though they themselves had escaped it by riding northward, a flurry of snow had come up that night from the sea, obliterating every trace of their encounter. Was the up-turned face in the mouth of the tree covered by the snow that night? If he lived, his breath would have melted it, but if he was dead, what better catafalque?

One effect of this curious commerce between himself and what he thought of as his errant soul was that he began to feel that to have taken a revenge like that was a proof that what the English said of him was true and that he *had* sold himself to the Powers of Evil.

During the first month of the New Year, however, this feeling had in its turn been transformed into an arbitrary desire to prove to Christendom that a spirit accused of such a monstrous deed and accusing itself of such a monstrous deed could yet be the liberator of a nation. Enforced, save for his recent raid, into an idle winter, Owen had used his monstrous revenge as a spur to goad himself into more definite schemes for the benefit of his country than he had as yet formulated.

In this task he found a ready supporter in his new adherent, Master Brut; and night after night, in this room with the three lancet windows opening upon the peaks of Snowdon, rebel Prince and rebel Evangelist worked out elaborate systems for the Reformation of Welsh Religion and the Revival of Welsh Learning.

Rhisiart would get sleepy as soon as these discussions began; but there were some occasions during these long winter evenings when the Prince would take it into his head to summon Philip Sparrow to join their consultation; and these were occasions when Rhisiart's sleepiness vanished and a pile of legal folios in the jargon of the Norman-French courts and of commentaries upon the Laws of Hywel the Good in ecclesiastical Latin forced Owen's books of magic to huddle together in dismay and aversion. Those indeed were gala-nights for the youthful admirer of Master Young; and it was all the Prince could do to prevent Broch's sarcastic attendant from leaving the chamber in a fury when his revolutionary dogmas were brought before the bar of so many Doctors of Jurisprudence.

The one point—and Owen made a mental note of this—where the Oxonian and Philip Sparrow seemed always to agree was in regard to the necessity, the moment the King of England's Writ no longer ran in the Principality, of summoning a Welsh Parliament. Master Sparrow, however, invariably became sardonic when the number of *lawyers* in Rhisiart's Public Assembly were found to outweigh every other type of representative.

Broch himself, with or without his belt of axes, seldom uttered a word till he and the Prince were alone; but as Owen insisted on his friend's sharing his chamber, the laconic giant had plenty of opportunities for expressing himself at length when he so desired.

As the winter went on Owen found the most difficult part of playing

Prince was this business of keeping the peace between high-spirited advisers, each with his own conflicting notion as to what ought to be done. Where he found he had to call to his aid the roving black eye and casuistical discrimination of Father Pascentius was when—and it was the Lollard who always started this ticklish topic—the discussion between them ran upon the delicate matter of the founding and endowing of Welsh Universities.

The Lollard wanted Owen, in creating these important adjuncts to his Sovereign-State, to make them self-governing; but Rhisiart pointed out from the legal, and the learned Father from the theological, point of view, that such Free Debating Societies would soon become even more turbulent and unruly than the notorious University of Paris, whose both teachers and students, as everyone knew, were always in revolt against King and Church.

"But it'll be *you,* dear my Lord," Master Brut would protest, "who'll be the King in this case; and enlightened and tolerant philosophers, like our good Father here, who'll be the Church! It is tyranny, it is oppression that leads to disturbance. The teachers and students of our Welsh Universities will be too free to feel the necessity for asserting themselves against authority. That was the whole trouble at Oxford over Master Wycliffe. If *you,* my learned Father, were the Archbishop of St. David's—"

But it generally happened at this point that Owen would hurriedly change the subject, for he hadn't forgotten his prophetic trance in the forest of Mathrafal and his imaginary interview with the anti-Pope; and it was clear to him that the best commentator in the world upon the *Summa Theologica* wasn't necessarily the person he would select as the head of his Welsh church. . . .

But he turned from the window now at the sound of a reiterated knocking at the door that partook of the character of a signal. Rhisiart hurriedly left his work and went to investigate. They had found by experience in this over-crowded citadel that young Madoc ab Evan—more reconciled to Rhisiart's presence since this latter had exchanged sword for pen—was alone incapable of deciding who among the stream of people that kept seeking an audience with the Prince should be admitted and who should be refused; so it had been arranged between them that, at a particular knock from Madoc, Rhisiart should rush to the door.

On this occasion it was the shaven poll and gleaming half-shut eyes of Father Pascentius that were the problem.

"I *must* see the Prince, my son. I bring a word for his ear alone."

"One moment, Father, I'll tell him, Father. But you *may* have to give your message to me. The Prince is writing to King Robert and I expect he's too busy to see you to-night."

Father Pascentius bowed. "Go and ask him, my son, if you please."

Rhisiart closed the door and found Owen standing in the middle of the room. The latter raised his eyebrows.

"It's the Father, my Prince!"

"Not Rheinalt?"

"Oh no, my Prince; Father Pascentius."

Owen sighed. He had begun to find the insatiable aplomb of the theologian's gaze irritating and exhausting. "Between me and God," he muttered now, "the man's a vampire! But let him in. When I can't stand it a moment longer I'll throw a log on the fire and you must get him away. A blood-sucking vampire! One day, when he makes me angry, I'll have those gloating little eyeballs burnt out!"

While the door was open for the entrance of the monk, Rhisiart and Madoc exchanged glances. The former had felt malicious joy in hearing his ruler's savage outburst. The substitution of this subtle casuist, who seemed to miss nothing that went on in that mountain-court, for the simple-hearted father of Tegolin, was as unpleasant to the younger element in the place as it was to their elders.

The Lollard alone, remembering with gratitude all the twists that this serpent of orthodoxy had made on his behalf round the English barons, felt no objection at having a subtle thinker as their palace-confessor in place of one in whom patriotism had killed piety, and passion logic.

"Sit down, Father," said the Prince, clasping his hands tightly behind his back, so as not to yield to his trick of stroking his beard.

But Father Pascentius refused to sit down; and though Rhisiart resumed his former position, and even ostensibly took up his pen, and though the Prince sank into the big chair by the fire, the man insisted

in shuffling in his sandals up and down the bare flag-stones and across
the clumsily-woven rush-mat which little Catharine had made for her
father. Thus and thus only, it seemed, could he reveal his news.

Owen unclasped his fingers from behind his back and proceeded to
clasp them resolutely together below the crossing of his knees. He
struggled against an uncivil inclination to shut his eyes so as not to
meet the other's gloating pupils as they dilated.

How queer it was to be looked at, and looked through too, for the
theologian was no fool, by eyeballs that were so totally devoid of
human feeling!

"What a relief it must have been," he thought, "not only to your
enemy the Abbot but to every monk in the place, when you put
Saint Thomas on your pony and left for the mountains!"

"So you couldn't *help* catching the drift of their conversation as you
walked up and down, Father?"

"As if in our cloisters, my son."

"And you heard something of importance to some of us?"

"To you, my son."

"And what was it you heard, Father?"

"It concerned Master Broch-o'-Meifod, my son," and the discreet
theologian gave a quick glance in the direction of Rhisiart.

Owen made an attempt to convey by his expression that he had no
secrets from his Secretary, but he was so shocked by this unexpected
mention of his friend's name that little else but this shock had room
to appear on his disturbed face.

"I gathered, my son," the Father continued, "that Master Broch and
his servant went to catch a few trout in the lake, and found down there
a messenger from Meifod, who's been hanging about, they say, for
some while, in the hope of coming upon his master alone."

"Well, Father?" But it was easy enough to say, "Well, Father?"
What wasn't easy was to keep his mind from the absurd problem as to
whether the shuffle of the man's sandals would *sound the same* on
Catharine's mat as it did on the bare floor.

"And Master Broch and his servant, my son, were seen in the stables
after that; and the stable-boys thought—"

"By my confession, Father!" cried the Prince leaping to his feet,

"Tell me the worst, and have done with it! Has Master Broch gone back to Meifod?"

The theologian stood still, one sandal on Catharine's mat, the other on the stone floor. He took in the yellow gleam from the fire, he took in the way the chilly breath of that spring-thaw added something that was at once balmy and acrid to the log-smoke, something that made the botanist in him think of the pink protrusions of that curious swamp-plant called butter-burr which shoots up so satyrishly through the chaste mould!

He met without the least perturbation Owen's angry stare. All he did was to allow his eyelids to narrow a little, so that what the indignant Prince was now questioning were a pair of shiny blacknesses peering out with indestructible vivacity from a thatched porch.

It was evident that to the brain behind those orbs the Prince's agitation was no displeasing portion of what they were enjoying; and they were enjoying so many things! Such things, for instance, as the shadow of the Secretary's Norman nose thrown by the fire-light on the back of a white-vellum quarto; such things as the voice of a bull-frog from the edge of the lake outside; such things as the charmingly-painted initial letter at the beginning of the very paragraph over which Rhisiart was pondering.

The young man's own ill-concealed concern over the Prince's mounting indignation, how it too fell into its place, among all there was for those eyes to savour as the beautiful spring-darkness, that tasted so different from anything else in the world, contended with the yellow fire-light!

"Speak, man, for Mary's sake, unless you want me to whistle you back to your Prior!" Certain drops of sweat which were running down Owen's cheek, and had reached his chin, and now seemed undecided whether to trickle to the left or the right must have struck Father Pascentius as even more significant of the nature of the Absolute than the spring-darkness that poured in through the windows, for he contemplated them with quiet joy.

"The stable-men told me," he concluded calmly, "that only one horse had been taken, but that Master Broch and his servant had not yet—"

Another knock and Rhisiart was at the door again. This time there was no questioning or delay, and the gigantic figure of Broch-o'-Meifod himself entered the room.

"Pardon me, Owen ap Griffith," he said, "but I've got Philip out there, on one of the black mares, waiting your leave of absence for a week. Morg ferch Lug has sent Llewelyn over to say that half-a-dozen Chirk foresters have encamped on the other side of the pond and have begun making themselves a nuisance, stealing sacks of corn and killing chickens. He says they haven't meddled with the maids yet, and that our girls are all right. But the pretty would never have sent Llewelyn all this distance if the look of things wasn't—"

"Six of 'em did he say?" cried Owen. "Let him take a dozen of our best Sycharth troop! But I'm not going to spare Sparrow. He knows your ways, my friend, just as Cousin Rhisiart knows mine! 'Twould be no kindness to your wife to let Sparrow go. Is Meredith at hand, Rhisiart? Go and find him—there's a dear lad! Tell him I want a dozen of our best men from home, and let Tom Evan lead them. Tell Meredith I can't help it, but Tom and his dozen must stay at Maen-y-Meifod till further notice. Tell Meredith they must all have ponies and must take meat and drink to last 'em till May. And tell him Tom Evan's responsible with his life for their good behaviour. No, better leave *that* out! Just tell Meredith about the demoiselles and the maids. He'll know the men to pick."

Rhisiart bowed without a word. But as he moved away he lightly twitched the monk's habit, whispering to him as he did so that he had a confession of mortal sin for his private ear.

As soon as the two friends were alone Owen earnestly enquired of the laconic giant what instructions he'd better give Tom Evan as to the future. "Suppose the English decide to do to Maen-y-Meifod as they've done to Glyndyfrdwy and Sycharth? Tom'll manage the foresters. But what if the Sheriff comes on the scene with his Shropshire levies? Could you bring youself, Broch, to let the place go, and have your family up here?"

The bald Hercules blinked. Then he made several guttural sounds in his throat and gave his belt such a jerk that the blades of the axes tinkled.

"The pretty—won't—like—it," he remarked slowly. "She's put her heart into that wheel. But I think I'll send her a word by your good Tom."

So saying he moved over to Rhisiart's desk and possessed himself both of the boy's seat, which creaked under his weight, and of a loose fragment of parchment.

Thus prepared, he covered his great visage with his hands, leaning his elbows on the desk and pondering. The Prince walked to the door and opened it.

"Don't let *anybody* in, lad," he directed Madoc, the sentry, "until Meredith comes." Then he discreetly returned to his seat by the fire and stared into its red depths.

The big man at the desk, meanwhile, was slowly and not without difficulty forming the following syllables:

Pretty of my heart, Owen ap Griffith is always ready and the Arglwyddes is always ready to welcome you and our girls to where they are now. He himself will soon be away, so you needn't think of the wheel. You can trust Tom Evan. He will bring you here as soon as it seems best. They may leave you in peace or they may not. If not, I bid you come before too late. Your old Badger—not yet "in the bag"—Broch-o'-Meifod.

The giant was so long composing this document—for the crucial word "bid," was only inserted after "beg," "entreat," "wish," "ask," "advise," "suggest," had each in turn been substituted for the one before it—that Owen had plenty of time to envisage in the red heart of his fire a surprise-attack upon Maen-y-Meifod by an overwhelming English force.

He passed his hands up and down his shins, while through his black hose the heat penetrated his whole being. What a thing fire was! And how curious to think of that upright corpse—a corpse *now* anyway —with its face buried in snow and the foxes barking round it. If he *did* turn the English out, would he have the power to do for his people what Charles the Great did for his, or Alfred the Great for his? "I doubt it," he thought. "We pure-blooded Brythons, as that woman said, are good at a pinch, but we can't *keep it up.*"

The warmth of the fire and the fragrance of that sweet alder-wood smoke seemed to make it possible for him to contemplate in calm detachment—he noticed this even as it was happening—the most outrageous and shocking things. "I shall turn them out," he thought. "Ffraid ferch Gloyw said that; and I've never doubted it. But when it comes to the Universities—and this Lollard says there must be two of 'em, a southern one and a northern—I don't know what to think! English Alfred had the genius of a commander *and* the learning of a monk; but who am I, who get so elated with triumph when I come back from a raid with fifty ponies' load of plunder!— Good Lord, Universities! There's a vein in you, *Owen the Irresponsible,* that's better adapted to burning markets and storming castles and making princes' courts on the slopes of Snowdon than to the founding of Universities! If only I had that man Young back again."

For a moment he gave himself up to the pure sensation of warmth. "How many rebel princes," he thought, "with their spearmen gathering, and their prophets prophesying, and their stars pointing the way, have let it all go in the warmth of a fire. It's a reversion with me, that's what it is, to the old cave-dwellers! A human skeleton squatting on its buttocks, feeling nice and warm, how can Universities spring out of that? And *one* won't content you, you learned rascal, eh? You must have two of them!"

And the evangelical lineaments of Master Brut took shape in the heart of the fire. "What a man! *He* cares nothing about the Percies or the anti-Pope! All *he* cares for are class-rooms of heresy, with a dozen Master Wycliffes to every Seraphic Doctor. But that fellow Young's the man. I *must* get him back. And yet Wales *could* be—only my bards don't harp to *that* tune—the centre of a new epoch for the whole of Christendom!"

And there came to him as he sat there—while the giant behind him erased with Rhisiart's green ink the word "advise" and substituted the word "bid" in a blood-coloured red—an indescribable feeling of power.

"I'm a medium of the gods for *something,*" he thought. "I wish to the devil they'd make it clearer to me for *what!*" It wasn't till towards eight of the clock that night that Owen, leaning upon the arm of his friend Broch and followed by Rhisiart and Madoc, entered, with a certain amount of feudal ceremony, the central hall of his motley court.

This was where the afternoon's banquet had been held, and well replenished it had been with fresh meats and viands pillaged from the rich Vale of Clwyd; but the tables had all been removed now, and the various members of the rebel headquarters, men and women intermingled, were seated in relaxed positions, as taste and etiquette dictated, passing the long spring evening as agreeably as circumstances allowed.

The Arglwyddes, portly lady though she was, and Owen was always sighing over her carelessness about her appearance and her reluctance to submit to any tire-woman who was an artist, was now walking up and down before a great loom, busily engaged in weaving, while, like a flock of starlings around a stately ewe, her maids chattered in high-pitched excitement. Quite often they fell into uncontrollable laughing fits and even exchanged ribald jests, for the mother of all those tall sons was the most indulgent of matriarchs, and there were many young pages to amuse them. Rhisiart's old acquaintances at Glyndyfrdwy had been recently increased by the addition of his friends from Dinas Brān as well as by several new-comers, so that that court in Snowdon was a paradise of love and mischief.

On this occasion the Prince's numerous sons left what they were doing and gathered ceremoniously round their father as he took his seat, each one in turn making the customary genuflexion. Owen looked round the hall while he listened sympathetically to the young men's stories, which were mostly about hunting and fishing, and he noticed that not only was Meredith absent, which had clearly to do with the provisioning of Tòm Evan's little troop, but his eldest son Griffith was nowhere to be seen.

"Where's your brother Griffith?" he enquired of one of the boys grouped round him.

The lad looked quickly at the others and hesitated. One of the pages broke in, "Griffith ab Owen has gone, my Prince, instead of Rhys Gethin to light the beacon on Carnedd Llewelyn."

The form of the Prince's visage changed and his eyes flashed. "But I told Rhys Gethin at dinner to get that done. Where has *he* gone then?"

"Rhys Gethin is over there, my Prince," said the page eagerly, while Owen's sons avoided their father's eyes. While the boy spoke he pointed to a secluded corner of the hall where the figure of a man and a woman could dimly be seen crouched over a fire of their own in deep and close conversation.

"Oh, I'm glad he's here," said Owen hurriedly. "I remember now it *was* Griffith I sent."

"He's been talking to Mistress Lowri ever since the sun went down," the page added, "and Master Simon's behind those soldiers. He always mends their armour when the torches burn well; and the torches are burning better than usual to-night."

"Mad Huw says, sir," broke in another page, "that the torches wouldn't be burning as they are if something weren't going to happen!"

One of Owen's sons, in order to dissipate their embarrassment over the matter of their elder brother, began to rebuke these officious pages, and even to push them away. "If the torches *are* burning extra bright to-night," he announced dogmatically as the pages sulkily went off, "it's only because Mother told the maids to put in some of the new oil."

The Prince rose to his feet at that, and crossing the room embraced his lady and complimented her on the brightness of the torches and on the progress of her weaving.

"No, that kiss wasn't meant for you, Mistress Sibli," he said lightly; but catching the look on the dwarf's face he hurriedly snatched at the little creature's hand. "What a dainty little hand!" he observed.

And while the small being flushed with pleasure and made a face at the giggling maids, "By my confession," he added, "the prettiest hand in the hall!"

Mad Huw now took the opportunity of coming up to him, dragging the Maid of Edeyrnion by the sleeve.

"She said I wasn't to bother you, my Lord," he cried earnestly, "but it's right for you to know, since you've given Him shelter, that He Himself told me just now that there's a sign on its way that when he sees it will drive the tyrant to despair. He said all the land would know of it, because— No! I *must* tell him, sister!"

"I know," said Owen, smiling at Tegolin who was looking especially lovely that night, "who it is who'd make Harry of Lancaster envy us, poor barbarians! No, but seriously, Mistress," he added, "I'm convinced the King of France himself hasn't such an ornament to his court!"

The Grey Friar's face lit up with pleasure. *"He's* told her, too," he whispered, coming close to Owen. "That's why she looks like an angel!"

The Prince surveyed him gravely, not humouring him but treating him like an obscure oracle. "What *kind* of sign is it that's coming, little Brother?"

But while Mad Huw was explaining that it was probably a fiery sign Owen noticed that Broch-o'-Meifod, whose movements couldn't very well be concealed from anyone, had seated himself among the troopers whose weapons the ex-Hog of Chirk was so industriously sharpening.

Simultaneously with this the Prince realized that Master Brut had been there all along, and was now turning from the amateur armourer to engage in a lively argument with the bald-headed giant.

A faint prick of jealousy assailed Owen when he took this in. But he upbraided himself for it. "I suppose you think, you dandified egoist, that because Broch's *your* friend he's not to be allowed to talk to anybody with a grain of intelligence! But oh, I'd like to know what those two are talking about!" He was still listening with half an ear to Mad Huw and still watching Tegolin as she now seated herself by Luned and took a corner of the latter's embroidery on her lap, when, amid the general murmur of voices, he became aware of the rich girlish laughter of his favourite child.

"Between me and God!" he said to himself, "the little one's talking to Rhisiart!" A vivid memory came over him, as he saw Catharine and Rhisiart standing together, of how when he'd first set eyes on the boy the lad had been standing side by side with the Maid of Edeyrnion. He glanced quickly at Tegolin. Yes, the red-haired girl was only half-interested in Luned's work. Her grave, steady eyes, whenever they were lifted from her lap, turned invariably towards Rhisiart and Catharine. He did his best to assume the expression of one too deeply absorbed in the Friar's words to see with intelligence what was going on before him.

But as he watched, with what he hoped resembled an unthinking stare, the look which Tegolin cast upon Rhisiart, "There's something—though God only knows what it is—" he thought, "between these two. Tegolin *may* not be in love with him—but she certainly is involved with him. Who can tell what goes on in her mind as she fixes that look upon him? But whatever the feelings are that betray her, her soul is absolutely calm. Even if she's caught that particular note in Catharine's laugh she's not going to let it torment her."

What Catharine and Rhisiart were doing while they were thus watched by Owen and Tegolin was innocent enough, for they were listening to the Nurse. The old woman was seated near the fire, with her feet on a foot-stool, engaged in winding a skein of purple wool with the help of Alice of Ruthin. And as she wound she sang in her faint, high, cracked voice; and Owen well knew what she was singing—one of those plaintive, mournful dirges attributed to Heledd, daughter of Cyndylan. He could see just what had happened. The English maid holding that purple skein round her white wrists had asked some stupid question of the Nurse, and the aged woman, teased by the girl's ignorance, had made an old wife's sly retort, at which the young people's eyes had met, and Catharine had laughed aloud.

"Thank you, Brother," he said as courteously as he could, "I will remember your words and watch well to-night. God be with you, Brother." But though Mad Huw moved away then, quite content, the Prince remained standing where he was, lost in thought.

Knowing his tendency to these fits of abstraction, none cared to approach him, though the Arglwyddes glanced at him anxiously more than once as she moved up and down in front of her loom.

Meanwhile the old woman's quavering voice rose and fell; some of the household turning to look at her, some murmuring the well-known words, others indifferent and heedless, continuing their conversation.

> *Stafell Cyndylan ys tywyll heno,*
> *Heb dan, heb gannwyll,*
> *Namyn Duw, pwy a'm dyry pwyll!*

> *The hall of Cyndylan is dark to-night,*
> *Without fire, without candle,*
> *And there is none but God to comfort me!*

To Owen both words and tune were so familiar that they were like the sound of the Paternoster at Mass, no more than a gentle February wind, moving among branches and twigs that were already feeling the stir of the sap within them.

But though in his crafty self-consciousness he didn't scruple just then, as he stood at gaze in the centre of *his ystafell,* to feign the approach of one of his trances, his thoughts had never been more cynical or more shameless.

"They're both mine," he said to himself. "She's mine and he's mine. I musn't, I *won't* spare them to each other. They're the best weapons I have. Shall I throw away my best weapons? That's what it would be if I let them melt together. It wouldn't be only one I'd lose."

There was rarely anything in the motion of his feelings, in the drift of his intentions, that Owen missed in himself. "You're a mirror-man—*drych dyn,*" old Iolo had often told him; and Broch himself had once said, and he remembered the very spot where he said it, that his was the only soul he knew that actually and without pretence obeyed the oracle "Know thyself." "But all you do," Broch had added, "is to push the unknown *further in;* and *that* only makes it darker than it was before. In fact"—Broch had gone on—"your lantern of self-knowledge only creates more darkness. 'Light the candle, and you'll see how dark it is,' as the old Powys proverb says."

He always thought of these words of "the Badger of Meifod" when there obtruded into his decisions motives so abominable that he would never have dared to reveal them to a living creature.

"I *must* have that boy body and soul," he thought, "and I *must* have a Catharine virginal and intact, to use as my grand tribute to destiny!"

These thoughts were expressed in unspoken words, but they were clear and definite. Nevertheless, behind these thoughts, just where the darkness seemed thickest, there hovered the will-o'-the-wisp of a suggestion that it wasn't because he wanted to use Catharine as a "castle" in his chess-game with Bolingbroke, but because the thought of her marriage was a torture to him, that he shuddered to catch that love-note in her laugh. It was one of his shameless concessions to his unholier instinct that in any raid upon a town or village he never interfered with his men's behaviour to the girls of the place; but no suffering any demon could ever inflict on him was worse than what he endured when taking him suddenly by surprise, his imagination conjured up a realistic vision of Catharine in the arms of a ravisher.

He had once been betrayed into supposing that the Arglwyddes would feel as he did; but when some reference to such a horror came he was confounded by the coolness of her tone. He shrugged his shoulders now and forced himself to look calmly and steadily about him. The sweet wood-smoke, rising in undulating curves and wavering wisps above the heads of that crowded assembly, mingled its wholesome scent with a new fragrance that night, the fragrance of the brightly-burning oil.

"Yes," the Prince thought, "that boy of mine's right. It's the oil we got from that rich rogue at Bryn Saith Marchog! I suppose *his* hall's as dark as Cyndylan's to-night—but he'd be alive now, the fool, if he hadn't resisted. To know when to strike, and when to refrain from striking—I shan't get the English out of Wales till I learn that."

Well! In the case of Rhisiart and Catharine his instinct told him that he must "refrain"; yes, and that was the word too in the case of Lowri and Rhys Gethin. "Time and chance and the envy of Heaven," he told himself, "are the powers that deal best with the attractions and repulsions of men. Lift a finger to intervene, and all's in a blaze."

Thus sobered, and cautioned too by something in his nature that his self-analysis couldn't altogether fathom, Owen disregarded the old Nurse and her young listeners, disregarded Lowri and Gethin, and sat down on a comfortable horse-block that somebody had brought in from the entrance-yard. Here he was near enough to the Lollard and his bald-headed friend to be able to join in their discussion; and here he could let the bitterness of his jealousy find a vent in harmless argument.

They were talking about Hell and Heaven; and it was no surprise to our Prince when he perceived that his own gravitation to a spot made somewhat noisy by the murmur of the troopers lying about on the floor while Simon worked was countered by the shuffling to the scene on his silent sandals of the ubiquitous Father Pascentius.

"Go on, go on, gentlemen," Owen begged them, as he took his seat. "No, no! I'm quite comfortable. What were you saying, Master Brut?"

"I was saying, my Prince, that what our theologians call 'the Fall' was in reality simply a wrong turn taken by our remote ancestors. They weren't altogether to blame; for it was only the continuance on this earth of a crack in creation that had begun much earlier, had begun in fact in Heaven. It's because it goes so far back that we feel, as Saint Paul says, that all Nature shares it. Coming down the mountain this very day spring-like though it is, I felt as I saw a mass of broken rocks and an old twisted thorn that they too were waiting and enduring. Enduring what?" He paused; then deepening his voice with intense conviction, *"Enduring Hell!"* he brought out.

There came at that moment such a curious expression into the countenance of Broch-o'-Meifod that both the Prince and the Lollard stared at him in wonder. The big man's face under the torch-light was transformed and his heavy lips twitched as if about to speak. But what startled and even shocked the men about him was the nature of the change that had come over him. Perhaps the best description of it would be to say that the natural human light in the man's eyes had gone out and a look had taken its place that resembled the endurance of rocks and stones and stumps.

"What's happened to your eyes?" Owen longed to interject, while Master Brut's words concerning the Fall, as they still hovered in the air, seemed to grow thin and brittle. They hung in that heavy-sweet smoke like the pitiful echoes of an oracle who had long ago been doomed.

But from Broch's expressionless face there now came a series of slowly-uttered but quite intelligible words.

"No . . . they don't . . . endure Hell, brother," he murmured. "You felt like that to-day because of the warm, loving glow in your own heart. I have no such glow. I have no such heart. The pretty often says, 'I don't believe you're any more human than my wheel, Broch!' And sometimes she says, and laughs and laughs as she says it, 'I believe you're a corpse, Broch, a corpse that's been dead a thousand years, and some great lumbering, lubberly devil's got into you and talks to me out of you—not a fire-devil, Broch, but a frozen mud-devil.' So that's what *she* thinks; and she's not jesting either. What was I going to say? Oh yes—that you're mistaken, Master, about that 'enduring.' And you're mistaken too about that 'crack in creation' and about that 'wrong turn.'

"You say things like that out of your warm, loving, human heart. You look at those rocks and you look at those stumps, Brut, and a chill goes through you! I know what you do. Sometimes you think to yourself, 'At this very moment there's a dead log in a frozen murky pool, where no one ever comes, or ever will come!' And your loving soul shivers to think of what that log feels, with no one, *not even a worm,* ever coming near it."

But the Lollard had recovered himself now. He had got more used to those deep eye-sockets in which the light had gone out. He could hardly keep his seat. "That's it!" he cried. "That's just what Saint Paul means! It's for the manifestation of the Sons of God that your log's waiting. And that means the Resurrection of Jesus and the Blessed Blood of Jesus. There *is* a crack in creation. We *have* taken the wrong turn; and it's only—"

But the face under that enormous bald head had now become so shockingly inhuman that his words died away before it. "Not even a worm," repeated Broch-o'-Meifod. "And the heart of Jesus is so full of love that it *can't* feel what that log feels. Jesus is like you, Master Brut. His loving heart calls all night and all day to that loneliness out there. 'Love me! Love me!' it calls. And like you it thinks—that warm, human heart—that nothing but a 'crack in creation,' nothing but a 'wrong turn' taken long ago, is holding back that loneliness. But shall I tell you"—his voice sounded now more like the dropping of icicles into black water than a human tongue—"the Spirit is moving already to another and a different Revelation. None of us will live to see it. But those lonelinesses that trouble your human heart, Brut, are its messengers; they may be 'enduring'; but as for Hell—"

The voice of Father Pascentius now became audible from where he stood leaning against a dark oak pillar. "If you'll pardon a poor monk, gentlemen," he said, and his words seemed to come from his burning eyes rather than from his mouth, "I would like to make one small animadversion upon what we've just heard. May I speak, my Prince?"

Owen bit his lip under his beard, but he bowed politely; and as for Broch-o'-Meifod everybody could see how humbly and patiently he swung his great head round towards the Cistercian till his lightless eye-sockets confronted the burning orbs of the other.

"I'm a theologian, not a politician," Father Pascentius went on, "but I must remind you, my sons, that King Harry and his Archbishop are burning many sincere men—and I fear Oldcastle himself will be the next—for holding views far milder and less subversive of our Holy Catholic Faith than what we have just heard. I humbly submit, my

Prince—though 'tis no more than the view of a poor scholar—that when the heresies we have been listening to begin to be bruited over the land, many patriotic Welshmen who are also good Catholics will say to themselves, 'What will become of our souls if Owen ap Griffith keeps such persons about him?' And for the King and his bigoted Archbishop this will be a supreme advantage! They already call our Prince a black magician. Now they'll be able to say he has people about him who are advocates of anti-Christ."

There was a frightened murmur of protest at this from among such of the troopers as had managed to keep their wits unfuddled; but Broch only bowed his head a little and made a groping gesture with one of his great hands towards the quarter of the horizon from which this spring-time thaw had apparently come.

"I have seen a letter to our Prior, now our Lord Abbot—may the holy saints long preserve him!—" went on the voice behind the eyes, "in which the sufferings of a recent heretic at the stake were described by an eye-witness; and I think, my Prince, and all of you, my Masters, it were well to remember that if, in the decrees of Providence, our cause was *not* successful—" He was interrupted by outcries from the men gathered about the industrious Simon. It was clear that he was troubling their minds! for there was fear as well as anger in their protests.

But the monk continued as obstinately as if he were in his own vaulted chapter-house in Valle Crucis, "Master Brut spoke of the desolation he noted in certain generated things, from which the creator had withdrawn his creative energy. But Saint Thomas clearly proves that the incorporeal agent by whom all things, both corporeal and incorporeal, are created is God, from whom all things derive not only their form but also their matter; therefore, what Master Brut saw, when he gave way to the sin of desolation, was simply an illusion of the Devil, an illusion representing corporeal things as they would be supposing that, with the cessation of the divine operation, they fell into nothingness."

Father Pascentius's Phorkyad eyes now turned from the Lollard to the Master of Maen-y-Meifod. "As to the words that you"—there was no need for him to name the bald-headed giant—"have just uttered, Saint Thomas refutes *them* in a logic before which every Catholic must bow. No new Revelation, Saint Thomas declares, even if it were possible for it to be known, *can* be known, because it is impossible that the end of the present Revelation should be revealed except to him who has received the Revelation of the whole of divine predestination, that is, to Christ as man, through whom the whole predestination of the human race is fulfilled; even as it is clearly said in the Holy Gospel: 'The Father loveth the Son and showeth him all things which—'"

He was interrupted by three shrill blasts of a horn from outside the main entrance, an entrance which opened straight into the banquet-hall where they were now assembled. Everyone's gaze turned instantly to the high folding doors, doors which in their massive portentousness nearly reached the beams of the ceiling. These great doors in their hand-wrought iron-work and blackened antiquity suggested that they had been brought from some old Snowdonian castle whose foundations existed before the departure of the Romans; but they also suggested by their surprising height that they had once defended a gateway through which riders could enter on horseback.

There is something about the concentration of a crowd of human beings upon some inanimate obstacle that dissolves the aforesaid obstacle into porous vapour, vapour through which the imagination draws forth out of the darkness monstrous images of the unknown event.

But the high doors were now being unbarred as if in response to a pre-arranged signal; and every soul in the hall strained forward to welcome the issue, some with dread, some with panic, some with dramatic exultation.

Half-a-dozen spearmen entered, led by Owen's eldest son, and as the Prince, without rising from his seat, straightened himself to receive bad news—for it had become a lodged impression, or if you prefer a settled superstition, with him that his eldest son always brought him bad luck—Griffith hurried to his father's side, carrying a large and carefully sealed letter.

Sinking down on one knee, though with anything but a courtier-like expression on his lowering and anxious face, he placed this document in the Prince's hands, and then with the words, "I expect you'll want to retire to your room with this," turned away from his father and crossed the hall to where the Arglwyddes was now seated by the side of her loom.

Such was the perpetual fretting discord and jarring contrariety between Owen and his first-born that it was quite enough as very likely Griffith realized it *would* be, for the son to suggest that this ticklish document should be carried out of the hall, to make the father decide that there was every reason why he should open it at once before them all. So while Broch-o'-Meifod resumed his conversation with the Lollard, and while the monk turned his devouring gaze upon what Master Simon was doing, Owen managed to catch Rhisiart's eye and made a sign to him to approach.

The boy obeyed at once; while the old Nurse, who, just as if the girl were still a small child, ordered Catharine, in some drastic nursery fashion, to go and kiss her mother before she retired for the night.

Lowering his head above the big document, so as not to see his daughter bid his Secretary good-night, the Prince broke the seals one by one with a vicious and malicious pleasure in the mere destruction of sealing-wax.

There was an outer cover of plain parchment wrapped round the contents of the document upon which the address, "To Owen ap Griffith, commonly called Glendourdy, and now in his Castle in the Mountains of Snowdon, *these,*" was written in French. Then there appeared a brief letter, also in French, signed "Henry Don of Kidwelly," which the Prince proceeded to read to himself, while both Rhisiart—now standing with grave attention at his side—and Father Pascentius, leaning against his wooden pillar, surveyed him intently. "My gracious Lord and most honoured friend," Henry Don wrote, "I received by word of mouth from your trusty servant, from whose hands your letter had been stolen, but to whom, in case of such an accident, you had communicated its contents, that by the will of God you had risen to liberate the Welsh People from the bondage of their English enemies. I write to inform you, my gracious Lord and most dear friend, that I am making my way by such stages as these troubled times allow with certain moneys and a considerable following, to put myself at your honoured service. One of my party, a Welshman from London, cognizant of affairs in that city, brings me his account of certain oppressive and unrighteous measures voted by the King's Commons in Westminster for the destruction of Our People. These insolent proclamations I am enclosing herewith for your gracious consideration and that of your Council of Worthy and Faithful men. May the God of our fathers be your Support in adversity and your Guide to victory. Your devoted and humble servant, Henry Don."

Still seated on his horse-block by the central fire of the hall, and watched in silence now not only by the Lollard and the monk but by the majority of that vast household, Owen handed to Rhisiart the new Acts of Parliament, referred to by his friend, and commanded him to read them aloud.

"Do you wish me, my Prince," enquired the young man when he had examined the legal phraseology of the document, "to translate it into our Welsh tongue, so that all here present can follow these monstrous and unheard-of edicts?"

"If you can manage such a thing, my dear boy," replied Owen smiling.

Put on his mettle by this, and using the resonant and official tone that he had acquired in his Sheriff's Court at home, Rhisiart proceeded, though with some natural hesitation here and there, to make that crowded hall echo to the following words:

Hear and obey, all good liege subjects, the will and pleasure of your Sovereign Lord King Henry: No Englishman may be convicted in Wales by any Welshman, but only by other Englishmen of good fame. No waster, rhymer, minstrel, or vagabond may maintain himself by making gatherings upon the common people. No congregations, divinations, lies, and excitations may be held in Wales, save in the presence of English officers. No Welshman, not loyal to our Royal Allegiance, may bear arms or armour in any town, market, or church or in any highway. No victuals or arms may be imported into Wales except for the use of English Castles and English Towns.

No Welshman, other than Bishops, may have castles or houses capable of defence beyond such as existed in the days of our gracious and sovereign Prince, Edward, first of that name. No Englishman married to any Welshwoman of the amity or alliance of Owen ap

Glendourdy, traitor to our Sovereign Lord, or to any other Welsh-woman after the rebellion of the said Owen, or that in time to come marrieth himself to any Welshwoman, may be put into any office in Wales or in the Marches of the same.

Owen rose slowly to his feet. "Well, men of Gwynedd and Powys," he cried in a ringing voice, "what is your answer to that?"

A terrific excitement ensued. The men-at-arms clashed their weapons upon their shields, and raised them aloft. Many of the women tossed their arms above their heads and loosened the bands of their hair. Some of the more excitable among the younger girls, not contented with setting free their flowing locks, bared their breasts in their emotion, a gesture of feminine feeling which the Prince had never witnessed be-fore, though he had often heard stories of such a thing being done when the women of Mōn flung themselves upon the Roman legions.

Curiously enough he himself felt a little puzzled by this display of passion in the presence of a few mean and vindictive measures passed by the perturbed commonalty of Bolingbroke's business-like kingdom.

"And what a dramatic hurry these English are in!" he thought as he stood in silence listening to the wild acclamations about him. "They might at least have taken the trouble to have a Welsh clerk look over their vicious statute. *Owen 'ap' Glendourdy!* What? Do they take me for a river-sprite, and the actual child of my Glen of Divine Water? But a good friend, a good friend, that Don is! Though I wish he'd brought *only money,* and not more of these curst mouths to feed!"

Never had he felt colder, never less stirred of any sort of racial emo-tion than at that moment. There! Catharine was only just going to bed now. "How young girls *do* hate to go to bed! I suppose it's different when they're married—but not for long; no, no, not for long." And he began to tell himself a story about keeping Rhisiart up, copying legal documents, half the night, so that he shouldn't disturb the sleep of a still beautiful wife whose heart had reverted to her father!

But he mustn't have her; never, never! She was his grand weapon, his "white queen," in his chess-game with Bolingbroke.

The clamour had died down now. But what was that? The old Bard playing on his harp? No! It was the sound of a pipe. And then he remembered that Lowri ferch Ffraid had been, ever since she arrived, anxious that the Arglwyddes should introduce the Dinas Brān custom, which had been dropped or perhaps had never existed in his more easy-going domains, with regard to the departure of the ladies from the hall. Yes, that was it! They were taking down the loom and collecting their things. But 'twas a silly custom! Much better were the homely border habits of the honest Hanmers. What put it into Lowri's head? Oh, no doubt a desire—he had noted this sort of thing in other cases—to make the Arglwyddes feel ashamed of her English blood— to trouble that simple lady's mind with the feeling that she ought to be grander in her ways, more ceremonious, more careful of the old Celtic traditions, now that her man was Prince of Wales.

A wave of vibrant tenderness for the mother of his children swept over him, and he cast a dangerous look towards the small fire at the extremity of the hall, which, when he had last seen it, had been monopolized by Lowri and Rhys Gethin. But they had disappeared. They must have taken advantage of that warm spring thaw to go out together.

He glanced quickly at Simon. The man was still hard at work, though the recent outburst of national feeling had deprived him of all spectators. Doggedly and obstinately he went on, polishing and hammering; using for his purpose the great central hearth of the hall when in his amateur labours as an armourer the heat of fire was necessary.

What had happened to the Hog of Chirk? Well, if it was Lollardry that had done this—"But she'd better not go too far! These convertites —I've known several in my time—if they're not mad, like poor Huw, are apt to burst out and risk Hell-fire! Rhys Gethin were wise to keep a weather-eye on you, my industrious Simon."

He couldn't resist a pang of jealousy when he saw how deep Master Broch and the Lollard had sunk out of hearing of all the world in their spiritual argument.

But the women were leaving the hall now, and though there was none but the family Bard to murmur in his quavering voice the traditional *"In Exitu Mulieres"* the old gentleman chanted the obscure words to the end.

Impatiently Owen strode across to the torch-lit stairway and was just in time to catch his wife in his arms as she was taking the first step.

The Arglwyddes was surprised, was even a little disturbed, by this unexpected demonstration; but she responded to it with an affectionate embrace, and as he watched her sturdy figure disappear leaning on Tegolin's arm, and with Mad Huw stumbling after them, he wondered if it were because she wished to conceal an unusual emotion that she didn't turn her head as she went up. Everything that this woman meant to him came over him now with a blind rush, and standing in the entrance to the stairs so that the maids couldn't easily pass, he fell into one of his queer reveries.

By the time he had shaken this off and was exchanging ribald jests with little Sibli he was astonished to see that pale English maid they called Alice struggling against the restraining arms of both Rhisiart and the Lollard, lost to everything in a violent fit of hysterics.

"Let me go to her—my mother, my dear mother!" the unhappy girl kept crying. "Let me go, I tell you! I *will* go; though I go through water and fire!"

"What is it? What's the matter with her? Tell me, child! Where do you want to go? Where *is* your mother?"

But the competent Luned came running up now with a jug of spring water, from which she mercilessly sprinkled the girl's face, till the young woman slipped down from the men's arms and sank in a heap on the floor. There she lay piteously moaning, but no longer insane with grief.

Owen turned to Rhisiart, while Luned remained on her knees drying the girl's drenched hair and neck.

"A messenger has come to her, my Prince, with terrible news. He was only a lad, and was too frightened to stay; but it appears that Grey got it into his head that this girl's mother—she's a Welshwoman, my Prince, though the father's English—had thrown witchcraft over the young Lord, and that the said young Lord was wasting away. In reality, my Prince, it is for love of Alice that the young man is pining. But Grey sent his people to seize the girl's mother and have her condemned in his Manor-Court as a witch taken in the act. Alice's father resisted these men and was killed in his own house; but no one knows what's become of her mother. And it's this *not knowing,* my Prince, that has set the girl beside herself. I watched her while the lad told her—it was just now, when you were standing at the foot of the stairs, or you'd have seen what was going on—and it was this uncertainty, this not knowing what was happening to her mother, that broke the maid down."

Owen's interest and his wrath, too, were fully roused by this recital, roused as it had not been by the vindictive Acts of Parliament.

Rhisiart saw what his master was feeling and he went on boldly. "Had he a legal right to arrest her and take her life, my Prince? For I seem to have read that to punish the sin of witchcraft is a privilege of the ecclesiastical, not of the civil, courts. Has Grey's Manor-Court, my Prince, the right to try a person accused of witchcraft? Has it the right to usurp the Bishop's jurisdiction?"

"It has no such right!" cried Owen fiercely. "This is the sort of thing that's been going on for the last two hundred years! They build their castles; they fill them with devils; they do what they like with our people. Oh, great God in Heaven!"—and his voice resounding through the hall made every man present leap to his feet—"if you'll strengthen my hand now, only for twelve months, so that I can clear the land of them, just clear the land of them, from Bangor to St. David's, you can do what you will with me afterwards, and with all I love!"

Something seemed to crack within him, something that hitherto, like the bite of a black frost, had made an ice-barrier between his soul and such wrongs. But now he felt pouring through him, as if from the outraged heart of every victim of every castle in Wales, a torrential strength that nothing could resist!

Rhisiart looked at him in amazement. The boy was awed, but puzzled as well as awed. What had happened to excite his hero so? The girl was an English girl; and he'd seen with his own eyes how she treated that feckless young Lord. From the way she's hypnotized Master Brut, too, he could well believe that her mother *was* a witch!

The lad wasn't old enough to realize how it can happen in life that a volcanic force that has been mounting and mounting for years, unseen and unknown, bursts forth at last under the impact of some minor shock with an explosion that shakes everything. And if he was astonished at Owen's unexpected emotion his Norman intelligence was no less bewildered by the response it met with among all these men.

Even the girl herself ceased moaning as Luned lifted her to her feet. She caught at once—ah! she was a witch's daughter right enough!—

the mood the Prince was in, and she rushed up to him and falling on her knees before him clutched at his hand, pressing it to her wet face.

"O save her, save her, Lord Owen!" she wept.

And the Prince raised her up before them all, and swore before them all on the handle of his sword that if her mother was still alive not a hair of her head should be harmed.

But what Rhisiart couldn't see or know was how, as the man stood there with his fingers meeting the English girl's fingers on the handle of his weapon, his curiously detached soul became suddenly icily remote from the whole scene. "Mortal men, mortal men *all,* whether Welsh or English!" he seemed to hear the voice of the great Oldcastle saying. "No more *real* difference between them than between your fingers and this woman's fingers!"

But it certainly seemed as if the absence of the Arglwyddes and her ladies had increased the nervous restlessness of the four-score armed warriors that filled the hall.

As Luned led Alice away—and the girl seemed greatly comforted, though it was hard for Rhisiart to see exactly why—Owen went back to his seat by the central fire where the Lollard and Broch-o'-Meifod had already resumed their blasphemous conversation.

Rhisiart settled himself upon a heap of dried ferns at his Lord's feet. Neither he nor Owen felt much inclination just then to listen to the daring and disturbing speculations of the two philosophers. Rhisiart had so much to think about that he found himself praying that his master would leave him in peace; and Owen was in the same case. But neither Prince nor Squire realized that in both the broad and the narrow skull the same image tyrannized.

It was therefore only with the surface of their minds that either of them became aware of the long series of enigmatic oracles that first one and then the other of these two sages uttered, between intervals of intense pondering.

But Father Pascentius was by no means content with such superficial attention. He had found a seat for himself now, at the end of a long bench occupied by the soldiery, and with his head propped on his two fists and his elbows resting on the angle of the bench, he had become one single exultant life-devouring eye. The countenance out of which this vision functioned was as negligible and commonplace as the Fa-

ther's figure was unwieldy and shapeless. But just as Nature sometimes
endows a blind man with senses of hearing and smelling far beyond
the average, so, in Pascentius's case, his *sight* seemed to feel and smell
and hear!

"Go on, go on, Masters!" his look seemed to say. "How full of sweet
odours is devilish heresy on a warm spring night!" Nor was the Father's portentous sense of sight devoid of its own special imagination.
He saw—and saw with the reverse of displeasure—Lowri and Rhys
Gethin amusing themselves under the conspiring heavens while Master Simon played the armourer. He saw—and saw without any pain—
that Welsh witch, the mother of Alice, stealing through the furze-
bushes and wading across the rivers, with Grey's men after her!

But Father Pascentius had other interests than the madness of human beings; and as he listened to what Broch was now saying, he
thrust his plump hand—the hand of a born commentator on Angelic
Doctors—into a little pouch under his habit, and brought out a tiny
withered stalk. This he held towards the fire-light, examining it closely;
and the curious thing was that if that small wisp of vegetation had
possessed consciousness it would have noted that over the pair of black
orbs regarding it so fixedly there crept a film of tenderness, a suffusion
of feeling, as the man stared. But since the stalk of a little rock-plant
divorced from its root can hardly be supposed to possess such an en-
dowment, it seems as if no one would ever know how different was
the gaze the man now fixed upon the realm of vegetation from the one
with which he regarded the realm of humanity.

Had the Father been damned for "botanizing on his mother's grave"
the only defence that could have reached his Creator would have had
to come from the sub-humanity of entities so minute and negligible
that even *the Philosopher,* as Saint Thomas calls Aristotle, could not
include them in *his Summa.*

But Master Broch was now revealing to the startled Lollard things
that no monk—not even such an inebriate of the madness of life as
this one was—could endure to hear.

"Saint Thomas," he interjected in a voice of such commanding authority that both Owen and Rhisiart were disturbed in their thoughts,
"Saint Thomas, quoting Saint Augustine, says that when a man thinks
his false opinions to be the teaching of godliness, and dares obstinately

to dogmatize about matters of which he is ignorant, he becomes a stumbling-block to others." Then seeing that Broch was silent and that the Lollard was beginning to smile, he added, for the benefit of the troopers who were listening and of the Hog of Chirk who had paused in his work, "If anyone here had read that account of a death by burning that came to our Prior he would keep guard over his wandering thoughts. None—not even our noble Prince—can be sure of the future.

"One thing is certain. Henry of Lancaster and his Archbishop, whatever else we may think of them, have resolved to stamp out heresy with pains unspeakable. Therefore it were wise—even while we support our brave Prince in defending our ancient liberties—to beware lest we confuse civil and national freedom with that dangerous revolt against the Holy Catholic Faith which not only imperils our immortal souls but gives an opportunity to cruel and ambitious tyrants—" He paused for a moment to gauge the effect of his words; but a stony and inscrutable mask had fallen upon Owen's face, while on Rhisiart's all he could detect was the familiar expression of an impatient young novice listening to a tedious sermon.

Be began afresh, turning his eyes this time towards the troopers, who in their respect for the power of the Church were looking not a little disturbed. "Why should we," he went on, "lend our ears to what our two greatest saints call the dogmatic obstinacy of wilful men? The moment, my brave warriors, you turn from that rightful liberty for which it is your glory to fight, and wander in these dangerous paths of heresy and schism, you strengthen the hands of our oppressors, you give them what they desire most, you—"

But Owen was on his feet. His mask had fallen. His whole form was trembling. He looked wildly round him; and it could even be seen that his fingers were clutching his sword. All the suppressed emotions which had just now flickered up over the Ruthin girl seemed towering into a fiery cloud of smoke and flame!

"Listen, monk!" he cried, "and listen all of you. When we have driven every Englishman in Wales back whence they came, who will decide what Pope we recognize and what rule we observe? *We shall decide for ourselves!* Wasn't there a Church in Wales before we bowed to Rome? Mend your words, good Father, mend your words, lest there be a Church in Wales again that acknowledge neither Rome nor Canterbury; no! nor Avignon either!"

He drew a long breath; and Rhisiart, casting a quick glance about them, saw that the soldiers were really disturbed and troubled. In the lad's practical Norman mind rose a feeling of angry contempt for all these doctrinal discussions. And here was the Prince himself taking a part in them! "It's Master Young he needs," he said to himself, "to stop this mystical jargon!" He felt more indignant than ever when he heard Owen suddenly gasp out: "Is there no power in Heaven or earth that can give me a clear sign?"

But at that moment everyone swung round, for a kind of a sign, though it could hardly be called a clear one, did present itself. A half-clothed figure was seen rushing down the women's staircase, flinging himself through the midst of the men, and laying a desperate hand upon the Prince's wrist. Rhisiart knew him at once as Mad Huw; but it was clear that Owen was bewildered at first about his identity from the fact that he wasn't wearing the grey habit of his order.

But "It's the Friar! It's the Friar!" rose from all sides; and there occurred an instinctive movement to cut off the theologian's escape. His recent words had frightened them not a little; and they longed to see him confronted by another spiritual authority, even by one crazed in his wits.

Everybody but Rhisiart, who was so new to Wales, knew that there was no love lost between the Franciscans and Cistercians; and all of them, as they crowded round, expected a fierce spiritual duel.

For a moment the man was too agitated and too much out of breath to speak. But as he clung panting to Owen's wrist it began to dawn on the Prince that this unusual night-attire covered the hairy chest and bony legs of the champion of King Richard.

"I've been telling them, Brother," murmured Father Pascentius before the man could speak, "how different civil liberty is from religious liberty. I've been telling them that it's only playing into King Harry's hands to defy the Archbishop. The Archbishop is the representative of Christ in these Islands; and though our Prince is liberating our bodies from an earthly King, no man can liberate our souls from their heavenly King.

"One minute, good Brother! I'm sure no follower of Saint Francis could have been silent under the monstrous heresies I've been listening to to-night; heresies that even"—he glanced at Master Broch whose head was sunk on his breast—"suggest aspersions upon the eternal procession of the Son of God!

"One more word, Brother; for you are under vows of obedience like myself! God, as Saint Thomas says, would not be perfect unless He were alive; and if He is alive we must attribute procession to Him, a procession of word and of love. And this—one minute I beg you, Brother!—this is the procession of the Son from the Father, for He is God's word, and of the Holy Ghost, for He is God's love. Brother, Brother, let me finish! Saint Thomas says that Athanasius most wonderfully declared at the Council of Nicea that what the Arians really implied was—since the Son and the Holy Ghost aren't consubstantial with him—that God is not a living and intelligent being, *but dead and unintelligent!"*

In his desire to stop the panting Friar from uttering a word till he himself had finished, Father Pascentius had pushed so close to Owen's side that it seemed to Rhisiart as if his Prince were being rumpled and tumbled by a pair of frantic jackdaws.

But in the monk's appreciation of the beauty of Athanasian rhetoric his voice was raised to such a pitch, as he uttered the passage about God being "dead and unintelligent," that Owen's nerves revolted.

The Prince straightened himself, shaking off, with an obvious physical repulsion, his too close contact with both the excited men of God.

But, as the Cistercian drew back, Mad Huw poured forth in a torrent of confused words the great news he had come to bring. "I knew it, Prince," he cried. And then he turned in rapturous triumph to the whole company. "I told him," he shouted, "I told him it was going to happen. I felt it. I knew it. And it *has* happened. Quick! Come and see, all of you, what God has done. It's in the sky over the sea! It's in the sky over Mona! The army of the angels of the Lord is marching against the Tyrant. Like the Assyrians from the walls of Sion the enemies of God's chosen will be scattered! They will be broken like potsherds. They will be driven from Wales like a pestilence. They will flee when no man pursueth. I see their carcasses on the slopes of the mountains. I see the smoke of their burning rising to heaven. Open those doors, Owen ap Griffith. Come forth, you men of war, with your spears and

with your bows. Over the forests of Mona, over the waters of the salt
sea, it has come! It has come from the west. It has come from between
the north and the west; the fiery army of the angels of the Lord!

"Open those doors, Owen ap Griffith. Come out, come out from
here, all you people! For the Lord has heard His servant. The power of
the Lord has justified His people. The angels of the Lord are moving
through the firmament. The host of the Lord is marching through the
sky to succour the sheep of His flock. My hero, my saint, my rose of
Britain, Richard my King, was the one who showed me. He woke me
from my sleep. He led me by the hand. He showed me the bright host,
moving, marching across the sky! He bade me call you forth, Owen ap
Griffith. Come then, come quick, and delay not; for the Lord has sent
his angels to help us; and the oppressors of his people are as the snows
that melt before the spring!"

So intense was the Friar's conviction, so prophet-like were his words,
that the whole company rose as one man. The Prince, the Lollard,
Broch-o'-Meifod, the Hog of Chirk, the commentator upon Saint
Thomas, even Owen's sluggish and sceptical eldest son, rushed towards
the door.

Here Rhisiart, who was the first to lay his hand on the great bolts,
was aware of familiar voices outside; and when the doors were opened,
there, grouped together on the hill-side and staring wildly towards the
north-west, were Meredith and Master Sparrow and Mistress Lowri
and Rhys Gethin!

Rhisiart's first thought when he turned his head towards the quarter
of the sky at which they were all gazing was of Catharine. "Is she
awake?" he said to himself. And then he thought, "But her window
looks to the East."

As for Owen he had become praeternaturally calm. All excitement
had left him, all anger, all passion, all ambition, all motive for living.
He looked quietly and coldly, without a pulse of emotion, at the
astounding spectacle before him. So calm, so collected had he suddenly grown that he was even able to turn his head aside, after the first
glance, and deliberately note the effect of this stellar phenomenon upon
his companions. He noted one curious thing, a thing that came back to
his mind several times later that night, the fact that Lowri no sooner
caught sight of her husband than she left Rhys Gethin and moved

quickly to his side. Not only so—and he couldn't be deceived, for Simon was quite close to him and the realistic Master Sparrow had seen fit to bring a great blazing torch into the miraculously-lit night—those ill-assorted partners had snatched blindly at each others' hands; and—so it seemed to him—the amateur armourer was making the woman's white face wince and twist with pain as he crushed her fingers in his hot fist.

But what a spectacle! A vast meteoric body of burning flame *was* actually—Mad Huw hadn't exaggerated its sublime appearance—shivering and quivering in a blue-black gulf of space just above the north-western horizon. And not only so, but it was trailing behind it a huge fiery train of lesser meteoric lights, lights that seemed to be bound together, like a swarm of fire-atoms, in some vast nebulous gonfalon of the awakened ether.

Owen turned quickly to observe Rhisiart's profile and to see how such a celestial apparition affected that hatchet-shaped projectile of Norman insouciance; and he smiled under his beard to mark, in the light of Master Sparrow's torch, the manner in which his young Secretary sucked in his lips, narrowed his eyelids, and glared at the comet as if he were putting to it a sequence of searching interrogations.

But he left Rhisiart now and walked over to where the Lollard and Master Broch were standing together. "Well?" he murmured, "so the Friar was right, eh? But, between me and God, what do you two mean by stirring up that monk to such a tune? He's no fool and we don't want—as he says—to give King Hal *every* point in the game."

The Lollard was silent. He had long recognized that there was a vein of unscrupulous secularity, and even of shameless cynicism, in Owen; but in face of that celestial portent sent by Heaven to the man's support he felt it an inappropriate moment to contradict him.

But Broch-o'-Meifod was less conciliatory. "Shall I tell you something, Owen ap Griffith?" he said. "For I've got my belt on to-night, and I feel as if I could make even the pretty listen!"

Owen scrutinized him closely in the darkness. He began to suspect that his formidable ally had been drinking too much. But he bade him say what he had to say. "But make it short, my Master; make it short."

"That great luminary," said Broch, "at which we're all gazing has nothing to do with you, nothing to do with the King of England. It has nothing to do with the Pope, or with the anti-Pope either; nor with what the good Father just now called the 'procession' of God. That trailing messenger has come from beyond all the Nine Heavens; yes, from outside both the *Primum Mobile* and the Empyrean. Do'ee know whence it is, Owen ap Griffith? From a new-born Spirit in unknown spheres it is pushing upon our old degenerate world; and foolish Broch, clumsy Broch, cowardly Broch, run-away Broch, is its voice to-night!"

In the darkness—for the precious oil from Bryn Saith Marchog had burnt out in Master Sparrow's torch and the Prince could see a whitish glimmer upon his friend's bald skull—the man's startling words sounded to his strung-up nerves like music played behind secure battlements to a man fighting for his life in a blood-stained mist. Yes, he must get off alone somewhere! When fiery dragons rush out of infinity to a person's aid, a person *wants to think*.

That great naked skull before him—didn't the man *ever* cover it? —seemed *always* able to think, and to think aloud too! And to-night, as that blaze in the west dimmed the stars and diminished the torches, the immobility of the face beneath the skull became monstrous. The face became a featureless part of the skull! It was *the skull* that had uttered those startling words about a dispensation that was to replace the Christian one. Broch spoke to-night like the corpse-god of those old mound-people, like the Head of Brān when it made years seem like seconds to those under its spell.

"I must get away by myself, get away by myself!" He remembered how he had uttered those words thirty years ago when he and his brother had been welcomed as boys by his mother's princely family in South Wales.

He did begin moving away from Broch and Master Brut; but he hadn't gone far before he was brought to a stand-still by the appearance of his old minstrel Griffith, whose heavy harp his own son Griffith was carrying behind the aged poet.

Owen's first feeling on encountering these two figures was that they might well have been strolling actors in some English morality-play entitled *Passionate Age and Dispassionate Youth*. But he was touched, in spite of his troubled thoughts, by his eldest son's consideration for the old man. He did catch himself thinking, "But the Arglwyddes must have sent him!" But he dismissed that thought as ungenerous and unworthy.

"He's a kind fellow at bottom, and a brave one—but I shall never understand him as I do Meredith."

Greeting the old and the young Griffith with almost effusive gratitude Owen despatched a trooper to bring a stool from the hall for the Bard. "And a torch, too!" he added, not realising that a harpist of Griffith's experience could feel those precious strings in pitch-black darkness.

"What do *you* think of this comet, lad?" he enquired of his son, using the profane word deliberately, though he saw the old Bard wince at the sacrilege.

"Do you care what I think, sir?" the man replied at once, grave and sad.

But Owen refused to be abashed. "Tell me, boy! On your allegiance tell me!"

"I think," said Griffith slowly, "that it's no more wondrous than fire, and no more miraculous than an ordinary sunset. I think a time will come when astronomers will predict these things."

"But they do, Griffith! They *have!*"

The man was silent.

"Haven't they, Griffith?"

"*Astrologers* have, my Prince, not astronomers!"

Owen was glad to welcome the arrival of the stool and the torch. Griffith was so fond of tripping him up like that. But hadn't astrologers always been the best astronomers?

Then the old Bard began to play and to improvise as he played. But a twinge of new vexation seized upon Owen as he listened. God in Heaven! if the man wasn't actually *improvising* in the tricky modern style! That was a thing he'd never done before. And it was too much. The troopers had begun to crowd round them. On those gleaming harp-strings the dragon in the sky seemed laying the flickering point of its prophetic tongue.

The clue to everything might have come to-night; the secret of his race's past, the mystery of Mathrafal, the sobbing cry full of a despair that wasn't *quite* despair of the dirge for Cyndylan—all these quivered on the verge of a new meaning between that light in the sky and those flickering strings! His own dim craving for something beyond battle and blood, and hearths made desolate—this might have been its voice, its solution!

But the Bard must needs let it all go; must needs balance his rhythms in this new tricky way and fill them with pious allusions to the star at the birth of Christ and the star at the birth of Uther Pendragon! He could have wept at a chance so lost. Huge, mystical, antique words, from the Songs of Aneirin in that sacred book of his, rolled like bruised and baffled thunder at the back of his mind. Yes, it was too much. He *must* get away by himself. Craftily he pretended to be overcome by emotion. He *was* overcome by emotion, but not by this damned modern cleverness. But with his hands clapped to his face and his head bowed he made his way out of the press. Oh, how well he knew the triumphant hopes which that fiery creature—it really did resemble a dragon now, all burning head and burning tail—would stir up from one end of Wales to the other, and the terror it would rouse among the simple English!

Why then did it only make him sad, him for whom all men would suppose that its beauty and its terror had drawn earth-ward out of the angelic spheres?

"It must be," he thought, "that at the bottom of my heart I was hugging a hope that some way of peace would be found, even at the last, between Harry and me. But if the very firmament is going to breed Pendragons, war to the end it is; war and a plunge, through a world on fire, into utter darkness!"

And then, still aware, behind everything else, of a smouldering envy of his friend Broch's detachment, he began to feel a longing for Rhisiart's narrow face.

"Where *is* the lad?" he thought. He turned from the sky-dragon and began moving among his excited followers, looking for his squire. Nobody dared to speak to him, hardly to approach him. With that symbol of his destiny before their eyes he had become a consecrated figure—unearthly, hardly human. "He can't have gone back into the hall," he said to himself. "He must have wandered up the hill to get a better view."

He moved further into the darkness, following the upward slope of the ground where the older portion of this rambling mountain-fortress lifted its confused bulk to the eastern quarter of the sky. Suddenly he saw a light, not the light of a torch, but the dusky reddish flame of a small fire of dead ferns and twigs.

Four human figures were bending over this fire, a man of dwarfish but powerful stature, and three young boys, one of whom was laboriously writing something on a fragment of parchment with a burnt stick.

Owen instantly dropped the prince and became in a second a hunted outlaw, a native of caves and forests! He became younger, too. A delicious sense of adventure, full of vague memories of old boyish escapades with his brother Tudor took possession of him. Clapping his hand to his sword and pressing it against his side, so that no metallic clink or jingle should betray his presence, he set himself to crawl forward on hands and knees towards the man, the three boys, and the fire.

No old mound-dweller could have squirmed on his belly through the primeval forest more silently! It is doubtful whether any other crowned prince in that civilized age could have played the cave-man as he did then. And the odd thing was that he felt happier and more himself as he did it than he had felt for years. Morg ferch Lug would have been surprised if she'd seen that forked beard thrusting itself between the dead stalks of the bracken! Had her pure Brython then, even he, a drop of the blood of the "older people"?

He was soon near enough to hear and see everything. He was so close to them that by stretching out his sword-arm he could have touched with the weapon's point the red flames of their small fire.

He knew now who the dwarfish man was—none other than David Gam! And it was clear to him that the fellow was terrorizing the boys; and he knew *them,* too. His own little page, Elphin, the prettiest child who'd ever served him, was the one whom Gam was compelling —the brute had reduced them all to a state of paralysed terror—to scrawl those letters with the burnt stick. The others—and he knew *their* names, too—were Rawlff and Iago from Dinas Brān.

"You're safe from me to-night," he thought, contemplating his enemy. "I'm not going to shed blood to-night." But he set himself to listen.

"Have you finished, you devil's imp?" growled the little monster, and snatching the fragment of parchment from the boy he surveyed the black scrawls that covered it.

"What does it say? Read it, you whimpering baby, or I'll—"

And Elphin read in a high-pitched tremulous voice, like the voice of a helpless girl, the following ungentle words:

To Owen ap Griffith Fychan:
Nothing in heaven or earth will save you from David's knife.
It is in every bush, in every tree, in every room, in every closet. If I have to sharpen it for twenty years it'll be between your ribs. *Live therefore in fear.*
From one who has never missed his mark.

There was a moment's silence, broken only by the low sobs of Elphin. Then the man's voice was raised again. "What will happen to you if he doesn't get what you've written? Stop that noise, and say the words!"

In a low gasping voice the wretched Elphin repeated his lesson. "If . . . Owen . . . doesn't . . . get . . . what . . . I've . . . written . . . my . . . my . . ."

"Go on!" growled David Gam.

"My . . . my tongue will be cut out!"

"Well, do it then!" said the man fiercely, "and do it at once. If it weren't for that thing in the sky he'd have had it to-night. But no matter—he'll have it; and so will you—and so will all of you, if you don't do what I've said!"

Thus speaking he jumped to his feet, stamped out the fire, and was gone.

It was lucky for him that he departed up the slope instead of down, for had he actually stumbled upon Owen it is doubtful if the latter's resolution could have been kept. But as it was, Owen waited motionless for a minute or two, while the three boys, too frightened to move, murmured to each other in whispers.

Then, still on hands and knees, he slid away, keeping his fingers tight round the sheath of his sword. But once arrived at the southeastern angle of the dark mass of buildings he leaped to his feet. There was the fiery apparition still flaming in the quarter of the sky under which lay the Isle of Mōn or Anglesea; and there were the dusky figures of his followers, still staring and wondering in scattered groups, while a hoarse susurration of low-voiced excitement rose up towards the comet-dimmed stars.

Humming audibly and casually a stave of that sorrowful dirge about the ruin of Pengwern he strolled back to where the pages were huddled.

Their aggressor hadn't succeeded in altogether quenching that small fire, and as its flames shot up again he could see by their helpless passivity, though they rose to their feet at his approach, how shaken the boys were.

"It's I, your Prince," he said in his calmest tone. "Something's frightened you children. Come tell me what's the matter. I'd forgive you, whatever it is! Only tell me everything."

They stood in a pitiful row before him with the revived flames between him and them; but he walked round the fire and laid his hand on the shoulder of the agitated Elphin.

"He rushed out on us," said Rawlff.

"We were up *there*," said Iago, pointing to a rocky crag above them where patches of snow still showed white in the star-light. Elphin, who still clutched the parchment, was too upset to utter a word.

"Please, sir, he made Elphin write a letter to you," said Rawlff.

" 'Twas a burnt stick, weren't it, Elphin, what he made you write with?" threw in Iago; and he nudged the effeminate boy's ribs on the side opposite from Owen.

"Oh yes! I thought you were holding *something,* child," Owen broke in, in his most matter-of-fact voice. "Here! let's see it!" And taking the scrap of vellum, upon which Gam had made his vow, from Elphin's numb fingers, he read it aloud as lightly as if he were engaged in a game of forfeits with the three boys.

"Well!" he said when he'd done, "I don't think I'm destined to live in fear of *that* little red man."

"Though his arms, sir, *are* like bars of Spanish steel," threw in the diplomatic Rawlff, evidently on the way to recover his usual poise.

"Shall I say our Dinas Brān motto to Elphin, sir?" added Iago in a superior tone.

A little piqued by the fact that Dinas Brān seemed carrying things off with more of an air than Glyndyfrdwy, the Prince forgot himself so far as to remind these alien refugees that upon neither of *them* had the intruder laid a finger.

Elphin brightened up at this, while the bolder ones stared at each other in dismay. What a magician the chief was. He knew everything.

"He pinched me cruel, sir," murmured Elphin. "Like hot irons his fingers were!"

But this was the first time the audacious Rawlff had ever been privileged to talk face to face with their leader. Obscure thoughts about becoming a belted knight swept through his ambitious brain, while like other youthful courtiers he suspected that the shortest path to distinction lay through flattering the great.

"I suppose, sir," he said, with his brightest and most engaging air, "*you* aren't afraid of the fire-dragon in the sky?"

"I tell you what I *am* afraid of," said Owen curtly, "and *that* is that three boys I know will get into trouble with Madoc if they don't hurry back into the hall. Take care of Elphin, you two," he added, "and let him show that bruise to Nurse if she's not asleep."

But as the pages somewhat reluctantly proceeded to obey him, he patted Elphin on the head. "Your Prince is a wizard, my boy. Remember that! He sees everyone you talk to and hears everything you say. But I can tell you *this,* child, between me and God: if you repeat your Angelus properly every night no little red man will ever touch you again!"

They went off; and Owen, standing where they'd left him, watching the flames of the bonfire, felt a sudden weariness of the whole game of life. Struggling against it, however, he threw the piece of parchment into the fire and let his eyes wander along the ancient walls of the castellated building above his head.

"I wonder," he thought, "if Catharine has seen the comet?" With his daughter in his mind he advanced a furlong or so up the rocky slope, still keeping an eye on the dark mass of buildings.

"*This* must be about where her chamber is," he said to himself. He stood still, letting his gaze wander over the half-ruined ramparts and broken buttresses of this most ancient part of the fortress.

And then he clapped his hand to his sword; while against all his self-control a trembling fury of rage tugged at his vitals.

For he saw at the same moment two things: things in an unmistakeable and devasting relation to each other. And what neither the blazing comet nor the curse of Gam could do these two things did. They made him pray. And he prayed as passionately as he had recommended

Elphin to pray if he wished to be saved from dwarfs with fingers like Spanish steel.

"Mary, Joseph! Mary, Joseph! Mary, Joseph!" he gasped in his beard, and thus he got the strength to turn sharply on his heel and stride back the way he had come.

He had seen a candle burning in a narrow arrow-slit high up in the dark wall; and he had seen the well-known figure of Rhisiart, gazing up at it, as if it were something more miraculous than any comet.

XIV

LOVE AND SHAME

THE MATERIAL disappearance of the comet by the end of March could hardly be called a complete departure. Unusual magnetic disturbances among the members of that Snowdonian court seemed to indicate that though the thing's visible presence had passed out of sight upon its spheric voyage, it had not altogether gone. Something of itself remained, a weight upon the atmosphere, a pressure upon human souls, a quickening of human pulses, queer criss-cross currents in the psychic air.

Coincident with an early and an exceptionally warm spring, after the cruel winter, there was a curious stir in that high retreat, that retreat which was at once a castle, a palace, an assembly-hall, and a camp.

And what made this stir in people's minds, this growing tension in their powers of will, a rather exceptional phenomenon, was the fact—and it is here that a meticulous observer might be forgiven if he detected the invisible wash of that meteoric vessel's wake—that the tension of purpose referred to divided the men from the women.

The pleasant relaxation brought by the balmy spring-airs, when that early April set in, in place of segregating the company into mutually-attracted couples, had the surprising effect of drawing together most of the women into one isolated gathering; and most of the men into another.

What the patient Arglwyddes felt in her heart when the whole feminine group—all except Tegolin, who with Brother Huw seldom left her side—fell into the habit of congregating, immediately the afternoon meal was over, in the agreeable little apartment facing the south which had been made the bed-chamber of Mistress Lowri and her husband, nobody knew, except possibly Owen himself.

The impetuous Catharine, who had grown attached to Tegolin,

scrupled not to express to the red-haired maid her suspicions of Mistress
Lowri. "Your mother *hates mine*," she would declare, as in the now
frequent absences of Alice of Ruthin the two young people combed
each other's hair in Catharine's turret-room, "and though it's wrong to
say it to you, I hate *her!*"

But Tegolin always sturdily maintained that these gatherings in the
south chamber had nothing to do with her mother's attitude to the
Arglwyddes. "I think," she would reply, "that she *is* lacking in proper
respect; but in *this* case I don't believe she's responsible."

"Who *is* responsible, then? For except for you and me and Myfanwy
and Gwen, mother's left alone with her weaving day after day!" But it
was generally at this point the elder girl changed the conversation.

A week of the loveliest April weather had indeed passed over them
before Tegolin was driven to defend her parent with evidence and circumstance and proof against her friend's suspicions.

"I've heard," she told Catharine one late afternoon as they stood by
the latter's twelfth-century window, surveying the sloping hill-side with
its patches of freshly-sprouting bracken-fronds, "I've heard that it's
Alice's mother they gather to listen to."

"And she a witch?" cried Owen's daughter, opening her eyes wide.

"Sit down, Catrin, and listen to me," said the Maid of Edeyrnion.
And pushing back the excited young girl upon the edge of the couch-
bed she lifted her hands to her own hair and proceeded to coil her
already-braided locks carefully round her head. "We have no right,"
she continued gravely, "to call Mistress Dilys a witch. She's a fortune-
teller, but so was my granny; and from what Luned says she and my
mother have devised a most important plot, a plot upon which all your
father's success may depend. Now listen to me, Catrin dearest," and she
took her seat on the couch by the younger girl's side and tenderly
stroked her flaxen hair, while she fixed her gaze on the other's eyes,
which in their nervous excitement changed colour as often as Owen's
did.

"This is between you and me and the Blessed Saints, dearest; and you
musn't breathe a word of it to the Arglwyddes, or to anyone else. Do
you understand? Swear to me you won't."

Owen's daughter solemnly crossed herself and gave the required
promise. The breath of that April afternoon crept in through the un-

glazed window and lightly stirred the listener's fair hair. The misty sun-shafts of the declining day had long since moved away to the westward; but their ruddy light, falling in a warm rich diffusion on the hill-side opposite, was countered, as that narrow window received its reflection, by a cavernous and mossy greenness, as if belonging to the interior of a cave, which hung about the heavily-pictured arras and about a clumsy wooden image of Saint Clare.

This austere piece of carving, which was of life-size, had followed the girl from her nursery at Sycharth to her bower at Glyndyfrdwy; and it now stared forth with its cold virginal eyes towards the yet colder peaks of Snowdon. The arras behind the wooden Saint Clare had also come from Sycharth, and as it caught a sudden glimmer from the fire, which all the year round the old Nurse had kept alight in that turret-room, its cave-like chilliness took on a motion of faint life. It became indeed the swaying branches of a green forest out of whose recesses the semblance of the antlers of a horned stag came forth.

That this beast was of no common lineage was proved by the fact that some faraway ancestress of Catharine had woven a rude cross between its antlers.

"You haven't forgotten," Tegolin was saying now, "how thrilled we all were when your father's men found Mistress Dilys half-dead in those Dyffryn woods, and brought her up here?"

"And *you* made Alice leave you," Catharine interjected, "though she didn't want to, and look after her mother."

Tegolin nodded. "Well, my precious, you know how we all love to hear our fortunes told, and poor mother"—Tegolin always spoke of the formidable Lowri since her return to her husband in this pitying tone—"has a passion for that sort of thing. But by degrees—I don't know who thought of it first, all of them together I suppose, but it's Luned who's told me—they worked out the most daring plot you ever heard, a plot to take both Grey and his son—the one who loves Alice." Catharine's lips opened so wide and her eyes grew so big that the red-haired girl kissed her anxiously; but after that, with one of her hands held tight in her own, she went on quickly.

"It's got quite far now, this plot of theirs; but they're waiting to tell your father till it's all absolutely ready. Mistress Dilys has lots of friends of her murdered husband—Englishmen they are, but men who hate

Grey—and she's got an Irishman too who's the—what do they call it?—
the messenger between them, and Luned told me last night that their
plot is to tell Grey how he can surprise your father when he's raiding
the Vale of Clwyd; but instead of your father being taken—you see,
my precious?—it'll be Grey and his son who'll be taken! Isn't—that—a
good plot? I think it's the best I ever heard of!" And Tegolin gave
a queer little laugh.

Not for nothing was Catharine Owen's daughter. In some things she
was hopelessly absent-minded, indeed her brother Griffith often called
her stupid; but where nervous emotions were concerned she was morbidly quick-witted. She rose to her feet now; so that it was her turn to
contemplate her companion from a superior height.

"Tegolin ferch Lowri," she began gravely. "I'm glad you've told me
this, and of course I'll keep my vow; but you're holding back something. You're *not* happy about this plot, and you must trust me and tell
me why!"

The Maid of Edeyrnion stretched out her hand, and possessing herself of some silver-headed bodkins, which had been removed when her
hair was combed, thoughtfully thrust them into her braided locks.

With her arms raised to her head her bosom looked as breathing-
warm in that April air as that of the huntress Artemis. Very different
did it look from the wooden infantile angles of the saintly form behind
her!

But Catharine could see she was strongly moved; and with a quick
glance, not at Saint Clare but at that horned head in the tapestry which
she could remember from her cradle, she pleaded with her again.
"Aren't we friends enough," she said, "for you to tell me everything
that's in your mind? I know Nurse treats me, and Mother too, as if I
was a child, but I'm *not* a child. I'm a grown-up girl, Tegolin ferch
Rheinalt."

Down came the elder girl's hands at this, and Catharine was quite
satisfied with the startled look she received, but she went on firmly.

"No, I'm grown-up, Tegolin dear. I think of a lot of things. I think,
for instance, how odd it is that we two should be such friends, when
we're both fond of the same person."

A rose-petal flush mounted up from the Maid's soft neck till it suf-
fused both her cheeks. She had that particular kind of ivory-white skin

that so often accompanies red hair; and it was in vain she covered her throat with one hand and smoothed out the creases from Catharine's pillow with the other.

"Brother Huw—" she began; but Owen's grown-up daughter looked so tall and dominant that she couldn't help meeting her eyes, eyes that kept changing in colour like the shifting lights in a rock-pool.

"No, not your Friar, Tegolin. I know about *that* too, though it's been different with me. It's—Rhisiart ab Owen I'm thinking of!"

Tegolin escaped the eyes above her for a moment by bowing her head over her hands, which were now clasped tight in her lap. They were large, strong, almost boyish hands, but she pressed them together in no boyish way. She longed to press them against her ears, against her heart.

But the clear young voice above her went on remorselessly. "You're older, you're better than I am, Tegolin, and you're cleverer too; but when anyone grows up thinking only of one thing, they see a great deal, they see *everything!*"

Slowly and calmly, though not without an interior struggle, the Maid lifted her head; and the two young people stared gravely at each other, not exchanging thoughts, but each using the other's eyes as an open gate to a long perspective of troubled speculation.

"Yes, that's what's so wonderful," Catharine murmured at last, "that we should stay friends in spite of him; and we *shall,* shan't we?"

"Does anyone else think," the Maid couldn't help enquiring of this terrifying young oracle, "what you think, about—all this?"

"No, no, no! Not a soul; except Father of course, and *he* doesn't count."

The Maid sighed, aware of a strange rush of conflicting feelings, one of which was a pang of blind prophetic pity. "Why doesn't he count?"

"Because, while he knows everything," cried the other eagerly, "he *never* interferes. If I were to go to him this very night and say, 'I want to marry Rhisiart,' he wouldn't scold or get angry; and if I knew we didn't have his blessing, I should know too we'd *never* have his curse!"

Once more the Maid of Edeyrnion sighed, and this time more heavily still. As she looked into those sea-coloured reckless eyes she got no comfort, no re-assurance, no premonition of peace or happiness for any of them—least of all for Rhisiart.

Catharine was the first to remove her gaze; for the steady direction of her friend's look, now that it was touched with sadness rather than with confusion, made her uneasy.

Was there more between Tegolin and Rhisiart than she had realized? Was the boy acting like an unscrupulous profligate, and playing with both their hearts? The daughter of Owen shook out the heavy folds of her brocaded gown, and catching them up with a sweep of her bare arm began crossing and recrossing the little room; a proceeding which was more ominous to Tegolin than anything else she could have done.

"He'd better not play with *me!*" the child was saying to herself, while her teeth pressed down upon her lower lip and her forehead grew distorted.

The only flaw to Catharine's beauty was the scantiness of her fair eyebrows; and this defect increased the youthful ferocity of the scowl she now assumed, as, forgetting Tegolin's presence altogether, she visualized an exposed and convicted Rhisiart cringing and shivering before the lash of her tongue.

By degrees, as the reflection of the sunset on the eastern slopes faded, Catharine's imaginary vengeance faded too; and pausing in her march, she relaxed her grasp of her heavy gown and, letting it fall over her shoes, gave it a few quiet kicks from inside to smoothe it out and keep it in order.

Then with a quick glance at Tegolin as the girl sat pondering, elbows on knees and chin on knuckles, she sank to the floor at her feet, and with extended arms, and Catharine's long arms always suggested the shape of her body, felt for her friend's fingers.

"Won't you tell me, now we understand each other, and don't hate each other as we might, considering"—all this was gasped out in one quick breath—"why you don't like this plot of Alice's mother and your mother to take Grey prisoner. It sounds to me as if it were a very good plot and *couldn't* fail; and I'm sure the men'll be delighted with it."

"Get up from the floor then. It's cold down there. And put some wood on the fire. And sit quietly by me here."

Catharine patiently obeyed her in all these details. "What a noise those crows are making," she said, as she sank down by the elder girl's side. "I expect they're young ones."

"What's troubling me is this," said Tegolin, disregarding the crows, and disregarding too, for neither of them could see it, the complete disappearance—into a moss-green enchanted forest that extended through the wall, through the fortress, through the mountain passes, through Conway and Carnarvon and Aber-Menai and all the Isle of Mona—of the horned beast with the cross between its antlers. Yes, deep into this mystic forest of Catharine's first imaginings did that horned head recede. It receded where Merlin long ago receded. It receded where the spirit of the old Iolo receded; and where the figure of a youthful Rhisiart, taller than human, braver than human, more single-hearted than human, was forever and forever receding.

"What's troubling me in this," said Tegolin. "We both have known well enough, though we haven't talked about it, that while the women have been plotting in my mother's room, the men have been plotting in the great hall. I expect Mother knows what they're plotting, *through that man.*"

Catharine tightened her grasp upon the strong, cool fingers of her friend, so that the latter should be aware with what grown-up perception this reluctance to mention the Hog of Chirk was understood.

"But how do *you* know about it, Tegolin dear?"

The Maid hesitated; and there was once more a danger of her telltale complexion indicating the fact that they were on dangerous ground. On no point in the world are deep-natured people more touchy than with regard to their relations with the man or with the woman who until now has been their ideal, when the irrepressible compass-needle of their heart shows that a different constellation is moving towards the north.

"The Friar goes in and out of the hall," she murmured gently, "and though on the subject of poor King Richard his mind does sometimes wander, in everything else he is wise. I've never known a wiser man!"

Catharine hastened to agree with this judgment. And indeed she did whole-heartedly agree; for Mad Huw had endeared himself, by his purity and courtesy, to every woman in that little court.

"Go on," she said, after a sad pause between them, in which the spring-air, as it breathed upon their tense faces, seemed to both of them like the breath of destiny.

"Well, it appears that some of the men, who have lately brought their ponies and spears to your father's allegiance, say that in the mountains of Maelienydd to the north-east of Radnor, or Maesyfed as we call it, there's a strong, though secret movement in our favour; a movement that would give us, if a few good leaders went down there, the best chance we've had yet for striking a real blow at the cruel King."

Catharine pulled her hand away and jumped to her feet. "But this is grand news!" she cried. "Why can't I rush to Father's room now, and tell him what a good idea this is!"

Tegolin looked so horror-struck that the eager girl grew grave at once, and remembered her vow. But she didn't sit down. A violent restlessness seized her. She went to the fire and piled it up with wood, till the whole little chamber glowed in the twilight and her own impatient shadow—distorted so much that it actually did look like that Queen on his chess-board to which the Prince had compared her—bowed mockingly before the immoveable Saint Clare and raced up and down the verge of that mystic forest.

But Catharine was the last person in the world to take any interest in the antics of a shadow, even if such a shadow possessed the power of locomotion without the aid of fins or wings or arms or legs. She turned to her motionless visitor, who had bent forward again, her chin propped once more against the knuckles of her boyish hands.

"I can't understand you, Tegolin," she said earnestly. "No, I can't! Here are two perfect plots, either of which would help our cause better than anything yet thought of in that 'magician's room,' and instead of being thrilled by such news you're sad about it, and—"

But she clapped her hands to her mouth in the old dramatic gesture of catching oneself in some outrageous lapse. "Is it because *he* is with my father in that room," she brought out, "and you think their plans will be disturbed by this Ruthin idea, or this Maelienydd idea?"

Tegolin rose to her feet at this, a frank smile on her full lips. "It's you who're the magician, Catrin, not the Prince! On my life, child, you must be a thought-reader, like Mistress Dilys. But if I *was* thinking just what you said, it isn't *only* that. Oh, I don't know. It's so hard to explain." She stretched herself and yawned, covering her mouth with one hand while she extended the other into the air with her fingers clenched.

"I think it's like this," she said, after a second's concentrated thought. "I feel odd and queer with these consultations going on and *they* not hearing anything about them. How do those Maelienydd men know, how do these Ruthin women know, what your father and Rhisiart ab

Owen have been planning for the cause, now that the warm weather's
come. And Broch-o'-Meifod and Master Brut, *they're* in the Prince's
counsels too; and I can't believe that thinkers and scholars like them
aren't better advisers to your father than my poor mother and Mistress
Dilys and Rhys Gethin and *that man!* And another thing too, my dear.
I know your father comes up every day to your mother's room and
turns us all out while they talk. Well! don't you think your father's and
mother's brains *together* are worth more than a conclave of ladies round
a fortune-teller, or a group of troopers drinking mead while *that man*
polishes their spears?"

Catharine looked at her sharply. They were facing each other now in
the fading light of the window and the growing light of the fire. "Isn't
a woman's instinct," Owen's daughter protested, "a better guide than a
man's reason? And when women are gathered together—"

"The devil enters into them! No, I don't quite mean *that*, Catrin;
though I've heard the Friar say it. But—oh, I can't explain the feeling I
have; perhaps it's Mistress Dilys and my poor mother—but of the two
plots I'd sooner trust the other one, for all the drinking, and *that man!*"

"Who's the Sheriff of Maesyfed?" asked Catharine, feeling a delicious
thrill of excitement to be discussing affairs of state, like the daughter of
a real ruler.

Tegolin frowned as she pondered. "The Friar *did* say his name. I'll
tell you in a minute! He's a famous English Bard, the Friar said."

"Does he compose to the harp like old Griffith?"

Tegolin didn't smile at her friend's simplicity. She was in no smiling
mood; but she hastened to assure her that in England poets only wrote
down in books what they made up. "I heard Iolo tell about it once.
They write for scholars and gentlemen over there. They don't play the
harp for the common people. Oh, I remember the name now—Thomas
Clanvow—and Iolo said he wrote about cuckoos and nightingales!"

"He can't be much of a Sheriff," commented the younger girl. "Rhys
Gethin would soon settle *him!*"

But there fell a silence between them then; while the air through the
window, blowing now, as darkness began to descend, with a gathering
force, made the flames of the fire flicker, and caused a faint ripple, more
like a movement upon deep water than the stir of leaves, to run shivering over the green forest on the wall.

Catharine broke the silence, but something about that sudden stir in the dim world of her childhood's imaginings made her speak in a low grave voice.

"Who is the Lord of those parts where Maelienydd is?"

Instead of replying Tegolin moved to an alcove in the room overhung with embroidered curtains and returned with a cloak which she wrapped tenderly round the other's shoulders.

"Who is the Lord—" the young girl repeated, still in the same low voice, and quite oblivious of the fact that this rising gust might be chilling her friend, too.

"Mortimer," said Tegolin.

"Mortimer," repeated Catharine.

There was another silence between them, during which the Maid of Edeyrnion went to the window and drew a heavy piece of tapestry across it. As she did so she felt as if she were shutting out the word "Mortimer" along with the night-wind.

"The Earl of March," she said more cheerfully when this was done, "is only a little boy. But he has a claim to the throne; so Bolingbroke keeps him with his own children. Some say the Mortimers are as restless as the Percies under this cruel tyrant. If *that's* true I don't know whether 'twould be good policy or bad policy to attack their domain. Hotspur himself's in Denbigh now; and I know your father was careful to leave Denbigh alone when he raided the Vale of Clwyd. So it *may* be he won't hear of attacking Maelienydd."

She paused for a moment, watching the wind make that little piece of tapestry flap like a diminutive sail. "It's cold up here, Catrin," she said, "let's sit close to the fire."

The two girls began pulling along the floor a cushioned bench and settling it in front of the blaze; but the rising wind, causing their little curtain to bulge inwards, whirled a cloud of smoke into their faces.

"It's always like that," cried Catharine impatiently, pulling back her friend. "I just go to bed when it begins. Let's go down to Mother. She's still got some of that Turkish sweet-meat—unless Sibli's eaten it. "Are there any others except the little Earl?"

"I believe there's an uncle," said Tegolin indifferently, "who's another Ed-mund," and she concluded with a yawn.

"Edmund *who?*" murmured Catharine peevishly, while with a shiver she clung to her friend, flinging a portion of her mantle over Tegolin.

"Mortimer," said the other. "And I expect he'll be more of a danger to us than the nightingale man."

"*Lord* Edmund?" whispered the child, still shivering.

"Lord, Count, *Sir*—I don't know! Plain 'Sir,' I expect. Catrin, I believe you've taken cold! Where's that iron guard? We oughtn't to leave the fire like this. Why did you put on so much?"

She found the protection required, and leaving that gusty and smoky turret, the two girls descended the stairs together. They were not destined, however, to reach the Arglwyddes's room as quickly as they hoped. They had to cross the big hall to reach it and ascend a different flight of stairs, but what they found in the hall completely paralysed all further intention.

There was an awestruck group of men, some holding torches, others pushing hastily forward between the torch-bearers, and then either drawing back in superstitious fear, or standing petrified and staring. The appearance of the two young women produced no little agitation on the outskirts of the group; though those in front were too awestruck to notice them.

"They've sent for the Prince," explained the officious Rawlff. "It's the old Crow from Dinas Brān."

But the nervous Elphin, white and trembling, and too panic-stricken to realize what he did, actually clutched at Catharine's mantle. "Don't go near!" he whimpered. "They daren't touch him. He's got a sword through him. He's all blood!"

"*Catharine!*" And Owen himself, with Rhisiart behind him, was at their side. "Away with you, child! Away with you! How could—" and he turned angrily to reproach Tegolin; but the Maid had already pushed herself between the torch-bearers. "Take her to her mother, boy!" And leaving his daughter with his squire, he followed the Maid into the centre of the group.

If Catharine hadn't been already un-nerved by the mortmain of that ominous wind in her green forest, it is doubtful whether she would have yielded to Rhisiart's pressure. But her flesh was weaker than her spirit, and she let him carry her, "he willing and she unwilling," as Homer would say, up the stairs to the Arglwyddes's chamber.

For a moment the Prince himself felt his stomach turn sick at what
he saw. Face upwards on the ground with a trickle of blood oozing
from his back and forming a little pool at some distance from him, for
the floor was uneven, lay the Seneschal of Dinas Brān. His face beneath
the torch-light was of a death-pallor but his eyes were wide open and
Owen could see he knew him at once. Indeed his lips murmured his
name. But what was so ghastly about it, what was causing even those
indurated warriors to feel sick as they gazed, was the fact that the man's
hind-quarters were actually *transfixed* by that monstrous relic of the
Bronze Age which he had insisted on preserving as the sword of Eliseg.

The Prince saw at once that this abominable weapon had been deliberately thrust through the old gentleman's rump; and as he lay there,
not mortally wounded but dying from pain and shame, his thin form
in its grey clothes made with the sword that pierced him the shocking
image of a bleeding cross.

Over him knelt the figures of Father Pascentius and Broch-o'-Meifod,
while the Maid, crouching on the ground, had succeeded in clasping
her hands beneath his head.

Owen knelt down too, bending low over the dying man; and no
sooner had he done so than the old gentleman in a very low but perfectly clear voice told him all that had happened. It seemed a comfort to
him to talk: indeed it had always been a comfort to him to talk; but
what troubled all his listeners now was that in every interval of his entirely coherent narrative his face took on an expression of unredeemed
despair. It was like a mask speaking, speaking firmly and clearly; but at
each moment when the voice paused the mask faded, and the image of
a human soul damned by shame substituted itself for that voluble medium.

"I wanted to—make peace—make a lasting peace, Owen ap Griffith,"
he said, "and I talked to the Constable and I found that he also wanted
peace between the two races. And so I took the sword of Eliseg out of
its chest, for I durst not leave it, and I rode to Denbigh to talk to Hotspur. And I found that Hotspur also wanted peace between our races.
So I rode on, carrying the sword. I had no other arms, and I had no one
with me, but I rode on to come to you; for I wanted to talk to you
about peace between the two races. I got as far as the foot of the moun-

tains. My horse was strong and my heart was strong. But his spies must have told Lord Grey"—here something like a faint smile flickered for a second across the mask under which he covered the despair of his shame—"and the young Lord, he whose wits are turned, followed me with a band. They knew the mountains better than I and they waited till I was near you—your watchmen didn't see them—and then—"

A terrible ruffling of the mask of his despair took place at this point, like the ruffling by a criss-cross wind of the surface of a dark stream. But he fixed his eyes on Owen's eyes, which were now close to his own, and after a few convulsive spasms of pain which hardly seemed to reach his consciousness he went on steadily. "He's out of his wits, the young Lord, from love or witchcraft, and 'twas he alone who thought of what to do. There was little light left, but enough for his purpose, enough to serve, enough to make the name of Adda ap Leurig a jest in men's mouths forever. His men wouldn't do it at first, but he threatened them with his father, and they—*did it*—at last."

Tegolin's hands were already pressed into her ears; while the Lollard, his eyes tight shut was muttering, "Jesus, Jesus, Jesus."

Broch-o'-Meifod, his head wagging from side to side like the pendulum of a clock, had completely lost all human expression. Into the sockets of his lost eyeballs there had descended from the peaks of Snowdon the endurance of primordial matter, matter that had not stirred in its vigil since the last Ice Age.

But Owen, his thoughts racing through his skull like the men described by Aneirin who rode drunk to Cattraeth, allowed his soul to exteriorize itself, till it crouched like a small white bird upon the handle of the bronze sword, where it surveyed, with an un-lidded stare, the blood and the excrement.

"They ran the sword sideways," went on that supine mask, "so that—it should—it should only pierce the flesh—and then they left me alone—and went away. And I walked—*like that*—till your people found me."

"Yes he did!" interposed Rawlff, "for I saw him! He walked with the sword through his backside. He looked like—"

"Be quiet, boy!" cried the Prince fiercely. But the old man seemed glad to have this corroboration of his words. "I did—didn't I, lad?" he repeated. "I walked—a long way—putting all—my life—to shame!" He paused and the men about him, and that one girl whose hands were tending him, drew the long relieved sigh that human beings draw when they know the worst.

But the worst was yet to be spoken as far as the proud old antiquary of Dinas Brān was concerned. "I couldn't hold back," he muttered in a low terrible voice. *"And my dirt's on the sword of Eliseg."*

This said, his mask fell away, and what those onlookers beheld were the features of a man who has desecrated his own idol.

"I wouldn't let them pull out his sword," this unmasked face now whispered, "till I saw you, Owen ap Griffith, with his belt."

At that the man closed his eyes and gave himself up to the thought that as long as the Welsh language lasted—which would be as long as Snowdon lasted—his name would be a by-word and a jest. His name would be *Adda y Gwman,* "Adam the Rump."

"Well," he said to himself coldly, "Adam the Rump's thoughts will end when they pull it out; it's right that the sword of Eliseg should lie in the belt of Eliseg."

And then with the calmness of someone whose life-illusion has been destroyed and before whose despair all is equal, the old peace-maker told himself that he ought to have gone straight to Bolingbroke with his peace-pact, and not merely to Hotspur.

Young Rhisiart meanwhile, who had been spared what the rest had endured, now re-appeared upon the scene, his face shining like a man who returns to earth after a vision of heaven; and indeed it had seemed more than heaven to him to carry Catharine in his arms, willing or unwilling, up all those stairs.

But Owen no sooner set eyes on him—the Prince was on his feet again now—than he despatched him to the "magician's chamber" to fetch the belt of the old king.

When the boy had gone the Prince turned impatiently to the three men who were still on their knees. "Shrive him, for Christ's sake, Father!" he cried earnestly to the monk. "He'll die when it's pulled out!"

Father Pascentius commenced automatically a deeply-intoned Latin psalm, to which the prostrate man paid no more attention than if it had been the tolling of a bell. But the monk interrupted himself and rose to his feet. "I must fetch the Last Sacraments," he muttered, rubbing at the blood upon him with the corner of his habit.

The result of this gesture was that not only one little rock-plant but several botanical specimens, along with a sprinkling of earth-mould, fell upon the body of the Seneschal.

But the Lollard—the monk once gone—snatched at this providential opportunity. "Jesus," he groaned, while the guileless earnestness of his imploring countenance held the old man's attention. "Jesus was humiliated worse than you! O think of it, my father, think of it, my dear lord! Think of *His* humiliation!"

But nothing save an infinite despair was in the flickering smile with which the old man responded. "Jesus was God," he muttered. *"What's that to me?"*

And Master Brut, choking in his helpless pity, for he had uttered *his all,* bowed his head and was silent.

Then it was the turn of Broch-o'-Meifod. Making a sweeping gesture with his hand which even the Prince obeyed, he made them all rise up and move back. "Listen, man," he whispered, so that Adam alone could hear. "I'm going to pull out that bit of rusty iron; and then you'll be dead before they come."

So startling were these words that for a second the ice of despair round the old man's soul cracked. Into this crack, before the ice could freeze again, Broch plunged his second bolt; aiming with Satanic insight, not at the man's despair, but at the life-illusion whose death-pangs were causing that despair. He appealed from Adam the Antiquary to Adam the Pacifist; and as he beat down the one fixed idea he lifted the other from beneath its corpse.

"Bronze and rust, that's all it is. A man's dirt and a man's blood are more precious than rusty bronze! And the belt—an old piece of saddle-leather! And Eliseg—rest his bones under his pillar—foxes and crows have vented on *him* time out of mind! Men in after ages, Master Adam, will think less of swords and belts than of blood and dirt. Is Edward of Carnarvon a laughing-stock because they killed him with a red-hot clyster? No! No! *He* died for Gaveston, his darling, and *that's* their tavern-jest, if there is any!

"And shall I tell you—" It cannot have been his words, for the Badger of Meifod was a blundering and obscure speaker. It must have been that those deep eye-sockets into which the dying man was staring seemed full of the blood and excrement of the whole world suddenly become *holy!*

At any rate Master Adam's expression had now assumed the look of a man who has disgorged a snake's head and can breathe again. There was hardly any need to go on; but Broch-o'-Meifod went on. "And what will you die for? That's what'll live as long as Snowdon! You'll die for believing that a Welshman's bones are the same as an Englishman's. You'll die for believing that men are men first, and Welshmen and Englishmen afterwards. You'll die, Master Adam, for a future ten times further removed than Eliseg's past. You'll die—"

But the old man stopped him. "Pull it out; and let me die," he whispered, "while you look like that."

And then, lifting his hand feebly towards his face, where Tegolin's hair was brushing his cheek, "Who's that? The Maid? Kiss me, Maid—and say good-night—and then off with you!"

His voice had the old tone of authority of the Seneschal of Dinas Brān, and for the next second nobody could see his face, so covered was it by Tegolin's hair; but from where he stood in the torch-light it seemed to Owen that from the head of that living cross on the floor there had blossomed a great fiery flower.

When the girl was gone, Broch-o'-Meifod and the Prince exchanged a quick look. Owen hadn't caught what they'd whispered; but he now heard the voice of Father Pascentius, as the monk re-entered the hall, and that decided him. He nodded to his friend. Even the most hardened of the troopers turned away their heads, and the Lollard shut his eyes. . . .

When it was done it was clear to all that the man was dying. The page-boy Rawlff, who alone hadn't turned away, whispered to his neighbour, "Who'd have thought that the Crow had so much blood in him!"

There was indeed only a little space left, close to the man's head, that was free from blood, and when at last Father Pascentius had finished his rites it was there he knelt. Broch-o'-Meifod, still on *his* knees, looked as he leant on the handle of the bronze sword like a Neolithic giant after some life-and-death struggle.

"Jesus, Joseph, and Mary, in peace with you I give up my ghost," murmured the monk, calling upon the Seneschal to repeat the words after him, but at that moment there was a disturbing movement among the onlookers, for Rhisiart had returned with the belt.

Supposing in his logical mind that nothing would make the old man give up the ghost more happily than to see these sacred objects re-united, the brave lad forgot for once to glance at his master. Advancing straight to Broch's side he held out what he had brought to the kneeling giant.

But Broch-o'-Meifod seemed completely oblivious of everything but the prostrate figure before him. It was old Adam himself who took in what was happening, and a most curious smile lit up his face. "Put them away, boy," he commanded faintly, "I—must—go—I must go now—to the King."

Thus speaking this treacherous custodian of the sword of Eliseg closed his eyes, and a minute later set forth unattended on his final peace-mission.

It was not much more than a week after the death of the Seneschal that the Prince actually departed to make trial of the bold stroke that those feminine conclaves had planned.

Rhys Gethin was unwilling to go. The less tricky and more purely military campaign against the Radnorshire lands of the Mortimers had by this time become an obsession with him. Owen did, however, swear on the hilt of Eliseg's sword, now safe in Eliseg's belt, that if he came back alive—with or without Lord Grey—his next move *should* be the one projected in the smoke of the hall-fire and under the inspiration of Nant Clwyd mead.

As for Rhisiart, his spirits had risen higher, and his confidence in himself had grown deeper, during these last months, than ever before in his life. This was not merely due to the spring, or even to the sharp, sweet, spring-time pangs of his feeling for Catharine. It was largely due to the fact that he found himself progressing fast—more to his own astonishment than might have been supposed—in those astute arts of statecraft and diplomacy which of all things he admired most in the world.

Owen's ways in these difficult paths exactly suited him. The master's imagination would go skimming between wind and tide, like a river-ouzel, while the servant's more practical intelligence would work out with the shrewdness of a water-rat the details of the scheme.

Where the lad *had* been a real statesman, and had every reason to be surprised at his success, was in the case of Father Pascentius. The monk knew everything that went on in that mountain-court, as much among the women as among the men, nor had he missed one psychic current of the queer disturbance left in all their nerves by the passing of the comet. Rhisiart, therefore, following some inspired hint from his Prince, had resolved after their return from Nannau that he would stop at nothing to gain the confidence of the enigmatic person behind those all-devouring eyes.

It first occurred to him to play upon the theologian's vanity as a confessor; but he quickly found that his most secret vices—even to that dark quiver he derived from certain forms of cruelty—were sins so trifling and childish to a confessor from a monastery that he was driven to invention; and it soon became evident that not only had Providence deprived him of the more labyrinthine forms of evil, but it hadn't even endowed him with the power of inventing them.

His next idea was to feign an interest in theological metaphysic; but he couldn't carry this design very far for the simple reason that when he began to study the Father's Commentary upon Saint Thomas he came bolt up against his old Oxford difficulties with Aristotle.

"The philosopher isn't logical," he would groan as he went to sleep. "He may have invented logic; but it isn't the logic of Roman Law."

But his chance came at last. Quite by accident he encountered the Father one day upon one of his botanical excursions. Anything more removed from the study of Nature than our young friend's interests could hardly be imagined; but by good luck, among her other girlish caprices, Catharine ferch Owen had welcomed that warm spring weather by instituting a little secret garden of her own in a secluded spot among the mountain-birches. Here she would resort, and here Rhisiart soon acquired the habit of finding her; so that when he stumbled on this one weak spot in his learned man's armour he joyfully exploited it, not only for diplomatic reasons, but inspired by the glamour of Catharine's vernal retreat.

And here was one occasion where the subtle confessor of men cared nothing for hidden motives. It was so wonderful to him to find at last another human mind with which he could share his passion that in his excitement he forgot his normal discretion; and the pupil of Snow-

donian flora began to tap little by little other secrets than those connected with the waywardness of rock-plants.

Thus it came about that Owen's secretary was not only acquainted
with the double conclave going on, but was even able, through the
medium of Luned in the one case, and of the officious Rawlff in the
other, to inject various timely modifications into both the schemes,
modifications that sprang from no lower source than the imagination
of Owen himself.

And all this, running parallel with certain paradisic moments in
Catharine's "garden," animated our friend's narrow features with such
a triumphant gleam that poor little Sibli was driven to show that she
too had her claim on him by sarcasms so lively that the laughter they
caused among the Arglwyddes's maids made him shy of going near her.

With Father Pascentius propitiated, and the Prince away on his wild-
goose chase, there was little to dread, during these warm mid-April
days, when the lad paid his visits to Catharine's hill-side refuge.

It is true that since old Adda's death the Arglwyddes felt a little
nervous of letting her daughter leave the enclosure alone; but she contented herself with insisting that when the girl went up the hill the old
Porter, Glew the Gryd, should go with her. But as Glew the Gryd was
on duty at night he generally found for himself a sheltered spot under
the birches; and though by his side lay the sharpest war-axe in the
fortress, his head would soon sink forward upon his leather jerkin in
profound unconsciousness.

Those were without doubt the happiest days in Catharine's life; and
with that self-protective instinct that great creative Nature has given
to girls in love she allowed herself to take the days as they passed
without looking forward or backward. She went to sleep thinking of
Rhisiart, and if her carved image of Saint Clare, as the fire-light
flickered upon it, stared coldly into the gulf of darkness revealed
through the arrow-slit window, she cared not.

Nor did she even care when the horned stag, with the cross between
its antlers, began gliding like a pale ghost in and out of the branches of
its green forest!

Rhisiart's presence was about her, his voice was in her ears, his arms
were round her. The one tangible object in her room upon which she
would fix her eyes as she knelt to tell her beads was neither her green

forest nor her childhood's saint; it was a silver bowl full of celandines. She had come to associate Rhisiart with these hard, bright, metallic flowers. Their glittering bodiless comet-heads with shining spatulate leaves were more independent and more defiant than other plants. It only pleased Catharine that their stalks should be so chilly and that they had no scent! They resembled young warriors, she told herself, and young chancellors too, with their piercing starry eyes held so straight, and their smooth, cool, dark, queer-shaped foliage—just like Rhisiart's inscrutable and far-reaching thoughts!

It troubled her a little, when he talked to her of all the things that must be done, when the last Englishman had been driven out of the country, to make Wales the pride of Christendom, that she had been so remiss in her lessons. She had begged him to bring up to their hiding-place a specimen of his work in the magician's chamber; but when he brought her a copy of his Latin letter to the Irish chieftains with its illuminated capitals and all its curlecues and flourishes, and when he showed her her Father's name as *Owynus Princeps* and translated some of his most eloquent appeals, in the style, he told her, of the best letter-writers in Rome, the shame of her ignorance made a little teasing cloud upon her exultant pride in his powers.

"Shall I ever dare to tell him," she thought, "that I can hardly write 'Catharine ferch Owen' without making a mistake; and that I've only read the first page of the *Consolations* of Boëthius which Iolo gave me before he died?"

The Prince had been away now for nearly a fortnight, and all manner of wild rumours about him kept rising up and dying down in hall and bower.

But Rhisiart remained cheerful and calm, always assuring her that Owen bore a charmed life, and that even if he didn't capture Lord Grey there was more danger of Henry invading Snowdon than of the Prince falling into the hands of his enemies.

One especially warm and windless day, about two o'clock in the afternoon, the boy and the girl were seated on their favourite log, overlooking the little natural spring that rippled from its grey basin like a real fountain among the mosses and fronds and nameless rock-plants of this happy retreat.

Catharine had so arranged her garden that this stream wandered between her stitchworts and primroses and cuckoo-flowers before it reached her favourite bed of celandines. On this occasion they were aware of an intrusive wood-pigeon, who rustling down upon a mountain-ash behind them began its melodious moan.

They were both so happy in their love that day that they were fearful lest even a kiss should ruffle the smooth deep tide on whose wave they floated. One hand was in her lap now, held tight in Rhisiart's fingers, the other was hanging loose at her side, twisting and untwisting a spray of ivy that had strayed from their log among the bracken-fronds.

"Rhisiart!" He turned his head towards her. How flaxen her hair was; more, he told himself, like the daughter of a Norseman than of a British Prince!

"This bird's *too* happy," she whispered. "Do you like it, Rhisiart, going on like that—over and over—and those last two notes always *left behind,* as if it were hiding them before it flies away so that they'll be all hoarded and safe when it gets back? How can it be so happy, and yet so hiding and hoarding? It's *too* happy! Oh, they're greedy things! They eat and eat!"

With a rustling so heavy that it was almost a clatter the wood-pigeon flapped off.

"It heard you," said the lad. "I don't see why it shouldn't eat all it can get, and I don't see why it shouldn't drag out its song if it wants to."

"Rhisiart!"

He knew that he was going to receive some disturbing shock from the way her fingers tightened on his own; and he knew it too from another little sign, from the way she lifted her free arm and mechanically brushed from her brow, where it must have been tickling her, a long-stalked primrose that with no little trouble and pains he had twisted into her flaxen hair.

The rejected flower, its brittle pink stem broken, fluttered down on the black sleeve of Rhisiart's scholarly tunic where it rested under his eye; but he dare not make the least movement towards it, because the girl's mood frightened him, and he'd already discovered that, like the Prince, Catharine ferch Owen had to be handled with considerable tact.

Neither the wise Luned nor the sharp-witted Sibli would have believed it possible that two young people could love each other with such an absence of ordinary amorousness. But they were both very young, and they were both fanatical idealists; and if now and then Catharine's mind *was* disturbed by natural girlish longings, the fact that any sensuality to be an overpowering temptation to Rhisiart had to be associated with domination, if not with cruelty, kept *his* feelings with regard to his little Princess on such a level of pure romance that she had no inducement to give way to this yielding vein.

But she thought of him day and night. She would wake early and watch the indescribable greyness of the hour before dawn as it touched the cold mouldings of her narrow window and poured itself like a presence round her sleep-warmed limbs. And always diffused in their grey light were the looks and ways and tones of the boy she loved. The cry of a hoot-owl at night was a menace to their love; the chattering of the starlings, when the sun rose in the eastern sky, was an omen of its prosperous issue.

During all this perfect day—the happiest of her whole life—they had only kissed twice, and these kisses had been quick and hurried and fleeting, free from all clinging passion. And yet there hadn't been a morsel of food that the girl had tasted, or a single voyaging fragrance that had come to her out of the earth, or one petal-ful of yellow sunshine caught on her bare arm that hadn't melted her in a floating ecstasy of happiness.

And just as Owen had prayed on his knees before he was declared Prince that thick darkness might cover his future, so day after day, and to-day most of all, did his daughter hide her joy under an iridescent mist.

A spell was upon her that every motion in her being guarded from the peril of thought. In a warm, dark, oblivion, oblivion to yesterday, oblivion to to-morrow, she hid her happiness and nourished her love, keeping them back, holding them down, so that like daffodil bulbs under the sheltering mould their green shoot might expand unseen.

And Rhisiart, as he gazed anxiously at her now, struggling to read the mystery of her mood, trembling, fearing lest some unguessed-at quiver in the air should threaten the towers of his new Dinas Brān, kept thinking to himself how strange it was that he should be content just to look at her, just to be with her, just to touch her—he who had had such wicked and sinister relations with other women!

"I shall tell her, of course, when we're married," he said to himself, "everything about Luned and Sibli and Mistress Lowri; but no need to do it yet! Girls are different from men." For some reason he felt it was no more incumbent upon him to tell her about Tegolin than about Modry or his mother. The Maid seemed a part of that natural background of a person's life that was outside Love's Confessional.

"Why do you think it is, Rhisiart," she burst out almost fiercely, "that I'm so afraid for our happiness? I didn't mean to tell you; but that greedy pigeon—"

The experienced profligate by her side drew an infinite sigh of relief. So after all it was only a girl's nonsense! He boldly replaced the broken flower in her hair and lifted her hand to his lips.

"*I'm* not afraid, Catharine. Your Father likes me. He depends on me. When we've driven the English out I'm going to see the great Master Young, and get *him* to be Chancellor to *Owynus Princeps*. Master Brut will be the head of our new Universities. But your Father will depend on *me* to revise the Laws of Hywel the Good. Hywel the Good was— What is it, Catharine? Don't you believe me? Why did you smile like that?"

But Owen's daughter had ceased smiling. "Just go and see—will you?—if Glew the Gryd is still asleep. I wouldn't like—" and she gave him one of those confederate glances out of her Glendower eyes that always enchanted him and reduced him to proud obedience. The minute he was lost in the tender green of the birches she jumped up from the log, tossed back her long straight hair, stretched herself, and uttered a queer whistling sound between her teeth that was neither a sigh nor a laugh nor a groan. What it really was was the body of a young girl lamenting to the birches and the stalks of the stitchworts and the spores of the mosses that the Laws of Hywel Dda couldn't beget children! But the mind of Catharine ferch Owen was too occupied in holding back the unknown future, against which she pressed her white arms as if against the scaly front of a dragon, to bother very much what her body was feeling. She did stoop down, however, and picked up the flower about which her lover had been so meticulous, hesitating whether or not to place it in her bosom.

As she held it between her finger and thumb she noticed that not only was its stalk broken but its petals were drooping. And it seemed to her as if that pale yellow flower, while it wilted between her fingers, began answering a complaint she had never uttered.

"Yes, boys are shy and difficult when they love," the yellow flower said. "When they *don't* love it's different. *Then* they don't care what blossoms they break."

Having delivered itself of this cold comfort, and comfort for a trouble of which Catharine, floating on the waves of her happiness, had been unaware, the selfish flower turned the conversation to its own affairs.

"I know," it said, "'tis a custom in stories for maidens to thrust us into their bosoms; and it's indeed a pure, soft, and fragrant death wherewith you're threatening me, Catharine; but I would far rather you threw me into the stream where I could enjoy the light of the blessed sun for a day or two longer!"

"But I'd have put you into the third page of Boëthius," protested Catharine, "where's there's an illuminated 'R' in three colours."

But the primrose was silent. The tiny hairs on its pink stalk leaned sideways. Over its beautiful eye there crept a misty film. Its calices changed their hue. One of its petals began to curl inwards at the edge.

"I'll put you in a glass by yourself—not with the celandines. No, I can't do that; for Tegolin'll see you and know exactly why you're there. Very well then! I'll put you into my fountain; and when Rhisiart comes to-morrow I'll show him how fresh you are!"

She did in fact hurry to her fountain's brink and there search about till she found a little miniature bay in its stone margin. Here she arranged the wilted blossom, with its head against the stone and its long stalk, twisted now by reflection as well as by accident, deep in the water. Her hair swept the water as she bent down, but this did not prevent a tiny but fierce stickleback from biting at that bruised stalk, which it doubtless suspected of biological kinship with the patient tribe of worms.

The violent movement of the stickleback disturbed a water-beetle from its afternoon sleep by shaking off a little group of vegetation-parasites which still clung to the primrose-stalk. These unarmed miniscules of the land now drifted, clinging to each other in shivering apprehension, into the watery gulfs of unknown regions, regions which to their simple minds must have been full of all the hungry monarchs and all the torture-loving archbishops of the aquatic world.

But having arranged the wilted blossom to what she felt to be the flower's complete satisfaction—and further than that how could the responsibility of the most beneficent goddess go?—she proceeded, still on her knees by her fountain, to remove various fragments of slaty stone that struck her as impeding rather than assisting the exploring tendrils of certain small rock-plants of which none but Father Pascentius could have named even the species.

Suddenly the ghastly thought struck her: "Suppose Lord Grey's men have been prowling about here ever since they murdered old Adda!" She scrambled to her feet and with difficulty restrained herself from running wildly down the hill in the direction where the young man had vanished.

"Suppose David Gam"—for *that* lurid tale, told with savage exaggerations, had reached every girl in the fortress—"armed with his dedicated knife, were lying in wait?"

But she *must* stay where she was. If she set off to look for him they might miss. Probably Glew the Gryd had changed the place of his afternoon siesta. But oh, how completely all obscure fears of the future had vanished at the touch of this immediate terror!

She saw him lying on the ground like that Englishman she'd seen Rhys Gethin kill, and like that glimpse she'd had of old Adda in his pool of blood. 'Twas a pity Rhisiart couldn't have stolen upon her at that moment as the Prince had stolen upon Gam and the pages! He certainly would have seen her under an aspect completely new to him. Each particular hair of her flaxen weight of tresses seemed stirred by an electric wind; and her eyes were as big and her cheeks as white and pinched as if she were gazing at a scaffold.

It kept growing upon her more and more vividly that she saw Rhisiart lying in his blood. He was calling to her for help. Oh, she must fly to him! But no; she *must* stay where she was. Suddenly her whole body stiffened. It wasn't Catharine, it was the statue of a paralysed wood-nymph that stood there. Yes!—again and again— distinct and clear through the misty sunshine—the sound of a horn!

Then, just as her rebellious blood was rushing to take her, whatever her reason might do, flying on the wind to her love, the birch-branches were moved aside. She leapt forward with a gasping cry—only to encounter the unwieldy form of Glew the Gryd, carrying his axe on his shoulder. How the sunlight made that bright weapon gleam!

"Don't be frightened, Missy," said the old man kindly, though Catharine could see he was trembling with excitement. " 'Twas Master Rhisiart what sent me to 'ee. 'A told me to say to 'ee that thee'd best get home-along, for the Prince be come back, and have brought with him, in good clanking chains, Lord Grey and young Grey, captives of his mighty spear!"

Nothing but the deep-instilled precepts of the wise Arglwyddes kept Catharine then from leaving Glew the Gryd in the lurch and running at top-speed to the castle-gate. As it was she reduced the Porter to breathlessness by the pace she set him. But it was with the panting old gentleman close at her side, bright-glittering axe and all, that she finally came upon the scene—and what a scene! Never to her dying day did she forget it.

The whole population of that mountain-court seemed to be assembled on the grassy slope in front of those great gates; and the cries of triumphant welcome that went up drowned all the eager questions and answers that kept passing from mouth to mouth.

There was her father; and oh! how magnificent he looked, mounted on old Seisyll, the long pennon of his tall lance fluttering in the sunshine, with the lion rampant of Mathrafal! And there was her Rhisiart —how glorious it was to meet his flashing eyes!—walking by Seisyll's side and waiting to help the Prince alight.

There was no sign of Broch-o'-Meifod; and there darted through Catharine's mind the thought, "He's Father's best friend; and yet he never comes on the scene unless there's trouble. I don't understand that man. He frightens me." She was surprised, too, not to see the familiar Cistercian habit of Father Pascentius. "I suppose he's off botanizing or writing his book; but I'm glad he's busy. He spoils everything with his staring eyes. Oh, there's Master Brut!" But in her eagerness to get a smile from the Prince she dodged asking herself the reason—perhaps her suspicion of "that witch's daughter," perhaps jealousy of his friendship with Rhisiart—why she was always so glad when Master Brut was *not* there!

"Room for the Princess Catharine!"

Who was it who had shouted that? It made her cheeks hot with excitement, and yet it gave her an uneasy feeling, too. It was the first time anyone had called her "Princess"; and she saw Lord Grey raise his head for a second in evident surprise. "Oh it's only that ridiculous Rawlff!" And she blushed again; this time for shame at her pleasure.

But the Prince had seen her now; he had dismounted, had given Rhisiart his lance, and was coming to meet her. Oh how proud she was as she embraced him before them all and helped him to unlace his helmet! And Rhisiart was only a few steps behind. Yes, she had them both to herself.

Such, however, is the tangled skein of mortal events that it's rare for one person's good moment not to be paid for by a bad moment for someone else. This absorption of the Prince in his daughter, for Griffith had gone, as he always did, straight into the hall to greet the Arglwyddes, and Meredith and Rhys Gethin were busy with the ponies and the plunder, made it possible for the captives' worst enemies to get close up to them.

Both the prisoners had their hands heavily manacled, but each of them was on horseback, the elder with his head sunk on his breast, the younger staring wildly about him. Lord Grey was a dark, gaunt-boned man of over middle age. He had a pale desolate face that this disaster had frozen into a mask of sullen hopelessness. Master Brut, as he looked at him, wondered what it had been in this gloomy unhappy man that had made him such a close intimate of the King's. When, however, the Earl lifted his head at Rawlff's unexpected cry of "Princess!" the Lollard got more light on the tyrant of Ruthin. Yes, he had the kind of merciless gaze into the blood-and-iron heart of things from which a usurper with his back to the wall might draw strength and support. But how different was this crazy youth!

Master Brut sighed, and told himself that it was the weakness of the heir to those unscalable red walls, more than any quarrel with any neighbour, that had embittered this proud man's heart. But what was the wretched boy so excited about now? He swung round and found himself at once face to face with the cause.

Alice and her mother! The two women were beside themselves with triumph and hate. They pushed past him without seeing him, without knowing him, and the elder one poured forth on Lord Grey such a torrent of imprecations as made the Lollard's blood run cold. The object of this savage vituperation seemed to disregard it completely as far as himself was concerned; but the Lollard could see from the troubled protective glance he threw on his son that what worried him wasn't the screams of the mother, but the deadlier whispers of the daughter, as she pressed herself against the young man's horse and toyed with the iron that bound his wrists.

The sounds that the youth himself emitted as he swayed about in his saddle and allowed his under-lip to hang down and his lower jaw to chatter made the Lollard think of those words that he knew so well on the lips of Jesus: "And there shall be wailing and gnashing of teeth."

"We know all about what you did to Master Adam, what you did to Master Adam," he heard the girl repeat in what resembled a low-voiced chant. "And they'll do the same to you; and they'll do the same to you!"

There had gathered by this time a most threatening crowd about the two prisoners, a crowd composed not so much of troopers as of men-servants and maid-servants from the fortress. Reckless and ungracious individuals among these latter began urging on the mother and daughter, and even adding to their maledictions appalling details of the manner in which—so they assured the men in chains—it had been decided they should perish.

But, as we know, it was not in the nature of the owner of Lyde Manor to see two fellow-creatures tormented without interfering. Had that "great gulf" divided him from them, to which Jesus refers in the story of Lazarus, it is probable that neither God nor Devil would have stopped him from attempting to jump across.

"Woman! woman!" he cried, seizing Mistress Dilys by the arm and pulling her back. "He's an old man; he's suffered much. Can't you see how much he's suffered?"

But the crowd's blood was up, and one of the cooks of the castle, a lusty fellow from Rhys Gethin's Conway, struck the heretic's arm with a skewer, compelling him to release the woman, who promptly returned to her post at the prisoner's side.

Master Brut then seized upon Alice, and, evidently supposing that his pupil in the doctrines of Wycliffe would be more amenable than her parent, proceeded to drag away the struggling girl; explaining to her, as he dragged, that it was the Prince alone who would decide the fate of his prisoners.

This was the first time in their acquaintance that her instructor in the Gospels had ever laid hands on her; and such was the response of her voluptuous body to his virile grasp—for she was a big girl and struggled vigorously against his compulsion, forcing him to take her in his arms—that when an indignant scullion began assailing him with coarse abuse it was she and not Master Brut who retorted to the meddling fellow.

In his simplicity the Lollard hadn't the least idea that to be treated by him in this rough manner and to struggle helplessly against his strength had been the very image that night after night since her mother had separated her from Tegolin had made this excitable girl toss about in a fever of desire before she could relax in sleep. He could indeed only attribute it to the miraculous influence of Master Wycliffe when she consented with complete docility to return with him and drag her mother away.

But the Prince himself broke through the crowd now, and gave authoritative orders as to where the prisoners were to be taken. To the surprise of both the surly young Madoc and old Glew the Gryd, who were the officials selected as warders to the two captives, it appeared they were only to be chained to the wall of a chamber not far from Owen's own.

For the purpose of rivetting these chains, however, it was necessary for Master Simon to be called on the scene; but Rhisiart, to whom the Prince delegated the task of supervising this sinister process, was unable to resist the panic-stricken appeals of the younger prisoner, and did his best, in spite of the scowls of Madoc, to re-assure the youth, and make him understand that no physical torture was to be his fate.

As long, however, as Master Simon, with Lowri's evil-looking servant Lawnslot to help him, was at work over them with his burning brazier and his hammer and pincers, it was clear to Rhisiart that it wasn't only the son who was uneasy as to the fate in store for them.

But when the Hog and his assistant had done their work and meat and wine had been brought and the captives had come to realize that not only was there a fire in their prison but that a channel of running water, to serve them for a latrine, flowed within reach of their chains, the countenance of the younger prisoner perceptibly brightened.

Lord Grey, however, though he remained seated on a wooden stool, with his back to the wall to which their manacles were attached, refused all refreshment save a sip of wine, and kept asking impatiently to see the "Baron Glendourdy."

Rhisiart, who couldn't help recalling how elated his Norman mother had been merely to offer refreshment to a "belted earl," felt that life was indeed an ironic procession of events. Here was he—but he broke off this thought to whisper to Glew the Gryd that it would be advisable if he took turns with Madoc to remain in the room, while the one not so engaged stood on guard outside the door.

It was curious how he himself kept making every excuse he could to stay longer in this room with the captives. He knew perfectly well that it was high time for him to dress for the banquet; and he knew that nothing annoyed the Prince more than lack of ceremony and formality in these old Welsh customs, especially in an adherent whose Norman blood might tend to make him supercilious towards them. And yet he *couldn't* tear himself away. Nor, down at the bottom of his consciousness, did he deceive himself about the cause of his attraction. It wasn't pity. It wasn't policy. It wasn't his dislike of "those Ruthin women." It was the sight of the chains! Yes, there was something about the idea of proud, well-bred men like Grey and his son being chained to the wall like dogs and having to manage with regard to the necessities of life like dogs that made that old dark nerve, which Lowri had discovered and played upon, quiver once again like the strings of a devil's fiddle.

How passionately he had poured out, in his informal confessions to Father Pascentius, his worst feelings in this kind! But never would he do this again. He had discovered that it is impossible to confess the particular evil with which our peculiar devil maddens us unless our confessor suffers from the same obsession. Short of *that,* it is as if we are uttering childish and ridiculous absurdities!

And all this while, as he made one silly excuse after another to postpone his departure, talking in English to the younger captive and in Welsh to the Porter, he knew well that the formidable intelligence of the Lord of Ruthin was weighing him up, wondering no doubt if this young Oxford fool couldn't be bribed. And there rushed through his own brain the thought that if only the great Master Young were here, what a chance this was to get such a ransom from this friend of the King that—

He felt so impatient to convey this statesman-like inspiration to Owen that he could hardly endure the thought of the triumphant banquet that he knew must be got through ere he had a chance to be alone with his hero.

"Was I lying to this terrified idiot," he thought, "when I said he was safe from death?" And an uncomfortable memory of how he had helped his master to dispose of *one* enemy in an extremely disturbing manner, and of the expression on the Prince's face as he went about this, caused a doubt to pass through him. "They'll all want him to put them to death," he thought. He now pretended to be taking from Glew the Gryd a few lessons in torch-making; but in reality he gave the old man a stern command, which he uttered as if it came straight from the Prince, that on no account must *any woman* be permitted to see the prisoners.

"That'll stop those two witches if *they* try their games!" he said to himself. "But I must talk to the cooks and scullions. Any real statesman like Master Young would take us for absolute madmen, if he heard we were thinking of killing these men. I wonder how much the Prince *could* ask? We'd keep the son as hostage, of course, while the father collected it. I suppose it would never do to ask a thousand marks? But why not?—for the King's friend—why not five, why not *ten* thousand?"

While he bent over the old Porter who had settled himself in a corner of the apartment with his materials for torch-making, Rhisiart couldn't help noticing the way the sallow-cheeked Earl, whose lips bore a clipped moustache as black as a raven's feather, and whose well-shaped teeth were as white as a wolf's, began at once arranging that part of their couch which was within reach of his son, so that as soon as the boy was so minded he could stretch himself out in comparative ease.

Our friend knew that it would be necessary for him to change his clothes before this triumphal banquet, when, as he sighed to think, he would certainly have to endure a prolonged improvisation by Griffith the Bard; and he decided, in order to do honour to his Prince, and incidentally to his own scheme on the Prince's behalf, to attire himself in a new suit of black velvet trimmed with silver, for the designing of which little Sibli, who scoffed at him on all such points, had made herself responsible.

How the small creature's eyes would shine when she saw him enter the hall! By reason of some quirk in his nature he cared nothing for pleasing Catharine in what he wore. It was by what he planned and dared that he wished to impress *her!* As to Tegolin—for the personality of his women always seemed to follow another in Rhisiart's thoughts, just as in his secretarial work one great legal name inevitably evoked another—he thought no more of how to please *her,* either by dress or achievement or daring, than he thought of pleasing the earth and the sky.

He couldn't imagine existence without being able to see Tegolin every day and receive her re-assuring smile. He left the prison-chamber at last, and the first thing that struck him, when, attired in his court-dress but too late to join the ceremonious entry, he made his way down the hall, was the fact that there were two new faces that afternoon.

One of these new-comers had been given the place of honour on the Arglwyddes's right, but it was a shock to him to see that the other was calmly seated in his own unalterable place by the Prince's side!

Owen, who wore what struck the Hereford boy as almost fantastically gorgeous attire, sat there like a golden image. But he had his eye on his belated squire; and Rhisiart, who knew his ways so well and with his Welsh-Norman blood knew so well how to handle him, had need to assume his most injured expression of woefully hurt feelings to induce the Prince to make room for him on his other side!

The guest of honour he saw at once was his old friend the Abbot of Caerleon; but who this spare, high-cheek-boned, hollow-cheeked, dark little man, with a neatly-trimmed pointed beard, might be, he had no notion.

He hadn't long to wait, however, for the Prince hastened to introduce them; and the syllables "Henry Don of Kidwelly" sank happily into the young statesman's mind.

"*That* means more money as well as more men," he thought, "and

the fellow looks a scholar as well as a soldier. I shouldn't be surprised
if Rhys Gethin's plan of campaign isn't changed a good deal now!
I've always thought it a mistake to antagonize the Mortimers."

He determined to postpone his communication to Broch-o'-Meifod,
who had moved to let him sit down, until the drinking began and the
ladies were gone; but he couldn't resist—for Rhys Gethin was sitting
opposite him and he greatly desired to convey to this fiery warrior,
who so nearly had murdered the finest intellect in Wales, the innate
superiority of the brain over the sword—the temptation of delicately
sounding Henry Don upon this nice strategic point.

It was clear that Owen treated Don with the utmost respect; nor
was this a surprise to our astute youth, for he recalled the letter they
had received from him and how pleased the Prince had been. "He
comes from as far South as the Abbot," he thought. "I hope he suggests
a raid upon *that* quarter."

"Some of us, my Lord of Kidwelly," he began, "have been specu-
lating as to whether it wouldn't be advisable to make a hurried descent
upon South Wales. Some of us feel it's important not to annoy either
the Percies or the Mortimers"—yes, Rhys Gethin *had* caught the word
"Mortimer"—"but in the South where you, my Lord of Kidwelly, have
so much influence—"

"Master Henry Don is my name, sir," replied that gentleman curtly;
and Rhisiart became aware—for he was addressing the new-comer
across the golden bifurcation of the Prince's beard—that his master was
smiling that particularly disconcerting smile which he knew by experience indicated disapproval. Oh, and worse still—what *had* he done?
—he was certain he caught an exchange of looks between Rhys Gethin
and the Prince.

This blow, a blow that was all the more bitter because it was so completely beyond his comprehension—had the Prince secrets, then, with
that headstrong soldier that had never been revealed? oh, for Master
Young, for Master Young!—threw Rhisiart into such gloom that when
the ladies *did* depart, and the drinking *did* begin, he felt too deeply
sunk in shame to carry out his plan of talking to Broch-o'-Meifod
about the ransom.

He was so hurt in his self-esteem that he scarcely knew how long
that monotonous chanting and harp-playing of old Griffith went on.

Why didn't the Prince come to his rescue? A few, friendly, intimate words would have been enough; would have soon shown both to *Master* Don and to *Captain* Rhys that there were brains, as well as men and money, in Owen's camp. To forget his bitterness he began drinking more than was his wont; so much more in fact that he hardly knew what to answer when in the height of the revelry he found his sleeve pulled by the pretty page Elphin.

"*Who* wants me?" he murmured crossly. "I can't come now."

"Mistress Tegolin sent Luned and me, Master Rhisiart, to fetch you," whispered the frightened boy in his ear. And then he added almost piteously, "You're not to talk loud. You're not to say anything. *You're only to come!*"

Rhisiart glanced about him. Broch-o'-Meifod, who was always the first to leave such revels, had already gone. The Prince was totally absorbed in what his friend from Kidwelly was telling him. Rhys Gethin was regarding Elphin with grim amusement.

Our friend pulled himself together, rose like a slim phantom in black and silver, and proceeded, though with steps rather stumbling than gliding, to follow the page out of the hall and up the stair-case.

"I know perfectly well what's happening," he said to himself. "I'm not in the least drunk; but I'm very unhappy. I'm too unhappy to think."

They came at last to a small landing where one of the two torches that usually hung there had burnt itself out, and the other was rapidly following it. Dim as the light was he had no difficulty in recognizing the beguiling form of Luned who greeted him with a tender smile.

"Well done, Elphin!" she cried. "But you'd better run up and bring us a light." Then she whispered in the boy's ear that the young gentleman would stumble in the darkness.

"Get a candle from Mistress Tegolin, child, and say he's just coming. She knows what these banquets are!"

It was partly the mead he'd drunk and partly the fact that to be alone with Luned upon a staircase leading to a Ladies' Tower brought back that night in Dinas Brān, but there was a yet simpler cause of his extraordinary behaviour, *and that was shame.* He had made a complete fool of himself before Rhys Gethin and before that fellow from South

Wales. The Prince had discarded him from his secret counsels. He had shown himself, once for all, no more like Griffith Young than he was like Archbishop Becket! He had better give up statesmanship and practise the long-bow. It had been in his wanton revolt against Brān the Blessed and Ffraid ferch Gloyw that he had formerly seized on this yielding cinnamon-scented body as the best means of asserting his independence. "Well!" the Devil whispered to him now: "Try squeezing a salve for your disgrace out of the same soft sweet fruit, ready to yield at a touch!"

Taking advantage of the dying gleam that revealed only a blur of filmy whiteness—whiteness that made him think of that summer night —he now seized upon the girl without a word; and without a word they swayed together there under the spitting and spluttering torch.

He pressed her so closely to him that it was as if his shame had been some diabolic essence that he was eager to transfer from his veins to hers. But Luned was still the wise one; and though she gave herself up with the old languid abandonment to this recurrence of *l'amour d'escalier* she listened intently for any descending steps.

But there come occasions when the wisest are fooled by the impulses of the reckless. What she couldn't hear she couldn't guard against. And the quick impatient feet of Catharine in their soft shoes fell like the feathers of a swan's neck upon those treacherous stones.

The "light" which Luned had asked Elphin to bring was not far away; for now the clearly-sounding footsteps of the page became audible, and also, though only Luned caught *that,* the shuffle of Tegolin's sandals behind him.

But though Rhisiart's arms fell to his sides and Luned uttered a rich, panting, unashamed laugh, they both knew that Catharine had seen them. It was with the final blazing up of its loyal flame that the enduring torch, as hostile to vice as it was protective of virtue, revealed to them the expression on Catharine's face, her wide-open eyes, her distorted mouth. But it was out of a darkness not yet broken by the candle that was descending the stairs that her voice came.

"Rhisiart!"

And it seemed to our hapless friend—from whose muddled wits the fumes of that fatal metheglin dissolved like smoke—that his protest was like the protest of a crushed worm, endowed in its destruction with super-human lucidity that now filled the darkness.

"Catharine, it's all a mistake! I was—I have—I am—"

But her voice came calm and cold, while the first flicker from Elphin's candle lit the staircase above her head.

"Will you tell Tegolin, Rhisiart, that I've gone to my father. I can feel my way down. I've done it before. *I don't want any of you.*"

Her final words rang out with all the pride and all the authority of the "Princess" Rawlff had called her; and they were clearly heard by both the young candle-bearer and the Maid; for when these two emerged upon the landing neither of them made any attempt to follow her.

Tegolin realized at once that the lovers had quarrelled; but she supposed it was only the renewal of some difference between them that had occurred earlier in the day. Luned greeted her with an innocence that had a touch of insolence in it, but Tegolin was too occupied with Rhisiart to give her any close attention.

She had never seen such a Rhisiart as she saw now! A lock of the lad's black hair had fallen across his forehead in his struggle with Luned, and his lips, in place of being sucked-in showed all loose in the candle-light, showed even bloody against his ghastly face, as if he had received a blow in the mouth.

The Maid gave him one long look, swallowing her saliva as she did so with a faint clicking sound like the turning of a tiny key in a silver lock. Then she told Elphin to follow them with the light; and taking Rhisiart by the hand led him without a word up the stair-case into Mad Huw's chamber.

Here there were the dying embers of a wood-fire, a lancet window open to the west, a couch of straw, with a crucifix on the wall above it, and an alcove, concealed by a heavy curtain, where the Maid herself slept. Squatting cross-legged on the floor by the dying fire, with nothing on but a garment of coarse un-bleached wool, sat the Apostle of King Richard. He leapt to his feet the moment they entered, and with the curious penetration he invariably showed where his obsession didn't arise he at once grasped the situation in its essentials.

He knew nothing of course of the part played by Luned, who with

Elphin had now discreetly withdrawn, but he divined that this mute, stricken lad, who now sank down on a stool by the embers and hid his face in his hands, had disgraced himself with both the Prince and his daughter.

Tegolin cautiously closed the door of the room, drew the curtains yet closer across her alcove, and, carrying some wood to the smouldering ashes, knelt down by Rhisiart's side and fell to re-kindling the fire.

She was still in her blue banquet-dress, but she had taken off her ornamental slippers with their turquoise-coloured *calch,* or enamel-work, and she had already braided her hair for the night. "He is unhappy," she murmured, lifting her head from her task and glancing at the Friar, who towered above them both with his thin legs gleaming white in the flames she was conjuring up, "so I brought him to you."

"You did well, daughter; you did well."

"How shall we make him understand, Father, that all of us—men and women alike—have to endure bitter shame, and yet go on living, go on struggling?"

Mad Huw shut his eyes and pondered; then he started pacing up and down the room. Then he stood still and stared at Rhisiart's bowed head.

"Well, Father," the girl repeated. "He's very unhappy, and I've brought him to you."

Mad Huw moved close to that crouching figure in its velvet and silver. The Friar's white legs with their black hairs brushed against the Maid's gown and were scraped by the silver tassels that Sibli had stitched to the lad's tunic.

"My dear son," he said, "do you realize that we two haven't been alone with the Maid since you saved me from that poor madman of Chirk?"

Rhisiart *did* raise his head at this. But he covered it again after one despairing glance at his comforter.

"*I* didn't save you," he mumbled into his hands. "And she knows I didn't." And then in a scarcely audible voice, "I'm good for nothing but to be a drunken bowman under Rhys Gethin."

Tegolin rose to her feet and gazed intently at the Friar. "Do you think, Father"—her lips formed the words slowly and gravely and her

forehead wrinkled itself into a deep frown—"that if you were to—to
pray to Our Lady—"

To her astonishment Mad Huw shook his head. "There *is* someone
who could help him," he said, "but he isn't—"

"Do you mean his friend Master Brut?" An angry light gleamed at
once in the man's eyes, not a mad light, but the obstinate sane light of
implacable orthodoxy.

"*That* perverter of our Holy Faith!" he cried hoarsely, "*that* taker of
our Blessed Lord's name in vain! Daughter, daughter, have you forgotten *all* my teaching?"

"*Who* could help him, Father? Tell me, oh tell me, for the love of
Mary!"

His flash of anger died down at once in the presence of her emotion.
But what he had to say didn't seem quite easy to him; and it was clear
to her, who knew him so well, that the difficulty lay in his conscience
rather than his wits. He began in a long roundabout manner that made
the girl sigh. "Alack! alack! It's King Richard he's leading up to!"

But Mad Huw, as sometimes happened at a pinch, was *not* leading
up to King Richard.

The Maid hadn't the remotest idea what he *was* hinting at, for he
was now explaining that ever since Saint Joseph of Arimathea brought
the Sangreal to Glastonbury, and Saint David built a wattle-chapel
for its worship, there were particular persons in Wales, not necessarily
priests, who had been given by the Holy Spirit certain miraculous
powers—powers that were neither condemned by Holy Church, nor
officially acknowledged—and it was his own secret thought that one
of such persons was none other—Tegolin's eyes opened in amazement
—than Master Broch-o'-Meifod. "Have you heard," he went on, "how
that insolent Cistercian, who hates us poor Brothers of Saint Francis,
goes about denouncing Master Broch? That alone proves him a man of
worth. Whenever you hear a cloistered monk, who knows nothing of
perils by land or of perils by water, or of taking the Lady Poverty as
his bride, abuse any man or any King either—"

"Blessed Virgin keep one king away a *little* longer!" prayed Tegolin.

"You may be sure that *that man* is inspired by the Most High. Do
you realize, my children," and the Friar began to stride up and down

the room with the tails of his woollen shirt flapping about his legs,
"that the old Welsh saints—such as Saint Collen, and such as Saint
Tysilio of Broch's own *cantref*—were much more like the little Brothers
of Saint Francis than these rich and learned cloistered monks! They
were soldiers, too, like our brave Abbot who arrived to-night—*he*
refuses to stay in the cloister—and many of them were quite unknown
to Rome and the Holy Father. Well, children, *that's* the sort of man
this Broch-o'-Meifod is! He doesn't quote the Gospel. He doesn't
pervert the Faith of our Fathers with human learning, like that son
of perdition, Brut. He leaves those matters to their proper custodians.
But I tell you the man's a holy man. I know it. I have seen it. And you
can't deceive a little Grey Brother in things of this kind! Holy Francis!
If I weren't in my shirt I'd go and fetch him myself. Yes, my unhappy
son," for the man's earnestness had made Rhisiart look up, "there are
moments—and I've known them myself—when God works better
through a layman than even through a begging friar, though begging
friars *are* in a sense the laymen of Our Lady. Well! compared with
cloistered monks they are!"

"I *did* have something," murmured Rhisiart—and perhaps it was as
well that Mad Huw didn't notice Tegolin's radiance when she heard
the boy's voice—"that I wanted to say to Master Broch. But I'd rather
say it here than in the Prince's chamber."

"But you'll find Broch alone there if you go *now*," cried Tegolin
eagerly. "All the men'll be at the banquet. Her father will be holding
Catharine on his knee and letting her taste the loving-cup. He did that
when she welcomed him a year ago, after his victory in Ceredigion."

Rhisiart turned his forlorn gaze from the Friar to the Maid. How her
eyes were shining, and how her blue robe suited her! A tiny sprig
of comfort began to lift its head, like the spear of a crocus, from the
bottom of his bruised heart.

"Yes," he muttered, "that was when I composed—for a pilgrim to
St. David's it was—my account of our rush down Hyddgant Mountain."

"That was before we came here," said Tegolin, "and I'm glad you
wrote it down, for you and the Prince usually keep such things so
dark."

Rhisiart could not help assuming the expression of one whose achievements rest in oblivion; and the little sprig of comfort waxed bigger.

"I think I *will* go and see Broch-o'-Meifod," he cried, jumping to his feet and pushing the lock of dark hair from his forehead. "May I come back—for a minute—before I go to bed?"

When he was gone, Mad Huw looked at the Maid with some uneasiness. "I wonder if I did right?" he whispered solemnly. "Do you think *He* would think I did right?"

"I know what *He* would think you ought to do now," said Edeyrnion's Maid with a smile. "And *that* is get to bed at once! You remember the Abbot wants to see you early to-morrow; and early with John ap Hywel *means* early."

Mad Huw's eyes shone. "He wants to ask me about the King. I saw it in his face. Did I say my office, daughter, before that sad young gentleman came in?"

The Maid lied to him like a mother, and kneeling for a second as she always did, to receive his blessing, withdrew into her alcove. Sunk deep in that unbreakable slumber that Nature grants only to her most favoured innocents was Richard's champion when the luckless monarch's namesake returned.

He knocked lightly and entered cautiously, carrying a lantern. The room was sweet with the mingling of cool night-air and fragrant wood-smoke. He found the Maid seated by the fire reading a French version of the *Adventures of Sir Percival in the Castle Perilous.*

"Well?" she murmured, as he took his place by her side, stretching out his thin wrists and long fingers over the blaze, while his embroidered sleeves fell across her lap.

"I told him everything, Tegolin, as I would tell you, but you never have to be *told;* and he said I must begin again from the very bottom. He said I mustn't think of anything but improving my hand-writing and improving my style. He said everything in the world, including fish and birds and rocks and stones, were only happy when they were all the time being what they *were.* He said I must think of nothing but doing what I *liked* doing, and doing it better and better. He said I mustn't care what Owen thought of me, or Catharine, or anybody. He said God was beginning to reveal Himself in a new way that wasn't the Church's way and wasn't the Lollard's way. He said a lot about that, but it all went out of my head, because the way he said it got rid of my shame and made me feel—you know— So, to tell you the truth, I *can't* tell you what he said! But I know he made me feel I must think more about my hand-writing and less about Master Young."

"Did he—say—anything, Gwion Bach, about Catharine?"

He drew away from her a little and clasped his fingers tightly together. "Who was it," he enquired, watching her face intently, "who sent Luned and Elphin to fetch me?"

She returned his gaze frankly. "*I* did, Gwion Bach, for I saw how things were; and I sent for Catharine, too. I didn't know she'd rush down the stairs like that. But I thought—I thought—"

Like a great salt wave that has drawn back only to advance again the whole memory of that fatal moment on the landing swept over him.

"Catharine—" he gasped; and then, just as if his proud young head had been severed at the neck, he let it fall hard and heavy against her knees and began to shake with deep-drawn sobs.

XV

BRYN GLAS

THE GRAND invasion of the rich territory of the Mortimers, inaugurated, as we have seen, as much over the mead-cups as was Aneirin's famous descent upon Cattraeth, threatened the ripening "bud of love" between Catharine and Rhisiart as if by a flash of David Gam's own knife.

Owen's mountain "Llys" was left under the care of his eldest son Griffith and his brother Tudor, aided by the imposing presence of the Abbot of Caerleon.

Against the Prince's wishes—but Rhys Gethin was obdurate; and in a sense this *was* his special adventure—Mistress Lowri, together with her husband, for none dared to meddle with the weird relations between those two, accompanied the expedition to Maelienydd; as did Broch-o'-Meifod, Master Brut, and our friend Rhisiart.

Henry Don of Kidwelly was to take a leading part in this campaign; but since he had a considerable body of horsemen with him he advanced separately from their main force, sometimes on one flank, sometimes on the other, and sometimes serving as a van-guard.

Rhys Gethin moved to and fro continually from one portion of their little army to another. The Prince himself walked by Broch's side, for he had left Seisyll behind; so that Rhisiart and the Lollard were once more thrown together, just as they had been at their first appearance in Wales. Both the young men were in low spirits; and both were in a mood to confide freely in each other.

It wasn't long, therefore, before Master Brut knew all about his friend's feeling for Catharine, while Rhisiart, not altogether to his surprise but to his no little dismay, learnt from the enamoured Wycliffite that he was already secretly affianced to the girl whom our friend in his heart styled "the witch-daughter of a witch-mother."

Round their bivouac fires in the long June twilights this small army of spearmen and archers and light-armed troopers found itself more inclined to sleep than to revel. Henry Don's horsemen, riding in loose formation till darkness set in, accounted for such a wide tract of country that they removed from every man's consciousness that disturbing sense of an unexpected encounter which tends to occupy the mind even if it doesn't upset the nerves. They had generally marched some twenty miles when evening fell, for everybody agreed with Rhys Gethin that the faster they moved the more contradictory would be the rumours that preceded them, and the more panic-stricken the King's subjects would grow.

Owen himself was for many reasons in a happier mood than he had been for many a month. He *had* taken his young Secretary's advice about the amount of ransom to be given before the two captives were released; and to his amazement he had already received half of this enormous sum; Grey himself being at large now, to collect the other half, while his son remained a hostage for its payment.

Everybody who had approached the two prisoners had been struck by the exceptional devotion of the father to his neurotic offspring; so that the Prince hadn't the least doubt that the remaining sum would be safe in his hands before the summer was over. He was thus relieved for the first time since he'd raised his standard of the most worrying of all his anxieties, the lack of money to pay his men; and though he still struggled to keep his vow not to consult "the spirits" about the future, he couldn't help being aware, as they advanced by these forced marches towards the Radnor mountains, that every omen they encountered was a favourable one.

The Prince never forgot this sequence of long warm summer days blessed by happy presentiments. Both he and Rhys Gethin were so sleepy with marching that when they encamped for the night there was little planning of any strategic moves for the campaign. Owen could see that his formidable Captain was in favour of taking things as they occurred, and trusting to luck; and this was the method after all that came most naturally to himself.

So all day long he and Broch-o'-Meifod philosophized together. Up hill and down dale they discussed the mystery of life; and so happily tired-out was Owen, both in mind and body, that every sunset after he had pledged his Captain in the best of the French wines the Arglwyddes had provided, he removed all his armour, save Iolo's mail-shirt, and sank at once in profound unconsciousness.

It was in the late afternoon of June the twenty-first, the Eve of Saint Alban, that Owen's adventurous force reached the village of Pilleth. Here the Prince was informed by Henry Don, whose horsemen had been scouting far and wide most of the day, that a great muster of English troops, led by Sir Edmund Mortimer himself, and accompanied by such knightly magnates of the border as Robert Whitney and Kinard de la Bere and Walter Devereux, not to speak of the Sheriff of the County, Thomas Clanvow, were on the march from Ludlow.

"There's a big force of Welsh archers with them, my Prince," Don's report concluded, "but I have a man here from the mountains—my people came on him and brought him in—who swears that if I release him and let him return to his fellows, he'll be able to swing them over to us at the first sign of success."

"Let him go, in the name of the Virgin, let him go!" cried the Prince at once, looking from Broch-o'-Meifod to Rhys Gethin. The former nodded, but the latter shook his head.

"He's a spy, caught in the act. 'Swing' *him* 'over,' *I* say; 'over' a stout branch of ash-wood!"

Owen surveyed his impetuous subordinate with that slow sad smile that always made Rhisiart think of his friend Meredith. That disillusioned young chieftain was absent at the moment, being occupied, as he so often was, with some of the less picturesque aspects of a campaign; but it was impossible for Rhisiart to hold his tongue. He felt that he had already incurred the hostility of Rhys Gethin, simply by being what he was, a scholar and a statesman, one whose intelligence inevitably kept hot-headed militarists in their place; but he couldn't listen to such brutal folly without protesting.

"My Prince, my Prince!" he broke in; "Master Brut and I were only saying last night that if every Welshman who's a tenant of the Mortimers were loyal to Wales, the King would have to go to Salop and Hereford and Gloucester for his men. Suppose this person *is* a spy, what matter? Any chance, however remote, of the archers of an army turning their bows on their own leaders ought to be snatched at! That the fellow suggests such a thing at all shows that there is, among *all* Welshmen, a feeling spreading fast. It's a matter of, a matter of—" The lad wanted to say it was a matter of mental seduction as against physical violence, but nothing save legal Latin terms came into his head; and to crush the Conway warrior with Latinity could serve no purpose.

But Owen *had* given him a sympathetic and understanding glance and Rhys Gethin had moved off with a shrug of his shoulders; so perhaps there was, after all, a place in the Wales that was dawning for intelligences who studied Aristotle and the civilized codes of Rome.

It was a triumphant moment for Rhisiart as he contemplated the haughty back of the retreating Captain; but the cup of his pride overflowed when their trimly-accoutred cavalry leader stepped up to him and congratulated him in a low emphatic voice upon his wise words.

It was indeed crowded with events memorable in the young man's life, that afternoon in the village of Pilleth; and on subsequent occasions he would call up in his mind every detail of its happenings. There was only one house of any pretensions in the place, a semi-fortified mansion from which the owner had fled at their approach; and it was here that the Prince had established Mistress Lowri and her husband, while the grassy slopes before its gates, leading down to the banks of the river Lugg, lent themselves to the repose and refreshment of the rank-and-file.

It wasn't till nearly six o'clock, much later than their usual hour, that the patient Meredith, always with the same disenchanted look in his eyes and the same life-weary smile on his lips, announced to his father that the meal was ready.

Between the little manor-house where Lowri, the only high-born lady in their camp, was quartered and the softly-murmuring Lugg there stretched nearly a quarter of a mile of grassy sward; so that from the hearths of the village-hovels and from the kitchen of the mansion, it was easy to supply the whole body of men with better food than any bivouac fire had offered them since they left their northern fastness.

Meredith's picked band of old family retainers from Sycharth, reduced in numbers though they were by the expedition to Meifod, served, under the young chieftain's direction, as the ministrants of this open-air feast.

In the matter of drinks there occurred a little friction that evening between the young chief and Mistress Lowri; for she, as the only court-lady in their camp, showed a natural feminine desire to humour the men by serving out from the stores so carefully prepared by the Arglwyddes headier and less diluted beverages than the cautious young man considered safe.

Rhisiart and his friend Master Brut were therefore given the privilege, when the gentlemen finally sat down to their meal at rough wooden tables under the walled terrace of the house, of watching at close quarters a fierce struggle to win the Prince over to one or other of these respective points of view.

As Meredith's opinion prevailed, and the pouring out of the headier drink was forbidden, our friend received a double impression; *first* that the mother of Tegolin was in a most reckless and dangerous mood, and secondly that the Prince was so wrought-upon and excited that it was all he could do to treat the woman with his usual courtesy.

Everybody's nerves that warm June evening seemed growing more and more tense. The loveliness of the hour as the sun descended, and as the sweet fragrances from the waving grasses and the white elder-blossoms arose, increased rather than diminished this tension; and when at last, as if with some demonic intention of making trouble, a great white owl came flapping over their heads, it was necessary for Owen himself to leap to his feet and forbid, under threats of dire punishment, anyone to draw a bow at the intruder.

It almost seemed as if the ungracious bird, disturbed and distracted by the confused assembly, understood the meaning of this command, for no sooner had it flapped away in its heavy unwieldy motion down to banks of the Lugg than it saw fit to return, and sometimes to the left, sometimes to the right of the men, grouped in their crowded companies on that sloping greensward, it went flapping, hovering now and then within a few feet of their heads, and producing the disturbing impression that with the great moon-daisy blinking eyes in its fluffy head it was surveying them all, and searching among them all for some particular person.

And though the Prince's command was obeyed there were many sullen mutterings, and even—so Rhisiart fancied—some uncivil suggestions that the ghostly visitor had a rendezvous with Father Pascentius! That ubiquitous confessor had ostensibly followed the expedition on the grounds of professional duty; but it seemed to both Rhisiart and Master Brut, between whom he was now discreetly seated, that his real motive in coming was to watch at close quarters the gathering dramatic crisis between Rhys Gethin and Master Simon in their electric relations with Mistress Lowri.

The Lollard kept assuring his friend that the converted Hog of Chirk was too steeped in the pure doctrines of Master Wycliffe to betray his feelings in any violent outburst; but Rhisiart, as he followed the botanist's Phorkyad eyes and contemplated Master Simon's expression as the fiery Captain flirted with his lady, was by no means convinced. The lad himself was aware, before the long meal was over, of a new and quite personal misgiving. His mind began reverting so vividly to Catharine that, as he sat there whispering to the Lollard and watching the owl, he began to feel that at any moment the girl herself might appear.

For some while, undeterred by any fear of attracting Master Brut's attention, for the Lollard was not very observant when Master Wycliffe's name was on his lips, he had been watching the curve of a white dusty foot-track along the side of one of the nearest mountains. It was along this track that he had already imagined Catharine riding. He had imagined her mounted on Seisyll and followed by the Abbot of Caerleon.

But it was danger, not love, that worried him now in connection with that track. Yes, he was convinced that his preoccupation with this far-away path had something to do with an imminent peril—not a peril to the Prince and his men; for there was no fear of the Ludlow army coming on them from that quarter—but a peril to himself. It could hardly have been the effect of the sunset that was now displaying itself in the west; for the great luminary had rejected any transformation into what is usually called "a ball of red fire" and was disappearing from the world in its normal splendour; but, whatever its cause, that faraway track had begun to outline itself on the green hill-side in a manner so emphatic as to suggest that the path itself were a serpentine creature advancing with a fatal intention!

Quite rudely therefore—indeed for some reason Rhisiart was always being ungentlemanly in his behaviour to his friend—he turned from Master Brut and enquired of Father Pascentius whether that particular path were the way any ordinary traveller would naturally approach the village of Pilleth, coming from the north.

The pair of fabulous eyes moved at once whither they were directed. "There's a horse and a rider coming now down your path," he said, "but to save the beast's feet they're using the grass by the edge."

What madness leaps up in a lover's heart! No sooner had Rhisiart heard these words than he felt sure he saw Catharine mounted on Seisyll "using the grass by the edge"; but he beseeched the eyes again, and the eyes, by means of the heavy jowl that was their only mouthpiece, informed him that the rider was very young and was holding something very carefully as he rode.

Rhisiart couldn't restrain himself. "You're sure it's not a girl?"

The Father didn't smile; and the eyes only screwed themselves up tighter. It was just as if the infatuated young man had been consulting some Chinese invention rather than a living theologian.

"It's a boy!" came the announcement at last, "and he's on a horse—not on a pony."

"Do you think it's a message from Snowdon, Father?"

The theologian lifted one of his plump hands from his wine-cup and made his accustomed gesture of devastating nescience. The movement was slight; but as the man made it the sun went down, and a dark wave of dejection flowed over Rhisiart's heart.

"What," he thought, "if this great host from Ludlow led by such a man as Mortimer cuts us all to pieces? Or takes the Prince and me and Walter Brut prisoners? Where would we be, then? In the Tower of London we'd be; or with spikes through our heads on London Bridge!"

Though the sun was gone, the twilight of that Eve of Saint Alban seemed interminable. A natural restlessness kept the men awake beyond their accustomed hour; while at the same time Meredith's stern resolve to limit their drinking on a night so charged with fate deprived them of the distraction of their usual carousal.

A crippled harp-player whose age and infirmity had kept him in the house, when his patron, fearful of the advent of war, had fled, was persuaded to display his skill; but it seemed to Rhisiart as if the wistful jauntiness of the blackbirds, whose notes came from nowhere, and went floating down long avenues of feeling, drew the heart out of those inanimate strings.

And the owl continued to be an ominous trouble. It was all very well for the ribald troopers to jest about its seeking the monk. To

Rhisiart's mind it was behaving like a lost soul among a company of threatened ones, and it was an indescribable relief to him when Broch-o'-Meifod rose from his place with the evident intention of relieving them from this flapping demon. "How on earth will he do it?" the boy thought, as he watched the giant stroll down to the bank of the river, while the phantom light of that strange evening made the axe-blades about his waist gleam like the water-drops of his wife's mill-wheel.

A pale mist was now rising from the surface of the stream; and it wasn't long before the figure of the man grew indistinct among the reeds and willows; and indeed after a while, as they watched, it vanished completely.

But the owl seemed disturbed. Rhisiart noticed he was flying higher and in wider circles. It was no longer possible to see that queer-shaped head, like the head of a minute air-whale, butting with its soft feathery weight against the air-waves.

Suddenly from the river-mists there came a low prolonged owl-cry, a sound so startling after the silent flappings of their visitor that the spell-bound warriors stared at each other and some of them rose to their feet.

Again came this unearthly sound, and after its third repetition, lo! the great bird above their heads wheeled round with evident intention, and in an impetuous flight quite at variance with its former movements flung itself down the slope and was lost in the mist. Once more, but from higher up the valley and with a perceptibly different accent, came the cry; but that was the end. None of the little army saw the bird again; and when the giant returned from the river-bank even Mistress Lowri, who had been shivering a little, and wrapping her cloak round her, and falling into fits of silence, looked at the man with an added respect, much as the sun-witch must have looked at Odysseus, when he returned from conversing with "the weary heads of the dead."

Broch-o'-Meifod's return and their feathery persecutor's departure broke up that troubled session; and each man began making what preparations seemed proper in his own eyes, either to sleep or to await the dawn in the best comfort of soul he could muster.

Rhisiart was following the others into the house, the lower portion of which had been reserved for the Prince and his advisers; Mistress Lowri and Master Simon had already retired into their upper chamber, while the crippled harper had been led back to his hearth, when Madoc came up to inform Owen that a rider with no password had been detained for hours by a group of his sentries.

The Prince at once despatched Rhisiart to discover what had happened and why Madoc seemed so furtive and taciturn about it. "They tell me," the Prince said to Rhys Gethin when Rhisiart was gone, "that your spy was a native of this place. So he may simply have been a deserter finding his way home! In which case it's possible that we *may* benefit by releasing him."

"I've never heard of any benefit, my Prince, coming from a serf of the Mortimers. All the men around here are cowardly time-servers. To get a stout and loyal Welshman you have to go to—"

"To Cwm Llanerch I've no doubt," interjected Owen; and he grasped his cantankerous follower's hand.

Rhisiart hadn't far to go, but he made that short way shorter by his eagerness; and he was rewarded by arriving at the very nick of time. He soon discovered that Owen's army was distinctly better adapted to rapid marching than to professional precautions when the march was over.

"Blessed Virgin!" cried the young lawyer in his heart, "if *this* is the way we prepare for the night before the battle there'll not be a castle in the country without the Royal Standard; and as for our heads—" and he experienced an uncomfortable sensation in the nape of his neck. He now found himself explaining with some warmth to a drunken group of Cadair Idris spearmen that he had authority from the Prince to see this boy and this horse, neither of whom had given the password. His position was less secure than it might have been, since he himself hadn't the remotest notion what the password was. It had been "Carrog" at their last bivouac; but Rhys Gethin changed it every night, and Rhisiart had been absent-minded when this had been done on their arrival at Pilleth.

There was a toll-gate and a high-walled enclosure where these unprofessional sentries were gambling with their half-groats; and it was peculiarly teasing to the anxious mind of an impatient scholar to hear the gross cry:

"Who'll *cover* her? Who'll *uncover* her?" repeated with monotonous iteration.

He gathered that both the boy and the horse must have been thrust into this enclosure; and all he demanded now was permission to enter and talk with them. "This ill-tongued young man has run away without the password and Crach Ffinnant says he must be tied up till morning. Tame enough I reckon 'a'll be if 'a be alive then. *Who'll cover her? Who'll uncover her?*"

Rhisiart lost his temper completely. "If you don't open that gate *this moment* I'll get the Prince to hang you in a row on Pilleth church-tower with your whoreson groats between your damned teeth!"

Rhisiart's own teeth gleamed so fierce in the twilight and his hooked nose looked so menacing that one of his hearers was reminded of how John Charlton of Castell Goch had that identical expression when he hanged fifty robbers on five oak-trees.

"Very well, Master, I'll let'ee see 'un. But remember 'tis Crach's done it if ill-tongued young man be past talking wi'."

"Where *is* that cowardly scum?"

"Drunk-asleep in pound, Master. 'A watched till ill-tongued young man ceased hollerin' and then he lay down snug and easy."

The fellow got up, took an iron key from a hook on the wall and opened the gate of the enclosure.

The first thing Rhisiart saw was his old piebald Griffin, who at once manifested vigorous signs of both recognition and indignation. But he hadn't time even to approach his old friend; for there, suspended in such an abominable manner that he would certainly have been dead before next morning, was his young acquaintance Rawlff.

With the aid of the now sobered gambler Rhisiart unloosed the boy's bonds and lifted him to the ground.

"Get some water, for Our Lady's sake," he commanded, "and some *eau de vie,* if any of you have a drop."

Whatever it may have been that the fellow produced, it had the desired effect. The boy opened his eyes, stretched his limbs with infinite relief, and smiled gratefully when his gaze met that of Rhisiart. Unluckily as his eyes wandered they lit on the hunched-up form of the Scab, who was lost to the world in a drunken coma. The mere sight of the disfigured prophet reminded the poor lad in a sickening spasm of what he'd endured at his hands and with a convulsion of his whole frame his consciousness was once more blackened out.

Rhisiart told his subdued companion to pour more of his liquour down the boy's throat and going up to the unconscious Scab kicked him furiously and repeatedly. This treatment having but small effect, he seized the prophet unceremoniously by the heels, dragged him to the gate and deposited him on a dung-heap outside.

On returning he found the boy's eyes open again.

"How could you people let that brute do such a thing to a servant of the Prince?" he whispered angrily, as they watched the lad's recovery.

The man looked extremely uncomfortable. "Don't'ee ask, Master, don't'ee ask! If us don't do what 'a tells us, he puts the curse of Derfel on's. Our cattle die, our girls have bastards, our crops fail! 'Tis when he's drunk he does things like this. 'Tis the spirit of Derfel taking him, I reckon."

"Well," said Rhisiart, "I'll do what I can for *you* anyway with the Prince. But I shall tell him the whole story."

The fellow pulled him aside by the arm. "If I were you, Master," he whispered, "I wouldn't say naught to Owen ab Griffith *till tomorrow night*. There be too many of we from old 'Cadair'; and Derfel's a mighty one for putting strength in our arms against the English."

Rhisiart gave him a long searching look. "What's your name?" he enquired. "You seem to have more sense than some."

"Ifan ap David, at your service, Master. Do'ee think, Master, us'll be all dead men by to-morrow night?"

"*You'll* be a dead man if you have anything more to do with that brute out there! Say your prayers, Ifan ap David; say your prayers to the Mother of God, and your women and your cattle need fear no Derfel, nor Devil either!"

Ifan crossed himself. "I've a-said that very thing many a time, Master; but 'tis hard to go contrary to them conjurers. There's a conjurer now up our way who do—"

But Rhisiart left him abruptly. Rawlff had risen to his feet and had managed to shuffle stiffly, though with several groans of pain, to the side of the old piebald.

"Master Rhisiart," the boy whispered. "Send that man away. I've got something for you."

Our friend signed to Ifan to leave them alone; and as soon as the fellow was gone the two youths faced each other, each leaning against Griffin's mottled back.

"Mistress Catharine sends you a letter," murmured Rawlff hurriedly; "and Mistress Tegolin sends you your sword." He paused, while our friend clutched eagerly at the familiar weapon laid along-side of Griffin's saddle; and then the boy added in the conspiring and significant tone of one whose life might have been spent carrying messages between high-born ladies and their lovers, "I've hid the letter inside the sheath."

Thus speaking he made a pathetic effort to unloose the withy-bands with which he had secured the sword to the saddle, but his fingers were so weak and his arms so bruised that he soon left this attempt to his excited companion.

Meanwhile old Griffin kept turning his head, twitching his ears, expanding his nostrils, evidently puzzled by his recovered master's lack of attention.

Rhisiart responded mechanically to these overtures, but the expression in the old horse's eyes said with unmistakeable plainness, "I've come all this way. I've brought you your sword. But you'll never be the same to me till that girl is gone."

But Rhisiart was hard at work pulling the blade from its sheath. Yes! there *was* a strip of the thinnest parchment he'd ever seen wrapped round the steel! It was no easy job to get the blade out, with that letter twisted round it, and once or twice he mentally cursed Rawlff's romantic device.

The parchment was torn clean across when he did separate it from the steel; but there it was! He held in his hand—the first love-letter he had ever received! Hurriedly, hardly glancing at it, he concealed it in the inside pocket of his tunic; but before sheathing the blade he couldn't resist brandishing it in the air and making slashes with it over Griffin's back at an imaginary Mortimer.

He insisted, however, on the boy's getting up on the horse again; and as he helped him to mount he enquired for whom he had picked the two huge bundles of bluebells that dangled head-downwards from the saddle, their stalks death-white and oozing with vegetable sap, just as when he'd first pulled them up in some shady recess of mountain hazels.

Rawlff smiled a grown-up courtier's smile. This was the question to which he had been longing to reply, even since he'd picked those purple-headed blooms. "I brought them for Lowri ferch Ffraid," he whispered proudly. "Mistress Tegolin said her mother would be pleased if I picked something for her on the way."

Rhisiart stared at the boy in astonishment. Had that devilish enchantress begun to play her games with *this* lad, no sooner than she'd finished with himself?

He felt certain the boy was lying when he said that Tegolin had told him to pick flowers for her mother. Tegolin knew the woman too well to throw any youth in her way. Bluebells for Lowri on the Eve of Saint Alban! Would she strew them on Master Simon's pillow or hang them from Rhys Gethin's helmet?

With Rawlff on the piebald's back and himself at his head they emerged from the Pilleth pound. "Cover her! Uncover her! Uncover her! Cover her!" And by some providential interposition the young rider became at once so fascinated by the gambling that this crazy repetition distracted him from a sound and a sight that Rhisiart, tugging at Griffin's bridle, prayed to the Virgin he wouldn't notice.

The gamblers had lit a torch; and this torch, creating little islands of glowings and flickerings in the falling night, made an outlying island of the dung-heap. Here, squatting on his haunches and relieving his bladder so shamelessly that he resembled the image of a beast-god in prehistoric art, sat the unholy Scab; and as he sat he swayed, and as he swayed he uttered sounds, and by degrees these sounds became articulate words. "Cover her! Uncover her! Uncover her! Cover her!" cried the gamblers.

Seeing Rawlff's intense desire to watch the game Rhisiart gave up his tugs at Griffin's bridle and lent an ear to the Scab's obscure chantings. He was past being shocked by the fellow. He had come to regard him as quite as sub-human as Derfel's phantom Horse neighing for virginities; but he was outraged all the same by the burden of this prophetic howl uttered just as the night was falling that could so easily be their last on earth.

To what particular demon the Bard was referring under the name Gwyn ap Nudd our friend had no idea; but the images called up by this oracle from the dung-heap disturbed him not a little. Everybody

—even the Prince—had a half-belief in the Scab's prophetic power.

"Cover her! Uncover her! Uncover her! Cover her!" cried the gamblers; but when at last he did drag Griffin away, it wasn't *that* refrain, it was what the Scab was chanting that rattled about his ears like a rattle of bones.

Who can strew whiteness in summer while rivers run red?
Can Gwyn ap Nudd counting his fishes and furling his sails?
No! They're for Derfel, for Derfel, these dainty dead;
Stripped of their armour, like mackerel stripped of their scales!

Long before silence had fallen upon that little army Rhisiart had learnt his letter from Catharine by heart. It was a very short letter and its spelling was infantile. It was written entirely in capitals. The word "love" was spelt "luf," and the words "never forget thee" were spelt "nef vorgat the."

The girl had evidently experienced especial difficulty with her own name; for the end of the parchment was covered with erased attempts at "Catharine ferch Owen"; and at the very last she had contented herself with "Cat-Rin" followed by the syllables "thy luf."

In the shock of his unexpected reception by the tipsy sentries Rawlff had forgotten his grand excuse for his daring ride, which was nothing less than a letter to Rhisiart from his mother in Hereford.

This letter the astute young lawyer held in his hand when he presented his messenger to the Prince; and he scrupled not to break its seal before them all.

It ran as follows:

By the mercy of God and the departure for Wales of a servant of the esteemed John of Mawddwy, a loyal gentleman of the Marches, I write to send you my blessing, my unhappy son. May Our Lady and all the Saints keep you in health and bring you to a right state of mind, and a speedy return to your allegiance to our gracious and merciful Lord, King Henry. I do you to wit, dear son, that by the blessed intervention of Our Lady I have recently taken to myself a second lord and husband, namely, the good Knight, Sir James Montfoison, a gentleman of French descent but as highly esteemed

in our City as in his native Provence. It is as much a grief to my dear
husband as to myself that nothing but our gracious King's pardon
for your unhappy errors will enable us to see your face again; but may
Almighty God and Saint Ann, my revered Patroness, keep you in
their merciful protection. Written at Hereford on this fifteenth day
of the month of May at the command of Laura, Lady Montfoison, by
Walter Hogpen, Clerk in Holy Orders.

Our friend, in his cunning craftiness, allowed it to appear that his
mother's marriage was a grievous shock to him. As a matter of fact
it was an immense relief; for more than once his conscience had
pricked him for leaving so lively and amorous a lady with no natural
defender.

It was only to Master Brut that he read the whole of this document,
but he hesitated not to give the Prince an eloquent summary of its
contents, and he nourished the hope that the pensive abstraction produced by Catharine's capital letters was put down to the clerkly penmanship of Father Hogpen.

Long after everybody else was asleep, at least trying to sleep, the
Prince and his advisors were discussing their plans for the morrow.
Bands of Henry Don's horsemen kept arriving with fresh news as the
night wore on; but all their news pointed in the same direction, namely
that the army from Ludlow was steadily pursuing the main highway
across the Mortimer country, and using no cavalry to try out the
preparations to meet them.

The impetuous Rhys Gethin was all for moving their force as rapidly
as possible towards the enemy, trusting that pure luck, when they were
near their foe, would provide them with some suitable ambuscade in
the overhanging woods from which to make their attack.

Broch-o'-Meifod, however, to Rhisiart's great relief, insisted upon a
strategy of a more concerted and calculated kind. The giant suggested
that their wisest course would be to draw up their men on the summit
of a long, slow-mounting hill to the west of Pilleth, a hill that bore
the local name of Bryn Glas, and then, by a skilful use of their Kidwelly
horsemen, to lure the Mortimer host to attempt the ascent of this
eminence; thus making the encounter between them, while nothing

was left to chance, an encounter between *men above* and *men below*.

"But surely, Broch," said Owen, who generally remained silent while these discussions went on, "surely Sir Edmund can't be such an absolute fool as to keep that great mass of heavy-armed men close together, following a track surrounded by hills? He must have *some* scouts abroad to keep their way clear!"

Henry Don broke in at this, somewhat piqued at his friend's distrust of his horsemen's news. "It's an army led by knights in armour; my Prince, I tell you! Heavy horses—heavy men. My people have watched them. They're riding so fast that their Welsh archers are running to keep up with them! It's a surprise attack. They hope to draw us down to meet them on their own level. They've no idea we have a cavalry arm in *our* force."

Broch-o'-Meifod wagged his great head. "There's never been an army led into Wales, Owen ap Griffith, since the days of Harold the Saxon, that wasn't too heavily armed. Harold chased us up the peaks of Snowdon with riders as fast as our own. But it's never been done since the Normans came. That's why the first Edward built castles. They trust in the thickness of their walls, these English, not in the nimbleness of their feet."

"What in the devil's name," cried Rhys Gethin, "are you fellows talking about? First you say they'll keep to the level, and then you say they'll begin climbing a great whoreson hill like Bryn Glas! Why should they climb it? What on earth would persuade them to climb it? How will they know we're waiting for them on the top? And if they *do* find out—by the beard of Dewi Sant, my good men, you're confusing Sir Edmund with his nephew, the baby Earl!"

"But doesn't the main highway go up Bryn Glas?" interposed Owen. "I took *that* for granted from the beginning. Is there any other track round here that heavily-armed knights *could* follow?"

Henry Don assured the Prince at once that the highway *did* ascend Bryn Glas and that unless the enemy had already taken a different route they had no alternative to climbing this hill.

"Well, gentlemen," said Owen, "what about dividing our men into three companies? Let one of them remain concealed at the top of the hill, let the two others wait in the woods to the left and the right; and wouldn't it be a good idea, Don, if your horsemen hid themselves in that thick fir-copse that we saw just now, on the other side of the Lugg, at the foot of Bryn Glas?"

"Does the Lugg cross the track they're following, Master Don?" threw in Meredith.

The cavalry leader looked blank. "God knows where the Lugg runs!" he groaned. "I know we had to follow its damned course for several miles before I'd trust a single rider among its rocks and pools!"

"If the highway crosses it," Rhisiart was moved to interject, "there must be a ford."

"Wise lad!" said Owen, while they all smiled. "But the point is, and it's the same whether Mortimer has to cross the Lugg or not, does that great fir-wood I saw down there border upon the track where it begins to ascend the hill?"

"It does! It does, my Prince!" cried the Lollard eagerly, "for Master Simon and I went for a little stroll at the foot of Bryn Glas after supper."

"To explore the country, Master Brut," threw in Father Pascentius, "or to refute Saint Thomas?"

"Yes, we'd all like to know," quoth Rhys Gethin, "what makes the Hog of Chirk swallow your God-damned heresies as if they were his native swill! I'm not as much for my beads as I should be," and the warrior crossed himself, "but if I don't confess myself to the Father *to-night* may the curse of Pelagius stick in my gullet!"

"Gentlemen! Gentlemen!" protested the Prince. "Master Brut has come all the way from his estate in England to fight for his country."

"A lot of fighting *he'll* do!" growled Rhys Gethin. "Why I know on good authority that his curst Lollardry won't let him carry arms. He said himself to Master Simon—"

"May I ask," interrupted Rhisiart, *"who* is your 'good authority,' Captain?"

There was a general laugh at this; and the enamoured warrior flushed angrily but held his peace.

"Well! it's decided then," concluded Owen. "We'll bestir ourselves before dawn, feed our men and our horses, and hear Mass. Then a third of us to the top of Bryn Glas with me! Another third to the left under you, Captain, and another under Meredith to the right. You, Don, will conceal your horsemen in that wood down there—letting the Lugg

run where it will—and whatever happens, and whatever accidents occur, don't let a man stir till I make the signal. I'll rush them down the
hill, Rhys and Meredith'll burst in on their flanks, Don'll cut off
their retreat at the bottom, and 'Saint Derfel for Wales' shall be our—
What's that you're muttering, Broch?"

"Nothing, nothing, Owen ap Griffith! Let those cry 'Derfel' who fear
Derfel. For myself I have no cry. But if I *had,* 'twould be some Gaer-
and-Gorsedd cry of the ancient people, the people of Mynydd-yr-
Gaer-yng-Nghorwen, and of the Gorsedd at Mathrafal, and of the
Dragon-Mound at Meifod."

Rhisiart watched the Prince's face with intense interest. "If I were
he," he thought, "I'd burst out at Broch for that. I'd cry, 'Damn your
ancient people! We're all Welshmen here to-night, fighting for a real,
living, modern Wales, a Wales with its own laws, its own clergy, its
own—'"

But fancying he detected on Owen's bearded lips that disconcerting
smile—so like Meredith's—he dismissed, for the time being, the thought
of the two Universities, and contented himself with suggesting in an
unassuming tone that "Saint David for Wales," or simply "Dewi
Sant!" would be a more suitable cry than "Derfel."

It was on the tip of his tongue to describe to them the lurid rhyme
of that ghoulish creature on the dung-heap; but he restrained himself.

Rhys Gethin, however, suppressed his whole suggestion in a moment.
"The men'll cry 'Derfel' to-morrow," he announced bluntly, "whatever
we decide for them!"

Owen called for a midnight "stirrup-cup" at this point, and gathering
round the great bowl in a less controversial temper they all began discussing the personal arms they would use. A vague notion that had
been hovering in our young friend's mind of charging down the slope
of Bryn Glas upon Griffin's back was soon dispelled by the Prince's
declaration that he himself would fight on foot with no weapon but
his two-edged sword. Rhisiart at once resolved to content himself with
his own antique weapon, now securely buckled round his waist, and
to offer his precious dagger to his friend, the Lollard.

"Why do you use nothing but those axes?" he permitted himself, in
the glow of this more intimate moment, to enquire of Broch-o'-Meifod.

" 'Tis a long story, child," replied the giant kindly. "But the gist of it is, I've practised with my axes so long—I *throw* them you know—that I never leave an enemy hurt or wounded."

"How *do* you leave them?"

"I leave them *dead;* but so quickly dead that they feel nothing."

The Lollard, who had been listening to this with the gravest attention, broke in eagerly. "You've no scruple, then, about killing—only about causing pain?"

The giant nodded. "You've got it exactly, my friend! I am partial to death. I don't regard death as an evil. But I regard pain as a monstrous and unnecessary evil."

"But aren't pain and suffering the basis of our religion?"

"Not of mine," said Broch-o'-Meifod. "Death is the basis of *my* religion."

"But isn't death the ultimate outrage, the ultimate defeat?" murmured Owen in a low voice.

Father Pascentius forgot himself so far as to lift the great bowl to his lips in place of dipping his flagon into it. "If death hadn't been the worst," he spluttered, replacing the bowl on the table while his eyes devoured, face by face, everybody in sight, "the Son of God wouldn't have died."

"It *isn't* the worst; it's the best," said Broch-o'-Meifod. *"He took the best,"* he added after a pause, and with a very strange note in his voice.

A silence followed this. Owen thought of his secretly cherished faith in his power of *externalizing* his soul. Rhisiart told himself a story of his mother, on the arm of her French husband, crossing London Bridge on her way to see the Coronation of Henry the Fifth; and how she would shudder at the sight of "mouldering head with a pike through it, not knowing that it was the head of 'her little monk.'"

The Lollard thought of the Florentine ring he had given to Mistress Alice, so choicely worked, and of how much she could sell it for if he were killed to-morrow.

"The Devil fly away with you all!" cried Rhys Gethin, rising to his feet. "I'm off into the fresh air to get a good sound sleep. If I'm not at your Mass to-morrow, Father, it'll be because I've got further to go than the Prince or Meredith."

"Not a string loosed, remember," Owen called to him as he went out, "till you see us rush on them."

"Don't shoot over their heads, Meredith ab Owen, as I've seen you do before now!" and with this final jibe the warrior went out.

Henry Don of Kidwelly was the only leader among them who made no attempt to sleep that night. After seeing his horsemen safely ensconced for the night, their unconscious forms stretched on the fir-needles close to their tethered beasts, he himself, upon his favourite white mare who had a touch of Arabia in her blood, rode silently down the valley in the direction of the expected enemy. There was a pallid half-moon visible now and again; but the warm west wind, driving great lowering banks of clouds before it, kept obscuring this troubled voyager, and Don rode slowly, pondering in his mind many anxious thoughts.

He felt thoroughly uneasy as to the result of all these preparations. That last bitter word of Gethin's about the shooting of Meredith's archers especially teased his mind. He knew, too, a good deal more about the fighting capacity of these tourney-trained knights in armour than did any of Owen's advisers or of Owen's men.

He knew how extremely difficult it was to induce men on foot, even if fighting with all the advantage of higher ground, to approach these steel-clad gentlemen with their shields and their mighty lances. A chance arrow—rarely a carefully aimed one—*might* sometimes bring down a horse or a rider. But these trained war-steeds were as well-armoured as their masters, and in any sort of equal contest their mere weight, with the long spears and armorial shields of the men mounted upon them, was enough to put panic into the hearts of all but the steadiest bowmen.

If the archers stood firm, he knew what the long-bow could do. But how rarely they *did* stand firm, when armed knights charged them with levelled lances and tossing plumes! Pensively and slowly Henry Don rode down that leafy glade. The cool night-wind stirred the heron's feather on his steel cap and blew through his trim black beard.

He felt, for all his anxious thoughts, a delicious relief in escaping from that noisy council-table and the fumes of that midnight bowl. Indescribably refreshing were the wood-smells that the wind brought as it rustled through the fir-branches.

When for a moment the half-moon swept into view, obscure shadows, that were themselves like sad and formless thoughts, not unhappy thoughts but thoughts with long vistas of memory, appeared before him.

Save for the rustling of the branches and the slow foot-fall on the mossy path of his white steed there was not a sound between earth and heaven. The thought did enter that trim head under the heron's feather that it was a pity that all this deep natural peace should be invaded by armed men bent upon a murderous struggle, but Don of Kidwelly was a practical though a lonely and thoughtful man, and his mind soon swung back to the matter in hand.

"They don't know," he said to himself, "none of them know, what they're facing to-morrow. Owen must be fifty; and his air isn't the air of a dare-devil patriot or a ruthless statesman. That Hereford boy's a typical Oxford scholar. Old Broch's a crazy mystic. The monk's little better. Rhys Gethin's a brave soldier, but you"—and he watched his mare's white mane as it stirred in the wind—"have as much intelligence as he has! Not one word have I heard from Owen as to the sort of princedom, if the common people *do* rise and help him, he'll establish in Wales. Has he given a thought, have any of them given a thought, as to what'll happen after his death? Will his eldest son succeed him? Or will he fall back on our fatal Welsh custom and divide the princedom between Griffith and Meredith? It won't last a year if he *does,* hardly a—"

His meditations were broken by the sight of a figure in front of him, the solitary figure of a man on foot with a bow drawn and an arrow on the string. Automatically he reined in the white mare, and horse and rider became one, the motionless image of a man upon a horse.

"A fine night!" he said quietly. "I am Henry Don of Kidwelly. Are you for Wales or for England?"

The figure in front of him unstrung his bow, returned the arrow into its quiver, and advanced without fear. "I thought it was you, Master Don," he said when he reached him. "Don't you remember me?"

Yes, the rider did remember him! It was the spy from Mortimer's army that he'd released that very day.

"You'd better ride back faster than you came, Master," said the fellow calmly. "They're not more than a couple of miles behind me."

"In what order?"

"In close array, Master. The gentlemen in front, then the troopers; and my mates in the rear."

"It's a surprise attack, then?"

"They know Owen's in Pilleth. They know he's waiting for them; but they hope to catch the fox asleep."

"It'll be dawn before they get there. It must be past three already."

"Dawn, yes; but it won't be light," remarked the fellow.

"They won't budge from the highway, will they?"

"I believe not, Master. They don't know the country. They think the village is the other side of Bryn Glas."

"And that Owen and his people are asleep in the village?"

The man nodded.

"Well, I'll be getting back," said Henry Don.

The two men stared at each other as the half-moon appeared between the branches.

"If—I—*can*—persuade my mates," said the fellow cautiously, "I suppose we'd better not join you till—"

"You mean you won't play *them* false till you're sure *we*'re the winners?"

"Something like that," murmured the spy sullenly.

"Well, well," said the other in a friendly tone, "I'll see you're well rewarded, if you *do* bring them over. And I'll leave the moment to you."

"*Master Don!*"

"Well?"

"I'd like you to understand one thing before you go."

"Well?"

"If I bring them over, it won't be for you, or for Owen, or for any other fine gentleman; it'll be for the common folk of Wales!"

The man on the phantom-white mare gravely inclined his steel-capped head, listened intently for a second, as if he could hear the march of the enemy, and then, lightly swinging round, rode off at top speed in the direction of Pilleth.

The peasant with the long-bow turned also, but more slowly. "*Will* it do us any good?" he said to himself. "Philip Sparrow swore to me— but they all hold together, these whoreson gentry. Welsh, Norman, English—they're all alike!"

Meanwhile, riding rapidly up the narrow valley, came the army from Ludlow. Hereford men, most of them were, but some came from Salop, and some from the broad Radnor lands of the Mortimers. Sir Edmund himself, with Thomas Clanvow at his side, rode in front. Both were heavily-armed, both carried mighty lances, both were tall, personable men.

Clanvow, a good deal the elder of the two, was less weary and very much the more voluble. *His* head was bare, revealing to his companion every time the moon appeared a massive brow covered with thick curls, laughing, care-free eyes, and a strong soft neck, surrounded, above his mail surcote, by a rich collar of beaten gold.

The lean, anxious profile of the young Sir Edmund, with the short Mortimer upper lip drawn back a little from his clean-shaved mouth, kept turning in polite but troubled attention towards the cheerful countenance at his side.

"Well, at any rate," Clanvow was saying, "there were no horses wading in blood when *I* was born. *My* stars are all in good aspect for this encounter—and since we're brothers-in-arms for the adventure, what happens to me must happen to you! You take life too hard, Edmund. You're tired out now with all the worry you've made for yourself. Why weren't you content with our good shire-lads, without dragging all these damned Welsh tenants of yours into it? That speech you made to them this morning—staying awake half the night, I warrant, to compose it!—why, my sweet lad, not half of them understood what you were driving at! And why the devil did you write all that stuff to Harry Hotspur? He knows as well as you what a stingy miser King Harry is!

"You *think* too much, Edmund, that's what's the matter with you; and your thoughts run too far ahead. I suppose you're fancying a time'll come when the Percies will turn against the King and put your little nephew on the throne. 'Hotspur the King-maker,' and all that sort of thing!

"I tell you, my dear lad, here and now, you'd better put that stuff out of your head! Two to one that precious letter of yours is in the King's hands already. Take things as they come, lad, that's the trick. Our affair now is to get hold of Glendourdy and pack him off in chains to London. Put out of your mind all these silly thoughts of getting a ransom for him. He's an outlaw, and must be treated as such. Who's going to ransom him I should like to know? King Richard's friends, the Franciscans? His estates are gone already, or soon will be. The fellow's a mere bandit, I tell you, from the caves of Snowdon! The King's mad to have let Grey buy himself off to such a tune. That's why Glendourdy's got such a rabble with him. When Grey's money's gone, *they'll* be gone. They're only a mob of Welsh thieves. There's not a gentleman among them.

"You say you're in want of money, and a good ransom for Glendourdy would pay your debts. But who was it I heard the other night telling Devereux that he oughtn't to evict his tenants? *That's* where your money's gone! What's the good of being a Mortimer if you can't collect your dues?"

While the lively poet was thus combining his enjoyment of the night's adventure with a little practical advice, a few paces behind them, the three robust knights, Robert Whitney, Kinard de la Bere, and Walter Devereux, were exchanging vehement hopes that their evasive enemy would show himself and give battle.

"The great thing," said de la Bere, "is to draw Glendourdy down from his hills. If we only once get him on level ground he won't have a chance. You should have seen the Shropshire levies under Hugh Burnell rush him into Vyrnwy two years ago. You should have seen John Charlton of the Red Castle hustle him when he came near Welshpool! The man's never once met any decent English troops without having to run like a hare. What worries me," and the lusty old knight disturbed the roosting-place of a flock of small birds by the brandishings of his long lance, "is that we're about as likely to get a sight of him this day as we are to get a sight of the gold that they say pilgrims have piled before the miraculous picture of Our Lady of Pilleth."

"How will you fight," enquired the portly Robert Whitney, "on horseback as we are, or on foot?"

"A good question, Master Whitney, a good question," threw in Walter Devereux. "I'll soon tell you how we'll fight. First call our people to us—each of us his own—and then wait their attack. Not too near each other though. Let 'em break themselves on us, like whoreson waves on goodly rocks. Keep to your saddles for Mary's sake, and run the whoreson knaves through with your lances! If your lance sticks and you've no one to pluck it from the varlet's ribs, let it go, and have at them with your sword!"

As he spoke, Devereux removed his helmet, and hanging it on his saddle-bow glared at his friends as if *they* were the enemy. He had the most grotesque features, this pure-blooded Norman. Nature had given him an enormous hooked nose, thin indrawn lips hidden by a straggly black moustache, and a pointed chin as sharp as a witch-wife's.

Old de la Bere just shrugged his powerful shoulders, and smiled in the man's face; but Whitney looked uneasily round as if to make sure that his retainers were within call.

Whitney was a new-comer among the magnates of the border. From the distaff side he did indeed boast a few drops of old Saxon blood, but his closed and clamped face, his crafty little eyes, his ponderous frame, all of them smacked rather of the justice's bench than of the battle-field. He had indeed been a mighty one for "adding field to field and house to house"; nor would he have joined this expedition at all had it not been that he was certain in his own mind that the Welshmen would vanish into their caves and that the King would reward so devoted a servant with many forfeited estates. The words "law and order" were the words most frequently upon the lips of Robert Whitney, and he had already managed to get it to the King's ears that he cordially approved of the policy of retaining all ransoms, especially of Scotch prisoners, in the royal hands; and that his tenants were always at the royal disposal if the Percies proved restive under this business-like treatment.

All this lively chit-chat by the way insensibly lessened the speed with which Mortimer's force progressed; and by the time they reached the place where the horsemen from South Wales were hidden there began to be recognized, at least by the leader himself and his poet-friend, certain faint but unmistakeable indications that dawn was at hand.

It was at this moment that one of Henry Don's younger followers, unable to sleep, and prepared to risk disobeying his Lord's command if he could only be the first to bring news of the enemy, caused a rustling in the fir-branches. He had seen what he wanted to see, and he got clear away; but the sound of his horse's hasty retreat reached the five knights simultaneously. The woods were thick around them. No better place for an ambush could have been found.

"Mortimer, a Mortimer!" cried their leader. "Clanvow for Clanvow!" cried the poet; and while the other two knights, for the judicious Whitney had no claim to a cry, echoed with "a Devereux for Saint Ouen!" and "a de la Bere for Saint Martin!" their retainers hurried forward in an excited pell-mell, and rallied in groups round their respective lords.

The main body of the shire-troopers followed more leisurely, while the Mortimer Welsh tenants, among whom was the friend of the revolutionary, Philip Sparrow, stood still to await events.

"Saint Mary! But *this* is foolishness if ever there was!" laughed Thomas Clanvow. "All right, John o'Dale, all right Peter Purvey— you can fall back again! Come on, Edmund lad. Tell 'em to fall back. We're a parcel of silly women. There's no ambush here. I've got a sixth sense for Welsh thieves. 'Twas a stag we disturbed. Those were a big animal's movements, not the feet of a horde of bare-foot scrubs! It was a stag, I tell you, or maybe a forest-pony."

So saying the curly-haired poet broke into a bawdy ditty, waved back his retainers with the steel helmet he'd been on the point of placing on his head, and proceeded to spur on his horse so fast that Mortimer had to gallop to keep pace with him.

The three other gentlemen glanced at one another with a smile and followed their example, while the heavily-accoutred men-at-arms who formed the main body of their force cursed freely as they quickened their march to a jog-trot.

The five knights, if the business-like Master Whitney could be called a knight, did, however, have the wit, if not the grace, to pause to breathe their horses, and to allow their followers to rest, when they reached the foot of Bryn Glas. The grey light in the east had now spread over the whole sky; and as they all rested there, many of the troopers easing themselves by removing the heavier pieces of their armour and some of them even sinking down upon the grass, there seemed to take possession of them all an unspoken desire to postpone ascending the hill till the dawn really began.

Clanvow was still restless; but Mortimer, as he watched the relief

with which the troopers took advantage of this pause, became obdurate
to his friend's impatience.

"I know, I know," he replied, when the poet urged the importance
of their attack being a surprise. "But men with no breath in their bodies
can't surprise anybody."

And as they all rested there it seemed as if the miracle of the dawn
drew their general consciousness towards itself, so that their life-sense
ceased to be an individual thing and became a common thing, a
multiple entity, that had grown spell-bound by what was happening in
the firmament.

Irregular blood-red streaks appeared now in the eastern quarter. One
second and there were none of these; another second and there they
were! And with the coming of these blood-red streaks the air that cooled
their faces suddenly lost a certain damp chill that characterized it
before; and though it didn't grow warm it carried with it a perceptible
quality of *livingness,* as if those red streaks in the sky, wild and sad
as they were, like a reflection from battle-fields of long-ago, brought
with them something familiar, something steeped in old earth-mem-
ories, that drove back the mortal death-chill of the empty night.

By degrees, as they watched, they perceived that these dark-red
streaks had changed their character. They didn't see them in the
process of changing, for it is forbidden to the human eye to catch the
actual movement of celestial presences, but where they'd been contemplating dark blood-streaks they were now contemplating rose-
coloured clouds! Nor was it long as they watched—and even the five
horses seemed to be expanding their nostrils towards the east—before
that rose-tinge had spread over the whole sky till it reached the zenith,
while in the quarter where the blood-streaks had first appeared it was
as if some vast magic gates had opened, leading into an infinity of
glorified distance, into a receding perspective of golden space.

It was still some while before the moment came for the orb of the
sun itself to appear when Mortimer gave the signal to advance. He
gave it as soon as he perceived that his Welsh bowmen, tenants of the
Mortimer lands in Wales, had begun to wind their way into the open
out of the gloomy umbrageousness of the fir-woods. These men, he
assumed, being more lightly armed and inured to these mountainous
tracks, would need no rest before ascending the long slope before them;

but when, half-way up the ascent of Bryn Glas, he turned to look back at his devoted array he was surprised, though not particularly disturbed, to note that the Welshmen *were* resting at the foot of the hill.

Anxious to keep his own and his friends' horses as fresh as possible for their assault upon the village, Mortimer continued to restrain the impatience of his poetical friend. All five gentlemen were now riding together; and they advanced so slowly that there was plenty of time for conversation.

"It's all the fault of Reginald Grey," announced Devereux, "that Glendourdy has made this stir. His own relatives are against him. All the most civilized of the Welsh aristocracy are against him. What the thing really is, is a peasants' revolt. It wants putting down with a firm hand, that's all! These bards are the worst. They're all for the common herd. What the King should do is to stamp out this curst gibberish they call their *language*. Language forsooth! Chatter of kites and crows it sounds to *me*. I can't stomach the whoreson tongue."

"That's what I say," acquiesced Robert Whitney sententiously. "There'll never be real law and order in these mountains till all the bards are hung and all the peasants forbidden to leave the estates they cultivate. Welsh gentlemen are like other gentlemen. I know many of them and they're ashamed to be heard talking this lingo of the common herd. Hang every bard in Wales *I* say."

"Sir Edmund don't agree with you," threw in Kinard de la Bere. "*He's* lived too long with these bare-foot savages. He's come to love 'em, as a man comes to love his hounds. No, no, Mortimer, you needn't try to deny it. But I tell'ee this, my boy; if your plottings with your precious brother-in-law—now don't look so sour for everyone on the border knows it—*did* put your nephew on the throne, you and your friend Hotspur would have to do exactly what old Hal and young Hal are doing now: burn these savages' huts till they know their masters! What do *you* say, Clanvow?"

"*I* say," replied the poet, "that a gentleman who treats his tenants *like* a gentleman and isn't ashamed to be on easy terms with a good simple man because he's a Welsh herdsman or a Welsh ploughman—"

Devereux interrupted him with a burst of rude laughter. "We know *you*, Master Clanvow! What about that 'good simple man' you caused to be flogged to death?" Here the outraged realism of this grotesque-looking aristocrat, more contemptuous of the poet's literary gentility than he was of Whitney's business gentility, caused his pendulous nose to droop over his moustache, his left ear to twitch under his helmet, and the inhuman tip of a saurian tongue to appear for a second between his toothless gums.

When his laughing-fit was over he winked so comically at Kinard de la Bere that that worthy knight had to clap his gauntleted hand over his mouth. The truth was that it was well known in Radnorshire that Thomas Clanvow's wife, wearying, as women sometimes do, of her lusty braggart of a poet, had played the wanton with his taciturn Welsh groom.

To escape their ridicule, from which Mortimer, who was watching intently a certain hill-ridge where the infinity of gold was rapidly thickening into a floating island of dazzling metallic brightness, alone remained aloof, Clanvow, for the second time that morning, spurred his steed forward, a move that made it necessary for Mortimer to follow him.

Thus it was brought about that though not a man throughout that whole English army, now straggling up the long half-mile slope of Bryn Glas, had missed one stage in the sun's premonitory approachings, its actual appearance was unseen by a single soul.

With a resounding shout of "Owen for Wales!" Glyn Dŵr and his men bounded from their shelter in the green bracken and swept down upon their enemy. Had a pair of ravens that were hovering above the crowded slope of Bryn Glas felt impelled to turn their eyes from the blazing orb of the sun and contemplate this onslaught it might have seemed to them as if Owen's little band was simply swallowed up as it charged down into the very centre of the Ludlow army.

To the Prince himself, who was tall enough to see what was happening beyond the immediate mêlée, it seemed like an hour, though it was only three minutes, before Meredith's division, though they scampered like demons along the side of the slope, joined battle on the enemy's left, while it seemed two hours before Rhys Gethin's band had time to reach the scene on the enemy's right.

Owen and Rhisiart were swept forward so fast by the rush of their own momentum and the momentum of the men following them that it wasn't till they were in the thick of the heavy-armed shire-levies that their primary impetus was stayed.

Here, however, it was stayed with a vengeance, for they had outstripped all but a score of their most eager friends, and this little circle of devoted Welshmen found themselves surrounded and hemmed in by the pick of the stout yeomen from the fertile plains round the Castle of Ludlow.

With shout upon shout these powerful troopers drove in upon them, shortening their spears and furiously stabbing at them, as if they were a small pack of encircled wolves in the jaws of the wolf-hounds.

The figure of Owen was unmistakeable. "Have at him! Have at him!" Rhisiart heard them cry out on all sides. "'Tis Glendourdy himself!" The voice of a young freckled leader among them was especially audible. "A thousand silver groats," he shouted, "to the man who takes Glendourdy—alive or dead!" This freckled youth himself did nothing but obstinately, constantly, and steadily drive his spear at the Prince.

Rhisiart watched his movements like a hawk, and at one second their eyes met, and to the astonishment of our friend he found himself actually exchanging a smile with this unknown Ludlow boy, just as if they'd been playing ball, instead of a game of life and death!

At last the boy's foot slipped where someone's entrails had strewn the grass and Rhisiart was on him in a flash with the first death-stroke he'd ever given. Thrusting straight at the freckled face that had smiled at him, he drove his great sword into the lad's panting mouth, drove it with so much vigour that the point of it came out at the back of his enemy's skull.

It struck him afterwards that he must have been in a kind of blood-daze; for he could remember putting his foot on that dead lad's chest without a flicker of hesitation, and remorselessly dragging out his weapon, while the Prince's Roman sword flashed above his head.

"We can't win! We can't win!" something in him kept repeating; but when he saw how Owen had perpetually to swing round he began to do what he saw Master Sparrow doing for *his* master—that is to say, guard at all costs the Prince's back.

Nothing of what was happening outside their own miniature battle-field reached him. Grimly, desperately, he set himself to that one sole task; and the result justified him; for, spared the necessity of swinging round on his heel, Owen with his practised wrist soon made a clearance of the press of spears in front of him.

The curious thing was that our friend didn't think once of Catharine. His brain was stupefied. But several times he thought of Griffin; and in some obscure way he felt as if Owen's back were a piebald thing, but a thing he had to guard while breath was in him.

This business couldn't, Rhisiart thought, last much longer. As a matter of fact it lasted for about ten minutes, after which they heard re-assuring Welsh cries from the bowmen at the foot of the hill and felt a certain "give" in the spirit of their opponents. Yes, the enemy *below them* were being assailed from *their* rear by flight after flight of sting-ing arrow-shafts! Ten minutes can, however, be a long time when death is at your throat; and thinking it over afterwards our friend acknowledged that if Broch-o'-Meifod hadn't been with them both Owen and himself, along with Master Brut and Master Sparrow, would certainly have perished.

Owen fought like a madman with his two-edged sword and Rhisiart tried to imitate him with his relic of the Crusades, but there was such terrific pressure all round them and so many blows struck at them at once from so many directions that our friend, till he realized that Mortimer's bowmen had changed sides, hardened his heart to meet his end.

Master Brut, who apparently had only accepted Rhisiart's dagger out of courtesy, showed incredible agility as a pugilist, and by his quick movements managed for a while to dodge the most murderous spears. But for an unarmed man to be in the centre of that stabbing and cracking and smashing was what Homer calls *hyper-moron* or a wilful rushing beyond the circle of your natural fate.

In the end Broch-o'-Meifod saved the Lollard's life in a very primitive manner. He brought down his own fist on the man's head with such drastic effect that he lay at their feet as though stone-dead.

But it was Broch's skill with his axes that really saved them all; for though the Prince's Roman sword turned its deadly point and swung its double edge faster than the Hereford boy had ever seen a sword move, there came moments, even in that short time, when he only just escaped a murderous thrust.

Two of these thrusts Rhisiart, at no small risk, beat off himself; but there came a moment when his arm ached so much with the weight of his great sword that if he hadn't tripped over the still unconscious form of Master Brut one of these spears would have pierced his own throat.

It was Broch's axes that saved them. The giant went on flinging them as if he were an iron engine of death rather than a man and Rhisiart saw only one of them sink into the earth without its victim. But Broch couldn't have achieved this if the revolutionary Philip hadn't been standing back to back against him.

Nor was Master Sparrow's method of fighting much less singular than his master's; for he kept whirling round his head in each hand, and both his arms seemed to have the strength of an ordinary man's right arm, a gleaming pole-axe; and under the slashing blows of this unusual weapon the heads of many vicious spears and the bodies of more than one spearman lay on the ground before him. Though his boyish muscles were growing so numb under the weight of his sword that each time he struck he felt that he could never strike again, Rhisiart was still not quite oblivious of the general nature of the life-and-death struggle round him.

He felt its primitive race-quality. He felt its primitive beast-quality. He felt it was body against body, though with iron in place of claw. Yes, he felt rising from these straining *Welsh* bodies one single blind, frantic, desperate obsession; an obsession to tear, to rend, to over-master these massive, struggling *English* bodies that by their sheer weight and oppressive obstinacy were beating them down.

It must, however, be confessed that when he tripped and fell, Rhisiart did, in his complete exhaustion, take advantage of his collapse across his stunned friend to remain on the ground for a perceptible breathing-space.

While on the ground with his face against a tuft of white clover he found himself sucking these honey-weeds, and as he sucked his breath came in spluttered gasps, "Hail Mary! Hail Mary! Hail Mary!" but in his mind he said to himself, "We may win yet! We may win yet!"

Just then a heavy weight fell against him, knocking for an instant all the breath out of him, and when he scrambled to his feet he saw it was Owen himself with an arrow in his chest. Blood was coming out of the chieftain's mouth and trickling down both forks of his beard; and to Rhisiart's horror their eyes had hardly met when the man fainted away.

"That's a Welsh arrow," remarked Broch-o'-Meifod in the dazed and confused ears of the recovered Lollard.

"Is he dead? Have we won?" gasped Rhisiart.

"He's *not* dead, little Master," replied Philip Sparrow, "and we *have* won. Their Welsh archers turned against them, that's what decided it! It's the beginning of the end. *It's the people's victory!* The people's victory!"

Rhisiart saw now that Master Sparrow was correct in both his statements. Piteous groans, wild cries for mercy, yells of pain rose up from Bryn Glas, and occupied the gap in space and time filled twenty minutes ago by that proud army from Ludlow. He could hear, dying away into the woods below, the clatter and curses of Don's horsemen, cutting off the fugitives.

And Owen's eyes were open again and he could speak now. "It's— under—my—collar-bone," he murmured. "I'm all right. We'll leave it there till to-night. My shirt turned its point."

"It's a Welsh arrow," repeated Broch-o'-Meifod with foolish iteration.

But the Lollard, pale, shaky, and though entirely himself again, totally ignorant as to what he owed his life, was extricating a bleeding form from among the victims of Owen's sword and Broch's axes. It made Rhisiart's heart cold to recognize in this piteously gashed creature none other than his faithful messenger, Rawlff.

The dying boy knew him. "I—shall—never—be—a dubbed—knight— now," he whispered, as our friend bent over him.

Rhisiart glanced at Owen whose eyes were also on the boy. "Lend me your sword," said the Prince calmly. Rhisiart obeyed. "Help me to get to him," he added. It needed more strength than Rhisiart's, however, to carry out this last mandate; but they moved him by degrees, one of his own hands nervously clutching the shaft of the arrow whose head was buried in his chest.

"I, Owen ap Griffith, Prince of Wales, Knight of the most Royal Order of Richard of England, Second of that Name, do in the name of the Father and of the Son and of the Holy Ghost dub thee, Rawlff

ap Daffydd, Knight Companion of my new Order of Dewi Sant. . . .
Rise Sir Rawlff!"

What "rose" was a spurt of arterial blood from the mouth of the
new Knight; but Rhisiart never forgot the look of radiance on the
boy's face as, murmuring something about "telling Luned," his soul
left its body. It was through a blood-stained mist, for his eyes, his ears,
his nostrils, his fingers seemed all sticky with blood, that Rhisiart
helped Broch and the Lollard to carry their wounded chief across the
dead and the dying till they got him to the summit of Bryn Glas.

The lad had to give up his place at one point to Philip Sparrow,
whose own long legs were dripping with blood from disregarded
spear-thrusts. What set him vomiting was the sight of Lawnslot and
Gwalchmai—both born executioners—moving among the rank and
file of the dying to give them their *coup de grâce*.

He had re-taken his place, however, at Owen's head when they
passed a hillock, slippering with blood, on the top of which beside his
dead horse the incorrigible Devereux was still fighting for his life.

Sick of the sight of blood, and unwitting who this fantastic gentleman might be who refused to give up his sword, our friend lowered
his eyes; so that it was from the Lollard he learnt later how the astonishing knight, his pendulous nose and insolent mouth twisted in one
final defiance of everything in heaven and earth, laughed aloud, as
with his death-blow he came near to cleaving poor young Madoc's
head clean from his neck.

On arriving at their headquarters the little group was jubilantly informed, though the Prince's critical state soon quelled all tumultuous
congratulations, that Mortimer and Clanvow, who had been surrounded
and disarmed at the first rush, were prisoners of war.

For the remainder of that day Rhisiart stayed by Owen's side. Indeed it was with his famous Teledo dagger, sharper than any knife,
that some Pilleth "conjurer," aided by the sobered Bard of Ffinnant,
succeeded at last in extracting the arrow-head from the Prince's collar-
bone.

How the lad longed for darkness to descend, the revelry to die down,
and Owen to fall asleep! He made up his mind that before he himself
slept he would read Catharine's letter syllable by syllable; and with
each syllable he would say seven "Hail Marys" for the Knight Com-

panion of Dewi Sant. This vow he meticulously kept, but for all his exhaustion of mind and body sleep refused to come to him.

Weary of tossing from side to side, while he kept seeing the blood spurt out from Rawlff's mouth, and kept hearing the groans of the anonymous victims of Lawnslot and Gwalchmai, he decided at last to put on his clothes and go out into the night. Once in the air he felt calmer, and for a while happier, as he thought of Catharine receiving the news of her father's victory.

But the shapeless moon, throwing a phantom light upon the aerial landscape, drew him on against his will in the direction of the battle-field. It didn't take him long to reach the summit of Bryn Glas; but once there, looking down upon that field of slaughter, he felt as if he had been turned to stone. The realization of what he saw and of what it meant was beyond mortal belief.

Only twenty hours had passed since the battle began, but what had been done in that short time! The women of Pilleth—and he knew at once who had roused them to it, for there she was still, like a were-wolf bitch among the dead—had, all that long summer twilight, been stripping the English corpses—and not only stripping them. *"Can* such things be," thought the poor lad, "and the Mother of God above all?"

He had vomited at the proceedings of Lawnslot and Gwalchmai, but *this,* the work of women, was an outrage beyond all *physical* reaction. Fiercely, desperately, for what he saw before him made a crack in his deepest faith, he tried to think the thing away by calling up the injury done to Wales by English oppression.

But *this* was beyond all human retribution, all human revenge. This was a work of insanity, of obsession by Satan. And that creature—surely she couldn't be human!—*was at it still.*

White with a whiteness like the whiteness of leprosy those hapless bodies, bodies that twenty-four hours ago were living Englishmen, lay now, under that shapeless moon, transformed into lewd mockeries of flesh and blood. Or were these white obscenities not corpses at all, but fiends from Hell, called up out of the pit by this ghoulish half-moon, to make monstrous sport of the mysteries of procreation?

The moon's power was upon Rhisiart. Do what he could to turn away from these silent parodies of man's nakedness, he *couldn't* turn away! Had the corpse-loving moon injected a drop of her perverse frenzy into his own veins? Would he, Rhisiart ab Owen, be soon leaping down among those snow-white images of life's obscene origin, adding a new bestiality here, a new monstrosity there, dancing in and out of that woman's work, as if he were an initiate at a witches' Sabbath?

No! No! Things hadn't come to that. He *was* fascinated; but he was also outraged to the bottom of his soul! What troubled him as much as anything was the shamelessness of the distorted moon. Why didn't she hide her face? Instead of that she seemed pouring her light down with an hysterical exultation.

Rhisiart's own nerves were so affected by what he saw that he began to regard the ghastly sight not so much as the reprisals of Welsh women upon English men as the reprisals of *all* women, led by this labouring moon, upon *all* men; women in their mad perversity working obscene and monstrous blasphemy upon the very secrets of creation!

It was as if that declivity of Bryn Glas had suddenly upheaved in a devilish parody of the Last Day, and a host of lost souls, white with the leprous scurf of sin, were mutely offering to the oldest witch in Nature their unspeakable transformations!

There must have been as many as twenty or thirty women down there with Lowri; and their were-wolf madness, as far as our friend could see, was increasing rather than diminishing. The men must have carried away all the Welsh bodies from the battle-field during the day; and none had felt it his duty to bury their enemies.

"It's because Meredith's wounded as well as his father," our friend thought, "that this bitch has got such a free hand. Rhys Gethin's probably dead-drunk by this time, and Henry Don thinks it's none of his business. Owen ought never to have let that woman come down here, but women have too many rights in Wales; and that's certain."

It struck his mind as a curious thing that the Scab wasn't serving *his* demon among these helpless English; but no doubt he was drunk too; "Besides a man would have to be pretty bold," concluded our friend, "to go down there among those mad witches!"

He had no sooner decided that even *living* men, and Welshmen to boot, might hesitate to present themselves before Lowri and her Maenads in their present mood when he was aware of two men running towards him. They ran so fast that they were soon near enough

for him to distinguish their identities. The man in front was Master
Simon and the man behind was Master Brut.

Rhisiart turned to meet them. His first emotion was a curious one.
It was burning shame. He felt his face grow hot. Had a blush on a
swarthy cheek and by moonlight too been a recognizable sight Master
Simon would have wondered at him.

But the ex-Hog of Chirk was past wondering at anything. The good-
natured Lollard, who had offered to take the place of the luckless
young Madoc, whose decapitation at one stroke had caused his slayer
to die laughing, had been disturbed in his vigil at Owen's door by the
furtive appearance of Master Simon. The reformed Hog was stealing
down the stairs from his wife's apartment without his shoes and with
a stare in his eyes so wild, so guilty, and so dominated by the Devil
that Master Brut jumped up in dismay. The fellow's explanations were
obviously lies and when the Lollard saw his back as it left the building,
it presented itself to his Pauline eye as a back unmistakeably ridden
by Satan; in other words as the back of a man possessed.

Dragging therefore into the house an extremely sleepy and sulkily
puzzled trooper to take his place, the Lollard, who hadn't removed any
article of his ordinary attire, which certainly couldn't be called a
heavy battle-array, started in pursuit of Master Simon, who, quickly
aware that his conscience was after him, ran like a rabbit.

It was Rhisiart's presence that facilitated the poor wretch's capture;
and it was our friend's destiny to be present now at one of the most
remarkable scenes he would ever be allowed to witness.

"She's my own wife," panted the obsessed prisoner, staring with a
devouring intensity almost worthy of Father Pascentius at the Satanic
charade revealed to him by the gloating moon.

Our friend's legal mind found it hard to resist this plea. "I don't
see, Brut," he commenced, "how you can very well meddle—" His
words died away in his throat; for in addressing his friend he caught
a glimpse of his face with the moonlight full upon it. The power, it
appeared, which controlled that gibbous moon forced it to throw the
good into relief equally with the evil; and Rhisiart, for the first time in
his life, was terrified of Master Brut. An authority shone forth from
this Hereford gentleman's face that was the flame of the Spirit. He
must have seen what Lowri and her women were doing. He must

have seen what they had done. But it was clear that his mind was so
overpowered by the image of his suffering Man-God that the hysterical
antics of these females were no more to him than if, gazing at his
Redeemer, he had noted in the *dulce lignum* of His Cross the obscene
proceedings of a few necrophiliast wood-lice.

Rhisiart now beheld an unseemly struggle between the two men,
each of them powerfully built, each of them possessed by a force completely outside himself. Master Simon's face was convulsed with an
emotion so great that its individual features in that pallid light seemed
to merge into one another, seemed to become one single feature, a
quivering, twitching, licking, straining *tongue*.

Suddenly Rhisiart saw his hand slide into his tunic and come out
again with a glittering knife.

"*Take*—" the lad cried out sharply; but the heretic had seen his
danger, and his method of "taking care" was as effective as it was
startling. He brought down his fist with the weight of an iron hammer
upon the head of his recalcitrant disciple.

Simon fell with a thud and lay as still as the Lollard himself had
done under the fist of Broch-o'-Meifod.

"Let's get him to bed," remarked the Wycliffite quietly, "before he
comes to himself. But his devil's left him. Didn't you hear it whizz past
us?" And then a little later, "Have you noticed," he said, and this
quaint remark was uttered in a perfectly calm and practical manner,
while our friend helped him to convey his burden back to the house,
as if the great victory of Bryn Glas had been no more than a riot
in the street, "have you noticed how Our Lord never came face to
face with a woman possessed by a devil?"

This was too much for Rhisiart, and he laughed aloud. "Do you
mean," he began; but neither then nor later, though as may be supposed his malicious mind often reverted to the Ruthin girl, did he
dare to pursue *that* question with his friend.

His mind was feverishly active all the same. "I don't believe I'll ever
sleep again!" he thought as they re-entered the building.

In examining his crusader's sword he had noticed two or three minute dents in it, several inches from its point, and had remembered how
a freckled, innocent-looking English boy had closed his teeth on that
blade as he had driven it home, clean through the boy's gullet.

"I *must* think of the two blows I've seen to-day *different from that*," he said to himself, "the one when Broch saved Brut's life, and the other when Brut saved—"

But though he tried hard to sleep it was always with the freckles on that boy's face who had bitten his sword that Catharine's letter kept spelling itself out on the darkness.

XVI

THE FORESTS OF TYWYN

THE NEWS of the victory of Bryn Glas spread at incredible speed throughout Wales; and to Master Sparrow's revolutionary delight vast numbers of armed peasants, many of them travelling at their own charges, gathered to the Prince's standard from every quarter.

Before August of 1402, though both Glyndyfrdwy and Sycharth had long been blackened ruins, Owen had several separate armies, amounting in all to over ten thousand men, whose bivouac fires, moving as if by magic through all parts of Wales, caused desperate appeals to reach King Henry.

From Abergavenny and Usk, from Cardigan, from Caerleon, from Carmarthen, from Newport, from Cardiff, and even from Gwent, these cries for help came.

Owen's own hopes were as much increased as Master Sparrow's, and his purposes as much strengthened and hardened, by this accession to the cause of what was practically the whole mass of the common people of Wales. It *was* a peasants' revolt, as Robert Whitney had predicted it would be, and though no castle of any importance had yet fallen into their hands, the local peasants of Glamorgan and Gwent and even of Cardigan had avenged themselves with delicious joy for three centuries of contempt by pillaging and burning every single mansion where the landlord was an Englishman or a pro-English Welshman.

Outside the walls of the great castles, and outside the walls of the great commercial towns defended by castles, this general rising of the common people gave Owen the feeling that he really *was* Prince of Wales, and Prince of a Wales that hadn't been so united since the days of that other Owen who, as Owen Gwynedd, brought the whole country together against Henry the Second.

Analysing, as he did with everything that happened to him, all the causes that had led to the victory of Bryn Glas, he was only confirmed more strongly than ever in his monstrous fatalism. Totally out of proportion, it seemed to him, was the *effect* of this victory to the victory itself!

And such vast results following from so small an occasion gave him the feeling that there were forces on his side, obscure, unfathomable, tremendous, to which, if he only accepted the trivial and casual accidents by which they worked, he might resign himself with impunity.

Such a casual chance had now arisen again in the fact that Mortimer, whose nephew had a claim to Henry's crown, and who was Hotspur's brother-in-law, was a prisoner in his hands. What if he married *him* to Catharine? Such a move would have a double value, forging a link with the Percies, and giving him an intimate interest in the little Earl's claim to the throne.

To let such a chance pass would be a sacrilege against the high invisible Powers that were using him as a medium. And it wasn't as if he himself would escape suffering. The girl and Rhisiart would suffer cruelly enough, but *they* were young. They would console themselves. But he would never console himself! It may seem strange to some minds that a person like Owen, whose intelligence was so restless, and whose consciousness of everything that went on within him was so clear, should have allowed himself to come under the power of an obsession of this kind.

But it must be remembered that his habitual attitude to himself was of such detachment that it only needed an extension of this detachment, till it included all those connected with him, to create a temper essentially dangerous to human happiness.

It wasn't only Catharine and Rhisiart he was prepared to sacrifice. As the struggle went on, and one after another of his sons were slain, the Arglwyddes was shocked by the calm he displayed. This brave and simple-hearted woman never to the end of her days grasped the depths of abnormality that lay behind the courtly façade of her husband's nature. He alone knew what a transformation of his inner being had occurred that morning before his proclamation, when he destroyed his magic crystal!

He gave himself up *then,* trimmed and combed and anointed, into the hands of destiny; and his cherished faith in his power of exteriorizing his soul had only increased the appalling passivity with which upon the image of fate, as upon a dark on-rolling tidal wave, he let himself drift.

In that one supreme moment, when he prayed on his knees to be given the power to embrace the darkness, he had carried down with him, as in a doomed ship, every human creature he loved. Since that moment there had been a curious gulf between his feeling *about* what was happening and what actually *was* happening. His power, if it were a power, his fantasy, if it were a fantasy, in this matter of exteriorizing his soul, grew on him more than ever after the victory of Bryn Glas.

In what Rhisiart thought of as his "attacks," but which were more often, though not always, *premeditated escapes* of consciousness, he would sometimes fling his soul into what felt like a vast cool empty space, an ethereal twilight of being, altogether beyond the tumult of the world; but more often he would fling it into some quite definite exterior object—like that hollow tree into which he had cast the living body of his enemy!

In the pursuance of what in his obsession he regarded as an inescapable obedience to the event, instead of accompanying his now formidable armies in the movements directed by the strategic Abbot of Caerleon, the far-sighted Henry Don, and the impetuous Rhys Gethin, he arranged for the Arglwyddes and Catharine to travel down to where, meeting them with his prisoners of war, he made use of the generous hospitality of a remarkable character of those parts, a gentleman who, whenever he put his seal to a document, signed his name as "Rhys ap Griffith ap Llewelyn ab Ieuan," but who was commonly known in South Wales as Rhys the Black.

Rhys the Black possessed in his daughter Elliw a child who was remarkable for two things: her extravagantly long hair and her disconcerting intelligence. Her father—for her mother was dead—had got into the habit of shortening her rather unusual name into the monosyllable "Lu." Rhys Ddu's dwelling, which was six miles from Cardigan-town, was no very spacious or commodious a mansion, much less an embattled castle. It possessed, however, an air of romantic antiquity, carrying the mind back—at least it carried Rhisiart's mind back—beyond the age of castle-building, to that remote epoch when few, even among well-to-do gentlemen, possessed moats or battlements. The outer walls, it is true, of the Rhys homestead of Tywyn were composed of a species of rubble into the composition of which plenty of small stones had entered, but it was the time-blackened ancient wood-work, almost entirely of oak, that gave the place its air of immemorial antiquity.

Glyndyfrdwy was modern compared with Tywyn, and even the castellated portion of Owen's Snowdon-fortress could hardly have been more than three hundred years old. Nor had Glyndyfrdwy any advantage of Tywyn in its mound or "gorsedd." Tywyn possessed a mound—though it was in the centre of the Forests—second only in mythical importance to the famous one at Narberth, and associated, like the Narberth one, with the unlucky Pryderi, the much-enduring tutelary genius of the whole district.

And while something about the modest dimensions of the buildings at Tywyn enriched and mellowed their appeal to the imagination it was the unending expanse of woodland, the vast and ancient Forests of Tywyn, that most enchanted Rhisiart and Catharine.

They had hitherto only seen woods on hill-sides and in narrow valleys where the gloomy magnificence was broken by hills and gorges and by rocks and rivers; but the Forests of Tywyn, since they extended over comparatively level ground, seemed, and perhaps *were,* the primeval woods of Wales, from which aboriginal herdsmen had had to flee for safety to the hills.

Strange and prehistoric were the legends that lingered among the woodmen of Tywyn. Wild tales had been handed down from the remote ancestors of the dwellers here, tales that told of ancient wrongs suffered by the mythical powers of this land, where there still lingered remnants of some great, long-lost, peaceful civilization that had been destroyed by force and enchantment.

Rain and mist and the wild winds of autumn were, it was said, the retort of these primeval Forests of Tywyn to their aggressors, to the cruel "magicians" of the Age of Bronze.

Such invasions of the ancient twilight of the Great Mother were assisted in their violence by the red glare of the sun and by the white glimmer of the stars. The invaders cut down the forest-people along with their peaceful groves; until at last, so much did the Forests of

Tywyn come to dread the clear skies, that that great white glitter of infinite disillusion which the classic races called "the Milky Way" was regarded in this region as "Caer Gwydion," the un-numbered hosts of the supreme enemy of the defeated race!

It was in this strange "Deheubarth" that Owen's mother had lived. It was in this land he had first seen *the two twilights,* those grey mists that he, life-lover though he was, preferred to either sun or stars.

The population of these dark Ceredigion Forests retained so lively a fear of iron and steel that they habitually expressed this instinct in the spontaneous cry of "touch oak," or "touch wood," when something ominous was toward.

Rhisiart himself had never been in South Wales; and though Modry's tales had been full of its glamour and of its peaceful twilight illusions, all his own romantic cravings had been for waving plumes and embattled castles, for banners and horsemen and flashing steel! This was natural enough. All that was Welsh in him belonged to the North, all that was Norman in him belonged to the North; and though his feeling for Catharine seemed strong enough to bring warm sunshine into this twilight land, he was aware from the start of a certain vague spiritual un-ease such as he had never experienced on the banks of the swift-flowing Dee.

But at first they were very happy. They had no idea how far the Arglwyddes realized the feeling they had for each other. They assumed that Owen knew; and they soon began to divine, with the quick instinct of lovers, this new devastating direction along which his imagination was travelling. But if he had really decided, why was he still so loth to meddle with their love? Well! They could only hope for some chance —perhaps Mortimer himself would reluct at such a ransom!—that might yet intervene on their behalf. One thing was clear to Rhisiart. Both the Prince and the Arglwyddes understood their high-spirited daughter far too well to tease her with any ill-timed restrictions.

She and Rhisiart went on meeting as usual. Indeed their encounters were made easier and less marked than in the Snowdon fortress by the friendship that quickly sprang up between Catharine and Elliw. The two young girls would stroll together down one of the Tywyn forest-paths, followed at a discreet distance by Glew the Gryd and an equally

aged serving-man of the Rhys household; and then on Rhisiart's appearance they would separate, Glew the Gryd following the lovers
down any leafy alley their fancy chose, while the old Rhys retainer
would remain with Elliw and her great wolf-hound, Corbyn.

Inside the house it was less easy for them to snatch any moments
alone; for the quarters were very limited, Rhys Ddu's hospitality being
strained to the utmost to provide sleeping accommodations for so
many guests.

But things went on happily enough through the warm summer-
months, which that year, even in those forests, were particularly free
from wind and rain; nor had the love between the two changed at all
from the high, romantic level of feeling that had characterized its first
awakening.

It would have been natural enough had it been quite otherwise; but
there was something in both these young people that predisposed them
to the more romantic and less earthly levels of passion. How far
Catharine would have yielded to her lover's emotion, had there been
less of this ethereal quality in it, it is hard to say; but they were so
intensely shy and proud that any sudden rush of ungovernable feeling,
or even any emotional note in their tone towards each other different
from the key in which their love had been originally pitched, seemed
out of the question with both of them. All July and all August went
by without any overt event disturbing the happiness of these daily
encounters in the forest.

It did sometimes enter Rhisiart's head to wonder—for with all his
courtesy to the proud girl and with all his romantic happiness in her
company he had what might be called a "wicked imagination"—how he
would feel and how Catharine would feel, if he gave Glew the Gryd the
slip, and carrying her off into the depths of the trackless forest overcame—and sometimes his wayward mind conjured up scenes of disturbing violence—his true love's haughty shyness; but the curious thing is
that it was always at night and when he was alone that these dangerous
thoughts came to him. When actually in Catharine's presence—though
of course it may be that the inescapable guardianship of Glew the
Gryd played its part in this—there would descend such a magical mist
of love upon him that he was more than content just to walk with her

and to sit with her in the heavy red-gold flickerings and the mossy green-blue shadows, watching the deer and the squirrels and the rabbits and listening to the wood-peckers!

When September came, however, it was clear to him that Catharine had something on her mind beyond the usual far-off cloud on the horizon. The girl's cheeks, never very ruddy, grew whiter than their wont; her swinging step dragged a little, and there fell a lethargy on the movements of her young body. He would catch her, too, in queer fits of abstraction. One September afternoon he said something to her to which she made no reply at all; and when he looked at her he found her eyes fixed on a loosened ash-tree leaf, among the Scotch firs and the spruce-firs, that having been the last to unclose its bud in the spring was the first to relax its hold in the autumn, and now was drifting in the air at some distance from its parent tree, drifting, indeed, where there were very few deciduous trees at all, and where it seemed reluctant to sink to the ground on an alien bed of pine-needles.

Rhisiart caught Catharine watching this leaf, which was only a portion of an ash-leaf, with a fixed gazed of such absorbed intensity that he was emboldened to ask her of what she was thinking.

They were seated together on a little mossy knoll at the end of one of these forest-paths, cut long ago by Rhys Ddu's ancestors for hunting purposes. Below them, several hundreds of yards away, they could see the reddish beams of the sinking September sun, turning the great axe of their venerable guardian into a flame of burning gold.

They could hear, not so far off, the deep-throated baying of Elliw's hound, and they could faintly catch, too, upon the sunset-air the poignant odour of peat-smoke from some woodman's hearth.

"Do you really want me to tell you, Rhisiart?" she said, turning towards him the same grave intent look that she had fixed upon the drifting leaf.

A deep cold fear suddenly grew up like a chilly mushroom in the centre of his heart, draining as it rose the blood from his swarthy cheeks and causing his arm to tighten round her waist. He felt as if like that ash-leaf she might go floating away at any moment down the sun-lit clearing. He nodded in silence.

"I'm sure now," she said, speaking slowly and in a very low voice. "I'm quite sure now."

"That the Prince wants you to marry Sir Edmund?"

"Worse than that, Rhisiart. We've known *that* a long time."

"That your mother wants it, too?"

"Worse than that! Oh, my dear, how can I tell you?"

Rhisiart drew his arm from her waist and leapt to his feet. "You don't mean," he cried fiercely and rudely, "that they've married you to him already?"

Catharine's sea-coloured eyes darkened with anger till they became almost as black as his own. "If you're going to say things like that," she retorted bitterly, "I shall feel that it's true, what Griffith says, that the old blood in you has worn thin."

"My mother's blood," cried the lad in a passion, "is the best Norman blood in all the—" But he couldn't go on. The sight of her there before him, with a wisp of her fair hair falling in unheeded disorder across one of her eyes and across her twisted mouth, melted his very soul. His knees loosened beneath him, and crouching there on the moss, not touching her, not looking at her, he began to utter those deep, dry, gasping sobs that in their men-children are, of all sounds, the most moving to women.

She bent forward and laid her hands on his head. "No, no, my only true love," she whispered in a broken voice. "I'm not married to him yet." Then, waiting for this, for this *at least,* to sink into his consciousness, she removed her hands, straightened herself as she sat a little above him on that green hillock, and repeated calmly, *"Not yet,* Rhisiart! The daughters of our race don't marry in darkness and hugger-mugger, as they say Sir Edmund's sister did, when Hotspur swung her on his saddle and dragged a priest from his prayers. No, no. Listen to me, Rhisiart, for Our Lady's blessed sake! What I'm sure happened a week ago, on Saint Matthew's day—for, remember, to-morrow's the Feast of Saint Michael and All Angels—was Sir Edmund asking me of my parents. What they said to him I don't know; but from the way my mother's treated me since—like a sick girl who must have things broken to her gently—I'm sure, I'm *certain,* that that's what happened."

Rhisiart, who was now swaying to and fro, hugging his knees and staring at her with a lamentable face, now burst out with a wounded querulousness that softened her by its weakness much more than his anger had hardened her by its rudeness.

"Why, oh why, didn't you tell me this at once? You've made a fool of me, Catharine, by letting me be happy—like I've been—all these days—and you knowing this all the time!"

In her pity for his childishness—and oh, how much older than this hurt boy she felt!—she set to work—shutting away, deep down in her breast, what her own heart felt—to restore, soothe, and quicken his devastated feelings.

She reminded him that between Sir Edmund's asking for her hand and the final issue of such a request there must be, considering her parents' doting fondness, a great gulf. They would never rush her or hurry her. With *them* there would never be any of those familiar threats—like the threat to put her into a convent—by which in the old uncivilized days girls were forced into marriages they loathed.

She reminded him of the troubled times in which they lived; and how in a moment the whole military and political situation might be changed. Plenty of things, she told him, might happen that would make such a marriage as hers to Mortimer totally impossible.

She called to his mind all that her father had said in respect of his Secretary's immense and irreplaceable value to him; and how it was still possible, if she and he *refused* to yield, that the Prince—if not the Arglwyddes and Griffith—would soften towards them.

While she went on in this hope-against-hope tone his countenance cleared perceptibly. Soon he began making his way on his hands and knees from where he'd been sitting till he was recumbent by her side; and then it was she who was invoked, sitting cross-legged like an image with a fixed stare, as in question after question he pressed her, in his naïve, eager, pragmatic way, to suggest what actually they could do if they *did* defy her parents. Could they take refuge in the kingdom of France, he asked her, or would the Duke of Brittany perhaps give them a place in *his* court? The truth is, however—only our friend's insight into the heart of a girl was hardly deeper after two years of worldly experience than it was when Tegolin slept by his side at the Tassel-farm—that though she had been forgiving to his manly rudeness and though her heart had melted at his childish weakness there was something in this eager chatter about taking refuge in Brittany that made her soul withdraw into itself and feel cold and alone.

She didn't altogether understand why his present tone—*and he wouldn't stop;* he even began to talk about that great continent beyond the seas that Prince Madoc had discovered—chilled her feelings so much and made her feel so lonely. She attributed it to her sense of outrage, to her pride of race, to his not realizing, as every Welshman did, that as the daughter of a princely house she belonged to her family; but what really chilled her about it was an instinct of which she was herself scarcely conscious, a feeling that all this cheerful talk of his didn't spring from the depths of his nature at all.

She kept giving him long, sad, puzzled looks out of her Glyn Dŵr eyes; but it seemed as if the excited lad couldn't bring to a close his airy projects for this happy future abroad, projects in which she got such cold comfort, and in which, deep in her heart, she doubted if he himself really believed.

Slowly up the glade towards them came Glew the Gryd, his axe-blade blue-black in the gathering twilight; and as in his quavering old voice he hummed a sad South-Welsh ditty he had learnt in Rhys Ddu's halls, whose lilt of flight and disaster and desolate resignation seemed to reach them like a troop of invisible mourners come to carry away the lad's false hopes, what must the old Welsh gentleman do but repeatedly pause in his track and turn about and lean on his axe as if his bones, or perhaps his breath, felt a need for rest.

"The dew is falling, Catharine ferch Owen," he cried in his high-pitched voice as he came near, "and Mistress Elliw awaits us. From where I stood I could see them, and Corbyn was straining at his leash."

The young people rose to meet him and no sooner were they on their feet than the great hound himself came bounding up the slope, trailing his leash behind him. He rushed at once to Rhisiart, as the person least familiar to him in the party, but having sniffed at him with several deep breaths as if he'd been a crack at the bottom of a closed door, he turned to Catharine and nearly upset her balance by his eager caresses.

The girl unfastened his leash and handed it to the old man, and as they moved towards his young mistress he kept rushing from one group to the other, as if they were two little herds of deer that it was his duty to round up and keep together.

As was their wont on these occasions the two girls advanced side by side towards the house, the dog bounding happily round them, while Rhisiart soon left the two retainers together and debouched by a rougher and shorter path to a small back entrance which connected with the particular portion of the old time-worn place where Master Brut and he had their private quarters.

"Lu," as Rhys Ddu called her, was a timid, retiring little maid, whom not all her father's doting care had been able to make striking in appearance or seductive in manner. She had lived a lonely life in Tywyn, for her mother had died in giving her birth and her foster-mother had run away with a Flemish pedlar, and none of the lively serving-girls by whom she was surrounded took the trouble to understand her.

Rhys Ddu's own aged foster-mother ruled the establishment; but as she had never really accepted his youthful bride it would have needed all those seductive charms that were so noticeably absent in poor "Lu" for that bride's daughter to have won her heart.

Angharad was the old housekeeper's real name, but this had been shortened by Rhys Ddu, who seemed from infancy to have regarded the nature of ladies as best expressed in single syllables, into "Rad"; and "Mistress Rad" she had become to everyone in the place.

Mistress Rad had always predicted that the frail bride her foster-child brought home would never have the spirit to give him a son, and it may have been her satisfaction at the truth of this prediction that made her kinder to Lu than might have been expected. But she was a competent and busy old lady, and what the shy little girl wanted was understanding rather than indulgence; and this she had never had, no not even from her devoted father, till Catharine came upon the scene.

How Catharine understood her and how Catharine, while understanding her, *could yet like her,* was a perpetual miracle to Lu ferch Rhys, but she responded with her whole heart; and Corbyn, who quickly grasped the happy situation, responded with *his* whole heart, too.

Towards Rhisiart the dog felt very differently; but he didn't always feel the same. There *were* occasions when he condescended to take the young man on long hunting excursions far up into the forest. But it was clear he wasn't sure of Rhisiart; and our friend certainly wasn't sure of *him*. Once the boy even told himself a story of how, caught by Corbyn in the act of stealing Catharine away from Lu, the great hound flew at his throat, and he was compelled to lay him low with his dagger.

With the beginning of October the weather changed; and gales of wind and rain, quite apart from more serious causes, made it increasingly difficult for Catharine and Rhisiart to meet on their old terms. They generally succeeded in snatching, between sunrise and sunset, for after all they were still under the same roof, some sort of hurried and agitated encounter; but fate, acting not only through the girl's parents but through an unpredictable concatenation of events, seemed to take a devilish delight in making these spasmodic meetings at once more brief and more disturbing as day followed day.

In the privacy of their thick-walled chamber Rhisiart and his friend, the Lollard, shared each other's troubles. This wet autumn in Rhys Ddu's domain drew them closer than they'd ever been drawn before. Their respect for each other increased with their deeper knowledge; and as time went on, even Master Brut's interpretations of Wycliffe ceased to get on his friend's nerves. Rhisiart's tendency to make daring and drastic plans, wherewith to cut the entangled knots of both their love-affairs, met with grave attention from Master Brut; and in the worthy man's speculations as to how Alice could be persuaded to leave her mother in the Snowdon fortress and join the light-hearted damsels who served Mistress Angharad Rhisiart noted with amusement that the geography of this rambling old mansion was as obscure to the lover of maps as it was to himself.

There were constant goings and comings between Tywyn and the Snowdon retreat and hardly a week went by without one or other of the lovers receiving some sort of written communication from Tegolin. The Abbot of Caerleon, though beginning to grow restless in so inactive a life, had taken complete charge of the fortress; and when Owen decided to keep quite a large army there as well as in Rhys Gethin's great camp in Cardigan the old warrior-bishop took heart.

Rhisiart couldn't help noticing how as long as they were discussing the chances of Alice's appearance among them the soul of the Hog of Chirk would dwindle in importance; whereas when Alice seemed irrevocably and hopelessly caught, in her caring for "that old witch up there," the spiritual perils of Master Simon, who was still with Lowri in Rhys Gethin's headquarters, grew more serious.

Rhisiart's penmanship—and he hadn't failed to take Broch's advice

as to becoming a clerkly expert—was in great request that autumn.
Closeted with the Prince and the Meifod giant for hours every morning,
he had to increase day by day the epistles that messengers kept taking to
one or other part of Wales, not to speak of communications with the
Percies and with France, and with both Rome and Avignon.

But in the long evenings, when the great meal was over, and Mortimer was playing chess with Owen and the ladies had retired, both the
young friends would compose letters to be taken to Snowdon, the
Lollard imploring Alice to be faithful to him and to trust him, and
Rhisiart confiding in Tegolin all his wildest hopes and fears.

The heavy rains of that wild October not only brought down the
leaves of the Forests of Tywyn but quelled any active movement of the
Prince's various armies. Owen was in possession now of the whole
enormous sum of Grey's ransom. He had also obtained no negligible
sum for the liberation of Clanvow, whose departure was an immense
relief to the little court at Tywyn.

Mortimer not only knew Welsh, but displayed a lively desire to be
initiated into every form of Welsh tradition; whereas the author of
The Cuckoo and the Nightingale behaved as did the famous poet Ovid
among the Goths, treating Rhys Ddu's minstrels with ostentatious
courtesy, but betraying in his handsome face such ironic condescension
at all their harp-playing competitions, that to see the last of those bright
curls and to hear the last of that boisterous laugh was as much of a
comfort to the bardic fraternity as the gold by which his genteel admirers restored him to civilization was a boon to Owen's budget.

But though he had enough money on hand now to support his armies
on the most liberal terms, certain fierce local quarrels between men
from districts so widely divided were constantly demanding his presence. He would saddle Seisyll, whom he had sent for as soon as he
got Rhys Ddu's invitation to Tywyn, and ride off alone, either to the
force under Gethin, or to the stationary camp under the Abbot of
Caerleon, or to Henry Don's troops in the further south. These lonely
rides were the only happy times for the Prince during that rainy
October.

As deeply set upon marrying Catharine to Mortimer as he was set
upon retaining Rhisiart in his service, life at Tywyn had become a

hair-shirt of such scraping jags and scratching tags that compared with it his harsh chain-armour vest was a silken luxury! Owen told himself bitterly again and again that until this fatal October he hadn't known what the pain of life was. He had known spasms and twinges and fits of suffering, both mental and physical; but he had never before awaked in the morning to find that his consciousness of life came near to containing a balance of pain over joy.

And there was no alternative. He had smashed his crystal. Iolo was lying in that stone sarcophagus in Valle Crucis. He had won the battle of Bryn Glas. He was committed to the event. Two of his younger sons had already been slain in his cause. Meredith himself remained in that house at Pilleth, still only slowly recovering from his wound. The young man was under the care of Crach Ffinnant the Derfelite, who allowed no other doctor or prophet or conjurer or priest anywhere near his patient; and the more the Prince thought of this the less he liked it.

In their hatred of the Scab, whom with some reason they regarded as second-cousin to the Devil, neither Father Rheinalt nor Father Pascentius would consent to beard him at Meredith's bedside.

"Little good it does me," thought Owen, every time he sat down to dinner and watched the two Cistercians conversing so happily with Rhys Ddu, "to be Prince of Wales, if I can't even compel a couple of cropped heads to go to my son's assistance!"

The Arglwyddes was no help to him during this dark October. What he wanted to do was to be honest with Catharine. He wanted to implore her to let him thrust the sacrificial knife into her bosom as he had decided once and for all to thrust it into his own. "When you consented, child," he wanted to say to her, "that I should be proclaimed Prince of Wales you consented to lie down by my side before the altar of our gods; you consented to let them cover both of us with the pall of death." He wanted to explain to her that since that day, though moments of exultation *had* reached him, the greater part of the hours of his life had been simple endurance, obstinate, uncomplaining un-self-pitying endurance. He would have liked to assure her that if she, *held to his heart as she always was,* would only consent to endure their sacrifice together, he could give her a love stronger, deeper, than

that of— But always *at that point* his incurable honesty of analysis cut
in two his self-justifications with an edge as sharp as Glew the Gryd's
axe.

What right had he to meddle with such a miracle as a girl's first
love? Was there, he asked himself morning by morning, as he combed
his beard before his metal mirror and watched the dead leaves whirling
in little eddies within the embrasure of his window, an evil jealousy
in his heart that he should force her to marry a man she didn't love
rather than the one she did? And then, when he watched her abstracted
eyes and cold, sad profile as she sat by his side at their daily banquet,
pain took possession of him, pain worse than any pain he had ever
known, the pain of one who can, but *will not,* give to the heart he loves
its one and only desire!

There was a particular morning when he thrust his head as far as
it would go through the narrow aperture that served as window in that
ancient wall of blackened oak, so that the wind and rain undid in a
moment the result of his elaborate toilet. It was one of Owen's nervous
peculiarities to poke his great fair head with its regal beard through
the window of every chamber he used. And as he did so now and let
the rain beat on his face he thought of the difference between his own
philosophy and that of his friend from Meifod; and how strangely the
giant's feelings seemed to blend with these falling, whirling leaves,
these groaning branches, these forests of death!

Life, not death, was what his own heart wanted, life that should
survive—somehow, anyhow—these mortal struggles, these sad victories,
this incurable pain!

And with the forks of his beard blowing in the wind, and wet now
as the dead leaves themselves, he began to play his accustomed trick
with his soul; letting it escape into the storm, through the storm,
beyond the storm, till it rested like a ruffled starling by his son's bed in
Pilleth! But he soon drew back both his head and his soul; for he
remembered that Catharine hadn't learnt to play these tricks! A
woman's soul was in her love; a woman's soul was in the very part
of her which *he* had set himself to kill!

And the Arglwyddes didn't help him. How *could* a mother not be
more affected by what they were doing to Catharine? The Arglwyddes
always answered in the same way. "Marriage and children," she always

said, "are the fulfilment of a girl's life. Love comes, love goes; but a husband and children remain." And then the wise lady would enlarge on Sir Edmund's good qualities, his gentleness, his courtesy, his patience. "And he is so sad," she would say. "I think *he* has had some love-affair that went wrong."

Certainly Sir Edmund was sad, at least he was sad for the accepted suitor of a girl as lovely as Catharine and the daughter of a reigning Prince—yes! he had noticed it himself. Had the young man detected that the girl's heart was already given? Was it *that* that saddened him?

But if this one particular morning was a purgatory to the Prince, there weren't many mornings of happiness for his daughter. Poor Catharine! She had another grief just then in addition to her love—too much, too much, coming together for a maid so young!—for her old Nurse, whom her mother had brought with her to Tywyn, was slowly dying.

The departure from Glyndyfrdwy had been more than the old woman could bear. She had hated that Snowdon place, and had shut herself up with her grief and her anger, seeing nobody but Mad Huw, letting all her interests and occupations fall away, and at last quite losing her old self and her busy spirit in helpless querulous complainings. The news that both Glyndyfrdwy and Sycharth had been burnt by the English was the final blow. They had tried to keep it from her, but the officious Rawlff, not yet a Knight of Dewi Sant, had blurted it out; and now in this mournful autumn, while those time-blackened buildings rocked under the wailing wind, she lay in her white bed, in her white coif and long white wimple like a marble figure in a church aisle. *She* knew well enough, the old Nurse, what was being done to her darling, and her wrath against the Arglwyddes, upon whom characteristically enough, for she regarded all *men* as children, she put the entire blame, was so bitter that she refused to allow her to enter her death-chamber.

Catharine would sit by her bed-side hour after hour, holding her bony hand, but rarely replying, except with silent tears, to her moans and her protests.

Several times she insisted on seeing Rhisiart, and these were the most distressing moments of all; for she would lie with one hand in his and one in Catharine's, making at intervals feeble and pitiful movements to join their youthful fingers together.

"Where is that Grey Friar," she would moan at such times. *"He* would end this nonsense by making you man and wife—and then, *let them rage!* They couldn't undo what the man of God had done. Why doesn't somebody go for the Grey Friar?"

Once, at a moment when the end seemed near, they brought Father Pascentius to her; but the old lady's fury at the sight of him was so extreme that she even rose in her bed.

"Take your staring eyes into the Hell they came from!" she shrieked hoarsely. *"My* confessor is a saint, not a devil—a sweet Brother of Saint Francis *he* is, and a friend of King Richard; not a monking monk from a monkery of mummers!"

One early afternoon in this wild month, some hours before the great meal of the day, Rhisiart and Master Brut were sadly contemplating the thin rain and flying leaves from the window of their little chamber, when they were surprised by observing the unmistakeable figures of Catharine and Lu, accompanied by Corbyn, but unaccompanied by Glew the Gryd, leaving the house by the men's side-entrance and setting forth, with dark cloaks over their heads, down a vista in the forest where a long perspective of dripping beach-trunks lost itself in the distance.

"Blessed Mary!" cried our friend. "Where in the devil's name are those girls going? You—don't—think, Walter, that they've got an assignation with Sir Edmund?"

"No, no, lad, and I'll tell you why," replied the Lollard—yes! she *does* step out like a boy; and look how the other's clinging to her! —"because I saw Sir Edmund a minute ago when I was down there with Father Rheinalt at the fish-pond; and he was standing on the balcony in front of his window—he's up there you know, just above our room, and that's why—but you don't like my maps of places!—but at any rate if he's watching them now just as we are, he's not the object of their walk."

"Perhaps we'll see him in a minute or two going after them!"

The Lollard shook his head. "You must remember the man's still a prisoner-of-war. I've never seen him leave the house unattended. But I'm sure he's watching them, just as we are. You're not a perch-catcher like Father Rheinalt and me, or you'd know his ways. He stands for half the day on that balcony. It's roofed-over, but it faces the rain. I didn't mean to refer to it, Rhisiart; but since you've brought it up yourself I may as well tell you. I think he'd be *glad* if he caught his death by exposing himself on that balcony! I don't like seeing his black figure forever standing there, nor does Father Rheinalt. And you can see it from such a long way off! Down the pine-avenue you can see it. Down the linden-avenue you can see it. And you can see it from Merlin's elm."

"Have you spoken to him?" enquired Rhisiart, aware of his friend's mania for talking to unhappy people. "Have you been up there to see him? I wish you'd told me this before, Walter—for there is—there are —certain things—which it is—behoveful to me—to say to him—sooner or later."

"There are *no* such things, lad!" his friend asseverated with stern emphasis; "and if there were, you'd have to find another emissary than Walter Brut of Lyde to—"

Their colloquy was interrupted by the appearance of Father Rheinalt from among the pond-reeds. Anxious and perturbed he looked, and wild and ungainly too, considering that his black tonsured head was uncovered, his legs naked to his thighs, all smeared with mud and duck-weed, a great pole with a line attached to it flicking the air in his hand, and round his bare neck, dangling against his habit, the striped forms of half-a-dozen perch, each about a pound's weight, strung together by their horny and tragic gills.

He evidently had caught sight of the young men's heads peering out of their narrow window, and Rhisiart—his brain full of Mortimer— fancied he saw him respond to a greeting from the balcony above. But when he reached the path, instead of following it, he crossed it and walked straight through the drenched grass and the thorny blackberries till he stood on a level with them, only divided from their two eager faces by the thickness of that incredible wall of solid oak.

"I've just been summoned by the Arglwyddes," he said. "Owen's away and Griffith ab Owen's away; and the Nurse is dying, and crying out for a priest."

"I *wouldn't go*, Father," said Rhisiart eagerly. "I wouldn't go! You've heard of the fury she got into with Father Pascentius, calling him a monking monk from a monkery of mummers? The Arglwyddes is mistaken; for I know—oh, dear Father, I swear to you I know! —she wants Mad Huw *and no other!*"

Father Rheinalt was silent. The puzzled bewilderment he turned on those two young heads was so touching that Rhisiart was hit to the heart. Something about the man's guileless and incorruptible integrity made him think of Tegolin.

"What a good man he is!" he thought. "*All* of Tegolin comes from him—nothing from that she-devil!"

"But, son," protested the strange figure before them, tapping the wood-work with his pole and entangling his line, "but, son, she's dying and calling for a priest; and I—my vows—my duty to Holy Church, my—"

"But wouldn't it be better," interrupted the Lollard, and to our friend's dismay he caught the familiar tone of controversy in his voice, "wouldn't it be better for her soul to go to its Maker unshriven, than to go in a tempest of ungodly fury?"

Father Rheinalt's swarthy face displayed such pure misery of indecision that Rhisiart felt inclined to advise him to go—even if the old woman *did* die cursing him. The young man was amazed afterwards to recall how some devil within him prompted him to repeat once more in the ears of this guileless fanatic those ribald words about "monking monkeries." This was something the Lollard would never have done.

But Father Rheinalt was too involved in his conscientious dilemma to notice either this spurt of Hereford malice or the controversial tone of Master Brut. He tugged mechanically at his line till at last he broke it, so that only a few yards of it dangled from the end of his pole.

At that moment they became, all three of them, aware of the presence of Broch-o'-Meifod. The giant had shuffled out from the house to obey a pressing call of Nature; and there he was, hooking up his leather belt, and listening to their debate. "Listen, Father," he said gravely. "Listen, children! I think I can arrange this affair. Come with me, all three of you! You're something of a physician, Master Brut, and the old lady loves Rhisiart. Come with me, Father. I think it's your duty to go."

The young men hurried out of their room and followed the two elder men up the winding staircases and down the intricate passages that led to the death-chamber. The door was ajar, and Broch-o'-Meifod, telling Father Rheinalt to wait on the threshold, went in, opening the door wide so that the torch above the old lady's head shone full on the extraordinary figure of the monk, still clutching the pole with the dangling line, and on the mud and the pond-weed still clinging to his bare legs.

"Have you brought him, Master Broch? Have you brought him?" quavered the dying woman, while two sturdy and not over-sympathetic damsels forced her back on her pillow.

Broch went straight up to the bed, his colossal form hiding the open door and figure on the threshold. "He has prayed to Saint Peter the Fisherman for you, Nurse—and the Saint has come himself!"

Something about Broch, as Rhisiart had noted long ago, was so native and endued to death that when the old woman met his inhuman gaze her confused brain accepted literally and without question what he told her.

"The Fisherman himself!" she murmured. "He's sent the Fisherman himself!"

Then Broch swung aside and beckoned to Father Rheinalt to approach.

The monk did make a fumbling movement with his hands, with a dim notion no doubt of propping his pole against some object. But there was no object except the bed, and on the bed struggled the departing soul. So to the bed he came, and standing there before her, began, without a second's hesitation, to call upon her to utter the words of confession so that he could absolve her from her sins.

Rhisiart was close behind him now and when he heard the familiar words—"In the name of the Father and of the Son and of the Holy Ghost"—issuing from the lips of that passionate and simple man, with five mud-smelling fish hung round his neck and his legs slimy with pond-weed, he was more religiously stirred than he'd been since that Midsummer Day when he heard Mass with Tegolin and Mad Huw

And in a way he couldn't explain, and never *was* able to explain, the authoritative apparition of this invoker of *"Pater-Filius-Spiritus,"* bursting out through the slime of a fish-pond and surrounded by the blood-stained gills of five perch—"all of them," as the good man was certain to boast ere long, "weighing nearly a pound"—added a new and paradoxical force to the irritable and inconsequential reactions roused in him by the convincing arguments of Master Brut.

How much the dying old woman understood of these magical words is doubtful; but they evidently seemed to her the sort of words that the Keeper of the Keys would naturally use; and when with a spasmodic jerk of her old bones the *rigor mortis* set in, Rhisiart, who was by Broch's side now, was convinced that he would never again behold a dead face so imprinted with the certainty of redemption.

They left the Father on his muddy knees while the astonished damsels closed the eyes of the dead; but as soon as they had shut the door the two young men turned towards the giant, each with a puzzled protest.

"The lie wasn't mine," replied Broch-o'-Meifod calmly. "*The lie was life's.*" What the man meant by this, and how he'd dared to do as he did, was the subject of many a long discussion between the two friends in the months that followed; but both the young men decided at *that* moment that they must get into the air as quickly as possible.

It was afterwards that the emotional effect of the old woman's death came upon Rhisiart; came upon him as though the half-plighted troth of Catharine's hands and *his* hands, held so tight in the beldame's clutch, was a covenant that had been ratified by the kingdom of death, ratified in fact by that innumerable company of the deceased whom a fragment of Homer in his college library called "the powerless heads of the dead."

Led—among other impulses—by a feeling at the bottom of Rhisiart's heart that he would like to be the first to tell Catharine of her Nurse's death, the two friends, wrapped in heavy cloaks, set out together down the avenue where the girls and their dog had vanished.

"Are the Prince and Griffith to return to-night?" asked the Lollard before they were a bow-shot from the house.

"God knows!" sighed his friend. And then laying his hand on the Lollard's arm he broke out, "Don't look round, Walter, for Christ's sake! I can't stand seeing that black figure on his balcony. Let's pretend he's not there! There's a couple of hours before dinner. We're bound to meet them. I hope Corbyn won't fly at me in this damned mist!"

Meanwhile the two girls, whose professed purpose was to meet Rhys Ddu returning from the hunt, had already gone several miles down that long clearing in the forest. The rain had subsided, and had been followed by a wet mist that clung to their mantles, in that grey light, like a phantasmal suffusion of some sprinkling from the Milky Way.

"If we don't meet him before we reach the Pryderi Tree we'll *have* to turn," said Elliw. "He won't like it for us not to have taken anybody with us—and if we're late for dinner too, I'm afraid he'll be really angry!"

"All right, my sweet," responded Owen's daughter absent-mindedly. "We'll turn at the tree." And then after a pause, "What's this legend about Pryderi, Lu?"

The other gazed at her in surprise. "Don't you know?" she said. "Why every old wife in these parts knows *that!* But of course you're from the North. Why Pryderi was the Lord of all this land before the Romans. His ghost rides on the rain in the Forests of Tywyn. But listen, Catharine—"

"Yes, dear?"

"You remember how you asked me just now what was the gossip about you among the girls of the house?"

"Not only the girls!" protested the other. "I wanted to know how your house-people and how all the peasants round here regard Rhisiart and me." She gave a little quick sigh. "It ought to help, to know *that!*"

"Help?" repeated Lu, puzzled.

"Father's always taught me," said Catharine gravely, "that none of us can afford to neglect the voice of the common people. Not long ago I heard that man Sparrow who looks after Broch—you know the person I mean?—telling one of your porters that the only reason why the common people are for Owen is that there's going to be no more gentry."

"When Adam delved and Eve span who was *then* the gentleman?" interjected Elliw.

But Catharine was in no mood that day to take anything lightly. "Certainly," she declared, swinging forward with long strides like a young Artemis, while her soft rain-sprinkled mantle clung in classic folds about her limbs, "certainly it's wicked to hold down the peasants and treat them like serfs. But when it comes to governing a country, and summoning councils, and planning campaigns, and sending embassies to foreign kings, the common people depend on the gentry."

"Wouldn't it," panted Lu, who was now clinging to the edge of her friend's cloak and almost running to keep up with her, "wouldn't it be truer to say that we all depend on the Church for these things?"

"What do you mean, little one? I'm talking about high state-policies and armies and navies and treaties and government and the making of laws. I'm not talking of religion. No, no, dear, no, no, darling," and the tall girl strode faster than ever.

"No country can get on without its gentry. The gentry have education; and it's education that counts."

Lu's panting became a long-drawn sigh. She thought of the good knight, her father, who could hardly sign his name. She thought of Catharine's brother, Griffith, who if he *had* education was certainly at wondrous pains to conceal it. She thought of Rhys Gethin whom she had watched in their private chapel, with the secret amusement with which she watched all men whether young or old, holding his prayer-book upside down.

And then she said to herself, "She's thinking of the Prince and she's thinking of Rhisiart! She hasn't lived, like I have, for ten years with hunters and bards"—and Lu panted out her weariness of both schools of experts—"who can't say a single word about anything interesting. *Educated gentry?* Gracious me! Why haven't I the spirit to tell her that when *I* want someone to talk to I go to the peasants' huts and listen to stories of Rhiannon and Pwyll Pen Annwn?"

"I'm afraid I interrupted you, Lu darling," Catharine now remarked, drawing her breath as quietly and easily as if she were seated before a warm hearth rather than striding through a wet mist. "You were going to tell me what your father's people say about Rhisiart and me."

Lu plucked at her friend's cloak and as she did so leant for a second against the dripping trunk of a beech-tree. "I don't—think—we ought to go any further, Catharine," she gasped. "I'm afraid of the darkness catching us before we get back. Father must have gone straight home a different way. Pryderi's Tree is further than I thought."

All the while she was uttering these innocent words the crafty little Lu was thinking in her heart, "She may forget about it; she may forget about it."

But though Catharine let her rest there, with her light weight poised against the wet beech-trunk, and though she made no attempt to override the decision to return, she didn't forget about it, and as soon as they began to retrace their steps she put her question once more to her reluctant friend, remarking that it was easier to talk, now they'd turned their backs to the quarter from which the mist came.

Lu's troubled little face under her hood began to resemble a crumpled leaf that had turned *its* back to the mist, but to give herself strength she took a firm hold of the tall girl's mantle, and thus supported drifted along at her side with swift-gliding steps, like an oarless boat towed by a ship in full sail.

"They say that Sir Edmund," she began, and her voice to her own ears, as she watched the ghostly form of her white Hound trotting in front of them, seemed like the squeak of a mouse in a great forest full of enchanted stags and fairy princesses, "may be King of England one day if anything happens to the little Earl, and that if he isn't King there's no grander title in all Britain than what you'd have as Lady Mortimer. You'd be a sister then, they say, to Lady Percy, and the only chance your father has of liberating Wales is to be allied with the Mortimers and the—"

"*Lu!*" The force of this interruption was accentuated by Catharine's suddenly standing stone-still.

"You told me to tell you," murmured the frightened heiress of Rhys the Black.

But Catharine's voice was quite calm and tender. "I know. I wanted to hear. I thought it might help. But listen, Lu," and the proud young face was bent down towards her in the growing darkness, "what would *you* do if you loved anyone and that person wanted you to go away with him, and be married to him, and"—she found these final words difficult to utter as she recalled her doubt as to the fullness of the heart from which they'd come—"and live somewhere—abroad?"

Lu met the beautiful eyes looking down into her own for one brief instant. Then she turned to her dog, and calling him to her side fastened the leash to his collar. It was a comfort to her to press her ungloved knuckles against his furry coat. She was so little that his head reached her small cold breasts and she hugged it against them.

"I have never loved," she murmured aloud; and then, "oh you fool, you fool!" she cried in her heart, when she realized by the salt taste in her mouth that self-pitying tears were running down her cheeks.

But oh! how old the childish directness of her friend's next words made her feel, as with the white hound between their black-cloaked figures they stood under the wet trees.

"What would you do *if you were me,* Lu?"

"Nobody's ever said that to me before," was the response to this; and unclasping her tight clutch on her friend's cloak the daughter of Rhys Ddu ran her fingers along her dog's rain-soaked spine.

"But what *would* you do?" reiterated Catharine mercilessly.

"I'd do—*nothing,*" whispered the other with bowed head. "I couldn't marry anyone I didn't love; and I would *never* run away from my father!"

Since Lu's face in the access of her discomfort was almost buried in her hound's fur there was nothing to prevent Catharine from giving way to her feelings. Biting her lip and turning upon the soaked twigs and the dripping branches above her with a look of savage desperation —such a look as her father had cast round him when those Salopian yeomen hemmed him in—she tore both her arms free of her cloak and raising them in the air above her head shook her young fists at the hoary sky.

Temporarily relieved of her throbbing tension by this unmaidenly gesture, for she had begun to feel as if there were none left, among gods or men, who weren't making mouths at her and wagging their heads at her, she gathered her cloak about her and they continued on their way.

"I sometimes think of asking my father," Catharine remarked presently, "whether he wouldn't let us go together—with a good escort of our people of course—to cheer up my brother at Pilleth."

Now for some while "my brother at Pilleth"—for Lu had never met Meredith—had been an inexhaustible topic between them. Catharine was always reticent about Rhisiart himself, though not at all about her love for him, but upon Meredith's intellect, beauty, originality, and recklessness, she had enlarged so freely and so often that the lonely little Lu had begun to take an interest in this romantic figure. It didn't happen at once. It happened after a certain talk they had one hot August evening in Lu's room when Catharine had admitted that except for herself there was no girl in Meredith's life.

After that, though she was too shy to ask any direct questions, Lu would hover round the subject, and almost always got some degree of satisfaction. Catharine not only talked of Meredith as other girls would talk of a lover but he was obviously her favourite of all topics! She couldn't think or speak of her father now without bringing up her own dilemma, but the image of Meredith had nothing about it save what was winning and fair.

No *man* could possibly have given the thousand and one little touches —many of them throwing into relief certain endearing weaknesses that only a girl would notice—with which Catharine painted the figure of the hero of her childhood.

The mirror in Lu's big chamber—for her father had long ago given her the best room in the house—was suspended at right angles to the window, and thus there could be seen in it, in addition to the shrinking little face of its owner, quite a few objects of the landscape below, chief among these being a fragment of the avenue leading to the main entrance of the building.

And it had become, long before that happy August ended, a morning habit with this little "bundle of fancies," as Rhys Ddu called her, to gaze at the leafy approach to her father's dwelling between the luxuriant cascades of her own brown hair.

The combing of Lu's hair, for she was too shy to allow any servant so much as to enter her room, took a very long time, partly because her hair was the most remarkable thing about her—indeed her nurse used to say that all her beauty had gone into her hair—and partly because she told herself such interminable stories about Catharine's Meredith, stories that always began with her suddenly catching sight of him in her mirror, between the dusky falls of her long hair, as in the flickering sunshine he rode up the gate.

Thus when Catharine suddenly uttered this bold suggestion about their going together to Pilleth it was as if the radiant mirror'd Meredith had suddenly turned into a pale, faint, pitiful Meredith, one to be protected rather than to protect. And this transformation was so serious to Lu that for a second or two she could make no reply.

When she *did* speak it was to merely mutter: "Thank you, Catharine dear. I should like it very much," and even these platitudes were overpowered by the sudden straining and barking and excited tail-wagging of the great hound.

Lu straightened herself at once and instinctively renewed her clutch on her companion's mantle; and then they advanced, the excited dog dragging them forward almost at a run.

"Rhisiart!"

"Catharine!"

And then, finding some kind of sanction in the presence of Lu and the Lollard, the lovers embraced more closely than they had done for many weeks. Whatever thoughts they were that went whirling about in his long and narrow cranium Corbyn took the opportunity of dragging his little mistress as fast as possible in the direction of home, and Master Brut hurried along at their side. The dog pulled and strained to such effect that they were soon out of sight in the mist.

Once again the lovers embraced; and Rhisiart became aware that the proud girl was in a softer, tenderer, more submissive mood than he had ever known. Her lips responded to his in a manner that sent an electric quiver through every fibre and nerve of his lean frame, and through both their cloaks he could feel that her body was given up to him as he had never known it to be given up before. This was the crisis in their fate—though neither of them knew it.

Catharine was a very young girl. She had lived a protected life. Proud and gallant as she was, she was like a beautiful spring-time shoot on the bough of her father's being. Her romantic love for Rhisiart had from the start been surrounded by a blank void; a void that as far as any future with him was concerned she had instinctively set herself to ignore, hoping blindly as the simplest child might have done, that the wizard father would find a way to give her her Love as he was giving Wales its Freedom.

Faced with the actual possibility of leaving her father in the midst of his great struggle, and of going God-knew-where, to live among foreigners, everything in her, even her romantic love itself which after all was for a Rhisiart associated with the life she knew, drew back, with panic-stricken roots, as a water-plant would draw back from transplantation to a desert. Rhisiart was the background of her *present* life, but this Rhisiart-and-Catharine living as forlorn pensioners of the Duke of Brittany was an image as cheerless at it was inconceivable, an image that held scant joy.

But what she'd never counted on, for she'd instinctively kept their passion on a high romantic level, was the treachery of woman's nature. The idea of giving herself to her lover, apart from marriage, had never crossed the threshold of her consciousness. She was a young girl in love; but she was a young girl with unawakened senses.

But she had all a woman's awareness of the weaknesses of her lover; and between the real Rhisiart who was so transported by her presence and this other Rhisiart of plans and schemes there seemed a wide gulf. The pictures he painted of what struck her as a pair of pitiful ghosts at the court of Brittany only distressed her. He wasn't the Rhisiart she knew when he talked like that. He himself became as unreal as his talk.

But what she didn't know, and what Rhisiart didn't know, was the difference between a girl in love and a girl who has yielded to her lover.

The exultant happiness that her unexpected response roused in the lad nearly turned *his* head. A new emotion such as he had never experienced before raced through his heart. She was his! She was his! He felt strong enough to defy all the world. He let her go, and drew a long deep breath, keeping his hands on her shoulders.

It was the crucial moment between them. Had his passion been ever so little greater; had it possessed ever so little more flame and less tenderness, he could have carried her then and there beneath those dark tree-trunks and made the rain-drenched leaves their bed.

But the fate of their diverse natures, the terrible power of that undertide of inheritance, was too strong. Her Welsh blood might cry out to his Welsh blood, "Take me! Take me!" But the forward-looking, clearheaded Norman in him—since this wasn't a case for brutal seduction—reverted irresistibly to practical decisions, to legal precautions, to well-laid schemes.

Alas! the only "scheme" that would have served him then was the prehistoric way of a man with a maid. But he dropped his hands; and under the pressure of three generations of sheriffs' clerks in the shrewd City of Hereford he gasped forth, eagerly, feverishly, hurriedly: "He's got another journey to make *after* this one! So we've plenty of time. I've thought it all out. We'll begin collecting our things at once. I've got a hundred silver groats. You've got your jewels. I've been making a few enquiries. Ships from France leave our coast every month, whenever the weather's calm. And there's a priest in Cardigan-town, who for—"

But she stopped him with an imperative gesture. The back-flow of her yielded blood, of her yielded life, reverting inwards, ebbing inwards, under the shock of the withdrawal of his domination, froze her whole being.

But not for nothing was she Owen's daughter. She might not—as her father in his remorse had told himself—possess his saving trick of exteriorizing the soul, but she was of the same proud race, and now at this crisis her will rose up, like a towering column of ice-cold mist from the crack in her heart.

"No silver of yours, Rhisiart," she said in a low voice, drawing her cloak with both hands round her, "no jewel of mine, will that Cardigan priest ever see." She paused for a moment, gazing at him as if from the other side of a gulf wider than that sea over which he'd said the ships sailed when the weather was calm. "Goodbye, my dear," she whispered hoarsely. "Kiss me and let us go. We have had— Kiss me and let us go— Rhisiart, my only love!"

Heart-felt and solemn as was her tone, final and hopeless as were her words, the impatient child in him refused to understand. Instead of kissing her he fell to staring at her in indignant wonder. Casting about in his mind for something to distract her, for in his innocence he took this new mood as a mere vagary of girlish pride, what must he now do but begin blurting out the news of her Nurse's death.

"And I wasn't there! I wasn't with her! Merciful God, what have I done? Oh misery! Why was I ever born! I bring unhappiness to everyone! Oh Nurse, darling, darling Nurse—and I wouldn't wait with you one little hour! Quick! Let's hurry! Let's run! Perhaps she *isn't* dead. Old people fall into these trances that *look* like death! Let me go to her. I want to go to her!"

Poor Rhisiart! If he'd fancied that an old woman's death would set free a young woman's heart from its unpredictable caprices, and bring it back to reality, he had blundered once again.

The girl was actually running now; and he was running by her side, explaining, imploring, consoling. Some women have room for more than one master-feeling at a great crisis; and if the dripping beech-tree trunks under which those two were running had been possessed of the power of reading thought they would have soon realized that the first shock of her nurse's death had already spent itself and that the boy's pitiful distress, as he panted out his explanations, was not without its effect.

The motion of her blood caused by her running was itself a redeeming agent in the un-freezing of that lump of ice which the too sudden withdrawal of his ravishing embrace had congealed in her bosom. She relaxed her speed. "Oh Rhisiart," she murmured. "Why weren't you and I born brother and sister so that we shouldn't ever have to be parted?"

"I'll never, never leave you!"

"Are you sure she died happily?"

"It was Broch's doing. But when we asked him why he did it he said it was life, not he, who lied. We couldn't understand what he said."

"I feel now that the sooner I'm married to Sir Edmund the better for both of us. I oughtn't to have let you love me. Deep down I knew it would come to nothing."

"I'll never, never leave you!"

Though the dark, dripping trunks of the beech-trees may have understood nothing of this dialogue, there was something in the girl corresponding to this dumb world of rain-soaked vegetation that didn't miss the curious effect of their voices as they hurried along. The wet vapours that moved with them were thinner and less palpable than rain; but they were chillier and even in a queer sense more watery. They were like the element of water in its essence, that essence through which all those vast Forests of Tywyn, with their dripping branches and fallen leaves, were compelled to endure whatever life brought.

And the voices of the boy and girl as they moved, sometimes running, sometimes moving as gently—so soft was the drenched moss—as if they were gliding without lifting their feet, struck this passivity in the girl with the effect of voices in a derelict boat, carried on a tide in which "near" and "far" have been drowned. There come moments in life when one accumulative aspect of Nature—in this case the drifting of rain-soaked leaves in desolate mist—permeates and possesses the human soul.

Catharine felt, as she glided along in that watery element, as if all the words she or her lover uttered were the murmurs of a couple of hollow straws floating on a dark tide. And although this feeling was in a measure due to the fact that they were both of them running, or almost running, it had the effect of bringing their souls together and of softening her heart towards him. And the further they went the tenderer did her heart grow; until it came to a point when she didn't dare to pause in their advance lest she should sink recklessly into his arms and feel again that blind, dark, sweet yielding which had so nearly decided their fate.

What impulse was it in her that gave her so wild a satisfaction in murmuring to him yet again, "It'll be best for us both that I marry him quickly"? Was it the vast, dumb acquiescence of those forests of rain-drenched vegetation? Or was it that as her limbs failed and her heart melted in the mist she was holding up between them, as a priest on the scaffold holds his crucifix to the lips of the condemned, that sad, black figure of the man on the balcony?

But what a long way she and Lu had penetrated into the forest! What if it were her destiny after she died—as a punishment for loving one man and marrying another—to run like this by Rhisiart's side forever, through an eternal mist, towards a "figure on a balcony" who eternally receded as they advanced?

"You are absolutely *sure* Nurse was dead when you came away?"

Rhisiart repeated what he'd told her already; but he began, as he kept glancing at the ghostly face above the wearily hurrying figure, to have an inkling that it was only to put the dead woman, as she had already put the figure on the balcony, *between herself and her life,* that she kept up this ridiculous running.

But the wet grasses dragged at her feet, and the soaked mosses like great undulating sea-sponges dragged at her ankles, and the gaping tree-roots full of jet-black watery mouths sucked at her knees, and the tall trees waved mesmeric arms towards her thighs, and the down-

sinking vapour drooped about her waist, and hung heavier and
heavier upon her bosom, and inserted itself between the hood of her
cloak and her bewildered brain: and—"Let him take you! Give up!
Sink down! Make all the Forests of Tywyn your priest of Cardigan!
Rhisiart is your life, your soul, yourself! Yield to him, yield to him!
Sink down and give up! The Forests of Tywyn are yielding to the
mist. The mist is about us, round us, in us. We have given up; and oh,
the deep, deep sea! Give up, you also, Catharine ferch Owen!"

It isn't only the vapour that's round your waist, Catharine! It isn't
only the mist that's heavy on your breast, Catharine! And as she
stumbled on, and as Rhisiart kept pace with her, measure for measure,
step for step, breath for breath, the proud virginal girl in the relentless
treachery of her woman's senses felt as though the waiting figure on
that balcony must wait forever and the waiting figure on that death-
bed must wait forever.

The Forests of Tywyn had yielded, the mist had its will of them,
their leaves had fallen, their trunks were encircled, their branches
were still, their sap was sinking, and the correspondency between the
element within them and the element without them was complete.

The girl sank down under an immense and absolutely immobile oak.
Scarce any foliage had this tree lost, but from all its twigs and from
many of its leaves the mist hung in whitish drops, drops that were
forever quivering to their fall but which never fell.

Her lover breathed long and deep, gazing down at the vaporous
blur that was her face and at the dusky shell-like curves that made up
her unresisting form.

"Kiss me goodbye, Rhisiart!" Her words were simple; but much more
so was the primordial appeal that rose up to him from that confused
heap of breathing darkness. The half-life which was the woman's called
dumbly from the mist-ravished earth to the half-life which was the
man's.

Why then did he go on standing there mute, motionless, like a
carved effigy above a tomb? Such was his nature that of these two
appeals it was only to the articulate one he responded. Had *she* seen
him as he now saw her in helpless weakness, or had she seen him
rob, pillage, murder, burn, commit hideous sacrilege, and even appear
like a gaping idiot before the execrations of a blind mob, she would

have felt the same identity between them. She would have felt it beyond all his crimes, beneath all his cowardice.

But he was not made after that fashion. Reactions, fears, scruples, doubts poured into his mind. The very fact that this relaxed, abandoned, desperate heap before him was so different from the proud, indignant Catharine whose strength had gone suddenly weak under his embrace left a troubled empty space in his mind. And into this space with the glint of armour and the gleam of gold rushed the figure of Owen, as he had seen it when, below the walls of Dinas Brān, he sucked that arrow-wound.

All his passion, all his devotion had seemed too little then to lay upon that heroic breast. And how he was going to betray him, now he was going to strike him a deadly, cowardly, secret blow, as from the blade of David Gam!

Between him and that heap of mist-drenched clothes and that white face that seemed to be sinking deeper and deeper into those tree-root hollows of black rain the figure of Owen appeared to Rhisiart, as he had first seen it, with that air of being the symbolic victim in a tribal ritual, decked and adorned for sacrifice.

The lad knew well—indeed his had been the hand that penned these intricate plots—all that depended on the marriage of Catharine and Mortimer. The liberation of Wales depended on it; yes, more intimately than upon twenty such victories as Bryn Glas!

It wasn't as if all these thoughts followed one another in a stream through the boy's head; it was as if they were revealed to him, instantaneously and simultaneously, from their pre-existence in some over-dimension.

"Aren't you *ever* going to kiss me goodbye, Rhisiart?" The words were followed by the descent of a couple of faded oak-leaves which fluttered down upon that phantom face; and, immediately afterwards, certain whitish-coloured bird-droppings descended into the centre of that heap of clothes.

"Love me once more, Rhisiart; and then we'll go."

But at that instant he had to give her his hand in haste, and she had to take it and struggle to her feet; for there were horses and voices and the barking of dogs close upon them!

"Who goes there?" cried our friend.

"Rhys Ddu of Ceredigion!"

And then came the voice of the Lord of Tywyn himself. "Catrin ferch Owen, can it be you? Master Rhisiart, God keep you in his caring! You've lost your company I see, my young friends, and your good men are all scattered, and your hounds all gone. 'Twas lucky I came upon you. *What's* that, Master? *What's* that, Princess? My little Lu has gone to find your lost people! Eh? Is that it? And under the protection of Master Brut? I hope, young sir, that Master Brut is as discreet and wise as *some* young men are—and not as fool-hardy as others! But perhaps one of you Fathers will give the Princess the use of your horse. We're near home now. You won't have to walk far.

"This is Master Griffith Young, Princess," he went on, "Canon of Bangor; and this is Master Lewis Byford, our Roman Pontiff's choice, he tells me, for the episcopal throne of the said city. They bring, they tell me, important messages from my Lord of Northumberland and Harry Hotspur, and I think from the Scottish lords, too. Will the Prince your father, Mistress, be home to-night? These gentlemen intend to remain here for eight days I believe, and then go straight to my Lord of Northumberland; and after that, it may be, to France; and this, Master Canon, is—

"But you two know each other already! What a blundering old fool I am! Forgive me, Rhisiart. Do'ee know Master Byford, too? No, not Master Byford? But you learned clerks of the great world have none of our rustic shyness. 'All chins without beards and all hearts without windows,' as our Cardigan saying is!"

All this while Rhisiart kept casting furtive glances at Catharine, fearful lest the shock of Rhys Ddu's appearance with these great clerics would prostrate her. But on the contrary! Never had he seen her more completely the proud, self-contained Princess. Such was his own contrariness that it was even with a certain pique at her easy manner and her refusal to meet his eye that he plunged into conversation with Master Young.

With Catharine mounted on the good man's sturdy palfrey it was natural enough for the former acquaintances to walk side by side; and they began by exchanging impressions of Rhys Ddu.

Catharine had long ago confessed to Lu that this chieftain with his black curling beard reminded her of descriptions Rhisiart had given

her of the Emperor of the East. Rhys's manners, though courtly, were
in the large, free, grandiose, old-world style; and what Rhisiart had
told Catharine about him—though *this* she had kept to herself—was
that he was a better huntsman than statesman.

It was clear as he now rode by Catharine's side, his three big hounds
sniffing at every patch of under-growth, that Rhys Ddu was glad
enough to escape from his recent companions.

Rhisiart and Master Young therefore walked quietly by the side of
the Rector of Byford, whose horse was a sluggish one, and it soon
transpired that the Canon was very anxious to get our friend's support
in the matter of his argument with his fellow-traveller.

"It may be, it may be, dear Canon," the Rector of Byford was soon
retorting, "and I don't deny that Benedict, as a man, is easier to handle
than Boniface. But what we have to consider in these delicate matters
is not the present but the future. Benedict may be easier than Boniface,
and his successor may be easier than Boniface's successor; but the fact
remains, and I'm sure our young master here will agree with me, that
it is impossible for any serious student of the history of Christendom to
regard the Avignon schism as anything *lasting*. It'll pass, dear Canon,
it'll pass; and what men like ourselves, who are the advisers of princes,
have to consider is the future, when there will be once more one flock
and one shepherd."

It was a considerable comfort to our friend to mark how straight
Catharine sat upon the back of Master Young's steed, and it relieved
him, too, when he heard her give vent to a quite natural little laugh at
something Rhys Ddu said. The black-bearded Lord of the Forests of
Tywyn seemed well-pleased to have Owen's daughter to himself; and
it wasn't long before their two horses had put a perceptible distance between themselves and the rest.

"You two," remarked the Rector of Byford, who had no difficulty in
keeping his horse to a walking pace, "are such old friends that I'm
sure, Canon, you won't hesitate to question Master Rhisiart as to the
interesting topic we were discussing just now."

Master Young turned upon his fellow ecclesiastic a very complicated
look, a look that Rhisiart was quick enough to catch; and having
caught it—for the situation was one exactly suited to his gifts—he
scrupled not to take the bull by the horns.

"You were speaking, reverend sirs, if I mistake not," he remarked in his best Hereford Law-Court voice, "about the rumours that are spreading through Cardigan as to a marriage between the Prince's daughter and Sir Edmund Mortimer. You are men of the world as well as ornaments to the Church, so that I can speak freely; and let me hasten to confess that I myself—unknown as I am—am an aspirant for the hand of Catharine ferch Owen. But the Princess and I are so devoted to the cause of Wales that we have already begun to wonder—all this, my learned Fathers, is, as it were, under the seal of the confessional— as to the particular direction towards which our conscience points."

Master Young—too sly to be twice caught exchanging looks with his friend on horseback—turned his toothless countenance towards this frank and straight-forward young man.

"What you have just told us, Master Rhisiart—you must pardon me if I omit any title that your distinguished courage in the battle of Bryn Glas may have added to your name—jumps with what we have heard as we travelled. You have been pleased to call us—humble priests as we are—'men of the world,' and as such we cannot conceal from you that it has crossed our mind that young people like you and this spirited child must often ere now have thought of escaping from Wales—no! don't interrupt me—and taking ship for France. Such a course would be, my dear son"—and he hesitated for a moment, as if searching for an appropriate word—"such a course would be—"

But Rhisiart's brain, keyed up to a fine point of self-defence, had considered and rejected at least five different lines of possible policy during that pause. The one he finally selected really did do his shrewdness credit.

"Not only ships for France, Father," he replied lightly and carelessly, "but ships to the unknown country to which Prince Madoc sailed, have crossed my mind; but Owen is a magician, and from beginning to end of my friendship with his daughter he has read every thought that flitted through my head. I can hide nothing from him. And since he has made no attempt to separate us, aren't I justified in concluding that he himself is still a little undecided about the advantages of this Mortimer match? Neither he nor I ever refer to it. It is true I've noticed once or twice that he speaks as if Sir Edmund had *already* given up all hope of being ransomed by the House of Lancaster. In fact, I myself copied out quite recently a letter from Sir Edmund to his tenants hinting at a change of allegiance."

"Has that letter gone?" enquired Master Young with innocent abruptness.

"Well, no," replied our friend quite unperturbed. "There's been no opportunity to despatch it yet; and, as I say, Owen knows so well his daughter's affection and my own loyalty that he recognises there's no hurry. He discusses everything, as you know, with Master Broch of Meifod, and I'm not sure that Master Broch wouldn't sooner see the Princess married to a devoted Welshman than to a Mortimer."

The ecclesiastics were silent after that, and so was Rhisiart. "How on earth," the latter asked himself, "did they guess that we'd thought of running away? I must be careful; but I must give these men confidence in me; and I must be as frank with them as possible, else I'll never disarm them, or find out what they're after. Both for Owen's sake and Catharine's I must be open with them and yet be on guard."

It was clear to him that his unabashed simplicity and openness *had* already nonplussed the two churchmen; for Master Young began explaining with uncalled-for minuteness and with engaging confidence all the high state reasons which made it essential that Catharine should marry Mortimer.

"How lucky I took the line I did!" he kept saying to himself. "Merely by admitting what they *already* knew I am now completely one of them. They won't say anything to Owen that they don't say to me first. Master Young recognized me as a kindred-spirit that day Mad Huw saved him from Rhys Gethin. He'll tell me everything now; and that'll be to Owen's interest as well as to mine."

It never occurred to this "kindred spirit" of Master Young to be "on guard" against himself; but the truth is, as the Canon of Bangor went on revealing all the threads of the elaborate combination, of which he held the secret, as to the part to be played by Mortimer *when married to Catharine,* and as to the part to be played by Northumberland and his son, by Scotland, by Ireland, by France, our friend's mania for political intrigue and legal niceties began to go to his head. This element in Rhisiart had always been Catharine's worst rival. The sandal-wood sweetness of Luned was a bagatelle in comparison.

Once having been, as it were, "broken in" to the odious phrase,

"Catharine and Mortimer," this "Catharine and Mortimer" ceased to have any vivid connection with himself and his love, but became simply a move in the great chess-game of World-Politics.

He was like a man who loves the chess-board so much that if during some desperate ride for life and death he were to find such a board by the fire of a wayside inn, he would be lost.

Lewis Byford's horse was of a dark chestnut, but on its left shoulder was a long curious scar upon which the hair had refused to grow. Upon this scar, when he got weary of Master Young's toothless mouth, Rhisiart now fixed his gaze; and as he gazed he began confusedly to wonder, for the scar was under the rider's nose, what the thoughts had been—thoughts rather concealed from, than revealed to, Master Young —which had associated themselves with this object in the mind of the Rector of Byford as he rode along.

Once or twice, as the Canon murmured his disclosures, he was sure he detected disapproval on the Rector's face—and what a face it was! Providence had given to Lewis ab Ieuan a square brow, a straight nose and enormous ears; but he himself by some ingrained habit of reticence had reduced his naturally capacious mouth to a downward-sinking curve of double-locked suppression.

It was from this locked-up mouth, which when it *did* open displayed quite a number of serviceable teeth, that the following words issued, the moment Master Young drew breath:

"As a Proctor in Litigation at the Roman court, Master Rhisiart, I cannot completely endorse our dear Canon's views. For my humble little church at Byford on the Wye—I don't know whether you're acquainted with the country round Hereford—the Holy Father has granted me so many privileges that I've been encouraged to take advantage of this recognition of my poor gifts and have dared to suggest that since the episcopal throne of Bangor is at present vacant it would be proper and seemly for His Holiness to 'provide,' as we say, a Welshman to it.

"As any friend here may believe, my first thought in these conversations with the Holy Father was to suggest *his* name. But since some crafty enemy of our race had apparently informed His Holiness of our friend's association with the anti-Pope at Avignon my kind patron, I may even say my benefactor, was so partial to his poor Welsh Proctor that he hinted that if I obtained Owen's sanction, assuming of course that our cause is triumphant, there might be a possibility that he would see his way to provide *me* to this vacant episcopal throne."

Our friend glanced hurriedly at Master Young; but the mist was too thick to see anything but a round orifice in a white blur. "You see, Master Rhisiart, how you and I are destined," were the words that now issued from this orifice, "to encounter each other on momentous occasions! In me, of course, Owen will meet only a humble candidate for the Archdeaconry of Merioneth, but in our learned Rector here he will find the Lord Bishop Elect of Bangor."

Rhisiart began to feel happier than he had felt for nearly an hour, happier than he had felt since Catharine so indignantly rejected all his well-arranged plans. He couldn't conceal from himself how perfectly he was equipped to cope with these two ambitious ecclesiastics.

"How much good and how much evil are mixed up in us all!" he said to himself. "Both the Rector and the Canon are patriotic Welshmen, but of course I can see that the Canon gambles on Benedict while the Rector gambles on Boniface; and that when it comes to bishoprics there's a deadly rivalry between them!"

"I'm myself a native of Hereford," he remarked aloud, addressing the Rector. "Perhaps you may be acquainted with my new step-father, Montfoison by name?"

The Rector of Byford shook his head; a gesture which brought very dark suspicions to our friend's mind. Was it possible that his susceptible parent had been deceived by some rascally French adventurer of no background at all?

"Did you hear anything," he went on, "of the trial of Master Brut for heresy? Master Brut is a great friend of mine, and has been appointed Owen's Librarian."

"My dear young gentleman," said the Rector gently, "you must realize that for several years I have been living in Rome. I assume this Brut you speak of was entirely acquitted of this deplorable obliquity?"

"At any rate he's high in Owen's favour," announced our friend proudly, "and even at this moment he is escorting the heiress of Rhys Ddu back to Tywyn."

"Alone?"

"Certainly, Rector, certainly alone!"

"May I enquire if the daughter of Rhys Ddu is affianced to any suitable young gentleman?"

"To none that I've ever heard of, Rector!"

"Really? Dear me! Perhaps then in *that* quarter—I have no wish to offend—a handsome young scholar like yourself might find—"

Rhisiart bit his lip in the darkness; and savagely transferred his whole religious allegiance from Rome to Avignon. Realizing his blunder the Rector of Byford took from his saddle-bow a daintily-carved flask, put it to his own lips and, courteously bending down as they moved, offered it to Rhisiart.

Naturally anxious to conceal the fact that he had in a single second selected a new Vicar of Christ, Rhisiart drank deeply of the fiery restorative offered him, a privilege which the cautious Master Young refused with a gesture.

Advancing in silence after this they all three became aware that with the deepening of twilight the mist had also thickened. It was only by the feel of the pathway under their feet and the density of the trees on both sides that they kept the track. But it was clear that if it got any darker the non-human senses of the chestnut-coloured horse with the scar on his shoulder would be their best hope.

Dazed by what he had drunk Rhisiart now began to reproduce in his narrow skull almost the precise feelings of the bewildered Catharine. He too visualized the black figure alone on his balcony. He too visualized the white figure alone in her bed. But in his youthful imagination he felt as if between himself and these singular harbour-marks there floated, over the waves of darkness, the shimmering *pali* in which he had first seen the form of his love.

Suddenly the horse stopped. They had reached a spot where the track divided.

"Are you sure we're going the right way?" said the Rector.

"Why has your horse stopped?" said Master Young.

And Rhisiart cursed the Forests of Tywyn as he had never cursed anything in all his life before.

"If we don't appear," said Master Young with grave assurance, "they'll send back to find us. But if we take a wrong turn it won't be easy to find us. I suggest we stay just where we are, even if an hour has to pass."

The Rector of Byford, whose form on the back of his horse had now become to our friend a darkness within the darkness, began to murmur the inspired words of Zacharias in the Gospel, in which the Canon reverently joined.

"*Ad dandam scientiam salutis plebi ejus,*" chanted the man on the horse.

"*In remissionem peccatorum eorum,*" answered the other.

"*Per viscera misericordiae Dei nostri,*" intoned the Rector.

"*In quibus visitavit nos oriens ex alto,*" continued the Canon.

"*Inluminare his qui in tenebris et in umbra mortis sedent; Ad direngendos pedes nostros in viam pacis,*" they concluded together.

The familiar psalmodic rhythm deepened rather than lessened the trouble in our friend's brain. His whole soul felt drugged, distracted, amort. He longed to be sailing over unknown seas with Catharine, and at the same time he longed to be resting his head, pardoned and at peace, on the golden breast of her betrayed father. But here he was leaning against a horse whose whole body was nothing but a hairless ghostly scar; here he was listening while the phantom echoes of ecclesiastical unction sank out of hearing.

It seemed to him as if in that dense darkness the ghosts of those resonant Latin syllables were uttering querulous moans and plaintive whimperings as they settled down among the expectant black slugs, waiting for them *on their balconies* on the under-side of the fallen leaves!

And he was aware, too, of a persistent and mortuary smell of funguses. The Forests of Tywyn were famous for funguses. Autumn lasted longer in the Forests of Tywyn than anywhere else in the world. Summer turned quicker into autumn and autumn more slowly into winter! The Forests of Tywyn patiently suffered the spring and the summer and the winter. But their inmost soul responded to the autumn. It rose up then and sucked at the autumn, it drained the autumn, it metamorphosized itself into the autumn! And since the extent of the Forests of Tywyn was so vast, the mass of vegetation with its sweet, sickly, autumnal smell, never *quite* obliterated by the other seasons, was correspondingly vast; and so now on this particular day, when the wild winds sank down and the persistent rains ceased, the whole forest became one all-dissolving, all-absorbing, all-unfathomable *fungus*.

Yes, the Forests of Tywyn were well adapted to suck the life out of young hearts. Elliw ferch Rhys was their natural and congenital off-spring. But what was *that*? Rhisiart's whole body stiffened and he listened intently. Ah! he knew what *that* was—the deep unmistakeable bay of Corbyn, the wolf-hound!

"You're right, Master," he cried joyfully, addressing the Canon. "They've not forgotten us! Mistress Lu's sent back her hound. *Corbyn! Corbyn!*—" and he raised his voice to its fullest pitch.

Contrary to expectation Owen *did* return that night; so that all the wanderers, at whose life-springs this Tywyn mist had been at work as though with the innumerable mouths of a colossal fungus, had plenty of time to warm themselves and to wash and change their clothes before the banquet began.

But all the days of that November were pitiable and shameful days for Rhisiart and indescribably tragic days for Catharine.

Owen reached such a point that though he wouldn't give in he couldn't look at her and could rarely bear to speak to her.

The Arglwyddes, however, behaved quite differently. Catharine's one desire was to get away and cry in solitude, but since the Arglwyddes persisted in making these escapes more and more difficult the girl's pride came to her aid. The one person from her earliest childhood before whom she had always refused to weep was her mother, and she felt the same about her brother Griffith; so that either of these persons had only to approach the door of her chamber, or of her friend Lu's chamber when she'd taken refuge there, and at once there was a cold, calm, cheerfully-smiling, though ghastly-white, Catharine ready to receive them.

Rhisiart supposed that after her formal troth had been pledged to Sir Edmund and their espousals drew near she would avoid him as the Prince avoided her. But the contrary of this proved to be the case. She managed—the Mother of God alone knows how!—to see more of Rhisiart than she had done before.

These encounters were pure misery and shame and embarrassment

to our friend; but he made it a point of honour to follow her cue and
copy her air as far as in him lay. Of their love she never spoke; and,
when he spoke of it, all she did without looking away or betraying
emotion was to slowly shake her head, while her mouth took on such a
lamentable twist when he tried to press her that he hadn't the heart to
persevere. He felt her eyes on him all the while. She treated him as she
had formerly treated Meredith, who was still too weak to leave Pilleth,
and she seemed totally unaware of the effect of this upon any onlookers. She kept gazing at him as if her marriage were to be her
death and she wanted to impress his image upon her mind so as to
carry it away with her into that unfamiliar realm.

One thing astonished our friend. She seemed to prefer the society of
her future husband to everybody's in the place except his own, nor did
it appear to cause her any particular distress, though Sir Edmund's
melancholy perceptibly deepened, when it fell out that she was alone
with the two of them.

From her parents, from the Rector of Byford who had been chosen
by the Arglwyddes as the officiating priest at her wedding, from Master
Young, from Broch-o'-Meifod and Master Brut, from the Fathers
Rheinalt and Pascentius, she seemed to be always escaping to her cold,
sad bridegroom, whose melancholy dignity had completely isolated
him from everybody. She would be always at his side, with her ungloved hand on Mortimer's black sleeve, standing in the covered porch
watching the rain, or seated together in some black oaken chair in the
library with some great illuminated folio on their knees, but both pairs
of eyes fixed upon vacancy.

Nobody ever saw them talk to each other. Catharine's eyes would follow Rhisiart everywhere, and would search for him if he wasn't there;
while Mortimer's eyes would be fixed on any object: a window, a door,
a fragment of tapestry, a picture, through which he could stare into
some receding horizon.

Mortimer's courtesy towards her was exquisite. Rhisiart saw him do
little things for her that he himself had never done. And though they
never conversed, they often exchanged a word, or a look, or even a
smile.

Once or twice it struck Master Brut, who hesitated not to observe
them closely and who was always troubling about how thin she was

growing, that Mortimer treated her with the tender reverence that a devoted servant would offer to a *mad queen*. It was the coming of the Rector and the Canon that hastened on the date of the wedding. And it was the presence of these much-travelled and political-minded men that kept Rhisiart from dwelling any more upon ships for France or priests in Cardigan.

Owen was naturally reticent with his Secretary as to the advantages to be derived from the Mortimer alliance; but the two ecclesiastics talked to the lad of nothing else. They soon found out that the deepest element in Rhisiart's life-illusion was his faith in himself as the guide, counsellor, minister, chancellor, secretary-of-state to an enlightened and civilized ruler of an independent Wales; and upon this they steadily, without pause or intermission, went on playing, till they felt sure that all furtive and reckless schemes had vanished from his mind.

As the fatal day drew nearer Catharine spent more and more time with her friend Lu. This young woman, indulged by her father in all her whims, had grown so eccentric and so much of a recluse that no-body, not even the Arglwyddes herself, who after all was only a guest at Tywyn, dared to do so much as to knock at her chamber-door. On one occasion when the well-meaning Mistress Angharad had presumed to go as far as this, the queer little creature had fallen into hysterics and shrieked down the passage that she must be "left alone, alone, *alone*"—or she would kill herself!

At the very last Catharine seemed not only to avoid all contact with Sir Edmund but to have torn her eyes away from Rhisiart. On the last day of all nobody saw her but Lu and Father Rheinalt. Father Rheinalt was the only priest she would allow to approach her. She made her confession to him. She had no concealments from him. She must have felt that with his tragic and passionate past he knew better than anyone what love was.

Owen was careful to keep Rhisiart close at his side and to cover the table at which the lad worked with rough drafts of eloquent letters to every potentate in Christendom who had ever quarrelled with the House of Lancaster.

A few days before the wedding Rhisiart had rather a startling surprise. Owen's most active leaders in the field, each with their separate army, the Abbot of Caerleon, Rhys Gethin, and Henry Don, weren't able to be present; but day by day various adherents kept arriving, who had either to be provided with tents under the trees or lodging in the foresters' huts.

It was when he was wearily and sadly ascending the front stair-case of the house to put himself in the dwarf's hands that this surprise occurred. The tiny creature had for some time astonished him by her understanding of what he was going through. Never before, since their strange covenant in Dinas Brān, had she kept such a check upon her sharp tongue; and she allowed him to unburden his heart to her as he couldn't do to another soul in the place—no! not even to the Lollard.

But on this occasion, while he had stopped for a moment to gaze out of a window that opened on that fatal forest-path up which he had followed his love after the Nurse's death, he heard himself addressed by name, and there at his side stood the beautiful page, Elphin! The boy was dressed in white silk that fitted tight to his girlish body; and round his slender waist was a crimson sash.

The sight of him brought back so vividly his first day at Glyndyfrdwy—could *he* too be wearing *pali?*—that he recklessly embraced him and kissed him on the lips.

But extricating himself quickly from this embrace, Elphin began in his familiar faltering and nervous manner—"Oh, how fate repeats itself!" thought Rhisiart—a timid request that he would be nicer to Luned when he met her and not go on passing her by without a word or look.

"She promised that if you'd only see her once, and be kind to her like you used to be, she would let me hold her for five minutes by the great clock in the library."

The perfume of sandal-wood swept over our friend with such an insidious wafture when he heard these words that he was forced to gasp and swallow his saliva. Was Providence beginning to imitate the ways of Saint Derfel? Was it *its* fault, or his own fault, that at every important crisis in his life, and *always on a stair-case*, this curst sandal-wood smell should stir his senses?

"Tell Luned—" he began; and he was going to say something bitterly cruel to both her and poor Elphin. He was going to command the boy to declare to her—but suddenly he saw in the beautiful eyes of the page a look that completely disarmed him.

"Why he's looking at me," he thought, "just as I look at Mortimer!" "Tell Luned," he said, "to come any day to the dwarf's sewing-room. I'll be glad to see her." And then he added, with a smile as melancholy as his rival's: "Will that purchase you your five minutes?"

"You—couldn't—possibly—see—her—*alone,* Master Rhisiart?"

At this our distracted friend did burst out, "No, I could *not,* you silly child! Oh, for Mary's sake, leave *me* alone!"

And as he ran up the stairs his mind reverted to Rawlff's last words on the battle-field. "Tell Luned—tell Luned—tell Luned," he muttered bitterly.

It fell to the lot of Mistress Angharad to arrange the details of the great day. It was the Arglwyddes who had sent to Snowdon for Luned and the dwarf, for she refused to trust any of Mistress Rad's maids in the delicate matter of bridal-dresses. Indifferent as to her own appearance, the good lady became more agitated than anyone had ever seen her over her youngest daughter's wedding. Sir Edmund's melancholy sweetness and courtly manners had made a deep impression on her and she alone of all the ladies concerned seemed conscious of the almost royal dignity of the proud House of Mortimer.

At one point there seemed a danger that Catharine might insist that Father Rheinalt should be among the officiating priests; but the poor man was so upset at the mere mention of such thing that the kind-hearted girl quickly put it out of her mind.

It was Father Pascentius who was Mistress Rad's right hand in all her arrangements. His insatiable black eyes and unwieldy figure moved here and there at the house-wife's bidding like some obedient Genie or Jinn from an Arabian romance. All the patriotic gentry of that part of Wales rode over mountain and moor to be present at this great occasion, for, though the marriage itself was to be celebrated in his little ancestral chapel, Rhys Ddu had caused to be erected a vast rain-proof pavilion outside his mansion where a sort of after-ceremony in the traditional Welsh manner was to take place.

There were all manner of wild rumours in the air. All agreed that Hotspur, the new Lady Mortimer's brother-in-law, was on the verge of raising the great Percy standard against the King. French ships in aid of the movement were, it was said, only held up by the gales. Messages of congratulation kept arriving from all sorts of unexpected quarters. Even John Trevor, Bishop of St. Asaph, had allowed his Prior to represent him, King's man though he still was.

Do what he could to escape, Rhisiart soon found his own costume for the occasion the object of the special attention of his little friend with the purple beard. He had insisted on black as best suited to his mood, but his small tyrant, whose fingers were as deft as they were tiny, soon managed to slash his scholar's velvet with so much sky-blue and silver that before she had done with him he had more resemblance to the dazzling Sir Gawain than to the grave Sir Peredur.

Owen himself, as at his proclamation, shone resplendent in gold; but he bore on his flowing mantle of scarlet the solitary black lion of his paternal house.

One thing our friend couldn't bring himself to do and that was to enter the chapel while they were being married. Side by side with Master Brut, whose own attire was as rich as it was simple, he stood in the front rank of the spectators who in a covered way awaited the passing of the bridal procession from the chapel to the pavilion.

A deafening clamour greeted Sir Edmund and Catharine as they emerged from the ceremony, and it was this roar of wild excitement that made it possible—while the bridegroom paused to acknowledge the crowd's salutations and to say something to Master Brut—for Catharine and Rhisiart to exchange a word.

The girl was as white as her dress. Rhisiart feared she was on the point of fainting, but she managed to look straight into his eyes which were burning-dry above his hooked nose; and as he pressed the bare knuckles of the hand she gave him against his clenched teeth she had the strength even to whisper to him. He could feel her breath as she whispered. He could even catch its fragrance which was like that of a crushed briar-leaf; and well—too well—could he catch her words. "I shall call my first boy Rhisiart," she said, and that was all. Then she tore her eyes away and passed on.

After the old Welsh custom they were to spend their bridal-night in the house of their marriage; and Rhys Ddu had resigned to them for this purpose his own private chamber, which was only a little less spacious, though a good deal plainer, than his daughter's.

How he endured the hours that followed our friend would have been hard put to it to describe. He lacked even the heart to drown his feelings in drink, though mead flowed like water that night. One thing he marked, and there were the wildest rumours concerning this: both the Prince and Broch-o'-Meifod vanished from the scene long before the bride and bridegroom went to their chamber.

But the terrible hours passed at last, as all passes, and Rhisiart found himself with the rest of that great assembly—only this time anything but in the front row!—watching those two figures, hers and that other's, grow more and more indistinct under the flickering of the torches, as they ascended the ancient stairs.

Then, frantically forcing his way through the gleaming crowd, that seemed to him like gorgeously attired dancers at a dance of death, he fled to the stables and buried his face in the familiar-smelling hide of Griffin. Deep blood-currents of comprehension and satisfaction quivered through those piebald sides at his having come to him and to him alone; nor was the old horse in the least astonished when, freeing him from his stall and wrapping his sack-cloth round his own finery, his master leapt on his back and rode him at a gallop down the nearest starlit avenue.

This, as it turned out, was the very one down which he and the Lollard had followed Catharine and Lu on that fatal day of the arrival of Master Young. How he had longed for the presence of that great statesman—and now he was reaping the benefit of his hero's far-sighted schemes!

He urged the old horse on, recklessly, heedlessly. It was lucky for both Griffin and his rider that the night was frosty and clear. How the stars glimmered through the bare branches, endowing each one of them in its motionless age with the monumental glamour of something withdrawn, unearthly, expectant!

A faint cool air blew upon his face, an air so light and noiseless that the sounds of the forest, the stirring of sleepy birds, the scuttling of rabbits over the dead leaves and pine-needles, the barking of dogs in distant wood-men's huts, the hooting of night owls, the scampering panic of wild-wood ponies, only intensified the spaciousness of the silence.

The stars were so bright and the branches so still that he felt as if he and Griffin were moving together through some celestial Forest of Tywyn, a forest older than the earth, larger than the earth, with its own gleaming firmament above it and the leaves of centuries piled up beneath it.

He had already gone a good deal further than Catharine and Lu went, in their search for Pryderi's Tree, when suddenly he pulled Griffin up, pulled him up so violently that the old horse nearly collapsed.

There in front of them, gathering what looked like toad-stools at the root of a beech-tree was Broch-o'-Meifod.

"Oh it's another of you life-lovers, is it?" said the giant calmly. Rhisiart perceived even by the faint light of the stars that the man was more upset than he permitted to appear.

"Ride on, if you want to find him, laddie. He's playing his tricks at the Tree."

"*Who* for Mary's sake?"

"Owen, *Owen*—I tell you. He's at Pryderi's Tree. He's punishing himself for this marriage. I can't do anything with him; but you're another of these—"

"But—Master Broch—how could you leave him? What can *I* do that *you* couldn't do?"

"Ride on, boy. It's not far. You'll soon see what he's been up to. I'll follow you in a moment. I'm getting something to stop the blood."

Rhisiart obeyed him without further protest; but his heart grew more and more ice-cold as his sweat mixed with Griffin's sweat. "This is the end of all," he said to himself. "Catharine gone, and now Owen gone. O Mary, Queen of Heaven, save him! It's for Owen, Griff; it's for Owen, old friend—faster—faster—faster!"

Though he had never seen them before, the mound and the Tree were unmistakeable when he reached them. They stood in a large clearing which itself lay above the level of all but the tallest trees; and as the clearing was above the forest, and the mound was above the clearing, so the Tree was above the mound.

Jumping off Griffin's back and leaving the old horse panting and exhausted, Rhisiart bolted up the bare hillock, scrambled up the mound, and then stopped, aghast and petrified at what he saw. On the top of the mound were the remains of a gigantic oak, an oak compared with which the one into whose heart he had helped his master to fling the Lord of Nannau was a mere sapling. Its girth, even in dissolution, was the greatest he'd ever seen of any forest growth. It was entirely hollow, and it gaped up at the stars like the jagged throat of some prehistoric monster than had upreared itself from the bowels of the earth to re-proach the heavens.

Down upon its gaping jaws shone the glittering hosts of stars; and all the multitudinous branches of that vast forest waited at its feet in spell-bound expectation. It was as if the Forests of Tywyn, burdened with the wrongs against which Pryderi had struggled in vain, were holding their breath until *that mouth* should utter its defiance of "Caer Gwydion," its challenge to the mocking immensity of the Milky Way!

Above the forest rose the mound. Above the mound rose the Tree. And out of the centre of the tree rose the figure of Owen. Pryderi's Tree was nothing but a ruined stump. The Prince had found no ob-stacle—save the superstitious fear of a whole country-side—in precipi-tating himself into that cavernous excrescence, the whole height of which could hardly have been more than five feet above the surface of the mound.

But Broch was right. The Prince had done something to himself! Only his torso was visible. He was leaning against the jagged rim of the orifice, his hands on its edge; but his head was flung back, as if, like the funnel in which he stood, he were lifting up a voiceless curse upon that starry expanse.

But what made our friend's knees weak and his stomach sick was that he could clearly see dark blotches upon that white throat under the lifted forked beard. Were they blood? He feared it, he greatly feared it.

"My Prince! My father!" he cried aloud; and his voice sounded so strange, so unlike any voice he'd ever heard, that the silence which fol-lowed it seemed full of ghostly echoes. Then something made him glance down to the ground. And there, just beneath the figure in the tree and just at his own feet, lay an object that he knew too well! He stooped hurriedly, picked it up and thrust it away amid the loops and embroideries of the dwarf's handiwork. It was his own dagger; and it came over him that he had left it in the Prince's room, lying upon his final copy of the letter to Mortimer's tenants: the letter that told them how Owen would place the Earl of March on the throne and how the border lordships of Maelienydd and Gwerthrynion and Rhayader and Arwystli and Cyfeiliog and Caer Einion must not be incommoded.

With a sick terror in his heart he now pressed his body close to the oak-stump and flung his arms about his master's shoulders.

"My Prince! My father!" he moaned hoarsely. "It's Rhisiart, my Prince—it's your own poor Rhisiart!"

Oh, Mother of God be thanked! Hail Mary, hail Mary! The man *did* bend down his head at this.

"Rhisiart?" The syllable came from his wounded throat like bubbles from a tree-root bole full of black water.

"It's I, my Prince, my father! It's your Rhisiart, come to bring you back to life, to Wales, to—*to Catharine!"* He knew the man had heard him, he knew the man had understood him; but the trance, or whatever it was, into which he had fallen broke under the too-sudden return of his soul to his body and his head fell forward, the blood from his hurt throat spurting against Rhisiart's face.

But a great human shadow rose up by their side now, and Broch-o'-Meifod, panting like a hunted mammoth, laid hold of the unconscious man. Together they dragged him out of the tree and laid him on the turf.

"Is he dead?" whispered Rhisiart. The giant didn't answer. He was busy with the wounds in his friend's throat into which he was pressing some sort of queer-smelling fungus-powder from the handful of toad-stools he had gathered in the forest.

At last he rose from his knees. "No, lad, he's *not* dead. Nor is he in the least danger of dying. He's only been play-acting for conscience-sake."

"I don't believe it!" cried Rhisiart indignantly.

"No, you don't believe it; because you love him without understanding him. He was only trying experiments! I know him. I tell you I know him better than I know myself. The man's a life-worshipper. He's *wickedly* alive!" He paused for a moment, staring at the silent figure on the turf. Then he said slowly, "What I can't get him to understand, with all his tricks, is that *this earth*"—and he lifted one of his great heels and brought it down again like the hoof of a centaur— "with all these loves and wars and plots and counterplots on it, is no more than a distorted mirage of the reality! There—he's coming back. Let's carry him to your horse."

At the moment when Rhisiart was setting off into the forest, Sir Edmund and the new Lady Mortimer heard the door of their chamber closed upon them.

"Turn away, if it please you, dear my Lord, till I'm in bed!" But there was no need for the Welsh bride to say this to her Norman bridegroom. A gentleman of the old tradition was Sir Edmund; and he was already moving to the small oratory concealed by heavy curtains, whither his personal possessions had been conveyed! Here, in almost complete darkness, he remained so long on his knees that a far less gallant girl than Catharine would have had all the respite she required.

As she lay in Rhys Ddu's great ancestral bed, her sea-green eyes wide open and staring at the steady candle-flames reflected in a shield above the smouldering hearth, she could hear the *click-click* of Mortimer's rosary as he told his beads.

"It won't be the pain I shall mind," she thought. "I'm *glad* it hurts. The more it hurts the better!" And she clenched her fingers into the palms of her hands as they lay at her sides, which was what Lu had told her—though it was entirely from that queer one's imagination— all girls did under the sweet pain of ravishment. "I shall think of you,. my only love," she said to herself, *"all the time!* Whatever he does I shall think of you. Whatever I endure I shall think of you. And I shan't cry out. Lu says all girls cry out, and that the maids will be waiting with bare feet outside the door to hear me. Well! Let them wait! They won't hear a sound."

"Shall I put out the candles or leave them?" he asked her. How grand and sad his head looked as he stood there in his long linen gown, a gown just like her own only of thicker stuff! She turned her head a little as she lay on her back under the wall—as close under the wall as she could get; for, for all the calm of her mind, her body kept yielding to curious little tremors and shiverings—and with her head thus turned to one side against the portion of the pillow that was covered with her flaxen hair she surveyed him with a thoughtful puckering of her brows.

"I hope my teeth won't begin chattering," she thought. "Lu didn't say whether girls' teeth chattered." And she began clenching her teeth just as tightly as she was clenching her fingers. But he *had* a noble head—and oh! how sad he looked!

This grave, melancholy silence, as he stood there in the chilly room, waiting till she chose to unclench her teeth and answer his question about the candles, now began in some fantastic manner to annoy her. It made her feel very lonely; and it made this clenching of her fingers seem childish and ridiculous. Why didn't he say something outrageous and obscene? Why didn't he say something sardonic and life-weary, as Meredith would have done? His grave, sad politeness made her feel as if she were going to give up her maidenhead in the chapter-house of Valle Crucis!

"Well, child," he said, "I'll put them out. I can easily light them again if you don't like the darkness."

Oh how silly her body was to shiver like this just because there was a man lying by her side! And he hadn't even touched her yet. The bed was so big, and she had made herself so small against the wall, that there must have been a dagger's length between them. A dagger's length? Rhisiart's dagger's length!

For a few wretched minutes, and these were certainly the worst of all she'd gone through that wretched day, they lay in Rhys Ddu's great bed without a movement, a word, a sound. The young man lay on his back staring at the unglazed window from which an air that seemed almost frosty was blowing in; and the young girl lay on *her* back staring at the tiny points of redness and the wisps of blue smoke of the extinguished candles, and at the fire-light shadows flickering about the walls.

At last she couldn't stand it a second longer. "Why are you so sad and so silent, dear my Lord? Do you hate it so much being married to a Welsh girl?"

"I'll tell you in a little while, Catharine," he said, pronouncing her name in the manner in which it was pronounced in France, "only you must let me do everything I want to first!"

Her relaxed fingers clenched themselves again and those tremblings recommenced. But this "everything" he wanted had apparently nothing to do with a girl's body, whether willing or unwilling; it had to do, it seemed, with re-lighting the candles, visiting the alcove where he had left his belongings and getting into bed again with a Provençal lute in his hand.

He now sat up in the bed, arranging his pillow behind his back and crossing his legs; and in this position, while the candle-flames were again reflected in the crusader's shield, he began playing on the lute.

Catharine's fingers relaxed, her mouth opened in wonder, her eyes got round, the blood returned to her cheeks. As he played—and she remembered with what interest he had listened to all their Welsh music and never breathed a word about his lute—he became a different person.

Flickerings of something resembling gaiety crossed his haughty profile, with its short upper lip, and its high retreating forehead passing into tight, small, dark-brown curls. One Provençal tune after another he played, and the faint smiles with which he became aware that with the motions of a timid bird, every time he began again, Catharine slid a little nearer, had a touch of mischief in them.

At last she was so near that as he commenced a melody known to all young people from Dublin to Constantinople, he felt her body touching his; and it was almost with the inevitableness of a movement in a dance that he slipped the hand that had been holding the lute round her form, so that when he grasped the instrument again it was in such a way that her breast was pressed against him.

One more ditty he played; and to the girl's amazement it was a tune that she had heard her Nurse repeat to her a thousand times when she was an infant at Glyndyfrdwy. This loosened the flood-gates. All those tears that her mother wouldn't let her shed and that she was too proud to shed before Lu began to pour down her cheeks.

Mortimer tossed the lute to the foot of the bed and drew her towards him till with her hair covering his chest and her face pressed against him she sobbed to her heart's content.

The candles were guttering in their sconces and Mortimer's nightgown clung about his throat as if he'd been exposed to the rains of Tywyn before that fit of weeping was over. Then settling his pillow in its proper position and sinking down in the bed with his arm still under her he began to speak. "Do you still want to know why I've been so sad—Catharine?"

Once more that French pronunciation of her name gave her a curious relief. She began to feel as if the Catharine who loved Rhisiart needn't be so stern with this other Catharine whose name sounded so different!

"Tell me, dear my Lord," she whispered.

"Do you mind if I let the candles burn themselves out?"

She replied by the faintest possible movement towards him.

"Well, child, it's a long story and a piteous one," he said, "but I'll make it as short as I can. Before my elder brother died there was a girl I loved and who loved me. She was—"

"What was her name?"

"Her name was Bridget, and she was fair like you, only her eyes were different. She was of the people, but she was very proud. She refused to be what we call my paramour, and what she wanted I wanted."

"You wanted to marry?"

"We *decided* to marry and escape to Scotland where I had many friends."

Catharine was silent, thinking of those ships to France and of that easy priest in Cardigan-town. Then she said, "Did your brother find out?"

"Yes," he said simply. "He found out."

"Did he make you leave her?"

A prolonged silence followed, in the midst of which the candles flickered down and were extinguished. Then she became aware that the man in whose arms she lay was making proud and indignant efforts to keep his self-control. She could feel his chest heave, and she clung to him the closer. But he recovered himself and went on.

"I don't know what happened. I never spoke to my brother again, and he died soon after; but she—she was found drowned in the Severn."

Catharine made no movement. She lay as still as if she were drowned, too. She saw this Bridget with the cold, proud face and the hair like her own and the heart that they'd broken.

"Whether she did it herself," Mortimer went on, "or whether it was done by my brother's orders I shall never know."

Once more there was complete silence in the marriage-bed of Tywyn; while the air that blew upon their faces from the window grew yet more frosty, and the last red embers faded.

Suddenly, when the room was quite dark, Catharine said, very quietly, "If we have children, dear my Lord, I shall call our girl Bridget and our boy Rhisiart. But it's been worse for you than for me; and I shall never, *never* forget your having told me this!"

XVII

THE GOOSANDER

THE TWO years that followed the marriage of Catharine and Mortimer were years of steadily increasing triumph both for Owen and for Wales.

The year of grace 1405, the fifth year of the Prince's assumption of his title, opened for all Welshmen with what looked like an irresistible wave of victory. It is true that Mortimer's brother-in-law, Hotspur, was dead, slain at Shrewsbury as he faced the King and his son, but Hotspur's father, the old Earl, was still in arms against the House of Lancaster; and a new adherent, and a very crafty one, had recently declared for Owen in the person of Thomas, Lord Bardolf.

This Bardolf was a King's man who had turned against his master with that undying hatred which Henry the Fourth seems to have had the power to excite; and his grand passion now was to unite the King's enemies in one triumphant pact.

The popular Bishop of St. Asaph, John Trevor, whose heart had long been wavering towards the Welsh cause, had now openly joined it; and though, in the North, the castles of Carnarvon, Beaumaris, Conway, Rhuddlan, Denbigh, Flint and Welshpool remained in English hands, the far more strategic fortresses of Aberystwyth and Harlech were securely in Owen's possession.

The fortunes of war still swayed up and down, sometimes with the most tantalizing chances lost by the breadth of a hair to one side or the other; as, for instance, when in the beginning of February the notorious Lady Despenser, who had actually kidnapped the little Earl of March, the Mortimer claimant to the throne, was only caught at the last moment with her convoy at Cheltenham, as she rode post-haste towards a sanctuary in Wales.

Owen had already summoned one of those parliaments of the commonalty, towards which both Rhisiart and Rhisiart's legal ideal, Master Young, had been steadily urging him; but our youthful friend was now arranging for a much more extensive assembly, modelled not only upon the parliament of Hywel the Good, but upon the parliament at Westminster.

For weeks he had been drafting and issuing writs to all the *cantrefs* in the principality, and he was in high spirits over the response. This second parliament was to be held in the castle in a few days so as to enable the free-holders, among the "four good men" of each *commote,* to return to their farms for the March ploughing.

Our friend's old acquaintance, the Rector of Byford, had by this time used the hold he'd acquired over Boniface the Ninth to get himself promoted, as he had predicted in the Forests of Tywyn, to the See of Bangor; but Byford's Pope was now dead, and the new Roman Pontiff, Innocent the Seventh, found it as hard as his predecessor had done to cope with the Great Schism.

It was no doubt this change among the successors of the Fisherman that encouraged King Charles of France to send his private confessor, Hugh Eddouyer, a diplomatic preaching-friar, to make a personal appeal to the new Prince of Wales to transfer that country's spiritual allegiance from Rome to Avignon. This crafty messenger from Charles the Sixth timed his visit to a nicety; for he caused it to coincide with the return of Master Young, now Owen's official Chancellor, from Paris, bringing news of a great French fleet on the verge of sailing to give him substantial aid.

The ubiquitous Lord Bardolf, urged on in his devious ways not so much by love of the Welsh as by hatred for Henry, had persuaded the new Bishop of Bangor to appoint to the archidiaconal office in his diocese a mysterious young Welshman who called himself Father Ignotus, and who was reported to be a somewhat questionable relative of the Bishop's own; and it was arranged by this shrewd pair of plotters, lest Bishop Byford's hand should be too apparent in the matter, that instead of the episcopal palace in Bangor, the private house of the newly-ordained Archdeacon should be the trysting place between any emissaries that Owen might wish to send and the representatives of the Earl of Northumberland.

It was Master John Hanmer, the Arglwyddes's brother, who had been Owen's lay-ambassador at the court of Charles; and it was he who now appeared at Harlech, in company with Brother Eddouyer and a couple of young French noblemen, to report on the success of the embassy to France.

Chancellor Young himself went straight to Owen's other headquarters, the impregnable castle at Aberystwyth, where he was to hold an ecclesiastical court of his own; but it was in Harlech that Owen's family, including Sir Edmund and Lady Mortimer, were now permanently established.

Almost all the devoted personal adherents of the Prince were gathered about him in these noble purlieus, the most ancient as well as the most romantic stronghold in the land; and it may well be that not only King Henry's Lodge at Berkhampstead but even King Charles's perambulatory court had less of the antique ritual of a royal residence than this great Castle by the Sea.

The vast space of its battlemented enclosure, the immense numbers of its chambers, its impregnable position, all these things rendered it an ideal sanctuary for a prince at war. Brān the Blessed himself, who was of such gigantic stature that no human erection could contain him, might have exercised his colossal limbs in the base-court; while the stairways and passages and banquet-halls and libraries and chapels with intricate ascents and descents everywhere, and with turrets crowded with arrow-slits looking across the water, made Harlech a world of its own, a world where dramas of love and birth and life and death could go on, and only the seagulls screaming about the battlements be aware of them, while from the infinite horizon where sea met sky any imaginary watcher on the ramparts might fancy he heard, when dawn rose or twilight fell, the far-off mystic song of the Birds of Rhiannon.

Rhys Gethin came and went, like an unpredictable thunderstorm, between his now well-seasoned army of spearmen and his perilous mistress if such she were. Nobody knew how far this affair had gone. All that could be said was that Lowri still clung, in her perversity, for none could sound that strange heart, to Master Brut's converted, or half-converted, Hog of Chirk.

Lady Mortimer had kept her word. She had now a son of two years called Rhisiart and a little baby-daughter called Bridget, and, managing both her husband and her lover with a dangerous skill that made the Arglwyddes regard her with puzzled wonder, she had already begun to take her mother's place as the Great Lady of the Castle.

Catharine, and she alone in that embattled princedom, broke every rule of the prehistoric ritual with which Owen and his bards and his prophets had surrounded themselves. She insisted on nursing her infants herself, whereas from time immemorial such babes of a noble house had been handed over to the care of a foster-parent. She insisted on leaving the women's quarters; and with little Bridget at her breast and little Rhisiart clinging to her gown would move freely, wherever her fancy led, about this huge and intricate pile. She was often with Sir Edmund, but she was quite as often with her little son's namesake. But such was the proud beauty of her blossoming womanhood that not a flicker of any uncomely rumour floated across her path.

It was Owen's way to get rid of *his* overpowering emotions by some weird penance inflicted upon himself; and even if his Meifod friend had been correct in his supposition that those stabbings at his throat with Rhisiart's dagger had been well under control, they and his whole abandonment between Pryderi's Tree and the "Caer Gwydion" of the firmament had been real enough to work their purpose. He *had* felt remorse, and he *had* punished himself; and his love of life had gone on.

The Arglwyddes did notice a certain reserve between him and Catharine; but she couldn't detect the least sign of such a thing between him and Rhisiart.

Catharine herself didn't forget her girl-friends in this new half-royal life. To the joy of everyone in the place she made the Prince send to Snowdon for Tegolin and her Friar; and since Rhys Ddu was now fighting for Owen at some distance from Tywyn, she persuaded her friend Lu to share her many-storied turret fronting the Harlech waves.

Whether there was a definite purpose or not in her choice of the moment of Lu's arrival, which coincided with a second convalescence of Meredith, wounded again in battle and again committed, but this time under the eye of his father, into the hands of the Scab, neither Sir Edmund nor Rhisiart could decide.

It became a sort of half-humorous link between them, the discussion of this nice point, a link that to the watchful eyes of Father Pascentius presented itself as pure masculine jealousy over a friendship between two women.

But whether intended by Catharine or not, the mere physical conditions of Meredith's second recovery, in a chamber adjoining the Mortimer turret, made it impossible for even Lu's shyness to create a barrier; and very soon the queer-looking little creature, her long hair floating about her frail form like the dusky smoke about a bonfire of weeds, was accepted by everyone in the castle as the natural and unquestioned guardian of the invalid's pillow.

How Lu dealt with the Scab nobody but Catharine was ever told; but the complete absence from her timid personality of every kind of ordinary feminine appeal made it seem, even to Father Pascentius, that unless the prophet had a mania for mouse-coloured hair it was unlikely that he would treat this intruder at his patient's bed-side with anything worse than professional indifference.

As a matter of fact a couple of weeks had hardly passed before the Bard of Ffinnant began to interest himself in transactions that drew him for many hours every day from Meredith's side; and it wasn't long before the whole castle, Father Pascentius included, took for granted that that so queer and eccentric young lady must have a knowledge of herbs and lotions and unguents and even of elixirs of life, hardly inferior to that of a real *conjurer*.

The Arglwyddes's brother, John, resembled his sister in almost every respect. In face and figure he was a middle-aged replica of her son Griffith, while in his calm, wise, unruffled nature he had the same power of steering his way through life as the Arglwyddes was destined to display to the bitter end.

John was on excellent terms with Father Rheinalt and he had equal respect for the monk's daughter whose presence in the castle he had welcomed from the first; but he could hardly bear the sight of Father Pascentius! He would complain to his sister that this spying monk from Valle Crucis spoilt Harlech for him. "I feel," he told her, "as if I were an heretical version of Saint Thomas that had to be revised from cover to cover!"

John Hanmer was heartily glad, too, when his fellow-ambassador to

France betook himself to Aberystwyth. He had got thoroughly weary of the smooth gabble of that toothless mouth; and he had a private notion that the knavish tricks of these incalculable Frenchmen were countered more effectively by a laconic reserve than by the voluble protestations in which Master Young loved to indulge.

The high-born young gentlemen—they were scarcely older than pages—whom Charles the Sixth had deputed to convey his promises of help to the Prince were two youthful cousins, Gilles and Jean de Pirogue. Jean was a big, blond, imperturbable young aristocrat, of whose personal characteristics nothing was betrayed, save a passion for hunting, a genius for hurriedly-invented lies, and an unconcealed loathing for his cousin Gilles.

This Gilles was more of an agitation to our friend Rhisiart than he was to Owen. Owen treated him with a grave punctilious courtesy from which every personal reaction was excluded. He compelled the lad, whether he liked it or not, to go through the long, wearisome formality of the presentation of certain ornamental pieces of armour, triumphs of the art of the Parisian goldsmiths, which he had brought from the French King.

This ceremony, Rhisiart assumed, was organized by the Prince solely to impress these young scions of a noble French family, but it was hard for him to imagine Owen going through such a tedious ceremony if he hated it as much as he himself did. And how could he *not* hate it? To our friend's Norman taste such ceremonies were simply tiresome and ridiculous. He could see the giggling fits against which his naughty mother would have had to struggle at the sight of Owen kneeling down so humbly while this repulsive young man hooked and buckled the pieces of armour about him.

The longer this young Gilles de Pirogue remained in the castle the more agitated did Rhisiart become. Only a very short space of time passed before he discovered that his own worst vice—that sensual ecstasy he derived from the thought of particular kinds of cruelty—was shared by this unpleasing youth to a degree that amounted to insanity. And yet the boy wasn't insane. In everything else he was crafty and cold and calculating. On this path only he seemed prepared to take the maddest risks, whether to his honor or to his reputation or to his life.

The culminating revelation he got of this young aristocrat's peculiar-

ity came, as might have been expected, from Father Pascentius. The
Father called him one day into the smallest and most remote of Harlech's three libraries, where he had collected the rarest of all the books
in the castle round his own desk. It was Candlemas Day, the second of
February, the day devoted to the Purification of the Blessed Virgin;
and Father Pascentius commenced by inquiring whether his fellow-
botanist had fasted from meat that morning.

"It's good to fast, my son, good to fast, good to fast," he repeated as
he pushed his visitor into a chair by the fire and planted himself upon
a wooden stool near him.

Rhisiart was amazed by the deft way the Father seized upon this
three-legged object, shiny as an axe-handle from the daily pressure of
his huge buttocks, and whipped it so neatly between his legs ere he
lowered his weight upon it.

"Good to fast, my son!" and it seemed to our friend as if over one
of those incorrigible eyes the eyelid perceptibly fell. Had the interpreter
of Saint Thomas winked at him? And then he remembered. Father
Pascentius was making sport of the present Abbot of Valle Crucis!

"My soul shall magnify the Lord and my spirit shall rejoice," was
his next utterance, half to himself and half aloud; and it was impossible
for Rhisiart, after five years of Master Brut's friendship, not to wonder
what the Virgin Mother, if she were watching this ungainly recorder
of her Purification squatting on his stool, thought of his rendering of
her Song of Conception.

"Well, my son, I expect you want to know what I bothered you
about"; and, seizing his stool with both hands while still seated upon
it, he caused it to hop along the edge of the cindery hearth, so that he
could get closer to his interlocutor. "The matter is this," and he cast a
cautious glance at the massive door of the chamber, "and it is an important—" And then quite suddenly, but not to Rhisiart's surprise, who
had long since grown accustomed to his vagaries, he thrust a hand
into his habit and brought out a tangled mass of minute plants. Dropping these into his capacious lap he selected one of them and held it at
arm's length in the shaft of sun-motes that fell across the room.

"You see the genus of course," he said. "Of course you do! But this
is a separate species. At first sight you mightn't think so, but I'm sure
I'm not mistaken. It's a *kind* of bitter cress. Of course you see *that*,

from the corymbose arrangement, but the common bitter cress never shows itself till March. I believe it will be necessary for me"—in his excitement he used a characteristic Welsh idiom—"necessary for me to 'put a name on it,' and I have decided to name it *Cardamine Pascentius*. And since it may be hereafter the only plant to bear my name, I would be glad, my son, if, when I'm dead, you'd be good enough to plant it— *Cardamine Pascentius*—upon my grave."

Rhisiart dutifully rose, took the *Cardamine Pascentius* between his finger and thumb, and walking to the window surveyed the small object carefully.

"Blessed Mary!" he thought, "it looks like little Lu!" And he held it in such a way, framed in that narrow window, that it made a tiny dark pattern against the golden sun-path upon the in-rolling tide.

Then coming back to his seat by the hearth he returned it to its complacent god-father, who without moving from his stool thrust it back with the rest into the pocket of his habit.

"I shall remember, Father," our friend promised him. "But, if the Prince allows me, I hope in the next campaign—"

He crossed himself hurriedly; but the monk was now with the familiar gesture of *his* hands reducing all such relativities as human promises to the indifference of the absolute.

"What's your opinion, my dear son," and, though Rhisiart attributed the impression to the dazzlement of his eyes by that bright path on the waves, the fancy *did* cross his mind that a quite human glance of affection had reached him from the unwieldly figure on the stool, "with regard to this young Pirogue?"

"Jean, do you mean, Father?" our friend hastily murmured. "I believe he's out hunting already; though what he'll find at this time of year—"

"No, no, my son, the other one, the other one! What's your opinion of *him?*"

Rhisiart might as well have looked for enlightenment into the bottomless depths of Llyn Tegid as into the orbs that now confronted him. "Oh, I don't know, Father," he brought out carelessly. "He's got an unnaturally pale complexion, and his mouth makes me think of that water-snake we found the other day swallowing a frog."

"You remember, son, how in one of your early confessions to me, before you loved Lady Mortimer, you spoke of the blood-lust—well! not exactly *that,* but in the same category of mortal sin—which you found to be such an agitating temptation?"

Rhisiart nodded without speaking.

"Well! this Gilles *lives* for that! Nothing else on earth has interest for him. Everything else is done mechanically, seen mechanically, spoken mechanically. The lad's like a perambulatory corpse, I tell you, *except for that."*

Rhisiart bent his head frowning, gazing uneasily at the Father's ragged sandals. "Father," he enquired, "why do you suppose it is that such horrible temptations reach us in these modern days? Do you think there's been some marriage in Hell since that star with a tail appeared?"

"Marriage in Hell, my son?"

"I mean a new type of devil, born to betray us, such as was never known in the earlier times? Or do you think, Father, it's because of the anti-Pope at Avignon? Or is the Christian Faith gradually dying out, as Master Broch says?"

"Every age, my son," the monk replied quietly, "feels itself to be worse and more wicked than the preceding ones. Our age does, as you say, suffer from the breaking down of faith and chivalry and from the grievous imputations implied in the mere existence of the anti-Pope; but you must remember that all great virtues carry their defects, I might say their *curse,* with them. Things were done under the urge of faith that sicken us in these enlightened days. Between ourselves, my son, I think the worse aspect of *our* age is the *intelligence* of its cruelty. King Hal, for instance, in his burning of heretics, is influenced by no old-fashioned wrath against blasphemies. It's a pure political move, to gain favour with the—"

"But I didn't come to lecture you, my dear boy, "I came to tell you that since Owen and Griffith and Sir Edmund have all gone hunting with Jean de Pirogue, there's no one left in this castle—for you know what Master Hanmer is!—that I can depend upon in the matter that's now come up. I don't want to go to Broch—"

Rhisiart leapt out of his chair with a bound. "You don't mean," he cried, "that Lord Talbot has rushed here from Hereford, or John Grendor from Glamorgan, and we've got to man the walls!"

"Tut, tut, lad! What are you talking about? Isn't the Abbot of Caerleon keeping at bay the last big army King Hal has the money to muster till his next parliament? You, the Prince's advisor, to talk so wildly!"

"But the Abbot may have been defeated! He may have been killed! Oh, for Mary's sake, Father, tell me what's happened! I'm only"—and the Secretary paused and groaned bitterly—"only a letter-copier, a clerk, a scribe, a wretched book-worm; but I *have* ridden a horse and drawn a sword in my time—and my horse is no fool either, though he *is* getting old. John Grendor's known to be the best captain in Christendom, and Lord Talbot runs him close. Our Rhys Gethin's a ramping madman compared with either! For Mary's sake, Father, what has happened? I'm sure it's John Grendor—I'm sure that's what it is. He must have raised the money and the men himself and decided to attack our main stronghold! It's just like him to have found out the day when the Prince would be hunting; for he always—"

But the Father had risen to his feet and in his impatience with his young friend had actually flung his stool against the wall. "*Listen* to me, Rhisiart, listen, boy! Your *horse* may be sensible enough, I don't deny it; but you yourself are a fantastical fool! Can't you believe me when I tell you that it's the doings of this damned French boy I've come about? So stop roaring of your swords and spears and your Talbots and Grendors! You're as touchy as an old bowman from Crécy, who can do nothing but talk of the Black Prince's horse-shoes. How can I trust you in a crisis when you behave like this?"

Rhisiart couldn't help smiling at the monk's reproaches. In his huge relief that it wasn't an English army—for of course there *was* serious danger of this, as he alone in that castle realized—he would have continued to smile if the Father had struck him with his stool instead of flinging it against the wall.

But the monk was in a very serious mood; and the most curious evidence of this was that his eyes had that same odd film upon them—like thin flakes of transparent horn—which they had when he was speaking of the *Cardamine Pascentius*.

"Something's happening that must be stopped, my son," he said gravely. "There's pain being inflicted in this castle that *cannot* be allowed. But I don't want to go to the Prince about it!"

"Why not?" asked Rhisiart. "The Prince wouldn't put up for a second with such things in Harlech."

The eyes of Father Pascentius came to life; and like two ferrets whom their owner sends down a rabbit-burrow they plunged into the young man's soul. "The Prince," said the monk solemnly, "isn't like you and me. He has himself in control *as a rule*—but not always! Cast your mind back, my son, and ask yourself, as others have asked themselves, what happened to Hywel Sele of Nannau."

"Let's go then!" cried Rhisiart impatiently. "Don't let's delay a moment! I ought to have a sword, though, oughtn't I?"

"Have you your dagger?"

The young man showed it to him and concealed it again.

"I've worn it bare," he said, "since we heard Davy Gam was on the prowl. 'Twould be out as quick as his knife if I saw him near Owen!"

"Come then," said the monk in a low voice. "But remember we've only got to stop *this*. You know as well as I do that nothing must happen to King Charles's envoy."

The theologian shook down his habit, pulled his cowl over his head and pushed back the curtain, for the door of this particular retreat was rarely closed, and went out into the passage followed by his young friend. Up and down endless corridors and endless flights of narrow stone steps Rhisiart followed the cowled figure. Sometimes the passages they traversed were nearly dark, in spite of the sunlight that poured down against the seaward battlements. More than once they emerged into the open air, and Rhisiart turned to glance at the fishing-boats on the glittering waves. He found himself growing more and more nervous. What kind of scene was awaiting them?

Rhisiart felt puzzled and sad. This great castle by the sea, over which now flew Owen's new standard, the four lions rampant of Gwynedd, had it been built for one kind of greed and cruelty, only to prove a protection for another, a subtler and a worse? Master Sparrow was still in good spirits; but what had the common people really gained by being free of the English? The country-side, he knew, was burnt and ravaged in every direction. And what had Owen himself gained beyond those ramping lions on his armour, on his shields, on his horses' trappings? In his imagination Rhisiart already began to hear the cries of that "pain" they were going to bring to an end. It must be something exceptional to have sent those deadly eyes of Father Pascentius voyaging down the sun-path. But what sort of a promise was it for the future when the Prince of Wales mustn't be told of what was going on in his own castle?

While he watched the cowled figure before him dive through a narrow arch, leading down from these high ramparts, our friend, who was no longer an impulsive boy but an eccentric and anxious man, cast a final look at the glittering distance. He was too high up to see the beach, or the rocks, or even the little stone-jetty; but he noticed how far the tide was drawing back, leaving a great stretch of yellow sand.

"In Brān the Blessed's time," he said to himself, "the waves must have washed against the wall. The sea's receded. A few hundred years more and all this sand may be tilled pastures!" He turned his head and glanced at the dark steps down which his guide had descended. The monk too had turned and was looking back at him. *That* meant they were at the end of their quest! He thrust his hand under his jerkin where he wore an unseen belt. Yes! he could draw his dagger at a glance from the monk, at less than a glance, at the flicker of an eyelid!

"I must go," he thought; but oh, how reluctant his body was to obey that command! Was he about to be seized by one of those attacks of black darkness, as when he drew his sword in front of the Chirk archers or followed the Lollard down that swinging rope? "But I did what I *had* to do," he said to himself, "even though I didn't know I was doing it! I killed that English boy at Bryn Glas—but *that* was with my sword. I've never stabbed anyone to the heart. Where *is* the heart? Under the left ribs? Blessed Virgin! I've become a monk myself with all my letter-writing!"

And as he bent his head to join his companion he heard the voice of his mother chaffing and laughing at him. "But what," he retorted, "did *you* want with a lousy Frenchman? Montfoison is he? Oh the sly son of a whore! Oh the lecherous pretender! And to get the prettiest lady in Hereford for a nod and a kiss and a French song!"

Yes—there *were* sounds now—strange, appalling sounds! Mercy of God! Was the Frenchman turning Harlech into—

But there was Elphin, the pretty page, with his hands full of wet sea-weed, trembling like a wisp of shudder-grass! And there was

Gwalchmai, that ill-favoured ostler Rhisiart had met when he first
arrived at Glyndyfrdwy and had always detested, holding the lad by
the wrist, while with his other hand he kept tapping at the bolted door.
The sounds from within the chamber, some of them human, some
sub-human, not only made these tappings inaudible but muted the approach of our two friends.

Father Pascentius gave Rhisiart a look which the latter interpreted
correctly. Leaping upon his ancient enemy, whom he'd suspected for
months of ill-using the aging Griffin, he seized his ugly head by its
thick locks and struck it—once, twice—with all his force against the
granite door-post. Gwalchmai fell without so much as a groan; a
stream of blood, blacker than the darkness, trickling from his skull.

Then Father Pascentius, who had clapped his hand over the page's
mouth, began questioning him.

"Who are with him in there? Whom is he tormenting? If you
scream—"

But Elphin, when the Father removed his plump hand, was nearer
swooning than screaming. His awe of Father Pascentius kept his soul
in his body, but it was in a gasping and piteous whisper that he revealed all they needed to know.

It was a stray hound Sieur Gilles had got in there, tied up for his
experiments; and there was a man too he was tormenting—a wandering Jew-pedlar, Livius by name.

"*He* said," and the boy indicated the unconscious Gwalchmai, "that I
was to bring him *these*—" and the sea-weeds slipped to the ground
beside the trickle of blackness.

"Who's with him?" asked the Cistercian.

"Mistress Lowri, Father, and Lawnslot's with *her*. And the Scab's
there too, and Mistress Sibli."

The monk and Rhisiart exchanged glances. "We must get the door
opened," whispered the former; and he turned with stern authority
upon the shivering boy.

"You're going to shout to them till they draw the bolt, Elphin," he
said; "but the moment it opens you're going to run as fast as you ever
ran in your life; and you're going to fetch Master Broch here. Do you
understand? And you're going to tell him to bring his poppy-drug. Do
you understand? His poppy-drug."

"Need I come back, Father?"

"You need do *nothing* but get Master Broch here! Do you understand now?"

"Yes, Father."

"Then shout your loudest, and say you've got the sea-weed!"

At the back of his mind during all that followed Rhisiart kept thinking, "Could *I* have done that? Could *I* have sent for my greatest enemy at such a crisis?" And his respect for the discoverer of *Cardamine Pascentius* mounted to a point from which it never afterwards declined.

Whether the Jew had suffered as much as the dog he couldn't tell, but the man hadn't bitten his tormentor as he was thankful to perceive Sieur Gilles's other victim had succeeded in doing. The sensation he got when he first entered the room was a revolting one. It was *the smell of pain.* Then the impression branded itself on his mind of *two vortices of pain,* vortices that issued screaming from both the tormented forms and filled the chamber, interweaving their fiery flukes, so that what was endured by the Jew, and had become the Jew's whole consciousness, mingled with what was endured by the dog, and had become the dog's whole consciousness.

Mistress Lowri had no need to give Rhisiart more than one quick glance; and after that, with the eyes of Father Pascentius boring—so it seemed to our friend—two livid holes through her yet shapely back she began to move to the door.

In a second Sieur Gilles made a bow worthy of a Lord Chamberlain and offered his arm to lead her away. But at that the Father rose to his full height, his ungainly figure made almost dignified by his Cistercian habit.

"A moment, a moment, my Lord de Pirogue!" he said. "*You,* Lawnslot, take the lady down; and remember, not a word—"

But at the opening of the door there came a groan from Lawnslot's prostrate mate; and seeing his fellow-servant bleeding so profusely the man paused irresolutely. Then a sudden wave of anger overcame him; for Gwalchmai was his only intimate in the place and they both came from Denbigh.

"It's you we've got to thank for this, you interloper, you traitor, you scribbler, you *Englishman!*" And advancing threateningly towards Rhisiart he made as though he would strike him. Something however about the look in our friend's eye and the quick movement of his hand into his tunic changed his intention.

"The Prince shall know of this," he muttered savagely, "and if Gwalchmai dies—"

But Mistress Lowri, who had taken the opportunity of examining her servant's hurt, now drew his indignant comrade away.

"I bid you god-den, Sieur Gilles," she said. "And I shall try not to forget the methods of your science. No, he won't die, man, he won't die. Master Rhisiart isn't brave enough to strike a real blow. Why don't you see to your precious infidel, Father? Or is the mongrel your concern?"

She had the grace to bend down after that and to arrange her veil under the groaning man's head; but this done she hurried off taking Lawnslot with her.

Rhisiart meanwhile was untying the dog who, bleeding as he was, resigned himself to his hands. But when the creature was free he sank down on his haunches with nothing alive about him but the look in his eyeballs.

The Jew was a different case. The "scientific method" referred to by Lowri had done less vital harm to him than to the dog. Freed from his bonds by Father Pascentius he was able to pull his cloak about him and to stagger back on the same bench where he'd been recently outstretched.

All this while the prophet of Derfel had been edging himself in silence inch by inch along the wall towards the still open door, where little Sibli was now on her knees, wiping the blood as best she could from Gwalchmai's hairy skull.

Then for the first time Sieur Gilles himself spoke, turning from the window to which he had nonchalantly retired after offering his arm to the lady.

"If you were of suitable rank, Master," he said with a bow, addressing himself to Rhisiart, "I should take pleasure in giving you the chastisement your interference deserves. But a de Pirogue—I must ask your pardon for the ridiculous rules of a civilized country—cannot enter

into personal conflict with—forgive me—a *petit clerc* or *sous-commis,*
like yourself. At the same time—no! calm yourself, *mon ami,* I too have
a bagatelle of a *couteau-poignard*—at the same time since you are a
little upset, how do you say it? a little *bouleversé,* and *quant à moi je
suis* cool—cool as—as *la glace*—you would be, apart from your lack of
habitude of the sports of gentlemen, you would be at a—how do you
say it?—at a *désavantage* with me."

Rhisiart withdrew his hand from his tunic. Past the white face, past
the dead-black damp hair that framed it, his eyes fixed themselves,
sadly, wearily, upon that wide expanse of yellow sand that he had
recently imagined converted into green pastures.

What vast spaces of non-human elements there were still in the
world, unaffected by the perversities and cruelties of men! It was the
raised voice of Father Pascentius that made him turn at last, and both
he and the young Frenchman surveyed with curiosity the scene that
was taking place.

The monk had caught the Bard of Ffinnant just as he was on the
point of edging himself out of the chamber; and concentrating upon
the man's roving blue eye the full force of his piercing gaze he was un-
loading upon him the accumulated indignation of a score of long
years. Shamed and disgusted with himself as he was, Rhisiart was still
youthful enough to be amused at this easy victory of the priest over the
prophet.

Derfel indeed seemed completely to have deserted his champion. The
Scab looked for help at the crouching figure of Lemuel Livius. He
looked for help at the cowering form of the dog. He even shot from
his single eye an appealing glance at Rhisiart.

But there came no help from any direction. He was compelled to
listen in undefended trepidation to a mounting sequence of supernatural threats that were of a kind not at all dissimilar from those of
his own armoury of holy terrors.

As Rhisiart contemplated these two singular figures, wondering
whether it was just a lie of the Scab's that—like Merlin—he was the
son of a nun, and observing with unpardonable interest how the rose-
marks on his face kept getting redder in various particular spots as if
his terrified soul were hurrying about, just under his skin, with a red

lantern, he thought how different from both these men the gigantic Broch-o'-Meifod was. "If *he* comes here now," he thought, "it'll be like the ghost of Brān come up from the sea!"

And then as he watched the Scab's unmistakeable discomfort while the monk drew shamelessly upon his erudition to describe in detail the proddings and pinchings, the scaldings and scorchings, the hookings and harrowings that were to be his lot the second his soul left its disfigured frame, it struck him as viciously typical of their modern life that in the breaking up of the old communal faith, everything had become personal, a personal mania, a personal obsession, a personal superstition! Here was the Scab who had blackmailed all the *cantrefs* of Ardudwy and Caer Einion; and for twenty years had crossed the Berwyns to gather his conjurer's rents, filled with just the very perturbation he himself habitually excited.

The wielder of Derfel's plagues was now learning what would happen to him at the hands of the Almighty the second his soul reached Hell. And the curious scene was made more significant by the unconcealed glee of Master Livius of Burgos, who as he stroked with his long Mesopotamian fingers the portion of his person to which Sieur Gilles had been applying his science gave vent to such low-voiced murmurs of approval as: "Father Abraham, it's the truth! Father Isaac, the holy man's read the Torah. Yes! yes! yes! To the good work, master devils! Don't let the false prophet escape! Father Jacob! see to it that he doesn't edge back across the gulf!"

But the final denunciations of the monk, as he drove the Scab into the passage, were attuned to the movements, not of a fly, but of little Sibli. Finding that Gwalchmai had ceased groaning, though whether this indicated his recovery, or the reverse, she had no idea, the devil in her small frame—and it was hard for our friend not to feel as if the combination implied more devil than dwarf—prompted the diminutive creature to cross the room and offer the sea-weeds, which Elphin had dropped, to Sieur Gilles de Pirogue.

This she did, while the full sunshine fell on her purple beard, with a mocking curtsey and a wicked glance at Rhisiart. The sea-brine that still clung about these slippery objects, was mingled here and there with the wounded man's blood, but it was the smell of the salt sea they brought into the room, and it seemed to our friend, as he watched

the Frenchman make a ceremonious bow and lay them on the window-
ledge, as if from the receding waters and the yellow sands there had
come a token of the obliteration of all the tribes of men and their curst
cruelties, a premonition of the end of an epoch, a hint of a new era.

At that moment Broch-o'-Meifod entered the chamber. The giant's
familiar weapons gleamed like sea-shells about his waist. He had clearly
come straight from the sea's edge, for his bare feet were caked with
sand and several seagulls' feathers had been thrust between the shining
axes in his belt.

"Mother of God!" thought Rhisiart, "he *does* look like Brān!" Broch
gave the merchant from Burgos one quick glance and went straight to
the crouching dog.

Rhisiart followed him anxiously. Had Elphin told him what to expect? Had he had time to get his drugs? But what the man first produced from his leather pocket was more necessary just then than any
drug. He—and he alone—had thought of *water*. Pouring this element
from a metal flask into one of his great palms he knelt down and held
it to the dog's mouth.

Lap! Lap! Lap! There was no other sound for several minutes in
that room. Twice, three times, four times, he filled his palm with
water; while each time he did so the dog gave him a look that our
friend to the end of his days couldn't forget. It was more, not less than,
a look of human gratitude. It was the look of one who finds God at
the bottom of Hell. It was the look of one who finds a crack in a universe where all is allowed and nothing forbidden. And out of this
crack water was coming.

Substituting at last a few diluted drops of what Father Pascentius
had called his "poppy-drug," Broch now spent some time in sending
his patient to sleep. Meanwhile Sieur Gilles, who clearly was unaware
of any crack in a world where all is permitted, was leaning out of the
window.

Something made our friend follow the Frenchman's investigations,
and he soon realized that this particular window, an unusually wide one
for Harlech, opened upon the roof of the castle chapel. He and Sieur
Gilles turned simultaneously; and standing side by side they both began, as any onlookers at any embarrassing scene might have done,
mechanically squeezing certain little slippery blobs in the sea-weed un-

der their hands, till they caused these blobs to vent the air they contained in inaudible pops.

The dwarf by this time had transferred her attention to the scene that now was proceeding between Broch and the Jew. Unlike his fellow victim, the merchant from Burgos showed no desire to accept the giant's aid; and when the giant produced his drug he thrust it away, summoning to his aid from their sepulchres in the desert the mothers of his people, Sarah and Rebecca and Rachel. The mention of these sublime names seemed to excite implacable fury in little Sibli. She endeavoured to thrust her purple chin into his pain-exhausted body.

"Jew! Jew! Jew!" she kept crying; and when Broch flicked her off, she danced up and down, making lewd gestures in front of the injured man and blaspheming those mothers of Israel he had invoked.

Broch drove her off mechanically till she worked herself up to such a pitch as actually to spit at the man's face; and even then he only brushed her away with the flapping hem of his leather jacket. But she was drawn from the Jew now, as was our friend himself, for Broch-o'-Meifod had turned his attention to the French envoy.

It was plain that the youth was staggered and puzzled by this queer friend of the Prince of Wales. Rhisiart who had gone out for a minute to satisfy himself as to Gwalchmai's condition, and had been relieved to find that Father Pascentius had effectually forestalled him and that both the Father and the wounded man had disappeared, returned to the room to find the Frenchman actually uttering a weird and monstrous defence of what he had been discovered doing.

There must have been something in the mere stature of Broch-o'-Meifod that awed him into this proceeding; and something too in the expressionless enormousness of Broch's face. Ever since as a child Gilles had begun his career of the infliction of pain, he had been put to it to harden his heart against the pity and wrath of others.

It was therefore in real desperation, though his hearers would never have guessed it, that he uttered this unexpected apologia. "It's that meddling *sous-commissaire,*" he cried, pointing an accusing finger at Rhisiart, "who brought that staring monk here! Madame and *le poète avec le visage de rose* were *très intéressés* in my little experiments. It is my *méthode scientifique,* Sieur Broch de Meifod. A little of pain I must give, that is true; but for what an end? That I may obtain the secret

of life, the secret of not-dying! What is the pain of a stray dog, of a
rascal Jew, if I can find by my *méthode scientifique* the elixir of life?
Consider the logic, *mon cher* Broch de Meifod; perhaps a little nothing
of pain, perhaps a little nothing of death even, to a useless dog, to an
infidel Jew, to some unwanted brat of a peasant-slave—but consider
the children of noble birth, so beautiful, Sieur Broch de Meifod, so
beautiful and tender, who will live long lives because of my *méthode
scientifique,* because of my discovery of the elixir! I give pain, yes! But
I give life, too. It is the logic, Sieur Broch de Meifod, it is the logic to
which I appeal!"

It was, however, as Rhisiart perceived, a "logic" that had scant effect
upon the person addressed. Broch-o'-Meifod moved a few paces nearer
to the envoy of King Charles. What the giant would have done when
he reached this vivisecting prolonger of life was not clear. What was
clear was Gilles de Pirogue's determination to risk no contact with
superstition on so large a scale. He whirled round and with one bound
was at the window, through which he had no difficulty in squeezing
his elegant form. In a second, agile as a young monkey, he was on the
roof of the chapel!

Broch himself had moved to the window now, so that Rhisiart missed
the spectacle of this messiah of science scrambling down a flying
buttress; but the youth's devilish laughter entered the chamber; and he
even had the gall to refer to Elphin's sea-weed.

"There's plenty of sea-weed upon the coast of France," he screamed.
"Enough for all my little experiments!" The truth is that the obsessed
envoy had long since permitted his eyes to wander during Holy Mass,
and he hadn't missed the fact that from any of the flying buttresses
outside, into any of the chapel windows, there was, for jackdaw or
devil, an easy entrance.

The state-banquet at Harlech that February afternoon was delayed
several hours. The great hunting excursion, designed for the pleasure
of the younger French envoy, had proved both tedious and disap-
pointing; and Owen had returned in no very amiable mood. Nor did
his spirits pick up during that long and formal meal. His friend Broch
was unusually taciturn. Rhisiart excused himself as soon as the ladies
retired, under the excuse of visiting the bedside of Meredith, while the

elder envoy, who had been feverishly lively during the repast, left the
hall before the drinking began, with an imperious request for a private
interview that same night.

Now it happened that the Prince had already arranged for a similar
interview with two other important persons. He had told Brother
Eddouyer, the emissary from Benedict the Eighth at Avignon, that he
would see him about the allegiance of Wales; and he had told the
Archdeacon of Bangor, who brought the terms of the secret pact, that
he would see him about the Tripartite Indenture. In regard to this
latter affair it was essential to have the presence of Sir Edmund; and
it was an added vexation to the harassed Prince when, on the top of
this untimely demand for an immediate interview by Gilles, Mortimer
announced that owing to some trifling indisposition of their infant
Bridget he and Catharine could give only very hasty attention that
night to business of state.

The Prince had been so diligently occupied in propitiating Gilles de
Pirogue, who sat by his side during the banquet, and from whom he
extracted a promise that his royal master wouldn't fail to send James
Bourbon, Count of La Marche as well as Jean de Hengest, Lord of
Hugueville, with the expected expeditionary force, that he felt it essential to agree to the envoy's request. After all, the French monarch
had sent this ambassador, whether he was a *persona grata* or not.

But even these trials weren't all. Fate indeed was set upon persecut-
ing him that night. For what must his Secretary disclose at this juncture but the information that he intended to spend the evening with
Meredith!

The Prince felt very indignant with Rhisiart for this selfishness.
Naturally a young man would prefer to exchange ideas with the
brilliant Meredith rather than to discuss a "Tripartite Indenture."
Heaven knows he would prefer it himself! But, after all, Rhisiart *was*
the Clerk of his Council-Chamber and he had no right to absent himself when matters so serious were in the air. The only flicker of irresponsible pleasure of which the Prince had recently been conscious
amid all these worries came from the presence in the castle of the
prophetic Bard of Gower, the famous Hopkin ap Thomas, whose
mysterious and occult poems written on the banks of the Tawy and
known by the name of *cywyddau brud* were being passed surrepti-

tiously all over Wales. These weird verses predicted the most startling events, from the crowning of a Welsh prince in London to the anointing of a great King by a girl in armour; while some of them even went so far as to hint at the imminence of a suicidal war in which humanity itself would perish!

But even this pleasure had been rudely shaken. At first when this extraordinary personage—called by many of his contemporaries "the divine Hopkin"—appeared at Harlech, the Prince would hardly let him out of his sight. Broch-o'-Meifod, on the contrary, got so little joy of him that in avoiding his society he remained completely in the background; with the unfortunate result that in these important questions, the pact with Northumberland and the acknowledgment of the anti-Pope, Owen began to follow the advice of his new rather than of his old friend.

"The divine Hopkin" treated the Prince not so much as a ruling potentate as a fellow-magician, and this brought back, in one great overpowering wave of temptation, all that dangerous dabbling with the unknown future, which Owen had shaken off when he destroyed his crystal.

Both the Arglwyddes and her eldest son were grievously troubled by the presence of this new prophet. Nor did the leaders of Owen's armies like it any better. They had grown accustomed to the peculiarities of the Scab; and since so many of them were men of Gwynedd and Merionydd it was one thing to accept oracles from Ffinnant, but quite another thing when they came from the Tawy!

But magicians are men; and men, when they acquire influence over other men, tend soon enough to carry matters too far. It was all very well to fascinate the Prince with *cywyddau brud* about the crowning of a Welshman in London; but when the present crowned King of that city sent the famous Talbot into Gwent, and Rhys Gethin's faithful troops had to oppose him, it was less of a pleasure to Owen to puzzle out riddling oracles to the effect that if the war ever approached the native district of "the divine Hopkin" himself, it would be the Prince, and not the prophet, whose life would be in danger!

This particular danger to Owen's life was—Hopkin ap Thomas kept repeating—to descend upon him under a *black flag;* and since Lord Grey of Codnor, a formidable namesake of the now impoverished Grey of Ruthin, did actually carry some "quarterings" that were, in heraldic language, *sable,* this "black flag" soon began to get upon Owen's nerves.

Grey of Codnor was as troublesome a King's man as were Talbot and Grendor; and it was upon this sable streak in the Codnor escutcheon that the Prince was meditating now as he sat in his "magician's chamber." He decided to let his son Griffith and his brother Tudor face the sable arms of the Lord of Codnor, while he himself took command of the forces collected by Henry Don and Rhys Ddu to oppose Talbot and Grendor.

It was towards the Usk rather than towards the Tawy that Codnor was now advancing; and it was due to this fact, as Owen sat alone, that there began to insinuate itself into his mind his first serious doubt as to the integrity of his new friend! "The divine Hopkin" had only yesterday informed him that he'd been inspired with a new prophecy about the victorious "virgin in armour." He had hinted that it *might* refer to some native Welsh maid; and Owen, as he gazed at his smouldering logs, conceived the not unnatural idea that it must apply to none other than the Maid of Edeyrnion. This idea, as soon as it entered his head, absorbed him so much that he completely forgot the passing of time.

As he gazed into his fire the image of Mad Huw's Maid—whose legend had now, though the girl herself seemed quite oblivious of it, spread from the north to the south—clothed in bright armour, mounted on his own Seisyll, leading his troops in their victory over these Talbots and Grendors, began to dominate his imagination. That's what he wanted, that's what Wales wanted at this juncture, some moving bardic symbol, at once poetic and religious! What was the use of being the acknowledged Prince of Wales from Môn to Gwent, when at a word from Worcester or Hereford these accurst Grendors and Codnors could penetrate as far as the Usk.

The Abbot of Caerleon, it was true, was there to resist them, and a great patriot was he, but if only by the Abbot's side could appear a figure such as his imagination now conjured up, the figure of a Maid in whom all the heroic traditions of Welsh womanhood were embodied, the English wouldn't have a castle left in the land!

"I'd be *then,*" he thought, "what I'm not *yet,* for all their flattery. I'd be a real sovereign of a free people!" He moved from the window and began pacing the room. "Dewi Sant!" he thought. "What a fool I've been not to think of this before! It'll enrapture Mad Huw. It'll bring the whole country round us! It'll do me more good than any pact with Benedict or any league with France. By God! *That's* what I'll do. Into your armour, Tegolin Goch! Into your armour, Tegolin Bach! So I'm not to put a foot on your damned Gower, eh, Master Hopkin? And I'm to perish under a black flag, am I? Well, we'll set word against word, and it shall be a Welsh virgin who shall drive the English out of Wales!"

He moved to the door and opened it. There sat Glew the Gryd, faithful as ever, silent as ever, and still, for all his fourscore years, polishing his great war-axe with an especial piece of holy stone.

"Anyone been here?"

"Only the Tawy man."

"What did you tell him?"

"I told him you were calling up such spirits as *he'd* never seen nor ever would see, and that you couldn't be troubled to-night."

"Anyone else?"

"Only that white-faced French boy."

"You didn't send *him* away—after what I told you?"

"No, Owen ap Griffith Fychan."

"What *did* you do?"

"Nothing, my Prince."

"What did you say?"

"Nothing, my Prince."

"And so he just went?"

"Yes, my Prince. When I looked up again there was nobody there, my Prince."

"Has the guard at the end of the passage been changed yet?"

"Twice."

"Mother of God, Glew! how long have I been calling up spirits?"

"I don't know, my Prince."

"Has the man from Bangor been here?"

"Three times, my Prince."

Owen stroked his beard. "And the Friar Preacher from France—what's his name?—Hugh Eddouyer?"

"Just gone, my Prince."

"How long did *he* wait?"

"An hour or so, my Prince. He sat with me and talked."

Owen looked down the passage. "Do you think he's talking to the guard?"

"Yes, my Prince."

"Go and fetch him, Glew. Tell him I'll see him now. And make them send up some more logs, will you, Glew, and some more wine and goblets. Let them be alder-logs, Glew; and tell them *the wine of Provence!*"

Owen wasn't long, as he sat opposite the much-travelled emissary from Benedict the Eighth, in taking a fancy to the man. "Jesu Maria!" he thought, "what a different fellow from that popinjay of an Italian who brought the indult from Rome when Iolo died!"

Hugh Eddouyer looked indeed, as he bent over the aromatic smoke of the alder-wood and sipped that rich wine of Provence, a rare specimen of his order. With a bright eye beneath a bulging brow, with thick lips forever twitching with ironic merriment, with a sandy beard that wagged as he jested, there was something in him, from his pilgrim indifference about his patched habit and frayed sandals to the careless way he rubbed his uncomely features with the palms of his hands, that inspired belief in his fundamental honesty.

It soon became clear to Owen that the man had a genuine respect for his master Benedict and an authentic belief that any nation that transferred its allegiance from Rome to Avignon would receive much more generous pontifical care than it could hope to get from Rome.

"You don't object, Sire," he was saying now, "if I show to King Charles—that is, if he's well enough to attend to business—these little points we've just jotted down for the Holy Father?"

"Not at all, not all! The most Christian King is, or soon will be, our staunch ally against this tottering House of Lancaster. Show him everything! Keep nothing from him! Is he, may I ask, a sensible man when his infirmity leaves him?"

Hugh Eddouyer rubbed his broad nose and corrugated brow. "I couldn't talk to him as I talk to *you,* Sire, if that's what you mean. But I can talk to him as one talks to an intelligent—to an intelligent invalid —with flashes of fine intuition. I'm not at ease with him, if you understand, as I am with the Holy Father; but I feel—what shall I say?—a *tendresse* for him, a—a pulse *sympathétique*."

Owen stretched out his long legs in their olive-green hose and surveyed his fantastically elongated slippers. A sprinkling of ashes had fallen upon one of these to which chance had given the shape of an "E," and Owen's thoughts rushed to the Maid of Edeyrnion.

"Read over the points we've agreed upon, Brother, will you?" he said.

The Friar, for he was short-sighted, lifted the document from beneath his wine-cup to where the light of the flickering lamp, swaying from the oaken beam above the hearth, helped his vision. *"One,"* he read out, in a voice intended to mock the gravity of a royal herald: "All oaths of obedience to the late Roman pontiffs Urban the Sixth and Boniface the Ninth to be annulled.

"Two: St. David's to be a metropolitan church and its Bishop an Archbishop.

"Three: All grants of Welsh parishes to English monasteries and colleges to be annulled.

"Four: A Welsh University—"

"Two Welsh Universities," broke in Owen with a chuckle, thinking of Master Brut.

"Hee! Hee! Hee!" laughed the travel-stained emissary. "Your gracious Mightiness has never seen a riot in *our* University!" But he duly made the correction and went on.

"Five: The campaign of liberation from the blasphemous destroyer of sacred edifices, Henry of Lancaster, to have the title of a Crusade or Holy War.

"Six: The Holy Father to grant plenary remission of all mortal sins, when, where, or how committed, for the duration of the war, to all those who fight on the Welsh side, provided they hold the—"

At this point Owen pulled in his legs with a jerk and interrupted. "Hold the orthodox faith, eh? But stop a moment, Brother. Suppose there arose—I don't say it's likely to arise, you understand; but suppose there arose a movement among us, a religious movement, perhaps in your own Order, for the Franciscans have always been our friends—a movement, shall we say, to greater freedom and simplicity in the worship of God?—would such a change, for Holy Church moves slowly in such things and Saint Francis had his opponents at first, *ipso facto* negate this blessed absolution?"

Hugh Eddouyer gave him a quick, shrewd, humorous glance, and turned his gaze upon the burning logs. Then, after a moment's thought, he lifted his wine to his lips.

"It is not," he replied slowly, replacing the goblet on the table, "for a humble Friar like myself to answer for the Vicar of Christ; but I can certainly say to you, Prince Owen, that if *I* were His Holiness, and I *have,* up to a point, a certain influence at Avignon, the fact that the *de comburendo* edict, with all its implications of undue Dominican influence, has encouraged Henry of Lancaster in his subservience to a meddling Archbishop, would certainly make me lean to a milder policy.

"And since neither the word Lollard, nor the name Wycliffe, has passed between us, we may, I think, assume that as long as my master lives there will be no Papal inquisition made into the orthodoxy of your Welsh subjects. And as long as this is delayed there can be no question of anything but paternal indulgence to reckless patriotic brains, too occupied in their Holy War with sacrilegious usurpers to exercise that control over our erring human reason, which—"

"Enough, enough!" interrupted Owen. "We follow you, Brother; we follow you. His Holiness will have no occasion for burnings among our people. I can promise him that! Oh yes! And there's one other thing you might add to the points we've named." He paused to replenish both their goblets, looking straight into the man's eyes.

"What a strange face he's got!" thought the Friar Preacher. "They talked in France of his golden beard. It's grey now, anyway. Power and success! Power and success! That's how things go."

"The Holy Father," Owen began gravely, keeping his eyes fixed upon the man, "won't of course forget his faithful and devoted adherent, our learned and pious Chancellor Young, Archdeacon of Meirionydd?"

The other uttered a rich chuckle, careless and roguish, straight in the Prince's face. "Archbishop of St. David's shall he be, my gracious Lord! Only I may as well warn you"—he paused and leant back, tilting his chair till his knees pressed against the table—"for I know the man as if he were my brother; once Archbishop, some of your good friends here had better leave the country!"

Owen tried for a moment to frown and tap the table and tug at his beard: but Master Eddouyer had seen too many hectoring princes of this world to be monarchized or brow-beaten; and his frank smile had its way.

" 'Tis my turn, dear my Lord, to cry 'enough' now!" he remarked. "But don't forget the words of an old observer of spiritual magnates. Have a watch on the tongue of your worthy Librarian here, the good Master Brut. If he can keep his mouth shut, all will be well. But if not —don't ask the Pope to make Young your Metropolitan!"

Owen stared past him at the closed door, and through the door down the passage, to where his men-at-arms were doubtless at that very moment talking gross Lollardry. Well did he know how there was that in Master Brut's doctrines to which his Welshmen responded like wildgeese to the waters of Llyn Tegid.

"Have you had time in your travels," he remarked now, anxious to turn the subject from episcopal peculiarities, "to note how few men there are without some irrational prejudice? You referred to my Librarian. Do you know, Brother, that wise scholar as he is, and good tolerant man, he can't abide our Castle of Harlech?"

"You astonish me, my Prince."

"Can't abide it; no, even though in a day or two his nuptials are to be celebrated in it."

At this the traveller couldn't restrain a sly grimace. "Perhaps that's the reason."

"Not at all. He adores the wench. The reason is that the place is soaked with sea-water legends. They say Brān the Blessed comes wading up with the tide when the moon's full. Yes! A great ghost he comes, carrying on his back the ghosts of half-a-dozen bards. By the way, Brother, the moon's full to-night, if my calendar's not mistaken."

Hugh Eddouyer shrugged his shoulders and turned to his wine. He had been warned on the Continent again and again that if he wished to please this strange new sovereign prince he would have to listen patiently to just such skimble-skamble stuff as this; but he couldn't do it! He could put up with many absurdities, and in his journeyings he'd done so; but cock-and-bull stories of Welsh giants carrying bards on their backs—as if there weren't enough of *them* in the place already!— were more than he could bear.

"I'll tell my master," he said to himself, "that if he wants to win this horned Welsh ram heart and soul to his flock he'd better send him, not indulgences, but a few books of magic."

But Owen, paying not the slightest heed to the Friar's lack of interest, rose from his seat and going to the window thrust his head through the narrow opening.

And in a second Brother Eddouyer, the Avignon Pope, Master Brut, and Chancellor Young, all were forgotten. What a sight met his eyes! The moon *was* full; and not only so, but the great brimming tide, carrying on its rippled surface what looked like an undulant highway to eternity, was bearing this moon-bright track close up to the castle-walls.

Owen could hear the splash of the waves against the castle-jetty. What this morning were rock-pools were now a portion of the sea's bed, and it was hard for a man far deeper versed then Rhisiart's Modry in the ancient tales not to behold riding upon that brimming tide the moon-lit sails of the fleet of Matholwch, with the Irishmen's great shields upturned in sign of peace, *a swch y taryan y vynyd yn arwyd tangneved!*

Peace? Peace? What prevented him now from making a final peace with Henry and ending this burning and despoiling? What prevented him? His own success prevented him! How *could* he stop now, when, if he went on a *little* longer—

But he had a strange feeling, as he stretched his head through this stone slit in the great wall and listened to the breaking of the waves, that all these blackened towns and ruined villages were the result of an enchantment, like that flung by the magicians upon the persecuted Pryderi; and that if only the clue-word, the exorcising word, could be uttered on such a night as this, all the waste-lands of ashes and blood would grow fresh and green again!

Moving his head, not without difficulty, for the masonry of the aperture grated against both sides of his skull, he gazed straight into that round orb of mystical whiteness. No, it *wasn't* whiteness! It was something for which there is no name. What he really felt was that there had been bored a great luminous hole in the swimming ether, a hole that resembled a hole in space; and that through this hole, and in his moon-mad fancies he felt as if the slit that was now scratching his ears *was* this mystic hole, it was possible to pass beyond space into whatever lay on the other side!

A real moon-intoxication began to seize upon him as he stared at that hypnotic rondure. No, it wasn't white at all! The night was white but this was different. There must be droves of gleaming fish below that moon-path drawn landward against all reason. What heavenly madness to plunge forward at the pull of that ravishing radiance!

There were certainly mother-of-pearl shells down there, deep down below those heaving undulations, who had fish within them, fish who were struggling to leave their protection, struggling to be caught up in that moon-tide, even though it meant death!

And how well he knew what the sea-weeds felt down there who were yearning, quivering, trembling upward; every drop of their oozy sap drawn upward, drawn with maddeningly-sweet spasms upward, to the moon-drenched ripples on the surface!

Tearing his dizzy eyes from that circle of circles, he could see in the moonlight some great somnolent sea-bird rocking up and down on the illuminated tide.

To his moon-drugged fancy the eye of this bird met his own. "What human greybeard is that," the seagull's eye seemed to say to him, "straining like the fin-backs in their shoals, like the shell-fish in their shells, like millions of sea-weeds, like millions of sea-worms, towards our goddess, our darling, the great Whore of Eternity?"

If that rocking seagull had been endowed with the eye of a sea-hawk instead of with the round, simple, greedy eye of a goosander, it would doubtless, after its fashion, have registered astonishment at the appearance of that protruding white neck and well-combed beard thrust out, *they alone,* from the huge embattled front of that sea-castle.

And if it caught the moon's white glint upon the golden band round the skull of that outstretched head, it might have whistled softly to itself: "Whirrraroo! It's Manawydan fab Llyr come to life again! Whirrraroo! Whirrraroo! We shall all be safe now from the clutches of Llwyd fab Kil Coet!"

To the round, mild, greedy-idiot eye of this simple goosander, whose personality reproduced to the smallest particular that of its ancestors of two thousand years ago, it appeared obvious that there was a sea-king

in Harlech. The bird regarded the phenomenon of moonlight in two
distinct ways; and it expressed this difference by the pose of its head.
With its head erect, its view of such a night as this was grossly realistic.
Shoals of fins and tails came crowding into the shallows that as a rule
fluttered and waved and flapped and squirmed in unfathomable depths.
Now the wakeful and contemplative goosander wasn't a fish-eater; but
there were certain small creatures that the fish wrought up with them
from the fathomless ooze, not to speak of certain minute sea-floor weeds
broken from their roots by this lunar migration and rising as if by their
own volition, which left an unequalled after-taste in its fastidious gullet.

But at this moment the goosander tilted its head a little to one side as
it contemplated the huge grey front of Harlech and that solitary human
skull projected from the centre of it; and the tilting of its head meant a
more recondite train of thought. For there floated into its simple intelligence race-memories of sea-castles and sea-kings of thousands of years
ago.

It had been driven from the north in search of unfrozen marshes and
estuaries; but it already was conscious of more warmth than it liked,
and it had decided a week ago that soon it would have to fly northward
again.

But that head with its strong white neck and its forked beard and its
golden circlet evoked strange, weird, obscure feelings in him. He didn't
make any attempt to tell himself that the goosanders and mergansers of
the early days of the world had seen just such persons, staring out of
stone battlements over moonlit seas; but an indescribable feeling quivered through the roots of his feathers.

And the goosander's ecstasy only increased, as long as he kept his
head tilted a little to one side, when the sea-foam swirling about the
rocks grew still whiter in the moonlight, when the sea-anemones in the
lost rock-pools, and the star-fish in the submerged shallows, and the
sea-weeds in the furrows of the sea-floor, all grew white, white with a
whiteness like the breasts of sea-queens, white with a whiteness that to
the goosander's arctic blood was a beauty so extreme that it resembled
the passing from love to death!

Thus did Owen's thoughts on that night of the Purification of the
Virgin mingle with the thoughts of the goosander, and the goosander's
thoughts with his.

And though the Prince forgot those eight hundred men-at-arms and those six hundred cross-bowmen, and those thousand and one light-armed troopers, that Gilles de Pirogue had sworn were already assembled at Brest, and though he forgot the envoy from Bangor with his "Tripartite Pact," and though he forgot the danger to Master Brut of a Welsh Archbishop, there was something in this white night that brought Hopkin's *cywydd brud* about a Maid crowning a King most vividly to his mind. He had been extremely impressed by the beauty of Tegolin when she re-appeared at his court. "Her skin," he'd quoted to himself when he first saw her again after those eventful years, "is whiter than the spray of the meadow fountains."

The Friar's Maid had indeed blossomed forth from a brave, athletic, boyish wench into a surpassingly lovely girl. He hadn't seen much of her since she arrived; but what he *had* seen had stirred his senses and troubled his mind. The girl puzzled him completely. What *were* the actual relations between her and the mad Friar? The man clearly worshipped her, depended upon her, watched her every movement. Could it be said that after his own crazy fashion he was in love with her? The Prince caught himself indulging, more often than his reason or conscience approved, in all manner of unbridled thoughts. What, for instance, were her relations with Rhisiart? Here again Owen found himself baffled. They seemed to understand each other perfectly—*that* at least was evident; and it was evident that the two were entirely at ease with each other, and that the Maid had a strong protective feeling for the young man. But the Prince didn't fail to notice that it was towards Lady Mortimer rather than to the red-haired girl that the Secretary's eyes would turn when the three were together.

But—for the boy was a man now—perhaps he realized that he was being watched! It was still Owen's habit to analyse every flicker of emotion that came and went within him. To his most scandalous and shameless thoughts he always allowed free scope, merely noting with an inward ironic comment where his reason or his conscience disapproved.

His conscience, not his reason, had protested in the matter of Catharine's marriage; but he observed with sardonic interest that the feeling for his daughter which had killed all other wandering thoughts, from the Snowdon days to the days in Rhys Ddu's forest, changed completely with the birth of her children. And how queer that was! Rhisiart apparently felt nothing of this reaction. *His* attitude, self-controlled and dignified as it was, seemed to have suffered no change; whereas— Yes! this moonlit sea, this white night, was certainly putting strange thoughts into his mind. A Maid in armour crowning a King! And that other *cywydd brud* of Hopkin's, of a Welshman being crowned in London. Well! He had sacrificed himself and his children for Wales. Did the gods of his race intend to reward him with a triumphal entry—he and his French allies—into Lud's town?

Were the Gwynedd lions destined to wave over that White Tower whither they'd carried Brān's head from this very spot? How white Tegolin's skin was—whiter than Catharine's! They say it often happens so with red-haired maids.

But *this* Maid's hair was more than red. *Couleur de flamme* it was! Red flame over pure snow! But to put those white limbs into golden armour; to have her riding by his side over the border, through Hereford, through Worcester, through Evesham, through Oxford—and finally over London Bridge—

And then to take off that armour; to unclasp with his own hands that cuirass, that gorget, those greaves—yes, yes, she should wear the very things King Charles had sent him. Never mind if Hopkin *were* a liar about the black flag in Gwent. There would be no black flags in Hereford, in Worcester, in Evesham, in Oxford! Hopkin was a great prophet; but all prophets could be false prophets.

Oh, when would the French come? That de Pirogue boy swore they were at Brest now, only waiting for the right wind. Well! he must conjure up a wind for them. But meanwhile—into armour with her, into armour! With her at his side he could defy even Codnor and his sable arms. Yes, she should ride with him to the help of the Abbot! She should—

It was the opening of his door, accompanied by noisy protests from Glew the Gryd, that made him withdraw his head not without some pain from that narrow orifice; and there before his eyes *was* that French boy, cursing Glew to the devil while Eddouyer talked to him as fast and with such a Provençal accent that it was impossible to follow a word!

To appease the indignant old porter and get him out of the room was the Prince's first task. Then turning to the intruder he found that the white-faced boy, when once he'd bent the knee and kissed hands in his foreign fashion, chose to leave his business to the genial Franciscan, while he himself paced in pregnant silence, his hands clasped behind him, up and down the room.

Owen signed to Eddouyer to be seated, and sat down in his old position opposite him, glancing now and then with some apprehension at this perambulating image of wounded feelings.

"He says your Secretary insulted him. He says he was experimenting on a couple of unwanted animals for the benefit of humanity—in fact to find the elixir of life—when Master Secretary set a monk at him, and when that didn't stop him, Master Broch also was sent for to bully him; and *he* bullied him so much that he had not only to disappoint the ladies who had come to study his *'méthode scientifique,'* but had hardly time to escape with his life by taking sanctuary in your Saint Chapelle. It was all Master Rhisiart's spitefulness, he says, because he caught this insolent clerk alone with the Maid of Edeyrnion. He doesn't blame Father Pascentius, he says, nor Master Broch de Meifod. They just believed the lies Master Rhisiart told them. He says Master Rhisiart drew a dagger on him, and if the man had been a *gentilhomme* he would have been forced—"

"Is this the truth?" cried Owen fiercely turning upon the perambulating envoy.

Gilles de Pirogue swung round, struck the heels of his fashionable upturned slippers together, and proceeded to make such a deep obeisance, bending himself so low from the waist, that his clammy black forelock hung suspended, while his slim form in its satin tunic took to itself the shape of a small but neatly-erected gallows, suitable for the execution of delinquent dolls. "By Saint Denis it *is* the truth, Sire!"

Owen made a haughty gesture with his hand as if dismissing to its play a tale-telling child, and the young nobleman, exchanging a quick glance with Brother Eddouyer, resumed his sullen march up and down the room.

It must have been by some leap of the devil's own instinct in one or other of these Frenchmen that they introduced that touch about the Maid. Either the Pope's envoy or the King's must have noted, with a

Frenchman's eye for such things, the way the Prince looked at the girl. One thing was clear to Owen even in his agitation and that was that the genial, frank, friendly Eddouyer must have known this all the evening, since they'd both been struggling to get an audience; known it and kept it as dark as if it had been the Pope's death.

So this jesting tippler had the power of being your honest boon-companion at one moment and the next of obliterating you from his slate! And although less interested in diplomacy than our friend Rhisiart, Owen did make a mental note that cynical and shameless bluntness could be the most effective of masks.

And what, in Our Lady's name, had made them bring in that tale about Rhisiart and the Maid? Was the castle seething with gossip about her—about Rhisiart and himself being both in love with Mad Huw's girl? Was this the price you had to pay for being a Prince, that every emotion you had was bandied about among the pages? "After Catharine, Tegolin!" Was that what they said? The Master and Man once again peering and spying and stealing marches on each other! Ho! ho! the Prince and his Secretary! Oh, the rare tale to spread through the *bythynnod* of Wales from Aberfraw to Gwent!

Tell me more of this, Brother Eddouyer, tell me more of this! Exactly *how* did you find them together? Was he combing her red hair? Was she sitting on his knee? *Clerk Rhisiart has free entrance where Prince Owen must pass by!* Dewi Sant! 'Tis like one of those bawdy ditties that that rollicking rogue of *The Cuckoo and the Nightingale* used to trilla-lirra on his sweet tongue, to tickle the kitchen-knaves at Rhys Ddu's!

While these disturbing thoughts jigged and jangled in his mind, the triumphant ruler of Wales was pretending to listen to all manner of further innuendoes about his Secretary, conveyed to him through the smiling wine-stained lips of the envoy of Benedict.

"I must never be fooled again," he was saying to himself, "by this honest, too honest, knave of hearts! This fellow looks me in the eyes like a downright truth-teller; but I *know* he's lying."

There came a moment presently, however, when—Owen couldn't have said how—the Pope's envoy and the King's envoy were standing side by side at the door. And then he realized what, with his head full of moonlight, he hadn't grasped before, what indeed was so serious

that he had pushed it to the back of his brain, namely that Eddouyer
had been for some while outlining in a most disconcerting manner
what he would have to report to the King of France's Pope with regard
to the treatment received by the said King's ambassador.

It was then, and only then, and not till then, that the full weight of
the blow fell, the full realization of the damage, perhaps the irretrievable
damage, that Rhisiart's quarrel with Gilles de Pirogue, whatever justification for it there might be, had done to this French alliance, this
alliance upon which so much—upon which *all* as far as striking a
crushing blow at the House of Lancaster went—hung and depended!

Never had Owen's mind moved faster than it did at this moment.
He was *de facto*—save for a few castles in the north and extreme west
—master of Wales. He knew at the bottom of his heart that if he
confined his ambition to Wales and performed the ancient *gwrogaeth,*
or homage to the crowned King in London, he could end the war; but
Hopkin and his dark *cywyddau* had upset all this, had aroused larger
hopes; and it was to these hopes—to the idea that with a great French
army behind him and the Maid of Edeyrnion at his side he himself
might be the destined Welshman to be crowned in London—that
Rhisiart's quarrel with Gilles struck such a blow.

But it was precisely at a point like this that the strange resources of
this man were quick to show themselves. In prosperity he gave way
to the most extravagant imaginations. In adversity he possessed what
was almost like the power of *cracking* the wall of one dimension of
life and passing through the crack into another! Perhaps it might be
said that he was too much in love with life, as a thing of more than
one level, ever to succeed in the manner in which his royal enemy
succeeded. He took life too seriously to take success seriously. Thus it
was the destruction of Glyndyfrdwy and Sycharth that had sent him
to Snowdon; and it was as an outlaw from Snowdon that he had
rushed, like the ramping lions on his shield, from victory to victory.

And now as he stood there, an imperturbable and incalculable figure,
towering above the two Frenchmen, he kept them both, by the mere
magnetism of his presence, waiting while he made up his mind.

Gilles de Pirogue shivered and looked down at his fantastic shoes.
Once again, as in the case of Broch-o'-Meifod, this strange young man's
soul melted within him. Indeed it spilled itself, through all his nerves,

like bilge-water seeping upwards from the hold of a sea-sick boat.

The "torture-insect" in him was too purely evil not to be as weak in the presence of a great life-lover as it had been in the presence of a great death-lover.

As for Brother Eddouyer, *his* mind reverted to an occasion when travelling in Eastern Europe to obtain help against the Turks he had met the Abbot of a monastery in the Aegean Sea. He recalled how this personage, by merely rising from his seat and surveying him as if he were insubstantial and immaterial, had driven all the irony out of him! This island-prince was doing the same thing now; and he remembered how an astrologer in Salamanca had told him that the *crossing of water* was unpropitious to French diplomacy.

All this while the Prince himself was calmly indulging in his old trick of "exteriorizing" his soul. He was thinking hard too, but he was thinking from some point in the moon-light outside the castle-walls. He felt faintly surprised at himself that he wasn't more angry with Rhisiart for this blow to his far-flung designs. "But I shall punish him," he thought. "I shall send him to the Usk with Griffith and Tudor; and I'll follow later with the Maid. *Rhisiart! Rhisiart!* Well, you shall mount your horse again and draw your great sword! You're a brave man and I've kept you too long at this lawyer's job. As for Master Brut, he'll have to manage his parliament and his bride at the same time! And now to unloose this knot by a little stage-play. Up from the void with your spirits, old conjurer! Turn your wheel, Fate, turn your wheel!"

The first motion the Prince made on releasing his envoys from the paralysis into which he'd thrown them was to cajole them back to the seats by the fire, and to pour out more wine. Neither of them wished to stay; but it was just as if they were in a real magician's cell, the exit from which was guarded by some cabalistical sign to which they lacked the clue.

Seeing them settled down to their drink and their furtive whispering, the next thing the Prince did was to open the door and give orders to the still deeply offended axe-bearer that he was to summon from the guard at the end of the passage as many pages as he could lay hands on. He himself remained on the threshold till the old man returned, bringing Elphin, now grown into a grave and comely youth, and a couple of younger lads.

"Tell the Archdeacon of Bangor I will see him at once," he directed Elphin. "Tell him to bring the 'Indenture' and all that's necessary for signing and sealing. Then go to Sir Edmund and Lady Mortimer and say I request *their* presence at once for a matter of the first importance. Tell Sir Edmund it concerns the Pact with Northumberland; can you remember that? *The Pact with Northumberland.*"

When Elphin was gone he despatched another lad for Rhisiart and Master Brut, and the remaining one for the Maid and her Friar. "And tell," he added to this final messenger, "tell Master Hopkin I wish to see *him;* and one thing more—tell him to bring his brazier and his divining-rod. Say our French guests would like to see a specimen of his art—do you understand?—and use just those words, boy. *A specimen of his art.*"

Spending a minute or two after these drastic orders in conversing so tenderly and frankly with Glew that the cloud lifted from the old man's face the Prince re-entered his chamber, glanced round to make sure there were seats enough for all these people, and walked thoughtfully to the window.

"I must rage at Rhisiart," he said to himself, "before them all. But I must give him—yes! and I'd better give Catharine too—a hint of what I'm doing, so that they won't take it too seriously."

Just as he'd done before he now squeezed his head through that narrow aperture and gazed out upon the moonlit sea. There was that same bird! Was it asleep upon the long in-rolling waves? "It doesn't look like a sea-bird," he said to himself. "It's a marsh-bird of some sort, come down the estuary. How queer it looks with its head sideways!"

But if the contemplative goosander looked queer as it rocked in the moon-light, Owen's own head, thus protruded from that vast grey pile, would have looked to any human eye more than queer. It would have looked grotesque. But neither for the organs of birds nor of fish, nor for the less complicated apprehensions of sea-anemones, can we conceive the category of the grotesque as an aspect of life.

Perhaps never again, till in the revolution of time Rhisiart's prediction of the retreat of the sea took place, would a grey forked beard and a forehead circled with gold confront from that mass of wave-defying masonry the round atavistic eye of one whose race-memory went back to Caer Sidi and Carbonek. But even so, even if a forked beard and gold-circled brow protruding from an arrow-slit and confronting a goosander never repeated themselves through all eternity, can we conceive such a sight presenting itself to the world-spirit as grotesque? The world-spirit and a moonlit star-fish on Harlech sands must share, we feel, the same attitude to such occurrences—*all* grotesque; therefore *nothing* grotesque.

"I'd better warn the Maid, too," he thought, as with more care than before he extricated his head. "I don't want her to think me an irascible tyrant at the very moment when—"

Thank the Lord! It was Master Brut who first presented himself; and since a frigid nod was all that French etiquette permitted a de Pirogue to bestow on a *bibliothécaire* of questionable theological views he was able to enlighten the worthy man in a few whispered words as to the whole situation; begging him to convey to Rhisiart, as well as to both the ladies, that the tone they would presently hear him adopt was political rather than personal.

The Lollard received these instructions with his usual equanimity. There was, however, a certain eager abstraction about his manner, as he lent his ear, which the Prince quickly attributed to the correct cause.

"I hope," he re-assured him with a friendly smile, "that the ladies will bring Mistress Alice with them. I know you would like in after years to be able to tell your children of the signing of this historic Pact. And this being so, you'd better hurry back to her. She was dressed very becomingly at dinner, so no change of clothes will be necessary, but remember she won't like passing the guard alone; so be sure Lady Mortimer waits for her. And tell Rhisiart and the ladies that this is a political, not a personal meeting." And then, as he pushed him out of the chamber, he repeated in tones so menacing that old Glew jumped to his feet: "No, no! We shall disgrace him before you all! We can't have guests of ours insulted in Harlech! We shall dismiss him from the castle. We shall send him to the Usk, where the Abbot is hard-pressed and the fighting's heaviest."

As Owen returned to the fire Brother Eddouyer remarked with an almost maudlin tenderness that it was a thousand pities such a useful civil servant's career should come to an end. "But better in battle than in—other ways. It's extraordinary how men who're not of *very* ancient descent show *some* bad breeding sooner or later. It's a very good custom in our French civilization not to allow a gentleman to cross swords with such people. We don't even execute them in the same way, do we, Sieur Gilles? 'The rope for the serf; the axe for my lord,' is the saying in Auvergne"; and the waggish Friar, fixing his clear, candid, confidential eye first on the Prince and then on de Pirogue, proceeded—for he had discovered what topics best pleased the clammy-haired boy during their tedious journey together—to relate in detail various public executions at which he had had the privilege of being present.

Owen himself, like a great golden cat, began to move stealthily about the room, lighting more candles and dragging out more chairs. His brain had never been so active or his nerves so calm. Whether he would be able to undo the damage done by Rhisiart he couldn't tell; but in some queer way he felt pleased rather than troubled by the incident. To be generous to Rhisiart while he publicly denounced him gratified some perverse irony in his nature.

"I'll indulge it now and analyse it later," he thought. The truth is that what Broch's elf-wife would have called his Brythonic pride had been outraged all along by King Charles having sent a couple of boys as his ambassadors; and whatever the quarrel may have been about, he wasn't sorry that this furtive youth with his dank hair and corpse-like skin had been ruffled in his composure.

"As long as he doesn't stop their fleet from sailing," he said to himself, "I don't care what he does. But oh, Rhisiart, Rhisiart! You've done me a scurvy turn over this business; and I hope you'll feel a *little* ashamed as you ride off to aid the Abbot. But I warrant you won't—with your old sword and your old horse!"

He paused in front of a polished shield in which he could dimly catch the outlines of his own face. "What are you smiling about now, old grey-beard? The 'Indenture'? The anti-Pope? The 'Maid in armour'? Not a one of them! But you're wrong, Broch, old friend, it's life, not death, that's the thing; and there's more in life than Hopkin knows, with his crowned kings and his black flags. If Hal Bolingbroke had all Wales at his bidding, the soul of Owen and the soul of that bird out there would still be at large!"

And there fell upon him as he stood at gaze, hypnotized by his own sea-green eyes, one of those singular escapes from the pressure of the moment that Rhisiart always thought of as his "attacks"; but when he did turn, it was to find Master Brut arrayed in a brand-new court dress—so Alice's lover as well as Alice had realized the historic importance of the "Indenture"—tugging obstinately at one of his flapping sleeves.

"Eh? Eh? what the— Oh they're here, are they? Well—let me think a minute, Brut! My grandfather—and they say it was the fashion at Griffith ap Madoc's court—used always to have a gentleman of noble blood at hand to call out the names of the guests at any great event. Do you think—would you mind—it wouldn't be hurtful to your dignity, would it, my friend"—and he laid hold of the Lollard's satin doublet— "acting as our herald to-night? You see I've played chamberlain myself in arranging the chairs, so it's only to open the door and call out the names as they enter. I trust you entirely about the order of their entering. You know how it would be on the Wye. Let's have the same order in Harlech!"

The Lollard bowed gravely and moved to the door while the Prince informed the Frenchmen that a Pact was now going to be signed between himself and the Percies and the Mortimers, dividing England into three parts.

This brought de Pirogue and Eddouyer at once to their feet, and had the innocent goosander observed the gleam in their eyes it would have undoubtedly concluded that "England" was a wicked dog-fish about to be cut up to feed meritorious mackerel.

"The signing of this Pact," Owen went on, "which of course will be in accordance with our own treaty with France, will take place at once; but the moment it's over you shall see our blundering and ill-advised Secretary dismissed in disgrace from our castle."

The Frenchmen glanced at each other. "These savages," their look said, "can do nothing without our aid. Well! they'll have to pay for it!"

Owen took his seat now beneath the window, and beckoned them to take their places beside him, Gilles de Pirogue on his left and the Friar Preacher on his right. But once more, as the door was opened by the squire of Lyde in his black satin, these exiles from civilization exchanged glances across the Prince. And perhaps on this occasion there *was* some excuse for them; for certainly in no court in Europe or Asia would ceremonious entrances into a sovereign's presence have been made as simple as Master Brut made them.

"The most noble and honourable Princess, the Lady Mortimer," announced the Lollard in the precise tone in which he would have preached before Master Wycliffe.

"The most worthy and puissant Knight, Sir Edmund Mortimer," he went on. "The most gracious and honourable Lady, Elliw ferch Rhys —the high and noble Ambassador from King Charles of France, Jean de Pirogue—his Reverence Father Ignotus, Archdeacon of Bangor—his Reverence Father Pascentius—his Reverence Brother Huw and the Maid of Edeyrnion, and—*and Mistress Alice.*"

Here there was a pause; while with many stately formalities and a good deal of what Broch-o'-Meifod would have called "bowing and scraping" this august company found appropriate seats.

The Lollard's bride, whose voluptuous figure was certainly shown to engaging advantage in a filmy rose-coloured gown, stood for a perceptible moment hesitating awkwardly by Tegolin's side; even going so far in her embarrassment as to imitate the shy little Lu, who in her bird-like fashion had taken a wisp of Catharine's fair hair between her finger and thumb. Thus Alice, with less delicacy but almost equal confusion, thrust her fingers into the flaming tresses of the Maid.

Even the two Frenchmen, however, were compelled to recognize a touch of civilized regality in the gesture and word with which the Prince directed the witch's daughter to sit down by the Maid's side.

"Hopkin ap Thomas ab Einion!" announced the Lollard now; and attended by Rhisiart, who, garbed in the robe of a student of civil law, was literally weighed down beneath the brazier and cinnamon-sticks and censer and inflammable oils of the great "Maister of Brut," there entered the chamber a figure so extraordinary that while Gilles de Pirogue drew in his breath, and Lu clung to Catharine, and Alice to Tegolin, a shiver of startled excitement ran through the nerves of them all.

The countenance of the "divine Hopkin" was of such a character that Rhisiart had long since assured the Lollard that the man's whole life must have followed the *tynghed,* or fate, which Nature had moulded into his physiognomy. He was as toothless as Chancellor Young, but he had a nose and a chin that were so prominent that the scurrilous pages of Harlech, watching him as he dined, swore that both these features plunged, in the manner of an open beak, into the meats he mumbled.

This singular countenance was now topped by a high-pointed cap upon which had been embroidered various terrifying symbols, while the black robe, through the slits of which his tight-sleeved arms emerged, was scrawled from collar to skirt with the signs of the zodiac. In his hand he carried a long ebony wand, the top of which bore a silver knob carved in the likeness of a serpent's head.

The Prince rose and indicated to this apparition the great oak-wood upright chair which he had reserved for his reception. Here the magician solemnly took his seat, his yellow-stockinged ankles and up-ward-curving slippers resembling the legs of a fantastic bird as he rested them on his footstool, while Rhisiart looking, as well he might, in spite of the Lollard's assurances, grave and gloomy, placed the man's paraphernalia in front of him and sat down by his side.

Meanwhile the Archdeacon of Bangor—whose face, as Rhisiart watched his proceedings, struck him as resembling the mask worn at Hereford Carnival by the impersonator of the Devil—had spread out upon the table, without bothering to remove either the wine or the goblets, a great fourteenth-century map of England and Wales wherein the projected dominions of Owen were painted red, of Mortimer green, and of the Earl of Northumberland yellow.

Rising from their seats Owen and Sir Edmund now proceeded to examine this map, asking as they did so, a great many hurried and pertinent questions of the Archdeacon, questions that chiefly referred to the winding curves and disconcerting debouchings—marked as blue undulations full of whales and dolphins—of the river Trent.

Father Ignotus, Archdeacon of Bangor, as Rhisiart watched him from across the magic instruments of Master Hopkin, not only had the face of a mask in a morality-play: he had the voice, too. "Where on earth," thought our friend, "did Bishop Byford discover this youngest of Archdeacons? Can he have been a 'by-blow' of his own?"

Rhisiart felt as though at any moment this young automaton might slip out from behind both his voice and his face, and vanish in a cloud of vapour!

Whether it was the trouble on his mind about Gilles de Pirogue, or his proximity to Hopkin ap Thomas, or some unprecedented magic that was being worked by Owen, our friend now began to experience a sensation different from any he had ever known.

"It's the Prince," he said to himself. "I know him better than does anyone in the world save Broch-o'-Meifod. He *has* magical powers. He has all the powers that Hopkin pretends to have. He's punishing me now—in his own way!"

Whether it was the Prince "punishing" him or not, there was one person in that assembly who began to be seriously worried by the expression on the young man's narrow Norman face; and that was Tegolin.

"Is that blackness coming over him," she asked herself, "that he said he had when he drew his sword that day and when he climbed down that rope? No, no, no! It *can't* be that. His eyes are so bright; and he's staring so intently at the Archdeacon's map. But he's staring without seeing it. He's staring without seeing anything—unless—but that's silly! What's the matter with me to-night? But he *does* look as if he were seeing a ghost!"

When later that night Rhisiart was trying to explain to Master Brut what he really had gone through, he kept using the word "timeless." "I felt I'd got out of to-day and to-morrow, and out of yesterday too and the day before yesterday," he told the Lollard, who, while quoting comfortable sayings of Saint Paul, had his own private explanation of his friend's psychic experience.

"Did you feel like that *before you saw anything* or only afterwards?" he asked him.

"Oh, before, before!" Rhisiart firmly declared. "I suddenly felt as if the Archdeacon, and his map too, yes! and all of us there, were puppets in a masque that I'd seen—I don't know where!"

The Lollard smiled and sighed. "We're all puppets of the great Predestinating Will," he said.

"Yes, but I felt more than that, Walter."

"Of course you did; you felt that our Lord—"

"I felt *nothing* about our Lord!" cried Rhisiart crossly. "I felt we were all parts of a—of a reality, Walter—that was like some—some timeless masquerade! There was a book in our library at Oxford, Walter, with bits out of Plato in it—not in Greek, you understand—in Latin—translated by a very dangerous scholar—so our lecturer said— but this was a piece about shadows on the wall of a cave; and it always gave me, when the man quoted it, the feeling that there was some hidden reality, of which everything that happens to us—"

"But who knows anything about this inner reality?" enquired the Lollard.

"That's the point!" cried Rhisiart eagerly. "Whoever knows about it, you can be sure of *one* thing; Hopkin ap Thomas isn't that man!"

"You mean it's religious truth, that we can grasp if we want enough to grasp it?"

Rhisiart frowned. This *wasn't* in the least what he meant but the worst of it was he wasn't absolutely clear himself as to what he meant; but it had more to do with bards than with priests; but not with bards like Hopkin, or the Scab, or even old Iolo—not with *cywydd*-makers at all; but bards more like Merlin and Taliesin, if *they* ever could come again.

And yet not exactly that! Bards so great that they could discover the immortal essence which—in the timeless—lay behind everything that happened in time, and was the truth of it, and the reality of it, and, if you only were a bard great enough to catch it, existed in both the future and the past at the same moment!

Both the young men, while they sat on their bed that night talking about all this, had queer feelings about each other. The Lollard's face showed the passing of time much less than Rhisiart's. Remembering the causes of worry the man had, and from his point of view must be even then concealing, such as the de-virginating of *that witch* and all the tales about his heresies that Hugh Eddouyer would most certainly convey to Avignon, it was astonishing how youthful Brut remained!

Rhisiart, on the other hand, struck his friend as looking ten years older than he was, and this especially when he cast down his eyes; for then, in addition to his heavy eyelids, there seemed to wrinkle and fold and crease and gather certain leathery corrugations—almost like the scales over a dragon's eyes the Lollard thought—that gave to this down-looking something far more subtle than ordinary modesty, something indeed that was very formidable, and suggested that, when next that geir-falcon gaze was lifted, the glare of a great judge would blaze out!

But it was—and this made a deep impression on Master Brut—with his heavy eyelids still downcast that Rhisiart told him that night how he *knew* before the Presence uttered a word what the substance of his word would be; and yet when he'd listened to him in Dinas Brān the man had never referred to *any* river—certainly not to the Trent. "How then did I *know*," Rhisiart asked his friend—keeping his heavily-lidded eyes still lowered, as though to talk seriously about such things abashed his pride—"that he was going to protest about that particular boundary? Of course the way he protested was the way he *would* have protested, for that was the way he talked; but why was I sure it was going to be the Trent? Do you know, Walter, what it felt like when he did it? Like seeing a ghost *out of the future!* No, not a ghost out of the future" —and Rhisiart bent his head still lower as if his fantasies grew more and more humiliating—"like the truth of the present out of the future!"

Thus, hours later, Rhisiart described his feelings; but as he watched this equivocal Archdeacon and his great map it was before the man had said a word about the Trent that the thought of Hotspur came irresistibly to his mind.

"And what a thing," he said to himself, "that when England is being once and for all divided into three parts under the complacent eyes of France, an event which affects our children's children for generations, it shouldn't be any Richard Cœur de Lion who conducts the transaction, or any Saint Louis either, but an Archdeacon of Bangor, a mask of parchments and seals!"

"By the terms of this everlasting Indenture," the mask was declaring now, "the aforesaid high contracting parties, my Lords Northumberland, Mortimer and Glyn Dŵr, undertake to defend this Realm of England against all men, saving the oath of alliance which the last-named mighty Prince has sworn to the King of France.

"'The map of the aforesaid Country and Nation of England, now displayed before you and before all men"—at this point the Archdeacon picked up from beside his map a little "sanctus bell" and tinkled it three times—"and henceforth divided forever before you and before all men and before Almighty God into *three parts,* never to be united again, shows clearly to all, and without question by any, how my Lord Mortimer's dominion stretches from all the southern and western seas as far north as the Thames and as far west as the Severn; how my Lord Owen's dominion follows the above-mentioned river to the north gate of the City of Worcester, thence to the group of ash-trees on the high road from Bridgnorth prophesied of by Merlin to his sister Gwenddydd and commonly known as 'Onennau Meigion,' thence by the old road running north to the source of the Trent, thence to the source of the Mersey and along that river to—"

But Rhisiart was suddenly too overpowered by what he now saw to pay any attention to where the Mersey ran! Apparently no other person present saw it, though everybody was staring at the Archdeacon's map. The roots of his hair tingled, the flesh of his body became what children call "goose-flesh"; he clenched his teeth to stop their chattering.

His first instinct was to suspect some trick of Hopkin's. No! the man's black wand lay across his knees. Then he said to himself: "The Prince is calling up his spirits to punish me!" And what was *that* out there in the moonlight? He was sure he heard a long-drawn cry from the sea. Was Owen really a magician? But there it was—clear before him— and no one saw it but himself. Between Owen and Sir Edmund it was —its point upon the outspread map—*the sword of Hotspur!*

He knew at once. It was the "kind sword" he had seen in the man's hand at Dinas Brān. "But he's dead!" his pulses pounded. "He died at Shrewsbury!"

He shut his eyes for a second, telling himself that he was feverish, that it was a false creation of his brain. But no! There it was still—as palpable as Owen's forked beard and Mortimer's proud profile! He straightened himself, straining his fixed gaze. He knew where it was pointing. It was pointing at those whales and dolphins by which the Archdeacon had depicted the great river of the Midlands! He began to shiver. "Yes," he thought, "he's calling up his spirits to punish me!"

But suddenly he felt quite different. His hair ceased to tingle, his flesh became normal again. Slowly, slowly, the sword was fading away. But what restored him wasn't the fading of the sword; it was the dead hero's own voice in his ears. And the strange thing was, this voice seemed to come from the future as much as from the past. But it was Hotspur's voice; it was full of the dead man's impetuous humour.

But it came from a dimension so completely beyond the revolving spheres of this distracting world that it soothed him rather than troubled him. He had been, it must be confessed, disturbed by the Archdeacon's map and by those tripartite greens and reds and yellows; for, after all, though he had sworn to give Wales her liberty, he hadn't sworn to divide England between a Percy and a Mortimer to the delight of a de Pirogue! If this *were* a turning-point in history, as the Archdeacon declared, it was a deep comfort to him that this great and gallant ghost from God-knew-where—from some Shrewsbury beyond space and time—should utter such wanton, such whimsical, such careless words.

They gave the whole business a touch of the unreal—as if time itself were unreal—and though he still smelt that mixture of an old bard's perspiration and an old magician's chemicals that emanated with such unpleasant actuality from the personage at his side— Well! whether that ghostly sword-point on the map and this ghostly voice in his ears were false creations of his brain or not, they certainly made—

> *See how this river comes me cranking in,*
> *And cuts me from the best of all my land*
> *A huge half-moon, a monstrous cantle out!*

—they certainly made this whole spectacle, as he watched it now—the fair hair of Catharine, the flaming hair of Tegolin, Mad Huw's bewildered face, Hopkin's fantastic cap and yellow hose, the morality-mask of the Archdeacon—fall back, fall away, fall into remote perspective, as if it had all happened before and would all happen again; while its real significance—

But the signing of the great Indenture had begun; and first the Archdeacon on behalf of the dead man's father, and then Mortimer on behalf, it would seem, not of the little Earl, but of himself and of—this made Rhisiart's cheeks grow hot—of Catharine's children, and finally Owen on behalf of Wales, put their names to this division of the Usurper's kingdom. Well! It was over now. "And now," thought our friend, "he's going to turn on me!"

But while the Archdeacon was rolling up his great map with the

Indenture inside it there came a series of violent but erratic knocks upon the door, knocks that seemed to be resisted even while they were delivered.

Rhisiart saw the Prince nod to the Lollard, who, this time without uttering a word of ceremony, admitted a figure staggering with exhaustion, his face bloody, his clothes disordered, his hair dishevelled, his eyes wildly staring round the chamber as he searched for the Prince.

Owen moved impetuously towards him and reached him just as he staggered and nearly fell. He *would* have fallen if the Prince hadn't held him up. There was first a deep hush, then excited murmurs, then questions and cries through the whole assembly.

It fell to Rhisiart's lot, for the Wizard of the Tawy had only seen the famous Captain at a distance, to explain to Hopkin that this scarce-recognizable figure of defeat and blood and fainting exhaustion was none other than the notorious Rhys Gethin.

"It must be a great disaster," he whispered, "a bloody battle lost, or he wouldn't be here!"

Hopkin ap Thomas began hurriedly asking where the battle had been. "I hope," he said, "it wasn't in Gower. For the Prince's sake I hope so. Oh! I hope it was anywhere but *there*."

"And for your own sake too, you old humbug!" thought our friend. But all he said to the man was: "Shall I help you carry your things back to your chamber?"

Hopkin ap Thomas surveyed him with angry astonishment.

"But Owen ap Griffith Fychan asked me particularly to bring my things! He said he wished to see a—a specimen of what he was pleased to call my—my art. You surely don't mean—"

But Rhisiart as he contemplated the feverish egotism under that peaked cap could no longer contain himself.

"I tell you a great battle has been lost!" he whispered savagely. "The King and the Prince and the Duke of York and Codnor and Grendor and Talbot must be marching straight for Harlech. There'll be some fine trials for treason here soon."

Meanwhile Owen himself, leaving the wounded man to the women, was thinking bitterly: "This finishes me in Môn! I know those Tudors —they'll rush for pardon to the King!" And his mind flew back over the years to his standard-raising in Edeyrnion and his visit to Mathra-fal. "*What* did the man tell me? That he'd brought that child Efa with him here? Mother of God! I'll soon have all the princesses of Wales in Harlech! What do they think? That Manawydan fab Llyr is going to rise up out of the sea to fight for us! He said something else, too. But how did he know *that*? John ap Hywel already out-manœuvred by Codnor, and his people deserting daily? No, no! Gethin thinks be-cause *he's* hit the whole game's up. But the French fleet—ah! that's the rub! A few thousand cross-bowmen, a few hundred men-at-arms, a few seasoned knights, and with the Maid in her armour we'll cross London Bridge yet. Rhisiart! Rhisiart! How could you betray me on such a night?"

Rhys Gethin had been conveyed to a recess by the fire, where no less than three of the women present were gathered round him; but Owen, standing alone, seemed unable to do anything but stare into vacancy.

The appearance of his wounded Captain—and a terrible instinct told him he was hurt to death—together with the news he brought, was a crushing blow on this night of all nights! The man had left the battle-front on the Usk to go to the aid of the men of Anglesea, as the English called the famous Druidic island of Môn, but Stephen Scrope, the King's deputy, had not only recaptured Beaumaris Castle but had defeated Gethin with such devastating slaughter in the battle of Rhosymeirch that every Welshman who bore arms in those parts had fled to Snowdon, while the Shrine of St. Cybi, the glory of Holyhead, had been carried off to Dublin!

"Well! it only bears out what the Scab's been telling them all, that by turning away from Derfel I've done myself a fatal hurt. But Rhisiart, Rhisiart, son of my secret soul, there's a double need for shaming you now! That fleet *must* sail—even if I have to make you kneel down be-fore this devil of a Pirogue! Well! I must announce the worst to them! But the worst is in that damned Frenchman's black skull! He's saying to himself now: 'I'll stop that fine fleet!'"

"But what on earth's my Maid doing? Leaving her Friar to talk to that *other* Frenchman! Things are getting out of control. The moon's gone over to Bolingbroke; and that bird, free as my own soul, has de-ceived me!"

But he began to address them all now, though Catharine and

Mortimer were in such deep colloquy that they didn't listen to him. "There's been a great defeat of our people in Môn," he said. "Beaumaris has fallen, and the sacred isle's declared for the Usurper. Not only so, but it seems that Codnor has already surrounded the Abbot's levies between the Usk and Severn. It'll be necessary to change many of our plans. We cannot postpone our parliament; so we ourselves must remain here for at least eight days; but neither the Usurper at Berkhampstead, nor his son at Hereford need think that these disasters will abate one jot of our resolution. In three days our parliament will assemble—such an assembly as has not been seen in Wales since the days of Hywel the Good, nearly five centuries ago! And our answer to these Grendors and Codnors and Talbots and Scropes, who deem that a few lost battles can quiet our determination, will be to have ourselves solemnly and before God—and in the presence of such envoys from France and Scotland and Castille as arè expected daily—crowned and anointed Prince of all this land between Môn and Monmouth, between Trent and Tawy! Yea, and we'll do more than this. We'll declare to the world, before all the nations and courts of Christendom, that Henry of Lancaster, falsely called Henry of England, is a blasphemous and schismatical opponent of the only true Vicar of Christ, our most reverend Father in God, Benedict the Thirteenth, now in exile at Avignon!"

He paused and then turned suddenly and unexpectedly upon Rhisiart. "There is one other matter which must be settled to-night. There has come to our ears an act of unpardonable discourtesy committed upon the dignity and honour of one of our noble ambassadors from France. I regret to say that it has been traced to some insane prejudice entertained against this esteemed lord by my own confidential Secretary, Rhisiart ab Owen. *Stand forth, Rhisiart ab Owen!*"

It now became clear that what Sir Edmund and Catharine had been so earnestly discussing had nothing to do with the wounded Captain's news; for simultaneously with our friend's shame-faced advance into the centre of the chamber Mortimer approached the Prince. But Owen —though treating him with the politest respect—wouldn't listen to a word.

Making sure that he had caught the full attention of the two Frenchmen, he went on, taking a tone that made his daughter's cheeks blanch and Tegolin's mouth grow round with indignation. "Rhisiart ab Owen, we must dismiss you from at.endance on our person as squire of our body and from attendance at our council-board. You have heard what we all have heard. Our Captain is wounded. The Abbot is in peril. The best place for an ill-advised adviser is at the front."

"He's talking like a Tatar or a Turk," thought the Lollard. "This is unseemly. This is degrading in a Christian prince. This is the sort of thing to which the Institution of Parliament was designed to put an end. No self-respecting Christian has a right to submit to such despotism. It's nonsense to think he can have it both ways! If I were Rhisiart I'd mount my horse and ride off to-night. Why doesn't Father Pascentius defend him? Rhisiart says he saw it all! And why isn't Broch-o'-Meifod here? By the blood, I've a mind to tell Owen that if Rhisiart goes *I* go, too! That de Pirogue—Christ forgive me—looks as if he were *predestined to damnation!*"

But Owen was speaking again now. He and Rhisiart were facing each other in the middle of the chamber and a curious psychic struggle was going on between them, a struggle which Catharine and Sir Edmund were watching closely; whereas the magician from Gwent, indifferent to everything but what he regarded as a personal affront, was sulkily gathering his belongings together and looking about for assistance in carrying them away.

As for Father Pascentius he had evidently decided that the wise monastic procedure was to postpone meddling with the course of events until they clarified themselves a little by their own momentum; for he had already vanished from the scene. Mad Huw, however, had *not* vanished from the scene; and although separated from his Maid many of those present heard him say, as if to himself: "He's asleep, he's asleep; but beware of him if he wakes."

"The envoys from our cousin of France," Owen was now declaring, "cannot be permitted to leave our court without witnessing a full reparation for the discourtesy of which they complain. We must there-fore require of you, Rhisiart ab Owen, a formal return to us of the Great Seal of our Chancellor's Court, with which we had endowed you, and with which the recent Pact has just been sealed."

As he spoke he pointed to the table upon which the materials for the transaction still lay; and from which the mask-like Archdeacon, for whom formalities of this kind were a second nature, promptly picked up the object in question and held it out for Rhisiart to take.

All this while between Owen's brain and Rhisiart's brain there was proceeding an exchange of telepathic communication. Owen's brain was saying: "Take it, take it, you idiot, and hand it to me on your knees—and *that* will end this absurd play-acting!"

"You took Catharine from me," Rhisiart's brain was answering, "but my honour you shall never take! This means an apology to that devil over there and I'll die before I give it!"

Like two thunder-clouds, full of electricity of equal force, the will-power of the Master was confronted by the will-power of the Servant. But the damage that would have been done by the discharge of these electric bolts was destined to remain forever obscure; for an intervention came from a totally unexpected quarter. There was one person in that chamber who hated Gilles de Pirogue even more than Rhisiart had yet learnt to do, and that was *Jean* de Pirogue, and it was Jean who now came forward.

"Our royal Master," he said with a cold smile, "appointed not one but *two* ambassadors to this court. *Quant à moi* I shall inform our Sovereign Lord that we had had *nothing* to complain of here; and what is more, I can assure you, most mighty Prince de Galles, that King Charles knew *very well what he was doing* when he gave your humble servant *lettres de créance plénipotentiaire equal* to those of my cousin!"

Both the Prince and his Secretary drew a deep breath. "Saved!" thought Owen. "The fleet *will* sail."

"Saved!" thought Rhisiart, "and I *didn't* apologize!"

It was, however, with a sigh of disappointment that the Archdeacon allowed his outstretched hand, holding the Great Seal of the Principality, to sink down. "They're like a pack of women," he groaned. "Not a thing, not a thing can they do in order and in decency. I was a fool to leave the King's service. *He* knew what business is, and that's why—"

A few minutes later as Rhisiart was hurrying down the passage he heard the voice of Elliw ferch Rhys behind him. The little lady was alone and beckoning to him. "They're all busy over their own affairs," she said, "and none of them thinks of Meredith lying there. Griffith ab

Owen and John Hanmer are with the Arglwyddes. Crach Ffinnant's with Mistress Lowri and Master Simon. Poor boy, lying there alone! He must feel the castle's full of rumours and alarms, and there's no one but me to tell him the news; and I never *can* get things straight. Please, please, Master Rhisiart, cóme with me to him! It's not behoveful anyway that I should wander about at this hour and the place full of refugees from the battle! Oh, why *can't* they leave us alone in our own boundaries, and we leave them alone in theirs? That's what puzzles me." And laying her infinitessimal leaf of a hand upon Rhisiart's arm and clinging so closely to him that her loose mass of mouse-coloured hair entangled itself in the dagger on his hip, she went on murmuring in her low querulous voice, that was like the wind in a wisp of grass on an exposed buttress, about how both she and Meredith thought that if only the Prince would keep out of England the King would keep out of Wales. "Why doesn't he sign a treaty with England? That's what *we* think. *We* think this wily Archdeacon's a mere tool of Henry's to lure us to destruction! What do *we* want with 'Tripartite Indentures'? Why can't the Prince do homage to the King, as they did in the days of Harold the Saxon and William the Bastard? Oh do look what's coming, Master Rhisiart—" and she pulled him back against the wall to permit a stretcher to be carried past. "The Maid sent for *that*—I heard her tell Alice to tell old Glew— It's for the Captain—he's got a bit of broken steel in his side—the Maid thinks he's worse than they know. She thinks of everything, the Maid does! Did you notice how she was talking to that fair-haired Frenchman before he came up to you and the Prince? What a world a great castle like this is! I've never been in one before. Do you think the White Castle in London's as big as this? You don't mind my chattering, Master Rhisiart? I never used to do it. I never spoke to anyone. But it tires Meredith to talk, and so *I* talk. Besides you're his friend. You and Master Brut are the only friends he has. And Master Brut's always with Alice now. Do you like Alice? Meredith and I haven't made up our minds whether we do or not. Oh yes, and I've always wanted a chance of asking you something, something very personal and very important, but I expect I'd better not ask you now; for you're— What is it, Master Rhisiart? No! no! Don't look in there!—that's where they put the dead before they know their names, before they take them to the chapel. Some of them are still warm. They came with the Captain. They *just* got here, and then *went*—like that! Father Rheinalt's been there all day keeping people off. They say he wouldn't let Mistress Lowri come near them. You don't like *her*, do you, Master Rhisiart? Meredith called her an *Ellylles* once, but I wouldn't have th'at—it's too like my own name!

"No! no! Take me on! I don't want to look any more. *He?* Oh *he's* nobody. *He's* not a person. It isn't *him* I mind. Catharine can't bear him, but I don't mind him at all! He's what I often used to think about at home. I used to think I'd *like* him to do *that* for me when I was dead! *There!* He's doing it for that dead boy! You needn't be afraid, Master Rhisiart. He's only eating bits of meat and bread laid on the boy's chest. With a girl they put it between her breasts. I've never thought I'd mind the feeling of it. He mustn't touch it with his fingers, Rhisiart! Look how he's doing it—bending down—just like a wolf! What's the matter, Master Rhisiart? You look ill. You're not going to faint I hope! 'Twould be no good my calling for the *Sin-Eater* if you did—unless you were dead; for he mustn't speak to a living person, ever again for the rest of his life; nor must a living person speak to him. I used to envy him when I was at home and people came chattering—like I'm chattering now! Rhisiart—*Master* Rhisiart—you're not going to faint, are you? Oh, please come on! I told you to come on before." And she pulled so hard at his black scholar's sleeve that she was fain to give a scream; for her hair was twisted round his dagger!

Her scream made the *Sin-Eater* look up from the bread and meat between the boy's bared ribs. He must have thought this hook-nosed young student had brought the girl here on purpose, to enjoy her the more in such a place. But the lifting of his face made Rhisiart certain of what he'd suspected before. The man thus regaling himself upon all the sins ever committed by this dead youth was the nameless pariah —"the Droog," as the lay-brother from Scotland had called him—to whom he'd given that bone of blood at Valle Crucis!

Hooted out of society for causing the living to sin, he now took upon himself up and down the land the sins of the dead. Reduced by the harshness of humanity to sub-humanity, he was now transformed from sub-humanity to super-humanity. From being a creature below human pity he had become a god-like being who bore human sins. From being a leper reduced by men to a condition lower than Hell, he now stood like Aaron between God and the Devil, turning the wicked into the innocent by taking upon himself their guilt.

And as Rhisiart stared into this wolfish mediator's eyes, and saw his mouth looking just as he'd seen it at Valle Crucis, he wondered how the creature had the spirit to move from one nocturnal orgy to another, being as he must be, weighed down by the sins of so many!

But as little Elliw, using all the strength of her thin arms, drew him away, Rhisiart's mind trembled on the obscure brink of something that made him feel that if he could only once more mount Griffin and draw his sword for Owen it would—

But at that moment a torturing, deadly thought came to him. Hadn't Father Pascentius been speaking with the very voice of God when he hinted that more good would be done by sticking his dagger into the heart of Gilles de Pirogue than if he cut off the heads of a score of Greys of Codnor!

And how easy to waylay the French boy in the intricacies of a castle as big as this! He could kill him and bury him. Nobody would be the wiser. The cousin would be delighted.

And all the future victims of the "elixir of life" and the *"méthode scientifique"* would be spared! He felt as though he could see a multitudinous procession of frantic eyeballs imploring him to use his dagger before such a doctrine of devils hypnotized the gullible crowd.

Why then did he know with an absolute certainty that to-morrow he'd be riding to Caerleon; and Gilles de Pirogue, *unharmed,* would be sailing for France? "There are certain things," he said to himself, "that for each man born *are impossible;* and to put my dagger into this vivisector's heart—though my deepest conscience bids me do it—is impossible to me!

"What then? Well! I must just forget him, and forget those frantic eyeballs left to their fate by letting him go. Life, with such as he abroad, has no defence, no justification, no redemption. Well! I must forget such a life in—"

They were moving along an arched passage now, just above the third line of battlements, for as Lu had justly remarked Harlech was more like a towering sea-city than a buttressed keep, and they came to an arrow-slit through which the full moon was pouring her radiance.

With the moonlight came a wafture of sea-scents, sea-murmurs, sea-brine. The girl stopped and pulled him to this opening. She had hoped to look out; but it was only her forehead that touched the base of the aperture.

"Lift me up!" she whispered; and then: "One minute! My hair's caught in something."

He obeyed her, and held her so tight that his narrow visage and sucked-in lips were lost in that mouse-coloured moonlit cloud. "She's in love with Meredith," he said to himself, "and I with Catharine; and yet—"

But he *had* forgotten Gilles's victims when he put her down. "Life," he told the next sea-window, "cannot bear thinking on. Broch is right —not Owen."

And then he said: "Mistress Lu, may I tell you what someone used to lull me to sleep with, when—you know how it is sometimes?"

"Say it to me, Rhisiart."

"Then they went on to Harlech—and there came three birds, and began singing unto them a certain song, and all the songs they had ever heard were unpleasant compared thereto; and the birds seemed to them to be at a great distance from them over the sea, yet they appeared as distinct as if they were close by—"

"Rhisiart!"

"Yes, Lu."

"Catharine told me that Tegolin's got a treasure-box that has only one thing in it."

It was his turn now to drag her by the arm and quicken their speed. For some queer reason he felt furious with Tegolin for showing her treasure-box to Catharine.

He vented his anger on the speaker. "That's what I can't bear in you girls!" he burst out in the very tone of the Rhisiart of five years ago who rode between the arrows and the spears. "You show each other everything!"

Lu laughed a little tinkling laugh like the sound of a reef-bell as far away as the Birds of Rhiannon.

"There's one thing we don't *always* show, it seems."

"What are you talking about now?"

"Our hearts, Rhisiart ab Owen, our hearts."

XVIII

THE MAID IN ARMOUR

THE WEEK that followed that eventful Candlemas, of the fifth year of Owen's proclamation as Prince of Wales, was a week long remembered by the people of Ardudwy and Meirionydd.

But when it was over and the second parliament of his rule had come and gone, the Prince's after-thoughts were anything but enviable. The great assembly only sat for three days; a hurried despatch of business that was due to the dangerous number of English troops now invading Wales and to the deadly strategy of the gentlemen who commanded them.

Both these disastrous facts were, as Rhisiart alone in the castle realized, due to the rapidly-growing military genius of the young Prince Henry, from whose headquarters at Hereford there emanated measures for harassing Owen that proved far more effective than any of the grandiose invasions of Wales led by the King.

The unfortunate issue of every one of the Usurper's own Welsh campaigns had begun to have a noticeable psychological effect on his English subjects. The impression kept sinking deeper and deeper into the popular mind that this mysterious "Owen Glendourdy" really *was* possessed of supernatural powers, and could call upon the elements at will to overthrow his enemies.

In many an outlying homestead all along the eastern coast, from Yorkshire to Kent, English mothers would make their children obey by the threat "Glendourdy will have you!" while terrifying rumours ran through all the shires that this incalculable Welsh wizard, in league with all the forces of destruction in the unseen world, had threatened to exterminate, by his devilish power over water and fire and wind, the whole English race from off the surface of the earth.

It was his friend Master Brut who postponed Rhisiart's departure for the front. The fearless Lollard indignantly rejected the Prince's suggestion that he should manage the parliament alone. He threatened point-blank to leave the lady who was now Mistress Alice Brut of Lyde and gallop off with Rhisiart to the aid of the Abbot of Caerleon if his friend wasn't kept at Harlech till the parliament had dispersed. For a moment Rhisiart feared that they were both going to be clapped into prison; but Chancellor Young, arriving post-haste from Aberystwyth, allowed his toothless gums to emit such a pontifical chuckle at the mere notion of dispensing with two such competent clerks, till their gifts had been exploited to the full, that the Prince became more reasonable.

It was Chancellor Young too who on the very eve of the coronation got rid of Hopkin ap Thomas. This he achieved by a method well-known at most European courts but not yet practised at Owen's; the method of warning the victim of a plot against his life. Hopkin believed and fled. Nor has any prophet ever rejoiced at returning in safety to the home of his birth more than this inspired but timid magician when he beheld the silver Tawy again.

Each of the young Frenchmen being anxious, though from very different motives, to return to France, they were the first of the envoys to leave; and they hurried off directly the coronation was over; the representatives of Scotland and Castille lingering till the roads to the coast should be less invested by Owen's enemies.

Neither the parliament nor the coronation created as much enthusiasm as the Prince expected. This was chiefly due to the impossibility of concealing from the natives of Ardudwy the melancholy processions of wounded men who kept pouring into the neighbourhood. It was also due to the fact that while the Prince's eldest son was away fighting, and his son Meredith was still confined to his chamber, Rhys Gethin's hurt proved to be a mortal one. The great Captain took long to die; but that he *was* dying seemed indisputable.

As far as Owen's own secret feelings were concerned there was one aspect of this sumptuous ceremony that hurt him far more than the presence of Bishop Trevor and Bishop Byford could give him pleasure, namely the absence of Broch-o'-Meifod. It wasn't that the giant had rushed off to visit his wife and children. It was, in a sense, worse and more startling to Owen than that. "If he had gone to Maen-y-Meifod," the Prince said to himself, "I could perfectly well understand it. He's not one for ceremonies. But knowing what I feel about it and the importance I attach to such things, it does seem really treacherous to the link between us to choose to remain *perdu* when such a thing was going on."

It soon became apparent that Chancellor Young's constant presence in the castle of Aberystwyth was indispensable from an ecclesiastical point of view. If Harlech was the base of the military operations of the principality, Aberystwyth had already become the centre of its ecclesiastical polity. And just now the proposed transference of Welsh devotion from the Pope to the anti-Pope, rumours of which were spreading through the country, was exciting a perilous agitation in all religious quarters.

The secular Welsh clergy were on the whole in favour of it; the monastic orders, with the exception of Owen's faithful adherents, the Franciscans, bitterly opposed to it. Benedict the Eighth had already discovered that it was easier to dominate bishops and bishoprics than to meddle with abbots and monasteries. He was helped, however, by the vein of cynical materialism in the character of the English King, which had led to sacrilegious despoilings on the invaders' side worse than any of which Owen was guilty.

The couple of days that followed the dispersing of the parliament and the scattering of the coronation-guests were days of weary anxiety to Owen and of violent altercations between his advisers in that still over-crowded castle.

The Arglwyddes kept imploring him to start at once for the Usk to aid the hard-pressed Abbot. Much as she loved her son Griffith, she had little confidence in his ability as a leader; and it was only the steadiness of her nerves that kept her from spending hours at her tower-window, watching in maternal anxiety the bands of fugitives who kept drifting to that sea-coast from the fields of battle.

Meanwhile all manner of messengers arrived at Harlech with news, some bad, some good, some obviously false, some with the very impress and seal of truth; and, by degrees, as he tried to sift truth from falsehood the Prince slipped into the cynical and fatalistic attitude of believing none of them, either good or bad.

Henry Don, he surmised, was still holding his own in Glamorgan, for the rumours from that quarter remained contradictory; and as long as he got no news of a definite reverse from Rhys Ddu he kept up his hope that that seasoned warrior was keeping the enemy out of Carmarthen.

Shropshire, left to its own devices by the King, who apparently had ceased forwarding Sheriff Burnell any further pay for his troops, had taken its affairs into its own hands and was now openly sending Owen money to keep his raiders from crossing the border; while Pembrokeshire where the English were especially strong had for some while been buying him off.

"If only the French would sail—if only the French would sail," was the constant burden of his thought. With the French army behind him all might still be well; for his English prisoners kept assuring him that the terror of his name had travelled from Durham in the north to Chichester in the south.

Mortimer had begun to be an anxiety to him, from his growing impatience to take the field; but in this point Catharine was proving curiously obstinate. She had heard of so many castles being lost from lack of an effective leader within the walls that imaginative ideas about being left alone in Harlech with her mother and her children till the garrison gave them up to the English kept obsessing her mind.

Owen himself was extremely unwilling to let his half-royal son-in-law, upon whose life so much depended, go to the front. When the French came, and they all marched upon London, it would be a different thing; but to risk Mortimer's life in some trifling skirmish in the mountains seemed ridiculous.

It did strike the Prince more than once, as he wasted precious hours analysing his feelings in his room overlooking the sea, that it was strange he should feel far more anxious about the fate of his brother Tudor on the Usk than that of his eldest son. Tudor was an elderly man like himself. Like himself he wore his beard forked. Like himself he was meticulously careful of his appearance. Like himself his favourite colours were yellow and green. Tudor ap Griffith Fychan appeared, however, some ten years younger, when in reality there wasn't twenty-four months between them. In the last five years Owen's hair had turned grey, while Tudor's remained as yellow as when they were boys. The chief difference between them lay in their eyes. Owen's were sea-green, mutable, equivocal, whereas Tudor's were a pure grey-blue, out of which a natural goodness of heart looked forth, faithful and unchanging.

Not only was the Arglwyddes made indignant and John Hanmer irritable by the queer lethargy which fell upon the Prince when his parliament and his ambassadors were gone; our friend Rhisiart was completely puzzled. Though the uncharacteristic rage he had fallen into with his Secretary and his Librarian soon vanished, Master Brut would often leave his bride's bed, both early and late, and visit Rhisiart's tower-room, where both the men tried in vain to get at the secret of their Prince's mood.

But the explanation came before a week had passed. The day was Friday; and Rhisiart in his almost *legal* superstition, that certainly was more Norman than Welsh, felt it was only viciously natural that he should wake on that chilly February dawn with anxieties going round and round in the revolving cage of his brain like a procession of agitated rats.

Some of these anxieties were purely political, some were very personal; and chief among the latter was a queer intangible estrangement that had made itself felt since her father's coronation between Lady Mortimer and himself.

And now in that dangerous clear air of the hour before dawn, when the nature-nourished *illusions,* upon which the life of all living things depend, grow thin and transparent, leaving nearly bare that naked reality which the Great Mother so tenderly pads and plasters with her imperishable pretences, Rhisiart beheld in sharp, cruel, self-accusing outlines the cause of this estrangement. The ignoble truth was that his own passionate love for the mother of Rhisiart and Bridget had cooled without his knowing it! But of late one of the results of this interior cooling had been an accession of exterior demonstration; and through this sweet treachery Catharine's sea-green eyes had pierced, as the Prince's lance might have done, to the heart of his false gesture; and it was *this*—not that his passion was less but that its romantic demonstration was more—that had given her tone this impalpable accretion of bitterness.

But as he lay there, inhaling the vague salt-water scents and enjoying the pre-dawn breath of the in-rolling tide, he began to be aware of

some unusual stir going on in the castle, a stir, it seemed to him, both
down in the base-court and within the walls. He listened intently,
throwing off his Oxford sheepskin, tilting himself up, hugging his
knees.

No, he heard no bugle, no trumpet, no word of command. It couldn't
be the English then. What the devil was it? Had he forgotten some
February saint's day, some local market? Had Lemuel Livius of
Burgos been the forerunner of a host of pedlars? They did come in
crowds sometimes, and not only Jewish ones; and it was quite possible
that the ladies of the castle had kept their knowledge of their coming a
secret, lest Father Pascentius or John Hanmer—or even the Prince's
Secretary—might, in their masculine prudence, have ordered them off.

But the stir continued and kept mounting up. "Curse your blood,
Walter!" he muttered viciously to himself. "You can leave your clip-
pings and cuddlings to tell me how your witch has learnt three words
in Greek; but now, when the whole castle's in an uproar, you must
turn her about, and e'en at it again. Oh, the witch, the witch! You're
lost to me, brother; you're lost to me from now on—and the Prince is
lost to me—and Catharine's lost to me. I'll have to botanize with
Father Pascentius! I'll have to add the hundred and fifth article to the
Tripartite Indenture and illuminate all its capitals!"

He jumped out of bed and rushed to both his windows. How many
times he had done this since his first coming to Harlech, only to find
that save for a strip of the sea's horizon from one of them and a couple
of mountain peaks from the other they revealed nothing at all.

With some trouble—for he was a bad fire-lighter, just as he was a
bad swimmer, a bad falconer, and no kind of an husbandman; fire,
water, air, earth, all throwing him back to his desk!—he lit a candle
and placed it in the window, wondering to himself, even as the flame
blew inwards against his hand, how many other lights in the arrow-
slits of Harlech could be seen at this hour from a boat at sea.

But the elements were, as usual, in conspiracy against the Secretary;
and his candle, quietly, obstinately, resolutely flickered out. Lighting it
again and placing it on a stone bracket out of the draught, he heard
the familiar cracked-metal sound of the old chapel bell strike the hour.
Was it five or six? He'd let the strokes pass uncounted.

But he began now hurriedly pulling on his black Oxford-scholar's tunic, his original faded one, half-a-dozen years old, and much too tight for him. Little Sibli—who had made herself responsible for his clothes —liked this costume the best of all he had. It must have been for that reason that whenever she saw him in it her wit at his expense became lacerating. She would run her little hands all over his body and call upon Luned to see how he was growing, as she declared, "out of his clothes."

And some instinct in him to-day made him not only put on black but reject every sort of ornament. His dagger, still without its sheath, was concealed below his tunic; and though he mechanically picked up a beautiful piece of red embroidery that Sibli'd told him she'd held against her body all last All Souls' night to bring him luck, he soon laid it down.

But since the sounds increased, and Master Brut didn't come, he decided to go down into the corridor beneath his turret and ask the sentry there what the stir was about. As he hurried down the winding stairs with the candle in his hand he thought of Luned, the damsel whom he'd come, by reason of so many queer experiences, to call his "stair-case girl."

"Mary, Joseph!" he muttered. "I'm certain she's in the corridor!" So certain was he, that there actually came to his nostrils that particular cinnamon scent which he always associated with this young woman. "She's like the one in Modry's stories," he said to himself, as he pushed open the turret-door; "only Modry made *her* keep changing, from ugly to pretty, and this one's always the same!"

No, there was nobody in the corridor—not even the sentry. "He must have gone like me, to find out what's up," and he stood still, listening, and guarding his candle-flame with his hand. Mary, Joseph! if there wasn't a woman, with a candle just like his own, coming towards him—and it *was* Luned!

The encounter was less astonishing than it seemed to him just then, seeing that the girl had come expressly from the other end of the castle with the sole intention of finding him; but when the actual cinnamon scent was really about him he could think of nothing else but this piling up of coincidence into what *couldn't* be coincidence!

"I was thinking of you," he blurted out, as they simultaneously moved their candles so as to envisage each other's faces.

It seemed so natural to Luned that the Secretary should be thinking of her at five o'clock in the morning that she didn't even smile.

"Kiss me, Rhisiart!" she said quietly. "You can kiss me as much as you like now, and—and anything else," she added significantly.

"What do you mean?" he whispered, when he had kissed her.

"Can't you see?" and she moved her candle again so as throw her figure into full relief.

Rhisiart might have been less stupid if Luned's figure hadn't always been so lavishly developed. But, as it was, he gave her one quick glance and then stared at the wall, where their candles were throwing two monstrous shadows. These shadows—one of which resembled a drooping heron with the head of a frog, and the other a tilted wine-cask out which an angel was peeping—seemed, as he stared at them, to have taken the whole situation into their hands.

"No, I can't," he replied. "But *do* look at our shadows, Luned!"

"I'm going to have a child, Rhisiart!" At this the angel's head sank back into the wine-cask, and the frog's head leapt up to the roof, where it transformed itself into a flying-fish. "Look at me, dear! Do you know whose child it is?"

He did indeed look at her now; for a wild rush of alarm shot through his heart. Was she going to father her bastard on *him?*

"It ought to have been Rawllf's," he remarked coldly and rather cruelly.

"Bend down your head, dear!"

It was clearly no use being bitter or unkind to this cinnamon-scented bundle of feminine confidences, so he simply obeyed her; and with what seemed to him an unnecessary amount of warm breath and of tickling locks the syllables "Elphin" caressed his ears.

"Does he confess to it?" he enquired, in his most business-like sheriff's-office voice.

She shook her head. "That's what I've come to you about, Rhisiart."

"He denies it?"

She nodded sadly.

He surveyed her from head to foot. How queer it was that just when the Russian's curst "insect" ought to have made all this engaging and exciting it completely deserted him and he could only feel towards her as if she were some great soft-scented peony-bud, ready to burst prematurely into bloom!

"You know what's done in—in some countries—to girls in my state when the man gives them the lie?"

"Don't be silly, Luned! We're in the fifteenth century not the fifth. The worst the Arglwyddes could do would be to send you back to Snowdon. You'd better go to Cath—to Lady Mortimer, and tell *her* about it."

"Rhisiart, dear—"

"Well?"

"It's not easy to say this, Rhisiart; but if the Prince is sending you to the war *anyway,* and taking Tegolin to the war himself, it wouldn't make any difference—I mean it wouldn't hurt you any more than you're hurt already—if you were to—"

"What—*are*—you—saying, girl?"

Luned now began to cry. Her candle went out, and she scrupled not to hide her wet face against his shoulder. "I've been lying awake," she sobbed, "thinking of this all the night."

He was unable to resist her tender gesture because of the absolute necessity he was under not to let *his* candle go out. Coldly, angrily, helplessly, he remembered the Ladies' Tower at Dinas Brān. How things *did* come round!

But her mention of Tegolin had profoundly disturbed him. "Listen, Luned," he said, almost beseechingly. "For heaven's sake tell me what's going on in this castle?"

She raised her head and stopped crying. It was an appeal to her discretion, to her superior wisdom. His tone was boyish and plaintive. Her protective instinct was dominant, and in a moment she was happy. She laid re-assuring maternal fingers upon his wrist. "It's Mistress Alice, not I, who's been helping her to pack. I've only helped Sibli with her armour."

In a single flash the whole truth revealed itself to Rhisiart. The Prince had out-witted him. He was going to rob him of Tegolin just as he'd robbed him of Catharine! He suddenly felt very old and very reckless. "He'd better take care!" he thought; and shaking off the girl's fingers he plunged his hand into his tunic.

"But Mistress Alice is so fond of her," he murmured, staring past Luned into vacancy. Nor did his hearer miss the implication that to fling the Maid into the arms of the Prince was anything but an act of fondness.

It came sliding into his mind how passionately Alice of Ruthin had courted Tegolin when they first met; and how he'd caught her that night at the banquet clinging to her form with a look of ecstatic adoration. It was incredible to him that so simple a matter as the virtuous embraces of Walter Brut could have turned her against her former idol.

"But perhaps they're *like that*," he thought, "and when once they've got a man they're ready to outrage and desecrate their girlish ideal."

But if Dame Alice's treachery was a thing to ponder on, the change that had come over Luned since she'd taken the control of the situation out of the hands of their shadows was quite as bewildering. And this change was such a relief to Rhisiart that he found he could endure quite cheerfully her feminine gossip.

Every tear she had shed had made him feel harder. If the Russian's "insect" had been roused ever so little it would have been different; for then he would have at least felt a wicked substitute for pity—something indeed that *could* have been transformed into pity!

But between the cold distaste her tears excited in him and every margin of pity a great gulf was fixed; and it was for this reason that the moment she began to gossip—even about Catharine and Tegolin— it was such a relief to escape the most unpleasant of all feelings, unsympathetic disgust, that he felt quite a friendly glow towards her, and was prepared to hear the most scandalous revelations without being offended.

He listened patiently, therefore, when she went so far as to assure him that Lady Mortimer was going to have another child, and that only a day or two ago the mere shock of encountering the *Sin-Eater* in one of the castle-corridors had caused her to faint away.

"I've always been unfair to this girl," he thought, as Luned went on telling him the most surprising things. She told him, for instance— while the imparting of such knowledge, as if by a clever mother to a stupid son, completely drove away her dread of becoming a mother— that the Arglwyddes was extremely upset by this whole project. There had been a dramatic scene, she told him, between the Prince and his wife only yesterday, with little Sibli as eavesdropper, but the Prince by a crafty appeal to his wife's patriotism had conquered; and the Arglwyddes had consented to allow the Maid an official farewell.

In the joy of telling him all this, Luned so far forgot her own trouble as to allow him to re-light her candle; and it was thus quite a harmless-looking conversation that the appearance of Master Brut finally interrupted.

With Luned's departure, and the men's ascent to the turret, candles proved no longer necessary; and by the time the two friends had got Rhisiart's fire burning the light of dawn was filling the room. They had just begun to break their fast upon beer and bread when they were astonished to hear a furtive knock at the door; and on the Lollard's opening it they were still more amazed to see the figure of the Grey Friar.

There had descended upon Mad Huw a state of emotional trouble quite different from any that Rhisiart had ever seen in him before. If his own appearance revealed the passing of time, the Friar's did so much more.

Neither of the men before whom he now presented himself had realized this change as they were compelled to realize it now. In that pale dawn-light Mad Huw looked like an old man. Before letting him speak Rhisiart took the precaution of descending the stairs once more and bolting the door at their foot. The chamber smelt strongly of a bitter-sweet aroma; for the wind blowing in through one window and whirling off through another kept the apartment clear of smoke but not of the *taste* of smoke; and this may have reminded Mad Huw of his youth. At any rate, in combination with the brown ale it certainly loosened his tongue.

The curious thing was—and both the men noticed it, though they took care to avoid each other's eyes—that the shock the Friar had received made it possible for him to keep the late King out of his mind. And once *He* was expelled Brother Huw could hardly be regarded as mad at all.

But if not mad, he was clearly very much upset, though his words were intelligible enough. Indeed their calmness alarmed his hearers more than the wildest incoherence would have done.

"It was in confession to Father Rheinalt—I couldn't keep it back—
for Saint Francis says 'keep nothing back'—and the Father said *I was
to tell you*. The Father said: 'Tell this to Master 'Rhisiart. He'll know
what to do.' But—God forgive me!—I couldn't tell you. I couldn't! I
couldn't! You remember when the Prince kept back the Maid after
Mass? No, no! You can't remember, for you weren't there. Nobody
was there but Father Pascentius and me, and the Father was thinking
of nothing but a plant he'd left in the sacristy—you know how he is—
sometimes he sees everything, but when he's got a plant waiting for
him— But the devil tempted me in the sacristy. He put his head out of
the wash-basin. He said: 'Are you there, Brother Huw?' And I said,
'I *am* there, Brother Devil.' And then he said: 'You can spy on the
Maid and the Prince! You can hear every word, too; if you stand on the
chair behind the story of Bel and the Dragon.' And I said: 'Is that
the truth, Brother Devil *Bach?'* And he said: 'It *is* the truth, Brother
Huw *Bach!'*

"So I did what he said. Father Pascentius was writing down like he
does, the place and the soil where he found the plant—I know what he
writes, for he showed me once, and got cross with me when I said he
oughtn't to write devils' names in the sacristy—so he didn't see me
go—but the Prince was holding the Maid's hand and making her cry.
He was telling her that Hopkin ap Thomas said she was to wear
armour. He was telling her he'd had Master Simon make that golden
armour the French King sent him smaller, so it would fit a maiden
like her. He told her that he'd had it taken to her room and that
Mistress Sibli was to help her put it on; and that when it was on she
was to come down and he'd bring a horse for her into the base-court—
and that when she could sit on the horse, all glittering and golden, and
the French were here, she should ride by his side all through Hereford
and Oxford and Worcester and over London Bridge. Then the Maid
said: 'Will Brother Huw be with us in Hereford and Oxford and
London?' And he said 'yes.' And then she said: 'Will Rhisiart be with
us?' And he said he didn't know. And then he whispered something
to her and held her hand.

"And he held her hand so hard that he made her cry; and when she
cried my knees shook so that the chair fell down, and when I'd got it

up again there was nobody there. When I told Father Rheinalt about it he asked me whether I thought the Prince loved the Maid, and I said 'yes'; and he asked me whether I thought the Maid loved the Prince, and I said 'no.' And then he said: 'You must go to Master Rhisiart and tell him all you've told me.' "

The two men stared at Mad Huw—this form so familiar to them that seemed suddenly to have grown old—and as his beautiful woman-ish eyes, now so unnaturally bright, met their own, they were afraid, not of his insanity, but of his sanity.

The Friar was now sitting hunched up by the hearth on a roughly-carved chair, while both the men were on their feet watching him. He had lowered his head and they were presently conscious that big silent tears were running down his cheeks.

Rhisiart's face had grown hard and stern; but his dark eyes were blazing. Thoughts, images, memories whirled through his head in rapid succession. Tegolin kissing his sword—Tegolin putting the orchid into her braid—Tegolin asleep with him under his sheepskin—Tegolin hand in hand with him entering Glyndyfrdwy—Tegolin's voice calling him "Gwion Bach"—Tegolin comforting him after the scene with Luned—Tegolin sending him his sword before Bryn Glas. And those words of Elliw ferch Rhys came to him: "Catharine says Tegolin has only one thing in her treasure-box." *What* was that one thing? He hadn't let himself think what it was! But he had known very well, all the while.

"You took Catharine from me," he thought, "and now you want to take Tegolin." All these thoughts, images, feelings whirled in such rapid succession through his brain that it was as if he'd been drowning. And when he came back to watching those silent tears of Brother Huw it was as if he *had* drowned—and then been restored to life.

The Lollard, too, was quite clearly passing through some interior mental struggle. When Rhisiart brought himself at last to glance at his face, it was anything but the calm, unruffled face to which he had grown so accustomed. It had gone haggard and drawn. It looked almost thin!

A silence fell upon the three of them now, a silence through which they could hear all manner of faint sounds. The silence seemed to mount up from the sea and sink down from the sky. It flowed around and around; buoying up the sounds that floated upon it, as if they'd been relaxed swimmers on a smooth tide; and the silence mingled with the sun-sparkles, too, that were rocking on the incoming waves, and with the rare sea-scents that kept entering that turret window. But the sounds were what the silence loved best of all; and *they* rose from all manner of different directions.

They were casual sounds, drifting sounds, accidental sounds, without order and without cohesion. But they were the music of life. Some came from fishermen drying their nets on the rocks, some from seagulls along the walls of the jetty, some from cattle and sheep in the castle-meadows, some from horses and hounds in the castle-yard. They were fainter, more volatile, more ethereal than the living things that uttered them.

A cock-crow was less and more than any chanticleer, a lamb's bleat less and more than any actual lamb, a horse's neigh, or a rook's caw, or a seaman's whistle, was a voice rising from generations of horses, rooks, and fishermen!

Fused together, these isolated sounds evoked a sense of the continuity of life by sea and land, a continuity simple, tranquil, universal, detached from individual hunger or desire or pain or joy.

Mad Huw, crouching by their newly-lit fire, lost the effect of this diurnal awakening; but in Rhisiart and the Lollard, as they stood staring at his silent tears, there moved and stirred an obscure home-sickness for the streets of their native Hereford and for the green banks of the Wye.

"Where is the Maid now? Is she still asleep?" enquired Master Brut.

Mad Huw scrambled to his feet and wiped his eyes with the back of his hand. "She's putting on that armour," he murmured hoarsely. "Mistress Luned and the dwarf are helping her; and the Prince is waiting for her with a big grey horse in the base-court."

Rhisiart's eyes had such a dangerous expression in them that the Lollard laid his hand on his arm. "Did you see the Prince in the court-yard?" he asked, clutching Rhisiart tightly.

Mad Huw nodded. "My black angel told me to look," he added, with a nervous glance round the room. "He's holding the horse by the bridle and walking it up and down. It's got that frontlet on with the black lions that Master Simon made for the coronation."

"It's Seisyll!" muttered Rhisiart. "Let me go! What are you holding me for? I must go down to him!"

But the Lollard only tightened his grip. "Was she willing to put on the armour, Brother?"

"She cried and prayed all last night. I would have come to you last night, but I dursn't leave her. She kept saying, 'Oh God, tell me what's right to do! Oh God, tell me what's right to do!'"

Rhisiart flung his friend's hand from his arm with a violent jerk. But he allowed Master Brut to put his back to the door without any protest. Indeed he didn't seem to notice what the other was doing. His burning eyes remained fixed on the Friar's.

"What else did she say last night?" he asked, in a queer, strained voice.

Once more Mad Huw glanced furtively about the room; and he did so with such an air of seeing more than his companions that they both automatically crossed themselves. "She talked of the shame. She asked me if it were not a shame for a maid to be seen of men in the armour of men."

"What did you answer to *that*, Brother?" enquired the Lollard, his back still against the closed door.

The Friar gave him a steady, resolute look. It was clear that they were now on familiar ground, the ground of spiritual discrimination, in the niceties of which every religious man is professionally at home. "I told her the truth," he replied simply. "Because—because I am a man, and she—is what she is, is that a reason why I should deceive her? I told her that the shame, if shame there were, lay in the lusts of the heart, not in what we put on or take off."

Rhisiart's feelings were in too dark a whirlpool of disturbance to evoke many clear thoughts, but he did say to himself: "That's where his honesty betrayed her! He should have told her that it *was* a shame. He should have remembered the damnable and lecherous wickedness in the mind of Owen ap Griffith!"

But the Friar's answer so greatly pleased the Lollard that in his fatal passion for theological controversy he went too far. "But if," he cried eagerly, forgetting that an advocate who had just slipped away from a love-exhausted bride was scarcely an unbiassed authority, "if the sight of a maid in armour should arouse—"

But the animal-like groan that this nice casuistical point, thus laid bare, drew from the smouldering bosom of his friend cut his words short; and he turned his innocent blue eyes, full of bewildered sympathy, from Rhisiart's distorted face to the Friar. "What did she say then, Brother?"

"She asked me if there was any danger of violence to her chastity from the Prince's love?"

Expecting every second that his friend would fling himself upon him in an unbridled desire to rush down and face this lecherous despot, the Lollard's cautious murmur: "What did you answer to *that?*" sounded like a violent and disturbing sneeze at the moment of the Elevation of the Host.

Mad Huw's throat was evidently swallowing something that resembled a large round marble; but once more his training in the cloister compelled him to pronounce the confessional truth. "I told her that a thousand angels of God guarded the chastity of a true maid; and that if she herself, in the frailty of our human flesh, weakened not, the heat of the wickedest passion would turn to ice."

"God forgive you!" broke from Rhisiart's twisted mouth; but the Lollard, from his position at the door, stared at the Friar in astonished admiration.

"He loves her," he thought, "and yet he can say that!" And the worthy man sighed heavily, knowing that he could never have uttered such things to his Alice.

The curious thing now, in that scene between the three of them, was the manner in which the Friar's companions completely discounted his insanity; and not only so, but from the moment he brushed away his tears with the back of his hand, it was Mad Huw who dominated the situation.

All Rhisiart's belongings lay about him in that turret-room; and though Master Brut had moved most of *his* possessions, which were not many, into his bride's chamber, he had begged him to leave him the *Consolations* of Boëthius. And as the Lollard went on questioning the Friar, Rhisiart's eyes moved from Boëthius to his crusader's sword and from his crusader's sword back to Boëthius. Boëthius made him think of Catharine. In fact the image of Catharine suckling her first-born possessed itself of the space—for in thought space is malleable—occupied by that parchment volume with its illuminated title. The crusader's sword, however, remained *in situ,* but its sheath disappeared; and across its naked steel lay the red braid of Tegolin.

And little by little his blind anger against the Prince receded, ebbing from his veins as if it had been his own blood. In fact he began to feel dizzy and faint, and, like the eclipsing form of the moon darkening a segment of the sinking sun, that curious "blackness" he had known once or twice in his life began again to invade his consciousness. But he struggled against this "blackness" and overcame it; and as he overcame it there swept through him, emanating from the Friar as the man answered the Lollard's questions, a feeling as though they all, Owen, Tegolin, Mad Huw and himself, were bound together by a fate that was larger and deeper than any anger he could indulge.

The Friar had never grudged *him* his share in the Maid—and what right had he? In the turbulance of what was happening in his own puzzled heart Rhisiart began to be aware of a childish humility before the victorious tourney that was reeling to its close under that grey habit—the victory of a faith beyond his comprehension over a love greater than his love! He suddenly found himself—just as he had always done with his trouble over Catharine—instinctively rushing to Tegolin for comfort and help, only to remember that it was *about* Tegolin that he needed this support!

"Does he want her to ride with him to the Usk," the Lollard was asking now, "or to the banks of the—"

But the unmistakeable notes of a horn, blown loud and clear in the court below, came through the window, breaking into the man's words; and simultaneously with this came a loud knocking at the foot of the tower.

It needed little insight on the part of Master Brut to realize that some sudden change had occurred in his friend's mood, and opening the door now without any apprehension he ran down the winding stairway. He returned with a handsome young man who was no other than the girlish Elphin, promoted, since the coronation, to the envied position of one of the Court Heralds.

"Everybody to the base-court!" this proud official declared in a

breathless and extremely important voice; though it was evident that
his surprise at not finding Rhisiart alone had chastened a little the
jargon of his heraldic office.

"Has He decided to show himself to his people?" cried Mad Huw;
and this reversion to the man's familiar mania seemed so pitifully
natural that it was down an almost unnoticed glacier-slide that his
madness merged, for Rhisiart at any rate, with the spiritual authority
of his recent tone.

"The Maid of Edeyrnion is going into the battle," announced Elphin.
And as he stood there with the light of the morning on his tabard,
and on its "four lions, rampant and sable," Rhisiart couldn't repel a
boyish surge of exultation, couldn't resist the triumphant thought:
"Now we'll drive them over the Usk, over the Severn, over the Wye!
Now we'll have a Wales for the Welsh!"

But immediately afterwards, when this resplendent young person
followed up his first news by proclaiming with more professional cir-
cumlocution than was necessary that the Maid's sword and shield were
now to be blessed by Holy Church and that all the liege subjects of
"Owynus Princeps" within the walls, who were not at present sick or
dying, were commanded on pain of their Prince's displeasure to be
present at this sacred scene, a ribald vein of Norman profanity in our
friend was stirred to its depths.

"You'd say your lesson to a different tune, my lad," he thought, "if
it were *you,* and not my Tegolin, who were going into battle!"

But when they were all gathered in the court; and Elphin had even
got Meredith himself carried down there on what, not very long before,
must have been a bier, not only Rhisiart's anger, but his Hereford profanity, dissolved and melted away. And the strange thing was that the
same effect was produced—save for one single exception—upon that
whole motley company.

Long, long afterwards those who survived the troubles that followed remembered that scene in the Harlech court. And whenever
they did remember it a curious mingling of infinite sorrow and proud
exultation came into their minds.

As for the soldiers and the old retainers of the castle, most of whom
had known the Maid before in her simple page's attire, none of them

had the remotest idea into what startling beauty she had blossomed forth.

The castle was crowded with wounded men and with refugees from devastated areas who had nothing to do but wander about in melancholy indifference, pining for burnt homes and murdered mates; so that there was not lacking in this crowd that weight of anonymous resistance to a magnetic current, which is always what lends volume to any electric wave, capable of over-riding such elements of opposition and of carrying them away with the tide.

But the most remarkable aspect of the occasion was the manner in which all the particular individuals connected with the Maid's life responded unanimously to this sudden apotheosis of her beauty and her character.

Even Mistress Lowri—and this was as amazing to Rhisiart as it was to the Lollard—had tears in her eyes as with her hand on Master Simon's arm she stood apart from the Arglwyddes and the other women, staring at her daughter as if upon a vision.

Had Rhisiart been in a less exalted mood he would have been absorbed by the sight of a vivacious and demonstrative girl to whom both Luned and little Sibli were clinging in fascinated admiration.

But, as it was, several minutes passed—for she had changed bewilderingly in five years—ere he recognized in this striking young person his old acquaintance Efa ferch Tudor of the Tower bed in Dinas Brān.

It was clear to Rhisiart that the Prince must have planned all this and sent his instructions through the castle after his Secretary had retired for the night; for though the custom at Harlech was for the inmates to break their fast at an early hour, the Arglwyddes was rarely visible till the sun was high and Mistress Lowri never left her chamber till noon.

Broch-o'-Meifod, whose stature alone made him an object of wonder to the crowd of refugees, who'd only seen him seated in the banquet-hall, looked even more of a cynosure than usual that morning, because in the bright February sunshine he had left uncovered his great hairless head. His own attention just then was a little distracted from the Maid in armour by the presence of Gilles de Pirogue's victimized dog, who,

though still weak and limping, insisted on following his rescuer wherever it was physically possible for him to go.

And as if the dog's presence were not enough, Broch-o'-Meifod's contemplation of this curious ceremony was further interrupted by the
presence of his revolutionary henchman, Master Sparrow, who, though
obviously impressed by the Maid's appearance, was anxious to compel
his master to admit that these archaic rites though they might have
their mystical interest were totally unsuited to a war like this, which
was a war of the common people against feudal tyrants armed with
modern weapons.

"Everybody knows," he was protesting, "that Prince Hal has got
several of these new pieces of ordnance-cannon, Master, *cannon* I tell
you, Master! And what could spear and shield do, even if blessed by
the Holy Father, against what cannon can fling?"

The ascendency which Broch had established over his revolutionary
adherent was proved by the manner in which Master Sparrow's realistic opinions were now expressed. The fellow looked chastened by these
recent disasters and by the sight of the refugees; but the absence of
contemptuous derision from his tone was not due to this. Broch had
been listening to him now for five years, and listening with so much
sympathetic interest that the man's pendulum-swing between sardonic
silence and bitter invective had changed to a more normal tone.

As has been hinted, all in the castle, save the watchers on the ramparts and the severely wounded and dying, were present in the base-
court; and only one of them—and this one was *not* Master Sparrow
for all his talk of overpowering ordnance—remained unaffected by the
startling loveliness of the Maid mounted upon Seisyll.

This one was Crach Ffinnant: and he was already making trouble.
Moving furtively among the rank-and-file of the crowd, joining one
group after another of the more truculent spirits among the refugees,
whispering bawdy jests to the castle servants and Derfel-threats to the
natives of Ardudwy, he was doing all he could, and none knew better
than he how to do it, to counteract the wave of enthusiasm that was
now mounting up.

Remembering what Mad Huw had said to him about Father Rheinalt and wondering how Tegolin's begetter could endure the presence
of the girl's fatal mother, Rhisiart kept looking about him to catch a

glimpse of the man; and at last he was successful. The monk wasn't in the court-yard, but he *was* looking on. He was high up above the whole scene, standing in the shadow of a buttress upon one of the narrow stone abutments used for flinging destruction on the heads of besiegers. He was too high up for our friend to see his face; but the way he balanced himself on that dizzy ledge, with his arms outstretched on either side of him, as his fingers clung to the projecting corbels, produced an uneasy impression on Rhisiart's mind.

As for Mad Huw, it was clear not only to Rhisiart but to all who knew him—indeed our friend could see from the way the girl kept turning her grey steed so as to keep as close to him as she could that she too recognized the danger—that the Frair was in the familiar state of excitement that usually portended an outburst.

It was Father Pascentius who represented the Church on this occasion, and he was supported by a group of choir-boys from the castle-chapel who chanted in their high treble voices the psalmodic responses to his solemn words.

"The Blessing of God the Father, God the Son, and God the Holy Ghost be upon this sword!"

And as the "sword-blessing" merged into the "shield-blessing," and as the "shield-blessing" merged into old Latin and Welsh war-prayers for victory, such as the whole concourse of people could join, it became hard for anyone in that assembly, save the unsubduable Scab, to gaze upon the Maid's figure without ecstatic awe.

And as the deep-rolling syllables chanted by so many voices rose and fell, in that queer blending of Latin and Welsh whose liturgical lilt, the bardic mystery embracing the Christian mystery, has such infinite seduction, the Maid herself seemed lifted up on the magnetic wave generated by the people's emotion. No one present had ever seen the beauty of a woman so heightened, isolated, thrown into intense and solitary relief, as Tegolin's beauty was then.

Owen had kept saying to himself all the day before: "No glory for you, old conjuror, but the glory of your Maid in armour!"

In his present mood, a mood that his subtlest introspection could scarcely follow, all the good in him and all the evil in him seemed to keep rising to the surface in one wild water-spout after another. What he was doing just now was making use of every mental art he possessed to reduce himself to non-existence by the side of Seisyll's new rider!

It is true that he himself was mounted; but he was mounted on the back of a horse he had chosen from the Harlech stables not for its significance but for its insignificance. It was a small dusky animal, hardly bigger than a Welsh pony, and though its back was broad and sturdy, it looked a commonplace nag compared with Seisyll. And not even content with this, Owen had rejected all armour, all weapons, and had attired himself completely in black.

Apparently he had tried to resemble some elderly master of ceremonies; but all he had succeeded in doing was giving himself the air—with his grizzled beard and ensorcerized eyes—of a demon-worshipping student of alchemy in some lonely tower in the Hartz Mountains.

Owen's mind had never moved with such pendulum-like alternation from pole to pole. The curious thing was that both these poles of psychic attraction were compounded of almost equally balanced ingredients. Nor for one instant was he able to stop the "tick-tick-tick" of his secret analysis of all he was feeling. He knew his longing to drive all these clever captains of Prince Henry out of Wales was as closely mingled with his passion for this girl as blue and yellow are mingled in the colour green.

He knew his Welshmen well enough too to be certain that he and she together would stir up a wave of sacred madness such as hadn't moved the country since Arthur's, or even since Boadicea's, time; and at the thought of this there surged through him a mighty afflatus of unconquerable power, as from the back of his dusky nag he gazed at her. He felt as if he himself were merely the medium through which some vast planetary force, that was absolutely irresistible, was pouring into the girl's form. He felt as if he were no longer a separate entity. He and his ignoble steed were melting into her and into Seisyll; they were endowing her and the grey horse with a supernatural strength that nothing could resist!

But what had he done with his soul—that live thing within him whose freedom from his body had been the secret struggle of all his days? This madness which was upon him, this dark power which was pouring through him into that white-and-gold form with its burning hair, took no more account of his soul than of a moth burnt in a torch!

He *had* no soul. But even as he moved closer towards her—his mind so deadly clear—it seemed to him as if against all his purpose and in spite of all his desire his will were bringing his soul back from God-knows-where!

"Yes, yes," he thought, coldly and cruelly, "if I had the will to let her go, and to let this supreme chance of victory go, it would be a proof to me forever that my soul *is* outside my body and *is* able to be as free as that goosander I saw on the waves!"

But if Owen's consciousness was playing these juggler's tricks within the circle of itself, Rhisiart's had never been more compact, more alert, more integrated. His narrow anxious face kept turning from the Prince to Tegolin, and from Tegolin to the Prince.

As for Father Pascentius and his beautifully attired choir of hand-some lads, they were apparently prolonging the religious part of the scene far beyond what had been originally intended. Rhisiart wondered what on earth the man was up to now. He had heard a bugle outside the gates and he had seen one of the porters hand a missive of some sort to the Father; but since the Father was always receiving furtive messages from one quarter or other this incident carried no particular weight.

But Tegolin's beauty as she held aloft that naked sword—and it crossed our friend's mind to wish it had been the one he'd just left in his turret!—was beyond all he had ever imagined. There was Cath-arine, leaning upon Sir Edmund's arm, with the little Rhisiart holding tight to his father's hand, and fair as a queen she looked; but though he had never until this moment allowed such a thing to cross the thresh-old of his consciousness he caught himself with the thought—and the thought itself was like a sacred bird, a forbidden bird, that he had dared to shoot, and now held warm and palpitating in his hand—that the Maid was the more lovely of the two!

The warm February sun fell full upon the loosened mass of the girl's flaming hair, hair so thick that it almost hid the gleam of her cuirass, hair so long that it flowed down in blood-red waves upon Seisyll's flanks; while the golden armour covering her breasts and guarding her thighs made all that was visible of her virgin flesh show white as the petals of wood-anemones exposed before their hour amid yellow leaves.

The bare arm that uplifted the sword—aye! but Rhisiart knew it now; it was the Roman sword the Prince had worn at Mathrafal!—passed through the leather straps of a heart-shaped, shell-bright shield, upon which was depicted, in vermilion enamel-work, the mystic Pendragon of Wales.

And it struck Rhisiart as he watched her that it needed all her strength to hold up that sword and shield. Her arm seemed quivering with the effort; and he felt—life-weary man as he was now, and one in whom the Russian's "insect" had long ago been scotched—that both he and the Prince, yes! and her mother too, and Father Rheinalt too, perched up there so perilously, all, all, except the Grey Friar, were, as in that sea-weed dance of five years ago, *clapping their hands* while she grew faint under the tension.

Yes, he felt as if the Prince and he were united now, united in keeping that bare white arm aloft, with its dragon and its sword! And suddenly he caught the eye of Mistress Lowri, and—Mary, Joseph!—a terrible revolution turned his whole heart round, as if on an interior pivot. He suddenly felt a spasm of ungovernable anger mount up from the pit of his stomach against the Prince. The eyes of the Maid's mother were quite tearless now. They were worse than tearless. No, no; this whole thing was wicked. They had no right to keep that sword and shield so tremblingly erect. They had no right to let the Prince use Tegolin so!

But Owen's dark figure upon that dusky, dwarfish horse seemed growing steadily more ominous and more dominant. The Father's chanting was now at its height. The choir-boys' responses were shrill and clear. But something else was happening. A power was emanating from Owen that he couldn't understand. Was that dark figure with those sea-green eyes, mounted on that squat, goblinish creature, really possessed of supernatural power? He had never quite lost, in all his five years' association with him, a feeling that the man *was* different from other men, that he had, in an obscure sense he couldn't define, something unearthly about him. He found himself moving closer and closer to Seisyll and his rider. That bare uplifted arm, holding both sword and shield—too heavy, too heavy! she *must* let them sink if he didn't help!—was fatally drawing him.

It was the look in Mistress Lowri's eyes, the look in the Prince's eyes

—oh, he must go to her help! One wild thought after another whirled through his brain. That witch-woman had thrust Alice just like this upon young Grey. It must be a mania with women to offer up their daughters—yes, a mania with them! Those tears he'd caught in the woman's eyes weren't for Tegolin at all. They were for Rhys Gethin, they were—

But his friend Brut was at his side now; and he too was angry; he too was outraged. In a moment he too would rush forward and help support that trembling arm. He suddenly felt impelled to glance up at Father Rheinalt. He was her father. How long could *he* endure to see the quivering of that white arm? Oh, the brave girl, the brave girl!

But somebody *must* rush in and stop it. Was Owen working some dreadful magic upon his enemies through that uplifted sword? Was the tide of battle on the Usk at this very second swaying, swaying, like a great sea-wave, uncertain where it would fall? Father Rheinalt couldn't—but *where was* the Father? Were his eyes dazzled by the Maid? No, he'd left that ledge. He'd climbed back—or fallen down. No! *There* he was, approaching them now, pushing his way through the crowd, saying something to the Scab.

And the Scab was coming with him now, and an angry tumultuous section of the crowd was following the two of them. Strange for him and the Lollard to be on the same side as the Scab! And Mad Huw too —Mad Huw was weeping again as he clutched at Seisyll's harness, that harness covered with gorgeous trappings across which the black lions ramped. Tears as big as wren's eggs were streaming down the Friar's face as he turned it now towards the Maid's begetter and towards the gesticulating prophet.

"He's fallen back. He's lost his vision," our friend thought. "If Owen takes her from him *now,* he'll resist. The man's as angry as I am! Yes, yes, .call upon your King, Grey Friar! That's right! Call upon him! Master Simon's watching you; but he can't hurt you. Lowri's eyes can't hurt you. They can watch the *méthode scientifique* of Gilles de Pirogue; but if Brut and her Father and the Scab and all these Ardudwy men were to join with him now in one great rush to rescue his girl—for what was Tegolin if not his girl?—they could stop Owen from riding away with her to the battle! What right had he to—"

But what was that? Two young heralds were bringing the Prince his armour, his helmet, his great lance; and the keepers of the castle-gates were dragging them open. Slowly, slowly they were forcing them open, with the harsh, strange, musical sound of vast hinges turning, and with the rush of sea-scents and sea-murmurs, and with the clatter and trampling of a host of armed men! Spearmen, bowmen, men-at-arms —an army was pouring in! And as they came they raised shout upon shout. "With the Maid to the Usk! With the Maid to the battle! With the Maid to London-town!"

There! The chanting had ceased; the responses had died down; and Tegolin had endured to the end. With her sword and shield laid across Seisyll's back, and her head so drooping that her chin rested against the front of her cuirass, she now allowed Mad Huw to possess himself of her numb fingers; and these the good man rubbed between his own in so besotted and pitiful a manner, wetting them as he did so with such a flood of tears, that there wasn't a damsel, save little Sibli, among all the Arglwyddes's ladies, but wept too, for very sympathy with so passionate a love.

But little Sibli, after giving her tearful friend Luned a glance of sharp contempt, transferred her small person and the insatiable "insect" within it to the voluptuous side of Dame Alice of Lyde, as the witch's daughter now insisted on being called. Rhisiart had taken advantage of the Prince's movement towards the in-rushing soldiers to take hold of Seisyll's bridle, thus enabling his rider to relax at her pleasure and devote herself entirely to the Friar; but he now became aware that the Lollard's wife was dragging her husband aside and whispering God-knows-what honeyed treacheries in his ear. That they *were* treacheries, to him, to the Lollard, to Mad Huw, to Tegolin, he divined easily enough, from the wicked delight which Mistress Sibli was manifesting.

Meanwhile the Prince, who had dismounted from his sorry nag, and had been armed by his pages in a resplendent suit of glittering mail, had leapt, all heavily armed as he was, upon the back of a horse Rhisiart had never seen before, a coal-black horse of menacing appearance and startling size. Thus mounted, and with his great lance in his hand, he looked indeed a formidable figure; and an involuntary cry of admiration and pride rose from the newly-entered troops.

"Owen and the Maid!" they shouted: "Owen and the Maid of Edeyrnion!"

It was then that Master Brut, breaking away from his bride, came up to Rhisiart's elbow. "He has thought of everything," he whispered. "Alice tells me all the Maid's things are packed on mule-back, ready to follow them. He's made up his mind to take her. Our last chance is Father Rheinalt. He's *her* father and a good man. Let him—let him say something to the people. Let him say something to *her!*"

Rhisiart cast a quick look round them, and then turned to Tegolin, tightening his hold on Seisyll's bridle. Something about the bend of her head and the way her hair fell across her cheek as she leaned down, comforting the Friar, brought back that Midsummer Day of five years ago so vividly that some inward band about his heart ripped and was rent, dividing itself like a strip of *pali*.

No! The Prince shouldn't have his will this time. He'd taken his love from him and he'd endured and lived. But Tegolin was more than his love. "She's part of me," he thought. "If he takes *her* away, if he makes *her* his own, *that's the end*. Blackness forever; blackness in this world, blackness in the next!"

The scene in that base-court of Harlech had certainly become a singular one. Our friend saw clearly enough that it had taken to itself the nature of one of those turning-points in life that are the heavier charged with fate, because, in the tragic tension, the good and the evil are by no means all in one camp. Owen with the Maid at his side would—both Rhisiart and the Lollard knew it well—raise such a tide of mystical loyalty that it might easily sweep these Grendors and Talbots and Codnors and Charltons out of the country once and for all!

And to clear Wales of the English—for what else had he left Oxford? But here he was—and the refugees from the Usk and the Tawy and Severn had already begun taunting the soldiers standing between Tegolin's mother and Tegolin's father, just as he had done five years ago! Here he was—and oh! how noble the Prince looked on his black horse and in his glittering arms!—prepared to put himself, his own life, which was Tegolin's, his own honour, which was Tegolin's, between his Prince and his one grand chance of saving Wales.

Why didn't Tegolin look up? Why didn't *she* speak and help him

and decide it all? It was always of the Friar she thought. It would be
of the Friar to the end. And yet he knew, and she knew that he knew,
what was the only thing in her treasure-box! Did she think the Prince
would respect her maidenhead? Owen ap Griffith prove another Mad
Huw? Or was she prepared for the sacrifice of *everything* to save the
country?

Father Rheinalt was at their side now and so was the Scab—a nice
partner to have in his defiance of his Prince!—and there was someone
else here, too. Yes, *he* was here, that traitor ancestor whose infinite remorse had looked out of the smoke at him from that ruined wall in
Dinas Brān. He became conscious now that his tight clutch upon
Seisyll's bridle was only with his left hand. His right hand was in the
folds of his scholar's tunic.

And if this crucial moment was a crisis in the life of Rhisiart, it was
hardly less so in that of Walter Brut. The Lollard had already been
troubled by his bride's attitude to the Maid's departure. He knew she'd
helped Tegolin to put on that rich French armour. And now as she
approached him and took her place by his side he sought in vain to get
at the secret of what she felt, as she gazed so intensely at the girl in
armour. Was it that she thought it was the grandest and most enviable
lot that could fall to any girl, to ride into battle by the side of Owen?
Or was it some subtle vicarious sensuality, some vice in women that
was new and strange to him?

The man's guileless soul had already received several startling shocks
from his intimacy with the witch's daughter; but what he saw now in
the look she fixed on Tegolin troubled him in the depths of his nature.

"She and I are one now," he thought as he watched her, "and her sin
is my sin." A curious and tragic sadness swept over him as he felt the
complete strangeness of this human creature from whose obliquity,
whatever it might turn out to be, he could never be separate again.
"What the Prince is doing is wrong," he said to himself, "and I shall
oppose him, if I die for it! The look Alice has got on her face now as
she watches her is an evil look. Well! we're one now; and if her
thoughts are evil and make her suffer—mine be the suffering! If she
creates worse evil by her thoughts—mine be guilt! I used to think that
a man who had a woman could save his soul alone. How little I knew
how it would be!"

With these thoughts pursuing each other through his mind he pressed her arm against his side. "You are mine," he thought, "and all the guilt and shame and suffering that such a look brings I must pay for; for you and I are one."

Meanwhile Rhisiart, as he held fast to Seisyll's bridle, felt a faint stirring of hope when he saw Broch-o'-Meifod move across, with Master Sparrow at his heels, to where, under the shadow of a buttress, the faithful little Lu was standing by Meredith's stretcher.

The Arglwyddes, with her ladies gathered behind her like so many murmuring pigeons, was talking gravely and earnestly to Mortimer and Catharine. Was she, Rhisiart wondered, begging Catharine to interfere—to hold her father back from this fatal adventure?

For some curious reason, deep, oh! fathoms deep in his secretest soul, he found himself hoping that it *wouldn't* be by Catharine's intercession that this thing was stopped! Mistress Lowri—alone now—had moved near them. Had she sent Master Simon to watch Rhys Gethin die? Was she going to give her daughter a Judas kiss?

And then he started back a step, still holding the horse's bridle, still clutching his dagger under his tunic; for Father Rheinalt had thrust Mad Huw aside, and—for the first time in his life completely disregarding Mistress Lowri—had thrown back his cowl and flung his arms round Tegolin's neck. So *he,* even he, had, in his burning patriotism, accepted the girl's supreme sacrifice!

Buried like that in her father's embrace, would she never turn, would she never give *him* a look?

But the Prince on his black horse was approaching to take her now; and Father Rheinalt had let her go. She settled herself on Seisyll's back, lifted up her sword and shield again, inclined her head beneath Father Pascentius's formal blessing and then, in the full sight of them all, bent down and kissed the Secretary on the mouth.

On seeing this, Owen jerked at the bit of his black horse with such unnecessary violence that the animal shook his head, scraped the stones with one of his front hooves, and clapped back his ears. "Oh mild and everlasting *Mare,*" he groaned. "Mother of Creation! Thou who has given thy servant the magnanimous docility of thine own patient and all-enduring heart, save me from the power of this Prince of devils!"

The only individual in that company who took any notice of the offended feelings of a being whose inner vision beheld the lustrous eyes and flowing mane of the Queen of Heaven was Broch-o'-Meifod's dog. He looked from the horse to his rescuer and from his rescuer to the horse in so emphatic a manner that the giant bent down over Meredith's stretcher, nodded to Master Sparrow to help him, and proceeded with this assistance to carry the wounded man into the open space that was still left between the opposing ranks.

And then as will often happen in a psychic crisis of this sort, when neither side wishes to take the final responsibility of precipitating the event, the electricity of action began to discharge itself in other ways.

For the crowd in that castle-yard *had,* clearly enough, divided itself into two indignantly tense parties; the newly-arrived soldiers clamouring to follow the Prince and the Maid, while the opposing ranks, led by Father Rheinalt and the Lollard, seemed resolute in their refusal to let the expedition start.

The Maid herself, after what she evidently felt to be her farewell gesture, began to make before them all a palpable effort to gather up her reins. This, however, she couldn't do; for Rhisiart had twisted the reins about one of his own hands, while he plunged the other into his tunic.

At the sight of his wounded son, thus placed—and placed by his best friend—between himself and the one thing on earth he wanted, Owen released his hold on his lance, letting its butt-end sink into the leather case in front of his saddle. Then bending his head over his horse's mane so low that the red feather in his helm pointed earthward he began talking to the prostrate man as if talking to himself. Breaking off this soliloquy he suddenly said in a low vibrant voice: "So you too, my dear lad, are against our one chance until the French come!"

"Not against our one chance, Sire," replied the man on the stretcher, "but against our Prince leading it." He paused; and then in a much lower tone, while the Prince strained every nerve to catch his words: "She loves Rhisiart, Sire! Can't you see it? Let *him* go with her, and the monk and the Friar, too. My father, my father, think of the honour of our house!"

"I *have* thought," cried the Prince, rising suddenly to his full height. "I *have* thought!" he repeated in a loud and terrible voice, "and nothing, lad, *nothing,* I say, can turn me back!" His words were heard and their meaning fully caught by all present.

There rose a ringing and exultant shout from the armed crowd behind him; and he beckoned sternly with his hand for Broch and his servant to lift the stretcher out of the way. "Why does he move his arm up and down like that?" he thought. "If he touches one of his axes I'll ride over them all and take her."

But Broch-o'-Meifod wasn't touching any of his axes. He was moving one of his great bare hands up and down; moving it with all the fingers outspread from where it hung straight by his side till his enormous fore-arm was at right angles to his biceps. It was a queer movement; it seemed a meaningless movement. The man's face expressed nothing as he made it. He did it as if it were the automatic gesture of a mechanical colossus. Was it a signal to someone?

But to whom could it be a signal, for the crowd was dense round the two horses now, and little Lu was bending over Meredith, while the figures of Mortimer and Catharine hid the Arglwyddes.

"I can do what I like," Owen said to himself, watching that hand go up and down. "It's all in my will. I can take her. I can give her up."

And then as he watched that moving hand, which only himself from his position above them all, could possibly see, it seemed to him as if that hand weren't a hand at all but *his own will,* his own will deciding everything—*up, down—down, up*—just as it chose!

"What I'll do," he thought, "shall be without cause, without reason, without motive. I'll do it just to prove to myself that I *can* do it. If I let her go they'll think I do it because of them. If I take her they'll think I do it because of my pride. But they'll be wrong. I'll take her because I want her *more than my free will.* But if I don't take her I'll prove to myself that my will can do—in a complete void—what it chooses—without cause or motive or reason! Just my will in a void, doing what it chooses! *Up-down, down-up*—like Broch's hand. They'll think I give her up because of them. But Broch will know—that's why his hand goes up and down like that!—Broch will know that I give her up because 'up-down' and 'down-up' are equal; and my will is my will, I could take her in a minute. She'd tell them herself she wished to come. She and I together could do anything. She'd know what love *was* if I took her, and there wouldn't be an Englishman left in Wales!

And when the French came we'd ride through Hereford and Worcester and Oxford and over London Bridge, until—playing off the
Mortimers against the Percies—and no one but I would take off your
armour, you lovely one!—but that would tilt the balance—*up-down,
down-up!*—with her for the motive, for the reason, for the cause! But
if I *don't* take her—*then,* in an absolute void, my will will please itself.
It will choose to sacrifice everything—everything but its own life; and
thus it will show the power of its own life! Yes, yes, that's what it'll
be—my will alone; my will where there's no 'up'—do you hear me,
hand of Broch?—and no *'down'!*

"*So be it.* And now, old conjurer, a little entertainment for you!" He
patted the neck of his black horse; he waved to Catharine as if he had
only just realized she was there; he made a quick gesture with his hand
for Broch's benefit alone, which evidently completely satisfied the
giant; and then, bending down over his son's stretcher, he uttered in
the rustic dialect of Powys Fadog an old nursery jingle which means:
"If you've won it's only because I've *let* you win!" Then he swung his
horse round and facing the excited soldiers behind him lifted his arm
for silence. So majestical did he look in his shining armour, with the
long heraldic pennon of his lance streaming in the sea-wind, that not
one of those war-fevered men, wrought up as they were, but lowered
his weapons in submissive silence.

"Before we set out to battle, my comrades, it were well if we all,
men and women, priests and laymen, gentles and commons, visit our
castle-church, and there assembled consecrate our cause to Heaven, in
the name of Cadwallader the Blessed, Brān the Blessed, Tysilio the
great Saint, and Derfel Gadarn, our Patron and Protector. My family
and my household will lead the way; and since it is the help of Christ
and Our Lady and the Blessed Saints that we shall now invoke, I
wish every man of you who cares to follow us to leave his arms behind
him here—my pages will look to them—and to join our solemn procession to the chapel, chanting the Battle-Song of Uther Pendragon."

It was one of those extraordinary inspirations of the man, that made
those who knew him best feel most astounded, that he should have set
them upon intoning this particular war-hymn. Almost every national
Welsh air had some local tradition behind it that would have clashed
with others in a crowd drawn indiscriminately from north and south;

but the deep Gregorian-like notes of this ancient Pendragon Psalm, familiar from childhood to every soul there present, was calculated above anything else he could have chosen to deepen patriotism to a religious intensity, and to draw upon a past so high and remote that all modern diversities and dissensions were lost in the unity of its ancestral grandeur.

It was none other than Father Pascentius—profoundly delighted at this twelfth-century turn given to what he had already decided to be a typical scene of fifteenth-century disorder and degeneracy—who promptly began intoning the harsh martial stanzas of this noble chant, whose rugged music might have risen to the Milky Way from the summit of Cadair Idris or of Eryri.

As soon as Broch-o'-Meifod, who seemed completely unperturbed by this new turn of events, had with Master Sparrow's help got Meredith and his little Lu safe out of the press, there was such a confusion around the black horse and the grey horse that Rhisiart and the Lollard drew aside. They still suspected the Prince of some sinister design but there was clearly no immediate danger of Tegolin being spirited away.

Rhisiart felt a most devastating sense of incapacity and helplessness. The sight of Catharine and Tegolin talking to each other, which was now what was happening, caused a queer disturbance to take place under his ribs. It resembled shame; and yet it wasn't shame. It resembled the feeling of the most miserable kind of blushing; and yet it was deep below the surface of his skin! He felt as he watched that fair hair in actual contact with that flaming hair, as the one young woman looked up and the other leaned down, that if they were to kiss each other he would hate them both!

If he had had even so much as a spark of divine power he would have ordered it so that never more on earth should those two converse together! But it was hard not to look at them side by side. Where else should he look? For the Prince, holding Mad Huw in a low-voiced dialogue, was delaying the procession behind Father Pascentius; while Father Rheinalt was being compelled to lend an ear to the Scab who in his excitement was actually clutching the monk's habit.

But never had Rhisiart reached such a level of humiliation. What had he to fall back upon. He had lost his position as the Prince's legal adviser. He had forgotten how to use his sword. And here were the

only two women in all the world he wanted to look up to him, to admire him, to watch what he could do, to listen to his knowledge, to
wonder at his courage, conspiring together to treat him with maternal
tenderness and consideration!

Inch by inch, like a sinking boat, all Rhisiart's passionate self-respect
began to go down. It was what he'd endured in the Tower at Dinas
Brān; but this was far worse. What was he? A nameless nobody, an
unwanted lawyer's clerk, the weak protégé of a couple of fair women!
Ah yes, of course! And here too was Luned; but he had no desire to-
day to prove the freedom of his soul by making love to a bundle of
sweet cinnamon! Who *was* the father of her child? No, no, it *couldn't*
be Elphin. Elphin could play the herald manly enough; but to think
of him— No, no! It was probably some soldier from the camp by the
sea.

What on earth was the Prince talking about to Mad Huw? He could
see both the flaxen head and the flaming head turned towards those
two, waiting till they should have done, so as to follow Father Pascentius and his choir. Could they hear what the Prince was saying? Mary,
Joseph! Both the girls' heads were turned towards himself now. No, no!
No response *while you're together* from Rhisiart ab Owen!

"I'd far sooner," he said bitterly to himself, "make Efa ferch Tudor
smile at me!"

But the Prince had beckoned to one of the pages who was pushing
his way through the crowd. Ah! He was giving the lad the bridles of
both horses; and both the riders were dismounting. *Dismount?* Let all
the world dismount; for Rhisiart's occupation was gone!

Oh, never would he forget that dragging procession through all those
same identical corridors and courts and balconies that he had passed—
and passed behind that same unwieldy figure too—when he went to
disturb the new ideal of knowledge through torture. "We scotched his
little game," he remarked to Walter Brut under cover of the Pendragon
Chant. "But he's up to some other mischief now. How clever the Scab
was to make trouble between those refugees and the Ardudwy men!
'Twas *that* that stopped him. He hates downright brawls. He likes the
ritual of power, not its—"

"Hush, lad! Hush, for Christ's sake!" returned his friend. "You're

being brutally unjust! He was led by his desire for beauty. Have *you*
never been? Have *I* never been? It was a sin; but he must have
suffered horribly when he was hesitating just then. Didn't you see how
he looked? Man, man! He was wrestling with the Devil! What's the
matter with you, Rhisiart? I've been watching him closely, lad; and I
saw him look at us just now with the face of an angel, over his old
forked beard!"

The hoarse, martial notes of the great Pendragon Chant echoed
round the two friends, as they moved forward together, their neat
Hereford clothes, faded during the last five years, separating them, as
did their English accent, from the careless, sumptuous colours and wild,
rich intonations all about them.

The crowd was so great that, though the austerity of what all were
chanting held the excitement in check, soldiers of one rank or another
kept pushing past them, most of them with a rough, casual greeting as
they went: "God be with you, Clerk Walter! God be with you, Clerk
Rhisiart!"—greetings which the Lollard answered spontaneously and
naturally, and our friend with a heart-sick effort.

"Clerk Walter" was certainly in the right of it over his companion's
mood. Rhisiart was puzzled by it himself when he thought of it afterwards; but keen lawyer by nature he was, and intelligent statesman as
he had become, he had all the average Norman's dislike of introspective analysis.

The truth was his emotional nature had only two natural outlets,
both of them very narrow ones. He could lose himself in idolatrous devotion for a man much older than himself, a man like the Prince; but
where women were concerned his romantic passion could be stirred
only when the sense of power rioted in him and a feeling that *if he
liked* he could be despotic and cruel! The only girl he had ever met
whose nature seemed to *beg* her lover to be despotic and cruel was little
Lu; but she was so obsessed by Meredith that he never let himself think
of *her* in that way.

But just because he was a man, and they were girls, he had *sometimes* had moments, both with Tegolin and Catharine, when this despotic craving had had its free fling. At such moments he had been mysteriously happy, and his soul had hurled itself upon this weaker soul

with an exultant abandonment; and, not only so, but even in retrospect, an indescribable tenderness had flowed through his veins at the mere thought of his relation with a girl who was at his mercy.

But now, as he sulked under his companion's rebuke and punished him by adding his bass notes to the chanting of the war-song whose archaic heathenism he knew displeased him, the sense of an understanding between the two girls, of which he was at once the object and the victim, tied an obscure knot of contrariety in his deepest soul against which he struggled in vain. Grown man though he was, he felt somewhere within him that blind, childish, angry humiliation, the only cure for which used to be to make Modry strike him; after which they would both burst into tears.

As may be expected this childish mood of his which could have been dissolved only by one of two things, either by risking his life for a man who was his master, or by becoming himself the master of a maid, was anything but lifted from him, when, as they overtook Tegolin and her Friar, the girl turned quickly towards him, and giving him one of her old steady glances, uttered the surprising words: "Well, Gwion Bach, what do you think of him now?"

All the Prince's household crowded into the chapel as soon as the Arglwyddes and the Mortimers had taken their places, and a considerable number of soldiers and refugees succeeded in getting in along with them and finding somewhere or other to stand and kneel. Some of the younger refugees from the Usk actually clambered up on the ledges of the high windows, through one of which the youthful Gilles had escaped from the chamber above; and in one way and another the building was soon so crowded with people that it was all Father Rheinalt and the group of parish-priests could do to force their way to where Father Pascentius was standing by the altar.

But the Prince kept back the Maid and the Friar from entering till Rhisiart and the Lollard arrived; and it was then, as the Master and Man met face to face, that Rhisiart realized the truth of his friend's words.

"We have decided, cousin," he began at once, "upon a little change of plan."

The blood rushed to Rhisiart's cheeks. They felt so burning—especially just above his cheek-bones—that, forgetting how swarthy he was and that no one could possibly see his confusion, he hung his head like a convicted school-boy.

There must have been something about the sight of this thin, lined, anxious face, with the dark moustache under the hooked nose, reduced to such an extremity of embarrassed shame, that was unbearable to Tegolin. She intervened hurriedly, begging the Prince let Brother Huw tell him everything.

Master Brut, who still detected in Owen's expression a look which, if it wasn't the look of an angel, was certainly a look of unearthly self-conquest, now noted—with his evangelical interest in all such spiritual phenomena—that no flicker of the faintest smile crossed the Prince's face as he responded to the Maid.

The Maid, on the contrary, didn't notice this. In fact, as the Prince saw clearly enough, she was in so radiant a mood that she had eyes for none but Rhisiart.

"Tell him, then, Brother Huw," said Owen slowly, speaking in the flat expressionless tone that an idol in a temple might have used, "what we've decided between the three of us—though I wish you could tell him what the soldiers will feel when they hear our decision!"

These last words, though uttered aloud, were more like thoughts than words; but so intensely alive at that second were all Mad Huw's senses that he caught their drift in a flash.

"Fear not, Owen ap Griffith," he said solemnly. "I will take it on myself to make the men understand that the Maid's marriage is a holy marriage, undertaken solely that she and I, a young woman and a witless preacher, should have an armed and clerkly man to protect us by night as well as by day as we march to restore the King!"

"But, Brother Huw, Brother Huw," cried Owen, while, like a sailor whose hands clutch the rudder as he watches the prow of the boat, Tegolin watched Rhisiart's face, "but Brother Huw, there's only one kind of marriage on earth, whatever there may be in heaven; and since this ordinary, natural, human marriage is a sacrament of Holy Church we mustn't—"

"I know, I know, Owen ap Griffith! But the Maid will be a maid still, though lawfully wedded, as she rides with us this morn to fight the battles of the King." Here he lowered his voice and laid his fingers on Owen's wrist. " 'Tis the King himself tells me—for the man's his

godson you see—they should be wedded before she rides! And the
King says—that—that"—here several big tears splashed upon the
Prince's armour and chased each other down its glittering surface, turning to gold as they ran—"that her Friar mustn't think of it *that way,*
else he'll go mad. 'Pray, Brother,' the King says. 'And when you pray
stop thinking! Saint Francis is here with me,' the King says, 'and Saint
Francis says, to love is better than—than to—than to thinl.l'"

Certainly it seemed that either the prodigal King or the poverty-
wedded Saint *did* come to the Friar's rescue at that moment. For Mad
Huw pulled himself up erect now, and calmly taking Tegolin's hand
placed it in Rhisiart's.

All this while Rhisiart himself had been like one whose mental consciousness is fatally active while all his feelings have been struck numb
and dead by a bolt of lightning. Once, however, his fingers clasped
Tegolin's, and behold! this numbness came to an end, and his life-
stream began flowing again!

And what was this? He suddenly felt as if he and Tegolin had always been holding hands like this, behind and beyond all that happened. He even felt that holding her hand he was beyond the bitter
humiliation of that knot of frustration that had been recently damming
up the channel of his spirit.

Meanwhile with exquisite punctiliousness, heedless of how Rhisiart
and Tegolin lost themselves in their union, Owen was following with
an ungauntleted finger the blurred track made upon his armour by the
Friar's tears. Then, as if it were somebody else thinking a tiresome
thought, he began vaguely wondering to himself what on earth the
people would make of a married Maid of Edeyrnion.

"I must get these two, and the Friar with them," he thought,
"straight up to the altar before this office ends! Better make one of these
parish-priests marry them, while Pascentius and her father are witnesses."

As soon as he had decided this he noticed quite calmly—as a drugged
sacrificial victim might notice the scent of the flowers round his neck—
that he was in a hurry to get them wedded, and in a hurry, too, to receive, like spears in his flesh, the looks of Catharine and the Arglwyddes.

"Cousin Rhisiart!" he found himself beginning. "My Prince, my Prince—"

But he spoke coldly, without giving either of them a smile. "Your wife must ride Seisyll, Cousin Rhisiart; and I'll have your things—the sword and the rest—put on my black charger. But I'll tell them to saddle *your* old horse; and then our friend here," and he turned to Master Brut, "or the Friar, as they please, can rest their feet. But you'll be moving pretty slowly, for all the troops save yourselves will be on foot. Rhys Ddu will meet you in Carmarthen and take command; and until then—"

"But my Prince," broke in the Lollard, "you're going with us yourself, aren't you? We shan't feel—the army won't feel—"

Owen gave him a quick startled look out of his sea-green eyes. No, the man *couldn't* be lying! And yet how could he possibly *not* be lying; for what could be pleasanter for the good man than to go to war alone with his friends?

"No," he said in a firm clear voice and a voice so loud that many of the soldiers at the back of the little chapel turned their heads. *"No,* we're not going to the Usk. We have *other* plans. And our other plans will hurt Hal Bolingbroke more than our going to the Usk. Kindly put your hand to *this*, will you, Master?" and turning a little as he spoke he indicated one of the fastenings of his helmet.

Master Brut's thoughts were singularly simple and direct, as struggling with this metal clasp he lifted both hands to Owen's neck. "This is Our Lord's doing, and it will give my little Alice the chance to go with us. But I don't think she *will* go with us! Some girls find travelling harder than others. Their bodies are softer and more delicate." He was careful to thrust to the back of his mind the formless, wordless thought that "some girls" had a much greater dread of battles than others and of being roughly handled by the enemy. "They're more sensitive about jolting paths and hard saddles," he repeated to himself; and without removing his fingers from the clasp with which he was busy, he stared with amorous guilelessness at Alice's sturdy and voluptuous back.

"She has her faults," were the thoughts that now kept twisting in and out of that obdurate fragment of gilded silver; "but any man who

reads the words of Jesus—*especially in Greek*—knows that we must be
indulgent without limit to others while to ourselves we behave as if we
were dogs on a string, pulling ourselves away with a sharp jerk when
we begin to feel—"

In order to unloosen this obstinate fastening Master Brut found it
necessary to push back from the Prince's shoulder the rim of his hidden
mail-shirt; and upon a couple of the links of this object, the morning
sun, gleaming through the red-and-blue dyes of a just-finished fourteenth-century window, threw a blaze of rich colours, colours that
spread across the scar on the man's neck, where, five years before, Rhisiart had sucked the blood.

The Prince himself all this while was explaining to Tegolin, gravely,
coldly, and in clear-cut detail, exactly where, without going too far out
of their way, they might get into touch with Henry Don. "I tell *you*
this," he insisted, while he felt as if it were Rhisiart's eyes that were
looking at him out of her face, and *her* eyes out of Rhisiart's face, "because my cousin may be far too gone in love or drink to see where he's
going. Oh yes! and remember that when he last sent us news Henry
Don was in the valley of the Monnow, with Grosmont as his goal. But
he'll have laid waste Grosmont completely by now no doubt. Most
troublesome King's men they were, though their homes are black
enough by now, I doubt not! Don does what he does right well; and
he's got the men of Morgannwg with him too; and *they* don't leave
much behind! Grosmont's in ashes; there's no doubt of *that*. You can
rest assured of *that*! Welshmen and yet King's men. Well, well. Their
homes are ashes now anyway. Black ashes!

"Hark'ee, my pretty, as Broch calls his mistress, and I'll hammer you
out a right clever *englyn* about black ashes and staunch King's men."

It wasn't only Tegolin and Rhisiart who now stared at the Prince in
startled trouble. The Lollard with all his guilelessness and goodness
had played the part of a lay-confessor to Master Simon and other neurotic spirits too long not to recognize this unbalanced note. His full lips
assumed the shape of a knot that is not tied tight, while a faint susurration, almost approximating to a low whistle, issued from his mouth.

But Mad Huw intervened. "Hush, hush, Owen ap Griffith Fychan!"
he cried, taking into his hands the Prince's helmet, now at last unfastened, and entrusting it to Elphin the Herald. "This is a day for a

psalm, not an *englyn*, a day for the priest, not the bard! Take them to the altar, Owen ap Griffith! The office is finished. The Fathers are ready. The King has spoken. A moment, a moment, Daughter of my Soul! The Friar and none else shall be *your* armourer!"

Thus speaking, and as he had done in Rhisiart's turret, dominating them all by the force of his pure spirit, the devoted man knelt down before the Maid; and there and then, while the girl, still with her hand in Rhisiart's, bent her head above him, unloosed the straps that bound King Charles's greaves about her shins.

This was the worst moment of all for Owen; for the Friar hesitated not in his spiritual ecstasy to unwind the linen cloth beneath the armour, leaving the flesh bare.

There was one flickering second when he might have broken down; but not for nothing had he played his games with his soul since he was a child. In absolute desperation he now went through the long-practised motion, the motion which, though none knew it but himself, was his real claim to being a magician. He did *what felt to himself*— though it would be easy to pretend he "imagined" the whole thing— like taking his soul, the entity within him that said to itself, "I am Owen Glyn Dŵr," and flinging it—through one of those open windows through which Sieur Gilles had skipped like a devil—far out to sea.

There, on the rocking waves, though there was no goosander to rock by its side, his soul floated now—free, detached, stripped of all desire— and yet capable, from where it floated, of directing with lucid precision every gesture of the glittering eidolon with the forked beard!

As they all five, escorted by the young herald carrying the Prince's helmet and the French King's golden greaves, pushed their way to the altar, the choir burst into a psalm that seemed to carry into the incense, into the rosy light from the painted windows, into the rich fourteenth-century carving, something of the wild Pendragon Chant with which they had entered the chapel. And in the exultation of his mood it seemed to Rhisiart that Tegolin's hand trembled in his own. She was his! She was his! And—like the first woman given up to the first man —she *was* troubled, she *was* bewildered, she *was* dominated! She was no longer the Tegolin to whom he'd turned to long for comfort. She was *his* now—passive and docile. He was a man, a master, soon to lift upon old Griffith's back the sweet captive of his sword and his dagger!

The one thing lacking to his complete happiness was the thought of the Prince. It wasn't that he pitied him for losing Tegolin. It was something deeper, more personal, more intimate.

As they made their way slowly through the crowd there came to him, along with the heavy sweetness of the incense and along with the fragrance of the girl's loosened hair, a strange salty taste upon his lips and palate, the taste of blood, the taste of that blood of his master, when he'd sucked at his arrow-wound beneath the ramparts of Dinas Brān.

"Oh Mother of God!" he prayed. "Grant me to give *my* blood for *his* blood before I die!"

But having made his prayer it seemed easy to let this silent figure at their side, this imperturbable ghost to whom he had sworn allegiance, fade into a cloud, a shadow, a pillar of smoke, a thing without substance, without feeling. This reduction of the Prince's presence to something so phantasmal that it seemed lawful to disregard it enabled our friend to turn his full attention to his bride.

And what was this? Was it the sun-rays falling through cunningly-painted windows, through all the modern foliated tracery that his Oxford friends so despised compared with the heaven-aspiring purity of the earlier style? Was it the stained windows that threw this deep rose-petal tinge on the soft curves of the Maid's cheek? If he had been excited before—this idea, this vision—imaginary or not—of Tegolin's sudden shyness, and shyness of *him,* made the pulses of his heart dance like the waves on those Harlech sands.

What a thing in the world—what a miracle such a blush was! That he'd caught this wise, strong, calm Tegolin, this unruffled second-self, whom he had leant upon, whom he had confided in, whom he had trusted for a thousand years, blushing like the little girl he'd once kissed in the unfinished cloisters of Tintern—oh! it made his blood race up and down his veins!—oh! it took that Russian's "insect" and turned it into a soaring eagle! So this was what the wisest woman was, when the primeval shyness in her was caught off guard and laid bare!

And as he stole glance after glance at that flushed profile, framed in its flaming hair—for the press was great and the Prince moved as if his mind were far away from the whole scene—he felt as if it were his prerogative and his privilege, his alone among all men alive, to catch in that rosy stain the aboriginal tremor of the female yielded up to the male, which made the very waves of the salt sea shiver and dazzle and redden to the power of their recurrent dawns!

Yes, he was sure the music he was hearing carried the lilt of that Pendragon Chant into the red glow from the windows and into the red stain on his girl's cheek!

It was fortunate for the whirling exultation in Rhisiart's narrow head that his romance with Catharine had remained on so rarified a level. The only woman whose body had ever lain by his body in the magic bonds of sleep was the woman now by his side. The Maid had known all the while the mystery of this bond, the fusion of their souls on that Midsummer night beneath the sub-rational, sub-passionate under-tides of sleep.

He had been oblivious of this. But it was this, and nothing less than this, that gave to his possession of her now this incredible feeling of recurrence, as if they were only returning, easily and naturally, to a link that had existed between them time out of mind.

Well! it was over now; and when the Maid of Edeyrnion, leaning on her husband's arm, but with her free hand twisted tight in her Friar's corded belt, emerged from the chapel, she noticed a squat, ungainly figure crouching by one of the door-posts.

The Prince, moving still like an abstracted armorial ghost, was on the further side of Mad Huw; the Lollard, with Alice at his side now, just behind them.

Then, in one blinding beat of time two startling things happened, and happened simultaneously. It must be remembered that our friend Rhisiart was the only one in that group of persons who could boast Norman blood. And the Norman in his narrow skull had been roused to its most alert activity by the ritual he'd just been through. His companions were absorbed, pre-occupied, remote, lost in their feelings. But never in his whole life had the Maid's young lord been more dangerously alive to all that was around him. The subtlest necessity of his life-illusion—his feeling of power—was satisfied. But the effect of this satisfaction was not to drowse, drug, daze, or benumb; it was to rouse and quicken. Rhisiart's temper was at the extreme antipodes to that of his chief. Success stirred his faculties to their liveliest pitch; whereas Owen's powers mounted higher and higher in precise proportion to the piling up of disaster.

It was the leaping into deadly activity of two separate human forms that now crashed through Tegolin's consciousness. One of these forms was the crouching figure at the chapel-porch; the other was her husband. The Maid found herself actually staggering against Mad Huw, so sudden was the impetus with which Rhisiart freed himself.

Two gleaming blades—a devilish hunting-knife and a Toledo dagger —made quick-cross lightning-flashes; but neither of them seemed able to bury themselves in human flesh. Both of them whirled and gleamed; but all they pierced was the air. This was due to the fact that Gam's leap at the Prince's throat had been so effectually countered by Rhisiart's leap at Gam that the two men were locked so closely in each other's arms that both their weapons were ineffectual. The gleaming flashes of white death whirled about helplessly in the air while their owners spun round; Gam endeavouring to crush his adversary's bones, Rhisiart endeavouring to throw the assassin to the ground.

Chance had decided, or perhaps Rhisiart himself had decided, for never had his wits been clearer, that the weaker of the two had the under-grip; and this fact enabled our friend to fling a quick glance around him and to gasp out in a ringing voice: "Back, on your lives— avoid! avoid!—this—is—*my*—quarrel!"

So nice, so punctilious were the new-fangled customs that had already spread into Owen's court that even the Lollard drew back; and although little Sibli—heedless of modern etiquette—skipped past the Prince and began dancing like a demented elf round the combatants, no one else dared to intervene.

In contests of this sort, the psychic mood of the opponents has an incalculable influence; and Gam who had counted on one deadly blow —and had seen himself, with or without his knife, forcing his way down the stairs into the base-court with a second wild rush—was reduced to his old stupid, bear-like, bone-crushing hug, his impetus checked, his mind befuddled. Rhisiart, on the other hand, was strung up to a power and spirit far beyond his normal state; and it wasn't long ere, by the use of an old Hereford trick with legs and feet, he'd tripped up his enemy and had him on the ground, the knife useless, and his own dagger at the man's throat.

At that point both the Friar and the Lollard intervened; and our friend, his un-blooded blade returned to its place in his tunic, rose from the ground, panting and radiant. Something in him kept up a drumming beat, a throbbing refrain: "My heart'll burst! Is it to me, is it to me, this moment's come?"

The kind-hearted Lollard, as he relinquished the prisoner to the Prince's guard, experienced the sensation of hot tears behind his eyeballs, as he noted his friend's happiness. "He deserves it *all!*" he thought. "He's never been satisfied till now."

Walter Brut was right. The two irreconcilable longings that had consumed the young man for the last five years were assuaged at last. He was the master of his own true-love and he had saved his Prince, and as in a few minutes, for news of this kind travels faster than any herald's voice, he heard the shouts of the army outside, acclaiming their Maid's marriage to the saviour of their chief, his heart would have burst within him if, as he snatched at Owen's hand and pressed it to his lips, he hadn't caught sight of Lady Mortimer making a step towards him, and then staggering, swaying, and falling heavily to the ground.

XIX

TILL THE FRENCH SAIL

THREE DAYS after the departure of the army, and at the very hour of day when Rhisiart had saved his life, Owen was standing at the narrow window in his chamber, looking across the sea. He was trying to recall every detail of the Maid's farewell to him, as she and her husband, with the Friar and Master Brut in attendance, rode off at the head of those troops.

How instantaneously the news had flown that day of Rhisiart's deed! It had been the one thing needful to reconcile the men to his own absence and to being led as they were now led! "I ought to have made him a Knight," he thought. "It was due to him. Why didn't I do it?" And then in his old inveterate way he set himself to analyse his motives in not knighting his Secretary. "Gam would have struck at my throat," he thought, "and if he'd struck downwards Iolo's shirt would have saved me. But if he'd struck upwards *nothing* could have saved me."

Pondering on this nice point he couldn't help recalling the similar insoluble doubt as to whether Hywel Sele was alive or dead when he left him in the tree. "My life," he thought, "is like crossing the *Eel Bridge*—every step's between fatal alternatives!"

He was beginning to follow his usual method of squeezing his head through his window, when the image of Tegolin as she looked when mounted on Seisyll seized upon him with such force that it severed the connection between his movement and its intention; and drawing back his head with an unconscious jerk he scraped his ear against the stone, breaking the skin and drawing blood.

Still unaware of what he did he automatically clapped his hand against his face, and feeling his fingers wet, stared at the blood upon them with a dazed, puzzled surprise. "What queer stuff blood is when you come to think of it!" he muttered. And then, forgetting about his ear, he picked up from the floor a letter he'd just received from France and had flung down in a rage.

It was a letter from the French Chancellor, Arnand de Corbie, and it informed Owen that that the said de Corbie was despatching to him from Brittany, under the care of two noble gentlemen of France, "a marvellous great ape," which he begged the Prince de Galles to accept as a token of his veneration. "I ask for an army and he sends me an ape!" Owen had cried as he read this; and he had become still more angry when the letter went on to say that the writer had begged this "Marvel of Creation" from his young friend, Gilles de Pirogue, whose purpose it had been to subject it to "pains unspeakable" for the prolongation of the lives of "high-born Christian babes."

Still mechanically putting his fingers to the side of his head and mechanically staring at the blood upon them, Owen listened to the wind blowing in from the sea, and to the sound of the waves breaking on the rocks by the castle-jetty. And with the sea-sounds and the sea-smell he thought of a dead porpoise he'd seen the day before, stranded on the beach, with the seagulls greedily devouring it; and it came into his mind what a gulf there was between sea-creatures and land-creatures, and how the gulf was only bridged when they were both dead and eaten by the birds of the air! "I suppose," he thought, "if this wondrous great ape, saved from the hands of my Lord Pirogue, were to fall into the sea the very fishes would refuse to eat it!" And for some reason the idea of a creature like an ape struggling for its life in the sea struck his mind with a curious pain.

Amid gills and fins and lidless eyes in jelly-like slime, and undulant slipperinesses gliding through ooze and silt, how painful to think of the struggles of a warm-blooded hairy ape!

And then, without any apparent cause, the solitary blue eye and rosy birth-marks of Crach Ffinnant came into his mind. "He's my enemy," he thought. "He's a danger to me!" And then he thought: "What's the use of being a Prince if I can't get rid of an enemy like that?"

Up once more to the side of his head went his fingers; and again he muttered: "*What* queer stuff blood is!" Then he searched in the folds of his jerkin for a handkerchief, and even thrust his fingers with the same intention up one of his wide-flapping green sleeves; but unable to find what he wanted he rushed to his mirror and proceeded to dab the bleeding scratch with the ends of his carefully-combed hair, which he now wore after the newest of all the fashions, no longer reaching to his shoulders but cut evenly all the way round.

The sight of his familiar visage in the mirror brought him to himself as it always did; and in his habitual manner—and the custom had grown more heavily on him of late—he began a one-sided monologue addressed to this mirrored double.

"Fifty-five years old, old conjurer! And until these last days you've not even known what the bards *meant* when they talked of unreturned love! By Saint Francis, you know what they meant now, and a good deal *more* than they meant! And yet, what madness! Come down to reality, Master, and think what a woman actually and physically *is*. Think of her organism! Think of what she's like—yes, *then*—yes, and *then*—don't shirk it! and *then* too! But God help you, old fork-beard! It's no use, and you know it's no use! We can see her so—and we can see her *so*—and we can drag down her beauty low and low. But—curse her sweet blood!—it's *not* her beauty. It's something else. God knows *what* it is! It's not our ideal of her. It's her actual self. *Isn't* it, old dotard? *Isn't* it her actual self? It's the turn of her head. It's the way her lips *don't* quite meet! It's that little triangle of freckles above the corner of her mouth. And there's a freckle by the side of her nose, too! That's what happens with skins as white as hers. But we *like* her to be freckled—aye, old grey-beard?—we wouldn't mind if she had freckles on her breast!" And as he and his double stared at each other the flicker of a smile passed between them; for they recalled a passionate obsession of theirs during these last days—a pure game of the imagination—in which they undressed her by this very mirror. But this smile of theirs soon died down; and the two masks of consciousness, the subjective one and the objective one, exchanged a grotesque grimace, distorting their features into the likeness of a pair of monstrous gargoyles.

The moment their features had relaxed, however, a quite different and still more complicated phenomenon occupied that portion of the magician's chamber. For if the power possessed by the body of Owen of seeing itself in a mirror created one "mysterious double," the power possessed by the mind of Owen of analysing its own thoughts created a second mysterious "double"; so that the Prince of Wales at that moment became a four-fold being, became, in fact, what might be called a *Quarternity.*

But the curious thing was that the existence of this four-fold Owen was of a very transitory duration; for it was not long before the soul of Owen in the absorption of its analysis of the mind of Owen reduced both the image in the mirror and the body before the mirror to complete nothingness. They would have been there had another person entered the room, but to the man's soul that was analysing the man's thoughts they were simply not there at all.

Without the least change of position, without any farewell being taken of one another, the body of the Prince of Wales and the reflection of the body of the Prince of Wales vanished away.

Owen's was the only consciousness in that magician's chamber, and to the consciousness of Owen there was now nothing in the mirror and nothing standing before the mirror. There was nothing there at all but what Owen was thinking and what was analysing what Owen was thinking. From a Quaternity the Prince had diminished into a Duality.

And what *was* the thought in his mind with which his analytical soul was then so busy that it had the power to annihilate both the man *before* and the man *in* the mirror? It was the thought of his enemy Gam, chained to the wall in a room next to his own.

So far he'd resisted the temptation to visit him; but such a dark, deadly, quivering sweetness rose up within him when he thought to himself, "He's absolutely in my power," that his soul was constrained to wonder why his giving up Tegolin should have left him vulnerable to so abominable an urge.

And pondering upon this he recalled a curious compendium of Roman history that with the aid of his friend Iolo he used to puzzle out, and he remembered how this chronicle declared that it was only when Tiberius was separated from the woman he loved that he discovered his appalling mania for cruelty.

Struggling against this devil's advocacy on the part of his analytical soul he allowed the red drops from his ear to trickle down disregarded, while to help him against such devilish excuses he deliberately called to mind an odd volume Meredith had shown him the night before which he'd bought from Lemuel Livius for fifty silver groats. The Jew, Meredith said, swore it was worth fifty ducats, but he'd let him have it at that low price because several pages of the script—itself only a portion of the whole work—had been obliterated by the blood of its former owner, on whose murdured body it had been found by the vendor.

Owen couldn't recall the title of the poem; but it was a fragment in the Tuscan vernacular about Paradise; and it accepted without question the orthodox theory of the revolving spheres. Owen had seen enough of the dark-rolling sea just now, before bloodying his face, to realize that the day was a wet and gloomy one; and as he struggled against his impulse to visit Gam he tried to imagine himself mounting, as this Tuscan pretender declared he'd done, by the help of his sainted mistress, through heavenly circle after heavenly circle, towards the Empyrean!

He was still staring into the mirror; but all he saw there now was a nebulous reproduction of the Tuscan's spheric heavens as he was whirled upwards! He imagined himself—and didn't this Florentine, or was he a Sienese, say his mistress did it with her eyes?—drawn up in ecstasy by the very smile—yielding, impassioned, provocative, ravished—of his Maid in armour; and she didn't stop at either the *Primum Mobile* or the Empyrean! Through both these divine areas Tegolin drew him—her red hair streaming across the firmament! —until they were—*mirabile dictu!—outside Space altogether.* He had always been a bold heretic in his magical astrological and alchemical studies. And he had often questioned this orthodox cosmology, so slavishly and ferociously reproduced in these Italian "triads." And now it seemed to him as if in pure reaction from this conservative poet's iron-bound universe he were exercising his old trick of *exteriorizing his soul* as he'd never dared to do it before. For he was exteriorizing Tegolin's soul along with his! *That* was a thing he'd never even tried to do with Catharine. Did Rhisiart note—as he gazed into her eyes— that her soul wasn't there at all? Yes, it was with Tegolin's soul that he was striding now along the spheroid back of the whole cosmic orb, feeling the wind of outer space on his face, feeling it dry the wet blood on his ear, feeling it heal his longing.

Faster, faster he must stride, for he felt her begin to stir, to struggle, to resist! Rhisiart was enjoying her on the small round earth, and her soul wanted to be enjoyed too, along with her body. Oh, how Rhisiart was enjoying her. He was made for the act of love, that boy—the lean, hawk-nosed, sinewy young rogue—made for overcoming a girl's resistance!

So there you are, soul of Tegolin—struggling to get back to him, struggling to join your body! Well! he must let her go. . . . Ah! there was his forked beard in the mirror again. But how he had loved that narrow-faced boy! Loved him more than anybody in the world except Catharine. Well! why couldn't he be pleased that the boy he loved had the girl he loved? It was the natural consummation—*youth to youth,* and the old man standing aside! Were they thinking of him at this very moment as they clung? Oh no! no! He didn't want them to think of him while they clung. Not like that—not as hunters think: "What a lovely creature he looked!" as they ate the venison. "Think of your Prince another time, maybe! but not while your kisses are so hot, not while your limbs are—"

His reverie was interrupted by the irritation of a violent tickling. Curse these whoreson fleas! If he'd caught *one* he'd caught a dozen since Hopkin ap Thomas had been so much in this room! *There!* He'd got *that* one anyway. How should he kill it? It was fairly caught. Safe between his finger and thumb. What a hard husk! It was in his power—just as Gam was in his power. What *was* it about lively independent things—fleas, murderers, or girls—being absolutely in your power, that had such a dark, delicious shiver in it?

Yes, he must visit Gam. A man oughtn't to be left cramped up like that so long. He must unlock the chain and let him stretch his legs. He hadn't had much water either. He must take him a drop of something. That cats' basin would do. Milk for cats, and milk for murderers! "All right my good flea, it's no use struggling: I've got you quite firmly! The question is, are you going to live or are you going to die? *You* don't know; and I don't know either; though I *am* your Fate, your Destiny, and your God. *What's* that you're saying, flea? That you want to live, because you have a lively and a skipping love? I had a love once myself—and I had a tall horse; but my horse is gone, flea, with my love on his back—and where is my servant Rhisiart? Aye? What's that? Talk a little louder, flea. You've got a faint voice for one who comes from the beard of Hopkin. Oh that's it, is it? Owen's between God's finger and thumb, as you're between Owen's? Well! And that's true too."

He moved to the door and opened it with his left hand. Glew the Gryd, grown heavy with years, had been permitted the privilege of a horse-block at Owen's door; and now, roused we might imagine by the indignant spirit of young Madoc, with his decapitated head hanging from its neck by a shred of ghostly skin, the old man blinked in bewildered astonishment to see his master flick something from his fingers into the air, while he uttered the enigmatic words: "May God do the same with me, then!"

"Herald Elphin has been here with news of battle, my Prince."

"Why didn't you let him in?"

"I knocked, but you didn't answer, my Prince."

"What did you say to him?"

"I told him you were engaged with the spirits."

"What else did you tell him?"

"I told him you might be back about noon."

"Back from where?"

"From riding with the spirits on the wings of the wind."

"Gryd—"

"Yes, Master Owen; yes, my Prince?"

"What do you think I am?"

The old man gave him a long, grave, drowsy, sly stare, screwing up his eyes as he did so. "I think you're the son of Griffith Fychan of Glyndyfrdwy, in the vill of Carrog, in the *cantref* of Edeyrnion."

"What about the spirits then?"

"The House of Powys Fadog has always been—"

"Speak up, old friend! Always been *what?*"

"Different from the House of Powys Mathrafal!"

"A lame conclusion, Gryd, and a foolish one; for as all the world knows, the belt and the sword of Eliseg—*Dewi Sant!* but what are you making me say? Off to the guard, my old friend, and tell them to send me Herald Elphin at once."

He closed his door and waited in the passage while the old man, leaving his axe behind him in his haste, hobbled off down the corridor. "The Maid's victory!" he thought. *"That's* what it must be. But can they have reached the Usk in less than four days march?"

It was soon evident—when the two figures appeared—that the old one was actually dragging the young one. The Herald of Victory seemed strangely reluctant to speak his news.

"Well, Elphin lad—out with it! A silver groat if the tidings are good!"

"A great battle on the river Monnow, my Prince. Lord Talbot, William Newport, and John Grendor have utterly destroyed our army from Morgannwg, and have retaken with great slaughter the town and *cantref* of Grosmont."

"On whose authority comes this news?"

"My Prince, the wounded are pouring into Ardudwy, and some have just reached Harlech."

"Thank you, Elphin. That'll do. Will you tell Master Broch to come to me at once."

As soon as Elphin had scampered away, which he did with a speed rather befitting a page than a tabard-bearer, the Prince turned to the old man. "When Broch comes," he said, "let him into my chamber." He pushed open the door. "Get me that basin of milk, Gryd."

"The cats' basin, my Prince?"

Owen nodded.

"For *him?* Is he to live, then?"

But the Prince didn't answer. Carrying the basin carefully so as not to spill a drop, he walked slowly down the passage, and entered the room where his enemy was chained to the wall. No sooner did Gam see the milk than he scrambled along the ground to the full length of his chain. He seemed to see nothing but the milk; and when Owen held the basin to his mouth he choked and spluttered as he gulped it down, spilling it over his hairy chest and making inarticulate animal noises.

"Gently, gently, man!" murmured Owen, moving back with the basin. But Gam, never a very human figure, continued to strain towards the milk with a countenance so distorted that it made the Prince think of the face of their Harlech *Sin-Eater,* whom it was the custom to keep only just alive until the bosom of some dead one served him as a table.

Owen let him scrabble for a second or two, not from cruelty, for *that* mood had passed, but in fascinated wonder. Then he approached him again and allowed him to empty the basin.

This time, the trusted servant of the House of Lancaster *did* glance up as he gulped and gurgled. "What arms he's got!" thought the Prince. "Except Broch's I've never seen such muscles!"

When the milk was gone, the man sat on his haunches and stared at his feeder. "You want to live then," murmured Glyn Dŵr, in an abstracted tone, more to himself than to the other. "Have *you* got a love like Hopkin's flea, or are you a married man with a family, like King Harry of England?"

And then he became aware that Gam was prostrating himself before him and tapping the ground with his head.

"What are you doing, man?" he muttered in a low voice. "Have you forgotten how I killed Hywel Sele?"

Gam raised his head. "It's just *because of that!*" He spoke in a husky grumbling tone, but without any particular emotion. His animal spirits had already begun to feel the good of the milk; and as if accustomed to address superior beings from a position like that of a leashed dog, he proceeded to shuffle to the wall so as to have something against which to lean his back.

Owen mechanically stepped up to him and arranged his chain to his comfort, touching the padlock as he did so as if to test its fastening. Then—this time quite consciously—he slipped his fingers into the pouch of his belt to make sure he had the key. Assured of this fact, he dragged a bench from the hearth and sat down over against his captive, whose red arms, red chest, and tousselled red head showed dark in the smoky light.

"What do you mean, 'Just because of that'?"

"I tried to kill you for it, but I couldn't. Your spirits were too strong. Now I know I never shall kill you. I serve the strongest. I served King Hal till your spirits drove him across the Severn. I served Hywel Sele till your spirits put him in the tree. I would have done for you, Prince, for I never strike twice; but your spirits saved you. And now it's *you*—not the King—not the ghost of Sele—who're my God." He was silent, stretching out his sturdy, leather-bound legs with a groan of physical relief, while the milk he'd gulped down made contented noises in his stomach.

Owen surveyed him thoughtfully.

"What do you think I'm going to do to you?" he asked.

The little red man shrugged his shoulders and made no reply. He seemed to feel that between a man and a man's new God silence was the indicated attitude.

"It's a curious feeling, Gam," Owen remarked, "to know you have an absolute power over another living person."

The ex-servant of King Henry settled himself still more comfortably; and only the faintest puckering of his heavy forehead indicated that he was giving this soliloquy of omnipotence any serious consideration.

"My Lord of Nannau," he brought out suddenly, "used to talk to me like a scholar—just as you do, Prince."

Owen sighed. It was clear that what might be called the metaphysical aspect of his relation to his prisoner was destined to remain a one-sided problem. He took a new line therefore.

"What would Hal Bolingbroke have done," he enquired, "if you'd tried to put your knife into *him?*"

David Gam's countenance brightened. This was talk he could understand.

"He'd have had fresh bread and fresh water brought to me every day," he replied, "and left just out of my reach."

Owen rose from his bench and regarded the man pensively for some moments. Satisfied by this scrutiny he drew forth the key from inside his jerkin and unlocked the prisoner's iron collar. Both collar and chain fell down with a loud metallic clang on the stone floor, and Gam after a second's pause made a rapturous but clumsy attempt to leap up into the air. Then he stood before the Prince with his arms folded; but he evidently had something in his mind to say which he found too difficult. Twice he began; and for the first second or two Owen thought the joy of life had turned his head.

But with the third attempt he delivered himself of his trouble. It appeared he had a vague fear that Owen's "spirits," in whose power he

considered himself inescapably to be, might begin tormenting him for
their private satisfaction, unknown to their master.

"No fear of that, Gam; no fear of that! I swear to you"—and the
Prince crossed himself—"on the bones of my mother, that any spirit
who dared to disobey me would have to come himself—and none
other—and tell me what he'd done."

"And then you'd make him suffer for it, eh?" And the ex-assassin
gave himself up to an agreeable vision of this rebellious spirit "suffering
for it."

But attended by his new "familiar," the Prince now returned to his
own apartment where he found his friend Broch awaiting him. Old
Glew the Gryd certainly gave this red-haired "slave of the lamp" no very
sympathetic stare; but he obeyed humbly enough when Owen told him
to take the man to the soldiers of the guard and explain that they were
to treat him well and give him arms, as a loyal adherent of the national
cause.

The following day the truth of the Grosmont disaster was most la-
mentably confirmed; and not only so, but an unpleasant incident occurred in connection with it, for when the Prince encountered a group
of these new refugees in the castle-yard, instead of greeting him with
the enthusiasm usually shown by the commonalty to their leader, these
unhappy fugitives actually burst into hostile and derisive murmurs, expressing the view that their new ruler from the north lacked the traditional valour and wisdom of their ancestral Arglwydd Rhys.

On the second day after the arrival of these indignant fugitives the
castle was thrown into an uproar of excitement by the appearance of a
distinguished-looking party of Englishmen bearing a white flag. This
party turned out to include not only Denis Burnell from Dinas Brān,
bearing Owen's tribute from Salop, but no less a personage than the
famous Lollard, Sir John Oldcastle, who, unknown to his master, the
King, had taken advantage of Denis's business to come on a private
mission of his own, which, when plainly put, amounted to little more
than pure philosophical curiosity.

Oldcastle had, it is true, been in the field against the Welsh for the
last five years, but he had the excuse of his ancient friendship with

Owen as a law-student at the Inns of Court, not to speak of a learned correspondence that had passed between him and Master Brut during the latter's trial for heresy before the Bishop of Hereford.

No news of any kind had of late reached Harlech from the Usk. Whether the Abbot of Caerleon was still holding his own with Tudor's and Griffith's help and whether the new army under the Maid of Edeyrnion and Clerk Rhisiart had reached the scene of action was still completely obscure. No word had come from Henry Don either, or from Rhys Ddu; and from what could be gathered from the sullen fugitives from Grosmont it appeared that the defeated Morgannwg host had lacked any competent leadership save that of local free-holders of small experience in arms.

It was characteristic of Owen that the mere reverberation of so many accumulated shocks, and the mere oppression of so much ominous silence, increased rather than diminished his power of mental detachment. Where Henry of England would have been acutely conscious not only of the balance, to an inch, of the swing of the historic pendulum, but of the attitude towards him of his own court and parliament and people, Owen Glyn Dŵr seemed completely indifferent even to what the Arglwyddes and Catharine thought of him and of the failure of his statescraft.

He received the murmurs of the fugitives from the Monnow with absolute equanimity. He disregarded with an amused smile the protests of both his son-in-law and his brother-in-law over this crazy "parole" allowed to the assassin Gam.

To crown it all he took no energetic measures, indeed he took no measures at all, to stop a movement of serious insubordination worked up by Crach Ffinnant. This ill-timed conspiracy came very near to actual insurrection. Jealousy of the spiritual leadership of the Maid was at the bottom of it. The Maid had always been an enemy of Derfel; nor was Derfel, to judge by the traditions concerning his cult, likely to be propitiated by the Maid.

At any rate Crach Ffinnant began to suggest both to the people of Ardudwy and to the soldiers of the castle that since Owen's handling of the Welsh cause had proved so ineffective it might be a good thing to take the leadership out of his hands and offer it to the Tudors of Môn,

especially since the young man, her cousin, to whom Efa ferch Tudor
was now affianced, had shown himself, though not a very successful
warrior, at least an extremely crafty diplomatist.

From this it may be seen that the reckless Scab had his eyes—or *his
eye,* to speak more exactly—still fixed upon this sprightly young lady,
once more sojourning among them, who alone among all damsels had
actually *wished* to be Derfel's bride.

Conspiracies of this sort, the Scab told himself, though rising from
small beginnings, could grow into world-events, if directed by prophetic
intuition; and he had found support for his idea that the Druidic
"Mona" rather than the Bardic Edeyrnion was the true soil of Welsh
victory in one of the mystic poems of the great Hopkin himself, a
cywydd that definitely predicted that from Môn would come the red
dragon who was destined to unite all Britain.

Everybody but Broch-o'-Meifod had been daily warning the Prince,
since the Maid's departure, of this dangerous activity of the Scab's; but
all the Prince did, as far as his little court could detect, was to devote
more time himself to this attractive young woman whose betrothed
was the heir of the oldest branch of the House of Tudor.

On the very day of the arrival of Denis and Sir John the besotted
Scab had actually persuaded the little Tudor lady, herself of their purest
blood and affianced to their craftiest chief, to accompany him to Derfel's
shrine, which was situated at Llandderfel in Meirion, a long day's ride
from Harlech.

The Arglwyddes protested in vain against this mad excursion; but
the Prince was obdurate. "If the girl wants to go," he declared, "let her
go. We were responsible for her as a child. She's a grown woman now.
Her betrothed knew what she was doing when she came to us. He sent
us no word. He let her follow her whim. Who are we to interfere?"

But worse—from the Arglwyddes's point of view—was to follow. For
when at early dawn, for the road was long and mountainous, the little
cortège set out, it was discovered that the Prince had deputed none other
than Gam—his late desperate assailant—to be of the party.

It is true that both Lawnslot and Gwalchmai, together with Herald
Elphin and the page Iago, made part of Efa's escort, and there was a
small troop of soldiers besides; but if it had been anyone but this in-

corrigible young Tudor the Arglwyddes would have implored Sir Edmund to accompany them.

Before they set out, however, the thing had been rumoured so far and wide that the expedition took on the shape of a formal pilgrimage from Owen's court to Llandderfel, for the purpose of consulting the oracle.

The late Abbot of Valle Crucis might talk of gods and demons; but as Father Pascentius said, when the Arglwyddes appeared to him, "No young Lord could object, even in *our* degenerate days, to his betrothed going on a pilgrimage." If rumour had been active throughout Ardudwy and Arwystli as to the organization of this journey it spoke with ten times more emphasis and with ten times more lurid unction when the expedition ended as it did.

The most popular version of the tale was that the great statue of Derfel itself had descended from the Horse and attempted to ravish Efa ferch Tudor; while Crach Ffinnant wrestling with the lascivious idol had been miraculously slain.

Another version declared that no sooner had Derfel's Horse caught sight of David Gam than he neighed like a thousand stallions and would have torn him limb from limb, and that, in the struggle between them, the Scab being concealed *within* the Horse, received Gam's dagger in his heart!

Herald Elphin was the only member of the party who actually *saw* what happened, and he saw it through so small a chink that the spectacle must have been presented to him in broken segments.

It wasn't till the ride back to Harlech through the cloudy spring night that Herald Elphin had a chance of unburdening his mind of what weighed upon it; and he couldn't have done this if it hadn't been that young Iago from Dinas Brān was his companion. Born in the racial confusions of the border, trained by his ambitious friend Rawlff to listen with discretion and keep his thoughts to himself, constantly watching the artful ways of old Adda, that dove-like pacifist with the guile of the serpent, not Father Pascentius himself—and the Father had never yet been able to coax or bully one single genuine confession from this youthful courtier—was a better confidant than Iago for dangerous secrets.

In his relations with his friend, though he was five years the elder, Elphin was like an excitable girl compared with this thick-skinned youth. Poor Elphin! he was more than excited that night. It was a crisis in his life. He underwent—and he realized it in a measure, too—a complete psychological transformation.

All the castle—as these agitating days came and went—began to recognize the change; but the person who got the greatest benefit from it was Elphin himself, for his shocking vision, even through so small a chink, into the under-flow of life, gave him what might be called the courage of his own timidity.

None but a born listener like the young Iago would have let him ramble on as he did, while they followed the wind-blown torches. Their track led them along a wild mountainous path, with the waters, first of Lake Tegid and then of the broad sea-estuary, lying dim and ghostly beneath them.

The cortege had to move very slowly; and, as it was, the soldiers who carried the corpse of the Scab were hard put to keep pace with the horses of the lady's escort, near whose person, acting as guide when they approached the estuary, strode the obedient servant of Owen's "spirits."

Elphin's listener soon discovered that there was to be no attempt by the relater of the weird tale that fell upon his ears, as the bare slopes and rocky ridges of Cadair Idris towered above them, to assume the heraldic tone of the professional announcer of dramatic events.

Elphin spoke simply and directly; concealing nothing of the less heroic moments of his behaviour or of his less honourable emotions. He explained that the curious Gothic *Betws* or Oratory, built near the Llandderfel parish-church, outside which everybody but Efa ferch Tudor and Crach Ffinnant were compelled to wait, was the prehistoric headquarters of the worship of Saint Derfel.

"Derfel Gadarn fought by Arthur's side at the Battle of Camlan," Elphin kept repeating. Indeed the excitable young man in his unending monologue used this majestic sentence about "the Battle of Camlan" very much as the compilers of the Psalter used the syllables "Selah" with the effect of a liturgical echo or muted antiphony after the Psalmist's more passionate notes.

For all his calculated detachment in human affairs, the vigilant Iago wasn't devoid of a certain lonely and quite special response to the sub-human elements in Nature; and it would have been an added shock to poor Elphin in his emotional confession had he realized the cold-blooded abstraction with which his hearer observed the majestical panorama of earth and sea. It was only at intervals, as they followed the estuary among the mountains, that with the lifting of the mist by some gust of south-west wind the unruffled stars of Idris, the Giant-Astronomer, rose into view above his rocky throne; but, when this did occur, the vision of that winding stretch of tidal water, as the dark mountain and white stars looked down upon it, appealed to something in him that he'd never revealed to anyone, and was convinced in his own mind that he never *would* reveal to anyone!

"Did they know Master Gam had entered the *Betws,* behind them?" enquired Iago, when the mountain mists once more swept over that phantom arm of the salt sea.

"I *told* you," replied Elphin reproachfully. "Didn't you hear what I said? I told you that I was *sure* Efa ferch Tudor knew that Master Gam was there! I could see her eyes shine when he first came in. He must have hidden behind a pillar. The place was full of pillars, like the dining-hall at Snowdon; only these were stone ones. He must have opened the door so quietly that the Scab didn't hear."

"No woman that *I've* ever known," threw in his cynical hearer, as if he were hoary with such experiences, "could see a man like Gam hide behind a pillar and not scream out."

"Luned wouldn't have screamed out."

"She certainly would," said the other. "Indeed she did."

"When?"

"Never mind when."

"You don't know anything about Luned!"

But Iago stared at the starlit water, as the wind once more swept the mist aside, and held his peace. He recalled without any sense of shame, but also without any particular feeling of pleasure, the occasion when he had completed the virile task from which his enamoured friend had shrunk.

But Elphin went on. The lad was shaking with so much excitement that neither the flickering torches nor the swaying corpse, no! nor even the horses and their riders, had any reality for him. He craved one thing only—to tell, to tell! He felt as if—until he'd told—something would burst in his heart and drown his life in blood.

"The *Betws* wasn't dark. It was only that I couldn't see anything but what was just in front of me. It was the Leper's window I think. The Scab couldn't take his eye off the lady. She was smiling at him. She was playing the whore with him."

The obscuring of the estuary had coincided at that moment with the disappearance, behind the next turn of the path, of the torches and their burden. *There*—the riders were out of sight, too! The lads were alone on the mountain-side.

Elphin laid his hand on his companion's wrist. "It's the eyes," he whispered hoarsely. "I can't get the eyes out of my mind."

"*Whose* eyes?"

"She was playing the whore with him. She was making him mad."

"*Whose* eyes?"

"I couldn't see the Saint's face—only his knees and his hands. He's on his Horse, you know. She was making him mad, I tell you! He was whispering to her—I couldn't hear—but he was wanting her to give herself up, to offer herself up."

"To *him?* And she a Tudor from Môn, and he—"

"No, no! It wasn't like that! Oh, *can't* I make you see how it was? *Won't* you see how it was, Iago? It's *the eyes* I can't get out of my head!"

"He's only got one."

"I'm not talking of *him!* I tell you she was making him mad. But it wasn't her. *She* didn't do it. And though I saw him strike with his knife it wasn't Gam who killed him."

"What in heaven's name *are* you talking about, Elphin? Hurry up and tell me! We can't stand here all night." As he spoke, Iago turned his head to look at the estuary beneath them. The wind was faintly moaning just then through the branches of a Scotch fir above their heads; and through his sturdy frame Iago felt a surge of a curious exultation. "It's the sea-tide," he thought, as he gazed at the grey waters; and for some reason the idea of this alien salt stream forcing its way so far inland gave him extraordinary pleasure.

"Tell me quick, Elphin," he repeated. "We can't wait here forever.

Did she lie down for him? Is it *her* eyes you're talking about—and she a Tudor of Môn and he—"

Elphin tightened his grasp upon the younger lad's wrist and tried to speak calmly. "It's not of *her* I'm talking, Iago, nor of the Scab. And I'm not speaking of the Saint either; for I could only see his knees and his hands and that great painted rod, like an axle-tree, which he carries. I'm talking," and here the Elphin's voice grew so low that his friend had to strain his ear, "about *Derfel's Horse*. Have you ever seen those fish they bring up from the Bottomless Hole, *pwll diwaelod,* a mile out beyond Madoc's Haven—what *eyes* they have?

"They're the eyes of *y faggdu* and *yr abred!* They're the eyes of the abyss! And they were looking at him, at the Scab, as she led him on, as she played the whore upon him. *Her* eyes drew him, mocked him, maddened him, but the eyes of Derfel's Horse swallowed him up. They were dead eyes. Yes, they were the eyes of the Devourer of the Dead. They were the eyes, Iago, of the *Sea-Horse of Annwn!*"

"Let me tell you something, Elphin," and the youthful seducer of Luned deliberately extracted from his pouch a sweet-meat of a particular kind the girl was wont to make for both of them, and breaking it in his fingers, offered the half to his bosom-friend. "You're as much of a fool as our noble Prince! Why don't you imitate Clerk Rhisiart? There *is* a man! The accepted lover, *one after the other,* of the two most lovely women in the world! And all got by his brain. Do you understand, Elphin, you trembling fool? Got by his brain! Nobody who lives could call Clerk Rhisiart handsome. He can't ride anything but that old piebald. He can't hold a lance, or handle anything but his pen; and yet there he is, going off with the Maid of Edeyrnion—snatching her from the arms of Owen! It's brains we want in this world, my dear; not chatter about wooden-horses with the eyes of—"

But at this point the incalculable wind rose with a rush and howl and revealed to the eyes of this sagacious youth the one thing that had the power of reducing *his* brains to complete non-existence—the sight of his nature-estuary in clear starlight. It was indeed the vision of Elphin dragging Iago from his obsessed contemplation of this scene that met the suspicious eyes of Gwalchmai when in obedience to Master Gam he came to find out why the lads were lingering.

But the same south-west wind that gave Iago that fortunate moment soon covered everything with such a cloud that it was only the dullest simulacrum of a red glare that indicated where the torches were moving; while the horses of Efa and Gam were completely obscured.

And Elphin took advantage of this cloud, as they went on, to make it clear to Iago how the girl from Môn played upon the lechery of the luckless Scab till it was aroused to a point so desperate that, shameless coward as he was, he was prepared to risk everything to satisfy it.

It was only when his friend arrived, in the course of his feverish narrative, to the moment when the one-eyed man had actually got her down and was fumbling at her garments that the impervious Iago began to manifest any interest.

"Was she frightened? Did she struggle?" he asked.

"I've just been telling you," complained Elphin crossly, "that to the very end she kept leading him on. I couldn't see Master Gam till the last, but I think he had his knife in his hand and had left the pillar. I think *she* saw him all the while and knew what he was going to do. Do you know, Iago, I believe it had all been arranged by the Prince beforehand! Well—perhaps not *all*—for I don't think the Prince *could* have believed any girl in the world would let a man like that go as far as she let him go before she made the sign. But what I don't think *any* of them counted on was Derfel's Horse. Of course I never saw the Saint's face, for I could only see his hands and his knees and his rod of—"

"If you go through that business again," interrupted his friend, "and say one more word about Derfel's rod being like an axle-tree I'll beat you like a dog!"

Elphin wondered what Luned would have thought had she heard this violent language uttered by a mere page-boy to the Castle Herald; he was himself far too girlish to take it amiss. He took it as a woman might take the threat of a blow from a rough but easily-managed mate. It endeared Iago to him, and indeed was one of the strongest links in the bond between them, that the latter should be able to threaten in that particular tone to "beat him like a dog."

The darkness at this point became so dense that they had to look to their feet as they went along; and the fact that the torches in front of them had come to resemble a number of blurred red bruises on the flesh of a troop of dusky tumblers indicated that the soldiers who were carrying Crach Ffinnant's corpse had had to lessen their pace and to change their position about their burden.

Unable to enjoy his favourite sight of the grey arm of the salt sea thrust between the precipices of the mountains, Iago began, one of his cheeks still bulging with Luned's sweet-meat, to press his friend as to how he was so certain that when her assailant's body was pulled away Efa ferch Tudor was still a maid.

"I think," replied the excited Herald, whose coveted rank was only indicated to-day by the now invisible black lions on his leather surcote, "I think that she *had* meant to make the sign sooner; but you must know, Iago"—and he addressed his companion in the superior tone of Luned's lover explaining matters to their boyish confidant—"that there comes a moment when to yield is such sweet abandonment to them that they *can't*—"

"I'm asking you whether—"

"If you interrupt any more, Iago, I'll never tell you another word!"

"One of the soldiers told *me*," threw in his companion, "that he heard Derfel's Horse neigh!"

"I'm the only person in this company, Iago, who saw *and heard* everything. She never made the sign, but Gam leapt on him; and I heard him go 'ugh! ugh!'—just like that—first when he struck him, and then when he flung his weight on the knife and thrust it in."

"Did his blood—"

"Don't interrupt me! What does it matter about his blood? She laughed as she got up."

The two lads were now so put to it by the difficulty of keeping the torches in sight, as their path wound its way down to the sea's edge, that they were forced to keep silence. And once on the level coast, with the lights from the fisher-huts shining on the shore-road their mood changed and they began to discuss the war.

"He'll go when he's got his storm-spirits ready, Iago. I know what he's doing. No one in the castle but Master Broch and me knows what he's doing. You can't hurry Beings as awful as the ones he's working with now. But you'll see! When he's ready, he'll go, and his spirits with him. And—you'll see!—there won't be an Englishman left in Wales. Why do you whistle like that, Iago?"

"Because you're such a fool, Elphin. He's waiting for the French—

they're the 'spirits' he's waiting for; and if they don't come soon—"

"Well? Go on! What if they *don't* come? Wales doesn't depend on a scurvy rabble of cross-bowmen from Normandy and Brittany and Anjou."

"You don't think so?"

"No, I *don't* think so! I think if the country goes on crowding to his standard he'll have the biggest force in arms in all Europe, and the bravest too! Wait half a year longer, and you'll see. We shall be march-ing over London Bridge before—"

Iago stopped whistling. "Elphin, listen. Do you know what Meredith ab Owen said to Mistress Lu the other night?"

"I don't know and I don't care! Meredith ab Owen can't walk half across the court-yard without having to lean against the wall!"

"What's that got to do with it? And only last night the dwarf told me that Rhys Gethin rose up in bed and said he saw the whole castle in flames and the Arglwyddes and Lady Mortimer carried away on mules."

"Why on mules? How silly you are, Iago! If the English *did* take the castle they couldn't burn it. Fire can't burn stone. And why on mules? Rhys Gethin would do better to say his prayers and die in peace. Only a man in a fever could imagine the Arglwyddes on a mule!"

Iago sighed. "Now Clerk Rhisiart's gone to battle," he thought, "there's not a soul in Harlech who uses his brains. I am the only one. Oh, Clerk Rhisiart, Clerk Rhisiart, what a great man you are! You're our only real statesman. The Prince will come to destruction without you. So will we all. But if *I* escape I'll imitate you, Clerk Rhisiart, in everything! I'll rise slowly and steadily, by brains and by women. Yes, like Clerk Rhisiart, I'll be the secret lover of several women at the same time and I'll take for my Master the ruler who has the most brains and for my—"

His enlightened and logical train of thought was interrupted—as it had been so often that evening—by the darkness clearing from the surface of the estuary. The estuary's mouth was now near; and a stone promontory could be seen with a lantern in its watch-tower, a lantern whose light flickered up and down on the waves along with a small boat, in whose stern a couple of fishermen slept, covered with sheepskin blankets. Iago's whole being was promptly transported with a rush of ecstacy. Something in his blood and in the pit of his stomach responded blindly to this sight, and then and there it made a furtive league with the sea, promising itself to outwit every rational decision of his brain.

The pit of his stomach uttered its own language in his ears, using blunt and illogical predictions. "You'll imitate no Rhisiart at all!" it said. "What *you'll* do is to imitate Prince Madoc, and sail the four seas! *That's* where Welshmen can get their liberty, whatever Welsh heads moulder on London Bridge! To sea, to sea, Iago ap Cynan!"

The morning that followed the death of Crach Ffinnant proved to be the darkest and most disastrous morning the Prince had ever known. Derfel's prophet lay in the already crowded death-room of the castle when Owen went to say a prayer for his soul. Here the corpse must remain till the *Sin-Eater* had been well-nourished from a capacious alms-dish on its breast. Then and then only it would be removed to the chapel. There was no Father Rheinalt to keep Mistress Lowri—whose passion for mortality was well-known in the castle—from visiting this temporary mausoleum; but for some reason best known to her own secretive and capricious Tudor heart Efa herself—the direct cause of the man's death —did public penance by remaining on her knees on the stone for more hours than any damsel of Owen's court had ever known a woman kneel, whether old or young.

She was there—a huddled young figure—when the Prince appeared; and she didn't move when he went up to the body; but it was at the moment when he lifted the cloth placed over the prophet's face, and in his imagination was beholding one of the eyelids raised, and that predatory blue orb fixing him with a ribald stare, that Owen first heard the uproar outside the walls.

He replaced the face-cloth, passed the girl without a word, and hurried to a high window in the passage, the very window out of which his Secretary had helped little Lu to look. Here for the flickering of a second it was his destiny to know what Mad Huw's rejected monarch must so often have experienced.

Half the population of the township seemed to be gathered on the beach, and they were shouting for him but shouting for him not with love or devotion, but with anger and contempt. The sea was calm and the tide far out; but it was a gloomy morning and the angry shouts of the mob took the place of the receding waters. Their clamour rose in waves against the grey walls; and the wild foam of their wrath beat against the buttresses and scaled the ramparts like the whirling wings of a host of screaming cormorants.

The Prince stood for one second watching and listening, while down the fibres of his thighs and legs ran an unaccustomed shiver, as if his warm woollen hose had suddenly been transformed into the scales of an ice-cold fish. But almost instantaneously his powerful will went through its mechanical gesture of recovery, a gesture which to his unconscionable self-analysis resembled the lifting of an interior dam.

"Well," he said to himself, "these are the experiences of all Princes! Gruffydd ap Cynan had to face worse things than this." Hurrying down the stairs he overtook Elphin and Iago, and caught the drift of their talk. Elphin was murmuring something about "the spirits," while Iago was regretting the absence of Rhisiart.

Arrived in the court-yard he found the Arglwyddes and John Hanmer already there. A crowd of soldiers about them were talking loudly and not very respectfully; and as they talked they perfunctorily armed themselves. Disregarding his wife and brother-in-law, he pushed his way to the postern that opened upon the sea-shore.

Here he found Meredith, unarmed and leaning on his stick; while at his side old Glew the Gryd was struggling with a great rusty bar that for years had been out of use, while the gate itself kept shivering from top to bottom with the blows it was receiving from outside.

Meredith and the Prince exchanged a quick look. Then they both smiled. "You'll risk it, I suppose, sir, and talk to them?"

"They won't rush us, my boy, will they?"

"It won't be *you,* sir, if they do!" and he turned to the old Porter. "Put down that iron thing, Glew, and open the gate. The Prince will talk to his subjects!"

The old man looked at his master in troubled dismay; but at Owen's nod he slowly removed what bolts there were and dragged the gate open. So suddenly was this done that the leaders of the mob who were striking at the door stumbled headlong into the court, while the billets of wood they carried fell heavily at the Prince's feet.

At the sight of Owen, towering there in that narrow entrance, their followers backed away, while they themselves, seeing the armed guards and the Arglwyddes in front of them, shrank in embarrassed discomfiture against the interior wall.

The foremost ranks of the crowd, however, though endeavouring to retreat, were pushed forward by those behind; while the howls from the rear rose unappeased and incessant. "Give us the murderer of our prophet! Saint Derfel for the Scab! Give us the murdering traitor!"

Owen raised his right hand. "Men of Harlech, men of Ardudwy—"

"Will he do it, will he, *will* he?" thought Meredith, propping himself against the open postern and trying to make out the nature and character of the rebels, and what local types they represented.

But even before the son had come to the conclusion that the leaders of the mob were a group of obstinate Derfelites who had been reluctant to follow the army of the Maid, fanatics such as Saint Jude calls "clouds without water," the Prince had hypnotized them into sullen, helpless, paralysed passivity. This, however, wasn't enough for him, and using the full force of his powerful voice and magnetic charm, he proceeded by a mixture of cajoling and pleading and threatening to change their mood into one so different, that as Meredith watched them they seemed to him like a great shoal of heaving porpoises, fascinated and allured by some majestic figure-head, upon a vessel sailing close to the wind!

This day of evil for Owen had, however, only just begun; for no sooner was the riot about the dead prophet quelled than far worse and far more devasting troubles began. The insurrection of the Scab's mourners had come from the sea-entrance to the castle; but now there burst in from the main entrance, straight into the base-court, encountering the Prince as he was making his way to the Arglwyddes's side where Sir Edmund and Catharine already stood, a ghastly and pitiful fugitive.

Catharine was the first to see this figure, and big with child as she was she staggered into its arms. The man she thus greeted looked like some victim newly risen from the scaffold; for his clothes were sticky with blood and there were wisps of straw and of dead bracken clinging to him, while the hairs of his beard, which were of a week's growth, had turned white with what he'd been through.

Owen at first glance didn't recognize him at all, nor apparently did Sir Edmund; and it was left to the dwarf to cry out in her piercing voice. "It's the Father! It's the Father!" Nor did the little woman content herself with this; for no sooner had she realized the condition of the Maid's parent than she began to emit the most heart-rending sounds that the Prince had ever heard. To *his* ears they resembled the screams of a hare when the dogs are upon her; though Father Pascentius, who was now entering the court along with the two Englishmen, at once began looking about for Broch-o'-Meifod's dog, so much did these sub-human shrieks recall to him the *méthode scientifique* of Gilles de Pirogue.

Certainly it was like an animal and unlike a person, the power the dwarf possessed of emitting these sounds without falling into blind hysterics. But though the syllables with which she interspersed her cries consisted of nothing but the name "Rhisiart," repeated over and over, the repetition of this name did humanize to some extent these painful howls.

It was no doubt the dwarf's repetition of the name "Rhisiart," conveying, as it did, to everybody present the notion that the man was dead, that made the Prince think it was one of her fainting-fits that left Lady Mortimer so long in the fugitive's arms.

This, however, was by no means the case. If she wasn't like her father, in his power of exteriorizing his soul, she was like him in being able to call up from some secret reservoir in her nature a spiritual force that seemed almost non-human.

And it was Catharine who now, disregarding both her parents exactly as the Prince was disregarding her mother, began questioning Father Rheinalt before them all. It was the monk who leaned against *her,* not she against him; and it was she, for his words were faint, who repeated them in a clear voice for the benefit of all present.

Herald Elphin was irresistibly reminded of the occasion when as a page-boy at Glyndyfrdwy he heard this same daughter of Owen rescue the last words of Iolo Goch from vanishing uninterpreted into the void. She held her head high while the exhausted monk clung to her arm, and she uttered the fatal words clearly.

"Our cause has had a terrible defeat. Codnor met our army at Pwll Melyn and drove it through the Usk into the forest of Monkswod. My— my lord Griffith—is—is a prisoner and—" But there rose a terrible cry from the Arglwyddes, a cry rather of wrath than of grief; wrath taking grief by the hair and whirling her among the rocks and nailing her to the rocks! Never from that time on, though she softened to him again more than once, did the Arglwyddes from the very bottom of her heart forgive the sacrifice of her eldest son. Her maidens crowded round her, but she thrust them back. "What else, Catharine? What else can there be, Catharine?" they heard her moan; and everyone near them saw the terrible look she gave Owen, though if she said anything to him it was lost in the ring of her daughter's voice.

"My Lord Tudor ap Griffith was slain in the battle. The Abbot of Caerleon was slain in the battle. *But he says further*"—here the girl had to make an heroic effort not to break down—"*he says further* that his daughter, Tegolin ferch Rheinalt, together with her husband, Rhisiart ab Owen, have been—have been taken prisoners."

While Lady Mortimer was playing her part as the messenger of death and ruin and captivity, Father Pascentius, leaving Oldcastle and Denis to the care of Elphin, in whose heraldic lions they pretended a protracted interest, himself moved heavily forward towards the girl.

It was of Rhisiart and of Rhisiart alone he thought as he listened to her words. Not a single soul in the place cared a farthing for him, now Rhisiart was gone! There was nobody now, in the whole castle, to whom he could even mention the *Cardamine Pascentius*. The Prince, he knew, disliked and misunderstood him. To Broch-o'-Meifod he was merely a clumsy gloss upon Saint Thomas. Meredith always put on his most ironical mask when he approached.

Yes, Catharine might faint when she thought of her lover; but she had her children and her husband. Owen too had his favourite Meredith. But if the Herald were to announce to-morrow, "Father Pascentius lies a-dying in his cell," not a soul in Harlech would as much as cross himself! How curious, when you came to think of it, that anyone who drank up the spectacle of life with the relish he did should be loved only by one person in the whole world!

"Oh, Rhisiart my son, my son Rhisiart! Will they torture you to get Owen's secrets out of you? Are you dead already on some Hereford scaffold?"

But if a film gathered over Father Pascentius's eyes as he heard this repetition of "slain in battle" and "prisoner of the English," the thought of his brother caused Owen's mouth to twitch like a child's, and big tears to trickle shamelessly down upon his grey beard.

"She's been ravished to death by now," he said to himself. "It's she who has perished under Hopkin's 'black flag.'" But though he told himself this, it was for Tudor not for her he wept; Tudor who had jumped that stream at which he himself had balked!

By degrees he became aware that Sir Edmund had carried Catharine away, that Father Pascentius had departed with Father Rheinalt, and that Luned—"How big *her* belly's grown! I'll be hearing tales of *her* soon!"—had managed to convey the heart-stricken dwarf from this arena of evil tidings.

The two English gentlemen, he now observed, not so accustomed as his own court to his reveries and abstractions, were slowly and sympathetically approaching him. He raised his hand to his beard—let it fall to his side—straightened his shoulders—and was preparing to greet them with a polite smile when the image of Rhisiart, torn from his bride to be horribly slain on the scaffold, so twisted his mouth that up to his face went his hand again, even as he made his bow.

But the forces of disaster—were they directed merely by some pure accident of planetary transit?—hadn't yet reached the culmination; for while the two Englishmen were still some paces away, the Arglwyddes rushed between him and them, her countenance transfigured by blind wrath.

In all her years with Owen this was the one sole time when she lost her incomparable self-control. And just because of the uniqueness of the occasion it was the more shocking.

Nothing in the world but the fate of her eldest son could have roused her to such a pitch. John Hanmer was at her side trying in vain to calm her. Sir John Oldcastle and Denis Burnell drew back. But their previous discretion was lost. They drew back in a manner that betrayed an indignant masculine free-masonry. *"Our* wives," their expression said, "are under better control!"

But looking straight in the Prince's face, and making no attempt to lower her voice, the Arglwyddes poured forth the whole torrent of the fury that swirled up within her portly frame. Even in the tempest of her emotion she kept her head—as the most angry women know well how to do—sufficiently to pierce him where the armour was weakest and the flesh most sensitive. In one sentence she'd broken his skin, in two she'd touched the quick of his master-nerve, in three she'd so transfixed his soul that it was outraged beyond escape. Her grand taunt was cowardice. "You didn't *dare,* you didn't *dare,*" she kept repeating, "to go to the Usk yourself because of Hopkin's prophecy. And so where you didn't *dare* to go you sent your son. No wonder King Harry

despises you! *He* goes to battle himself and the blows he gets he takes
—like the man he is! You're *not* a man. You're a false-prophet and a
preacher of vain words! Oh yes! When it comes to lifting your hand
and stroking your beard and acting the great monarch, you can do it
to perfection. But when it comes to leading your men to the battle-
field—*you let your son do that!* Why haven't you long ago put off that
circle of gold from your well-combed grey hairs and let my brave unadorned Griffith be Prince? Then he'd be safe now, and not in Henry's
hands, and you'd be in a cloister playing Saint Francis with that—*with
that girl* as your holy Clare! But oh no! you won't do that; you'll be
that conjurer, you'll be the magician— Ho there! Spirits of the Pit, rise
to the aid of Prester Owen!—" and the poor lady, overcome by a flood
of hysterical sobs, turned her back upon him, and supported by her
brother moved off to the castle steps.

That night there was held a most lively discussion in Herald Elphin's
chamber. He had persuaded Luned—for the Arglwyddes had retired
early and the Prince sat long over his wine with the two Englishmen
—to come and taste a special bottle of home-made cordial that had
been sent him by his parents from Crūc in Edeyrnion. Iago ap Cynan
was there too, and the young men were listening to a warm defence of
the Arglwyddes from their girl-friend.

It was hard for Elphin to grasp the full import of the tragic news
that had come that day. His mind kept wandering to what he had
seen through that fatal chink in the Llandderfel *Betws*. He was also
feeling proud of his new quarters; for the Castle Herald had an
official chamber all his own, and upon its walls he had hung a rough
picture he had himself daubed upon wood, of Luned caressing a
unicorn. He had learnt the rudiments of painting at a monastic school;
and in one of the castle libraries he had found a book devoted to the
history of unicorns. And now in some vague and even mystic manner
he had hesitated not to endow this beast, whose head was lifted to the
sky, with an extremely human expression, an expression resembling
that of a celestial Herald.

To this work of art he had endeavoured to call his companions' attention; not directly but indirectly, referring several times in the course
of their discussion about the scene in the base-court to the general
subject of heraldic beasts. He found it much easier, however, to draw

Luned from the topic of mothers and sons by reverting to Efa ferch Tudor's prolonged vigil over the corpse of the Scab, and by alluding to the psychological question as to whether, when a maid has reached the very edge of yielding to a rape, there comes to be established between her and her assailant some dark, sweet, fatal passion-link that lingers on, long after she has escaped the actual peril to her virtue. This seemed a topic that gave a more piquant flavour to their Turkish sweet-meats and Crūc wine than the problem of the part played in heraldry by legendary beasts.

But Elphin's room that night seemed exceptionally appealing, to the lad's own sensibility. A rough sketch upon parchment of a second unicorn, this one with its head between Luned's knees, lay upon a table under his window, and on the window-ledge, a rare possession in a Harlech chamber, was a flower-pot with snowdrops in it. He'd thrown some cedar-wood on his hearth under the excuse of entertaining a lady, and he felt like the Herald of all Britain when he rose from his seat to snuff the wicks of his two candles.

Luned settled herself luxuriously in her host's big embroidered chair by the fire. She threw back her mantle and stretched out her legs towards the hearth, making no attempt to conceal the life-bearing promise of her rounded belly. She joined in their talk, which grew every moment more wilful, critical, and passionate; but under all her prudent strictures upon Elphin's idealism and Iago's cynicism there ran a deep, undulating, brimming tide of unspoken exultation.

She didn't formulate her *Magnificat* in any definite thought, far less express it in words, but her inner consciousness kept setting the palpable weight of this new life within her, as if upon some invisible, planetary scales, against the lurid horrors of her companions' talk.

The more comfortably did she settle herself, and the more luxurious did she feel, with the wine on her palate and the sticky sweet-meat on her lips, the deeper grew the delicious unease of her child's movements within her body.

Without being aware of it, both the lads, as they argued with each other and showed off before her, drew the magnetism of their self-assertion from that gently-breathing, calmly-resting rondure above her dwindled lap. Her great belly, as the fire-light fell upon it, seemed to throw into a diminished perspective the tragic disasters the lads were discussing.

Without their knowing why it was so, the spread sail and lifted anchor of Iago's escape over the sea, and that fabulous encircling of heraldic beasts by multitudious spring-flowers which was Elphin's ideal, kept waxing more and more dominant in the young men's secret thoughts, for all their discussion of the "drawing and quartering" of Rhisiart, of the ravishing of Tegolin, of the death of Tudor, and of the last stand of the heroic Abbot of Caerleon.

This orbic promise of the unconquerable continuity of life, resting there heavy with the future between Luned's diminished lap and expanding breasts, threw round every image that was evoked in those lads' talk a muted remoteness, a softening of emphasis, a recession into far-off vistas of perspective. The girl's own mind, as she sipped Elphin's cordial and let the sweet-meats dissolve against her palate, languidly travelled back over the years of her life. She thought how she had always longed for a child; how she had loved Rhisiart; how she had hoped against hope that he might be her child's father. She thought of poor Rawlff, how devoted to her he'd been, but how his ambition and his boastful arrogance had made a barrier between them.

And then as she listened to Elphin's talk about Owen and his familiar spirits a curious smile parted her lips. Many an amorous scene with this pretty lad floated across her mind. She had never loved him, she told herself—she had loved none but Rhisiart—but so much had she longed for a child that if he'd only been more of a man she would have let him do it. And then, still with the same vague maternal smile, the real recipient of which was the unborn being within her, she glanced at Iago. "If Elphin hadn't tantalized me so," she thought, "and stirred me up so, I'd never have yielded to *you,* you little know-all sailor-boy!"

And she smiled a rich, wine-scented, sweet-meat-sticky smile, as her eyes met those of her young seducer. It was a much more equivocal smile, however, than the bold Iago supposed, as he thought to himself with treacherous satisfaction that she was his, and not his friend's. "No," her smile *really* said, "I used you, my good boy, to get my child, but if you think I love you, or that I'm your victim, mightily are you

mistaken! Oh Rhisiart, Rhisiart, what are they doing to you as we sit
here?"

But the queer thing was that she would envisage even Rhisiart's
death without anything more than a gentle pity. "I suppose," she
thought, as she puzzled over this, "that when a girl's like I am, and
has these feelings within her, it's *you*," and she apostrophized her unborn, "who are the one—*you, you,* my darling, and nobody else!"

Meanwhile Elphin was assuring them with vehement words that it
was impossible that Owen should ever really be defeated. The lad had
removed his official costume and stood before them in white tunic and
white hosen; and as he lifted up his impassioned face, with the curls
falling upon his bare shoulders and the candle-light throwing into relief
his rounded hips and slender thighs, it crossed Luned's mind that he
looked more like a Herald of Saint Gabriel than of any earthly prince.

"But a girl doesn't want beauty in her child's father, does she, my
pet? She wants courage and wisdom, knightly courage and clerkly
wisdom!" and she sighed deeply, thinking of Rhisiart on the scaffold.

"Owen's great year," declared Iago dogmatically, "was the year after
Bryn Glas, the year *before* he took this castle. This castle's been his
ruin! There's something about this castle that's enervated him and
turned him from war to magic. And I'll tell another thing. Having a
castle has given him a conventional court with a retinue and a sly
Archdeacon Young, or Archbishop Young or Bishop Young, as he'll
soon be. And having a court he must needs listen to wind-bags like
that rascal Hopkin, who's far worse than poor ol l Crach"—and the
lad crossed himself—"and he must needs think of Tegolin ferch
Rheinalt; God guard her red hair! When we Welshmen are great is
when we've got a leader who can move like a dark storm up and down
the land—hit them here, hit them there, harry them day and night, and
never meet them in formal battle-array. He's thinking *now*—you mark
my words!—of nothing but these damned Frenchmen. 'When the
French come,' he's thinking, 'we'll march on London.' But I tell you
this, you two. What he ought to do is leave this curst Harlech, where
there's a spell and a *tynghed* on every stone, and go back to the wild
woods and play the game he played at first—rushing about the country
and rousing the common people and looting the greasy merchants of
the market-towns. What we want is a thunder-and-lightning leader

in the field, not a magician in a closet! Never mind the whoreson castles, is what *I* say! Keep to the mountains; dodge their lumbering troops. Rule Wales from the good green-wood, until we tire the rogues out!"

He had been pacing up and down the room in his excitement; but, "Why does she smile at me like that?" he thought, as he sat down, leaving the whole chamber vibrating to his bold tones.

But though it was Iago and not Elphin who'd given her her unapproachable superiority, it was Elphin and not Iago who gazed with awe at that great belly, as if it were a planetary orb, heavy with fate. She was wearing a garment of light green, very much like the leaves of the snowdrop in his flower-pot, and this particular colour intensified the rotundity it concealed.

Whatever the girl's own feelings were for the living creature that was the burden of her noble amplitude, to Elphin it wasn't so much the child within it, as the actual rondure of her belly itself, that was so beautiful, so miraculous. In the strength of his idealism he had from the start been trying to persuade himself that his own ineffectual embraces were the cause of this miracle; and his head was so full of unicorns surrounded by thousands of flowers that this miraculous rondure seemed like a great water-lily in bud, and the girl's equivocal smile like a ripple upon a sacred pond that was his and his alone.

He grew more and more fascinated by the spacious curves of the serene convexity opposite him. And yet he thought, "How unashamed she is! I thought girls always wrapped mantles round them! And this thin green stuff's as filmy as a flower's calix! She feels like me when I've done a good piece of work and just sit back and think. I'm an artist as well as the cause of that big belly; and though I *may* be the youngest herald in 'Ynys Prydein' I'm the best heraldic painter north of the Severn. I can't, I know, compete *yet* with Master Trundle of Shoreditch"—and the lad recalled specimens of this expert's work that he'd seen at Saint Matthew's Fair—"but once let Owen's spirits give us peace and I'll soon challenge him!" And Elphin's thoughts ran upon all the rich artistic achievements of the flamboyant century just over.

"I was born too late," he thought. "This modern age has no taste for art! All it cares for are the quarrels of Popes and Princes and the Inventing of Heresies and the Burning of Heretics. Oh! those exquisite windows in Valle Crucis! Who can do work like *that* to-day? Why didn't Father Pascentius let me go on with the choir-stalls? Because he's a perfect example of the science and logic of this age! He thinks of nothing but confuting Lollards."

Gazing rapturously at the girl in the chair, and thinking of her form as his handiwork, he recalled certain beautiful grotesques he had designed for the chapel choir-stalls, but had never been allowed to use. Luned's maternal curves in their green vesture began to assume for him symbolic shapes—shapes of life's fecundity from all the elements of Nature. The girl's belly became a capacious gourd in a rich stubble-field. It became a great satiny puff-ball carried over the fields on a warm south wind. It became an iridescent bubble, mounting up from a fern-shadowed fountain. It became a floating Nautilus, bright and gleaming, luring him towards a fairy estuary, where by the reeds of salt-marshes that were neither land nor sea, calm, tame, beautiful-eyed heraldic creatures grazed upon sea-grasses and horned poppies.

But if life under the girdle of Luned and in the enclosed garden of Elphin's fancies seemed timeless and immortal, in the magician's chamber of the Prince of Wales it was dark with fatality and sprinkled with the foam of all that rushed away.

Owen had exhausted his will-power in adjusting his mind to the death of his brother, and to the more lurid fate of Tegolin and Rhisiart; and he had no spirit left to play his last card with his wandering soul. Here it was—still the unconquerable soul of Owen—but there was a troubled doubt upon it to-night, debarring it from leaving his tall frame and his imposing presence, "adorned," as Rhisiart would have said, "for sacrifice."

For an hour or two he had lingered over the wine with his English guests; but when he felt it was entirely polite and proper to do so, he let them pay certain state-visits; first to the apartment of the Mortimers and then to that of Meredith and Elliw. This last incorrigible pair—while the Arglwyddes was too stricken by Griffith's death to take the least interest in what she regarded as the irresponsible selfishness of her only surviving son—had persuaded Father Pascentius who at least was no wanderer from his post, whatever his private griefs might be, to consecrate their union by a formal wedlock.

Catharine and Sir Edmund were the only witnesses to this lover-like retort to the ills that had descended upon the House of Powys Fadog; for though Father Pascentius duly informed the Prince of what was going on, it proved impossible to get from him, in his present unapproachable mood, anything more than an absent-minded blessing.

A piece of news that apparently troubled Owen a good deal more than his favourite son's marriage was the fact that Morg ferch Lug, Broch's tricksy wife, together with their three daughters, had suddenly arrived at the castle. Maen-y-Meifod had been burnt by the English and it had been all their Welsh guard could do to bring the ladies safe to Harlech. Thus it appeared that the disconcerting Lady of the Mill-Wheel *had* proved obedient, after all these years, to the giant's command from Snowdon, so carefully written with Rhisiart's red and black pigments.

On this particular night the Prince was in such a dark mood that Father Pascentius, who was pining for Rhisiart, thought bitterly of King Saul bereft by his own fault of his servant David.

Old Glew the Gryd noticed with astonishment that instead of dismissing "Brith," one of the castle cats, a taciturn being of dingy tortoise-shell hue, after its accustomed dish of milk, the Prince allowed the creature to climb upon his knees and curl itself up to sleep.

Lady Mortimer who was worried about her father had implored her old friend to keep an eye upon him; and Glew the Gryd obeyed her literally in this, opening Owen's door at regular intervals and peering shamelessly into the room. Hard of hearing in his old age the devoted Porter could only note, as a bad sign to report to his young mistress, that he found Owen, each time he spied on him, talking aloud to the animal on his lap. What he was saying to the cat, though Catharine would have given much to know this, the old man couldn't hear.

The wind had dropped now and the rain had passed, and it was a calm starlit night, this night of Owen's accumulated disasters. As he stroked the soft fur of the sleeping Brith he could just see through his narrow window, for he had extinguished his candles in the flickering fire-light, a single bright star. What was that star's name? It shivered in its burning, so it wasn't a planet. Was it part of the ruling constellation of his enemy Bolingbroke, triumphing over him across the waves of Brān the Blessed? His mind kept reverting to Broch's wife. It was surely an evil day that had brought *that* woman here. "She's come to fetch him," he said to himself. "I feel it in my bones. First Rhisiart and then he! And Tudor's dead and Gethin's dying and the French haven't sailed."

It was curious the comfort he got from Brith remaining so sound asleep on his lap. Steadily he went on stroking him, for the calm of the cat and the vitality of the cat seemed to pass with a perpetually increasing power from that variegated fur into his own nerves.

Then he suddenly remembered that his brother had always made a pet of this particular cat. "Brith!" he murmured, "Brith! Where is he then? Where is he?"

And all at once he began to feel that Tudor ap Griffith was actually with him in that darkened room. But he went on stroking the cat and did not lift his eyes, for he felt that the presence so near him was no ghost that he could see, no ghost at all, but the consciousness of his boyhood's companion close to his own consciousness, without form, without shape, the familiar identity of the man he knew so well impinging upon *his* identity.

He began to talk to Tudor now; though old Glew, whose head kept appearing round the door, like the man in the clock recently invented by a Glastonbury monk, thought he was talking to the cat. "I'm glad I didn't play any games with my soul to-night, Brother. I must have known you'd come."

The trouble was that instead of letting him enjoy in peace their closeness to each other, this presence which was nearer to him than his own hands and feet must needs compel him to use the new strength he'd got through the mediumship of Brith in a manner most distasteful to him. Matters were amiss in the castle that night, he seemed to gather from Tudor, or from Tudor's pet animal, and it was his affair—so it seemed intimated to him—to deal with what was wrong.

He stealthily slipped his fingers beneath the sleeping cat with the intention of placing the creature on his bed. But a flood of devastating weariness came over him at that instant. He felt as if to sink forever, far deeper than Brith, under a thousand fathoms of forgetfulness was the most desirable thing in the world! But even as he relaxed in his chair, with his fingers under the cat's warm body, and stretched out his legs, covered so smoothly in olive-green, he knew very well he would be soon exploring every part of the castle and facing just the very people he always found most hard to face.

"You lazy trickster!" he muttered aloud, apostrophizing himself. "Forgive me, Brother, if I find this quest you've put upon me too heavy for me to-night. I feel as if I could sleep, Brother, sound and still, for a thousand years!"

Then he thought—still holding his fingers under the sleeping cat— "There *must* be, in all the revolving worlds, a place where the soul can rest *and be conscious that it's resting!* Are *you* in such a place, Brother? Old Broch talks of death. But death's not what I want. Death's not rest. Not unless you're conscious of being dead! Are *you* resting, Brother, even while you make your Owen bestir himself?"

Very slowly, though under his olive-green hose he experienced what children call "pins-and-needles," but with the cat still held between his loose, flapping, scarlet-lined sleeves, he did rise now, and, walking gingerly to his bed, deposited the unconscious animal in the centre of it.

Then he looked round the room. "I'd better take my sword," he thought, "for you never know. Joseph, Mary!" he thought, "I must have left my sword in the hall. The stars are certainly against me to-day. It only needs Hopkin's black flag!"

He unhooked an unscabbarded weapon from the wall and tried its point and edge. It had been his grandfather's sword, and it was only a little less old-fashioned than Clerk Rhisiart's. But at the moment it suited him because its blade was so long and its handle terminated in such a spacious knob that an old man could have used it to support his steps. Owen felt like an old man as he moved to the door, emphasizing as he did so the clattering sound of the weapon's contact with the flag-stones.

On opening the door he was confronted by two figures. Father Pascentius was conversing with Glew the Gryd; and the Father looked unusually disturbed.

The Prince had never felt less inclined to encounter their castle-confessor than he did at this moment.

The two men looked at each other, and the torch that burned above the door revealed their unwonted agitation. As they looked, Owen's sea-green eyes dilating against the coal-black orbs of the other, an ir-resistible wave of antagonism passed between them. The monk thought: "Here's the moody despot who's robbed me of Rhisiart"; while the Prince thought: "Here's the cunning priest who'd be glad to see the Broch desert me!"

"Well, Father," said Owen, leaning on his sword, "I suppose you've come to tell me of some wench who's in trouble, or of some lad who hasn't been to Mass."

For a moment the Father was compelled to swallow his saliva and utter a swift prayer to Saint Thomas for self-control. "Would it were no worse, my son," he said sternly. "Is it your pleasure that we enter your room; or—" and he gave a glance at the Porter.

"It's 'my pleasure' to hear what you've got to say, Father, in the fewest possible words. We have no secrets from our trusty servants."

"There's great dissatisfaction, my son, throughout the castle. The soldiers are murmuring that the slayer of their prophet—God be kinder to that rogue's soul than he deserves!—is treated at your command like a belted knight. But it isn't of the soldiers I've come to speak. There's a scene going on now over Rhys Gethin's death-bed that makes it impossible to give him the last rites. The man's end's come. Dead he'll be before morning; dead and unshriven, unless you interfere."

Owen wrote something with the point of his sword on the floor; but he didn't raise his head. "It's been going on for years, my son, as we all know; but some influence—God working in some roundabout manner for His own purposes, has brought it to a head, just as the man's dying."

"*It?* Brought *it* to a head? Stop speaking in riddles, man. Brought *what* to a head?"

"Simon's jealousy! And if you must have it in plain words, my son, I think Mistress Lowri's mind has broken down."

"Do you mean the woman's gone mad?"

"I don't think she knew me when I spoke to her just now, my son."

The Prince smiled. "There must be many in this place," he said bitterly, "who have good cause not to know their spiritual confessor."

"Do you wish me to tell you what I heard between her and Master Simon by Rhys Gethin's pillow?"

"*I don't wish*—" but the Prince broke off abruptly, and began drawing squares and circles on the stones with his sword's point. His nervous prejudice against this man changed at this single moment into a violent distaste and an implacable determination to get rid of him. "I've endured his tale-bearing and his spying long enough," he thought. "If I'm to be driven out into the mountains I'll begin by clearing my path."

Father Pascentius contemplated the movements of that sword-point and gave the folds of his cowl several quiet twitches as if to shelter the back of his neck from the chill of the passage.

"You took Rhisiart from me," he thought. But such was his relish for every aspect of the visible world that he couldn't help drinking up as he did so—as if the Prince were offering him a cup of golden wine instead of this angry hostility—the curious lights and shadows, some of them soft and dim like rich velvet, some of them opaque and hard like polished silver, that the torch-light above the door drew from Owen's embroidered tunic, from his scarlet-lined sleeves, from his antique weapon, and even from the forks of his grizzled beard.

"You took Rhisiart from me," his hidden heart repeated, like the striking of a muffled bell, while with his eyes on Owen's he obstinately went on. "There's another thing you ought to know, my son. Since the news came of our defeat on the Usk my Lady's dwarf has taken possession of Clerk Rhisiart's chamber, and the girls tell me she refuses to leave it. They say there've been lights burning all night, and they even say they've heard wild supplications up there, addressed, not to the Holy Trinity, but to the three most potent Devils in Hell, who have—as you know well, my son, and as several angelic doctors attest—taken upon themselves to simulate the Divine Persons. They also say—"

"*I* also say," cried Owen, stepping back several paces from the man, and jerking up his arm in its flapping sleeve, and pointing westward with point of his sword, "that to-morrow morning, Father, you'll choose any horse you like from our stable and any escort you like from our men—they'll be glad enough to leave us if what you say is true!—and ride off to pay our respects to Chancellor Young, Bishop-elect of Bangor. You'll find him at the Castle of Aberystwyth where our flag still flies, and you'll find plenty to do among his colleagues, both secular and religious; and you can take all the books you can carry, whether they deal with the Trinity *above,* or with the Trinity *below.* God speed you, and good luck to you, Father!"

And Owen strode off; holding his sword this time so that its point was at an obtuse angle to his flapping sleeve.

When he was gone the monk and the Porter looked at each for a moment without a word. Then Glew the Gryd shook his head sadly. "I told'ee how 'twould be, Father. I told'ee how 'twere with Owen ap Griffith. He's been a different man since the Maid went. She hurt the heart in him, that woman did; and Clerk Rhisiart turning on him killed it. I shouldn't wonder if 'tweren't not thee but him himself what sets out to-morrow. 'Tis this curst castle to my thinking what's done it! 'Twere better for us in the rocks of Snowdon; better in the Forests of Tywyn. Some say Harlech has never been the same place since they took Brān's head to London."

"Do you think he'll come and beg me to stay, after he's slept on it, Master Glew?"

"He may; and again he may not, Father. Owen ap Griffith be wonderful stubborn when 'a's done what 'a knows 'a shouldn't do. But so be all the High Ones of the earth I reckon. If I were you, Father, I'd get a lantern and ramble round the stables to-night. They be tricky devils, these Lawnslots and Gwalchmais, and no mortal person can tell what they'll up to. Like enough if they hear you want a good horse there'll be none in Harlech to carry your weight till they've taken gold off you. But I wouldn't count on Owen ap Griffith's changing his mind. I've known him stubborn in times past; but his stubbornness, since Tudor ap Griffith have been slain, be past talking of! You saw yourself, Father, how he took umbrage at what you said touching that Trinity of Devils. That's because ever since Clerk Rhisiart and the Maid went he's been talking to devils; and there's not a trinity of their horned heads he doesn't know as well as we know him."

Father Pascentius wrinkled his nose, caused his upper lip to protrude by pressing his tongue against it, and scratched his ribs with his thumbnail.

"Silver groats are heavy when a Servant of God is travelling in haste, Master Glew," he remarked, "and gold nobles are heavier; and I expect I'll be leaving a few of such oddments to the friend who helps me to a good horse and picks me out a couple of trusty men on good horses, if the weather *don't* change to-morrow. So bear it in mind, Master Glew, and Saint Thomas make you die rich."

While this conversation was going on outside his room the Prince was proving the truth of every one of the monk's words. He felt as if his recent hours in that darkened chamber, wherein he had used the sleeping animal as a link between himself and his brother, had lasted for many years, and that it was as a *revenant* that he came back now, wandering with his naked blade through a generation that had forgotten him. Had he, like Pwyll Pen Annwn, been living for twelve months in some over-world of enchantment?

But Pwyll's people had been ruled in their lord's absence by an eidolon wiser than their lord, whereas to-night he was aware of grim silence and averted looks, of murmured insults and conspiring whispers. He passed guard-room after guard-room—for the castle was crowded with soldiers—where not a man rose to his feet to greet him; and where if he addressed them he was answered with silence.

By degrees he became aware that he was being treated as if he were already discrowned, dethroned, rejected; and as if the whole castle were only waiting in angry and sullen expectation the triumphant arrival of an English Prince of Wales.

In the last guard-room he entered, before ascending one of the flights of winding stairs to the passages above, he found David Gam sitting by himself over the fire, his heavy features wearing an expression of stupid bewilderment not unmixed with an animal-like dread. His fellow-soldiers had moved away from him as far as they could go, treating him like a leper, like the Sin-Eater himself! This palpable and visible sign of his commands being disregarded and his will flouted struck Owen the worst blow he had yet received. Wasn't it the essential prerogative of princes to raise up whom they pleased and to degrade whom they pleased?

Well! he had just degraded the most learned scholar in Wales. Now he would advance to honour the most unscrupulous bandit in Wales! He had sent his faithful Rhisiart to be cut to pieces on an English scaffold. He had sent the girl he loved to be ravished to death in an English camp.

And these things he'd done without explanation, reason or cause— solely to prove that he could *will what he liked,* even to the destruction of Wales, even to the death of his brother. He replied half-mechanically to Gam's greeting, though the little red man rose up at once to do him homage; but the sight of the way his men were isolating his new adherent in defiance of his will flung him down to the lowest depths of shame.

But the rock-bottom of pain and defeat and humiliation was always Glyn Dŵr's sounding-board for testing the resources of his spirit. The metallic tappings he now made with his sword-point, as he paused to speak to Gam, were so emphatic that they actually struck sparks from the stone; and even as they did this the living waters of his own defiance of fate spouted forth from the stony floor of his soul.

Gam was probably the most superstitious man of his brains as he was certainly the strongest man of his hands in all Wales. In a battle he would have been invaluable, because since it would never have occurred to him that the supernatural could take part in a battle he would have no fear of anything. What is commonly regarded as the magic of personality Gam interpreted as *impersonal magic;* and here in Harlech he was at once threatened and protected by the innumerable hosts of Owen's "spirits." He now felt—as his new master smiled at him as he left the guard-room—so completely indifferent to the hatred of his fellow-servants that his very insouciance imparted to his own personality something of the awe that he felt for Owen. They would have been reckless warriors, even from the Scab's own district, who would have dared to meddle with the little red man from Brecon.

Continuing his ghostly round, and feeling more and more like a ghost as he made it, the Prince ascended one of the main stairways of the castle. As he passed the entrance to the Mortimer apartments he caught, through a half-open door, a glimpse of his daughter, in the loose robes of her pregnancy, conversing with a young woman in a becoming black gown whom he recognized at once as Dame Alice of Lyde. He couldn't help being struck by the clinging, adoring and infatuated look with which "the Ruthin girl," as Rhisiart used to call her, was tending Catharine.

"Is it nothing to you," he thought, "that your good man should fall into the King's hands and be burnt at the stake?"

Holding his sword horizontally now, and treading softly on his pointed deer-skin slippers, he advanced down the long dark corridor at the end of which Luned had implored Rhisiart to take upon himself the paternity of her child.

As it happened, Rhisiart's old enemy Gwalchmai was the torch-bearer in this passage to-night, and Owen was so struck by the fellow's surly response to his greeting that he grimly took his torch from him and bade him practise his scowls upon the darkness as he found his way out.

"If I can hold Harlech," he thought, "and if Rhys Ddu can hold Aberystwyth, *till the French sail,* all may yet be well. Our people are still free. From Aberffraw to Gwent our mountains, our forests, our moors are free. I wish the Usurper would raise money enough to invade us himself. It's these Codnors and Talbots; yes! and that boy at Hereford, who're the trouble. There's a *tynghed* on Henri Père whenever *he* crosses the Wye or the Severn."

He stood pondering, the torch in one hand, the sword in the other, and the feeling stole over him that if only he could make the ghostly heroes of his land *understand* where the danger lay, the invaders would be helpless. "They think it's the foreign King we have to fear, because it was foreign kings in *their* time. They don't understand how everything has changed; and how it's strategy and skill and trade and money and swiftness of attack—not huge armies with royal banners and royal tents—that's our trouble to-day."

His mind reverted to Father Pascentius. "He'll be all right at Aberystwyth," he thought. "Young'll use his learning and his staring eyes to better purpose than I can."

And then he realized that he had intended all the while to visit Rhisiart's tower-room about which the monk had told such tales. He tried the door at the foot of the steps. Yes! it was open. Very softly on his deer-skin shoes he crept up the stairs, the sword's point in advance, the torch behind his back. Arrived at the top of the stairs he found a rusty iron sconce, a century old, driven into the wall. Into this he inserted his torch; and with his sword gripped tight and it must be confessed with a nervous twinge in his stomach, as if that organ contained a hidden hand that clutched and unclutched its fingers, he softly opened the door.

Not a sound greeted him; and his first impression was that the chamber was empty. Save for a faint whiteness from the starry sky, the only light in the place came from above the half-opened door from his torch outside. It took a second or two for his eyes to get accustomed to the obscurity, for the torch-rays from above the door had the effect of darkening rather than illuminating the rest of the room.

But when he *did* get his vision—that is to say when he saw the bed and what was in it—he received such a shock that 'twas a wonder he didn't cry out. For Rhisiart himself lay on the bed!

Had Morg ferch Lug seen her "pure-blooded Brython" at that juncture it is hard not to think that she would have been compelled to admit that the new Prince of Wales had at least *some* drops of the blood of the "older people."

Nothing—one might surely argue—but the prehistoric self-control of a race that had tracked mammoths and sabre-toothed tigers through the Forests of Tywyn could have prevented him at that moment from betraying his presence! But Owen ap Griffith didn't even draw his breath in a sigh that was louder than natural. He lifted the point of his sword about four inches, while his scarlet-lined sleeve entered quickly and left more quickly the wavering path of the torch-rays from above the door.

And then it *was* given him—largely by reason of this neolithic self-control of which none but a race with the blood of *the aboriginals of the locality* in its veins could have the secret—to take in the true reality of what he saw. It was—and was not—Rhisiart. It was *his clothes;* it was that gorgeous silver and blue costume that the dwarf herself had made for him to wear at Catharine's wedding; and she had stuffed it out with a long, thin straw-bolster. The little creature herself lay fast asleep by the side of this image—this image of the only man who had ever seriously kissed her—her tiny little arms, like the arms of a doll, tightly clasping its neck, while her disfigured chin was buried in its breast.

The head of the image was a mere blob of rags, but its bed-fellow had drawn so cunningly over this featureless rag-head the neat scholar's cap the man always wore at his clerkly labour that the Prince was astounded at the thing's likeness to what he had so often seen—his Secretary asleep!

The moment Owen took in the full meaning of what he saw a transformation took place in him. He ceased to be an aboriginal. He became not only a "pure-blooded Brython" but a representative of the most courtly ruling house west of Constantinople. Automatically inçlining his head, he swung round on his deer-skin heels and left the place as hastily and reverently as if it had been the bridal chamber of the Maid of Edeyrnion.

Having closed the door as silently as he'd opened it, he mechanically re-possessed himself of his torch, and scarcely less mechanically, as he descended the stairs, lifted the chilly handle of his sword to his distorted face. He was of a far too introspective turn of mind to be long in shaking off this emotional mood, but the almost ghastly glimpse he had been given into the love of women found a crevice in his mental armour that a less grotesque exhibition would have missed.

What he had just seen had indeed one extremely practical effect upon him. It made him resolve that at whatever cost to his masculine pride he would effect on the morrow a reconciliation with the Arglwyddes.

At the moment, however, carrying his now smoking torch less carefully than before, and once more using his naked blade as a staff, he made his way to the death-chamber of Rhys Gethin. Before reaching his defeated Captain's room it was necessary for him to pass an unfurnished and unaccommodated cell, usually devoted to the commoner sort of prisoners. From this place, reaching his ears through the heavily-barred door, there issued a long-drawn, moaning monotone, in a voice he recognized at once as that of Lowri ferch Ffraid. His torch was nearly out, but he could see a light streaming across the passage at the corner where it turned.

He beat with the handle of his sword against the barred door. "Lowri! Mistress Lowri!" he shouted. The monotone within went on just the same. It wasn't the voice of wrath or despair or misery. *It was the voice of reason,* that ghastly monologue of pure reason with itself, when all the humble, natural sub-streams of life's irrational flow have been *mentalized* into a horrible avalanche of glacial logic.

He struck again at the door, and again shouted the woman's name. But no end arrived to the interminable monologue within; to this monstrous stream of crazy assertion, wherein the reason confided to the reason the causes and effects of irrational passion.

And then the Prince made a grimace at the closed door which separated him from that voice, that high-pitched argumentative voice of the *mathematics of passion* which he felt would soon sound to him as if it were the pendulum-tick of the whole cosmos; for he suddenly realized that it was barred only *from outside;* and that all he had to do was to push the bolts and enter!

He hastened to do this; but as he did so the draught between the door he'd opened and the window of the cell extinguished his torch and at first there was only blackness and the voice of the woman. But since there was light at the turn of the passage there was a dim glimmer in the place, which increased when the smoke from his dead torch floated away.

And he saw that there were two figures here, too; but whereas in the other sleeping-place of his nocturnal visitation one was a dummy and one a dwarf, here one was mad and the other a corpse. It didn't take him long to realize that the corpse was that of Master Simon; and he soon understood, too, what it was that the delirious woman was justifying to herself in this one-sided dialogue, while she piled on the Hog's bare chest every scrap of the food that had been thrown into her cell. She was proving to her victim with irresistible logic that their love was sealed by his death.

The curious thing was that in that dim light and with her loosened hair and exposed bosom the mother of Tegolin had never looked more beautiful. She had the look upon her face that women have when they are listening to the passionate words of their first lover. There was a rope lying by her side, but it had not been used; and it flashed upon Owen at once why it was that contrary to the new custom with mad persons—so different from the old way of letting them wander about to the terror and inconvenience of sane folk—Mistress Lowri had been allowed not only the privilege of mourning over her dead but the privilege of neither being chained nor bound.

The only armourer left in the castle was the dead man lying there before him, while the authority responsible for her restraint was the father of her child.

What had the most weird effect on Owen's mind, as throwing down his extinct torch he addressed her by name, was the fact that while she knew him perfectly well and kept calling him "My Prince" she never stopped for a moment her stream of monotonous argument addressed to the dead.

She knelt erect over Simon's body while one logical necessity followed another from her lips; and even in that obscurity her beautiful eyes seemed caressing, cajoling, and hypnotizing the dead man to accept without question this rational and inevitable seal upon their love.

How Simon had perished was as transparent as the reasons she gave for killing him; for if Father Rheinalt had forbidden them to touch her with cord or rope he must have also forbidden them to tear from her victim's heart the small Spanish dagger that had caused his death.

For the second time that night, but on this occasion with full consciousness of what he did, Owen inclined his head as he stepped backwards to the door. Realizing he was going, the woman made a slight gesture with her hand, and he even fancied he caught the whisper of a hurried benediction; but the logical argument with the dead went on; and it was going on without intermission when he closed the door, shot the bolt, and walked slowly away.

"If only I can hold this place and Aberystwyth," he said to himself, "till the French come, all may yet be well." And then he thought, "I'll drink some of that Malmsey presently Sir John brought me. I'll be able to sleep after that, and forget Rhisiart on the scaffold and that girl. If I can hold out till the French come I may win yet! He's never been able to get into the heart of Wales. Twice he's been half drowned in the Wye; thrice he's lost everything in the Severn. Pull yourself together, old conjuror! This is what you embarked on; this is what you were to expect when you raised your flag. You've got to go on, on, *on*—till every head you've trusted lies low, and every heart you've loved is broken!"

But by this time he was leaning heavily on his sword, and as he turned the corner of the passage where a blaze of torches streamed out from Rhys Gethin's crowded death-chamber, he found he needed something more than the spirit to go blindly on. "I shall see her early to-morrow," he said to himself, thinking of the Arglwyddes. "I've taken away from her all but Meredith; and that little *ellylles* has got *him* now. Love? Let it come! Let it go! But if you don't, to-morrow morning, take every shame she can pile up on you, till she melts in your arms, a miserable magician *you* are, Owen Glyn. Dŵr!"

Oh, this room of Gethin's long dying, how well he knew it! He had made a point, during all these troubled days, of visiting for brief, painful, embarrassed moments his dying Captain.

Well! it was over now! He could see at once from the look of the figure on the bed, and indeed from the unrepressed relief on the faces of everyone there, that the great warrior had gone to his account.

He stood for a moment in the open doorway, leaning silently on his long sword. Then growing aware by the sudden hush that fell upon the people—and there were representatives there of every level of life in the castle, even of merchants and craftsmen from the town—that his presence had been perceived, he waited for some murmur of recognition, some sign of greeting and welcome to their Prince.

But no such sign was forthcoming. It was only too evident that the mysterious murder of Derfel's prophet, and the more mysterious enlargement of Gam, and now the spectacular decease of Gethin, had added the last bundle of fuel to the great smouldering bonfire of popular discontent which the disaster upon the Usk, the Abbot's death and the capture of the Maid had already ignited.

What was really going on in that death-chamber was a sort of Lying-in-State; an honour rarely given in Wales to any but lawful Princes of the blood of Cunedda and Rhodri Mawr.

Owen recognized quickly enough that this popular honour paid to the dead Captain wasn't without its implication of dishonour to the living Prince; but he made up his mind to disregard it, and disregard it he did so completely that it would have been hard for anyone to believe he noticed it at all.

Making no claim to any precedence therefore, he quietly moved up to the dead warrior in the patient line of those paying homage; though it is true that when he reached Gethin's bed he took advantage of his height and stood back a little, looking over the heads of the people as one by one they pushed past. The women who had washed the hero's body and closed his eyes had evidently had great difficulty in composing his features. They had forced the dead man's jaws nearly together, but they'd been loth to sever the stiff fingers with which he'd clung in his last struggle to an iron ring in the wall at his side.

It was the expression of his mouth, however, rather than that clutching hand, which most arrested the Prince. Owen had seen more dead men slain in battle than he could count, but he had never seen on any human face a look like the look on this man's.

He *had* seen it somewhere though. And where was that? Ah! he had it! It was a great pike he'd caught once in the river Dee; a pike that in place of leaping up from the grass, as most dying fish do, had straightened itself out and clenched its teeth and fixed its eyes upon the sky with a look of such abysmal fury of defiance that those gnashed teeth locked together had remained in its killer's consciousness for more than thirty years.

In addition to the fingers and the mouth, the women who had "laid out" this Hector of North Wales had had difficulty with the eyes.

The warrior must have been roused to such a pitch of passion by the behaviour of Lowri, who, it was said, scrupled not at the last to caress the Hog of Chirk in his presence, that his eyes seemed actually to retain the imprint of that shame as the Prince gazed upon them.

Owen was assured later that it was the visits of Lowri—and several times, they told him, she was accompanied by Simon—that had made Rhys Gethin's hurt incurable. The verdict of both bower and kitchen, of ladies and serving-men, was identical in this matter; namely, that had Crach Ffinnant tended him, and, as was his custom, kept everybody away, the warrior would have recovered.

A base and unpardonable impulse began stirring in Owen now; the impulse to turn from his old friend, the man who above everyone else was responsible for the victory of Bryn Glas, and depart without kissing him.

It was partly the desperate ferocity of the look that had been frozen upon the man's face that tempted him to shirk this natural courtesy. The cause of this look had been the woman he'd just seen; and there seemed something horrible in pressing his lips to such a look. And although he was the reverse of a squeamish person there were two other things that militated against this gesture. In the first place the skin of Gethin's face wasn't only whiter than is usual with the dead but there were drops of death-dew still upon it that normally should have dried. In the second place the women who "laid out" this obstinate corpse had not been able to close the eyelids completely, so savagely had they been fixed upon the sight that killed him; and in the crevice, out of which the eyeballs peered, certain excretions of rheumy glue had formed themselves, that now, catching the light of the candles, gleamed like fragments of sardonyx.

The strain that was making the Prince's inmost will vibrate like a cord at breaking-point brought it about that he was more sensitive to such things than was his wont; but nevertheless muttering "Mary! Joseph!" in his beard, he did at least make the sign of the cross over that scowling forehead.

"I *must* see Father Rheinalt," he said to himself as he made his way through the murmuring crowd.

He enquired in vain of one person and another; but at last a little page from the hills, awed and delighted to be able to help the ruler of his land, directed him to the chapel.

Here in the vestibule he found the man he sought. Father Rheinalt was seated on a wooden bench, holding a large rough crucifix in his hands. He rose when Owen approached him and signed to the Prince to sit down by his side. A low-voiced murmur was going on within the chapel where several priests from the neighbourhood were muttering psalms over a row of pall-covered coffins; while from a chantry just within the edifice where a host of candles had been lit a stream of wavering radiance fell upon their two figures and upon the crucifix in the monk's hand.

The Prince was astounded at the man's self-control. He had intended to question him as tactfully as he could about Simon's death; but he had never expected to find a person less wrought up, less confused, and much calmer that he was himself!

"I did what I could, my son," Father Rheinalt said. "It was pain to me to see what she was doing to herself as well as to those two. I think, after her fashion, she loved them both. I think Simon understood her; the other never! How could he—a simple soldier like that?"

"What made her kill him?" Owen didn't dare to look at his companion as he asked this question. He looked instead at the crucifix; but no sooner had he done so than it seemed to him that the face of the figure upon it resembled that of the man to whose words he was listening.

"What—made—her—kill—him?" repeated the monk slowly. "I think I can tell you *that,* my son, after all we've gone through. Knowledge comes at last, Owen ap Griffith, if we suffer long enough and deep enough. She killed him because with the best that was in him he *wanted* her to kill him! He understood her, my son—Christ have mercy on him!—as I never have, and as *he* never could. He thought—Simon I mean—that she'd lost her wits forever; and he couldn't bear to see it and live. I don't think she *has* lost her wits forever. I think if Denis Burnell takes her back to Dinas Brān she'll recover; but whether her heart'll change, Christ who knows all hearts alone can tell."

Owen lifted his eyes from the other Rheinalt, with the arms stretched out and the nail through his feet, and stared at his companion in amazement.

"Burnell doesn't think of taking her back, does he?" He suddenly felt as if he had been sleeping for a whole Platonic year, and had just awaked into all these people's lives—only to find he had lost every clue.

"I've been talking to Burnell, my son," declared Father Rheinalt, "and he says it was with the hope she *would* go back with him that he brought the tribute-money himself."

The Prince closed his fingers over the hilt of his sword and, pressing its point against the ground between his knees, gazed at the monk with the expression of a child who has turned the page of a lesson-book and found a picture of a boar-hunt. His grey-blue eyes became round with wonder and his bearded chin sank down on his clasped hands as if the monk were telling him something that transformed the bones of his skull to lead.

"And you—" he began. He longed to say, "How can you, who're the father of this woman's child, go straight from the murder of her husband and the death of her lover to encourage a fourth man to take her?"

But like an open psalter the monk read his thought; and having done so, he quickly moved his crucifix so that the candle-rays from the chantry flickered upon the figure's face.

"I like *this one*," he said, "better than any I've ever had. It belonged to Abbot Cust and on his death-bed he sent it me. The lay-brother who nursed him brought it—unknown to the present Abbot."

The sea-green eyes above the beard that covered the sword-hilt grew still more like those of an astonished child; for it was apparent to him that across Father Rheinalt's ravaged features there had actually flickered a smile.

The Prince turned back to the pain of the crucifix from this kindred pain that had the power of smiling.

"I don't—see," he whispered hoarsely into his beard, as if rather to the hilt of his sword than to his companion, "how the sight of suffering like that—even if it *is*"—and he muttered the syllables "Mary! Joseph!" —"the pain of the cross—could help anyone to go through what you've gone through."

Father Rheinalt bent his head and was silent. For some reason the unfathomable life-force that emanated from those glaucous eyes was harder to bear just then than what was in his mind.

"I don't suppose," he said, without looking up, "that I can make it clear to you, my Prince; for"—and the man actually smiled again— "God hasn't given me the gift of our good Pascentius. But when you take pain as the—as the basis of human life—and—and—as—as *the life of God*—there comes up—for it isn't *the whole* of God—something from underneath—that is—but what am I saying? Who am I to talk like this?"

And to Owen's astonishment the monk lifted his head, clutched the crucifix as if it were a weapon, and striking its foot against the bench between them, uttered the identical words that Owen himself had been hearing in his heart all that night. "If only the French come, my Prince, all may yet be well!"

They rose simultaneously from their seat after that; and the Prince said with his old authority, "Go back now, Father, and see if she sleeps, and if there's water and wine where she is. If it's well with her, I wish you to spend the night with me in my room. Don't fail me, Father. We've got to decide what's to be done if—if the French *don't* come!"

It turned out that Lowri ferch Ffraid had fallen asleep, fallen asleep even while they'd been talking about her in the chapel; and it wasn't long before the two Welshmen's blood-and-iron discussion of new methods to deal with the enemy ended with the Father's falling asleep, too.

So heavy a drug was the wine Owen forced his temperate guest to drink that he had no difficulty in lifting him, unawaked as he was, upon his own bed, and covering him with as many "black lions rampant" as could warm the most ascetic bones!

The following morning broke with radiant sunshine over Harlech and the sea; and the Prince, though his bones were stiff and cramped from his bivouac on the floor, could feel the spring-warmth pouring strength and vitality into his blood. It was in the power of the sun and of the dancing sun-sparkles on the inflowing tide that he entered the Arglwyddes's room.

Father Rheinalt had passionately entreated him not to risk everything in some wild uncalculated move against the invaders, but to wait for a week or so. "At least," the Father had said, "till news comes from Rhys Ddu."

And this advice, proceeding from the most uncompromising Welsh-man in the castle, had had its weight with him. Indeed it had jumped shrewdly enough with his own instinct. "There'll be a time," he thought, "to avenge our dead, when we know for certain the French are *not* coming!"

Never in all their life had the heart of the Arglwyddes been more difficult to soften than it was that day. But he managed it at last, such was the power and vital force given him by that dazzling sun and those dancing waves.

As with Odysseus, when the goddess had made him "taller and fairer in form and in face," it was hard for the mother, even of all those lost sons, even of her lost eldest-born, to resist the man she loved when he wooed her as if she were a young girl, when he courted her with all the magnetic concentration of their first love.

It was characteristic of the Prince that his pleasure at being reconciled with the Arglwyddes ran like quicksilver through his veins and added yet another vibration to those which poured through him that morning from the sun and the sea.

Feelings, emotions, sensations such as he hadn't known since his childhood radiated through him; and his spirit felt so light, so integral, so compact and free that what had hitherto been a patient cult became a spontaneous joy. He kept flinging his soul—or, if you will, *imagining* that he flung his soul—far out to the horizon, where it seemed to hear clear and sweet, from a yet *further* horizon, the mystic song of the Birds of Rhiannon!

He even began to feel happier about the fate of the Maid and Rhisiart. Henry of Lancaster *had* his generous moments, and perhaps— Whereas where his dead brother was concerned, he felt his presence so vividly that it seemed to him as if he were eating for him, drinking for him, losing himself in the elements for him! His brother's nearness seemed to double his delight in the multitudinous sun-sparkles upon those in-rolling waves.

He had the feeling that something had broken—some dam, some barrier, some rampart within him—and that he could draw on a reservoir of power the depth of which he had never even suspected.

So boundless was his feeling of power that he didn't hesitate to snatch his friend Broch from under the very hands of the man's elfish wife; nor, with the assistance of Broch, did he hesitate to entertain Oldcastle and Denis by taking them to the rock-pools beyond the jetty where there were a number of sea-anemones of startling and incredible beauty. Whether it was due to the fact that a large portion of Owen's exalted mood came from the glittering sunshine and dazzling sea, or whether the spiritual forces he was drawing on were non-moral forces, the fact remains that his feelings were by no means all noble or righteous as with his bald-headed friend he escorted the two Englishmen along the shore. He felt outrageously thankful that he *had* instructed Gam—not without a hint to that unscrupulous young woman from Mōn—to use his knife upon the Scab at any serious pinch.

It even occurred to him, and without a flicker of shame, that as he sat with Father Rheinalt in the porch of the chapel, and contemplated that row of coffins, he had completely *forgotten* that under one of those palls the single blue eye and the ruddy disfigurement of Derfel's prophet were already beginning to revert to the anonymous monochrome of the dust. Nor did he repent for a moment—but on the contrary stroked his beard with grim satisfaction—when Father Pascentius, mounted on one of the castle's best horses and attended by two of the castle's sturdiest guards, not to speak of a baggage-mule loaded with the most precious books of the castle libraries, came jogging and swaying past them along the shore-road.

Father Pascentius looked to him in no sense a pathetic figure. It would have needed the more sympathetic eye of Rhisiart to note the clumsy attempt of the man's plump fingers—entangled as they were with the reins he held—to make his familiar metaphysical gesture, reducing all the changes and chances of this mortal life to the infinite indifference of the Absolute.

Let us hope that the tremendous shade of Saint Thomas himself noticed that blundering attempt of the hands that had composed the great Cistercian Commentary to bid farewell to Harlech with an appropriate gesture. Some of the most piteous things in life are these same brave whistlings and drummings and hummings wherewith, when our stars are crossed, we mechanically save our faces and cover our retreats; and those of us who feel tenderer to the weaknesses of an orthodox Scholiast than Owen did may be permitted to hope that before getting very far on his road to face the toothless sarcasms of Chancellor Young the Father's roving eyes may light upon a wayside plant even more uncommon than the *Cardamine Pascentius*.

It was not long before the two Welshmen and the two Englishmen were seated upon a sun-warmed ledge above the now ebbing tide, listening to the gurglings and gaspings of the water as the inflowing waves alternately brimmed and emptied the cavernous recesses below them, and covered or left exposed the jagged shell-bitten surfaces of the rocks.

The talk between the four men turned to the fate of Master Brut. "I suppose I'd recant in his place," Sir Thomas Oldcastle was saying, "for the Archbishop's as fond of the smell of burning flesh as he is of basting peacocks. But a man never knows! As a matter of breviary," he went on, with a whimsical glance at the retreating figure on horseback, "and in the Blessed Order of Holy Reason of which I'm a humble Brother, my *Credo* is to enjoy such wine as you gave us last night, to savour the heavenly essences of meats and fishes, to get drunk on the raptures of Venus and Priapus—and be ready to believe whatever the Archbishop believes! But, gentlemen, when I saw one of his Grace's latest burnings, I found myself worshipping not the correct theology of that cruel old time-server, but the divine spirit in any poor human breast that could bear such pain and yet not yield! On my life, gentlemen, that burning may be the cause of *my* burning! Till then, and this was but a few months ago, I was only a Lollard in what you might call a Platonic sense; that is to say, as a matter of ideal intellectual truth. But after watching those two faces—the face of that ambitious, selfish, soulless old man, and the face of that angelic young martyr—shall I tell you what I decided? I decided that even though the Archbishop's belief was *true* and the other's false, I was *all for the other!* I decided that it was better to die for the wrong than to torture for the right."

"Wouldn't the Lollards," interjected Denis Burnell, "torture us Catholics if they had the power?"

"Very likely," returned the other, "but not the young man *I* saw suffer. And *that's* the whole point. It isn't the Lollard's 'truth,' or the Catholic's 'truth,' that's the important thing. *Truth itself's* not the important thing. The important thing is the spirit to defy tryanny and pain. I can imagine"—he paused and chuckled—"only I'm such a whoreson coward! But I can imagine swearing I believed what I didn't believe and swearing I doubted what I didn't doubt, simply and solely to defy to the death *the kind of person* our present Archbishop is, and even the kind of—"

"This ledge you've brought us to, Sire," interrupted Denis Burnell, fearful lest Sir John—who had already had several flagons of old metheglin—might say something indiscreet, "is such a striking spot that I'd like to know if it has any particular name?"

"It has indeed, Master," replied Owen; and he looked quickly round to see if he dared, in the presence of his friend Broch, give full rein to his mystical pedantry. But Broch was staring at the two vessels in sight, each of them engaged in elaborate tacking movements against that difficult wind, so that neither encouragement nor disapproval could be got from him.

It wasn't only that the Prince delighted in letting his imagination, which was considerable, and his learning, which even little Lu respected, have their free fling; he itched to impress Oldcastle, whom of all living Englishmen he most admired, with the superiority of Welsh legends over those of England. So he explained to his guests that this rocky ledge was called "Cadair Brān" and that it was here that the mysterious god of their fathers beheld the fleet of the King of Ireland. And, he went on, for the temptation in his present high spirits to dilate on this topic was irresistible, arguing that the only way, as you pursued the long reversion of demigods, by which the true Immortals could be reached, was to follow their traditional pedigrees *to the end*.

"Where," he went on to explain, while the forks of his beard trembled in the listening breeze, "the pedigrees become silent—where, in fact, a name has no 'fab' or 'ferch' affixed to it—we touch the depths. I used to beg my friend Iolo to make a litany of the names thus reached, so that we might invoke them with the more reverence *just because* they have no father and no mother! I often think that the saints of whom we know least are the most powerful; and in the same way—"

But Broch-o'-Meifod hesitated not to interrupt him. "One of those ships is from Mōn," he announced. "I know her build. Those Tudors are the best ship-builders we have. I fancy, my Prince, she brings young Efa's betrothed."

But here Sir John broke in. "If Master Broch," he said, "knows yonder fancy-rigged vessel that's as high above the water as a church-porch and has a poop like a whoreson whale, I can tell you, Prince, what the other is. 'Tis a Frenchman or I'm no Englishman! Do'ee mark the height of that mast, Denis? And the weight of the sail they're hauling down? There! They've got her! And in good time too, or over she'd have gone! Look, look, Masters, there's her ensign going up! 'Tis as I said. She's a French maid and a royal one too! Oh, that old Jack Horne of Deptford were here with his funny little—but what am I saying? Pardon me, Prince Glendourdy, but I never *could* look at a French ship without laughing. But 'tis the truth before God. This Western Sea don't suit the cut of a French craft as well as it does ours, whether Welsh *or* English. Christ! They're both off again! And if this breeze doesn't drop they won't be into harbour, no! by Christ, not your Welsh one *nor* my French one, for an hour yet! And even then, if yonder mole's the best welcome you can give them—though I can't speak about the ship from Mōn for I don't know that build of bow or how she answers to the helm—I can swear to you the boat I call French —though she *may* be one of those heavier Portuguese craft—I forget their fancy name!—will be mighty put to it to get near that jetty of yours or to cast even a long hawser on't."

"Sir John knows what he's—" began Denis; but Broch-o'-Meifod cut him short with an involuntary: "Well done, lads!" as both crews with equal success swung their vessels to the wind and sailed off on another tack.

The Prince tried to catch Broch-o'-Meifod's eye, for he wanted to warn him that there was no reason why they should betray to their visitors the extreme importance to Harlech just now of any news from France. It was unlikely that Sir John, at any rate, could be ignorant of the assembling of that fleet at Brest; but he *might* be, and if there were a chance he was, it was silly to refer to it.

But Broch-o'-Meifod was a very difficult person to communicate with by looks. In the first place his eyes were so deeply set in his great bald head and were so peculiar in themselves that it was hard to exchange any quick glance of understanding with them. The chief peculiarity of Broch-o'-Meifod's eyes was that both the pupils and the irises were so small in comparison with the white convexities out of which they appeared that when the least mist or watery film blurred them they assumed a dull, opaque, neutral tint, and became completely devoid of expression.

But since from the look of things there was, as Oldcastle had said, little chance of either of these ships reaching land for some while, Broch-o'-Meifod now proceeded to climb down from Brān's Seat and, sinking on his knees, began to examine the contents of a rock-pool from which the retreating tide had only just withdrawn. There was evidently plenty of water still in this pool, for the Prince, who was seated between his two guests, saw his friend pull up one of the leather sleeves of his jerkin and plunge his arm between the glistening rocks.

Presently he held up a star-fish to their sight, and while the sunshine danced and flickered in gleaming points of dazzlement up and down his great dripping muscles, "Dead!" he cried. "It's dead!" And rising on his knees and making a tremendous sweep of his arm he flung the creature far out above the breaking waves, where it sank with a splash.

"What is it, Sir John?" the Prince allowed himself to ask; for Oldcastle's shoulders were shaking with laughter.

"What is it this time, Sir John?" echoed Denis in the tone of one who had been a little longer than he liked in the society of such a Democritus.

But Broch-o'-Meifod relapsed into a sitting posture on his heels, his bald head gleaming before them with a veritable aureole of sun-sparkles. "Out with it, Sir John!" he panted, for he had used most of his breath in disposing of the star-fish, "or I'll tell them myself, if you can't speak!"

"You're enough to make an Archbishop laugh!" gasped Oldcastle. "I've seen plenty of people in my time fish for live things in the sea and shout when they've killed them; but I've never seen anyone fish for the dead."

"Broch's got a mania for death, Sir John," explained Owen, thoughtfully pulling at his beard. "It's an old story with us who know him."

The visitor contemplated the squatting sage before him and hummed a tune. Wondering what the man was thinking, and a little ashamed of having dragged his old friend's eccentricity into the open like this, the Prince gazed at Sir John as Sir John was gazing at Broch.

"What a face he has!" he thought. "And it's the same face—but it's aged a lot more than mine!" And as he looked at the man scene after scene came back to his memory of their student-days together in London at the Inns of Court. "It's all that stubbly hair," he thought, "that makes him look old!"

Indeed Oldcastle's unruffled brow, full lips, and ruddy complexion were offset by a short rough growth of grey hair, hair that was almost too sheep-like to be called curly, but which, though it served the purpose of beard, moustache, and whiskers, gave a curiously harmless expression to his physiognomy; gave it, in fact, the look of a humorous and philosophic sheep-dog, from whose woolly visage a pair of whimsically-affectionate brown eyes looked forth upon the world.

"So you're a death-lover, are you, Master Broch?" he said, leaning forward from Brān's Seat, with his sun-burnt hands on his knees. "I've heard of such men in China and Cathay and I met a hermit once in Muscovy who spoke to the same tune. I take it that by 'death' you don't mean the loss of your identity, Master Broch, but rather the passing into—"

The great blurred head and gigantic torso in front of him composed themselves into an opaque and featureless monolith, out of which issued words, as if out of the statue of Memnon. It was only by blinking and screwing up their eyes that the three men on the ledge were able to face the dazzling sunshine which the sea-sparkles multitudinized into myriad pin-points of blinding radiance.

"I *do* mean the loss of my identity!" were the words that now issued from the haloed rotundity on the top of this dusky plinth. "That's exactly what I *do* mean! By worshipping death instead of life I worship the *opposite* of life; and since the essence of life—ask my Prince over there!—is the thing that's forever crying, 'I! I! I!' death must be the extinction of this 'I'!"

Sir John's full lips emitted a low whistle, and his woolly countenance wrinkled itself into a courteous attempt to suppress a profane chuckle.

The Prince sighed, and stroked first one and then the other of the forks of the beard. *"Is* that a French vessel?" he thought. "And if it is, will it bring news from Brest?

"But isn't it possible," remarked Denis—while in his mind he thought, "How tiresome all these grand dogmatisms are! We know nothing of life; how can we know anything of death? The more time these two waste in discussions of this kind, the sooner their rebellion'll be over"—"isn't it possible, Master Broch, that life and death are as closely connected as night and day, man and woman, good and evil? Isn't it possible that the reality of things includes them both and explains them both, just as what you call 'nothingness' *is nothing,* unless there's something to compare it with?"

The sun so dazzled the eyes of the three men seated on "Cadair Brān" that it was impossible to see the effect of these metaphysical subtleties upon the figure before them.

The Prince, however, as he turned his head towards the speaker caught the fact that what Denis *said* was on a completely different plane from what Denis *thought.*

As for Sir John, he was keeping all this while a shrewd weather eye on those two tacking vessels. But whether it was that both the handling of the ship with the crew from Mōn and the handling of the ship with the crew from France were so different from the English way that it tickled his fancy, or whether it was that the spectacle of that dusky torso in front of them, with its dazzling halo, advocating death when it looked so preposterously alive, struck him as comical, the man never ceased his low chuckling laugh.

It needed all the respect he had for him to keep the Prince from feeling irritated by this unseasonable merriment; and as it went on the sensation grew upon him that not only he and his friend Broch, but their whole race, their whole cause, their whole country were being subjected to a detached and unsympathetic amusement.

"Mary, Joseph!" he groaned in his beard, and he prayed that Broch would stop philosophizing even if it meant that he had to move out of hearing and hunt for dead star-fish among remoter rock-pools. Above all he prayed that the giant wouldn't punish him for starting this unfortunate conversation by any reference to his own mental peculiarities.

"We shall never understand these English," he thought, "and they'll never understand us. What a pity all civilized nations don't talk Latin!"

Several seagulls were whirling about the men's heads just then, their wings irradiated by the sun-glare and their wild screams reaching in *sound* the same pitch of quivering intensity reached by the sea-sparkles in *light;* and the fantastic notion crossed Owen's mind, while Sir John began answering Broch, that those scintillating birds, that kept darting down and sheering off above them, were feeding on the shoals of thoughts rising from their four heads, spitting out the English thoughts like the bones of dog-fish, and digesting his own and Broch's like fresh mackerel!

"Don't you see, Master," Sir John was saying—and the shameless thought entered the Prince's wrought-up mind that the worthy knight as he leaned forward with his hands on his knees might have been using Brān's ledge as a close-stool—"don't you see that the bountiful Creator has been pleased in his inscrutable wisdom so to construct our mortal intelligence and fashion the frame-work of our terrestrial minds that all ultimate reasoning is impossible? How could we live, Master; how could we enjoy our meats and our wines and our venery, or the classic authors, or the Holy Scriptures, or the blessed light of the sun, if our Creator hadn't *blackened out* for us with the celestial juice of the sweet grapes of his divine *Nescience* all knowledge of these remote things? When we say 'Life' we might as well say 'Blub-a-Blub,' like the Shoreditch idiot. When we say 'Death' we might as well say 'Ding-a-Dong,' like the great bell of St. Martin's. All that is permitted to our intelligence, Master, all that our minds are made for, is to fear God and forgive— But pardon me, gentles all! Pardon me, Prince de Galles et Prince de Bon Compères, there's another ship in sight—and—by Christ —if she isn't—" and even while he uttered the words he was clambering eagerly, for all his portly figure, up the side of a slippery rock a little to the right of them and more seaward than Broch's pool.

"By the fig of the Pope if she isn't—yes! by Jesus, she *is!*—old Jack Redcliffe of Bristol and his *Merry Moll!*"

But if the sight of the Bristol buccaneer—for Master Redcliffe was at once a King's man and a high-seas pirate—was a mischievous joy to the gallant knight, the sight of this group of personable gentry standing exactly where he had intended to land was evidently disconcerting to the Bristol captain. He was sailing close to the wind and near to the shore with the·intention of carrying off what booty he could while bad news and local dissensions kept the Welsh court within its walls, when the sight of these four formidable gentlemen, apparently guarding the very landing-place for which he was steering, changed his intention. Straight out to sea, therefore, with the offshore wind filling her sails, he steered the *Merry Moll,* only to find himself in the direct sea-path of the high-bulwark'd French vessel, which was now, though very slowly and under thin canvas, working her way shoreward.

The redoubtable commander of the Bristol ship evidently regarded this foreign craft as a prize sent him by a sympathetic Providence, and from the stir on board it was clear he intended to show his gratitude.

As to the vessel from Mōn it was soon obvious to all who were watching that she was hauling down the few sails she could use in that difficult wind; and indeed a minute or two later she dropped her anchor.

"Little Efa's betrothed," thought Owen, "it a true Tudor. He's decided to watch events!"

Meanwhile several local fishing-boats, that had been launched before the *Merry Moll* appeared, hurriedly put back to land; while, led by Broch-o'-Meifod, both the Prince and Denis joined Sir John on his high rock of observation.

Here the four tall men were in full sight of both French and English vessels; but it was soon plain that the two crews were far too occupied in their personal encounter to pay any attention to spectators.

"There she flies, the Fleur-de-lys of France!" cried Sir John; "ha, yes! And d'ye see *that?* Do ye know what *that* is, my Masters?" He turned to the Prince, as he spoke, and Owen smiled back in response; and then he sighed heavily and a lump rose in his gullet, for what he now saw on that queer-shaped unwieldy vessel brought all his adventurous youth into his throat.

Up to the top of the highest mast of the ship there now slowly fluttered, till it waved well above the Fleur-de-lys, a long streaming pendant of rich *couleur de rose*—the royal oriflamme of Saint Denis!

"*That* means we're at war with France," said Burnell quietly.

But the incorrigible Sir John had begun laughing again. "Look! Look!" he cried. "By Cock and Crish! if Jack's not nailing up his old

Bristol shop-sign, straight from the water-front by the town-bridge! Think of the rogue's gall—taking to sea his old city merchant-mark! No! No! We know you're no pirate, Jack. We know you're a huffing and scruffing rope-maker of Bristol-town! *You* can't see what he's nailed up, Prince Owen; but I can tell you I've heard that piece of Gloucestershire pine-wood groan and creak and whine in the wind when you couldn't smell the mud for the tide! He's one of *us,* is Jack, the rope-merchant! I've heard him read a tract of Master Wycliffe's from cover to cover in the old Bull's Head at Bristol docks, and not a gospel-point did the man miss! 'Twas the Bishop's Court that made a sea-thief of him. You watch, my Masters, you watch how he tumbles the Frenchmen!"

The Prince couldn't help glancing at the great bald head at his side to see how his fellow-Welshman received this lively information; but Broch was too intent upon the exchange of bow-shots and catapult-shots and oaths and curses and howls of derision and yells of pain and triumph, and upon the ominous splashes in the water and upon the hideous scraping that the wooden sides of the two vessels made as they grated against each other, to give any heed to the talk of his fellow spectators.

Denis Burnell had been aware for some while of a crowd of armed men collecting at the foot of the castle and of a noisy exchange of shouts between them and the fishermen who were dragging up their boats; and it didn't now fail to cross his mind as he saw a group of these men rushing towards them, following what looked like a human butter-fly, all black and red and brandishing a silver trumpet, that it was within the bounds of possibility that the bitterness against the Prince had culminated in a successful insurrection; in which case the chance that the rebels would respect the lives of Glendourdy's guests was small indeed!

But it wasn't only the bald philosopher of death who was watching what was going on in front of him with such spell-bound interest. Both the Prince and Sir John were far to absorbed in the struggle between the ships' crews to concern themselves with what transpired behind them.

To the Prince there was something painful and repulsive about this fight. It wasn't only that he regretted the Frenchmen's defeat, but

Jack Redcliffe's men were such a rough piratical set, and so well used to this sort of attack, that the French noblemen, of whom there were several on board and Owen even thought he recognized the arms of two of them, namely Gascoigne de la Roche and Varge-Deslormes, found themselves at a disadvantage that was distressing to see. "There must be something essentially gross about English humour," he thought, as he heard Sir John's chuckles when both these courtly gentlemen, ·unable to use their weapons at such close quarters, were overpowered by the Bristol crew, who with jubilant shouts were now clambering from one ship to the other.

And what was this? What in the Virgin's name were these ruffians doing now? His eyes beheld what was happening; but it was too monstrous, too grotesque to be real!

Down were coming both those haughty gonfalons and up was going every stitch of sail on the straining rigging of the *Merry Moll;* until Sir John's words, "With the breath of the Lord behind them and a good gospel-rope round the neck of my Lady," Jack Redcliffe steered out to sea with his rich chance-given prize!

Owen heard the shouts of his men behind him, but he heard them as sounds that were irrelevant and meaningless, like a chorus. of humming midges on a hot day. The insolent triumph of those Bristol rogues dragged down his spirits till they sank in a moment as low as all that day they had been mounting high. He *saw* the ceremonious words on the special parchment used by Charles the Sixth. He *saw* the familiar Royal Seal of France fastened to the document in the delicate way the French Court always did such things. And he saw them being chuckled over by this scurrilous Jack, just as this equally profane Sir John had made sport of their distinguished bearers. They lacked all reverence, these English, whether high-born or low-born. All they could do was to take and to keep; and laugh while they took and preach while they kept!

He now became aware of an object in the water, about a bow-shot from where he stood, that resembled a human head. Yes! it was a man in the sea. Suddenly it disappeared, but, a moment later, appeared again. It was certainly a swimmer, and a swimmer nigh to the limit of his endurance.

He surveyed this struggling "ego" on the verge of perishing, and he couldn't help glancing at Broch to see whether *he'd* seen it.

To his surprise, the giant, who was unable to swim, was deliberately advancing into the water; and while he glanced he waved his arms to encourage the swimmer to make a final effort.

Irritated by the cries behind him, for he wasn't in a mood just then to deal with his subjects, Owen swung round on his heel and fiercely ordered the crowd to stay where they were. Then he turned his eyes to the swimmer; and from him to his friend's bald head, which was all that could be seen of Broch-o'-Meifod, who was now standing in seven feet of sea; and in a flash there rushed into his mind the description of Brān's power of wading—*nyt oed uawr y weilgi yna, y ueis yd aeth ef:* "There wasn't much water there, and he went wading."

No one but the Prince himself caught the quick imploring look that reached him from that bald head; but he obeyed it without question and hurriedly began taking off his clothes.

Even while he did this—so quick is thought—he said to himself: "Owen is Owen still! Never dead nor alive shall Hal Bolingbroke, or any other Hal, or John, or Jack, tow *me* after him! *And what I am my Welsh are!* They can out-sail us, out-fight us, out-trade us, out-laugh us—but they can't *out-last* us! It'll be from our mountains and in our tongue, when the world ends, that the last defiance of man's fate will rise!"

Stark naked now and stumbling over the slippery weeds and the sharp rock-jags and the cutting rock-shells he could see the bald skull of his friend like a shimmering bell-buoy in the water and far out beyond it the head of the swimmer whose strokes had now become those final black, blind, automatic motions of a life-pulse at bay, crying *no! no! no!* to the down-sucking fathoms of salt-swallowing death.

Denis Burnell, who oddly enough was nervous of the water and unable to swim, watched with interest the deliberate movements of his fellow-Englishman at this juncture: for, divested of his leather boots and his brocaded tunic, the burly knight, panting for breath, but still chuckling in wheezy gasps, was now himself in the sea and swimming with the easy aplomb of a porpoise.

The crowd from the castle, heedless of their Prince's command, had begun to swarm over the rocks; but Denis took no notice of them. What absorbed his attention just then were the events taking place in that element from which he himself couldn't help shrinking.

He glanced at the two ships—the French prize and the Bristol pirate —and it struck him as one of the most disturbing attributes of this dazzling expanse of sea-water that it should blend the two vessels into one—one fantastically-shaped sea-monster, heading for the horizon. Another phenomenon that arrested his attention was the inhuman appearance of certain exposed portions of the drowning creature now being dragged to land by the Prince. Could that be a human head? Could those hairy arms belong to a human being? The water around the two figures was kept in a perpetual turmoil by the Prince's struggles not to lose hold of his treasure-trove and yet not to be dragged down by its insensate struggles.

But there! They were both in contact with John now, whose rotund form seemed to be prepared, like an air-blown wine-skin, to support any number of exhausted swimmers.

Panting and spluttering and slipping many times on the sea-weed-covered rocks, Sir John no sooner found his feet than he began making attempts to shout to Denis, but each time he reached some particular point, he would fall into such a paroxysm of laughter that, rocking and swaying as he stood, he would find it impossible to retain both his balance and his power of speech.

Nor was his merriment—though not very polite at that moment— without its excuse; for with mutterings and gabblings and chatterings and many disgorgings of swallowed salt-water, there sank down, on the first dry rock he reached, an enormous, almost human-sized chimpanzee.

The crowd from the castle, by no means all soldiers or even all grown-up people, now began to gather in a nervous fascinated circle round this unusual object on the rock; and the sight of their stupefaction started Sir John off upon a renewed laughing-fit.

"*Dyma,* Maitre Jacques Bonhomme!" cried a cook from Brittany; and several more daring children began throwing stones at the frightened creature, but ceased at once when it uttered a jabbering defiance and rose on its hind-legs.

The Prince and Broch-o'-Meifod had both joined Oldcastle now, but

Denis hesitated to approach them till the Prince had re-assumed his clothes. He felt a little ashamed of himself with his dry hair and un-ruffled garments in the presence of these dripping heroes, even though they *had* rescued nothing but an ape.

He bent down and picked up a seagull's feather and began mechani-cally stroking it. He had a queerly complicated nature and he experi-enced no mental shock nor did it strike him as at all inappropriate when from the rescued pet of the French nobles his thoughts fled to Mistress Lowri. "I shall get her," he said to himself, "and when the war's over I'll take her abroad for a while. I'll tell the King it's a pilgrimage." And he began for the hundredth time imagining what he would feel when he showed Mistress Lowri the wonders of the Continent.

While he was lost to all his surroundings in these thoughts of Mistress Lowri the third vessel of this gathering of swift keels had been cleverly and expeditiously roped to the jetty, and a fashionably-dressed young chieftain, with a countenance as crafty as it was intelligent, was at this moment advancing straight towards him, evidently taking him for one of Owen's adherents.

Still a little ruffled in his self-respect by not being able to swim, and pondering whether, if he'd been in Owen's case, he would have let that monkey drown, he found himself instinctively taking Owen's part against this Tudor from Anglesea who had come to claim his bride. He had heard on all sides in the castle rumours of Crach Ffinnant's choice of this man, as the one destined to take the Prince's place; and as he scrutinized him now he seemed to detect in his face every quality needed for remorseless but infinitely cautious ambition.

He turned his head. Ah! the Prince was being helped into his clothes now by that fellow Gam who'd become such a slave of his. *There!* He was handing over to *him* the rescued monkey! And it certainly looked as if the poor beast understood that henceforth he was to be as much a slave of Gam as Gam was a slave of Owen! "Were Gam as naked as the other," thought Denis, "they'd make a fair pair!" And as he moved forward to greet the young chieftain he decided to hold him in conversation as long as possible, so as to give Owen a breathing-space. He was in complete possession of himself now; and as he greeted the man in the airy, frivolous manner that had become the fashion in place of the old chivalric courtesy, he said to himself, beneath his conventional words: "How anyone as sensible as Sir John *can* go off into such vulgar guffaws just because a beast's saved in place of a man! Mother of God! As if we weren't *all* monkeys with our chatterings and our antics!" And while he kept his cold inscrutable grey stare fixed on the restless eyes of this proud youth, his mind reverted to the loosened hair and exposed breasts of the woman *he* had come to fetch—no wilful young Efa, but a mad sorceress—and his spirit faced his future with this strange being in perfect calmness.

"I shall subdue her again, as I did before," he thought, and all manner of intimate passages between them rose up in his mind. "It's because I'm neither excited by her, nor afraid of her. It's because I *like* her. It's because I'm *fond of her*. And I don't suppose anyone else in the world—certainly not her daughter—could say *that!* The monk loves her, but he doesn't *like* her. Think of only being *liked* by one person in the whole world! She becomes a young girl again with me. Nobody else does that for her. And *that,* after all, is the thing with a woman that outlasts *everything else!*"

"Exactly, my dear young sir," he was now saying; and there was something about his neatly-trimmed, pointed beard and about his Saxon *sang-froid* and his cold, detached, indifferent stare that made the Tudor feel as if the prow of his proud boat had struck an iceberg. "Like yourself," Denis went on, having made sure by a glance at the man he had left that Gam had gone off with his fellow "familiar," and that Owen's fantastic Herald, in his tabard of black lions, was delivering his message, "like yourself I am on my own business here. The Baron of Glendourdy has just picked up from the water a valuable present sent him by the King of France. From what I've seen of this treasure-trove it ought to prove a most interesting addition to the castle's bestiary. Have you chanced to see in your travels, sir, the talking Ape of the Emperor Manuel? No court, of course, can be considered civilized without *some* rarities of this kind. Even King Harry has a white mule at Berkhampstead that breaks wind to each letter of the French King's name. I believe, if the word 'Glendower' is uttered in its presence, it—"

But it was no longer necessary to block the young man's audience with the Prince. Owen seemed completely himself now. He was apparently holding the Herald and the crowd at arm's length while he said goodbye to the sea-drenched Broch. Queer that he should be shaking hands with the man and giving him his blessing when the fellow was only retiring to the castle to change his clothes! Had Denis been nearer, however, he would have been astonished to see how calm two Welshmen can be when they are trying to break each other's hearts.

"So this is the end," Owen was thinking, "a monkey instead of a fleet; and my friend deserting me! Well, well, old conjurer, you've got to swim alone to land now, or sink forever! You knew what was coming when that woman arrived, and now it's come!"

But his words to Broch were calm. "No, no—it's all right, old friend. You needn't say anything. There are times when we're forced to make our choice. I made mine at Glyndyfrdwy when I broke my crystal. You made yours just now when you were tempted to let the sea cover your old skull and have done with it once and for all. Goodbye, my only friend. I fully understand. I know what you feel about Morg and the girls. No! no! Don't say any more. Take what men you need and off with you to Snowdon! In Snowdon you can defend your women against King Hal, forever! No! we've discussed it enough. We part as we've lived—nearer to each other than any Welshmen have been to any other Welshmen, since Arthur disappeared!"

The salt-water dripped from every curve and every angle of Broch's figure; and for some queer reason he'd been trying, ever since he came out of the sea, to make a great slippery sea-weed ribbon remain in position round one of his huge wrists.

But now he gave this up and threw the thing away. "You're being as cruel to me as you can, Owen ap Griffith," he said, spitting some brine out of his mouth. "But remember this, my love and Prince! We may be play-actors before each other, night and day, for fifty years; but a time comes when we have to act our part *for ourselves alone.* We shall meet again, my Prince—*once again;* and then—"

If there were two kinds of brine on Broch's face, as he pushed his way through the crowd, past the Herald, who tried to hold him back, past Gam and the monkey, both of whom gave him an obscure greeting, to where Philip Sparrow awaited him at the postern-gate, there were three kinds on the face of the Prince, for the monkey, either in love or in bewilderment, had bitten his cheek as they struggled in the water, and the tears that flowed from his eyes were mingled with blood as well as with sea-salt.

But the impatient and agitated Elphin was now at last permitted to hand to his master the travel-stained letter, the foreign bearer of which, riding post-haste from Milford Haven, had already excited the castle to fever-pitch.

The Prince could see at once—as he raised his head after reading this hurried but ceremonious scrawl, signed by the famous names of Patrouillart de Trie and Robert de la Heuze—that the temper of his subjects had completely changed. He was their venerated leader again; and both Crach Ffinnant and his Demon-Saint were completely forgotten.

"May I announce it in the presence of these English noblemen, my Prince?" asked Elphin.

"You may announce it to the Irish Sea, my lad," laughed Owen. "All Ardudwy seems to know it already!" And in the most resonant voice that had ever been heard on that Harlech beach the young man proclaimed: "To the Principality and Dominion of our high and mighty sovereign Lord, Owen ap Griffith Fychan, and to the Realm of England lately subject to the noble and gracious Prince Richard, the Second of that name: be it understood and known of all men in both these nations and in all the countries and provinces and continents and islands abroad that the royal army conveyed by the royal fleet of the Royaume de France has safely anchored in Milford Haven, to aid and assist to the best of its power in the downfall of that sacrilegious and treacherous usurper, Henry Bolingbroke, falsely called Henry the Fourth. *God save Prince Owen!*" And so deafening was the shout that went up from the soldiers and people that it was only Denis, to whose side the dripping, fish-smelling Sir John had now shuffled, who heard what that incorrigible jester said.

"God save the King!" the old Lollard retorted. "And God confound the King's Archbishop!"

XX

KNIGHTS AND BISHOPS

THE SPRING had passed and most of the summer, when on Lammas Day, August the first, in the year of grace fourteen hundred and five, Herald Elphin and his young ally, Iago ap Cynan, stood together in the door-way of a large shepherd's hut, or *bwthyn,* overlooking the castle of Haverford West. The cottager, or *bwthynnwr,* to whom the hut belonged, was at their side, engaged at present in a political argument with Master Philip Sparrow to whose care, for both the Arglwyddes and Lady Mortimer had implored him to keep an eye on the lads during their first campaign, Owen had entrusted the two young friends.

It had been at Broch-o'-Meifod's express wish that Master Sparrow had remained with the Prince when he himself with his wife and daughters departed for Snowdon; and all the ladies, with whom the beautiful Elphin was such a favourite, had been delighted when the Prince—always indulgent in matters of this sort—had assigned the formidable Master Sparrow as body-guard to the Court Herald and his friend.

Elphin had just that moment turned to Master Sparrow, whose pre-cise position with regard to them had not been made very clear, and had petulantly enquired how soon he supposed the professional summons, to announce the capture of the castle to the burghers of the town, might be expected to arrive.

To this question Master Sparrow had seen fit to return no answer; and the impatient Herald and his friend could do no better than listen to the argument that was going on between the two men.

"Penfro's more English than Welsh," the shepherd was declaring, "and where her's not Welsh her's Flemish; and what *I* say is—"

"But *you're* a Welshman as much as I am," protested Master Spar-row, his high-pitched Powys-Maelor accent rising sharper and shriller the more his feelings were aroused. "What you people of the South don't see is that Owen ap Griffith is fighting for something larger than just Wales against England! He's fighting for the common people against the gentry in all Ynys Prydain! Your Flemish weavers will gain by his victory as much as we. When once the red dragon flies over every castle in the land—when once—I tell you!—Wales is what Owen wants to make her, with her Parliament for the Commonalty and her colleges for poor scholars, these curst gentry behind their stone walls will have to come to terms!

"We'll have *then,* Master Twm-o'-Bryn, what we've never had yet in the world, a real nation of the common people! I don't care how many foreigners there are in Penfro. To the Devil with your foreigners! If their sweat fattens our soil, and their fingers weave the wool of our sheep, they're our brothers. They're born of women like us, aren't they? They eat, drink, sleep like us, don't they? And when they're dead they stink like us. What do they pay tribute to Owen for, save to be kept from the malice of the men of the castles?

"Do'ee think I'm proud of these French knights, with their fol-de-rols and *garde-à-tois,* their trilla-lirras and fleur-de-luces? I'm ashamed to the marrow of my bones that we had to have them! But Owen knows what he's about. He's using knighthood to crush knighthood and chivalry to end chivalry! He's going to Tenby next, they say; then off, over the Usk, to Caerleon and Llantarnam! You've got to take a long view, Tom Shepherd, when it comes to this war. It'll go on, I tell you, even if Owen fails. It'll go on as long as there's a shepherd or a herdsman left in the land!

"These Frenchmen won't do us any lasting good. *They're* not workers like your Flemings. They're just the old love-your-lady and couch-your-lance gentry that the long-bows have un-saddled already!

"Times have changed, Twm-o'-Bryn, times have changed. Owen's doing more than he knows—bless his fork-beard! He may fail—Dewi Sant grant he don't!—but he's already lit such a beacon in this old land that *nothing* can put it out! It may be lost for a season—buried under the cinders of your Penfro *bwthyn* and of my Meifod *bwthyn*—but once lit it can never be extinguished."

"Gently, gently, Master Sparrow," protested the shepherd, winking at

Iago ap Cynan who had begun to give ear to their talk. "My wife's dad
in there," and he jerked his thumb towards the interior of the hut,
"can mind the Black Death; and the day when labouring men, such as
we, were beat and tormented and hanged by the neck for leaving their
masters' fields. *He* says—of course he's old and dotty, but I've listened
to 'un since I were a *bachgen* and I've never known him wrong—*he*
says that the land-serfs rose in many places and killed their lords, but
naught came o't, he says, save a speechless hatred, lying like a mill-
stone at the bottom of our hearts. There've been, Dad says, poor men's
revolts, since thousands of years before Jesus—but not a one of them
have done no good! Them as has got the land has got the souls of them
as has to live upon the land!"

"Master Sparrow!" interrupted Elphin who hadn't listened to a word
of this talk, so intent were his eyes on the extremely obscure and bewilderingly confused segment of the skirmishing below that the morning mists were alternately revealing and concealing. "Do you think,
Master Sparrow, that the time has come for us to go down and find the
Prince? It seems to me that there's hardly any more resistance. He'll
want me to announce his terms to his prisoners; as well as to those who
aren't yet his prisoners! I'd hate not to be there when he wants me."

Both Master Sparrow and the owner of the *bwthyn* turned upon the
young man faces of scorn. "Where are your eyes, lad?" the shepherd
remarked, revealing, Elphin thought, a deplorable ignorance of the
great world, and of how heralds were esteemed there. "Don't you see
that that wall you're looking at, between those trees, isn't the town wall
at all, but the *castle* wall! They've a-took the town hours ago—afore you
gentlemen were awake! Didn't ye hear what *Taid* said to little Olwen a
while since, when ye were making her cheeks so red by praising her
cakes?"

"No, Master, I didn't hear," cried Elphin eagerly; and he approached
closer to the shepherd, who regarded his excited young face with less
sympathy than if it had been the face of a well-horned tup.

"What *did* the old gentleman say to Mistress Olwen?" the lad repeated.

"Said young David came along here afore dawn, wi'all his pigs, and
'a told 'n town were took—took in the night. Didn't ye hear? But 'twere

when ye were asking little Olwen for more of her *bara brith* and her
were toasting at the coals! 'Twere little Olwen's curls ye were thinking
of, I reckon, more'n her grand-dad's talk."

Iago came forward at that point, casually and nonchalantly. He
hadn't hesitated himself, during this eventful night, when the town of
Haverford West was being pillaged, to lift aside the curtain of the
alcove on the left side of the hearth where little Olwen slept. But the
old *Taid* was as uneasy a sleeper as any amorous youth, and before the
girl was even aware that the most unscrupulous page in her Prince's
court was peering down upon her pillow a significant movement from
the ragged deer-skin on the other side of the hearth had sent the discomforted amorist back to his place by his sleeping friend.

"I must *not* play the fool," was what crossed the boy's mind now,
"with any more Luneds! I promised myself I wouldn't. It was only because—" And he tried to persuade himself, as he listened to Olwen's
father repeating what the swineherd had said, that the girl had "given
him a look" as she drew her curtain.

"No, it's you, it's you, Rhisiart ab Owen, that I must keep in mind.
First the Princess and then the Maid in armour! No light-of-love could
turn *you* aside. Nothing could turn you aside! They think the King has
caught you. Not a bit of it! Or if he has, he's caught a Tartar."

So absorbed was Iago in the competent steering of his life that as
soon as Olwen's father ceased mentioning the girl who had un-loosed
her black curls behind that curtain, after "giving him a look," there fell
between him and the confused mêlée in the valley below a kind of pictured glass.

A parallel intervention, only this was a muting medium rather than a
dimming one, rose between him and what Twm-o'-Bryn and Master
Sparrow were saying to each other. These subjective transparencies—
for a portion of his consciousness pierced through them—contained a
procession of moving images and grandiose sounds that weren't very
different, for they too were full of blood and iron, from the drama that
was now being revealed in the more objective medium of the morning
mist and commented upon by the men at his side.

It was thus through fluctuating projections of himself in various commanding situations that Iago heard the men's talk, and watched the
mist-magnified weapons and the rising and falling pensions, as be-

siegers and besieged struggled for the possession of that fragment of wall.

"I can tell ye, Twm," cried Master Sparrow, "who that tall knight is —there! he's down! No, he's up again! It's from the back of the castle he's trying to get in! He must have bridged the moat—it's narrow there —not more than a ditch! He'll do it! No he won't—he won't!"

Iago's mental mist was all gone now and his pictures of future glory gone with it. He was staring at that gap in the trees as eagerly as Elphin. Neither of them had ever seen such a desperate fighter as that tall knight, or one so reckless of wounds and death.

Presently the owner of the *bwthyn,* without displaying any particular emotion, said something in a low voice to Philip Sparrow who turned at once to the two lads. "Into the house with ye, gentlemen! My orders was clear—to keep ye both out of harm's way till we're on the march for London town! *Then* ye can show your mettle as ye will!"

Tom the Shepherd, or "Twm Bugail," had already entered the hut and his voice could be heard talking to his bed-ridden wife; but Master Sparrow, recognising that this was a critical test of his authority, had to go about the task of getting his young charges into shelter with considerable tact. But the truth is the man hadn't lived for five years cheek by jowl with Broch-o'-Meifod without noticeable modifications of his former cantankerousness. Besides, he himself found difficulty in withdrawing from this exciting scene, for he knew the *bwthyn's* one small window would be a wretched substitute for the open hillside.

Thus he kept pulling Elphin by the sleeve towards the door while all the while his own head was twisted round towards that narrow stage of desperate battle.

"Yes! It's Patrouillart de Trie, their chief French champion! I know his black armour. Like all those fool-knights he's been itching, ever since he came over, to do some mad impossible thing. *There!* They're making a sortie against him—coming over the wall with ladders! *Fool!* If they begin *that* he hasn't a chance. He'd better get away while he can. There's not a Welshman with him, look you! It's Patrouillart right enough. Can't you see his black armour? 'Tis the very mail he had on when we found them encamped at Milford. 'Tis a pretty suit. Our armourer can't hammer out all that fancy work. *There!* he's down! Yes, they've got him; and his men are running! Twm here knows the garrison well. Three were herdsmen from Somerset, he says, not to mention a dozen from Exmoor. Stout men of their hands, he says; and not over-fond of King Harry either. But they'll fight with any *coup de Dieus* or *grâce de Maries* like cur-bitten badgers! Don't like the cut of a French beard, he says. Into the house with ye, gentlemen! Those were the orders. No, there's not a Welshman down there. French and English; nothing but *them;* so what's it to us *who's* prisoners?

"Patrouillart must have thought he could take the castle alone if he got in from the back. There! All quiet. How his household ran! He must be a prisoner. They made a sortie and finished his little game. Well! he's a man anyway. Fair play to him; he certainly is a man! Think of trying to take Castell Haverford West by his own strength! Into the house with ye, gentlemen; and bear witness how I kept my word to the Prince.

"Fight like a devil that Frenchman did; and what armour! Our armourers don't bother with all those fol-de-rols. But 'twas a pretty sight; and he's a prisoner now! A tirra-lirra gentleman—curse his whoreson soul!—but, fair play to him, a man for all that; and a prisoner. Who'll wear that armour now? His magnificence Francis de Court, no doubt, King Harry's pet! And Lady Joan will have those black orna-ments made into bangles. Heigh ho! The great Patrouillart a prisoner! Into the house with ye, gentlemen, into the house!"

As they stooped to follow him under the low-hung lintel our two young friends had very different thoughts. Elphin said to himself: "Oh, that I'd been sent by Patrouillart to tell the Prince of his plight!" While Iago thought: "Our worthy Sparrow's torn between his peasants' revolt and his love of heroes. He hates Patrouillart on principle and adores him in practice! This is what might have happened to me if I hadn't ac-quired the philosophy of Rhisiart, that profound and penetrating man!"

Forcing himself, therefore, on the strength of what he considered his hero's principles, to avoid the peril of those "looks" which he was cer-tain Olwen was giving him, Iago deliberately sank into a concentrated speculation about his future life. The sight of the sea at Milford, though there were only a few French ships still anchored in the bay, had been not a little upsetting to him; and it was upon this overpowering attrac-tion that he now brought to bear the full force of what he had come to call "Rhisiart's philosophy."

How could he find these highly-placed damsels—by whose aid he was resolved to rise to power and glory—if he yielded to his longing to go to sea? It is true his friend Elphin often spoke of mermaids; "But I might as well ride to success," he thought "on the back of a unicorn, as on the tail of a mermaid."

The famous Prince Madoc had left the warring nations in disgust and had found some huge continent beyond the setting sun; but none had sailed there since, and even if he followed the example of that great man it was likely enough that there were no more continents to discover.

It almost seemed then that if he pursued the relentless path of Clerk Rhisiart he would have to give up not only the dark curls of the maidens of Penfro but the dark horizons of the sea as well, and this thought troubled him not a little.

"I feel," he said to himself, "as if this campaign were the crisis of my life," and he gave a quick sideways glance, full of the irritation of a person who is *suppressing* himself with a person who is *expressing* himself, at the illuminated countenance of his friend Elphin who, as they sat side by side on a bench that, by the notches upon it, had evidently served the purpose both of a butcher's block and a carpenter's table, was clearly absorbed in one thing only, the penetrating charm of this *bwthyn* interior.

The great Patrouillart, whether dead or alive, had passed completely from this young artist's mind. He too was forming resolutions; but these had only to do with certain changes he would make—when this campaign was over and he had proclaimed Owen's victory—in his Herald's Chamber at Harlech.

He had no idea that the shepherds' huts ever held such perfect specimens of twelfth-century carving as was the low bed, only raised a foot from the floor, upon which the sick woman was lying.

There were very few modern objects in the *bwthyn* of Twm-o'-Bryn. Indeed perhaps only one could be called so; and that was a particular kind of shepherd's crook, a kind that was now being made in Dorset in considerable quantity, and conveyed from Poole Harbour to Milford Haven by that enterprising burgess and ship-master, Dick Hussey of Wareham.

It was by marrying the old man's daughter that "Twm Bugail" had entered into possession of this homestead, whose name—"Ty-uwch-y-

Lyn"—indicated that it had stood for centuries on the hill above the castle-moat.

It was spacious enough, this single room round which Elphin's eyes now wandered; and to the lad's mind it possessed a special dignity and beauty, for it reminded him of his own home, "y Grug" or "the Mound," bestowed on his ancestor by Griffith ap Cynan.

The mist-distorted image he had glimpsed just now of that tall figure in black armour hurled back into the moat and deserted by his men had sunk deeply into his imagination.

This was the first vision of real war he had seen except for that Bristol pirate and the French ship, and his heart leapt up to think that it had been his privilege to see the great Patrouillart, singly and alone—like Peredur ab Evrawc, or Owain ab Urien—assaulting a whole castle!

The worst of it was—and how mixed up the events of life were!— whenever the heroic Patrouillart appeared between him and all these gracious objects that revived memories of his home in Edeyrnion a pulse of shame beat in his soul and a hot interior blush, though his friend couldn't see it, burned in his cheeks.

He ought to have rushed down the hill to the help of that noble knight, instead of letting himself be hustled into shelter along with these peasants and these women!

But Elphin's passion for a symbolic atmosphere soon overpowered his shame. "This scene," he said to himself, as he listened to Master Sparrow's prediction that the English labourers would throw off their lords' yoke the moment Owen crossed the border, "is a scene I'll never forget to my dying day. It'll most certainly affect the whole arrangement of my room when I get back to Harlech. And if only I could—oh! if only I could!—see all these heads as the heads of heraldic beasts!"

But whether he could give them an heraldic twist or not, the clear-cut classical lineaments of the sick woman as she rested immobile on her high pillows, the tumbled curls and mischievous mouth and restless eyes of Olwen, the long pointed nose and rough red hair of Twm, the familiar lanky black locks, pinched mouth and sunken eyes of Master Sparrow, along with the bowed grey head of the old man bending over the pot, made up a group of living creatures that roused an indescribable feeling in the lad's breast.

The walls were hung with old-fashioned bows and arrows, intermingled with the still carefully-polished harness of horses long since dead. A massive distaff and weaving-frame stood at the foot of the woman's bed. On the heavy oak-table in the centre of the room was a large wooden-bowl, surrounded by smaller ones of the same dark oak, rubbed smooth by a century's use, and each containing a battered wooden spoon.

There was a great bundle of dried furze-stalks piled up against the inner wall of the *bwthyn;* and every now and then the girl would cross the room to this pile and fetching a little bundle of these inflammable sticks throw them upon the hearth where the glowing bricks of peat caused them to break into flame.

But Elphin's artist-eye soon appreciated the fact that the real centre of the whole place wasn't so much the hearth itself as an enormous iron cauldron which stood on a tripod in front of the hearth.

Some extremely savoury stew was boiling in this cauldron; and the grandfather, armed with a long wooden spoon, was engaged in stirring this steaming brew.

Elphin soon became teased by the fact that Tom Shepherd, the master of the house, kept approaching the cauldron, as if distrusting the competence of the old man. Elphin himself cared nothing about the brew or its stirring. All he desired was for everything and everybody to remain where they were forever. "This is life!" is what his whole nature was crying; though he made no attempt to put this feeling into words.

With a vague delicious sense of majestical far-off times, when cauldrons like this were mixed and stirred by beings of supernatural power, he would have liked to have immobilized this spectacle and shown to the world its immortal significance.

But Tom Shepherd suddenly cried out, "Take care, Grand-dad! Those daisy-eye bubbles be rising and bursting! Take care or broth will spoil!"

"See to't theeself, Twm!" muttered the old man, without lifting his head. "Stir'un theeself, if thee can't trust one as has stirred cauldrons in Castell Merddin avore thee were born!"

Elphin watched with intense interest these "daisy-eye bubbles" rising to the rim of this huge receptacle, which was so arranged on its iron tripod that the flames kindled by Olwen ardently licked its belly.

He soon perceived what the grandfather's dim eyes, made obstinately dimmer by his son-in-law's interference, had missed; namely, that a thin foam of broth was trickling down the side of the cauldron upon the hearth-stone.

The girl, however, also saw this, and running for a cloth was soon on her knees wiping up the steaming drops; while, with the dying down of the flames she'd been feeding, the boiling in the pot subsided too.

"Why do women," thought the young Court Herald, "always go on so long scrubbing the place where anything's been spilt, after they've got it up?"

But Elphin was soon aware of a fidgetty unease on the bench beside him, where his friend was having some difficulty in following his recent adherence to the Rhisiartian philosophy of self-control.

Elphin himself was not indifferent—though being an artist his emotion was more diffused—to the engaging spectacle of Olwen scrubbing the floor at their very feet; but the whole scene was giving him such exquisite pleasure that the kneeling girl became only the final touch in a natural work of art so perfect that it was impossible to isolate any of its elements from the rest.

The whole *bwthyn*, with all its human figures, was grouped to the Herald's mind round the cauldron; and the longer Olwen scrubbed at that stone, and he began to wonder now if she weren't purposely tormenting Iago with her proximity, the more the scene lost its prosaic reality and became the kind of symbolic truth that he had long longed to eternalize in some form of art.

Elphin had already been made obscurely aware of the presence in this great western promontory of something that answered a craving in him that he was unable to define. It had to do with a peculiar quality, a hidden virtue in the very texture of these rocks and marshes and mists and headlands; and it seemed to him as if this great cauldron that he now saw bubbling before him, with the girl kneeling beneath it and the old man bending above it, held the very secret he sought.

He even found himself wishing that he were the youngest in the place; so that in accordance with what he had heard was a custom in these parts he might be given the first taste of this magic brew!

His mind had just reverted to Luned and to a fantastic hope, a hope that grew more plausible the further off he was, that he might really be the father of her child, when the white-faced woman suddenly lifted herself up into a sitting posture and brought them all to their feet with a terrifying cry.

"*He's at the door!*" And Elphin realized then that ever since they had entered the *bwthyn,* they had all been expecting this, and that every word they had uttered and every gesture they had made had been a mystic prelude to this consummation.

With the woman sitting up straight in bed, with Olwen standing at her side clinging to her hand, with the old man crossing himself and muttering, "Mary, Joseph! Mary, Joseph!" they were all certain now—though no knock had come and no appeal had been made—that the tall figure in black armour was outside.

"Shall I bar the door, Nest?" enquired the man of the house, in a low husky voice, of the woman in the bed.

"*Bar* the door, do you say? You fool, you fool! Open it quick, for Christ's holy blood, or I'll do it myself!"

Twm of "Ty-uwch-y-Lyn" obeyed her without question; and there, on the threshold, and now stumbling forward into their midst, with bare head bent to enter, was the man who had fought alone against a castle! His long narrow face above his black gorget was white as death. He held a broken sword in his hand, which slipped from his fingers as he stood swaying there before them, and fell with a metallic ring upon the floor.

Iago ap Cynan moved stealthily past him and took upon himself, unauthorized by anybody, to close and bolt the door. He even went to the window and looked out. "They've gone back," he said, addressing nobody in particular.

Patrouillart de Trie lifted his hands, both of which were bare, to his long death-white face and covered his eyes for a moment as if to give help to his bloodless brain in formulating its last and most difficult thoughts. When he removed his hands there were bloody smears across his thin forehead and it seemed to Elphin, who watched him in spell-bound awe, that these crimson stains arranged themselves into a mystic monograph, like the mysterious name written on the foreheads of the army of martyrs in the Book of Revelation!

Elphin never forgot that moment. It was the culmination of all. He felt the presence of the wooden bowl in the centre of the table. He felt the presence of the smaller bowls each with its wooden spoon. He felt the presence of the great cauldron on its iron tripod. And now here was the Black Knight himself, the dedicated subject of all the romances he had ever read!

Elphin could not be called belligerent; but in his heart he cursed Iago just then with a ferocity that surprised himself. He uttered this vicious malediction on his friend's head because, while everyone else was awaiting in hushed expectancy some word or sign from Patrouillart, whose right hand was up once more at his head, while his left was scrabbling grotesquely and impotently at his armoured breast as if the trunk of his body were a wire cage containing a fluttering bird, what must Iago do—and oh! how he hated that puckery face and those small black eyes! —but kick over a bucket of swill which Olwen, interrupted by their entrance, had forgotten to remove!

And as if this weren't enough the insensitive lad proceeded to save himself from a fall by touching with his hand the almost supernatural figure of the Black Knight.

Everybody but Iago was completely under the spell of this tottering and swaying form; and there quivered through Elphin a faint shivering fear, *not* of Patrouillart, but of the power of his friend to treat Patrouillart so calmly. The spilling of that bucket caused a sour garbage smell to pervade the place; and the unconcerned manner in which Iago was now actually assisting Patrouillart in his advance to the woman in the bed played the same part in the human dimension as the bucket played in the inanimate one, both of them joining to drag Elphin's enchanted moment heavily to the ground.

It was an indescribable comfort to our young Herald when his friend, having so grossly presumed to meddle with this tragic apparition, did at last fall back, letting the figure sink on its knees at the side of the woman's pillow.

Olwen too fell back; and it was a surprise to Elphin, though from the expression on that square face it was no surprise to Iago, when the girl's fingers tightened upon that rogue's wrist.

"*Aux blanches mains—aux blanches mains!*" murmured the Frenchman hoarsely; and then, "*Tiens!*" he groaned. "*Désarmez! Délacez! Arrachez! Souffrez-moi que je meurs! Par l'amour de Dieu—cette pointe de lance!*"

Whether the woman understood his words Elphin couldn't tell, but that she understood his meaning was plain to all. Very gently she un-

laced his gorget and laid it on the bed beside her. Then with more difficulty—but none of the onlookers, not even Iago as he stood by Olwen's
side, dared to offer help—she unhooked his breast-plate and pulled aside
from the ghastly wound his blood-soaked shirt.

"She'll faint now," Elphin thought. "She *can't* pull out that spear-
head!"

But the man kept beseeching her; and it was clear that the pain was
almost beyond his endurance. *"Arrachez la pointe de fer*—for the love
of God!" he kept repeating. "Your hands are so small," Elphin heard
him moan. *"Mains petites—arrachez la pointe—souffrez-moi que je
meurs—vite! vite!—aux blanches mains!"*

And then in the view of them all—those two faces, the man's and the
woman's being as close as they were white and wide-eyed—she clenched
her teeth and forcing her fingers into his bleeding flesh, while a choking,
long-drawn, shuddering cry tore itself from *both* their throats, she
wrenched the spear-head out of the wound.

Following it, in a dreadful spurt of red, his life-blood poured over
her; over her arms, over her breast, over her pillow! His last words
seemed to sink with his blood into the inmost being of this woman he
had never seen before.

"Vièrge de Chartres!" Elphin heard him gasp twice over; and then:
"Pour le Royaume de France!" and with this the head of Patrouillart de
Trie straightened itself, jerked backward, jerked forward, and sank
with the death-convulsion of the man's whole body against the carved
edge of the woman's bed.

The days that followed this event passed through the brain of Elphin
like heraldic pictures embroidered on canvas by the hands of the Fates
themselves.

"I don't care *now*," he thought, "even if we don't crown Owen in
London where Brān the Blessed was crowned! I have seen honour in
in the flesh. I have heard *honour* give its triumph-cry. And though it
was its death-cry also, *that* doesn't matter; *that's* a bagatelle. *N'importe!
Ce n'est pas grand' chose."*

Elphin held fast to the end of his days to this revelation of the spiritual
character of French chivalry. He held fast too to his belief in his own
capacity for heroism, though this latter faith was now to receive a considerable shock. The allied army—and it was a wonder to see that

enormous host; for there must, all told, have been nearly fifteen thousand men embattled there under Owen—moved from Haverford West to Tenby and besieged the castle there. While thus engaged the King's courtier-captain, Francis de Court, who had managed by the help of his wife Joan to wheedle himself into the great Lordship of Pembrokeshire, brought into action against the allied host a curious and terrifying weapon.

De Court was a personable young favourite, frivolous and fantastic, and full of end-of-the-fourteenth-century disillusionment; but he took a lively and wanton interest in scientific experiment. Thus no sooner had the enormous allied host, with its numberless banners of France and Wales flaunting in the air, its emblazoned shields, its thousands of bowmen and spearmen, its masses of heavily accoutred men-at-arms, made its first assault upon the walls of Tenby than, with calm assurance and incredible levity, this same unconscionable de Court, perched upon a rampart that seemed impervious to all missiles, ignited a monstrous charge of gunpowder that caused to be flung for a distance as far as a stone's throw projectiles of such size that it was as if Jove himself with his thunderbolts were aiding the defenders.

But this was not the worst. For no sooner had the noise and smoke of this alarming cannonade drawn all the bravest commanders, including Owen and de la Heuze, the one-eyed French champion, to this menacing angle of the fortress than a far more agitating event struck panic-terror into the captainless rear of the allied army. This was nothing less than the appearance of a great fleet of English ships—thirty to fifty in number—in full sail for the landing-place!

The sea was calm, the wind was behind them, their decks were crowded. At the prows of each ship there waited dare-devil desperadoes, armed to the teeth, who looked as if they would leap to the shore the moment the ships touched land. But it was the horrid silence with which they approached, it was the absence of ordinary battle-cries, it was the lack of all the civilized paraphernalia of modern warfare, that made this fleet so terrifying.

In a few moments all the advantage that Owen had snatched from the reckless de Court by a bold defiance of his cannonade was lost to the allies. The unfortunate thing was that this new attack threatened the less experienced portion of the straggling Welsh army. Their best men were all gathered under the castle walls; and it was their leaderless rear, trailing along the harbour's edge, that confronted the approach of this fleet. Sailing in on a favouring wind this armada looked larger than it actually was. The whole water seemed covered with swaying masts and swelling sails.

Elphin himself, it must be confessed, was among the first to take refuge in flight. The others followed him; and very soon the whole of that portion of the army was seized with a wild panic. It was as if this frivolous young de Court had countered Owen's "spirits" with some appalling kind of *hud* or *lledrith,* some devilish illusion or enchantment, calculated to throw the noblest host into confusion!

As Master Sparrow and Iago ran by Elphin's side, and as it became evident that the Prince and his vanguard had been compelled to follow their panic-stricken army, Elphin heard his friends breathlessly commenting on this untoward event. Their comments struck him almost as painfully as the phantom-fleet itself; for they both were presuming to criticize the Prince's whole management of this great campaign. With gasps and groans Master Sparrow, who sweated freely as he ran, for he was no longer the lean and taciturn husbandman whom Broch had lured to Meifod from the Tassel Inn, hesitated not to accuse Owen of truckling to the Frenchmen's love of display.

"Why the devil," he panted, "aren't we now half-way to Hereford, instead of parading our ridiculous pomp round these castles? Owen thinks too much of castles. It's his curst gentility! He ought never to have left the mountains and forests. Above all he ought to have kept away from the sea. We're not meant—"

But this aspersion, by a simple rustic, upon the element over which Prince Madoc had sailed to discover new worlds was too much for Iago; and Elphin, who could think of nothing just then but the unheard-of shame of a herald running away, was compelled to listen to a completely irrelevant defence of the fine seamanship of Welsh sailors.

"By Crish and Saint Ffraid!" groaned Master Sparrow soon. "I can't run a step further. There, there! Enough my masters! Enough i' God's name!" They stopped and looked back. " 'Tis as I thought," the breathless fellow gasped. "Owen's got 'em under control. There are his black lions! There's his flamingo-feather!" He paused and rubbed his face with both hands. But the flamingo-feather had excited his spleen. "What *does* the man want, I ask ye, with all that flummery? To astonish the Frenchmen! That's all it is. Oh these gentry, these gentry! Here, sit ye down, masters, sit ye down," and he indicated a fallen tree. "I've a pretty little poppet of news for ye, if ye can bear any more."

The two lads were glad enough to take his advice; and all three sank down in the bracken with their backs against the log, watching the flamingo-feather of their Prince and the white plume of the one-eyed de la Heuze flit about amid the disorganized ranks like a couple of majestic butterflies.

But neither of the young men felt the smallest desire to hear their companion's "poppet of news." Elphin had been out of sympathy with this champion of the people all along. The man's tone made him feel like a pampered page rather than the youngest of the ancient and honourable Order of Court Heralds. It was an insult to his discretion as well as a slight upon his courage that he should have to put up with this cantankerous and crochetty body-guard.

As for Iago, *his* mind, as would soon have been detected by an observer more on the alert than either of his present companions, was almost oblivious to the impressive scene before him. It is true that his small, deep-set black eyes stared at those tossing banners and glittering spears just as his small, well-shaped ears listened to the shouts and the clamour of the re-assembled host; but both sights and sounds were to him just then a negligible background, against which he saw the detestable red hair and inquisitive nose of the owner of that *bwthyn,* as these objects intruded themselves upon his farewell interview with little Olwen.

"It's dark chestnut her curls are," he thought, "not black as they looked in that smoky hovel. Mother of God! What a sneaking devil, to come round the house spying on a person!"

" 'Tis a wonderful sight, gentlemen, isn't it," Master Sparrow was saying, "to see all those spearmen and bowmen from the land of our fathers ready to march upon the city of London? Well! I'll tell you what reached my ears last night, as I had a cup of mead with certain old mates of mine who've friends over the border. It seems there's a real revolt brewing in Hereford and Worcester against the gentry. They've only to catch a glimpse of our people to hail Owen as their deliverer!"

Thus speaking he turned to his companions with the air of an oracle. But the young egoists at his side received this information with complete indifference.

Elphin said to himself: "Will my voice *carry* in the middle of those tall houses, when I proclaim to the London merchants that their lives and possessions will be respected?"

And Iago thought: "He must sometimes have snatched a *little* pleasure, on the side as it were, as he pursued his master-purpose. Besides, *my* princess, *my* maid in armour, hasn't yet appeared; and even *he* must— have allowed himself—before he met the women he could use—an occasional—"

But their body-guard from the plough hadn't lived with Broch-o'-Meifod for nothing. In place of falling into sardonic silence in the presence of these insolent young springalds as he would certainly have done at the Tassel, he contented himself with asking them if they'd heard why it was that the French knights had so few horses.

Both the lads turned quickly to him then; and having secured their attention he explained that several hundreds of their horses had died at sea from lack of water.

Elphin shuddered. His imagination pictured the heavy bodies of these dead and dying animals as they were thrown to the fishes; and he suddenly found himself yielding to a dark and chilly doubt as to whether he would, after all, lift up his voice in London-town.

"What do you think," he enquired, "has become of those terrible-looking men we saw on those ships? You don't suppose they've landed, do you, and gone off by some long detour to intercept us?"

Iago gave his friend a quick glance. It was strange what practical thoughts *could* come into that girlish head!

But Master Sparrow re-assured them both. "English sailors," he said, "never go far from their ships. Besides, gentlemen, not even the crews of fifty ships would dare to attack a whole army."

Pondering on the peculiarities of English sailors, Iago decided that it would certainly be with a Welsh crew that he would sail to discover Prince Madoc's continent and the hidden retreats of its eager princesses.

"How did the Black Knight come to be left so entirely alone, Master Sparrow?" Elphin now enquired. As he spoke he cast round the neighbouring hills the glance of a seasoned campaigner. He hadn't missed his friend's surprised look, and his tone was now the tone of one man with another, in the presence of a well-meaning but totally inexperienced youth.

The ex-herdsman of the Tassel found this question entirely to his taste. "These French gentry," he explained, "are as different from ours as ours are from the English. Their chief desire is to win personal glory by performing some startling feat of arms. The Black Knight was alone for the simplest of all reasons: because he *wanted* to be alone. Nobody knew—neither Owen nor the others—what he was up to; and so of course they couldn't—"

"But I have often heard you say, Master Sparrow," Iago broke in, and there was a contrariness in his voice that made the herdsman's fingers itch to give those little shining black eyes a resounding buffet, "that all gentry are *the same;* and that our campaign is as much to liberate the common people of England as the common—"

But the malicious lad now scrambled to his feet quite as precipitately as his listeners. None of the three, as they stretched out their legs in the sweet-scented bracken, watching at their ease the stirring spectacle before them and listening to the Welsh horns and the French trumpets, had noticed the approach from their rear of a little group of Harlech guards.

Well known to them all, these stealthy new-comers hesitated not to enhance the shock they gave them by considerable merriment at their expense; and thus when, under instructions from the Prince, our three friends were gathered into the Ardudwy contingent not far from his own person, and falling into their places were swept forward in the general advance, Elphin at any rate was aware of a dull throbbing bruise in the depths of his self-esteem which considerably spoilt the excitement he felt at having at last really and truly started on this historic, this memorable, this longed-for march to London.

As may be imagined the various disturbing episodes, some romantic and marvellous, some shocking and painful, which that great march evoked, obliterated by degrees the youth's chagrin at having led—for in his heart he knew that he was *the first to run*—that panic-flight from those ships.

It took some days, all the same, to free his mind from that awe-inspiring sight. He may, he thought, have a *little* exaggerated the ogrish ferocity of the sailors, for of course they were too far-off for him to see their faces; but there must have been *something* weird and unnatural about them, or Master Sparrow and Iago wouldn't have run, too.

Hadn't Rhisiart told him a terrifying tale once, in their Snowdon fortress, about the great enchanter Gwydion ap Don calling up from the abyss a fleet that was pure illusion to over-awe the crafty Arianrod? Elphin remembered how Rhisiart had pinched his arm as he told him this story and how he'd said to himself, even while the tears filled his eyes, that the pain of the pinching was nothing to the awfulness of the vision described.

But if Elphin's feeling about the ships gradually died away as they marched, Iago's memories of the *bwthyn* of Ty-uwch-y-Lyn and those curls that were "rather chestnut than black" grew more and more obsessing.

Iago found that it was pain to him even so much as to speak to any red-haired Welshman in their troop because it brought back to his mind the red hairs that grew between the eyebrows of Twm-o'-Bryn; hairs that had presented themselves to his attention when he had almost decided that it wasn't necessary to have a purpose *quite* as clear-cut as that which suited such an unusual character as Rhisiart. "We can't *all* be Rhisiarts," he had said to himself on that occasion, with Olwen's dainty chin already between his finger and thumb.

But it was all spoilt by that whoreson foxy nose, with the red hairs above it, sniffing round the house! So absorbed in these thoughts did Iago become that Elphin decided again and again, as their victorious advance led them through many famous places, that when he returned to Harlech he would relate to Luned the whole engaging story of their boyish friend's initiation into the joys and pains of love.

"She'll have her child by then—*our* child!" he would say to himself; and he even went so far, when necessity compelled him to fall out from the ranks, as to fit the words "our child" to a wistful little ditty full of the old Welsh *cynghanedd,* or alliteration.

This production, which he kept scrupulously from Iago, who was naturally too young to associate romance with children, he would hum to a tune of his own; until the love of Luned and Elphin took the place, in many a border-forest, of the birds-songs that had died away in that summer-heat. The further he went from Harlech the easier he found it to thrust from his mind the teasing doubts of his paternity.

He would tell himself again and again that the importance of all those physical details, so distasteful to his nature, those details about which the dead Sir Rawlff so loved to discourse, was probably greatly exaggerated.

The most memorable pause the allied army made ere it left the confines of Wales was at Caerleon-upon-Usk. Elphin was moved more than he expected, when lingering behind the Prince's guard he watched the impassioned ardour with which the French knights—mounted on Welsh ponies and cursing themselves for letting their own good steeds perish at sea—contemplated the famous earth-works where Arthur held his Jousts and his Round Table. Several of the foreign gentlemen displayed as lively an interest in our romantic-looking youth as they did in Arthur's Table, but Elphin astonished his ambitious friend by the cold civility with which he received these flattering overtures.

Both he and Iago paid a dutiful visit to the grave of John ap Hywel in the precincts of the Abbey of Llantarnam; and as the two lads knelt side by side before that new tomb, as yet unmarked by any head-stone, they both thought of Rhisiart and the Maid, and prayed ardently for their safety whether in this world or the next.

If Iago was surprised at his friend's reception of the courtly interest taken in him by several famous French knights, Elphin in his turn was amazed by the deep abstraction that fell upon Iago when they were ferried across the tidal Usk and scrambled up its muddy banks. Not a word could he get from the boy on this point, not even when they were well away from that fatal river; and if the one lad was kept in ignorance of the birth-song to Luned's offspring, the other certainly never knew of the deep, tearless heart-cries that went up from those mud-banks: "Rhisiart! Clerk Rhisiart! What has become of thee? Rhisiart, greatest and wisest of men, where is thy proud soul now?"

Perhaps the most glorious moment for both the young men was when this great host of Welshmen and Frenchmen entered in triumph the outskirts of the City of Hereford. With a grand fanfare of trumpets they marched in, and in one of the outlying parish-churches the longed-for deliverance from the usurping House of Lancaster was intoned by various rebellious priests. The leading clergy, the Bishop among them, had already fled to join the royal forces in Worcester; while from the ramparts of the impregnable Old Town, with its towering Norman Cathedral and castellated Keep, Owen and Robert de la Heuze wisely turned away. They were anxious to reach Worcester before Henry's shire-levies had time to assemble; and they were reluctant to waste their strength in a tedious seige, merely for the satisfaction of hearing Mass in a Cathedral.

"Well, we are in England at last, lads," Owen cried, as he rode past them one morning, a day or two later, in his daily inspection of his Welsh forces, "but we must see to it we don't leave our bones in England! *That* might suit our ladies in Harlech—eh?—ha?—better than it suits us!"

"What made him say that, do you think?" said Elphin to his friend when the Prince had ridden on. "Doesn't that seem to you rather an odd thing to say? About our leaving our bones, and our ladies being glad? I tell you, Iago, I don't like his having said that! There's something funny about it—and his voice—didn't you notice his voice, how unnatural it sounded?"

Iago shifted his spear from his left to his right shoulder, and surveyed his friend across its polished shaft. Elphin had never carried a spear in his life, and now as a Court Herald he would be indefinitely excused from carrying one; but the down-right soldier-tone, so blunt and unaffected, assumed by Iago, *simply because of that spear,* had been irritating him all that morning as they marched together. The fruit-orchards of Worcestershire, with their blue hazy distances and their windless foregrounds of quivering heat-waves, seemed to be absorbing Iago's attention to the destruction of all serious conversation; and to this remark about the Prince's unnatural excitement, and his strange quip about bones and ladies, he returned no reply at all.

Elphin glanced at the stocky figure at his side, plodding along with that great spear over his shoulder. He himself felt tired and sad. There had been little resistance so far to the advance of the allies; but he couldn't get out of his head one Worcestershire hamlet where requisitioning had been opposed, and where they had left behind them blackened ruins, unburied bodies, wailing and cursing, and cries to heaven for vengeance.

One horrible sight he had seen, a dead woman with a living child at her breast; and he found himself tormented by the thought that whenever in future he worked at his favourite subject of a unicorn surrounded by thousands of flowers some devil would force him to depict *that* woman in place of an idealized Luned!

They were following an old Roman road now and the horizon was misty with heat and each step they made sank in heavy dust. Elphin began to find Iago's way of making a cheerful little skip or hop every few steps almost more than he could bear. His friend's manner of breathing annoyed him too. Iago seemed to delight in breathing as loudly as possible and making whistling sounds as he went along.

"How *can* he go on staring in front of him," Elphin thought, "when there's nothing but dull lines of mud-coloured clouds over there; and nothing between them and this dusty road except a welter of blue heat? He marches along like an animal; yes, like a beast! I've often seen horses and cows stare in front of them just as he does. That's where I'm going to suffer, being with Iago; and I know, when the order comes to rest, he'll just sleep like a log!

"What *can* he see in this dull flat country to make him whistle? *I* have to have some *real* scenery, romantic, exciting, distinguished, like our mountains and moors, before I can invent my heraldic symbols and compose my *cynghaneddion*."

Meanwhile Owen, riding now by the side of Robert de la Heuze, and listening to the Frenchman's elaborate plans for their strategy when they encountered the King's army, was giving way, at the back of his mind, to a discouragement profounder than he had ever known. What he now felt was even worse than what he'd suffered when he first heard of his brother's death. How was he to feed this great army advancing daily into a hostile country? The villagers, as it moved, kept driving their herds further and further a-field, and butchering and burying what they couldn't drive off; and when he *did* meet Henry's forces face to face, and the grand encounter of his life *did* happen, what were his chances of a crushing victory?

The Frenchman at his side kept talking of the necessity of dividing their troops before the shock came. "We needn't," the man was assuring him now, "take any measures till our scouts bring us word he's within a few miles. *Then* all our *mounted* men must make an extensive detour and get behind him. That's the great thing, Sire! I've learnt it from a thousand historic campaigns. Without it there's no science of war at all, though there may be plenty of bloody skirmishes. We must take them in the rear, Sire. The whole art of strategy lies there. The rear, the rear! *That* puts it in a nutshell."

And Robert de la Heuze caused his heavy charger, one of the few that had survived the voyage, to caracole like a filly.

"That's exactly where it *does* put it," thought Owen savagely. "In a nutshell of neat words! But it would put *us* on spikes on London Bridge. *Divide?* Mother of God! And your French knights, I suppose, would be the mounted ones! A grand detour *you'd* make through country you're absolutely ignorant of; and can't I see my Welshmen's faces when they watch you prancing off!"

They presented a curious contrast, these two leaders, as they rode at the head of their motley host. Owen had given up, since meeting his allies, the modern Continental way of cutting his locks. Some deep instinct in him, perchance going back to the days when they buried Brān the Blessed's head in London, with its face turned to France, not as a friend but as an enemy, had effected a singular change in that portion of a man's life-illusion—and, as we know, this was a large portion in Owen's case—wherein his mood is reflected in his regard for, or disregard of, his personal appearance. This was indeed, and all the Prince's body-guard noticed it, the first time in his life that he had ever neglected to comb his beard or to trim his hair.

They noticed too, and Elphin regarded this with romantic delight, that since he'd left Harlech he'd ceased bearing on his arms the four black lions of Gwynedd, and in their place had substituted, and Elphin believed he'd found these arms in that ancient Caerleon Abbey, a shield and breast-plate and golden helm that bore the mystical red dragon of the old *gwledig* or chief ruler of Britain.

He rode a tall, gaunt white horse and carried a lance of a totally different kind from those carried by the French knights, much heavier in its shaft and with a head of bronze in place of steel. He still wore his famous flamingo-feather, but in the retaking of Merlin's citadel at Carmarthen half of this airy plume had been torn away, with the result that the golden circlet fastened round the golden helm—the metal of the one being very pale and of the other very glistering and burnished—carried with it, combined with the tangled forks of his now quite grey beard, an almost Arthurian look.

The man had grown much older and much sterner, and in the presence of these lively French nobles he had an expression that was almost ravaged, an expression as of one who was *outliving his heart*.

Robert de la Heuze, on the contrary, riding a dusky-coloured Arab charger, that was all curves and curvettings and archings and prancings, was a swarthy little man with a bristling moustache and restless black eyes whose shield and pennon and horse's trappings were covered with such complicated armorial symbols that he resembled a figure from one of the newest stained-glass windows in some seignorial chapel of Auxerrois or Blois.

Owen kept inclining his massive head and golden helm towards the lively gentleman, who apparently was completely satisfied with the impression his strategic plans were making on this courtly *revenant* from the Round Table, but the thoughts that revolved beneath that torn feather and pallid circlet were wistful and sad.

The Prince was recalling the day he had ridden from Glyndyfrdwy to Mathrafal with his devoted Rhisiart behind him and little Efa on the back of his saddle; and he was thinking of other things too as he kept up his, "Yes, my dear Baron; yes, yes! *Vous avez des desseins à outrance*. You are a born Belisaire, my dear Baron! You invent such super-plans that I can hardly keep pace with you. Yes, of course. *Ma foi!* I never thought of *that!* Of course we must— Well, I shall give your words the most grateful and careful consider-ation!" He was thinking for example of that tombless grave of the Abbot of Caerleon. Aye! if he only had John ap Hywel by his side to-day! How that swarthy face would burn, and how that plain Welsh accent would ring out, in protest against all this fantastical *guerre gauloise!*

"What a fool I was," he thought, "not to have realized how it would be, between my mountaineers and these flowers of chivalry."

He sighed bitterly into his untrimmed beard, as, bending his head to learn yet more about the art of campaigning in enemy territory, he decided that Robert de la Heuze had the expression of a one-eyed rat, licking its whiskers before gnawing through the final barrier to a well-stocked granary!

The truth was that there had always lain in Owen's nature a vein of the arbitrary and the incalculable. He "followed his demon" in the old irrational sense of trusting the impulses and urges that came from the depths of his being rather than any rational motive.

Well might his body-guard from Ardudwy and his picked band of troopers from Edeyrnion wonder when they saw their leader, who had always been so punctilious in his courtly attire, revert to this primitive mode.

But they loved him for it! It pleased them more than anything he could have done. It fell in exactly with their own instinctive reaction from these sophisticated French gentlemen.

But Owen's sadness had other causes than mere contrariness. For one thing he had never felt more lonely. His Meifod friend had left him. His brother was dead. Rhisiart and the Maid were lost. Catharine was absorbed in her children, Meredith in his bride. And for another thing, unless he consented to take the advice of his ally and sack every town through which they passed he was at a loss to see what would happen when their supplies were exhausted.

Nor was the French force composed, as he'd hoped it would be, of a vast host of light-armed, quickly-moving soldiers, against whose advance, till they reached London, all resistance would be impossible.

The new tactics of young Prince Hal, under the competent, unromantic leadership of his English captains, had shown fatally enough how a country should be invaded; and yet here were these proud fantastic knights, just like the ones he had defeated at Bryn Glas, planning the campaign as if it were a war against unarmed serfs instead of against the stout yeomen of the shires!

How sure he had felt of ultimate victory as he marched, by Rhys Gethin's side, over the mountains, before that successful battle!

Where had he made his first mistake? Where had the tide *begun* to turn against him? The men behind him, Welsh and French alike, felt exultant and elated to-day. He alone was sad. And the mere fact that he, the leader, was the only one distrustful of the event, just when outwardly his fortunes were at their highest peak—how like fate it was!

Yes, he had had his dark moods before; but he had never felt quite as he did now. Something about the fact that he was staking everything on one grand throw of the dice deepened his congenital fatalism;

and he began to be aware, too, of another curious psychic oppression. He had never—not even when he served in the late King's wars— been at the head of such a host; and there came over him, from the very weight of his responsibility, from the very immensity of the mass of human emotions behind him, a feeling that no "tricks" with his individual soul, no tapping of supernatural powers in his own mind, could affect the practical issue. *He* might never submit to Hal Boling- broke, nor to young Harry either, *but what of Wales?*

He felt just then like the only powerful swimmer on a ship doomed to sink. "Where did I make my mistake?" he kept asking himself; and as he struggled to find an answer he could only see the peaked wizard's cap and long ebony wand of the unconscionable Hopkin. "But that's absurd," he thought. "I was only playing with that old idiot's predictions. I never really took them seriously."

And then, all in a moment, he made up his mind where he had blundered. It was in that thrice-accurst "Tripartite Indenture"! But even *that* was not an isolated event. It had its own train of secret causes, one of which was his alliance with the Percies; and, by Our Lady, another was his marrying Catharine to that man! What he ought to have done after Bryn Glas was to have drawn back into Snowdon, left the Barons in their border-castles, and made an offen- sive and defensive alliance, *not* with the enemies of England, but with the crafty King himself!

They had now arrived at the summit of a small eminence; and he was disturbed in his ponderings by a change in the tone of his com- panion, and by the Frenchman's suddenly fixing his one eye upon him with an exultant gleam and pointing with the end of his lance to a large compact village that lay, with a church in its centre, in the peace- ful valley beneath them.

There was a considerable area of arable land about this village, land that was now composed of stubble-fields, upon which, as they looked down on them from above, the sun shone in a rich golden haze.

The disturbing thought crossed Owen's mind at that moment, as he encountered the Baron's excited gaze, that one-eyed men were the cause of all his troubles! He suddenly felt an unholy pleasure in the Scab's being safely under the sod and a shameless wish that his present companion had perished with the noble Patrouillart. "Yes," he thought, "one-eyed men are my danger. If *you* were dead, you vicious little rat, I might have a chance still!"

He lifted his helmet from his forehead and wiped away the sweat, trying in vain to follow what the other was saying. "Sparrow *may* be right," he thought. "There *may* be a rising of the peasants. But that young Harry's my danger. He takes after his great-grandfather. Oh, Patrouillart, Patrouillart, why did you go and get killed? You're the one we'll need when we're face to face with that young fox! I'd like to see you challenge him to a single combat!" And as he stared at the golden stubble-fields the old French proverb came into his head: "In the kingdom of the blind the one-eyed man is king—*Au royaume des aveugles les borgnes sont rois!*" But he fell, after that, as he brushed a cloud of summer-flies from his horse's neck with the helm he still held in his hand, into a daze of wonder as he thought what a maniac for glory and honour the deceased Patrouillart was. "There's no soil in the world," he thought, "like France for breeding such men. They die for honour as trout for flies! And yet you're a Frenchman, too, you one-eyed rat!"

At that moment, without any warning, his consciousness of the passing of time began to grow blurred. He recognized the sensation at once and knew what it portended. It was the usual prelude to what Rhisiart called one of his "attacks." He had taken off his helmet and held it in his hands and he now balanced it on his saddle-bow before him and looked round. Yes! There were those two lads. What a Providence at the particular moment! He heard his own voice calling, "Elphin! Iago!" just as a man might hear himself calling "Help! Help!" if he were drowning at sea.

Both the boys came running; and at the same instant, with a regular tourney-clatter and a jingling of accoutrements, the whole band of Frenchmen rode up. Robert le Borgne, after a quick glance at Owen and his attendants, advanced to meet the new arrivals. He had seen this happen to the Prince before; and the two lads didn't fail to mark the satisfaction with which he welcomed his compatriots, pointing his sword first at the helpless village below and then at the motionless figure on the white horse.

Meanwhile our two young friends, as they supported their chieftain, conversed in awed whispers across his horse's back. "A person can't," Elphin explained to Iago, "don the dragon of Uther without *something* happening. But I'm glad he did it, because it means we'll reach London and I'll proclaim him on Tower Hill, but it's a terrific strain for him. You heard what Master Sparrow said about his vomiting every night when the army-watchman calls twelve? Well! that's how it is! You remember what that monk said at Llantarnam—about Merlin in the shape of a pig-dealer conversing with him as he watched his arms by the Abbot's grave? Well! a man can't be visited by Merlin in these modern times without suffering for it."

In reply to his friend, Iago whispered that he'd heard at school about some ancient general who would remain for hours in the middle of a battle standing on one leg.

"But look, look! What are those French soldiers doing? They're entering the village without orders! Where's Master Sparrow? What's become of Master Don of Kidwelly?"

Elphin looked; and as he looked he became so agitated that his hands shook as he pressed them against the Prince's golden armour. "They're going to burn the whole place!" he thought.

But Iago went on. "They're going to loot every house down there! Elphin, look! This is a real war. This is a real— *There!* Did you hear *that?*"

But Elphin couldn't look; and he longed to stop his ears. He thought of Luned. He thought of his parents in Edeyrnion. And then, as yells and cries increased and the smell of burning rose from the foot of the hill and he tried to harden his heart, fumbling with the Prince's accoutrements, he suddenly recalled a terrifying scene in the great hall at Snowdon. "Iago! Iago!" he whispered, fearful lest le Borgne should hear him, "he's got on Eliseg's belt and Eliseg's sword!"

But Iago, who had less of the Prince's weight to support, and was wholly absorbed in the confusion below, answered roughly, not troubling what he said, "The more fool he! Isn't the bronze lance enough? Look! Look! This is real war. We're seeing a real battle! Look! It's burning! It's burning! Can't you smell the burning? Look, Elphin! Why don't you look? They're dragging some prisoners up the hill!"

But if Elphin hadn't been supporting the Prince he would certainly have put his hands to his ears and shut his eyes. The only comfort he got as he countered the chieftain's massive weight with all the strength of his thin arms was to rub his throbbing forehead against the handle of the bronze sword, and to shuffle his feet, in their leather thongs, between a clump of knapweed and a mole-hill to where his heels could touch the bronze spear.

Robert de la Heuze and his group of knights were watching the scene beneath them with as much interest as Iago. They had by this time grown used to these "attacks" of their formidable ally; but never before had the Prince become *hors de combat* at so convenient a moment as this! They decided at once to give him no time to shake off this providential seizure. The plundering of a place like this, lying amid its over-flowing granaries like a rustic queen among her golden locks, was too tempting.

And the Prince sat on, motionless and still, supported by his pages on his white horse, with his shining helmet on the saddle before him, and the dragon pennon of his antique lance trailing amid the yellow hawkweed.

Nor was Iago mistaken about the prisoners. The three chief men of the village they were: Father Bertram, the Priest; old Sir Andrew Courtyce, the Justice of the Peace; and Master Staniforth, the Tanner; and as they were dragged before le Borgne, with their hands tied behind them, to be questioned brutally and cruelly, they stared with wonder at this bare-headed figure on his tall horse, his forked beard flowing down over his breast-plate, his dragon-helm clasped between his motionless hands, and his lance-point resting among the flowers.

"*Everything,* from every barn in the place, Master Justice," Robert de la Heuze was saying, while his confrères with gleaming teeth and shining eyes swore their confirmation of these wholesale words; "and *everything* from your good larder, Father, and *everything* from your rich store-house, Master Staniforth. And what's more, you three gentlemen must guide our men from house to house—we shall send our wagons—and you must give us—that goes without saying—*everything* in your stables. And you, Father, must bring us all your church-plate; and you, Master Justice, must open your chests to a learned clerk we'll be sending; and especially we shall require any letters you may of late have received from your pretended lord, Henry of Lancaster, showing the disposition of his forces; and further we shall require—"

All this was spoken in tolerable English but was accompanied by so much ferocity from le Borgne's single eye that each of the worthy men he was addressing felt that the worst was still unsaid.

"And what," replied old Sir Andrew, "will follow, if we refuse these monstrous demands, unheard of by the Law of Nations?"

"In the Holy name of Christ and His Mother," broke in Father Bertram, "I, God's humble priest, *refuse,* here and now—*whatever follows!"*

"And I am with you, Father," added Master Staniforth, struggling to loosen the cords that bound his hands, "and in the name of King Harry I protest—"

"What will happen, do you ask?" cried Robert le Borgne. The *droit de guerre* will happen. And you know what *that* means! There won't be a house, there won't be a woman—*there!* My worthy friends, you're too late already! You should have agreed at once; and not put us to the trouble of all this. *À la guerre comme à la guerre!* Our brave archers from Auvergne I perceive have taken things into their own hands! Here, Raoul, Sebastien, Jacquot! Take these men and keep them close—close I say!—till we've finished with their larders and their—"

It was now plain enough that it was not only the Frenchmen from Auvergne who had anticipated the *droit de guerre* referred to by le Borgne; for clouds of black smoke were beginning to roll over the roofs of the village, and presently there reached that hilltop from the heart of the smoke one single piercing feminine scream that had a blood-curdling effect not only upon Elphin and Iago but upon many other young Welshmen who were within hearing, and who, though reckless enough in their own way, had not until now been permitted the privilege of witnessing Continental warfare.

"My girl! My girl! Devils! Oh devils! Stop! stop! I'm coming, my child; your father's coming! Let me go, I say! Devils! Oh devils!"

The desperate yells and savage struggles of Staniforth, the Tanner, were seconded in a yet more effective way by old Sir Andrew, who, when there arose a new series of feminine screams, not so piercing perhaps, but even more heart-rending, hesitated not to use both head

and feet in a furious attempt to escape; and this he did with such unexpected alacrity that bound though he was the fellow who was holding him was laid by the heels; and since nothing more than a brutal
laugh from between the teeth of le Borgne followed him down the
hill, his hoarse shouts of "Nell! Nell! Wait, wait, you devils!" weren't
silenced till they were lost in the tumult below.

Aroused at last to what was going on, Glendower's wits returned
to him as fully armed as were his powerful hands. In an instant he
took in the whole situation, and it was with wildly-beating hearts that
both his boyish attendants rushed, tumbling and leaping, after the
flying hooves of the white charger; and as the Prince, thundering out
his commands, rode down the hill at break-neck speed into the smoke
of the burning village he was followed by a crowd of Welsh troopers.

Whatever the campaign may have gained in material supplies by
the plunder of this place, as the march towards London was resumed,
both our young friends agreed, as they discussed the episode during
their evening bivouac, that nothing would ever really heal the rift that
had yawned that day amid the smoke and the looting and the treatment
of the women between the Welsh and their Continental allies. The
lads had caught enough of the foreigners' fury at having their *droit de
guerre* plucked away from under their very beards to realize that nothing but some resounding triumph over the Usurper would really unite
them again. "It's London or nothing now, Iago!" Elphin assured his
friend, as they shared in the chilly dews of the August twilight the last
of the Turkish sweet-meats with which Luned had provided them.

"I tell you Owen had to prick one of those lecherous devils with the
point of his lance three or four times before he'd stop his game; and
the woman he'd got down was no daisy neither! She was as old as
Lady Mortimer, and she'd more children than *she* has; for I saw them
myself beating at the fellow with their fists when their mother was
giving up.

"But Owen would soon have done more than prick that itching
rogue; and you should have seen how he treated the woman when
the man had gone. He lifted her up and dried her eyes as if she'd *been*
Lady Mortimer! And she was an ugly wench, too. If that bronze-head

had been sharper—whew, lad! how he'd have made that son of a whore skip! Shall I tell you something else, Iago?"

"No, for Jesus's sake! Can't you see I'm saying my prayers?"

"You don't often do that, Iago! It's *because of to-day* you're doing it. I'm older than you; and, as I've told you before, women—"

"If you say another word—"

"I know what you're thinking. You're thinking of *that girl*. There! Did you hear? That was a fox! I didn't know they had foxes here. Mary, Joseph, how cold it is in England! Lie closer, Iago—closer! closer!—like you did last night."

But if this youthful pair, about whose safety the ladies of Harlech had plagued the Prince for days before he set out, were uneasy that evening, the Prince himself was more than uneasy. He had come to le Borgne's tent to discuss their approaching encounter with the royal troops, and as he looked about him he decided that no painted window in any French cathedral could be more resplendent in armorial bearings than this knightly pavilion.

"They'll undoubtedly come out of Worcester to attack us, Sire," asseverated le Borgne. "Our prisoners confessed as much in my hearing."

In the depths of his heart Owen had an instinct that the two Henries would *not* come out; but so painful was it to him to contemplate a repetition of those *droit de guerre* scenes in a crowded town that he automatically suppressed this premonition.

"But of course if they don't come out," muttered the French leader in a lower tone, "though we have no siege-engines, I have Gascon troops here who'd stand on one another's shoulders and fight like a pack of demons for the chance of a gala night of looting and raping in an English city!"

It seems to a superficial eye as though the whole course of human history often depends on the turn of a hair, on the tilt of an eyelid, on the fall of a feather; but to a more philosophical mind these trifles are only the instruments of what we call fate or destiny, a force for which in our nescience we have no adequate name.

Had Owen at that moment heard the words of his ally, uttered in that lower tone, it is probable enough that his pride in his Welsh followers would have reluctred at their being regarded as less daring than le Borgne's Gascons. Providence however—to use the popular term—saw fit just then to incarnate itself in an extremely blood-thirsty gnat, whose attack upon the Prince's face was so fierce that it caused him to leap from his seat with an oath, an oath that completely drowned his companion's words.

The crucial proposal passed therefore unheard; while le Borgne's pride in his own certainty that the King *would* come out forbade its repetition. In one sense thousands of lives depended upon the fact that from its shelter beneath a painted shield this ferocious insect attacked the Frenchman's guest; but in a deeper sense we may conjecture that if the gnat had failed its purpose fate would have found some other instrument, no less trifling, to carry out its shameless purpose of allowing Henry of Lancaster to die in his bed.

Yes, there come moments, even in the decisions of commanders of such a host as this, when a pressure, light as the impalpable air and ubiquitous as grains of sand before an invisible wind, urges the course of events in a certain direction, a direction either contrary to, or favourable to, drastic action.

The anxiety of a Worcestershire gnat to taste Welsh blood was only one manifestation of the impalpable force that was exercising its pressure upon these two men. To a superstitious mind it might almost have seemed as if the dead bones of King John, repentant for the injuries which during their life they had inflicted on that monarch's people, were projecting some numbing and drugging spell upon those who were conspiring against the walls that guarded his tomb.

At any rate as Owen lay that night upon a heap of rugs in his own tent, listening to the sounds his horse was making outside, he thought how strange had been the way he'd interfered with le Borgne's treatment of those villagers. In his young days, he thought, he had never felt such squeamishness.

"Something's come over me," he said to himself, "but what it is—Dewi Sant! *I* don't know! I feel as if Bolingbroke and I were tilting at each other in one of Richard's fancy tourneys. I feel as if even the crown in London wasn't worth—"

He hoisted himself up and listened intently to his horse; and there seemed to him something more *real* about the way it was cropping the grass out there than about all this marching and counter-marching; yes! more real, and with more life in it!

To whatever curious conclusion, however, the sacking and burning of a Worcestershire village in his march upon London might lead the eccentric mind of the Welsh leader, it was he, and not his one-eyed tutor in modern strategy, who finally got the allied army safely encamped at Woodbury Hill in the parish of Great Witley, over against the ancient city where lay the bones of the destroyer of Mathrafal.

Into Worcester itself the Usurper had already hurried; hurried with that amazing speed which was his chief characteristic as a warrior, and the summons had gone out to all the surrounding shires to rally to his support. Luckily for the burgesses of Worcester, and for their wives and daughters if le Borgne had his way, the two Henries, the father advancing from the south and the son retreating from Hereford, got safe within the walls of the city before the allied army reached Great Witley.

There was a grassy valley between Woodbury Camp and the walls of Worcester, and for over a week Owen behaved, as the scholarly Rhisiart would certainly have observed if Exeter College possessed that particular Homeric passage among its Latin translations, like Achilles sulking in his tent.

It was indeed the most miserable stretch of days that the Welsh Prince known since he was a little child in the time of the Black Death, more than half a century ago. It made little difference that in his meticulous analysis of events he was unable to include the gnat. His conclusions were correct enough without that officious insect. His one chance of victory, he told himself, would have been to storm the walls of the city in overwhelming numbers the moment they reached the spot. It was too late now, with the sturdy shire-men gathering from all sides and his supplies failing. Why *hadn't* he stormed the city at once? He knew very well why he hadn't, though he shirked telling himself so in plain words. The savagery he'd seen in the burning of that unlucky village had bruised something in the depths of his nature; and it was this bruise, though he dodged it and avoided facing it, that had covered up *that* road, when they reached the cross-ways of their fate, with an impenetrable darkness.

They had far outnumbered the King's troops at first, though they didn't now. Why hadn't the French knights themselves insisted on storming the city without delay? Ah! for a very simple reason. For all their talk of strategy they were just mediæval adventurers. A campaign to them meant tilting chivalrously against armed equals in the field, while they lived mercilessly upon the country they were invading.

But Owen couldn't keep his imagination from following the road he *hadn't* followed. The old bearded chieftain as he sulked in his tent caught himself in fantastic tales about taking both the Henries prisoner, and demanding as their ransom the crown of England. But it was all over now; and in his heart he knew it. It would be fortunate if he got his Welshmen safe back across the border without any appalling catastrophe.

One night he awoke just before dawn, for it was a peculiarity, a *cynnedf,* with all the descendants of Griffith ap Madoc to get their best inspirations at that hour, and he had a vision of besieging the King and his heir, however long the siege might last, till he starved them out! But not for long did that vision last. What of his own supplies? And what of the shire-levies in his rear? No, it was over! His chance had been given him; and something in his own nature had balked. He thrust his hand under his pillow of rugs and touched the rusty bronze that had been the death of that old peace-maker of Dinas Brān; and as he did so the impression came over him out of that vast stillness, a stillness unbroken even by a sentry's tread, that he and his people *could afford to wait,* could afford to wait till long after his bones were dust and Henry's bones were dust. He knew how his own soul could escape, escape without looting cities and ravishing women.

And was the soul of his people, the oldest of all the races where the sun sank into the sea, *less able to wait* than the soul of its leader? Well! his allies had had their taste of their *droit de guerre;* and he would leave them a day or two more to enjoy their chivalrous feats of arms in this play-acting tourney-ground of theirs between camp and city!

And then—God give him the grace to get his great army back safe into Wales! *So be it.* At any rate there'd be no wailing and weeping in

Edeyrnion and Ardudwy, in Gwent and Morgannwg, for Welsh corpses left to English crows!

He drew his hand away from old Adda's death-weapon and stretched out his arm so as to feel the central support of his tent, from which, suspended by a nail, hung that queer fragment of ink-black leather, ornamented with golden studs, that he'd been taught from his infancy to call "Eliseg's belt." Merely to touch this ancient object—and how well he knew its cold, damp, slippery texture, like the skin of some extinct amphibium!—was a comfort just then, and he felt happier as he pulled up the bed-cover.

"Three-score years I've lived, come Michaelmas," he thought. "And who'll remember me in three-score years to come? Well, we've certainly killed some Englishmen in these fantastical single combats. Like the old Knights Templar tilting with Saracens, they are; and how the Frenchmen love them! Mary! Joseph! And no wonder they love them! King Hal hasn't any such champions. A dozen English knights killed in a couple of days! Well! They'll have some pretty tales to tell when they get back to France; but all the tilting of all King Charles's court won't get us to London. Too many long-bows, too many yeomen! Aye, Master Sparrow, and where's your peasants' revolt now?"

He let his head sink back, thrust his fingers beneath his grey beard and carefully spread it out, as if over the edge of a shroud, above the blanket he'd pulled up to his chin.

So untrimmed had he let his hair grow that this beard of his could scarcely be called a forked beard any more. It was just any old man's beard; and as he lay on his back Owen felt as if he himself *were* any old man, "feeling," as they say, "his age." But the folds of his tent hung open about the width of a man's hand, and between them he could catch a glimpse of two small stars belonging to one of those northern constellations from which Ffraid ferch Gloyw had predicted that he would fail in arms but triumph in spirit.

Revealed between the hangings of his tent, with nothing but blue-black space above and beneath them, they seemed to him like the eyes of Destiny watching to see what he would do in the hour of his defeat.

"What did Arthur do to the Twrch Trwyth," he said to himself. "There's a smell of the mud of the Severn upon the air. It must come

up with the dawn when the tide draws back." And without a movement, save only the movement of his breath, he defied those small
intent watchful eyes. "Eyes of Twrch Trwyth," he said to himself.
"Pig of Hell," he said to himself, "Arthur drove you down the Severn
into the deep sea!"

And it was brought about at that moment by the power to which
some give the name of "chance" that a cloud swam across those glittering pin-pricks in the dome of immensity; and the immediate effect of
this was to cause an indescribable relaxing of the tension of the man's
brain and at the same time to apply to his consciousness a gentle pressure, light as the fanning of a butterfly's wing, a pressure towards the
slippery water-shoot of sleep. But, ere he slept, memory after memory
crossed the swaying light-ship of his mind. He remembered the very
occasion, on a sweltering August day, when Ffraid ferch Gloyw had
uttered her enigmatic prediction. "Over your body, Cousin Owen," she
had said, "our people will pass to their triumph; but it will be a
triumph in the House of Saturn, not in the House of Mars."

And then he forgot Ffraid ferch Gloyw, and across his closed eyelids
floated the image of Rhisiart's narrow Norman skull, as the lad's lips
sucked at his arrow-wound. "I've dragged you all down," he thought,
"and we sink together—so many—so many—down the tide into the
deep sea. But over us—over us—"

If the Prince himself found it hard, after all his clear realistic analysis,
to understand why he hadn't risked everything in one grand fling, and
hurled his ten thousand Welshmen and his two thousand Frenchmen
against the walls of Worcester, it was much harder for Rhisiart and
Master Brut to comprehend the cause of his unexpected retreat.

They knew of course, in their room in the Bishop's prison, what the
allies could only guess at, namely, the small number of men that made
up the royal garrison. The younger Henry was more alarmed than he
allowed his father to see, when he welcomed the King into the city.
He'd hoped for an army; but the Ruler of England had only his
private guard, and a handful of horsemen he'd picked up as he rode
through Oxford.

But the walls of the old city were strong, its gates massive, and it was unlikely that Owen and his Frenchmen had brought any siege-furniture with them. Scaling-ladders, catapults, and assault-platforms, not to speak of the new ordnance inventions for explosive cannonading, were awkward things to convey through a hostile country.

And every day that passed—every hour even—was so much gain to the English. The thing that puzzled Prince Henry was that the enemy made no attempt to surround the city. The gates to the east, the roads from the east, were never in any danger; and it wasn't long before considerable bodies of shire-yeomen, already summoned post-haste by the King from every county through which he'd passed, began pouring into the town.

To an enterprising strategist like the younger Henry it seemed hardly short of a miracle when instead of either attacking the city or surrounding it the allied army contented itself with occupying an·impregnable position on Woodbury Hill.

"They act as if *we* were the aggressors and *they* the defenders," Prince Hal told his father; but the weary old campaigner only replied caustically that all wise leaders were "defenders," unless like Hotspur they preferred to die in their glory.

At this the long white face of the young Prince had flushed; and after muttering something about badgers and mole-runs he enquired how many *more* men from the shires they must await before assaulting Woodbury Hill.

"There'll be no assault of Woodbury Hill while *I'm* in Worcester," the King had said; "and what's more, Hal, if you ride down again into that valley, I'll send you home with letters to the Parliament."

"But their tourney-tricks, Sire, their prancing tourney-tricks! And we not able to find one knight—"

"After tomorrow, Hal," said the King, *"no one shall go down that hill."*

"And let those popinjays wave their lances at us, and call us—"

"Hal, Hal! What has come over you? Ask Cousin York, ask Captain Shirley, whether, when a host like that is deliberately starving itself instead of attacking, there's any reason to throw away loyal men's lives for nothing. Let 'em tilt against the walls! Let 'em make their jongleur ditties for their ladies! What's the matter with you, Hal? I'll be think-

ing soon that all your Welsh victories *came by accident*—as indeed—
God help me!—all the victories I've ever seen *have* come. Shut the
gates, lad, and man the walls. Our good Commons will soon be voting
their thanks again to the most puissant and renowned Prince, Harry of
Monmouth!

"And remember this, boy, for the day when I'm gone. If you invade
France, as these men are invading England—yes! and march into Paris
with twice as many men—you'll never win. Sooner or later, *out* you'll
go! Don't you see, boy, that the Lord himself is fighting for us against
Sisera? Any morning now we may wake up and find them gone. Let
those Frenchmen tilt against each other! Shut the gates, shut the gates.
Let them tilt against the walls! Woodbury Hill will soon be as bare as
a tennis-ball! Never mind their tilting, Hal. Let them play, let them
play! We'll to business."

But the King was almost alone in all the City of Worcester to take
this view of the situation. The people crowded into the churches.
Monstrous images of Glendower, as a Devil with horns, were burnt in
the squares. Wild rumours spread through the streets of horrible
cruelties habitually practised by the Welsh.

But there was a minority who held the view that since there'd been
no attempt to stop the influx of loyal yeomen from the neighbouring
shires it was clear that the number of the enemy had been ridiculously
exaggerated. 'Twould make a bad impression upon the country, these
hot-heads argued, if the King of England let himself be shut up in a
walled town while a party of French courtiers and a rabble of Welsh
serfs made sport of him in the heart of his own kingdom!

Prince Hal always spoke too freely in the taverns, and since there
was a group of lively young squires who followed him everywhere, the
rumour quickly spread through the town that though the King was
sick and troubled with superstitious fears the Prince would soon on his
own authority be making a desperate sortie upon Glendower's camp.
Nor were there lacking plenty of tale-bearers to make trouble between
the two Henries; and as is usual in such cases the elder man completely
misunderstood what was in the mind of his son.

And if his father misunderstood him, his tavern-cronies did so still
more. As a matter of fact the daring young warrior had worked out a

shrewd and startling plan of campaign, including a pretended frontal attack, followed by a pretended retreat and a second devastating sortie, while the escape of the huge disorganized host was cut off by the best long-bows in the kingdom!

And this soldierly plan of his might have resulted, so his best captains, Crosby and Shirley, argued, in the death or capture of Glendower; had it not been that in his pique at the King's tone towards him he let it all evaporate in the fumes of the city's wine-shops.

It may be well imagined what wild stories of all that was occurring around them reached Rhisiart and Master Brut. The Bishop's Palace was miles outside the city walls, but the Bishop's prison where they were held was in the old castle-keep, and had a moat around it. Only a couple of days before the allies moved their camp from Woodbury Hill and began their orderly but melancholy retreat, the unfortunate prisoners were discussing their chances of rescue with unusual fervour; but had Elphin and Iago seen their former friends at this moment they would have been hard put to it to know them as the same men.

They possessed only one suit of *outer* garments between them, and to-day it was Rhisiart's turn to wear these rags of his old scholar's suit. He himself had grown a straggly beard as black as his hollow eyes; and the effect of this, combined with the dark dishevelled locks that hung down over his ears, gave to his narrow face and drooping moustache a desolate dignity that would have broken the heart of Lady Mortimer. Master Brut, on the contrary, had persuaded their jailer's child to steal for him a pair of scissors; and with this—though unable to shave—he had managed to reduce his beard to the limits of a hairy fringe round his smooth moon-face. This hairy fringe did, however, and in a very curious way, alter the man's whole look. The Lollard's left arm had been broken, and only hastily and improperly set; so that often, though not continuously, it caused him considerable pain, especially since he had had to have it bound tight to his waist with a strip of his shirt.

The two friends were securely though not heavily manacled and they had plenty of bread and water and even sometimes, when their jailer was in a good mood, a cup of wine and a fragment of meat. There was no latrine in the Bishop's prison; but as the chamber was an extensive one, and they were not chained to the wall, they were spared any intolerable unpleasantness.

Master Brut's books had been taken from him, but their jailer, who couldn't read himself but who had an avid thirst for the sort of knowledge that comes from sensational chronicles, soon acquired the habit of bringing into their chamber various roughly-copied parchments describing the most blood-curdling of recent events, richly interspersed with pleasant though incredible marvels. These it was the privilege of our prisoners to read aloud by turns, a thing that Walter Brut did as eloquently as if in the presence of a crowded congregation of Gospelmen; while Clerk Rhisiart did it in a high-pitched, mock-judicial manner that had the double effect of relieving his own feelings and impressing the jailer with awe and reverence in the presence of such forensic power.

On this particular morning the prisoners were sitting opposite each other on wooden stools, with a third stool between them on which were the remains of two half-loaves of bread and two earthen-ware mugs of water. The Lollard had drawn on this third stool, with his unhurt hand and a burnt stick, a map of Woodbury Hill in its relation to the city walls, and it was at this map that the two men were now earnestly gazing.

"One thing is certain," said Rhisiart. "Owen'll never retreat, now he has once made the plunge! Besides, he must have an enormous army" —here he groaned and made an impatient movement on his stool; for he had a wound in his hip, which, though it had ostensibly healed, gave him now and again a lively twinge. Though he kept it to himself, for he knew his trouble was a pin's prick compared with what his friend endured from his broken arm, Rhisiart had come to indulge a morbid fantasy that his wound was a malevolent entity to whom had been given the power to plague him. He even went so far in his secret mind as to baptize this enemy with a Christian name. He called him "Sele" in honour of the Lord of Nannau.

"Even discounting Master Giggleswick's dramatic turn," he continued, when "Sele's" twinges diminished, "we can't put the allied army at less than twelve thousand men. Of course what I would do myself if I were Owen would be to pass by Worcester altogether, and rush forward by forced marches, living on the country as best I could, till I reached London. I'd dodge Warwick and Oxford and Banbury, too. In fact I wouldn't bother *what* towns or castles I left behind me. I'd get to London if I had no sleep for a week!"

His friend smiled and, having erased a section of his map with a crumb of bread, proceeded with calm deliberation, still smiling, to flick this missile out of their open window, where, falling into the Bishop's moat, it was instantaneously devoured by a watchful carp. It had been a natural custom for nearly a thousand years for the Bishop's prisoners to throw scraps to his carp. The Bishop in the time of King Stephen used to throw the prisoners themselves to these plump fish; and ever since his day the more waggish of his successors would exchange with their chaplains every Friday a somewhat lurid but entirely ecclesiastical jest about this custom, in which the Latin for corpses and the Latin for nourishment were felicitously sprinkled with parsley and washed down with Malmsey wine.

"Rhisiart!"

"Yes, Walter."

"Do you remember that story about Pharoah's two servants in prison?"

Rhisiart sighed; uttered a curse under his breath; and, as he had done a thousand times since they'd been together, swore affectionately that he remembered the story well.

"You'll be pardoned, but *I* shall be burnt," said Master Brut in a decided voice, "but I wish, before they separate us, which may happen any day now, that you'd admit," and he put his finger upon a particular place in his charcoal map, "that I was right and you were wrong as to the position of Woodbury Hill. That child assured me the wind's in the west; and you know how clearly we've heard the French trumpets to-day. Well! *that* means—you're not looking, Rhisiart! Yes, *there*—just *there!*—there's been no interference with the English yeomen coming in. That child said they've been pouring in through what she called 'East Gate' for the last two days. Owen isn't besieging the city. But neither has he left the city behind! He's challenging them to battle, from a position chosen by himself. If the two Henries are clever enough to wait behind their walls, and if Owen *has* encamped as I've got him *here*"—and moving a piece of crust to a black spot in the surface of the stool between them, he showed it complacently to his friend—"there'll have to be a battle, *or*—"

"Or what?" sighed Rhisiart wearily, for as generally happened when the Lollard discoursed on his map his mind was reverting to Tegolin.

"Or he'll have to retreat!"

This *did* arouse the man in black tatters; and he gazed with consternation at the unruffled countenance of the man in white rags. He did indeed sit up with such a start at the word "retreat" that he was forced to utter a sharp cry as "Sele" took the opportunity of giving him a twinge.

"He'll *never* do that!" and Rhisiart's voice rose as it used to do when he was disputing in his room at Oxford.

The Lollard smiled and rubbed at his map with his piece of crust.

"Jesus Christ!" shouted Clerk Rhisiart. "I believe you'd sooner be right in your whoreson opinion than see the red dragon waving over Worcester gate!"

But before that day was over our two friends had been reduced to a graver mood. Their jailer, for one thing, had brought into their room an appalling account of the recent burning of a Lollard, when Prince Hal, still too young to understand such things, had had the heretic removed from the flames to give him a last chance of recanting, but had been forced by the Archbishop to see the already blackened body thrust back there again. They had also received a startling visit from Mad Huw bringing the news from Tegolin that she herself had obtained permission from the Bishop to have a brief interview with her husband after sunset that night.

This wasn't the first time Clerk Rhisiart had been allowed to see his wife who was now lodged by judicial consent in the house of the famous Worcester armourer, Master Dickon Shore. Room had been found in the same kindly quarters for the Mad Friar; but it had recently become doubtful whether this privilege would be continued—and for a sufficient reason.

The truth was, the poor Franciscan's mania had suffered a disconcerting change. Something about the present appearance of Rhisiart, with his straggling black beard, his tangled elflocks, and his hollow eyes, had so worked on the Grey Friar that he got it lodged in his brain that the prisoner in the Bishop's prison was none other than King Richard himself. Both Tegolin in the armourer's house and Rhisiart in the castle-keep had done their utmost to disabuse the poor man of this new illusion; but Mad Huw had received so many shocks of late that his feelings had been driven inward; and though he no longer burst out into fits of wild excitement his mania in this new secretive and hidden form was less than ever open to reason.

The interview between Rhisiart and his young wife had been timed to coincide with a final examination of Master Brut before the Bishops of Worcester and Hereford. The latter magnate, fleeing from his residence on the Wye at Glendower's approach, was delighted beyond measure to find the heretic who had so cleverly escaped him five years before safe in the power of his fellow-prelate. Indeed, like Pilate and Herod with another Prisoner, the two pontifical inquisitors, who before this had been inordinately jealous of each other, became, from this day on, close friends.

Nothing is a stronger bond, whether with time-serving prelates or with murderous foot-pads, than the sharing of a guilty conscience, and for several nights after dealing with the Lollard both ecclesiastics slept a sounder and less troubled sleep than they had done since they broke their vows to King Richard.

It had been by Master Shore's influence with Prince Hal that this particular interview between husband and wife had been permitted; and it was by the influence of the rich armourer's largess that the jailer had gone a step further in locking them up alone.

Master Shore, though not a Lollard himself, was an easy man where religion was concerned, and a good friend of both Sir John Oldcastle and the youthful Prince. He might indeed—as far as the taverns of the city went—have been called a boon-companion of these two. He was a widower with no official feminine dependent save his small daughter Julietta, between whom and little Nance, the jailer's off-spring, there existed a childish friendship.

Julietta was ten and Nance a year older; but when Julietta came to play with Nance in the castle garden it was always she who took the lead in their games. Mad Huw had hardly appeared upon the scene than he won both the little girls' hearts, and the children would listen to him for hours as he would tell—with many mysterious hints as to

Rhisiart's identity—how kind the renowned captain, Lord Grey of Codnor, had been to them all, and how he had despatched them, as prisoners of the Church, under the escort of his own guard, to be judged by the Bishop of Worcester.

"He must have guessed who *He* was," the Grey Friar would whisper at this point, as the children made him tell them the story for the twentieth time, "and he knew he had to be tender to the Mistress and her poor Friar for His sake!"

But it was only when the two little girls were alone that Julietta explained to the awestruck Nance how it was that the beautiful lady and the holy man had come to their house.

"I *know,* for I heard Sir John ask Father to take them. Sir John laughed a great deal; and Father looked like he does when he sends me to bed because a lady's coming to supper with him."

"One's white and one's black," Nance would reply when Julietta pressed her with questions about the two prisoners. "But sometimes the angel one's black and the devil one's white. I like the angel one best because he's like my Spanish doll. I lent him my scissors to cut off his beard and I never laughed once when he did it. They both want sewing up; but they haven't got no one to sew them up."

On one unfortunate occasion when Julietta broached the subject as to what was going to happen to her friend's angel and devil, little Nance began to cry.

"They're going—to put—*my* one," she sobbed, "into the fire—because he won't say his 'Ave, Maria.' Father told me *that*—when I wouldn't say mine because there was onion in my broth! I hate onion, don't you?"

It was curious how the relations between Rhisiart and Tegolin remained unchanged after all they had experienced since they'd been married. She'd brought needle and thread with her, and though after they'd hugged each other he wanted her to sit on his knee she insisted on kneeling by his side and doing at once, as fast as her fingers would work, what little Nance had called "sewing him up."

While she stitched she talked to him gravely and quietly, just as she'd done so many times when he was unhappy about Catharine or about his prestige with Owen; while Rhisiart, watching her with his mournful eyes through his tangled hair, thought how much more precious she was to him now than that Midsummer Day so long ago when they slept together under his sheepskin.

"I wish I'd put something," he suddenly burst out, "if it were only a heap of stones—on his grave!"

"But you did—you *did,* Rhisiart! You put your dagger into the earth. I can see how its handle looked now, all dripping with the rain! *That* made a cross; and a cross is better than any stones."

"But *he* wouldn't know it *was* a cross! He'd think I'd just forgotten. He'd think I'd be coming back for it. And I never *have* gone back! Besides, anyone seeing it there would steal it. They couldn't steal a heap of stones. How long do you think his skin will stay—like it was—?"

Tegolin thrust her needle through the piece of his shirt she was mending, and leaving the thread swaying there between them, like a gossamer across a narrow lane, possessed herself of his hand and pressed it to her lips.

"He had some happy days," she said gently, "before he died. He was the least tired of all of us when we first saw the Usk. Think, Rhisiart, how fast he trotted down that hill. Everything on his back *rattled*, he went so fast!"

Rhisiart sighed and repeated secretly, not caring that even Tegolin should know what he was doing, a solemn prayer for the soul of Griffin the piebald.

She went on with her sewing again then; and the flesh of her rounded arm, as he hung his head above it as it drew the thread, smelt so sweet to him that he thought in his heart: "Would it spoil it all for her if I lifted her up from her knees?"

But he didn't dare to do this. Nor was it only for fear of breaking her thread that he refrained. Upon his long thin features and emaciated cheeks there had come to be imprinted, during this fatal summer, lines of tenderness, such as his face had never displayed before. So he confined himself to caressing with the tips of his fingers the warmth and softness of her neck.

Lightly up and down, and cross-wise again, his fingers moved beneath her chin; and he thought in his heart: "I feel as if I'd lived with her for years; and yet I feel as if I'd only found her to-night!"

But he *had* been holding her in his arms—and the pain that it had given his wounded side to do so had been an excruciating sweetness to him, like a pain that passion demands ere it can reach its furthest tidal-mark—when at last with a long-drawn sob of weakness he let her sit down on the Lollard's stool beside him and allowed his hand to sink heavily on her lap.

"Gwion Bach—"

"Yes, Tegolin ferch Rheinalt!"

"Do you know what I've brought for you?"

His expression at that moment was so like his look, when he used to await her decision about Catharine or the Prince or Mad Huw, that her eyes filled with tears.

But she drew from her bosom a tiny phial, which she had fastened round her neck by a long black ribbon, and without drawing its silver stopper held it out to him. He surveyed it with widely-staring eyes.

The Bishop's prison was well lighted. Earlier Bishops had no doubt found it advisable to throw into relief under unusually strong illumination the faces of their victims when the necessity for calling back to the One Fold the perilous reasonings of the human mind made the infliction of pain indispensable.

"What is it?" he asked in an awed whisper.

"Death," the girl whispered. "Master Shore sent me to an alchemist's to get a sleeping-draught for Julietta when the child was sick; and I gave the man—well! never mind what I gave him. But *he* gave me *this!* It's the surest and quickest there is. It's only like water to look at. I had to buy this phial from him too. He was poor. He was grasping. But he swore, by the heart of Mary, that this was certain death. 'Death in thirty ticks of a French clock,' he said. And he said he could be hanged for giving it to me. Smell it, Rhisiart! It hasn't any smell at all."

Rhisiart took the thing from her, lifted the stopper, and bent his Norman nose over it, snuffing vigorously.

"Does it taste as little as it smells?" he asked her, still holding the little bottle to his nostrils and staring at her above it with feverish eyes.

"The man swore it had no taste at all and no colour at all. He said it could be put into water or wine or milk or anything and the person would be dead in thirty ticks of a French clock."

Rhisiart replaced the stopper, laid the phial on its side on the third stool, and asked her with a certain irritation in his tone why it had to be a *French* clock. "Can't we even take poison in our own way?" he said.

Tegolin flushed and tears of vexation came into her eyes. It was only a trifle; but since, as a woman would, she had repeated the shopman's exact words though there was no particular significance in them, there was something annoying in being caught up in a casual phrase like this.

Instead of dropping the topic Rhisiart must needs go on harping on it. The unspoken dread of their separation, that lay at the bottom of "the lake of his heart" like a drowned animal in a sack, sent up these bubbles of contradiction.

But she had something else in her mind to say to him, something that lay as heavy in her consciousness as an infant within a womb; but it was so hard a thing to say that she was now struggling with the temptation to leave it unsaid just five minutes longer, while he went on being cantankerous about the French clock just as he'd been about the way she wore her page's dress on that long ago Midsummer Day, when she rode to Glyndyfrdwy on Griffin's back.

"Put it away!" she burst out, pointing at the phial. "For Mary's sake put it in your belt! It'll go in there, won't it? It *must* go in there!"

Since he still remained inert and motionless, just staring at her with an expression as if he had to make sure that another Rhisiart, already in a different world, was correctly imitating him, she snatched at the phial herself and tearing open the shirt she'd been mending, squeezed the thing impulsively between his body and his belt.

What she did was painful to Rhisiart in every conceivable way. It caused him anguish in his wounded side. It gave him the sensation that he was her helpless infant rather than her equal mate, and it seemed to emphasize their parting in a manner that was like a push down a precipice.

But the hurt look in his eyes, together with that very emanation of outraged childishness which his whole attitude betrayed, reminded her so irresistibly of the Rhisiart she had loved in secret in those early days that she flung her arms round his neck and desperately clinging to him gasped out a spasmodic succession of endearing words.

But she quickly saw how weak he was—far weaker than she had expected—and she realized too, for he could no longer conceal it, how vicious was the pain in his hip. Quickly she let him go. Quickly she made him lie down on his bed of straw; and while the tears trickled from her cheeks upon his beard she flung herself down by his side and stroking his face whispered half-inaudible murmurs of love into his ears.

"Don't look at me while I tell you something, Rhisiart," she said at last, after they had lain together in silence while time flowed over them as if it were made of something lighter than air and swifter than thought. "Shut your eyes, my only love, while I tell you what I *have* to tell you."

Rhisiart needed not her fingers pressed on his eyelids to make him obey her now. He felt weary of everything in the world except her presence. He wished in his heart that she would tell him nothing; that she would but shut *her* eyes too, so that they might sleep side by side forever!

But by slow degrees her terrible words, each one sounding like a moaning plant torn up by the roots, pierced his drugged intelligence. It was about Master Shore she was speaking; and she told him that the armourer was a great favourite with the young Prince, that no one in the kingdom, save Sir John Oldcastle, had more influence with him. She told him that the man was a widower and had grown enamoured of her; that she herself felt no repulsion for him, and *did* feel considerable gratitude. She told him that Julietta had come to cling to her as to a mother, that she felt sorry for both father and child; and finally that the man had sworn by the heart of Mary that if she *did* consent to live with him he could obtain from Prince Hal, not a complete pardon, for the connection with Glendower was too public, but a mitigation of the sentence from death on the scaffold to imprisonment in the Tower of London.

All this she told him in a flat, even voice, and very rapidly. It was a voice Rhisiart had never heard from her till once or twice of late he had heard her say her beads aloud. And when she'd finished she still kept the fingers of both her hands pressed upon his closed eyelids. She was crouching above him now, with one of her knees on the straw of his bed and one on the flag-stones; and as she bowed over him, the bodkin that held her braid about her head became unloosened, and the familiar coils slithered down like a living serpent across his face.

The touch of her hair, with its familiar fragrance, sent a sharp shudder through his frame, while its fall caused her to liberate his eyes from their enforced blindness. Then it became Tegolin's destiny to stare without blinking—for she'd always been one for straight and steady looks—into the eyes of the person to whom she had just offered the supreme test, the most crucial that a girl can put to a man, namely, whether he considered his life more important than her honour.

Rhisiart lay without a movement; you would almost have thought without a breath. She felt as if his eyes were swimming like dark fish steadily, irresistibly, through wave after wave of her secret being.

Without removing her own eyes she now rose slowly, lifting one knee from the stones and the other from the straw; and even in the tension of that worst moment retaining such calm of nature that the curious thought flitted across her mind: "Do nuns have straw to kneel on, like cows in a shed?"

But she rose to her full height now, lifting her hands to her head to coil up her braid. To do this she removed another bodkin, and, because her fingers were busy, held it in her mouth till its time had come, staring at Rhisiart from above the tightened lips out of which it protruded. She had thrown her mantle aside when she first entered, and her pale blue gown, caught up below her breasts by a gold band, displayed to their best advantage her soft white throat and rounded arms, and even those tiny freckles on her skin of which Glyn Dŵr had made so much.

But though the eyes of these two were searching each others' souls like divers in deep seas, they both remained absolutely ignorant of what the other was thinking. So little did Rhisiart understand his wife that he hadn't the faintest suspicion that this whole tale of hers *was retrospect,* and she had *already* saved him from being hung, drawn, and quartered by going up into the armourer's bed.

And if it was no more possible for Rhisiart to imagine his wife's lying to him than it was possible for him to imagine her naked in bed with a man he'd never seen, it was unthinkable to Tegolin that a Norman-Welsh gentleman, who had been to Oxford, and whom she herself had seen advancing on his fantastic horse in front of a line of arrows pointed at his heart, would be able to fish up from the shifting sands of moral casuistry a sufficient reason for the sacrifice of honour to life. She had expected a violent refusal and a pitiful struggle between them. What she hadn't realized was how far below all casuistry he had sunk in his weakness.

Tegolin was a warm-blooded girl, and she never had been a girl of morbidly virginal shrinkings. But save for her romantic idealizing of the Friar she had given herself to Rhisiart, body, soul, and spirit, to such an absolute tune that it would have been hard to make another woman—even Lady Mortimer—understand what she felt when she climbed those stairs to the armourer's open door.

The worthy man had rallied her the next morning about the candle-grease with which the stairs were sprinkled; but she didnt confess to him how many times she had descended, before the final blind rush that took her to the top.

But the truth was that Rhisiart from the first time they met had been conscious of something in Tegolin that was stronger than him-self; and upon this stronger power he had always unscrupulously leaned. And this leaning upon her had reached a sort of culminating ecstasy as he longed just now, in his weakness and his pain, to go to sleep forever upon her breast.

Thus when she talked of "giving herself" to armourer Shore, this "giving herself" didn't call up any image of his actual Tegolin, with her red braid pressed between her white shoulders and a strange bed, submitting to the final outrage. It rather called up a comfortable vision of Master Dickon's hearth with a great bowl of venison stew—for the Lollard and he had been vying with each other lately in the images created by hunger—and with the lively Julietta, of whom he'd heard Nance talk, keeping a place for him too at the table; and only a dim benevolent cloudy *blur,* resembling God the Father, to show that Tegolin had "given herself" to anyone!

It was the weakness of his famished body that formed these dis-honorable visions; and it was the escape from the barrels of tar and the red-hot prongs, and from the time it took to get it done, for he'd seen it at Hereford as a child, that made him sink into her strength as a tired seagull into an ocean-wave.

And as he looked at this beautiful being upon whom his life depended, and who was prepared to give him his life, he felt as if he were absolved by those soft breasts and those white arms from the whole burden of choice, from the necessity of any decision at all! A deep in-sucking tide of infantile gratitude drew all the manliness out of him; while the expression in his eyes made so great a contrast to his hollow, emaciated cheeks, his straggly beard, his pinched hawk-nose, his narrow forehead, that the girl began to feel as if a Rhisiart, younger even than the one who had allowed her to kiss his crusader's sword and had teased her about her page's dagger, was begging her to take him on her lap, to hold him to her breast, to save him from the wolves!

Without a quiver of his mouth or a movement of his manacled limbs, the big tears of absolute weakness began to form in his eyes and to trickle down upon his beard; and she knew that whether he understood or not the price she'd paid he accepted the life she'd given him.

Two days later Master Dickon Shore was seated with Sir John Old-castle in the snug inner sanctum of the Rose and Crown talking of the unexpected retreat of the allied army from Woodbury Hill, when their host, with the self-conscious lack of ceremony that the Prince insisted upon, announced the presence of the heir to the throne. "Let him in then, you whoreson herald of woe!" roared Sir John. "Let the sweet lad in, without making such faces! And bring some of that *Lacrima Christi* of yours he praised the other night, and—mark you, Martin Glum!—write it down to *me* this time—dost hear? Master Shore and I aren't like those whoresons they tell of who tap royalty and hiss treason! Let the boy in, and then open a bottle of *Lacrima Christi* and keep both Hal and the wine from these burning logs. He brings news, or I'm a Polack! Put a chair for him away from the fire. His blood tingles enough as it is; keep that wine cool till he calls for it."

Dickon Shore, who was a man of caution, nodded significantly at his knightly friend when Martin was gone. "It'll be as I said," he remarked. "He wants to rush you off in pursuit of those French prancers and their bare-foot Merlins! But beware of the old fox when you run with the young one! Well, well. A word in the nick is snuff for the wick! The Lord gives and the King takes. He may bring news; but I can tell you what he *won't* bring; he won't bring the head of Owen Glendourdy; and that's all *I'd* thank him for!"

"Let him—" But there was no need to ask their landlord to "let him," for Prince Henry came bursting in a state of intense nervous excitement. There was a peculiar vein of the neurotic in the whole Lancastrian House. It showed itself in Henry the Fourth both outwardly and inwardly. Outwardly in his desperate forced marches and inwardly in his religious superstition. No captain could get his men quicker from one end of England to another. Since Harold Godwinson there'd never been such an adept in the rapid movement of troops. But Harold understood the Welsh as Henry never did. Henry's invasions were the laughing stock of that nation; while Harold penetrated even into the fastnesses of Snowdon.

The Prince entered the room dressed in full armour. There were drops of sweat on his long white face and burning fever-spots on his cheeks. His hazel eyes, which were not unlike his father's, gleamed with a consuming excitement, and his mouth above his narrow pointed chin was twisted awry, and even when he ceased speaking his thin lips kept up a queer twitching. Sir John and Master Shore had often been put to it, as they discussed the Prince, to account for this twitching; while the whores of the house, Madge Howlet and Bess Bolt, who were both girls of some poetic imagination, indulged in quite fanciful comparisons. Madge maintained that when he spoke it was like a moorfowl crossing a stream: "The ripples go on spreading after the bird's flown!" Bess had a less homely comparison. She said it was like *seeing an echo*. "His lips," she assured them, "echo every word he utters, only without a sound!"

As Sir John and Master Shore now rose to greet Prince Henry, they did so with an anxious exchange of glances, the burly knight's ruddy cheeks distorting themselves like a face in a concave mirror, while the armourer's visage paled a shade or two, like a flagon of wine suddenly diluted with water.

Prince Hal addressed them as if they had been twice as far away as they were. "To horse, to horse, Sir John!" he cried. "I stopped at your lodgings. Your man is here with your harness. Not a moment to spare! Off you ride with orders from me to Codnor, to Grendor, to Talbot— Mother of God! to any man of them! orders to Beelzebub—as long as you get out of *here* with a whole skin! The Archbishop's arrived—hot on the trail of heretics. He's with my father now. He's going to burn and burn and burn! That young stiver of Lollardry we took along with Glendower's Secretary is to suffer to-morrow. They're already piling up the bonfire in the market, and the next thing will be my father's warrant to have you taken! I'll ride with you for a mile or two—'after Glendower' we'll tell the guard at the gate; and you, Dickon —you, Dickon"—he paused while his lips moved in that same silent twitching that Madge and Bess had noticed even while he was making free with them—"and you, Dickon, had better get your wench's husband out of that place at once and pack him off to London."

He paused and bit his lip. It was clear to his friends that there was something on his mind more personal than Sir John's escape. "I've been talking," he said, "to the Archbishop. He thinks my father won't live many years longer. He thinks this worrying about his soul will kill him. He's very bad to-day." Two or three seconds passed while he thought how bad the King was. Then he began again. "The Archbishop says that when—that when my father's gone—I ought to invade France and end all this. He says I have a claim—a very good claim." And he began pacing the room in his clanging armour with the springy step of a young player at quarter-staff.

"Take Tom Crosby and his whole company— Here! I'll give you the order in writing—Martin! I say! Martin! No! By Crish! I've no time for liquour. Take the stuff away and give it to the wenches!—and bring me a tablet. Let Crosby put the fellow in the Tower along with Glendower's son!"

While Prince Hal with ostentatious penmanship—for the bravest Prince in Christendom was prouder of his clerkly ability than of his prowess in arms—was laboriously inditing his commands "to our trusty and redoubtable captain, Master Thomas Crosby," the most perturbed personage in the Rose and Crown was certainly its landlord. This careful man saw the best customers he was ever likely to get in his lifetime dispersing like swallows in September. His only comfort lay in the thought that even if the Prince did call for Madge or Bess again the girls were such poor judges of wine that he would never know what had been substituted for his royal bounty.

At the very moment when Prince Hal was laboriously displaying his

clerkly gifts at the Sign of the Rose and Crown, Rhisiart and Master
Brut were having a poignant discussion in their spacious prison-house.
They had come to understand each other with an understanding deeper
than that of brothers; and their love had grown so diffused as to spread
through them like the sap in the kindred branches of one tree-root.

When they had first got fond of each other at Glyndyfrdwy and
Dinas Brān the relation between them was crude enough. Master Brut
was a religious prig in those days and our friend Rhisiart a romantic
egoist; but after all they had gone through, these peculiarities had been
so modified and mellowed that in addition to the Lollard's indulgence
to his friend's touchy pride, Rhisiart's maturer interest in religion endowed their friendship with many tender refinements.

In their earlier relation the boyish conceit of the young Oxford
student had obscured what might be called the *feminine element* in his
soul; but, as their love deepened, this element grew more and more apparent, until to-day, as they talked together about life and death, it was
the man whose beard had been untouched by little Nance's scissors
who played the woman's part, while the soul of the soft-cheeked Lollard
showed itself both in its weakness and its strength to be masculine
through and through.

The golden August sunshine, as heavy and mellow within their
prison-chamber as it was outside, threw upon every object in that large,
low room a peculiar kind of glory. But to Rhisiart's nerves there was
something malign and dreadful about this reddish glow, especially
when it fell upon an enormous life-size crucifix which occupied the
middle of the wall opposite the door.

This great crucifix, which extended practically from ceiling to floor,
hung at right angles to the window on one side, and on the other to
that portion of their chamber which had been perforce converted into
a latrine. The heavy sunshine had a curious effect on the facial expression of this hanging figure; converting the pain it was suffering into
an un-earthly desire to inflict pain upon the enemies of God. The
words: "And many are called but few are chosen," together with the
words: "Wailing and gnashing of teeth," were what to Master Brut at
any rate this object represented. But in the downright virile manner of
a sturdy Wycliffite he hesitated not to utter rough and even gross
ribaldries in the presence of this dreadful figure, comparing it very un-

favourably with what he assured his excitable friend was the *real* Saviour of the world, whose form emerged, like a blessed Jinn, out of the un-sealed bottle of the original Greek.

The agitated sympathy of Rhisiart, who to do him justice forgot his own trouble in the worse horror that over-hung his friend, had the opposite effect from what his wife's presence had had upon himself. It simply steadied the man's courage. But Rhisiart found it impossible to take in the full import of Tegolin's words. In his feverish weakness he kept thinking of Mortimer and Catharine; but there was nothing in him now of the jealous realism of a grown man's natural emotion towards this shadowy Master Shore by whom she was to be dishonoured and he was to be rescued.

One thing puzzled him. Why, if he were not to be executed, had his wife brought him that little phial? He had been vividly aware of it, all these two long nights and days since her visit, pressing against his side; but a deep instinct, totally beyond any rational explanation, had caused him to say nothing to his friend of this death-bearing draught, "clear and tasteless as water."

What amazed him about Master Brut was the way in which the man kept reverting to that revolting description of a fellow Lollard's burning which their illiterate jailor had made them read aloud.

"I know," Master Brut was saying now, after expressing what was to Rhisiart an incomprehensible concern as to the fate of "that damned Ruthin witch," "I know I shall lose my mind in the flames. But I've decided to cry, 'Jesus! Jesus!'—and that isn't *you*"—and he made a profane gesture towards the figure hanging above them—"as long as I don't go mad with pain. And my idea is"—and a look so curious crossed his smooth round face that it made Rhisiart think of the smile of the Man in the Moon—"that even if I do go mad, I mean if I become nothing but a blindly-shrieking pain, I shall *mechanically,* if you know what I mean, go on with that same cry."

This was too much for Rhisiart and he stumbled to his feet. He had been lying on his straw-bed most of the day. Indeed, ever since Tegolin had lain down there by his side his bed had grown precious to him. He had caught on that occasion the shape of certain particular pieces of straw that were larger than the rest and had the empty husks of wheat still adhering to them; and these he had avoided disturbing, fearful lest they should be crushed or lost among the rest in their special position against the wall.

But he scrambled to his feet now, and shuffling up to his friend, whose turn it was that day to wear their only suit of clothes, he hugged him to his heart. "You'll—turn—me—into—a whoreson heretic soon!" he groaned as he hugged him; and to the end of his days he never forgot the grotesque expression of shy embarrassment that distorted that smooth countenance. How was it, he wondered, that a man who was going to be burnt alive could feel such discomfort, such embarrassment, such obvious misgiving, at being passionately embraced?

But what was that? Hurriedly they drew apart, both praying they would see the face of little Nance. But it was her father; and never had Master Giggleswick, since they'd first been brought here, showed so much agitation. To their amazement he waved them aside and, going hurriedly towards their extempore latrine, began fumigating it with burning charcoal, sprinkled with incense, that he was carrying in a brazier.

"The King is coming!" he muttered presently, turning towards them a face out of the midst of his fumes that was a convulsed image of horrified awe. "The Archbishop arrived this morning and they're both coming to see you. The King is in one of his moods."

"What do you mean, *his moods?*" asked Rhisiart.

The man stared at him in astonishment. Then a look of anger crossed his visage. "*You'd* be in a mood I reckon; if *you* hadn't slept for nigh a week!"

The Lollard's round face assumed once more the accustomed mask of patient placidity that his friend's burst of womanish emotion had disturbed.

"There's a stake being set up in Market Square," said Master Giggleswick, giving them a look of terrified commiseration, "and a scaffold, too," and with these words he went on resolutely swinging his censer above their piled-up excrement.

When he was gone, the Lollard shuffled over to Rhisiart and offered his unhurt arm to help him to rise. Neither of them could move faster than this awkward shuffle, for their ankles were bound by short chains about a foot long; but Master Brut helped the younger man to reach his accustomed stool, and then sitting down by his side began picking up with his finger and thumb various fragments of bread with which, on the stool that served as their table, he had been showing how the land lay between Glendower's camp and London.

"Jesus! Jesus! Jesus!" Rhisiart caught him muttering, as he mechanically placed some of these fragments in his mouth and flicked others, in little neat pellets, against the legs of that oppressive and inquisitorial crucifix.

"He's thinking what he'll do," Rhisiart said to himself, "when the pain's unbearable."

And then he noticed that their jailer, in his fumblings with his brazier, had dropped upon the floor that filthy bit of parchment containing the lurid popular account of the burning of the last London heretic. He prayed Master Brut wouldn't notice it lying there. And then he began comparing—and he was pleased with himself for having such thoughts which he felt were worthy of an imprisoned diplomatist— what they'd been hearing of the casual ways of Henry's "entourage" with the stately formality of Owen's court. "And how different must be," he said to himself, "this 'mood' they talk of, compared with those strange trances of Owen's. Everybody seems to understand the caprices of this King; whereas I've lived with *our* Prince all these years and he's as mysterious to me as he was at the beginning!"

Presently as he watched the Lollard obliterating his map, Rhisiart found himself trembling. "It's not the prongs and pitch this time." he thought. "It's seeing the King!" And in spite of himself the old traditional Norman respect for his feudal sovereign made him straighten his body as he turned his head towards the door. *There!* Voices and steps were now audible outside. The two men's eyes met; and to Rhisiart's relief his friend ceased muttering the name of his Saviour and remarked quite calmly: "I don't want you to intervene, dear lad, whatever the Archbishop says to me, or I to him. Do you understand?"

Rhisiart had only time to nod when the door was flung open.

Both the prisoners rose to their feet and made the best obeisance they could, considering their chains. Behind the King and the Archbishop there entered, along with the jailer, a grotesquely-attired dwarf, and behind the dwarf, evidently uneasy, evidently disobeying his Master's command, a small white grey-hound. Our friends had been told of this white dog who belonged to a breed brought from abroad by

John of Gaunt; and little Nance had often talked to them about the dwarf, who, derisively called Hercule, was a privileged creature in the royal camp, as well as in Henry's lodge at Berkhampstead.

The Archbishop was dressed in the plain garb of a monk, and after acknowledging the two prisoners' genuflexion, he fell back with priestly propriety, leaving the situation in the hands of the temporal ruler of the realm.

Rhisiart was startled beyond all expectation by the appearance of England's monarch. The words of the jailer: "If *you* hadn't slept for nigh a week!" returned to his mind. To say he was shocked would be a mild expression of what he felt. He had heard rumours about Henry's strange illness, which some said was a form of leprosy, but the haggard and disfigured features that now regarded him with an expression of intolerable nervous tension from under their helmet—for this Prince when once he took the field rarely removed his armour—horrified him so much that in spite of his prejudice, and in spite of his loyalty to Wales, he felt a pang of painful pity.

Henry of Lancaster had an extremely long face like his eldest son, but there the resemblance between them ended; for Prince Hal's physiognomy conveyed a sense of vigorous and lively youth, whereas the King's countenance was haggard with premature old age.

As Henry looked round him now, after giving a hurried glance at his prisoners, Rhisiart made no attempt to conceal either his student's interest in an unhappy man or his inherited respect for England's monarch.

The King certainly had an eye of terrifying authority. Indeed the first impression our friend got of him was as startling as it was horrible. The man made him actually think of a corpse, in the early stages of decomposition, tottering under a suit of glittering steel. "I can understand the Battle of Shrewsbury *now*," he thought. And he had reason for the thought; for the energy that emanated from this sick and world-weary man was over-powering.

But if Rhisiart caught the unconquerable vitality of the English King, Master Brut, who, as we know, was more of a psychologist, detected at once the man's spiritual secret, the secret that was like a charnel-house rat gnawing at the tissues of his soul. "He's got a devil," said the Wycliffite to himself, "and its name is *Remorse*. And only the words of the living Jesus, not *you,* you monstrous parody!"—and the bold blasphemer made a motion in his mouth that brought his saliva to the tip of his tongue—"will ever cast that devil out!"

As for the Archbishop, upon whose face Rhisiart now turned his attention, no emotion that *he* called up could possibly be associated with pity. Nevertheless, none could deny that the successor of Anselm and Becket was a handsome old priest. But had a child made a comic picture of everything most antipathetic to childhood this crafty and cruel face—like that of a horrible old woman employed in the punishment of whores—would have been that picture.

It was the face of the eternal Enemy of Freedom from the foundation of the world. His features struck our friend as being entirely composed of sinister and enigmatic *curves.* His massive nose resembled the bulb of an evil plant, while over his almost invisible eyes that seemed to be perpetually sucking at the nerve-centres of heretics there hung heavily-curved folds. These folds were repeated *below* his eyes, and hung suspended there like fungus-growths beneath wood-pecker holes. His cheeks, his forehead, his chin—all were a series of equivocal curves. There wasn't, our friend hurriedly decided, from the top of that shaven poll to the bottom of that shaven jowl, one single honest straight line!

"You don't happen to know, Master Secretary," began the King, addressing Rhisiart, "how many Welsh gentlemen, of any note or quality, were with Glendourdy on Woodbury Hill?"

"No, Sire," replied our friend looking straight at the distressed and restless eyes which rested on him only for a moment as they turned from the grey-hound to the dwarf and back again to the grey-hound.

"Have you any idea how long this foolish rebellion is likely to last?"

"No, Sire."

"About how many men could Glendourdy count on if we ourselves were to march into this unhappy country to restore order?"

Rhisiart began to take heart. If there was anything, as we know, that he prided himself upon, it was his legal acumen. The only doubt in his mind was whether it was better to emphasize or to disparage the Welsh powers of resistance. He knew well that the one thing Owen *wasn't* afraid of was a formal invasion by the King in person. "It's just what he wants," he said to himself, as he pretended to be undergoing a painful mental struggle as to whether or not to betray his master.

He hurriedly decided that the larger Owen's forces were, the more likely was it that the King would come.

"I believe, Sire," he replied with gloomy intensity, as if the words were drawn out of him by the presence of a scaffold, "that the person your royal question refers to could raise at a pinch about *twenty thousand spears.*"

Master Brut wouldn't resist a gasp of astonishment, which wasn't lost upon the Archbishop; but at this moment the entrance of a couple of soldiers with chairs that resembled judgment-seats for both Church and State postponed any comment he might have made.

If it was a relief to the prisoners to have their judges seated it was a positive joy to the dwarf and the dog. The sinking down of that troubled figure, in his unadorned breast-plate and polished greaves—for Henry, out of a deliberate and shrewd policy, wore the royal arms only on state occasions—proved too tempting an opportunity to be resisted by these devoted adherents.

Dressed entirely in blood-red the little Hercule held in his hand an enormous wooden sword, the tip of which, painted an ominous blood-colour, he now proceeded to use as a jumping-pole, and began hopping about the chamber, ostentatiously approaching the Archbishop, and then, with no less fantastic ostentation, hopping away from him in pretended panic.

Master Giggleswick, without waiting a sign from Henry, had seen fit, in his discomfort and uneasiness to take himself off along with the soldiers, so that the King and the Primate were now seated alone before their prisoners; while round and about them, and round and about the men in chains, who stood together in the fumes left by the brazier, hopped the restless Hercule, his proceedings resembling, had the frowning crucifix possessed the power of vision, the antics of a blood-red flea.

"What in your own opinion, young man," began Henry again, "was the motive of these unhappy rebels in advancing so far into our realm? Surely they didn't—"

"The King of France with thousands of his men," chanted Hercule, pausing for a second as he leant on his wooden sword, "climbed up the hill and then climbed down again!" And immediately afterwards in a low wistful voice: "You are sad, Sire Gossip, you are sad."

"We *are* sad," said the King, smiling at him and glancing meaningly at the Archbishop. But the effect of this smile was to throw into such appalling relief the ravages of his strange disease that the dwarf skipped away with a gnat-like wail.

"I thought you were!" he shrilled with an hysterical scream. And then he went off hopping again, repeating in a weird crescendo: "I thought you were! I thought you were! I thought you were!"

It was at this point that the Archbishop intervened. "With your permission, my royal son," he began; and Rhisiart noticed that he didn't use his lips to speak. Indeed he seemed to have no lips. His cheeks had the power of folding themselves, without the mediation of lips, into the indrawn orifice of the mouth out of which the words came.

"With my royal son's permission I should like to say one word to *you,* Master Walter Brut of Lyde in the County of Hereford." As he spoke he made a slight movement of his fingers *upwards* as if in an automatic blessing; but as soon as they reached the height of the cross on his stomach he projected two of them—and they were the whitest and most shapely hands our friend had ever seen—in the manner of a pair of *horns* towards Master Brut. This gesture terrified Rhisiart on behalf of his friend more than if he'd rolled out over the Lollard's head a volley of priestly curses.

"I wish the King to hear me offer you, my unhappy son, a last opportunity to reconcile yourself with the Church of Christ. Are you still obstinate in your blasphemous opinion that the Sacred Element used in Holy Mass is *not* the living Body of the—"

But Rhisiart couldn't help intervening at this solemn point. "Oh, my Lord Archbishop!" he cried eagerly. "My friend has often said to me, while he's been reading the Scriptures, that the centre of the Catholic Faith lies in the Holy Mass. I can testify, my Lord, from the bottom of my heart, that no one has ever attended Mass more reverently than Master Brut, or has lived a more good, a more kind, a more unselfish life!"

The Prelate's eyes, as he heard this startling suggestion that mere human goodness could counterbalance an improper view of the Blessed Sacrament, sank so deep under the curves of his eyelids that their cavities came to resemble those round holes of in-sucking sand made by sea-worms.

"Do you still adhere, Master Brut, to your blasphemous opinion?" he said, taking no more notice of Rhisiart than he did of the antics of Hercule the dwarf.

"I do, my Lord," replied the Lollard calmly.

That the reply was much more satisfactory to the zealous supporter of the Statute *De Heretico Comburendo* than would have been any tendency in Master Brut to recant was proved by the triumphant tone in which the Prelate now addressed the world-weary monarch, the droop of whose ravaged face against the metallic edge of his gorget suggested a longing rather to sleep forever himself than to vex the sleep of others.

"You see how it is, Sire!" he said loudly, while Henry gave a queer galvanic jerk as if he'd been pricked by a bodkin. "The same conceited tone, the same air of self-righteousness, the same contempt for tradition and authority! It was a happy day for the Church, Sire, when you were crowned King; and since the King rests on the Church, and the Church rests on God, you may be sure that our dear young Prince will live to walk in your steps; and *his* son to walk in *his*. I can see before me, Sire, your son's son—a third Henry of Lancaster—reigning over a kingdom, Sire, wherein all heresy and all treason and all rebellion, together with all the malice of man's wicked mind, have been crushed *out!"*

The Archbishop was not one for impulsive gestures. He moved his eyes without moving his head. He moved his hands without moving his arms. He moved his fingers without moving his hands. But when he uttered the syllables "crushed *out!"* he placed one clenched fist upon the other in his capacious lap, and as though they were "the upper and the nether mill-stone" of the Scriptures, he caused them to rotate, not rapidly, but quietly, slowly, irresistibly, as if they were crushing by leisurely progression the reckless soul of Master Wycliffe to powder.

As if mesmerized by this visual exhibition of the Mill of God to which it was his task to lend his weight, the King turned to the Lollard, and it seemed as if his words had no personal feeling behind them at all. He made a weary motion with his hand for both the prisoners to come nearer as he began to speak; and Rhisiart, who experienced a childish fascination for the patches of repulsive scurf that disfigured the royal features, felt as if *they,* and not the man behind them, were uttering judgment. "You have heard what the Archbishop has said, young man, and you'll be wise to spend your last night on earth in remorse for your sin, for your most grievous sin, against the Laws of our Realm, against the Religion once for all delivered to the Saints, and against the Vicar of Christ. We condemn your body to be burnt with fire until it is utterly consumed; and as for your unhappy soul, if the pangs of—the pangs of—" But at that point there was a complete change in his intonation, and he uttered the word "remorse" with such a ghastly emphasis, and fell into such a strange muse the moment it had been uttered, that the dwarf who had been watching him intently came with three long hops to his feet, and crouching down there set up a moan like the howl of a dog.

"Hercule," murmured the King, "Hercule." His voice was so tender that the men in chains exchanged a quick glance and a longing to fall at the side of the dwarf, and clasp the knees of a prince who could speak like that, passed through both their minds.

But the small creature had scrambled to his feet again. "Sire Gossip!" he cried. "Can you answer a riddle?"

"Put it to us first," said the King; and Rhisiart had a vision of this corpse in armour clinging to the jests of his fool as he swung above a dizzy gulf.

The dwarf picked up his wooden sword and after several attempts managed to insert it so firmly and deeply between two of the flag-stones that he could play the acrobat upon it and with one hand on its cross-hilt could dangle his legs and point his finger at the seated church-man.

"Why, Sire Gossip, is an Archbishop like a grid-iron?"

There was a jingle of chains as both the prisoners drew a step nearer. They all became aware now of excited voices outside the door and some kind of violent altercation. But Henry took no notice of this; and the Archbishop, though he moved his eyes and clasped his fingers, remained immobile.

It was clear to Rhisiart that the more his fool made sport of the Archbishop the easier it was for the King to forget his need for sleep. "His piety's all politics," thought our friend. "He's got Richard on his brain as badly as Mad Huw; but he can forget all when Hercule's at his tricks."

"Why a grid-iron?" asked Henry softly, giving his chair a jerk so that he had his back to the crucifix and his face to the dwarf.

"Because," began Hercule, who now bore a striking resemblance to a monkey on a pole, "because—"

But there he stopped; for the King had swung round towards Rhisiart. "As for you," he burst out, turning his sick man's gaze upon our astonished friend, "*you* may thank our good Dickon, and not us, that we've decided on the Tower for you, and with a whole skin!"

"Sire Gossip?"

"Well, Hercule?"

"An Archbishop is like a grid-iron because so much good gospel-meat goes in red, and comes out—"

But the door was flung open at this point, and Jailer Giggleswick appeared, clinging desperately to the excited form of none other than Mad Huw.

"*What's this?*" cried Henry angrily, struggling to his feet with his hand on the hilt of his sword. "I told you we were to be left alone. By my father's soul, Master Jailer—"

But no sooner had Mad Huw set eyes on the angry monarch, now standing close to the figure in chains, who to the Friar's demented fancy was no other than the dead Richard, than he shook off the hands of Master Giggleswick, glanced with a Welsh Franciscan's contempt at the Archbishop, and, after inclining his head humbly and reverently in the direction of Rhisiart, began to pour forth a torrent of prophetic eloquence.

As Rhisiart had long ago discovered, there was a magnetic hypnotism about Mad Huw, when he let himself go, at once so tender and so terrifying that few hearers were able to do anything but hold their peace in awestruck silence.

"What will they do now?" our friend thought, glancing from the King to the Prelate.

But the Archbishop did nothing; though his eyes moved in his motionless head towards the troubled monarch and gave him one penetrating glance. Then they turned to their contemplation of the feet of the crucifix.

The white dog, after sniffing at the Friar's legs, settled himself on his thin haunches, and watched him intently, his delicate pointed head drooping a little to one side. "He acts," thought our friend, "as if it were Saint Francis himself."

But the Lollard had eyes for nobody but the King. He seemed to forget that this conscience-stricken figure had just condemned him to be burnt. The pathologist in him was touched to the quick; and well it might be! The extraordinary thing was that in his self-lacerating mood Henry was exerting his own powerful will to draw the speaker on.

An appalling reciprocity rose up in that Worcestershire prison between Richard's murderer and Richard's idolater. The same superstitious mania in the monarch that made him helpless in the Prelate's hands made him equally helpless before his accuser. And mingled with this nervous confederacy in his own indictment, there was, as both dog and dwarf seemed perfectly to understand, a malicious satisfaction in the discomfort which the Friar's words must needs be causing the Archbishop. That portly figure in the monk's garb, however, gave neither to Henry nor to Hercule the least sign of being disconcerted. All he did, while Mad Huw's words rang through the prison, was to assist the King to sink once more, with a dull metallic tinkle of his heavy armour, into the chair he'd vacated; but this done he quietly resumed his own seat, folded his hands in his lap, and fixing his eyes on the crucifix above him assumed the expression of inscrutable piety, with which in his cathedral throne he was accustomed to await the close of some prolonged anthem.

The door of the Bishop's prison had been left open; and poor Master Giggleswick, whom Providence had intended rather for the rôle of a town-crier than a jailer, now beheld—as the last straw to his shame—the fair head of little Nance, accompanied by the fairer head of Julietta, peeping in with spell-bound curiosity!

Frantically the good man gesticulated to the children to go away, but instead of obeying him for they were both the motherless darlings of indulgent men, they sidled into the room, and stood there, hand in hand, staring with delighted awe at the King, at the prisoners, and above all at the gesticulating Friar.

Rhisiart kept saying to himself: "Why doesn't he stop predicting these woes for the House of Lancaster and say a word for Walter here?" He glanced at his friend. Was the man praying for a miracle under his breath? Was he anticipating his struggles, his pain, his cries of "Jesus"? He himself shook off as if it were a mortal sin the stir of sweetness in the depths of his nature at his escape from the prongs and the pitch. The thought came to him: "Mightn't the sick King, in his present remorseful mood, cheat the Archbishop in return for some real information about Wales and its Prince?" And then he had a diplomatic after-thought: "Couldn't I buy Walter's pardon by *inventing* a master-secret that would do Owen no harm and cause this sick King intense satisfaction?"

But what a man Walter was! Why wouldn't he let a person catch his eye? Was he fearful of anyone, even the friend of his heart, peering through the bloody sweat of his soul into the pain-dance within?

But what was this? The astonishing man was actually watching Hercule with lively interest—and, by Jesus, if he wasn't smiling! No, no, no—this smile of Walter Brut's, and how it had baffled him from their first encounter! rising to the surface just now, just when Tegolin—no! he refused to think of it!—*it was too much*. It made him angry. It almost made him hate the fellow. Oh blast, oh damn this skipping red flea! What *was* the whoreson up to now, just when the whirling predictions of the Friar were warning that corpse in armour that nothing, *nothing* he could do, could conquer the Welsh nation?

But it wasn't only to Rhisiart that Hercule's behaviour seemed inexplicable. Little Nance and Julietta were staring at him in an ecstasy. Indeed it looked as if they would soon be clapping their hands! What he was pretending to do was to catch in his cupped fingers the prophetic words that issued from the mouth of the Friar and then to convey them in that same imaginary receptacle to the abstracted Archbishop, and having made as if he'd emptied them there like burning coals, to go skipping back to Mad Huw where he held out his hands as if to obtain another handful of these scoriac words.

In this performance, to the children's delight, and apparently not to the King's displeasure, the butterfly-like little dog took a lively part, leaping up at the dwarf and exhibiting a moving vignette in scarlet and snow-white!

Had Elphin been there he would doubtless have caught the full effect of this weird picture, sketched by the heraldic artist, chance, for his masters, the fleeting hours; but, as it was, the particular way the sun shone across the chamber, making the King's steel armour gleam like glass and throwing into ghastly relief the yellow sores and grey scurf upon his ravaged face while it caused the grime upon the unwashed skin of the two prisoners to be transformed into beaten gold, found no human eye to note it. Master Brut had never been one for aesthetic effects; and though he might smile at the antics of a little white dog, his friend knew well what *must* be going on in his mind—the chain—the stake—the writhing flesh.

And all for what? All that one handsome old monk, without a straight line in his face, should get the Holy Father's blessing upon the House of Lancaster!

"Oh Richard, oh my Saint!" Mad Huw was intoning again; and Rhisiart began to feel that there was no parallel, in philosophy, or law, or politics, for the situation he was now compelled to confront. It was the monarch's business to stop the Friar; and yet all he'd done was to make a signal to the jailer to let the man alone! He *must* be getting some monstrous satisfaction from having his tormented conscience objectified in the cries of a madman.

Meanwhile the wretched Giggleswick, helplessly watching those little girls at the door, made up his mind that he would resign his job and sweep the streets before he ran the risk of another scene like that.

But it wasn't over yet; for though something, some psychic emanation from his victim-accomplice, had in a curious way muted the Friar's tone, both the dwarf and the dog knew what the King was suffering. They had indeed been, so to speak, *inside his nerves* to a degree forbidden to any human creature and they knew that the man was approaching the verge of an hysterical outburst. They were unable to stop this outburst; but they could show what they felt by anticipating it. And this they did with a wild rush, leaping to his side, crouching at his feet and setting up simultaneously such a heart-rending howl of pitiful sympathy that the children fled, the Archbishop changed the position of his fingers, and Mad Huw, pointing at the crucifix, upon which the sun was certainly playing curious tricks, murmured in an awestruck and hoarse voice: *"Who has done this?* Who has put *horns* upon Christ's head?"

This final word was too much for the over-wrought King. Rising from his chair, while his emotion caused several dark blood-drops to appear amid the sores on his face, he moved a step or two towards the

Friar, and very quietly, while the terrified jailer shut his eyes and the Archbishop changed the position of his feet, uttered the surprising words: "It's sleep you want, Brother Friar. Let's go and look for it together, Brother. It's sleep we all want. Richard has it. Hotspur has it. The Duke, my father, has it. Hercule and Seamew will have it tonight. He," and he made a gesture towards the Lollard, "will have it to-morrow. But who will give it to Henry of Hereford, Brother? To Henry of Lancaster, Brother? To Henry of England, Brother? Give me sleep, I pray thee—a feather of it, a grain of it—one little tiny fly's head of it, Brother! Sleep's an easy thing to find. It's cheaper than ale. It's commoner than bread. Sleep's everywhere; isn't it, Brother? Isn't it, Grey Brother? Sleep's as wide as the air, as deep as the sea! What have they done then with poor Harry's sleep? The King's tired, Brother. A man can't live and be as tired as the King. You're all my subjects! *Aren't* you my subjects? Then I command you—on your allegiance"—here the wretched man shook Mad Huw frantically by the arm—"go, hunt, look about, search! Say it's the King who sends; say it's the King who must know, and by night-fall too, who it is who's hoarding all the sleep in the world! Go and look, I tell ye! There must be *somebody* who's stolen the King's sleep!

"*You* there! Crosby! Denton! Talbot! Send out, and hunt him down! He's stolen the King's sleep and hidden it in a little hole! Yes, yes, good Seamew! Fetch it! Fetch it! Fetch it! Fetch it!" All this while the little white dog was leaping up at his master and pawing at his armour, as if he were fain to find his hurt and lick it.

As for Hercule, he seemed set upon one thing only—to break his wooden sword! With his foot upon it, groaning and panting, he had already broken it into three pieces; but the wood near the handle was too tough for him. Like a child with a baffling toy he now began furiously beating it against the wall. Nobody else dared to stir or to speak. The Archbishop had gone as far as to thrust his hand into his habit to find his beads. But evidently fancying that the eyes of all Christendom were upon him, he let it remain there, and contented himself with a murmured, *"Miserere nobis!"*

But there must have been something in the outstretched hand with which Mad Huw now boldly touched the sick monarch that carried a healing power. And the little dog at last succeeded in doing what it wanted to do. Its wordless distress reached the man's heart; and Henry took it up into his arms.

It was the turn of the two prisoners now to receive a shock; and a shock that they alone in all that place *could* receive. His hated enemy's remorse had done for the Friar what neither Tegolin nor Rhisiart had been able to do. To say that he no longer confused Rhisiart with King Richard would be going too far; but that Henry's hysterical outburst had restored to the former his association with Glyn Dŵr was proved by the calm and collected manner in which he now begged his life of the King. "The lad's no Lollard," he said. "He's a good lad and a true Catholic. He has been—"

The way in which the King interrupted him—though since Seamew was licking his master's face the prisoners heard nothing—must have satisfied the Friar, for he now was seen to make the sign of the cross over both monarch and dog; and the prisoners clearly heard him utter the words, and utter them in a tone of the most convincing authority: "To-night, at least, Henry of Lancaster, *Saint Francis will give you sleep.*"

Rhisiart's mind at that moment became so absorbed in an internal struggle of his own that what went on before him grew suddenly indistinct. He felt faint and dizzy with standing so long, so much so that it was almost with a tearful relief that he took the support of the arm his friend now offered him; but it was the contest in his mind, not the hurting of his wound, or even the danger of that old "blackness" overtaking him, that made him respond to Mad Huw with hardly a sign, when the jailer, mentally withdrawing his resolve to change his occupation hustled the Friar away.

Yes, our friend was thinking of that little phial of death, "colourless as water and tasteless as air." Mightn't he have desperate need of it if they decided after they got him into the Tower to extract some *real information* from him about Owen and about Wales? But what of Walter? Nothing they could do in the Tower could be *worse* than what Walter was to suffer—*and suffer to-morrow!*

But had he a right to give away what Tegolin had brought him? Dewi Sant! but he was past thinking of that. His mind gave a queer jump, as if the pit of his stomach had become a single pulse of horror.

So this is what it had come to. There was no other way. Obscure memories of Roman and Greek heroes rose up in his mind.

But he felt anything but heroic. He felt odiously calm and clever. He felt as though he were the incarnation of cold-blooded practical common-sense. Was there any way he could dodge this calm, clear-headed, inevitable decision? No, there was no way. Walter would never kill *himself* and so—yes, he must do it. He loved him; and he must do it. "Thank God," he thought, "I'm an unscrupulous Catholic, and not a fussy gospel-man!"

And then quite suddenly the old "blackness" did sweep over his wits. He seemed to see them chaining his friend to the stake— *"Walter!"*

When his consciousness returned he found himself alone with his friend. The Lollard's round moon-face was bending over him as he lay on his straw bed. And the man was actually looking happy because he'd opened his eyes! Christ! This was rather a moment to look happy when you *couldn't* open your eyes—when you'd *never* open your eyes again! But the jailer must have come and gone, and brought them their bread and water. There was the pitcher; there were their two mugs; all just as usual! There was the stool they used for a table.

And he found that he'd absolutely made up his mind. He must have made it up while the "blackness" was on him. Yes, his brain had never been clearer. And not for nothing had he his mother's unscrupulous Norman wits! He called up the image of his mother. Lady Montfoison! Well, at any rate *she* wouldn't hesitate. Walter had to die anyhow; and he'd die now without ever knowing. Yes, yes—but he must do quickly what he had to do.

"Shall I bring you your supper, laddie?" It was Walter's voice— just his ordinary, kind, even voice. How he would hear it when he was in the Tower with Griffith ab Owen!

He pretended that he could only answer faintly. God! he felt strength enough to shout the place down. "Bring—the whole—thing—over here —my—dear," he whispered. "We'll have our—our last supper."

The Lollard turned his back and began his jangling shuffle towards the bread and water. In a second Rhisiart extracted the phial, tried its stopper, and held it under his rags. How slow the man was! He found it necessary to shut his eyes. Those slow, awkward movements were maddening. And what if—doing all this with his one hand—he dropped and broke the pitcher! Oh, he would never be able to carry that precious water balanced on that ricketty stool!

But there!—he'd done it at last; and the stool, with their mugs and their half-loaves, rested safely by his side.

"Get—*your*—stool!" he whispered, with the air of a man who might faint again at any moment.

Shuffle—shuffle—shuffle! How cleverly he'd managed! He felt so pleased with himself that he even took the time to kiss his hand to that familiar back as he poured out the water into their two glasses and emptied the phial into the one further from his bed.

Having replaced the little empty bottle in his belt he took the precaution to possess himself of his own mug. But he didn't lift it to his lips. He waited. Here was his friend jangling back; and clutching his mug he closed his eyes.

At last the man was seated opposite him and he could breathe freely. Not *quite* freely, all the same; for there was an odd sensation in his throat. He felt as if *he* were the one going to escape the Archbishop. "What shall we drink to?" he found himself saying in a loud and resonant voice; not at all the voice of a man who at any moment might faint away. Oh, the whoreson fool he was! He should have *whispered* that; for the innocent eyes opposite him opened wide.

"To Owen!" he murmured as quietly as as naturally as he could; and he lifted his mug. But his heart was shouting. Surely Walter must hear his heart. "Drink—drink—drink—drink!" thundered his heart, as if they were both inside the great horologe, invented by that Glaston-bury monk, when it was striking the hour! *There!* the hand that he knew so well—every line and mark on it!—had taken the mug—was raising it—*had* raised it—to his lips—"Hail Marry! Hail Mary! Hail Mary! —'tasteless as water.' Drain it, for Christ's sake! No! no! Don't look at me over the rim, like children do! Don't—"

"*To our wives!*" And the Lollard put down the mug—empty. "I've been wondering," he said, "how soon a person faints with the pain; and whether—" He stopped suddenly, evidently mistaking the expression on his friend's face for unbearable fellow-feeling. "How selfish I am!" he cried, and stretched out his arm across the stool. But their fingers had barely touched when the man's face, body, limbs drew in upon themselves, self-locked in a deadly, constricting, stiffening spasm. Up, up his figure rose, as if there were a galvanic propulsion beneath it, and for one tick of that time-clock, inside of which Rhisiart, like the Glastonbury monk's automaton, was empty of all feeling, the convulsed form balanced itself on his toes; and then, for Master Brut died as erect as if he *had* been chained to a stake, it fell forward across the stool and across Rhisiart's knees.

When Master Giggleswick entered the prison at midnight along with the executioner whose official duty it was to measure his victim for the iron band that was to encircle his waist, they found both prisoners extended on the same bed; but thanks to the precautions taken in Worcester that the Bishops might see the faces of their victims, the place was so easily lit up that it was soon clear that only one of them was enjoying that temporary cessation of consciousness that Mad Huw had promised the King. The other was in a deeper sleep.

For a short while, as the two men questioned him, it seemed as though a danger, quite unforseen by our astute friend, was on the verge of arising; namely, that there had been a quarrel in the prison; but so free from any bruise was the Lollard's corpse, and so realistic was the survivor's account of the shocking access of panic-stricken blasphemy that had resulted in this providential stroke, that the worst our friend had to endure were the long-winded accounts of similar incidents in that place exchanged between the two cronies.

"Well, Master Clerk, I'll be getting home along," remarked the executioner at last, "and you, Ned, I can see are ready for Mother Goose's feathers. Give my love to London-town, Master, and accept a good Christian's congratulation! Of course, as a professional man—which is, as you might say a good Christian writ backwards"—and the fellow gave Rhisiart an indescribable leer that was at once sympathetic and avaricious—"a man *might* complain, and Ned here knows it well, at having to rise with the cock to take down an unblooded scaffold *and* as pretty a pile of dry withies as this town has ever seen. But, as I've always said, 'tis the hand that signs the warrant, not the hand that piles the faggots, that keeps the smell of the burning in his beard."

Well, they were gone now; and Rhisiart, who never analysed his feelings, was quite unconscious of anything ironic in the fact that, as he lay with his arm across the body of the man he'd killed, his mind fretted so much because he'd lacked the silver groat that, as "a Christian writ backwards," the executioner had evidently expected; or that he was so worried because he had only these rags—even if he carried off their single outer garment—to ride in to London.

With his head full of the groat he hadn't possessed and of this problem of his rags, he kept staring at that monstrous crucifix, till, like a forest-ranger hanging dead hawks in sight of a heronry, he left these annoyances suspended on those wounded feet; and fumbling with his hot fingers till he got hold of the icy hand by his side, he began at last to think of Master Brut. But, really and truly, there was nothing to think about. He had met him by chance; he had killed him by intention; and let fate be the arbiter! What he really felt was that Master Brut had gone off altogether, goodness knows where, but *very far away!*

This ice-cold flesh he touched had no connection with his familiar friend. As for Walter's *soul* being in danger, it no more crossed his mind than it crossed his mind to regret killing him. The only positive feeling was a deep complacent malicious satisfaction at having robbed the Archbishop of at least one man's weight of protracted pain!

But though his emotions seemed to have grown as dead and numb as the ice-cold fingers he continued to clutch, there was one problem, as he heard the watchman beyond the moat calling the hours, round which his mind hovered like a tethered and blinded falcon.

"He must have quarrelled with the French," he said to himself. "It was too splendid a chance for him not to have taken it! He could have burned the gates, sacked the town, and captured both the Henries! He could have done it after the second day he camped on Woodbury Hill. Later than *that* I doubt it. From what Nance said, the shire-men were—"

But the affection that had grown up between Master Giggleswick's little maid and Walter called his thoughts off *that* speculation as if it had been a bell-buoy.

The jailer had left several well-oiled torches burning in their sconces and this illumination inside his room made it hard for him to see the stars outside; especially since the flamboyant end-of-the-century window that recent episcopal taste had inserted was partly concealed by the projecting crucifix; and the law of association of ideas made it impossible for him to see the feet of this figure without thinking of the executioner's groat-less face and of his own ride to London in rags.

Between the numbness of his heart and the number of things he had to avoid thinking Rhisiart must have slept again; for when he was next aware of the "realities," as we call them, of this somewhat limited dimension of life, he was offered two noteworthy phenomena.

For one thing the light of dawn was endowing the torch-flames with that peculiarly mystic and consecrated effect that any Promethean light displays when it humbles itself before the presence of the sun; and, for another thing, from the dead body at his side there now emanated, faintly but unmistakeably, unlike any other smell in the world, the dreadful sweetness of human mortality. He found also that in his sleep his friend's fingers had so stiffened about his own that it needed an effort to disengage his hand. Scrambling over the stiff form at his side he got out of bed.

But he was shocked to see that neither of the men who'd examined the corpse had thought of closing its eyes or its mouth. It was too late now to do either of these things decently; but while he did what he could he kept murmuring aloud: "Don't'ee mind, Walter; don't'ee mind, Walter dear!"

He was thus engaged when he heard voices and steps outside, and then the noise of the key in the door. He sat down on the bed, one hand straightening the edge of the blanket he'd pulled over his friend's chin, the other making sure that the empty phial was safe back in his belt. He must have appeared a sorry spectacle to the persons who now entered, with his black elf-locks, his ragged beard, his staring eyes.

But the Rhisiart inside these appearances was the same sagacious disciple of the diplomatic Master Young, now my Lord Bishop of Bangor, as he was when he helped that worthy to keep his seat on the piebald back of Griffin. This he showed by the dignified and self-possessed manner in which, with a polite apology for not rising, he received his visitor.

The gentleman who entered was as striking a figure as he was a completely unknown one. Master Giggleswick, who ushered him in, came straight to his prisoner and kneeling down without ceremony

proceeded to free him from his fetters. Once more our friend had to
go through the indignity of having nothing to offer the man save his
hand to shake; and he felt convinced that the hasty glance which
Master Giggleswick threw upon the dead said in plain words: "If *you'd*
been alive there'd have been at least a gold noble forthcoming!"

Little Nance, whom her father now left behind as he went out,
showed more interest in the new-comer than in her late friend's
survivor; but this interest Rhisiart soon began to share. The gentleman
was carrying a large bundle; but he laid this down on the chair recently occupied by the King and proceeded to introduce himself.

"Palamedes Playter, of the County of Suffolk," he announced with an
inclination of his whole body; "Knight of St. John and officer of the
King's Guard, and, if I may add, the sworn and devoted servant of
the beautiful Lady Tegolin. The Lady Tegolin has sent me," he went
on, "to bring you these clothes; and to tell you that she has had permission to bid you farewell; and will very shortly be here in person.
Captain Crosby, whom in my military capacity I serve, is, I have to inform you, already mounted, his charger stamping, his men cursing, his
banner raised. It is my privilege to invite you, with this little lady's
leave, to put on without further delay the—the contents of this poor
bundle."

"Please give me your rose!" This request was made in quite an impassioned tone by little Nance, whose cheeks were flushed, her blue
eyes wild with excitement, and both her small hands clutching one of
the Knight of St. John's elaborate sleeves.

Rhisiart stood up, made the sign of the cross over the Lollard's half-
closed eyes, and shuffling with his feet, as if the irons were still about
his ankles, bowed to Sir Palamedes, and advanced to the chair that
held the bundle.

But lively as was his interest in his own new attire he couldn't help
pausing to take in the fantastical garb of the gentleman from Suffolk.
Sir Palamedes wore the most elaborately up-turned shoes our friend
had ever seen on human feet. His hosen reached upward from these
shoes to the joints of his groin and were so tight in their fit and so
thin in their texture that every muscle of his limbs was visible. "What
a dancer he'd make!" thought Rhisiart.

The colour of Sir Palamedes's hose was pale blue, his sleeves were silver edged with black; and his tunic was so short that though his cod-piece was punctiliously treated according to the dictates of the most exquisite modesty it is likely enough that Father Pascentius would have found his attire a flagrant example of the degeneracy of the age. He wore his hair rather after the Italian than the French manner, cut much lower behind the neck, for instance, than was the fashion at the French court; and treated as if for hair to *curl,* even with the smallest ripple, was a barbaric lapse from gentility.

He held a small hunting-cap in his hand whose wild-goose feather tickled little Nance's bare arms as she clung to his sleeve; but what so attracted the child's notice was a fresh white rose, of rare beauty, which he had pinned to his tightly-fitting embroidered collar. He smiled at Rhisiart over the little girl's head now; and our friend who was standing awkwardly before the bundle with his feet a little apart— exactly as they would have been had the chain been still there—was conscious of something about him that reminded him of the glimpse he'd had at Oxford of the Emperor Manuel.

"You must give me a red one in exchange," said the Knight of St. John, tossing down his cap and unpinning the flower from his throat; and then, while little Nance frowned in bewilderment, he raised her chin with the tip of a finger and kissed her on the lips.

The child having obtained her desired treasure became so occupied with the task of fixing it to full effect upon her small person that the two men took the opportunity of opening the bundle; and before Nance had succeeded in discovering even the palest reflection of the white rose among the sinister objects in the room, our friend found himself, with the deft help of Tegolin's messenger, dressed in a becoming black suit, with the professional velvet pouch suspended from his belt, of a well-to-do Student of Civil Law.

Drawing together the chairs left by the royal attendants the two men now fell into a friendly talk, and Rhisiart learned that it *was* from Constantinople that his new acquaintance's ancestors drew their paternal lineage.

"Tell me, Master Secretary," the young man enquired, delicately altering with a couple of pointed finger-nails the outline of his smooth brown hair across his unwrinkled forehead, "what you think is going to be the end of this Welsh war? I was a lad when it began—is it five years ago?—but I begin to grow weary of it! It seems to me that all it does is to deprive both our nations of their bravest spirits, and to hasten our good King's end by rushing him about in these mad campaigns."

"That's what Owen's son, Meredith, thinks!" cried Rhisiart—delighted to find himself discussing state-affairs again with a person of the great world—"but you must remember that even if the war *were* brought to an end by a peace satisfactory to both sides, the trouble's certain to break forth again in another reign—I beg your pardon!—I mean under a different King of England."

"But what in your opinion," repeated Sir Palamedes, *"would* bring this unhappy struggle to a satisfactory close?"

Rhisiart gazed at the man's fantastical attire and at the mournful negligent brown eyes that were fixed upon him and a curious irritation seized him. What right had these elegant triflers—endearing though they were—to speak in this airy tone of matters that needed the experienced brains of the greatest statesmen? "Oh, if only," he thought, "I were back again in Harlech in the full confidence of our Prince!"

Under his tangled locks his narrow face contracted into an intense faraway gaze, and the vision of an independent Wales with a well-directed chancery-court issuing orders to competent captains, compared with whom poor impetuous Rhys Gethin was a mere outlaw, flitted across his mind.

But the sallow oval face of the gentleman whose ancestors came from Constantinople wore such a mocking expression, and had by nature such wantonly-lifted eyebrows, that, as our friend caught the man's eye, everything came back to him. He became aware of the smell of mortality from the bed behind him. He remembered that he was to say goodbye to Tegolin. And with a spasm of pain that until now he had held at bay the price of his escape from the scaffold clutched at his heart.

Thus when his wife did come and, by the tact of the Knight of St. John who carried Nance and her rose away, he and she were left alone, he broke down completely.

"Don't, Rhisiart, don't, don't!" she cried, as he clung to her like a sobbing child, his head buried in her bosom. "Oh my only love," she murmured, her own eyes as dry as if all the fountains of tears had been drained away into that Worcester river, "don't, don't be like this! Rhisiart, Rhisiart, lift up your head and look at me! This may be—oh, we don't know when—and I want you to be—I want *to look at you,* Rhisiart!"

But he still went on sobbing. And he couldn't have told her why he sobbed, why he let himself go like this, or the indescribable relief it was! But it was as if the breasts he clung to had been the breasts that had nourished him as a child. To them his sobs told everything: told how he came to Wales on Griffin; told how he had planted his crusader's sword in the earth, how he had ridden between the spears and the bows, how he had served the Prince, how he had lost Catharine, how he had killed his only friend, how he ought never, never, *never* to have let her save him like this!

But he was wasting these unreturning moments. In the warmth of her breast he was forgetting everything, forgetting what he had to say, what *she* had to say, forgetting that it was the end, that it was the last time.

And the man who resembled the Emperor Manuel was already knocking at the door, and he hadn't even spoken to her, he hadn't even looked at her, and their time was over.

"Kiss me, Rhisiart!"

Who had said *that* to him before, and he hadn't done it; and he didn't do it now. He just clung to her, seeing only deep, lovely, in-finite darkness, feeling only deep, sweet, infinite release.

But the knocking at the door had changed its character now. It had grown loud and violent. Captain Crosby had come himself, furious, relentless, impatient. Tegolin tore herself from him; thrust him back, for he had no strength left, into the chair that was full of his rags, and going over to the bed bent low down above it, and pressed her dry eyes and her cold mouth upon the face of the corpse. She did this on an impulse she couldn't have explained. It was as though from the weakness and the unreality of life she turned for help to the strength and the reality of death. Life gives a fictitious warmth to the poor thin covering of a living skull; but when our lips touch the ice-damp of a dead face we know, by the feel of *that skin,* which we recognize now for the first time to be what it is, that this cast-off shell, this husk of matter, this puppet of shame, this moment of corruption, has no connection at all with the indestructible spirit we have lived with and have loved.

But it was, on this occasion, from what had perished, not from what survived, that Tegolin drew strength. She used the body of this heretic as priests used the relics of their saints.

"Rhisiart," she said, coming back to him, collapsed upon his cast-off rags and breathing the long gasping breaths of a man who has sobbed his heart out, "Rhisiart, will—you—remember this?"

He gave her a desperate look out of his dark blurred eyes and formed his lips into a whispered consent.

But speaking quite quietly, almost as if she were speaking to herself, "I am going to the church by the East Gate now," she said, "to pray for his soul. Whatever happens to us to the end of our lives, I want you to remember that you're with me—*alive or dead*—and I'm with you. Will you remember this, Gwion Bach?"

This time he made his reply clear and distinct and in the Welsh tongue; and she, going to the door, with her head held high and without turning again, called to the men outside to enter.

XXI

DIFANCOLL

One wild autumn day towards the middle of November, in the year of Our Lord fourteen hundred and sixteen, the youthful parish-priest, newly appointed to the village of Corwen in the district of Edeyrnion, was seated in the commodious entrance-room of his school-house, occupied with his solitary pupil.

By an arrangement between the Bishop of St. Asaph and the Abbot of Valle Crucis the old ecclesiastical domicile attached to the Church of St. Sulien had been recently converted into a local College for the training of such lads of the neighbourhood as were anxious to enter the priesthood; but it had not been till the general amnesty proclaimed by the young King that these spiritual authorities had come to an agreement as to the most fitting candidate for the directorship of this new institution.

How far the Father they had finally appointed would be able to fulfil the chief requirement of the post—namely, the recruiting for the Church of promising and clever pupils—remained still to be seen; for the boy he was at this moment teaching was his own ward-in-chancery, whom he had brought with him little more than a month ago when he took possession of the newly-erected "College."

"You've forgotten what you promised, Father!" the boy in question was now protesting in an injured voice, as yet another page of the great illuminated volume before him was turned over.

"It's *you* who've forgotten what I told *you*, Rhisiart," said the other gently, laying his hand on the page to prevent the child's closing it.

"That you painted *this* one, Father, like you did the last?"

The youthful priest smiled. "Well, I *did*, as it happens, paint this one too; but it wasn't of *that* I was thinking. Don't you remember what I told you about the great Doctor Pascentius, how he bequeathed this

867

book to the Abbey on condition that I might use it? It was the Doctor on whose grave—what did I tell you, Rhisiart?—your god-father planted that cress."

The boy's eyes lit up with interest now. As long as the Father told him stories about the great Commentary he was quite happy. It was when he had to follow the book's contents that life seemed to lose its savour.

"Wasn't it he who made them open the castle-gates," cried the child eagerly, "when Owen cut off the head of Rhys Ddu of Cardigan!"

"Cut off his head? How can you say such things? Rhys Ddu lived till six years ago! He wasn't taken till Owen's last campaign; and you know when *that* was because I've often told you how old you were then."

"How old *was* I?"

"Rhisiart! Think a little. I told you how to remember. It was when I took you to see old Glew the Gryd, who died in his sleep with his axe under his pillow."

"I'll be thirteen at the end of this month."

"Well?"

"Seven! Seven! Seven!"

"That's the lad! And when were you born?"

"I was born two years after the Great Comet," repeated the boy in a dull mechanical voice, as if by constant repetition the words had lost all meaning for him. "My father was a brave English gentleman. My mother was a beautiful Welsh lady. I was born in wedlock. I'm an orphan of good family; and I'm the ward of Father Sulien. You weren't christened Sulien, though!" he added in a more interested tone. "Your name was—"

But at that the Director of the College of Corwen closed the great Commentary himself; and did so with a display of emotion that overwhelmed the boy.

"If you ever say that again, Rhisiart—"

But it was clear from the tears in the lad's eyes, and the passionate quiver in his voice as he expressed his repentance, that a repetition of this lapse would be unintentional if it *did* recur.

Father Sulien softened at once. "My name in this earthly world *died,*

Rhisiart dear! That's what you must say to yourself. And you must think of it as a secret between us. Do you see, my child? A *deep* secret."

The word "secret" caused the boy to snatch at his friend's hand and kiss it devotedly, as if sealing a memorable conspiracy.

"Is the man who said he was my god-father coming again to-day?" he asked, glancing first at the closed work on Saint Thomas, and then at the window.

The Head of the new College looked steadily at his only pupil. "They're *all* coming to-day," he said gravely, "and this time you must be a *real* gentleman and as polite to Lord Talbot and to Meredith ab Owen as you were to Master Rhisiart."

"Can Lord Talbot and Meredith ab Owen talk Latin like my god-father?"

"They've no need to, little son. Talbot's a soldier of the King, and Meredith ab Owen is on the King's business. Your god-father's a great Doctor of Law. It's his profession to talk Latin."

"He can *write* Latin too, when he wants to, as easily as Welsh or English!"

Father Sulien sighed. It was one of his constant humiliations that in their lessons together he found this writing of Latin almost as difficult as his pupil did.

A priest's life had many advantages over a herald's, but it had its disadvantages too; and one of the worst of these was the Church's mania for Latin.

"Master Rhisiart's the cleverest man in Wales and Scotland and France!" declared that gentleman's namesake roundly.

The Father made no attempt to deny this; but as if anxious that proficiency in Latin shouldn't retain the sole place of honour in his pupil's mind he asked him if he'd remembered during Mass to pray for Iago ap Cynan, the famous sailor, whose ship, following the traditional direction taken by Prince Madoc, hadn't been heard of since the spring.

"I can see you forgot, lad"; and he added sadly, thinking how foolish it was to try to convey to another human creature all those imponderable touches and colours and lights and shadows that go to make up a living person we ourselves have loved: "It was Iago who brought me that icon from Cyprus which I have above my bed."

Rhisiart made no comment upon this. He had come to know too well the particular vistas of memory that made the Father sad, and he had learnt caution. "Shall I go and see if there's anybody in the church?" he asked a moment later.

The ex-herald's mind came back to Corwen with a jerk, came back to it from a castle-turret overlooking the sea, where its owner was pensively rocking an infant's cradle with a baby-girl in it, a girl whose features were the living image of Iago ap Cynan.

"Yes, yes! Run off and count them, lad! If there are more than half-a-dozen we'll chant the office in the Lady chapel."

He stood at the window, watching the boy thread his way through the graves till he reached the cross on the Druid Stone. *"There!"* he said to himself. "That's what he always does! And I've told him a hundred times to wait till he's in the church!"

The slender little figure had indeed paused at the great circular stone and had gravely dipped his fingers in one of its hollows and had touched his forehead with the rain-water it contained.

"What makes him do that?" thought the Father, as he watched the boy disappear into the church. "Children are funny creatures. You can't tell *what* they get into their heads."

But the boy came flying back in great excitement to say that there were several English soldiers in the church. "And all Mother Mali's maids from the Inn are there too, and Mistress Gwerfil's there, and Sir Hugo's man from Gwerclas. I *say,* Father! you don't think it's possible there's any news of *him*—to bring such a crowd?"

The priest shook his head. "I should have heard, sonny—I should have heard. If Meredith ab Owen knew anything I should have heard yesterday. You don't think he'd let Talbot's men find him before his own son, do you?"

Rhisiart bowed to the wisdom of his superior; but in his own heart he thought: "If the Father would only let me do what I want, I'd be the one to find him!"

But neither the priest nor his pupil, when their psalms were said, and their talk with the Inn maids and with Mistress Gwerfil and with the man from Gwerclas was over, had found out any new clue to the hiding-place of the lost hero.

"In my opinion," the man from Gwerclas had dogmatically announced, "he's not in the north at all. And Sir Hugo agrees with me. Sir Hugo thinks he's hidden in the Forests of Tywyn, where the foresters and swineherds were always loyal to him."

"He's with Lady Scudamore in Herefordshire," affirmed Mistress Gwerfil. "There are no two opinions about it. That's why he married his girls off as he did—every one of them to some great English lord!"

Talbot's soldiers declared that he'd been dead and buried for *four years*. One of them went so far as to declare that he'd seen his grave in Bangor Cathedral.

It was only Mistress Mali's maids—Myfanwy Goch and Mair Wen—who dared to uphold the view of the common folk of Edeyrnion in the presence of all these competent authorities, the view that Owen ap Griffith Fychan was playing chess with King Arthur in the heart of Mynydd-y-Gaer. The girls first only giggled when Sir Hugo's man rallied them on this wild fancy; but upon being ordered by Mistress Mali to tell Mistress Gwerfil what they'd told *her,* they declared that they'd picked up a white knight and a red knight in a cornfield at the foot of Mynydd-y-Gaer.

There was such rude hilarity among Talbot's soldiers at this substantial evidence that Father Sulien gave his blessing to the ladies and led Rhisiart away; but the little boy was so bitterly reluctant to leave such an exciting discussion that the gentle-hearted priest suggested that since his visitors weren't expected till the evening they should then and there ascend the famous hill themselves. "We shan't find any chessmen I'm afraid," he said. "But we *may* see the beacon-fire on Bryn Saith Marchog. Do you remember why they always light a bonfire there at this season?"

But Rhisiart refused to search his brain at that moment for anything so remote as the Seven Horsemen.

The priest had to return to the "College" to change his clothes; and while dutifully helping him in this process the boy suddenly dropped the garment he was holding and stared at a carved chest by the side of the fireplace in a self-forgetting reverie.

"What is it, lad?"

"You know what you said you'd do next time we went up Mynydd-y-Gaer?"

Father Sulien followed the boy's gaze. "I know—I *know!*" he replied with obvious distress. "I've been thinking of that myself. It certainly *is* the place for reading it. It's a great, great secret; and you ought to open it far away from everybody. I wish the Hermit still lived up there so that we could open it in his cell!"

Rhisiart's eyes flashed. "The—Hermit—*does*—live—there—still!" he whispered solemnly.

Father Sulien stared at him in amazement, one arm thrust into his priest's under-coat, and the other hanging loose in his white shirt. "*What's* that you're saying?"

"He *does* live there still!"

The Head of the new College hurriedly finished dressing. Then, all prepared for their walk, he looked round for his house-key, found it, together with a stout staff, which latter however he laid down as soon as he'd taken it up, and moving to the chest at which Rhisiart had been staring, removed from above it several parchment-scripts, and proceeded to lift its heavy lid.

Rhisiart had an opportunity now of showing both his breeding and his training. He took full advantage of it. He remained absolutely motionless; displaying no curiosity as to the contents of the receptacle his guardian was ransacking, making no attempt to approach it, no sound to interrupt its exploration.

At last the priest turned to him, holding up a small leather case. "I oughtn't to have left it there," he said, "with the lid unlocked. Think if robbers had got in! But there it is. It's yours now. May I keep it for you till we're at the top of Mynydd y-Gaer?"

The boy was too excited to utter a word. He nodded gravely, staring at the priest as he carefully concealed the leather object in an inner pocket. The word "robbers" had had an electric effect on him and had caused so many thrilling images to rush through his brain that his curiosity about the contents of the case receded for a time.

For some reason the occasion seemed a suitable one for asking a question that had been on the tip of his tongue ever since they'd come to the College.

"The last Corwen priest," he remarked, "was a Father Sulien, too. How was that?"

His friend smiled and drew a deep breath. "But I *must* find out," he said to himself, "how he knew about the Hermit."

"Whose church is it?" he enquired of the boy.

"St. Sulien's."

"Well then, what better name could any priest have?"

"For luck?"

"For luck—if you like, little son. But now I've answered *your* question, won't you tell me how you knew that the Gaer Hermit was still there?"

"Myfanwy told me—but I knew before *that!*"

The Father wisely decided that this wasn't the moment for disparaging the talk of Mistress Mali's maids.

"*Before* that? Dewi Sant! And what other fairy told you?"

The boy frowned. "*Nobody* told me," he said. "I can see his fire up there, from the top of Pen-y-Pigyn."

Once again the Father showed a discretion belonging rather to the court than the cloister; and he asked no question as to how it was that his ward should be exploring the rocky eminence above the village at an hour when it was dark enough to perceive a fire across the valley.

"Well—off we go!" he said; and then, glancing at the slender figure before him: "Get your leather jacket," he commanded. "It'll be chilly up there."

Rhisiart scowled, and used under his breath an improper expression, learned this time not from Myfanwy but from Mistress Mali herself. But he went off to their sleeping-room at the back of the College, and soon returned, sulkily pulling on the detested garment.

"When did Meredith ab Owen and Master Rhisiart say they'd come to-night?" the priest asked his companion, as they crossed the wooden bridge over the swollen Dee.

"After dark, Father."

"That's what I thought. I asked to make sure."

"And my god-father said you weren't to keep dinner for them, because they would leave their horses and have their dinner at the forester's house in Carrog."

But the Director of the College was still uneasy. "What if they come earlier than they said, and find the place locked?"

"They'll go to the Inn, like they did last time. My god-father"—this was added with profound complacency—"drinks five beakers of Malmsey before he gets drunk."

"There's not much that goes on at the Inn, young man," thought Father Sulien, "that *you* don't know!"

Their path became steeper after crossing the river; and burdened by his winter coat the little boy began to flag. To distract him from the effort he was making, our friend the ex-herald—who well knew how exhausted the body *can* get when the spirit has gone too far ahead—plunged without preface into one of his interminable tales of the recent war.

"The question was, of course, how long we could hold out after the meat was gone. But Aberystwyth is as strong as Harlech. Its *walls,* lad—aye! aye! you should see how thick they are! And you must remember, child, Prince Henry had the Duke of York with him, as well as such captains as Talbot, Carew, Audley, and Grendor. Yes, and there was Sir John Oldcastle, too! But they could do nothing, for all their cannonading, but starve us out. Oh yes! I forgot about their getting the Chancellor of Oxford University. It was he, really—Courtenay was his name—who thought of the terms of the truce. We were to have a six weeks' armistice; and then Owen was to have a week; the last week in October it was, and weather just like this! He was in the north, they say, somewhere round here, in Edeyrnion. And if he didn't come in that week's time, we were to give up the castle and do homage to—"

"You've forgotten about Rhys Ddu!"

How well the boy knew every word of this tale! He must have heard it so often that it had become *his;* but it was clear it didn't *come to life* for him, didn't take flesh and blood for him, unless the Father related it. Only it must be related without the least change! It must be a reality independent of the relater and not to be tampered with by any human agency.

Father Sulien admitted that he'd reached the point in the story where a description of the strength and courage of Rhys the Black was called for. But he forgot that he'd never explained to the boy that when Chancellor Young, Owen's Bishop of Bangor, sailed for France in the company of John Hanmer—and as far as he knew they were still in Paris after all these years—Rhys Ddu of Ceredigion had no one to counsel him; and if anyone had ever needed wise advice it was this brave but short-sighted warrior!

Rhisiart knew everything about Rhys the Black. He knew the particular way a single lock of hair fell across his forehead; he knew the rough, abrupt, careless manner of his speech; he knew the tears that would always come into his eyes when he spoke of "little Lu"; for our friend Elphin, for all his priestly anonymity, had remained an artist in verbal draftsmanship. The one thing his guardian had never disclosed to him before was the warrior's helplessness when Owen's Chancellor sailed for France.

This addition to the story was at once a painful shock to Rhisiart and a thrilling vista of new conceptions. The boy began to look so white, and so hot in his leather coat, that Father Sulien, who was quick as a woman in his perception of such things, made him sit on a mossy stone to rest, while he himself, leaning over the wall at his side, surveyed the undulating landscape below them.

"Owen had substituted Master Young for Master Byford as Bishop of Bangor," he explained wearily, as his eye followed the recession of bare, round, grassy hills that flanked the entrance to the Vale of Clwyd. "But the Holy Father soon afterwards appointed a man of his own choice, a simple parish-priest like me, whose name was Benedict Nicholls. *He* was the priest of a village in Dorset no bigger than Corwen—Stourbridge it was, or Stalbridge—and he proved in many ways a better—"

But whatever the rector of Stalbridge may have proved in the registry of Bangor he proved infinitely wearisome to the small figure seated on the stone.

"Go on," he interrupted, "to when you were eating dog's flesh, and to when the English were feasting over their fires, and when you heard them singing *The Rose of Northumberland,* and to when it was beginning to get dark, and to when you heard Owen's trumpets far away in the woods and saw his men come rushing down from the mountains, and to when he swore he would cut off Rhys Ddu's head if you didn't open the gates, and to when the English marched off when they knew he had come, and to when you had meat and wine again, and to when Owen was—why are you laughing at me, Father?"

"I'm not laughing, my son."

"Why are you screwing up your mouth like that then?"

"I was thinking, Rhisiart."

"What about, Father?"

"Just thinking—that's all."

"*I* know what it was! It was about Owen's other castle being taken. Why don't you ever tell me more about *that?*"

The once youngest of court-heralds certainly looked at that moment the saddest of parish-priests. Scene after tragic scene flashed with piteous rapidity through his mind as the child's figure melted under his fixed stare. He saw the wasted form of Sir Edmund and his hollow eyes, as he lay dying in his turret, looking over the English camp, over the English ships, to that far-off horizon of the sea, where the Birds of Rhiannon had sunk into silence forever. He heard the voice of the Arglwyddes weeping and refusing to be comforted. He saw the calm tragic eyes of Lady Mortimer, as she gave up to his care this same little boy whose form in his leather-coat was now the mirror of all this.

He saw the tender-hearted captain from Taunton who had sworn by Saint Mary of Glastonbury that he would save Luned and her child. He saw the looks of excited pleasure—yes! actually of pleasure—with which Mistress Brut of Lyde greeted the besiegers.

He was standing with the little Rhisiart outside the walls on that terrible day, wrapped in a clock to hide the "lions rampant" on his tunic, when he saw what looked like the body of a large doll fall from the ramparts upon the rocks beyond him. He daren't attract notice by making a move at once from the buttress that concealed him, but he knew in his heart what had happened. Many a time had he heard Mistress Sibli swear in her wild fits that no English soldier should touch the true love of Rhisiart ab Owen; and later when he did examine the dwarf's corpse he found that her tiny body, under her clothes, was wound about with parchments, bearing Rhisiart's script.

While these memories were racing through Father Sulien's brain, his pupil had risen to his feet.

"There, there!" the boy now cried in a shrill voice. "Do you see, Father? *There's* his fire!"

The young priest looked in the direction indicated. Yes! In the autumn greyness there certainly was—rising unmistakeably from the crest of Mynydd-y-Gaer under the great prehistoric wall—a thin wisp of smoke.

The wild hope rushed through the ex-herald's heart that it might be his destiny and none other's, led by the instinct of the man's own grandson, to discover the lost hero! He snatched up his stick, took the boy's hand in his excitement and led the way, with rapid youthful steps, up the steep face of the aboriginal *mygedorth,* or fortress.

They climbed so fast, and both their hearts were beating so fast, that their first vision of the Hermit's fire, *and of what else was there,* was a blurred and confused one.

"There are *two* Hermits!" cried the boy. "No! only one—no! It's not a man at all—look, Father! It's only a rock!"

There was no need to conjure Father Sulien to look. His very soul was in his eyes. Was it a rock? It was rounder, smoother, less jagged, than any part of that ruined wall he had ever seen up there. But there certainly was a fire; and it was against red flames in that grey mist and greyer masonry that the round stone, so like a human head, projected.

If it *was* the Hermit, he must be seated with his back to them facing the fire. Whether rock or man, the figure they were approaching wasn't only motionless, it was very upright. How could a living man, even a man about whom such awestruck rumours had been circulating through all Edeyrnion, have a head like a great smooth, round granite ball, balanced on a pedestal?

But Rhisiart suddenly jerked at his friend's hand; and not content with that, tugged at his arm till he got the priest's head low enough— in spite of the gusts of wind that seemed to be sweeping round the Gaer like supernatural sentries—to be able to whisper in his ear.

"It's the Hermit!" he whispered. "It is, it is! I *know*—by his bald head! Myfanwy told me about his head. It's as bald as a stone!"

The Hermit must have been deaf as well as bald; for he permitted the intruders to approach so near that they were compelled for very reverence to stand as motionless as he was sitting.

But Father Sulien felt ashamed to be caught spying upon a holy man; and incontinently he lifted up his voice. "The Lord be with thee!" he cried above the whistling of the wind.

"And with thy spirit," answered the figure at the fire, rising to his feet and facing them.

Rhisiart's fingers tightened upon the hand he held. Myfanwy had never told him that the Hermit was a giant! As for Father Sulien he felt like one to whom it is permitted to be present at the Resurrection from the Dead.

Edeyrnion was his native district and Powys Fadog his tribal *talaith,* or province. His ancestral home, the *Cruc,* or "the Mound," was even now facing the risen Hermit across the valley; but twenty years had passed since he had served the Arglwyddes at Glyndyfrdwy and he was now a stranger in the place. As preceptor of the newly-established College he held a position that repelled local confidence and gossip.

It flashed through his mind now: "I'm the one single man in Corwen who didn't know that *you* were the Hermit!"

"Mother of God!" cried the giant limping towards them. And to Rhisiart's complete astonishment, there was the holy man hugging and kissing the priest!

"It's little Elphin turned monk! It's our baby herald turned shaveling!"

"Master Broch, oh, Master Broch!" and the young preceptor's cheeks under the Hermit's kisses grew wet and hot. "Who—would—have—thought," he panted, as all the old days rushed back under this overpowering hug, "that we should—meet—here!"

While the two men were thus greeting each other, Rhisiart was aware of a desire to sink into the earth. He was used to being corrected; he was used to being punished but he had never before, in all his experience of life, been ignored. But as he surveyed the slender form of Father Sulien almost disappearing in the huge embrace of this *Cawr-y-Gaer,* this giant of the prehistoric *mygedorth,* it was precisely to this condition it was now his destiny to come. He was ignored to such a tune that he became non-existent. Where a minute or two ago two persons had been spying upon a third person there were only two persons left; and he, the centre person, wasn't one of them.

His short upper-lip, drawn back a little from his teeth in the true Mortimer manner, quivered violently.

Faint memories of the bald giant began to slide back into his own mind; but they were too vague to restore him to his self-respect; and in any case, between the shaven head and the bald head, one had totally forgotten him and the other considered him as nothing. Hurt to the heart, the little boy shut his eyes and endeavoured to call up the narrow face and hooked nose of his god-father. To *him* at least, he would always exist. No apparition from the dead would make his god-father forget him.

"Didn't I see someone with you just now, Master Broch?" asked Father Sulien as they seated themselves by the fire and the Gaer Giant began pouring out wine into leaden mugs to warm and balancing a row of Spanish chestnuts on a half-burnt furze-root.

Broch chuckled. "Quick as ever with your eyes, Father Elphin! Yes, you *did;* and if our little master here would run away as far as that fir-wood and back, I'd tell'ee of *somebody* of whom many in these old islands would give—"

He had no need to finish the sentence. With burning tears in his eyes and without a glance at his guardian, Rhisiart scampered off, the flaps of his leather coat, which he had unlaced in the heat of the fire, flying behind him as he ran. When he came to the fir-wood he found it enclosed by a high fence; but by the simple method of removing his coat and leaving it on the larch-needles that strewed the moss beneath this barrier, he was able to force himself between its planks.

Then, scrambling to his feet, he began pushing his way deep among the brown larches and the green pines, the latter scratching his face and hands, and the former leaving their needles in the creases of his tunic and even between his shirt and his skin.

At last he came to an open space in the wood where there was a great pile of loose stones. Even in the midst of his desolation and his outraged feelings he noticed that these stones had recently been moved; and it vaguely crossed his mind that it was odd that people should have been moving stones in the middle of a thick coppice.

But he was too young and too unhappy to give the phenomenon more than a passing glance, though what he saw might well have struck a boy's mind as the sort of attempt to build a primitive "home" among the fir-trees that a boy playing at being a hunted outlaw might with some difficulty and some industry have succeeded in constructing.

But what attracted his attention much more than this erection of stones was a clump of funguses growing on the northerly side of the enclosure. To these he now directed his steps; and falling down on his knees set himself to inhale their curious smell.

To do this was a more significant impulse of that small wounded heart than Father Sulien could possibly have understood. One of the things that the boy remembered most vividly of his childhood was a certain occasion when playing outside Harlech walls Lady Mortimer had scolded him for smelling funguses. He had vigorously protested; and during their altercation the Prince himself had approached and had expostulated with his daughter, justifying his grandson's queer caprice.

The peculiar smell of funguses—especially the kind that grow under fir-trees—always brought back this scene. He could see even now, as he scrabbled on his knees at the task of clearing away the larch-needles from those damp strange-smelling stalks, his grandfather's forked beard and the band of gold round his forehead and the black lions on his breast-plate.

The Prince had launched out, in justification of his interference, into the tale of Gwydion the son of Dōn, and how by magic and sorcery, by *hud* and *ledrith,* this terrifying enchanter, whose memory still clings to the Milky Way above our heads and the wildest oracles of Taliesin under our feet, not only carried off the pigs of Annwn, but by his transformings of sea-sedge and fungus deceived and slew the mighty son of Annwn's king.

The child never forgot the deep pity in the great man's voice as he spoke of the victory of the magician from the north; and the smell of these particular funguses had become a secret passion with him ever since that day. It was almost as if, in his childish fashion, he dimly realized that everything in life is a symbol of the unseen and that the smell of funguses as much as anything else could be a writing on the wall.

"They sent me away," his heart kept repeating, as his face touched those chilly phantom-heads that were like things fallen from the moon. "They sent me away. I'm nothing to them. I'm nothing to anybody. *They've sent me away!*"

He uttered this last lament aloud; and for a second he thought that some tremendous echo had caught up his moan and was repeating it, and the strange thing was that when he lifted his head and saw the tall tottering figure coming out of the wood towards him the remembered feelings of the child merged so completely into the present feelings of the boy that all fear, all amazement even, was swallowed up. A vast indescribable sense of refuge, of escape, of sanctuary, lifted him up and drew him forward; and long before he was in the Prince's arms his tears of desolation had been transformed, as if Gwydion's magic had been undone, as if the cold snouts of the recovered herds were all about him, as if the lost hero were alive again, into the sobs of one who out of a long darkness finds himself on the threshold of his home.

"*They've sent me away,*" his grandfather repeated as he hugged Catharine's first-born to his heart. "They've sent both of us away; they've sent us all away."

Rhisiart could feel the old man's heart beating under Iolo Goch's chain-armour. But it was enough for him to catch the faint scent, bringing back all his childhood with it, like some far-flung aromatic incense, of the white beard that tickled his face; and he gave no heed to the murmured words that followed: "But—we—shall—all—come back—again."

Snow-white was the man's hair, for the Prince had endured so much and had wandered so far that he was prematurely old, but he had reverted to his former scrupulous tending of his person, and the forked beard was as meticulously trimmed as it used to be sixteen years ago, and the golden circlet round his forehead looked just as it had looked in the patriarchal days at Glyndyfrdwy, only the curls that fell around it were white instead of yellow.

Owen was bare-headed; and he wore the leather tunic, the leather belt, the leather bands twisted about his legs, of any ordinary farmworker; but the contrast between this simple rustic attire and the man's majestical lineaments enhanced his air of primeval dignity.

It may be imagined how tightly, as the Prince tottered slowly back to the men they had left, Rhisiart clung to his hand! The little boy had no fear that his grandfather would fail to take his part, whatever reception he got. It wasn't *for that* he clung to him. It was because he was home again, home with his lost parents. It was because he had got back his pride, his self-respect, his rightful place in the great, callous, hostile world.

"I mustn't call him grandfather," he was saying to himself, as the old man led him through a gate in the fence he had missed in his flight and told him to pick up his discarded jacket. "I must call him Sire."

"*Sire!*" he therefore began, and his voice had the proud confidence of one who is certain of the gravest attention. "Wnere hast thou"—he said "thou" rather than "you" from an instinct that the more formal pronoun went better with "Sire"—"been hiding from thy people all these years?"

Owen paused and leant heavily on the long shepherd's crook he was using as a staff. It was still light enough for him to see the child's features. "He's more like him than her," he thought. "Catharine's voice in a Mortimer body. 'Thy people' is Sir Edmund all over! *She* would have said 'from us.' 'Twas the Norman in him gave it that legal touch. He's Rhisiart's god-son right enough!"

"Art thou the Hermit Myfanwy said lived in Mynydd-y-Gaer? Or is the bald giant the Hermit—Sire?"

The old man stroked the forks of his beard as he would have done twenty years ago. His infirmities had been so heavy on him of late that he rarely smiled; but he did smile now.

"Broch and I are both hermits, Rhisiart. But look, child! Do you see *that?*" As he spoke he pointed with his crook to a just perceptible curvature in the grass, like a magnified mole-run; only this particular ridge was covered with grass.

"I see it, Sire!"

"And you saw those stones in the wood?"

"Yes, Sire."

He gazed at the boy intently, and as he did so a delicious shiver ran through Rhisiart's veins. "It's the secret! It's the secret!" his heart cried. "*He* knows I can keep secrets!"

"Well," murmured the old man hesitating; and it was almost as if he were thinking aloud. "I'll be gone before winter, as far as I *can* go"— and Rhisiart thought he had never seen such a strange look in anybody's face as his Prince had then—"and my son says Elliw can never have a child. It breaks the family law to tell you, little one, the law that's come down among us *ym Mhowys* since Brochfael ab Eliseg, but I'm dying, and you're my child's son, and so I'll tell you; and let it be on my own head! You must know that there are three hiding-places of our race that are indestructible and indiscoverable. One is under the mound at Glyndyfrdwy. One is under this fortress. And one is at Mathrafal. There weie secret passages too; but most of these have fallen in and been lost. All these hiding-places and all these passages were dug by the ancient people conquered by Cunedda. Those ancient men were cunning in such digging, for they lived in underground dwellings. Iolo once told me—you've read his poems, I hope, Rhisiart? —that there was an entrance once to such a passage at Mathrafal but that when King John—"

"*Mathrafal*, Sire? Where is Mathrafal?" Now if Rhisiart ab Edmund was good at *keeping* secrets his power of discovering them was sorely limited by his years.

Here was a secret that he never found out to the end of his days— namely, that his grandfather's heart received a dagger's stab when he learnt that Catharine's first-born had never so much as *heard* of the royal "Llys" of his ancestors!

"Have you heard of the 'Halls of Cynddylan?'" he enquired, not without an under-tone of sad bitterness.

Rhisiart hastened to recite at random from the famous elegy in his best choir-boy's voice. "Ystavell," he chanted; and he made a little stiff movement to illustrate abandonment to hopeless grief. This he did by lifting one thin arm till it was bent at right angles at the elbow; and at that point sawing the air with his hand, while his small fingers remained stiffly outstretched like the indignant claws of a cat when it has wetted its paw; "Ystavell Cynddylan," he intoned, exactly as the children in the monk's school at Valle Crucis were taught to chant.

"Ystavell Cynddylan," answered the echo; while the sound of his boyish voice went drifting down the valley, following the scanty wisps of smoke from the Hermit's fire, following the forlorn deciduous leaves as they were blown across the larches, following the tattered banners of the mist as they streamed over the twenty-thousand-years-old masonry of Mynydd-y-Gaer, carrying the dirge, "It is darkness to-night!"—*Ys tywyll heno!*—carrying the undulant dirge for the children of Cyndrwyn—"for Cynan and Gwion and Gwyn"—over church, over college, over cross, over rain-soaked meadows, till it sank into the flowing of the dark water, of Dyfrdwy, the divine water, where it disturbed the yellow-bellied salmon as they rested in the shallows, and troubled the white-breasted ouzels as they drooped their wings at the roots of the alders.

The effect of his grandson's voice upon the old man—so young a voice and so sad a burden!—was to make him murmur into his beard the dead-leaf moan of Llywarch Hēn; but, digging his crook into the earth and leaning on Rhisiart's shoulder, he shuffled on, and they were soon in the warmth of Broch's furze-stalk fire.

"Room for Owen ap Griffith and Rhisiart ab Edmund!" laughed the giant. "Did you find each other where I predicted you would?"

But it was clear to the boy that Father Sulien was too shocked by the Prince's state to join in any jest. He poured out wine for him at once, and both Broch and he made the old man as comfortable as they could, with his back against the foundations of some prehistoric guard-room, and the dead bracken piled up beneath him and about him.

But his comfort was short-lived, for the wine as it quickened his pulses brought on a horrible fit of coughing, which when once it had started seemed as if it would kill him before it ended.

When it did at last end, and the old Prince sank back exhausted against the wall, he began, in spite of the roaring bonfire before him, to shiver so pitiably with cold that Broch hurrying into his "hermit's cave," which was really the entrance to the secret passage of Cunedda's mound-dwelling captives, brought out several Moorish rugs and also brought his Prince a flask of spirits so fiery that Owen choked and spluttered as he swallowed.

"How heavy these stones are!" cried Father Sulien presently, anxious to turn away their thoughts from topics gloomier and heavier than palaeolithic masonry.

As he spoke he made the gesture of weighing in his hand one of the smaller and rounder of the rain-washed pebbles about them. "Dewi Sant!" he cried, "but it's as heavy as a thunderbolt!" This comparison of the Gaer-men's masonry to thunderbolts was highly agreeable to Rhisiart's mind; and sitting on his jacket instead of putting it on, for Broch's great bonfire warmed him through and through, he began throwing these meteoric objects into the blaze, an occupation that so absorbed him that the men fell to conversing together as if his presence were no more palpable than a small phantom-shape risen out of the mound-dwellers' passage behind them.

The giant's fiery cordial, whatever it may have been, soon loosened the old man's tongue, and the ex-herald, who asked questions that in former days he would never have dared to breathe to the wearer of four black lions rampant, listened to strange matters.

"How long, Sire, did you hold Davy Gam a prisoner?" was one of the least bold of these eager enquiries.

"*Prisoner* do say, boy? *Prisoner*? Why I've never— No, my old friend"—this was to Broch who looked not a little uncomfortable— "I've *never* had a more faithful and devoted adherent!"

"But I heard he'd been ransomed, Sire, for two thousand marks!"

The great white head with the golden band amid its fleecy locks lifted itself erect with a leonine gesture. The old chieftain was clearly as proud of this singular prisoner's behaviour as of any triumph in his whole life. "You heard correctly, boy; you heard correctly. The worth of those marks—two thousand as you say—was brought to us in current coins of the realm of England and the realm of Castille, together with certain moneys of the Royaume de France."

"This was before he went to the French wars?"

"Naturally, boy, naturally. But look ye! This is the point; and I can only say it shows what can go on between two Welshmen when they're hunted like the 'Twrch Trwyth' from one end of Wales to the other. Gam was ransomed, you say; and correctly you say it! He *was* ransomed. Those who brought it saw him lay it at my feet and saw him armed, unshackled, and free. But would the man leave me? No, my boy-father, no, my little priest, he *wouldn't* leave me! We used that money to hire safe and trustworthy labourers to open up the passage here. We worked at it for years, I tell you! Gam was as strong as a bear. I was strong myself then; and we had good faithful men to work for us. Some of them died in grievous pains rather than to betray to these new Lords of Chirk and Ruthin and Castell Goch what we were about or who we were.

"There have been many staunch Edeyrnion farmers—yes! and many honest craftsmen too in Corwen and Carrog and Bonwm—who knew our hiding-place. Do'ee think one of them betrayed us? Not a one, my pretty boy-father, not a one! The story of Glyn Dŵr will be a story for all the Welshmen who come afterwards—to the end of time! And in no other land in the wide world save Wales could it have happened. That's what we Welshmen are! They may conquer us in arms, they may out-wit us in trade, they may out-mode us in fashions of science and art. One thing they *cannot* do. They cannot *catch our souls!*"

"Sire!"

It was the shrill voice of little Rhisiart. The child had ceased for some time throwing thunderbolts into the fire; and now with his impassioned eyes fixed on his grandfather's face the secret of his swelling heart burst forth.

"If I say I won't do homage to King Harry shall I be killed for the sake of Wales? I *want* to be killed for the sake of Wales!"

The Prince turned to Father Sulien. "Does he know who he is?"

Our priestly friend hesitated, glancing from the excitable old man to the excitable little boy with some apprehension.

"*Do* you know who you are?" he said at last in a low nervous voice.

A crafty look, more characteristic of Rhisiart ab Owen than of either Catharine or Sir Edmund, came into the boy's face.

"Will you read to—to the Prince," he said, addressing his tutor, "that letter you've got in the leather case?"

Though our ex-herald was not possessed of an exceptionally penetrating mind he gave his pupil a quick startled look. "He's opened that chest and read that letter!" he said to himself; and then as a second thought, "but after all it's his own property and she's dead now!"

Glyn Dŵr leaned forward with an expression of intense interest in his sunken sea-green eyes. "Read it, Elphin—Father Sulien, I mean. Is it from her? Is it from Lady Mortimer?"

"It's from *my* mother to *me!*" cried the little boy, leaping to his feet and standing by his tutor's elbow. His face gleamed with pride; and he glanced at the old Prince with a look of exultant complicity. His heart was bursting with indefinable emotion. He felt as though the words of this message from the dead isolated them from the others and bound them together forever.

The bald-headed giant stared unheeding at the wide landscape spread out before him. It had long ago become a necessity for him to detach himself from the old man's turbulent and multifarious moods; and this vast autumnal expanse of rolling hills, sweeping away in one direction towards Cadair Idris, and in the other towards Snowdon, and

narrowing itself in the immediate vicinity, eastward to the valley of the
Dee, and westward to the valley of the Clwyd, was just then peculiarly
adapted to his habitual train of thought.

The blaze of their bonfire had created a circle of light and warmth
in the midst of a segment of the earth's surface which at that hour
seemed to be reverting to what it must have been when the old inhabi-
tants of Mynydd-y-Gaer gazed across it, thousands upon thousands of
years ago! Reverting, so it seemed to Broch, in his strange yearning for
the impersonal, for the non-human, to the primal supremacy of the
grey slate, so unique among terrestrial formations, that familiar landscape had become during the early weeks of this sad November intensely congenial to his mind. He liked the way the grey rocks alternated with the patches of pale stubble and red bracken. He liked the
way the whole landscape seemed to converge at this season towards
some austere rock-bound ideal of its own secret engendering. It gave
him a grim pleasure to see the rounded grassy hills forming themselves,
as they rose above the leafless tree-tops, into vast terraces of green
stepping-stones, along which the majestical spirits of the past might
move in tremendous procession towards the far-off mountain-peaks,
where not only trees and grass would be left behind but all the turbulent human lives as well; lives that sought their nourishment and contended for their feverish masteries among the sheep and the cattle and
the horses and the swine that fed upon the fatness of these less purified
places.

It was only by moving a little distance out of the blaze that Broch
was able just then to satisfy his insatiable longing for the calm of the
inanimate; but when he *did* manage to get the fire-light out of his eyes
he was rewarded by a cold deathly chill that came up the slopes of
Mynydd-y-Gaer from the flooded river below and as it came precipi-
tated itself into a clammy vapour that settled on his naked skull in
minute drops, each drop a perfect microcosm of all that desolate and
de-humanized world, of wet mists upon grey rocks, towards which his
spirit yearned.

Meanwhile the Prince was listening to his daughter's letter. "To my
grately loafed leetle boy," began Father Sulien in his resonant heraldic
voice; and though a furious protest surged up in the old man's heart

against this emphasis upon Catharine's lack of scholarship, it was so precious to him to hear the actual words she had set down that he restrained himself from interrupting.

As for Rhisiart, his original surprise that his mother should be less skilful than himself in the difficult art of writing had long ago been dulled by familiarity. Like the elder Rhisiart on the bloody field of Bryn Glas with a similar document he knew every syllable of this production so completely by heart that he had come to take its peculiarities for granted, very much as a lost fledgeling might take for granted some familiar hoarseness in its parent-bird's distracted call.

"Thy father died by Our Lady's Mercy before our fall, which cannot be far off: or send his blessing he would. Be honour; be courage; me leetle boy; say thy prayers to thy Mother in Heaven and remember gentilhomme Toujours. Writ by me very hand in Castell Harlech. Trust God his Mother—C. M."

Father Sulien preserved a double professional aplomb while he read this letter, the aplomb of a court-herald and the aplomb of a parish-priest; but the instant he concluded his task both these complacences fell away and he became once more the shy and sensitive youth with whom our friend Rhisiart had flirted when he first arrived at Glyndy-frdwy. And it was doubtless this relapse into the diffidence of a page-boy that suddenly made him unable to look at the aged Prince. But there is nothing like extreme physical suffering for the mitigation of the emotionally poignant; and the Prince had been afflicted of late by increasingly acute spasms of pain.

By a devotion of the commonalty of those parts unparalleled in the history of nations Glyn Dŵr's *incognito,* if such it could be called, which was only a secret to his foes, had been scrupulously respected since he returned, for the last five years of his life, to his Powys-Fadog patrimony. The element of the supernatural, or, let us say, of popular terror of the supernatural, had doubtless played its part in this miracle of concealment; but without the man's own incredible vitality the thing would have been impossible. It would have been impossible too if the Prince hadn't from his earliest manhood made a cult of those queer fits or trances which Rhisiart used to all his "attacks."

These he had developed to such a point during his years of *difancoll,* or "disappearance," that neither Gam nor Broch had any compunction about leaving him, when such was their wisest move, in a condition to all appearance like that of a dead man, in the mound-dwellers' hiding-place beneath the mystic walls of Mynydd-y-Gaer. The danger that any enemy might light upon him in these prolonged trances had been reduced to a minimum by the traditions of the supernatural which surrounded this prehistoric camp.

No doubt even this accumulation of conspiring elements would have been insufficient to guard against the invasion of his Merlin-like *esplumoir,* if he hadn't been the man he was; that is, if he hadn't been one of those singular persons who appear only at rare intervals in our human tribes, and then only among those that have clung to the same foothold upon the surface of our planet from time immemorial.

Broch-o'-Meifod's disconcerting wife had upbraided Owen as a "pure-blooded Brython," and this may have been a legitimate accusation as far as his paternal ancestry was concerned; but as Catharine had instinctively felt in the Forests of Tywyn there was another strain in his blood, a strain that went back to those prehistoric "Lords of Annwn" beyond whose rumoured presence at the beginning the boldest speculation cannot pass.

It may well have been from his mother that Owen inherited not only those strange magnetic powers that made poor Davy Gam believe he could call up spirits from the deep, but also those more realistic and less spiritual endowments which enable their possessors to alternate so bewilderingly between hunting and being hunted.

In the legends of no other land do these weird pursuits of something that cannot be caught play such a part. After the spore of the "Twrch Trwyth" and behind the panting of the "Questing Beast" all Welsh history trails!

The very geography of the land and its climatic peculiarities, the very nature of its mountains and rivers, the very falling and lifting of the mists that waver above them, all lend themselves, to a degree unknown in any other earthly region, to what might be called the *mythology of escape.* This is the secret of the land. This is the secret of the people of the land. Other races love and hate, conquer and are conquered. This race avoids and evades, pursues and is pursued. Its soul is forever making a double flight. It flees into a circuitous *Inward.* It retreats into a circuitous *Outward.*

You cannot force it to love you or to hate you. You can only watch it escaping from you. Alone among nations it builds no monuments to its princes, no tombs to its prophets. Its past is its future, for it lives by memories and in advance it recedes. The greatest of its heroes have no graves, for they will come again. Indeed they have not died; they have only disappeared. They have only ceased for a while from hunting and being hunted; ceased for a while from their "longing" that the world which *is* should be transformed into Annwn—the world which *is not*—and yet was and shall be!

But just now it was his physical pain that deadened for the old man the poignance of his daughter's broken words.

"Put it away," he said to Father Sulien; and then after a pause, during which he groaned several times and changed his position against the ruined wall, he commanded his grandson to come to him. Although his pain had muted his own response to the pathos of Catharine's letter, it had not hindered him from watching with close attention the boy's attitude to his mother's words. Nor had he failed to observe—for he had always been one to notice these little things—what an easy, give-and-take relationship existed between the priest and his pupil. He had noticed how spontaneously the boy had leaned against the Father, and how naturally and irritably he had shaken off the Father's hand from his waist as he listened, shaken it off as children do only when they take for granted the affection of the grown-up person they treat so touchily.

"Come here, Rhisiart!"

He was obeyed at once; and it was clear to Father Sulien that the child hadn't the least fear of his grandfather. All he seemed to feel was a proud and confident trust in the old man. The Prince made him stand between his leather-bound knees; and in that position laid his hands on his head till his outstretched fingers hid completely the boy's compact skull.

"May the blessing of the Holy Trinity," he prayed, "and the blessing of Our Lady, and the blessing of the Souls of all the Faithful Departed, be with thee, my little son."

After that, he made an effort to rise and it was evident to the young Father as he hastened to help him that he was in serious pain. For this he now apologized as the former herald supported him. "We've got many comforts *in there*," he explained in reply to the priest's anxiety. "Davy Gam made them for us. With Davy to help, and my own people, it's all been easy, and the years have passed, Elphin, the years have passed! Prince of Annwn I've become, they'd say in my mother's *cantref*. It's quite warm *in there*, Elphin, and we've plenty of light. *She*"—and he glanced at Broch—"would be content with her 'pure Brython' now. Prince of the mound-dwellers I am! Driven to earth, Elphin, driven to earth. Broch's my fire-lighter under there. Broch can chop wood faster than Davy. But Davy was a good log-man though he's dead and rotten now. He was as good a captain to the King as he was slave to me. Slave to a Prince, Elphin, and captain to a King! But he was a man-royal as a horse. Derfel's horse neighing for maidenheads was a whoreson nag compared with Davy.

"And now—dead and rotten, Elphin lad, dead and rotten in the French Wars!"

"My Prince!"

"Well, boy-father?"

"Are you going to accept the King's pardon?"

Glyn Dŵr flung away the arm that was supporting him and rose to his full height. "Dare *you* say that to *me?*" His voice was so hoarse and threatening that Father Sulien drew back a step, while Rhisiart, who had been listening intently, yielded to a fury that corresponded with the old man's and actually struck his tutor with his fist.

"Forgive me, Sire!" the priest cried hastily. "Forgive me, Rhisiart ab Edmund!"

For a second it looked as if neither the grandfather nor the grandson would ever forgive him, as the child clutching at the Prince's belt and the Prince supporting himself against the child's shoulder glared side by side at him. But the sensitive ex-herald's remorse was so plain that their anger subsided as quickly as it had flamed up.

"No, no, boy—but you meant no harm," murmured the chieftain; and then to Rhisiart, while he allowed the repentant priest to take the fierce champion's place, "Run and fetch Broch to me, sonny, will you? He's had long enough with his mists and rocks; and I want to ask him something."

They watched the boy scamper off to where the man's gigantic figure rose out of the mist. "I—think—I would—like you," whispered the Prince faintly, "to *see*—how—we—*accept*—King Harry's pardon."

"I am at your service, my Prince. Only as I shall meet both Meredith ab Owen and my Lord Talbot—yes, and Clerk Rhisiart, too!—at the College to-night, it would seem—"

But the approach of Broch and the child interrupted him. The giant saw at once that the old man was near the limit of his endurance and he said as much to the priest in no roundabout manner.

"How unfair he is!" thought Father Sulien. "He's used to managing the Prince, and he's a powerful man anyway. What does he think *I* could have done?"

"I—was—telling—the Father," gasped Owen—while between his words a spasm of pain forced him to cry out sharply—"that—I would— like him to bring—Catharine's boy—to see how—how we receive our —pardon—from the House of—Lancaster."

Broch-o'-Meifod shot at the nervous ex-herald a look of uncompromising indignation from within the folds of his leathery eye-sockets. "Do you wish them to come *here,* my Prince?" he asked, slipping his powerful arms round Owen's tottering form.

Glyn Dŵr gasped something that the others couldn't hear.

"The Prince says," Broch interpreted, "that you're to come up here with the gentlemen you speak of, to-morrow about noon. Let Meredith ab Owen bring his horn and he's to blow the Mathrafal call—*not* the Powys-Fadog one—do you understand?—when you reach this spot."

But though Father Sulien was a timid man and Broch-o'-Meifod, supporting his groaning master, was an awe-inspiring sight, the sense of duty in the young priest's heart was stronger than his fear.

Coming up close to the two men, while Rhisiart watched his proceedings in astonishment, he whispered in Broch's unsympathetic ear how he felt it would be deplorably unwise to give so young a boy the kind of shock he must necessarily receive from such a disturbing scene.

"One minute, my Prince, one minute!" grumbled the giant. "I've got to *make* this fool obey you!"

Saying this he gently lowered the old man, who had now quite collapsed in his arms, on the bed of bracken, and pushing the boy towards his grandfather, incontinently seized Father Sulien with an ogre's grip and led him some paces aside.

"Don't'ee mind our ways, laddie," he said in a totally different tone, when he saw how troubled the priest was. "My Lord and I understand each other—but we've had a queer life—too much for both of us— this last year; and we're both unstrung. He's at the end, Elphin my lad. I do what I can, but he moans in the night for Davy. Davy loved him with a dog's love—more than a man's, I tell you, more than a man's! He's got this crazy rejection of the King's pardon on his brain. He was always one for ceremonies and scenes—mad life-lover as he is!—and he's bent on carrying through *something*—I can't tell you what—I'm a simple man compared with him; and what's more, little Father, he and I take different views on this whole business of being alive on the earth. I think we might just as well before we die, Scots and Welsh and English together, hold hands like the children at Martinmas Fair and dance round the fire with the old song of the *baban* being washed:

> *Cover your eyes and pinch your nose!*
> *And tell me which way the water goes!*

"I know what you feel about the child, little Father. But the child we've got to think of now *is the one over there;* and I tell you this rejection of the King's pardon is—"

He was interrupted by a long clear note on the wind, the sound of a hunting-horn in the valley, and the two men stared at each other. "Meredith ab Owen!" murmured the younger man; and then he hurriedly added: "I'll bring him, Master Broch, I'll bring him to-morrow. But you'll remember how young he is; and keep your—" The giant touched him on the arm. Rhisiart was at their side, his small face a white blur in the darkness.

"He's asleep," he whispered softly. "But he keeps lifting up his arm and dropping it; and pulling up his leg and stretching it out! I think the pain hurts him in his sleep."

The giant turned. "I'll see to him," he said; and he made a sign for them to be gone. Then, while they hesitated, "You *that* way—I *this* way," he repeated, in a queer intonation that Father Sulien never forgot, "but the same wheel carries us round."

They had begun to move away when they heard him calling after them. "Tell my Lord Talbot," he cried, "that he must be the only Englishman here!"

Lord Talbot was at any rate "the only Englishman" among the group that gathered that night round Father Sulien's fire. The little Rhisiart clung so passionately to his god-father that the soft-hearted priest couldn't bring himself to send the boy to bed. "I'll get him back to his proper routine," he thought, *"when it's all over";* and then feeling ashamed of the sinister implication of this thought he substituted the mental phrase: "when we're alone together again."

But it was a memorable evening for the little boy as he sat on his wooden stool in his black satin suit enjoying the Moorish sweet-meats that the great Doctor of Civil Law had brought for him from London.

The priest soon perceived that it was a wonderful comfort to Clerk Rhisiart to talk freely to the child about the death of his mother and sisters; while to the young Rhisiart—as the ex-herald shrewdly noted—the death in the Tower of Lady Mortimer and her little girls was just an exciting story. He was too young to remember them with any detailed vividness or to feel any tragic emotion about them; but he wasn't too young to derive a proud and delicious satisfaction from its being *his* mother and *his* sisters to whom the great Lawyer referred with such dramatic respect.

Just three years had passed, the elder Rhisiart explained, since he had been honoured with the privilege of attending the dying lady. The King had been in her case more liberal than usual, he told them with a humorous glance at Lord Talbot, and after being released from the Tower she had received each year, at her lodgings in Westminster, a substantial sum for her maintenance.

"Is—my mother—buried with—my father?" interrupted the little boy, jerking himself along the floor, with the aid of his own legs as well as those of his stool, till he was close to his god-father's chair.

The great Doctor of Law continued for a few minutes describing minutely to the rest of the company how Lady Mortimer and her little girls—one of them named Bridget—were buried in Swithin's Church; but when he'd finished he turned with the gravest politeness to the child at his side and explained that it had been at his own advice that

Lady Mortimer had decided to lie in St. Swithin's Church rather than be conveyed to Montgomery to rest by her husband.

"Your mother died of the Plague, Rhisiart ab Edmund"—and his voice changed its tone as he bent down over the child—"and your sisters too; and there were"—he drew a deep breath—"there were difficulties about their interment."

At this point he seemed to forget the boy's presence altogether in his self-complacent memory of a fascinating legal problem; for he lifted his head and addressed the whole company in resonant professional tones. "By the mercy of God I was able to exercise a little *pressure* upon the Rector of St. Swithin's, owing to certain legal help I'd had the privilege of giving to the King's Council on the complicated problem of the—well! to tell you the truth—of the Salic Law."

To Father Sulien's horror the little Rhisiart leapt to his feet at this. "Haven't I some claim," he cried in a voice that rang through the chamber, *"to my father's estates?"*

Lord Talbot began fidgetting uneasily in the great carved chair in which, as the King's Special Messenger, the ex-herald had placed him. He was a lean, weather-beaten gentleman, taciturn in speech, reserved in manner, and with something about his build and expression that brought irresistibly to the young priest's mind an image of the animal known in heraldic language as the Wyvern.

The uneasy creaking of the chair of the King's emissary caused a faint smile to flicker across the face of Meredith ab Owen, who all this while had been staring into the fire as if he saw depicted there some faraway scene completely different from that which was now working itself out before him.

The scene he beheld was indeed one that rarely left his troubled memory. It was of his little Elliw mounted on her Cardigan pony, with the aged Angharad in a litter by her side, driving away the seagulls from a ghastly relic set up there in the eyes of all, whereon a few bleached hairs waving in the wind beneath a human skull were all that was left of the once majestic coal-black beard of Rhys Ddu of Tywyn.

But the great Doctor of Law turned his long thin face, with its hooked nose and drooping white moustache, towards his fellow-ambassador. Then he surveyed his excited god-son; and his expressive countenance took on a look of such formidable judicial authority that both the heavy-lidded Wyvern stare of Lord Talbot and the proudly-lit Mortimer gaze of young Rhisiart were compelled to give him their full awe-struck attention.

"Oh, if only Iago were here!" thought their priestly host. "How he would be impressed by this learned Judge."

"The puissant House of Lancaster," announced the elder Rhisiart in measured tones, "whose present representative is our mighty and merciful Lord, King Henry, has, I am sorry to say, many reasons for regarding the Mortimers with less than confident trust. Renowned through Christendom for his clemency to the conquered, our God-appointed Sovereign of the Realm of England, France, and Ireland is bound in the interest of both his Welsh and English commonalty to weigh with studious caution those spontaneous impulses of magnanimity towards the ancient Border Houses to which his natural instinct predisposes him.

"You must remember, dear child"—and though he addressed the puzzled boy beside him his hawk's eye was fixed on Talbot—"that the elder branch of your renowned father's family is at the present moment more than suspected of making various claims that are inconsistent with that Established Royal Succession upon which the peace of our two nations depends."

Having made this resounding declaration, which echoed through the new College with as many hollow reverberations as it did through the head of the institution's single pupil, the learned Judge stretched his hand to the refectory table and possessed himself of his goblet of hot spiced wine.

Over the brim of his silver mug, as he raised it to his lips, he contemplated his god-son, and although no one knew it but himself a sharp pang shot through his heart when the younger Rhisiart, quite as much hurt as he was puzzled, deliberately left his side and crossed over to Meredith ab Owen.

Meredith received him tenderly and put his arm round his waist as the boy settled himself on the edge of his uncle's chair. "That's right, lad, that's right," he murmured softly, "Aunt Lu is sure to ask me how you've grown and what books you read now-a-days. We hoped once you'd have a new little cousin, but Our Lady hasn't yet—"

And then again, as had been happening so often to him of late, the child became aware that the thoughts of his uncle, like all these other men's thoughts, were only waiting to leave him in the lurch, only waiting to float away like the ravens that so often hovered over his head on Pen-y-Pigyn, after leading him by their repeated croakings to fancy they had some oracular message to deliver.

He began to experience a feeling he had come to know so well that it presented itself to his mind as a necessary aspect of life, as something that life *could not be conceived without.*

It was the feeling that there wasn't, really and truly, one single human being in the whole world who would care if he were dead, or would care if he ran away to sea, like Iago ap Cynan!

And they were all the same. Father Sulien had let him stay up; but he might just as well be in bed! He really *had* thought Judge Rhisiart would be different. That's why he'd asked him about the Mortimer estates. He never expected that all he would get from him would be a speech about the Lancastrian Succession.

And now no sooner had Meredith begun to tell him that Aunt Elliw might *still* give him a new cousin than his uncle's arm grew limp and lax about his waist, and the man stared in front of him, apparently forgetting that there was such a person in the world as Rhisiart ab Edmund.

It was lucky that he *had* sat up so much later than his usual time; for sleepiness was the one thing that could make a man not care whether he was in the world or not.

But how clever uncle Meredith was! How *could* he know, and that too without being told, that anyone wanted to go to sleep? But here he was letting a person slide down upon his lap. And here he was changing his position in his arm-chair so that a person's head had something to rest against.

"I believe," said Meredith ab Owen presently, turning his head towards their host, but taking care not to disturb his sleeping nephew, "that there's some disturbance going on in the church-yard."

They all listened intently.

"Yes, you'd better see to it, Father—or, if you'll take the child, *I* will."

The head of the College for the Priesthood put down his cup of wine and rose unwillingly to his feet. He knew, better than any of his visitors, how many disturbances could occur in that consecrated enclosure, due to its proximity to the Inn, such as it were wisest to allow to die down of themselves!

But he snatched up his clerical traveller's cloak, wrapped it untidily and anyhow about his shoulders, and let himself out.

The second he was gone, for Rhisiart Junior was lost to the world and all his claims upon it, the three men began talking quick and fast.

"It's Sparrow's revolt," sighed Meredith.

"I'm afraid that's what it is," agreed the Judge. "What'll *you* do, my Lord, if his peasants *have* managed to capture Dinas Brān? Denis has but a handful of men, and the walls are so ruinous, that his only chance, in my view, would be to rush them down before they got to the top of the hill."

In the absence of their heraldic priest there was nobody to notice the Wyvern-like contortion of the leathery visage of the King's Pardon-Bearer.

"I wish to God we'd heard nothing about it," Talbot groaned. " 'Tis a Fitz-Alan affair, or a Charlton affair. 'Twould never have happened if the King's orders had been obeyed."

Meredith's eyebrows twitched and he tried to turn towards the window. Very gently he moved his limbs, for they were growing stiff under the boy's weight.

"What *were* the King's orders?" he asked wearily. "Do *you* know, Judge? Some greater folly still, I warrant!"

The grey-headed Rhisiart looked at his friend's swarthy face and the lock of black hair that fell across his brow; and there rushed through his mind a vivid memory of a scene in Glyndyfrdwy sixteen years ago when Master Brut and himself admitted this evasive spectator of human unwisdom into their youthful counsels. "Oh, Walter, Walter," he thought, "how you'd smile to hear your innocent pupil in the gospels called 'Judge'!"

But after listening for a moment to the wind moaning in the new college-chimney, he glanced at the brightly-coloured tapestries that reflected the fire-light, and tried to explain to the son of Glyn Dŵr the attempts that the youthful monarch was making to limit legally, and above all *judicially,* the arbitrary tyrannies of the great barons.

Meredith softly stroked with his finger-tips the dusky head of the slumbering child. "But didn't Master Sparrow," he said, "marry one of old Broch's daughters? He must be an unusual man to risk losing that snug Meifod mill for the sake of his former friends."

"Once a peasant—always a peasant," threw in Lord Talbot, "and what's more, I'll tell you this. The King's policy of propitiating the burgesses at the expense of the rest of us will upset everything. *I* don't blame this Master Swallow of yours for making trouble! If he's married a miller's daughter he's been able to see for himself the difference between a peasant and a tradesman! The Guilds and the Crafts and the Master-Merchants are the great ones to-day. And as long as the House of Lancaster's on the throne they'll *be* the ones! That's what none of these whoreson pretenders have the. wit to see. If *I* were a great-grandson of Edward I'd do what Richard did, flout the Guilds and the Crafts and the City of London, and pay court to the peasants!"

The Englishman's words met with an unexpected response from Glyn Dŵr's son. Indeed he cried "bravo!" with such lively conviction that the little Rhisiart on his lap waved one of his hands in the air.

But the grey-haired Doctor of Civil Law, who bore the courtesy-title of "Judge," though he wasn't yet upon any circuit, showed by the expression upon his face what he thought of this chatter of ignorant neophytes. The nostrils of his great hooked nose quivered, his moustache twitched, a big vein in his neck expanded. "Sirs!" he burst out, and it was only the fact that his god-son was asleep that prevented his voice assuming a tone more adapted to Westminster Hall than a priest's refectory. "What neither you nor our good Master Sparrow understands is that the real Government of these Nations—I don't speak of France, because no sensible man—we're all friends here!—believes that the English Conquest will last like the Norman Conquest—the real Government, I say, of England and Wales is no longer a government of the Crown, or of the Barons, or of the Guilds, or of the Commonalty! It is a Government of—"

Our old friend's eyes were flashing so fiercely in the light of Father Sulien's candles that Talbot and Meredith exchanged whimsical glances. "Of the Church?" the latter interjected; but Judge Rhisiart swept this aside as dogmatically as Clerk Rhisiart would have done sixteen years ago.

"Of the Law!" he concluded in a tone worthy of Justinian. Whether the word "Law" roused to revolt the Mortimer blood in the younger Rhisiart or the blood of Catharine ferch Owen cannot be said, but it certainly wakened the child from his sleep. He opened his eyes, thrust aside his uncle's arm, and struggled to his feet.

"Where's the Father?" he asked in a querulous tone. "It must be time for me to say my prayers."

"Didn't I tell you, Judge?" sighed his uncle softly. *"That's* not the Crown or the Commonalty or the Law. That's—Mother of God! What's the matter, boy?"

The little Rhisiart was now standing where they could all see his face; and they all watched him in consternation. His eyes were wide; his mouth was open and twisted; his breath was coming in gasps. He was staring wildly at some point in the chamber that was mid-way between the window and the fire.

Meredith leapt to his feet. The elder Rhisiart clutched the arms of his chair. Lord Talbot muttered a blasphemous curse. But at that instant the old massive door that had belonged to the priest's house before the new college was built swung inwards, and Father Sulien appeared, supporting a panic-stricken, bare-legged young herdsman. Their appearance brought the boy to his senses in a moment. "Father!" he cried, rushing to his tutor and throwing himself weeping into his arms, "oh Father! oh Father!"

"Give this man something to drink, my Masters," said Father Sulien hastily; and then to the sobbing child: "What have they been doing to you, Rhisiart? What's the matter with you? Come, come, come. If you're a brave lad and can say your prayers I'll stay with you till you're in bed. Come, child! Come, my dear son!"

When the two of them had retired into their bedroom and both doors were shut, Meredith proceeded to obey the priest. He thrust the frightened and trembling youth into his own chair and poured him out a beaker of the spiced wine from the bowl on the hearth.

Talbot began questioning him at once; but Rhisiart intervened. "Let the fellow recover himself a bit. He's all *égaré. Il s'effraie de peu de chose."*

The three men, who were now all on their feet, moved together to the further side of the hearth and began discussing the little boy's trouble. "The child saw *something*—that's clear."

"Not at all! Children are often like that when they're suddenly waked."

"No, no, he had *some* kind of vision. There's no doubt of it. The question is, what *was* it he saw?"

It was Judge Rhisiart who at last drew up his chair close to the young herdsman. "I can't help thinking," he began, "that I've seen you before, my lad."

"I don't—know—Master. I've lived in these here parts all me life and I can't exactly, if you understand me, recall *what* gentle-folk I *have* seen down St. Collen's way; but I do seem to mind when I were a scrub—"

"By God, Meredith, I know him!" cried the Judge, forgetting both his dignity and his position in the wondrous sweetness of recalling the adventures of long-ago. " 'Tis the goose-boy I met on Midsummer Day, when with Tegolin and Mad Huw I was finding my way to Glyndy-frdwy! Listen, my lad, don't you remember, when you were little, being put once in charge of your sister's geese, and meeting some people with a beautiful horse, near St. Collen's Church—a horse of wonderful colours, a grand, tall, *old* horse, a law-abiding, obedient horse, the sort of horse that—"

But the young herdsman's shy face had lit up and he nodded vigor-ously. In some queer way the mere memory of Mad Huw's intervention on his behalf made him feel happier about his present situation. "Yes, sir, I *do* mind me of a strange Man of God," he declared hurriedly, speaking in Welsh and in the high-pitched accent of Powys Fadog, "who went about the land in them days. I were the only one that saw him close; to speak to—as you might say—and to touch his clothes. My dad wouldn't have been surprised if it 'tweren't King Richard himself! But it's the truth I'm telling'ee—I were little enough in them days but I talked to him, and touched him I did, with this very hand, same as I might touch you, sir!"

The learned lawyer from London fell into a muse as he stared at the world of memory behind the furtive eyes of this rustic lad. It was clear to him that in the passing of time the piebald horse, the geese, the girl,

yes! and he himself had all sunk into oblivion—all been annihilated—
while Mad Huw enjoyed a relative immortality. The warmth of the
fire, together with the fumes of the spiced wine, soon created, now
that his immediate fears were allayed, an irresistible tendency to nod
on the part of the youth from the *Llan* of Saint Collen.

Nor were the three friends any longer in a mood to converse. Judge
Rhisiart inserted the finger and thumb of his right hand into the
capacious travelling-pouch that he wore beneath his stately velvet tunic.
He saw the hilt of the dagger he'd thrust into the sod above the piebald
horse; he saw the red braid of his wife and her lifted arms as she stood
above him in the prison; he saw Mad Huw make the sign of the cross
as he promised sleep to the sick King; and under his breath, while his
fingers touched Tegolin's letter, he repeated the precise words that,
if the saints were merciful, would take him to Worcester when this
business of the pardon was done.

No lawyer in the kingdom had a better memory than Judge Rhisiart.
But what puzzled him was Tegolin's fluency. He little knew how
studiously she had shared all the lessons of their child. "I have been
bereft," her letter ran, "of the kind friend you wot of. Julietta, dear my
Lord, was wedded last Lammas Day to the worthy knight, Sir
Palamedes. Brother Huw died a week after Master Shore; the one of
a fever caught from the foul mud while fishing in the Severn, and
the other from a surfeit of fish bred in the same. Our little Catharine
can both read and write. Brother Huw taught her till within a few
days of his death. Will you have time to see my poor mother? Dear
my Lord, your last messenger reached me in four days. He says the
roads are less dangerous than they were. I marked well what you said
about my comeliness. Oh, Rhisiart, my dearest Rhisiart, what will you
think when you see your Tegolin as she is? To her you will always be
—Gwion Bach."

The Judge drew his fingers from his pouch and looked about him.
There was a faint liturgical murmur from the room at the back. Father
Sulien and the little Mortimer were evidently repeating the psalm for
the night. What *had* the child seen? Well! Well! The visions of children are as hard to catch as the foam of the sea; and he had trained
himself to avoid insoluble speculations. Let it go! And he set himself
to ponder on an interview he'd had that morning with Father Rheinalt

at Valle Crucis. The monk's sanctity, his guilessness of heart and single-
ness of brain, had overcome even Abbot Bevan's hostility; and the
fierce old patriot had talked freely to his daughter's husband. And
strange indeed was the tale Rhisiart heard!

The monk told him that Mistress Lowri was now obsessed by a
morbid infatuation for Denis. Such was the peculiarity of her nature
that ordinary love—as we say, "natural" love—was impossible to her;
and her mania now drove her to be the submissive and docile odalisque
of the man who had brought her back to Dinas Brān. Every beat of the
perilous perversity with which her veins pulsed had been quickened,
the monk explained, into a new life by the thought of being Denis's
helpless slave.

Judge Rhisiart had found his interview with his wife's father far
less painful than he expected; but as he recalled it now, watching with
half his consciousness Meredith's melancholy broodings over the fire and
Talbot's dazed, wine-fuddled astonishment at their host's tapestries,
a dim mist-like feeling did fumble for entrance into his narrow skull
that there were levels of human destiny totally outside his ken!

For all his learning in matters of law Judge Rhisiart was hardly
more skilled in the perilous sphere of human aberrations than when
he kissed the dwarf at the foot of the Ladies' Tower; and he now
began to feel obscurely uneasy as he thought of the sagacious legal
questions he had presumed to put to Tegolin's father.

But the monk had been strangely frank. He had even smiled once
or twice at the questions put to him. He admitted freely that Mistress
Lowri came frequently to the Abbey. He admitted that she forced him
—in spite of the fact that she knew he loved her still—to listen to the
wildest outpourings of her last obsession. He had gone so far—and
that also with a smile that staggered his questioner—as actually to
confess that in his love for this beautiful and tragic creature—"She's
simply a she-devil," thought Judge Rhisiart—he had had to do penance
for the fathomless pleasure that her coming to him gave him.

And the Judge, as he watched how the former goose-boy kept disturbing his own sleep by the noddings of his heavy head, recalled the
gracious but jerky manner in which Abbot Bevan had entertained him.

"Walter, Walter!" thought the Judge. "How you'd have chuckled if
you'd heard the way he told me about meeting Glyn Dŵr on the hill-

side above the Abbey and assuring him—you may depend with his usual self-echoes—when the Prince commented on his early rising, that it was *he* who had risen too soon by a hundred years. But I certainly said a good word for Father Rheinalt! I'm glad I had the opportunity to do *that;* and I think I made the fellow open his eyes when I defended Welsh patriotism by appealing to the Abbot of Caerleon. How lucky I knew that Valle Crucis was one of the monasteries that applied for his canonization; even though it was, of course, for the sake of the Order."

It was in the midst of thoughts like these—and indeed the Judge had begun to decide that, if he hadn't accompanied Talbot, this ticklish business of the pardon would have been a complete fiasco—that a shock of supernatural terror, giving him the sensation of having his stomach plucked out of him in a rush of ice-cold air, forced him to jerk his chair backwards with such violence that both his companions leapt to their feet while the goose-man spilled his wine over the burning logs with a sound like the hissing of salamanders.

"My Prince, my Prince!" cried Judge Rhisiart. And he uttered this cry in such a tone that it made Meredith leap to the door, Talbot rush to the window, and Father Sulien, pallid and trembling, come flying out of his bedroom.

But, as we have already seen in the course of his turbulent career, Judge Rhisiart was always at his best when he was well pleased with himself. It was in disaster that his powers became less conspicuous. At this moment with the news in his pocket of that providential catch of fish his wits were as lively as the wits of Lady Montfoison when she paid her momentous visit to London to beg her "little monk's" release.

Probably in the whole history of Corwen, from the days when Mynydd-y-Gaer was the centre of its life, no man, woman, or child has ever been so little *bouleversé* by an apparition. Was it the mixture in his veins of Norman and Welsh blood—the former making him naturally sceptical, and the latter making him so addicted to marvels that they were no overpowering shock? Whatever it was, the change for the rest of them was amazing when the convulsed image of terror that had a second before confronted them was transformed into a narrow-faced, grey-haired gentleman, smiling at their concern, putting his own agitation to the most realistic account, and with the utmost nonchalance thrusting his arms into the sleeves of his travelling-cloak.

"I must have been cold, Father," he said lightly, "in spite of your good fire! *Cold;* I must have been cold." Then, nodding kindly at the timid goose-man who had made a motion to relinquish his seat, he proceeded to place his foot upon a brazen fire-dog, pulling up the skirt of his cloak as he did so, so as to keep its lining of rich grey vair from being scorched.

"It's an extraordinary thing, gentlemen," Judge Rhisiart now announced, including all his three friends in the same piercing gaze of his dark eyes, "how *cold* can affect the human body! And the cold here, of course, is something different from what it is in London. It's a more *supernatural* cold, if I can use such an expression."

His listeners didn't dare to exchange glances under the fierce stare he kept upon them.

But not one of them let him off.

"I've never seen your Honour so disturbed," hazarded Father Sulien.

"This whoreson cold of yours, Judge," remarked Lord Talbot, "seems to have affected your god-son too."

"What did you see, cousin?" Meredith asked him point-blank. *"Was it my father?"*

This made Rhisiart turn his hooked nose and flashing eyes upon the Prince's son; and the instant he did so Lord Talbot began whispering to the priest. There was a pause; during which the Judge collected his thoughts by taking in every detail of Meredith's appearance.

Elliw's husband had retained his dark locks untinged with grey. He was dressed in a tight-fitting black tunic with violet-coloured hosen and he carried in his silver belt not only the horn that had brought them down from Mynydd-y-Gaer but an exquisitely-mounted hunting-knife in a purple sheath.

"It isn't sadness—not exactly *sadness*," thought Rhisiart. "I've never seen a human expression like it. He looks as if he knew the worst that could happen and was always cheerful when it didn't happen."

"Yes," he admitted gently, as if his scrutiny had taught him to hide nothing. "I *did* see the Prince. He was in chain-armour. His beard was white, but not unkempt. I suppose," he added turning to the priest, "our lad saw him too?"

Father Sulien nodded.

"Does this mean," broke in Talbot brusquely, "that Glendourdy's dead, and the King's pardon—wasted?"

His words instantaneously, without so much as the flicker of an eyelid between them, turned every Welshman present, including the goose-man who had understood the syllable "dead" though Talbot had spoken in French, into one single multiple personality. This composite Being withdrew, without a groan or a sigh, into a "secret passage" far deeper than that made by the mound-dwellers.

But Meredith smiled; and his smile caused Rhisiart to think of Sir Palamedes and his white rose.

"No, no, my father's *not dead.*" He spoke with such conviction that the spell was broken and there were four separate Welshmen again, one of them a courtesy Judge of the King's court; and though he couldn't have explained it, a curious discomfort was lifted from Lord Talbot's mind.

"I'm glad you say so!" he declared heartily. "It would have been a great pity if the pardon—"

He was interrupted by a series of heavy impatient blows at the door of the College.

The goose-man displayed extreme nervousness and looked wildly round the room as though seeking a hiding-place.

"It's the Chirk men, Father—it's the Chirk men, your Honour! They must have dragged him from the altar and killed him—and are now come for me!"

Father Sulien didn't hesitate. "If you don't make a sound so as to frighten the boy, *you can go in there.* Don't go near the bed! Stand behind the door till I call you."

He waited until all was silent in the College bedroom, then he flung the door open and three archers in the Fitz-Alan livery burst in dragging with them the redoubtable Master Sparrow. The peasants' champion had only received a few scratches during the struggle to drag him from the church, but he was in a dangerous temper and indeed had no scruple in the presence of this notable company about denouncing his captors roundly.

"They've taken me from sanctuary, my Masters!" he shouted.

"They've committed sacrilege, my Lords and Gentles! It's Master Hardy who set them on—Master Hardy from Wessex. Yes it is, you Saxon pig!"

"One minute," began Judge Rhisiart, "let us get this clear. *You* are Master Hardy I presume?"

Never was there a more turbulent conflict of emotions on the face of an elderly bowman than those that contended with one another on the visage of the man from Wessex. "I be, Mëaster; but such a rogue as he baint to be found between Orkneys and Land's End. Hold him, mates! Hold him fast!" he added, addressing his companions; and then looking round stubbornly and sheepishly. "He's a desperate man, my Lords! He's a murderous and mutinous rebel, my Masters!"

"All lies! All lies! your Honour," cried Philip Sparrow appealing directly to Judge Rhisiart. "This man's the most vindictive and narrow-minded liar in the kingdom. He knows as little of Shropshire as he does of Wales. He comes from a part of England that my wife says is still heathen!"

"Who is your wife?" enquired the Judge.

"Pardon me, Master Doctor, but you're asking what you must know already. My wife is Morg ferch Broch and our child John is heir to Meifod mill."

"He's a traitor to the King, my Lords," cried the man from Wessex, appealing to Lord Talbot. "We caught him in the act of stirring up the people. He's a cunning trouble-maker!"

"If this is true, Judge," threw in Talbot, "they were in the right of it. Many a time have I seen men dragged from sanctuary when—"

"They were *not* right!" cried Father Sulien indignantly. "As God is above the King, so the Church is above"—he caught himself up—"above all temporal power!"

Judge Rhisiart turned again to the man from Wessex. "What were you going to do with him?"

"With thee's permission, Measter"—it was clear that Master Hardy was less impressed by the furred robe than a Shropshire herdsman would have been—"us be tëakin' of 'un to Chirk."

"You'll never take me *there!*—not *alive!*" panted Master Sparrow.

"Is your charge," enquired Judge Rhisiart, "that he's an agitator

against the King made on account of his saying in public that Owen
Glyn Dŵr, formerly called Prince of Wales, will return and claim his
rights?"

The Wessex man's eyes gleamed with unappeasable hatred and he
fell at once into the trap prepared for him by our crafty friend.

"Eees, Mëaster," he blurted out. "He do say and he do swear to all
and sundry that this here conjuring devil, this here Mëaster Glendourdy, when 'un *do* coom back, wull cut the weasand of every rich
man in our wold island!"

The Judge looked significantly at Father Sulien.

"Kindly make a note for us, will you, Father, of the declaration just
uttered!"

Father Sulien hurried off to get his tablets and pen; and, on his return, fell to jotting down as fast as he could the churning torrent of
hatred that burst forth from the old Wessex archer. For sixteen long
years had this avenging wrath burned unappeased in the man's soul,
burned there since in the banquet-hall of Dinas Brān he had seen
Glendower's arrow pierce the throat of his girl's dad.

It was by one of those queer lapses of memory that are totally unaccountable that Rhisiart didn't recognize this fellow, while the goose-
man's lineaments, which were those of a child at that time, came back
to him so vividly.

It had begun by this time to dawn on the political wits of Master
Sparrow that this Welsh Judge and this Welsh priest were up to
something in his favour, so that, though the pain it cost him was
great, he restrained himself from hotly declaring that the peasants'
rising for which he'd been agitating was entirely un-racial.

For the thousandth time in his life he told himself that "gentlemen"
were the same all the world over, and that it wouldn't be till there
was found some way to unite the *gwerin,* the common people of every
race, that their tricks would be ended.

At this moment, however, these "tricks" were being exercised in his
favour; and because life had grown sweeter to him of late, and to be
dragged to Chirk meant death, he held his peace.

"A Wyvern! A W.yvern!" thought our heraldic priest, as he glanced
at the leathery countenance of Lord Talbot, who, with Glyn Dŵr's

pardon in his pocket, was evidently hesitating as to his proper cause of action.

There was indeed a serious conflict going on at that moment in this great Englishmen's mind. "Oh these curst border-barons!" he thought, "it's just like them to hunt their rebels and pursue their private quarrels when the King has all he can do to hold his own across the Channel. You look as sturdy a rogue as ever I've seen, Master what's-your-name! But—*nom de Diable!*—how am I to persuade the arch-devil to accept the King's grace when these fool-barons go on hunting his nameless devilkins? God help me! but I'm loth to let you go free, Master Obstinate, with your sulky airs; but I'm the King's representative here, and no Fitz-Alan or Charlton of them all shall over-ride *me* with their hired bravos!"

With all this, and more than this, in his mind, the conqueror of Harlech turned sternly upon the devoted exile from Wessex and made it clear to him that the King's present purpose was propitiation, not punishment. "Leave the fellow here," he said, "and off with you to the Inn! Here's a couple of silver groats for your charges—which is more," he muttered to himself, as the indignant archer withdrew with his companions, "than any Fitz-Alan has ever given a man in *my* service for a night's tippling!"

The early hours of the following day seemed deliberately conspiring, as the dying Prince sat by a fire of furze-stalks at the entrance to his hiding-place, to give him, as far as the elements were concerned, the right conditions for the ceremony he had planned. Broch and he had already broken their fast in their usual manner, drinking mead and eating cheese, and the Prince was wondering, as he sat there, from what direction his death-stroke would descend. He knew his hour was near; though whether his death would come from his heart, which had been his most menacing trouble of late, or from his lungs, which had been racking him all this damp autumn with exhausting spasms of coughing, or from what one Edeyrnion "conjurer" had diagnosed as a cancer in his stomach, troubled him not a whit.

It was a comfort to him, rather than the reverse, that his gigantic vitality should be thus beseiged from three directions at the same time.

It removed those teasing speculations always so fretting to an insatiable life-lover, as to whether if he'd taken this or that precaution all might yet have been well! If Death's legions were scrambling over his defences from three sides at once it was clear that what was coming upon him came, as Homer would say, "according to Fate," and not "contrary to Fate."

This confluence of a triad of enemies closing in became something larger and more majestical than any one of them could possibly have been alone. In itself the growth in his stomach might be un-malignant, the cough that was wearing him out merely bronchial, and his heart-trouble not of a deadly kind. But for their attack to be as simultaneous as this, Death must have got fate and chance and the will of the gods, all, all, all, as his irresistible allies!

The secret of the mound-dwellers' chamber at Mynydd-y-Gaer, handed down from father to son among the descendants of King Eliseg, just as it had been handed down to Eliseg himself, must now, the Prince decided, be lost forever—lost as he himself must be lost! Dead was his son Griffith who knew it. Dead was Davy Gam who knew it.

It would be against the whole nature of old Broch or of young Meredith to reveal what he wished should be concealed; and with them the secret would perish!

He was seated now in a comfortable old-man's chair covered with soft deer-skin; and his seat was so arranged that he could see the far-receding convolutions of the sacred river, twisting and coiling—as though its very flowing were a symbol of the Mystic Serpent of the mound-dwellers—towards Valle Crucis and Dinas Brān and the Shrines of St. Collen and St. Tysilio.

On his left, however, he could see the entrance to the well-kept "secret" of the long line of his ancestors. The chamber which served as a porch to the mound-dwellers' passage was a wide, low, rock-hewn cavern, with nothing of interest in it save a roughly-carved stone object in its centre; and even this at a first glance might have been taken, so confused were the markings on it, for a natural product of some remote glacial or volcanic antiquity.

A careful scrutiny would, however, have revealed that some of these markings were the runic straight lines of "Ogam," the Druidic alphabet, others criss-cross ribbon-patterns, like the intertwining of flattened-out snake-skins, other clumsily-carved reproductions of the foliated festoons of classic ornament; while various mediæval attempts had obviously been more recently made to turn the thing into a Christian altar by the super-imposition of dagger-like crosses.

An altar of some sort it may well have been, a relic perhaps of a race, of a religion, earlier than the mound-dwellers, and the portion of this stone palimpsest, which had most arrested Owen's attention, when as the heir of his House he had first seen it, was a crudely-shaped coil of mouldings at the back of the stone bearing a vague resemblance to the head of a serpent.

One thing had always struck Glyn Dŵr's mind about this queer piece of antiquity; namely, that there was no scooped-out hollow *for blood!* At the present moment, when the Prince turned his eyes in this direction, what he saw was the enormous figure of Broch-o'-Meifod, upon whose broad back the late November sun threw a long straight beam, causing the single axe which he still carried in his belt to gape and glow like a bleeding wound in his side.

Broch was busy just then replacing one of the small wooden wheels Davy Gam had fixed to a species of truck, by means of which that "slave of the spirits" had carried furze-stalks up the hill's side.

"Broch!"

"Yes, my Prince."

"Are you still sceptical of what I told you last night?"

The giant groaned, straightened his back, propped up the truck with its row of rattling wheels against one of the posts of the chamber, and coming to Owen's side stretched himself out on a heap of straw. If they hadn't been a pair of old countrymen, long accustomed to such bivouac blazes, there would have been a danger from sparks. As it was they both quickly measured in their minds the distance between the fire and the straw.

"I told you you'd tire yourself," said the Prince querulously. "I wish you'd let that thing alone. It won't have any more journeys to make! You'll be at Meifod and I'll be under the sod."

With his eyes half shut and the sun turning his bald head into a great lump of gold, the giant was silent for a minute. Then he remarked obstinately, "I'm not going to meddle with fate, Owen ap

Griffith Fychan. If you think I intend to help you to die, much as I want you dead, you're mightily mistaken. I wouldn't do it, even if by the lifting of a finger I could annihilate you without a second's pain! I tell you it's contrary to my whole nature to kill a man, except in battle, before he reaches his allotted destiny."

Owen looked down at him lying there on the straw, and as he looked he pondered, and as he pondered he stroked first one and then the other of the forks of his snow-white beard.

"Broch, old friend."

"Say on, my Prince."

"Why did you say just now you wanted me dead? So that you can go back to Morg ferch Lug?"

"Of course! You're my *other* self, Prince; but Morg's myself. But there's another reason, too."

"What's that, Broch?"

"I don't like *pain*. I never have, and I never will! I accept life and I accept death; but I *don't* accept pain!"

"But we *have* to, Broch, we have to!"

"Oh, of course! In *that* sense we have to—I mean we have to get through it somehow, as best we can. But in the case of life and death it's much more than just going *through* them! It's making them part of us, it's becoming part of *them!* I refuse to become part of pain. And I want you dead because when you're dead I shall have you without your pain."

"Have I showed it so much then? I was under the impression—"

Broch sat up and looked him in the face, and for some minutes the consciousness in the colourless orbs of the one lost itself in the consciousness behind the sea-green orbs of the other.

"Do you think, Prince," the giant burst out, "that I don't know every pulse and twitch and twinge of your old, soft, corrugated face? You don't have to wince and squirm and wriggle, you don't have to groan and squeal for me to know when the pain-devil's in possession! You can endure about twenty times what most of us can. But it's not a question of enduring. You can't *share* your *elixir vitae* when the pain-demon's draining it. Yes! you may sit there, stroking your old beard and looking like King Arthur; but I know very well, though you got over your coughing-fit pretty cleverly just now, and though you managed to do nothing but grind your teeth when your heart nearly stopped before dawn, I know very well, even as you're looking at me now—I know it by a pulse in your cheek—that your cancer, or whatever it is, is at this very second hurting you so much that the only strength left in you is just enough to play the dying actor with picking fingers. You're like a figure in a Martinmas Show, Owen ap Griffith Fychan, turning your head and smiling at the people, while inside of you the sawdust's already burning!

"Yes, you may smile and smile, dear my Prince; but if I didn't know that it was your destiny to hug your old life-bride till the death-rattle shakes you both, I'd—I'd use my last axe on you!"

Owen left stroking his beard, and slipt his fingers under his tunic till they reached the place where his cancer hurt him. At this spot, by long working at it, he had weakened and bent one of the links in Iolo's chain-armour. " 'Twould be a pity to do that, Broch," he said, "before I find out whether any of them saw me last night."

The giant struggled to his feet and stood before his friend, literally swaying with wrath. "So you're at *those* old tricks again, are you? Isn't it enough to be torturing *me* with your endurance that you must go and paint your twitching face on the air of poor Elphin's College for God knows how many generations? *Saw* you? I pray to God they *didn't* see you! Why can't you spend your time getting used to being dead, Owen ap Griffith Fychan, instead of trying to break the only merciful law in the universe?"

The Prince grasped the arms of his chair and leaned forward a little, looking up at the unwieldy form above him with a majestically secretive smile. "I've got another trick, too," he whispered hoarsely. "I've been practising it ever since"—he turned his hands against his ribs and forced his knuckles into his side while his words came in gasps—"ever since Davy went away. Come nearer, Broch, nearer! I want to tell you."

Broch-o'-Meifod knelt down, so that his great shoulders hid the whole perspective of the flowing of the Dee, while his bald head hid half the wooded slopes above it.

"Let's have the worst," he murmured grimly. "I suppose you're plotting to give that horrible phantom of yours some sort of monstrous longevity. You say you saw your son in that room of Elphin's. *That's* no proof; for you knew he was there. You must give me better proof than that, my Prince."

Owen shut his eyes and spoke very slowly. "I—saw—my—grandson."

The bald head came nearer him. "Tell me, Owen ap Griffith Fychan, *what's the use of all this?* You saw your son. You saw your grandson. It's like a rhyme my girls used to sing when they played hide-and-seek.

"Tysilio sat on Tysilio's throne: His son and his grandson were all alone: Cry spy and catch me before I'm home!"

"He wasn't—in his bed—he was—on Meredith's knee—and—I saw—Clerk Rhisiart."

"My Prince, my Prince—"

The man's voice was so troubled that Owen opened his eyes. Then very feebly he raised his fingers from his side and stretching out his arm drew his friend's head towards him and kissed him on the forehead.

The giant scrambled to his feet with a groan and went back to his heap of straw.

"Before I die," and Owen spoke more rapidly and firmly, now that the bald head was further off, "I shall take my soul and mix it with *all this*"—and he waved his hand towards the horizon—"so that every Welshman from Ruthin to Llan Collen and from Carrog to Lake Tegid shall feel me in his bones."

"My Prince—" began the other, still in the same troubled tone.

And it gradually dawned on Glyn Dŵr that Broch-o'-Meifod was afraid for his sanity. This was more vexing to the old man's mind than any attitude his friend could possibly have taken. Hurriedly he tried to re-assure him. "I must make this clear," he thought. "If once I make him understand me he'll see what I'm going to do."

"Listen, Broch," he said. "If, by sinking into Glyndyfrdwy and Dyfryn Clwyd and into all the land of Edeyrnion, I increase rather than lessen my power, why shouldn't the whole race of Welshmen increase its power by sinking inwards, rather than by winning external victories?"

"It's power, my Prince? Do you say it's *power?*"

"It's life, it's life, Broch! Why shouldn't we be the one single race—along with the Jews, of course!—who *win by losing?* Hopkin prophesied that a Welshman would be crowned King in London; and you remember Crach's prediction about the Tudors of Môn? Well, my friend! Listen to your old Owen prophesying to a different tune."

He leaned forward, as he spoke, bolt against the sun-rays, and Broch was impressed once more, as he had been several times of late, by the fact that the old man's sea-green eyes hardly blinked at all as they faced the sun. They even seemed in his excitement to gain more colour and more depth from the blaze they encountered, as if there existed between those eyes and that great furnace of light some fabulous reciprocity!

"Never mind," he went on, "whether I sent my soul to the College last night or not! *That's* not important. *That's* nothing! What I'm doing now, and doing all the while, even when the pain's at its worst, is what all Welshmen can do who've got the least drop of what your Morg calls the ancient people's blood in their veins; sink, that's to say, into the 'Secret Passage' of our race." He paused, and fumbling among the folds of the deer-skin, between his wasted flanks and the back of his chair, he lugged out a leather-bound parchment book.

"I've found several passages here," he announced; and his tone was so youthful that Broch suppressed the groan of weariness with which as a rule he listened to his chief's obscure renderings of yet more obscure rhymes, "that bear out exactly what I mean. No! you needn't make that face! I'm only going to read you what Taliesin says happens to us Welshmen when we sink down into our spirit, down below all these wars. Listen now; and if you don't like the word 'God,' you old Death-worshipper, you can substitute Annwn. When *I* read 'God' I read 'Life' not 'Death,' as you're sick of my telling you! But I'm talking of our *people* now, not only of you and me! One minute—here it is—*just* this, Broch darling, and then I'll stop. He's talking of our people—three, five, *seven* centuries hence."

He held up the book against the light, so that all Broch could see of his head was the gold band around it, a band that at that moment shone as bright as the great Bard's own "shining brow." There certainly had been little need to warn the husband of Morg ferch Lug that the word "God" was to be taken in some special sense. If the strange words held any piety at all it was clearly a piety that might have come up from the bottom of the Atlantic!

> *A weleist darogan dofydd?*
> Hast thou seen the prophecy of the Lord?
> *Buddyant uffern Ef dillyngwys.*
> Hell's prey He hath set free.
> *Y thwryf kaethnawt Ef kynnullwys!*
> Its captive host He hath gathered together!

The final words of this singular chant, especially the words *uffern* and *kaethnawt,* "hell" and "captive," the old man intoned as if they were part of some liturgy of the lost Atlantis.

Broch was sulky with him for dragging in that book just then. He was sulky with him for raising his voice and getting excited. "He could spit blood at any second!" Broch thought. But those words of Taliesin seemed to shake off, as Glyn Dŵr hurled them over Edeyrnion, everything that was weak and hopeless. They seemed to Broch just then to take to themselves quadruple wings and to become like flying fortresses of eternal escape, wind-blown bastions of the sort of refuge suggested by the old Brythonic words, *Mygedorth* and *Pedryollt,* that a travelling scholar once told him had been stolen from the ancient people.

The Prince himself seemed to be staring after the words he'd uttered, as if they'd been emanations from the peaks of Snowdon or had come up the salt estuary out of the open sea, and were returning whence they came. But he had replaced the book in the folds of the deer-skin and was speaking quite gently and reasonably now.

"Don't misunderstand me, Broch. I know how right our old Abbot was when he cursed us as a race for our tipsiness and amorousness. Le Borgne was astonished when he found we'd more bastards in Gwynedd and Powys than in all the Provinces of the Seine! But I'm not talking about our vices or our virtues. I'm talking about our *souls.* And I tell you this, old death-lover; our souls from the beginning have been"—here he was taken with a spasm of pain so acute that it distorted his face and caused him to jerk and twist in his chair, as if he'd been a great bearded fish that some devil-fisherman had hooked with a double barb; but pressing the links of Iolo's mail-shirt against his side with one hand, with the other he waved back his friend—"have been," and his voice seemed to shake the pain from it as Lleu-Llaw-Gyffes shook the rotting flesh from his eagle-bones, "have been able to escape into Annwn, into—into the"—his voice seemed shot like a quivering bolt from his jerking body; and Broch felt it whizz past his bald skull, as if it had been aimed straight at the sun—"into the world *outside the world!*"

The spasm subsiding, he sank back gasping, both arms hanging down on each side of his chair, like useless oars in a tide too strong for them, but he had something else he was trying to say, and Broch restrained himself from touching him. "Tell Morg," he murmured, "that I've got the—the blood—of the ancient people—in my veins—the people *we* conquered, as the Saxons did us, and the Normans *them*. It's the voice, tell her, of the ancient people that spoke through me just now—when I said—not by the sword—but by the—by the—" But a horrible paroxysm of coughing seized him then, and staggering to his feet he clutched his friend's arm, while with bowed head and with blood and phlegm pouring from his mouth, he set himself to endure, while thought, feeling, identity were momently lost in the down-sucking drag and drain of unconscious matter.

But it was over at last; and the first thing the Prince did when he recovered was to inform his friend that he was worried by the fate of Griffith Llwyd, his ancient bard. "You heard what that man said, Broch? That he's at the Tassel, and they're using him for money? Oh Broch, Broch! And I can do nothing—and he the bard of my house! He's a bad poet, I know, a tricky modern poet; but he's like a baby in any rogue's hands and as proud as the devil! Oh, Broch, to think of him at the Tassel; and so old—so old and helpless!"

The giant muttered something about going down there himself one night; but he could see from the tears on his master's cheeks that he took such talk as of no value.

But what a beautiful November day! And how peaceful the two of them could have been, if Owen's mania for this accurst ceremony hadn't spoilt it. Broch himself detested all ceremonies; and yet it was his destiny under the Prince's peevish instruction to do just the very things for which nature and inclination had most unfitted him.

It had especially pleased Glyn Dŵr that the prehistoric mound-dwellers' altar possessed no hollow place for blood; but it made the tips of Broch's great fingers tickle with nervous tension when it became his destiny to prop up and balance beneath those serpent-coils an appro-

priate selection of inflammable sticks and twigs. When their preparations were complete, and they had eaten their second meal, and had
piled up such a fire that it became necessary to remove their heap of
straw to a safer distance, the Prince fell, as was always happening in a
moment of rest, into a heart-rending coughing-fit.

So violent was it that when it was over he lay back in his chair so
ghastly-white and motionless that his friend was driven to put his
hand against Iolo's mail shirt. This gesture, however, so amused, so
touched, so roused the Prince that, though his lips under his moustache
scarcely moved, Broch could detect by the lines about his eyes that he
was smiling.

"I must have a mighty heart," he whispered, without opening his
eyes, "if you can—feel it through an iron shirt!"

Broch begged him to let him take off this hidden armour once and
for all; and his irritable refusal struck the Meifod giant as the most
crazy of all his inconsistencies. "Who does he think's going to stab
him in this precious ceremony of his? Lord Talbot? Clerk Rhisiart?
Father Sulien?"

But after this period of prostration the Prince's irrepressible life-force
began pouring into him again and he sat up in his chair. "Give me my
mirror, Broch. Give me my comb."

The giant obeyed him; but the weight of the polished metal, and the
effort it required to use the comb, were beyond his strength; and his
friend was forced in his blundering fashion—and it was the first time
they had come to this—to attempt it for him; with the result that there
were bitter tears in the Prince's eyes, and both objects were flung away.

"Sit down, for God's sake, man; and let me talk to you! If this goes
on you'll have to do more than curl my beard!"

With the patient bald head obediently bent forward, like a great
fossilled shell, Glyn Dŵr now began a series of detailed instructions.
He told his friend he wished his body to be taken to Mynydd-y-Gaer
and there burnt. "If you can't get a blaze hot enough to do it in twelve
hours, Broch, there'll be the spine and the shanks and the skull and
hands left; but the flesh'll be off them. They'll be just bones. And I
want you to break *these* in pieces with your axe, and strew them—*little*
pieces mind!—round the walls of the Gaer. But I want you to keep

back a handful, say half-a-dozen bits; and of bone, remember, not cinders. Have you caught the drift of what I'm saying?"

Broch made a sound that resembled the noise of his wife's mill-wheel. "*Drift,* eh? It'll be *you* who'll be drifting off in smoke, Owen ap Griffith Fychan, while I'm doing what you're telling me! But go on, for Christ's sake! This is just what I was wanting to know."

Owen tried to localize in his mind the mischief that was causing the Fisher-King's hook to tug at his vitals. He felt if only he could communicate to what Gam used to call his "spirits" exactly where the trouble lay, these powers could deal with it. But he had to content himself with feeling his soul to be a twisting and curling feather, lying on the lid of a cauldron of pain.

While he spoke to Broch the feather rose and fluttered a little above them both. "I'd like you to take a bone or two—just a few, Broch!— and go down to Corwen where there's that cross in the centre of the Druid mill-stone. Go on some dark night, Broch. Give yourself plenty of time. But take a spade with you and a mattock. Dig a hole—no bigger than a rabbit's—*under the stone*. Dig till you're below the centre of the stone and below the pillar of the cross; and there leave what you've got in your hand! Spit on them first, Broch old friend. They'll rest the better for that. And then back with the earth-mould and stamp it down! Afterwards will come the hardest part of it—and perhaps you'd better get little Elphin to help. For I want you to put grass-sods where you've disturbed the earth; so that only you, or only you and that boy-priest, will know there are bones under the stone.

"Trust nobody, Broch—do you understand?—who isn't *entire Welsh!* What happens to my flesh'll be the secret of Mynydd-y-Gaer; what happens to my bones'll be the secret of Broch-o'-Meifod; what happens to my soul"—and a light came into the old man's glaucous eyes that was boyish in its roguery—"we'll leave to the little priest of the College; but what happens to my spirit will be the secret of all *entire Welshmen* to the end of the—" Here he was taken with a spasm of pain of a new kind; of a kind that made it necessary for him to slide down from his chair upon the ground; and as he twisted there, like a king-salmon with a spear through him, he got his foot-stool under his belly; and this, for some reason, mightily eased him. In fact it eased him so much that he commanded his friend to let him lie; and Broch noted that though at first he scrabbled in the ground with his fingers, a second later, after he'd got the stool under him, he lay without a movement.

"That Cross in Corwen," Broch heard him mutter, in a voice to which the nearness of the earth to his mouth gave a low rumbling tone, like the sound of a bumble-bee in a broken ram's horn, "has the same snake's skin ornament as our mound-dwellers' altar—a mat of flattened-out snake-skins it is, woven like a basket! The sort of 'mat' it is that the Berbers in Marakash sit cross-legged on, and are transported whither they will!

"Iolo—used to say—can you—hear me—Broch?—that it was 'Mercian' —and not Welsh at all—but—but—what do *you*—think, Broch?"

He was silent after that; and the bald-headed giant, who was now on his hands and knees by his side, was fain to place his head against his head to catch the sound of his breathing.

"Mercian!" the giant groaned in his heart, "Mercian, Persian, Tertian! O these life-lovers, these life-lovers!" Then after a pause Broch scrambled to his feet. "He's asleep," he said to himself. "He's worn-out with his pain and his fancies."

But glancing at the long diminishing perspective of the road that led towards Corwen he perceived afar off three men and a child approaching. "I'll have to rouse him," he said to himself. "He'll be furious else. Oh these ceremonies, these ceremonies!"

But such was the Prince's supernatural vitality that even this brief surcease of pain gave him renewed spirit.

"Come, Broch," he cried unexpectedly, after the giant had carried his chair up the couple of stone steps in front of the altar, "let's cross our water, as Tudor and I used to do, when we vowed to be friends for-ever!"

Broch-o'-Meifod had no scruple about obeying him; and the two elderly chieftains proceeded, solemnly and deliberately, to invoke the friends of their childhood in the manner suggested.

"How Morg would laugh!" thought Broch-o'-Meifod; and he recalled innumerable cases in their life together when he and his water-sprite-wife had shocked their "pure Brython" neighbours by their aboriginal unfastidiousness. "They don't understand," he said to himself, as he re-settled Owen in his chair—and his "they" applied to the Brythons and the Goidels as much as to the Normans and the Saxons—"what we ancient people know right well, that it's only by accepting the maggots and the rats and the gob and the spue"—he was talking to himself in Welsh now—"and all the other 'after-births' of Nature that this 'spirit' they talk about can float clear away."

"Are they near, Broch? Go and look *once* more! Tell me when they've got to the wooden bridge!"

Broch came to announce that they were even then crossing the wooden bridge.

"Listen, my friend!"

"I *am* listening, my Prince."

"Do'ee know what I'll do? I'll make Rhisiart throw his King's pardon into the fire."

Broch lost his temper completely at this; and the outburst that followed had behind it all the suppressed irritation of their long clash of opposite temperaments. The giant never forgot how the Prince opened his sea-green eyes; opened them till they were, as children say, "wide as saucers," under these unexpected reproaches.

And well might the old man open his eyes, for Broch at that moment was a disturbing sight. In the course of his incoherent out-pouring, the bald head kept wagging from side to side and the enormous body kept swaying backwards and forwards; both body and head being composed, as Owen gazed up at them in the sunshine, of dazzling surfaces and dusky shadows.

Broch was trying to explain to the incorrigible old rebel that this whole business of burning the King's pardon on the mound-dwellers' altar was a ridiculous hocus-pocus.

"All this race-ritual's just child's play!" he shouted. "Life goes on being swallowed up in death; and death goes on spawning new life; and the reality is hidden by their struggle. What you've done all your days is to fight death; and the more you fight death the stronger death grows! *You'll* make Clerk Rhisiart skip, you will! *You'll* make the King's messenger stare! *You'll* turn young Elphin from priest to herald again, you will! *You'll* make little Mortimer clap his hands! You'll love, you'll hate, you'll laugh, you'll cry, you'll make Gam your slave and Rhisiart drink your blood! I—I—It's—it's—it's more of life and love *than I can bear!* I—" and then, without a pause, and still muttering something that Owen couldn't catch by reason of a noise that reached him like the sobbing of a wounded Behemoth, Broch collapsed towards him, whether to strike him or to embrace him the Prince never knew, for at that moment there resounded a familiar voice from the ruined court-yard outside, the voice of a priest and yet the voice of a herald.

Both the men became their natural selves in the beat of a pulse. Morg ferch Lug would certainly have clapped *her* hands at the sight and cried aloud: "The ancient people! The ancient people!" For thus, and in that manner and no otherwise, would the aboriginals of Mynydd-y-Gaer have dropped their quarrels and "touched wood" at the approach of the invader with "the pitiless bronze."

Experienced courtiers as they both were, Father Sulien and Judge Rhisiart wouldn't allow either the little Mortimer or Lord Talbot to advance a step—though they must all have heard the giant's incoherences—until Meredith ab Owen's hunting-horn had been duly sounded.

"Get the torches lighted! Get your axe handy, in case the Sais—get the mead out and the flagon—the stirrup-cup, Broch, the stirrup-cup, not the loving-cup!"

When the Prince had settled himself in his chair, which now stood upon the dais with its back to the altar, he glanced first over his left and then over his right shoulder to make sure that the torches were properly burning in their iron sconces.

"They'll think he's as sound as a bell," said Broch to himself, "but the pain's got him again. He's making faces."

"The most worthy and worshipful Knight Gilbert, Lord Talbot of Goodrich!" Father Sulien was now announcing; for the temptation to unfrock himself in the presence of that prehistoric altar and that Arthur-like figure was too much for him.

The little Rhisiart clung to the Judge's hand while the conqueror of Harlech—looking to Elphin at that second so like a Wyvern that it would have seemed quite natural if he'd carried the royal pardon in his mouth—made a brusque soldier's bow and paused in extreme discomfort.

Seasoned warrior as he was, and battered campaigner, he now most heartily cursed King Hal for sending him on this fool's errand. He'd seen too many Welsh patriots, too many French prisoners, too many ambassadors from Scotland, not to feel convinced, as soon as he set eyes on that forked beard and that weird altar, that he had landed himself in a ridiculously false position.

"The devil fly away with you all!" he cried in his heart; and he tried to catch Judge Rhisiart's eye with a suggestion that it was desirable they should *not* offer the pardon.

But Meredith was too quick for him. Risking his father's anger, he respectfully but boldly climbed upon the dais, advanced to the old Prince, and kneeling on one knee kissed his hand.

Owen was just then, though he concealed it from all but Broch, suffering abominable pain. His forces were so absorbed in simple endurance that there was scarce any magnetic quicksilver left over with which to force to a conclusion the startling anti-climax upon which he had set his heart. All he had strength to do was to enquire of his son, in a tone that had more courtesy than feeling in it, about the Lady Elliw.

Now it had happened that since the execution of her father, little Lu had been subject to many wild fancies; and one of her fancies was that Owen himself, and not the King at all, was responsible for Rhys Ddu's death. Instantly aware therefore, though the pain. he was enduring caused a curious-tasting foam to burst in minute bubbles between his lips, that he had blundered in some way and hurt Meredith's feelings, the Prince laid his hand tenderly on his son's wrist and pulled him towards him so that he could whisper in his ear.

He soon allowed him to rise erect after that; but they all noticed that the two of them never again completely lost hold of each other. They didn't exchange another word, nor did so much as a look pass between them, but such was their electric affinity that Broch as he observed them felt as if all that was needed to give them the power of *thinking in common* was that they should be, or at least their *clothes* should be, in some kind of physical contact.

Owen's pain lessened now; and though this lessening was accompanied by a new interior sensation that made the old man say to himself, "I know what *that* means! *That* means I'm done for," the relief to him was incredible. So intense was it that he began to feel happier than he had felt for months. It was as if his body, having received its journey-money from death, had made a present of it to his mind. He felt a sudden glow of affection towards this whole little group of people; especially towards the two Rhisiarts, whom he beckoned to come nearer.

Catharine's child, however, seemed curiously unwilling to release the Judge's hand. There was something about that pair of torches throwing weird shadows upon those serpentine coils—for Broch had by this time shut out almost all the light of day—that troubled the boy's mind; and he felt, without knowing why, the unnatural vibration of his grandfather's mood. The serpent-coils were very roughly carved; but one of the effects of this blend of torch-light with faint day-light was to give them a resemblance to the curves of a feminine body.

With the instinct of courtier rather than a priest, Father Sulien now approached their Wyvern-like guest, who kept looking round him in sullen uneasiness, and began thanking him for his chivalrous behaviour to Mistress Luned on the occasion of the taking of Harlech. Whether it was the curves of those prehistoric mouldings or whether some primitive matriarchal aura emanated from that bloodless altar, it now became the destiny of all of them to think of the women of their lives.

The younger Rhisiart thought of his mother. The Judge thought of Tegolin. Meredith thought of Elliw. And it wasn't long before the Prince himself, in his mood of unnatural elation, followed Father Sulien's lead and began thanking Lord Talbot with grave dignity for the consideration he had displayed towards the Arglwyddes.

"I believe," he said mischievously, yielding still further to the hypnotic influence that was affecting them all, "that this old-fashioned welcome we're giving to the ambassador from London would have been more acceptable to him if our beautiful cousin, Mistress Lowri from Dinas Brān, had been able to be present. It is," he went on, and his voice began to assume such an unusual tone that Broch, who all this while had been idly lighting the twigs of furze-stalks and extinguishing them as soon as he'd lighted them, advanced a step or two towards him, "it is, I think, a recognized fact that our women of Wales have always—have always—"

He ceased abruptly; and there ensued a scene that not one of those present were able to forget. Supported on one side by Broch and on the other by Meredith, Owen rose slowly, painfully, menacingly, to his feet.

"It is, therefore," he gasped, "in the name of Arianrod ferch Dōn, in the name of Branwen ferch Llyr, in the name of—of—of—" Here his words became incoherent, like the falling of winged creatures, blind with blood; but some of those present thought they heard Catharine's name, others Tegolin's. All of them, save the little Rhisiart who had hidden his face in the Judge's furred sleeve, felt as they gazed at that uplifted white beard that they had suddenly come close to a crack in the visible; a crack through which the invisible was blowing an ice-cold blast on its phantom horn.

But Owen was now standing erect; and with out-stretched arm was beckoning to Judge Rhisiart.

The Judge seemed to know what he meant; for gently disengaging himself from the little boy, who promptly clapped his hands to his face and began silently weeping, he moved across to Talbot, took from him the King's pardon, and with this in his hand gravely and deliberately ascended the steps.

But the Prince, supported by Meredith and Broch, made no sign that he had seen him, and acted now as if he were pushing away with that out-stretched arm something different from the King's pardon.

Meanwhile Judge Rhisiart paused quite naturally, as if he were certain of receiving further orders; while swinging from the parchment roll in his hand there swayed to and fro a massive seal. The tension in that low-roofed chamber of the ancient people grew almost intolerable. And it was suddenly accentuated by a curious convulsive jerk that Owen gave; a jerk that flung back his head so far that the forked white beard concealed his face.

At last, just as Rhisiart was saying to himself, "The blackness—the blackness," and, after that, as if he'd been a youth again at the foot of Dinas Brān, "I want to suck out the poison," there came a voice that reached them all.

To Father Sulien, who had laid his hand upon the shoulder of the little boy, it didn't seem to come from the Prince at all, but to Talbot it did, and to Judge Rhisiart it certainly did.

But Glyn Dŵr still had his arm out-stretched. "Prince of Powys—Prince of Gwynedd—Prince of Wales—" and then in a tone that made the boy stop crying and made even Lord Talbot cross himself, "Prince of Annwn!"

A deep silence followed and Father Sulien said to himself: "He was dead before he spoke. *A spirit spoke through him.* They're holding up a dead weight now."

If they were, Broch-o'-Meifod was powerful enough to do his part with one hand while with the other he deliberately removed one of the torches from its iron sconce and set light to the dry furze-stalks on the altar. These instantaneously burst into flame; and as the flames rose Judge Rhisiart was aware of an irresistible compulsion.

Lifting the hand that held the pardon high above his head, he flung it lightly, easily, and without effort into the heart of the fire.

"Where is my god-father and Lord Talbot?" enquired the little Rhisiart of the priest, some ten minutes later, as they took the road to Corwen.

"God knows," was Father Sulien's answer. "God have mercy on us all, and forgive our sins—our most grievous sins!"

The gentlemen in question who had mysteriously hung back, so as to separate themselves from the child and his guardian, were now settling together a nice point of honour; and settling it in a manner that would have seemed strangely fantastic to the two Welshmen they'd left with the dead Prince on the top of Mynydd-y-Gaer.

Rhisiart was, as we know, only half a Welshman, and what Welsh blood he had was less mixed than his princely cousin's. It was, therefore, with complete understanding that he recognized his fellow-ambassador's duty to exact from his person at the point of some equal weapon the blood-debt he owed to their royal master. He was too proud to plead —as he might well have done—that the force which compelled him to burn King Henry's seal had been a supernatural one; but all the same his was the lighter heart of the two when he faced his scrupulous opponent in an already darkening *llanerch* or clearing, among the gorze-bushes.

Talbot gave him the choice of the pair of daggers he always wore and which, when meticulously measured, proved of the same length; and the fact that his challenge was understood and accepted banished in a moment from the great captain's mind all personal feeling.

The matter could only sink into oblivion, however, after the insult to their sovereign had been atoned for in at least a *few* drops of blood, and he felt a glow of chivalrous admiration as well as satisfaction when the Judge hung his vair-lined mantle upon a gorze-bush.

But his complacency turned to surprise, and his surprise to gravity, when he found that the river-mist which accentuated the November twilight instead of bewildering his antagonist seemed to endow him with the eye of a lynx.

Though one of the best soldiers of his age as a strategist and commander Lord Talbot was not only an elderly man but somewhat stiff of his joints.

Had the contest been with swords, our friend the Judge, whose life had been for the last ten years entirely pacific, would have been at the other's mercy; but a dagger is, of all weapons, as even women are aware, the least professional and certainly the least exacting of any special technical skill.

Thus, though Rhisiart's muscles had grown slack from want of exercise, the two men were on fairly equal terms; and for several moments, as they circled round each other and dodged and parried and shuffled this way and that in the growing dusk, there was no sign that any furred or feathered identity in the vicinity felt that instinctive premonition which we may assume most creatures of the earth feel when some tragic shedding of blood is imminent.

Something, however, about his cousin's death had revived in the Judge's nature that old romantic spirit that had driven him to leave Oxford; and the fact that this lean, wizened, war-battered veteran, whose artful attacks and well-counterfeited retreats showed a long experience of sword-play, wasn't only far less sharp-sighted than himself but was clearly playing with him and trying to draw his blood in some un-vital spot threw him into that vein of exultant alertness that he had displayed when he saved Owen from Gam's knife.

"I'll teach you to play with me!" he thought; and taking advantage of a yet darker cloud of mist rising from the river he made use, in one swift, well-timed rush, of his more flexible limbs, closed with the man, and pierced his dagger-hand with a neat downward stroke.

That was the end of it; and it was to the tune of what would have struck Broch-o'-Meifod as the silliest fol-de-rol of fantastical courtesy that the two gentlemen embraced each other and the rebellious lawyer's silken handkerchief was produced to staunch the flow of loyal blood.

"What in God's name, man," enquired Lord Talbot, as, the matter of the pardon thus chivalrously if not amicably settled, they took the road to the forester's where they'd left their horses, "did you cry out as you leapt at me like that?"

Our friend's cheeks flushed hot in the chilly darkness; for well he recalled the scandalous lapse from all the rules of the "Court of Love" of which he'd been guilty. In his excitement he had outrageously and harshly mixed together the musical syllables of Catharine's and Tegolin's names!

But not for nothing was he the son of the wittiest romancer in Hereford; and it was entirely in the spirit of Lady Montfoison that he gravely invented a paramour in Eastcheap whose name was as unusual as her appearance was bewitching.

Both the men fell silent after that; the indiscriminate charms of Dame "Catholin" having whirled their thoughts away, down secret passages as strange and as well-concealed as any in Powys Fadog.

Judge Rhisiart's mind went back to the first time he trod this road between Glyndyfrdwy and the Church of St. Collen. The figure of Tegolin returned to him as she looked when mounted on Griffin with Mad Huw by her side. Again and again he slipped his fingers under his fur robe, as if only by the actual feel of her letter could he realize that ere a week was over they would be together again!

But the thoughts of even the most honourable of lovers are wayward and shameless; for, as he went along in peaceful amity with the man who had captured Harlech, the image of Catharine as he had first seen her in that robe of glittering *pali* took the place of the pitiful prisoner in the Tower and the care-worn matron in that sad lodging on Ludgate Hill.

How *could* he have mixed up the names of the two loves of his life in that victory-cry with which he had, for all he knew, cut forever the fighting sinews of the best sword-hand in England?

Women were so separate from each other, dead or alive! He had loved two of them and lost them both. But one was found again. And now that he was on his way to *her,* why should his mind keep reverting to the other?

"Would it be like this," he thought, "if they weren't Welsh? Why did he call out to those great dead ones at the last? But mine were his,

and his were mine—Catharine and Tegolin, Tegolin and Catharine
—and *that* day I drank his blood, and *to-day* I've drawn his enemy's."

That same enemy began indeed to feel a little uneasy just then as to
the amount of blood he had drawn, for as he crooked the tips of his
fingers so as to touch the Judge's handkerchief he found that the blood
had already soaked through. He was puzzled by the abstracted silence
which had fallen upon his late adversary. All he could make out of
Rhisiart's profile in the darkness was his hooked nose; but as he glanced
at the grizzled blur that represented his eyebrows and at the second
blur that represented his moustache he received the impression that the
great lawyer was walking with his eyes shut and mumbling to himself
as he walked.

The truth was that our friend was wrestling with a problem for the
solution of which neither Nature nor Providence had provided him
with any clue. There was something, he pondered, about the mysterious
beauty of a certain smile, of which all Welsh women seemed to have the
secret, that suggested *a common origin.* Could it be that that was why
Owen, while he thought of Catharine and Tegolin, cried out the names
of Branwen and Arianrod? Were the women of Wales, in their closer
affinity with the original "Mothers," possessed of some love-charm,
especially revealed in their smiling, that the younger races of the world
had lost.

Both the wayfarers were relieved when at the village of Carrog they
were able to mount their horses; but Talbot's attendants had been
directed to await them at the Tassel, and with his hurt hand the Englishman had to ride with caution.

By the time they approached the spot where, sixteen years ago,
Rhisiart and Tegolin and Mad Huw had enjoyed their meal of Midsummer cakes, the wind had risen behind them, and the air had grown
chill with a vague prescience of snow.

Rhisiart noticed that his companion had begun to sway wearily and
painfully in his saddle, once or twice raising his wounded hand to his
lips and perceptibly shivering as the chilly gusts whistled about them
and whirled the dead leaves round their horses' hooves.

So warm was his own blood and so sweet to him was the thought
that his face was already set towards Worcester that when Talbot
confessed that the blood had soaked through the handkerchief and was

dripping from his hand, and that he felt a whoreson chill in his bones, he stealthily changed the hiding-place of Tegolin's letter, and with *that* to warm his own blood, snatched off his fur robe and wrapping it round the other's shoulders kept their horses neck to neck, while with his free hand he steadied the swaying form of his friend.

Thus they went along; Rhisiart repeating a few "Mary, Josephs" and a few "Hail Marys," but concentrating his invocation upon the soul of his friend Walter, whom, combustible heretic though he was, he'd privately and unofficially canonized. But whether it were the Mother of God or the noble husband of that witch of Ruthin, our friend felt an imperative necessity to pray to *some* super-human power that night.

"Oh soul of Mad Huw!" was his final ejaculation, "for mercy's sake, let's get to the Tassel before he collapses!" But having relieved his feelings by these impulses of piety he fell to meditating upon his favourite topic. It was *his* turn now to feel the snowy wind, but in spite of his impatience to reach the Inn he suddenly felt inexpressibly happy. He was far too cold to analyse these feelings, nor in any case was the process of mental analysis one of his strong points; but he was just then seized with a new kind of exhilaration that had nothing to do with the sight of the Tassel's lights ahead, nor with the letter in his pocket.

It may seem natural enough that when a Judge of the Realm felt a stir of pleasure in his vitals it should have to do with the idea of universal justice.

But Rhisiart was still—though indirectly—harping upon the pardon he had burnt. "The Law," he assured himself, "is above all this race-enmity and all these national contests. The Law is beyond all religions, all governments, all races, all peoples, all languages. The Law represents the human race; and is the voice of our common humanity. A time will come when it won't be any more a case of Welshman against Englishman, or Frenchman against Spaniard, or Hungarian against Bohemian. It'll be a case of universal Justice and the power and authority of universal Law!"

With this triumph of justice whirling through his brain and his wife's love-letter pressing against his ribs Rhisiart's spirits rose so high that they shook off, as if they were nothing, the various untoward

events in his exciting life. The chief of these events was the fact that
Griffin died by violence rather than of old age.

Thinking of Griffin, as with the familiar sound of the murmur of
the Dee in his ears, they approached the Tassel, Judge Rhisiart was
seized—it was probably the effect of the smell of the Tassel-stables—
with a vivid sense of the presence of his old horse just behind him.

Risking the discomfiture of Lord Talbot he swung round, mechanically extending his free hand. He touched no warm piebald
back; but, for all that, Griffin *was* there, and not only Griffin. Clear
before him under the northern constellations rose as of old, magical
and majestic, the towers of Dinas Brān; and he couldn't help muttering
a sort of prayer for that tormented spirit still enclosed in its walls who
had fed with such deadly sweetness the "insect" within him.

He thought of Griffin again that night as he went round with a
lantern to the Tassel stables to make sure that their horses would be
fit for the morrow's journey. They were to ride together as far as
Hereford; and Rhisiart had the mischievous intention of leaving the
famous soldier under Lady Montfoison's care, secretly hoping that the
man's nation-wide renown as the conqueror of Harlech would so fascinate my lady that Monsieur's nose—if nothing more—would be put
out of joint.

What with warm cordials and home-made ointments Lord Talbot's
spirits soon returned to him that night; and indeed it wasn't long before
the gallant soldier, looking anything but heraldic as the avaricious landlord plied him with expensive liquor, was all for exchanging bawdy
ditties with anything that could breathe, from the great Tassel sow to
the old blind falcon.

Rhisiart, however, in his black fire-side suit and buck-skin slippers,
was in no vein for such frivolities. He was in a curious mood that night,
a mood in which the romantic feelings of youth seemed to blend with
the fantastic intimations of old age. All the wine he drank turned to
tender retrospect and all the mead to vague reverie.

But in the end he became restless; and the figure of the Prince, with
his out-stretched hand rejecting the pardon, and his voice, if it *were*
his voice, calling to him from another world, began to trouble his mind.

In his lordly tipsiness Talbot took no more notice of the old landlord of the Tassel than if he'd been an ale-drawer at an Eastcheap tavern; but the Judge couldn't help recalling Master Sparrow's indictment of this smug rogue, when, sixteen years ago, he and the Abbot forded the Dee.

The landlord's dame was just such another too, with her pinched mouth and snatching eye; and remembering how these people had catered for Owen's enemies in those old days it sickened him that such rats should be prospering still when the lion lay dead.

His disgust quickened to wrath before midnight came. Talbot showed no inclination to go to bed; nor, as long as these wretches laughed at his drunken tales, did he seem to care who or what they were. When he became too fuddled to proceed with his own follies, however, what must they do but use another devise to keep him drinking.

The Judge fancied he caught them muttering a name familiar to him, and—*nom de Dieu!*—if they weren't hauling into the room a great antique harp, and along with it, borne in a chair by two serving-men, none other than a ghastly simulacrum of his old acquaintance, Griffith Llwyd ap Dafydd ab Einion, whose voice he had last heard fourteen years before on the night of the comet.

If the old Bard had looked to him on that occasion like a withered grasshopper, he struck him now as something even less human. What was visible of his face was of the colour of ivory; but so preposterously had they allowed his hair to grow that when he was first carried in, and placed in the centre of the room, our friend was uncertain which was the front and which was the back of that pinkish skull covered with silky locks.

Subsequent enquiries revealed the fact that these miserly wretches had taken advantage of the immense age and failing intelligence of Owen's Bard to enrich themselves at his expense while pretending to offer him a charitable asylum.

That they would eventually have to bury him at their own charges didn't deter them. Old men had many infirmities; and when *no* device —and they spared few—could make him perform, there would be no necessity for further outlay.

The woman *did* have a few instinctive qualms that night about the attitude which the restless gentleman in black might take; but the man scoffed at her fears. Her feminine foresight proved, however, to be completely justified; for when their visitors left they not only carried away the ancient harpist; but they left behind a disturbing document; a document which was declared, though nobody at the Tassel could read it, to be a summons to appear in the Shrewsbury court in the following spring, to answer a charge of so dark a character that apparently it could be expressed only in the Latin tongue.

But if the Judge suffered while he watched the soul of this lamentable cadaver being summoned by repulsive threats and vulgar entreaties to return to earth from its happy euthanasia, when at last with pains like the pains of a frozen creature brought back to life old Griffith Llwyd lifted up his croaking voice and plucked at the strings, the sight became intolerable.

He left the chamber while the old man was still playing, and ascended the stairs to his bedroom. Here, walking impatiently to the window, he could still hear from the floor below the sound of the harp-playing and even the old cracked voice accompanying it; both harp and voice, though all the Tassel was listening with a silent unspoken dread, became, when he reached the window and leaned out of it in the starlit night, something more than the evocation of a pantaloon-Samson, making sport for the enemies of his Lord. Those broken harp-notes and that old cracked voice became indeed a true death-dirge, a real *marwnad,* for a sovereign prince of the Cymru.

For there in the northern sky, beyond St. Collen and Glyndyfrdwy and Carrog, where he knew Mynydd-y-Gaer must be, there was a red light in the sky; and Rhisiart knew that this red light came from Glyn Dŵr's funeral-pyre.

And as he gazed at this light in the sky and listened to those pitiful notes he realized how he had loved what was dissolving in that red light. Faint was the light in the sky, but fainter still were the tones —like sounds from the other side of Lethe—of the old man's playing.

And very slowly a portion of Judge Rhisiart's consciousness that was neither his love nor his intelligence began to respond to that faint glow and those feeble sounds. Owen's body was dust; but a light came out of that dust. The tormented wraith of the old Bard made those strings weep; but the weeping was not the weeping of despair.

Rhisiart leant out of the window, staring at the glow in the sky while the harp-tones sank to a dull repetition, the heavy breathing of a dying man, whose consciousness, like the fin of a fish in shallow water, is already in another.

Why did Owen call himself *Prince of Annwn?* And Rhisiart suddenly thought of Modry, and how she would talk sometimes of what she called "the harrowing of Annwn" by King Arthur. While Owen lived, there had always been something about him that for a narrow legal skull was hard to understand; but this dull thrumming of the strings and this fading glow in the sky were like a simple childish hand copying the Commentary of some planetary Pascentius!

And he felt that no success or prosperity, no crashing disaster or devastating ruin, would henceforth ever make him forget he was a Welshman or that he knew with Welsh knowledge that the things which are seen are un-essential compared with the things that are unseen. And he put it to himself, quaintly and characteristically in his secret colloquy with that red glow and those notes' dying-fall, that he was drawing up a new "Tripartite Indenture" between his soul and the soul of his master! And indeed for the rest of his days it was remarked of Judge Rhisiart, by foes as well as by friends, that it was to the over-tones and under-tones in a human controversy, to the pitiful prejudices which qualify and complicate a clash of opposed interests, rather than to the more obvious causes of quarrel that as an interpreter of the law he gave the most patient and most penetrating consideration.

It was not till the grey dawn, cold and sad, and full of the weariness of the outer spaces, began to fall upon Mynydd-y-Gaer that Meredith bade farewell to Broch and proceeded to descend the bracken-covered slopes that led to the forester's house in Carrog.

The giant had assured him that he could follow without assistance on the ensuing night all the Prince's instructions about the "handful of bones" to be buried beneath that strangely-shaped pillar, by some called a cross, and certainly bearing a cross on its side, that rose from the centre of the Druid stone in the church-yard of Corwen.

Meredith had left his horse as had the others, at the forester's house, and he was impatient to be gone. He had indeed a difficult quest in view—nothing less than an attempt to persuade a pro-English cousin of Rhys Ddu's, to whom the Tywyn estates had fallen, to hand over to Elliw and himself at a substantial price—for the man never came near the place—the ancient dwelling and its immediate surroundings.

Whether he could persuade little Lu to leave the vicinity of that ghastly spike on London Bridge which still supported a human skull, he doubted; but he played with the hope, since he had himself received the King's pardon of obtaining permission to convey that sacred relic to its old Cardigan home.

Troubled were his, thoughts as he descended that long dark slope in the grey dawn. Should he, or should he not, visit for the last time the blackened ruins of Glyndyfrdwy? Should he, or should he not, put his ear to that great stone placed by his father's grandfather at the entrance to their family-mound? Probably it was overgrown now with grass and ferns. Perhaps the very site of it was obscure, if not lost forever. Aye! but how well he remembered little Catharine stealing down that long corridor, past the Saracen's chamber, to listen to those strange sounds! Did anyone ever go there now to listen? Did the spirits of the dead *themselves die* as the world rolled on? No! he would let it go. He would ride due south; first along Lake Tegid, then over the mountains—straight to the Forests of Tywyn!

It was very dark still beneath his feet. He had to move cautiously because of thorn-stumps and furze-stalks and rabbit-holes. But when he lifted his head, there was the eastern sky beyond Dinas Brān growing already golden! He couldn't distinguish the castle itself yet. But it had been always like that. Rising as it did at the valley's entrance, that ramparted hill-top *ought* to have been seen from many a hill above Corwen. But it rarely was! Indeed he himself had seen it only once from here. And yet it was there all the time. But the puzzle was to disentangle it from the Eglwyseg Rocks that rose behind it. Brān the Blessed! How characteristic of that *Deus Semi-Mortuus* that his dwelling should be visible and yet invisible—a true *open secret* of "the Glen of the Divine Water"!

Aye! How many human feet had come down this hill since the days when the people of Mynydd-y-Gaer waited for that golden light! All gone—gone as his father was gone. What a man Broch-o'-Meifod was! None but he could have done what he'd done all that interminable night. But that body in the fire. The fire licking it before devouring it. The fire—but he must get certain sights, visible through those red flames, out of his mind now. Life had to be lived. A person had to go on. To force yourself to enjoy endurance—*that* was the pleasure of life!

Yes, you must bear the day's burden, thankful when the day ended. Yes! certain things *had* to be forgotten, else the sad play couldn't proceed; but the dead needn't be forgotten—they *couldn't* be. They were in us! While we lived *our* half-life, they lived *their* half-life. Dark, dark, dark—the life of the living, the life of the dead! And how dark it was under-foot! But the East was transforming itself now into receding gulfs of golden light. It was as if some huge planetary portcullis had been lifted, and the base-court of the Infinite exposed to view! Night and dawn! So the cycle revolved, so the wheel turned.

Yes, he was beginning already to forget "certain things"! Oh blessed, oh divine forgetfulness! Forgetfulness was greater than that dawn in the sky, than this darkness under his feet. Into this darkness his father had gone, and was there still; so that henceforth when either of the two twilights covered the earth—for the night blotted out all but itself! —he would find him.

But comfort from that golden light was an illusion. He knew *that* well enough. And yet he was comforted! What was it about such golden transparency that drew the soul out of its body and carried it down such an infinite regression!

Illusion! Illusion! But why should man be so made that the mere *sensation* of the boundless in this particular depth of transparent gold should have such an effect? The effect was upon him now; and what did *he* know? Perhaps the *effect* was nearer the truth than the cause! His path now led him through a small group of fir-trees; and he was just emerging into the open again when he suddenly stopped, awe-struck and spell-bound.

Absolutely motionless—with its head lifted as it sniffed the dawn-air—there stood before him on an isolated rock a magnificently-horned stag. Meredith was enough of his father's son to turn himself, in a single pulse-beat, into a figure of such immobility that the forward gestures of foot and hand with which he was advancing remained frozen in the very act. That horned head, dark against infinite golden space, stamped itself upon his mind forever. Years after, through all the Forests of Tywyn, his wife's people knew him, in their curious parlance, as *yr Arglwydd heb saeth,* "the arrow-less Lord."

He waited there breathless, till, by its own volition, the creature bounded away; but, as he went on down the hill, there gathered in upon his interior vision, summoned by that stag, a random crowd of kindred impressions from the misty shores of memory. A broken grey wall with a solitary mountain-ram nibbling the grass beneath it; the out-stretched branch of a wayside pine upon which as a child walking with his father he had seen a great buzzard taking its rest, red-brown as the branch beneath its folded wings; the sight of the double peaks of Snowdon, Wyddfa, the nameless tomb, and Carnedd Llewelyn, as he caught them once, towering up, forty miles away, above a white sea of undulating fog; the leap of a salmon from the dark swirl of the Dee-waters beneath Glyndyfrdwy; the wild "tu-whit" of the owl he used to hear from his nursery at Sycharth—all these things came now with a strange comfort upon him, and he thought: "Like us, like *him,* these creatures of our land rise up, live for their hour and pass away, but our land remains; and while our land remains, as the prophet said, our speech will remain, and with our speech our spirit." Meredith moved more lightly after this, but it would have been impossible for him to explain to anybody—aye! not even to Elliw ferch Rhys—the real under-tone of what he felt.

From his birth he had been without any illusions about human life. Neither the faith of the earlier times nor the Lollardry of his own modern world had ever affected him. When he was first seen as an infant Owen had cried aloud: "He's a changeling! Look how *triste* his eyes are!" But though his eyes were *triste* it was Meredith's *cynneddf,* or "peculiarity," as both Rhisiart and Walter Brut had often observed, to possess the secret of smiling a strange secret smile that seemed to come from outside the whole visible world!

And now, as the sight of those majestic horns against the dawn brought back memory upon memory, he felt that each one of these images—else why in the confusion of his days had they remained? —was much more than an owl's cry, a buzzard's vigil, a salmon's leap, a mountain's summit above the mist. What were they, what did they have in them, that they could bring such comfort?

"It's their impersonality," he thought. "It's the fact that they're the visions of thousands of generations of men living in these hills. They're mine; and they're not mine! With a host of other, commoner, simpler things they're the experiences of our people throughout the generations. *Something* stores them up; a spirit that is more than just ourselves; and each one of them brings more than we know to what that spirit stores up!"

But there came over him now a vision of Arthur's ship *Prydwen* sailing between Hell and Heaven, and yet motionless in the depths of a single soul, its great dragon wings reflected in fathomless water!

"Oh, my father, my father! A greater Welshman has never been; but greater than your greatness—"

"What is that sad-faced man smiling for?" cried the oldest winged creature in Edeyrnion, the croaking raven of Llangar, to his aged mate, as they swooped down over Meredith's quickened steps.

"Nis gwn! I don't know! *Nis gwn!"* croaked the other; and as the pair rose on their heavy-flapping wings and sailed away eastward, mounting up in huge spiral circles higher and higher as they followed the river's flow, it seemed to the man watching them as if there were something in that vast broken landscape that had echoed that hollow answer in his ears as long as he could remember.

But the great birds soared on, heedless of the echoes; soared on till to Meredith's vision they were dots and specks in the remote distance. He knew not where they were flying. But in his thoughts they were flying over the rocky crest of the Berwyns; they were flying over the fallen roof-tree of Sycharth; they were flying towards the mounded turf and the scattered stones that were all that was left of Mathrafal.

THE END

ARGUMENT

EDWARD III had been King of England for half a century; and after his death Richard "the Redeless," the son of the Black Prince, was crowned King. This was in 1377 when Richard was a boy of eleven. When he was sixteen he was married to Anne, sister to the King of Bohemia who was also the Holy Roman Emperor. Anne died childless in 1394, and two years later he married Isabella, daughter of Charles VI, King of France. "She was at the time," says Wylie, "a girl of eight years old, but she was formally crowned at Westminster as Queen of England and lived with the King as his wife." The King was beautiful, charming, wayward, moody; as unscrupulous as he was reckless. Being childless he declared his heir apparent to be Roger Mortimer, Earl of March, grandson of the third son of Edward III.

But in September, 1399—exactly a year before the rising of Owen Glyn Dŵr in Wales—Henry Plantagenet, named Bolingbroke from his birthplace in Lincolnshire, with the consent of Parliament and the support of the Commons deposed "this second Absalom," as the chronicler calls the ill-starred Richard, and usurped the throne under the title of Henry IV.

Henry was the son of John of Gaunt or Ghent, who was the *fourth* son of Edward III, so that the Mortimer claimant, descended from the *third* son, had the prior right; but at the critical juncture this Mortimer claim had fallen to a child. Shakespeare's description of the forced abdication of the unhappy Richard follows the facts as closely as the laws of drama allow. Wylie quotes from the chronicler the actual words of Henry's first speech from the throne:

"Syres, I thank yow, espirituelx and temporelx, and alle the estates of the lond, and I do yow to wyte that it ys nought my wil that no man think that by wey of conquest y wolde desherte any man of hys heritage, fraunchis, or other ryghtes that hem ought to have, ne put hym out of that he hath had in gode lawes of this reiaulme except hem that have ben ageyn the gode purpos and the commune profyte of the reiaulme."

There is no doubt that Henry's most formidable supporter in all this was Thomas Arundel, Archbishop of Canterbury, a personal friend of the Pope at Rome. And it was he who became the new King's Chancellor.

The circumstances of Richard's death, which probably took place in Pontefract Castle in 1400, remain obscure to this day. Our best historian of Henry's reign, Mr. James Hamilton Wylie, thinks it probable that he *was* murdered and that the body subsequently displayed and buried in London *was* his body. According to one account Henry had him starved to death. According to another he died of voluntary starvation. In Shakespeare's version, which came from a French source, where because of Richard's young French Queen there was every reason for giving the fullest details of a revolting crime, a certain Sir Pierce of Exton was Henry's tool.

All this happened sixteen years after John Wycliffe died in 1384. His writings and sermons were of so bold and revolutionary a character that they set the minds of thousands of people questioning not only the theological but the social and moral conventions of the time. To quote Wylie, "He opened a new well of authority in his translation of the Scriptures into English; and by his strictness of life, his courage, his subtlety in wit and argument, he set ablaze a fire in men's minds that could not be put out."

The word Lollard means "tares," or dangerous weeds sown by the Devil; and "under the common name of 'Lollards' were gathered together every species of religious malcontent."

Henry's father, John of Gaunt, had been favorably disposed to the Lollards, but the extraordinary power the Archbishop exercised over Henry's conscience turned the King into a religious persecutor.

On his accession to the throne Henry appointed Henry Percy, Earl of Northumberland, to the position of Constable of England. This office, after the Chancellorship now held by Archbishop Arundel, was far the most important in the kingdom.

The family of Percy was supreme in the North of England and the hereditary enemy of the kingdom of Scotland. It had received its lands from William the Conqueror; and Wylie describes the Earl—and the description includes his son, Henry Hotspur—in these words:

"In his own country his will was supreme. He lived apart from English life, keeping court at Bramborough, Warkworth, Newcastle, and Berwick; a border robber, holding his lands by his sword; rough and unlettered himself, he loved the flatteries of his own bards and rhymers; a bitter hater or a steady friend, generous and faithless, merciless and brave, a loyal Englishman, not from love to England, but from hatred to the Scot."

The safest authority on the "documented" events of Owen Glyn Dŵr's life is Sir John E. Lloyd, the historian of Wales. He speaks of Owen as a student of law at Westminster at the end of the reign of Edward III; and later as a knight-at-arms in the Irish and Scotch wars of Richard II. He was a middle-aged man between forty and fifty in 1400; and it seems clear that the immediate cause of his taking up arms was a quarrel with Reginald Grey, Lord of Ruthin. His friend, the poet Iolo Goch, has described in detail the quiet patriarchal life which he led in his Sycharth domain. His wife, Sir John Lloyd tells us, was the daughter of Sir David Hanmer, one of the most distinguished Welshmen of the day; who in 1383 was appointed a Judge in the Court of King's Bench. The Hanmer family itself was of English origin, but had long been settled on the border and had intermarried with the Welsh. Sir John Lloyd seems to think it doubtful that Glyn Dŵr would have raised the standard of Welsh independence if he had not been so unfairly and unjustly treated in his fierce personal quarrel; but on the final page of his careful biography we come upon the following words, which may be taken as indicating the position Glyn Dŵr holds, not only in the popular legends of Wales, but in the mind of a trained and judicious modern historian.

"He stands alone among the great figures in Welsh history in that no bard attempted to sing his elegy; this we must attribute, not merely to the mystery which shrouded his end, but also to the belief that he had but disappeared, and would rise again in his wrath in the hour of his country's sorest need."

In considering, however, the full scope of Owen's background—for as Shakespeare reminds us he was one of the most cultivated figures of his age—it is necessary to give a brief glance at the general condition of Europe and the western world at the beginning of the fifteenth century. Now the period that formed the immediate background to the dramatic events related in this tale—1400 to 1416—saw the beginning of one of the most momentous and startling epochs of *transition* that the world has known: the transition from the more or less federated Christendom of the Middle Ages to the turbulent evolution of our modern sovereign states.

The fifteenth century, of which our story covers a little more than the first decade, witnessed the gradual rise of that individualistic spirit of commerce which did so much more than the religious Crusades of an earlier epoch to bring the far-flung continents of the world into relation with one another.

America seems to have been already discovered by the Norsemen, and according to Welsh tradition, re-discovered by Prince Madoc, the son of Owen Gwynedd of North Wales, who so successfully resisted the invasion of Henry II; but the adventures of its more "documented discoverers" were yet to come; and before these occurred the path of navigation was eastward rather than westward. After the Norsemen's explorations and the more legendary voyages of the Welsh Prince, it was the new kingdom of Portugal that took the lead in these heroic if self-interested voyages; and in Portugal's rise to sea-power the kings of England played no mean part. Portuguese navigators were, however, always more interested in reaching the East than the West Indies, but whatever Indies they aimed at it was Henry IV's grandfather, Edward III, who by a royal proclamation commanded his subjects to abstain from all harm to the Portuguese; while only fifteen years before Owen Glendower's rising an English army assisted in repelling from their commercial allies at Lisbon the peril of a Spanish invasion. A few years later King John of Portugal married Philippa, Henry IV's sister, and what was called the Treaty of Windsor was signed between the two countries; after which, in the words of Mr. Saunderson, "the policy of Portugal was to maintain a close friendship with England and a cautious neutrality in Spanish affairs."

At the time of Owen's struggle for independence, however, it was the republic of Venice that dominated Europe's eastern commerce and defended the trade-routes from the attacks of the Turks. At the very time when, according to my reading of his end, Owen was rejecting Henry's pardon, Venice was defeating the Turks in the battle of Gallipoli. All this, it must be remembered, occurred more than half a century before the cessation of the wars between Castile and Aragon brought Spain to the front.

As for France, during Owen's struggle, in spite of the spiritual patriotism of her common people, she was passing through one of the most unhappy epochs in her history. Several of her provinces, including the famous towns of Calais and Bordeaux, were in the possession of the English, and she was not only constantly menaced by Burgundy, whose Duke exercised a feudal lordship over the riches of the Netherlands, but was weakened by quarrels between her own royal princes and by the intermittent mental prostration of her King Charles VI.

Russia had been overrun in the thirteenth century by hordes of Mongols under the Tatar conqueror, Genghis Khan, and not long before Glendower's revolt Moscow had been burned to the ground by one of this potentate's Mongolian successors.

This was the epoch that saw the rise to power of Poland as a formidable nation; a rise that took place under the rule of Ladislaus II, Grand Duke of Lithuania, who by his marriage united the two countries.

It was 1410, when Owen's family had just been taken prisoner at the capture of Harlech, that there was fought one of the most bloody of all the battles of the early fifteenth century, in the marshes of Tannenberg. It was here that the Poles, aided by the Czechs, under their famous Prague leader, Ziska, and aided too by a vast host of Letts and Finns and Russians, defeated with a slaughter so horrible that all Europe was shocked and scandalized the powerful German Order of the Teutonic Knights. This defeat of a mediæval religious order, designed to protect Christianity from the pagans, by the sovereign of an independent state, supported by formidable mercenaries, some baptized and some unbaptized, is as clear a symbol as we could find for the startling change that was passing over Europe in the beginning of the fifteenth century.

It seems that the Czech leader Ziska, who did most to crush the Teutonic Knights, used a novel military device that makes us think of what today are called "mechanized units"; for he invented "wagon-forts," or chariots linked together by strong iron chains. "These vehicles," I quote Mr. Saunderson's account of this famous battle, "were covered with steel or iron; and on each of them the best marksmen were placed next to the driver." In addition to these "wagon-forts" Ziska made use of the same sort of cannon and gunpowder with which Henry's captains were eventually able to overcome the Welsh defenders of Harlech. Mediæval swords and lances had already been out-dated by the long-bows of the yeomen, and the appearance of gunpowder was yet another milestone on the road along which Fate was marching.

The English merchants owed at that time considerable sums of money to the great German Hansa, or Hanseatic League, that extended from Hamburg to Danzig; and these sums were needed by the Germans to pay the huge indemnity to the King of Poland. The defeated Teutonic Knights demanded Christian sympathy because of Poland's use of unbaptized heathen at Tannenberg; but the astute London merchants retorted that if the enemy were really unbaptized it would be contrary to the interests of religion to hand over good Christian money to infidels. It is not without interest that we learn that the most powerful nation in central Europe during Owen's boyhood was Hungary. Hungary first became formidable under Louis the Great; while after Owen's *difancoll,* or "disappearance," the Hungarian monarch, Matthias Corvinus, played the rôle, in his heroic yet intellectual patriotism, of a fifteenth-century King Alfred.

The great new nations of the early fifteenth century were, therefore, Portugal, Poland and Hungary; while Burgundy, by reason of its hold upon the Netherlands, was as formidable a menace to the kingdom of France as were the English themselves. As the religious feeling that had made an imponderable unity of Europe slackened, the spirit of national sovereignty grew stronger and less scrupulous.

But the age of Owen Glendower was not only the age of the decline of feudalism; it was also the age of social upheavals. Wylie's superb history points out that when Owen was a young man in the service of Richard II there were democratic popular risings in Ghent, in Languedoc, in Florence, in Paris and in Rouen. In England itself the House of Lancaster leaned more heavily upon popular support than any previous government. In a sense it might be said that Henry IV was the first of our Parliamentary kings. The middle class had supported him against Richard; and all through his reign the Mortimers represented, according to primogeniture, a nearer claim to the throne than his own. Indeed, it was the steady support of the merchants and yeomen of England that carried him through the almost incessant treacheries and troubles of that distracted time. The King of England got his revenue partly from custom-duties on exports and imports, partly from direct taxation, and partly from his own great landed estates. The chief products exported from the country at that time were corn and honey and cloth and wool and sheepskins, along with salt and tin and lead. These products were sold to Lombard, Genoese, and Catalan traders. "Wool," Wylie quotes from a contemporary, "was the sovereign merchandise and jewel of the realm." A single sack of wool was worth from five to six pounds, each sack weighing twenty-six stone, fourteen pounds to the stone. From the earliest times, Wylie reminds us, the King claimed half a mark—six shillings and eight pence—on each sack exported. This claim was never disputed.

It is a queer and a significant thing how it was the Commons themselves who—as long as it could be done without being taxed for foreign wars—urged the King to violent patriotic measures. In earlier days all noble children in Britain were taught to speak French, but as the King and the Commons together began to encroach upon the ancient feudal courtesies, the emotion that we now call *nationalistic* began to take the place of the old crusading zeal and the old religious unity. The hatred formerly directed against infidels was now directed against aliens. Parliament itself was always taking the lead in this: violently petitioning the King to enter upon a serious campaign against the menace of resident foreigners. The Commons even went so far as to quarrel with the presence of foreign ladies in the Queen's household; and a statute was passed forbidding the use of French in the law-courts.

In the year 1406, when the French fleet sailed to the help of Owen, the English King was sore put to it for funds. His resources were sufficient in peace-time; but it was different in time of war, and in 1406 things looked very dark for the House of Lancaster. "The country," says Mr. Wylie, "seemed at a low ebb in all respects and the Commons began vehemently protesting. Poverty was everywhere. Merchants were ruined. The counties were drained of archers in this incessant warfare. The French were sailing up the Thames." In this serious situation the Commons debated so long that their turbulent session received—as did another famous sitting two and a half centuries later—the name of "the Long Parliament." They actually sat, though not continuously, for 158 days. The Speaker of the House in this eventful year, when with the French to the south and the Welsh to the west the situation was so critical, was Sir John Tiptot of the county of Cambridge; and Parliament had never been bolder in the language it used. And well it might be. There was chaos in Ireland where many of the English settlers joined with the native Irish against the government. Ireland was at that time governed by a deputy of the King, but his writ didn't extend beyond a narrow strip of country on the south and east coasts. The native Irish of the north, west and centre did not recognize his authority. Owen must have heard rumours in his childhood of Edward III's "Statutes of Kilkenny," whereby war with the natives was enjoined as a duty for the English colonists, and marriages between the two races were forbidden. But these statutes were constantly disregarded. Many famous families among the English settlers, with names familiar to us now as Irish names, such as the Butlers, Powers, Gerardynes, Bermynghames, Daltons, Barretts, Dillons, intermarried with the native chiefs and adopted the attitude, if not their customs, of true Irishmen.

In addition to this chaos in Ireland there was no security upon the seas where piracy was plundering lawful trade. Things were so bad that the Commons spoke of the King "otherwise than they ought." Peace, they declared, was what they wanted when they put him on the throne; but there had been nothing but ceaseless war. They demanded an account of all public moneys; and when they got the curt reply, "Kings don't give account," they answered, "Then their officers must." In the end an agreement was drawn up between the King and his Council, on the one hand, and the "Merchants of England," on the other. The merchants, seamen, and ship-owners were to put their ships at the disposal of the country, armed with 2000 fighting men to protect the sea. They insisted that all prizes taken should be theirs and should be dealt with by themselves.

Now it must not be forgotten that in the last decade of the fourteenth century and the first of the fifteenth the craft-guilds and trade-guilds were still the arteries of English life and kept the community sound and healthy. This remained true even after the exports and imports of the rich merchants had begun to inaugurate the rudiments of international capitalism. Each separate craft formed a fraternity of self-defence. During the years of Owen's retreat to the mountains of Snowdon and of his victory at Bryn Glas, the city of York alone, Wylie discovers, possessed no less than 96 organized trades. Each of these craft-guilds wore its own "livery," elected its own masters, managed its own affairs. The strength of each guild lay in its monopoly. In London, which was reckoned the wealthiest city in western Europe, a man must be a member of one of the "misteries," as these guilds were called, before he could keep a shop. By this means the public was guaranteed, Wylie explains, against bad workmanship. The workman was sure of his holidays and his wage; while the regulations against night-work secured fair play to the poorest who could not afford to pay for candle-light. The guilds were not only an insurance against old age or mischance by fire, water, robbery; they formed a buttress for the Church against free-thinking innovations. In London, Wylie says, there were no less than 90 guilds closely connected with parish-churches. So complicated were the guild-laws, that the ordinary law-courts sometimes had to intervene and set their ordinances aside.

Second to wool and cloth the most important commodity handled by the merchants was *herring;* and the herring fishery, owing to mysterious migrations of the fish themselves, moved during this epoch from the Baltic to the North Sea. English trade with the German cities of the Hanseatic League was enormous. Wylie's researches into old account-books prove that no less than three hundred English vessels cleared from Danzig alone in the year 1392 with cargoes of corn, honey, salt, wine, skins of Russian beaver and ermine.

In one important respect the age of Glendower resembled our own—in the extreme variety of its seasons. While Owen was fighting his final and tragic struggle there came, with the season of 1407–08, the worst winter for a hundred years. From December to March the country was covered with snow; and the merles, mavises, fieldfares, plovers died off by the thousands. The official scribe, Wylie tells us, "could make no entry in his register; for the ink froze on his 'pointel' at every second word; though he kept his little copper *chafer* beside his chair."

It was only a year after this in the early spring of 1409 that the famous schism between the Roman Pope and the Avignon Pope, the schism

that caused John Huss to utter language resembling the language of
Rabelais' Friar John, reached its culmination. The majority of the Car-
dinals decided to end the scandal by electing a third Pope. And the
French Chancellor, Gerson, took the lead in this movement. Pope Bene-
dict thereupon fled to Spanish protection at Perpignan, while Pope
Gregory left Rome, a penniless fugitive.

The mediæval system of European life implied a loose kind of federa-
tion with the dual authority of Pope and Holy Roman Emperor at its
head; and it is clearly a sign that this system had begun to break down,
under the combined pressure of nationalism and free thought, that not
only should there be three Popes in that fatal year, but two Holy Roman
Emperors, in addition to the one in Constantinople.

We are permitted to wonder whether our hero Owen, as he desperately strove to ward off his fate, heard through his Chancellor, Bishop
Young, of the summoning of the General Convocation to Pisa by the
dissentient Cardinals. This Council of Pisa in 1409 does indeed deserve
our attention as a notable sign of how the whole organism of mediæval
Christendom was breaking up. Wylie's incomparable narrative of this
epoch gives us many arresting details. The Council opened on March
25, 1409. There were present 160 archbishops, bishops and mitred abbots;
120 doctors in theology; 300 doctors in civil and canon law; 22 cardinals;
4 patriarchs. An indictment under 37 heads against both Popes was
read, and two of the cardinals walked through the building asking three
times in a loud voice if Benedict and Gregory were there. On receiving
no reply, both of the two absent Popes were declared contumacious.

Later, on Wednesday, June 5, in the cathedral beneath the leaning
tower, the Patriarch of Alexandria mounted the pulpit and pronounced
both Popes heretics, schismatics, enemies of God, excommunicate from
the Church.

And if this revolutionary attempt to restore the dignity of the Papacy
was a sign of the changing times, still more so was the remarkable intellectual movement of that epoch to which might almost be given the
name of the "National Renaissance," as distinct from the better-known
Classical Renaissance which came more than half a century later. If
Glendower was a disciple of the Welsh bardic lore, Henry IV was no
mean patron of national literature. Wylie reminds us that he had the
friendship of the poet Gower, old and blind; and that not only did

the dying Chaucer receive an annuity of 40 marks, but that Thomas Hoccleve, then a young clerk in a government office, got a pension of 10 pounds for life. Nor was the English King content with this. He even went so far as to make vain attempts to attract to his court the famous French poetess, Christine de Pisan, whose learning and wit were one of the wonders of that curious age. In her own person Christine de Pisan was a notable symbol of what I have presumed to call the "National Renaissance." She might almost be called the first of the feminists. Wylie emphasizes the passionate appeal she addressed to the French Queen and Council against the civil war that was ruining France. And if in that nationalistic age a woman like Christine could reach such prominence by a mixture of patriotism and learning, it must not be forgotten that the supreme path to distinction for any man of genius of humble origin was still the Church. This is proved by the result of the Conference at Pisa. The 23 cardinals went into conclave in the archbishop's palace and after 11 days announced that one of their number had been elected Pope. This was Cardinal Pietro Filargo, a man of such extremely humble birth that he used to say he didn't know who his parents were. He was picked up by a Franciscan friar as beggar-boy in the island of Crete. He was sent to Oxford, and in 1381 to Paris. He was now seventy years old and Archbishop of Milan. "He was crowned Pope at Pisa," Wylie tells us, "on a high scaffold, July 7, 1409, with the title of Alexander V. Gregory and Benedict were burnt in effigy. The Grey Friars were wild with delight that one of their order had been elected." The new Pope was a Greek and was interested in the question of reunion with the Greek Church. It was Chancellor Gerson of France who among the dignitaries was most keen on this reunion. He knew that the Greeks hated the Latins worse than the Turks, and that it would be asked what right had France to talk of peace with all the world when she couldn't even live at peace with England. But, nevertheless, when the news of the election of Alexander V reached Paris on the evening of July 7, the cry was: "Long live *our* Pope!" The new Pope did his best. He wrote to Henry remembering his studies at Oxford, and to the French King urging him to make peace with England; but the war went on. And in spite of the Pisan Conference making so good a choice, neither Benedict nor Gregory would give way; and the schism was left unsettled till long after Owen's disappearance from that dramatic stage.

Matters were complicated by the fact that a serious crack had yawned in the *other* unifying principle of Christendom, the Holy Roman Empire, the one about which Dante had been so eloquent. In Owen's time there were two claimants for this distinction, both of them "Kings of the Romans," namely the German Rupert, Duke of Bavaria and Count Palatine of the Rhine, and the Czech Wenceslaus, or Wenzel, King of Bohemia.

But a much more serious menace to the unity of Christendom than the existence of the rival Popes and rival Emperors was to be found in the growth of startlingly new religious opinions at home. Wycliffe had not been dead many years before his revolutionary doctrines spread like quicksilver among the more progressive spirits. Oxford was riddled with Lollardry, and boldly defied the authorities; while the movement grew so rapidly that the Archbishop initiated the notorious statute, *De Heretico Comburendo*—"concerning the suppression of heresy by fire." But Wycliffe's ideas found no Oxford disciple as devoted or sympathetic as John Huss of Bohemia. And the Czechs as a nation followed him, especially the citizens of Prague. Huss himself was betrayed and burnt, but his ideas—which were Wycliffe's—survived him; survived to tear a living limb from the body of the Spouse of Christ.

And if this extraordinary epoch was characterized by individualism in religion and nationalism in politics it was remarkable for its unscrupulous diplomacy. One aspect of this particular unscrupulousness shocked certain minds, even then: the marriages of children for diplomatic reasons. Both Henry IV's little daughters were married—just as Owen's youngest daughter was—to further the political aims of their parent. Some of the quaintest revelations in Wylie's *History of England under Henry IV* concern the precise expenditure upon the trousseaux of these brides. Henry's youngest daughter, Philippa, was married, for the most purely political motives, to the new "elective" King—for he was no Norseman—Eric of Denmark. Thirteen years ere Owen proclaimed himself Prince, Olaf III, King of Denmark and Norway, had died at the age of sixteen. His mother, Margaret, at once became Regent. She was the widow of King Haakon of Sweden and soon became ruler of that country too, after conquering the German Prince, Albert of Mecklenberg, "who sent her"—Wylie mischievously records—"a stone to sharpen her scissors and needles." But she succeeded in uniting the three kingdoms together under her great-nephew Eric, with the little English Philippa as Queen.

If the Middle Ages had been passionate and poetic, the fifteenth century was fantastic and bizarre. At the very time when so many Welsh students at Oxford were flocking to Owen's standard a far more rare and exciting personality arrived on a visit to England than any Holy Roman Emperor. This was Manuel II, Emperor of the East. Officially he came to beg the help of the western nations against the Turks who were besieging Constantinople; but actually his visit gave rise to a sequence of the most fantastical pageantry ever recorded. The day of the old authentic chivalry was over; but its ghost pranced and caracoled and jousted in a Masque of Death. Manuel came from the most romantic city in the world. The Welsh bards called the place Taprobane; and they felt that Manuel himself must have had some drops of Constantine the Great's Welsh blood in his veins even if their own remote ancestors hadn't actually come from the fairy-city in the "Land of Summer." Along with the Eastern Emperor came his Greek teacher, Chrysoloras; and here indeed we encounter a personage who, in the midst of what I have presumed to call the "National Renaissance," was a true forerunner and precursor of the more famous classical one.

The figure, however, that captured the imagination of the poets of a later time was not the sophisticated Christian Emperor, but the appalling old heathen who gave the City of Civilization a brief breathing-space from her pre-destined doom. This was the blood-thirsty leader of the all-conquering Tartars, Tamberlaine the Great.

In the East of Europe Christianity was at the time of our story fighting for its life against Islam. Asia Minor was lost to the Turks already, and their hosts were now gathering round the Bosphorus. In his desperation Manuel had made peace with the Pope of Rome, but only four years before Owen raised his standard at Glyndyfrdwy, Sultan Bajazet I crushed a vast Western army at the Battle of Nicopolis. Henry of Lancaster was actually present at this defeat and barely escaped with his life. As the danger grew greater year by year the Pope called upon Christendom to help with money if it could not do so with arms. Wylie tells us how there were mayor's funds and collecting boxes in all the English cities. After the first lull in the Welsh trouble, Henry—now the recognized monarch in Richard's place—subscribed a thousand pounds for the rescue of Constantinople. At the very time when Owen was taking prisoner Lord Grey of Ruthin the Eastern Emperor was being fêted in Paris like a creature from another world. Meanwhile one old ferocious nomad easily accomplished what all the princes of Europe had been unable to do: "Timur the Lame," or Tamberlaine the Great, made one of his famous mountains of human skulls out of the heads of the dreaded Turks. Having thus saved civilization, the godless old man promptly despatched letters to the King of England from Samarcand, begging English traders to visit his dominions and promising them protection from all interference.

The beginning of the fifteenth century may justly be described as an era of degenerate faith and degenerate chivalry. It was an age of unscrupulous individualism but also an age when *national self-consciousness* under independent rulers superseded the old feudal ideal of a united Christendom under Emperor and Pope. The dominant note of the epoch was what might be called the cynical use of the masks and symbols of lost ideals to advance shameless personal ends. A simple religious faith had "kept the strong in awe," but the simplicity of that faith was gone; and as yet no secular moral public opinion showed any sign of taking its place. And the age of Owen Glendower had to get worse before it could get better. In its strange recurring spirals of advance and retreat our tragic caravan of human progress was taking just then one of its most dangerous "horse-shoe curves." It was an age of restless adventure rather than of practical achievement; an age of fancy and imagination and ideal passion. Orthodoxy burnt without conscience; and heresy blasphemed without decency. But those mysterious movements of destiny that neither the strong can retard, nor the crafty side-track, were at work all the while. What happened, as we see it now, was what none of the parties concerned expected, hoped, or imagined. It was what Fate intended; and whether we force ourselves to "love" the issue, as Nietzsche does, or sink beneath it to the life within, as Blake does, we can at least in either case do as the blind bard in the *Odyssey* did and take all these things as having happened in their beauty and in their pain "that there might be a song for those who come after."

JOHN COWPER POWYS

Corwen
* North Wales*
*   May, 1940*